T0244122

Song of the Mysteries

By the same author

Sorcerer's Legacy
The Master of Whitestorm
That Way Lies Camelot
To Ride Hell's Chasm

The Cycle of Fire Trilogy
Stormwarden
Keeper of the Keys
Shadowfane

With Raymond E. Feist
Daughter of the Empire
Servant of the Empire
Mistress of the Empire

The Wars of Light and Shadow
The Curse of the Mistwraith
The Ships of Merior
Warhost of Vastmark
Fugitive Prince
Grand Conspiracy
Peril's Gate
Traitor's Knot
Stormed Fortress
Initiate's Trial
Destiny's Conflict

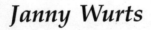

Janny Wurts

SONG OF THE MYSTERIES

The Wars of Light and Shadow

VOLUME 11

Harper*Voyager*
An imprint of HarperCollins*Publishers* Ltd
1 London Bridge Street
London SE1 9GF

www.harpercollins.co.uk

HarperCollins*Publishers*
Macken House,
39/40 Mayor Street Upper,
Dublin 1
D01 C9W8
Ireland

First published by HarperCollins*Publishers* Ltd 2024
1

ISBN: 978-0-00-865390-3 (HB)
ISBN: 978-0-00-731036-4 (TPB)

Typeset in Minion Pro by Palimpsest Book Production Ltd, Falkirk, Stirlingshire

Printed and bound in the UK using
100% Renewable Electricity by CPI Group (UK) Ltd

For Larry Fast
Whose inspired invention scored more than music,
but abandoned constraint and conventional instruments
to compose his orchestra by the limitless synergy
of imagination—
this story embraces that challenge
to venture beyond the familiar.

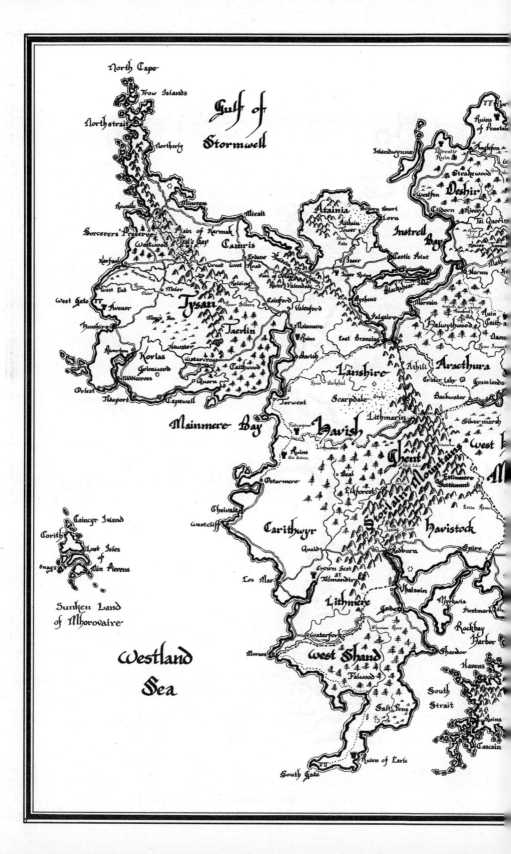

Athera

Continent of Paravia

Age of the Mistwraithe

North Ward Grimwood
Fallowmere
River Valstayn
East Ward
Plain of Araithe
Werpoint
Perlorn
Crescent Isle
Ithamerin Mountains
Etarra
Valleygap
Minderl Bay
Rathain
Tier Rocks
Darkling
Eastwall
Ithilt
Minderl Strait
Ramon
Ithamon
Minderl Ruins
Shelsevrie
Valhearp
Saint's Point
East Gate
Vastrait
Mhar Ruins
Bay of Eltair
Narms
Norfastor
Tharidor
Whitehold
Narse
Castlair
Shipsport
Tirans
Perdith
Atwood
East halla
Tirans Ruins
Atlain
Cildein Ocean
Midhalla
River Adleith
Alestron
Kalesh
Tiriac Mountains
Adruin
Mirthvain Swamp
Los Lier
Orvandir
Methisle
Durn
Methlas Lake
Methlas River
Ishlir
Ganish
Six Towers
River Tal Tal
Elssine
Third mark
Shand
Athera
Telzen
Scimlade Tip
River Ippash
Merior
Forthmark
Sidhe Bay
Shaddorn
Junish
Desert of Sanpashir
Selkwood
Southshire
Sanshevas
Ruins

South Sea

0   10   25   50   100

	Town		Grimward
	Ancient Ruin		
	Unvanquished Town		
	Worldsend Gate		
	Paravian Marker		
	Kingdom Boundary		
	River		
	Forest		Preserve
	Marsh		
	Waste or Desert		
	Roads		
	Mountains		

© 1984 Janny Wurts

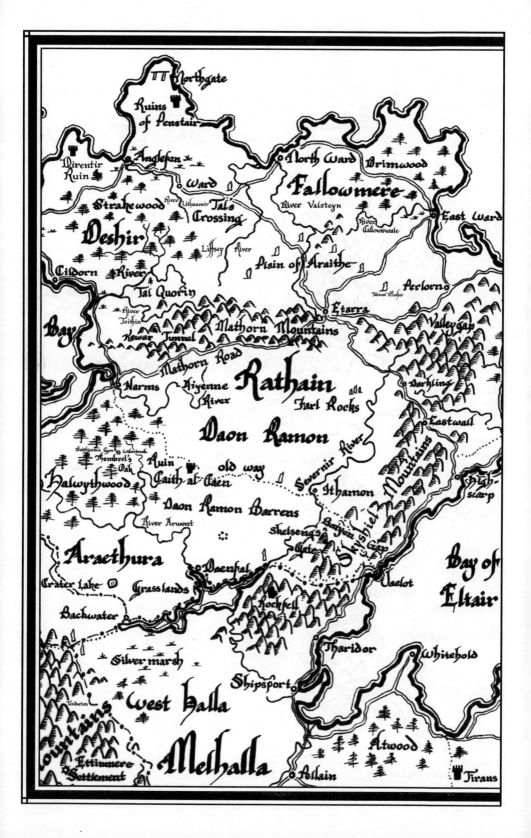

Acknowledgements

While writing is solitary, the milestone of a fifty-year work does not happen alone but surrounded by the loving support of many.

First, my husband Don Maitz for a marriage that survived this journey.

Invaluable thanks to my draft readers, for feedback and proofing: Andrew Ginever, Brian Uri, Blaise Ancona, Jon Moss. I could not have done without your support.

My agents, in New York and London, Ben Camardi, Sandy Violette, Anna Carmichael.

My long-term partners in copyedit, from the ground floor, Bob and the late Sara Schwager.

My editors, Natasha Bardon and Vicky Leech, and for support at Harper 360 in New York, Jean Marie Kelly.

The earliest enthusiasm of video reviewers for making it happen: Under the Radar Books, Page Chewing, A Critical Dragon, Philip Chase, Johanna Reads, Angie, the bookaholic, Niko's Book Reviews and so many more unmentioned just coming on board.

Last, and sadly, for the friends who have passed before this series was completed: Mike Floerkey, Wayne Mcalla, Jonathan Matson, Abner Stein.

Deepest thanks to the musicians whose work continues to inspire.

Contents

Song of the Mysteries
Time line with relevant dates

—5637 Exile from Dascen Elur brings Arithon and Lysaer to Athera.

—5638 Defeat of Desh-thiere and containment by Asandir.

—Failed coronation at Etarra sees the half brothers entrapped by the Mistwraith's curse.

—Mistwraith's collective wraiths prisoned under wards in the vault at Rockfell Peak.

—Massacre at Tal Quorin, first war between Arithon and Lysaer under the curse.

—Arithon apprentices to the Masterbard Halliron sen Al'Duin.

—Lysaer swears to unify the towns to destroy the Master of Shadow.

The Ships of Merior

—5643 Asandir assigns Dakar to Arithon's service.

—5644 Lysaer's false claim to inheritance rebuilds the royal seat at Avenor.

—5645 Healing of a fisher lad establishes Arithon and Elaira's gestalt rapport.

—Lysaer executes Maenalle, *Caithdein* of Tysan for robbing his caravan.

—Allied war host to destroy Arithon is stalled by the burning of the fleet at Minderl Bay.

Warhost of Vastmark

—5647 Lysaer's pursuit of Arithon to Merior brings an encounter with Ath's adepts but fails to ameliorate the Mistwraith's curse and entrenches his determined campaign.

—Talith's abduction by Arithon to stall the war estranges her marriage with Lysaer.

—Arithon's horrific tactic of slaughter at the Havens fails to forestall the battle's engagement at Dier Kenton Vale.

—Lysaer's resounding defeat hardens his curse-driven resolve to found a religion.

—s'Brydion change coat and ally with Arithon as undercover spies.

Fugitive Prince

—5648–9 Lysaer establishes the Alliance of Light at Avenor and is expelled from the Fellowship Sorcerers' compact for inciting slavery and making a false claim to divinity.

—After the unsuccessful search to find the Paravians, Arithon's plot at the Riverton Shipyard goes wrong when the Mistwraith's curse is triggered by a Koriani fetch, and his sword stroke fatally wounds his liegeman Caolle. Flight into the Scarpdale Grimward destroys a troop of Hanshire guard, with Sulfin Evend, the sole survivor, installed as Lysaer's First Commander.

—5653 While Lysaer is diverted offshore to Corith by Koriani machination, his wife Talith is assassinated by the conspiracy of Avenor's council and the Light's priesthood.

Grand Conspiracy

—5654 Lysaer marries Lady Ellaine and their son Kevor is conceived.

—5669 Arithon's innocent double, created by Koriathain to entrap him, is arrested and accused of Arithon's crimes as Master of Shadow.

—5670 Arithon's rescue of the innocent arraigned in his place corrupts Lirenda, who is demoted from rank as First Senior.

Peril's Gate

—Morriel Prime details Elaira to track Arithon's flight for his life, and bind him under an oath of debt should he lean on her help to survive against his closing pursuit.

—Lysaer is tainted by necromancers in a blood rite by a corrupted priest when the Grey Kralovir cult infiltrates Avenor's council and the Religion of Light.

—Prince Kevor s'Ilessid crosses the corrupt High Priest Cerebeld, who plots his death by Khadrim fire, but the boy survives transformation as an adept of Ath's brotherhood.

—5669 Koriani plot to overthrow the Fellowship Sorcerers rips Athera's etheric web, whereupon Morriel Prime seizes the diversion to take possession of Selidie to effect an irregular succession and salvage the secret assets held by the order.

—5670 Arithon's narrow escape from Lysaer's Alliance cordon costs Jieret's transcendent death and great losses to Rathain's war band, and drives him to perilous refuge in Davien's Maze at Kewar, where he achieves mastery of the Mistwraith's curse and restores access to his blocked talent.

Traitor's Knot

—5670 Lysaer returns his war host to Tysan in defeat. Sulfin Evend discovers Lysaer's corruption by necromancers, bargains with Enithen Tuer for the Biedar knife and the rite to free Lysaer from enslavement, which sets them in dangerous conflict with the corrupted faction entrenched at Avenor.

—Princess Ellaine flees Avenor to escape the corrupt factions who killed her son and finds haven with the s'Brydion, leading to her protective custody with Ath's adepts and enabling the abandonment of her marriage, which unleashes Lysaer's virulent fury upon Alestron in retaliation.

—Arithon binds Jeynsa by a mage rite under his protection at her father's dying behest; the tryst by the Willowbrook with Elaira is halted by the Fellowship Sorcerers.

—5671 Arithon eradicates the Grey Kralovir at Etarra, stirring the Alliance and the Religion of Light to shoulder Lysaer's war and the siege of Alestron.

Stormed Fortress

—Jeynsa mistakenly believes Arithon is delinquent of his crown obligation and runs away to Alestron to remedy his lapse, well aware her presence must draw Arithon to the town's defence.

—Siege of Alestron engages, before Elaira and Sidir's attempt to extricate Jeynsa.

—Arithon's appeal to Merevalia Teirendaelient from the King's Grove in Alland frees him from the Mistwraith's geas.

—Siege of Alestron, Sidir is wounded defending Jeynsa from a s'Brydion conspiracy, Arithon's call for peace through Alithiel's power stalls the war, enabling Sulfin Evend to turn Lysaer away from the carnage and distance himself from cursed influence before the defences are breached.

—5671 Sethvir is failing at Althain Tower, worn down from holding the grimwards damaged by the Prime Matriarch's meddling. His collapse forces Davien to shoulder his obligate bargain with Seshkrozchiel, then rescue Asandir from a grimward, where a twist of the dragon's dream empowers Davien's reincarnation.

—Vengeful destruction of Avenor by Seshkrozchiel's drakefire eradicates the dragon-skull wards buried under the rubble.

—Parrien s'Brydion's assassination of Arithon is thwarted by Kyrialt's death, leaving Glendien widowed, while Elaira and Talvish complete his escape as he is wounded and comatose.

—5671/5672 Dakar the Mad Prophet invokes Fellowship authority, attaching Rathain's crown with an oath of debt to the Koriathain, that Elaira can invoke her initiate training to recall Arithon's strayed spirit.

When she alters the ritual to comply with free will, the form replicates the original construct stolen from the Biedar tribes by the Koriathain, allowing the crone to intervene through the ancestry, lay claim to conception of a child, and reincarnate the ancestral spirit of a tribal ancient as Arithon's daughter, born to Glendien at Althain Tower.

Interim events

—5672 Birth of Teylia to Glendien at Althain Tower.

—Elaira returns to the Koriathain under summons.

—5674 Arithon is betrayed and taken captive by the Koriathain, ignorant of Dakar's oath of debt to the Crown and all that occurred at Athir to spare him.

—When the Prime threatens Elaira's life to break him, Arithon sequesters all of his memories of her, together with his perilous knowledge, into the emerald signet ring of Rathain, which is protected under Fellowship auspices and guarded by Elaira as his handfast beloved.

—5674 The Fellowship Sorcerers gamble with extreme risk to halt Arithon's immediate destruction at the hands of the Prime Matriarch. Kharadmon collapses the star wards that are holding back a mass invasion by Marak's free wraiths, forcing Prime Selidie to negotiate or see the world become devoured, since only a Masterbard's art can ameliorate the threat.

—The Koriani Prime's final bargain stays Arithon's execution only until the last free wraith is settled, appended to the demand that Sethvir surrenders guardianship of Teylia to the sisterhood.

—5676 Teylia swears initiate's oath to the Koriathain but fails in training to fulfil the prime succession since every focus crystal she touches shatters on contact.

—5683 The Great Schism: Lysaer abandons the Religion of Light in Tysan and retires to the mayor's seat at Etarra, dividing the faith.

—5688 Reform Years in Rathain, as Lysaer's justice establishes a Treaty of Law, bringing a truce with the clans of Rathain.

—5691 First Book of Canon Law establishes the True Sect High Temple at Erdane.

—5867 Drake War fought to a standstill by Fellowship Sorcerers at Penstair.

—5902 True Sect zealots in Tysan and the Crown of Havish reach a tenuous accord, to expire upon the death of the reigning queen.

Initiate's Trial

—5922 Free wraiths from Marak are redeemed, and Arithon's stay of execution is forfeit. Teylia assists his release and strips him of memory so Koriathain cannot track him.

—Asandir relinquishes charge of Arithon's fate back to the Prime Matriarch, but her spell to destroy Arithon claims Teylia's life in his stead.

—Arithon takes refuge with Tarens on the family croft in Tysan.

—Now a Master Spellbinder, Dakar is summarily discharged from Fellowship apprenticeship and evicted from Althain Tower.

—Asandir swears Daliana sen Evend to Lysaer's service to curb the effects of the Mistwraith's curse.

—5922–5923 True Sect priests raid the crofters' home under suspicion of heresy. Tarens kills the examiner and takes flight with Arithon under close pursuit.

—5923 Arithon wakens the wardings of Caithwood to stall a True Sect invasion, blending ancient magic of the Paravians, the Fellowship Sorcerers, and his bard's arts, which makes him a source of knowledge coveted by the Koriani Prime Matriarch.

—A resonant intersection in time/space bequeaths High Earl Jieret's memories to Tarens.

—A plot by Koriathain and True Sect priests triggers the Mistwraith's curse, causing Lysaer to abdicate the mayor's seat at Etarra to raise the True Sect host for invasion of Havish.

—Elaira holds audience with the Biedar crone and is assigned bearer of a flint knife with arcane properties.

—Clan children Siantra s'Idir, Khadrien, and Esfand s'Valerient steal the sword Alithiel and seek Prince Arithon but run into the perilous verge at the border at Athili and are rescued by Asandir.

—Having fallen out with Arithon during the escape from True Sect captivity at Torwent, Tarens parts company to escort a band of refugees to safety with the High King of Havish at Fiaduwynne, and Arithon escapes eastward, hiding in plain sight as a healer in the True Sect war host.

—The great drake, Seshkrozchiel, enters hibernation, and Luhaine, as a Fellowship discorporate, assumes the burden of Davien's bargain to allow his reincarnate form to survive.

—Battle of Lithmarin: the Hatchet's campaign against Havish sweeps across Lanshire, pinning Arithon against the shores of Lithmarin, where a heroic stand wrests the opening for his escape at the tragic price of High King Gestry's early death.

—Asandir's loose horse delivers the sword Alithiel as Arithon flees into Melhalla.

—Dakar and Daliana spirit Lysaer off the field at Lithmarin and sequester him under duress in Scarpdale.

Destiny's Conflict

—5923 Lysaer repudiates Daliana for intervention, and Davien shape-shifts her to male form to serve him undercover as valet and continue her effort to temper the Mistwraith's curse.

—Arithon's flight from the field at Lithmarin runs afoul of a Koriani trap, with Elaira's imprint laid on Vivet, with her son Valien's birth hooking him to the Ettinmere shamans by his oath of child-right as his ward.

—Lysaer seizes Miralt's dedicates to overthrow the True Sect, and loses his eye in defeat by the Hatchet. His convalescent recovery at the True Sect Temple at Erdane forces Daliana to bind a shady glamour on him to spare him from intractable madness.

—5924 Cosach dies in Daon Ramon under assault by True Sect forces, who march unchecked for expansion.

—5925 An offshore storm shipwrecks Arithon's sloop on the Paravian refuge on Los Lier, where he unravels the stasis holding Ciladis before his release to return to the mainland.

—Arithon defeats the Ettinmere shamans and restores the rogue hostel vortex to Ath's adepts, and in the process unravels all oaths and bindings held over him.

—The True Sect makes war on the clans in Rathain, but stops the assault under influence of Koriani conspiracy to take Arithon captive through Vivet's betrayal.

—Vivet's death by decree of the True Sect Canon, and Valien's execution as Spawn of Shadow at Daenfal, where Arithon is narrowly spared the same fate by intervention of Dakar, Tarens, and Elaira.

—Lysaer recoups sane awareness in terrifying straits, held under duress at the heart of True Sect power in Erdane's High Temple.

—True Sect zealots witness the Fellowship Sorcerers' removal of Arithon from the scaffold and turn apostate to the faith.

—Ciladis returns to Althain Tower.

Song of the Mysteries

The season is late winter, Third Age 5926

Late Winter 5926

ERA OF CREATION
Birth of a primal world above the threshold of entropy.
ERA OF DESTRUCTION
Dragons wrought wilful chaos unto the brink of ruin.
ERA OF REDEMPTION
Ath gifted the Paravian races to heal the balance.
But not all Elder Dragons agreed. Some rejected the
Treaty Accord to defend Athera's Great Mystery . . .
—Cianor, Keeper of the Records, Second Age Year 902

I. Estrangement

Stars like luminous dust, thick as glittering smoke, hazed the jagged crack in the rock ceiling high overhead. Sight recorded the image, as awareness resurged after red rage and a virulent explosion of pain had hurled living consciousness into a caul of oblivion. Arithon gazed upwards, enveloped in stillness. Braced by a cold, desert night, he breathed in the desiccate scent of volcanic sand. These surrounds were familiar. Once before, this cavern in Sanpashir had sheltered him through the recovery that followed a primal wounding of spirit and flesh. He remembered, unwilling, a traumatic assault on his being sufficient to rend the veil at the turn of Fate's Wheel.

But this moment differed. His reflexive extension of mage-sense lacked all grounded sensation of form. Instead, Arithon grappled the ephemeral half world of dream traversed on a spirit walk. Nor was he alone. The well of poised silence at arm's reach to his left held a dread, female presence he dared not refuse to acknowledge.

Though her deep silence burned him, he would not speak first. Power acknowledged true power. Impeccably trained, his tenterhook deference stonewalled the nascent entanglement of her imposed obligation.

The rooted claim on him held no animosity. Only the patience of ages that walked hand in glove with the wisdom bestowed by a passage that trod the realm past the boundary of death.

The crone, in life revered as the Eldest Voice of the Biedar people, declared finally, "You have kept the hair-splitting edge on your etiquette."

Arithon inclined his head in respect. "You foretold I would visit the far side, twice again, and warned of the hour I must meet the venerable pillar of your tribal ancestry. You'd prefer the more earnest snipe of my helpless impertinence?"

The crone wheezed a laugh, her shade a substanceless shadow beside him, still overwhelmingly perilous. She need not respond. Rebuke surfaced from his recalled experience: of her tender hands cupping his face, while the sheen of spilled tears striped her cheeks for the upcoming trials hedging his future. What else moved her to weep, he preferred not to know. His refusal to ask, then or now, did not signify. His implacable claim to autonomy never had been sufficient to shield him.

The ancient presence commanding this audience was a force strong enough to bend nature. When she spoke, her husked warning came laced in riddles that predated Mankind's settlement on Athera.

"You are Mother Dark's Chosen, of Requiar's lineage. Blood inheritance binds you to the oath sealed upon Scathac's world, that swore surety for Jessian Oathkeeper's legacy. She died unbroken and true to her word. Yet the price of her integrity unleashed the baulked fury of her oppressors against our tribe. Their might prevailed, to a terrible end. For the Koriani sisterhood's coercive theft of our heritage begat the vile perversion of necromancy."

"A horror defanged," Arithon tested, in reference to his recent destruction of the order's Great Waystone, and the recovery of Elaira's personal crystal.

The crone's reply swept those triumphs aside and struck him like a fist in the gut. "Do not succumb to self-blindness! The threat to *all* you hold dear has redoubled. The dead prime was cagey. She kept duplicate imprints of your associates' records, and held more than one rear-guard play up her sleeve. The secretive sting of her vengeance awaits you. Aligned enemies of your lineage, and ours, will spare none from her use in brute leverage against you." In accusation fit to freeze his blood, she affirmed his dire fear without flinching. "Make no mistake! You cannot shelter behind naïve complacency, or rest on the blindered assumption Althain's Warden's oversight is unassailable. Elder powers are at play, with you the unwitting spark entangled in old tinder ripened for a hostile conflagration."

Arithon gave the Biedar shade his skewered attention. "What in Sithaer's seventh pit do you know that eludes Sethvir's earth-sense?" But he already guessed the battlefield underlying his ignorance. Besides the opportune opening seized through the past misuse of Elaira's personal crystal, his harrowing traverse of the archive stored within the Great Waystone's amethyst matrix had sketched the breadth of a canvas far beyond mortal scale. The provenance of Mankind's offworld history was unknowably vast, a deadly trove kept proscribed by the ironclad terms of the Fellowship's compact.

The crone's shade hedged her answer. This lifetime's untried potential must rise to level the ancient score of tribal obligation. Cut the head from a tainted legacy's snake here and now, before the corruption at large broke loose to seed worlds with another cycle of suffering. The weaker lineage had failed to stem the warped practices spawned from stolen knowledge: Hassidii's culpability remained unredeemed. Requiar's integrity therefore stood alone to meet the cost of redress.

Pared to cryptic reference, she said, "*Anshlien'ya's* promise, you are not the born fool. A storm is coming far greater than you. Your destiny threads the core of the gyre, whether you triumph or fall. Fate will tread the course of the abyss. Either become consumed, or stand steadfast and steer by the light of your only inviolate beacon. You bear the graces of all of your forebears, and the hour for their entangled reckoning draws nigh. You must return to the realm of the flesh. Go back, awaken, and be the forged sword born of Requiar's issue."

The crone left him then, her departure a void that brought bleak foreboding to roost upon his unsettled equilibrium. The stars shining through the rock rift overhead were the diamantine constellations of winter, undisturbed by his tormented past and his latest horrific lapse of a sworn obligation. Ahead lay the turbulent promise of pain, whetted by the dread cry of urgency thrust upon him by the Biedar ancestor's eldritch counsel. '*The threat to all you hold dear has redoubled.*'

The beguilement of the setting's false peace chafed against the flayed impetus of his emotion. He could not step aside and quit the arena. The untenable choice was defeat, uncontested.

Arithon, once more Teir's'Ffalenn, bent his head in consent. He would shoulder the stakes on fraught course towards peril sufficient to break him. Acknowledgement keyed his path to release. The cavern the desert tribes called by the name of the Air, and before them, the Paravians named *Inshidik en Vayar*, the Great Crack in the World, lost dimension. As the battening weave of the dreamscape gave way and shredded around him, he beheld the hallowed vista swallowed up by a rampart of cloud black as ruin . . .

* * *

The web of unborn probability shuddered into change when the Eldest
crone of the Biedar opened her protective fist. Time's referent realigned
like jerked cord as the marked spirit cast forth at her bidding tumbled free
in the nadir of the night. In the moment Arithon Teir's'Ffalenn embarked
upon his gradual ascent from the dreamless haven of comatose oblivion,
the Warden at Althain Tower shivered where he perched, sketching a
freckled, brown thrush's egg in the quiet fastness of his top-floor library.

His dipped pen nib froze between strokes. A poised droplet of ink
trembled in arrested suspension.

Across the stone table, welded in the stilled darkness scented with
musty books and new parchment, Ciladis glanced up from the page pinned
under his lean, ebon finger. Profound survey of his colleague's untidy,
hunched form let him plumb the nuance behind the abrupt stillness.

The tempest nothing might stem had begun.

Sethvir rinsed his quill in his half-empty mug of cold tea before a
splotch marred his manuscript. "Beyond recourse, the critical moment's
upon us."

Small words, to encompass the momentous sweep of event, while more
than one era of overdue reckoning merged into a relentless confluence.

Ciladis bookmarked his chapter with silk ribbon. Shadow cast by the
room's only lit candle stub scythed across the illumined, miniature script
of a sunchild's hand as he eased closed the boards of a frail volume,
centuries preserved. "Asandir's committed past recourse at Northgate?"

"He's en route." Wide glance rinsed blank by thoughts fanned over
distance, Althain's Warden laid aside the wet pen and cradled the bird's
egg as though the world's precarious course lay inscribed in the mottled
shell. "Close enough, barely, to change course at speed and shoulder the
needful side errand."

Polished sepia beside Sethvir's ivory pallor, Ciladis arose, spare of
movement as wafted smoke. "Then handle the summons. I'll ease the
transition as best I may."

"Little more than a gesture within our Fellowship's power," the Warden
admitted, aggrieved.

Gloom swallowed Ciladis's form in retreat. His whiskey-grained baritone reflected his heartache as he reshelved the irreplaceable book. "What
use, if I never tried?" From the start there had been no sound avenue
open for consolation. The brunt could not be softened by regret, or
altered in form under the Law of the Major Balance: only weathered

in dogged, precarious trust, until the convergent impact of unresolved choices forged the path through the thickets of latent crises.

Asandir, backed by Chaimistarizog's oversight of the Northgate Accord, no longer stemmed the floodtide of on-coming contention. The ancient, bitter score would come to be paid, while the mighty of more than one world collided, and continuance of the Paravian presence and the precarious terms of Mankind's future survival became blown chaff in the onrushing winds of conflagration.

Cleared long since of the sick-room taint of wound salve and steam from the exhaustive boiling of linen bandages, Althain Tower's second-floor guest chamber brightened under the milk tint of midwinter dawn. Elaira perched in the bolstered chair by the hearth, another night's quiet vigil of many throughout the months her handfast beloved had lain unconscious in convalescence.

Routine never blunted the cruel strain. The enchantress scarcely could bear to regard the slack form on the bed. Too long quiet, the exquisite, musician's hands remained stilled as a sculptor's masterwork. The combed gleam of raven hair on the pillow, unrumpled, a jarred statement set against the chiselled bone armature clothed in immobile flesh. Life imprinted the bedclothes less than the scene woven into the Paravian tapestries that softened the chamber's stone wall. Rich dyes and silver-gilt thread depicted a waterfall in a woodland glen stirred in the fresh draughts from the cracked casement, more movement than the slow rise and fall of the breathing man's chest.

Time had knitted the worst of the damage. The ugly, gaping sword wound in Arithon's solar plexus left a whorled, pink scar, while the ruin inflicted by severed nerves, torn muscle, and ripped organs had progressed into healthy recovery.

Elaira swore for the second time in an hour. She unlocked her white-knuckled grip on the chair's arms, ruffled by chills of unease. The signs of restored function, so desperately awaited, augmented her persistent anxiety. Healer's wisdom failed to steady her poise. The instinctive rapport shared with her beloved worried her hollow with reason. While a Fellowship Sorcerer's longevity spells mended Arithon's body with flawless precision, free-will choice governed the invisible wounds. The festering shock of an apparent betrayal yet wreaked untold havoc beneath the shattering blow of near death to the psyche.

The inevitable, brutal reckoning approached. Elaira dreaded the moment when wakened awareness unsealed the Teir's'Ffalenn's shuttered lids.

The strident pitch of her foreboding drew notice. Or else some other intrusive concern brought the soft footsteps approaching the door from the outside stairwell.

Elaira acknowledged the respectful knock but did not arise when the tall, dark Sorcerer tripped the latch and crossed the room's threshold.

"Ciladis?" Training tempered the troubled reproof in her query.

Yet his smile acknowledged her inner disquiet. Transfixed by a survey that pierced her crisp composure and neat, auburn braid, Elaira surrendered the pretence. No matter how far removed from her care-free penchant for the practical disarray of mud-caked hems and bramble scrapes gained in the thickets while foraging, and despite the rigorous, initiate use of artful concealment, she could not outflank a perception that ranged past the veil. Before Ciladis's probe broached the intimate source of her stress, she blurted, "He cried out before dawn."

First sound, from a throat rendered silent by the sword of the Light's executioner.

"I heard." Elucidation came, tendered in the compassionate restraint of the Sorcerer whose return to the Seven had lit Althain Tower's obdurate gloom like a beacon. "His Grace's awareness has surfaced into lucid dreams."

Unlike the determined, flint edge of enquiry proffered by Asandir, or the scintillant genius that electrified Davien's presence, Ciladis sheathed the might of his being within a serenity vast as the ages. His calm defied scrutiny like staring into the sun.

Soothed by the benison of his influence, Elaira's flagged spirits and jagged nerves melted into rueful honesty. "You're here to say when Arithon wakens, he's going to be furious."

Shadow flicked through the shafted light from the window as Ciladis crossed to the bedside. Today's damascened robe was slate blue, wide sleeves lined in saffron, rolled back as he laid an eloquent, ebony hand on Arithon's forehead. "Our Fellowship's custody's not going to sit well."

"He'll survive to be testy," Elaira declared, her arid jab an admission the alternative had been unviable. "How long do I have before the explosion?"

"Very little." Master healer, perhaps unsurpassed on Athera, Ciladis withdrew his touch. His carriage retained its unconcerned elegance. Not his steady regard as he turned. The eyes in deep-set sockets no longer reflected limpid tranquillity. The enchantress's trepidation met a hawk's stare, yellow as moulten ore.

Unbeguiled by her effort to humour the subject, Ciladis addressed the initiate will behind her unswerving intelligence. "Is there aught you require, beforehand?"

Lent his assurance her preference for privacy would be honoured, Elaira measured the question. Unblinking before the restraint of an implicit warning, she said, "Find Iyat-thos Tarens."

Ciladis inclined his head, unforthcoming as knapped obsidian. "Asandir has shouldered that summons already at Sethvir's request."

That Althain's Warden foresaw the necessity stunned Elaira like a kick in the gut. She stifled the sudden burn of welled tears. Fellowship interests ranged beyond her depth: Ciladis's unvoiced concern encompassed far more than the trivial bother of her trepidation.

Raked by a sharp grue, she demanded, "This is an appeal to my courage, in fact?"

Her outcry met the Sorcerer's silence, which compelled introspection on her own merits.

Few spirits alive could be trusted to uphold Arithon's interests. If she failed to check the brunt of his outrage, one liegeman's loyalty must ride the whirlwind and stand unflinching at his Grace's shoulder.

Haloed by the glare from the casement, or perhaps the rare, fleeting flare of his unshielded aura, the Sorcerer took his leave with spare words. "You are more than you know. Let your heart guide your actions. In strength or defeat, remember the Fellowship's resource remains at your back."

"That's what I'm afraid of," Elaira declared, which burning admission welded the air for the fact that the Sorcerers' diligent interests had seized Arithon's fate and stranded his spirit on the present-day shoals of jeopardy.

The blaze of Ciladis's smile flooded the chamber and ignited the spectrum above the range of visible light. "*Affi'enia*," he murmured, the same Name bestowed on Elaira by the Biedar crone in Sanpashir. "Your Sight is clear as a beacon, and worthy, though your course may lead your firm step into darkness."

A prickle of gooseflesh doused Elaira's skin. For the tribal ancient had said much the same in past closure to a private audience. '*For Prince Arithon's fate is entwined with your life-course. Mother Dark's mystery walks in his tracks. But you, Affi'enia, are the shining Light on the path come before him.'*

In uncanny echo of that dread hour, as abruptly as the crone's harrowing presence had released her, the chill passed. When Elaira looked up, Ciladis had just as silently left her.

The needful moment was forfeit to quell her rattled nerves and ponder the riddles of greater entanglements: for the beloved face on the pillow before her no longer reflected the peace of repose.

Tension hardened the line of Arithon's jaw. Sculpted hands long settled at rest on the coverlet closed a split second before his lashes quivered. Then his shuttered eyelids snapped open. The conscious awareness of initiate discipline stripped the dross of confusion at fearful speed.

Elaira had no attention to spare. No thought, as green eyes sharpened to measuring focus swept across the sequestered chamber. Swift assessment encompassed the tapestried forest scene, and by the singing swirl of the flux, acknowledged the signature of Paravian artistry. The narrow casement, stamped by winter's clear daylight, threw the brass-cornered chest and restrained, antique desk into naked relief. The heaped books, pages crammed with marked notes, bespoke her frenetic activity, alongside the comb and brush, stranded with the glint of bronze hair. A flicker of hesitation inflected the discovery he was not alone.

Paralysed in the room's only chair, Elaira waited, unflinching, until that keen scrutiny plumbed the one corner in shadow and encountered her steadfast presence.

Expectant, perhaps, for his studious pause to record the subtle changes imposed throughout centuries of separation, from the pensive frown graven by desperate care and forced solitude, to the peaked, indoor pallor at odds with her character. Then the oversight, apparent in hindsight, that caught her clad in a pastel robe adorned with Sethvir's distinctive embroidery. The belated mistake provoked the whiplash recoil a split second sooner.

Nothing braced Elaira for the impact of Arithon's undilute horror: not Ciladis's caution, or the near-to-infallible instinct refined through her extensive rapport. Her beloved's blaze of emotion seared through and torched the joy of reunion.

She found her tongue despite anguished dismay. "What's to fear? My vows to the Koriathain have been renounced. The Seven themselves secure my protection."

Her words stabilized nothing. Only redoubled the pure terror that threshed him. The storm ripped into her shocked equanimity. Battered to raced pulse, she spoke quickly, before he mastered the visceral onslaught. "You don't trust the Sorcerers."

"No." The rasped renouncement was final as death: a severance as ruthless as the executioner's sword that had pierced an innocent's heart, paid in forfeit to salvage his life.

Elaira stifled her unconsoled grief. Graphic recall of the slaughtered child crumpled in pooled blood on the scaffold had resurged with swift and vengeful clarity. No kindly forgetfulness blurred the unreconciled sting resurrected by Arithon's return to consciousness.

"If you doubt the Seven, can we not rely on ourselves since the sisterhood's leash has been broken?" Her appeal floundered against arctic silence. His turned glance dismissed her with surgical brevity. Elaira throttled her panic, forced to regroup. *Ath! She knew him too well.*

Further pleading on her part was futile. Reasoned argument based upon pithless necessity could not ease the emotional wound of betrayal that had endorsed Valien's sacrifice. Likely no power at large on Athera might blunt Arithon's rage, or breach the armoured determination forged in the crucible of his inflamed mistrust.

Fear lifted the hackles at Elaira's nape, gouged by the flame of his fury. Her intimate love yielded no crack in the mask. No quarter, as he said, "Leave me!"

When demand to forsake him left her unmoved, he shoved off the impeccable coverlet with intent to enforce his adamant autonomy.

Her heartbeat slammed under the impact of pity. "Arithon, you can't!"

His glance scalded her with contempt.

She argued, regardless. "I cannot abandon my stake in your future. You know this!" To thwart his stubborn folly, she did the unthinkable: wrested off the ring given to her in pledge, then clawed the flint knife from the thong at her neck, left in her custody by the Biedar Eldest. "If you're going, these belong in your provenance."

Arithon might dissolve her personal stake and reclaim his royal signet to end their betrothal. But only an ignorant madman would cross the will of the crone in Sanpashir.

The stark import of Elaira's warning glanced off. The spurned bedclothes slid to the floor in a heap, topped by the crisp sheet that had decently covered his crippling weakness. Exposed, the nakedness of wasted flesh, and the wracked posture of compromised balance. Selfless love had tended his insensate helplessness throughout the arduous months of recovery. Day upon day, Elaira had nursed the drastic toll of injuries that still ravaged the body's innate vitality. Arithon's anguished struggle to rise should not shock the experienced healer.

"Keep on, and you're likely to fall on your face," she snapped with acerbic impatience. "You've been laid low by a severed spine, and your atrophied muscles aren't fit to bear weight."

Arithon's stony expression crumpled into a rictus. With fixated effort, he wrestled his wasted legs to the edge of the mattress. He pummelled dull reflexes until his hitched frame accomplished the graceless shove that slid his feet towards the floor. Dauntless will failed him when his soles struck the carpet and gelid limbs buckled beneath him.

Elaira shed the knife and the ring on the side table, lunging for his elbow to steady him before he measured his length.

He evaded her grasp, collapsed to his knees before suffering her touch. Clammy sweat beaded his skin. The breaths straining his ribs flushed the hideous whorl of scarred tissue welted over his sternum.

Hazed off, and too wise for the fatal mistake that would seek to gainsay such adamance, Elaira stepped back and tossed him a nightshirt. "You've never bowed your stiff neck since your birth." She regarded him with fond exasperation as he fought his way into the garment. "When you pass out I'll be here to pick up the pieces."

Arithon's white-knuckled grip on the bedstead propping him upright, he snarled, "What difference to me, as the Fellowship's tool or the blunt instrument of the Koriathain?"

Masked pain *always* fired his choice to lash out. Elaira matched his viciousness with gentle reproof. "Were that true, you would have rescinded your handfast bond and accepted my return of Rathain's seal ring."

Which proved the wrong tack.

His rejection slapped the seized air between them before the blast of his inimical glare raked her. "Keep the Crown's token! Since you've traded my life on the coin of Torbrand's legacy, let the formality stand as your signal test of the Fellowship Sorcerers' feckless priorities."

Driven at bay against granite integrity, Elaira engaged the ferocity of her initiate's training. Against the choked outcry of her kindly spirit, she levelled her best strike against him. "You dare to spurn the Biedar tribe's knife?"

The razored flash of his teeth was no smile. "Mother Dark's business is not my priority."

Elaira returned that flung gauntlet, knowing: the canker left by the child's demise snapped the tatters of civilized reason. "If you are hell-bent on destroying yourself, I won't help."

Love's fidelity would *not* lift a nurse-maid's finger to abet the annihilation of better sense. If Arithon planned to repudiate Sethvir's hospitality, he would accomplish the feat by himself. Anchored in place, arms folded at her breast to contain her appalled apprehension, Elaira watched, dumb-struck, as he gathered himself, trembling, the carpet's sumptuous pile rucked under his tormented struggle.

The chamber was twelve strides across for a hale man. He would not succeed. Depleted by months of prostrate coma, he should not be capable, far less own the stamina to drive himself far enough to reach the threshold.

Hand over hand, gasping, Arithon proceeded undaunted. Elaira witnessed his unbearable exertion, her shaken resolve hammered firm by the raw gratitude he was alive to be suffering. The maimed body cut down from the post at death's door had been too far gone for her adept skills. Fellowship sorcery had cheated mortality, a salvage come too late for the victimized child passed beyond the veil. The enchantress believed she knew Arithon's limits, as surely as she set rooted faith in the probity of his spirit.

Arithon Teir's'Ffalenn would not give way, though he crawled belly down like a dog. Under discipline ruled by initiate mastery, surrender defied the straight grain of his nature. He never backed down, no matter the arduous toll exacted by his tortured progress. Elaira could do nothing more to deter him. Intervention would seal his enmity. Her helpless regard marked the throes of his labour, gauging each bout of dizziness as short breath and palsy thwarted his creeping pace. The adamant depth of his measure made her shoulder the inconsolable patience to wait until bodily punishment exacted full due and the weakness of overreach felled him.

The drastic strategy defeated her hope in the end. His hitched progress brought him to the postern, with the upright stretch for the latchkey past his reach unless he laid desecrate hands on the heirloom tapestry to haul himself upright.

She played her last card. "Don't even ask me to open the door."

Blank as rinsed glass, the quartz pallor of his expressionless features. "You won't." Though he shook with fatigue, his schooled voice retained a Masterbard's lash of satire. "But the Fellowship must, if their founding ethic still binds them to honour free will."

Elaira gasped, her appalled disbelief backed against the brazen scope of his audacity. For the glittering edge on his challenge woke the threat of Shehane Althain's wrath if the tower's Warden breached the Law of the Major Balance to interfere. The last frail thread of denial snapped. Brutal evidence stared her full in the face: she confronted a rogue power, perhaps every whit as unbiddably dangerous as the compromised initiate once shackled by Desh-thiere's curse.

She mustered aplomb from the wreckage of her discomposure, hauled a next breath into her seized lungs, then lashed her stunned intellect to fathom Arithon's motive. *Always, the shock of his hair-raising ploys stemmed from his most desperate agony.* From an airless space that sucked the spark from her soul, she wrested the ghastly gist. "You want me to demonstrate who holds my loyalty?"

"My dearest! Sit down." The edge on his contempt slashed for the jugular. "Your impeccable keepers have spared you the test."

Arithon had detected the step on the outside landing, before her; or else, all along, Sethvir's steadfast watch had expected the impasse erupted within the closed chamber. The latch clicked, and the released panel swung open, wafting the spill of cold draught from the stairwell. The gloom framed the upright serenity of Ciladis, who surveyed the wretchedness sprawled at his feet with a tenderness huge enough to outface a thankless prodigy's insult.

"You know what you must do," the Sorcerer said, the burled grit in his tone clean of censure. Then he stepped aside and let Arithon pass without stooping to offer the dignity of a blanket.

Elaira wept then. The flood of withheld tears spilled over and blinded her. Groping for the chair at her side, she was caught by warm hands as her gutted strength failed her.

Ciladis guided her to the seat and set her down, his murmured consolation inflected as though to soothe a whipped horse. His shielding form and the sweet fragrance of herbs ingrained in his robe softened the wrenching view of Arithon's belaboured passage over the threshold. The Sorcerer offered no more than his presence while Elaira swiped streaming eyes and fought back the semblance of her composure.

When she glanced up at length, the same seamless efficiency had pushed the door silently closed. Compassionate forethought saw Ciladis returned with a towel plucked from the washstand.

"Damn the finicky man and his sterling ethic!" she railed, while accepting the linen to blow her nose. "Though, Ath wept! Should that ornery principle change, I'd no longer recognize his Grace from a stranger."

"The explosive tempest was not unexpected." Ciladis's regard correctly outflanked the cogitation behind her pinched scowl. "If the chill in the stairwell concerns you, Sethvir chose his moment to dry laundry in the arcade at the first-floor landing."

Astonishment widened Elaira's glazed eyes. "The Warden of Althain has rigged the Paravian statues in the Chamber of Renown *as a clothesline?*"

"No less." Ciladis's merriment successfully raised the ghost of her smile. "Though the irreverent scapegrace himself might insist that tweaking the heat off the memorial flame was the least bothersome ploy to counter the damp that breeds mould in the storage rooms."

Elaira let go and slouched in her chair, her sodden grin almost spontaneous. "Bless Sethvir's conniving interest in an ingrate's uncivil behaviour. The temptation to pilfer what lay within reach might have worked, if his Grace wasn't hell-bound to spurn handouts."

The Sorcerer laced his sculpted fingers and perched on the vacated bed. "Be sure we Seven have centuries of experience dealing with s'Ffalenn recalcitrance."

"But wouldn't we be a mite *happier* if nobody needed to juggle that magma bare-handed?" Elaira's caustic levity bit as she skewered the implied reproach.

"Did you actually think I could not discern the infallible heart behind the hurtful rhetoric? Arithon's vicious attacks are transparent! I allow for the back-lash when he is fragile. His flaying tongue always defends the arena where he feels he is vulnerable." She added, "The stinging thorn in the problem's the same. We're left second-guessing his secretive plans at the redoubled risk of direct provocation."

Behind the enigma of his mild manner, Ciladis pressured her platitude. "How far into the murky unknown will you maintain your unreserved trust in him?"

"Until Arithon demonstrates proven basis for doubt." The glimmer of the emerald signet on the side table would not have passed unobserved. The treacherous current not mentioned in fact could undermine the probity of her beloved's unshaken faith in her.

For a well-guarded quagmire founded the reason Elaira had let Arithon go: veiled ground where even the Fellowship Sorcerers were chary to tread. Given Arithon bore Valien's death as a branding atrocity, how might he respond to Sethvir's kept secret concerning her part in the past crux at Athir? Justified *also* for the critical salvage of his royal heritage, her surrogate union in coitus, enacted through Glendien's body by means of an old Biedar rite, could have resulted in a conception. How would Arithon Teir's'Ffalenn respond to discovery if he had fathered a bastard of direct descent?

Davien's unequivocal counsel had cautioned Elaira never to ask. Infallible instinct chose not to pursue the damning particulars spun from the outcome. Her inner self, knowing, shrank back in foreboding. The gravity of the consequence should her beloved plumb the buried extent of such concealed repercussions defied probability. For Arithon was the last of Torbrand's lineage. Dread faltered to imagine the vicious recoil if a second child's fate had been seized in the weave of the Seven's long-term machinations.

"The will of the dragons is not forgiving," Ciladis demurred, past question aware of the seething concern battened beneath her strung silence.

Elaira skirted those perilous waters, afraid beyond measure to plumb the uncharted depths. "You've shown reason to hope. At least no one's rushed to invoke the blood oath his Grace swore at Athir."

The delight that triggered Ciladis's smile shone brilliant as the moon. "You refer to the fact we sent him off half-naked?" A burst of musical laughter, and then, "He will not reach the outer doors until dusk, and Tarens will be there to meet him. His Grace cannot brave winter's chill in a nightshirt, far less stand erect on his own. More, if Valien's death fuels his pique, he won't have the gall to reject Earl Jieret's debt without stripping the threadbare cloth of his hypocrisy."

Elaira's spontaneous chuckle at last signalled a genuine spark of resiliency. How apt, that his Grace's adamant ideal locked the jaws of the Sorcerers' fiendish entrapment! "Remind me never to earn the retort dealt by Sethvir's innocuous cleverness."

Ciladis retrieved the mangled towel from her slackened grip. He stood and draped the used linen on the washstand, which released the pressure of his direct scrutiny as he remarked, "Arithon's motives are seldom straightforward or simple."

The oblique reference did not escape Elaira's canny perspicacity.

"Don't claim his Grace acted in my behalf!" Furious at the prospect his rejection might stem from undue concern for her safety, she snapped, "I don't need his protection, far less at such cost!"

"He'd be first to agree," Ciladis confirmed. "Though I suggest his committed love in that regard is not malleable."

Ahead of Elaira's stiff protest, he added, "Valien's loss is the scale demonstration none of us dares to repeat." Whether in dire warning or subtle rebuke, the Sorcerer redirected her towards the future before unwise questions probed into the ominous implications. "Since Arithon's chosen his course, what will you do?"

Elaira weighed the changed subject, taken aback. "To fill the time while we strive to make sense of the motives his Grace won't admit into anyone's confidence?" She displayed the mettle of her courage then, in the spirited strength of her independence. "I would beg leave to ask what you would require to grant me a healer's apprenticeship."

"My pleasure, lady, you had only to ask." Ciladis extended his lean hands in welcome.

Her surprise at his swift acceptance was short-lived. The Sorcerer did not escort her down the stairwell to temper Arithon's adamant estrangement, or broach the advanced techniques to speed the course of a complex regeneration as wishful logic expected. Instead, steered by his light, irresistible clasp, Elaira found herself swept upwards to the third-floor vault repurposed as Althain Tower's still room. There, couched in fragrant air and deep quiet, Ciladis deposited her on a stool at the corner work table claimed as his own.

The non sequitur to her request escaped words. Elaira stared in heart-torn, tactless dismay at the brazier and glass flasks, stoppered philters and racks of bundled, rare herbs, too distressed to seek solace by perusing the labels inscribed with his meticulous script.

Ciladis salvaged her deflated dignity before she rallied her shredded wits. "On the topic of infusions for restful sleep with sweet dreams, I insist we begin immediately."

Far removed from the crisis at Althain Tower, Iyat-thos Tarens rode into a blinding storm in the desolate wilds of northern Rathain. Gusts off the frozen coast matted ice into his mount's mane and whipped the crusted folds of his mantle, the brute misery a necessity as snow devils spun off the peaked drifts erased the rumpled furrow of his backtrail.

No woodwise stealth could conceal a track carved by two headstrong pack mules and a moody jennet harnessed to a sledge.

Born blessed to the Light as a westlands crofter, Tarens snugged down his hood, too late. Another trickle of wet snaked underneath his soaked collar. He had never imagined his destiny would entangle him with the clanfolk who guarded the proscribed ground of the free wilds.

Better years at this season, he had been shelling nuts for his sister's solstice cakes, an endeavour set back by two pilfering nephews, and the soulful sighs of the sheep dog begging for scraps at his stockinged feet. The cosy warmth of that kitchen hearth was behind him. Both little boys lay five years in the grave. For a fugitive hunted by Canon decree, the cheer of the close family in Kelsing forever lay beyond reach.

The beasts under his care shared his hardship. Baulked with rolling eyes, all three resisted his tug on the lead rein. "Flop-eared carrion! Move along. Or belike you'll wind up on a headhunter's spit, with my scalp flayed for a temple priest's bounty, and your shaggy carcasses rendered for horse glue."

The creatures responded by stretching their necks, ears flat and legs braced where a senseless delay threatened ambush and slaughter. When the blizzard slacked off, he would lose the tenuous pretext of cover and safety. Yet tried as he was by the danger of running supply for the clan refuge concealed in the frozen desolation of Anglefen, Tarens preferred the harrowing risk of league reavers to the uncanny peril of braving his liege's convalescence at Althain Tower. Sore consolation for maudlin reflection, he had salt taffy and honey sweets stashed in his pockets for children who may never have tasted the wonder of town-made confections.

Insult to injury, the saddle horse under him joined the ranks of the hoofed rebellion.

"Get up, dog-meat!" Past question, the freebooting leaguesmen's patrols had increased with the influx of tithes levied by Etarra. Tarens dug nettled heels into his mount's barrel flanks, his easy nature reluctant to cut a bare branch for a switch.

But the ornery marsh pony planted his feet.

Hair rose at Tarens's nape. He peered forward. The instinctive drive of Earl Jieret's old-blood heritage jabbed to urgent alert, he cast flux-trained awareness into the murk for the signature of a stalking predator.

Yet no crouching wildcat lurked, poised to spring. Instead, the silhouette of a horse emerged through the scrim of swirled snowfall. Not a soldier's mount burdened with cumbersome tack, curb chain muffled and strap leather creaking. This black wraith arrived, blowing steam in the flesh, its hoofbeats eerily silenced. Reined in with scarcely a hand on the bridle, the creature's ghost eye and stark stillness identified the cloaked rider.

"Asandir." Trepidation overset the traditional response. The ex-crofter no longer required the prompt of a dead clan lord's heritage to break into a sweat. Rumour's whisper insisted that trouble trod in the steps of Fellowship Sorcerers. Made witness to the incomprehensible power unleashed on the executioner's scaffold at Daenfal, Tarens had justified cause to worry: the expedient focus imposed during the Teir's'Ffalenn's urgent rescue *almost* had overshadowed the ruthless sacrifice of an innocent.

The irony dawned late across wrenching ambivalence. Asandir's presence suggested the suspended brunt of that crisis had slammed against the impasse of Arithon's character at long last. Hackled nerve and the vengeful thrill of served justice spurred Tarens to reckless joy. "His Grace has awakened and left you," he blurted, just missing a crow of stunned awe. "Why should I commiserate?"

The gust died. The Fellowship's field Sorcerer resurged from the white-out, his squared posture in the saddle unflinching and his steely eyes just as ruthlessly frigid. "If you'd rather death ended two lives, by all means."

Which stony riposte wielded truth to eviscerate: for of course, Arithon would not be reconciled to a survival bought at the bloodprice of the child's demise.

Tarens recovered his sensible reason, the Sorcerer's statement measured against Jieret's reliable grasp of the cross-grained temperament of his liege. "Truly, I'm expected to sympathize? Your Fellowship's betrayal of humane expectations would prompt s'Ffalenn fury, not suicide."

"An oversimplification of catastrophic proportion," allowed Asandir, not tipping his hand.

When Tarens's cagey brass weathered the scorching silence, the Sorcerer relented. "We're challenged by a crisis of ethic, magnified by the royal bent for compassion, and compounded by shock, since Arithon woke to the bewildered shame of the atrophy that impairs his lower limbs."

"He can't stand or walk?" Tarens was horrified. "Why hasn't your Fellowship healed him?" Fear shredded discretion. "Don't claim his injuries could thwart the acumen that sheared the progression of time at Daenfal!"

"No." Asandir looked uncomfortable, the human frailty inflected on his stark facade terrifying for the implication of helplessness as he dismounted. "His Grace has refused us permission. We preserved his life by the tenets of crown law. But the delay imposed upon our response at the scaffold until Valien's spirit departed also deferred the ignition of Davien's seal of longevity. The lapse forestalled a clean-cut reversal of the body's crippling damage. Not permanently!" The Sorcerer hastened to qualify, "Hale restoration of Arithon's etheric imprint requires more time to manifest."

Tarens grasped the uncomfortable gist. "No more can be done to hasten recovery without Arithon's free will consent."

Asandir sighed. "How we wish the extent of the quandary stopped there."

Snowfall hissed through an awkward pause, while the wind caught its breath, and a black horse unlike any foaled out of a flesh-and-blood dam blew a restive snort through flared nostrils. Moved to sympathy for the sufferance of ages pinked by the gadfly sting of s'Ffalenn temper, Tarens laughed. "Let me guess? The wee man's prickly neck would not bend for the civil gift of Sethvir's hospitality."

"Beyond that." Unburdened by the crofter's capitulation, Asandir released his stallion's looped reins and let fly in exasperation. "His Grace has refused even basic necessity! Came to us in bloodied rags fit to burn and left without taking even a blanket."

The next risen gust bit to the bone, bitter with the glass edge of winter. "Has the stickling cockerel lost his last wits?"

"No, more's the pity." The Sorcerer eased the lead ropes from Tarens's numbed grasp and stripped off the harness mule's headstall. "That's your liege doing his vicious best to provoke."

Tarens frowned, unsurprised. "Arithon's insufferable when he's been wounded."

"Yes, well," snapped Asandir, deft efficiency moved on to run the long reins from the harnessed mule's terrets. He stowed the shed bridle under the tarp in the sledge. "Don't swallow the hook in the woebegone flummery. Watch instead for the purposeful motive. We've seen Arithon aim a strategic attack on our Fellowship's probity before. Expect he will jeopardize what we value the most as crude leverage to test our integrity."

"His life being the best weapon in his possession," Tarens surmised from the prompt of Jieret's experience.

"Quite." Asandir's direct stare drilled through the veiling blast of the gale. "Welcome to the match stake on the counterplay we have to win." Taut reserve broken by stark practicality, he continued, "Your pony's not needed where you are bound. Secure its tack and free the beast on my guidance to make its own way."

Resigned, Tarens yielded his propriety over the resupply under his charge. "Why are you sure I can make any difference?"

Economy ruled the Sorcerer's movement, brisk as his scathing honesty. "Sethvir has parsed the range of probabilities. The debt owed to Earl Jieret is the only hold Rathain's crown prince might choose to honour."

"Dharkaron forfend!" cracked Tarens, appalled. "That's your last flimsy straw? You know his Grace ditched me at Torwent for exactly such arch interference."

"In that circumstance, yes," Asandir acknowledged, hooded head bent in communion with the surly beast in the traces. "Though we hope, not this time." Arcane ministrations complete, he smothered impatience while Tarens emptied his pockets and stowed the packeted sweets for the children to go with the dry goods. Then the Sorcerer traced a shining glyph between the mule's rolled eyes and bestowed a Paravian diminutive addressed to his mount. The black stud sidled clear of the path, ears pricked with eldritch interest, while an affectionate slap on the draught animal's shoulder broke the mollified devil into a trot, towing the sledge on its way without further rebellion. The pack mules duly followed. Trailed by the shaggy marsh pony, their forms dimmed and vanished into the storm.

"Tarens?" Asandir vaulted astride his dark stallion, with the near-side stirrup left dangling. "The provender will reach the clan enclave without you, and our urgent mission turns north." An extended, strong hand invited the crofter to set foot in the iron and swing up behind him.

Tarens accepted the fork in his path. Wrung clammy by Jieret's distrust of grand conjury, he took the Sorcerer's clasp. Contact woke a tingle that coursed through his flesh. The effortless lift that pulled him astride accompanied a dazzling flare of white light. Deluged by an explosive power his reeling mind could not grapple, he scarcely heard Asandir's hurried apology.

"Forgive the disruptive haste! I'll need the focus circle at Direntir if you're to reach Althain Tower by eventide." An immutable deadline barely possible given the time-shifted advantage, travelling westward. "Stay on!" cracked Asandir. "Once begun, the flux-shear raised by a rushed transit will not be forgiving." Warning delivered, he closed seamless forces that walloped the air into thunder-clap recoil.

Tarens clung like a burr thrashed in the maelstrom, dizzied as the stallion lunged forward beneath him. Disorientation scrambled his senses in waves that clobbered perception. Snowflakes appeared to drift in stopped motion, while memory recorded the passing landscape in vistas that changed in the eye blink between the stud's mighty strides. Space and distance compressed to the drumroll of hoofbeats, stretched into after-clap echoes that wailed in eerie glissandos behind.

Too fast for credibility, the ancient ruin jutted through the grey murk of the flattened horizon. Tarens barely registered the sight before the shock of curbed motion brought Direntir's massive, obsidian spires towering overhead. The sheer face of the Second-Age masonry raised by the centaur guardians millennia past remained flawless, except where the scars inflicted by drakefire had slagged the stone's mirror polish, or melted gaps in the symmetry of the terraced buttresses. The black horse never faltered, where human nerve cringed with stupefied wonder. Asandir's bidding drove the stud through the desolate wreck of the hall, the shorn pillars of the breached ceiling vaults left open to winter's bleached sky. Shod hooves clattered down a cracked stair, where the roused focus coiled the fourth lane's transmission into a vortex of cracking static.

The virulent resonance of the flux spun Tarens to the brink of unconsciousness. Thrashed witless, he clung, while the spate swelled to a roar that hammered through mortal cognizance. The Fellowship Sorcerer relented for nothing but reined his uncanny mount past the threshold of upstepped harmonics with a crisp word of farewell.

"We part company here, since my business lies elsewhere. Sethvir will meet your arrival. If he offers counsel, at your peril, pay heed."

Sane thought flinched from the gravity of the Sorcerer's cry of appeal. Last moment for questions already lost, the gyre spun to peak resonance. Cohesive consciousness frayed into sparks, ripped asunder by the galvanic wrench of a lane transfer that hurled flesh and spirit away across latitude.

Reunions

Tarens emerged through a white dazzle of light. Solid ground firmed his dislocated stance as the pinpoint focus of the lane surge delivered him to the dungeon vault at Althain Tower. The carrier energy released his true Name, heightened frequency downstepped through the spectrum of blue, then faded through transparent violet. Marble walls and stilled air replaced the gusty blizzard that buffeted the forest in northern Rathain. Reeled under the after-shock, Tarens swayed, braced by someone's grip on his shoulder.

The touch steadied his traumatized senses. Settled back into his natural faculties, he shivered in damp clothes, breathing the mineral scent of close stone, laced through by the storm taint of ozone.

Shorter by a head, Althain's Warden peered up at him, eyes keen as the filed edge on a blade, and his flyaway hair tangled in tufts. "Bless you for coming. We haven't much time."

Towed by the Sorcerer's badgering grasp, Tarens stumbled up the circle's slight incline, blinking under the milder glow of a fluttering torch in a gargoyle bracket. His tread echoed off the black agate floor, reverberations whispering into the narrow stair shaft ahead. Althain's Warden led upwards, expounding upon the particulars of the binding ties invoked by traditional guest oaths.

Jieret's heritage parsed the nuance of sworn obligation, where townborn wits stumbled, slower to grasp the abstruse bent of the conversation. "Did Arithon drink the cup of amity under your auspice at Althain Tower?"

"Never." Sethvir's sidewise glance could have vaporized quartz. "More's the pity. If he had, our Fellowship would not have a problem and you would be shivering in northern Rathain, mobbed for sweets by clamouring toddlers." Remanded by his visitor's chattering teeth, the Sorcerer pursued in banal deflection, "Refined hospitality's wanting, I know, but at least you won't lack for comfort. I've a cantrip in place that will dry your clothes and banish the leftover chill."

Indeed, warmth permeated the ground-floor chamber beyond the trapdoor. Tarens stepped into blanketing heat, fragrant with the wistful scents of baked earth and midsummer's cut hay. Ahead, etched in gloom held at bay by a flickering pine knot wedged in a sconce, he beheld the Chamber of Renown with its majestic ranks of commemorative statues. Coronets and caparisons teased the eye with the glint of gold braid and the gemstone sparkle of emerald, ruby, and sapphire. Beneath the pale sheen of Sethvir's subtle craft, the mighty defence wards laced through Althain's granite walls rattled raw nerves like distant thunder. Tarens's unstable vision kept splintering. Fractured rainbows flared off solid objects, while his perception of sound shimmered into distortion that rang in his ears like brass chimes.

Sethvir's steering hand guided him through the memorial array raised to the Paravian races. Among them, the grand weight of history stopped thought. Speech died. The irreverent intrusion of footsteps became a desecrate violation. Seized in the chest, fighting tears for the sorrows past reach of Mankind's comprehension, Tarens faltered.

"We walk here by permission," the Warden allowed in solemn reassurance. At due length, his lead brought his visitor to the bronze-panelled doors that accessed the buttressed arch to the sally port. There, the Sorcerer offered a bundle strapped up in weatherproofed fleece.

Tarens unlocked his seized throat. "Arithon's unlikely to bend his stiff neck for the charity of your provisions," rugged honour obliged him to point out.

"Indeed." Sethvir winced, aggrieved as he thrust the burden back into Tarens's arms. "But I dare his Grace to show the effrontery to reject a gift granted in amity by Maenalle s'Gannley, and held in his name all these years for safekeeping."

The package in question was surprisingly light. An item of frail antiquity, tagged by traces of wax polish and linseed ingrained under the rancid taint of the fleece. "You're tempting sore luck that I don't break his royal head with this."

Sethvir raised a bushy wool eyebrow. "By all means do, if the threat will contain him."

Tarens shouldered the cross strap, careful not to entangle his weaponry. Glancing up from adjusting his baldric and buckles, he discovered himself left alone.

The Sorcerer had deserted him without sound, a last-minute list of cryptic instructions left impressed on his bewildered consciousness: 'Stay at your posted station, come what may. Don't give Arithon help. No matter how harsh the temptation, though the cry of necessity rends your heart, let his Grace cross the distance! He must come to you.'

Abandoned to wait, Tarens leaned against the high polish of the Paravian frieze. The Warden's admonition seemed a moot point. He lacked the resource to meddle with anyone, dizzied as he was by his ungrounded faculties. Try his legs, and he risked falling flat. Besides, no way under the hazard of Dharkaron's Black Spear did he care to repeat his past mishandling of Arithon's interests at Torwent.

While the mild air and pervasive quiet settled the trauma of his cross-latitude transfer, Tarens surveyed the venerable sculptures backlit by the sconce at the base of the stair. Even shrouded in gloom, the stilled host radiated a haunting nobility, exquisite form scribed in the gleam of alabaster, and the glimmer of ceremonial trappings and armour.

No witness sustained the exposure, unmoved. All Paravian artistry inflected the flux. Yet at Althain Tower, where the third lane crossed an electromagnetic nexus, the enhancement of amplified resonance afflicted the emotions. Carved stone acquired what seemed the reactive semblance of life. The figures enshrined in the Chamber of Renown bespoke courage that defied indelible loss and despair: the terrible scope of blood sacrifice that preserved the mysteries across the turbulence of three Ages. The towering might of the centaur guardians reared with raised lances against the monstrous scourge of Searduin, and predatory swarms of winged Khadrim. Storied heroes, distanced by legend, depicted the triumph of peace, muscled forearms crossed in salute over the peacock enamel of their blazoned breastplates. Others bound to safe-guard the forests stood foursquare, antlered heads lifted to wind the clarion blast of their dragon-spine horns. The endurance chiselled into stern features mapped the bygone millennia prior to Mankind's inaugural settlement.

The circles of sunchildren tugged at the heartstrings, captured in step as they danced the lament for the fallen slaughtered by the Great Gethorn, or plying their delicate, crystalline flutes for the hallowed Mending that rebirthed Cianor Moonlord.

If sight of them tightened the throat, mortal eyes flinched to behold the undying exaltation of the Riathan, unearthly grace captured in translucent quartz. Their lost presence poured chills of awe down the spine and pebbled the skin to raised gooseflesh.

Tarens unlocked his paralysed lungs. Too late for regret, he shivered, aware of how far he had strayed from his pastoral origins. How Arithon Teir's'Ffalenn had encountered such creatures, *living*, and survived the impact beggared his imagination.

No turning back from the plunge off the precipice. Committed, Tarens wondered how deeply his Grace might have changed, emerged from the trial that once had defined, even killed, the crowned strength of his s'Ffalenn forebears. He would find out shortly. Faint noises disturbed the inviolate hush. A tortured shuffle from the upper stairwell scattered echoes across the vaulted chamber.

To a scout tracker's acuity, the halting approach bespoke brutal effort sustained by raw will.

Dread redoubled, Tarens understood he would not be greeting a lost spirit, stripped of identity and half-broken from an extended and cruel captivity. No prior experience prepared him. His abrasive exchange with the prince last encountered at Thunder Ridge had brought failure, no improvement after the searing quittance provoked by his miscall at Torwent. Frayed trust provided a treacherous foothold upon which to grapple the lash of a volatile rage.

No helpful vision sparked the latent gift of s'Valerient prescience as the tormented rustles subsided to obdurate silence. The swathe cast by the single lit sconce fell away, with the stairwell cast into darkness. Minutes passed, with no further suggestion of movement. While anxiety shredded to grim apprehension, Tarens agonized over Jieret's recall of another fraught vigil in the winter wilds, when under night's cover in Daon Ramon Barrens, a stalker's patience had intercepted his liege under extended pursuit by armed enemies. The wary creature chased into his *caithdein*'s arms had been all but stripped of cognizant humanity, survival reduced to the lethal reflex of a hunted animal.

Tarens shed his suffocating winter mantle. Precaution urged him to guard his sheathed weapons from Arithon's adversarial temperament.

The hiss of an intaken breath and the laboured struggle resumed, tortuous as trap-wounded game. Earl Jieret's blood-bonded perspective gleaned no advantage from such intractable vulnerability. Arithon's aggressive response under weakness spanned the unholy gamut, from the flaying tongue wielded to gut interference to the withering honesty that undercut commonsense argument under the white heat of crisis.

Tarens withstood the inhumane pressure though his tender heart bled. Sethvir's instruction forbade intervention, while the dragged scrape of forward progress faltered again, relapsed into exhausted quiet. While the world's need commanded his stoic inaction, he ransacked Earl Jieret's vantage for the intimate levers to unseat an initiate master's indomitable will.

And the merciless weapons fell into his hand: first, the debt left by a dying liegeman, struck down by his cursed crown prince's blade. Second, the blight of the abject defeat, when Jieret's steadfast love had defied an oath-sealed bequest and embraced annihilation to draw the Light's war host as Arithon's decoy. That impetuous, brave sacrifice had brought the Teir's'Ffalenn to his knees in their bitter, last hour of parting. The horrific price suffered in consequence demanded full redress. For Jieret's fate had not been clean. Degraded by abuse in captivity, he had snatched a transcendent triumph in death, when his final appeal raised the spirit of a centaur guardian to bolster the realm's defence. More, the after-shock had grounded the mystical interface that delivered Arithon's requital from his near-fatal trial in Kewar cavern.

Ath forbid the dread moment of final resort, if Tarens must call the last card and invoke Valien's name as the innocent played to buy quarter for the royal bloodline saved from extinction on Daenfal's scaffold.

The crux drew nigh. The griped sounds of approach inched across the vast chamber and at last emerged into view. Clenched knuckles appeared, latched onto the pedestal beneath the rampant defiance of an Ilitharis warrior, carved in marble with raised sword and targe. Shaking with strain, the invalid prince dragged his recalcitrant flesh another excruciate span closer. His extended arm followed, splayed fingers rigid against the worn flagstone floor. Black head bent above a crooked elbow in the wretched fight to gain traction, Arithon pushed his undivided attention with a ruthlessness Tarens found frightening.

The lifted hooves of the Riathan circle let him haul himself painfully upright. He staggered onwards and crashed. Sprawled in a bruised heap of wasted muscle and bone, he lay panting in half-stunned collapse.

Tarens throttled his pity. Jieret's cold-cast eye for survival weighed the setback of extreme fatigue against the rigours of outdoor chill and spent resource. Wisdom damned the folly of shepherding such severe disability through the winter wilds of northern Atainia. Stunned by the reckless scope of that prospect, Tarens stared down the charged moment when Arithon Teir's'Ffalenn rallied his stamina, glanced up, and recognized his unsolicited witness.

Torchlight hid nothing of the wretched frailty bundled, bare-limbed, in the rucked nightshirt.

Yet the fierce emerald glint in that wary regard retained the acuity of the initiate master. A far cry from the emotional husk brought to grips under Jieret's impeccable loyalty, Tarens confronted a spirit poised at the honed edge of distrust.

The hair-trigger response in the breach was not Jieret's, but the crofter's countrybred kindness. "You look awful," Tarens blurted, and extended his hand. "Come on. Get up. Your bid for freedom's scarcely worth the dregs of your personal dignity."

Arithon's inimical wariness broke, astonished to naked relief. "Ath wept! Forgive me. I expected another Fellowship shill with a lecture." Hoisted onto his feet, propped shamelessly upright, he accepted the enveloping warmth of Tarens's cloak. His mercuric rebound suspiciously cheerful, he added, "Not to wallow in sentiment, I don't suppose Sethvir loaned you the key to access the outer portal?"

"No." Tarens risked honesty. "Althain's Warden left this instead." Poised for the bristled objection, he said, "Save the stiff-necked embarrassment. Sethvir insisted the possession is yours, gifted under guest oath by Maenalle s'Gannley."

That formality silenced the vicious rejoinder. Outmatched by the Sorcerer's devious countermove, Arithon surveyed the nondescript sack, stunned to transparent disbelief. "Let me down. I must see."

Tarens eased his liege's tremulous frame to the floor, then settled the wrapped package into Arithon's arms. Too light for weaponry, the bared content revealed an antique lyranthe of plain, battered hardwood, restrung to pitch with shining, wound wire.

Arithon stroked a finger over the fine silver inlay laced into the ebony fretboard. Then his reverence snapped. Breathless laughter folded him double. "Remind me," he gasped, "never again to pit mortal wits against Sethvir's devious character."

While Tarens gaped, clueless, Arithon gave rein to his effusive, rare pleasure. "This lyranthe is Elshian's priceless work, salvaged from the destructive violence provoked by Desh-thiere's curse." The same instrument, subject to a half brother's blind rage, once had been smashed in pieces amid the disastrous throes of his failed coronation at Etarra.

Suspiciously garrulous, Arithon qualified with flushed enthusiasm. "I wondered why Ciladis failed to upbraid my ingratitude. Lighten up! We'll avoid testing my half brother's nerves, and skirt Erdane at a wise distance. Better, you won't be tasked with an invalid in the wilderness. Instead, we're bound for a sheltered roof at Rathain's royal seat in Ithamon."

Blank with puzzlement, Tarens neglected to challenge the effusive elaboration.

"If you're up to hauling my carcass downstairs, I can sound out the resonant notes to raise the lane focus here for a translocation."

Tarens's tone-deaf ear made no sense of the plucked measures that picked out and built the primal chord to awaken the Paravian circle beneath Althain Tower. Fallen into an uncomfortable drowse on cold, concave stone, he missed the first flicker of opalescence that flushed the quartz pattern beneath him. Refined music woke a billow of energy that flooded his nerves like a tingling current. A piercing tone followed, ranging to a whistle that climbed beyond hearing and burst into a flare of white light. More notes, blended, seeded a second harmonic that rocketed upwards. The world flipped upside down. A shocked breath sucked frozen air into his lungs, sharp with the scent of fresh snow.

Then his consciousness plunged into the primal, black caul of the void . . .

. . . thought resurged, thick as syrup, perhaps under the after-shock, scrambled disruption incurred by a second transfer across latitude. Or, Tarens presumed, the rough dross caused by lane forces channelled without the finesse of a Fellowship Sorcerer. No clue revealed how much time had passed. Fragmented fact dredged from Jieret's clan heritage recalled the old circle at Ithamon lay in the open atop the windswept escarpment where the Compass Point Towers still standing centred the ruined defence. The focus itself nestled amid the riven foundation of Daelthain, the fifth spire for justice destroyed since the Second Age.

A winter arrival on that exposed site should have frozen them both to the bone. Arithon's wasted strength could scarcely stand up, far less drag his companion's more substantial bulk into shelter. Tarens inhaled the scents of sandalwood and dust, and the fragrance of birch coals in a grate far removed from Althain's dank, vaulted stone. Ruby light warmed a Narms carpet of rich green, flourished with a stylized motif of silver geometry. The claw legs of an ebony side table striped shadow across cedar wainscoting, varnished panels carved with an exquisite interlace of laurel and stylized animals. Earl Jieret's recognition identified the distinctive wardroom in Alathwyr Tower at Ithamon.

Murmured conversation threaded the quiet, a familiar disturbance at first overlooked, cosy as Tarens had been with close family crammed under a croft cottage roof. But the deeper voice in discourse with Prince Arithon was a stranger's, clipped by the precise inflection of power that phrased information with ringing exactitude.

". . . I cannot shift circumstance. Whatever I say will seat your actions all the more firmly."

A sudden draught streamed the candle. Intent features obscured by flickered flame, Arithon entreated, "You will reveal *nothing?*" Scraped to a fraught whisper, "Is my half brother's destiny already sealed?"

"All roads converge at this crossing," the speaker insisted. "Fore-knowledge will not avail you."

"*Tell me,*" Arithon implored. "I will face the price."

"No doubt, you shall," the remorseless consultant responded. "I can offer you counsel, instead, ahead of your foolish objection. True steel does not shy from a blow. I would not stand in your way, or prevent the one step that might spare you. Choice maps your fate, Teir's'Ffalenn. If you must put yourself through the forge, you will do so without interference."

Alarm nettled Tarens fully awake.

He rolled over, gouged by his baggage of weaponry. A cot with straw ticking creaked under him, entanglement with his blades hampered further by the heavy mantle returned since the loan made to remedy Arithon's inadequate nightshirt. The garment thrown across his shoulders bespoke the unknown hand that had brought him to safe haven from his unconscious delivery to the focus circle outside.

The same presence, no doubt, had led Arithon here, which implied someone's informed expectation.

Across the wardroom, the candle's pooled light revealed Arithon, propped on a crude wooden pallet with a fine blanket draped over his knees. The animate flush on his peaked features suggested the on-going stress of contention. Back turned, with one negligent elbow hooked on the back of a straight wooden chair, the taller male figure lounged opposite, long legs clad in rust breeches and dark brown boots crossed at the ankle. A burnt orange doublet, cuffed in fine lynx was obscured by a stallion's mane of white-and-red hair.

The colouring matched Davien's description. "You know what needs doing," the Sorcerer probed. "Are you braced for the task? There are limits to which I can go to protect you. Not without invoking the unwanted yoke of the Fellowship's stakes."

"My guest oath was sworn to you at Kewar cavern, you'll recall," Arithon responded with razored delicacy, "which somewhat changes the ground under my ancestors' roof at Ithamon."

Davien laughed, the swift bite of his humour resounding an echo that struck Jieret's clanbred roots to unease.

The Sorcerer unfolded his relaxed posture and rose, the candle thrown into eclipse plunging Tarens's view into darkness. "Then fly free, my wild falcon. Heal on your own merits and do as you must."

"I don't hold you to blame," Arithon finished evenly, not in reference to his crippling wound but to the murder of a blameless child; or not: the guarded alternative thrust chill through warm flesh like a dagger.

Jieret's cautious nature prevailed, that after the brutal, late round of blood sacrifice, Arithon was wont to stay secretive.

Tarens armoured his vulnerable heart, regretful to have missed the core of the discussion as the Sorcerer moved. The gaunt face of the invalid in the flame's restored glow confirmed the bitter dearth of close confidence. Likewise, the trained grace of the Masterbard's courtesy shielded the vulnerable source of his sterling sincerity. "Ath grant I live up to your trust in me."

Davien's unreserved smile was tender as he rose to depart. "You already have, Teir's'Ffalenn. You might resist the inheritance I would have spared you at any cost. But you will not shame the crown you abhor. You have owned the courage to shoulder your fate. I wish you the bright guidance to master it. Whatever the outcome, I cannot think less of you. Three times from the crucible, I've tested the steel. Each pass through the fire has reforged you, unbroken. Fail or not, claim your path with my blessing."

Tarens tossed off his mantle. Sword and weapons chimed with metallic urgency as he stood to full height and blocked Davien's way. "How far from the Fellowship's aims have you strayed?"

Matched eye to eye, man and Sorcerer locked stares. Though the ex-crofter possessed the more muscular build, the challenge levelled against his defiant loyalty was nothing physical.

Then the studied, uncomfortable moment swept by, the accusation of Kamridian's tragic end a live spark left unspoken on the tensioned air.

Renowned as the Betrayer, Davien stirred first and demolished rejoinder. "By all means, stand firm as the realm's staunchest liegeman. Though for how long, I wonder? You've plunged into deep current beyond your mortal wits. When the next moral short-fall sticks in your craw, how far can your upright limit be stretched before you discover you've lost the strong stomach to swallow the recoil?"

Late Winter 5926

Turnover

Two dragons duelled in the night sky of Sckaithen Duin, the splinter world beyond Northgate. Asandir observed their titanic battle at safe remove on Athera, lent the shared stream of Sethvir's earth-linked awareness. Even at secondhand witness through the mind's eye, the mighty contest evoked the raw power to intimidate. The murderous arcs carved by armoured hides sliced the turbulent air like the stab and riposte of matched scimitars as the agile wyrms wheeled and dived. Flame plumed from their fanged maws in scorching blasts fit to sear granite to magma.

Within moments, or hours, one or both of the great drakes would perish. The silver-scaled elder, Chaimistarizog, fought yet another upstart claimant, the bronze shimmer of pre-sexual adolescence changed at mated maturity to banded gold. From head to spiked tail vane, the youngster's length measured beyond fifty spans: a sinuous package of muscle hell-bent to upset two Ages of established order and break the authority restricting access through the Worldsend Gate to Athera.

As the lone sentinel sent to guard the breach, the Fellowship's field Sorcerer had left his black stallion sheltered inside the ruin at Penstair. Exposed, he stood vigil in the open, while the conflict joined on the splinter world raged past the pale of human imagining. Gusts off the ice-ridden Stormwell coast lashed his face and shredded the banked storm cloud to indigo rents sequined with constellations. Before him, the Gate's weathered pillars loomed in silhouette against jetted spume as the combers smashed into the desolate, rocky shingle.

The roar of the elements gave voice to the ominous thrum of the excited flux. The shimmering interface that spanned the void between worlds quivered like ruffled mercury, disturbed by the violent contest on the other side.

Asandir waited, braced for the worst. The last bid to rend the Treaty Accord had left Chaimistarizog near to mortally wounded. The drake war which followed that fraught victory had forced Fellowship resource to hold the drawn line, while the scarred Gatekeeper laired up in recovery. Barely, the lane currents' aberrant, whiplash recoil had been contained in the aftermath. The peninsula under his feet wore a jagged hellscape of scars, cratered and pocked with tide pools rimmed with the glassine slag seared by drakefire.

Chaimistarizog had not recovered hale fitness before rising to reclaim his duty. Although Sethvir's archive held no record of a restorative hibernation for five millennia, the supreme wyrm's might appeared undiminished. The power of Chaimistarizog's bellow stupefied even a Fellowship Sorcerer's wits.

Channelled at distance from the planet on the far side of the Worldsend Gate, the concussive blast of stress-heated air boomed with a deafening thunder to paralyse thought. Bass echoes rolled through the shriek of recoil, where the shifted waves of altered realities clashed in chaotic collision. Drake battles waged over ocean hammered shock ripples outwards, wracking Sckaithen Duin's cratered terrain. Mountains erupted from once-verdant plains. The raised peaks of new ranges belched lava, carved and recarved as their flanks ran moulten red, summits flattened or ripped into chasms, then flooded under frothing tsunamis that shredded into titanic tatters of steam.

Asandir tracked the broadscale display, alive to the danger. Historic battles between great drakes had remade the features of continents on Athera. Kathtairr was laid waste by two warring flights, devastated to ruin that ended an Era. Dragonkind then had ceded their pre-eminence at First Age Year One, when Ath gifted the world with the Paravian races as the first tempered stay of restraint.

The outbreaks of damage inflicted after the centaur guardians' stewardship transferred to the Fellowship invariably burdened the taxed shoulders of the Sorcerer tasked in the field. Faced again by the cataclysmic threat of a drake war, Asandir trod the gamut of thorny concerns he had scant resource to remedy.

Sethvir shared his turmoil. *'Traithe's report, and my vision, shows Seshkrozchiel's heart rate at the nadir of her comatose hibernation.'*

Asandir's grim mouth flexed, his alarm unappeased. Today's reprieve surely foreran tomorrow's frustration, with Luhaine's entwined consciousness held hostage by Davien's prior pact with the dragon, and the Fellowship again left critically short-handed.

'All news is not dreadful,' Althain's Warden temporized with his unlikely, ebullient optimism. *'Arithon managed the lane transfer to Ithamon. He's supping with Tarens in Alathwyr Tower, which was made habitable and stocked in advance under the astute eye of Davien.'*

Asandir's surprise cracked his taciturn poise. "For what guarded intent? We might come to rue the redoubled odds of combined mischief from that quarter." But the prospect pleased him. Davien's brazen meddling, even on the grand scale, lightened the shadow of horrendous portent. Perish the dread thought, should a drake's acquisitive nature become entangled in fascination with the royal offshoot of Dari's descent.

"Sufficient potential for mayhem to gripe the crone in Sanpashir," Sethvir grumbled, then launched into a tangential account of a riot provoked by the shore-leave tax imposed upon the waterfront dives in Southshire. Asandir took sharp stock, never fooled by his colleague's breezy obfuscation. Eyes closed, the field Sorcerer on site by the Worldsend Gate in Athera assessed the drake duel's progress upon Sckaithen Duin.

A bolt silver streak, Chaimistarizog rose. Glimmering speck above the chopped waves of a violet sea, the wyrm darted through a wingover and arrowed into a corkscrew stoop. The crack of opened wings levelled him with his rival and whiplashed his serpentine length into a coil. Yet the lightning riposte of his fanged strike lagged by a fraction. The flicker of the golden challenger's dive evaded with flaunting ease.

Chaimistarizog was tiring.

Broad-ranging vision grasped the tide's turn, foreshadowed under the ranging severity of multiplied, probable outcomes.

Asandir interrupted Sethvir's smoke screen of chatter point-blank. "How long have you known?"

'The question's moot.' Althain's Warden sighed. *'The end will reach closure in moments.'*

The advantage of altitude sacrificed, the elder dragon twisted in midflight and banked. The gust clapped off his stressed wing leather blasted spray off the face of the deep as he climbed. Above, the young challenger flipped end for end. His gout of streamed flame hissed downwards, while Chaimistarizog sideswiped the shear of the slipstream and snaked into a contorted spin. Too late: his avoidance sliced through the incendiary plume. Blind on one side, raked by showering sparks, the Gatekeeper roared with earth-shaking fury and death-rolled. The barbed fluke of his tail sliced an arc through the glare and clouted his cocksure opponent. Spines bristled like a star mace snapped the fanned structure of extended wing vanes, slashed the webbed flesh of the young dragon's undersail, and thudded into the scaled flank beneath. Ribs caved under the bone-smashing blow.

Both combatants drifted in the black air for a hung instant, the rush of their striving suspended. Then injury claimed its crippling due. The vanquished wyrm kited off-balance and tumbled. The trumpeting cry of the victor resounded over his defeated adversary.

Chaimistarizog soared into a glide, while beneath him, the fatally fallen burned and blazed, immolated as crushed lungs ignited. The meteoric rush of descent in extremis sliced across the starless sky and plunged into the sea. Impact spewed up a geyser, the diamond glitter of back-fallen spray wisped through tatters of steam and spent smoke.

The flux ripple of the wyrm's final agony quenched in salt water, and cleared the destabilized after-shock. Battle fury and death trauma released in requital left behind no raging remnant. Another great dragon was lost to the worlds. That absence spread over the face of the deep, profound as the silence before Ath's Creation.

Chaimistarizog had prevailed by a whisker again. Asandir awaited the Warden's linked summary to tally the cost of the reckoning.

Yet the summons Sethvir relayed instead committed the Fellowship's field Sorcerer to cross through the Worldsend Gate for a direct audience.

The unexpected command prickled Asandir's nape. Weathered face to the wind, white hair whipped against his squared shoulders, he accepted without protest. "Hold Athera secure at my back."

Three strides brought him to the shimmering film that spanned the stone pillars, rimed in winter's opaline mantle of ice. Another resolute step took him through.

His footfall on the firmament of Sckaithen Duin broached a strand of trackless cream sand. Placid breakers of ruffled lace whispered and ebbed, exposed shellfish foraged by wheeling flocks of small reptiles. The howling gale that strafed Rathain's northcoast gave way to baked heat and the volcanic tang of wet pumice and sulphur.

Dragonkind revelled in flight through the crystalline chill of the stratosphere. Grounded, they detested water and cold, wont to mince and lash tails with feline distaste. Yet that evocative grace was absent from Chaimistarizog's gliding descent. He came down from aloft like a damaged raptor, right wing drooping and slant snout crooked sidewards. No more feather-light, his landing shook the beachhead where he alighted. Asandir regarded a single, gold eye, bright and terrible as the sun. But the burned socket opposite reeked of charred blood, the cooked flesh peeled back from exposed bone. The platinum scales of venerable age, once buffed to a mirror polish by the ice-crystal clouds of high altitude, were smoke-tarnished and pitted by cinders.

Worse than physical, the damage to the azure curtain of the drake's aura. The lustrous auroral brilliance had dimmed, blown ragged and rifted with holes. Asandir's steady gaze took stock of the damage. Frail witness, he beheld a prepotent agony forced into ruthless check. Even in ruin, Chaimistarizog's presence wielded the raw force to pulverize form. His flicked thought could smear land and water alike to cosmic dust in the giddy span of an instant.

The wounded serpent drew himself up, maimed head towering over the toothpick stance of the Fellowship Sorcerer. Left the scraped semblance of once-mighty dignity, Chaimistarizog spoke. '*This day's triumph has secured my right of succession. My choice, ratified by the elder Protectorate, grants Ozvowzakrin, pale gold in years, to stand forward as Northgate's posted guardian. I would cross the veil from Athera, old friend. Let my fire be quenched in the sea on the world of my birth.*'

Asandir crossed his wrists at his heart in salute. His dispatched, tacit contact forewarned Sethvir. Then he acknowledged the dragon's bequest. "Your passage shall be mourned with honour."

The great wyrm hissed. The massive wedge of his marred head dipped downwards, spiked jowls poised at ground level. The three-span radius of his gold eye fixed on the Sorcerer, whose upright frame was diminished before his monstrous, slit pupil.

Asandir stilled his thoughts. Marked and measured by the wayward mind of one of the world's most fearsome powers, all breathing existence weighed up as a cipher, the most wise chose to wait. Under a dragon's pinpoint regard, the least stir of intent might spark ruination. No Sorcerer tempted the risk of becoming a mote figment embroidered into the caprice of a great wyrm's expansive dream.

The tattered flame of Chaimistarizog's aura flickered, the more dangerous in volatile ebb.

'I leave your Fellowship with due warning,' the behemoth declared before parting. 'Our kind deems that the unruly rambunctiousness of our young exceeds the dissent of those factions chafed by the Accord. An incentive appears to be seeding the flare, from a source undisclosed by our persistent search.'

Asandir acknowledged with delicate care. No surprise, that the fractious temptation stirred by Davien's unorthodox bargain with Seshkrozchiel should taunt the whirlwind. But disquiet rode the least possibility the unrest might stem from another disturbance.

The Sorcerer shielded that unquiet concern. Too perilous, to broach the suspect quandary Sethvir held altogether too close to his chest. Beyond worse, if the aggravation of an outside influence sought to erode the vulnerable interface binding the precarious treaty with wyrmkind. Any hint of Mankind's ignorant complicity would enrage the Dragon Protectorate and torch off a holocaust fit to reduce Seshkrozchiel's immolation of Avenor to the paltry blaze of a dropped match. Whatever murky threat vexed the Warden's earth-sighted faculties, glib subterfuge would not withstand a drake's narrowed scrutiny. The Gatekeeper's precaution ramped up the stakes, with who knew what mischief under the thumb of a hidden meddler tilting the balance.

Chaimistarizog did not deliberate. 'The foundation of our Concord with the Paravians relies upon the solidarity of the Fellowship Sorcerers. Woe betide humanity's fate if the compact that defends Athera's mysteries should fail.'

The field Sorcerer averted the fatal mistake and sealed his unequivocal promise without hesitation. "We Seven are steadfast. Cross the veil at peace on my explicit assurance. The charge uniting us shall be upheld. If the day ever dawns on the gross violation that calls for executive action, our Fellowship will respond first."

'You are bound,' the great drake reminded, his timbre the rumble of doom.

Chaimistarizog arose, wings unfurled to extension in readiness for his final flight. Asandir gave the behemoth's wounded majesty his last homage. No trace of stress marred his mask of serenity as he backed clear of the curved talons arched over his head. He crossed through the Worldsend Gate, harried by more than the colossal draught as the great drake coiled his sinuous mass and clapped down the eighty-five spans of taut wing leather that launched him aloft.

The slap of the icy gale, Athera side, had lost none of its murderous bite. Asandir gripped the whipcracked folds of his cloak, lent a scant handful of seconds to field the crisis. Sethvir's immediate reach from Althain Tower could not help cast the urgent buffer required to stabilize the electromagnetic pulse of Athera's fourth lane.

Drakes and the offshoot spawn quickened by their eldritch faculties were archetypal beings. Their inherent awareness did not discern through self-reflection. Dreamspun creation was not sourced by love. Interaction with their kind conformed always to their rigid view of existence as a solitary projection. Chaimistarizog and the Protectorate that co-founded the Accord to ensure Paravian survival had never conceived of an independent reality worthy of co-existent respect.

Only one wyrm, ever, had wrestled the extended concept, that life by nature owned sentient consciousness. A single dragon had dared to test the idea of another frame of identity. That daunting leap of evolution could herald a fracture to the limitless glory of Dragonkind's wild existence. For a notion that restricted their absolute freedom of expression must birth the dialogue of an inner conscience.

"Cry havoc," Asandir muttered as he wrought the dire seals to temper the on-coming resonant back-flash. For great drakes were the eldest power on Athera. Their finicky temperament met expansive change with querulous unpredictability. Some, roused to ire, would seek to annihilate the least possibility of a rival entity. Others would seize the irresistible challenge and contest with human consciousness for novel amusement as playthings.

Above everything else, for equilibrium's sake, Chaimistarizog's impetuous flourish must not be allowed to disrupt Seshkrozchiel's hibernation.

Late Winter – Early Spring 5926

Precursors

The meteoric descent of a dragon's death dive scores Athera's night sky, the shock of annihilation doused in the cold waves and calved icebergs off the northern coast, and the cry of Chaimistarizog's passing resounds across the etheric continuum, an inflection that ripples the dreams of the prophets yet leaves undisturbed the great serpent cocooned in suspension at Scarpdale . . .

In strict isolation behind a sealed door, the mind-stripped husks of condemned Koriathain pore through library shelves of fusty scrolls and obscure records compiled in crystal, then catalogue the forgotten fragments of history for the exclusive perusal of their Prime Matriarch . . .

Within the dark vault beneath Rockfell Peak, watched by the mineral heart of the mountain and sealed behind rings of the mightiest wards actualized by grand conjury, the wraiths of Desh-thiere brood, while their covert effort to defeat the Fellowship Sorcerers ripens towards a long-term fruition . . .

II. Short-falls

Eight months after the True Sect's staged execution failed to torch the remains of the Spinner of Darkness, the after-shock crisis of faith that challenged the Canon still convulsed the High Temple at Erdane. Fragility strained an atmosphere tense enough to cut with a knife. Dace Morley weathered the religious recoil at remove, imprisoned within the high tower belfry converted to secure Lysaer s'Ilessid during recovery. Daily, their confined quarters reverberated to the deafening clangour as the peal of dawn carillons shattered the quiet. Another spring sunrise arrived, smudged by the oily smoke off the pyre roasting the latest of many apostate priests.

The on-going cleanse of Shadow's corrupted curdled the air, the sickly aroma of scorched flesh billowed upwards from the walled courtyard below. There, the top-ranked offenders condemned by tribunal were executed with clandestine ceremony. Commonplace heretics ferreted out by zealot diviners, or flushed from the countryside by the headhunter's leagues, were arraigned under an examiner's inquest, with mass immolations cleansing the taint from Backwater to Jaelot, and southward to Shipsport. Dace kept his perilous vigil as enfleshed divinity's valet, close held by the high priesthood at Erdane. For his master posed more than the temple's prime asset. His service attended the most dangerous suspect of sacrilege positioned with the irrefutable standing to subvert the writ of Canon Law.

At present, the cripple sequestered in kid-glove duress scarcely troubled the four sentries posted outside his locked door. Lysaer sat in state splendour in a high-backed chair, tidy in a gentleman's doublet and voile shirt, tastefully trimmed with pale ribbon. Hands shorn of rings lay clasped in his lap, atop button breeches tailored without loops for a belt. His ravaged eye socket was swathed in muslin, too sheer for damaging mischief. A profile impassive as a cut cameo faced the current blasphemous abomination to burn for the Light's omnipotent glory beneath the bell tower's silled casement.

The glass stare of his exposed, arctic eye showed no flicker of conscious thought. Fair features expressed no outraged revulsion. Even to Dace's trusted regard, no cue suggested the impulse of Desh-thiere's renewed curse might stir vengeful mayhem, or sow a campaign of righteous retaliation if s'Ilessid justice opted to dismantle the weapon of dogma and gut the Light's entrenched covenant.

Day brightened the lock-stepped course of routine. Below, where the crisp snap of the flame stitched the song chant, blue shadow gripped the flock of pigeons startled on the wing. The Lord High Examiner's choreographed panoply proceeded, unmarred by crass gore or agonized screams. High-Temple victims met the Light's executioner drugged senseless. The dose stopped their hearts ahead of the sword thrust, before the ceremonial torch lit the faggots beneath their chained ankles.

The caged avatar bore silent witness to the blessing invoked for the damned shade just dispatched, at each moment relentlessly watched. The stone lintel that fronted the outer landing was embedded with spy's nooks fitted with prisms. Both sentries' embrasures had slotted murder holes and curtained niches for discreet observation. Night and day, an avid clerk scribed a record of movement and conversation. But the servant's impeccable protocol, and the blank poise of the god-sent statesman yielded nothing to such diligent oversight. Not a clamped muscle twitched Lysaer's clean-shaven jaw. Immaculate from trimmed hair to his slippered soles, only the bodily failure of weakness flawed the impression of remote indifference. Always, Lysaer wrestled the lopsided carriage afflicting his painful recovery.

The novel miracle of his survival encroached on what remained of his privacy before the coals of today's heretic crumbled to ash.

The guards dressed their weapons in smart form for the latest august party inbound from below. The clang of the lock on the iron grille and the brisk jangle of the watch captain's keys scattered echoes through the squeal of the hinge.

Dace Morley's circumspect glance peered downwards at the parade beneath the arched window. "The usual delegation of priests, with attendants, and several consulting physicians," he soothed, a pretentious courtesy staged to reassure a seemingly infantile helplessness. The cagey warning in fact alerted his master the attached faces were unfamiliar. Yet another pilgrims' tour, made to impress the outlying districts before the unpopular news of raised tithes satiated the constant demand for war revenue.

The wrinkle that tightened Lysaer's visible eyelid evinced his signal displeasure.

Since propriety expected a valet's retirement in the company of his betters, Dace withdrew to his stool in the nook overshadowed by the carved armoire. Trust had not earned him the untoward liberty, but the lowly need for those tasks too demeaning to soil the scented hands of superiors.

Prepared with a fresh towel draped over his arm, Dace tracked Lysaer's deportment with wary reserve as the despised invasion trooped up the stairwell, chivvied by a fatuous lecturer.

"Indeed, yes. Verified experts have documentation. A crossbow bolt to the eye, always fatal, demonstrated the omnipotence of Divine Light beyond question."

Through scattershot murmurs, the overawed party tramped upwards, commingled steps shod and pattened, trailed by the individual with the asthmatic wheeze Dace dubbed 'the whistler.' The rear-guard included the martial grate of matched pairs of hobnailed boots.

Dace smothered dismay, disturbed by the addition of armed dedicates at mid-watch.

The officious speaker's diatribe dimmed, aimed down the stairwell to field someone's query. "Coherent speech? Barely." A huffed pause for disparagement, then, "Slurred phrases, symptomatic of the aftermath incurred by apoplexy."

The High Temple's presiding physician elaborated. "I assure you naught's amiss with his lungs. Our Blessed Lord wailed like a traumatized horse early on, while his fouled dressings were changed."

Someone's cough quashed an untoward interruption. "Time alone will determine whether his functional cognizance will be restored," the offended authority rebuked.

Armour chinked at the landing. The posted sentries snapped a formal salute to the crowding arrivals. The worthies stuffed at the threshold gawked at Lysaer's back-turned chair, while others crammed behind craned their necks, jostled by their less-privileged peers, jammed on the risers behind.

Dace's basilisk stare fixed on the temple's Master of Healing, beaked nose like the prow on a boat, and his forehead crimped into a jaded squint. Bunched at his back with rolled sleeves, two pasty attendants hauled his chest of tinctures and implements. The barracks surgeon brought his smocked lackeys, huddled in whispered conference. More panoplied priests wafted in on a gust of incense, gold-and-white vest-ments and dazzling gems jostled by a prim secretary laden down by a lap desk and a folding stool inlaid with ivory. Last came the Sunwheel dedicates in full arms, whose bulk at parade rest quenched restive nerves like the banked chill off a snowdrift.

Dace stifled his alarm at the numbers, afraid for Lysaer, who had no other recourse but patience.

The displaced arrivals reshuffled themselves by tedious order of prece-dence. None seemed eager to disturb the Light's avatar until the pre-eminent priest nodded at the resident healer. "Shall we start?"

The physician's assistant minced up to the back-turned seat with its motionless occupant.

Lysaer thrust to his feet, disinclined to be docile. The rocked chair jabbed the luckless subordinate in the midriff and doubled him, whooping, while the clustered dignitaries gasped and swayed back-wards.

Incarnate divinity gave their chorused dismay his regal indifference. His vacuous gaze through the lancet windows never wavered. The awkward pause stretched, until the walloped assistant recovered his seized wind and barked at the sidelined valet. "Strip your master's raiment to the waist."

Dace bowed to the thankless demand without fuss. Lysaer suffered his handling, arms rag-doll limp throughout the removal of his corded doublet. The padded left shoulder no longer masked his atrophied stoop. Infirmity bared to public review, Lysaer withstood the humiliation in shirtsleeves, while Dace unlaced the points at collar and wrist. No deferent care salved the on-going indignity of the recited indoctrination on the particulars of divine regeneration.

The inevitable cynic expressed disbelief, while the quietly sceptical tittered. Emboldened, the curious edged closer to stare, which obliged Dace to cede unwise ground and withdraw his tacit support.

Lysaer swayed, unbalanced. A rankled, cold fury sparked in his single blue eye, as the offence against royal prerogative tested his last semblance of poise.

Dace tempered the fractious impasse with the accustomed steadiness of faultless care. He eased off his master's fine shirt. By intimate touch, he soothed nettled nerves throughout the physician's expounded remarks on the curved spine, the shot hip, and disfigured impairment of wasted musculature.

Lysaer sat for the summary list, a skin-and-bones figurehead, passively enthroned, while the agog audience spouted questions, and medical peers whispered in consultation. Dace endured his station, constrained by the shed clothing draped over his forearm when the priest's curt instruction moved the dedicate stalwarts forward to grip the lame subject's wrists.

Overpowered, Lysaer bridled as the master healer whisked the muslin blind off his face to affirm proof of his immortal divinity. Daylight lanced into the weeping, raw tissue crumpled within his maimed socket.

Lysaer bellowed in pain, spurred erect. His wrenching surge butted the shorter man-at-arm's nose, and knocked a glancing blow to the other's chain-link chinstrap. Both dedicates reeled, bloodied, through smashed cartilage and bitten lip spitting murderous threats.

"Take charge!" The temple physician cried, shamed. "Damn your ineptitude to the Dark! A head-injured subject who's deranged should be strapped immobile for handling!"

Dace despaired amid the unfolding disaster, aware Lysaer could be forced to submission no longer. The avatar's levin bolt loosed in retort struck down the physician and blistered the bystanding gawkers. Panicked officials recoiled, singed and beating out sparks, their scrambling flight jammed willy-nilly into the scared ranks behind.

The packed rout surged in reverse, scattered loose pens, and trampled the scribe's upset box to matchwood. The collective, volte-face egress to escape tangled elbows and heaved, compacted at the narrow threshold. Dace watched, coughing through the swirled smoke, as the pileup burst, hammered through by the dedicate guards, whose surcoats and helmet plumes trailed livid sparks in their stampede down the stairwell.

"You will take due note!" shrilled the high priest pummelled like a rag wedged amid the routed descent. "Whether or not our Blessed Lord recoups his lost eyesight, behold, he still wields the Light's power, incarnate."

Lysaer presented his back to the commotion. Unspeaking, his daunt- less valet snatched the moment, dumped the burdensome clothes, and knelt by the fallen physician. Since the meddling idiot still breathed, a sensible call for help roused the rattled soldiers stationed outside. Dace withdrew, meek, and waited, while the brutes mustered their courage and entered, and duly collected the unconscious casualty. The instant they exited with their burden, he trod over the splinters and puddled ink and swung the broached door gently shut. His astute survey meas- ured his liege, then stepped softly and granted wide berth as he closed the casement curtains down to a slit.

Gloom cloaked the strained pause. When Lysaer let down and sank into the chair, Dace readied a dampened towel and fetched clean gauze from the hamper.

"May I?" he murmured.

A resigned gesture granted him leave. Lysaer suffered the aftermath without flinching. His savaged temper withstood the ministration that blotted the streaming tears from his sunken right cheek. A hissed breath through clenched teeth met the swab that that mopped the congealed serum from the collapsed folds of his inflamed socket. Nestled within, Davien's sealed conjury had begun to regenerate an embryonic, dark orb the size of a pea. The lancing pain caused by exposure to air and light would subside to an ache underneath a protective, fresh dressing.

Yet the shudders that swept Lysaer's frame did not ease. His flash- point rage simmered, denied the surcease of a ready target.

Dace could do nothing, trapped in the breach, except keep the chamber shuttered in gloom. Safety for them both was precarious under the vigilant prying of temple surveillance. Lysaer's convalescence exacer- bated his vulnerability. Constant threat left Dace naught for defence but a clothespin against armoured men. Impatient folly at this pass invited shackles and chain to keep his liege muzzled.

Day upon day of weary restraint taxed the straight grain of a man whose innate drive for justice was not wont to pander.

Dace deferred the urge to tend his liege's dress and tidy his hair. He secured the muslin dressing and stepped back, prepared for the thrust that shot Lysaer upright, then the piqued snatch for the shirt, which his liege yanked over his head with little trace of ineptitude. Dace stood, hands laced at his back, while Lysaer paced like a predator, driving recalcitrant muscle and nerve back to fitness.

The guards outside would hear his gimped stride as the scribbling spy took dutiful note of his weakness. Yet the shut door obscured what occurred in the dark. Lysaer's foot did not drag on his bad side, but he faked disability on the leg *opposite*. The determined ruse let him rebuild hale strength with the priesthood's oversight none the wiser.

Neither master nor servant questioned that covert necessity. Lysaer's imperative need to hide his recovery ran the unholy gamut of peril. For the Master of Shadow was once more abroad. The nettlesome pressure of Desh-thiere's curse increased, responsive to the least stimulation. Let the temple discover their avatar's mended health, he would become the Light's beacon to steer the next campaign under flags of righteous conquest to banish Darkness. Or beyond worse: Dace himself lacked the sure means to decipher what secretive bent of intention seethed beneath the irascible mask of s'Ilessid reserve.

Adamance stiffened Elaira's frayed nerves through her wearing recoil from Arithon's scathing rebuttal. Always, her patent insight had untangled the strength of character behind the deliberate sting he inflicted for sleight-of-hand misdirection.

But this trial mauled her quietude as never before.

Doubt whispered that the execution of the child at Daenfal may have warped his integrity. Despite the supportive perspective of Sorcerers annealed by the wisdom of ages, Althain Tower's Fellowship resource granted Elaira little reprieve. She had one life to live. One love to cast into the crucible of free choice. Blindfolded virtue's endurance wore thin. While her uncertainty thrashed through the thickets of thorny anxiety, she wrested sanity from the inadequate solace derived from skilled healing. Her current pursuit involved a basin of water, cleared under a refined set of precepts, and a thirsty lavender sprout potted in a clay jar.

Behind her, garlanded in the flit of small birds, Ciladis laced ebon hands and withheld the warm touch of sympathy that might shatter her dogged poise. Above all spirits living, he understood the pressured conflicts afflicting Arithon's choices. If the Sorcerer dared not break his silence, even to broach the appalling scale of the stakes, he could lend his compassionate balance to steady Elaira's courageous response.

"You are well practised in the foundation of active permission to engage your medicinal cures in willing partnership." The Sorcerer dispersed his feathered admirers through the sunlit casement, and qualified, "Let's expand that foundation. Suppose your individual herbs, as themselves, could be addressed by invitation to lend their conscious participation by Name."

"That's possible?" Wonder flushed the etched strain from Elaira's face. "You're saying I might entrain herbal cures through identity for their cooperative assistance?"

Ciladis displaced the last perched wren from his shoulder and baited her freshened enthusiasm. "Such access begins with profound attention to detail. You must learn to cultivate the rapt focus a Masterbard applies to listening."

Artfully hooked by the nuanced comparison to Arithon's training, Elaira pounced. "How do I start?"

"You'll develop the subtle connection in stages, starting with your natural affinity for water." Ciladis turned to the filled basin brought to a boil and neutralized to energetic equilibrium by an infusion of chipped ice. "Blend your consciousness with the cleared element, the same way you prepare for tranced scrying. But instead of expanding your attentiveness outwards, bring your connected Sight into absolute calm. Quiet your expectations until you can sustain the null poise to hold water's volatile properties without striking an electromagnetic response. Then pour the crock onto the lavender shoot and map the flow that unfolds."

"I'll be reading the plant's individual charge by the impressed reflection?" Elaira pondered the daunting concept of a signal near-to-vanishing small.

"Like threading the eye of a needle in darkness, you cannot rely on the senses you know." Ciladis tracked her absorption, his tactic affirmed by the strayed wisp of hair she tucked behind her ear out of habit.

"Arithon studied under Halliron for half a decade," she mused, not quite able to curb the quaver of intimidation.

"At the time, you'll recall, he was mage-blind," Ciladis side-stepped, well informed the demand on her self-command would be difficult.

Elaira punctured his sop with wry humour. "I'll take that pearl of wisdom in partial good faith, that you're not proposing the brutal exercise for distraction."

"If only I could," Ciladis allowed.

For no such wistful palliative existed, as Elaira's staunch urge to stem Arithon's plight became swept up in the onrushing avalanche. From the bronze plait fretfully twirled into wisps, to fingernails trimmed relentlessly short, and the foot laced through the chair's rungs to quell her impulse to fidget, the brave facade she imposed over heartbreak bespoke a torment too harsh to bear. Ciladis slipped away before his stifled distress frayed the calm she required for study.

Gloom followed him with the dank air swirled from the stairwell as he entered the sunlit haven of the tower's top-floor library.

Pen in hand, Sethvir glanced up from the inked page of his manuscript. He blinked, shot up straight as the absence of birds strafed the daft mist off his distanced awareness. "What's chased you in here like a scalded cat?"

Ciladis explained nothing, his response the shot spear against the sharp inrush of grief. "Tell me where Dakar has laired up."

Sethvir blotted his nib on his sleeve and laid the quill flat on the table as if the stout goose feather might snap. "You don't quite trust Asandir's faith in Arithon's planned course of action?"

"I do with regard for his Grace's adamant character." Ciladis paced to the window seat, too driven to perch. "But not the determined face of a rage fierce enough to inflame his volatile temperament."

Sethvir required no dread validation. The grim gamut of probabilities had been sown well before his colleague's concern broached his threshold. Trepidation made him loath to ask if Ciladis sought something beyond a wild-card talent's fixed augury. "You needn't go far afield for an interview. The Mad Prophet's holed up in the squatters' warren infesting the rubble that's left of Avenor."

The scar caused by a dragon's wrathful vindication as a rule did not crater the afflicted site with annihilation. Great wyrms endowed with the manifest power of creation and destruction vented their fury in swathes of broadscale havoc, both in blackened vistas scoured to flinders, and through a territorial ferocity that enshrined their cherished recollections in spiteful rebirth.

Avenor's focus circle at seaside at present replicated the original, interlaced pattern fashioned by the Paravians in the First Age. Ciladis emerged, sheened in violet light, as the lane force coiled back to quiescence. The stone inlay under his footstep was seamless. Nothing remained of the coarse brick paving last installed overtop by Lysaer's fanatics, or the upstart, gilt cupola erected as a Sunwheel shrine. The square-towered guildhall of the vanquished Sunwheel's false regency might never have existed, nor the doubled arches of the walled barbicans Mankind's Third-Age crown tenancy had raised earlier over the harbour gate. In place of a winding road chock-a-block with steep cornices, and dormered roofs tiered with merchants' look-outs and railed balconies, the downward slope to the shoreline wore rustling dune grass skeined by the crab-trappers' footpaths. The Paravian founders' stone landing, with its jade pillars and gargoyle mooring rings broke the surf inside a carved breakwater, a serene anachronism bathed in the golden reflection left imprinted from the faded glory of Cianor Sunlord's ascendance.

Uphill, tinctured in shade, the grand edifice raised by centaurs in Marin Eliathe's reign scalloped the morning sky. Yet past the soaring, pillared facade, the structure within lacked the lofty chambers and stairwells of old. The fortress warren that once had sheltered the ancient races from horrific predation by Khadrim and Searduin was reduced to a folly, an external front replicated in solid granite where no dragon's perception had deigned to trifle with bothersome, irrelevant detail.

Further exploration encompassed a devastation to make even a Sorcerer flinch. A levelled expanse whorled in slag marked the remains of the spires adjoining the pretender's demolished council hall. Water sparkled and lapped the vast rim of the crater, where the dungeon beneath once had imprisoned a cabal of Grey Kralovir necromancers. Smelted stone, scoured clean, obliterated the remnant of the warded, locked chest, instantaneously vaporized. No safe-guard survived the punitive retribution called down by a dragon: none whatsoever for an aberrant tool cobbled from the skulls of four murdered hatchlings. The cautery wrought by Seshkrozchiel's revenge had scythed down man and beast, Lysaer's tenancy and a teeming populace flamed to magma and ash at a stroke. Naught remained but a rimwall of half-gutted shells, open to sky and crumbled by weather.

Ciladis picked his sober way, without birds, through the glassine detritus. But for Davien's secret, brave pact to mediate Mankind's transgression, Seshkrozchiel's blast of eradication might have razed humankind from Athera.

Across the pocked wrack left of Sunwheel Square, the sterilized aftermath gave way to a straggle of derelict buildings, gapped windows abandoned to disrepair. Haze smudged the view from open-air cook-fires. Clogged gutters brimmed with scummed puddles. Vermin scuttled in daylight and starved curs snarled and scrapped over garbage. Other raggedy, two-legged scavengers scarpered into dim crannies at the Sorcerer's approach.

Ciladis strode under the eaves of patched roofs and passed doorways tacked with frayed tarpaulin. The genteel, crumbled walls of the past's courtyard gardens sheltered makeshift shacks, scumbled over with thatch. Eyes watched from the nooks, dulled by apathy or agleam with restive suspicion.

No beggars loitered in the sunlit corners. Denizens here preyed on each other before seeking handouts. Ciladis's saffron-lined cloak of grey wool drew covetous stares of appraisal, until malign interest met his direct glance. Then the shady practitioners and huckstering charm sellers skulked, cowering, back into their lairs in the shadows.

Isolated from the sanctioned trade route and girdled by free-wilds territory, the most vicious flotsam cast adrift from society dared not cross a Fellowship Sorcerer.

Ciladis's business led him into the tumbledown booths of a seedy market, where dubious commerce and rickety stalls were centred by cockfights in a boarded pit. Cheap ale sold in tin jacks for a halfpence, and open fires roasted fowl snared with lime and poached game on improvised spits. There, in an abandoned booth, Dakar lay in a drunken sprawl with shut eyes when Ciladis's shadow flicked over him. Choked awake mid-snore, he rolled over, his galvanic surge to escape yanked up short by the Sorcerer's planted foot on his tunic.

"Pox and mayhem!" The Mad Prophet shielded his face with a pudgy hand, squinting through crusted lids. "A man can't get happy on gin without being plagued by the arse clap of doom." Aware of whose ebon figure had pinned him, he groaned. "What have I done that's summoned you like damnation ahead of the afterlife?"

But his cringing distemper bespoke a man sick with remorse from his toll of appalling mistakes. The stale reek of alcoholic neglect stunned decency at twenty paces.

Ciladis weathered the noxious assault, while wisped clouds framed his dark silhouette. "Try me with another delusional fable." But his tender compassion drew the sting from the accusation. "As if you haven't fled straight to ruin for an untenable quandary." When Dakar crumpled, he lifted his foot. "You'll wallow in your self-imposed muckheap until you free yourself from imprisonment."

Dakar winced, his greying beard pasted in strings to his double chin. "I'm the puppy dog pissing myself with excitement. Fawning to grovel at Asandir's knees, or worse, tug my forelock through a flaying evisceration for the mawkish effort to mollify his Grace of Rathain?"

Sarcasm failed before stripped incredulity. The damage wrought by the gross misstep at Athir, exacerbated by two horrendous betrayals, before the fool's ploy with the lightning at Caith-al-Caen had cost lives and bashed over the Fellowship's ordered prerogatives. "Why under daylight should I bother to move?" Inertia ossified his dauntless contempt, voiced through the thump of a bucket girl's clogs past Dakar's unsavoury refuge. "Daenfal's spilled blood has bequeathed a sufficient reward. The venal hoard I stripped off the Light's priests at the scaffold should keep me in bliss for a century."

The comment floundered, while spring's fickle gusts buffeted through the cheep of the nesting sparrows tucked in the warped stringers above.

"I am here asking for Arithon's sake," Ciladis admitted, his cast-iron grip on the subject pitched for endurance. "His Grace needs your service as never before."

With reason, Dakar shied from the abyss. The unfolding, dangerous future woke elder powers with rooted entanglements older than Athera's ancient history. Arithon Teir's'Ffalenn stood at the crux, against desperate stakes that outstripped his foundational training.

"Why appeal to me? If Asandir's taken the matter in hand, his Grace has Tarens to stand at his shoulder." Hounded from smug oblivion, Dakar sat up and let fly his resentment. "Granted the redoubled endowment of Jieret's loyalty, surely your prodigy's moral devotion won't snap."

But Ciladis gave specious excuses short shrift. "That's fallacy, based on a *caithdein*'s inflexible ethic, and reliant upon the close confidence Rathain's prince refuses to share."

"To protect his friends, keeping them at a safe distance." As though pestered by flies, Dakar added, peevish, "We've all had our self-esteem shredded, if not given life and limb for the cause." The heroic roll call had claimed Caolle first, then Jieret, and by far not the least in self-sacrifice, Feylind and Teive. The Seven did not disown the truth, no matter how stark or excoriating.

"Cosach died forgiven," the Sorcerer agreed with surgical sympathy.

Leftover guilt from that tragedy rankled the muddle of Dakar's giddy malaise.

But Ciladis had no cruelty in his nature. "Asandir never banished you from his apprenticeship as a reprimand."

"One suspected." The Mad Prophet heaved a gusty sigh, flicked splotched bird guano off his threadbare sleeve, and relented. "My release became the Seven's made tool." The Fellowship had required him as a free agent when the Koriani oath of debt strapped their hands. "No surprise, they would scapegoat the maladroit fool who created their ugly bind in the first place."

Patience rebuked in the velvet-grained sorrow no Master Spellbinder had the crass guts to defy. "There is an alternative view much less damning."

Dakar cradled his tangled head and moaned outright. "That I was selected instead for my trustworthy competence? *Try again!* A more plausible tack that doesn't leave wrecked credibility high and dry on the rocks of ineptitude!"

Ciladis did not humour the graceless dismissal. Instead, his raptor's gaze ruthless, he broached further unsettling facts. "Arithon already has given Elaira his most vicious repudiation. Her generosity of spirit will honour that choice above her own pain. She's altogether too strong, and wise enough to his temperament not to give way. Yet the disastrous lengths her beloved might undertake to spare her from harm's way may well test her exceptional fortitude."

The gravel bite to that prospect made Dakar take pause. "You think he's gone too far."

The Sorcerer admitted, stressed past the pale of his innate serenity, "In this case? I don't."

"There's *worse*?" Dakar glowered, incredulous. "His Grace has entrusted you with his long-term strategy?"

"No." Ciladis's fretful uncertainty showed. "Since my insight extends into his most intimate self, I cannot become the party to pry. Nor could I, against ethic under the Law of the Major Balance."

In bolt-struck epiphany that shattered all precedent, Dakar shoved backwards into cracked boards with a wallop that panicked the nesting sparrows to flight. "You require my ham-fisted bungling to trample the boundaries of human decency?"

"Our willing surrogate must be someone whose reckless love will not swerve for respect." Ciladis's presence quelled the flushed birds, which circled and swooped in return, pelting their winged shadows over him.

"Ath's tears cleanse the Spear of Dharkaron's Vengeance!" Dakar flared in whipped misery. "Twice burned, Arithon's lost every last reason to trust me!"

"Precisely why you are best suited to become the thorn in his side." Ciladis did not sweeten that logic with nicety. "Your contentious relationship has no facet left intact to break, which gives you free licence where no other ally might venture."

"When does faith cross the line into criminal murder?" Dakar loathed the reamed hollow punched through his belly. "You expect Arithon's reprehensible countermove may stem from a moral foundation?"

"Elaira believes so." Evasion or tact, Ciladis would not commit. "Sethvir's backed my appeal to you in her behalf, not least for the sake of her shielded protection."

That statement spawned hair-raising avenues Dakar lacked the grit to pursue. Tongue bitten to quash the bitter grue of incipient prescience, he blurted his question before sounder sense dropped the subject like a hot poker. "What nasty angle of possibility is your Fellowship's covenant concealing?"

"If Sethvir knows in full, he's not saying." Ciladis glanced away, then said with reluctance, "On my own account, I've shouldered the errand on more than the faith of conviction: Arithon confronts a gathering storm beyond your imagined experience. He knows he's outfaced. Against brutal odds, his path carries risks that extend beyond his personal destruction. He'll expose no one he values to hazard: only there, an old friendship damaged by perfidy might test his intent. You could try his will, impose on his private affairs where another might flinch from the back-lash."

"Nor am I the tamed sop haloed in the virtue of your Fellowship's impeccable creed," Dakar argued. Acid fear wrung him pithless. "Forgive my hesitation to volunteer as your stalking horse. My choices have bollixed your purpose before. Why are you Sorcerers sanguine? Surely Tarens will stay planted at his liege's back as Earl Jieret's infallible proxy."

Though debate on that point ran contrary: an honest man standing shadow for Arithon might not bear up under the dread pressure. A stout heart would baulk, driven to go where straight-grained sensibilities were hell-bound to shatter. Foreboding backed Ciladis's exigent request. "Because, Dakar, you may hound Arithon's footsteps where even Davien the Betrayer won't dare to tread!"

"Fire and fiends!" The fat prophet scowled, gobsmacked. "You're suggesting his Grace might break his royal covenant to the point where charter law might oblige his vested *caithdein* to condemn him?"

And, *yet again*, Ciladis ducked candid disclosure. "We have only the power to act in the present. His Grace doesn't undertake half measures. Even his short-term goal defies convention."

"Fairly drives a body to cussedness," Dakar agreed. "Not to mention, the craven's escape in the wine jug." Knees curled to his chest, he clasped obstinate knuckles over his shins. "What has the green-eyed devil planned this time?"

The hammerblow fell as though muffled in velvet. "He's embarked on a course to restore the purified resonance required for Paravian reproduction."

Dakar uncoiled too fast. Reeling, he regarded the Fellowship harbinger, eyes ringed white in sheer disbelief. "But that task at scale means wresting humanity out of the Mathorn Pass, then razing Etarra to rubble. And, avert Dharkaron's Black Vengeance, releasing the Severnir's diverted reservoir above Darkling!"

Ciladis's smile was nightfall under clear sunlight. "You don't think Arithon's wiles are sufficient to strategize the attempt?"

Dakar coughed, the throb of his mauled temples nursed in sweating distemper. "I was not born with the nerves to withstand that prince's perpetual busyness." Nor was the Warden of Althain immune to anxious palpitations, where the massive impact of the proposition assuredly must have flipped the equilibrium of all seven Fellowship colleagues. "Then you want me to serve in the breach as his Grace's checkrein, in fact," Dakar fumed.

"No." Ciladis rescued the fat prophet's staggered shock from jellied collapse in the gutter. "Actually, I want you to keep his Grace alive! At least for long enough to complete the ambitious agenda he's starting."

"Easier to bag desert vipers, bare-fisted." Dakar yanked his rucked tunic to rights and untwisted his belt with laborious focus. "Best to die quick for the brazen effrontery." Heedless of splinters, he parked his slump against a weathered slat and groused sidelong, "You know that's why Asandir put the knife to his royal wrist for the binding at Athir."

The sullen retort packed a venomous jab, since a blood oath under Fellowship auspice should have stiffened his Grace to defend his survival at all costs. Through a comfortless pause, the hustle of the stews' ragtag populace carried on, oblivious to the worldwide ripple of impending disturbance. A scrappy matron broke up a dogfight. Slop water splashed from an overhead sill, and the ale seller's boy cursed to clear the way for a rolling barrel as if the morning's routine were unshakable.

At reluctant length, Ciladis admitted, "We Seven have not made the critical hitch common knowledge, but Arithon passed through the Ettin vortex under the White Brotherhood's influence."

No need to elucidate the rife repercussion: the adepts' inflexible creed of release rendered forfeit all imposed bindings.

Icy wind gusted through the brief, appalled silence. In fact, the unmalleable stay upon Arithon's conduct had been revoked! Dakar's queasy stomach turned over. Sapped spineless, he gripped the warped post and swore with invention until his lungs emptied.

Spent breath recouped, he found Ciladis gone.

Then free will warred in earnest with the ill-starred whisper of increased responsibility. Dakar shuddered, blistered by fuddled resentment. The delusional veil of his peace had been rent, and his quietude shattered past remedy.

"Should I mess up again, and another grand failure inks my name on the Fatemaster's reckoning," he railed, "where under Athera's forsaken sky can I find a refuge from penury?"

If the attentive conduit of Sethvir's earth-sense tracked the spellbinder's festering anguish, no guided response eased his straits. Forbye, the hag-ridden question was moot. A hedonist's lot sank no lower than the squatters' stews at Avenor.

Whatever measure of doom threw the outcome, the drastic change kicked into motion must upset the precarious stance of the clans in Rathain. The Light's dedicate war host rose again from the ashes of last year's defeat. When the fervour of a fresh provocation ignited the next chapter of self-righteous war, the thunder-clap repercussion would consume Lysaer s'Ilessid's frail poise at Erdane and trigger the resurgence of Desh-thiere's curse. Arithon's dicey undertaking could backfire and void Mankind's charter right to inhabit Athera.

Dakar scrubbed his temples, thumped by an acute headache. Gathered cloud overhead foreran a shower. While the pranking spring breeze razed chills to the bone, the scintillant shimmer of nascent prescience threatened an uncontrolled surge of wild prophecy.

"No," the spellbinder snarled through clenched teeth. "Not this time!

I won't play the string-puppet mouthpiece for the sweet grace of Ath's bleeding mercy!"

The old wounds ripped to the quick at Daenfal still were altogether too raw. Come Sithaer and Dharkaron's filthy Chariot, Dakar refused to be dragged feetfirst into the next catastrophic explosion.

Bent on oblivion as never before, he shoved off and tacked down the derelict street. The nearest wine shack welcomed him in, where a half-silver delivered a gallon of rotgut gin. He drank in gulps until he was stupefied, drowning the whine of his conscience while the shower outside drummed in torrents and splashed through the leaky roof.

Reprise

One month past his eighteenth birthday, Esfand, designate *Caithdein* of Rathain and titled Earl of the North, sweated waist deep in the Anglefen bog, his square face smeared with muck to forestall swarming midges.

Beside him, astraddle a plank skid stacked with poles of waterlogged oak, his rangy, redheaded cousin scratched his welted arms, carping in nasal complaint. "Nobody's seen hide nor hair of a headhunter's foray for months." His sly glance flicked towards the high ground, where their dark-haired companion sat motionless, immersed in a watcher's trance. "Siantra's flagged no intruders all morning, besides."

No capricious dismissal: her keen Sight was above reproach since their harrowing encounter with the dire vortex at Athili.

"Sure," Esfand scoffed. "No reason, blessed with her dazzling gifts, why we're laying a sunken log track in this brackish sinkhole to start with."

"You always wallow on the grim side of everything," Khadrien grumbled, half-gagged by the noxious scum stirred up by their labour. Truly, who needed another escape route crafted in trail-wise concealment? A league scalper would have to be mad to prowl where the summer doldrums brewed up virulent outbreaks of fever. "Likely your gloomy fancies will curry favoured from Iyat-thos Tarens."

"Sometimes I wish we still thought you were dead." Esfand extended an exasperated hand. "Might stuff your tiresome chatter and finish while we're still young."

Khadrien laughed, an unlikely deep rumble split to a reedy tenor. "Come on! You can't *imagine* enticing some gullible lass to singe the feeding leeches off your tender bits?"

"Say that again when Siantra's awake!" Esfand flashed a combative grin. "I'd watch for the entertainment. Your winsome admirers surely would cheer while she hog-ties you in public and gelds you."

"You always stomp joyful wishes to flinders." Khadrien swiped back his sodden braid, slid off his bobbing seat with no splash, and rolled the next pole off the sledge. While Esfand lifted the opposite end, he resumed, "If not for me, you'd arse-kick yourself into a dotard. Provided we're not tasked to an early grave, first." Maintenance of the covert byways was filthy, gruelling work foisted by lottery on the unlucky. "Pox take the Light's bountymen straight to Sithaer, riddled with morbid disease. Another year gone to ground in this bog, we'll be mauling each other from rabid insanity."

Esfand notched the pole, then grimaced and bent shoulder deep in the pool and noosed the submerged timber with twine. "Keep on, then," he grunted, his hazel eyes serious. Once last summer's disarrayed enemy regrouped, the next True Sect purge would unleash a fresh war host against them. "Waste your blowhard breath, whining."

"You say?" The ripe temptation became too sweet. Khadrien yanked on the pole with muscular strength.

Esfand stumbled, overbalanced facefirst. His conjoined weight staggered Khadrien backwards. Both of them smacked into the turbid, foul water with a walloping splash.

The mud fight that erupted between them was glorious, the high jinks of frisky young men too long stifled by the grind of subsistence survival. If their muffled exuberance irked the posted sentries, the slosh as they wrestled like rams ducked them under and brought them up, spluttering.

Neither noticed the warning, when Siantra roused, or heeded her urgent wave from the sidelines. "Ath almighty, you oafs," she snapped, forced to stand, then to scold like a harridan.

A sleek head, dark-haired, surfaced from the fracas.

"—riders are inbound!"

"What?" Esfand clawed off the marsh reed plastered to his lips. "How many? From which direction?"

Then Khadrien's elbow slammed into his ribs. Plunged under again, the tussle resumed in vicious earnest, with Esfand determined to thrash sense back into his cousin ahead of a hostile threat.

"Fiends plague! Will you stop your asinine brangling and listen?" Splattered in the teeth by a poorly aimed kick, Siantra shed her dry leathers, waded in, and clamped a merciless grip on two plaits of soaked hair. "I *said* the Prince of Rathain, not diviners! His Grace and Iyat-thos Tarens are coming! I caught the lane ripple of their arrival from the focus circle at Direntir."

Met by stunned wits, she qualified, brisk, "They're mounted, en route for the chieftain's lodge tent. Want to take Arithon's oath stinking wet? Then keep larking off like brainless toddlers."

"That's not fair!" Yet Khadrien's irreverent curiosity triumphed. He paddled through the hummocks, declaiming, "Hasn't his Grace stalled our case since forever? Lady Jalienne's been owed his state condolence for over a year! If Cosach's death meant so little, his royal nibs could sit for a day, cooling his heels for the rank discourtesy."

A thoughtful step behind, Esfand shoved the log skid into hasty concealment. As the heir burdened with the *caithdein's* succession, eager speculation for him became tempered by the realm's obligation.

"We've no status to tackle the stickling problem while we're underage." Siantra caught Esfand's wrist in steel fingers and towed him towards firm ground in Khadrien's wake. "Forbye, we'd best push the pace, or your steward's oath will be usurped in proxy by the council, and we forfeit our chance to witness his Grace's reception."

For notorious contention marked Arithon Teir's'Ffalenn's relationship with Rathain's feal clans, the onus of crown duty abrasive as sand against his mage-trained perception and the profound sensitivity sprung from bardic insight. Past record of his encounters was turbulent, smelted in the crucible of livid crisis, and by ruthless necessity, forcefully brief.

The legend writ large in the lines of old ballads once inflamed the brash ideals of adolescence: Esfand, Khadrien and Siantra had ventured the breadth of the continent, determined to serve a prince hounded to flight after centuries of cruel captivity. Three years wiser, their keen fascination unslaked, they raced like the wind for the covert encampment, the s'Valerient cousins grimy and wet to the skin, and Siantra's willowy slenderness bare-shanked, her doffed leathers and boots slung over her shoulder.

Bedamned to the briars and razor-sharp tussocks of sedge, propriety must be recouped on the fly. While the designate steward ransacked his quarters for his black tabard and a horn comb, Siantra and Khadrien rushed to plead their claim to attend the formalities. After their part in delivering the heirloom sword Alithiel to Arithon's hand, they deserved a rightful place to observe the kingdom's affairs in the lodge tent.

The uncanny range of Siantra's Sight foreran the vigilance of the elder seers. Caught aback, the signal relay could not respond in time to convene a full session of Rathain's council. The loose children were rounded up, curtailed from their boisterous licence to set upon strangers, while their titled elders scrambled in haste to meet their sanctioned crown prince.

The momentous arrival occurred after dark. Not as a displaced community wished under starlight beneath the lofty oaks of Halwythwood, but on a peat mound in the clammy aftermath of a summer shower. Misty overcast lidded the flutter of moths, darting like ghosts through the tarry smoke of the cattail punks lit to suppress swarming insects. Sound carried as the inbound cavalcade approached. Hooves muffled by mud, the chink of bridles sliced the felted quiet when the riders reined in and dismounted before the peaked frame of the lodge tent. Mingled footsteps squelching across sodden ground, the prince, his chosen attendant, and a joined escort of scouts reached the curtained entrance.

The moment hung, heightened by uncertainty despite the flurried preparations made for the assembly. Elder representatives of the named bloodlines summoned in frantic haste packed the confined space, the crammed air fragrant with swamp cabbage oil anointed to thwart midges. None wore jewels or ornament. A scout captain's bald head gleamed among the drab flotsam of workaday leathers and clan braids tied off with rawhide. The central trestle's board was swept bare to accommodate the dead High Earl's unsheathed sword, a hip flask of brandy, and someone's matched drinking horns scrounged for the ceremony. Seated behind, Esfand's tigerish form wore the traditional *caithdein's* black tabard, his tender inexperience flanked by the aged lore mistress to his left. To his right, a small, sun-browned sparrow, Laithen s'Idir perched on a raised stool as the council's appointed speaker.

Before them, honoured with precedence, Cosach's widow Jalienne stood painted in flame light. Her finery jarred, set apart from the clan elders' subdued forest dress. Her white chemise and watered-silk overdress was outshone by the silver-blond hair, swept up in carved walnut combs and backlit by the staked tallow dips.

Persistence had triumphed over adult protocol. Recognition for their past, courageous foray permitted the two eager youngsters their place at the sidelines. A lean slip beside Khadrien's unfinished frame, Siantra garnered an untrammelled view as the prince heretofore seen in visions crossed the lodge threshold, a half pace ahead of his irregular liegeman. Dark-haired as a crow, the man in the flesh was refined beside the fair crofter's straightforward tread. His Grace of Rathain stood three hand-spans under Tarens's muscular strength, an impression that did not reflect kindly. Arithon had been gravely ill for some time. His careful balance and the hitched stride he tried to conceal unsettled Siantra's keen instinct. The recalled grace of movement, tonight, lacked the fluid symmetry of thoughtless reflex. Damaged nerves may have knit. But hale flesh had not yet recouped agile fitness.

Danger infused his Grace's presence regardless. Nothing blunted the Sorcerer's focus inflecting those wide-lashed green eyes. Coal hair tied at the nape revealed the steep, angled features of Torbrand's lineage. Sheathed in a calm that deflected intimacy, Arithon yielded no expressive insight to ease the assembly's avid expectation.

Only Siantra's fey acuity pierced through the pretence, layer upon shocking layer of leashed turmoil unmasked to her uncanny review.

The emotions locked fast behind his self-command unravelled all semblance of quietude. Beneath the frail ice of mannered civility, Arithon's racing thoughts moiled in flashback: centuries past, compelled to his doom, crown obligation had met him headlong within the s'Valerient lodge tent.

Then as now, his step had been dogged by an escort of scouts, ushered into the same palled atmosphere haunted by the spectral miasma of bloodshed and violence. The familiar fust of mildewed canvas and hot oil raised a visceral shudder, viced still. Siantra flinched, wrung by the ferocious revulsion clamped under his desperate silence.

More than his muted restraint stunned her faculties: the void imposed by his initiate discipline stifled the reactive flux like a thunder-clap sealed into vacuum. Such forced self-command held no vestige of peace. Where no ripple inflected the ambient web, *nothing* might stem the Fellowship's direct seal of attunement that joined a living crown prince with the land. Rathain herself thrummed to her sovereign's numbed anguish, a sustained note too deep for most clanbred awareness to fathom. But not past a talented seer honed by the prepotent shift imposed by a close brush with the mysteries.

Siantra stared into the storm's eye throughout Prince Arithon's deliberate approach: *his step did not squelch in soaked boots across woven Narms carpet. This time, hands free, he carried no sorrowful burden concealed in his cloak.* Though the small child infected with gangrene as a captive conscript in the knacker's yard had been dead for millennia, town law at Etarra still enabled abuse that scoured his heart and shredded the present-day masquerade of equanimity. Too many horrors flocked home to roost, till the onslaught of past obligation threatened to crush even schooled equilibrium.

Siantra reeled, dizzied. Her grasp on Khadrien's forearm steadied her, while the tightening gyre sown by the living rustled around her like wind, overlaid by the cries of the deceased multitude that gibbered unseen in the dark. *Past two centuries gone, the Names of those fallen haunted this prince's return.*

The toll of their losses had not diminished. The breathing man saddled with Rathain's royal mantle came marked and measured by slaughter. The added debt of Deshir's recent casualties compounded old anguish and trampled the rags of his personal preference. Fate's requiem churned once more into reprise, no matter the faces before him were different. Duty trod the same vicious gamut. Tonight, Arithon faced the direct descendants whose ancestors' trials still clamoured in chorus.

The widow due his consolation this time was tall, fragile as sculpted glass under candleflame. *Not diminutive, not battered to frailty by grief, or fretted by a grown daughter's rebellious bitterness.* Siantra shuddered, wrenched by the inward effort required to distance the crown prince's invisible turmoil. She watched Arithon Teir's'Ffalenn muster the ironclad wits to winnow the desolate ranks of his ghosts and address the agony of Cosach's bereaved.

Khadrien's elbow dug into her ribs. Siantra slapped him off, annoyance eclipsed by the strident awareness of incipient peril. The ceremonial encounter yet unfolding before her wrenched her entrained vision wide open.

Iyat-thos Tarens filled the traditional role of liegeman at the prince's back. Fair hair tarnished with damp, his affable temperament subdued, he minded the gravity of Earl Jieret's heritage and halted an arm's length behind. A royal condolence bestowed for crown service was always shouldered alone.

The Teir's'Ffalenn paused, isolated before Lady Jalienne's ice-crystal poise. Insubstantial as shadow before her erect pride, he bowed his head and saluted her with crossed wrists at his breast. Unflinching before a scrutiny that had shed no tears through the news of her spouse's death in Daon Ramon, Arithon delivered his opening line, impeccably cadenced. "I come before you in High Earl Cosach's behalf."

Siantra bore riveted witness as courtesy lifted his gaze. Full bore, Arithon matched Jalienne's hostile regard.

Then he said, pitched to carry, "Lady, I claim the charge for your husband's demise on my own account." Shock stunned the assembly. Their riveted astonishment skewered the prince, who presumed, and reached out, and gathered the widow's clenched fingers into his own.

"Mourn the hour your man's impetuous courage sparked my unconscionable loss of temper. Cosach's recoil outstripped my prearranged plan. Had your beloved been less than the hero let down by my weakness, he would be alive still."

Empathy failed. The magnanimous force of compassionate honesty shattered like noise against Jalienne's stony facade.

Arithon continued, regardless. "Cosach crossed the veil under my personal care with all error forgiven and reconciled. For you, for your youngest child and grown son, today I stand before you empty-handed. Yet when my act of redress is complete, if my endeavour succeeds, I will gift your daughter Cordaya the bolt of scarlet cloth that her sire dared not allow for reasons of safety."

The detailed assurance he *had* known their departed by Name raised a rustle. More than one onlooker swiped brimming lids. The alchemy of a Masterbard's finesse cracked the most ossified heart: except Jalienne's.

Arithon Teir's'Ffalenn maintained his tender clasp nonetheless. Head tipped aslant through her desiccate censure, he pursued, "My promise was given, once, to Caolle at the memorial ceremony for the clan fallen after the massacre at Tal Quorin, and repeated on the terrible hour my cursed stroke cut him down in the faultless course of his service."

An intent, twice spoken, a third time sealed his oath. Siantra understood he saw all of his ghosts through the solemn conclusion. "You will see Ithamon restored in your lifetime."

Gasps erupted. Above the amazed outburst, through the upended tumult of nerves braced against the anticipation of renewed war, Arithon's closure rang adamant. "Cosach's name will be inscribed in tribute, alongside the names of others, on the keystone of the arch when the main gate of the citadel is raised from the ruin."

The excited stir streamed the flames on the wicks. Flickered light wheeled, as Lady Jalienne narrowed her lustrous eyes. "That will happen the unlikely day the wild rose in Daon Ramon blooms bitter black in remembrance!" Forged in fury, her deprecation served him a contemptuous reckoning, "Our clans have endured kingless since the red slaughter that upended the royal seat in the rising. Throughout seven centuries, we have not forgotten. An arrogant presumption on your part, to deem Mankind's work is fit to defile a hallowed foundation crafted by Ilitharis Paravian artistry."

"I should have imagined you'd be a match for your husband's cantankerous spirit," said Arithon with irreverent bemusement. "Else you wouldn't have tamed that roaring bear, but dropped him on his arse and rejected the marriage." Then, smiling at last, he laid her fish-cold hand overtop his beating heart.

No artifice spared the explosive intimacy of his response. Siantra Saw the glimpsed glory, exposed: for a fleeting moment, his aura flared with subliminal light, pure as the midwinter stars during the flux crest at solstice. This prince had witnessed the grace of Ath's gift to the world, and survived the encounter, still sane. The clarified echo of harmony stamped into his being whirled Siantra into a disorienting cascade of ecstasy. She grounded her trembling flesh, before the thundering pulse in her veins shattered under the deluge.

"For my arrogance and presumption," Arithon's voice continued unshaken, "you have already broached the nefarious business that's brought me."

"You propose a preposterous breaking of dams?" Jalienne's scorn mocked, her oblique retort in reference to the wasting drought incurred by the dry river course in Daon Ramon.

"Yes, my habit of breaking things being an infamous specialty." The quiver that threatened her brittle reserve did not prompt the demeaning impulse to gather her close. Arithon's assured stillness nailed the drawn pause.

Until the abstruse implication of a Paravian return burst the snap-frozen atmosphere like an avalanche.

For Siantra, the revelation smashed the known horizon of her existence: for Arithon implied nothing less than the complete restoration of the suppressed flux that blighted Rathain. More: a moment's flare of white radiance established the incontrovertible proof. This prince wielded the power for absolute change. Past argument, he could tap the well of the mysteries and reforge the land's ancient, unsullied connection. The expansive jolt to fey faculties threatened to buckle Siantra at the knees.

Then someone's cheer ripped away collective decorum. Disbelief scattered the resonant flux, while the lodge tent's kingpost rattled under the upswelling racket. Unswerved by the seethe of overset protocol and shouted acclaim, Arithon spoke to Jalienne's distress. A private exchange, had Siantra's unworldly Sight not rent the curtain of decency.

Spontaneous vision displaced her perception again: this time to a bygone night in a ditch, where Cosach s'Valerient lay in extremis. Savaged by his shared agony, his last moments commandeered her swamped faculties as he fought sodden lungs to draw breath. Death's approach stole hope in suffering and regret, until the desolation let in by three arrows became rendered meaningless by the warm fingers that closed his slackened hand over a pebble. Spirit all but unmoored by the contact, Rathain's High Earl forgot his traumatized flesh, lifted past the veil by the crystalline melody sounded by Athlien flutes. Pain dissolved, sheared away by the fiery surge of awakening once unfurled for the Riathan Paravians' seasonal migration. The cold and the immanent dark came unravelled, banished forever by the intoxicant joy called to earth through the living bridge to Ath's mystery.

Rushed out of her senses, Siantra swayed, snatched back from the maw of a black-out faint as Khadrien's grip braced her upright.

"Fiends plague!" His alarmed whisper sliced through her confusion. "Sian, what's wrong?"

"Wild talent." Spun out of altered perception, Siantra leaned into his anchoring support. "Stay close. I'll manage."

She clung, reorientation distorted by the febrile ring in her ears.

Before her, yet standing, Jalienne had recoiled. Still the frost matron, too upright to hide her welled tears, she marshalled her grief. A Masterbard's release might have freed her to mourn. But straight shoulders proclaimed her resistant contempt. No lofty promise forgave the lapse imposed by the royal absence. That echoed resentment scalded the clans. A derelict duty, deferred almost four years, suggested the negligence of an abdication.

Wary, while the widow's baleful regard dissected his unregenerate presence, his Grace moved on to address the titled head of the council. Tarens, repositioned beside him, introduced Laithen s'Idir, shaded by the inflected echo of Jieret's legacy.

Siantra's frayed attention snapped back to sharp focus as the striking emphasis placed on her mother's ancestral name raised Arithon's flinch. He would have known Sidir's elder daughters, nurtured under the maternal claim of their kin ties in Fallowmere. *Laithen's evolved surname therefore must spring from the mature liaison with Jieret's widow,* a late-blooming, vigorous love formalized by a subsequent marriage.

Arithon faced that union's descendant: a diminutive woman whose level regard measured him as Feithan's once had, without prejudice. Yet there, the uncluttered script between strangers unravelled. The charged instant he met Laithen's brown eyes roused the liminal flare of his repressed emotion.

Laithen inclined her head. Linebred to shrewd insight, she contained her surprise and spoke first. "The tried man in such company might welcome a drink. As you see, we're not haltered by history's mistakes. The vessel before you won't threaten your dignity."

"Provided that flask doesn't hold the fell poison your scouts dub Dharkaron's Redress," her gaffed target quipped.

Her adroit handling, then as now, chained them both in lockstep to the mores of tradition.

Apology, not malice, acknowledged the storied breach of his trust that occurred, long ago, during a past state visit to Halwythwood. Laithen's steady poise masked no artifice as she lifted the goblet and decanted an exquisite peach brandy. Strong and sweet-natured as the aged liquor, she drank half, then offered the civil diversion of ritual.

Arithon accepted the cup. Siantra watched like a hawk as he quaffed his share and laid the drained vessel rim down. He recited the renewal of his vow of amity with surgical diction. Every raw nerve smoothed back under control, he moved on to the naked blade on the tabletop.

No pause ensued, not for polite courtesy or the formality of introductions.

"Yours?" Rathain's prince asked of Laithen point-blank. No direct glance, but a nod dismissed as a child the seated young man attired in *caithdein's* black. Esfand bridled, incensed. That fast, his Grace clipped his injured protest with the trained edge of a Masterbard's censure.

"You have suffered war. You may think you know hardship. But nothing in your extremely short life can bend my knee to accept the crown oath from an underaged stripling." Lest the adamant statement should be misconstrued, Arithon nailed his ultimatum. "However indignantly you insist, your mother, as guardian, will take the pledge of fealty until you come of age."

The outrageous manoeuvre was going to succeed: a ploy that won Jalienne over as his immediate ally. But the cruel delivery stopped Siantra's breath for the blow to Esfand's fresh loyalty. Khadrien also resented the sting. Bruised by his irate punch on her arm, Siantra deflected his incensed retort with a head shake. "Later!"

She watched Arithon strangle the argument outright by seizing the unsheathed blade on the tabletop. Face averted from Esfand's crushed fury, he tested the edge, then unloaded the grip into Tarens's ready hand. "This weapon is adequate. Quite sharp enough to provide lethal surety if Laithen s'Idir will put forward her dagger. One should suffice, if she's able to step forth as the council's representative?"

The move leveraged the oath swearing to a swift closure. Arithon extended an expectant palm, his testy impatience an affront to taunt fate.

Charter law left no recourse. Laithen surrendered her belt-knife as the legal proxy for the kingdom's clans, binding the royal claim of crown service and selfless defence before the clan elders.

Bristled objectors were free to walk out. Anyone with the straight gall to cry challenge faced Tarens's poised blade, obliged to draw blood to annul the reciprocal grant of feal obligation. Arithon knelt without qualm before witnesses. He crossed steady hands on the haft of the knife. Back turned to Laithen in defenceless trust, he reaffirmed his vow as crown prince for the weal of Rathain's land and people.

Siantra looked on with strained concentration. Again, she hushed Khadrien's clamour. Fey senses alert, she strained to detect the insincere note, or a duplicitous undertone of callous mockery.

Yet no such disparity flawed Arithon's delivery. The flux current rang pure with earnesty throughout his timeworn recitation. "I pledge myself to deliver justice according to Ath's law. If the land knows peace, I preserve her; war, I defend. Through hardship, famine, or plague, I suffer no less than my sworn companions. In war, peace, and strife, I bind myself to the crown charter, as given by the Fellowship of Seven. Strike me dead should I fail to uphold for all people the rights stated therein. Dharkaron bear witness."

Closure accomplished, Arithon surged erect. Tarens backstepped, a driven recoil to avoid a collision with the levelled sword. Laithen's dagger, relinquished as though the grip burned, came with the brisk assurance his Grace would confirm his commitment to those left unsatisfied on the morrow.

Finished without courtesy, the prince shouldered past, intent to depart before the startled council waylaid him.

"Fiends plague and Dharkaron's Almighty Vengeance!" Khadrien swore in repulsed admiration. "There's a man who thinks his bollocks hang to the knees! Shown Torbrand's temperament in the flesh, no wonder Cosach exploded!"

"No." Siantra stayed entrained, wary of the unfathomed nuance behind Arithon's vicious retreat. "Don't misread the appearance. His Grace showed only what he wished us to see based on our established presumptions."

"I don't care!" Khadrien snapped over the wasp hum of affront as the gathering shuddered into motion around them. "I'd rather slam the bastard in the face for insulting my cousin without cause!" Impetuous, he shoved off for a heated tangle with Rathain's sovereign prince.

Siantra blocked his way on scared instinct. "No, Khadri! Don't interfere!"

Furious, the taller boy fended her off. Unbalanced, Siantra staggered backwards into the fast-striding muscle of the royal party behind her.

Agile hands snatched her short. One heartbeat, in tight quarters, she confronted the expressionless features of Arithon Teir's'Ffalenn. Her grey eyes met his, of sheared emerald. The lean fingers grasping her shirt and dark clan braid snapped tense, as past remedy, his impervious mask of indifference slipped.

"*Laerient*, Sidir!" Arithon exclaimed, as through that exposed instant, fey insight on both sides saw more than either one of them wished.

The Paravian phrase attached to her dead forebear's name implied a life debt no measure of mortal integrity could ever repay. Siantra sensed the ferocious mastery that curbed the riptide of his resurfaced memory. She understood, fully, how profoundly Arithon kept himself shielded. Her gifted talent slammed hard against an armoured core he would torch the very scaffold of decency rather than breach.

Not quite all of his personal thought could be hidden. Siantra stared into a desolate loneliness leagues beyond her tender vantage to encompass. Then, like the after-shock of crossed swords, Arithon's adroit reflex ended the encounter. Imperious in recoil, he thwarted Khadrien's aggressive remark, proffered a polished apology, then seized his desired escape.

Threaded like a wraith through the crowd, his smaller frame fell into eclipse behind Tarens's solid protection. "Don't follow," Siantra begged, clinging to forestall Khadrien. "For Ath's mercy, please! Flag Esfand's attention instead. Help me stop him. I can't. Not alone against both of you."

Respect for her prodigious ability quenched the surge of justified outrage. Khadrien smothered his badgering questions and signalled his cousin, then watched slit-eyed as the spurned *caithdein*'s hurt pride whiplashed against their allied restraint. Yet the bed-rock trust of long friendship prevailed. Esfand forewent his headlong pursuit, quenched to ice-water patience.

"Service to that prince will be worse than a vicious dare involving bare hands and live serpents," he surmised, breathless as he re-joined his companions.

"His Grace taunted you to pick an immature fight," snapped Siantra. "No credit to him that you refused the lure."

Khadrien expelled a scathing oath. "Liege or not, he's a flaming arse! Nobody breaks Jalienne's nerve down in public or swats Laithen off like a lapdog."

Siantra was loath to divulge an opinion. Her quelling clasp on Khadrien's wrist doused the injured outburst of chatter.

The purpose driving his Grace stayed too guarded, the spiked bastion of his secrecy a blockage too steep for her Sight to surmount while her rattled instincts shrilled warning. Whatever impelled the prince's close strategy, risk trod the razored edge of the abyss. Something far deeper than personal preference scoured his royal nerves beyond bearing. The close prospect of state interaction with clansfolk presented a threat to have sparked such aggressive aversion.

"We can't stalk the meat of this problem tonight," Siantra allowed at drawn length. "I can't shake my impression the proposal to restore the Paravian presence barely scratches the surface as a first step."

Whatever came next, Prince Arithon's intentions were annealed by harsh losses he dared not, for sanity, gamble bad odds to repeat. To provoke the desperation behind his defences posed a frightening challenge, mined with pitfalls beyond their experience.

"Let's take the matter outside," she implored.

Esfand and Khadrien exchanged a barbed glance, then moved with the press through the tent flap, unspeaking. The pleated frown on Siantra's forehead informed her best friends her precaution meant business.

"I don't have answers," she fretted, while the clamour receded behind, and night's chorus of frogs filled the windless, black air. "Nothing is clear but the certainty we're poking a firebrand into a hornet's nest."

Esfand yanked off his oppressive black tabard and wadded the garment between furious fists. "Whatever you ask, we'll give you the space. Only for your sake. Not his."

Khadrien chose not to object. All of them needed to digest the affront just flung into the council's teeth with the implacable viciousness of a hurled gauntlet.

Summer 5926

Inheritance

Lirenda shut the door and turned the key in the lock of Selidie's private study at Whitehold, eleven months after her bid claimed the matriarch's seat bequeathed by a tainted heritage. None stood, who dared to dispute her accession. A ruthless culling of rivals had exhausted the fractious dissenters who questioned her absolute right to steer the sisterhood's course in the aftermath of the Great Waystone's destruction.

The chamber she broached had remained sealed since the former Prime's premature death. Lirenda stepped into shadow, cut by a spear of grey light flocked with dust, and cloyed by the taint of parchment books and a trace of her predecessor's floral perfume. She crossed the wool carpet stitched with copper-thread patterns of ward and parted the cracked curtain. The paned casement, unlatched, let in the sea air, shrill with the squabbles of gulls scavenging the fish-market midden.

As wretchedly forced to glean from the mouldered leavings of the order's legacy, Lirenda squared her elegant shoulders, determined to comb the available salvage from the deceased Matriarch's personal effects.

The Prime had hoarded secrets. Her hostility towards the Biedar in Sanpashir was legend, the feud shrouded in guarded obscurity. The whiplash of Selidie's temper after her failure to thwart Elaira's audience with the tribal crone three years ago had peeled everyone's nerves. Of a thousand unanswered conundrums, that signal thread topped the troublesome list.

At first glance, the Prime's closet held nothing momentous. A plain chair, a small desk, swept ascetically bare. The crisp quill and capped inkwell in their stand of wrought swans looked unused, though the pearl-handled penknife was sharp. The wax stick was new, and the bronze seal with the order's cartouche, lightly tarnished, evidently not handled for routine correspondence. The glass-front cupboard nearby held sand pillows sewn from black velvet, with the various tripods and hoops to support active crystals. Also spooled copper wire, the tin blanks and wood stylus for stamped wardings and *iyat* banes, with rolled swatches of leather and silk kept for veiling stored in the drawers underneath.

Cold light gleamed on furnishings unwelcome to visitors. No cushions softened the decor. Only two blackwood coffers rested against the bare walls. The old Prime's clandestine effects had been warded behind ominous sigils coiled with traps, which implied the contents were not innocuous. To the eye of an advanced initiate, the protections laid into the carpet alone raised trepidation that prickled the nape.

Lirenda blotted damp palms. An attempt to broach those sealed chests must disarm a lethal array against trespass. She had served the past Prime long enough to have seen similar chains of ciphers. The stamped rune on the trigger carried a death seal, the unauthorized meddler's drained life force subsumed to strengthen its fatal potency.

The posed challenge raised a fluttered thrill of excitement. Why fear, after all? Arithon had breached Selidie's personal coffer by force, smashing the wood that anchored the hinges on the hour his machinations shattered the Waystone and slaughtered the order's most powerful Senior Circle. Whether his impunity stemmed from superior knowledge, or the outsider's edge that evaded the order's master sigil, no clue had survived to lend insight.

Lirenda confronted this trial alone. As claimant to the matriarch's seat, her necessity forced the question. If archives existed to reconstruct the course of her interrupted succession, answers would be worth any risk to recover. Lirenda slipped off the Matriarch's signet ring, knelt before the larger coffer, and pressed the amethyst carved with the prime sigil against the spelled lock.

Contact woke a sequence of true Names sequestered in the heirloom setting. The unreeled array confounded Lirenda as the imprints of a thousand past lives met and matched the dire query raised by the construct. The last cipher was not Selidie's, but Morriel's, inlaid by an occult ritual above the threshold of an eighth-rank initiation.

"Coupling fiends!" How Lirenda resented the bitter reminder! The acumen of her predecessors thrust her into treacherous waters fathoms over her head.

No living memory existed to mend the damage inflicted by the Teir's'Ffalenn. Beyond forgiveness, that Lirenda's deliverance from an intractable term of enslavement had extracted the cost of Selidie's untimely destruction.

"Grant me the tools to bring Arithon's ruin for his irreparable harm to our order."

Raw rage palled by dread, Lirenda replaced the seal ring to her finger. She flipped the latches, lifted the trunk lid, and exhorted the shades of past matriarchs for means to redeem the magnitude of her short-falls. Leverage must exist to recoup the Koriathain's rightful, autonomous primacy.

The trays of silk-shrouded bundles masked gemstones, their cut and polished facets tuned for electromagnetic enhancement. Koriathain stored their sensitive information in crystal matrixes mined off world, outside the purview of Sethvir's earth-sense. The quest to amend the sisterhood's tattered fortunes began here.

The smallest item seemed the most recent, wrapped in silk unfaded by time. Lirenda's tentative touch probed the content, a rough-cut shard too slight to seem dangerous. Yet the past Matriarch scarcely would sequester a trinket with a warded lead seal on the drawstring.

Lirenda used the penknife, slit the packet, and bared the clear quartz fragment inside. The imprint she assayed made her gasp: a pristine copy taken from the original pendant worn as Elaira's personal matrix. A boon unexpected, preserved by Selidie against need, which might seed the rogue enchantress's downfall.

"Sweet sister!" the Prime exclaimed in delight. "What other gifts did my rival bequeath me?" For if Arithon harboured a weakness, the infallible route to his doom ran through Elaira.

Engrossed, Lirenda thumbed through several delicate wands, bypassed two rows of squat points, and selected a swathed sphere a handspan in diameter. A sandbag fetched from the cupboard nestled the veiled stone on the barren desk. Then she snapped closed the thick curtains and seated herself on the hard wooden chair.

Stilled in darkness, she calmed her breathing, eased her tight nerves, and waited for absolute clarity. The oldest archives in crystal were precious and fragile, subject to attrition under exposure to ambient electromagnetics. Lirenda perfected her neutralized trance before she stripped off the masking fabric.

The clear quartz inside was unknown to her, sliced with gossamer veils and the shimmer of rainbow inclusions. Gazing into its depths, she embraced the immeasurable plunge into silence as the mineral warmed and awakened from inertial sleep. Piezoelectric current stirred through the matrix, activating the interface to bridge consciousness.

The eerie sense of displacement bespoke extreme antiquity. Lirenda suppressed her primal excitement. The trove she tapped here predated the Third Age by orders of magnitude! Morriel Prime had insinuated the order had an ancient past prior to Mankind's settlement on Athera, and vast knowledge proscribed by the Fellowship's edict. But just how far removed from the known annals of history, Lirenda had never grasped until the sphere's deluge of cached information upended the frame of credibility.

Vistas opened to her review, vision after vision unfolded like pleats in a painted fan. Her shocked cognizance, receiving, scarcely mapped the torrential cascade. Rationality staggered, shown revelations beyond *anything* revealed to the seasoned sisters of administrative rank. The indexed repository packed the quartz lattice to capacity. Astonishments riffled past like turned cards: of massive cities whose tiered towers sparkled with lights under a lavender sky with five moons; of Koriathain crowned in gemmed diadems and regaled in shimmering metallic fabric; of mighty engines stacked like spinning rings, adrift against the dusting of stars in the deep; of gargantuan canyons carved by magma where poisoned vapour spun roaring turbines like beads strapped in lightning on a tensile string. Lirenda beheld sleek capsules that flew, and bubble dwellings that coasted on sails above methane clouds swirled in whipped patterns like feathered marbling. More, so much more, until her shocked awareness stuttered and gaped and lost focus.

Dizzied by the gamut of her smashed assumptions, Lirenda gasped, overset by the inconceivable scope of a history prime authority had kept suppressed. The chasm that yawned underfoot defeated *every* concept of power, and paled her prior aspirations to a pittance. The vast reach of the order's former influence extended beyond comprehension. *Nothing* had prepared her! The stupendous archive curated by her predecessors reduced her to a worm's-eye view, buried under the depth of her ignorance.

The magnitude of the succession, unveiled, utterly crushed her grasping ambition. The burden she had seized in trust spanned *tens of thousands of years, and encompassed countless worlds epochs older than humankind's residence on Athera.*

Lirenda smothered the maddened urge to pound her fist on the desktop, as, like the whipped horse, she laboured to assimilate a responsibility that demolished her self-esteem. She realized, floundering, her disastrous strait single-handedly preserved the salvaged diversity of human achievement. Humbled, she understood, finally, what Morriel had smashed moral precepts to save. The glimpse of *just one crystal's repository* recast the tenets of prime service, and refigured every exigent priority.

Once a secret society, the Order of the Koriathain had been dedicated to humanity's welfare. The original founders had enshrined the historic knowledge, intact, that encompassed *whole cultures* and civilizations before the upheavals of war and cataclysm razed them to destruction. The sweeping range of Mankind's accomplishments beggared the primitive industry permitted under the Sorcerers' compact.

Lirenda scrubbed the grey hair threaded at her temples, her triumph curdled to dust. Choked on the bitter brew of humility, she barely warmed the Prime Seat as a crippled imposter.

She had been a rank fool, prideful and deaf to well-warranted censure. Her pathetic tissue of delusion destroyed, Lirenda wrestled her inadequacy against a purview that demanded a dedication above mortal humanity. A ruling Matriarch's directive survived intact only through iron devotion.

The Waystone's irretrievable loss now silenced the tongue. Lirenda might strive and never surmount the critical gaps shorn through an incalculable heritage.

The servile knock on the outside door interrupted the excoriating flush of her shame. Nettled by the lane watcher, come bearing the scheduled report of Athera's developments, Lirenda snapped, "Do you bring anything momentous or new?"

"Nothing of consequence, Matriarch." The rebuffed sister departed, obedient, her dutiful list deferred to the sundown shift.

Left fuming in solitude, Lirenda faced a position that lacerated her nerves like ground glass. The pruned ranks of her subservient seniors availed her with too little seasoned experience. Just four loyal, sixth-level peeresses spread the order's operant knowledge precariously thin. With the irreplaceable passage to ninth rank undone, that had transferred the Prime's legacy intact across worlds for untold millennia, Lirenda grappled a quandary to bankrupt the capacity of her lifetime. At best, she had two centuries left before her longevity failed. The merciless rush of each moment, passing, now chafed her with relentless urgency: the hag, after all, had been wise to seize every cruel expedient to prolong her survival.

Lirenda cupped the ancient crystal and sank into trance, seeking clues to the order's most advanced initiation . . .

The exhaustive search yielded only a fragmentary conversation exchanged between a nameless past Prime, and an applicant groomed for the trial of accession: *'Our order suffers more failures at the ninth initiation, a peril that cannot be addressed before the test is administered. You will encounter the absolute truth. What would you do for the sake of your order? How much are you willing to yield to defend the tradition our creed has held constant for thirty thousand years?'*

Then, warnings plucked from a later chronicle: *'Aspirants die because they cannot do the necessary. They baulk, or they hesitate over a principle. We lose them because they are slow to respond at the split second when consequence overtakes them. Others snap under pressure and perish. More, because they shy off from pain, or flinch out of weakness. But most stumble because they will not face their own death – or in the fullness of ninth-rank surrender, give over their will for the greater good of the order. Trust must be absolute in the moment, or the transfer of prime power fails. For the retired Matriarch bequeaths herself, flesh and spirit in perpetuity. When the successor receives the keys at accession, the living essence of her predecessor passes into crystal, her memory and her lifetime's experience sealed and bound to our order's purpose thereafter.'*

The appended instruction involved an advanced cantrip engineered for enhanced scrying. *'Use this refinement to review your precursors' preparedness, and sharpen your talent accordingly . . .'*

Lirenda's assay of the crafted extension yielded an elegance of function that outstripped her prowess, *again*. Just how far had Morriel augmented her innate command of trained observation? How often her curt disparagements had savaged ignorance, stripped through dissent, and undercut subordinate arrogance with overbearing, surgical intimacy.

Lirenda ached in hindsight, deprived of the polish granted to earlier candidates.

The tidbits found here only tantalized her. Too many centuries under the compact's bucolic strictures saw her stranded in a gap as wide as the ages. An insufferable impasse, that Mankind's creative potential should be sacrificed for the sake of Paravian survival; and how acid the price rendered in trade for the worldly refuge granted on Athera. *Who else remembered the searing explosions flared in the black deep, as one after another the great engines that had ferried humanity between stars were destroyed, landing the refugee remnant in permanent exile under the screws of the Seven's directive?*

Clearly, the terms imposed upon reigning Primes by the Sorcerers forced a desperate gamble with fate, the losses of time and attrition traded against a future chance for rebellion.

Lirenda steamed in volcanic frustration. She was the spark of the phoenix buried amid the cold ashes. A full restoration of the Koriathain demanded the Seven's defeat. With their tyranny the immovable object thwarting the order's advancement, the inestimable value Morriel's judgement had placed on Prince Arithon's life now made chilling sense.

Thwarted malice needed no further incentive to justify an unslaked thirst for vengeance. Lirenda returned the wrapped quartz to the coffer and reset the dire lock with the amethyst signet. Consolation now rested with the quartz pendant strung on fine chain at her neck. Not her personal crystal, tainted beyond recourse, but another impressed with the vicious comeuppance dealt to Fellowship interests on Daenfal's scaffold.

Lirenda cradled the delicate point. Awakened, the matrix unfolded the captured image of Arithon the instant before the Hatchet's blade had slammed home through his heart. Prized access through the new invocation heightened the detail of his excoriating ordeal: the rigid wrists shackled to the post, and the sword in mid-thrust, clotted with the heart's blood of a blameless child. Lirenda tingled, rushed by the addictive thrill of her archenemy's agony. Satisfaction drank in his fury at the nadir of helpless despair and savoured the suffering that had subsumed his last vestige of clever intelligence.

But the difference revealed by the cantrip's enhancement sprang stark to the eye in review: rage beyond quarter had ruled the rapt stillness that received the killing blade's impetus. Arithon's expressionless features were anything but razed blank in defeat. The spirit behind those emerald eyes blazed unvanquished unto the final spark of drowned consciousness.

Lirenda measured a volcanic ire seized in black ice, the murderous glint of a promise unquenched at the threshold of death. The man fought his doom with steeled purpose, a resolve so deeply defended, *so hidden*, he would embrace wrack and ruin to achieve his completion.

Price would be exacted for that hour on the scaffold. Lirenda beheld the cold-struck certainty of her downfall. For the manipulative murder of another innocent, and for the twisted use of Elaira's imprint as decoy, and not least for the discard of Vivet's warped fate to the provenance of the Light's priests, the Order of the Koriathain would be struck off the face of Athera. Arithon Teir's'Ffalenn would be coming for them – all or nothing, he would answer their violation of his integrity.

Cry havoc, Lirenda saw her most urgent directives compounded. She must plunder the most potent weapons at speed from the order's store-house of secrets, then revitalize her subversive use of the True Sect fanatics. Spearheaded by a new-minted tool selected as the Hatchet's replacement, she would bring disruptive pressure to bear from all angles. Not only to break the Fellowship's sanctions, every resource at hand must be turned to thwart Arithon's reprisal and lay the trap for his final demise.

Foresights

Apprenticed in safety at Althain Tower and unaware the new Prime retains a remnant crystal with the potential to forge a hold over her, Elaira scatters bread crumbs on the stone sill for a scrapping flock of brown sparrows, and her wistful request for a meaningful task prompts Ciladis's loan of a book copied from the Second-Age archive at Methisle Fortress . . .

Encased in warmed stone where the mudpots and fumaroles of the Scarpdale Waste abuts the crumpled fault at the Storlain foothills, and oblivious to the seething unrest sown by Chaimistarizog's violent succession, the great drake Seshkrozchiel curls in hibernation, her dreamless sleep partnered yet by the bound shade of Luhaine of the Seven . . .

The interim governor appointed to Lysaer's vacant seat at Etarra dictates yet another complaint, exhorting the Light's High Priesthood at Erdane to bolster the town's garrison, undermanned since the mass apostasy that afflicted the troops dispatched to Daenfal for the unsuccessful demise of the Spinner of Darkness . . .

III. Objectives

The scandalous rebuff meted out to Rathain's northern clans by the delinquent arrival of Rathain's sanctioned prince had no chance to settle. Heated talk battered through sober assessments and made shreds of the sensible plan to salve last year's war wounds in protected seclusion.

Esfand nursed his bruised loyalty, shunted aside in dismissal along with his best friends.

"As if we're the stickling thorn in the arse, and not his Grace, who's shat the nest like the pestilent scours," Khadrien grumbled into the teeth of Siantra's reserve.

His provocative comment floundered, ignored. The encampment's collective nerves were snappish enough, strained by the harsh conditions endured in close refuge at Anglefen. Under the humid blanket of heat, spiked by the nuisance of biting insects, Arithon's aim to restore heightened resonance fit for the Paravian presence ignited sufficient alarm to rock settled habits and upend security.

No one living could grapple the radical scope of such change. Not only the ancient resiliency of the clan heritage had lapsed, untested throughout generations. A release of the blighted flux across Daon Ramon would disrupt seven centuries of complacent human settlement on the grand scale. The flash-point recoil would demolish Etarra with the shock of an earthquake. Disaster wreaked on a terrified populace would whiplash the True Sect into frenzied reprisals.

The camp's grizzled war captain worried out his last strands of receding hair. "As though the great upshift years back didn't sow mayhem enough to plague the free wilds with diviners and tracking dogs."

Argument raged, uncontained by the thin canvas walls of the lodge tent. "Where will we go to flee the red purges when the Light's priests demand more culling of talent to sate their faithful with burnings?"

From youngest to grey eldest, Deshir's clanborn reeled, raw from the abrasive sting of s'Ffalenn temper, then puckered to discord by the debates sparked like brush fires in the aftermath.

Siantra favoured Laithen's tacit view, that Arithon's proposal mapped the foundation of a shrewd strategy. "How better to secure our beleaguered defence?" The centaur guardians' inhabitancy would deter wanton trespass. "Weapons can't protect the dedicate war host that advances through an occupied territory." No faith and no prayer would spare the stricken ranks as they succumbed to unshielded exposure.

Amid wracked uncertainty, a bid to reinstate the old races in the free wilds offered a buffer the Light's fanatical war hosts dared not cross. Yet the temperamental strife raised dissent, that the high risks involved promised the chieftains no guarantee of Paravian reciprocity.

Disgusted enough to have shed his *caithdein's* black for yesterday's muddied leathers, Esfand clipped the bark off a partly turned arrow shaft with irritable strokes of his knife. "They'll scrap all day long, like foxes gnawing off their own legs in a noose trap."

Siantra's frown tightened. "Actually, they're about to adjourn."

High summer in Anglefen was too wretchedly hot to badger cantankerous adults for information. Impatient, Khadrien crammed up his sleeves, mouth flexed in devilish provocation.

"Are you dozers ready to grub in the dirt? We'd overhear plenty, up close." Not waiting, he flipped back his clan braid and slid belly down through the thicket, leaving his red-faced companions behind.

"Dharkaron Avenger trample the hindmost!" Esfand slid his sheathed knives to the small of his back, as quick to jettison his mature dignity. "Hang back, and I'll lose my new arrow to Khadri's extortionate barter for sensitive news."

Siantra shed her dyed tunic. A brief crawl through the sedge, and she also lay prone, chin propped on her wrists, elbow to elbow with her fellow conspirators.

The first elders dispersed from the lodge tent, rankled by discontent that continued apace. "Etarra will never cede the Mathorn Pass. They'll fight tooth and nail and orphan their children before they dismantle their reveted walls!"

"Old Dogtail," Khadrien murmured, "out front and yammering in full cry."

But the deadlier threat raised by the summer muster quashed any impulse to laugh. The rancoured town garrison smarted yet with shame from the faith's mass defection to apostasy at Daenfal. Ranks swelled by a fresh crop of fanatics would be primed to whet their new steel on clan-blood for vainglory. The Light's rolls acquired signatures before last year's grave mounds greened under the promise of eternal reward and salvation.

With the plight of the northern free wilds at stake, a resolve to break the dam diverting the Severnir must replenish a riverbed siphoned dry for six centuries. Back-lash over the loss of water rights would ignite turmoil from the Skyshiel notch through the trade towns downcoast to Shipsport.

Objections continued in yammering chorus. "Provided the glib royal bastard can accomplish such feats. Fail, and he tosses our lives straight to Sithaer, and our children to conscript labour and beggary."

Esfand snorted. "There's the old chieftain's nephew, pissing his breeks." That canker had smouldered since Cosach's day, lest the Light's interest should target the redoubts in Fallowmere. "Well due cause fuels his nattering, now."

Siantra thumped ribs to stifle their frivolous noise before her mother's relentless perception sussed out their covert vantage.

"You'd beard his Grace to denounce his plan?" Laithen flared to the loudest detractors in rare irritation. "Then corner that leopard at your own risk! Won't be my hand that hauls your flayed hide from the bloodbath."

Halwythwood's battered war captain scraped at the stubble rash of his razed beard. "A bootless gesture for a lost cause. The past ways are gone. Are we not better off? No looking back once the elder races reclaim their foothold in the northern territory."

Truth weighted the prospect. No one alive had served under the constraints of the Paravian heritage. Old law precepts faded into misty legend could not measure the impact of direct experience. Three insep-arable friends were in position to know, having witnessed a high king's attuned power unleashed alongside Iyat-thos Tarens in Havish. Crowned sovereigns died young, without able heirs to enable a rapid succession and timely retirement. Untested, no referent existed to guarantee today's reduced bloodlines had bred true. Parents wrestled the uncertainty held in common: how would the clans' stewardship fare, once again subject to an *inhabited* etheric web? How many could surmount the trial of the living Paravian presence, unshielded?

The ancient haunts in the deep glades under the surge at full moon were as pale shadows. Nothing near the expansion of flux tides flushed into the crested resonance unfurled by a circle of Athlien dancers at solstice.

"Whatever's decided, we'd better pack up," Esfand whispered. "Before somebody with an unfinished task looks askance and nabs us as lay-abouts."

Siantra snagged the idea as inspiration. "Actually, that's a foolproof strategy. We volunteer to pot boil the drinking water."

Khadrien rolled over and groaned. "I'd much rather scheme holed up in the shade. Why sweat buckets for privacy in plain sight?"

Esfand scrapped back in earnest. "Sia's right! We can talk without interruption. And did you forget? The water brigade Tarens collared for spying is unlikely to rat us out if we take over their assigned punishment."

"You'd trust the weasels that far?" Khadrien muffled a cynical grunt, in the lead nonetheless as the trio slipped out of cover.

Siantra ducked the branch his crass antic released in her face. Falling into stride like a panther, she splashed shin deep through the pools with her shed tunic draped over her shoulder.

All awkward angles, a rash step ahead, Khadrien sawed into their strenuous strategy. "We're not larking fools? You saw the tucked tails of that water brigade when they tangled with Iyat-thos Tarens."

"Dead as the aim on Dharkaron's Vengeance!" Esfand grinned through the virid smear of crushed moss acquired while vaulting a rotten log. "The brute ploughman snared the numbskulls in a noose trap when they sneaked up to ogle Prince Arithon's scars as he bathed."

"The worst of his Grace's wounds left no visible mark," Siantra stated with quelling calm.

"Well," Khadrien enthused, oblivious, "You saw the shackle weals on his wrists, not to mention your crack at a close-up view of the welt on his palm from his half brother's light bolt!"

Siantra stifled that comment with silence. Cheek slashed with gold by sunlit dollops struck through the scrub willows, she wore her innate dignity with her skin, more reserved than her fellows. Under the glued blaze of noon heat, naught stirred in the hummocks but the cellophane flit of the craneflies. The humid air clung like damp wool, dampened buckskin chafing skin spangled with perspiration.

"Let me list all the ways we're going to regret this," Khadrien grumbled.

But Esfand's squared shoulders rebuffed second thoughts, and Siantra withheld her opinion.

Through the sluggish pools of dark, tanbark water, they slogged across the looped creek that drained the sheet flow from the bog into the northbound river course. On a dry knoll with a stoked firepit, a muddy pack of youngsters tended the steaming vat to render safe water for drinking. Of mixed ages, the rogue lot were stripped down to their clouts, bold ebullience and banter wilted by the heat. Iyat-thos Tarens indeed had set guard on his liege with Jieret's infamous noose traps, evinced by the livid score of their rope-burned ankles.

Swift parley with Esfand had the taller boy stirring the cauldron laughing over his wooden paddle. The pair who knelt, straining marsh water, dumped their cloth sieves and scarpered with glee. Another, detailed to split wood, hailed the smaller boy and stringy girl gathering fuel. Their laden sling, dropped with a clatter, signalled the rest, wading knee deep to drag buckets from the sluggish current. Tow string shed with a splash, they scattered on pumping, bare legs.

"All yours," mocked the hindmost, amused as Siantra flung her shucked tunic aside and scrambled before the slack sank in the sludge.

The ringleader at the cauldron surrendered his paddle to Khadrien with a smirk.

"Enjoy the feeding gnats." Teeth flashing through smudged soot, he vanished into the marsh grass after his fellows.

"No spying!" Siantra warned through the rustle of their retreat. "I'll know if you try."

"Mind you don't perk up the ears of the watch!" Khadrien tossed the wood paddle aside, swore, and attacked the laces on his sodden leggings. Before the young men had stripped to their smallclothes, Siantra secured her dumped tunic, then knotted her shirttails and splashed into the shallows. She hauled in the filled bucket and set to with the sieve. Esfand hefted the axe to split wood, while Kadrien stirred the cauldron as the sundial's crept shadow measured the interval for the cured water to be poured off to cool.

"Do you credit his Grace's cavalier claim that we need hardening to face the Paravians?" Khadrien opened, once assured their discussion was private. "If the refired flux cannot build that foundation, who among us is able to challenge the question?"

"Who else would know?" Esfand murmured. "Arithon's met the old races in the living flesh. He survived intact with his sanity."

"Is he?" Khadrien smirked. "Sane, I mean." His scathing remark met s'Idir's stark incredulity.

Black eyebrows bunched, she broke her silence at last. "Rash fool! Don't imagine you'll stalk his Grace to find out."

"Then you fear him?" Khadrien mocked, lashes fluttering.

And Esfand and Siantra retorted in unison. "Yes!"

"Whatever he guards," Siantra declared, as a shudder resurged from her moment of contact, "the mere thought of testing his boundaries scares me witless!"

Before Khadrien pressured her nerve, the stretched tension broke to the rustle of foliage.

Tall, blond and scar-faced, Iyat-thos Tarens emerged, primed to dress down the japes whose effrontery had subverted his punitive assignment. "I came to check on my scamps, only to catch you lot hell-bent on conspiracy!"

"How long were you listening?" Khadrien accused, blushing under his freckles.

"Long enough. Whose idiotic folly toys with the disaster of trying to shadow your liege?" Tarens served them a blistering glare, astonished that last summer's war had not excised the impulse for such feckless exploits.

"Still playing the nurse-maid yourself, I see." Khadrien's shameless mockery trampled prudence. "Tell me, do you also wash Arithon's smirched linen?"

Esfand ditched the axe, shouldered Khadrien aside, and declared with stiff dignity, "Iyat-thos, our grievance is not without cause. You witnessed our liege spurn my rightful place as the realm's appointed *caithdein*."

"What did you expect?" Tarens reverted to broad, townborn accents, run out of patience. "Merciful Ath! His Grace saw his infant ward put to the sword by Daenfal's priests. The factions that hunt him sow death without quarter. Why else do you think he shuns a starry-eyed following, and won't brook your naïve idealism? How many times can a man lose all he holds dear? How long, before the tender lives of the fallen he failed to protect drive him to grief and despair? You want to attach yourself to his fate? That's asking his Grace to treat you as a cipher and let me assure you, that's not as he's made!"

For a space, nothing moved but the flip of a fish in the stream. The eddyless current sluiced through speared sedge, to the burbled hiss of the cauldron. Khadrien and Esfand waited, uncowed, while Siantra stared down the blond townsman, her fey eyes fathomless as a fogbank. "That's exactly what his Grace wants you to assume." She bared her concern, fingers clamped on the hide bucket. "Our liege will not share his confidence. You know him. Tell me I'm wrong to fear worse! Prince Arithon has set himself on a course that will brook no interference. *Nobody* knows the dark depths where he treads. That's why someone has to pursue, not just to keep pace, but to flank him."

"Don't imagine he will suffer a keeper." Tarens cringed from bitter experience. "This time, you can't go where he's bound."

"Though you will," Siantra insisted, not blind to the empty waterskins slung from the crofter's broad shoulder. "You came to provision for leaving, not to chide your impish miscreants."

"Perhaps." Tarens shut his eyes, honest face ridden by dread.

Yet Laithen s'Idir's daughter was more than the willowy, serious girl bucking adult authority. "You, Elaira and Dakar did not pause for permission when you risked the Light's war camp to run interference." Brazen steel, she tackled the subject that daunted the Fellowship Sorcerers. "Tell us, did his Grace even want to come back from his demise on that scaffold?"

Thought staggered under the surgical slice of her uncanny, seer's insight. For the brutal card of the innocent life played in sacrifice at Daenfal had not been the first spent to salvage Rathain's royal line. No surprise at this pass, that Arithon rebuffed the self-imposed escort thrust into his path. *How far would his Grace go to protect what he loved? What extreme lengths, to secure his interests from the hands of his enemies, or worse, how might he retaliate for the violations incurred by his most loyal friends' interference?*

"Beware," Tarens cautioned. "You have no concept of the back-lash you court."

"Then show me," Siantra insisted. "Give me a reason why we should back down that has substance beyond the pretext of our immaturity."

Her challenge to his bleak reticence sparked the livid remembrance of midnight's disquiet, when Tarens had sheltered within haunted stone walls amid the desolation of Ithamon's ruin. When the confluence of the fifth lane with the moon crested the bore of the flux currents, the ancient site wore the resonant presence of history like a siren's call across time. While Arithon slept in oblivious exhaustion from the brutal effort to recoup his fitness, Tarens had mustered his nerve and confronted Davien . . .

The fire in the grate had settled to embers before the Sorcerer tendered his response. "The answer you seek is not forthright. Arithon claimed his freedom to fly in the maze, and afterwards, I granted him the keys to my library. Because I won't ask, and because I've not tested the implied assurance his personal choices are sacrosanct, he'll work with me up to a point. We tread a fine line. I won't press his privacy, and he will not ask me to cross the Fellowship's interests." A pause, then, "Concerning his shadowed intentions, here's truth. The one who might know is Ciladis."

The lack of evasion punched Tarens to visceral dread. He gripped the arms of a chair that, perhaps, had once seated a past s'Ffalenn high king. The carved wood, worn by centuries, reminded him just how far he had strayed from his origins. Jieret's ironbound charge as *caithdein* alone spurred the dangerous enquiry. "Can't we rely on the royal gift of compassion to checkrein his Grace's motives?"

Davien stared back, black eyes levelled with drilling contempt. "Has the clans' oral history neglected the purposeful reason why I fashioned Kewar's maze in the first place? Put straightly, the passage was designed to test the virtues of the royal lineages and disprove the probity of crown succession. High King Kamridian died, you'll recall. Prince Arithon surmounted Torbrand's generational binding under the same extreme pressure, and he accomplished far more than survival!"

Tarens met that rebuttal, sweating in stout refusal to quail. "Then you lured Arithon to the emotional abattoir, knowing, in that case. Or else for some reason you gambled upon the singular force of his ferocious tenacity."

"I was forging a weapon to root out the abomination of necromancy based on a hunch with grim odds." Davien smothered the rife urge to pace. "My candidate bore up to be tempered. Grey Kralovir perished. Two more extant factions remain to bring down. In the upcoming tumult, we'll see if the finished blade turns in the hand or shatters outright under contest."

*   *   *

"Or stands fast to strike true," Siantra interjected, rending the flashback like windblown smoke. Tarens blinked, befuddled, while Esfand's and Khadrien's fixated interest suggested his spontaneous moment of vision had induced a confluent burst of s'Valerient Sight. The seeress meantime kept talking apace.

"His Grace still has support from staunch friends. Since the Fellowship Sorcerers haven't seen fit to revoke their crown sanction, you lean upon the blindfolded hope that a fortunate future still steadies the balance?" Smelted in the forge fire of Athili, she grappled the glaring omission. "Exactly how far do you and Davien intend to humour him?"

Exasperation tinged Tarens pink. "The compact's directive backs his Grace's measure to rekindle the viable resonance for Paravian reproduction." Honesty shrank from disclosure of the rogue Sorcerer's subsequent promise.

Siantra's uncanny Sight rent through shrinking reluctance and plucked Davien's statement point-blank from memory: *After that, the jesses stay off.*

Like the wild falcon released from the hood and the leash, his Grace would stay freed to carve his own destiny.

Khadrien huffed a wisp of red hair from his teeth and piled into the loaded exchange. "Maybe his Grace figures he won't survive the course of his planning."

Siantra's engaged stare slid like the glass edge of fear under raw skin: more likely, their liege might be terrified he would live to witness the fallout. The moment for detailed analysis vanished as a slithered rustle parted the grass and disgorged the elusive subject under their rapt dissection.

Coal hair tied back, green eyes alight, Arithon Teir's'Ffalenn stepped into the shock of a suspended silence. Through the steam winnowed off the neglected cauldron, his ironic, blistering glance raked the party of four caught aback by surprise.

Tarens stifled a choke, tensed for the vicious rejoinder his Grace tendered towards gossips enamoured with his affairs. If Siantra's facade stayed remote as chipped ice, Khadrien's violent flush kept no secrets, and the wicked bent of Esfand's slighted rage aimed to strike for the throat.

Rathain's prince spoke first, self-possessed to indifference. "Time to go." Fox features angled towards Tarens, he added, "Our horses are saddled and ready."

"You're right quick to duck our feal hospitality," Esfand lashed out, undaunted. "The ungrateful pattern's entrenched. Come as you please, throw our clans into uproar, then sneak off without basic courtesy. One might say you're a coward."

"Stripling!" exclaimed Arithon with wicked delight. "I am turning tail to unshackle the forces of mayhem, though not here." Hilarity poisoned by sarcasm, he jabbed, "You're able to whet your grudges with reason? I'm thrilled. Such cheeky verve will age in the cask until you reach your majority. I don't plan to wait for the vintage to ripen. My outstanding, rancorous score's overdue with the pedigree squatters behind walls at Etarra."

Esfand folded his arms, as unfazed by testy rhetoric as his s'Valerient forbears. "The war band will be notified."

"The *remnants* of Rathain's feal defenders will stay clear." The prince did not acknowledge the crofter's prudent, backstepped retreat from the bared teeth of altercation. Quick to resume the lapsed task of filling the journey flasks, Arithon bladed his attack with a Masterbard's satire. "You don't imagine the most black-hearted criminal on the continent can raise a sufficient disturbance to frighten town children and terrify a sanctimonious passel of priests? Natter on and split hairs over titled prerogatives until you choke. I will not lead the strength of the clans out of cover. Or entice anyone to the glory of slaughter exactly as you lost your father."

Objections dispatched, the last flask corked brim-full, Arithon turned on his heel. "Iyat-thos? Since I'm back from the scaffold primed for frisky business, you're the luckless dupe strapped with the invitation."

Gone as fast and quietly as he had come, Arithon left the harrowing question still dangling: exactly how much of their embarrassingly personal discourse had he overheard? In prime position to guess, Tarens gathered up the remaining waterskins without comment. Then he seized fierce charge of the simmering scrap and hung back instead for a warning. "Don't try to follow his Grace at this pass. This isn't about underestimating your crown prince's capability but knowing what Ath-forsaken lengths he won't attempt while beset under extreme provocation."

Tarens shouldered his burdensome load. "When Arithon digs in, you'll suffer the rough quittance I faced when I tried to meddle at Torwent. Not only will you squander his trust, you'll loose the kraken and be left in the dust empty-handed."

Esfand slapped the stout paddle against his palm as though testing the heft as a bludgeon. "You've the nerve to suggest we allow the s'Ffalenn royal lineage to plunge headlong into jeopardy?"

"Hound his Grace now, and he'll do that himself." Tarens measured the threat with the tried resignation of a cornered man short of rest. "Without a look back and beyond second thought, he'll drive in the wedge to buy distance. The moment may come to break his intent and sleep with your drawn sword at his threshold. But as you love mercy, please Ath, not today, if you value the worth of Earl Jieret's experience."

The noon sun blazed down, the resentment wrung to a standoff punch-cut amid the breezeless air. No one moved when Tarens departed, steps drowned by the sawing churr of cicadas, and blond head vanished like sunken gold into the humid welter of greenery. Esfand stared after, jaw clamped to the throb of bulged veins at his neck.

"Blow this!" Khadrien surged to follow, jerked short by Siantra's yank on his wrist.

"Don't, Khadri!"

Khadrien wrenched free, furious under the scruff of red stubble spiking his chin. "Are we piddling puppies, cowed when we're told to sit tuck-tailed on our arses?"

"We do nothing." Siantra stayed planted before her outraged companions. "Tarens is right." She scrubbed down a blanched rush of gooseflesh, suddenly shaking. "I *Saw*, do you hear? Townborn or not, that man bore upfront witness to the horror on Daenfal's scaffold! Not only in person with Dakar and Elaira, Tarens carried the foreknowledge unfolded by Earl's Jieret's true vision!" The gestalt imprint received through proximal charge reeled her dizzy. "His Grace suffered that child's death under empathy, shackled in duress and bled to the verge of collapse! You have no concept to measure the anguish inflicted through Arithon's birth-born compassion. The scar has forged him an obdurate mask. We can't stay his Grace's exploit at Etarra. Davien's involved directly, forbye, which sanity should shrink to mention. When Tarens and that Sorcerer cannot rein in his Grace, if our cross-grained liege sends them packing, *then* we take today's impasse to trial. In that hour, we're going to be needed."

"Two more years," Esfand allowed, hoarse with revolt. "Dharkaron Avenge, on the day I turn twenty, I will bind his nibs under kingdom law and serve his cavalier ways a *caithdein's* due reckoning."

That moment, the cauldron boiled over and doused the coals to a hissing shriek of white steam. "Festering pox!" Khadrien leaped back from the scalding droplets that spattered his shins.

They could pursue nothing further in any case. For their sins, they were stuck pot-tending all night to maintain the encampment's potable water.

Tarens thrashed off a garrotte of willow fronds, pushed to chase after Arithon's abrupt departure. Annoyed, not quite grateful for the salvage Siantra's foresight had raked from disaster, he unsnagged the strap of the gurgling flasks and plunged knee deep into sucking mud. Lose a boot in the mire, and he would be left behind without a pang on the royal conscience.

"Blinding powers of daylight and damn all to that stickling bastard's impatience!" Tarens hacked through a shed blizzard of cattail fuzz. Likely, Arithon would be mounted by now, and Sithaer's blight take the hindmost. "Ploughing frozen ground with blistered heels was less toilsome."

Temperamental rebuff taught a man to be cautious. Aware of raised voices, the big crofter slowed down before he charged into the acrimonious brangle that embroiled his liege at the horse picket.

A woman's pert reprimand sieved through the percussive thuds, as a third saddled mount sidled against Arithon's harried thrust to set foot in the stirrup.

"I'll stand for no evasive language, your Grace! No excuse!" If her forthright language made Tarens wince, her following line stopped his breath. "The historical record has muzzled your case. How often have you spurned the charge of your birthright? Flitted in unannounced like the will-o'-the-wisp, thrown our ranks into turbulence, and gone with chaos sown in your wake? Last autumn's toll of shed blood demands an accounting beyond the caricature of state courtesy."

Tarens unlocked his seized chest and crept forward on eggshells.

The baulked prince caught short while gathering his reins stared downwards at upright defiance: Laithen s'Idir, her diminutive frame clad for rough travel, and self-equipped with a snorting, provisioned mount steadied in expert hands. Cool poise matched the bristle of his royal temper, fearless under the risk of equine maceration.

Jieret's instinct drove Tarens's hand to his sword. The blade slid, half-drawn before reason curbed reflex. Slight as she seemed, the woman required nobody's upstart male backing. Beside feisty resemblance to the former high earl's departed wife, Feithan, Laithen had inherited Sidir's steel nerve and infallible insight. Tarens watched the frayed thread of past obligation stay the galled brunt of Arithon's anger. Astute wits were not fooled: the riveted fury beyond his stiff-backed calm strained the quivering verge of explosion.

"I will not be pressured," Arithon stated. "Not under the burden of Sidir's debt, or by my long-standing liability to s'Valerient. Level dead scores against my priorities, and you'll burn your last bridge beyond salvage."

Laithen straightened, the fluffed sparrow braced on the twig rattled by pending storm. "Who's looking back? Where's your responsibility for Cosach's death? You think your word to Jalienne held you accountable? Today's *living*, feal clans need your oathsworn protection. No, don't toss me the pap you won't expose children to hazard! Esfand's underage, unfit, you insist, to serve the realm as *caithdein*. After blooding his sword in Strakewood's defence, and as Asandir's Named choice for his sire's succession, that's a gutless pretext to ditch the due censure of charter law's oversight!"

Tarens shivered. He dared not intervene. One wrong move, and the disaster, unfolding, might repeat the fatal misstep sprung on that cold dawn atop Thunder Ridge.

But Arithon stroked his restive horse, settled into the deadly, expectant pause that invited his opponents to spout off their passionate list of admonishments. Laithen's hurled tally included the armed threat posed by the Light's summer muster, spiked by the rash endeavour partnered with Davien. Relieved, Tarens strode forward. He had exhausted the very same arguments, including the point every headhunting bountyman would be abroad with a True Sect diviner frothed white for the burning of heretics.

"Also Koriathain, bent on arcane revenge," Arithon ripped in advance. "I agree." He swung into the saddle. "Life's been too abysmally tame, strapped in bedclothes with atrophy."

If the pat reference to his infirmity suggested the altercation would stop short of violence, the ploy failed to reckon with Laithen s'Idir, whose shrewd claws were well sharpened by motherhood. "An arrogant blow-hard might misappraise Esfand s'Valerient, your Grace."

Arithon fielded her sally, his downward stare not blinking. "Did I ever suggest the pup was not grown, or that his fanged prowess required my shelter? Sword-wielding baggage and green youth are not, in this case, the obvious hindrances."

Laithen spurned his denouncement. "Then prove out the flaw in your character, Prince. Ride me down. Debase every hope our forebears placed in your trust to redress the oppression that sells us out for league bounties."

The assault went too far. Arithon's features hardened to glass. Tarens rushed forward. His snatch missed the reins as Arithon's agile horse-manship wheeled his savaged mount sidewards. Mud divots spattered, thrown by gouged hooves as he tipped his dark head in sardonic salute. "First dart to the lady, had the contest involved my base disregard for Rathain's crown heritage." Against Laithen's courage, he struck with venomous clarity, "Your daughter, and Esfand, and his rascal cousin, all three, have suffered a transfiguring back-lash from their exposure at Athili. At their tender years, did you take pause to think my affairs might shift the course of their lives past recovery? Lady Jalienne's lost quite enough without my landing that callous offence at her feet."

"I hate to deflate your self-importance." Laithen snapped through his withering scorn. "But those youngsters crossed the continent for your sake on their own initiative. You flatter yourself to assume any one of them needs our adult supervision."

Rathain's crown prince glanced aside. On a changed note to stymie combative annoyance, he destroyed the camouflage of misperception. "The difficulty keeping your precocious get at home in fact stems from the dangerous prospect of resonant overload."

Tarens lost wind, seized by the soundless echo of music fit to rend spirit from flesh. In Arithon, unshielded, the unearthly blaze of Los Lier's hidden glory spoke in the shimmering gap between thought and language, an ephemeral brilliance shed into the flux stream for a fleeting instant past able senses to fathom. No one possessed the depth of experience to gauge the shifted perception imposed upon human flesh. Straight black hair and green eyes, the Teir's'Ffalenn in that moment wore the living embodiment of yesteryear's high kings.

Shaken, the true liegeman would bend the knee and beg Laithen s'Idir to stand down. Except her resilient mettle withstood the demolition of her integrity. Against a seized stillness where no leaf or grass stem dared tremble, she shrugged. "The return of the Paravian presence will subject us all to the perils of that lofty threshold. Or indeed, the tenure of charter law fails. If the charge laid upon our endowed heritage proves too heavy to bear, we are lost."

Tarens winced, braced for the next ruthless retort; yet Arithon met her interference with the sweet release of his laughter.

"I've been thrashed to capitulation upon sovereign ground. Very well, lady. Come ahead. Bear direct witness since you're inclined. Such dauntless pluck deserves the chance to give the clan council your best informed advice on the matter. Mount up with my blessing. We're leaving directly."

Wise example, Tarens slipped the knot and untethered his horse. He set foot in the stirrup, swiftly astride before Arithon dug in his heels, wheeled and departed at a whirlwind clip.

Small Laithen might be, and burdened with weaponry, yet her huntress's vault cleared her strapped pack roll and saw her seat settled in time to flank Arithon's haste. The same ironclad competence matched a pace aimed to ditch laggards and chafe seasoned callus to blisters.

Together, unspeaking, they crossed the fens, riding south as the crow flew. Across the trade-road to Tal's Crossing, they veered due east into Strakewood. Arithon kept the lead, melted into deep shade as the forest closed over them. Laithen and Tarens kept close, wary of softened ground where the mirror-smooth rims of the sink pools lapped a treacherous cover of moss. They reached rising ground without mishap, the horses' hooves thudding over laced roots, muffled by leaf litter and pine needles. The dim canopy swallowed the last gasp of breeze, the shrill of cicadas beating through stillness that trembled with heat-waves.

Arithon slowed at last to ease their lathered mounts, reins slackened without comment. No obvious effort masked their fast passage.

Yet the nettled furrow upon Laithen's brow implied his reckless haste should not have evaded the clan sentries at Strakewood's verge.

"Your chieftain's scouts are not remiss," Tarens remarked.

The offended glance Laithen flicked his way scorched his upstart effrontery. "You suggest after seven hundred years, we've forgotten the protocol granted to a sanctioned crown prince?"

"Never." Tarens grinned, at practised ease with prickly attitude after family spats with his younger sister. Arithon's access to the free wilds engaged the royal prerogative, his rightful grant of permission allowing their passage through the hidden ways. "If you recall my rough handling by the patrol at the Arwent Gorge, I've reason enough to be chary."

Wry amusement tugged Laithen's mouth. "Our people have in fact forgotten too much, even before Earl Jieret's lifetime." Motivation supported her adamant choice to travel in her liege's company.

A wistful gamine overshadowed by Tarens, Laithen peered up at his good-natured face, scarred livid by his broken nose.

Kindness shamed him to outspoken embarrassment. "You can't want to be here."

Her sparkling glance showed arch astonishment. "That's a specious remark for a fellow seen lurking behind the lodge tent to share a cosy farewell with the Duchess of Fallowmere's cousin."

The blond crofter flushed. "Since headhunters murdered her sister last winter? Yes." Focused on the sturdy knuckles laced through his reins, he admitted, "But helping, not courting. Her two weans remind me of my deceased nephews."

Laithen's wicked insight demolished the pretence. "Kyrwen's remark on the matter agreed. You're a family man to the core."

The blush drained from Tarens's face. His wary gaze sized up Arithon, drawn a tactful distance ahead of eavesdropping interest. "This isn't the moment to encourage a romantic attachment."

Laithen's shrug rattled her shoulder-slung weaponry: not sparrow today, but the taloned sparrowhawk. "Don't count Kyrwen's mettle by your west-lands outlook, or demean her by misplaced protection. Clan women take their mates as they come, or our lineages would have perished."

Tarens chuckled, sweet humour banished as he nodded towards the baleful royal beyond earshot. "I'll hold my peace until you've tamed your crown prince's will on the ticklish subject."

For nothing about Arithon's abandonment of Elaira made sense. Her selfless love, that had delivered him from execution, matched the gener-osity of spirit Tarens had known in the man, reduced by penury to wretched homelessness after his escape from Koriani captivity. The appre-hensive dread would not rest: that the creature revived from the scaffold might have lost the heart-deep character once committed to spare a child's life above the needs of a kingdom.

The uncanny talent of Sidir's lineage understood his foreboding. "I came as much to mark the change as the resonant upshift impacts the known landscape, if that's any comfort."

Tarens weighed that determined platitude, not fooled. Had sureties existed, Arithon's armoured silence gave none. Laithen tracked the same concerns with open eyes, braced in the cross-chop of jeopardy. At least her knowledge of the scouts' markers lent warning if Arithon's course ran them afoul of a set noose or a spring trap.

Yet the hidden way through the guarded terrain threaded the trackless glens near the hallowed groves forbidden to Mankind's intrusion, farther into the verge than clansfolk fared unaccompanied by a royal escort. Here, mortal intellect lost cohesion, half-unmoored by the current of Athera's mysteries. The dazzle of flux shimmered off disturbed greenery, as heightened awareness flooded the mind with a splendour encountered in dreams. Past haunts purled like floss through the hollows, their left imprints like mother of pearl in dim shade as the crest surged the lane tide at sundown.

Tarens travelled, light-headed, clocked by the bellows breaths of his horse. Laithen seemed least afflicted, her mount scarcely sweating under her supple balance, while Arithon laboured, wrung pale by strained stamina after extended hours astride.

They camped without fire, a cold meal of jerky and dried berries, refreshed by dipped springwater. Tarens languished, unaccustomed to the dearth of chores after rubbing down tired horses. Laithen sat, maintaining her trail gear, while the cold, dappled moonlight gleamed through the trees, and the sheen raised by flux flare shattered perception in waves to the whispered drip of fallen dew. Arithon rested, his head tucked on crossed forearms with a delicacy that suggested his skin hurt. Perhaps he quelled nerves fretted raw from the surfeit of uncanny experience: time spent at Los Lier had burnished his talent at the penalty of hyper-refined sensitivity.

Nor was Tarens deaf to the bewitching allure endowed by Jieret's extended senses. The quiet sang, the reactive texture of the mysteries alive with the shimmer of consciousness stretched towards the verge of the veil. The expansive presence weighed on the heart, far from familiar country for a man estranged from a close-knit family.

Arithon's posture rebuffed conversation, and Laithen, clan-raised to strict discipline, seemed intent to keep her own counsel. Or so Tarens assumed, until she provoked with a candour that challenged her crown liege's male reticence. Not as the sparrowhawk, but the scavenger kite flown to pick the rank bones of contention.

"Why is Elaira not at your side after the trials she's endured without stint?"

Tarens bit down a gasp through locked teeth.

Arithon Teir's'Ffalenn appeared not to bridle. Cloth rustled as he regarded the woman whose perspicacity had ventured the question no Sorcerer at Althain Tower dared broach. Then with studied indifference, he struck. "Does a man ask a woman he's barely met how many times she's miscarried a pregnancy?"

Then he watched, unabashed, as Laithen's face paled. "Sometimes the seed takes," he added, and twisted the knife, "and sometimes the gift is rejected."

Uncoiled, he stood with the hitch that yet marred his fluid balance. "I'm going on watch without need for relief."

His retreat vanished into the dark at a site where the pretence of vigilance was a wasted pursuit. Tarens froze. Nothing had prepared him. Jieret's experience had never witnessed so callous a wounding. He shrank, unwilling to watch while Laithen reeled in stifled agony.

Eyes helplessly shut, he was startled when her steely response turned upon him in dissection.

"Why are you here, Tarens? What binds you to a dead man's duty when, plain as daylight, you are happiest with laughing toddlers clamped to your knees?"

Tarens shoved erect and stalked off without answer, knotted by fury beyond expression. His skin tingled, then burned, licked by the raw flame of disrupted resonance. Warned nearly too late, he recalled where he trod. Nerve storms amid a heightened flux stream posed a grave liability. He throttled his angst. Jieret's skills as a stalker let him centre in stillness. Yet the acuity that sharpened wily clan instinct was not required to locate his liege.

Arithon stood a short bowshot away, on his feet and braced, straight-faced, to meet him. Moonlight dappled the birch trunk beneath the hand that steadied him upright. Ink hair against darkness a hole in the night, his features beneath were blurred into shadow. Whether from arid impatience or infirm ennui, his barbed resignation gave Tarens no civil opening.

The crofter chose not to probe the enigma. Though he had intended a tongue-lashing, speech died, strangled off as his gorge rose. The square fist he launched hammered into Arithon's cheekbone and jaw.

The slighter man went down like a stone. Bashed flat on his back, he uttered no sound, though consciousness darkened no more than an instant before a shocked breath shuddered into his lungs. Recrimination stayed absent. Arithon lay still. By Sorcerer's training or adamant affront, he gave the punishing censure not even a visceral groan.

"You earned that, and worse," Tarens rasped through a clenched throat. Then he spun on his heel. Blond hair pale as flax swallowed into the wood, he stalked off, past remorse and unwilling to offer a placating hand.

The split knuckles he nursed through a soak in the spring lent too much space for unwanted reflection. He had argued with family, but never like this. His affable nature pined for a sibling to stem his upwelling despair. No human comfort extended that grace. When he reached the campsite, Laithen seemed asleep, curled tight as a squirrel beneath her spread cloak.

Sunrise revealed the purpled bruise swelling the royal jaw. Tarens flushed, warmed by just vindication, until his sideward glimpse caught Laithen's warning headshake. She waited to elaborate until after Arithon slipped off to wash in seclusion.

"You may not be informed by Jieret's shared memory. But only two liegemen survived of the three called to serve during Arithon's campaign of slaughter at Vastmark. Their witness became an established clan legend. But Sidir's peerless insight saw the truth. My forebear's fist knocked our prince on his fettlesome backside only because his liege let him." Brazen, she overran Tarens's disgust. "His Grace provoked the comeuppance you gave him! More, he allowed you because his primary purpose had been met."

"To gag our enquiries, and shuck off rightful restraint, no matter the grief we stand to avoid by clipping the wings of his bullheaded arrogance." Tarens worked his jaw. "The devil! Arithon's nasty temperament isn't forgiven. I'm sorry, lady. I don't buy the excuse."

"That obstreperous behaviour is his Grace's pressured defence when he's most vulnerable?" Laithen's locked glare skewered the crofter without quarter. "My forebear Sidir forgot just that once."

Tarens raked exasperated hands through his hair, his wince for the flex of grazed fingers. "Spare me from the weapon of decency. Your ancestral insight leaves too much slack. Since I wasn't born to your cussed heritage, the plea for my sympathy doesn't cut bait."

Too quiet, Laithen broke off abruptly, hell-bent to tidy her trail gear. "The meat of the matter can't be watered down. Torbrand's lineage cannot inflict pain to no purpose. Ask instead, since we urgently need to know, what appalling pitfall is your liege hiding?"

Tarens shied off from that brutal enquiry. Smarting under the misspent rags of his gallantry, he snatched up the saddle no clanbred woman needed assistance to heft. Courageous enough to broach the unthinkable past, he challenged, "What secretive plot was his Grace hatching when your forefather tested his boundaries?"

Force of character brutalized Laithen to yield against the grain of her ethic. "The unconscionable tactic that torched all restraint, unleashed on the Light's host at the Havens."

"Sky and earth!" Tarens strangled on horror. "We cannot let Arithon forfeit the grace of integrity instilled by his royal gift. After Kewar, and the upstepped awareness kindled by his exposure to the Paravian presence, the wilful repeat of a bloodletting atrocity at scale would destroy him."

Laithen jerked her final knot tight and rose with the pack straps slung over her shoulder. "Then woe betide us, and him, if we fail to breach his Grace's adamant solitude."

Ancient Claim

Rain spat through the north casement in Sethvir's quarters, chased in by rank gusts that rattled and slammed the latched-back planks of the siege shutters. The Sorcerer's step squelched across the moist, scarlet carpet beneath, the wet-dog smell of his fur buskins blended with the miasma of old horse trappings, raspberry leaf tea grounds, and oak galls lately powdered for ink. His daft inattention and packrat housekeeping dismissed summer squalls that did not threaten the books. Yet this inundation did not stem from neglect. Windows stayed open at Althain Tower with Ciladis in residence to allow for the birds that flew in to roost.

A hawk currently snoozed atop Sethvir's branched clothes rack. Two fluffed sparrows, a finch, and a drenched crow perched on the vacant hooks underneath. Hospitality for avian guests had spread seed grain and diced suet in a chipped saucer, and a frayed mat of cerecloth to catch spattered guano.

Welcome for winged visitors did not include bats, whose desire to nestle a colony in the eaves above Ciladis's rooftop balcony stuffed up the ventilation of the top-floor library. To thwart the creatures' domestic instincts, Althain's Warden sat, pen in hand. Written in runes that streamed volatile light, his precise script composed a plea to the gravid females to keep the tower off-limits. Sincere concern detailed alternative sites. Suitable dry caves fit for a maternity roost on the fells threaded through the on-going stream of Sorcerer's expansive Sight, spiked by the restive urges of live dragons and the dreaming, mad rage of their unrequited dead.

Sethvir tracked the magma flows roiling the ocean deeps and the slowed heartbeats within the encapsulate stone of Seshkrozchiel's cold hibernation. He traced the corked fury, as dangerous, that seethed behind Lysaer s'Ilessid's unclouded, blue eye as an officious tailor took his measure for jewelled vestments decreed by the priests. Beyond the crippled captive cosseted on puppet strings at Erdane's High Temple, Althain's Warden ached for the birth-born emotion reft from the mute husks of the Koriathain's condemned peeresses. In particular, three who perused the dusty archives at Highscarp, scroll upon scroll, and shelves sagging with musty tomes yet to be slavishly catalogued under their Prime's directive.

Sethvir's observation mapped Arithon Teir's'Ffalenn in eastbound pursuit of a mission kept viciously guarded. While the flux stream re-echoed last night's provocation that had earned the fresh bruise on his royal face, Laithen s'Idir and Iyat-thos Tarens maintained their determined escort beyond the patrolled cover of Strakewood. The Plain of Araithe unrolled before them, taupe vales of rustling grass and sheltered thickets of hazel and willow: as fair a vista as once clothed Daon Ramon, when the mighty Severnir's waters ran free. Wild oats, sweetgrass, and lace aster had gilded those southern hillsides in mythic beauty before the rank invasion of thorn had choked the meandering streamlets.

Sethvir's extended recall encompassed the imprint of the bygone Paravian presence overlaid like a faded dream: when the untrammelled flux had sparked summer's storms and purpled the sky with anvilhead squalls. Gusts razed keen by the bite of ozone had crackled with speared lightning, striking the natural fires that suppressed the scrub, swiftly quenched by torrential downpours. A cycle of renewal that might rekindle, if Arithon successfully cleared the obstructions choking the fifth lane . . .

The Warden of Althain flourished a signature on his request to the bats. He rolled the sealed parchment, when, without warning, a disturbance shredded his wistful reverie. The resonant patterns that sequenced the probable future shifted momentum, jostled into kaleidoscopic change . . .

. . . while his snagged awareness altered course in lockstep, he viewed *the squalid shacks tucked into the ruin at Avenor, where Dakar the Mad Prophet shuddered, roused by the tingle forerunning an onslaught of prescience . . .*

*   *   *

Sethvir snatched the instant to lay down his quill. Thrust erect by nascent alarm, he faced the casement as the owl glided into his quarters. The arc of her flight momentarily eclipsed the wan daylight. Suspended on silver-barred wings, her arrival was silent to human perception, a suggestion of movement melted into the cloudburst. Except the surge of her etheric presence shocked through the flux with a bang like a thunder-clap. Ranging shadows spun off the moment of contact when she alighted.

Light and shade shimmered, then shifted. No avian being perched on the soaked carpet. Come to confront the Warden of Althain, the visitation took the shape of a crone mantled in tatterdemallion black. No frail granddame born of flesh-and-blood motherhood, this wizened creature was beyond ancient, spindled full length by an aura that glittered like moonlit ice.

Sethvir checked, hollowed out by a qualm. At first glance, the creased, walnut features of the old woman before him might appear mortal. Not her gaze, which reflected the wisdom of ages, infused by a perilous, mighty tradition wielded by forebears whose steps marked the soil of other worlds than Athera.

This entity came and went as she pleased, an elder power without regard for locked doors or polite invitation. Shehane Althain's watchful oversight granted her entry no challenge. Whether the dedicate Paravian shade owned the main strength to deny her was a contest no Fellowship Sorcerer wished to provoke. Sethvir therefore extended the wary respect that suggested her business was genuine.

In place of the transient name given to Glendien's daughter, the Warden's formal greeting acknowledged Teylia's greater identity by her aspected title, wrists crossed at his breast in salute for her recent incarnate sacrifice. "Mother Dark's Shadow, Ancestral Grandmother of the Biedar people."

The crone's nod acknowledged his courtesy. Yet the ripple raised by her silence pealed outwards, shivering the tapestried web of the flux across shimmering threads of alignment:

. . . bound on horseback across the west verge of the Plain of Araithe, Laithen pursued Arithon's resolute back, disturbed by the stiffened discomfort that marred his ease in the saddle.

"He's not recovered from last summer's ordeal," she lamented, reined in beside Tarens to resume the morning's bricked standoff.

Through the drifted milkweed down thrashed by their passage, she attacked the fair liegeman's complacency. "His Grace is vulnerable. Seize on the opening. Mark my word, you'll rue what occurs if you defer the smart intervention."

Tarens stared, his earnest fibre offended. "You want a sneak's ambush to take your prince down . . . ?"

Pinned as ruthlessly by the unflinching candour of the crone's uncanny jet eyes, Sethvir winced to the lash of Tarens's rebuttal as, remorseless, relentless, the breadth of his vision exposed the conviction behind Laithen's loyal appeal . . .

"Whose hand will stay the cascade to disaster? Rathain's *caithdein* is a callow young man, where you hold the referent of Earl Jieret's mature resolve. Would the realm's past high earl have let Arithon break the sterling adamance of his integrity? Stand aside, and you will enable his Grace to destroy the redemption achieved at such harrowing cost in the maze under Kewar!"

Tarens glowered back at her, beyond aggrieved, his wheaten hair whipped against his sunburned cheek as he steadied his horse. The clan problem that moral imperative laid on him outmatched the kindly soul of the crofter. "Could we stop him, in fact?"

"Better to have tried!" Laithen slapped her mare's flank to keep pace. "Whether the effort proves moot, curse the day we refused to take action. I know this! Jieret's experience never bore witness to the terrible means Sidir once required to keep your liege sane, nor did he endure the hideous morass of remorse that followed the Vastmark campaign . . ."

Yet the crux come to roost at Sethvir's lonely post made a pittance of Laithen's anxious case to override Arithon's autonomy. Enigmatically still, the ancient before him broached the purpose that brought her to Althain Tower.

"Sorcerer! Do you acknowledge our signal claim on the spirit you name Arithon Teir's'Ffalenn?" A shade limned in white fire against the rain's fallen gloom, the crone spoke in words that struck air like a bell. "Will your Fellowship honour the line of our Biedar heritage and accept the price of the blood debt between us?"

Sethvir bowed his head, without grounds to refute that cruel obligation. He must bear her demand. The terrible burden of Teylia's gift sprung from the tie of matrilineal kinship: when Requiar's issue had fatefully crossed in descent, through s'Dieneval. Blessing and rue marked the hour when young Meiglin's commitment to thwart the Mistwraith's conquest had invoked the starborn pledge that birthed Dari s'Ahelas to salvage the royal lineage of Shand.

The crone seized her due for the outstanding balance. "By our rightful charge, Arithon must stand or fall upon his own merits."

"Only by his sacrosanct claim to free will!" Sethvir dared to insist.

"Our terms rely upon clean-cut intent!" The crone's rebuke was the scrape of dry leaves. "My people are not barbaric, or unlearned, or ignorant of your Fellowship's origins."

The backwaters of history ran too murky and deep. Sethvir skirted that quagmire and kept his own counsel. Whether the wrath of Mother Dark's Aspect might rival a dragon's, the prospect had never been pushed to the test. Her moral prerogative was not his to debate. The force of nature before him grasped all of the perilous ciphers in play, as past human transgressions strung between worlds and the oldest conflict spanning Athera's bygone Eras collided.

"You must at all costs, regardless of risk and no matter the price, leave his Grace's fate in our hands." Eyes the starless black of eternity swallowed the light without blinking. "If your prince cannot resolve the consequence placed on his destiny, another of Requiar's bloodline must rise to shoulder the burden."

"Will we retain the viable lineage?" Sethvir asked, moved to plead. Whether or not the Teir's'Ffalenn won the restitution imposed by Jessian's ill-starred legacy, Rathain's royal succession must not fail, nor endanger the prospect to wrest the Mistwraith's defeat to full closure.

The ancient spirit cocked her head, her farsighted vision perhaps keen enough to pierce the bleak mist of the future. "Maybe." A pause gripped the storm-freighted air, between gusts. Compassion and sorrow gentled the grief of a shared understanding. "If, in the coming hour of trial, you allow the *Affi'enia*, Elaira, her unfettered liberty. Else the bloodstock for our purpose, and yours for s'Ahelas, must derive from Lysaer's issue, or better, the alternate family branch still alive on Dascen Elur through Westgate."

"Elaira's part anchors the fulcrum in fact?" That implication sparked the foreboding gravity to wring Sethvir to his knees. "At what cost to s'Ffalenn integrity?" While the query struck, hammer to anvil, against the sensitive web of unbirthed probability, the crone opened her empty palms. "All beings shape their own path through the Dark."

Her strength of purpose was not unassailable. Across thankless ages, her heart still bled. Love muted her cry beyond bearing. Sethvir beheld hands just as savagely shackled as his by the warp thread of on-coming conflict. The shock wave rippled beyond Althain Tower. His earth-sense tracked the Mad Prophet's stumble in the stews of distant Avenor, not caused by drink, but reeled under the broadscale repercussions spun off by the crone's visitation.

Sethvir firmed his frayed nerves, fused his scattered perception, and tested with surgical delicacy, "You place our Fellowship under a painful conflict of interest. For while Elaira holds Rathain's signet ring as Prince Arithon's betrothed, she's entitled to our protection. More, Ciladis gave his personal bond to his Grace that he would keep her safe from all harm."

"Then choose," the crone declared unequivocal.

"To break our guarantee of crown covenant and forsake Arithon altogether?" Sethvir fought not to weep as the shadows of possibility diminished, sucked towards the grim narrows of an irreversible nexus.

The crone extended no shred of false comfort as she brought the audience to firm closure. "*Affie'enia's* mate holds the very flame of our people's hope, the long-awaited promise of reprieve from the unconscionable theft and perversion of our ancestral legacy. Also, flesh and blood, Arithon is the embodiment of compassionate empathy your Fellowship nurtured to master the reckoning." Tears sparkled and spilled down her seamed cheeks. "Love does not breathe or survive without risk. Freedom's nature is wild, else it withers, extinguished. Your prince cannot be smothered in shielded protection. He must grapple his doom without interference. Triumph or tragedy, no safe-guard exists. Only the bitter wisdom of courage, brandished like a torch in the night."

A gust spattered rain drops across the stone sill. Draught whipped the crone's tattered form like a bird's, huddled to ward off the tempest. "You Seven shall be granted due warning. When the critical hour draws nigh, our seeress will speak through the mouth of your prophet."

But Sethvir did not ache for Dakar's woebegone guilt, or denounce the freak connection that channelled his black-out fits of prescience.

Instead, he staked his appeal on behalf of Rathain's sanctioned crown prince. "The man you have placed at the cross-roads can endure only so much before he snaps!"

But the owl had flown, leaving a cryptic silence laced with the scent of drenched stone. The Sorcerer's warning dwindled to echoes, received by naught but the natural flesh-and-blood birds in a desolate room.

Sethvir shuttered his anguish behind ink-stained fingers. "If we come to this, then by every known measure of care, we Seven will have failed our Teir's'Ffalenn."

Summer 5926

Overture

Days later, south of the rutted scar milled into the Plain of Araithe by the retreat of last year's dedicate war host, Prince Arithon and his anxious escort of two splashed their horses into the riffled shoals at a bend in the River Liffsey. A strenuous swim breasted the span of swift current and disgorged them into the sandy shallows a turbulent distance downstream.

"Sweet sister!" remarked Tarens. "I'm decked out in weed like the *Talliarthe*'s suitor, dragged up half-drowned from a reef." He swiped the strung garland from his streaming hair, and from the lacunae of wet clothes, released several stranded tadpoles.

The farmhand's big callused hands just as tenderly delivered Arithon's discomfort from stoic penury in the saddle. Laithen untied the bedrolls and spread them to dry in the glaring afternoon sunlight while their spent mounts were hobbled to graze. Tarens muffled his concern by working the soaked leather supple with goose grease. Laithen's tactful stealth slipped away to set game snares in the shaded thickets.

Arithon sat on the turf in tucked solitude, his bent head a coal blot flecked with grass seeds. The eggshell curve of his shut eyelids suggested a catnap beneath the slashed ink of an untroubled browline. Yet repose never tamed his aggressive awareness. Experience granted that innocuous appearance the wide berth of a coiled viper, even when the ache of stressed nerves and exhaustion should have dropped the man prone for recovery.

Tarens was no longer the affable, innocent fool, rescued in terror from condemned captivity. The clicks of summer's insects and the flutter of foraging butterflies painted a false picture of tranquillity atop the plucked tension cast through the flux. Displaced awareness rankled Tarens's warmed skin, no minor offshoot of Laithen's dissent or Arithon's clamped isolation. His tuned faculties responded with nettled malaise to the Light's annual muster, as martial drills elsewhere hazed the etheric web into subliminal recoil.

Tarens weathered his rampant unease, fixated on cleaning the gear in his preoccupied hands.

Then Laithen returned, the unused cord snares looped to her belt and her sun-browned cheeks flushed from exertion. "I've encountered fresh signs of trespass." In no mood to cater to dicey male temperament, she qualified with lashed ire, "Flux disturbance, still crisp, and also tracks recent enough that the edges aren't crumbled. Ten horses, at least, with hobnailed boot prints in the mud banks a scant bowshot upstream, leagues away from a passable ford."

Arithon stirred, his opened eyes of sheared emerald too dreadfully focused. "The dedicate captains have had outlying patrols on reconnaissance in the vicinity for a fortnight."

"As far west as the Liffsey?" Laithen slapped a fist to her belt-knife, appalled. "Not for an exercise to season raw recruits! Just how large an invasive armed force do we have encamped this far into proscribed territory?"

Arithon unfolded his cramped posture and arose, hitched by pulled scars and discomfort. "At last count?" Laithen's dawning, grim spark of temper roused the suspect glint of his hilarity. "Sethvir's summary record for Asandir said eight thousand greenhorns have signed onto the Light's rolls. They train under the five thousand dedicate veterans retained by the garrison at Etarra." Through her paralysed after-shock, he added, "By Davien's updated estimate, that number excludes the companies wintered over at Darkling and Narms, sent on sealed orders to join them. We're bang into a countryside thick as hopping fleas on infested linen."

Laithen blanched. "How long have you known?" Reeled yet by the toll of last summer's slaughter, Deshir's winnowed survivors forgot at their peril: only a fraction of the enemy's seasoned troops had marched from the past battlefront to cordon Daenfal.

"Correct me if my assumption's misplaced. Wouldn't your war band ditch caution and break my warned constraint not to stray?" Arithon served his conclusion, unperturbed. "Convince me otherwise. Your lodge council at Anglefen would forego their sensible vigilance and remove the dependent families from sequestered retreat."

"Surety would have delivered the facts," Laithen chided. The gambit failed, if Arithon imagined she would reverse her course to report the incursion. "Your Grace, you cannot possibly thread the eye of the needle through what amounts to occupied territory!"

"The thicket and thorn of my tasked intent," Arithon admitted, unfazed by bad odds and a debilitating impairment unfit to bear weapons beyond a skinning knife. "I have an outstanding score to be answered. A cold bath for the traumatic clamour of nerves. Are you faint at the prospect?"

"Try harder!" snapped Laithen, galled by his insolence. The jut of her chin stiffened her commitment beyond any question of cowardice.

"Stand on your rooted choice, not my argumentative viciousness." Arithon spurned the pretence of hiding his limp, caught the reins of his loose horse, stripped the rope hobbles, and girthed up for departure.

Tarens winced, braced for an explosion, certain the sharp woman who stabilized clan policy must rise to her prince's excoriating bait. Yet the perspicacity of her lineage, or else bed-rock dignity curbed Laithen's rowelled temper and stayed the acrid reproach once used to check Cosach.

Trailing as she sprang to recapture her mount, Tarens almost missed the evidence his liege had not yielded to weakness without purpose.

The grass stems where Arithon had rested were left woven into an intricate knot that flicked chills across his sun-warmed skin. Conjury quickened the peculiar construct. Tarens lacked the foundation to fathom the working. Denied Laithen's counsel, and sore for the loss of Dakar's erratic insight, Tarens caught up his gelding. He checked the hang of his weapons and swung into the saddle, homesick for the honest blisters that plagued the yokel driving the plough.

Eastbound through open country, Arithon eschewed the evasive measures to foil a hostile patrol. No vigilant town outrider raised the alarm though they topped the hill crests in brazen sight. When Laithen's vexed frown shifted to arch disbelief, Tarens risked her snappish mood to point out that small songbirds and flushed game were not put to flight by their passage. That uncanny aberration defeated sense, until the belated thought dawned, that the peculiarity had been brought to her notice with disingenuous calm.

"You've seen this before?" Laithen accused, bristled enough to eviscerate him for complacency. "Smug creature. You might have spoken up sooner."

"Were you ready to listen?" Tarens inclined his head with suggestive amusement, blue eyes lit with the teasing crinkle that once foiled his older brother's disgruntlement.

In fact, Arithon was singing, a melody subtle and soft as the whisper of breeze through tall grass. Laithen repressed a snarled oath, looking hot. The theme had eluded her sharpened senses, blended at one with the natural surrounds until a townborn man cued her awareness.

Not wont to cloud her mind with a grudge, Laithen harkened to sound the result.

Where a trained scout with astute talent could inflect the flux to minimize sign of their presence, Arithon's invoked appeal cast a resonant sphere addressed to earth element. His influence raised tone to an upshifted octave, until their mounts' hoofbeats trod lightly on the land as a cloud's shadow, passing. The lulled eye of the observer might see no movement beyond the expected shimmy of brush in the wind. A sanctioned crown prince who invoked his attuned tie to the realm through a Masterbard's consummate artistry shook Laithen to swift reassessment.

"Contact with the Paravians will have refined his touch," she remarked, her awed wonder beset by a shiver. A keen glance backwards noted the unsettling fact no swathe of bent stems marked their beaten track. "Was your liege always this stealthy?"

Fear, before awe, spiked her rattled nerves. *Dharkaron's punitive Spear reap the hindmost, if this prince ever received coronation and the consummate ritual invested him with a high king's sovereign power.* Attunement to three additional elements, air, fire and water, commanded at scale by his grasp of initiate knowledge outstripped the concept of terrifying.

"Surprise digs at the cuticle are his nasty style of candour," Tarens allowed. His wry grin kept no secrets. He had cached a brandy flask in his bedroll for the unabashed purpose of consolation. "His Grace's trustworthy pranks are done in plain sight. Dread the moment when we're sent packing."

Laithen lapsed into critical silence, all the more chary of the naked pitfall yawning under her feet. Rathain's prince was beyond dangerous. Without means to grapple the audacious breadth of his invention, the worrisome duty of ethical oversight was the shepherd's crook poking the kraken.

Yet the afternoon progressed without incident. Gilt sunlight deckled the hilltops and pooled the vales in cerulean shadow. No movement flagged the nearby activity of True Sect men-at-arms. Arithon rode at a pace that spared horseflesh. Still the sapped weariness of his infirmity drained his complexion to whey.

He drew rein and dismounted five times before sundown, brief pauses snatched to weave more of his enigmatic, swirled-knot patterns into the vegetation. Laithen seized the intervals to scout and determined his laconic assessment of enemy numbers was accurate. Dedicates ranged at strength across proscribed ground in shameless defiance of charter law. Despite plentiful sign of their trespass, no sight of the mass intrusion broke the horizon before Arithon called for a halt. They unsaddled under the first stars at nightfall. Laithen weathered the cracks pressured through her equilibrium, satisfied as the horses were hobbled where no chance silhouette against sky would draw notice. Their fireless camp straddled the nearby notch, while darkness deepened, and the glimmer of orange northward and south revealed the fires of the armed encampment. The officers' horn calls threw clarion echoes, and the changes of breeze carried the whiff of smoke, fragmented voices and outbursts of laughter.

That uneasy proximity compelled a cold meal of fresh greens, dried berries, and cured jerky. Laithen's covert foray to map the terrain brought her back frothing to pick a fresh fight.

"You'll know we're surrounded." The testy fist on her weapon itched to flense royal flesh to the bone. "Tell me, your Grace. How do you stage your plan for a massacre given just two swords between the three of us?"

"Massacre?" Her affronted victim reclined on hard ground, his mage-sighted regard resharpened to flaying intensity. "A sorry idea, overrated by history, ancient as dust and as painfully dull." The bard's inflection pierced the descant scrape of the crickets with acid contempt. "Try harder?"

The weight of that bearing gaze lifted, heavy lids bruised by exhaustion. Laithen's sense of fair play baulked at hounding infirmity with a righteous kick in the ribs. Against her stiff grain, she left the contentious score to her nemesis for tonight.

"But tomorrow's another day, bucko." Midsummer morning came early in the far north. Determined to seize her deferred moment of reckoning, royalty's distraught keeper backed off and claimed the first watch from Tarens forthwith.

*   *   *

Laithen brooded over the spattered, coal glimmers of the enemy's spent fires from a hilltop vantage, tucked into a crabbed thicket of hazel. Hours crept, beyond measure in the moonless dark. No townborn sentry patrolled the far slope. Hostile forays, if any, ranged elsewhere. Night's studded diadem of stars wheeled over the Plain of Araithe and winked out, sunk behind the pleated line of the horizon. The wind backed and turned, freighted with the winnowed char of cooked meat and wood ash. Laithen's relief arrived without incident. She nodded to Tarens and retired, clothed for quick flight, her blades laid ready to hand. She drifted into light sleep, primed senses wary, one ear pressed to ground for the drum of unfriendly hooves, and the other keyed to the scrape of the undisturbed insects.

Instincts tuned to the rhythm of the free wilds woke Laithen in the hush before daybreak. A late gibbous moonrise winked through the inked tangles of brush. The mercury gleam sketched the humped form of Tarens, recumbent with his blond head pillowed on a crooked elbow. The exhaled fumes of metabolized spirits implied more than his country-bred preference to sleep until cock's crow.

Laithen muttered, "The devil!" and scrambled erect. Her narrowed glance confirmed the telltale hollow left vacant in the pressed grass. Arithon Teir's'Ffalenn was already abroad, and bedamned to her trust in the crofter's due diligence.

She poised to deliver a kick in the ribs, until the quiet admonition in town accents shredded her presumption of drunken delinquency. "His Grace isn't alone. He's in perilous company. No more than I, you won't thwart him."

"Won't I just?" Laithen twitched her leathers to rights and shoved off towards the crest where her annoyed survey seized on the furtive flicker of movement.

The oath gasped through a scrambled commotion behind her bespoke the alarm that launched Tarens out of his blanket. "Lady, beware. Ath on earth, you're obsessed! Or stark mad if you try to cross what's afoot."

Beyond futile, to protest Laithen's firmed will, birthed from a lineage that could, and had, confronted death before breaching straight principles. The woman slipped like a hazed deer through pitch-dark. Her lead lengthened apace and pushed Tarens to a tipsy jog, marked by bungling noise as he tripped over bushes and thrashed to stay upright.

"You don't know whom you're facing." Disadvantaged by the rough ground and steep grade, snagged and slapped by dense vegetation, Tarens fell back in breathless disgust. "Go your bullish way, then. Don't hear me through. When you live to regret, may the vengeful bite of Dharkaron's Spear show you mercy."

But Laithen s'Idir feared nothing and no man under the hackled drive of her integrity. Nor would she stall for deliberation. The hilltop above revealed Arithon's stance against naked sky in the open: a ripe target for enemy archers from all sides, if but one townbred sentry was alert.

"Larking daisy," she snarled, the wrist snared by thorns raked free to the sting of torn skin. Halfway up the rise, wrung breathless as she raced the pearl advent of dawn, she seethed to forestall the insufferable prince from his daft crack at extermination. "Reeking cess to bad stock! Should I regret if this morning's lunacy rids us of your cocky descendants?"

Ducked left to avoid a looming boulder, Laithen rammed into a muscular arm that barred her impetuous mission. Impact drove the wind from her. The *rock* that had hoodwinked her faculties was warm flesh, immovable strength packed into an angular frame muffled under a nondescript cloak. Male, but no mortal: the banked well of self-contained power bore the stamp of a Fellowship Sorcerer.

Not Asandir, whose obdurate presence wore the sturdy, broad-shouldered might of a quarryman; nor Sethvir's quicksilver air of distracted reverie. This ascetic, steel grasp obstructed her with a brittle restlessness as hazardous as the gleam on spring ice. No raven companion disqualified Traithe, and a pale complexion eliminated Ciladis.

Default left Davien engaged, fair or foul, for an undisclosed motivation.

Laithen's exasperation outstripped prudence. "What murky purpose draws you to the bloodbath?"

The Sorcerer also called the Betrayer swiped back the hood that contained his tumbled mane of frost-streaked hair. "I serve here as the errand boy. Your liege wished a particular black mantle and an heir-loom sword retrieved from his sloop, left sequestered under sealed wards off Myrkavia."

More than suspicion hackled Laithen's nape. "Alithiel. Why?" But her truth sense understood, sure as freezing water poured down her back: the sword's virtue wakened only for a just cause, which implied a live gambit dangled as bait.

Davien plucked that strident concern directly from her harrowed thought. "I cannot protect him, nor should, given his chosen alignment with the fourth lane. Sethvir would yank himself bald if I risked undue notice from Northgate's unseasoned new guardian. The interest of the dragons," he qualified with razored delicacy, "poses a greater threat than a few rampaging Sunwheel dedicates."

"I'm glad you think so," Laithen declared, her tart distress more urgently centred on crossbows. "Forgive the rest of us for the foible of our mortality."

Davien's amused admonishment flashed even teeth. "Choose to blunder ahead as you will, though best watch where you place your next step." His pause, like the crocodile's, invited her to avoid the uncanny feature overlooked in her path. A construct fashioned from laced grasses and pliable twigs, interlocked whorls braided into a spiral, turned widdershins. This intricate pattern was larger than yesterday's weavings, knotted in daylight en route.

Laithen studied the artistry, stunned by a complexity evident even amid charcoal gloom. "His Grace would have laboured all night to complete a such working. I remain unconvinced of the wisdom."

"Your moment to meddle is already forfeit," Davien allowed without sympathy. "Also, your final chance for retreat. Too late, now, to reach a safe distance."

Laithen scrubbed the gooseflesh that pebbled her arms. "The killing field merits a sober clan witness."

The Sorcerer ceded no ground before sarcasm. "If you came to spare bloodshed, you'll be disappointed." His rapt expectation glued the dense silence spare moments before the first liquid birdsong opened dawn's chorus.

No abstruse prompt, this time, was required to grasp how roundly her critical interest had been outflanked. Already the on-coming lane tide fired a riffling eddy through the ambient flux. The amplified current caught Laithen aback. Raked through by a sudden, sharp tingle, she gasped.

Atop the ridge, the grey pall of daybreak revealed Arithon's cloaked figure crouched on a bent knee, the unsheathed sword Alithiel placed point down against earth with his clasped hands on the emerald-set pommel. The keen ear poised to listen picked up the metered beat of his incantation. Immersed, almost singing, he recited an appeal with flawless control, phrases unreeled one after the next in cadenced Paravian.

"... *da Am'n, tur itieren gries s'en e'dael i'teir, Ei dasil fiathen muir ahe liernmien eth saerlieth ahe kadi ankiorath liessiad* . . ."

His pealing command rang through in translation: *'By Name, under sworn obligation of my royal lineage, I claim true cause to centre the gyre to quicken the natural balance . . .'* Struck spark for a ripple of change, the groundswell built towards an etheric awakening of the land's dormant mysteries. The petition's audacity rocked credibility and made even the Sorcerer bend his head in silenced respect.

". . . tehal ple eth skyrion s'el ro'anii skyrient, av wherin ahe eth li'era tierent tur cuelii'n itieren'jia huellient ot analtient . . ."

Meaning stung Laithen's eyes with welled tears. *'. . . speak for the plight of a people beset, and peril to the free wilds sealed under their oathbound protection in perpetuity . . .'* Awareness quivered, grazed as the fired catalyst sounded the prelude to a mounting salvo. Seized into suspension, the enhanced seconds stretched, while sight, touch and hearing spun into painful acuity.

The scrape of the crickets ceased in the grass. Dawn's pregnant hush on the region intensified, stilled like a pent breath. Then, like a snap in the pervasive calm, the horn call of a dedicate officer wailed. Voices yammered in electrified discovery from the far slope of the rise.

The poised target at risk of attack never wavered. Rooted as though under enthrallment herself, Laithen watched a crown prince's enabled attunement to the realm call Athera's electromagnetic properties into flower: with no other artifice but naked voice, and nary a Crown Jewel to bind the connection.

". . . amalind ahe eth thiere s'Kadierach, laeren da dasil'iel s'ielten diereng roth, rissay lin'dass al eth ayient avar'n paraient . . ."

'. . . appeal to the spirit of Kadierach, graced by permission of his living brother, rouse the echo of ancient memory's full glory . . .' Under bold summons, the flux purled and rang, an entrained peal of resonance that belled through Laithen's talent awareness. The raw elements answered. Breeze teased from no natural source combed through the braided constructs near at hand, and the others twined elsewhere in the free-wilds grasses.

The esoteric flood quickened the fourth lane in response. Laithen shuddered, hurled into spontaneous joy that thrilled every nerve to sweet ecstasy. For a belated instant, she envied Tarens's sensible refuge in excess drink. Then the cascade thrumming through flesh and bone exceeded the threshold of subtle awareness. The rising swell snared all living consciousness swept haplessly up in the cataract.

Arithon's seamless phrasing flowed onwards, the staked lightning rod before the storm front.

More horn calls answered the first cry of alarm. The hysterical summons to arms clamoured from every direction, with the citrine flush of on-coming sunrise fast dissolving the cover of darkness.

Laithen's helplessness mounted to agony, at no safe remove where she stood behind Davien's unperturbed shoulder. Arithon's silhouette on the hilltop exposed him. Yet his planted form was not static. Faint as the glint of flung water, the building nexus flicked a glimmer through the argent embroidery on his draped cloak. He clasped the sword, steadfast, orchestrating the torrent as the flux tide climbed towards peak. The phrase of his closure claimed the hushed register above Mankind's frenzied commotion.

"... *kia av dacelios eth amlient ahe lithmierent eth Paravia'n am'era!*"

Comprehension wrung Laithen weak at the knees. '... *lift and restore the harmonic register to preserve the Paravian presence!*'

An enemy crossbolt whined overhead, air parted like a muffled scream. The missile sliced a miniscule rip of dissonance, engineered for the precise moment the flux tide rushed into full crest. Narrow miss or grazed strike, the first salvo opened the breach for the concerted sally to follow. Laithen braced for the slaughter, pulse pounding, her outcry overset as the shattering blast of the arcane release blazed across the surrounding terrain. The channelled explosion wakened the lane surge in force, and unreeled heightened skeins of moulten-silver energy like transcendent lacework through the worldly landscape. The concatenation seared into unbearable brilliance as the starspells laid into Alithiel's black blade ignited like vengeance unleashed.

The erupted flare deluged Arithon's person. As the airborne flux poured through his grounded sword, the chord that Named the winter stars joined the raised shimmer of confluence with a hammering blast to unravel the senses.

Laithen swayed, overwhelmed. Unmoored, cast adrift by the pervasive chord of refined vibration, she had no measure to grapple the impact inflicted on the True Sect townsmen. The percussive peal of the elements ignited the sheet of gold light that whirled upended reason to rarefied ecstasy. Then a second horn call blared through the tumult, nothing like the tinny warble of a human officer's bugle. This deep, sustained note swelled to earth-shaking might, a wave of rolling reverberation overlaid amid dazzling illumination. Nothing prepared the frailty of mortal flesh. No concept encompassed the grandeur of the dragon-spine horns wielded by the centaur guardians of old.

Laithen's knees buckled. A split second's glimpse through the burgeoning blaze showed an antlered form twice the height of a man, crowned in jewels and scalding light. She never felt Davien's embrace bear her through the collapse of her flooded awareness.

Spiralled downwards into the well of unconsciousness, she lost grip on her clay faculties and wept.

A Sorcerer's words chased her meteoric descent into velvet oblivion. "Brave lady, you'll thank me tomorrow."

Groundswell

As the explosive surge from a crown prince's appeal to Rathain's dormant powers subsides into a dull orange sunrise, and the silvery shimmer of excited flux flickers and fades from the Plain of Araithe, the after-shock drops three Koriani on lane watch unconscious, and collateral earthquakes rattle the Mathorn Pass, stressing the mortared masonry at Etarra . . .

Roused to the feverish sweats of raw blacklash under Davien's astringent care, Laithen's complaint that due warning might have allowed her the oblivious refuge of the brandy flask earns the Sorcerer's galling rebuke, "You cannot follow your liege where he's bound, and as rough consolation, you have certainly validated the endowment of your traditional lineage . . ."

Midday, in the shattered encampments of the Light's summer muster, while delirious recruits and veteran dedicates suffer seizures and deranged senses, and their talent diviners languish in raving insanity, a rampaging scourge of overcharged fiends breaches the arrays of tin banewards left uselessly stripped . . .

IV. Tinder and Spark

Messenger pigeons sped news of the widespread upset in Rathain's free wilds. Word of the etheric quake stirred concern through the priest-governor's seat at Etarra, compounded by the unsettled accounts brought in with caravans from Tal's Crossing. Fearful whispers described an eldritch horn call that shocked sober men from their senses. Eyewitnesses spoke of Paravian haunts glimpsed in shadow alongside the trade-road. Truthful citations, or scaremongering embellishments, the disturbance sparked more than conjecture. Dispatches from the Light's summer muster languished, overdue from the outlying encampments westward on the Plain of Araithe.

On the fair morning Etarra's garrison pursued the True Sect's directive to investigate, the urgency of their northbound patrol smeared plumed dust in the sweltering heat. Their double-file column bypassed without notice two mismatched riders headed through the foothills. Travelling light, the pair joined the congested commerce jammed chock-a-block in effusive complaint for the mandated onus of questioning.

The clamour by then fumed amid the clogged air, stalled industry tinted sepia in silhouette, while argumentative carters' oaths clashed with the wilted dedicates conducting the tiresome inquiry. The two horsemen slipped through the milling confusion, as overlooked as the breath drawn ahead of on-coming disaster.

A feathered hat broad as a platter overshadowed the slender man's face. Not inclined to blend in, his attire was ostentatious, the impression of excess wealth reinforced by the conspicuous shine of blood horse-flesh. Chin high to the stalwart beside him, just as exquisitely mounted, his broad-shouldered companion sported a livid, scarred nose and an eye patch.

Every unhurried stride, Tarens wished himself elsewhere, discomfited by flagrant trappings too colourful for the toiling traffic upslope.

Routine horsemen would dress for rough country as messengers, or serve in arms as protection for the ox-drawn freight rolled on rumbling wheels. Bundled charcoal and lumber, or seal oil in barrels, salt fish and baled wool, raw hides and cut hay trundled in the slat wagons that moved resupply for the field troops. Pampered luxury favoured the southside approach, where more exotic cargo off seagoing galleys brought spices and silks, the peacock bolts of Morvain brocade, and netted citrus from Sanshevas. Wealth come to Etarra by the Mathorn Road flaunted banners and outriders, with the factors' road masters in their lacquered wagons shaded under hooped canvas.

Here, a one-eyed veteran and his pedigree charge without a liveried entourage perked interest. Curiosity measured their minimal saddlebags, fastened with gilded buckles.

Skewered by the wide-lashed stare that dissected unease as if thought was transparent, Tarens winced when his liege chose to comment. "Is your stomach weak? Don't forget I encouraged your return to Ithamon in Davien's company."

Hot retort rose too fast to the bait. "Your taste for subterfuge in plain sight is mayhem ripe for a suicide."

"Incompetent idiots earn contempt, not suspicion." Head turned, Arithon sideswiped his companion's forehead with the ridiculous feather.

His fretful mount sidled, champing the bit as the scrum of congestion caused by quake fissures crammed forward-bound progress up short. The outside track had collapsed into rubble where Mankind's bricked-up shoring expanded the access for carriages. The inside track's mighty blocks and spanned arches held firm, stabilized since antiquity by the harmonic affinity practised by centaur artisans.

Sweating under his eye patch, Tarens raked a jaundiced glare over the restive column of stalled summer transport, his countrybred origins at home with the bawling oxen and fragrant manure. Nostalgia chafed at raw odds, after months of wilderness isolation. The unnatural burden of his heightened faculties forced him to cruel acknowledgement: normalcy was forfeit wherever he went. Condemned to the scaffold by the True Sect Canon, he weathered the loss of his innocent honesty. But not the wrench into disjointed conflict, as Arithon's abrasive reticence tangled with the imposed instincts from Earl Jieret's heritage.

The tasked purpose that led to this pass challenged sense. Tarens grappled the pith of those perils headlong, rooted by a mind-set moulded and forged under bloodshed befallen in Jieret's time. Etarra's first campaign against Shadow had been gutted to a standstill by massacre in Tal Quorin's ravine. Three centuries since, the embittered aftermath refortified the walled town above. Blunt ramparts of granite loomed overhead, their stolid strength unintimidated by the upheaval fore-promised by the Crown Prince of Rathain.

Foreboding seemed absent, despite the subliminal clamour of etheric wrongness. Puffed cloud drifted shadows across the taupe slopes and rock outcrops, where the road coiled in looped descent into haze on the sweltering plain.

Tarens nursed taut nerves and stressed horseflesh, fenced by the grind of spoked wheels, while crawling progress halted again to the plink of pickaxes and the scrape of the conscript labourers' shovels. The choked, two-way traffic traded off forward passage by turns, pleated into the switchbacks beneath the outer gate.

Unrest livened the farm gossip meantime: of freak lightning and cloudbursts brewed up out of nowhere, or squalls that blackened the sky without rain, and white-out fogbanks blanketing midday. The unsettled tremors that rattled the mountain lent weight to such bizarre signs and portents, until one inquisitive ox driver questioned the finicky horsemen's reluctance to mingle. "Came from upcountry, didn't the pair of you?"

Tarens scratched his scarred nose, while the languid creature beside him aimed a supercilious glare from the shade of his hat brim.

"Well?" Thwarted curiosity bore in. "Some folks claim there's been unrighteous doings afoot."

"My nephew's with the Light's couriers," called a matron, downhill at the reins of her drowsy mule team. "He's days overdue. Come down from Tal's Crossing, did you see what's upset the messenger's relay?"

"How the Dark would I know?" Tarens flipped off a gesture to avert evil. "D'you see me attached to a Sunwheel blazon?"

The bravo beside him stared down his nose, scorn packaged in lofty accents, "Yon's my hireling bodyguard, discharged for injury from the ranks of the blessed last year."

Yet rebuff only whetted the bystanders' attention. "Pardon, but your armsman's not blind in both eyes. Nor you, despite the sponge-headed arrogance swelling that dandyish hat."

Sweating, Tarens twitched his plastered collar from his sunburned nape, forced by his employer's superior silence to spin lies and embroider on the deflection. "Didn't see past the refuge sucked neat from my flask. Rotgut dinged my skull like a bell and wrung my tripes inside out for three days. Hurled enough puke in the ditch not to guzzle that poison again."

An aproned brewer upslope brayed with laughter. "If your spirits came from an apothecary, you've survived the raunchiest hangover of your born life."

"Who knew?" Tarens grumbled. "The swindler hawked the swill as a rub that did squat for my aching scars."

When his shamefaced confession failed to divert the badgering woman's interrogation, the languid dandy puffed his ostrich plume off his tickled cheek. "Boorish hussy. Ignore her."

Insulted motherhood shrilled, "Light spike your filthy tongue in the afterlife! Were I your dam, I'd welt your pansy behind with my mule switch!"

Outraged aristocracy spurred the elegant horse, curbed up short by Tarens's yank on the bridle. "Blithering idiot! Don't bash into a heck-ler's fight."

The hat swivelled, indignant. "Wallow into a scrum? Wouldn't soil my hands!"

"Mincing gomerel!" another bystander yelled. "Picking on a skirt?"

The goaded horse tussled against Tarens's sensible strength.

"The matron just wanted news from the west," interjected a reasonable onlooker. "Why not let your milksop patron ease her concern for a kinsman's safety?"

The hat brim tilted. Sunlight sliced the overbred chin underneath, before pouty lips parted, flashing white teeth. "Should I waste my breath?"

"Too lowbrow, are we?" The brosy chap from the brick kilns cracked a smirk, while his grinning mate atop the stacked cargo puckered, took aim, and spat.

The gobbet splashed the cockerel's cordovan boot.

Roared laughter carried. More heads swivelled, across the switched-back turns. Tarens wished himself buried and dead as his splattered comrade yelped in plaintive pique, "Lout raised in the sump of a hog's wallow! You'll pay to replace what you've sullied."

"Will I?" The craftsman's surge to pulp pampered flesh captured the onlookers' sympathy.

Tarens forestalled the brawler by seizing his insolent charge by the collar. "Act out again like gold-plated royalty, I'll toss your runt carcass over the brink."

The hat's extravagant cockade twitched sidewards. "Unhand me!" Peevish contempt gathered volume. "I'll take down that guttersnipe scum without your crass interference!"

Tarens rolled his long-suffering blue eye. "Of course."

Sarcastic applause erupted from the idlers.

"Laddie!" the mason's driver crowed, grinning. "D'ye fancy a wager? That dagger o' yours with the flashy pearl handle, staked on an arm wrestle, or double its worth for a throw in the dirt?"

Another provocateur tossed a pebble that stung the dandy's mount on the haunch. Bucking like a tossed hinge, the hot-blooded animal careened off the thoroughfare and plunged downhill amid a ploughed slide of clumped furze and clattering rocks.

"Light bless my salvation!" swore Tarens. "The sumph's belike to break his fool neck before I collect my earned pay." He reined off in pursuit, engulfed in the ochre billow of dust, just as the flagman's signal restored right of way.

Upward-bound teamsters yipped and cracked their whips. The stalled column shuddered and rolled. Tarens's shouts drowned in the bass grind of wheels, while the hat with its fluttering plume sallied downslope with the runaway horse. Debauched onto the next switchback, the uncontrolled scramble of hooves and bent hocks pistoned into the orderly plod of a freight hauler's caravan. Clubbed sidewards, a sun-broiled carter in no mood for antics flicked his goad. The lash clipped the scatterbrained horse on the muzzle. An equine shy that evaded both hands on the reins dislodged the hat, which kited away on the breeze.

The horse lost its wits. Nostrils flared scarlet, eyes rolling white, it reared and tossed its flapped rider like a hurled chicken from his expensive saddle.

"First fall to the nag!" howled the mason, folded with mirth.

Lordly epithets echoed in salvoes between the rock-cliffs as the injured bravo stamped to his feet. Fist clapped to his sword, he drew the blade only halfway, fouled by his hopping effort to unhook his knee from the twisted scabbard.

"Split me!" yelped the mason. "The fancy pants daisy's primed for a duel!"

"Duel!" Incensed fury shrilled upwards and swivelled the helmeted heads of the gatehouse sentries.

Threat from their enforcement of civil decorum drove Tarens to hurtle his scrambling mount down the grade. A vault from astride tackled his bristled employer from behind and pinned his snarling fury into a bear hug.

The fop howled still when the trio of gate guards arrived, primed to bash skulls, including Tarens's, despite his contribution of muscled restraint. "Duelling is a criminal offence in Etarra."

Tarens grunted, staggered by the maniacal fight clamped in check. "Cuff the runt as you please. Let him cool his tantrum behind bars. When the magistrate's bench delivers his sentence, I'll pay the fine and collect him."

"Well enough." The officer's clipped nod moved his men to seize custody.

Their gauntleted grasp galvanized indignation. "Louts! I'm cited for duelling? That's rich! Choke me, before I'd cross blades with a hireling."

The prosaic sergeant tipped back his peaked helm. "Hold the nuisance still, can you?" Eyes crinkled by macabre enjoyment, he dealt a brisk tap on the prisoner's nape. The scofflaw sagged. Amid restored silence, the strong arms of authority hauled their limp trophy away.

Tarens watched, the expression under his eye patch chipped flint as the gate's shadow swallowed his feckless master. The staged ploy proceeded according to plan, aside from the whack that delivered his liege to the gaol unconscious. Since a thumped skull did not call for a nurse-maid, Tarens shouldered the practical bother of chasing down the strayed horse. Throughout, the bystanders yelled good-natured advice and ribald cracks in commiseration. Invited for beer in ebullient company at the Red Cockerel, Tarens laughed and re-joined the uphill creep of traffic through the late morning.

Anvilhead squalls gathered when he dragged the jibbing, riderless mare into the cavernous gloom of Etarra's outer gateway. Arched overhead, vaulted Elssine granite cast back deafening echoes, the clatter of hooves undershot by the rumble of iron-rimmed wheels. Froth white in the gloom, he trailed the bent hat plume, the crumpled booty crammed atop the bald head of the kilnsman.

Disgorged into the racketing jam of the bailey wedged between the doubled wall, Tarens breasted the press to place his inquiry on criminal process at the gatehouse.

The garrison's laconic officer directed him to the magistrate's hall. "Ask for the recording secretary in charge. He arranges the docket for petty infractions."

Tarens firmed his grip on the horses, re-joined the stream of afternoon commerce, and sized up Etarra's defences. Moss-splotched brick had long since replaced the original stockade and tollbooth erected when the rogue traders incited by Baris sen Etarra first occupied the pass in opportunistic defiance. Today, the entrenched trade town built in his name elbowed for dominance in the confined space between squared-off crenels, pegged by blunt turrets with verdigris cupolas. Marksmen with arbalests manned their outward-facing posts, the notched roofs of the four-storied guild ministries and their streamered flags silhouetted beyond.

Then the mouldering gate arch sundered the overhead view. Ahead, sunk in shade, turreted mansions with tiled roofs lined the street, echoes slapping off corniced balconies, and striated facades garnished with gingerbread like layered pastry. The walled compounds with arrow loops were not relics of the infamous days when mercantile enterprise seized the pass: riots and feuding rivalries bloodied a history of tumultuous dissent. Here, the factions behind the Third-Age revolt that destroyed the crown seat at Ithamon still nourished deep-set, restive roots. Etarra crowed in its brash, squatter's roost, flaunting old charter law and intransigent wealth with unchecked bravado. Its vigorous populace blustered and teemed with a scofflaw tenacity unique to the setting.

Tarens wended his way through the crowded streets, immersed in the fragrance of patchouli and pine, birch smoke and sweets from the confectioners'. The matrons and children, artisans and shop boys rubbed elbows with seamstresses, weavers, and lackeys. Replete cats lounged outside the butcher's for scraps. Street brats and beggars pestered, whining for handouts. Gaudy life from all backgrounds walked unwary of Shadow let in through the gates.

The single man cognizant ached to behold the lively, oblivious faces.

Tarens suffered the rift in his background as never before, jostled as he crossed the bustling markets, pulverized by the din of the stonecutters' mallets and the huckstering chants of the hawkers. The hubbub surrounding him bared the harsh reckoning; the shoes of his origins no longer fit. Sensitized instincts tuned to the free wilds cringed in recoil from the eddies of misaligned lane force. Where the crofter in him might have lingered, entranced, the prickle of inbound storm flux gadded him onwards to stable the horses.

Tarens paid the livery's fee without bargaining. Coin slipped to a garrulous street urchin directed him to the magistrate's hall. Past the grandiose entry, enveloped by the blurred voices re-echoed off marble floors and a vaulted ceiling supported by pillars, he threaded the gamut of stuffy clerks to reach the appropriate desk.

"Name of the offender under arrest?" The bothered scribe peered through his smudged spectacles, and thumbed pages in a voluminous ledger. "Ah. Here's your plaintiff." He sighed with ennui. "Infraction for inciting a duel, compounded by insolence, flouting authority, and five charges attested by citizen witnesses for belligerence. Your fellow's slated to be heard on the seven day. Present yourself for the assize that morning and wait on the associates' bench until the docketed case is called up for arraignment." A splay finger stabbed into the notated entry. "Appended here, stamped and sealed, the plea has been formally entered. '*Guilty, with prejudice*' means judicial debate is suspended, the pending sentence to be determined."

The clerk's mournful stare lingered.

When Tarens chose not to pillage his purse for the Etarran custom of bribery, the clerk slammed the book shut. "Any questions?"

"None," Tarens lied. Since Arithon had imprisoned himself by design, he would languish to fulfil his purpose.

The hall's lancet windows dimmed under the on-coming storm. Outside, chased by the pattered droplets forerunning the cloudburst, Tarens located the Red Cockerel Inn, where he spent without stint and secured private lodging. Led upstairs to the room, he flipped the lamp boy a silver for candles and heated water hauled from the kitchen. Then he washed and changed in the stuffy gloom as the fastened casements rattled under the squall.

Descended to the tap-room, Tarens encountered several fellow travellers packed into the boisterous company on the benches, a hat of distinctive flamboyance among them. He ploughed through the press: tradesmen in stained aprons, seamstresses, a rambunctious pack of caravan guards, one of whom dealt him a brotherly backslap in commiseration. Shy of notoriety and grateful the noise forestalled conversation, Tarens ducked the bawdy, muscular women who kneaded the bakers' dough. Eased ahead, snagging buttons, he passed liveried coach lackeys, then the dour, smocked secretaries planted like blight amid their peacock factors. He side-stepped the table of scruffy academy students, hot conversation bent close over scraped plates and used beer steins. Around him, the hot grease of cooked meat, summer sweat, and the stale aroma of stewed onions congested the air like a blanket.

The hat welcomed him in, waved above the mason's florid grin. "Does your master want his filched property back?"

Tarens eyed the squashed felt, almost speared by the bedraggled, extravagant plume. "Spare me the torment!" Laughing, he sat with the carters, if only for the coarse jokes and camaraderie to divert Earl Jieret's cantankerous instincts.

Dusk brought the off-duty guardsmen, also flagged by the infamous hat. Their hobnailed bulk jostled the cardsharps, and disrupted a cutthroat contest at darts. Outspoken contempt for the day's pedigree fool gained momentum when the gaoler's turnkey swept in, and hilarity oiled the on-going account of the milksop's incarceration.

"Posed a bother, did he, the insufferable gnat."

"Didn't thole our polite tradition of tribute," the gaoler admitted with relish. "Oh, and he bites. Our fellow who drew the lucky straw to confiscate those prettified rings got a mangled thumb during collection. Our second-place winner had a knee slammed into his nose when he bent to claim the gold buttons off them prissy breeks."

"The best entertainment came afterwards," enthused a smiling friend, paused to hook a tankard off the barmaid's tray. "Our sergeant stepped up to coldcock the problem. That pipsqueak lordling moves like a snake. Knocked our bloke out with a kick to the jaw, before we ganged on and pulped him."

Tarens choked behind the drumstick in his fist.

A neighbour's jab to his chest cleared his airway. "Worried you'll lose your employment? A touch bruised, aye, but your wee blighter's undamaged. Nobody'd risk the docked pay. Loss of criminal fines to rough handling riles the brass something wicked."

"Besides," the gaoler shoved in, "the pawn of yon fancyman's rapier squared the healer's fee to salve his injuries."

"Didn't quiet his ruckus over the jakes!" a jocular colleague interjected. "His squeaky nibs threatened a riot over the waste pail not cleaned to his liking."

Tarens cradled his head in his hands. A sympathizer saw his beer stein refilled, while the rollicking laughter exploded around him.

"So we dragged in the slop boy. Sent the crusted old pail to be polished with our respectful instructions. Back it came, brim-full o' the prisoner's dinner broth." The tap-room crowd pummelled the trestles, clutching seized ribs, to the turnkey's shouted finale. "Don't muck with the cook, let me say, when your sorry lot's under his oversight."

"Ha!" wheezed another. "The devil's work lands on the night watchmen now. Those brutes nip the uppity into righteous shape. Else a troublesome pest turns up peacefully drowned in his jurden come the next morning."

Beer flowed freely. Embraced by the jocular crowd until dusk, Tarens weathered the tidal surge of the flux, rattled by the belated discovery that Jieret's inherited instincts had been heightened by the sanctioned crown prince's late act of conjury. The coarse company played havoc with his sensitized nerves after nightfall, no relief gained by the polite withdrawal to seek his room. Long after the hour the packed tap-room emptied, he lay wakeful, threshed to prickles by the whiplashed eddies of Etarra's warped flux. The ingenious subterfuge forced his acknowledgement: not even the True Sect diviners connected the swanking dandy caged under lock and key as the responsible culprit.

Day began brisk and early at the Red Cockerel. The great shuttered casements were latched back before dawn, and the streetside door wedged open to air. Trestles scrubbed down yestereve quickly filled to the clomp of the hireling escorts and drivers in for a bite ahead of their outbound caravans. Tarens braved the clamour, enticed by a hot breakfast after months of jerked trail fare. Unease distanced by baked pastry, stewed pears, and boiled eggs with steamed sausage, he listened as change flowed around him. The first patrons moved on, replaced by yawning grooms and sleepy apprentices, then the genteel drawl of the trade factors, red-cheeked seamstresses, and the hatters, the dyers, and the robed scribes, blotted like sober shade amid the gaudy livery of the coach boys.

Midmorning admitted the transient customers funnelled by inbound trade. "We're always busy," chattered the lissome girl who collected the emptied plates. Leaned in with a swayed hip, she asked if the strapping man wanted a tankard.

Tarens paid for his leisurely meal, tweaked to a smile by the flirtatious wink the wench gave his dismissal. How his sister Kerelie would have seized brusque advantage, released from the stuffy propriety imposed upon women in Erdane.

Yet the town ambiance of harnessed horses and soap, candle wax, and wet flagstone trampled by bustling humanity did not bring him complacency. The vociferous arrivals burst in as he stood up to leave shocked a grue through his inherited instincts.

Their shrill agitation also stalled conversation and turned heads the breadth of the Cockerel's tap-room.

"Bring gin!" The rattled shout floated over the din. "Straight up from the bottle! We've a powerful need to shake off the creeping taint of the uncanny."

Barraged by questions, the front rank yelled loudest. "West road to Anglefen's polluted with haunts!"

A seasoned traveller in rugged dress vented through the stunned clamour. "Light dispel the rank powers of Darkness, our mule train came in chased by *iyats*!"

A watch bell tolled the alarm from outside. The uproar flushed through Etarra's streets would not rest: the cascade spun by the crown prince's formal appeal on the wild fells had arrived to unravel established obstructions.

Tarens snagged a fresh beer stein and reclaimed his seat. Compelled to lie quiet until the day of the magistrate's scheduled hearing, he must watch the disruptive wave as it crashed. The Red Cockerel's forerunners were but the first to be routed by the etheric upheaval. Soon to follow, the troops from the summer muster would pour through the north gates in flight from the outlying territory.

Tarens blew the foamed head off his drink, resigned to contain his chafed nerves and endure the phenomenon.

Few townborn owned the faculties to recognize the chaotic recoil imposed by misaligned flux current. Anxiety spread like contagion, then burgeoned to panic. Brawling fights irrupted as stray energy sprites abandoned the squall lines to feed on the excess charge of human emotion.

By noon, the tuned bells to repulse *iyats* gave tongue. When nightfall brought sightings of witch light and haunts, their tolling, dissonant treble rove through the bass note of the sacred horn winded from the temple. The racket strained tempers throughout day and night, while incessant reverberation punished cast bronze beyond tolerance, and cracked metal thumped, deadened under the strike of lead clappers.

Crying infants and yammering dogs frayed equanimity until disrupted commerce scrambled to join the first trickle of exodus. The True Sect's ordained priests prayed themselves hoarse, then dispatched white-robed acolytes to preach in the square. Distribution of shadow-banes and blessed tokens failed to salve the beset. Nor did the candle-lit vigils convened at the site where the avatar's Light had unmasked the Spinner of Darkness and routed the Fellowship's coronation.

Rumours eroded the Word of the Canon, hysterical whispers that Etarra's prosperity had been cursed in retribution for the demise of evil on Daenfal's scaffold. Primal fear fanned the flames of more ritual burnings, decreed by the hallowed examiner.

Tarens's kind heart overruled better sense. He prowled the back streets, primed with coin for the hungry. Mobbed by ragged waifs, he encountered the destitute industry too poor to bundle their belongings and move. The pinched faces where the frenetic clack the looms underscored the desperation of back-alley shoptalk, and hardworking folk bewailed the ebb of good fortune, helpless before the inexplicable change that had upended their respectable lives.

Nights, Tarens tossed, restless, his humble origins at odds with the role his turned fate had bequeathed him. Fitful sleep brought on nightmares, perhaps from trammelled flux or bleed-through from Jieret's past bond with Prince Arithon. Or he started awake, to the ringing echo of song haunting him from the darkness. An etched prickle of flesh suggested arcane patterns traced onto the bed-rock floor of Etarra's dungeon. But without initiate knowledge, he could not discern the prompt of true talent from hallucination.

Dawn found him wrung limp. Amid summer's close heat, he persisted, while the raised flux tides peaked at the solstice full moon, and the ebb at last slackened the grip of disruptive resonance.

When the hour arrived for the magistrate's hearing to sentence Arithon's case, no one connected a fop's picadillo with the subliminal crackle of tension. Scoured by the atmosphere of malaise, Tarens withstood the pompous tedium of the arraignment. He paid the extortionate fine for release, then waited in silence while the wretch he delivered was fetched and relieved of his shackles.

Filthy and battered, shoved downwind of the guards, the Crown Prince of Rathain stumbled to freedom through the prisoner's gate and crashed to his knees at Tarens's feet. Daylight exposed the rifled clothes, shorn of buttons and laces, and the rank hair crocheted in tangles matted with straw.

"A bit worse for wear, I'm afraid," the rueful reprobate husked.

With fury that implied he preferred to be strangling civets bare-handed, Tarens exclaimed, "They abused you for singing?" Innate kindness triumphed. He extended a hand and hoisted his reeking, rag-bundled liege upright onto shaky feet.

Wicked irony glinted the muddy brown that masked Arithon's natural eye colour. "No." Gimped steps and a wince clipped his genuine laughter. "There are easier methods of provocation than gadding a turnkey's louts to retaliation."

Tarens muffled his nose, trailed by offended glares as he steered his reeking companion past the faithful thronging the priests' kiosk in the main square. Shade lapped the verges beneath the ornate facades of the trade factors' mansions. Guild banners flapped, and sun gleamed on the lozenge cartouches of the established house blazons. Amid the whiffles of flushed pigeons, and two chattering girls turned to stare, the awkward quiet of poisoned camaraderie settled like mist in broad daylight.

Arithon expelled a hitched breath, and said carefully, "You have not been party to acts of foul practice."

"Haven't I?" The brittle retort sliced the cries of the hand-cart hawker selling grilled meat spiced with cloves, two for six coppers.

Amid the customers' recoil from the dungeon stench on his person, Arithon stopped. Amused by the offended flurry of scented handker-chiefs, he regarded Tarens's suppressed disapproval. "Etarra is built upon bed-rock, an obdurate blockage wedged bang overtop of the fifth lane's main channel. Any subtle working would twist awry in this place, and worse, draw ruinous notice."

Anger spurred Tarens's thoughtless retort. "Do I need to know?"

"For the peace of mind you require to raise children? Yes." Forbearant as he had not been since Daenfal, Arithon confided, "Arcane ritual is binding by threes. For Etarra, my prior score stood at deuce. One hostile count short of full measure, I had to bleed inside these walls once again to set an unbreakable seal on the record."

The singing would come later, Tarens surmised, careful to strike before peerless empathy could soften the knot in his gut. "Don't pretend you needed a week to arrange that!"

The wolfish creature beside him could exasperate with a glance. "Credit Etarran zeal for excess."

Tarens bristled, stung by more than the trickle of sweat from his eye patch. "I gather your unsavoury purpose is met?"

Arithon's equanimity was not seamless as he also side-stepped direct enquiry. "Maybe, if your long face says we haven't the coin left over for a private bath?"

Tarens ground out a laugh. "In your state? A respectable inn wouldn't open their door. What's left in your purse will cover my lodging, and share a sparse meal between the two of us."

Arithon shouldered ahead, his smile insouciant. "Then I'll settle for a dunk in the public horse trough. And don't waste your annoyance. We have honest coin left to spare because I've paid off my infractions, and everything else, with what Davien refers to as dragon's gold."

Tarens's entrenched frown raised a chuckle of hilarity that stole Arithon's breath before he elaborated, "Honest coffers stay filled unless the accounts have been padded. For an overcharge past the value of services rendered, the excess payment will dwindle to compensate. I suggest we visit that horse trough, retrieve your belongings, and ride out before the magistrate's clerks tally this morning's collection."

Jieret's experienced recall knew every hidden fold in the vales where the trade route ran northeast through Perlorn towards Werpoint. Turning off the road before the narrows at Valleygap, Arithon's lead wound through the trackless hard scrabble and stunt fir that peppered the rock spur adjoined to the Skyshiels. Their path seemed innocuous. Until the rough qualm that shook Tarens's nerves came upon him out of nowhere.

He drew rein, a wary glance cast down their back trail. Naught seemed amiss. Gusts tossed the scrub grass overgrowing the scar of an ancient avalanche. Whirled dust palled a darkened sky threatening rain. His alert survey found nothing suspicious. No glint of metal betrayed human presence. No movement, beyond the hawks tossed like rags on the high thermals. Naught explained the sourceless unease that scraped chills over his endowed instincts.

Facing forward again, Tarens noticed Arithon's tensioned reins. "How long have you recognized something untoward?"

Rinsed decently clean, and reclad in the trail garments from his saddle pack, Arithon had stripped his disguised colouring along with the affected dandy. "You've noticed we've picked up a follower."

Tarens swore, squared off for a fight.

Arithon bypassed the interrogation and hailed an unseen party farther downslope. "You might step out where Tarens can see you."

A bush rustled, scarcely a stone's throw away. Stealthy enough to startle clanwise talent, a lithe figure emerged, dark-haired, brown-eyed, clothed in drab motley, and barefoot. A sheepish grin split a deeply tanned oval face, the cocksure expression of braggadocio beardless and sprinkled with sienna freckles.

"The devil!" Tarens glared. "That's Jackal." The slinking, disreputable street waif had tagged him like a lamprey throughout his stay in Etarra. "You scamp," he scolded. "My gift of a meal didn't seal an adoption. What do you imagine you're doing here?"

"That's no boy," Arithon corrected. The hard twist to his mouth tendered warning. "Nor a stray child, had you known his race lacks facial hair at maturity." Head tipped in respect, he appended a guttural phrase of apology, then switched tongue to accommodate Tarens. "I gather you act by the will of your elders?"

"Protection," snapped the prickly person, incensed.

Arithon's level temper showed strain. "How many, and for what threat of endangerment?"

His query stirred tremors of surrounding movement. On silent feet, robed and hooded, eight more dartmen slipped from cover on what until now had seemed a barren slope. To a man, their bleak gaze and raised weapons fixed on Tarens.

"Don't move!" Arithon's gesture forestalled the surge of the blond crofter's startled response. Outflanked too swiftly to deflect confrontation, Arithon said carefully, "I have no cause to doubt my companion."

The warrior appointed as speaker advanced. "The big man's will is not in alignment with yours."

Arithon looped his reins on his horse's neck with demonstrative calm. "I don't believe our difference of opinion amounts to a lethal betrayal."

The peppery fellow spat in contempt. "We are the hands serving Mother Dark's truth. A knife in your back while you sleep, maybe not. But a message sent on the sly will befoul your course one bad moment when you are not watchful."

The frosty regard Arithon fastened on Tarens was inflected by exasperation. "I lack the authority to relieve the gravity of your situation. Take care how you answer. Biedar perception extends to your thoughts. They'll know by the nuanced conflict of detail if your words fail to match your intentions. Insincerity will see you condemned. Their aim is deadly, and the envenomed tips on their darts have no antidote."

Tarens flushed. "Do they know in full what you plan for Etarra?"

"Everything. Yes." Arithon inclined his head. "I have nothing to hide from Mother Dark's purview."

If that whiplash reprimand aimed to provoke, Tarens succumbed, a fortnight's measure of strangled emotion abruptly too fierce for restraint. "I'm expected to stomach a broadscale slaughter? I realize you grapple stakes that require an entire town razed to rubble! What you propose to level are homes. Livelihoods, upholding decent folk and their blameless families! I have walked their streets while you laid your furtive spellcraft in the deep! Nowhere, come the day, did I sign up for a red-handed massacre!"

Arithon firmed his demeanour, inwardly plagued by who knew what personal demons. Then he said, expressionless, his phrasing addressed to the rapacious dartmen. "We have a misapprehension, easily cleared, since at no point have my arrangements involved the potential murder of innocents."

Tarens cried out, "But Etarra—!"

Arithon's scathing impatience arrested the disastrous objection. "Etarra must be levelled to restore the resonant flux current, yes. Except to reach that end, nobody dies, unless by willed choice as a suicide! My aim, start to finish, has been arranged to empty the town in advance. The unsettled populace shall have ample time to pack up and relocate."

Nothing broke the standoff but the wind and the crickets. The dartmen stood motionless, waiting. Then, his impervious gaze distanced, Arithon finished his statement in metaphor. "The lone khetienn stalks, cloaked under impeccable silence. Her stealth impenetrable as the nadir of night, she strikes but once to annihilate."

The Biedar spokesman held out through a weighted pause. Seconds seemed to stretch in eerie suspension until he placed his steadfast enquiry.

"Whom do you serve with your heart? Whose loyalty binds your body? What cause rules your mind?" Deliberate phrasing directed towards both men in equal measure, the tribesman waited for answer. Eyes keen as knapped obsidian, and the relentless aim of his fellows tracked their blond target, unremitting.

On the slope, under sunlight, Arithon shut his eyes. *At what point does the strong heart falter? When, tested to breaking, should steadfast character shy off and preserve itself from self-destruction?*

Tarens wrestled with similar thoughts, pierced by fear beyond his experience.

Then Arithon pressed the question of loyalty, his emptied features fragile as spun glass. "Are you with me, or set against?"

Death rode Tarens's answer, by the dartmen's swift judgement. Or perhaps Arithon's query had challenged the stalkers in turn.

For today, the cruel finality of decision yet retained the marginal grace of ambiguity.

Through the flicker of hesitation, the grey-robed tribesmen melted from sight. Nothing moved. Not a thorn leaf trembled. In their uncanny wake, the barren surrounds of the Mathorn slopes shimmered under noon heat, the rock outcrops and scrub fir emptied as though the encounter had never occurred.

And of the Biedar warning delivered, its searing questions left dangling, Rathain's crown prince and his townborn liegeman measured their individuality with separate meanings: interpretations both directly personal, and diametrically different.

Darkling Dam

Five days after Sanpashir's escort of dartmen vanished into the brush, Arithon hobbled the horses in a remote mountain vale fifteen leagues farther east. Predawn murk masked the peaks when he cached the stripped saddles and provisions beneath a weathered marker engraved with ancient characters crusted with lichen.

Intent upon covert business afoot, he allowed, "You need not come along."

Unswerving, Tarens flanked his lead without comment.

At high altitude, chill lingered even in summer. Fog cloaked the peaks well past daybreak. Far removed from remembrance of sun-scalded sweat at the scythe, Tarens skulked on the ridge overlooking the site of Arithon's interest. Emerged like sketched charcoal through the thinned overcast, a steep ravine sliced the gap where the eastern spur of the Skyshiels joined the greater, spined range that buttressed the shelf of the Eltair Bay coastline from north to south. Past cataclysm had riddled both walls of the chasm beyond their position with cavernous holes.

Tarens shuddered, disturbed by more than cool weather. "Looks like the warped ruins of some behemoth's nightmare."

"In fact, yes. The caves were scoured under those mountains to harry trapped prey into monstrous lairs in the deep." Arithon regarded the cheese-holed rock face, stretched flat with his chin on crossed forearms. "The wyrms' mazes were tunnelled by spawn of a dragon haunt's vengeful dreaming. First-Age legend described them as eyeless, scaled, with acid saliva and vicious teeth. Their mindless slaughter afflicted Paravians long before Mankind's settlement."

Yet the daunting vista that loomed in the present required no lurid embellishment to sap Tarens's equilibrium. Through breezeless, damp air and filmed mist, the gargantuan defacement erected by humanity engineered the Third-Age edifice that throttled the springs at the Severnir's source. The brute mass of the dam baulking the river's egress through Daon Ramon spanned the sheer cliffs above the empty, gouged seam of the riverbed. The mighty, stepped structure was compacted from the debris of titanic rockfalls, sheared off the undermined scarp by tinkering industry, then stabilized by braced tiers of rubble, shored up with patchworked repairs. The concave accretion of stone abutments and zigzagged retaining walls had been doggedly strengthened over the centuries, the towering tonnage of mortared block and rammed earth a high bowshot from base to crest.

"That structure's not righteous," Tarens murmured, shaken.

The scent of fresh water saturated the alpine air. Freak acoustics carried the slap of brisk waves at the rim of the far side's drowned vale, a furlong away. Logic faltered to measure the baulked force held in check, or fathom the frigid, stilled reservoir, incomprehensibly deep, that reversed the Severnir's outflow over a spillway, to thrash in white-water spume down the Skyshiel divide to the east.

Arithon said nothing, immersed in his grim survey, while scudded cloud wept a silver-grey mizzle that veiled the skeined snow laddered over the summits. Riffled draughts off the glaciers made their covert reconnaissance unpleasant, while the early hour sent labourers in shivering gangs to plug the seep of sprung leaks. Abusive directions from their overseers rove through the ragged plinking of pickaxe and mallet.

"Poor wretches." Tarens assessed the virid marsh at the base of the dam, cratered with soupy, black mud and pools coated green with stagnation. "Besides ague and pustules from biting insects, they must drop like flies from swamp fever and squits."

Yet Arithon's preoccupied focus quartered the defile beneath, where the last, shredding fogbank revealed a dull flicker of movement. Mounted lancers in paired columns patrolled a raised causeway through the marshy apron below.

"Rot the dastardly claptrap of merchants!" Tarens swore upon a plumed breath. "Someone's sent word ahead of us." His irritable tally tagged additional horsemen, threading the undulant trail from the service shacks nested in a notched ledge on dry ground. "Seems like we're expected given the double dozen sent as reinforcements."

"Maybe." Arithon swiped back the stuck hair dripping through his narrowed lashes. "Could be a routine relief, detailed to nab deserters. Lazy sods, too. Huddled out of the wind with their weapons at rest? They resent the short lot for their watch in the open."

Extended review of the anthill activity disclosed drab wooden sheds placed at intervals along the banked dam. Under the occupants' comfortable oversight, the exposed workers were roped into coffles. "Convict labour?" The fine point scarcely mattered by Tarens's assessment. "Slovenly gaolers or not, those riders' lances are sharp. Worse for us, not to mention the luckless dupes in coercion who can't help being stuck in your way."

Arithon sniped back without turning his head. "Serve your complaint to the Fellowship Sorcerers. Or better, pack up your squeamish concern and leave with my blessing."

Tarens succumbed to a visceral shiver. "That's posturing nonsense! Were I not saddled with Jieret's stiff conscience, I'd stay for the heart I recall in the beggar who spared me from a True Sect examiner."

"Did you truly know me in either persona?" The barb struck with a savagery aimed to curdle warm blood in the vein. "Don't bank on the surety."

No civilized retort existed to blunt a sally aimed as a weapon. Tarens dug in for the thankless duration. "You'll have come with a plan." Yet the creature reprieved from Daenfal's executioner could nip camaraderie quick as frost in the bud. Nor had Arithon defrayed the possibility the mounted squad pacing the perimeter below might have been tipped off ahead of their business.

"I'll be snatching a nap." The Prince of Rathain scuttled back from the brink, sought a sheltered cranny, and hunkered down, uncommunicative.

Tarens dealt him the contrary disregard once granted to an older brother intent to pick fights. He frittered away the dull hours that followed keeping a pointless watch, while the rain sank its insipid ache to the bone, and unnerved dismay fed the vicious suspicion that Arithon was not sleeping. Tarens fumed on tenterhooks, while the guardsmen dawdled the afternoon through on their assigned picket. Nothing stirred but the sweat of forced industry until the dreary day faded to dusk.

Arithon uncurled from his tucked repose without urgency. Flattened against the ridge beside Tarens, he regarded the fresh torchlight kindled in the redoubt, then eyed the stirred movement of the clustered lancers. "Watch change," he surmised. His keen gaze flicked sidewards. "You didn't rest earlier? Best snatch a catnap while you still can. No sleep tonight, if you're with me."

"You couldn't have mentioned that detail before?" More than ever, the untoward secrecy chafed. The scowl stitched over Tarens's tight headache lidded venomous thoughts of Sanpashir's dartmen, perhaps lurking invisible at his back.

"The Biedar escort left us two days ago," Arithon stated, unperturbed to have directly addressed his companion's stifled anxiety.

"The fact you've dismissed their uncanny protection is a lunatic's reassurance!" Out of sorts, Tarens fixed his disquiet upon the enemy guard, whose numbers alone stacked the radical list of bad odds. "What are we doing? Precisely."

"Sapping," said Arithon, inexplicably forthcoming. "Or at least, laying the groundwork for a swift demolition of that hideous dam."

Tarens girded himself for the thankless attempt to champion the plight of the shackled convicts.

But Arithon's sardonic glance gutted speech. "The prisoners are locked in the stockade overnight. Watch. They'll be marched into the keep before dark."

In fact the dispirited gangs on the dam broke away, their misery shuffled under shouted orders into a ragged column. The downtrodden shamble tugged heartstrings enough to raise the perverse question: such a pitiful lot might be better off spared from another day of manacled purgatory. The affliction of Arithon's on-going influence wrenched the precepts of human decency, until Tarens felt like the blindfolded dupe asked to piss on a flagstaff in a lightning storm. At wit's end, he nestled his forehead on crossed arms and drowsed, until a tap on his shoulder rousted him to move out.

The loose scree on the open slope past the ridge grew scant vegetation beyond clumps of weed and scoured lichen. Tarens skulked after Arithon's heels, unsettled by the inadequate cover. Yet no alarm sounded. Cloud sooted the wan, silver of the crescent moon. The hollow where daytime's mounted lancers had loitered retained only fragrant manure. Across the pocked scrim of hoofprints, Arithon picked a furtive course through a sucking bog, where forced seep from the reservoir pooled in noisome pockets. To the right, the mossed crevice of the Severnir gorge funnelled the south wind into their faces. Above, the bedded embrasures of the Darkling Dam curtained a pallid sky filmed by a grainy layer of precipitate fog.

In the dank cotton gloom, with meticulous care, Arithon mapped the trickling fissures riddled through Mankind's edifice by the Severnir's trammelled headwaters. Close-up inspection revealed where moist mortar had pressure-cracked under assault by frost, and the loosened remnants of quakes let the relentless greenery pry fecund roots into stolid retention walls. Switched-back rain gullies guttered the storm-fed overflow, until the fearful, held gallons bound into check by human determination burdened the hushed air in pregnant suspension.

"A cheerless place," Tarens whispered, slogging ankle deep through slurried muck that made his slow progress a ready target. Taut nerves goaded on his perverse urge to argue.

"Not to douse the excitement of your righteous rage, but take warning. Your bitterness might not be genuine. You haven't sensed the gadfly provocation?" Prompt met by a glower, Arithon added, "The flux here is jammed to a fare-thee-well. A bait feast to fester a rife plague of *iyats*, hell primed for a rampant catastrophe."

Tarens lashed out, regardless. "Has the day ever come when you don't have pat answers?"

He had overstepped: the glaring, poisonous exception had birthed the unconscionable horror let in innocent blood at Daenfal.

Yet Arithon peered upwards, groped for a handhold, and climbed. "Mind yourself. Keep pushing that angle, and you'll find the ascent something more than treacherously slick."

Tarens grunted, more concerned that loosened debris might unseat a rolled boulder and crush him. He absorbed the back-lash from his aimed dart and pushed into the upward course without flinching.

The scrambling effort disgorged them on the tiered ledges carved by the maintenance labourers. Ominous bulges buckled the retention walls, skirted by narrowed footpaths where displaced masonry was rammed stable by the angular jut of winged buttresses. Tarens looked up, appalled to misgiving. The enormous dam overhead rimmed the zenith, more than ever a folly of pebbles and toothpicks cobbled together with spittle.

"Are you here for the thrill of the view?" prodded Arithon.

Boots mired in clotted mud, every step, Tarens grumbled, "Reeks worse than a hog byre." An improbable bliss in pig-ignorant hindsight; he found little use to cry sentiment under straits well beyond turning back. He grappled upwards, ducked a dislodged rock, and secured his next hold. "Given the instability of this heap, no surprise we're not plagued by a night guard."

From his agile ascent a few yards above, Arithon warned, "Don't bet your life on that. We don't know the charges that sentenced those convicts, or what criminal background merits the precaution of stationed lancers."

Yet the work site they traversed under darkness and sounded, each level, with rapacious thoroughness seemed untenanted, the shored logs and stacked revetments without movement. Ditched hand-carts and dropped tools gleamed under the glimmer of stars, pricked through fuzzed haloes of mist. Or so Tarens believed, while their arduous climb splashed through boggy nooks and scaled gullies choked with debris from old slides. Arithon's focused search scoured every niche, his paused assays enacted for who knew what obscure purpose. Tarens lagged, yawning into the wee hours. He scrambled through a patched-over crevice, and carelessly tripped on a bundle of rags that yelped an indignant protest.

Startlement nearly pitched him head over heels, until rational thought overcame rushed adrenaline. Evidently the face kicked in the teeth by his stumble was not attached to a corpse. Contrite, Tarens dropped to his knees, sympathy roused by the plight of a convict slipped through authority's oversight.

"Arithon!" he exclaimed. "We can't leave this sorry fellow to suffer." No person of conscience would abandon a malnourished labourer, maybe ill, perhaps hurt, to the further cruelty of oppression.

His liege reappeared, arrived soundless and swift as a wraith from behind.

"Help me get the wretch up," Tarens begged, a forearm thrust under one prostrate shoulder, and his balance centred to lift.

But instead of assistance, Arithon pounced like a predator. A slammed blow to the nape knocked the dazed victim cold senseless.

"Merciful Light, have your lost your wits?" Tarens cried, stung to horrified rage.

"Quiet!" Arithon dropped the stone just used as a bludgeon. When his hurried inspection encountered no blood, he added, remorseless, "Stop fussing. Your forsaken rescue is going to wake up."

Numbed by distress, not finished with anger, Tarens attacked. "Why'd you wallop a helpless fugitive? The poor fellow presented no threat. For your senseless abuse, I'm not leaving him."

"I expected as much." Arithon stood, quick to smother the tinder for argument. "Lay off spouting virtue and heft your stunned prize. Fast!" A scalded gesture towards the stockade showed torches swarming like fireflies at the fortified gateway. "We have to bolt. Now! Or we won't live to see daylight."

Tarens shouldered his inert charge with a grunt, staggering under the unwieldy weight. Cooled logic caught up with inflamed emotion. The body he hefted was far too well fed. Not likely the malnourished frame of a convict. "You think he's a decoy?" Chin tucked, yet unable to quench his high temper, he bent to necessity and soldiered ahead.

"Run!" Arithon exhorted. "And, yes. Only worse. I counted the convicts. This morning's round number left intact, under guard. Whoever you're packing has just flagged the garrison. A gifted talent, beyond any doubt. Also female, had you troubled to notice her build. You've bagged one of the temple's talent diviners who picked up our trail, most likely tipped off by prescient faculties. I've suspected for days. That's why I bashed her unconscious, and also the reason we need her alive."

Glib assessment aside, the alarmed clamour raised at the keep killed debate. A streamed column of lights disgorged from the stockade gate, the night quiet shattered by iron-shod hooves clattering over the causeway. Then the wail of a lance captain's horn gave tongue with the watchtower's alarm bells. The mounted sally snaked down the terraced switchbacks at speed, backed as swiftly by a rousted company of reinforcements.

Tarens firmed his regretful grip on the nuisance slung over his shoulders. The initial climb had been nightmare itself, jagged masonry set in rotten mortar and switchbacks potholed with sinks to turn ankles. The steep pitch edged by the sheer drop gave him cold sweats, pressured over slick footing by hostile pursuit and saddled with the peril of a True Sect diviner. He resisted the murderous reach for his dirk and plunged skidding in reckless strides downwards. Ironic, that the born crofter in Tarens would never be sanguine with entrusting his safety to the bona fide powers of Darkness.

That uneasy thought fled as a turned stone threw his balance. He staggered into a sickening lurch, his burden like a sack of wet sand on his neck as he skated beyond recovery.

A snap sheared the air. Inhaled breath stabbed a lance of dire cold through his chest, and his sliding boot sole stuck at the brink, seized fast in snap-frozen ground. The sharp wrench stopped momentum and fetched him to his knees.

Arithon snagged his elbow and yanked him back upright to a gasped apology. "Wrought shadow. I'm sorry." The subsequent warning bristled like ice. "Mind the *iyats*. They're a mite stressed by the upset of my leisurely schedule."

"You plan to wreck the dam early?" Tarens wrenched his trapped boot. Wedged leather tore free, the virulent sting to his toes an unpleasant assurance he suffered no frostbite.

"Keep moving," urged Arithon. "Fiends in their natural state are not biddable. Enjoy the thrill and praise glory, their antics don't thrive in the cold." Amid slithered descent of another retaining wall, he choked off a snatched snort of laughter. "Chaos to the enemy."

The mounted charge from the garrison recoiled into contorted agitation across the ravine. Irate epithets, lagged by distance, swelled into blurred echoes, punched by the staccato rattle of pebbles skittered off the overhead cliff face. The loose missiles bounced helter-skelter downslope, pinged and cracked in malicious ricochets that pelted horse-flesh and spanged off steel helms. Tarens grinned as the lancers' column unravelled. Then something hurtled, whistling, past his exposed ear. A mud divot splattered into his calf, almost collapsing his leg. No random mishap, but the capricious mischief an *iyat* unleashed to harry nerves and gorge on the frustration of man and beast.

Except a fall from this height would be fatal. Goaded to hurry, Tarens crunched over paned ice. He eased over a redoubt, chest pressed to the wall, and scraped down the far side. That instant, the flaccid lump on his shoulders woke, struggling. He jounced the disgruntled creature hard in the gut and called softly, "Ware prisoner!"

Arithon shed his jerkin. He shredded the sleeve off his shirt. The twist of cloth wedged between snarling teeth gagged the captive's groggy outcry, while Tarens gritted a banged jaw and pitched in to contain his misfortunate catch. Female in fact, though built slim as a boy, she delivered a wildcat tussle. He locked her flailing limbs, pinned her struggle under his knee, while Arithon trussed her at hands and feet, then noosed her neck in ruthless subjugation.

That brutal handling raised second thoughts. "Liege, you're certain we've bagged an enemy talent?"

Arithon yanked the final knot tight. "You didn't sense anyone's spying presence in the flux? Well, neither did I. Not until I was all but on top of her. Backed by my crown attunement to earth, that means a talisman crafted by Koriathain or the finesse of a temple initiate."

The same wicked alliance had seen Arithon trapped in duress at Daenfal. Tarens swore. He hoisted his mewling parcel, braced to resume the precarious plunge downwards.

"No. This way." Arithon bent their course sidewards across the rutted tier towards the sentry's outlook on the far wall of the ravine. "Make for secure ground as fast as we can."

Tarens ran, shocked by the burn of drawn breath in his lungs: not from overexertion, but the deadly wave of dire cold risen off the infirm ground that shuddered ominously under him.

"Shadow!" he gasped, horrified. "You've flash-frozen the seeps." The explosive expansion shoved, stone on stone, and heaved the buttressed tiers out of alignment. Something let go with a rumble, above. Cubic yards of held water trembled, a brute surge poised to burst the rim of the dam and unbridle the riptide of rampant catastrophe. Blunt mass and gravity would weaken the rest, a debacle of high-pressure erosion poised to smash everything in its path.

"I can't stop what's started," Arithon confessed, charged to madcap exhilaration. "The guards on the causeway likely will survive. We're away clean, provided we're quick and if they don't carry crossbows."

The rumble beneath Tarens's pumped strides gained dimension. Then a glottal gush splattered through the earthworks from behind. Spouted mud geysered. Water jetted like a scream through the gap, built to the throaty roar by the falls toppled over the brink as the dam breached. Boulders caromed downwards. Impact slammed into wracked fragments of wall. Debris shuddered and gave, propelled by an avalanche of slumped slurry, then frothed foam, and a grinding millrace of sheared granite slabs.

Tarens sprinted. Panic lent him unnatural strength. The strapped witch on his back might as well have been thistledown. Cramped and winded, he reached the northside vantage post, his shredded boot slapped onto safe ground. Arithon arrived with a light buffet behind, just as all the furies of hell poured through the defile behind. Like Sithaer unleashed, the might of a river eight centuries suppressed burst restraint with a howl of doom that thudded tremors through deep Skyshiel bed-rock.

Human voice drowned under the gargantuan roar. Spray showered the cliffs to the summits above, while dirty, taupe gallons rampaged and leaped, tier to tier, caving bastions and bashing retaining walls to bristled clots of inundated rubble. Across the weltered expanse of the chasm, the armed riders were bucked from their saddles by terrorized mounts. Tarens stared, agape, shivering from excess adrenaline. Past question, the violence of the Severnir's course cut off the armed chase at their heels.

Yet the squirming bundle of malignant rage burdened them with the live peril slung over his back. Prepared to unload the rank bother forthwith, he was stopped by Arithon's insistent grip.

"I'm sorry. We're not shut of your hostage just yet." Shouted into the roar of the falls, the unpleasant instruction went further. "Like it or not, stand her upright. Not for cruel caprice, but necessity."

Tarens glared. No escape was possible, except by scaling the overhead ridge. The parallel trek down the adjacent valley implied a rugged, roundabout hike to retrieve their sequestered mounts. "Curse your weasel's invention. We're taking the long way out!"

Arithon nodded. "The best choice, unless you'd rather swim."

The unfettered waters crashed downwards with scouring violence, limiting their option to the steep ravine which, thanks to Shadow, was slicked by white rime and sheeted in glare ice. The sheer walls above instead offered a harrowing ascent upon unstable rock fraught with peril. Tarens shouted through the battering din. "Well, I can't make the vertical climb while shepherding hostile weight hell-bent upon murder."

"There's a crude stair of sorts used for routine inspections." Arithon drew his knife with intent to release the prisoner's lashed ankles.

"Leave her free, she'll dog our trail like fell fury," Tarens grumbled. Provided they surmounted the circuitous egress before dawn made them quick pickings for archers, they had only two horses between them.

"Yes." Arithon's teeth flashed, whether smile or grimace became moot amid thundering darkness. "Your lissome prize, bless her duty-bound faith, will be coming along."

Tarens stiffened in flabbergasted dismay. "You've thwarted the hornet's reprise out of Darkling. Dare I mention the dastardly thorn in the rose?"

"Oh, the bit where yon talent broadcasts our location?" The bright smile, without mirth, evinced wicked irony.

A careful breath steadied Tarens, barely shy of a swung fist. The path shook underfoot. Before the avalanche thrash of white foam, they were puny as ants, doused in chill spray on a precipice. Though nothing alive would be crossing a river course hurled into rampaging spate, the cantankerous, spooked garrison penned up at Etarra faced no such lethal constraint.

Tarens measured his language. A man condemned by Canon Law might rather drown than cuddle the threat of a True Sect diviner. "We'll have murder itself tracking us within days." Armed dedicates numbering in the thousands would be lured in full cry after prey that had slipped the punitive sword of the Light's executioner. "I'm not risking the scaffold for your sake again."

"Then we'd better scat." This time Arithon laughed. "Good thing I'm practised at leading the chase. As the advance payment for my evil game, we'll be drawing the might of the whole northern muster behind us."

"On purpose!" gasped Tarens, punched to wit's end.

"Always." Arithon sliced off the makeshift rag bonds, then gadded the priesthood's prized hound to her feet. After that, the vertical pitch of the climb robbed the will to pursue conversation.

Chain Reaction

Dace Morley snapped awake in his servant's cot, hair prickled erect at his nape. The quickened rasp of his liege's breath shouted warning: some disturbance more troublesome than a bad dream had invaded his master's sleep. Past the flimsy privacy screen, the lit candle's buffeted flicker tossed distorted shadows across the chamber's sparse furnishings. Then Lysaer rolled over with a fraught cry. His tumultuous thrust to arise tore the sheets and snuffed the flame to a sullen spark. Darkness swallowed the momentous surge as he kicked free of his entangled bedclothes.

Peril charged a pent atmosphere at the brink of murderous violence. Burning threat lit the warded spirit-mark branded on Dace's chest. No refuge at hand offered safety. The barred door thwarted the sensible urge to take flight. Yet to cower before the impending calamity would strand Lysaer at the crux.

Dace armoured his nerves and eased from his blankets.

Movement proved a mistake. Light shattered the darkness. The actinic levin-bolt flare dazzled sight and slammed the tower's stone walls into after-shock reverberations. Stunned deaf and scared witless, Dace wrestled the horror. Desh-thiere's curse had broken through, rending the delicate core of protection he had nurtured on tenterhooks throughout three years of bleak isolation.

Somewhere, for who knew what insane purpose, Arithon s'Ffalenn forsook prudent restraint. One wanton act of spun shadow snared Lysaer's cursed awareness and woke fury that torched every tenuous grip that remained on his self-control. At a stroke, the precarious ruse that stalemated the True Sect's bid for a resurgent expansion smashed the pretext of convalescent infirmity. Lysaer's charade of frailty was undone. Worse, the dedicate guards on duty below risked their lives if they stirred their righteous backsides to investigate.

Dace acted first. He shoved off the cot, barked his wrist on the nightstand, and groped for the striker. Breeze fanned his cheek. A half pace away, his liege paced the closed room with a gadded tiger's ferocity. Savaged by Desh-thiere's geas, Lysaer would kill without conscience.

Dace socketed a fresh candle by touch. The scrape of the flint seized Lysaer in his tracks. Deadly as a hazed viper, he spun towards the spark that ignited the wick.

The flare of caught flame recorded the inhuman gleam of his single, undamaged, blue eye. Frost paled in comparison. Terror hurled Dace prostrate. Lysaer's attack lashed over his head to a tortured shriek of stress-heated air. Rolled sidewards to snuff out his smouldering nightshirt, Dace slammed against the washbasin's marble pedestal. Cornered, he ditched the suicidal attempt to unsocket the towel bar as a bludgeon. Marked as prey, he had a split second before the next strike brought his incineration.

"My liege!" Exhortation cracked through a dry throat, Dace shouted, "Lysaer, look at me."

Inane words, perhaps useless. But speech invoked the wrought glamour engaged through Kharadmon's past instruction. The blood-bound beguilement forged against extreme need energized Dace's aura. The resonant connection steadied instability and seeded a ripple of calm like oil spread on troubled water. "Lysaer," Dace repeated. "I'm here at your side. Whatever comes, my loyalty is unshaken."

Hung at the cusp of primal assault, the paused moment stretched, measured by trip-hammered pulse and sawed breath. Dace held his ground. Nakedly helpless, choked by the reek of burned hair and scorched linen, he crushed down dismay and ignored certain ruin. Alarmed shouts drifted up from the courtyard below. Outside intervention would loose a disaster, with the volatile creature poised for violence already beyond all containment.

Lysaer's crazed regard swerved from skewered fixation on his pinned target. Dace froze, while the drum of his heart shook his chest.

Yet catastrophe stayed suspended, as moment flowed into moment without retaliation. By a tenuous thread, the crafted enhancement on the valet's person divided the geas-bent impulse to kill the obstructive servant out of hand.

"Hold on, liege," Dace encouraged, flushed to clammy sweat.

A shudder harrowed his master's locked frame from seized fists to the sag of his atrophied shoulder. His battle for balanced recovery trembled at the precipitous verge. Reason stayed absent. Blond hair raked into tangles by tormented fingers quivered to the grisly tic that spasmed his damaged eye socket. Lysaer looked, every inch, the demented berserker.

Dace lost his wind, gut-wrenched. "You are not lost. This I promise."

"I see no salvation," Lysaer grated, shattered. "Not while my nemesis lives."

"That doesn't mean no recourse exists." Dace quashed his frightened urge to look away. "Hope is not futile. Nor is ruin a certainty, though in your present straits you cannot see a solution."

Lysaer unclenched his fists and shuttered his wracked face. "You haven't been party to my inner turmoil, or the onslaught of cunning, warped blandishments stalking my every thought."

"Look at me, liege!" Dace dared the impertinence and stirred without leave. "I serve in good faith."

In that wretched instant of candid uncertainty, the ringer's tug from the rope loft creaked the pulley mounted one level below. The great bell in the tower swung on its yoke, the lead clapper struck, and a half-ton of cast bronze sounded the alarm with a clang that eviscerated the quiet. Lysaer broke his fraught pose. Dace saw his tentative progress undone. Past sorry tears, deafened by the tumult, he cursed the vigilant dedicates assigned the night watch belowstairs. Permitted another second, or ten, he would never know whether Lysaer's lapsed self-control might have been coaxed back to sanity.

The glamour's fragile attraction dissolved, shredded outright by Desh-thiere's design. Lysaer spun towards the doorway, stilled as a starved predator, his unnaturally triggered awareness hypersensitive to movement. The racketing bell masked the rushed footsteps inbound from the stairwell until the key turned the lock. The iron-strapped portal wrenched open to the sulphurous glare of lit torches. Four Sunwheel sentries in chain mail escorted a disgruntled sortie of temple dignitaries. Dace watched the superior outrage crammed at the threshold sort itself out, the discomposed worthy insistent on precedence pink as a peony in the gold-rayed regalia of a grand high priest.

Met, nose to nose, by his avatar, he jammed to a stop, dewlapped jowls wedged in the starched braid of his collar. The temple's gaunt chancellor blinked, just behind, whiskers still gouged into tufts from his pillow. Awake and inquisitive in his napped nightshirt, the cadaverous ferret appointed as the True Sect's premier examiner stalked behind.

Dace silently damned the parade of Canon authority to the red spear of Dharkaron's Redress. His station hobbled his last, outside chance to salvage the unfolding calamity. Worse, the invasion delivered enough righteous brass to wring fullest advantage from what seemed a full blown, Light-sent miracle.

Dace ached in dismay as Lysaer's majestic bearing destroyed the painstakingly kept semblance of weakness. Slurred speech abandoned, he took the crisp offensive and claimed his unquestioned command of the crisis. "Evil has risen! Darkness returns, and the Master of Shadow has emerged to sow havoc in eastern Rathain."

The True Sect priest gasped and sank to his knees in fatuous reverence. Over the battering din of the bell, he prayed, "By the Light everlasting! May our devout faith vanquish the scourge that defiles the innocent."

"On your feet! I've no time for platitudes!" Impatience augured through the examiner's questions, Lysaer cracked imperious orders to the dedicate guards at the doorway. "Silence the bells, straightaway." Next, he accosted the kneeling priest before the dumbstruck chancellor's awe reverted to calculation. "Since the temple precinct is wakened, I want every ranking official assembled. Half-clad or in nightshirts, they'll come as they are. I'll be down directly to address them." Snapped fingers dispatched Dace for basin and towels, while the avatar bent the beady-eyed examiner to his will. "Take down the names of any man who arrives late and those who fail to answer my summons. Put them to the question. Sympathizers with aspects of Darkness will burn. Turn the innocent laggards out in the street. I have no use for faint hearts and slackers."

The watch officer received Lysaer's grilling stare last. "Report! What uncanny practice has overset my lawful prosperity in northern Rathain?"

The accusation sheared through stricken quiet, the swing of the bell fallen still. The sergeant assailed in the breach groped for words, caught outfaced, while Dace placed a stool for his liege and applied his attention to soap suds and razor.

Only the High Priest braved the tableau of cowed inertia. "Be sure our divine lord will have the summary update from the temple's high council. Meantime, fetch his Blessed Lordship's state dress from the lower wardroom. While the Light's avatar is made presentable, assemble the parade guard for his escort forthwith."

Lysaer quashed the upstart arrangement, incredulous. "I gave no such command! Nor will I bestow the grace of my presence before my question is answered in full."

The checkreined priest flushed. "Due your Divine respect, the True Sect High Council should stand first witness to honour the sacred recovery of your hallowed person—"

Light slashed the air. The burst cracked across the stone floor, the bystanders hazed backwards by the flash-point blast of seared air. The insolent priest was hurled off his feet like a rag doll, his hair and scorched vestments smouldering, and both blinded eyes poached white as creamed milk.

Desh-thiere's curse pervaded an atmosphere galvanized to petrified fright. Sober panic at last rooted the standing party into paralysis. Nothing moved, no one spoke, while the scalded priest on the floor writhed in whimpering agony. Lysaer's icy stare flickered across the subservient entourage. Enthroned on his stool, he let Dace's deferent hand finish shaving, then blot his jaw dry with a towel toasted by the flare of his gift.

"Carry on, soldier." The regal dismissal jolted the stupefied silence and unlocked the stunned guardsman. "Fetch my state vestments as you've been tasked." Startled to be called forward by name, the two dedicate sentries who quailed past the entry were detailed to remove the stricken priest. "See him dispatched to a surgeon, then inform the captain on duty I want a veteran squad in full arms at my disposal." Last, to the intimidated examiner, "Deliver the news from Etarra unfiltered. From your lips, here and now, or I will tread over your ashes to question the messenger's scribes in the pigeon loft."

Spinelessly humbled, the scared talent talked fast: of haunts unleashed upon the summer muster, of earthquakes and lightning-struck fires, and a terrorized town populace driven to riot.

The relentless toll of troublesome news cranked Dace to a frantic anxiety that must not, at all costs, mar his bearing. He emptied the basin into the slop jar. Cleaned and stropped the razor with fragrant oil, then trimmed the candle lamp with the immaculate semblance of calm. He dared do no less. The coiled bundle of animosity under his care was a victim possessed, while Desh-thiere's directive alienated the innate pattern of his birth-born humanity.

Dace combed and trimmed the fair hair of exalted divinity as though he handled fragile, blown glass. Then he accepted the weighty, jewelled vestments brought forward, and clothed the Mistwraith's feral automaton from head to slippered feet in gold-embroidered white silk studded with diamonds. He fastened the fitted cuffs and high collar without fumbling, smoothed priceless brocade to sartorial perfection, his quaking dread and sick grief choked for a downfall past his helpless reach to avert.

Lysaer endured his valet's ministrations with magisterial indifference. When the faithful servant bowed and stepped back, he arose without smiling. His aggressive stride clipped past the trace of a limp, he marched towards the door, his prepotent ascendancy re-established in full for who knew what insatiable agenda subsumed by the Mistwraith's design.

Dace snatched his livery coat and trailed in attendance with recklessly loyal determination.

The incensed examiner bridled at the bold pretention. "Where by the Light do you think you're going?"

Dace tugged his forelock, pinned with no glib excuse.

"The Light's grace seems able enough to preside on his own merits!" The examiner puffed up his narrow chest to vent. "Mind your place and tidy this chamber before I have you turned off and whipped bloody for sacrilege!"

Lysaer's rebuke snapped across the tirade. "My personal valet's not yours to impugn." His brisk nod to Dace seemed addressed to a stranger. "The used linen is not your concern. Instead, pack for travel. My train will be on the road to the east before nightfall."

Dace understood which master to serve. He side-stepped the fuming examiner, ignored the soiled towels, and bypassed the ripped snarl of sheets on the bed. Yet beneath the deportment that arranged the trunks for the avatar's apparel, he seethed. Craven necessity demanded the charade that pandered to Lysaer's suborned interests. Dace embraced his meek role and began sorting garments. Skewered by the upstaged diviner's steamed glare, he selected the appropriate finery for a gentleman's impeccable wardrobe. Practice stifled his rebellious insolence: though Daliana, given a handful of darts, would have pinked the sanctimonious weasel in the breast of his pompous insignia.

The boring display of lowly servitude soon dismissed the onus of critical scrutiny. Unremarked, Dace wrapped the white doublets crusted with seed pearls. Pleated cuffs of silk lace and gilt braid remained flawlessly crisp under his delicate handling, while the wretched penury of his powerlessness lashed him invisibly raw.

Lysaer's headstrong intentions unfolded apace, his called escort arrived at the double. Their armoured bulk whisked the glitter of his divine person through the outside door, beyond benign oversight. No one's concerned sympathy helped the avatar negotiate the steep, spiral stair to ground level. No kindly hand from his browbeaten, worshipful officials would dare presume to steady his compromised balance.

Dace raged as though shackled, forced to maintain the lonely post of rear-guard. Ears ringing from the after-shock of the bells, he breathed the nauseous cloy of temple incense mingled with the lingering char of roasted flesh.

"Damn all to the Avenger's Black Spear!" The stickling pinch of his duty roped him down in strict isolation, while the juggernaut avalanche he could not stop caromed towards the shoals of disaster. Dace fretted, gnawed sick by his desperate uncertainty, while the distanced tumult beyond his tower eyrie mapped the meteoric course of events. Too quickly, the chorused meter of adoring plainchant became disrupted by fractious cheers, the glorious sight of the restored avatar fanned hotter by a speech that unleashed the roaring thunder of mass adulation. Lysaer's masterful gift of charisma excited the crowd into fervent commotion that boiled outwards from the public square.

He had snapped the True Sect's gilded leash holding him in duress. The enormity of his transcendent return fuelled an incandescent momentum, a thousand throats hailing him as the living proof of Divine Light's omnipotence. The electrified ardour of the faithful beat off the tower walls and rang from the spired domes of the cupolas, a manic frenzy crescendoed like gathering storm re-joined by the ecstatic clangour of the bells. Pummelled to a shattering headache, Dace slammed the lids on the clothes trunks. Forced idle, he paced in caged agony. The courtyard view from the casement lent him no vantage to parse the directive launched by Lysaer's peremptory bid for command.

The night hours waned, swelled by relentless noise, while the enforced privacy of seclusion granted the servant no surcease. Dawn came and went. At mid-morning, the racketing tumult subsided. Uninformative silence was harder to bear, till the multiplied tramp of inbound footsteps mounted the tower stair. Dace had the door open, the chamber behind restored to perfection. At last, his exhausted, strained hearing picked out the lagged inflection of Lysaer's overtired tread.

The man met by his bow at the threshold was ruled by Desh-thiere's curse no longer. And yet: the sharp eye of astute assessment revealed more than the stuffed martinet underneath the jewelled stiffness of costly attire. Royal bearing surmounted the test of endurance. The brisk consonants of Lysaer's autocratic dismissal packed off the fawning cling of his worshipful escort.

Dace was not fooled by that faultless comportment. The instant the massive door thudded shut, he sprang forward, prepared when the semblance of dignity shattered.

Lysaer stumbled. Caught by his valet's firm hand, he crumpled against the ready shoulder that braced his collapse. Harrowed features reflected the stark change at a glance: Arithon had ceased weaving Shadow. Provocation removed, intellectual clarity should have grappled the spectre of ruin in the self-poisoned sanity of the aftermath.

Except a deep-set tension still thrummed through the tender flesh steered into a chair by Dace's support. Lysaer sank into the seat, worn-out but not quite diminished in the dazzling splendour of divine appointments. "What have I done?" he ground out, his stripped note of horror underslung by a dissonant strain of contrary satisfaction.

"Freed us of these walls for a start," Dace allowed. Bent to salvage the dregs of initiative, he now strove to shore up what else might be spared from the buried threads stitched through his master's curse-tainted motivation: if anyone could.

"At what price?" Lysaer clamped his face behind tortured palms, to every appearance inconsolably gutted. "You may as well hear what the priests have withheld."

"That a freak surge of earthquakes is mauling Etarra?" Dace shrugged, bemused. "Or that an outbreak of sorcerous haunts has scuttled the Light's annual muster?"

"Both, more's the pity." Lysaer dropped nerveless hands, marring the silk swathed over his mangled socket. "You *knew*?"

Drilled by a blue eye whetted to accusation, Dace sighed. "I didn't say, because gossip overheard on the servants' stair isn't exactly reliable."

Nor could the damning, unmentioned developments alleviate today's welter of conflicted anguish. Unrest in Rathain had been gathering impetus, incendiary fuel for another campaign well before Arithon's ill-starred meddling reignited the hot spark of religious fervour. Dace regarded the first of the tragic casualties to be torched by the fires of consequence.

"I cannot countenance another massacre cloaked under the sham of false faith." Lysaer's voice split, distraught. "I'm not Mankind's born saviour! The ethical right to unchain human destiny from Fellowship compulsion deserves an honest rebellion to break the unnatural strictures of sorcery. Not the fake creed of a hidebound religion wont to stifle invention and tyrannize thought."

Scared witless, Dace set his teeth against comment. Though his liege's damning recrimination seemed just, the upright choice to baulk the might of the religion trod the unstable rim at the chasm of double-edged peril: for already the havoc of armed violence aimed to obliterate the Master of Shadow and condemn the free wilds' mysteries had been pressured irretrievably into motion. Honesty ruled the bittermost truth, however the murderous cleaver of fact came to slaughter the shining ideal. For Lysaer, the insidious threat to self-control remained yoked by the Mistwraith's curse. By the end, that warped drive stranded him with no honourable recourse but the craven's exit of suicide.

Cornered there, Lysaer's deepest motivation would not show through the facile acumen of the seasoned statesman.

Dace froze, stunned analysis strangled by his preoccupied failure of oversight: next to the basin, the honed razor beckoned, altogether too near to hand.

"No!" Attuned to his valet's distress, Lysaer rejected the morbid temptation, his agony harsh as ground glass. "I cannot shirk accountability for my weaknesses, or abdicate what remains of my responsible power."

"Then we will bear this," Dace promised, hollowed out by the dreadful trajectory of Kharadmon's prior, foresighted warning. "We accepted the difficult path would be harrowing. Nor are you alone. Together, we'll take each day as it comes. Ride the whirlwind however we can, and strive for the merciful chance to prevail."

Lysaer mastered his dignity. His offended glance surveyed his costly regalia, disgust primed for murder outraged by the peacock excess of bullion buttons and jewelled cloth. "For starters, let's beggar the treasury's war chest." Ingenuous self-deprecation blighted the sting of his irony.

"Canon hubris can't begin to imagine the extravagant retinue the faith's risen avatar will see fit to demand!"

"The bankers will rip themselves scabrously bald." Dace extended his arm and raised his liege for disrobing, empty-handed amid the battle to come beyond naked wit and lame humour. "How large a campaign did you wring from the treasury's purse?"

Lysaer choked. Upright and stiffened to wry resolve, he indulged in the irreverent refuge and quipped, "A divine writ to sweep conscripts from every village enrolled under Canon Law. Expect the burden of tithes and logistics to gripe hidebound digestion aplenty and muzzle the trade guilds for years."

Dace slipped off the glittering weight of the over-robe, appalled by the stoop to his liege's bad shoulder. While he cringed inside for the scale of the muster glossed over by painful, light words, s'Ilessid acuity doggedly parcelled the measures to meet the terrible challenge.

For the after-shock of surprise slipped away, second by second ceding the precious advantage wrested away from the True Sect's initiative.

"I'll need armour and weapons." Astute enough to usurp swift command of the Temple precinct's dedicate troops, Lysaer ran on apace. "Rid me of this obscene regalia. Then step outside and dun the Sunwheel guardsman nearest to my size for his kit."

"Very well, liege," Dace admonished, "Hold still." Before the dazzle of state diamonds dissolved under the blur of welled tears, he snatched the razor and slashed through the frogged fastenings and the diamond-tipped cord of laced points.

The captive spirit he served never flinched. The sly gleam of Lysaer's lofty indifference covertly applauded the vindictive score exacted for months of excoriating humiliation.

Yet the slick poise of the statesman never deceived the eyes of a friend. Dace ached for the fine-grained tremors raking the flesh underneath his impersonal touch. The venom of Desh-thiere's latent influence galled the entrenched canker of wounded regret, cruel price behind the stacked bargain that tilted the Fatemaster's scales towards the bloodbath of redress.

Servant and master, they were complicit in a dangerous bid to blunt the radical fury of another armed conflict. Dace nursed the venomous sting of fresh hatred. Whatever had prompted the s'Ffalenn bastard's unconscionable outbreak of Shadow, no motive justified Lysaer's torment in the silenced straits of defeat.

Conscience could but weep for the horrific consequence. The unravelling cascade to ruin began, with no certain guidance to ease the cold course, and no visible path towards a blameless redemption anywhere in existence.

Offshoots

As the white water flooding the Severnir gulch rampages down country towards Daenfal Lake, the stones of a riverbed parched lifeless for centuries tumble and sing with exuberance as pent-back energy erupts in release, and the etheric pulse rippling the web of the mysteries brightens the rapt awareness of Athera's Paravians . . .

While courier pigeons wing westward from Darkling with urgent news of the dam's demolition, Lirenda Prime's conniving exploitation targets the humiliated diviner seized captive by the Spinner of Darkness, just rescued spitting mad in the Skyshiel foothills, stripped to her pink skin and left destitute on the dry bank above the frothing spate . . .

Amid the unsettled precursor to war, Sethvir's concern tracks a Koriani messenger southbound from Highscarp, and among the news packeted for her anxious Prime is the archival record of a vault concealed in the sisterhouse cellar, forgotten for millennia and laid under seal by Athera's first Matriarch of the Order prior to her death at retirement in Third Age Year 450 . . .

V. Windup

Fresh upheaval pealed through the world's flux currents, the vectored inflection of myriad events braided into Athera's great lanes, a planetwide web of electromagnetics driven by the gyroscopic spin of her iron core. Elaira shielded herself from the clamour, strained discipline challenged as Althain Tower's fey attributes thrummed to the turbulence forerunning the momentum of change.

Few sites were as energetically volatile as Atainia's desolate ground. Bedded deep in the earth, a torrent of resonant confluence transected the free-wilds peninsula, an unruly channel sourced by Isaer's quickened mysteries, quenched at last in the restive grey brine off Tysan's north shoreline. Mankind shunned these windswept downs, where the gusts keened aloud and spectral echoes of past ages resurged like blown mist under daylight.

The cascade peaked to puissant clarity at the Paravian focus under the tower's foundation, fed by the fulcrum array sited southward at Isaer's Great Circle. Near autumnal equinox, under the waxing moon, the harmonic surge saturated perception, fired by the flare spun off by the Severnir's explosive release.

The impact frayed more than Elaira's peace. The barren vales teemed with the phosphor wisps of Paravians, slain in their stand at the Bittern Field as Ath's living gift for the drake spawns' redemption. Entangled with their translucent sorrow, the actinic stamp of a dragons' revolt reprised Ischarivoth's fiery death in the waste. For days, the shimmering echoes roiled the pulse of present-day transmission.

The flood ought to have drowned out everything else: yet Elaira's empathic connection to Arithon pierced like a needle through dross. She knew, as she breathed, his southbound course through Daon Ramon: the thrill of his laughter, when in flippant conspiracy with Tarens the True Sect diviner's stripped clothing was strapped to a rock and hurled into the river; then the arduous flight after daybreak, as yells of dismay from the disrobed victim launched a vicious pursuit across Daon Ramon.

At dusk, stumbling on foot with exhausted horses on lead reins, her beloved rejected her contact. The rueful amusement once shared in rapport met an impermeable wall. If Arithon knew his subversive activity had sprung Lysaer's relapse into Desh-thiere's cursed directive, her urgent forewarning went unheard. Near the end of his secretive flight to Ithamon, he might not expect the renewed campaign from the west on the march to upset his delicate strategy.

Perhaps she muttered her anguish aloud.

A dark hand closed over her furious grip on the pestle, mindlessly pounding a styptic to pulverized dust.

"Peace," said Ciladis, his arrival soundless despite the indoor dress exchanged for stout boots and leathers. "Overwork won't settle a burdened mind. The mizzle has lifted outside. We have time before sunset for us to gather the late-season bloom on the cailcallow."

The practical foray to replenish the supply for a commonplace decongestant checked her brooding with velvet-gloved tact.

"The ungrateful harridan tenders her apology." Elaira tipped the powder into a jar, then fetched her satchel and knives, the steel and the knapped flint for those plants with virtues adverse to cold iron. "Will I need my mantle?"

"I've taken the liberty." Ciladis proffered her heaviest cloak, his own bundled and strapped at his shoulder. The oiled wool on an overnight field trip would double as open-air bedding. "We'll also harvest a rare lichen found at the Attin's source before snowfall."

"You think I've been cooped up for too long." Elaira twisted her braid into a knot, head aslant to hide her embarrassment. "By your grace, I've accepted a master's instruction. Reason enough not to fluff like a hen and bolt into the fox's den with Davien."

"You? Display the white feathers of cowardice?" The lilt to Ciladis's chuckle was musical. "Never, brave lady. Not in my company or under the anguish of Arithon's absence."

"Like the well-mangled bolster, the down stuffing inside stays obscured by the trappings." Elaira accepted the impersonal touch that prodded her towards the doorway.

"Your concern is not frivolous." Though Ciladis stayed reticent concerning the threshold about to be crossed at Ithamon, Sethvir's earth-sense perceived the penumbral shade of probability writ large by Arithon's affairs: when thoughtful diversion would fail, and the empathic cry of Elaira's true heart would drive her to seize the initiative. Until then, the Seven did what they could to alleviate her conflicted anguish.

The dim stairwell ahead spiralled downwards, sliced by unshuttered arrow slits with crudely knapped stone that reflected the haste of the original centaur masons. Worn, shallow risers descended, the draughty air thickened with candle soot, dust, and deep secrets, freshened by the outdoor pungency of witch hazel and evergreen as they reached the base landing.

The unworldly splendour enshrined in the Chamber of Renown ever brightened the dullest of spirits. Today, the statues of the Riathan Paravians shimmered, limned by a nimbus of translucent indigo Elaira had never seen. Her amazement prompted Ciladis to qualify in his velvet-grained baritone. "The quickening's real. A reawakening caused by the Severnir's release, and the first sign of Daon Ramon's restoration."

Wonder hallowed body and soul. Hushed by awe, Elaira plunged into the semblance of dream, the distraught fuss of mortality diminished by gleaming gold and the sparkle of jewelled caparisons. Majesty spoke in the horned grandeur of centaurs, with the ethereal Riathan captured in marble, their unearthly beauty ringed by the joyous grace of diminutive sunchildren, dancing. Three races original to Athera wove the tapestry threaded through the deep pulse of the mysteries.

The bronze doors beyond were rolled open, filtered daylight seeped in from the doubled gates of the sally port. Breeze slapped through, brisk with north-country chill, the metallic tang of the windlass chain a grounding influence on bemused senses. Fear pierced through elusive hope like a knifepoint, that Arithon's effort in Rathain could fail, and the vanished glory of Ath's gift to the world might dwindle and fade.

Reproved by Ciladis's mild glance, Elaira nipped back her anxiety. One forgot at one's peril the peerless perception of a Fellowship Sorcerer.

Yet the presence that flanked her step into the embrace of late afternoon was human. Ahead, the north downs of Atainia unrolled, sun-drenched and mottled in cloud shadow, the crags tinted pale blue with distance.

Elaira trod the warmed earth and let the obdurate strength of the tower's warded walls and Shehane Althain's rapt, guarding presence fall away. Yet delight and distraction were not consolation.

She blurted. "I know you mean well. But, please, stop trying to shelter me!"

Ciladis paused, dark features fierce with surprise. "Sweet lady, don't rush to the reckoning." Did compassion have the words to admit that the upcoming trial would test her more severely than Arithon's ordeal by the sword on the scaffold? Already the Light's muster galvanized Erdane. The scour unleashed by Daenfal's taint of mass apostasy demanded fresh recruits, with troop rolls filling the dedicate ranks in the westlands against custom open to women.

Lest his stricken silence extend, the Sorcerer resumed his long stride, his direct query tendered with a gentleness to crack brave pretence down to the quick. "What would your beloved not do to protect you?"

Elaira tripped over a rock. Steadied by a kindness that melted the sting, she swallowed. "Everything." The admission uncorked her throttled anxiety. "His Grace might not entrust his own fate to your hands. But mine? I'm not cast off so much as sequestered like a fragile treasure cocooned in cotton and locked in a vault."

The Sorcerer regarded her, eyes the limpid, pale sienna of a trout pool in sunlight. "You grasp your beloved's true nature, precisely." Ciladis's patience attracted delight: melodious songbirds surrounded his person, swooped in to halo his bare head. "And what would his Grace do if you left our protection?"

Elaira's gut clenched. For Arithon's original answer in Merior rejected equivocation: *'Give me torture and loss, give me death, before I become the instrument that seals your utter destruction.'* Repercussion wrought consequence, brutally stark.

"Everything," she repeated, afraid. "Arithon would defy every intractable risk and bedamned to whatever cost met his action."

He would baulk at nothing to defend her safety, no price too steep, unto the bitter exhaustion of power and strength. Sidir was gone, whose inveterate insight had anchored his liege after the horrors of Tal Quorin and Vastmark. Nor was Tarens's tender heart tempered to match the forged resolve of a forest-bred *caithdein:* sooner or later, his stretched nerve would snap. Elaira sensed in her mate the adamant wall raised against sharing his confidence when crisis demanded the unthinkable.

"Do you trust Arithon?" Ciladis prompted.

"With my life!" she exclaimed before thought.

The Sorcerer's smile blazed blindingly bright. "Then you perceive your part very well, and the terrible range of your choices."

For he grasped the horrendous precipice before her. His support would not advocate by direction. The grey mantle billowed by the fretful breeze clothed no pretention. His keen regard gave her uncertainty nothing but unconditional acceptance.

Chills stabbed Elaira to gooseflesh for the pitfall of hazards too hurtful to count.

Ciladis raised a tapered hand. The sparrows fluttered down and alighted on his fingers. "Frost waits upon no one. Are you game for rough weather? The most potent herbs grow at altitude."

His musing let Elaira blink back suspect moisture. "More antidotes for Methspawn poison?"

"Partly." Enigmatic as a worn map, Ciladis loosed his winged escort, then resettled his satchel and set off at a clip that forced her to hustle to keep up.

Five days later, equinox eve at Ithamon fell muffled in fog, with opposite forces primed, thrust and counterthrust, to spring a baited snare. Arithon's lathered pursuit whipped spent horses, at wary pitch for a pitiless reckoning on their quarry's chosen ground.

Which was the hunter, and which the marked prey, stacked an encounter cocked for an upset.

Within the wrecked shells of Ithamon's triplicate walls, felted mist blurred the scrape and flurry of dry leaves through fissured stone. Greatness had walked here, where the Severnir's liquid voice lisped through the choked overgrowth of twisting byways, flecked by the tarnished gleam of tossed slate shattered under the jackstraws of caved roof beams. Against stillness freighted with ghosts and the bones of historic catastrophe, the chink of furtive footsteps echoed up slope towards the old citadel crowning the heights. High above, the fuzzed yellow star of a candleflame fluttered in the square of a vacated casement.

The Sorcerer laired within Kieling Tower tracked the uphill approach from the threshold at the ground floor. One man, not two, ascended the switchback towards the upper-tier wall, the broken ramparts the diadem surrounding the intact majesty of the four Compass Point Towers.

The early arrival was burly and tall, blond hair and soiled clothes dripping.

Obstructed at the postern by Davien's braced arm, Tarens glared, stitched by cramps and corked anger. "My liege is behind me," he gasped. "Hell-bent, setting ugly traps to wreak mayhem on the enemies at our heels. He stayed deaf to mercy though I argued. If he wants a massacre, he can bloody his hands without help from me."

Davien's pause curdled the chilly air like a harbinger. "Did his Grace of Rathain use those exact words?"

Implied accusation made Tarens wince. "I was told in stark language I'd regret if I stayed at his back to bear witness."

Implacable granite, the Betrayer bored in. "Hazed you off, did he."

The memory drew heat. "The tongue on him peels skin to the quick. But don't lash yourself breathless. Before I was sent packing, his Grace said to tell you his plan would unfold before midnight."

Davien's teeth glinted briefly in darkness. "And you let him shave his timing that fine?"

"*I allowed?*" Tarens's injury clashed with the Sorcerer's deprecative amusement.

"You're scarcely the first to be flensed." Davien's backhanded censure struck home. "His Grace is unpleasant defending his interests, but did you consider his vulnerabilities?"

Tarens flushed. "Under barbed assault by a master of satire?"

Davien augured in without quarter. "Yes. Words are Arithon's ready weapons. He will inflict hurt to convince the world he's devalued a friendship."

"There are limits!" Tarens bristled, scoured by the grief raked up since the gut-wrenching, near-fatal sword stroke incurred at Daenfal.

"Indeed?" Cloth sighed as Davien yielded the entry. "If the consequence of your sister tossing his Grace out of her door at midwinter means nothing, ask Sethvir what Arithon once suffered to spare his associates from a sea borne attack by Koriathain."

That comment strained the inimical pause, until Tarens snapped. "What I think hasn't mattered one whit for some time."

Davien's punitive cross fire subsided. Not his combative tread, which crunched over the layered grit of desolate centuries. "So we'll see." Disdainful of Tarens's weary, hitched stride, and at ease without light, he extended a gesture of truce. "For a start, try the view from the top of the tower."

Agile as a weasel, the Sorcerer led the ascent, silhouetted by turns against misted sky punched through arrow slits embroidered with ivy.

Tarens followed, bone-weary and chafed by soaked boots and damp leathers. The turnpike stair spun his orientation, alive with the echoes of past and present, textured by emptiness that smelled of weathered stone slathered with fecund moss. He crossed a flat landing. An eldritch inlay of agate runes rang with etheric vibration as he passed through the archway to the next course.

Cracks faulted the layered masonry where the original risers repaved for Mankind's lesser stature had been sprung by the mighty resonance ingrained by the dragon-spine horns of Ilitharis guardians. The flux trembled yet with the remnant harmonies of the sunchildren's crystalline flutes, a wistful descant that flicked human flesh to spurious thrills of ecstasy.

The banked mist thinned away higher up, routed by daylight's cached heat. Stars gleamed through the casements, the latched-open siege shutters still left intact twined in the flowering clockvine that laddered Kieling's outside wall.

Another turn, past the next level's spooled railing, vacancy gave way to the inhabited tang of waxed cedar and antique tapestries. Tarens walked on a polished floor inlaid with black agate, green jasper, and pearlescent quartz. Davien's tenancy added the wisped fragrance of dried herbs, oak-gall ink, and leather from the filled bookshelves that framed his work trestle.

Above, potted plants filled an airy, groined gallery, more overhead balconies accessed by a narrow stair with balustrades of cut cypress. An incised frieze of dragons and unicorns framed the trapdoor to the spire battlement, with Ithamon's stepped ruin unfolded in vista below.

Tarens flanked Davien's stance at the crenel overlooking the scars of past siege and the shattered spans of the bridge causeway. The tower eyrie commanded the anvil face of the scarp, punched upwards by the fist of past cataclysm. Three tiers of the walled citadel fell away into mist, the skeletal arches of the upper precinct swathed like graveclothes, and below, the roofless squares of the old craft quarter sunk into the combed-cotton fog veiling the plain of Daon Ramon. The vantage revealed no sign of movement. Ithamon's labyrinthine ruin lay darkened. No glimmers of torchlight pricked the sundered windows, or flickered in the scrub-choked maze of gaping cellars and toppled chimneys. The hooked loop of the Severnir flowed like poured glass against the western riverfront, its mills and wharves long since demolished. Placid water lapped at ramps that once bustled with Mankind's commerce, shivered into riffles under the cliff where the current spooled over sheer falls past the bend, roaring white through the gouged potholes under the breached lower wall.

Silence undercut the moan of the wind. No intrusive disturbance seemed evident beyond the restive haunts of past ages.

"Here they come," Davien remarked.

Tarens saw nothing. His inherited knack for extended perception strained into vertigo amid the dazzle of heightened flux.

Then came the low rumble of hooves, pocked by excited shouts. An officer's horn gave tongue, trailed by a kindled flare of streamed flame. One torch became many. The on-coming line of lancers blossomed like a wound in the felted dark, fanned into a charge towards the citadel's gapped outer wall. Whether they coursed prey or a feint had waylaid their pursuit, Arithon's flight stayed invisible.

Davien's poise seemed bloodless, but for the rapt jut of his profile.

A scream pierced the night. Tarens started, rattled. Yet the shriek was not the dread outcry of violence. Too pure to be human, the shrilled note was joined by a second, then a third, blended into a harmonic salvo.

"Whistles." Davien qualified without heat. "Ones carved with a Masterbard's tuned ear for sound, laid down and triggered by spring traps of green-bent brush."

"Scarcely an effective defence for a mounted assault," Tarens remarked in distemper. "The armed foot ranks carry crossbows as well." Only fog reduced their efficacy. Once Arithon's racketing handiwork diminished, fallen quiet would isolate the furtive scuffs of a hounded fugitive.

The riders swept through the broken wall, marked by clustered torches and clattering hooves on heaved stone. The vanguard reined back, hampered by obstacles, while a winded horn sounded the rally.

"They'll dismount and split forces," Davien said, laconic. The company rearranged and peeled off in flanking formation, undaunted by the piercing chorus set off as they narrowed the chase.

The crafted diversion seemed pointless. The onslaught of noise might have shocked a few nerves and unsettled the horses. But the troops sent ahead minded orders, unfazed. With cressets doused, the poor visibility masked the threat to Arithon's furtive evasion. Denied the advantage of Sighted vision, Tarens parsed the enigma of Davien's untoward satisfaction.

"He's inside and unharmed," the Sorcerer confirmed, reassurance undone by the spanged release of a crossbolt. Tarens swore. The quarrel cracked into rock, a clean miss. The ratchet as the bowman spanned his discharged weapon chattered through the wasp whine of a concerted volley. Multiplied strikes against flint-bearing stone spattered firefly sparks in the darkness. The flat cracks of chipped masonry brought no relief: a live target hit would be silent. Small advantage to Arithon, the maze of tumbledown stonework at least hampered a reckless pursuit.

"Your trust is as flawed as your premise." Davien's shrewd remark lifted hackles. "On one hand, you fear Arithon's ability to stage a tactical massacre from the high ground. Or worse, you think his crown penchant for empathy might cozen him to his doom."

"Perhaps the stark opposite!" Sapped by fatigue, Tarens blunted his unwise rejoinder. "I'll admit Jieret's recall from Tal Quorin and Daon Ramon inflates the traumatic concern. If you care to debate, the ugly debacle salvaged at the scaffold makes a fatal self-sacrifice more likely."

"So we'll see." Curdled to contempt, Davien continued, "Will your bullheaded pride hear insightful advice? Those fanatical dupes nose-led by their Canon have drawn breath without self-preservation since birth. And only the fool with a stick in both eyes measures Arithon's interests by the scars from his past."

Argument lagged, as muted orders below cut through the jingle of weaponry. The advance moved in squads, picked out by the screech and echoes of whistle notes swathed under grey flannel gloom.

Then a counterpoint shrilled in response from higher up slope. Last plaintive tone of a delicate chord, the Masterbard's plucked harmonic raised Ithamon's latent majesty to piercing resonance. The uncanny pulse sieved through the arcane bindings laid into Paravian masonry. Tarens felt the subliminal tingle course through the tower beneath him.

Light bloomed. A phosphor glimmer brightened the ruin, indigo ignited to translucent aqua that shimmered, brilliant as gas-fed flame. The invaders below pressed their advance, oblivious. Their methodical pursuit trampled onwards, blind and deaf to the etheric corona of actu-alized power that purled over the shattered stone block of the lower precinct's gapped defences.

"Flux fire," Davien murmured, entranced.

The foundation tone scaled rapidly upwards, plunged into the rarefied octaves above mage-wise hearing, but still vibrant when the second prepotent note sounded. The combined frequency intensified the inau-gural ripple sown by the whistles and sustained, augmented by a third intonation cast ringing into the breach. The impact ignited a charge like a beacon, burgeoning flickers of visible light brightened to the actinic sear of white lightning.

Tarens gasped, awed. Before him, the palled outline of Ithamon's foun-dation gave rise to the spectral architecture raised by the centaur masons of old. Pearlescent brilliance took shining form, walls and crenels and spired roofs limned upon velvet night as though scribed in refracted starlight. The dazzling wonder of beauty beyond dreams wrenched the flesh like a mortal blow. Human senses shuddered out of phase. Time hung trembling like the cling of a droplet in defiance of gravity, while the surreal peal of unbearable joy diminished Mankind's affairs to tawdry insignificance.

Thralled pithless, Tarens swayed. Davien's grip caught his arm as he buckled, shattered in witless surrender to the unveiled cloth of the mysteries. Drowning in song, he thought he glimpsed armoured centaur guardians standing vigil at the compass points on Kieling Tower's height.

The dutiful voice spouted from Jieret's heritage exclaimed at the bitter-most edge, "Who will stand watch for my liege's protection?"

Davien's glower pierced through ebbing consciousness. "I do recall giving my word on the matter."

The Sorcerer steadied the crofter's collapse, and did not add, as he might have: that Rathain's prince may have cut his margin too short.

Snug at Althain Tower, feet propped on a footstool, Sethvir savoured steaming tea and regarded the night through the casement, immersed in unfocused reverie.

Asandir, folded into the stuffed armchair opposite, sheathed his resharpened field knife. Controlled as he pocketed his whetstone, impa-tience honed the grim spark in his grey eyes. "Under Shehane Althain's protection, would you care to elaborate why Ciladis diverted Elaira on an herb-gathering jaunt through the high country?"

"Divert?" Kharadmon swooped, seething, from the beamed ceiling. "His daisy plucking's a tad more than distraction!"

Sethvir blinked. "Windy shade. Is the topic germane?" Engrossed in the slipstream of worldwide event, Althain's Warden stifled the disquieting gossip within Asandir's predacious hearing. Ciladis had shortened his foraging stint in Atainia. Not to expedite his return for the equinox convocation, but to hare off on a roundabout tour of Melhalla, for what seemed a cosy hobnob with Mirthlvain's Guardian. Whether to test his novel antidotes for efficacy, or if his apprenticed enchantress required instruction from Verrain on the particulars of Methspawn, Sethvir preferred not to speculate. Not amid the cascade yet unfolding at pitch within Ithamon's derelict citadel.

Asandir's fierce interest stayed piqued nonetheless. "Why the added concern for Elaira?" he probed, alerted by the irregular tidiness of the library table. Heaps of thumbed books and penned manuscripts had been swept aside to make way for a locked coffer of Second-Age antiquities. "She's never yet succumbed to the folly of nurse-maiding Arithon's interests."

Sparks spluttered in the fireplace, huffed by Kharadmon's recoil from Sethvir's subvocal warning. "Nails."

Unenlightened, Asandir waited. Composure, from him, scotched complacence like dynamite, given the voluminous power he held in continuous check.

Sethvir's sleepy gesture side-stepped explanation. "Kharadmon refers to the True Sect diviner given that tag by her underlings."

The field Sorcerer's iconic regard showed no quarter. *"Nails?"*

Static charged Kharadmon's testy retort. "A fearsome talent with a vile tongue and the ill temper of a dockside fishwife. The witch nags her dedicate companies to shreds. Unsubtle as hammer and nail, the new temple recruits tend to forget whose hand aims the spike before they cock up and try swinging."

"She bears sigils, infused, from a book stored at Erdane," Sethvir temporized, "and string ties to the Koriathain. A nasty surprise brewed by Lirenda's galled desperation."

Asandir's seamed face stilled to quartzite alarm. "Against what provocative odds of fresh bloodshed?"

"Under current projection? Too scattered to forecast." Sethvir frowned at his teacup, laced with sudden hoarfrost by his discorporate colleague's intemperate irritation. "The dedicates' trajectory of lethal intent is a blur, diffused yet by uncertainty. Before the extent of their threat has matured, earth-linked farsight cannot fathom which facet of character may drive Arithon's unformed response." The s'Ffalenn penchant for empathy annealed a will that survived Kewar's maze, smelted and reforged in the fire of betrayal that met the red sword of the Light's executioner. "He might flip in any direction."

Kharadmon careened ahead on blind reckoning. "When do we tackle the inadmissible fact he's becoming too dangerous?"

Asandir tapped restless fingers, disquieted more by Sethvir's cagey reticence. None of them wished to be first to suggest Ciladis's faithful attachment might be too personal. The chewed bone in contention jammed everyone's craw. Arithon's core motive as ever remained *by far* too desperately shielded.

Meanwhile, the phenomenon of Ithamon's spectral past unfurled through the mist in Daon Ramon, resurrected from history like an architectural rendering sketched in translucent phosphor. Enmeshed in the splendour of his own making, Arithon heard a faint scrape of movement. Opponents on foot hedged him from behind. How that feat had been managed through the flare of a flux storm could not be fathomed.

The resonant crest of wild conjury heightened apace, a chord upscaled beyond human hearing that amplified the confluence of natural forces. Harmonic registers scored to engage the ephemeral mysteries intensified with the on-coming equinox surge. Derangement should have stalled the intrusive advance.

Yet the vituperative voice of female argument slashed like a blade through a painted masterpiece whenever the True Sect dedicates faltered. "Here's another who thinks his prick swings to the knees!"

Male protest rumbled a bitter rejoinder.

"Raving idiot, we're done!" bawled the incensed diviner. "I don't care squits how far you've shoved your empty gourds up your arses! Light's scripture says we fight Darkness on earth. This cesspit of sorcery gets reamed out! Whaup-nosed cowards, belt up! Or you'll kiss my whipping post for desertion."

"Well, sweethearts!" the lance captain barked. "You heard the boss mare. Forward march, and bedamned to the hindmost."

Seconds passed. The plink of grazed armour drew nearer. Low-grade distortions riffled the flux as the shamed company pressed their blundering search through the hazard of Ithamon's proximal boundary.

Arithon had to move. As the frequencies peaked and the tidal flux quickened, he shared the pitfall of deadly entrapment. Sobered judgement admitted his deterrent had failed. Superstitious fanatics who should have bolted came on, unaware they marched their sorry lives into endangerment.

Arithon retreated. Into the ruin, cloaked in stealth and shadow, he made distance his ally. Amid the prepotent spiral of upshifted forces, the most fervent dedicate must succumb in due course to sensory disorientation.

Instead, a loosed quarrel shrieked overhead.

The point glanced off a corbel, too close. Surprise prickled Arithon's nape. Bad odds to worse, he realized someone's arcane training was shielding his benighted pursuit, too likely augmented by a more powerful foe's interference.

"Hell hath no fury," he grumbled, annoyed. Evidently, the temple diviner capriciously ditched by the Severnir craved her blood taste for revenge. A talent advanced enough to withstand threshold resonance, and more, her able knowledge of wards so far appeared sufficient to defray her company's afflicted derangement. The miscalculation would cost him dearly unless he reclaimed the advantage forthwith.

Arithon ducked through a crumbled courtyard, enveloped by the phosphene imprint of formal flower beds and phantasmic moths. The resurgent ignition of electromagnetics flushed his surrounds, flexing time into fluid distortion. Exposed as a blight silhouette in the flood, Arithon hastened ahead. A horn blared at his heels. Someone's shout of discovery incited a snapped-off volley of quarrels.

Running as chipped masonry pattered his shoulders, Arithon rifled the gamut of his lifelong discipline, pushed to improvise under a deadly range of reduced options. *All over again, must he render the sacrifice for altruistic stupidity?* These zealot fumblers stalked a crown prince upon sovereign ground, yoked to their blindered cause by self-righteous temple authority.

The lancers' advance muscled onwards, hell-bent, while their safe haven past the outside wall fell farther and farther behind.

Even asleep, Ithamon's ruin did not welcome trespassers, the wrecked stone imbued with a corrosive miasma of loss. Agleam in the remnant blaze of lost glory, the traumatic spark of an ecstatic surrender might unhinge the unwary mind. Beguilement threatened the laggards who strayed away from sheltered protection.

"Close ranks, you daft cravens," snapped a harried officer. "Piss off the whining and hustle up! Want your unhallowed bones gnawed meatless by haunts? Then crack on! Damn all if you forfeit your chance for salvation and succumb to an eldritch enthrallment."

"Feckless death!" a nervous compatriot groused. "This accursed place is infested!"

Embedded like sunken wreckage in glare, ragged foundations and tumbled masonry belaboured the dedicates' progress. Bruised shins and stubbed toes pitched them to grief, sheeted in translucent illusion. The glassine shimmer of timbered floors and patterned tile masked the yawning pits of overgrown cellars. Riled tempers and frazzled complaint griped the ranks, while spooked marksmen discharged their crossbows at nothing.

"Look smart!" The sergeant of archers squared his shoulders and spat. "Here's Nails."

Sunwheel surcoat belted over her boyish hips, the diviner tramped up, her livid profile keen as a cleaver. A suspect, worked talisman tied to her belt cast a murky pall of stagnation through the dazzle of excited resonance. Men shrank from its morbid proximity, suggesting her craftwork tapped into black practice.

"Gormless bitch." Evidently the paunchy young officer feared Darkness and Shadow far less than the leaden thumb of the diviner's command.

Yet her Sighted guidance delivered on point. The blanketing volley she directed flushed quarry. Arithon broke cover, set to an uphill flight within lethal range.

The officer forgot his disaffection. "Span crossbows, you louses! Aim high and loose!"

Showered steel blocked the fugitive's line of retreat, while the front rank pounded in full cry up the avenue frothing hot for the kill.

Under candlelight at Althain Tower, Asandir's cobra-quick fist caged Sethvir's slackened grip before his tea mug sloshed over. Direct contact opened up a shared view of the hunt ranging through Ithamon's ruin, the upset afflicting Arithon's design driving the Warden's anxiety.

Cold iron, the field Sorcerer's exasperation pierced the pause as he rescued the canted crockery. "You see cause for alarm?"

Kharadmon's singed contempt attacked first. "By Daelion's record! Did we sanction a crown prince or a rabbit? My call says to reinstate the blood oath Arithon swore against fatal risk. Stand idle, and who wants to stomach the mess? We can't have another religious charade with a sacrificial goat on a scaffold."

"But by lengths, this isn't a desperate case." Asandir's regard bored through the shade's gusted angst and accosted Sethvir. "His Grace is still taunting the lot of them, isn't he?"

Althain's Warden blinked. "Maybe." Arithon's pulse rate reflected exertion, not the frightened spike of adrenaline.

"The man owns the agency to salvage his straits," Sethvir temporized. Yet the gamut of probable offshoots tied into Ithamon encompassed the world, as the etheric expansion spun upwards excited the entire fifth lane incandescent. "His Grace can seek outside help, if he asks, much nearer than Althain Tower."

"From *Davien*?" Kharadmon's recoil frisked a folio of unfinished manuscript airborne.

Asandir's lunge captured the flyaway leaves before they plastered his shins. "Of the volatile pair, right now I'd suggest Davien is the more stable spirit."

Kharadmon ranted on unappeased. "Not to stickle the subject, but that's setting a wicked bit too much trust in the virtues endowed by the Five Centuries Fountain."

Sethvir winced. Pained by the snatch that snagged the last errant sheet from kiting into the fireplace, he regarded the singe on his immaculate penmanship with less fuss than the foibles of bickering colleagues.

Yet no Fellowship Sorcerer ever misappraised the Warden's vigilance, entrained across worlds at rapt strength . . .

. . . strained hierarchy contorted the Treaty Accord binding the dragons on Sckaithen Duin past Northgate. The voracious circle of rivals still testing Chaimistarizog's claimant successor postured for battle. Their mighty wings knifed through the brimstone taint of drakeflame laced on the wind, and stitched through the restive, subsonic rumble of the lesser sirens prowling the Westland Sea's chasmed deep on Athera. Trouble on both planets mounted apace, with the Matriarch's entourage lodged at a wayside inn on the Eltair trade-road, and their sleepless Prime avid to delve into the mouldered stash of secrets uncovered at Highscarp. Waking nightmares distressed Lysaer's psyche at Dyshent, the imperative pressure of Desh-thiere's curse whetted for the armed muster to scour Rathain . . .

*   *   *

Causation for the gathering conflict arrayed from the cat-and-mouse ploy at Ithamon, strung along for who knew *what* further aim under Arithon's purposeful wiles. Sethvir raked white knuckles through his mussed beard. Too much power centred upon Rathain's prince. Earth-sighted vision could not parse the volatile thrust, far less interpret the probable, overlaid patterns hurled into rapid-fire motion with certainty. The crown prince's evasive interference thwarted even the Warden's prodigious reach.

Nails's ill-starred retaliation charged onwards meantime, a straight-forward engagement *ostensibly* shielded from resonant beguilement by her suppressive talisman. Her determined dedicates streamed uphill past the Second-Age memorial to honour the valiant slain by the Great Gethorn. The flame in that monument, and the ghost-scape of ephem-eral architecture that *should* have deterred her invasion dissolved like blown floss dispersed by a cyclone. Too readily, Ithamon's resonant imprint faded, erased from her path.

The bard sprinting ahead was not anxious. Methodically stripped of his artful cover, he exerted himself only enough to maintain a short lead.

An unwonted chill disturbed Althain's Warden. The grounding effect of the diviner's talisman *was being augmented by a delicate trace of wrought conjury, worked with subtle care by a whisper of sound and a gossamer veiling of Shadow.*

Lysaer's tormented unrest tonight was no accident; nor did Sethvir's grue evade Asandir's insight. "Arithon's working the elements to encourage the chase. To what end?"

"I don't know!" Sethvir shuddered.

"Ath wept!" Kharadmon's snarling passage this time tumbled an unshelved book. "The rough consequence could spin out of control!" Lysaer thrown to the curse, with a dedicates' war poised for a renewed assault on the free wilds: Daon Ramon's clan survivors could not sustain another invasion. "*Does yon royal mountebank realize he's dicing with humanity's collective future?*"

"Avert!" Sethvir clapped down the reverberation of fear. Woe betide them if ever the s'Ffalenn bent for empathetic compassion devolved into staring madness. Should Arithon forswear conscience to embrace a deliberate course of annihilation, a disruption to threaten the mysteries must invoke the Fellowship's charge to react in prevention.

"We should pinch the upstart menace in the bud!" Kharadmon fumed into the appalled stillness.

Asandir shot erect, the rescued sheaf of papers still clutched to his chest. "Not without Ciladis's word on the matter." Dauntless, he pressured Sethvir's stricken quiet. "Unless you believe as Althain's Warden that our colleague has withdrawn in retreat. Is Ciladis guarding his own tender heart, or worse, might he blindside Elaira to free our hands for that fatal consequence?"

"*I don't know!*" Sethvir expelled a taxed breath. "The resonant cascade entrained for the equinox peak is not dismantled in any case. If Arithon means to destroy his opponents, the Light's holy war became inevitable when last spring's harmonic upsurge galvanized the Plain of Araithe." No longer myopic, the Warden's gaze fastened upon Kharadmon's turbulence. "You once challenged Davien with a specious accusation. Take due care, at this pass. We deliberate over a subjective murder, set upon dangerous ground. Please don't trigger Shehane Althain's protections with another rash argument."

"Davien's involvement concerns me, exactly!" Live sparks jumped and grounded to Kharadmon's agitation. "I'll not be caught gobsmacked in hindsight. Don't wail to me when we hang for the questionable motives stuffed hand in glove with the Master of Shadow."

Asandir sequestered the loose manuscript, fetched the dropped book, and reclaimed his skewed chair from the tempest raking the chamber. "The probable outcomes remain unclear."

Sethvir bowed his white head, the gnarled hands rested loose in his lap uncharacteristically frail and helpless. "Dare we render a verdict on Arithon in the absence of proof? No firm evidence exists beyond guesswork to condemn an initiate master. Nor has any lawless infraction occurred, sprung from defective morality. If his Grace demolishes this diviner's trespass to save his restoration of the fifth lane's etheric resonance, we Seven possess no sound case. No possible justification supports a summary execution."

That brutal point put the torch to their own hard-won grace, and recast the Fellowship's absolved claim to peace as pretention: *what were the lives of a handful of fanatics worth, and even, the teeming obstruction of Etarra's rooted population, balanced against the moral rectitude of Paravian survival?* The healing of Rathain's impaired mysteries aligned with the Seven's tasked purpose, an essential precursor to stem the decline of the old races' fecund reproduction. No blameless resolution answered the tenets imposed by the Dragon Protectorate. The binding laid on the Sorcerers demanded the remedial sacrifice if Paravian survival became threatened.

Human lives on Athera were ever expendable. The Seven must serve compact law without flinching upon free-wilds ground within Rathain's sovereignty.

Acid sorrow founded Sethvir's conclusion. "The vector of tonight's actions cannot bend. If our sanctioned crown prince forswears his integrity, he must first reject mercy and denounce the principled virtue of his royal lineage. Or he dies, since the leverage imposed by our blood oath at Athir was broken."

"We lose him both ways," Asandir whispered, hoarse, and no voice arose to contest him.

A whizzed flight of quarrels smacked into rubble with Arithon pinned down underneath a leaning stone lintel. His antagonists swarmed the adjacent alley, marked by the plink of spanned weaponry and spurious footsteps bolting for cover. Delay cost him too dearly. Arithon shoved onwards, snagged by weeds and waylaid by a cracked horse trough, repurposed from a Second-Age scryer's font. His stumbling flight barked a shin on the pedestal of a candle shrine once pledged to Ath Creator. The chink of smashed roof tiles in the littered enclosure betrayed his rushed passage. More quarrels sheared past. Hostile forces flanked the streets on both sides. A wrong turn would see him surrounded.

He dared not draw Alithiel, even at lethal risk if the enemy cornered him. The disastrous impetus of a just cause would unfurl the star spells forged into the blade, a transcendent chord that would augment the prepotent surge already in motion. Sited on the fifth lane's nexus at Ithamon, the mighty peal of recombinant harmony must ignite an annihilating cascade. Explosive transmission on that scale threatened a catastrophic unbinding: all the primed stays in tuned place at Etarra would tear asunder in spontaneous back-flash.

"Merry hell!" Arithon swore. Irony poisoned the Fatemaster's jest. The minimal shadow required to finesse the diviner's talisman, coupled with his person as the baited enticement to lure her company onwards towards safety, played hob with his artful interface. Miscast by a hairsbreadth, and the caul that dimmed the blaze of Ithamon's lit glory within human limits could fling his larger strategy into chaos. Unavoidably worse, the aggravation inflamed Desh-thiere's geas and unbalanced Lysaer's stability. The collateral penalties courted ruination if he over-spent his deadly hand.

Arithon darted into the derelict craft quarter, where invention yielded plucked shoots from a stand of overgrown basketry cane.

The diviner's dedicates scrambled hard at his heels as he nipped through the stump remnants of columned supports. Undampened flux flare scribed what had been the groined facades of the Third-Age guild warehouses fronting the old commerce street gate, the dockside wharves for the river trade a filmed imprint, long since rotted away. Forlorn in their absence, the cobbled ramps for the teamsters' drays, sloped towards the mercury gleam of the Severnir. Downstream, the current thrashed white against the wracked remnant of the lower battlement, hazards the dedicate hounds might attempt, with their prize in close flight before them.

Arithon left his draped cloak as a decoy, scooped a handful of gravel, and dropped belly down into a caved culvert. His stalkers converged on the movement, bunched in silhouette against the phosphor gleam of yesteryear's vanished shop fronts. Their drawn swords and the grounding influence of honed steel carved a swathe through the cobweb glimmer of ancient remembrance.

Arithon loaded his tube of cut cane with grit, aimed and spat, and peppered the nearest dark alley. The sharp cracks of impact wheeled the on-coming armed men and spurred them, shouting, to a full gallop.

"Good hunting and rue!" the live quarry muttered, and bolted flat out like a weasel. He dodged through their gapped line, overlooked as an enemy's frustrated steel hacked rents into his abandoned cloak.

Arithon slipped the milling recoil and eased through the pearlescent scrolls of a wrought-iron grille. Beyond, clogged in burdock, the roofless colonnades of the customs house fenced the fluorescent shimmer of clerks' nooks fronting the exciseman's office. Arithon vaulted the broken foundation and emerged through the ephemeral walls into a back-alley close. A bad step on debris flushed roosting pigeons from a fractured dome. The panicked whiffle of wings snagged a crossbowman's aim and drew pressured pursuit once again.

Arithon sprinted uphill into the craft-quarter smithies. Traps for the unwary littered the courtyards: mouldered brick furnaces, chock-a-block with crumbled stone benches for anvils. He leaped over quenching vats choked with leaves, baulked by the sunken grottoes of store cellars linked into a warren festooned with roots. Compelled to swing wide, Arithon shifted his harried offensive to gaming the bounceback acoustics with shied stones.

The reverberations misdirected his opponents, a drawback that also muddled his own clear perception of his opponents. And no trick with tossed rocks swerved the focused Sight of the wretched diviner. Arithon checked his bearings. Uphill, the spectral frames of the weavers' lofts pleated a pallid geometry of translucent beams. Downhill and leftwards, the bygone mill's ghostly wheel spanned the oxbow loop of the race diverted from the riverbed.

A man's voice downslope turned the patter of on-coming footsteps, led by the cankerous blot of the diviner's benighted talisman. Their distortion pocked the dazzling flare of the tidal bore's immanent crest.

Arithon sprinted, galled to frustration. Inconceivable, that an impeccable conjury leveraged by the river's release and the clockwork precision of seasonal equinox should be fouled by upset timing. Scant moments remained before his concerted plan came unravelled past reach of retrieval.

Mist fuzzed the creped sheen of the second-tier wall, curved breastworks and smashed parapets skirting the crag. Above reared the summit of the promontory, the intact redoubts of the third-ring defences speared heavenward by the spires of the Compass Point Towers. A fleck of lamplight pricked Kieling's height, where Davien maintained steadfast vigil.

Arithon faced that marathon climb, dogged by a diviner subversively compromised, and at rabid heel, her pack of dedicates at lethal risk of exposure through a grand confluence. Let the equinox tide take them in the open, they would go mad as the flux crest ignited the Second-Age imprints. Rushed beyond self-preservation by the heightened register, Mankind's mortality could not withstand the torrential harmonics galvanized at the resounded chord of First-Age glory. When the Song of the Mysteries roared into full flower at midnight's peak resonance, human consciousness would be flayed, even the initiate spirit stripped from breathing flesh by the surge. Or the ruthless opposite: Arithon could wield shadow and snuff out the entrained event at the crux.

One stubborn lance company might be spared at the ruinous price of his half brother's afflicted sanity. That exacted cost anchored the entangled plight of Paravian survival, with the fate of Etarra's hapless populace also slung into the tilted balance.

The hiss of a crossbolt spared the agony of further deliberation. Most risky of all, Rathain's crown prince weighed the drastic third option that chanced everything at a single throw.

What did one man owe to a world whose consumptive demands had bought and sold the heart of him in betrayal?

Arithon spun and sprinted *downhill*. His twisted course angled back through the market, offering the enemy marksman the ripe temptation of an easy target.

First Discharge

At Althain Tower, Sethvir pinched his shut eyelids, auger focus renewed by the sharp shift in the earth-sensed range of current probabilities. "Rathain's prince has doubled back."

"Into harm's way, and for what?" Kharadmon needled, his brooding intensified by suspicion. Too likely, the tectonic shift underway at Ithamon deflected the primary purpose behind Sethvir's peremptory summons. "The overripe question's still moot. Why haven't you winnowed a clear-cut motive from yon royal weasel's bent for live chess?"

Asandir dissected the fractious remark, keen to unmask whose game of deception was the more devious: the concealed strategy wrangled by Rathain's prince or the Warden's inclination to outbluff dissent with a thornier problem stuffed up his sleeve.

"What else aren't you saying?" he ventured.

"Just now?" Sethvir raised a wizened face innocuous as a drunk pixie's. "That particular vicious addendum will keep until midnight's crest sweeps through Ithamon." The bland stare that deflected the field Sorcerer's adamance sparked a war of strong wills that riffled the candleflame.

Even Kharadmon's prying interest could not crack the Warden's adamant reticence.

Unmoved, Sethvir deferred the bricked impasse by peering into the tea mug cradled in his lap. His jaundiced survey dissected the dregs, as if the kaleidoscope patterns of augury mapped impending destiny in the tepid sediment. Whether the future lurched into jeopardy, he was not ready to speak. "You might as well nip to the pantry and eat. We're testy enough without the rude edge on your ravenous appetite."

Asandir understood when to beat a retreat. Despite the anguished suspense at the precipice, patience at least let him brew a fresh pot for Sethvir. Any gesture of solace to ease the raw wind blown through the frayed weave of Athera's affairs. If disaster broke loose at Ithamon before-time, Kharadmon's flighty disposition would chase him down with ghoulish relish to share the alarm.

Arithon at that moment stretched prone in a cracked storm sewer that sloped towards the arched sluice of the ancient millrace. The muck underneath him seeped wet through his clothes. Salvation perhaps, or a dog's grave, if hag's luck dealt him a merciful downfall. Listening, he gripped a corroded gnomon rifled from the beseeching arms of a nymph. Denuded of love's arrow, not ten yards away, the ornamental sylph wept verdigris tears, bare feet thatched in twigs by the bird's nest enthroned on her sundial.

The baited diviner swallowed the blandishment steering his tactical ruse. Her thwarted dedicates trampled overtop of his entrenched cover, swearing in martyred complaint through the toppled statuary smothered by vines in the courtyard above.

"Balefire!" a man's nasal discord carped on. "We're expected to scour that drain? Motherless bastard! I say we've earthed a slinking clan scoundrel. Cowering in a bolt-hole doesn't cut teeth. Not for the wiles of a murderous, Dark-dealing Sorcerer."

"Well, whining won't solve the clinch any faster." Further reprimand corked the conjecture. "Light blast the wicked. Nails wants the rat bagged for the sword and the faggots."

While the dedicates drew lots for the noisome prospect of routing him out, Arithon slithered ahead, caked in mud to blunt his etheric signature. No remedy for the diviner's keen sight, but a stopgap feint to enable the strategy birthed at wit's end under stark desperation.

The lancers gave chase, trained hounds starved for slaughter. Arithon wished them a clammy reception, and wormed into the branched conduit beneath the old drains under the communal laundry. Caved stonework and detritus skinned him at hands and knees. He groped forward, until his touch located the jointure where kiln-fired terra-cotta gave way to

hewn bed-rock, and a widened artefact of centaur workmanship. A groined
ceiling lent space to clamber erect. Underfoot, clean polished stone transmitted the silken whisper of subtle harmony. Ages ago, this repurposed
warren had connected the tunnel to a concealed boat landing. The warded
vault built during Perehedral's reign once provided safe egress for Paravians,
when Ithamon lay besieged by Vissoncharizel's drakefire.

The hidden stairwell to the upper citadel was obliterated, never
restored since the repeated defeats that wracked the defences before
Mankind's tenancy. Today's critical hope involved his s'Ffalenn heritage,
reliant upon the precarious assumption the craft-work of the ancients
belowground had bided the centuries intact. No time left for surety,
Arithon scraped an edge on the arrow. He nicked the back of his wrist,
binding an invocation to seal a blood construct amplified by the copper.
Eyes closed, immersed, he tapped the resonant forces imbued by the
First-Age Paravian artisans.

A second of clarity shaped his appeal: permission, intent, and
demarked limitation, founded on his claim to birthright. Then he wielded
his consecrated instrument and stabbed the arrow point into the seamless stone at his feet.

Impact exploded a starred burst of light. The etheric shock inducted
through flesh crumpled him to his knees. Accepted like vengeance, his
plea sank the copper shaft deep into stone. The flux ripple unleashed
resounded through the vault and whirled outwards in reverberation . . .

*The cascading change dashed through the arc of probability shot Sethvir
erect with a gasp at Althain Tower.* His turquoise eyes locked in naked
distress with Asandir's, of flint grey, wide open and steady.

"You've fathomed Prince Arithon's motive," the field Sorcerer surmised
with tart irony.

"I have, the rank madman." Sethvir ripped to the meat. "Before you
ask, yes, the ethic is clean. Though by every permutation of mayhem,
the outcome we dread might befall nonetheless."

"Who's surprised?" Kharadmon's fitful retort crystallized hoarfrost
across the latched casements. "Confound the loss of our imperative to
survive imposed upon his Grace at Athir! Can nothing we do prevent
him from playing the cardsharp with everyone's equilibrium?"

"You're welcome to try," Sethvir temporized. "Provided Nails and
her lancers don't finish him first." For his earth-sense tracked the

twofold invocation aimed to shape Arithon's endgame. The first, a lit beacon of his live proximity, seized hold of the entrained temple diviner. Like grounded lightning, talent and zealot faith fused into manic addiction. She whipped on her lancers like coursers, and set them upon Arithon's location as though overtaking him sealed their survival. Since in fact it must, provided the innocents reached his broadcast position prior to midnight's confluence. Warded stone engineered to quench drakefire, under the rightful prerogative of royal request, also could spare helpless subjects from demise by etheric incineration.

"The nasty catch in the weave is a doozy," Sethvir admitted, point-blank . . .

Arithon shoved, reeling, back to his feet as Ithamon's latent power awakened at his needful command. His specified outcome *would* happen, whether or not he moved swiftly enough to uphold his part of the bargain. Minutes remained for his secure escape, *both* threats against him still viable: the dedicate enemies hell-bent to kill him, and the unstoppable, fatal electromagnetic flare coming on at full confluence.

He stanched his cut and doubled back, dizzied, into the pitch maw of the Ilitharis labyrinth. Dropped prone, he scrabbled through the dank conduit but turned at the branch, scoured smooth, that sloped downhill towards the river course. A diviner enthralled by an amplified construct might ignore the wet-dog trace of his progress. If not, the miscalculation undid him. Arithon clambered forward, aware he was finished if the passage ahead had given way or become jammed with debris. Neither could he protect his benighted pursuit, should they fail to cross over the seals of the warded vault before midnight.

Ordered thought lay beyond him. Egress splashed him into the black gush of the millrace. He tumbled, submerged by the maelstrom and flushed like thrashed flotsam over the spillway into the white-water froth of the Severnir.

No alarmed shout met the shock of his plunge. Teeth chattering, pummelled by perishing cold, Arithon breasted the moiling current. He fetched up downstream in the eddy swirled by the rickled breach in the lower wall. Above, a sheared crack angled into the scarp permitted a chancy ascent. Soaked numb, now racing the onset at nocturnal equinox, he scaled a treacherous spill of smashed stone, and scrambled across the fosse underneath the sheer face of the second-tier wall. The cleft staircase to the broken keep that accessed the promontory had eroded over the centuries into a nearly vertical storm sluice. Sparked static arced over his skin. The advent of confluence neared, by the second. His chance for salvation relied upon speed, with the flux shimmer risen in dazzling auroras around him.

Arithon hauled himself upwards, clawed over the rim wall, and sprinted for the dimmed arch of the postern. Brush and briar noosed his ankles. Shattered stones turned underfoot. Wrenched muscles, and scraped shins, and abraded lungs burned, punished to tortured exhaustion. He ran, every fibre of his taxed being immersed in the siren song rendered in sound and light – *and time slowed* – past and present merging towards pinpoint simultaneity as the ignition of the resonant peak charging Ithamon's harmonics neared the octaves beyond incarnate survival.

Dazzled, he stumbled. The tunnelled ramp through the gatehouse engulfed him, illumined reverberation like ripples in transparent glaze overlaid upon howling, stygian darkness. He pelted up the broken turnpike's gapped treads and ploughed into the gutted guardroom. Razed towers on both sides, torn open to the elements, now soared aloft reclothed in phosphor that dazzled his vision and stung the unsheathed marrow of nerve and viscera. Blued glare sheeted across the inlaid floor. Beyond, the ancient grace of Paravian workmanship sheened the rock scarp like translucent crystal, the zigzagged streets in between like sliced canyons.

The rarefied air roared, vised into fast silence.

Arithon forged onwards, wrung pithless by glory. Each stride, he wept for the forethought that had dispatched Tarens onwards ahead of him. Fate only knew if the dedicates' chase had been saved from etheric enthrallment.

Kieling's guarded portal loomed perilously near the peaked source of magnified resonance: the focus circle that fired Ithamon lay inside the remnant foundation of the King's Tower. Arithon reeled into a thundering chord fast upshifting past mortal endurance. Before him, impenetrable to human sight, the white flame of the spire's structural imprint speared skyward, relict monument to the age before the warped influence of Methuri possession provoked Marin Eliathe's heinous murder. That plangent horror on this night lost voice, swept under in the keening torrent. The glass-clear harmonics on the promontory sieved bone. Breath and heartbeat spiralled towards nonexistence. The electrified atmosphere reeked of ozone. Hallucinating, Arithon had no wind left to scream, no strength to drive through the viscous lag of stretched motion.

Then someone's insistent grip seized his arm. He was bundled, hard, against a warm shoulder that blanked his stressed senses and dragged him headlong into shelter before he crumpled.

"Well done, your Grace!" said Davien, careless of the muddy water smutched on his immaculate sleeves.

Arithon sank onto quiet stone in safe haven, grounded one saving step past Kieling Tower's warded threshold. "I'm sorry," he gasped. "The sewer was fulsome with rats." Yet the spark in his eyes acknowledged the Sorcerer's feral amusement.

"Well, yes." Davien wrinkled his nose. "Evidently the price in public embarrassment that let you relieve the diviner of my involvement. A bravura performance, though unfit for company. Have I your leave?" His profligate flick of neat spellcraft scoured the stench from his hands, then, permission received, freshened Arithon's person and set abused clothing to rights.

The flare discharged by the working whiplashed the flux and swiped Arithon to flash-blinded prostration. "Dharkaron's Redress! You set no containment."

Davien raised his eyebrows, chagrined. "Didn't I just. Is the recoil unfair after all?"

Thrashed between aghast bemusement and reproof, Arithon choked. "Then you've cross-fired my amplified conjury, I presume. Blown out that temple pawn's blighted talisman and landed her on her arse. If that's your sneak touch to complete my flawed plan, I gather the lance company's just won their lottery chit to walk out alive?"

"Indeed." Davien laughed. "They'll stay put where you led them if the zealot recovers with the born sense given to a hatched tadpole."

Arithon suspiciously eyed the altered raiment foisted upon him by his disingenuous benefactor: not any longer the sturdy leathers suitable for the wilds, but linen adorned with green ribbon, and a sable jerkin lined in grey silk befitting his royal station. "I ought to remember your bargains carry a backhanded slap. You've levelled my scales with a meddler's thumb and a hair-raising exhibition."

"The messy loose end needed to be rectified," Davien agreed without blinking. "Now the ascendant position is yours, how would crown justice care to dispatch the game pieces snagged in the cross fire?"

Rathain's prince shoved upright and propped his exhaustion against the comfort of a solid wall. "Your sense of humour is evil."

The Sorcerer returned a triangular grin. "The comeuppance is worth a wee favour, I think. Provided you wish my assistance to send yon parcel of bigotry packing?"

"Not exactly." Mirth erupted to laughter, despite rankled weariness. "Much better, given your willing connivance, here's my preferred salvo to finish this."

The resounding crash from the top-floor library above reverberated down Althain Tower's stairwell, pocked by a descant tinkle of smashed ceramic and the tap and ping of sundry antiquities and spilled needles. Asandir peered upwards, stalled amid his burdened return from the larder. Surprised reflex jettisoned the laden tray. Jounced silverware clashed against Vhalzein lacquered plates piled with bread, cheese, and hard cider, and the steaming teapot just saved from harm's way. A cobra-quick snatch trapped a lone, stray projectile, ricocheted downwards in bounding arcs from the gloom of the upper landing.

"Sethvir?" The field Sorcerer's query echoed upwards through cavernous silence. "Plague your doddering foibles! You implied the probable outcome at Ithamon should have mitigated the crisis."

A wheeze filtered down from the chamber above.

Wary, Asandir uncurled the knuckles clenched over his catch. A seed pearl nestled in his seamed palm, drilled with a pinhole for thread.

The gaunt Sorcerer grabbed his ditched tray and ascended apace. Sped through the open doorway above, skidding over an opalescent swathe of spilled beads, he winced at the crunch of fragmented porcelain from the upset vase that lately had contained them. Casualty of Sethvir's laconic housekeeping, the rifled coffer on the table had disgorged a folded length of white silk, spooled lace, and a stuffed sock bristled as a pincushion. Hunched facedown, crinkled forehead nestled on his tailor's shears, Althain's Warden snorted into the tangles of beard wadded over his bony wrists.

Not fallen ill, but folded helpless by laughter. Pinked erect by his colleague's arrival, Sethvir gasped, while the nexus that defined Kharadmon wafted in chilly hilarity from the window embrasure.

"Dare I guess?" Asandir placed the rescued tray on an aumbry and slung himself into a chair. "Arithon's dispatched his pursuit in Rathain with signature style?"

Sethvir swiped his streaming cheeks. "I daresay. To bald-faced embarrassment and tomorrow's woeful chorus of blasphemy."

Disembodied without any breath to recoup, Kharadmon cut in, "His Grace had Davien's conniving assistance. They seized shameless advantage of the explosive surge when the grand confluence peaked. While the stalwart lancers trembled on their knees chanting prayers, their pleas for deliverance were granted in full."

The rich silence dangled. "And?" pressed Asandir.

"Nothing happened!" Sethvir guffawed. "The equinox flux crest passed over Ithamon while they were shielded by the active conjury Arithon worked inside the Paravian vault. Since Davien's flourish negated the Koriani charm driving their diviner's talisman, they won't be free to emerge until daylight the morning after tomorrow."

Overcome, barely able to straighten, Sethvir chuckled, while Kharadmon snorted.

The field Sorcerer recovered the antique lace unreeled over the table's edge. Then, out of patience with playful suspense, unwavering, he glared like the heron that jabbed for a fish and skewered a viper.

Althain's Warden recouped his sobriety. "The dedicate company will surface unharmed to find the ruin deserted. Davien engaged Ithamon's focus and whisked Arithon and Tarens away to his preferred nest in Kewar. The upstaged diviner can harry her True Sect dupes and search until she goes barking mad. Her frustrated company will tramp home empty-handed, blistered to their sanctimonious reward by their worn-out boots."

"Their spooked horses broke loose from the picket?" Asandir chuckled, versant with the terrain. "That's a brutal hike to the pass into Jaelot, or an even-more-desolate march southward over the lowland flats to Daenfal."

"Well, the weather in Daon Ramon is mild." Sethvir eyed the rickle of fabric piled like storm wrack before him. "They'll straggle in distempered and hungry as stoats. The punitive brangle that refits their equipage will demolish their pay and sour morale for a year."

Asandir assessed the clutter of notions spread over the library table. "If the jumble stall's meant for Queen Ceftwinn's nuptials, you're a little behind on your sewing."

"Plagued by distractions." Sethvir plucked the stashed needle nipped through his sleeve, slipped a knot in silk thread, and retrieved the gown's waistband, basted at the seams and chalked for the flourish of beaded embroidery. "The sweet news runs cheek by jowl with the bitter."

Mirth died. Kharadmon's shade contracted as the upbeat atmosphere suddenly dimmed.

Dauntless point of light against fallen darkness, the pearl cached in Asandir's palm shimmered like a beacon.

The treasure's joyful aspect raised hope like a torch before present uncertainty, percussive with the after-shock memory of ancient sorrow. Thoughtful, Asandir scraped back his chair to recover the antique trove spattered over the floor like droplets of sea foam. Althain's store vault had sequestered the priceless cache since the Westland realm of Mhorovaire subsided beneath the waves. Golden, pale purple, fired blue and opalescent green, such pearls were the harvest of Athlien divers from the oyster shoals beyond Carithwyr, their like unsurpassed since the scourge of greater krakens savaged those shores and wreaked slaughter in the First Age.

Paravian high queens of old had been adorned by such exquisite splendour.

Large hands occupied with the fruit of his salvage, Asandir shivered, then restored the fragmented vase: a cloisonne piece inlaid with gold wire wrought for an Elrienient high king's Second-Age coronation. Unspeaking, he admired Sethvir's fillip of intrepid defiance. Stand or fall, these times rode the precarious cusp. Whether Athera's fair legacy saw defeat or triumph, the Mistwraith's grim legacy had not prevailed. Paravian grace still illumined the world, a feat that surmounted the sorrows and strife of three ages. Heroes mourned in the distant past, and the tumultuous defeats endured since Mhorovaire's grievous demise had not dimmed the annals of history forever.

The compact's threatened stake in the free wilds yet preserved the wellsprings of the mysteries, with the freed spate of the Severnir rushing the threshold towards sweeping change. The resistance of deadlocked factional tensions soon would topple, with or without the rebirth engendered by a Paravian restoration.

Asandir tipped the rare pearls back into a vessel warmed by the forces of etheric mending. Surrounded by the tower's bastion of old books, he set his precious burden at prudent remove from edge of the tabletop.

Dark felted the latched casements beyond the lit candle, hours before the blush of dawn woke daylight's chorus of birdsong. Night's silence gripped the Paravian continent. In Rathain, the sapphire sheen of raised resonance drained from the imprint of ancient Ithamon, while distanced leagues to the east, stars paled above the restive waves of the Cildein. Sethvir hunched like a wizened gnome, stringing pearls into luminous patterns of blessing on the waistband of Ceftwinn's wedding dress. Asandir scrounged a needle to finish a seam. Kharadmon spun in cogitation by the window seat, loath to badger his colleagues while earth-linked vision streamed into the cataract of the after-shock . . .

. . . the arc of the terminator raced into the hemisphere cloaked in darkness. *Iyats* cavorted in Athir's foamed surf as the seventh lane surged into dawn's crest. Fishing luggers, tanbark sails lit to red, caught the blustering gusts off East Halla. Ashore, tinted by early sunrise, the port towns woke to the crack of shop shutters opening, and work chants from the dockside longshoremen. Light chased the narrows at Vaststrait, the sixth lane ignited as daybreak sparkled across Eltair Bay. Rose tinted the snow-clad peaks of the Skyshiels above the misted vales of Daon Ramon.

Sethvir threaded beads when the first quiver of the equinox upset bore down on Etarra. Penumbral shade swathed the grey battlements yet, guarded by a veteran watch crowded out of their barracks by the displaced recruits from the northern downs. Slop carts rumbled through the quiet streets, pedestrians flitting like shadows past orange-lit windows where bakeshops and taverns stirred earliest. A bell tolled. Prayer lofted echoes off the spired guildhalls, and pigeons rustled beneath recessed eaves.

Nothing seemed amiss. Except alley cats did not prowl for mice as the swell begun by the Severnir's release gained momentum unseen. The Light's priests chanted their routine prayer for deliverance when the tidal bore cresting at equinox dawn pealed down the fifth lane. Dogs barked, a split second's forewarning before the charged flood swept Etarra. Set stone and bed-rock belled to the octaves past hearing. Percussive vibration shuddered the ground, and dimmed streets bloomed with light like a comber. Ethereal phosphor, the spirits emerged: ancients who once marched through the Mathorn Pass before Mankind settled Athera. Giant Ilitharis, antlered heads crowned in gemstones and glory, and tiny, graceful Athlien dancers circled to the unworldly melody of crystalline flutes.

Joy fired the resonant imprint, a primal resurgence that stormed the unwary town like a tonic. An exalted vibration met, not with welcome or wonder, but by screams from a terrified populace. Fear flared the charged flux. Static arced between flag staves and roof peaks. The actinic discharge sizzled over damp cobbles and spanged fractures in glass, and stressed, groaning, the wooden frames of stout doorways. Casements buckled and splintered in recoil.

Anywhere the cascade jammed on its course, the baulked current growled and shuddered the strata of bed-rock. White-capped summits shed plumed snow and boulders, as earthquake rattled the compromised pass and toppled flowerpots off tenement balconies. Stacked barrels tumbled like dice in the warehouses, milled under the roar as the shored-up spans of the carriageway crumbled and carved furrowed slides down the notch.

No lives were lost, though a miller's draught team broke loose when firm footing caved under their hooves. A few injured parties wailed in the markets, pummelled beneath collapsed awnings. None came to harm in the open, with the sparse traffic too thin for a mass stampede.

Tousled councilmen shaken out of their beds waded into the turmoil with emergency orders. The garrison watch closed the roads, while work parties pressed into mandated service roped down boxes, barrels and bales to stem further havoc.

Quakes had shaken Etarra before, a predictable inconvenience that swarmed the hired masons to survey the damage. Levied taxes under-wrote the repairs. Temple priests with lit censors banished the haunts and blessed the afflicted homes of the faithful, dispensing shadow-banes and sanctified candles.

In days, or a fortnight, unrest would subside. Etarra had straddled the Mathorn Pass uncontested since the mountebank's shantytown had extorted illicit tolls at the cross-roads. Stables and taverns and craft sheds in turn brought the guilds, entrenched behind walls at the coveted hub of humanity's lucrative commerce. Mankind's rooted tenancy expected to outface the spectres dispersed under sunlight.

But not this time . . .

Althain's Warden tracked the initial reverberation shocked through the etheric web in Rathain. Shifting probabilities mapped a revitalized future as the next crest at equinox noon reprised the upheaval at redoubled scale. Shining shades would become a persistent phenomenon in the path of a resonant shift soon to render the town in the notch uninhabitable.

One victory gleamed like found gold in the balance, offset by uncertainty elsewhere.

Kharadmon succumbed to his simmered impatience. "How long will you keep Elaira in the dark?"

Asandir marked the deft pause, while the Warden threaded another pearl bead and qualified, circumspect, "No conspiracy on record supports your accusation the lady's been hoodwinked."

Discorporate agitation whirled a wind devil through the scattered snippets of scrap cloth. "Don't claim Ciladis lacks the dauntless insight to fathom Arithon's intentions. Or that Davien's wicked intellect hasn't grasped the problematic scope of the back-lash."

"Unwise speculation might sour the pot." Sethvir's owlish stare parsed the conundrum, an interlocked tangle not hypothetical, and most vexing, beyond metaphorical.

Unrest among dragons rumbled a continual, ominous refrain underneath the frantic pulses of human activity. Nothing yet troubled the seasonal rhythm slackening trade into autumn. But an eastbound pigeon fluttered down to peck grain on a temple rooftop in Narms was collected with the inaugural message of panic affixed to its leg. Already, hysteria sown in Rathain spurred the blessed's renewed cry to muster.

The forerunning drumbeat of war knotted other threads, fast unreeling. The crone in Sanpashir would seize her hour, forepromised by the Reiyaj Seeress's immutable reckoning. Sparked warning clapped a gust off a dragon's wings, and a sudden, subliminal draught blasted through the fast stillness at Althain Tower.

Asandir shot bolt upright. "What ill wind from tomorrow caused that?"

Sethvir sighed and unbent. "The snag we don't need rides the Eltair trade-road, with my assignment for Kharadmon's oversight." Forced at last to lance the worrisome canker, Althain's Warden confessed, "The Koriathain's exhaustive inventory at Highscarp has unearthed her predecessor's sealed vault. The one with the casket containing the forgotten, bad chapter of history our Fellowship interests would rather disown."

Prime Secrets

The sealed vault discovered in the Highscarp sisterhouse cellar bore a worn inscription in a dead language. Lirenda crouched on a stone floor razed from seamless bed-rock, original to the Second Age. Centaur masons had worked the merle granite, the bayside battlements first erected against sea worms, Khadrim, and lesser kraken. Today, massive timber beams scaffolded the human-made edifice above, the old dungeon accessed by dusty plank stairs and platform lifts with rope pulleys engineered to muscle the stockpiled supplies.

Koriathain had claimed the cliffside fortress and established a sisterhouse during the fourth century of Mankind's tenancy. Lirenda knelt, perhaps in the footsteps of the earliest prime on Athera, whose rule had directed the order's affairs until the extended, ripe age of five hundred and twelve. The date carved on the capstone preceded her death, two decades before she yielded her seat through the initiate rite of accession.

Whatever her sequestered legacy held, the content had bided in shrouded secrecy for thousands of years.

Lirenda surveyed the site, her shadow distorted by the flicker of torchlight. The dank gloom wore the must of cobwebs and rot, enriched by the oak wine tuns in storage, and tubers sacked in coarse burlap. How many sisters sent to fetch candles and flour had trodden heedlessly over this clandestine aperture? Lirenda peeled off her calfskin glove. Excitement suppressed, she traced the engraved foreign characters. The bronze loops of two handles, set flush, were corroded in place, incised sigils gummed by a crust of patina. A rank fool would be careless. The deterrent stays against an unauthorized entry yet sustained their dire charge at full strength. Untoward haste already had killed an unwary novice.

Undeterred by the casualty, the sisterhouse peeress gushed over the Matriarch's shoulder. "We combed the back-closet archives to translate that archaic cipher." Enthused, she recited from memory: *'To my prime successor, should the traditional chain of initiate succession come to be broken.'*

Lirenda smothered a jealous pang, curdled to angry resentment. She needed no avid witness to plumb the desperate straits of her ignorance. Here, at last, rested her hope of reprieve, and a counterthreat to the agency bestowed upon Arithon by the Biedar crone's accursed heirloom knife.

Thrust erect, Lirenda cracked a querulous order. "This area will be cordoned immediately." None would usurp her pre-eminent right to broach the former Prime's legacy. "I'll have no attendants but the husks of the condemned. Make certain your resident sisters adhere to stringent protocol and ensure my inviolate privacy."

"Your will, Matriarch." Banished, the peeress departed in haste, with none but the cowering, white-ribboned initiate left awkwardly holding the torch.

Lirenda inclined her head to the glitter of pins in her coiled hair. "Tell the sisterhouse kitchen staff I'll want a hot meal with good wine. Then brush down my cloak and unpack my wardrobe." She extended a ringed hand, snapped the torch from the underling's grasp, and bent to her work without pause to acknowledge the girl's obligate, obedient curtsey.

While the staid routine of the Highscarp sisterhouse convulsed to accommodate the Matriarch's residency, prime fiat saw Highscarp's cellar sealed under triplicate rings of containment. The crafted warding capped by Lirenda's invocation was mighty enough to deflect the meddling interest of Fellowship Sorcerers, elevated by the forceful protection of eight black tourmaline rods. Once the interlocked sigils had meshed, Lirenda's rigorous sweep guaranteed her absolute isolation.

"Now we get to work." Her smug satisfaction died without echo, swathed under oppressive quiet. Battened down under impervious wards, the cobwebbed ceiling beams and soot-grimed walls smothered even the subliminal, harmonic traces inflected by the Ilitharis masons.

The three witless attendants poised near to hand, their empty features and vacuous eyes unresponsive since their arraignment. Black-clad and reft of voice and identity, one steadied the candle lamp, while the other pair waited like furniture.

Knees cushioned on her mantle, Lirenda crouched, questing finger-tips trailed over the vault's capstone. The flat surface yielded back no sensation, no tingle of active conjury. Not even the slight gradient of warmth or chill suggested the latent presence of any craft-worked design. Yet a rank fool had perished for her false belief the ancient defences were discharged.

Lirenda scraped the small indentation found at the centre, and bared a concave depression. A hairline seam rimmed an inlay mounted flush with the granite floor. "Bring the lamp."

Stronger light speared a sullen glimmer through the insert, a fitted piece exquisitely cut from a prepotent black quartz. Wear had dulled the exposed, outer surface. Visible through the ingrained scrum of scratches, the high polish remained intact underneath. Cut facets flashed back, agleam with the sheen of an aligned focus. Lirenda spread her palms overtop, surprised by the tepid contact. A matrix left purposefully guarded should be cold, inert, and unresponsive to a casual touch.

Or else, dreadful thought, the ancient gem had been damaged, either by a past defilement, or worse, from careless hands inadvertently salting dried fish, unwary of the vault's presence.

A word to the husk swung the light closer still. Lirenda chipped out the rimed dirt. Excavation revealed an oval cavity, inverse fit for a cabochon seal ring. Only one jewel defended a prime's secrets: Lirenda twisted the Matriarch's signet from her finger and inserted the amethyst setting.

Contact struck a spark that awakened the black quartz. A sharp surge of power sheared through her. The blast branded letters of fire into her consciousness, virulent as the induction that had slain the tinkering, subordinate initiate. Eighth-ranked, and once titled as Morriel's First Prime in the past, Lirenda sustained the harrowing jolt, the violent onslaught of vertigo curbed by the reflex of her advanced training.

Or so she believed. Until the crystal's directive snapped shut and ensnared her. The rune for 'death' seared across her mind's eye. Beyond her volition, the ominous character yoked her into rapport through the socketed seal ring, with the dark quartz beneath attuned to her being in wait for an unknown riddle's response.

Her very life hung in suspension, gripped by an imperative stronger than the master sigil that shackled subordinate sisters into surrogate obedience. No recourse would avail the unprepared spirit linked in thrall to the vault's warded matrix.

Lirenda sweated, afraid. She dared not raise her arm, or lift the seal ring's enmeshed setting. Break the engaged prerogative, the entrapment would shred her conjoined consciousness and strip her of sentient identity. Her husk might breathe. But her self-awareness would stay caged within the dark jewel's implacable grip.

The witless could not help, denuded of the autonomous will to utilize their initiate training. The sisterhouse peeress lacked the advanced proficiency, and no one else could access the cellar without broaching the adamant stays against outside intrusion.

Clammy chills prickled Lirenda's spine. Immobile and aching, she wrestled the spectre of childhood shame. Born to privilege and wealth, she had been reared by strict parents, her conduct incessantly scolded for unseemly pride and ambition. The same flaws deemed likely to lead her to ruin instead married her to high office as the Koriani Prime Matriarch. Adult, and now past volition to change, she let acid reason prevail.

A derogation designed to thwart imposters would test the standard of integrity fit for the matriarch's burden, with fatality the unmalleable penalty to cull the unsuitable and the weak. Mineral's inexhaustible patience did not acknowledge flesh-and-blood mortality. The spelled sigil noosed to her incarnate existence ranged through tissue and bone, and paralysed animate movement. The conundrum she wrestled must be resolved before she succumbed to exhaustion.

An incalculable prize relied on her merits, with no quarter given for failure.

Eyes shut, Lirenda confronted the pitfall of her irregular elevation. A matriarch served for a lifelong term, her passage prerequisite to the transfer of prime power. Yet the shock incurred when the Great Waystone shattered left carnage, Selidie's slaughtered corpse sprawled untimely along with her inner circle. No allowance forgave the disruption of precedent. Yet the meaning implied by the first Matriarch's inscription suggested the faulted heritage was not intractable.

Thought itself triggered the seal ring's connection, a barrage that lanced into Lirenda's mind. The interrogation ransacked her privacy, her personal memories of facts and events sieved from the dross of self-deceit. Thrashed by the whirlwind, her bid as Prime claimant was exhaustively cross-checked and verified: that she was, to the fullest extent of her knowledge, the most able of the initiate seniors enrolled on the order's roster. Her standing had been legitimate, even before she put down her close rivals: Lirenda was the last eighth rank alive, and the only sister groomed as First Senior.

The probe's next challenge relied on experience, a grand sigil's unbinding that demanded a sequential cancellation of enchained ciphers and proven command of the forms of high mastery. Difficult, truly, but equal to the rigour of Morriel's training. Lirenda executed the exacting steps. She threaded the fraught course through the quadrangle runes of chaotic destruction, the unstable sigils of counterward matched with the correct runes of closure.

Balance bought her requital. The black quartz subsided to dormancy, the clamped hold through the seal ring released. Battered limp, too shaky to crow, Lirenda chafed sweaty hands, whirled giddy by her flushed triumph. The ancient vault lay open before her, its precious cache of secrets hers to pursue.

In Althain Tower's top-floor library, a stinging, cold draught ruffled Sethvir's white head with a snap that frosted his eyebrows. "Insolent shade! Back so soon?" Muffled through tousled wisps of fanned hair, he added, cross, "You're forgiven, provided the fast turnaround brings me a conclusive report."

"Ath wept!" Kharadmon's irritation sheared across the obsidian tabletop, now crammed with inkpots, parchment, and books, as though last night's indulgent affray with rare pearls and wedding lace had been dreamed from another existence. Dragon's business, gleaned in translation from Chaimistarizog's chronicle, replaced the nuptial garment, efficiently packed in a saddlebag and bound southward to Havish with Asandir.

"You have the short list in troublesome summary?" Sethvir's clipped acerbity lidded an impatience rare enough to drive fidgeting worry.

"Don't take me for Luhaine!" the miffed shade blustered back. "That nitpicker henpecks his tasked assignments long enough to crack rock from sheer boredom." Through the flap of loose papers pegged by Sethvir's fist, and the cellophane vibration of mica sheets scored with the cryptic spirals of Drakish ideograms, Kharadmon huffed, "That windbag would have possessed a dust mote and malingered to spy, whereas I—"

Sethvir quashed the tirade, in no mood for bombast. "While you propositioned one of the Matriarch's husks to serve as your eyes and ears? I saw your exchange of permission before Lirenda's exclusionary defences locked down."

Kharadmon's airy retort rattled the bookshelves. "My mawkish butty, sincere gallantry works. The victimized ladies granted me, at their pleasure, a direct line of access through their puppeteered flesh, without strings." Pity softened his rage to a whisper. "The poor dears' denuded spirits were bored! Severed untimely from warm flesh myself, I could sympathize with the desolation of their benighted condition! Susceptibility ferments amid savage cruelty, and loyalty withers, soured to vinegar bottled up in the isolation of a wretched long life. Experience ought to have made Lirenda wary of the weapons such resentment breeds at her back!"

Sethvir rescued the feather pen snagged in his cuff. "We owe your volunteer sisters a healing, if they should ask."

Kharadmon snorted. "They have given names, and no, they won't. The bitter harpies prefer ice-cold revenge above wistful nostalgia. Curse the creed of an order that cripples their child victims under an unnatural regime of austerity!"

Althain's Warden stemmed the ranting disparagement of the sisterhood's mandated abstinence. "How much bad news survived, sequestered for centuries inside Prime Hennishe's damnable crypt?"

"A trunk full of books. Most of them thankfully mouldered to rot and illegible. Four shielded coffers of crystals, crammed to capacity with the worst kind of stored information. Diagrams of pre-settlement technology drawn in engineer's jargon that lost translation has also rendered incomprehensible. We've Arithon to thank, since the codes to access their meaning were obliterated with the destruction of the Great Waystone."

"Copies existed," Sethvir contradicted, arms clutched to his chest with the unfinished manuscript at hazard of breezing aloft. "Significant extracts, though if we stay lucky, most of those burned to ash with the archive at Mornos in the aftermath of the crown rebellion."

"Well, Dame Fortune's forsaken our case with the rest." Kharadmon rampaged onwards. "Several large quartz points hold historical records. Texts from the annals before Mankind's settlement, and quite enough to pack us a backhanded wallop of damage."

Sethvir stuffed his rescued sheets in a cupboard, one finger poised to rifle his cache of fresh parchment. "How many pages are needful for a transcription?"

"That stack should suffice." Kharadmon's tempestuous impatience tweaked the heaped books and flaked sheets of frail mica still left at large in his path. "Best tidy up the antiquities, first."

"Your tempest's not helping." Sethvir abandoned the spare quill winnowed sidewards, and pounced on the oldest rare volume just rudely snapped shut with a smack. Then he tucked the mica inside the vellum slip sheets of a strapped leather folio, shelved a miniature volume of Athlien verse, and arrested with a muttered stayspell the tipsy pile of scrolls that threatened to avalanche.

Housecleaning accomplished, Althain's Warden honed a new nib and peered through deepened gloom at old furnishings sunk into the shadow of Kharadmon's graphic brooding. "You might as well summarize the evil gist."

"First of all," Kharadmon snarled, "our offworld association under your birth name as Calum Quaide Kincaid."

Sethvir sat, unsurprised the broadscale genocide attributed to the Fellowship's prior activity should surface from oblivion. He had assumed for millennia that reprehensible story of blame lay buried somewhere in the Prime's proscribed archive. "One matriarch or another was likely to unearth the damning link. A warning snag for the future, since the disclosure has yet to be read. You imply something worse?"

Kharadmon unloaded the scathing addendum. "Far more, and in full as we've never encountered, a treatise that describes the frightening power imbued in a consecrated instrument wrought by the Biedar ancients. The worked severance, created to right Jessian's legacy of bad debt, overseen by the crone in Sanpashir."

Sethvir froze, the readied leaves of parchment beneath his poised pen swiped into the shade's restive gyre, at remove in the centre of the cleared table. "That dreadful flint knife, at present foisted on Elaira."

"Quite." Kharadmon's accusation settled a piqued chill through the lofted sheaves and the workaday scents of ink and waxed leather. "How long have you known? Who else suspected?"

When cornered, Sethvir plumbed the frightening depth of apparently transparent innocence. "That the warded stone blade was created to nullify *all* bindings without discrimination?"

"Don't imagine bland words can gut the fell import. That weapon, wielded through the initiate awareness of informed intent, could sever us from the dragons' bound obligation. Or tear the Koriani Order asunder, negating the life-term vows of every initiate sister by shredding the Prime's master sigil at a *single stroke*."

"That's accurate," Sethvir allowed, reluctant to embellish the ticklish corollary: that the heritable traits of Athera's royal bloodline were as vulnerable, coupled with the dread fact that when the dagger was drawn, its profound influence shifted the balance of *everything*.

But Kharadmon trampled past fainthearted reticence, ever unflinching. "You chose not to mention that knife's puissant properties sparked the unrest behind the last drake war! Each time that blade leaves its warded sheath, that latent, wild power flags perilous notice. I'd hazard the insane provocation inflames the rogue drakes, fanning their rebellious desire to erode the Accord holding them in restraint beyond Northgate!"

Sethvir buckled into his chair, glazed to limpid surrender. "I've known since I handled the flint blade for a thorough assay at Elaira's request," he confessed. "Asandir very likely has an inkling, since he instructed Enithen Tuer to sever her vows to Koriathain with that knife on her personal initiative."

"You'll say Davien shied away from an informed involvement, and Ciladis, most likely, has guessed." The stiff wind of Kharadmon's ire deflated, his blizzard of parchment released to resettle into a disorderly wrack. "Why am I last to find out what's afoot?"

Sethvir thumped the flyaway pages to rest. "Because as a discorporate, any knowledge you carry poses too fractious a risk under scrutiny by a dragon." His nettled shove slid the heap into the library's focal point, where the third lane's current transected the obsidian table.

Prodded incandescent, Kharadmon took the hint. He coiled his ephemeral presence around the jumbled leaves and riffled the mismatched corners into squared perfection. Then, by aligned will and surgical intent, he fired the flux current and branded the stack with ruled lines of characters, top to bottom, at a single stroke. When the wafted coils of smoke swirled clear, Sethvir thumbed through his finished archive, completed under the flash-point imprint.

"You're welcome!" Before Althain's Warden acknowledged the favour, the Sorcerer's shade circled back and retrod the sore subject with a terrier's persistence. "Eventually Lirenda will research that poison. How long do we have?"

Sethvir grunted, bent on scrounging through oddments for waxed twine and the awl he preferred to stitch folios. "Who knows, given the tangled array of potential diversions."

"You don't plan to forestall the explosion," Kharadmon accused like a thunder-clap.

Althain's Warden curbed his impulse to jab sharpened steel to haze off his colleague's incessant badgering. "Would you care to lock horns with the Biedar crone, or meddle into the deadly agenda she's woven through Arithon's destiny?"

Kharadmon prowled a disgruntled cat's-paw of breeze through the ominous, fallen silence. "Well," he puffed finally, "let's hope for our sake his Grace exhausts his stickling temper beforetime. Best he tackles the hag's business before our ugliest chapter of history crosses Lirenda Prime and resurrects her antecedent's thorny agenda."

Sethvir offered no shred of encouragement. The Koriathain's inveterate hatred of their archenemies extended back to the chaotic wars that tore apart interplanetary civilizations. Demonized by the great weapon that made ashes of Mankind's starfaring empire, the research cadre formed by Calum Quaide Kincaid had been targeted under their tireless pursuit. Plucked in midflight during an interstellar transit by wilful dragons, the fugitives had been reforged, committed to the weal of Athera's mysteries as the Fellowship Sorcerers. If knowledge of that prior origin surfaced from distanced obscurity, how much hotter the fires of vengeance would burn? How much more corrosive, spurred by the recognition the Seven were one and the same, whose adamant fist on the compact yet thwarted the sisterhood's coveted bid for unbridled expansion?

All buried grudges and secrets came due, with the crone in Sanpashir's long-sought restitution poised to level the scales for the age-old theft and abuse of the Biedar's cultural arcana. Athera's future and Paravian survival aligned at the cross-roads of fate, reliant upon two mortal lives at the eye of the vortex.

Late Autumn 5926 – Winter 5927

Failure and Stratagem

Baulked when the Master of Shadow eludes a scouring search of Ithamon's ruin, Nails and her dedicate troop march southwest before the onset of winter, and the grim report brought back to Daenfal describes an onslaught of fell sorcery that forced them to the penury of an ignominious retreat, hunkered down for three days belowground . . .

While the holy remedies of blessings and prayer fail to stem the resurgent earth tremors and haunts erupted since the lane crest at solstice, Etarra's trade hub suffers an attritious decline, as master craftsmen pack up their shops and their tools, with uprooted apprentices and close family crammed into wagons to seek an untroubled start elsewhere . . .

While the restive pressure of Desh-thiere's influence bends Lysaer's seizure of the True Sect war host towards Etarra's relief, the jilted high priesthood at Erdane formulates their redress, first to redeem the Light's chosen co-opted by his rebellious corruption, then to cage him as their irresistible gambit to recoup their usurped hierarchy at any cost . . .

VI. Sleight and Riposte

The first time reckless avarice led Avenor's sly riffraff to snag the temple bounty for a Dark-touched soothsayer, the hopeful conspirators decided to lure their fat prize with a spiked crock of rotgut. Gin laced with soporifics made Dakar easy pickings. Quick work, to bundle his insensate bulk in a grain sack, sling him over a mule, and pack him off to Hanshire's examiner for a speedy arraignment. The plotters planned to divvy up the reward before their besotted mark woke up chained to the scaffold.

Inveigled into jocular company by night, their brosy target chugged down their dosed bait. "Suckered like a babe at the teat!" The jubilant ringleader of the affray smirked. "We'll have the whoreson triced up like a ham. He'll be kissing the puckered arse of a priest soon enough, pleading in vain for redemption."

No one allowed for a slinking snitch. Or maybe dumb luck fouled their net during their quarry's staggering course towards unconsciousness. When their bagmen crept in for the pounce on the hulk laired up in his noisome straw bed, the pinned quarry seethed and unravelled, squealing, into a horde of live rats.

Panic ensued. Grey, vicious and agile, the four-footed decoys sank vengeful teeth into two-legged meat. Routed humanity flailed backwards and roared, to the wakened anger of the whole neighbourhood. The stymied kidnappers pelted, nipped at the heels by vermin ensorcelled to give vicious chase.

For three days the culprits cowered and slunk, subjected to ambush by unnatural fury from drainpipes and culverts and middens.

The plump soothsayer responsible reeled on his way, whistling, trailed by a mongrel assortment of urchins who had pesky, sharp aim with flung stones. Misfortunate lurkers were picked off at whim, in particular those whose scabbed hands sported rodent bites and lacerations.

Intimidation failed to gag freebooting rumour. Hanshire's True Sect diviner paid anyone with perked ears for the tipoffs that exposed suspect practice. Canon Law cut no slack. Amid raw winter weather, the right-eousness of the devout mustered a lance squad of ten. Their immaculate zeal clattered into the ruin with a sealed temple writ for arrest.

Dakar viewed the commotion, flat bored. Damn his carcass to Sithaer's seventh pit before he let a sorry flock of fanatics breach an obstinacy unmoved by appeal from a Fellowship Sorcerer. He dodged arcane notice with snide finesse, more concerned by the venal surveil-lance of the informants. Pudgy mitts stuffed elbow deep in holed pockets, he watched True Sect brutality scour the stews: beggars and whores ousted from their cribs, and hapless squatters bludgeoned into the snow to the tearful shrieks of their ragtag weans. Dakar masked his signature presence in the roil of resentment raised by the victims upended from their sorry lives. The Light's searchers were not adverse to seize perks. They rifled the pathetic, jumbled belongings for loot and torched the spurned refuse.

Dakar took their cruel measure. Inspired, he staged a volatile distur-bance, primed by the nudge deployed earlier to harness the instincts of feral rats. His laid craft-work struck by night under snowfall, while the diviner's sentries snoozed at their posts, and drowsiness gripped the religion's encampment, abetted by torpid fumes winnowed off the smoul-dering coals of smashed furniture.

Dawn wakened the faithful to an outrageous tally of pilfered gear, stolen boots, and stores filched by scavenging curs too wily for their marksmen's crossbolts.

By noon, three head of prime horseflesh were snatched from two grooms hoodwinked into an idler's dice game. Public whippings failed to trim discipline. Past nightfall, the diviner's acolyte was exhumed from the latrine ditch, presumably knifed and robbed to the skin while he crouched to relieve himself.

The provocative spellcraft inciting harassment exacted a toll: Dakar languished in bitter sobriety at the mercy of clear faculties that destroyed his oblivious peace. Sleeplessness served him with grim visions spun off the titanic disturbance sweeping Rathain. The diviner's persistent hunt for his hide forestalled his alcoholic relief. Dakar made his pique felt. He sloshed a tweak through the ambient flux that amplified the leaked dissonance of emotional overload.

Distortion spiked the diviner's sensitive assays. Whiplash eddied outbursts of static, until grounded contact with metal and weaponry stung every lancer deployed within range. Men called to bear arms yelped, cringing, and swore, loath to lay hands upon chain mail and sword. Hot tempers leveraged the moil, till snappish frustration also infested the Light's patrol squads with scavenging fiends.

Avenor was riddled with volatile ground, even off the peak tides at solstice. The destitute and the dispossessed skulkers in residence tended to weather such flares hunkered down, resigned to outlast the fraught storm in stoic privation.

But this round, the well-heeled temple lancers tempted them with the opportune chance to poach horsemeat. Mounts vanished to butchery on the sly. The poisonous angst provoked by the sneak thievery in turn attracted fiend-driven dousings with seawater that soaked bedrolls and spoiled stockpiled provender. The diviner's quest faltered at swords' point, finished off by the pinch of starvation, chilblains, and threatened revolt.

Slit-eyed, Dakar watched the lancers' clattered retreat through the broom towards the trade-road. His spite ripped the sullen stragglers with a fare-thee-well gift that cycled their mares into heat out of season. Wind carried the raucous barrages of squeals and thudded kicks back to his vantage atop the tower abandoned to crumbling brick since the exodus of the portmaster's excisemen.

"Good riddance to bad cess, and may septic pox rot your sanctified ball sacks." He plonked down, satisfied, and popped the cork off the brown jug cradled like a newborn to his breast. "Soak all to oblivion," he murmured, pestilent talent and nattering conscience consigned to the joy of inebriation.

His intended celebration triggered chaos instead, his alcoholic libation milled under by the rogue torrent of his suppressed prescience.

He saw: *Koriathain's hooks driving a female diviner called Nails,*
summoned from the rough end of a failed campaign and dispatched
northward by the high priesthood's clandestine orders.

At full bore, the fit rolled his eyeballs and pitched his usurped
consciousness to black-out oblivion.

The Mad Prophet woke flat on his back. Someone's heels drubbed his
ribs. A second parcel of mayhem parked like deadweight atop his
squashed chest. Bleared sight swam into reluctant focus. Two filthy
urchins straddled his torso. To drummed kicks and an earsplitting spill
of invective, he gathered he owed recompense for three pokes of shied
stones, scurrilous services rendered.

"Fatemaster's list spare my blighted score till the afterlife," he moaned.
His furred tongue tasted like yesterday's fish. Worse, the steaming
warmth soaking his breeks was not the embarrassment of incontinence,
but the prank of the freckle-faced brat he caught shamelessly lacing
his britches.

Dakar roared. Levered up from the splashed puddle of urine, stabbed
at palm and knee by potsherds, he folded over and threw up.

The insufferable street gang darted past reach, shrieking with laughter.

"Pay up," lisped the sexless mite prancing nearest.

Dakar wiped his clotted mouth on his sleeve. The sprayed pocket he
turned inside out yielded lint. The glare he transferred from his ransacked
person redoubled the chortling gales of amusement. "Filthy liars. Seems
you've squared the account by helping yourselves."

"Didn't," the boss hussy huffed through gapped teeth.

Dakar measured her brazen insolence, backed in force by her spiteful
conspirators. For a bread crust, the lousy weasels would turn and prey
on his interests.

"All right," he agreed. "Keep what you're owed, though beware! My
vengeance will lay a scourge on your privates, a cluster of warts for each
penny you cheat."

The grimy pack scattered, pelting him backhand with the purloined
coppers cached in their fists.

Of course, he had hired the thieves for their aim.

Dakar cursed his welts, too fat to give chase. He salvaged his scattered
coin from the piddle, engaged Sethvir's better housekeeping cantrip to
freshen his clothes, and slumped in despair. Slack living no longer

impaired his initiate faculties. Spontaneous bouts of vision still tainted his waking perception.

"Fiends ding me senseless," he grumbled. A psyche that wasn't worm-holed like a sieve at least could stay blissfully ignorant. Forehead pillowed upon his crossed arms, he rued the implication his days of depraved hedonism were foredone.

Shallow living had been his indispensable mainstay until Arithon s'Ffalenn had dismantled the fallacy. Nettled conscience befouled his quietude since, to the ruination of his digestion. Brutal stakes clouded his destiny, while corrosive awareness kept shredding the gauze of rosy evasion to cobweb.

Come spring, the bane of his prescient surety spelled disaster for the Crown Prince of Rathain.

"Damn all to the screws of the Fatemaster's reckoning!" Dakar heaved upright and tacked down the stairwell. He acquired another flask. Swilled spirits through the night in futility, raw drink insufficient to hammer him witless. When daybreak arrived like a gouge in the eyes, only luck's happy throw had spared him from the next punter's bid for an opportune bounty.

Temples squeezed between his moist palms, Dakar shivered. The ranged echoes from northern Rathain trounced his stubborn resistance and mangled him to desperation: from the pent whisper of the embedded catalyst seeded in the dungeon at Etarra, to the nasty, recurrent remorse saddled on him since Darkling's burst dam had freed the flux tides in Daon Ramon, his avoidance had not stemmed the onrushing chain of event. Dakar howled. Defeated, he wept, mauled prostrate as the Masterbard's patterned strategy seared him through like the cry of glory unleashed.

For the linked chord that refired the fifth lane after last autumn's equinox wakened more than the magnified charge of past resonance at Ithamon. Latent vision eroded through his armoured nerves, until sorrow's denial sliced Dakar's bruised heart into ribbons.

He knew, *oh, he knew, as the Fellowship must:* the shift set underway in the east breached a threshold beyond reversal. The unstoppable rampage of change galvanized Mankind's deepest insecurity, inflamed worse as the ancient, imprinted haunts drove scared families to exodus from Etarra. *The wise on Athera foresaw the back-lash spark to conflagration:* soon the scintillant crescendo achieved through high art *must* unleash the inevitable recoil.

No engineered care could smother the balefire of on-coming war.

Arithon, by his nature, took action on clear-sighted ethic, unswerving before the punitive rage aimed against him. The doomed lines of augury promised no victory. *No clean course existed to stem the savage retort sprung from Mankind's terrified ignorance.*

Desh-thiere's curse smouldered always. Lamentation and death keened and swirled like dense smoke through the stacked templates of probability.

Dakar drowned in the cross-chop of unglued perception: *saw Ciladis, dark features stone-cast by the profound sorrow Sethvir hid behind dissembling guile. Nonetheless, the shepherd's touch of the Fellowship's healer mentored Elaira in a sequestered retreat with Verrain at Methisle.*

'You foresaw everything when you came to bedevil me,' Dakar blurted, reckless with outrage. When Ciladis raised limpid, golden brown eyes, aware of the spewed accusation, the Mad Prophet railed into the Sorcerer's teeth. *'Do you plan to give warning before the axe falls? Or will you continue to shield Elaira in cosseted ignorance?'*

No answer emerged. Either Ciladis rebuffed the effrontery outright, or Dakar's unruly faculties fumbled the tenuous contact. The Mad Prophet collapsed, while Avenor's pernicious damp ached his bones, and the pelt of falling sleet on the sea wind hounded him into shelter.

No haven existed for storms of the mind.

When, trapped in nightmares as wrenching as these, did a man's pummelled spirit snap under the morass? How long until, broken, he forsook breathing life? Ugly sobriety grounded the reckoning. The clown's masquerade that flirted with lancers and temple diviners clothed the skeleton of a death wish.

Barefaced, the unmalleable pain stared Dakar down.

Arithon s'Ffalenn laid the perilous groundwork to manifest the impossible, surely aware his dauntless stance laid claim to the high ground alone. Twice over betrayed by Fellowship interests, he leaned upon Davien's devices. Naught guarded his back but an honest field hand's born kindness, fatally flawed by the ideological hope of a former *caithdein's* crown obligation.

Yet a seer's view encompassed the perspective of ages: the Seven spared no man's mortal preferences. Not where a ruthless ancestral consent bound this moment's flesh-and-blood royal cipher. And assuredly never, while Arithon's effort reframed the grand arc of renewal to salvage Athera's Paravians.

Dakar shivered, brushed by the finger of destiny. He was made of no such stern stuff, to wrestle the harrowing breach; not when the cruelty of true-sighted prescience rang like a bell to the thunderous chord surging upwards. The world-weary habit of dodgy retreat threshed him into a barricaded state of surrender. Guilt condemned him past mercy. For Valien's sacrifice had not found him innocent. Whether he dared to broach Arithon's estrangement, reconciliation on any terms might not exist.

The squalid hideout in the old, seaside tower no longer provided a surrogate refuge when the quickening sweep of the lane surge embroiled affairs in the east. Resigned as the struck spark ignited disaster, Dakar pulled on his holed boots and departed.

The first hammer tap tested the anvil while Rathain's northern trade-roads dried to hardpan clay under the grind of iron-rimmed wheels and the bedraggled tread of Etarra's migrant refugees. Clumped thorn at the verges still flowered when the select True Sect company tasked to corral the Light's renegade avatar debarked from a berthed galley at North Ward. With them came Nails, vexed by the sway of fresh sea legs, and hell-bound to amend her smirched record. Savage ambition cut no slack with her subordinate, whose pragmatism lidded the slow fuse of a temper scatheful as pressurized magma. Their ill-matched partnership dropped the pretence of cohesion past the town's landward gate.

There the temple's priority mission ground to a crawl, gummed by the multitude dispossessed by the plague rash of haunts grown endemic since solstice. The old, sanctioned thoroughfare alone granted townborn wayfarers an untroubled passage. Every benighted league was overburdened. Not only from Etarra's destitute traffic, but by seasonal trade displaced by the tremors that wracked the unstable cross-roads through the Mathorn Pass. Loss of the town's seizure of way rights struck nerves, the established convenience taken for granted throughout the centuries after the uprising.

"Worse," the lance captain drawled, "Lord Lysaer's self-indulgent tour of the northcoast sends us backside of the barbaric hinterlands." Grinding the sunburned jut of his jaw, he vented, "Damn all to black Shadow! Might've side-stepped this rumpus had Erdane's jilted council not fumbled the priesthood's tight leash at the start. Could've nabbed the almighty deserter before he dug in like a tick with the Light's war camp at Narms."

Nails mashed the bloodsucking fly lit on her mount, disinclined to nurture any man's hindsighted carping. As put off by the pathetic stream of humanity that hamstrung her urgent advance, she preferred to redress her hampered agenda through gaming the lancers' impatience.

Their bearded captain obliged her and stood in his stirrups, craning his neck. To no use: the shimmering heat-waves and pancake-flat countryside spoiled his vantage. Relapsed to fuming, he received in due course the apologetic report returned by his lathered outrider.

"We're at least a league distant from Callowswale's ferry." Reined in, flocked with dust, the man unclipped his helm and scrubbed gritty sweat from his forehead. "Got families bearing strapped bushels of infants. Urchins gadding baulked livestock, and mules overladen with craft tools and furniture. A plodding mess that makes the ox-drawn caravan here a ringside seat at the circus."

The lance captain seethed. "We've a river to cross before nightfall." Scaled gauntlet pointing, he cracked, "Carry on! Get a detachment busy ploughing a bypass."

The task squad deployed, jingling bits and accoutrements, while Nails spat stirred dust, looking bored. Welted by midges off the delta marshes, the stalled company behind her jostled and groused, sweltered by the delay and resigned to supper chewed cold under the haunted shadow of Fallowmere.

Idle pessimism compounded when the mounted advance floundered to a standstill, thwarted a long bowshot short of the riverbank.

"A carking shambles!" ranted the harried rider sent back through the press. "Can't go around. Every pesky refugee family's staked out their patch on both sides of the thoroughfare."

Nails's riveted interest mapped the cocky jut of the captain's chin.

"Light-blasted nuisance!" The man's corked temper scrapped the enervated dregs of decorum. "As if a two-legged menagerie griped at both ends doesn't pose us enough aggravation! Send the armoured lancers ahead."

"Why not unfurl the standards in front of the vanguard?" Nails frothed the stirred pot. "Our Sunwheel pennons should make a sufficient impression."

The dedicate lancers reordered their ranks. Shining white as the edge on a cleaver, the standard-bearer led the mounted company into the mire of animate motley. Grim purpose whipped them onwards for half a league: through staked livestock in various states of stripped harness, shrieking infants, bellowing donkeys, and yapping dogs herding skittish sheep. Amid the stewed fetor of fry fish and mutton smoked over open fires, the awakening dawned too late for dismay. This ragtag encampment sprawled unabated all the way to the riverside.

Steaming underneath their fine armour, the Light's horsemen snaked a jostling course past women with rolled sleeves bearing buckets. Parade dress dragged askew, they fetched up at the waterfront, impeded by farmwives with kirtled-up skirts pounding laundry in the rocky shallows.

Chatter stalled their barked order to clear the way. Over bonneted heads, past obstructive, sopped linens heaped in baskets, a jam in midstream at the Callowswale ford revealed the devilsome source of the impasse.

Several bare-chested men wielding barge poles sloshed waist deep to clear three canted wagons snagged to the axles. The bogged vehicles bucked the swirling current, an awkward flotilla ripe for an accident. One soaked draught team stood unhitched, switching flies on the far shore. The others strained, collared to a rope and tackle purloined from the ferry shed, and jury-rigged to the landing's stout bollards. Goaded and cursed by their sunburned drivers, the animals jostled in uneasy partnership, while the immersed helpers strained to lever the largest stuck dray from the submerged pothole.

The warp was drawn taut. The involved labourers had no attention to spare, nor apparently, a swill pail's inclination to pander to a temple cavalcade.

Needled by Nails's superior smirk, the lance captain's patience expired. "Take us through by whatever means necessary."

Erdane's coffers could settle for damages later. Righteously justified, the unmuzzled lancers jabbed spurs into their fractious mounts. The horn's blast for the charge trampled civilian outrage. Equine momentum shouldered forward, punched through screeching female obstruction, and dashed into the shallows to a silvered explosion of spray.

Nails curbed her palfrey. Hanging back with wolfish anticipation, she let the captain's blunder unfold.

Mid-river, the men minding the wagon's extraction straightened up, braced against the green tug of the current. Their turned heads ignored the on-coming horsemen, focused instead on the sodden fellow among them, who tossed his pole to a deferent henchman. A common farmhand dismissed at first glance, his tanned arm sheathed in muscle, and his folded headband knotted from sackcloth. Except for the inborn, peremptory demeanour, and single eye, arctic blue, that assessed the hapless plight of the folk caught up and milled by the melee.

No empty gesture, that man's raised fist loosed a crackling sheet of white light. Scattered droplets scalded, shrieking, to drifts of puffed steam as the surgical strike arced over the bystanders, grazed the air above the destriers' flattened ears, and sheared into the on-coming lancers. Their foray unravelled. Shocked into plunging disorder, blinded riders clung to their saddles, the luckless front rank thrown and trampled to maceration by their berserk mounts.

At safe remove from the havoc, Nails watched the paragon planted in the ford leave the jam of wrecked wagons. His damp headcloth, torn off, revealed his pale hair, plastered against neck and temple. Also a fury seared to full bore as daylight pinched the injured right eye to a murderous squint.

Then Lysaer s'Ilessid served his flaying rebuke on the armoured wrack of the Light's savaged casualties. "I will hold the officer in disgrace whose callous recklessness has endangered the helpless!" The decree hurled across the threshed roil of water sliced through turmoil with sovereign command. "Before my hearing addresses the guilty, every temple dedicate will be stripped of their weapons and badges of rank. Those hurt will be treated for injuries. Then the hale lancers under the Light's oath will soil their hands in reparation. No man rests until this wanton damage has been righted and tallied at law for punitive recompense."

The robin's egg sky of late day tinted the Callowswale ford's ruffled shallows when the corrective tour of duty wound down at long last. The True Sect veterans emerged wrung like rags, exhausted into shamed silence.

Surrounded by the flotsam of refugees, none had envisioned the sizeable war camp tucked under the eaves of the forest. Lysaer's officers suffered no slackers. Except for the diviner sidelined under restraint as a noncombatant, the stoutest veterans ached, muscles stretched to slack taffy.

Sundown flamed the horizon over the marshes when Lysaer's promised assize began. Lanterns on poles glimmered through fallen dusk, smoke laced by pungent oil to repel biting insects wafted through the darkening trees. Frogs chorused under the slats of the ferry dock, where the avatar's draped chair of state overlooked the cleared mud at the shoreline. A board trestle seated the True Sect company's spindly scribe, and an armed cordon flanked a parked dray stacked high with the spoils seized in forfeiture: an exquisite collection of armour, blazoned surcoats, and superior weapons. Grooms minded the picket of destriers, those lamed surrendered to the finicky care of his Lordship's Master of Horse.

Order prevailed. A liveried herald in Etarran scarlet called the hearing to order. The accused lancers lined up, unkempt and sunburned as the common folk come to bear witness or submit complaints. Discipline dressed the career elite like a plumbline. Raised chins and bare-knuckled pride endured the seeping pain of scalded, blind eyes, while the miserably sighted among them awoke to their disastrous peril. Too late, they recalled Erdane's senior commander had been supplanted. Lysaer owned the loyalty of the crack companies holding them to account.

Their lance captain faced the exalted Lord's judgement, not standing, but roped on his knees, his collarless neck scalded pink, and his freckled shoulders stripped naked. Outrage chiselled his leathery jaw, clamped in the constraint of a sullen man forced to swallow green bile under an upstart.

Then the avatar made his state appearance. Impeccably clad, devoid of jewels, his bare head the sole shimmer of bullion about him, Lysaer s'Ilessid claimed the raised seat with iconic majesty. His frosty regard swept the supplicants, a presence of impartial justice cold as bared steel amid the abrupt, fallen hush. Most arraigned for chastisement went weak at the knees, cowed to trembling remorse.

Not their hardened captain, whose murderous rage stunned even the most seasoned onlookers. "Incarnate divinity you may have been before you fell prey to corruption. But the human part of your nature's gone rogue, confirmed by this assault on my lancers. The Law of the Canon shall annul your exalted status. Let the record declare you an apostate."

"Lord of Light, without nominal godhood will suffice," Lysaer denounced without heat. "Your offence on my docket is criminal assault, unembellished by ideology. Upright integrity never runs amok over innocents. Responsible ethic does not forsake principled equity. Nor does honest cause grant the licence for the roughshod brutality witnessed today."

"For what stakes?" The disgraced captain spat. "How many blameless Etarrans have been driven from their homes by the vile incursion of Shadow?" Stiffened to revolt, he challenged, "Were those worthy folk put to flight of less merit? How many more must suffer the brunt for your sorry failure to lead? Is the uncanny havoc sown in Rathain by the Dark's reign of terror to go unchecked until such horror afflicts all the world?"

Lysaer's cameo expression stayed pitiless. "I will curb that wild threat. Forget at your peril! Your blessed Canon is no law of mine. The temple's avowed purpose might seem to align. But now, then, or ever, I'll not have my name or my choices attached to anyone's fanatical worship. Faith turned as a weapon breeds vicious contempt. An unquestioned doctrine debases the value of others, with mercy degraded as means to an end that abandons morality. Justice must be served. On my own terms directly, speak again out of turn, and my bailiff will gag you."

Lysaer dispatched further discussion forthwith. "I'll hear the cases, starting with the injured civilians."

The first petitioner entered the torchlight, a sturdy goodwife with country skirts and two grubby toddlers. The clerk's crisp recitation presented her straits: a brother harmed by a lancer's horse while he watered their yoked oxen at the riverside.

"Dislocated his shoulders when the upset beeves bolted." The woman accused in hoarse anguish, "Who's to manage the wagon, except for myself? We have no paid hand, nor any grown sons."

Lysaer made disposition. "A soldier wounded in the Light's service is cared for at temple expense until fit for duty." The elevated comparison stirred sullen mutters throughout the dedicate assembly. "Recompense will be paid to your family, underwritten by the lance company's treasury. Give your name to the scribe." Snapped fingers set the terms into record.

The bound captain glared daggers to no avail. The avatar's seal on the verdict would be honoured, unless an appeal to the high priesthood at Erdane denounced today's sham as a venal pretention.

The wronged matron accepted her stamped writ, eased on her way by Lysaer's personal word of regret. The next petitioner's case was advanced, and the next, an onerous procession that ground inexorably into the night. Whether pleaded in labourer's dialect or the languid vowels of Etarra's pedigree elite, Lysaer heard every detailed complaint, and allotted them fair compensation: for maiming, a pension or convalescent care paid in coin. For torn clothes, crippled livestock, and mild contusions, a gold Sunwheel button stripped from an offender's confiscated accoutrements. For families afflicted with loss of livelihood, missed wages were accounted to the penny.

No petty distress was dismissed. No plaintiff left empty-handed. The tedious process dragged on in formality, to the last mangled goose and burst egg in its crushed osier basket.

The scalded lancers were kept standing throughout. None had been fed, though a stableboy hauled a filled bucket to quench their thirst. Those too proud to drink from cupped hands stayed parched, while the torches burned low and fizzled to embers.

Lysaer showed no fatigue. The lamed shoulder perhaps less than trim beneath the sartorial perfection of his state dress, he turned off the servant arrived with fresh cressets. "No. Dispensation for this militant lot will be quick."

Hope for reprieve died. Lysaer's imperious survey measured the cashiered men without quarter through a strained stillness surreal against the routine of the settled encampment. Voices and laughter wafted through the dwindled smoke of the campfires. Stars pricked the black sky, backdrop for the avatar's golden facade, flawed only by the livid welt that pulled his scarred socket askew. None dared interpret that half-lidded gaze. The offenders' fates were weighed under a scrutiny that compounded their excoriating indignity.

Then judgement spoke, the stern sentence aimed to break the most hot-blooded ambition. "The lancers struck blind are already punished. They shall be turned off empty-handed, forthwith. Let them beg in the streets, or better, seek menial labour to redress their disrepute in humility. Their noncombatant servants and squires are blameless. They are free to fare onwards or stay for hire to whomever they please. Lancers left sighted are offered a choice. They may join my ranks with their seniority forfeit. Tasked as of tomorrow, they will train my green recruits for a penalty term of five years, after which they may earn an advancement by merit. Each man keeps his boots and the clothes on his back. Their temple kit, all the horses, armour and weapons will be redistributed to the striplings signed onto my rolls who have none."

A grim pause extended, pregnant with dread, until Lysaer saw fit to continue. "Under wrongful orders, today's reckless action reviled decency and violated the covenant of due process. The honourless who spurn to redeem their good name will be branded tonight, marked by hot iron as outcast and forsworn."

The fate decreed for their commander forgave nothing. "Your captain pays with his life, come the dawn. For no blowhard's self-righteous authority can be trusted, nor will I condone the cavalier arrogance that forgets mercy and oversteps the restraint of humane accountability."

A nod signalled the bailiffs, who closed with armed enforcement. At weapons' point, they herded the sentenced lancers into custody.

"Rot damn you in Darkness for treason," shouted the condemned captain hauled off in chains by compatriots suborned by Lysaer's charisma.

Impatient, mailed hands divided his disbanded company. Some, winnowed separate, signed on for reassignment to a common soldier's billet. Rage and argument contorted the shuffle, where the stiff-necked and the furious brokered their future with resentment and disbelief. Their bluster changed nothing. Embers glowed in the blacksmith's forge, the nestled iron awaiting the foreheads of any too prideful to bend.

The captain's scarred sergeant reviled the summary dismissal that beggared his lot. "How dare you disrupt a True Sect mission pledged to uphold the beacon of the everlasting? An egregious act at this critical hour, while the taproot of Darkness arises once more!"

His shouted objection pushed equanimity too far: Lysaer's sharp astonishment curdled the outburst. "Light's grace, do you truly believe I'm that craven? I aim to address the fell crisis in person. As the profligate cause of today's delay, how galling to hear your baseless claim, sprung from an empty creed that insinuates otherwise."

Skewered to flushed embarrassment, the discharged dedicate blazed back with clenched fists. "You realize your seizure of True Sect authority cannot bear up under scrutiny."

"No?" Lysaer s'Ilessid vacated his lofty seat, blistered to caustic amusement. "Is Erdane's priesthood too shallow to finger the actual upstart? A Mayor Elect holds his office for life, a point of town law established for centuries before fatuous men scribed the temple writ that defines the pages of True Sect Canon!" *That fast*, he crushed the retort in contempt. "How do you imagine your adulterated faith should resolve a dispute vouchsafed by the vetted miracle of my immortality?"

Lysaer's acid closure levelled the scales. "Let death itself test your piety's worth. The burden is yours to arrange the last rites for your condemned captain. Coin will be allotted to pay for his burial, along with the courier's fee to inform Erdane's High Temple of his demise."

* * *

For Dace Morley, the night's extended anxiety stemmed from the tedium of genteel service. As the lowliest cog in the staff attached to the war camp's pavilion, a valet had little influence to bend the discourse of greater affairs. The fine, trodden line was more viciously dangerous, since the volatile thrust of his liege's cursed motives had seized fractious command of armed strength. Dace raged under the guise of constraint, the urgent, close contact he needed to temper the quandary too often forced back at remove. Lysaer had annexed squires for daytime attendance and practice at arms. Eager pages polished his weapons and kit. Lackeys hauled buckets and heated his bath, and a steward managed the provisions, the cook, and the civilized table appointed for his titled guests.

Left with oversight of the wardrobe and jewels, the linens, and the tagged hampers shuttled to the laundresses, Dace fretted under the isolation imposed by his covert role. Idle chat breached the mores of domestic protocol. Lysaer's morning shave and the attendance that dressed him stayed silent, unobtrusive efficiency maintained in propriety while officers bustled through with their reports, and runners and scribes received messages for the couriers. Untoward speech incurred risk, even during the master's retirement, when canvas walls and the cover of darkness encouraged loitering eavesdroppers.

Dace tracked Lysaer's moods through acute observation, and measured the nuance that inflected his manner by touch. Outside his purview, he gleaned word of his master's affairs at second hand, omissions sketched in by gossip.

Tonight, caged by duty under the pavilion's guttering lamps, Dace fretted against mounting unease. An unknown delay stalled his liege in the aftermath of the formal assize, although filtered noise from the riverside suggested the assembly came to an end. The screams of the branded faded to fallen quiet against the backdrop rush of the Callowswale's torrent. The restive movement of torches winked out. Whoops from rough horseplay and laughter wound down as the off-duty troops sought their bedrolls.

The calls of the checkpoint sentries marked Lysaer's two older pages, excused to retire. The drooping boy squire set their lord's arms to rights, while Dace fretted beneath stern deportment, his empty hands left with nothing to do.

Such unnatural deportment pinched the youthful spirit crammed into eclipse, the hindsight malaise of regret come too late. Lysaer's long convalescence may have seemed at the time a clear path through the nadir of hope. But naïvete shattered upon his release, once affairs in the wider world bestowed prestige and power, inflected by Desh-thiere's curse. Temperamentally volatile as never before, Lysaer's condition became unmanageable where class barriers gutted a countermeasured response.

The wait dragged. Dace fumed, unauthorized to send an enquiry. The last, wakeful staff were long since in bed. Posted since sundown, the guards by the entry knew nothing. Dace suffered the worrisome vigil alone, nerves sawed by the tremolo descant of nocturnal insects. The wilds were not his natural element. Clad in livery, not skirts, the pleasure of crowded warmth in the taverns and the piquant thrill of wagers at the dartboard felt remote as a wistful dream. Remembrance of human fellowship in female persona opened the floodgates of useless nostalgia.

No going back to that care-free life, or those illusory friendships. Not since a public trial for witchcraft had made kin turn their backs, and acquaintances swear damning testimony. The long days on the march only salted the wound. Even while alienated, Dace's burdened heart could not disown the refugees' misery. Mass flight from Etarra might afflict distressed family, each weary face he passed by the wayside a possible, chance-met encounter with a dispossessed relative.

Apprehension salved nothing. Not while his servile existence hung on the singular voice, at last returned within earshot. Dace picked out the bearer's lit torch through the trees. Then the master's distinctive blond head and immaculate bearing, shoulders stiffened by the suppressed hitch of a limp.

A stranger's voice partnered Lysaer's discourse. Not that of a discreet retainer, but a piercing soprano whose vehemence exuded an overbearing authority. A woman: one uncowed by magisterial force, and forthright in her steamed disagreement. Consonants sheared to exasperation bore in at a clip that tingled a warning through s'Gannley instincts.

Dace reacted on foresight and kindled the lamps. He rousted a servant to prepare refreshments, then readied the partitioned guest quarters reserved for state visitors. Time allowed nothing more. Composed on return to his post by the entry, Dace peered past the stolid stance of the night guard and surveyed the indignant arrival. Captive, not visitor, she came in duress, wrists bound and prodded in the small of her back by two reliable Erdani veterans.

Their irruptive charge seemed a mere slip before their armoured bulk, her awkward, emaciated angles gadded by a rapacious energy that tussled with their martial tread. The oddity jarred, that adherents distanced from the High Temple's influence managed her with wary reluctance. Her person lacked the visible means to intimidate: cropped ash-brown hair fringed a seamed forehead steep as a cliff, and her blade-thin posture draped the fabric of Sunwheel trappings like grave-clothes over her papery skin. Nearer, the fluttering torch illumined the gold sash and insignia of a certified True Sect diviner.

Dace averted his glance. The Sorcerer's mark on his chest twinged under the talent's scouring scrutiny, which thankfully noted his servant's livery and flicked away, unimpressed.

Lysaer's dour guards, deemed more worthy of notice, received their prisoner's brazen contempt. The hawked gob of spittle she splashed towards their boots uncorked a spate of vituperative rancour.

"Light's blinding glory! I don't jump at the bidding of conscripted lackeys." Her staccato annoyance shrilled higher. "Did I escape Shadow's filth and a rampage of haunts to be thwarted by a backwater puppet show costumed for philanthropy? Damn the rot of subversive apostasy! Resurgent evil takes hold, root and branch, while the True Sect council sits on its collective arse, breaking theosophical wind and nitpicking the particulars of the Light's Canon. And you!" she added to Lysaer, unfazed, "Shame us for sheep, that we fawned over the marvel of your convalescent decrepitude!"

Her target side-stepped the withering blast with the burnished aplomb of the statesman. "Dace?" Yet the note of appeal adroitly suppressed bespoke Lysaer's besieged tension. "Have wine brought. Fruit and cheese only for two. My wardens at arms will remain outside for the interview."

The pavilion's paired guards accepted the irregular arrangement, closed ranks in lockstep, and blocked the diviner's reverse at the threshold. Dace offered the comfort of private seating, where refreshment laid out on a lacquered tray awaited the master's pleasure. The disgruntled subject of enquiry threw her trussed frame into the cushioned camp furnishing, which creaked under the cavalier usage. Her demonstrative gesture of outthrust, lashed wrists received Dace's impervious bow. Dead to the indiscretion shoved into his path, he poured claret in goblets, while Lysaer took the upright, carved chair he preferred when confronted by a hostile challenge.

Dace trod lightly, his sense of Desh-thiere's latent influence ominous as the unsounded stress on an overcranked string. The absence of jewels concealed the slight tremor that flawed his master's self-contained bearing, making a valet's circumspect assessment more difficult.

Lysaer sipped to stall, his marked disinterest intended to goad equilibrium. His testy prisoner resisted, until the clapped lid on her indignation boiled over.

She banged down her bound forearms to a jounced clash of crystal. "Free my hands. Now! Then explain why you've dragged me in here."

The raptor's gleam behind Lysaer's focus intensified, grim forerunner to the active prod of the curse. The goblet set aside became the stalker's prelude to a laid ambush. "Because, my dear, I suspect you wanted this audience private. Or did you finagle your chance and invite capture for some other end?"

A flush splotched the diviner's gaunt cheeks. "I'm no one's dearie. Don't test the mistake."

"Nails, then," Lysaer allowed, equable, his informed use of her dedicates' nickname a jab to unseat a seasoned ambassador. "You guided the company that strayed into Shadow at Ithamon's ruin on the autumn equinox. Let's ditch the theatrics. Surely your True Sect superiors have brought you here under assignment. The astute question follows. Have you seized the opportunity to manipulate your own agenda? The lance captain sentenced to death deserved better. Shall we discuss that bare-knuckled byplay under truce as my guest?"

Cued, the left-side guard by the door drew his knife. Freed by his deft cut, the diviner chafed circulation back into her sinewy wrists. Outside, the camp slept in oblivious quiet. The canny opponent in her position must realize her official standing did not exist; only the trusted eyes of Lysaer's wakeful servant and four guards of impeccable loyalty witnessed her contentious fate. Dace watched her calculate what her survival was worth.

Determined, where prudence should have scared the starch out of anyone courting the predation of the Mistwraith's geas, the diviner leaned into the gambit. "You detest Shadow as I do. Would that be your purpose for dragging a vested temple talent under your roof?"

Lysaer pounced, smiling. "Darling! Did I seem so naïve? Your uncanny endowment isn't exclusive, or rare. Far from the provenance of the blessed, the arcana sequestered in Erdane's library was written centuries before your religion saw birth."

"But not the knowledge stored in the locked crypt at Hanshire." Her curled lip the vixen's bared glint of white teeth, the diviner taunted, "Proscribed texts and heresy quite unfit for the righteous are held under the provenance of our priests." Agile fingers spurned the untouched wine and instead shaved a sliver of cheese. Like a gobbet savoured blood-wet from a sacrifice, Nails bit down. "Also treatises on chartered restrictions and land use, secured under interdict for thousands of years."

"And yet, you're aware of them. Sent here quite likely to dangle forbidden knowledge as a bargainer's bribe." Lysaer twirled his goblet, reflective except for the tension that sculpted his jaw.

"Of course." Nails chewed and swallowed. "Those books source the techniques that enable our arts of divining. Also information scribed by Koriathain, that empowers the examiners' sanctified practice of compulsory interrogation."

"You assume I'd traffic in the sisterhood's secrets?" Lysaer's distaste seeped through, his hatred of sorcery and his brush with the Grey Kralovir's necromancy a horror beyond banal concealment.

"I assume nothing," Nails insisted.

Dace dissected Lysaer's rapt disquiet, cognizant of the perilous undercurrent, but helpless to thwart such an expertly curated overture.

Nails stretched, pleased to toy with her wicked ascendency. "Why else broach the unsavoury topic at all?"

Lysaer's riposte was oil and honey, prelude to the venomous sting. "Because you survived the ruinous conjury that swept through Ithamon and witnessed the launch of the spectral cascade that's disrupted trade and savaged the peace." He raised his goblet in tribute, composed as ice sheathed in a snowdrift. "I plan to reclaim that scourged ground by right. As Mayor of Etarra, I won't need the clinging petticoats of religion to banish the throwback taint before the incursion takes permanent root."

"Then you need me, past question," Nails rebutted with unblinking ferocity. "Our interests align. Yours to reclaim your governor's seat and mine to expunge the stain on my career caused by the Master of Shadow. But without my contribution, you must reckon the severe disadvantage you face on your enemy's turf in Rathain. If you want to take down Arithon s'Ffalenn, I hold the sure key to defeat an attuned crown prince upon his sovereign ground."

And the laid snare primed by the named enemy snapped closed.

Dace inwardly wept, ignored in his dim corner, as the quickened spark of enticement struck tinder and kindled Desh-thiere's directive. Lysaer succumbed to the irresistible blandishment aimed to leverage his half brother's demise. Whether Nails was the agent entrusted to further the True Sect quest for expansion, or a lone-wolf fanatic obsessed with revenge, the proposal the diviner's malice concocted froze the loyal s'Gannley blood in Dace's veins. Any amassed campaign to enforce way rights through the Mathorn Pass threatened an avalanche of disastrous consequence: for no mortal interference with Athera's primary network of electromagnetics escaped the Fellowship Sorcerers' censure.

First Repudiation

Lysaer's revised strategy cascaded fresh change through the probable range of Sethvir's earth-sense. Overwhelmed by the multiplied impacts, he caught his shocked balance by starlight at Althain Tower's north-facing casement. The qualm shuddered through him and disrupted the critical line of his immersive incantation. Flickers of refracted light juddered through the glass-tipped harpoon bridged between his spread hands. Paravian mariners had crafted such weapons to slay meth-spawned monstrosities that preyed on their keels from the deep. Tonight, his custodian's care of their legacy went for naught: the critical conjury to harden the edge would not be retuned into stable completion.

A failure of paltry significance, since the greater krakens, long dead, threatened no one. Their lesser kin, exiled through West Gate to the oceans of Dascen Elur, kept their accord with the Fellowship Sorcerers still.

Else, Sethvir grumbled, vexed, "History would have seen Karthan's freebooting mariners devoured, and two *particular* royal exiles could not have survived to knot their blood-feuding trouble through Athera's contrary mangle of problems."

Swearing in six languages, none of them native, Althain's Warden flexed ink-stained fingers and rested the harpoon against the stone sill. "Devil take the fell spawn of the devil!"

For the onrushing ripple of consequence mapped an upset at horrific scale. Drastic measures in repercussion demanded a cross-continent contact with Asandir . . .

*   *   *

The urgent call overtook the field Sorcerer at Queen Ceftwinn's court, his seated breakfast with Traithe crammed like stolen warmth in the black hour before a daybreak departure. An infrequent pleasure, curdled when the raven perched on the adjacent chair back fluffed its raised hackles and cawed in strident alarm. Asandir froze between bites, long legs in knit stockings extended beneath the antique lacquer table.

The shock that drained his cragged features elicited Traithe's concerned sympathy. "Daelion Fatemaster's nitpicking list! Can the crisis not wait through the course of one meal?"

"No." Plate abandoned, Asandir thrust to his feet. "Sethvir's dispatched an adamant summons."

"You'll be leaving directly?" Traithe laid down his fork, dashed to resignation. "I'll have a page fetch your leathers and boots."

Asandir shook his head. "No need. Our Warden's en route." Amid the sudden, unfurled corona of his unshielded power, he stretched out a hand and snapped, "Reach!"

Sethvir's inbound step from Althain Tower brought a sharp shift in air pressure that slopped the filled teacups. Ruffled, the raven swivelled its head as porcelain and silverware chimed in complaint, and a book tumbled with a smack off the adjacent shelf.

Arrived in haggard state, wreathed in a spitting crackle of static, Sethvir lamented, "Some days I'm tempted to toss Mankind's leave to inhabit Athera into oblivion as a lost cause!"

Traithe yielded the host's place at the table. Braced for a problem with casualties, he rescued his overset tome, then dragged up a stuffed chair to ease the chronic pinch of his scars.

"What's Arithon done this time?" raged Asandir, the perilous, unspent charge on his person not yet furled into containment.

"Not Arithon. *Lysaer!*" Sethvir raked down his flyaway hair, aggravated beyond his indulgent taste for refreshments. "Damn all to the ignorant absence of training that leaves the man wide open to manipulation."

Traithe shoved the spurned seat with a suggestive toe. "Koriathain are aiming to play him, again?"

"Hand in glove with the fresh round of impetus well poisoned by slighted True Sect ambition, we have a reprise of premeditated conspiracy aimed to derail our primary directive." Sethvir blinked as though dazzled by a bull's-eye lamp. "Desh-thiere's geas was ignited by ruthless design. S'Ilessid swallowed the bait and committed his ardent followers. They'll be on the march by tomorrow, intent to salvage the squatters' hold at Etarra by razing the array of Paravian megaliths on the Plain of Araithe."

Asandir's astonishment broke into profanity. "Of all the Ath-forsaken, *brainless* acts born of pulverizing stupidity!" Beyond stark madness, the effort to unseat the ancient channel that upstepped the fifth lane would uproot the anchor that stabilized the axis of the continent's major fault-line. Tectonic forces would rupture. The catastrophic recoil invited a sundering past the pale of the First-Age cataclysm that drove Mhorovaire's subsidence under the Westland Sea. "This stroke of dim-witted destruction takes the eternal prize!"

Sethvir's confirmation dismembered pity. "We haven't the grace to prevaricate, even for blistering language."

"The hammer's fall will occur before solstice?" Asandir deduced, beset.

"Countermeasures must happen sooner. I'm sorry." Sethvir lamented the incorrigible bind, that Lysaer's fate remained ousted from the compact's protection. Nor would the flash-point pressure of Desh-thiere's geas permit the valet in his service the safe margin to try a tactful intervention.

Already Asandir's anguish mapped out the collateral ramifications. "We cannot leave Daliana unwarned." Her s'Gannley mettle would not shirk the futile attempt to deflect Lysaer's disastrous strategy.

Sethvir's broadscale vantage had vaulted ahead. "Kharadmon's been sent to forestall her." Scarcely the worst diabolical upset, Rathain's crown prince would be ousted from his headstrong seclusion straight into a frontal collision with a war host. "A curse-bent entanglement now would see Lysaer destroyed."

How wounding a sorrow to gut the moral fidelity behind the Masterbard's meticulous planning: the gradual upshift to vacate the Mathorn Pass before the peak surge fulfilled his bid for a restoration required six more months to mature. The slow build of raised resonance, spun up by the solstice tide, had been entrained with precision to uproot Etarra's persistent inhabitants. By autumn, the last refugees should have packed up and fled, well before the frost at midwinter pried into the stress cracks stitched through their cemented masonry by repetitive quakes. Next spring's cumulative structural weaknesses would be ripe for the tuned note to crumble the bulwarks and buckle the upstart settlement into collapse.

Every masterful stroke of Arithon's finale built on the fifth lane's transmission, the might of the flux current tempered at full bore through the Ilitharis markers on the Plain of Araithe.

"Ath wept!" Traithe exclaimed, his shooed deterrence ignored as the raven swooped down to rifle the cream. Their Fellowship could not stand idle. Not while stone rendered conscious by the centaur guardians faced a profane demolition to violate the sovereignty of an attuned crown prince. "Too much rests on Prince Arithon's shoulders. A man can be driven too hard for too long."

Asandir's fury transcended speech. How bitter this hour's descent into havoc, wreaked in malice to weaken the compact. The brutal irony stabbed to the quick, for an upset spawned by the same vengeful diviner just mercifully spared from Ithamon's lethal harmonic.

"Hell's finger has already poisoned the brew." Sethvir waved the plundering bird off the breakfast tray, dispatched the tepid dregs of the tea, and sank into the hard chair at the head of the table. No choice, ahead, but to brazen the course and task his colleagues for a last-minute salvage. "At best we've a fortnight to resolve this before bloodshed erupts in the recoil."

His expanded faculties perceived no concrete warning of other factors afoot. Nonetheless, Althain's Warden stayed guarded, pricked by elusive unease. While the Seven formulated the delicate handling of their response, the hollow foreboding persisted: that somewhere, a stalker's pre-emptive move from the shadows flicked the touch match into the tinderbox.

The latent storm gathered, poised for the sparked catalyst as Rathain's ruined crown seat cast pooled shade upon stone, serene under fair sky at late morning. Past the sentinel height of the Compass Point Towers, spring sunlight buttered the lush vales of Daon Ramon, the storied grassland once beloved by the Riathan in resplendent bloom for the first time in eight centuries. Arithon savoured the view from a sheltered niche, shoulders braced sidewards between two carved merlons atop Kieling Tower's upper battlement. Unguarded solitude found him at ease as he finessed the final tuning of the lyranthe nestled in his lap.

Desolation no longer keened like a dirge through Rathain's ancient capital. Breeze chipped diamond reflections off the Severnir's current below and flicked Arithon's black hair into elf locks. The ruin wore the seductive fragrance of wildflowers, shattered stone garlanded in pallid lime runners of ivy and bramble.

No untoward warning riffled the Masterbard's tranquillity. The sweet glide of the tensioned string he adjusted climbed gently under his applied torque. Contentment infused his rare moment of calm. A shudder of joy ran over and through him as the note achieved perfect pitch. Arithon locked the ebony-and-abalone shell peg head, then proceeded with the next course, minutes before the noon flux crest swept the focus site in the King's Tower's shorn foundation.

Each fortnight, at the full and the dark of the moon, he engaged his high art to augment the melody guiding the cascade to upshift the fifth lane. Immersed, his initiate talent in fugue with Ithamon's electromagnetic signature, he glanced up, startled, as the cliff swallows' aerobatic gyrations exploded into arrowed flight. Silence muffled their cheerful chirps.

Then the rush of Ithamon's wind paused, seized into suspension, the held breath before a powerful burst of actualized lane force stunned every wide-opened nerve raw. Pain jangled senses attuned to a land's pulse suddenly wrenched into dissonance. Voice gasped, short of outcry, while the instrument under the musician's hands thrummed an atonal wail, disharmony transferred through sensitive wood from the wasp hum of silver-wound strings. Arithon launched from the battlement. Running throughout his descent of the stair, he refounded his unseated discipline, steadied his faculties, and slowed his raced heartbeat.

Sound was his trained element. Close in proximity, he traced the shock wave's source to the King's Tower circle. Yet no answering tremor recoiled through Kieling's laid stone underfoot. His aghast recognition awakened too late: an uncharted, prepotent assault on the lane current had upended the metered progress of his engaged strategy. The graduated build of high resonance he forged into alignment with such care to empty the squatter population from Etarra thundered into confluent unity *here and now,* impelled to peak prematurely.

Instantaneous, the impact released an explosive peal of harmonics: tonal frequencies fit to raze any edifice caught out of phase with the precipitous surge.

Arithon registered the catastrophic consequence in bursting, white rage. When the heightened blast combed over the Mathorn notch, walls and buildings haplessly built out of true would be tumbled into collapse.

Devastation would macerate everything trapped in the breach: people, animals, works of fine art. An instant's interference summoned the might to displace the controlled arc of his cautious working. This explosive completion, closed at pressured speed, destroyed the prearranged, measured pattern begun at autumn equinox, and harnessed by increments parsed to span the next eighteen months.

No hostile upset: only one wilful power on site at Ithamon was capable of the feat.

The Masterbard's headlong rush burst in upon Tarens, busy punching down bread dough at the pantry trestle.

"Here!" Arithon thrust his priceless lyranthe into the crofter's floury grip. "Take her! The fleece cover's tossed on my bed. Bundle her up and secure her in safety."

Tarens clutched the antique instrument in gobsmacked consternation. "You intend to bolt *down there?*" He side-stepped, decisive, and thwarted his liege's impetuous path. "For a head-on confrontation with *Davien?*"

Scorched by Arithon's incandescent glare, Tarens puffed bristled cheeks. "More fool you, then. The Sorcerer stormed out in a vicious temper. You imagine you'll beard that tiger bare-knuckled?" Singed a pace backwards, deflated, he cowered behind the lyranthe as a shield. "Man! You'll get butchered to dog-meat. Welcome to that mauling, all by yourself."

"I am in much worse than a terrible mood," Arithon snapped. "Block my way at your peril."

Tarens held his ground, mulish. "Whatever's been done lies beyond your control."

That blunt admission checked Arithon cold. The fury that smoked off his stillness was murderous. "*You knew?* That the Sorcerer meant to level Etarra stone from set stone by the ruinous might of a convergent harmonic surge?"

No need to elaborate. Tarens looked ghastly peaked under the flour dusting his nose. Unreconciled to the mass casualty of innocents, he deflected the interrogation. "What could I have done? Davien's not forthcoming. Damn all, neither one of you lends anyone the civilized grace of forewarning."

"Then what deadly intent has the Sorcerer kept hidden?" Arithon bulled past to ransack his quarters. "Mankind's affairs devolve to crown justice. Under law, in accord with Rathain's royal charter, I have not been consulted! Moreover, a Sorcerer who invokes the Fellowship's superseding authority must honour free will under the Major Balance!"

Light through the casement blued Tarens's petrified pallor. "Davien expected that argument. His testy remark insisted he was not acting by Fellowship agency."

"Then whom does he serve? And for what murky motive?" Arithon snatched his baldric and sheathed sword from the armoire. "By Ath, on that score, I'm due a straight answer in behalf of Rathain's injured subjects. No chance I'll stand down and see a hapless people ploughed under by broadscale massacre."

Tarens swallowed, the lyranthe cradled against his stricken chest. "That wanton damage is done." He ventured the dangerous ground and tried reason. "Nothing under my power or yours can salvage the outcome in motion."

"Sithaer take the awareness, I know! Which leaves the affray in my hands to finish." Consumed by haste, Arithon slung the Paravian blade at his hip. "I can, and by Dharkaron's Black Vengeance, I will challenge my usurped right to royal authority."

The nerveless effrontery jerked Tarens up short. He said, desperate, "What if the Sorcerer refuses to answer? Sky and earth, Arithon, nothing good can be gained!"

Green eyes met blue in glacial rebuttal. Then Arithon stated, "I can abdicate."

"Mercy avert!" Tarens pealed, blindsided by a past *caithdein*'s echo of outraged astonishment. "Not so easily done without a due-process petition for Sethvir's release."

"No?" Irony glittered in Arithon's glance, flicked askance to contain the incisive promise of a lethal retort. "Then Jieret's lack of imagination on that score confounds the perversity of flat rejection."

"The very suggestion you'd gainsay a Sorcerer is raving insanity!" Ruthlessly outmatched, Tarens resorted to pleas. "Liege, you're needed as never before. After-shock will reap a groundswell of blood fury such as your feal clansmen have never seen."

Shoved aside, the ex-crofter snapped, "Then by Ath, have your tantrum alone. I'll stay uninvolved while Davien knocks you to your senses." Wiser to sane limits, he backed off and left Arithon to his irrational sprint down the stairwell.

"Grant my plagued bones their sweet peace in the afterlife!" Tarens blurted to the vacated room. Shaking, beyond scared, he buffed smeared flour off the heirloom instrument's lacquer polish, then restored the fleece cover with rattled hands and stomped back to the pantry trestle.

His violent punch at the unfinished dough skinned his knuckles against the plank underneath. "Daelion Fatemaster's immortal witness!" he yelped. "Geld me under a True Sect examiner's knives before I take the brunt of s'Ffalenn temper."

He did not mean to waver. But his ironclad resolve spun away, undone by an onslaught of dizziness. Tarens lost the wind for ripe langue, hurled headlong into the spontaneous throes of Jieret's inherited s'Valerient Sight . . .

The same spring sunlight glittered like foil off the snowcapped summits of the Mathorns, where block walls and doubled brick revetments cupped Etarra's chock-a-block jumble of peaked roofs. Devastation came wrapped in stunned quiet, the mountain breeze strangled breathless. The red-and-gold banners and blazoned trade pennons sagged and draped limp on their poles. A scrape against fallen hush like cast glass, a dog barked. Then another, and another, until the panicked chorus racketed over the distanced, ants' lines of the mule trains baulked on the switched-back causeway.

Then sound swelled, a mighty bone-shaking chord of raw noise, offset by the shrill scream of harmonics. Earth and stone shuddered as a bothered horse would dislodge a swarm of biting flies. The din burgeoned and shrieked, as hammer to anvil, the resonant assault spidered cracks through mortared walls and half-timbered buildings. Masonry shimmered into collapse, shuddered flat in an instant to a strewn rickle of tumbled debris. Palled dust plumed over the wreckage, not one standing structure left upright.

Thin as the crying of gulls, anguished screams threaded the rumbled grind of settling rubble.

Tarens recovered his horrified awareness, slumped with his cheek pillowed in squashed bread dough. The tower beneath him buzzed in sympathy with the shock of the etheric transmission, whiplashed the entire length of the fifth lane. Reason strove and failed to assimilate the gut punch of cataclysmic event. Disbelief stumbled before the widespread scope of the unbridled disaster. All the gaudy, teeming life packed into the streets of Etarra, gone in an instant, levelled at who knew what agonized price in snuffed lives.

Sensibility lost to incandescent, galled conscience.

No matter, now, whether Earl Jieret's imprinted priorities jammed in a countrybred craw: reft of grounds to fault Arithon's impetuous motivation, argument caved before straight-laced decency. Tarens mustered the brave will to reap the whirlwind, at least to bear brazen witness to Arithon's response in the aftermath.

The fool's errand spurred the crofter out of Kieling Tower and into the eroded, desolate avenue that accessed the high courtyard, thrice ruined since the First Age. Arithon would have gone straight to the King's Tower foundation, where the engaged might of the Paravian focus now subsided past the shimmering flare of maximized resonance. Backwash lane current rippled yet in titanic reverberation.

Tarens had experienced the after-shock recoil before, though never while conscious, and not at this magnitude. Discharge spun off the excited flux lifted his hair and jumbled his senses to the verge of black-out derangement. The residual electromagnetic spike reamed him with shudders and arced static between his finger-tips.

Ahead of him, Arithon also must be obliged to take pause, mortal frailty compelled to maintain a safe distance while the heightened frequency dropped back within range of human tolerance. The slipstream dizzied Tarens to nausea. The weathered stone paving underfoot lost all semblance of firm continuity, rendered dissolute as the dimensional seep bled his surrounds into an oil-film veil of hallucination. Sight burned, infused by the forgotten glory of Athera's ancient inhabitants, wrestled into disorientation by the shimmered imprint of architecture long since vanished and reduced to dust.

The tidal rush of the ephemeral ebbed, each stretched second releasing the overburden of upscaled energies. Artefacts warped into the present bled off, filtered by the return of natural senses. Tarens walked under blue sky and sunshine, through the present-day ruin whose artistry still graced a beauty fit to stun Mankind witless with awe. Lore dismissed lightly elsewhere could not be silenced here, where the distant past imbued even the most battered carvings with emphatic eloquence.

After extended months spent in Ithamon's desecrate shadow, Tarens still reeled under a loss to raise tears for an absence beyond worldly description. All comparison suffered. The moonstone shimmer that glanced across centaur masonry dulled the finest of polished gemstones. Lyric sound spoke from these battered walls, too refined for the ear, but accessible to a bard's gifted perception.

Yet Arithon's fraught haste would not have bypassed the sorrows of ages under the moment's goad of provocation, however sorely the residual intonation flayed his emotional equilibrium.

Tarens passed through the memorial archway. Opened before him, the round plaza echoed to his frantic steps, heaved paving scored by the glassine scars of past siege and the wanton depredation of the legendary Great Gethorn. Burdened by the age-old whispers of tragedy, and gut sick with foreboding, he leaped the remnant foundation of the King's Tower that centred Ithamon's windswept top tier.

The focus circle's seamless inlay spanned the concave declivity, laced yet by the revenant, gossamer form of the turret razed by the Second-Age trauma of Marin Eliathe's murder. Emerged from the luminous wisps that dispersed under brazen, full sun, Davien's erect figure strode off the mother-of-pearl gleam of spiked power not quite settled into quiescence. His carriage exuded the clipped impetus of instigation, damning as the ozone reek of unshed lane charge wafted off his tumbled hair and extravagant dress.

Rathain's prince met the Sorcerer's advance, defiant of consequence. Intrusive as autumn in burnt orange and black, the Sorcerer faced off, self-possessed to a reptilian indifference that stopped Tarens cold on the sidelines.

Courage faltered, locked mute as two powers met in contentious collision.

"What's changed?" Arithon accosted point-blank.

The bristled query made Tarens wince, a cry of betrayal that harrowed echoes through the forlorn wreckage of Rathain's crown seat. "I formulated a merciful strategy to clear the Mathorn Pass and dismantle Etarra's obstruction without bloodshed. You've broken the covenant of charter law. Trampled roughshod over blameless crown subjects caught in the breach when a merciful parcel of patience would have seen them safely away! What possessed you to shred my studied plan and destroy a walled town without warning?" Etarra's inhabitants were innocents under Rathain's sovereign protection. "We're speaking of people, promised a level scale and a just measure of their birth-born right to exist in free will. Equity has no defensible caveat. The choice of who lives and who dies for a principle does not signify when this realm is not under attack!"

Davien's silent reproof yielded nothing.

Tarens cowered in speechless dread, as Arithon stiffened in recoil. Torbrand's true descendant would not back down: even if the Sorcerer's stare bored him through and dropped him senseless on the pavement.

His Grace's incandescent outrage spurned caution. "Why was I cozened by the patent belief Fellowship Sorcerers hold our mortal lives sacrosanct?"

"Indeed, the quaint premise prevails, bar the caveat in exception." Davien's mockery scorned the honest retreat, fanned under the flame of the royal rebuttal. "Mankind's permit for inhabitancy lies forfeit should a destructive collapse harm the mysteries that sustain Paravian survival."

"No such threat is extant, today," Arithon insisted, uncowed.

The Sorcerer's drilling stare lost none of its blistering insolence. And yet: such brash arrogance had been misappraised, even by his own colleagues. Exchanges with Davien demanded the utmost restraint, sharp intelligence, and icy exactitude. "Human lives may be declared inviolate in Fellowship hands under the founded writ of the royal charters. But you would be well advised to take heed, Teir's'Ffalenn. Not every power alive on Athera is subject to the compact under the Seven, nor bound by those terms when we swore surety for Mankind's harmless settlement before High Queen Tierendieriel Merevalia."

"Then what transgression has prompted this untoward violation?" Arithon attacked with the savage edge of a pain not yet tempered through anger to aggrieved acceptance.

Davien elected to qualify. "An army of overheated, religious simpletons marched to fanfares from North Ward to bolster their ill-starred tenancy at Etarra." The verdict that followed bared razor teeth. "Unswerved from their canting, misguided folly, they aimed to topple the array of standing stones that channels the fifth lane's transmission across the Plain of Araithe."

That profound implication crackled the tension between prince and Sorcerer.

Then Arithon said, "Timing left me a fortnight to defang that menace. What gave you the licence to disbar my chance to enact a direct intercession? By Ath, how many townfolk have *died* out of hand? What made you side-step the Crown's prerogative for an advance consultation?"

Davien's abstruse posture suggested a shrug. "Other extant causes overshadowed your claim."

"Then, under my sovereign oath, let's test the issue of just cause directly." Arithon firmed his grip on Alithiel, resolved to let the drawn sword impose the starspell for an unimpeachable arbitration.

Yet Davien granted royal justice no quarter. His swift reverse backed him into the central ring of the Paravian pattern. A Fellowship Sorcerer required no pause to wield the lane's focus at strength. Electromagnetic forces coiled to peak in an instant. The hammering spiral unleashed at close quarters buffeted Arithon into retreat.

"Then consider my royal vow null and void!" Arithon yelled, pitched onto his knees past the range of lethal proximity. "Not just to abandon the realm at this pass, I will give you a fight to upset your intentions."

Regal fury bought no satisfaction. Only Davien's last word, bestowed through the singing implosion that whisked his presence away from Ithamon. "Beware my promise made real, Teir's'Ffalenn. Your absolute freedom comes at a price. Dread the moment I side with the Seven against you."

Too late: the metallic slide of Alithiel's bared blade met vacated space, without adversary. Fair trial was denied to answer the wrong imposed on Etarra's populace. Ithamon's ruin abided beneath sunlit sky, with the King's Tower pattern quiescent and empty.

The day, begun cursed, chose not to relent. Tarens missed his timely cue to withdraw. Countrybred wits stunned past common sense collided with Earl Jieret's wounded outrage and caught the rebound as Arithon's furious exit rammed headlong into an eavesdropping witness.

Private agony infused the glare levelled over the unsheathed sword still gripped in his hand. "Move. Clear my way."

"I can't." A liegeman's loyalty fixed Tarens's resolve. "Not unless you hold to your promise to sire the blood heir laid on you by Caolle's dying words."

Which rebuke struck a canker too deep, attached to obligations stretched too grievously far. "My will cannot be gainsaid, damn all to Crown heritage."

No more the crofter, Tarens stood fast. "Jieret's love won't see you forsworn."

Rune-marked steel gleamed, obdurate black metal and enchanted, pale inlay unresponsive: true reason enough to risk altercation against the hot-tempered threat to abandon Rathain.

"No, Arithon. I'm sorry." Tarens blocked the shouldered attempt to shove past. "I won't let you destroy every principle you and others have sacrificed lives to keep sacrosanct."

"Stand down or bleed, damn your lapdog effrontery." A flicked turn of the wrist whined honed steel through the air. The warning transformed to aggression, *that fast*. Naked reflex impelled the defensive draw that cleared Tarens's blade from the scabbard.

His shocked protest drilled through the clashed thrust turned aside by his vigorous parry. "Dharkaron wept, Arithon! Stop this madness at once!"

"I'll brook no interference." Steel screamed against steel. "This is not your affair!"

"Isn't it?" Tarens deflected the next vicious lunge. "Who else is left to steer you from the folly of crossing the Fellowship Sorcerers?"

"I'll offend whom I please." Sword to sword, ruthless, Arithon bore in. "By no means will I play the patsy for a backroom intrigue that enables the wanton slaughter of innocents."

Yet the ferocity that snarled in rebuttal mired on the festered scar of brutal recrimination: Tarens's greater reach and muscular stature made avoidance of injury difficult. The pernicious conundrum spurred Arithon's recklessness, this exchange the reprise of a tormented past, when he had fought Caolle to a fatality. Stroke on stroke, he opposed a *caithdein*'s shade, backed by the stubborn loyalty of a field hand: but one whose adamant, deadly technique encompassed the lifetime of Jieret's skilled experience.

No harmless closure was possible, even had either combatant spared the breath for dismay. The savage shock of steel meeting steel stung the palms numb, the retort of armed animosity become the replacement for language.

Arithon's ferocity drove Tarens backwards, then back yet again, sure footing harried into the treacherous clutter of broken paving and moss-choked debris. Tarens hooked his heel. His left wrist bashed on stone as he stumbled off-balance. He landed on a braced elbow, bruised and winded and stunned helpless with fear.

Arithon's lunge did not follow through for the kill. Instead, steel screamed on steel, hooked through the looped quillon a hairbreadth shy of Tarens's clenched fist. A wrench with the vicious force to snap bone twisted the locked weapon out of his grasp.

The freed sword sailed, flashing, and skidded with a clang that scared up a brown sparrow nested in the tangled overgrowth.

Disarmed, still alive, Tarens nursed his sprained hand in defeat. His hurt met a creature turned cold, realigned as his antagonist.

A Sorcerer's uncanny regard stared him down, terrifying for the uncompromised depth of perception. Whatever Arithon Teir's'Ffalenn *Saw*, the true spirit raked over by his scathing survey harboured no enmity towards him. Only the sincere dedication born of steadfast caring and straightforward kindness.

Arithon broke off, widened the gulf one brisk step, and spun away.

The swift shock of that severance seethed Tarens's blood, and demolished the last of his patience. "You are not the same man who risked all to spare me from the True Sect scaffold. Not any longer the person who steered a friend off the shoals of stark madness, and yet again, yielded his life to the sword for the sake of a child condemned at Daenfal."

"Do you think so?" said Arithon, back turned. Each word shocked the noon stillness, precise as the mason's chisel tapped to shear granite.

Tarens had no stomach left to lay hands on him. Nor could he weather the wreckage headlong, that laid waste to a friendship as Arithon walked away.

This hour, he knew, *oh! how sorely he knew!* The breach lay too far beyond mending.

'This place is one Word,
and all other Words, living,
contain the whole Arc of Eternity.'
—Biedar tribe, concept of existence

Second Repudiation

The Biedar elders brought their song to completion. The shimmering pause that was absolute Silence seized the transdimensional gap rifted through the fabric of Athera's existence. Ringing, the reverberation of their melodic invocation faded, the blurred whisper unleashed by grand conjury beyond knowing subsided back into fast quiet. Deep belowground in Sanpashir, an ephemeral after-shock of rainbow ripples licked through stone, the translucent overlays of solid form multiplied through infinity for a stretched second longer.

Then the phenomenon flickered and died. Aligned focus restored, the recent swathe carved across time and space reintegrated into seamless fusion, with the crone's select strands plucked from parallel probabilities merged back into a singular continuum. Earth's tranquillity abided in the hallowed chamber where the tribe's revered eldest sat in centred solitude. Composed, she waited in expectation for the just ire of a Fellowship Sorcerer's visitation.

Dripped water plinked dissonant echoes through the carved tunnel that accessed her lair. The pervasive scent of dank mineral rode the dense air, baked by the clay pot of coals by her knees. Radiant heat threw rippled distortions across the patterned floor, the diamond-scaled coils of spiral-carved serpents lent the eerie semblance of sinuous motion.

The detonation of Davien's arrival gusted into her presence, a thunderclap without sound. A blast of seethed magma, his scathing annoyance razed through sacred space, primed for a stark confrontation.

"I've completed the circle at your behest," he opened without pause for courtesy.

"No violation occurred." The crone's wrinkled expression stayed unperturbed before the ferocity of his overture. "Free will prevailed."

"Under rank provocation!" Davien rejected her rooted detachment. Abrasive, unflinching before the dire certainty her elder singers shared every word in communion, his eyes bored into hers, inscrutable as jet dropped into the starless nadir of night. "Premeditated, by glory! Of course the Teir's'Ffalenn snapped."

"Then your prince let his volatile temperament blind him," the ancient agreed. Embers hissed a sulphurous refrain through her complacent censure. "Will you do the same?"

Davien froze, incensed, sharply caught aback. "Your point being?"

The crone unclasped her gnarled fingers. The minimal movement chimed the glass fetishes looped through her wool bracelets, struck notes that were not random, but a warning to calm the bridled offence of the dartmen who communed in avid attendance upon her. "Arithon did not pause to engage his initiate wisdom against his overheated assumption. Had he done so, considered reflection might have revealed the altered course of the manifested response."

Yet hindsight left the fixed choice unchanged. Beyond useless to wring sorry hands in regret, that a rational moment of clear insight may have discerned the inviolate trust kept intact behind his Grace's grounds for dispute.

Davien vented, a rare outburst of exasperation. "The adage that Fellowship Sorcerers do not kill? Or the charter's foundational promise, that human lives in our hands are held sacrosanct under the terms of the compact?" Eyes narrowed by the pinch of fraught nerves, he heaped scorn on the crone's bloodless premise. "The flash point today demanded a prodigy beyond the pale of human endowment!"

The adept perception that enabled Sethvir's enhanced Sight *might* have yielded the provenant range of deduction to question. Even then, the profound intervention twined through the cataclysmic event at Etarra beggared even a visionary's imagination. The odds laid against such unlikely acumen were vanishing small, clinched amid the thrown levers of crisis. Few minds could encompass the scope of the Biedar singers' exchange, far less comprehend the crone's powerful reach. Split to the millisecond, her workings stopped *all* in suspension, while simultaneity shuddered, rearranged, and recombined. The precipitate concatenation actualized a deliverance that asserted a doomed populace had been spared in full.

Gifted as Arithon was, and masterfully schooled to practise grand conjury, his self-command during that overwrought instant demanded a heartless, dissociate reserve beyond anyone's emotional reflex.

"His Grace could not fathom the paradigm at scale." Nettled, Davien nailed home his point. "Nor have I ascertained the count of the survivors displaced from harm's way!"

The crone waived the moot surety of confirmation. The Reiyaj Seeress's vision had verified proof, backed by the unimpeachable record of Sethvir's earth-sense. Her handling had not erred in dividing the slipstream of existence, the multiplicity of parallel probabilities recast as one braided whole and folded back into the present moment. No victims had perished in the resonant collapse that annihilated Etarra's disruptive construction. Misjudgement did not skew the collective might of the tribe, when singular inflections of reality were plucked from the infinite reflections strung through the grand chord of creation.

But the ingenuous assurance did not blunt the dangerous quiet edging the Eldest's spare words. Biedar interests thumbed the world's scales beyond question, with Arithon's path kept darkened by purposeful ignorance.

Davien fumed without recourse. "Yon's a brutal play of misdirection at best, hinged upon the sterling character that endows the flower of Torbrand's lineage. Ciladis should weep!"

"Your Fellowship owned their share of direct cause," the crone corrected in pristine contradiction.

And there, Davien was obliged to concede: Etarra's rogue settlement in fact *had* posed a direct violation to the compact. Yet no clean-cut declaration of law excised the layered nuance imposed by the crown charter's prerogative. Rathain's royal heritage inflected all choice with the inborn drive of pernicious bias. The motive behind the Teir's'Ffalenn's distress was not flawed in the grain, but steered in force by compassionate mercy.

"I accept no excuse." Davien swallowed the venom of self-accusation. "Denied your express leave, I did not do other than fail to correct his Grace's blindered initiative. Ath wept! It's the same confounded tragedy Asandir enacts every time a mortal sovereign accepts the Fellowship's attunement to the elemental attributes at coronation."

The crone lent no credence to that cry for solace. Painted in red by the glare from her fire pot, enthroned in the aura of power within an underground cathedral of stone, she let the earth swallow the clamour of outrage and smother the Sorcerer's torment to null quiet.

Gooseflesh plucked skin before the walled adamance of her rejection.

"You'd better know what in creation you're doing," Davien lashed back, clipped prelude to a challenge clapped under advisement. "I earnestly hope the strategic delivery's concocted the outcome your purpose requires."

His veiled threat made no impact. Sanpashir's crone remained disinclined to share confidence. Nor did she yield what elusive insight she gleaned through her mystical link with the Reiyaj Seeress. Davien bowed before the inscrutable impasse. Biedar's people remained a law unto themselves. A force perhaps answerable to Athera's Paravians; but under the standoff of wary respect, a wilful power beyond the constraint of the Fellowship's mandated purview.

Not even the Seven grasped the prerogative central to the linked mind of their tribal consciousness.

The adage of myth stated Mankind's provenance encompassed four powers, two granted by Ath Creator, and two more forged by the impulse of human invention: the Chalice and the Knife, and the Ring and the Coin. Biedar acknowledged only the Chalice and Knife, symbolic of birth and destruction. The Ring, also known as the cyclical wheel, and the coin of commerce were shunned by the way of their kind. The Biedar path had branched from humanity's course millennia in the past. Beyond Fellowship reckoning, their people had inhabited other worlds for countless generations. Ancient in memory of their ancestry, and ever set at odds with outsiders' objectives, they had been an enigma far and long before the pursuit of Jessian's breached legacy called Hasidii's descendants and the accountable bearers of Requiar's lineage to seek due redress upon Atheran soil.

"Well, I never liked being the fly in the bell jar," Davien cracked in dissident conclusion. "You'll agree, my term of service is finished?" Without asking her blessing, nor beholden to her for permission, he twisted off the citrine ring worn like a shackle and chain for nine onerous centuries.

The cold, offworld jewel that had kept his intentions concealed from six colleagues dropped into the crone's upturned palm.

The moment shivered the air like a struck bell unswathed from muffling felt. A crushing weight lifted from the Sorcerer's spirit. Perhaps the crone's circle of singers had realigned something more profound than the fate of Etarra's compromised inhabitants. For a pocketed parcel of veiled history resurfaced into the world's hoop of remembrance, signal missing connections restored intact to the heightened stream of over-arching consciousness . . .

The subtle adjustment did not evade Sethvir's vigilant notice at Althain Tower. Presently on his knees by the access hatch cut through the inside wall of the pantry, he fiddled with the laid-open guts of the pump that lifted fresh water from the underground cistern.

"Never a flagstaff that doesn't draw lightning," he groused through the snarled wisps of his beard. "Why ever not while we're strafed under crisis?"

Diverted as the pulse from Sanpashir swirled through the greater flow of his earth-sense, he sat back on his heels. An irritable snatch bunched his left sleeve for convenience, the moth-eaten cuff utilized as a rag. He mopped off crabbed knuckles clotted with grease, and short-changed his effort to replace the worn leather gasket. The rushed patch he replaced on the persistent leak fell back on the same unreliable cantrip: consent for spells laid on the hides of dead animals were twitchy, and stays exposed to running water defied the natural grain of electro-magnetic attraction. "Always ten things at once. And Sithaer's fell fire! Can't Asandir ever stay here long enough to overhaul this relic of Second-Age engineering?"

'*What?*' Engaged in rapport for remote consultation from a lofty vantage in the Mathorn Pass, the field Sorcerer's seared exclamation crossed distance and upbraided his maundering colleague. '*I've been diverted at speed from the Plain of Araithe for a sightseer's view of Etarra's total destruction, only to be asked to flit back to Atainia to fix yesteryear's rotted plumbing?*'

Sethvir blotted smeared grit off his cheek and shoved aside the anti-quated wooden housing that coupled the dismembered pipe valve. "Not at all. Carry on." Sunk onto his hams, bony wrists draped over drawn-up knees, he listened, while his on-going stream of awareness tracked the curious quirk just emerged from the recoil of the appalling reverses that drove Arithon's precipitous departure from Ithamon.

'*Why would Davien opt not to tell his Grace the crone's intervention forestalled loss of life from the scour of the fifth lane?*' From Asandir's overlook, filtered through the dust cloud wafted aloft by the catastrophic onslaught of harmonics, the titanic demise that had excised a prosperous town's trespass stunned sense. Amid wreckage smashed to violent ruin, tiny human figures straggled through the crushed rubble. Shaken, dirty, and bruised, the distraught survivors emerged from the wrack of disaster, little the worse beyond minor contusions. Asandir's survey bore witness. If no stranded inhabitant sustained crippling harm, the galvanic rage brewing for a murderous retort broke the fertile ground for a bloodbath. *'Do we cling to blind trust that Davien had a justified reason for this debacle?'*

For whatever bleak terms attended the errant, black bargain the reclusive Sorcerer once struck with a great drake, this day's feat outstripped rational sense. Not under the tinderbox threat of Desh-thiere's malice, with Lysaer's cursed nature aligned at the spear's head of an armed campaign primed by terror to reap the whirlwind in retaliation.

Doubt preyed on Asandir's obdurate patience. *'For too long, Davien's tucked his precocious motives too viciously close to the chest.'* A ridden pause poisoned the lag as Sethvir's broadscale vision mapped the multiplied shocks of percussive realignment. *'Davien might have stayed his infernal meddling,'* the field Sorcerer steamed on in distemper. *'At the least until I had the grace to stall Lysaer's war host and secure the array on the Plain of Araithe from desecration.'*

The Warden answered through distraught reverie. "Your assumption is flawed. Seshkrozchiel's not involved, this time. Davien fulfilled the terms of the dragon's pact long ago."

Asandir's mercuric intellect reframed his snap deduction, referent to the abused skulls of four murdered hatchlings, and the murderous scour by drakefire that had laid waste to Lysaer's capital at Avenor in wrathful reparation. *'Fatemaster's nitpicking judgement bedamned! If Davien's done being puppeteered by a wyrm, then what other infernal provocation would make him cross the line and bait Rathain's prince into open rebellion?'*

Sethvir stalled, beyond words. He could not unravel the convolute motive stitched through the past tangle of bitter betrayal. Not yet. But against lethal stakes, Davien's inexplicable behaviour at the least supported a stay of opinion. Nuanced insight suggested a secret charge bestowed by the Reiyaj Seeress. A cruel conundrum, perhaps sprung from the forecast of an egregious infraction. An incorrigible threat to Mankind's survival well might explain Davien's scheme to abet the historic assault on the compact brewed in deadly conspiracy by cult necromancers, Hanshire's mayor, and Koriathain.

"Davien's move to trigger the last Crown revolt perhaps suggests a cold-cast strategy aimed to spare our Fellowship from the consequent enforcement of humanity's eradication," Sethvir allowed, beyond afraid to tweak for the hidden ties knotting the present. "The desperate sacrifice of the monarchies may have side-stepped a wider disaster, had the plan's execution not turned awry." The Warden's musing trailed off, stalled by the expansive ripple stirred by the crone's finger thrust into the weave. Revelation redefined the horrendous price paid in blood under Davien's twofold pact with the world's elder powers.

'He's been a pawn silenced under a terrible vow, I grasped that much,' Asandir agreed. The wasted urgency that had driven him cross continent from Havish gritted his steel-clad resignation. "Davien will answer our enquiry, hell take his discretion, come the day he decides to return."

The rancorous wounds of disaffection that yet savaged their two discorporate colleagues did not bear mention. Aggrieved tears flowed too late for the bloodbath founded in subterfuge Davien had carried out in service to a ruthless covenant. Sethvir's earth-sensed vision recalibrated the ill-starred round of disastrous inquiry gone wrong at Althain Tower in Year 5129. The current severance at Ithamon recast Davien's harsh dialogue then under a different light: each past, hurtful word deployed as a weapon to crush sympathy, break ties, and secure his safe distance through enmity. The crass sarcasm that alienated Kharadmon, and the baiting engineered to inflame Luhaine's stupendously phlegmatic temper – each unforgivably brutal retort had beaten down all appeals for solicitous understanding. Davien's systematic attacks had been most exactingly tailored to demolish the sacrosanct trust of his colleagues.

Nerves armoured for the role of subversion had withstood the blistering course, to shred even Ciladis's indefatigable compassion.

Naked insight, reft of Davien's personal testimony, sketched an enormity fit to harrow Sethvir beyond all remorse. Worse than vicious speech to demolish empathy, *Davien's cornered move to unleash Shehane Athain's protective wrath had never been thoughtless, but surely impelled by bare-knuckled courage and frigid calculation.*

'Your string-puppet accused will not dance for the question,' Davien had declared in a defiant fury that clothed desperation. 'You don't need my presence to bandy conjecture. Carry on, by all means. Enjoy your salacious dissection of character without the bother of my protestation . . .'

Sethvir muffled his face in his palms, castigated anew as Asandir shared the punch of remorse through across distance. *'Ath wept! You imply Davien chose his fate? He took that drastic, appalling step to trigger his downfall?'*

Sethvir's stricken silence confirmed, past conjecture: flesh, blood, and bone, Davien had chosen to defy the Tower Warden's drawn line. Eyes wide open, he had shouldered the cost, seized that last, irreversible ploy to avert certain ruin at the hands of his *misappraised, well-meaning* colleagues.

As enforcement to salvage his guarded privacy, Davien had wrenched open the King's Chamber door on that bleak hour and walked out. One fateful stride broached the warded threshold, a deliberate act that crossed his impetuous will with the sentinel shade whose unmalleable provenance defended Althain Tower.

The agonized scream harrowed the etheric web, still, as Shehane Althain's roused might marshalled dire forces beyond comprehension. Seized and rendered discorporate, Davien's deathless spirit had been shredded in excruciate pain from his living flesh.

"Ath forgive!" Sethvir scrubbed his wet cheeks, the bother of faulty pipe gaskets forgotten. "Our Seven's integrity was never betrayed." Nor had Davien's loyalty for one moment abandoned the steadfast ranks of his fellows.

Asandir added his stricken acknowledgement. *'I suspected we might not be privy to everything after the transformation that restored our scapegrace exile in the crucible of Scarpdale's grimward.'*

"Nothing close to this burden of misunderstanding!" Sethvir retorted, beyond aggrieved.

'No.' Asandir's admission was not insensitive, or deaf to the Warden's torment. Too pragmatic to dwell on past errors before an uncertain future, he regarded the scar of Etarra's wreckage and resolved to extend his forbearance for this day's upset at Ithamon. *'Let's hope for the sake of Prince Arithon's trial, Davien's remained true in more ways than we know.'*

Sethvir coughed behind his grimed sleeve. "Very likely, the sly fellow had his hand forced. The long game at this pass is the crone's, and by measure of the exchange in Sanpashir, he has just dealt her association his most bitter quittance."

The Biedar ancient was at that moment seated in stillness, the colourful yarn fringe on her garments rippled in the turbulence sown by Davien's unquiet departure. Glass fetishes chimed as she lifted her hand, plucked select herbs from a pouch at her waist, and tossed the dried leaves in the fire pot. Crackled sparks whirled aloft as the sprigs ignited, flurried in the eddied smoke. The pungent fragrance infused the close chamber long after the greens burned to ash. The crone breathed in the exotic mélange, sheathed in telepathic communion with the singers aligned with her consciousness. Their awareness steadied her purposeful course as the perceived bounds of the veil thinned like gauze and unfolded her vision into expansion.

Jet eyes set agleam with the lit coals' reflection bent her extended gaze across time and distance, a perception drilled through the span of generations, unborn, living, and dead. Sight melded at one with the ancestry parsed the shadows of present and future. Couched in the nadir of Mother Dark's void, and unified with all being, Sanpashir's eldest contemplated the latent inflections of volatile forces released into play. Knowing, she embraced the grand arc of unformed possibility, then measured which select moments emerged from the deep with the crystalline clarity to achieve fusion . . .

. . . lengthened shadow crept over the vista of Etarra's uncanny destruction. Where late-day sunlight shafted the plumed dust veil over the Mathorn Pass after Asandir's thoughtful departure, the crone's interest tracked Davien's more assiduous tally of the displaced survivors, still crawling unscathed from the wreckage. Shaken, distraught, no person spared grasped the stupendous sweep of the feat that had averted their annihilation.

One instant had shimmered in arrested silence. No mindful review might encompass the number of select probabilities Biedar power had threaded from the infinitude of a catastrophic mass event. Yet Davien identified each dazed individual plucked whole from the parallel streams of unmanifest form. His exhaustive count tested the continuity of each living fate spun out of harm's way. *A death trap of slaughter that had not occurred, each concurrent strand seamlessly re-joined with no viable being, man or beast, bypassed as a casualty.*

"Two departed," Davien concluded, unremarked where he paused, dusting off his abraded hands. He tipped a nod to the crone's matchless touch, cognizant of her ephemeral oversight. Neither of the deceased had crossed the veil untimely: one lonely old man expired, asleep, and a stillbirth conceived with a fatal deformity slipped the mother's womb without a heartbeat.

Both spirits had passed by free-will accord, death arrived at the moment of natural choice.

The Sorcerer lingered, while twilight fell over the vista of rubble and extinguished the afterglow from the high peaks. Full darkness under the first glimmer of stars silvered a vale reclaimed from humanity's frenetic commotion. The pearlescent shimmer of the fifth lane rang untrammelled, a resonant current resurged to enrich the upper registers beyond hearing. A tasked victory exacted at a terrible price: both the Fellowship Sorcerer returned to autonomy, and the Biedar ancient whose long-sighted vision spanned worlds and epochs understood where the outcome must lead.

Within days, early word of Etarra's destruction would reach Lysaer's burgeoning war host. The enraged cry would compound, fuelled to conflagration by the hysterical embellishment of eyewitness accounts. The wise on Athera assessed the cost meted out. Already, the appalled groundswell dimmed the bright avenues of probability. Etarra's demise by whatever means, had been destined to rouse the juggernaut of human hostility . . .

Yet the crone in Sanpashir prioritized other concerns as her regard left Davien. Focused elsewhere, she weighed the critical, covert shift at Highscarp, where the Koriani Matriarch cloistered herself, poring over the content rifled from the sisterhouse cellar's sealed crypt . . .

. . . an intensive survey ground into tedium after six gruelling months. Lirenda rubbed exhausted eyes gritted by hours of labour by candlelight. Night and day blurred together, closeted in the privacy of a shut room. The current, flocked page beneath her smudged finger was a treatise, expounding upon an ancient weapon of destruction that destabilized stars into catastrophic collapse. The yield from such fireball explosions had laid waste to an empire inconceivably vast, civilizations eradicated wholesale under scorching assaults launched to sterilize worlds.

Lirenda deciphered a fragmented text from a context vast beyond comprehension, where cryptic lines reduced Athera to a dust speck at the margin of human history. The knowledge left at the order's command was outmatched, pathetic as hen scratchings, and simplistic as dirt before yesteryear's trove of technology. Only one field of expertise had advanced through the backwater penury of their exile. Lirenda sat back, a tigress's gleam in her tawny eyes. The Koriathain of old would have been covetous of the magical practice enabled by Paravia's electromagnetic web. Burned to fresh rancour by the compact's restrictions, she clenched her teeth in frustration.

Come the hour, she would break the Fellowship's tyrannical grip and restore Mankind's rightful claim to the inheritance sequestered by her distant forbears.

But that dream required an opening impetus to ripen the plan to fruition. Smutched with soot from a primitive candle lamp, Lirenda detached the sealed envelope found tucked into the rolled leaves of a crumbled manuscript. Dogged, she pursued the cryptic translation without second thought for her overdue meal.

The lamp's steady flame melted the chamber in shadow, the hiss of hot wax the sole sound as the packeted quartz wafer slip-cased inside settled into her palm like a promise. Lirenda warmed the crystal pane with her breath, closed her eyes, and settled in trance to plumb the content . . .

. . . a speaker's voice, imprinted tens of thousands of years past delivered a brief introduction. 'Today's lecture concerns the new, advanced theory on accelerated fusion funded by Meta-Veriarch's research grant to a task squad of seven pre-eminent physicists, chaired by Calum Quaide Kincaid.'

A spatter of appreciative applause greeted the scholarly genius who stepped up to the lectern . . .

Struck cold by the recaptured image, Lirenda gasped. *She knew that face!* The white hair and svelte beard, distinguished by an air of daft curiosity and disarming, blue-eyed, innocence – she beheld a younger, less-weathered Sethvir, perhaps in his fifth decade. The stunned moment hung, as her astonished discovery gave rise to elated excitement.

Sethvir and Calum Quaide Kincaid were the same person, with the piquant identity of his associates revealed as the Fellowship Sorcerers themselves.

"I have plumbed the bottom of their bag of tricks at long last!" crowed Lirenda in breath-taken joy.

Their unspeakable, criminal history provided the ruthless advantage she could exploit. *Finally!* The leverage was hers to expose the Seven's appalling hypocrisy.

Past and present, Koriathain always had battled the same inveterate enemy! For when Calum Kincaid and his close colleagues went rogue, they had fled a relentless battle for supremacy between bitterly polarized factions. Chased by flouted authority, record stated they bequeathed their legacy formula for annihilation to a network of underdog rebels. The breakthrough discovery in subversive hands had upset a deadlocked balance of power, catalyst for the unravelling war that consumed the pinnacle of Mankind's starfaring civilizations to ashes. Scuttled to their remote refuge on Athera at the dawn of the Second Age, the Sorcerers were the same branded fugitives whose specialized feat of molecular engineering had enabled the great weapon that caused the wholesale destruction of worlds.

The shocking truth fitted like a worn glove. Lirenda reeled in giddy revelation as the overarching particulars bridged the gaps in known history. For the engine that carried the Seven between stars had been seized en route, waylaid by the dreams of Athera's dragons expressly to wreak destruction upon the drake spawn that threatened Paravian survival. Athera's first Prime Matriarch had known Sethvir's infamous identity. The secret had been gagged under seal by an interdict imposed by the Seven themselves.

These nefarious, unprincipled authors of mass murder at scale without parallel were the very same, bound in alliance with the Concord's Dragon Protectorate, and conjoined by fiat to smother the potential greatness of humanity's intellect in perpetuity. All for the sake of Athera's Paravians, whose choice to abandon their native ground should have ceded the continent to Mankind's ascendancy.

Lirenda rubbed her pounding temples, infuriated. No matter the means, regardless of cost, she vowed on her life to reclaim Mankind's usurped autonomy and exact overdue restitution . . .

. . . in Sanpashir's deep cavern, the Biedar crone stirred. She lidded the clay pot and quenched the sullen coals, the uninterrupted stream of her consciousness joined into communion with the Reiyaj Seeress. The etheric ripple sheared up by their melded vision breathed outwards, slight as the drop of a pin in the restive currents of the actualized present.

The whispered deflection did not pass undetected amid the tumultuous cross-chop threshed into oscillation by the quickened frequency of the fifth lane. With the delicacy of a feather's brush across a precisely tuned sounding-board, Dakar the Mad Prophet staggered to his knees, ungoverned talent seized by a black-out fit of unconsciousness. Sighted power shot through him. Channelled into the resonant wave of a triplicate chord of completion, the unstoppable vision reforged his awareness with the dazzling shock of a levin bolt.

Seen true on that hour, two horsemen parted ways at Ithamon. One of them, fair, reined northward to re-join the clans in Deshir, heartsick and burdened with momentous news. *How to convey the ruin of their most cherished hope?* That Rathain's sanctioned prince had vowed to reward their steadfast patience with callow desertion.

The second, dark-haired and royal, turned his mount due south. Two days' ride, and a span of tormented reflection ended with a night vigil at the site of Cosach's deathwatch in Daon Ramon. Where the great man's mouldered flesh and bone greened the damp moss in the gulch, Arithon Teir's'Ffalenn placed a single red rose for remembrance. Then he tuned his lyranthe. The grand requiem sung in apology embraced the memories of Jieret, Caolle, and Cosach, Sidir and Feithan and Jeynsa, and many more lost through the years.

There and then, upon closure, he declared fulfilment and quittance to his promise to uphold the tradition of their clan legacy. Unequivocal, he renounced his sovereign oath and declared his abdication of Rathain's crown obligation. Masterbard, at the focused pinnacle of his art, he concluded his poignant lament, and the moment empowered an imperative summons, made consummate by a grand fusion that seized the etheric web.

. . . and a shimmering pause that was Silence hung over the Arc of Eternity . . .

Sanpashir's crone heard that plucked note. Her extended vision Saw the resonant imprint of *all* that was flowering as it *rose* in myriad form across epochs and worlds. From all of eternity's manifest shapes encompassed within that expanded frame, she recalled a species native to an arid planet called Scathac; and others, perceived through Paravian eyes; and still others: an infinite, prismatic overlay splintered from parallel universes where humanity's footsteps had never trodden. She embraced the Masterbard's aggrieved cry set in motion. The reflection amplified through her circled singers re-echoed, a descant song line that transcended the pliant illusion of linear time.

Creation and Destruction were a single thread: the dirge of regret and the rekindled flame of renewal twined one with the other, inseparable. For Biedar, the unrequited grief had cankered the tribal mind for millennia. An intersective reckoning come due, when Mother Dark's Chosen of Requiar's lineage stood poised at the ripe crux of destiny.

The crone veiled her features. Cheeks damp, she wept with sorrow and joy: for the longed-for deliverance was never assured. Davien's cryptic question yet hung in the balance, hope's shining potential unanswered. Free will would prevail and forge a result to annihilate or illuminate.

She had done her part. Now the pieces aligned, choice and agency poised to seize the day and determine the endgame.

Ricochet

Change peals across the etheric web, a reverberation that shivers the dimensional intersection of time and space in the chambered skulls of Athera's dragons, living and dead; and laired in sealed stone, warmed by a caldera in Scarpdale, Seshkrozchiel stirs to the quickening flicker of dream amid the deep stasis of hibernation . . .

On the uncharted Isle of Los Lier, veiled behind wards, the same ground-swell prompts Tehaval Warden to convene the High Queen Regent's council, and by Teirendaelient Merevalia's decree, dawn sees the Ilitharis fleet raise sail for the first time in eight centuries: along with Avileffin's kin and Ffereton's descendants go the builders and masons of matchless expertise unsurpassed in the world for Three Ages . . .

High summer's eve in Rathain, at the surge of the midnight crest, a gentle rain falls infused by the melodic cry of a Masterbard's dirge sung in heartsore regret, and every budded wild rose in Daon Ramon unfurls into full bloom with each velvet petal jet-black . . .

"Davien the Betrayer shall hear no reason,
nor bow to the Law of the Major Balance;
neither shall the Fellowship be restored to Seven
until the black rose grows wild on the vales of Daon Ramon.
The briar will take root on the day
Arithon s'Ffalenn embraces kingship."
-Black Rose Prophecy, by Dakar in Third Age Year 5637

"There can be no remedy for Etarra
except to raze it clean to the ground."
-Lady Maenalle s'Gannley

VII. Reverberations

The morning Ciladis took abrupt leave and fared east on an unspecified errand, the Master Spellbinder Verrain bent his back at the oars of the skiff after setting the Sorcerer ashore beside Methlas Lake. Elaira occupied the broad seat in the stern. Tucked like a barefoot waif between her host's stowed bundles of drop nets, she rested crossed ankles amid the jumble of tarred leather buckets, a crab rake, various wooden tongs, an immaculate skinning knife, and rested athwart, the Guardian's ash staff, scored by the teeth of swamp denizens slavering for hot-blooded flesh.

She appeared at ease. Canvas knee breeches, too large, and a belted linen shirt clothed her elfin stature in place of a tunic. The wide-brimmed straw hat with faced ribbon perched on her auburn hair had shaded another estranged princess before her. The lady was not the first to shuck feminine dress and decorum while in sheltered retreat at Methisle Fortress. Suited to the rough setting better than most, she was not the only one anguished by the fractious rebuff of Atheran royalty.

Verrain's kind regard and matchless finesse understood women, in particular when they were under pressure in difficult straits. "You look primed to spear something nasty with fight for a tasty meal in the supper pot," he remarked to lift her sombre spirits.

Elaira's immediate, silvery laughter restored the sparkle to misted grey eyes. Yet her agile quip was upstaged by a surprise interruption: a jet-black rose tumbled out of clear air, fresh as though plucked an instant before. The bloom struck the skiff's floorboards between Verrain's boots, the scrape of barbed thorn a testy accusation.

Kharadmon's presence blasted in with a gust that etched hoarfrost under the glare of new day. "You were made aware of the strand casting that prompted Dakar's most infamous line of prophecy?"

"I was not." Verrain's caustic correction stemmed from his snap-frozen cuffs, left damp from the wade to relaunch his craft through the bull-rushes. He winked towards Elaira, and deflected Kharadmon's prickly overture with his raised oar blades poised between strokes. "At the time, I was here. Sick with overextension, you recall very well, from a harrowing sweep by grand conjury to eradicate venomous meth-snakes. Why not state what brought you without the snide angling?"

But Elaira had the claws for her own self-defence. "If you've breezed in to ask after Arithon, I'm sorry. I haven't a clue."

That arid rebuff bit, cut off as she was from the cherished connection of initiate rapport. Yet no enchantress trained to scry for the lane watch could have missed the altercation touched off by Davien, or the vicious severance dealt out to Tarens. Not while Methisle Fortress sat bang overtop a Paravian focus whose axial current aligned with Ithamon, and by no mistake, lent the further insight of Ciladis's dead reckoning.

Kharadmon's nettled enquiry, keen enough to pierce lead, braved her unperturbed stare without satisfaction. Then he said, "Sethvir knows where Arithon is."

That pregnant, veiled threat bared the rampant pitch of the Seven's concern.

"Ah!" Wide-lashed beneath the straw hat brim, Elaira's gaze returned tepid sympathy. "The wee stubborn man's turned his back on your gameboard? Well, then. Happy hunting! Your Fellowship's earned his adverse retreat. I won't pry into his private affairs, or share his motive since he hasn't taken me into his confidence."

Verrain coughed and averted the bristling standoff. "I gather Sethvir's nerve storm stems from another quarter."

Kharadmon snorted. "Yon's a mouthful of understatement given the weasel's air of sideways misdirection thrown into our teeth! Our Warden's cornered blindside this time, mark you. The upset's not feigned. Sethvir's not alone, uprooting his hair in yanked tufts! We'd all banked upon the *infallible* Sight Dakar blurts in his unconscious seizures. The promise has enshrined the hope for nigh unto three hundred years that our Fellowship's crippled ranks would be restored when a black rose, *which did not exist*, bloomed wild in Daon Ramon."

Emphasis dramatized, the manifest, funereal bloom on the floorboards gusted into a widdershins spin.

"The broached caveat's dropped the brutal last straw," Kharadmon continued. "Our glimmer of faith to unite at full strength hinged on the provision the Teir's'Ffalenn *on that day* would embrace the high kingship in full."

"And he's abdicated!" Elaira blurted, flushed to perverse excitement. "Though you have to admit, the provocation's been richly earned, and to Arithon's credit, thrice over delivered by justification."

"On formal terms, yes, he's abandoned the crown with his signature jab of vindication." Kharadmon's agitation rocked the flat-bottomed boat with the frustration of a teapot tempest. "We were hoping you could illuminate us, since your betrothed has bolted the coop with nobody the wiser as to his intentions."

"Sethvir can't read him?" Verrain broke in, shocked enough to fumble an oar. "You fear the s'Ffalenn heir has used his offworld birth to advantage and learned how to blindside the Warden's earth-sense?"

"Maybe." Through the splash, Kharadmon's testy warning whip-cracked a ruffle of white water to squelch that angle of possibility within Elaira's altogether too avid earshot. "Arithon's mixed into the crone's long-range business. Threshed by her design, the span of probability tends to get muddled."

Elaira rubbed the sunburn peeled off her nose, and tacitly lent thoughtful insight. "He's never consented before to carry the Biedar tribe's torch."

"Does anyone volunteer for that privilege?" Kharadmon snapped. "The old besom came to Athera and settled her people on her own agency. Even the Paravians bent to her bidding."

Elaira smothered her smile with a deadpan blink. "For a start, perhaps read me in on the page, starting out with the sacrosanct prophecy Arithon's flouted."

"Not here." Verrain dug in, at guarded pains to conceal Ciladis's close instructions to scale up the threshold of Elaira's electromagnetic tolerance. Steady stroke resumed, he propelled the skiff homeward towards Methisle. "If the world's turned upside down, we'll hold our discussion where no one's distress might contribute to heatstroke."

Yet the Spellbinder's strategic tact failed to quell the mercurial seethe of discorporate impatience. "I've no more to say past the imperative question." Kharadmon narrowed his prying interest upon Elaira's combative wariness. "If your beloved should cross our Fellowship's directive, come the hour we're forced to alliance against him, whose side are you going to choose?"

"I don't know." Elaira's vexed frown unravelled presumption, that she had ever forsaken her agency or wavered from self-possession. Thrust on dangerous ground, she resisted the hook for a negotiable partnership. "That rather depends on what Arithon does, where the battle lines are drawn in the sand, and whose stand on the high ground demolishes compromise. If you'll hear the reminder," she summed up, tart, "my beloved never acts without purpose. If he plays his strategy close, be advised. Most often, his unassailable secrecy defends a legitimate cause."

No murmur gainsaid her, and no sound interrupted the rhythmic creak of the skiff's battered rowlocks. Morning sunlight sheared down with what seemed unnatural heat, Kharadmon's frigid presence having departed.

Days later, a great ship from Los Lier broke the Cildein horizon, inbound from the eastern ocean. She reduced sail off the coast of Melhalla, came about, and aimed her tall, painted prow through the narrows towards Alestron's cove harbour. Wind at her back, varnished spars gleaming, she entered the strait to the peal of a centaur's dragon-spine horn. The sound swelled on the air, shaking earth and sky for first time in human memory: folk in Kalesh and Adruin clapped terrified hands to their ears and cowered behind bolted posterns.

The same hour the Paravian vessel dropped anchor in the sheltered harbour beneath the vacated fortress of Alestron, the first panicked strings of town messengers galloped north- and southward upon lathered mounts. The momentous hysteria furled under the mayors' seals with their dispatches was rescripted at speed, cryptic text on rice-paper strips dispersed farther and faster by carrier pigeon. Word touched off panic at Perdith, New Tirans, Durn, and Ishlir, the shattering spike in the lane current entwined with the celebratory greeting sent to the Fellowship by the ambassador of High Queen Regent Merevalia Teirendaelient. Ciladis and Kharadmon met her delegation's oared tender upon landing beneath the gapped tumble of the outer wall breached two hundred fifty-six years past under siege.

The keys to the Mathiell Gate drum towers, yet intact, were ceded back to her crown, returning the upper ward of the citadel long held under entailment into the massive hands of the Ilitharis builders and masons.

When in full ceremony the Seven's white star and cross-slashed blue pennant was run down and replaced by the crescent moon and oak diadem of Imaury's lineage and the High Queen's triaxial pennant of emerald and silver, the moment found Tarens well away from Ithamon, en route to the northern clan enclave. He had ridden the sixty leagues to the Farl Rocks, heavy-hearted with news, and turned wide of his course by resurgent, lightning-struck fires, as storm patterns reverted by the upshifted lane balance burned back Daon Ramon's overgrowth of scrub briar. Suntanned and dusty, he pressed on to the trade-road, where his birth accent finagled a hired stint with a westbound caravan short of outriders.

News of the momentous landing at Alestron by then fed the hysterical fears already ignited by the beggared survivors who fled the demolition of Etarra.

Their eyewitness accounts staggered incredulity: the Mathorn notch was impassable. While Jieret's inherited Sight had envisioned the ghastly extent of the wreckage, arcane awareness did nothing to blunt the lurid descriptions delivered by firelight, or the rumours spread far and wide by the venturesome scavengers who scoured the rubble for salvage.

"Nothing's left," a long-faced prospector complained, tattered and scuffed to cracked nails and scabbed knuckles. "Buried beneath shattered stone, it's uncanny. All trace that anyone lived there is gone, down to the last spoon and cached gold piece, everything, milled under a scar like a rockslide. Not a keepsake remains in that desolate heap, though some have broken their legs, even perished, while searching."

Salacious accounts bent towards speculation. Some forecast the Lord of Light would wage bloody war to eradicate Shadow and sorcery. Others entertained the more grandiose scheme of rebuilding, underwritten by guild persuasion and taxes, with raised tithes for funds by the True Sect Temple. None knew for certain. The choked pass throttled reliable news.

Information by pigeon from Narms lagged up to four weeks, with the dovecotes destroyed that had guided their homing.

Tarens chose not to wait. Pressed under the onus of Arithon's contrary standing, he cashed out his pay to saddle up and veer north across the high ranges through Leynsgap.

"Barbarian territory!" The caravan's grizzled road master spat in gloomy disparagement. "You won't get through alive. The clan scouts who set snares against trespass are demons. Split your guts on a sharpened stake, or snag a trip wire that dead drops a log on your noggin. You might languish for weeks, and wind up pecked to shreds as a snack for the buzzards."

Tarens waived the earnest advice, unoffended. "I've a cousin's map from a smuggler to guide me upcountry."

The excuse marked him outright for a rank fool, unworthy of curiosity. Nothing evaded the net of clan scrutiny. Challenge waylaid Tarens a bowshot off the verge, expected since the patrol's covert reconnaissance watched all movement on the Mathorn Road.

"East to west, Rathain's infested with couriers primed with war-bonded dispatches. Nervous authority can't rest for a day without urgent reports." The squad captain snagged Tarens's water flask and slaked his parched throat, tongue loosened as his surprised welcome devolved into back-slapping banter. "Towns are stirred up like hopping fleas ever since the resonant onslaught ousted the squatters' nest from Etarra. You saw the desolate wrack in the pass?"

Tarens's silence varnished over the brutal disparity, that his crofter's heart grieved for the families disrupted by the debacle.

"Ath wept!" the scout captain enthused. "Not a brick nor a joist left standing upright. More, Asandir came through like the whirlwind saying the Ilitharis Paravians have reclaimed Alestron."

Astonishment on Tarens's part did not obscure the unease that sobered the tenor of the discussion.

"No way we thought we'd see that in our lifetimes," the scout tracker mused. "Never mind the thrawn upset cranking a hitch in the breeks of the trade guilds' dawp. They've had their jaws clacked to gnashed teeth already by lamentations and resentment."

"Merry hell and go lucky," a gaunt archer swore, stoked to perverse admiration. "Ware the poor mark wont to cross Torbrand's lineage. That wee s'Ffalenn bastard's kept his fell promise. Sharp to the mark as Dharkaron's black Spear, and bedamned to the vengeful consequence."

Tarens slipped away to water his horse. Such fierce pride and bright-eyed expectation crushed his honest soul, the burden of the bad news he carried made unbearable by the next hopeful question. "Surely you'll have word from his Grace?"

Tarens fended off his mount's dripping muzzle. "For the realm's *caithdein* and the high council, yes," he admitted, evasive.

"Aye, well, then." Disappointment came tempered by the blunt courage bred into a hardscrabble life, pared to fatalism. "Sent alone with crown orders, you won't want to tarry. We'll tack a fresh horse straightaway, and speed you along with an escort. Are you hungry?"

"Only for news," Tarens admitted. "Rumour on the road had nothing recent from anywhere north of the ranges."

Amid loaded glances, the taciturn elder paused, slit-eyed. "Pot on the boil's frothed up, sure enough. Leaguesmen have their dogs out in droves, with the town mayors scairt to pissed linen. The clamour's pitched for a fight, although the augury says not quite yet. Whittles down to the s'Ilessid upstart, and which way he'll jump as the lapdog of the Sunwheel war host."

A stringy girl with a scabbed knee arrived, leading a surefooted hill pony better suited for altitude. She took the reins of Tarens's blown horse, wary as a hunted creature within the big man's proximity.

Her feral timidity earned his wide smile. "Easy, pip. I don't bite."

"She's skittish of your town accent, don't try her," advised the rawboned woman whose helpful efficiency transferred his bedroll, then secured a hefty pack to the cantle rings, shared out from their common supplies. "Lost her auntie last spring. Dharkaron's curse on the temple gold that funds the headhunters' bounties."

Aggrieved, Tarens curbed his impulse to ruffle the child's hair. He remounted, also wise enough to stifle his thanks, such acknowledgement for the gift of provender sure to be taken as insult. His slight hesitation was noticed, regardless.

"We're thick with pigeon-pie morsels between here and Narms," came the laconic admission. Shown the crofter's blank face, the speaker grinned. "A pie morsel's a messenger bird, shot down for tally points by our archers. Poor birds wind up on the spit. We prime the fire to roast them with the seal wax and parchment nicked off their legs."

Set off with the scouts' relay, Tarens tightened his belt on trail rations of jerked meat, mint leaves, and dried berries. Across the high pass at

Leynsgap within the fortnight, he reached the northern plain, where fresh information became more reliable.

Subdued by the patter of rain, and intent on the sharpening stroke of her whetstone, the lean runner reported the latest unpleasant development. "S'Ilessid plans to set up headquarters at Perlorn, with other towns requisitioned for billeting troops over winter."

A courier's case waylaid on the road through Tal's Crossing had yielded a prize sheaf of the enemy's updated orders. "Temple's busy amassing their troops, sure enough," the man leading the raiders related in summary. "But the plan seems extended at cautious, long range. It's a gang-up rush for popular support, well greased by resettlement incentives for the vagrant Etarrans."

"The religion's in no position to dole out largesse for indigent reparation." Last to weigh in, the laconic clan elder tossed the stiff grass stem just used as a toothpick. "For a quick grant of asylum for skilled craftsmen, dangled alongside of the promised expansion of trade? The commoner's got motivation aplenty to sign onto the Sunwheel campaign if his weans and his kinsmen are roofless and hungry."

Tarens mulled the notion from Jieret's perspective. "Townfolk won't win back their access by road through the Mathorns, no matter how large the armed force fielded by Lysaer's silver-tongued statesmanship."

"Oh, aye. The Sorcerers don't negotiate." The fellow braiding a new leather hackamore spat on his hands and spliced the hemp noseband. "Doesn't mean the devilsome fanatics won't slaughter us, trying."

The relay riders resumed their circuit, the sweat-caked misery of late-summer dust given paltry relief by the swim across the slack current below Tal Quorin. Reports from the east came in with the hunters ranging to forage in the shortening days towards the season's end. "War's spoiling, hatched on the grand strategy for next spring."

The gloomy assessment drawn for the long term shaded the warning dispatched in conclusion. "Lysaer's building a unification across the northern kingdoms not seen since the siege of Alestron first cemented the Sunwheel Alliance."

"True Sect religion will burrow in for the course." Late night, over a stirred glue pot to mend damaged gear, the boy tasked to trim fletching echoed his elders' disquiet. "They'll be chary to waste the momentous incentive with Alestron repossessed by Paravians."

Apprehension on that score strung clanborn nerves to fraught temper, with the old rites of passage demanded of their blood heritage no longer a matter for idle conjecture. No one knew how the surviving lineages would withstand the fresh shock of exposure.

Talk shied from that question, the redoubled threat to clan progeny stiffened by the bandied word the Elssine quarries had been commandeered for five years by a Fellowship mandate.

Laughter met Tarens's poleaxed astonishment. "Where'd you think centaur masons would mine their granite? They've settled in, starting with restoration of the seagate landing at Alestron. Quality block with quartz in the matrix is preferred to repair the breach in the Wyntok battlement."

Fireside conversation filled in the particulars, clan reaction divided between electric excitement and dismay, strained to apprehension over the vacant royal seat at Ithamon.

Hopeful eyes fixed on Tarens. "You'd say whether the Teir's'Ffalenn might be ready for his coronation?"

Tarens deferred the unbearable enquiry, his ruddy countenance a blank wall. "For the council's ears, when I get there."

"Sithaer take his Grace's absence!" The speaker jabbed a reckless stick into the banked coals, lofting a fugitive flurry of sparks.

The taciturn squad captain ignored the transgression, more disquieted by the prospect of a dawn departure with a town-blood liegeman in tow. "We'll pass through the charged ground in Deshir for five days. Are you hardened enough to surmount that?"

"I should hope so." Tarens slapped dust from his leathers and set foot in the stirrup, grateful to straddle a gelding with stature after days astride mountain ponies with sledgehammer gaits. "Held my own by way of the secret paths through Strakewood in your liege's company before this."

"The flux current has upshifted since," the scout warned. "The etheric web in Rathain's reconfigured entirely, with the surge at full moon beyond the range of anyone's prior threshold."

"We'll see, then." Tarens shrugged off the uncertainty by proposing a lively wager. "Should I fall to mewling madness, you win." After his residence at Ithamon under the deranging hallucination of electromagnetic flares, and subject to the tuned resonance impelled by the Masterbard's music, his extended tolerance ought to suffice. "If I can't withstand the ambient threshold in Strakewood, I might as well throw in my lot with the evicted Etarrans."

A rangy teen acclaimed for his prowess eyed Tarens sidelong in dubious assessment. "Don't bet you're the exception. Had a lad with clear descent back to the founders who collapsed, blind with fever and raving. Not just him. My own cousin puked up her guts and delayed our patrol for three days."

Tarens tipped his farmer's straw hat with scant sympathy. "Anyone have a flask? On Davien's advice, I found getting soused on neat spirits knocks the worst edge off a harmonic back-lash."

The suggested remedy sparked no enthusiasm. "Too late. We finished last season's cider when the Darkling Dam fell and unyoked the Severnir."

Sober and thoughtful, the relay scouts spurred their horses, while a fast rider sent word ahead to assemble the chieftain's council for Tarens's arrival.

Frost came early to the far north. Flame red and gold, the turned leaves in Strakewood met the call to clan gathering, a disruptive nuisance at season's end during the exigent rush to stockpile stores before winter. Insult to injury, Tarens sent as the mouthpiece for Rathain's truant prince tested even Laithen's intrepid patience.

Esfand s'Valerient resolved this time to claim his place at the chieftain's council.

"The seat's a moot point, if the greybeards won't grant your due as the kingdom's invested *caithdein*." Cinnamon braid as frizzled as his squirrel cap, just rakishly jammed on askew, Khadrien worried the blister gouged by the awl to pierce heavyweight leathers for stitching.

The pair sat with Siantra at an open-air trestle scattered with tools: the punch just cast down in demonstrative pique, several quality knives to slice buckskin laces, and the worn stubs of charcoal and chalk to mark patterns. The cured pelts for jackets draped the wooden moulds to shape high-top buskins for snow.

Furrier's work was a brutal chore nobody loved. Not while bracing wind stole the last heat of summer, and stags in clattering rut made an autumn hunt the more lively enticement.

Yet warm garments were needed as never before, with the lodge tent's encampment pitched in the far north, and expeditions planned far afield to meet the urgent requirement for resonant hardening. Scout parties would travel to Deshir and Halwythwood to weather the upshifted tides at equinox and solstice, wary of increased patrols on the Mathorn Road and the grim bent of Lysaer's renewed grip on the temple's intentions.

Siantra broke her opaque silence, likely a peacekeeper's move to deflect the griped canker of Esfand's thwarted standing. "Would a hood lined with grey fox or red suit Kyrwen's youngest daughter?"

"Wolf, rather," remarked Khadrien. "The pesky minx bit my wrist. Drew blood, too, when I took away the sharp stick that belike would have gouged someone's eye out."

Less prone to diversion, Esfand glanced up from the jig he employed to drill deer antler buttons. "You know that crofter's packing bad news."

Siantra doused his impatience with caustic rebuff. "We'll hear soon enough. The relay scouts will come in before sundown."

Her abalone-shell bracelet chinked as she reached for the fox pelt, a gifted match for the drop earring that glinted through her raven hair. A courtship trinket, likely from a hopeful admirer, since teasing had not pried out the shy flirt's identity.

Curiosity caught Khadrien staring, again.

"Pest! No way I'm telling." Siantra dealt him a slap on the wrist. "Lay off! You lot could badger a gadfly to exhaustion. Pity the swain's tongue-tied misery. He, *if he's male,* scarcely deserves your gang-up rowdiness. Forbye, I'm not ready to settle for pairing with anyone. Which also is none of your business."

A fellow pricked by Siantra's reticence understood when to stand down. Moreover, emphatically, she had placed both sensitive topics off-limits to speculation.

The scout relay arrived as the young seer had forecast, though Tarens's blond hair and distinctive height was not amid the trail-weary company. The squad captain accosted by Esfand's bunched frown shrugged off his pointed enquiry. Cornered by Khadrien's importunate persistence in the dappled shade by the hitching rail, she slung her mare's stripped tack overtop the withy hurdle that penned the camp's herd.

"He's damned well a grown man, and I'm not his mother!" Staggered as her blaze-faced mount stropped her side as a scratching post, the exasperated woman rescued her bashed quiver and swore over the mussed fletching on her best arrows.

Siantra stepped up and led off the hot horse. Grateful, the tired scout smoothed down her rumpled shafts and relented. "Tarens abandoned our company yesterday. He had pay in his scrip. Shoved off to Anglefen, so he said, for supplies he wanted from the market."

Before Esfand's scowl blackened, she added, tart, "The bullheaded farmer scorned the idiot risk. Insists he blends in with town folk without bother. Still, we warned him thrice over. If such carelessness sets headhunters onto us, we'll be right quick to gut his corpse for the scavengers."

Khadrien's obstreperous manner jammed her tirade in midstream and raised a wry laugh. "Sorry, whelp. All the news from Ithamon's been clapped under seal for the ears of your elders."

"The man's frivolous delay won't wrangle him any favours." Esfand winced to contemplate the steamed reception awaiting the delinquent liegeman. "Laithen's temper's been sharp enough to flay skin since her recovery from the Teir's'Ffalenn's last mettlesome foray."

But that gloomy conviction proved to be premature.

Tarens slipped through the encampment's patrolled boundary on foot three days later, his arrival announced by the shrieks of the ecstatic children. They surrounded him in a voracious pack, the smallest clutched like lampreys to his legs, pawing into his pockets for sugar treats. The largest ones, grinning with stuffed cheeks from behind, led his laden mount, bundled with merchandise like a pack mule. The bulges roped under tarpaulin swiftly quelled the adults' offended animosity. The most hardened eye facing the hardship of winter melted to eagerness as the pleased recipients pounced on the luxuries sequestered inside: three bolts of flannel, fine linen, waxed thread, steel needles, an iron cauldron, two sacks of wheat flour, wool fleece, refined salt, a keg of molasses, and four pokes of dried apricots, currants, and citrus peel.

"Naught here couldn't have been snagged in a raid," a sour scout carped from the fringes.

Tarens met the disparagement with an infectious grin. "Honest coin hurts far less than blooded steel. Can you truly want to live on the edge as society's outcasts forever?"

"Look, he's brought tailor's shears!" Reticent pride came unravelled: too many palms were welted from the knife handle after the exhaustive tedium of slicing buckskins. "Beats the dumb luck haul from a caravan."

"Bribes and chicanery," Laithen allowed, waded in expecting to quell the controversial acrimony over his feckless jaunt and in turn, subdued to mollified resignation. Swarmed by celebration and genial gratitude, and apt to face revolt from the hungry eager for baked biscuits at dinner, she rested her case and forgave the big-hearted crofter's transgression.

Better sense deferred the more serious business for the high council's formal review. Astute s'Idir wisdom parsed the tactical sense behind Tarens's brash generosity. Laithen kept to herself the grim implication, that the guarded news brought from Ithamon was best broached after the youngsters had been sent to bed.

Her affectionate backslap snagged Tarens's attention through the boisterous clamber of his small admirers. "Get cleaned up. I saw the bear hug you gave Kyrwen's weans. Seek her out, Iyat-thos. You've got time. Just don't mention I noticed she missed you."

The chieftain's council assembled by late evening, crowded into the lodge tent before the dismal threat of rainfall swept in off the northern sea. Where a less formal session would have seen every able hand busy stitching garments or mittens under the flickering torchlight, solemnity faced the immanent upset of change with undivided attention.

Staked cressets threw the head table into swooping shadow. Laithen s'Idir presided, flanked on her left by the aged hunch of the clan lore mistress. Jalienne's pale hair loomed like a ghost's, the honorary grant of the head chair bestowed upon her as Cosach's widow. Esfand sat as the *caithdein*'s heir at her side, bulwarked by the weaponed bulk and seamed scowl of Deshir's grizzled war captain.

Restlessness settled to expectation as Tarens, clean-shaven and refreshed from the trail, assumed the speaker's stance before the high trestle. If Kyrwen's affection had made his afternoon memorable, the sweetness of reunion no longer eased the anxiousness riding his countenance. Nor the capable hands, at unrelaxed rest on the pommels of knife and sword.

The role of the crofter was not his tonight, Siantra determined from her earned vantage with the clan seeress in the front row with the northern chieftains. A clamped fist on the warming blanket spread over her lap bridled an irritation that had naught to do with the chill. Khadrien's sneak presence crouched underneath the plank bench, concealed by the demure wool draped over her shins.

The invited assembly inclined towards surly, with individuals bone-tired from duty since dawn obliged to stay alert after hours.

"Council is called to hear of the Teir's'Ffalenn." Jalienne's ceremonial opening deferred the speaker's prerogative to Laithen s'Idir, whose leadership eschewed words with a crisp nod of leave towards Iyat-thos Tarens.

The scar-faced liegeman straightened to his full height, flushed by disarming embarrassment. The fierce attentiveness trained upon him intensified to discomfort under his evident wish to be elsewhere.

"I bring difficult news of the sanctioned crown prince to whom you swore your feal oath." Resolved, he plunged on through the punch of the gusts that billowed pegged canvas. "When the Fellowship Sorcerer, Davien, unleashed the harmonic surge that laid waste to Etarra, the compassion that founded the realm's royal line rejected necessity. Arithon has broken with your liegemen's commitment and declared his abdication."

Siantra's bashed heel clapped down Khadrien's oath, while around her, a collective gasp took the brunt of the blow in shocked disbelief. Then the clan war captain slammed to his feet. Shouts and uproar shredded decorum. Against rage that surged the incensed crowd forward, Laithen slapped the board with a whipcrack report.

"Sit down! All of you! Are we a scrofulous rabble? Or can we show decent restraint and not sling uncivilized rocks at the messenger?" Her scorn lashed across the emotional upheaval and quenched the outcry to ashamed silence. "Listen to what Tarens has been charged to say! Your inflamed objections serve nothing, before we have the facts laid before us for an ordered discussion."

Shaken, his blue eyes vivid blue against his creased, sunburned skin, Tarens gathered his courage before a fallen hush as tensioned as the seized calm before the black front of an on-coming squall. "Arithon did not wait on the Seven's formal acquittal of Rathain's crown obligation. He turned his back and departed, no matter the standing for his release might be held in defiance. I don't know where he's gone. He shared none of his plans. With heartfelt regret, I attest that his fury was heated past measure by his birth-born s'Ffalenn conscience. Who knows what he'll do? Given the talented power he wields, I stand here terrified to admit my trust in him has been shaken. I suggest you confront the rough possibility the realm may be saddled with a rogue prince."

"Arithon's movements are dark to our Sight," the clan seeress confirmed, unchallenged by the raptor's keen vision behind Siantra's masked silence.

The unthinkable sank in through a gravid pause, repellent disbelief broken by Esfand's unexpected statement of legal authority. "Arithon s'Ffalenn has done nothing criminal to substantiate a *caithdein*'s trial of character."

"Not yet," Tarens allowed, pained to sorrow. "On the contrary, I can corroborate the probity of his Grace's actions in favour. He has delivered upon the promises witnessed by your people last autumn. The Severnir Dam was released with no casualties drowned in the flood. His plan to restore Ithamon's raised resonance was studied, a clean execution aligned by his cautious intent to deliver Etarra's subjects from harm's way. The premature closure triggered by Davien disrupted that strategic care. But the prince's purposeful task did not fail: the flux lines that furnish Rathain's mysteries are secured beyond desecrate jeopardy. No longer hindered, the fifth lane has been realigned to support the return of Athera's Paravians in our time."

"Centaurs have landed to rebuild Alestron," Laithen reminded. "The fiery temperament of Torbrand's lineage is well-known, besides. Our primary obligation remains. We guard the free wilds. Leave the Fellowship Sorcerers their sovereign charge to release Rathain's prince or pursue his reconciliation."

Tarens tipped his head in acquiescence. "Your straits with your prince may yet bend to reason. Yet wishful thinking is dangerous under the pressure of momentous change."

Deferent, directed to Jalienne's frigid reserve, Tarens framed his tacit appeal. "Unrest from the townborn will not subside. War may ravage Rathain before the Athlien High Queen Regent gathers her singers and dancers to re-establish the Paravian court on the continent. If Riathan herds return to Daon Ramon to breed, the ancient charge falls to your clans to fend the rest of humanity clear of endangerment. Are you prepared to shoulder your ancestral lot and reclaim the legacy peril of that burden, based only on legend and guesswork?"

"Now, see here!" interrupted the lore mistress, galled. "Our spoken record has been preserved with utmost diligence for generations. More, the Seven have not abandoned us!"

"Your historical expertise is impeccable," Tarens allowed. "But where are the Sorcerers now?"

"We have only rote knowledge!" a scout called through the groundswell of muttered uncertainty. "No mentors with living witness to guide us."

"We cannot speak for Havish, ruled at strength under an attuned sovereign," another declaimed.

Example weighted the outbroken argument: Melhalla's crown steward had been forced to step up from the moment the Ilitharis mariners' great ship hove in and dropped anchor. Both Shand and Tysan were kingless. Absent a royal heir, the onus of active liaison with the Paravians devolved to the *caithdeinen* wearing the black.

"Are we prepared for the sacrifice of our youth if Rathain's royal lineage abandons us to our fate? Will you risk the sanity of your kinfolk, when the directive attached to clan heritage falls on your best and brightest?"

No parent heard Tarens's warning without a pang. All had witnessed Laithen's fraught recovery from her bout of resonant back-lash. She had returned, changed, from her sojourn abroad on the Plain of Araithe. Despite Davien's patent charge, she had suffered for days, wracked delirious after exposure to the upshifted frequency keyed by Arithon's pealed cry to the land. The signal experience altered the mind and marked even the most resilient survivor.

Tarens's appeal presented a last patch of firm ground in the cross-chop of hesitation. "Maybe the hour has come to revise the royal charters that dictate the terms of land use, with the stakes of town welfare buffered in separate from the mystical dangers of arbitration."

Against rife agitation stirring the scouts, Tarens raised a hand. "Hear me through, if you please! My perspective is uniquely placed to lend nuanced insight into the impasse from both sides."

When the wasp hum of protest rose to a growl, the ex-crofter shouted, "How many town families have been dispossessed, or lost kinfolk for the sake of way rights through the Mathorn notch? Etarra has *died*, a whole thriving populace rendered destitute for the priorities of charter law. Are those people's lives worth less than your own, exposed to madness, or dead of starvation and slaughter by the predation of headhunters?"

While clamour arose in heated dissent, Tarens persisted. "I see every hand here worked to the bone to meet the privations of a lean winter. Is this what you want for your children unto the next generations?"

The clan's lore mistress interceded. "Elder times, before the rebellion saw our kind split off and hunted under persecution, the benefit of civilized comforts were equally shared. We gave birth under snug roofs in the towns, with free-wilds patrol assigned to the scouts and their families in rotation. The Fellowship's imposed duty never consigned us to exile, nor to the penury of a subsistence clawed from the forest in bitter hardship."

Jalienne was not unsympathetic. Second wife, after Cosach lost his first marriage to a malnourished childbirth in a lean year, she had carried two pregnancies to term under the adverse rigours of outdoor exposure. Conviction rooted her passionate advocacy that Tarens's proposal should merit serious thought.

"No momentous decision will be reached today," Laithen declared with finality. "Everyone's too tired to thrash over the precedent, nor is a hasty call necessary. Winter's freeze will mire the wheels of town mischief and war. We have time to deliberate, and to prepare, while we wait upon the verified course of development under oversight by the Seven."

The storm broke as the lodge meeting came to a close, the staccato spatter of rain punctuation to risen wind and a darkened morass of uncertainty. The chieftains dispersed to dissenting opinion against the urgent problem ahead: without landmark, they had no established path and no compass to steer their old-blood customs through the shoals of momentous upheaval and change.

Long after the acrimonious gathering dispersed, with the watchfire's sultry coals doused to plumed smoke beneath driven rainfall, Siantra, Esfand, and Khadrien slipped through the black, dripping trees, and struck a sly bargain with the four youngsters assigned to the rat watch. The serious business of chasing marauding vermin from the bundled stores in the root cellar provided them with the convenience of shelter to huddle in privacy.

Crouched under low eaves with a candle, equipped with net slings and a bludgeon, Siantra shivered beneath her soaked blanket, the qualm of distress that chattered her teeth not due to the foul weather. Touched fey ever since the encounter at Athili, she endured her fraught gift, whipped like a rag in the gale wind of visions strung between present and future. Her friends understood when not to disturb her. She never divested a word out of her high-strung silences before she was ready.

"They're scared to death of tradition. The whole council," Esfand fumed in disgust.

"And you're not?" Khadrien hugged his drawn-up knees, and blew off the droplets seeped from his plastered hair. "Faced with the Paravian presence, any one of us could flip off the edge and die pissing ourselves, raving crazy."

"Never mind that," Esfand countered, impatient. "The Teir's'Ffalenn has the lot of us cowed until nobody dares to tangle with his personality, far less corner him for close questioning." His considered pause gauged Siantra's clamped reticence. "What does Laithen think? She's the only one besides Tarens who's spent significant time with him."

"She doesn't say." Siantra glanced up, eyes a troubled, cool grey. "If I had to guess, she's afraid of him."

"Well, who isn't? His kind of will is the sort that wrecks mountains." Khadrien shied a cracked nutshell at the pattered rustle of something furtive lurking in the shadows. "Not to mention he's got the striking, ill temper of a scalded snake."

The frown that furrowed Siantra's forehead made her underlit features look ancient. "It's all too convenient," she declared, steadied at last to pose an opinion. "Arithon's alone because he doesn't want anyone else finding out what he means to do next."

"Well, who listens to us?" Esfand's tucked brows bridged his nose like black iron. "Jalienne sides with Tarens because he is townborn, and not wholly wedded to our clanborn ways. Laithen looks up to him for a *caithdein*'s wisdom on the basis of Earl Jieret's memories."

"They all hear what they want," remarked Khadrien, surly. "As if you don't exist, and Rathain doesn't already have a vested steward to stand shadow and speak for Rathain's crown interests."

"Until next summer," Esfand agreed, and slapped the wooden bat into his palm with emphatic resolve. "The charade can last only as long as I remain underage."

Calculations

After the hectic months of logistical urgency inflamed by the destructive collapse of Etarra, a march expedited at punishing speed saw Lysaer s'Ilessid's fevered interests relocated for winter, headquartered at Narms. His household settled into a furnished mansion just as powdered snowfall whitened the roads, and ice closed the high notch through Eastwall to the Eltair coast. Instrell Bay's sheltered ports kept the westbound passage open, though rough weather made crossing by galley to Tysan an irregular misery of inconvenience. Off campaign, Lysaer retained his pavilion staff, a skeleton company of his elite officers, and armed troops pared down to the summer's green recruits with a select roster of veterans to trim their shambled ranks into discipline.

Lured on by the opportunity to secure a trade town without fortified defences, the guild merchants grovelled and scoured their deep coffers to make their turf indispensable. The lavish grant of facilities for martial activity and use of the mayor's hall for the state sessions imposed by diplomacy saw Lysaer's schedule crammed to capacity.

More than ever, the role of a domestic servant left Dace partitioned at the sidelines.

Messengers came and went dawn to dusk. The upheaval and delays that snarled the relief sent to appease the voracious straits of Etarra's destitute exiles demanded the master's nuanced attention. Where his appropriations met parsimonious fists, the wrangling negotiations parlayed in formal sessions stayed off-limits to the master's personal staff.

Dace exhausted his meagre pay share to compensate.

Other eyes witnessed what transpired between Lysaer and his field officers. Scribes recorded bills of lading, and underlings copied the archived sheets from his meetings with temple ambassadors and town delegations. A discreet bribe in silver might loosen the tongues of the smug pages and squires bullied by their dedicate overlords. Or, at the risk of fanciful embroidery on a story, a gin flask slipped to a frozen sentry, or a thrifty penny might wheedle bored coach boys and garrulous stablehands for eavesdroppers' rumour.

Most reliable sources lay beyond reach. Administrative hauteur kept the secretariat too busy to cultivate, with clerks and post couriers and the pigeon loft's fowlers constantly pressured to punctilious haste.

At remove, Dace watched the genius of deft leadership cement the affairs of town interests into a broadscale coalition. Help received, and near-term advantage welded disparate partnerships at long range. Fear and uncertainty were Lysaer's practised tools to shape the foundation for future alliance. The Paravian claim to Alestron, and Etarra's appalling demise stoked the frenzied clamour to garner his favour, driving the obsequious scramble for his contracted support. The bit player's hustling grasp had to peck at the crumbs to glean Lysaer's planned intentions.

Yet what purposeful aim the Light's instrument moulded from the ashes of his Etarran sovereignty stayed shrouded from the arena of outside speculation.

Menial placement at last gave Dace Morley's vantage the unusual backhanded edge: for the clandestine directives nurtured in quiet gestation at first stayed confined to the master's private quarters.

Maps, geography, and the inveterate pursuit of Arithon s'Ffalenn obsessed Lysaer s'Ilessid to exclusion throughout the grey months of winter. Constant, tinkering manipulation kept the Mistwraith's geas engaged, with Nails installed at his Lordship's side at all hours. The gaunt diviner flanked his state chair in and out of his meetings with officers. Her temple standing and crafty manoeuvring made her privy to the brokered promises that smoothed the ruffled feathers of commerce. Yet no inveigling influence could displace the active intelligence guarding Lysaer's person. Her subversive persistence failed to dislodge the valet who minded the master's chambers.

Deadlocked rivals, both watched Lysaer's generous incentives for skilled craftsmen sway the influential magnates and ingratiate the mayors of three kingdoms. Savvy wits noticed the nuance, that s'Ilessid foresight retained the best and most well connected at lavish expense. Cryptic calculations penned on his maps decoded the choice to feed idle mouths over winter alongside his troops, and illumined the scaled dexterity expanding his strategic alliances. The invidious, cursed enmity that Nails's sly handling kept chafed on the raw drew the backroom interests of less savoury accomplices to the gentleman's suite under Dace's exclusive domain.

The overcast glare of midafternoon burnished the cartographer's parchments draped over the table in his Lordship's personal study, a cramped room attached to the valet's closet adjacent to the master's bedchamber. Dace lived with the smells of oak-gall ink and scraped parchment, of charcoal and rice paper, finished with turpentine varnish. Here, Lysaer's finicky preference forbade the steward's staff entry. The fresh-faced coterie of pages and squires ventured no further than the anteroom where he doffed his armour. Dace cleaned and tended the innermost sanctum himself, a confidence not to be squandered.

He touched nothing. No matter how sharp the temptation to snoop, he left Lysaer's internal affairs as they lay, from the sensitive town correspondence stacked on his desk, to the ships' rutters and charts left unrolled in plain view. The annotations complied there with exactitude showed a detailed analysis of port access and trade routes, with known impediments to travel culled from experienced road masters. Penned notes on free-wilds terrain jammed the margins, gleaned from the seasoned league headhunters who scoured the remote wastes and expanded upon by reclusive freebooters of dubious character.

The stiff-necked steward bowed to the master's instruction and admitted such uncouth informants, unquestioned. Come whatever hour, regardless of their rough appearance, they were installed on the bench by the armour rack in the anteroom, and made comfortable with wine and refreshments. The current pair fidgeted, ill at ease, awaiting his Lordship's pleasure to receive them.

Dace minded the suite's inner chambers, while the coarse jokes and braw laughter common to the backcountry outposts and stews styled the ruffians as rootless adventurers. Behind closed doors, the valet built up the fire. His efficiency saw the plain wooden chairs rearranged as replacements to spare the costlier ones with brocade upholstery from oil stains and grimed charcoal. Prepared when the guard at the entry dressed weapons, Dace positioned himself for Lysaer's return, Nails in tow at his heels.

Inbound, her inflected consonants punctured the constant, needling patter she employed to prime Desh-thiere's geas. ". . . of your true enemy the longer you dally with placating trade guilds."

Dace strangled annoyance. Impassively placed for smart attendance, he doffed and hung his Lordship's fine mantle, the unsullied polish on the master's boots noted in passing. Proper etiquette deferred to the unlikely foursome crowding the study: Lysaer in Etarra's heraldic red-and-gold thread, tasteful jewels selected to impress, but not to outshine the peacock wealth of the merchant magnates; and his pet diviner, an icicle decked out in temple regalia, her cropped hair, steep forehead, and scrawny neck stark as a post, collared in white velvet beaded with pearls.

Dace snubbed the creature's glare of resentment, obligated to usher the lowlier visitors to their seats, both clad for the backwoods, beards jutted like unwashed wool over leathers and gamey jackets redolent of log fires and grease off the spit. The buck knives strapped to the taller one's belt identified him as a free-wilds trapper, while the other sported a fancy stiletto, throwing blades favoured by upcountry guides commonly hired by smugglers. Beer breath suggested the dependable steward had furnished them with topped flagons, sufficient to loosen their talk without turning them crapulous.

Lysaer assumed the head chair, backlit by the mullioned casement. Nails perched in shadow at his right hand, a mantled hawk in restive, keen charge of poached territory. Eyes pallid as weak tea stared daggers at Dace, who minded the tingle of Asandir's spiritmark and kept his hostility shielded.

Neither prevailed in this deadly game. Posture and bristle like dogs as they would, the wrangle for Lysaer's attention doused the outbreak of overt hostility. Dace stewed in muzzled forbearance, hamstrung as Sulfin Evend had been when unclean insinuations were the weapons deployed against his liege's cursed vulnerability. Counterweight to that abrasive manipulation, the valet's intimate loyalty manned the redoubt through unshakable trust.

Impervious to Nails's animosity, Dace accepted Lysaer's doffed gloves. A stressed seam marred the fine, kidskin leather, which retired the garment for mending. He was back in his unobtrusive, servile place when the master's flicked gesture requested pens and ink from the escritoire.

The smuggler tilted his chair backwards, a booted heel propped on the table's edge bracing the other leg, crossed at his ankles. "Are we clear? There's gold royals paid out for spilling tips brought from the forbidden ground in Daon Ramon."

Lysaer disregarded the uncouth abuse of his furniture. His apparent, arctic indifference instead plumbed the trapper's abrasive defiance. "Two royals, yes. More, based upon the quality of your information."

He leaned suddenly forward, peeled back the top map of Tysan, and slid another sheet from underneath. Spread flat, the chart depicted the southern principalities of Rathain, east to west from the coasts below the Mathorn ranges and down to Daenfal Lake in the flats. "Why don't you show me everything that's not marked, including corrections."

Forced to right his slouched posture, the trapper dropped his chair legs foursquare. The smuggler's flinched recoil saved him from a pinched toe, as both burly men craned their necks in rapt eagerness to divulge their illicit experience.

They talked. Chapped hands with dirt-rimmed fingernails swept over the parchment, collided, recoiled, then reverted to civilized turns since Lysaer's penmanship could not inscribe suggestions from both at once.

Dace observed the familiar routine: the initial gush of gruff voices followed up by Lysaer's careful questions. Precisely where had the trapper forded the Aiyenne? If summer's lightning-struck brush fires persisted, was crossing Daon Ramon possible after spring thaws? Did the smuggler know more than one path of ascent to scale the high cliff by the Arwent? Might his recall specify which sinks to avoid on the elevated plateau in Araethura? Where was clan vigilance wont to be slack, and when? Were the haunts on the Old Way through Ithamon much worse since the Severnir's release, and had any bold spirit attempted the ancient gap through the Baiyen?

Nails interjected with prickling remarks over bolt-holes wont to conceal minions of Darkness, while Dace gritted his teeth and served tea to ease the fresh tension elicited in Lysaer's bearing.

Between the veiled thrusts of underhand byplay, the afternoon overcast drained the light from the sky and ushered in evening shadow. When the woodsmen had nothing further to add, Lysaer dried his pen and sweetened the happy pair with five coinweight in gold apiece. The steward was summoned to see them out, then dispatched with an excuse to defer a scheduled engagement. "And ask the cook to send up a supper tray."

Lysaer stretched his back and reclaimed his seat. Nails's irritable, insistent complaint, that the valet ought to have shouldered the errand to the kitchen, met his displeasure.

"The fellow saved my life more than once." Lysaer weighted the annotated map flat to resume the business under review. "Do I need further proof? Dace carries my interests as close as the beating heart in his chest."

Nails fanned herself, her offended scowl increased by the redolence of sweaty fur and the sour, lingering reek of smoke char from green oak. "I'd go myself for the breath of fresh air." Her pretence of capitulation included the sidelong barb. "Though, I warn you such sentimental indulgence comes at the risk of unthinkable setback. Our campaign against Shadow might fail if your untoward faith in the lackey's misplaced."

Dace smothered the furious urge to drop something fragile. Deliberately busy refreshing wax candles, he gauged Lysaer's response to the provocation. Not deaf or blind, the valet lived in dread of the meticulous strategy being hatched in sequestered secrecy. He had watched since the orchestrated first steps: the hopeful forays for salvage that confirmed Etarra's recovery as a lost cause, the unstable debris field too massive to shift. Gone, the deep cisterns carved into rock. Demolished to rubble, the dungeon storage vaults stocked for supply to frustrate a siege. From wrack and ruin that stunned comprehension, the master's avid review of geography fomented a compromise plan.

Dace sparked the desk lamp, the flounce of flame under his unsteady fingers a telltale of his suppressed dread, and a mistake, had Nails's avid eye not been diverted.

Light bloomed, Lysaer's fair head gilt against gathering gloom as he leaned over the trestle on a propped arm. "Passage through Araethura's the long way around, making Caith-al-Caen the best site for an alternate trade hub."

Nails reclined, her knee cocked over her chair arm, and half-lidded lashes masking the predator's fixated stare. "A bold bid you can't win. Not unless you raise the armed strength to prevail against clan resistance from Halwythwood."

"Allied support from Morvain can arrange that." Lysaer tapped the strategic choice on the map. "Moreover, the First-Age track's established already." Linked through the Baiyen, trade could reach the Eltair ports via the notch above Jaelot, also convenient for the needful alternative when winter ice and avalanche closed the high peaks. "The attractive advantage also connects with the southern passage by river out of Daenfal."

Trade clamoured for a cross-continent route that stayed open year-round, the contingent priority critical to logistics and resupply of an armed campaign.

"You have arcane backing," Nails allowed, a cat sharpening claws for the hook that secured her temple's prerogative.

A valet endowed with s'Gannley insight dared show nothing beyond the blank mask of feigned ignorance. Dace lit the next lamp, his hardened nerve frightened witless: for the enormity of the proposed transgression was hell-bound to cross the imperative grain of the Fellowship's interests. Nails egged on the fatal embroilment, knowing: the danger posed by a charter law trespass well served the True Sect's pre-emptive aim to bend their rogue avatar to subordination, or goad him to his destruction.

"Seize command of Ithamon, and you advance your cause to put down the Dark." Motivation shone through the blunt-force insinuation: Nails baited the drive of the Mistwraith's curse for entrapment. "Best to make sure Shadow's lair remains empty."

That purposeful prompt, paired with the lure of the map, muzzled the teeth of vigilant protection. Nails's vitriolic leer flashed in sidelong triumph as Lysaer ordered the bowl and the pendulum brought to enact a divining.

Dace swallowed the scream that raged in his chest, forced to fetch and carry the items as bidden. Desh-thiere's addictive taint enabled the temple diviner to ply her insidious persuasion into the night.

Teased by warped desire, Lysaer forgot caution. He fell prey, while Dace's ancestral heritage exposed the perilous thorn in the fever dream centred by town-based prosperity: the Paravian presence returned to Alestron must rise.

A lethal threat if Lysaer's coalition tried an unsanctioned expansion into Daon Ramon. Inconceivable disaster awaited the cream of Mankind's war host should their proud ranks answer a rallying cry to drive an incursion into the free wilds. For Lysaer's ambition contested the ancient Riathan breeding ground and abrogated the charter from Third Age Year One, with its sacrosanct grant of Paravian entitlement to rebuild the Crown seat at Ithamon.

Trapped witness, Dace endured in powerless silence. Kharadmon's harsh precautions, and Davien's forewarning crumbled the dregs of complacent denial. Naught else could be done but hold out upon the fragile hope for an opening that might never happen.

Dace laid out the meal the steward delivered. He removed the congealed sauces and meats left untouched in the heat of Desh-thiere's warped obsession, then replenished the candles burned down to stubs. Lysaer's captive attention could not be swayed. Never while the diviner's artful use of the pendulum crossed and recrossed the plotted points of campaign on the maps.

Dace withstood the exhaustive course, reduced to wan desperation and prayer that the s'Ffalenn bastard's whereabouts would stay elusive. To speak out, even to pose the suggestion the master might wish to retire, would provoke a summary eviction. Reason could not shake a mind locked in spellbound thrall by the Mistwraith's directive.

The session wound down only when the diviner's talented stamina wavered, the seeking arcs of her pendulum marred by the tremors of incipient back-lash. Exhaustion alone compelled Lysaer to break off and release Nails from duty to rest.

The door closed upon her departure at last. Privacy restored, Dace poured warmed wine. His gentle touch undressed the master for bed. Impeccable valet, he dried the despised bowl and returned the limp pendulum to its padded case. Then he tidied the chairs and snuffed all but one of the lamps.

Afterwards, he settled in silent vigil while Lysaer lay wakeful. The relentless quiet would wear him nightlong, the black shackle of his affliction tightened by Nails's dark influence. Morning light would not alleviate the necessity of maintaining diplomacy with the True Sect Temple. Genuine justice spurred his s'Ilessid care for a dispossessed people and gaffed sterling virtue on the barbed hook. For his committed campaign to rebuild Etarra's displaced sovereignty must suffer the brunt, if expulsion of Nails soured Erdane's high priesthood and aligned the Light's faith as an enemy.

Hobbled anguish rowelled that canker of cold recognition, but never acceptance. Dace resisted the pit-fallen whisper of reason, however insistent. The cursed impairment that flawed his well-meant resolve to defend Lysaer's ridden autonomy had no other champion, should he fold in defeat. Another day, another hour, he nurtured the unconditional calm that made him indispensable.

Give way, or give in, he must stay the course at the side of his liege, *perhaps* to find means to divert a disaster. No reprieve would come from the Fellowship Sorcerers. The Seven's hands remained tied since Lysaer's outcast status abrogated the protective terms of the compact.

Scheme

The Prime Matriarch of the Koriathain endured the bitter discomfort of winter at Highscarp, icy feet muffled, and nerves frayed by the rattle of salt-crusted casements besieged by the gusts off the Cildein Ocean. Ithilt's exposed peninsula made old bones enspelled for longevity ache in the pervasive damp. The sisterhouse peeress's insatiable curiosity torched even the threadbare pretence of civil tolerance.

Behind a locked door, into another year, Lirenda continued her survey of the exhumed records by the ragged glow of a tormented candleflame. If speedier means and less risky relief for her quandary existed, her last hope for vindication lurked here. Chapped hands cupped to cold quartz to assay packets of cached information, and nursing cramped fingers callused as a clerk's, she transcribed curated notes onto stiff parchment.

Yet the miserable search extended without better remedy, while seasonal drifts choked the pass through the Skyshiels, and the westerly gales snugged the trade galleys down in the harbour. Few coastal captains bucked the green rollers of Eltair Bay with a severe blow wont to brew overnight and send their wrecked keels to the bottom. Weather crowded the taverns on the frozen roads, and packed travellers four to a room in chilblained discomfort, bed and board priced for extortion.

Since Etarra's demise, the volume of goods trapped in limbo exacerbated the grinding tedium of the slow months worse then ever. Cryptic news flew by pigeon, the bulkier sheaves of trade documents bundled with the sealed letters in strapped cases borne by mounted couriers. Even sensitive packets entrusted to the order's own messengers ran the gamut of highway theft and disclosure. The imperative for absolute secrecy tied Lirenda to paper and ink, defended by warded ciphers, while her patience with Highscarp's insular society galled her brittle temperament night and day.

"We could be worse off," the peeress enthused, unaware how narrowly she escaped censure to mute her garrulous tongue. No matter the ignorant woman's blithe optimism sanded the skin with a harsh grain of truth.

News for the Koriathain moved unhampered throughout the snowbound months of isolation, the world's affairs tracked at remove through the vigilant eyes of the lane watch. Critical word sped from the four quarters by crystal transmission arrived tainted by the evident drawback: such sophisticate means were seldom secure from the Warden at Althain Tower. The most sensitive matters unearthed from the crypt were too momentous to delegate. Since the tool required for the hour her plan ripened must be shaped in advance, the efficient deployment of resource commanded the service of Whitehold's most experienced senior.

Lirenda timed her summons for the still hour past midnight. Admitted to the sealed chamber alone, the wizened sister bent her stiff knee in obeisance, silk mantle pooled on the patterned carpet.

The Matriarch voiced her impatient demand to the yawning ancient, still myopic with sleep. "Time is nigh to select a worthy candidate to be groomed for the initiate passage to secure my succession."

Shocked alert, the elderly enchantress awaited instructions.

"I want an immediate summons dispersed to all peeresses by crystal transmission." Lirenda narrowed the cogent particulars for brevity. "Each will review her pool of young resident talent. The elite with the highest potential must report to Morvain or Hanshire by midsummer, where I will hold personal interviews to assess them at my convenience."

"Your will, Matriarch," the ancient sister rasped. Offered no wine to blunt the malaise of her broken rest, she accepted her abrupt dismissal.

Biting chill from the hallway lingered after the doorlatch clicked shut. Lirenda tucked her raw fingers beneath her wool wrap and rose from the Prime Seat. Candleflames streamed to her pacing, while her hooded eyes glittered with calculation. Let Sethvir discern her intent to induct a gifted prospect for training. His meddler's interest would not know, nor should, the deeper purpose shrouded behind the rigorous process of elimination.

Lirenda's restive rage stirred echoes like whispers from humanity's forgotten, scorched dead, lives by countless billions imploded to ash with the ruined suns of a starfaring empire. "Calum Quaide Kincaid, I know who you are."

The gloves would come off! She would deal the destroyer of worlds and his colleagues their overdue, vicious comeuppance. Throughout every wretched hour exhausted in painstaking machination amid Athera's toilsome arena, Prime directives had marched sister initiates like ants, mocked in contempt by the vantage of eagles. The Seven's affairs spanned immeasurably more than the cockfighting spats on this planet. Their invested interests through the Worldsend Gates redefined the expanded reach of Lirenda's plot to destroy them. Mankind's factions and pawns became her small-scale feints, her manipulative ploys with Nails rescripted to support a more deadly, ambitious design. The wider game-board now encompassed the biggest of the restive perils forced into exile on the Fellowship's splinter worlds.

"Fair play, in war," Lirenda murmured as the wicked glimmer of her hatched inspiration took inaugural shape.

Tonight's summons staged her first test of the steel required of her loyal peeresses. The players she needed to build her cabal must be forged and tempered under the gall of faultless, subordinate obedience. Any who baulked in resentment, or dragged their superior, recalcitrant feet could be discarded without explanation. Last, her plans secret, Lirenda would pluck from the best and the brightest one young initiate endowed with precocious intelligence. That green talent would become the shaped decoy lured in by the ambitious enticement of the titled rank of First Senior.

Timing could not be rushed. Lirenda curbed her impetuous antici-pation. She sat down. Prodded by pent-up momentum too long denied other outlet, she snapped the wax seal off the last box of papers and took up her pen. She had months on her hands to perfect her assault. Highscarp's tedium caged her like a denned bear until winter's white chokehold released in the spring.

Sea travel eased the deadlocked ports earliest. While thaw bogged the low country with melt puddles and rivulets chopped to mud beneath the iron-rimmed wheels of impetuous commerce, the wet, heavy snows relented to cold showers that no longer impaired the oared galleys. News from hardy seamen arrived first at the docks, bandied accounts of sailors gone mad, strayed too near Alestron's closed harbour where the horned centaur masons were said to be rebuilding Alestron's wrecked landing.

"They claim the stone block's cut and shaped by uncanny forces, too massive to raise by the timber lifts fashioned by Mankind," gushed the rawboned kitchen girl who banged down the Prime's laden break-fast tray.

Too early yet for the spring milk, nothing spilled. Lirenda ascertained the pastries and gruel were hot before waving the chatterbox off in dismissal. A Prime had access to better information than foolish tales washed up with the galleymen's rowers on shore leave, and no Matriarch in her natural mind would dare the risk of proximity to the Paravian presence.

The overland route across the Skyshiels through Eastwall after thaws better suited Lirenda's exigent security.

Two hopeful candidates from Whitehold and Jaelot, meanwhile, brought letters from their peeresses requesting shared travel arrangements for the scheduled testing at Morvain. Lirenda served them both her rejection forthwith, their names as swiftly forgotten.

"A string puppet won't do." The Prime's applicants needed the verve to push boundaries. Amid the chaotic upheaval of packing, Lirenda found her matured understanding in sympathy with the former matriarch's tolerance of Elaira's impertinence.

Had such renegade sentiment not provided the opportune chance to forge the order's best instrument against Arithon, Elaira's path might have ascended the ranks. She could have made an exemplary choice for the perilous challenge of ninth-level initiation.

Weapon she remained even still, mused Lirenda, no matter the pawn believed herself exempt from an oathbreaker's penalty, sheltered by Fellowship auspice under Verrain's coattails at Methisle. The day would come when Lirenda would wield every lever at hand to achieve her vengeful requital in full.

The Prime Matriarch's train snaked through the Skyshiel passes, flanked on both sides by the towering drifts carved by the advance riders. The narrow road zigzagged in descent upon glare ice, the gates at Darkling cleared without incident, despite baulky pack mules buffeted to a near standstill by the winds that keened through the notches at equinox.

Downcountry, her progress suffered delay at the Severnir, where no bridge yet spanned the old, crumbled pilings, and the tumbling roar of spring spate battered and shook the crude, flatbed ferry erected as a stopgap to compensate. Travellers reached the far bank with wet feet and damp baggage, harried by the whipcracks of the drovers sorting their milling bunches of wild-eyed livestock.

Everywhere, the industrious, massed movement to launch Lysaer's upcoming campaign afflicted the traffic across Rathain.

"The need to outbid his Lordship's quartermaster is leaching our coffers," complained the sister minding the purse strings.

Time had not blunted the timbre of fear touched off since the fall of Etarra, though nothing but theory suggested where the Master of Shadow had gone to ground after leaving Ithamon.

Lirenda crossed Daon Ramon. Smoke hazed the horizon from the fires set off by the seasonal squall lines. Potent lightning strikes had intensified since the Severnir's release, the virulent weather fronts suppressed by centuries of drought restored to their natural patterns. Smouldering brush routed more than the invasive, scrub briar. The scorching, swift outbreaks of wind-driven wildfires also suppressed the True Sect advance. Rather than roast on an ill-advised march, the officers garrisoned at Narms turned the additional year of delay to hard use, perfecting the coordination of their armed drills.

The battle for the Old Way would strike off with men trained to a lethal edge.

The retrenchment taken under advisement, Lirenda's train pitched her pavilion downwind of the ammoniac reek of the dye pits, then packed up and turned south by the coast road to Morvain. Air felted in soot from the armourers' forges belched scud under the fresher wind off Instrell Bay, pungent with sawdust carved up by the timber cut green at the Aiyenne sawmills. Oxen for haulage were traded like gold, and fodder costs soared in price-gouging proportion, while the Prime hosted the Light's priests at their ease under the amber tint of her staked lanterns. She probed the morass of True Sect disaffection with Lysaer's wayward independence, soothed distrustful feathers to re-anchor alliance, and refired the subtle ties of affinity that furthered the stealthy pursuit of her business.

No diviner detected her mercuric influence, nor suspected the subversive trajectory planted for Nails when at length the Koriani Matriarch moved on.

*　*　*

The initiate candidates presented at the Morvain sisterhouse left her savagely disappointed. "Timid as rabbits, when what I need is a blood-thirsty weasel," Lirenda confided to the disgruntled peeress forced to lick the wounds of disappointment.

Lirenda looked forward without regret. Desperate stakes required fearless innovation, not a tittering flock intimidated to sweating nerves before the gloved fist of highest authority. Perhaps the old prime in her morbid despair had come to regret the stifling mould, hobbled for too long by the order's tradition of absolute, unquestioned obedience.

Away the next morning from the ancient compound with its carved arches and cavernous, groined cloisters, the Matriarch boarded a hired galley and crossed the salt water to Tysan, rowed under the mercury sheen of flat calm.

She slept poorly, landed at Dyshent, oppressed by the toilsome pace of her baggage train in the dust bloom of summer heat. Past Erdane, the desolate road across Camris offered scant amenities and paltry incentive to linger. Pared down to her trunks and her handpicked coterie of ranked seniors, Lirenda endured the high pass over the Tornir Peaks by post coach, jolted through the last, rainy leg of her journey, and arrived discomposed by the clinging reek of wet horse.

Tysan's sumptuous welcome made the protracted hardships of travel worthwhile. The entrenched sisterhouse at Hanshire was a commodious amalgamation of residential suites and airy libraries crammed with rare volumes pillaged during the uprising, for centuries the most unassailable seat of the order's influence. Here, Koriathain flourished with the unstinted support of generations of mayors inimical to crown rule and old charter law. The stone hall, with its honeycomb of closeted chambers, had been laced through the years with elaborate wards of protection, long established as a haven for the order's most clandestine work, and proof against prying eyes for Lirenda's interview of the presentable candidates.

Only three individuals received the accolade of her private attention. Behind closed doors, sealed under the triple sigil of secrecy, she asked each of them the same question.

"How would you solve the imbalance of power to put down the Fellowship Sorcerers?" From her raised chair in the windowless gloom, flanked by pillars topped with bronze candelabra, the raven-haired Prime in her deep purple mantle posed herself with the iconic majesty to intimidate. "Can you offer a bold avenue of initiative to elevate our sisterhood's prospects, and if so, how would you dare the attempt?"

The last called forward, named Ceynnia, proved to be a pert, brown-haired creature, pigeon-plump curves squeezed into the narrow wooden chair isolated before the Prime's dais. Lids like pale shell stubbed with coarse lashes veiled eyes dark as Morriel's, held downcast before her superior. Humility moulded the soft, pillowed hands nestled in the grey-silk lap of her skirt.

Lirenda's eighth-rank perception peeled back the tender innocence implied by a pert nose and apple-round cheeks. Young yet to aspire to the red ribbons of advanced training, the girl presented a demure facade beyond most initiates of the third rank. Nimble curiosity simmered underneath, scarcely contained as the clever aptitude pressed under query ignited to passionate flame.

Ceynnia harnessed her bold intellect, raw enthusiasm tempered into an avid recitation of historic fact. "Second-Age history says the Sorcerers' power was bestowed by Athera's great dragons, who bound them in summons by their Protectorate in liaison with the Paravian Crown Conclave assembled in Cianor Sunlord's regency."

"Yes?" The Prime packed her prompt with ferocious scorn. If the character under examination lacked guts, if she caved, too timid to exercise her nimble genius, her latent potential was useless. "Do go on."

Ceynnia caught a shocked breath. Her lifted glare sharpened. "Not every dragon embraced the Protectorate, or acknowledged the treaty made in Concord with the Paravians. Restless factions persist, some risen to recent rebellion. I daresay the fury that sparked the last drake war stemmed from the discord of wyrms who regard the Sorcerers' enforcement with enmity. Their opposition might provide fertile ground for dissent." Shown no encouragement, the girl owned the brass to deliver her theoretical conclusion. "If we make contact with the disaffected, they might join forces with us to upset the Treaty Accord and lift their oppression. If shrewd negotiation persuaded such dragons, perhaps they would endow our Koriathain by the same blood ritual that elevated the Seven to their superior strength."

At last, a spirit with spark, unafraid to broach established boundaries! Yet Lirenda's surge of approval did not blunt the predatory glint in her tiger's eyes. Early promise must not soften her to untoward temptation. If this untried talent did not measure up, better that the prime candidacy should stay vacant. The architecture of her clandestine plan would keep through the next generation, however the wait rasped her patience.

Lirenda displayed the blank face of autocracy, remote as carved marble in the cowled robes of her high office. "Fetch me the chest from the shelf that contains the Skyron aquamarine."

Ceynnia paled, spirited enough to fear the consequence of her outspoken premise. The Prime waited, impassive through the tortured seconds. A girl who faltered under merciless scrutiny was worthless, without spine on the prongs of uncertainty. Yet this shaken creature stood up. Her step firm in the yoke of subordinate standing, she demonstrated the grit to respond without crumpling.

Lirenda watched, devoid of sympathy. She had suffered such rigorous trials herself in the crucible of Morriel's oversight. Alert for the first sign of weakness, she pressured the mettle of untried nerves well past an unfit candidate's breaking point.

This girl walked, unswerving, to the closed case. She unfastened the glass-paned doors and did not fumble the awkward weight as she lifted the bronze-bound coffer inside. Her deliberate tread returned with a burden that sapped courage and eroded the rooted assurance of birthborn identity.

Lirenda's brisk gesture directed the initiate to the black-lacquered side table.

Ceynnia deposited the chest as directed. She accepted the key from her Matriarch's gloved hand, betrayed only by the film of moist fingerprints as she unlocked and raised the varnished lid. No murmured plea for reprieve passed her lips. Life or death in the hands of her Prime, she freed the dark silk swathed over the contents. Dread chill pervaded the room. The aquamarine focus seemed to drink in the wan light cast by the fluttering candleflames.

"Sit," Lirenda commanded.

Ceynnia sank into her chair, the wood frame creaking under her weight. If her knees buckled, the tremor of dread that wrung her person stayed constrained. Head bent, hands clasped, her form stayed immaculate, an ironclad control well above white-ranked status capped over a volcanic fury that scalded her scarlet.

Lirenda waited, avid, while the girl dissected under a skull-cracking examination flexed her trained strength to maintain deportment.

The magnificent show of fine discipline flicked the Prime to covert excitement. She had found her choice vessel! Lirenda broke the tensioned silence at last, sated by the sweet thrill of anticipation.

"Swear in on the Skyron crystal as my chosen First Senior. As of this moment, you assume the pre-eminent title as my successor. Finish the task laid out before you, and you will undergo schooling for the advanced trials of initiation to ascend to the privilege of red rank, followed by select preparation to assay an accession to the Prime's mantle."

Ceynnia expelled a pent gasp. Startled giddy, without staged modesty or coy posturing, she shook off stunned disbelief and recouped the assured composure to meet the drastic shock of her changed fortune. "I'm expected to forge an alliance with the dragons opposed to the Protectorate's Concord?"

"We think alike." Lirenda reclined, ringed hands relaxed on the carved swans that adorned the arms of the high seat. No longer impassive, she praised the disciplined, guileful woman before her. "Your proposal to leverage the fracture between dragons to drive the wedge that destroys the Fellowship Sorcerers becomes your overture to pursue. But carefully. We'll withhold the announcement of your elevation until you have completed your mission."

Pert colour heated Ceynnia's cheeks as the Matriarch's wily acumen dawned. "For an ambush laid for covert surprise, I understand. As a charitable sister in grey rank, I can travel to Anglefen beneath anyone's notice."

Clever girl. Flared to savage impatience, Lirenda gathered the Skyron crystal from the nested silk in the coffer. "Swear to seal your commitment to greatness. But yes. You'll go as a wandering independent, shrouded under impenetrable protection. As the Koriathain's ambassador, you'll bear a crystal imbued with my tailored invitation to the drakes discontented with their exile on Sckaithen Duin."

No need to elaborate on the danger that chancy directive entailed, or doubt the tactical decision to place this exceedingly delicate charge upon innocent shoulders. Ceynnia's rapt posture radiated flattered excitement to be selected for the momentous assignment.

"Summer will speed your passage by ship around the north cape." Lirenda finished her crisp instructions, head bent to veil her deceit and awaken the Skyron focus. "Your venture at Northgate must be timed for the critical moment the Fellowship Sorcerers are paralysed by distraction."

Ceynnia's coral lips parted, sharp teeth gleaming white as a ferret's. "Your will, Matriarch. With pleasure."

Not ungraceful for her generous flesh, the girl gathered her unassuming grey skirt. She laid eager palms on the crystal's cold facets, and spoke the solemn words to seal her commitment.

First Senior to an ascendant Prime, no insight suggested her keen intellect grasped the double-edged import of her elevation. Accession to rank in fact made her expendable, the honour a noose dangled over thin ice and high jeopardy for a prize with world-spanning stakes. The girl would meet failure and certain destruction, or else rise to enable a meteoric success without parallel in the order's history.

By Moonlight

Dappled beams at full moon stream through the night oaks of Strakewood when three fast friends filch a flask of cherry brandy from the marriage feast for Tarens and Kyrwen, and laughing in wild celebration, they sneak off to commemorate Esfand's coming of age and full investiture as Rathain's *caithdein* . . .

Farther south, shafted in argent rays speared through the canopy of Atwood, a clan scout asleep near the deep glades dreams without lasting recall upon awakening: *the magnificence of a centaur guardian towers over a slight, black-haired man who kneels in rough dress, a leave-taking in fair words exchanged before the next leg of his journey begins* . . .

Moonset darkens the face of the Westland Sea before dawn, when armoured dedicates under a temple diviner revisit Avenor to storm the harbourmaster's derelict tower, where wards tattered to cobweb by summer lightning yield to forced entry; yet the redoubt of the fabled prophet lies empty, his nefarious person departed . . .

VIII. Trespass

The paired servants on duty below her lofty spire allowed the solitary male visitor to pass, against form: the Reiyaj Seeress did not serve Mankind as an oracle. She who had issued summons to Fellowship Sorcerers did not counsel mortal petitioners. Certainly none who presented themselves at her threshold without invitation. How this brash applicant convinced her attendants his question was urgent, or why they elected to waive the brazen ignorance of his entreaty, did not matter.

His introductory plea had been courteous and his words, addressed to an impeccable ethic. Had the sentries consulted the blind ancient in her high seat, she would have permitted the upstart liberty: she had Seen this claimant's intent to seek guidance years before he arrived.

He mounted the tower's exposed, outdoor stairs with a quiet step that bespoke caution before hesitation. With him came the bracing scent of the sea, a balm wielded to heal the rifts seared by a fevered bout of back-lash derangement. Although blind since her birth, the ancient's etheric vision discerned the residual sheen instilled by the cause. Like crown royals of old, he had recently invoked the risk of close contact to importune an Ilitharis guardian.

The Reiyaj crone's Sight encompassed all that could not be hidden: individual Being appeared to her mantled in the raiment of true Name. Nuanced insight revealed the clean lines of consent: empowered humility had stripped his core self to her view voluntarily.

Shielded or not, this spirit would cause impact however lightly his feet trod the skin of the world: the blaze of a master initiate's aura shone like a star through his presence, inflected with the stamped-foil gleam of the six-pointed imprint of Asandir's crown sanction. Patterned like music, arcane faculties parsed the flame of his inherent compassion, an innate attribute sealed into lineal descent by Ciladis's gift of shared resonance. The profound change in that ancestral dynamic all but seared perception, where the ruled strength of mature character outshone the infusion embossed like a watermark across generations.

Long before Davien, the Reiyaj Seeress had foretold the double-edged weapon sheathed in the living matrix standing before her. Though latent as yet: the struck calm that preceded the gathering storm encompassed her wizened form without staring. Genuine poise did not shrink in revolt from her shrivelled flesh, though the sheer, azure silk that draped her lent sparse grace to a crabbed form weathered by immense age to skeletal bone and mummified leather. Fingers splayed like bleached twigs gripped the ivory chair that enthroned her, immobile as though bonded by the ages to the inscrutable dance of her solar communion.

Keen hearing marked the neat movement by which he claimed deferent space. Seated on the swept stone before her slippered feet, the petitioner sustained the spanned silence, as the geared clockwork rotating her gimballed chair clunked through the ponderous seconds and kept the marble orbs in her sunken sockets faced sunwards. His reverence acknowledged the glory that crowned her: white as the coiffed head beneath her jewelled diadem, cirrus clouds fanned the indigo zenith above like the combed hair of a goddess.

He never spoke. Realized, surely, language was superfluous. The query he sought, of an alternate choice, vibrated on the continuum like the cry wrung from a plucked string. Since he understood not to broach his request, the Reiyaj ancient rewarded his wisdom with answer.

"The change you want offers no other way." Reedy as a thrummed filament, her spare counsel continued. "Success demands what the heart knows already. You must stay the hard course. Perception confirms the forked path of your dread. No second alternative exists to be found. Act with the needful courage to break things, and forge your fate without surety. Or else abandon the effort untried."

The geared wheel chunked. He pleaded for nothing. Stark still as he remained through the wounding impact of his disappointment, her tuned ear detected the scream stifled under control as he tempered his breathing.

Then, true adept, he embraced his decision. The sigh of his clothes as he rose riffled under the gust whipped across the spire's exposed platform. The supplicant who had garnered no succour, who owned a Masterbard's gilded tongue and the full measure of Dari s'Ahelas' rogue farsight, did not demean her vision with pretty thanks. Nor did he depart without veneration, although the sweet gesture he advanced to bestow might be an effrontery.

She felt the near sweep of his shadow, with scrupulous care taken not to cross the direct sunlight streaming into her milk-quartz eyes. Balance steadied, he bent over the carved, ivory arm of her chair. His kiss brushed the back of her shrivelled wrist, a caress there and gone, insubstantial as the fall of a moonbeam but for the splashed tear he had not intended.

Unlike the practical touch of the attendants who bathed and cared for her withered flesh, this grace bestowed, like a ghost, the lover's endearment he assumed she had never known through her decades of mystical service. Her amused smile and wheezed laugh forgave the mistake, never noticed.

The draught let in by his vacancy tickled her side, footstep quiet in leaving as he had come.

He had earned the diviner's forethought that looked after him. Tactfully summoned, one of her dedicate servants waited at the stair-head as bidden: a firm hand safe-guarded her rare visitor's fraught descent from the dizzy vantage of her presence.

Mindful of his limits, the grief-stricken petitioner did not dismiss the favour that escorted his shaken balance down the narrow stair, until her farewell blessing saw him onto firm ground.

Had Arithon s'Ffalenn taken the interval to recoup his composure as he crossed the spire's shadow into the glare of morning sunlight, he might not have tripped over the lumpish hulk lodged in his path. Recoiled shy of barking his knee, he stared stupefied as the kicked rags underfoot yelped with indignant injury.

When the shambles unfurled, a grey beard and a thatch of mussed hair streaked with cinnamon marked the detritus as human.

Dakar the Mad Prophet cleared the gruff cough jammed in his throat. "You know," he declared, "how damned narrowly close you missed being scorched to a cinder?"

"Hell hath no fury," Rathain's rogue prince quipped, his startled nerves not agreeable. "Except for the bit where I wooed the wisewoman with grace, and unlike you, she didn't scorn me." A breath restored his equilibrium, with sting. "What brings you here? Star-crossed courtship or, cry mercy, the role of the misguided chaperone? How brilliantly apt. You reek like a bilge rat just rousted from a fortnight's binge in a midden."

Dakar opened and shut moistened lips like a fish. Lamentably gullible, inept at rejoinder, he flailed to stem the barrage. "Good day to your vicious defensiveness, too."

Impenetrable emerald, the ironic stare widened, unhelpful as the Mad Prophet floundered onwards, "Abdication won't bestow the bootless licence you hoped. Sethvir hasn't chosen to grant the stamp of his acknowledgement. Lacking the Seven's lawful release, don't imagine you can do as you please and go hell-bent for slaughter against Lysaer's religion."

Arithon relished, unscathed, a ferocious astonishment, while the north gusts strafed the taut chill stretched between them. "Demolishing a frocked batch of dullard priests wasn't the murderous fun topping my list."

Spine bristled, Dakar dug in his heels. "Well, whatever scapegrace collision you're planning, you won't hunt alone!"

"Really?" Slick as butter, Arithon ducked past. "I don't recall asking for company. The strenuous challenge might fell you, forbye. Unless, unlovely as warts, you've raised the pluck to appreciate sailing?" Amid the hitched pause, he laughed, crowing, "I'd thought not!"

"You can't impose terms on the True Sect at sea," Dakar grumbled, his wheezy effort at forward momentum scarcely sufficient to stay abreast.

"No," Arithon agreed, deceptively fast. "I've a nasty task slated first. You won't approve. And you haven't addressed my devilsome question. What makes you think I'm inclined to let anyone else tag along?"

Met volte-face, slammed still in his tracks, Dakar found himself skewered by the critical focus of green eyes that missed nothing. Squirmed to red embarrassment, he felt the prickle of every caught twig in his snarled hair, and the unravelled stockings poked through muddy boots scuffed to holes. Forget mention of clothing fit to shame a corpse, gaped seams patched, and salt-stained from stowaway passage and forceful evictions into noisome, wharfside gutters.

"I do need a wash," he allowed, without the bother to excuse his negligent hygiene. "Once I'm clean, we'll resume conversation."

The site by the trout pool was not far, where earlier Arithon had sequestered his bedroll and tidied his person. Immersed in the steam of his own trepidation, the Mad Prophet trod the line he was given, and quite failed to suspect a resistance that crumbled too easily.

That mistake overtook him as he rose, spluttering, from the brisk shove that plunged his rotund frame underwater. Through streaming eyes, blinking in riled disbelief, Dakar absorbed the walloping ignominy: that the opposite bank was deserted. The yellowed carpet of leaves nestled under the willows, empty also, his raggedy bundle of clothes whisked off elsewhere, and likely scattered to the four directions. A scrying to locate his trousers would cost him an irreparable delay, while Arithon and his strapped blanket roll vanished without trace, slipping farther away by the instant.

Stark naked and furious, Dakar smacked a fist into water, dousing spray up his nostrils. Folded, sneezing, he sloshed through the shallows, in ripe language reviling stubbed toes with the fervour to resurrect a speared corpus from Dharkaron's Vengeance.

Kharadmon chose that moment to reveal his eavesdropping presence. "Next time maybe you'll learn when to watch your back."

The fat spellbinder startled backwards and tripped with a gargantuan splash on his rump. Roaring as his pale hide puckered to gooseflesh, he accused, "You were here all along! Wretched shade. Couldn't you have bestirred your vacuous self to side with my pathetic interests for once? A fillip of warning would've hobbled Arithon's bid to give me the slip."

The discorporate Sorcerer's snort whisked up a gyre of fallen leaves.

"Stop laughing, at least!" Dakar righted his bulk and stumped back up the bank, nursing an ear filled with liquid and a skinned elbow. "You could help find my sorry clothes, knit a patch or two over the rents, or offer some other solid encouragement." Runnels puddling from his streaming hair, the spellbinder located his frayed, whipcord breeches and doggedly set about towelling himself off. "I didn't spend months chasing yon royal wretch only to let him skip through my fingers."

"Might as well finish washing before you go on," Kharadmon recommended with snide practicality. "You smell raunchier than a wet hound, and your quarry has thoroughly covered his tracks."

Head poked through his collar, Dakar glared at the nexus of air that harboured the Sorcerer's essence. "That's not possible. Not that fast, and not past the worldly reach of Sethvir's earth-sense."

The shade's dearth of comment implied a smirk.

Dakar cursed, hopping, one chubby calf jammed halfway into his crumpled garment. "Stop playing coy. I'll shoulder the laundry after you tell me where Arithon's bound. He's up to no good. Else you wouldn't bother to run the embarrassment of interference."

"Excuse me?" A windy cough pocked Kharadmon's irritation. "You truly don't want to follow where Arithon's going. Be well advised not to embroil yourself. The endeavour's hell-bound to unleash crazy mayhem fit to rattle the gateway to Sithaer."

"I knew it!" Dakar shivered, his puckered buttocks half-clad. "The cocky pest's up to far worse than no good."

Wind-driven, the scurry of dry leaves scratched the pause. The fat spellbinder sheathed his opposite leg. Waistband hiked over his ample belly, he swore breathless murder for the critical button gone missing and cursed his lackadaisical dearth of a belt. Rush off anywhere, and his forsaken britches would slide down to his ankles and trip him.

He gritted his teeth and filched his cuff tie to rig a slapdash closure for his gaping fly. "You underestimate my distrust of Arithon's motives. I'm cranky, besides." Since activating a lane focus gave him the squits, he had ducked the despised repercussion of transit and taken the long route to get here. "Months of travel without civilized food or a lissome tart warming the bed fairly raddles a man's constitution."

"I wouldn't remember," Kharadmon scoffed, sarcastic before he relented. "I know where Arithon's pleasure sloop's berthed. If I give her location, even teach you to disarm her master's set wards of protection, would you recover your patience? Bide aboard *Talliarthe*, and I promise the odds favour your chance to catch her master up without breaking a sweat."

Dakar stared. Then he crouched and slapped his thighs in delighted epiphany. "The bastard's outfoxed you. Ath wept! You haven't a clue which direction your wicked loose end plans to jump."

"Sethvir's narrowed the field to a stickling hunch," Kharadmon snapped, beyond nettled. "I'll repeat myself with some stringent advice. Don't be anywhere near to the infamous scene if the Warden's unsavoury theory plays out."

Dakar's heaved sigh brightened to speculation. "What I wouldn't wager to see yon royal cockerel get his arse kicked in comeuppance." His jaundiced regard shifted back to the trout pool, lit by an inveigling gleam. "You've asked me to wait. The sloop's moored off the southcoast in a concealed cove, along with Arithon's lyranthe and sword? Then by all means, I'll clean up and shave. If time permits a night's romp at Ithish, I'll accept your breezy counsel with pleasure."

"Take a fortnight." Kharadmon chuckled, a frontal blast of disparagement that flung the spellbinder, windmilling backwards. "Just keep enough coin in your pocket to lay in provisions. I suggest stores sufficient to outlast the long haul from a midsized apocalypse."

Dakar's plunge off the streambank into cold water stole the wits to regroup, far less cogitate on the shrewd change just observed in his glancing encounter with Arithon. Smacked by the colossal chill of immersion, the Mad Prophet surfaced and spluttered through Kharadmon's vexing, last comment.

"Just have the foresight to air out your rank trews. Unless you want to attract carnal pleasure that's raddled with the Avenger's black dose of the clap?"

If fierce demand before the season's turn caused a scarcity of hired hacks bound northwest on the trade-road from Ithish, a slight man skilled astride found ready employment as a mounted courier. Newcomers earned their pay by their merits, first allotted the ugliest mounts and the hardest routes across distance. Shown a quiet fellow with the sensitive touch to manage the worst-tempered horse on the string, the short-handed post captain assigned his fresh applicant the lonely ride across Vastmark that grey dawn under driving rain.

"You'll have a fresh remount at each wayside shack." The head hostler shifted the chewed straw stalk pinched between his seamed lips. "That's seventy-three leagues, lad." His squint lingered as he handed off the rider's dispatch log, sealed in a weatherproof sleeve. "There's the record by which you'll sign off at each stop. Reach Thirdmark in three days, and if you don't want your hide peeled, don't lame the horse underneath you. Plenty's broken a leg or their necks by night, run afoul of a gulch in the foothills."

Arithon tucked the cerecloth envelope into his shirt breast, then strapped the message case to the saddle. His vault astride measured by critical eyes, he settled his oiled wool cloak, while the brute chestnut under him sidled and pawed, gathered reins met with a tossed head, flattened ears, and bared teeth.

"Kicks like a mule, does Murder, stay canny!" The head hostler grinned and loosed the animal's lead with a snide grin that marked his approval.

"Hits whatever he aims at, no messing around. Sure you're up to his nasty tricks? Aye, then, off you go! Get 'im out of my yard before someone gets hammered."

Away without hindrance, Arithon set about handling four-legged magma without coming to grief.

He reached the first post station in adequate time. Skin wet beneath streaming rain, he handed the frothed horse to a miserable groom, and submitted his courier's case and documentation in the lit shelter of the messenger's shack. There, steaming by a fire, he bolted hot soup, while the relay's man verified the integrity of the seals, then snapped open the pristine page in the log packet.

"Rode Murder in, did you?" A keen glance noted the grip on the spoon displayed no tender evidence of welted blisters. "Eat fast. I'll have Echo saddled up for you, meantime."

"Echo? Don't tell me!" The choked snort beneath the sopped hood evinced humour. "Because he bounces back?"

"She, as it happens." The relay's man warmed to the plucky, new hire. "That mare chucks her riders however she can. But she's fast in the mud. Stay astride, you'll earn a cash bonus for speed."

A scratched notation marked the hour, alongside the name and condition of the retired mount. Arithon exchanged the emptied bowl for his filled case and updated paperwork, then shoved outside to step into the stirrup and plunge on through the stormy night.

Echo's antics failed to unload him. Next post station, under the breaking cloud of a rose-gold dawn, he snatched four hours' sleep and a meal. When he reclaimed his packet and outbound dispatches, his knack for sharp timing sparked rival jealousy that earned him a slab-sided gelding called Pig-iron.

Arithon declined the whip offered up by the groom. "If he needs a prod, I'll pluck a green switch off a tree."

No such encouragement would be needed. The indolent animal quickened its stride by free will under a master initiate's tactful incentive. Yet the notated log when the horse was brought in without welts mentioned no suspect methods condemned under interdict. Slight stature spared the wear on good mounts, and nowise did this fellow suggest the Shadow-bent Sorcerer reviled by the True Sect Canon.

Moreover, the next leg's completion at Thirdmark established the most coveted of credentials: no post captain or hostler in his right mind tossed the gift of rapport with the most ornery animals attached to his string.

"How soon can you contract another assignment?" The slouched relay clerk tipped his bald head towards the pigeonholes crammed with back-logged correspondence. "If you don't loll about on your perks, I've got an elite run bound to Firstmark at speed. Fifty leagues, and only one station en route begs for a man with the sweet gift for horseflesh."

Arithon gave the proposition the pretence of thought. "One night's rest and I'm ready to go."

"Very well. Report back before dawn." The relay man yawned and stretched his cramped legs, held on duty himself after midnight. "A priority badge will be ready along with your documents. Light knows, we're short-staffed." He rummaged into a drawer, snagged a wash-leather purse, and tallied the rider's allotted share from his cash box. "Rathain's brewing for war in the spring, trade and requisition both vying against the temple's order of precedence. It's jump here and hop there like fleas, with every reliable horseman we have getting pinched for the routes north of Pellain."

"Stay off the drink." Earned wages changed hands with a haphazard toss. "The Cockerel's Perch won't overcharge for your lodging."

Arithon shouldered the dispatch case at predawn the next morning. He spurred out the stable-yard gate, well aware he would not be returning southbound as a courier. The temporary position lent him the anonymous convenience of swift transit across Melhalla. His total earnings at Shipsport would purchase a sturdy hill pony for rugged travel upriver. No slack remained where he was bound, before winter ice halted safe access to the high country.

Failure was no option. Arithon had no course *except* to succeed, else betray his own Name forever to infamy.

The journey across the flats of West Halla to Daenfal Lake's southern shore in late autumn raced the gloaming of early dusk, starless under the summit cloud battened like wool over the snow-clad teeth of the Skyshiels. Gusts whistled a forlorn canticle by night, mild prelude to the snarling gales and white powder that pummelled the ranges by solstice. Few folk fared beyond the game trails worn into footpaths by hermits and charcoal men. Fewer still ventured into the seamed wilds, where hardy, crabbed oaks scrabbled roots where they could between the knurled granite bed-rock poked through the bald crowns of the foothills. All trail-wise trappers shunned the steep gulch that ascended to Rockfell Vale. Even in summer the zigzagged, rocky track broke horses and mules. The stepped climb towards the heights defeated the sternest sinew of endurance. Talent-trained clansman on remote patrol came rarely, loath to go where even a Fellowship Sorcerer passed under driven necessity.

To tread in the fell shadow beneath Rockfell Peak, with the towering pinnacle sunk like a fang into the pearl billow of the lidded overcast was no feat for the fainthearted, never mind a challenge pursued under bittermost risk at the end of the season.

Arithon s'Ffalenn spat into the eye of indifferent fate. He quenched his sparse fire, stowed his bedroll, and shouldered his pack, and for one moment only regarded the course he embarked on that frigid morning. Hereforward, there could be no turning back. Glimpsed through a torn gap in the swirling clouds, Rockfell Peak knifed the heavens, a honed dagger of glittering ice and black iron scraping the azure vault of the zenith. Then the fugitive view narrowed and closed, the bleak vista swallowed back into the purled-cotton mist.

Arithon set off upslope. Mindful of the mountain's inimical presence, he trespassed: dared the ribbon-thin seam gouged in tentative switch-backs up the precarious flank of the scarp. The gorge below fell away as he climbed, a cleft sunken beneath a vast ocean of air, where hawks circled and cried on the thermals. Shoulder pressed to the slope, on cracked footing scoured clean but for mustard and pepper blotches of lichen, Arithon balanced with care, reminded of peril by the ping and crack of dislodged gravel that ricocheted down the sheer face of a fourteen-thousand-foot drop.

Stone did not welcome Mankind's presence, here.

Snowfall whipped like scrim off these baleful heights. Thin drifts covered the hidden, blue ice polished slick by glacial seeps, where the cushioned step might skid into a dizzying plunge to the hardscrabble boulders jumbled far below.

Tissue-thin air burned the lungs, and the ruthless glare of high altitude dazzled eyes watered by battering turbulence. Of the luckless fatalities sent to their demise, few were storied in fable and legend. Most vanished, forgotten from memory. Entrenched rumour insisted the ensorcelled peak gainsaid an unauthorized intrusion outright.

Arithon inched upwards against Rockfell's grain through the wary use of his initiate senses. He surmounted the harrowing, vertical ascent, at last come before the incongruous staircase carved into the cliffside by Davien's immaculate artistry.

Late afternoon waned. The shadowed vale had long vanished under the dross of grey cloud beneath. Sunlight glimmered through the wisped cirrus above, slashed by Rockfell's tooth summit, erased now and again under rolling, ice-crystal mist. Gilded as fool's gold, the chiselled risers rose upwards, by turns dimmed by lashed snowfall, and rendered ghostly through mantling fog. Carved into black rock skeined and cobwebbed with cracks, each narrow step sliced the face, flanked like gateways with opposed pairs of gargoyles.

The dizzying cliffs on both sides reared upwards, an impregnable, impassable barrier surmounted by no other way.

Warning prickled Arithon's nape. The statues' ominous presence confronted his wayward incursion, their deathless oversight impenetrable, and their immobile stance upon weathered granite staid with an indifference to outlast the ages. Their fixated stare might seem vacant, inured to the transience of warm-blooded life, and deaf to the tumultuous elements.

But Arithon surveyed the ranged pairs of sentinels, unfooled. Davien's wards were lethal beyond compare, their deceitful appearance a foil for their implacable vigilance. If the Betrayer regretted bestowing the keys to his library, the access to knowledge now offered the intellectual leverage to disarm his interleaved defences. Yet insight into the wards lent no surety. Execution of the feat would be contrary, exactingly difficult, and by default, diabolically likely to be crushed as an act of brazen effrontery. Arithon shivered. The unbinding required to claim his untoward passage risked fatality, as assured as the freezing exposure he courted should nightfall catch him in the open.

The test before him posed the lesser trial. Far worse awaited if he survived. The access to unlock Rockfell Pit would be fraught: a danger to outstrip all endeavour compiled over a lifetime spent mage-wise.

Arithon shed his rucksack. Grounded amid a half world between sky and earth, he centred himself in the moment and *listened* with a Masterbard's tender perception. Patience encompassed the precise sequence of notes to drill through and negate the adamant resonance laced into Davien's guardian protections.

All or nothing, Arithon steadied his breath. Yet his shaped execution
of the tempered harmonic imploded, plucked from his throat without
sound.

The whipcrack flash sheared the face of the mountain from *nowhere*,
ripped across the desolate rockscape like elemental lightning
unchained. No thunderous, booming report slammed back in retort.
Untouched, only dazzled, Arithon confronted the Sorcerer come to
arrest his transgression.

The Seven's taskmaster was formally clad. Stern height and gaunt
frame unmistakable, he stood with squared shoulders mantled in
midnight blue. The unshielded might of his presence outshone the silver
braid glittering in bands on the sleeves of his formal mantle, and the
starred reflections scalded off the talisman bracelets engraved with black
runes that encircled his wrists.

Asandir, arrived with apocalyptic displeasure, barred his path to
Davien's warded staircase.

The contested passage failed to surprise. Arithon had made no attempt
to blindside Sethvir's capital oversight. Nor had he harboured the naïve
delusion his intrusion was inconsequential. The sealed entrance to
Rockfell Pit was forbidden, a baleful charge minded by Fellowship
Sorcerers beyond any mortal's purview to question.

Devious subterfuge served nothing beneath Asandir's steely regard.
Ruthless perception stripped the rebellious spirit transparently naked.

"I don't care why you've come." Cold iron, the Sorcerer's rebuke split
the shriek of the wind without emphasis. "Don't try me with prevarication. Quit this insane venture at once! Turn back under my given
word for your safety, and no harmful accident will befall your descent
after dusk."

"No." Arithon's flat refusal flared the stone eyes of the gargoyles that
flanked Asandir's planted stance sultry scarlet.

A shocked pause spun the elements into alignment. Unseen force
polarized the clear air to the stickling verge of incandescence. Naked
power at the Seven's command need not shout to rivet attention. Asandir's
rebuttal was the sword's edge, poised to fall without quarter. "You have
no idea—"

"But I do," Arithon interrupted, uncowed. "Too well, and too late,
over innocent blood sacrificed without mercy or conscience. I'll adhere
to my earliest promised commitment, first sworn to your Fellowship on

Atheran soil. I vowed to battle the Mistwraith to victory, or perish in the attempt. High time I finished the burdensome obligation, wouldn't you think?"

"You are outflanked, outmatched, and far out of line!" Asandir's quarried features displayed no expression. The swoop of a gust off the heights flurried snow, sharp with the tang of ozone whipcracked off Asandir's streamered cloak. "Beware, Arithon!" True Name wielded with the mailed glove of compassion, the Sorcerer pressured for the vulnerable breach. "Prince, you overstep your royal purview by lengths. Desh-thiere's prison will not be broached at your whim, and our grant of Rathain's crown sanction is revocable."

But that assault, too, shattered against a bulwark reinforced by cynical expectation.

"By all means! I agree." Arithon's fury did not take the knee. Determined, he applauded the Sorcerer's censure with sulphurous rancour. "Let's not baulk at slinging threats. My oath to the kingdom's already forsworn. Seal your legal severance to what I have started."

The impertinence of the hurled gauntlet smashed scatheless against Asandir's bed-rock calm. His tempered judgement was not to be hazed. "Attuned royal, served under my sovereign charge! You've rejected the choice to leave by free will. Go you shall under charter law by main force!"

The thunder-clap struck beyond sound, without movement, a concatenation of poised might unfurled in a millisecond's hair-trigger release. The hammerfall split the continuum, an explosive cry from the elements ranged throughout the sound-and-light realm past the veil. Above silence, the concussion raised nary a puff of changed wind, nor deflected even one gossamer snowflake. The wave of unsheathed power crashed, spent, the last heightened vibration struck still.

The swept rock at the foot of the stairway to Rockfell's sealed threshold stood empty, one nettlesome man and his bundled pack removed as thoroughly as though erased from existence.

Asandir regarded the actualized vacancy, brought to his knees on the stair. Paper white, a crooked elbow buttressed against the nearest impassive stone gargoyle, he lifted his silver-white head, then drew breath, right palm raised as though movement pained him.

"Reach!" he rasped, grey eyes pinched in anguish.

Not a ripple marked his departure in transit.

Time suspended. Distance collapsed. Then his angular frame was caught and propped upright by Sethvir's sinewy grasp at the faraway focus in Methisle Fortress.

Behind, the swept scarp of Rockfell's looming pinnacle blurred as fresh snow sifted down and erased the footprints of the trespasser and the defender lately met in contention. Nightfall shrouded the mountain, while the tireless wind keened to winter's cruel prelude, and Desh-thiere roiled, fast imprisoned behind thrice eightfold rings of the Fellowship's coiled wards of containment.

The gentle tap at the still-room door interrupted Elaira while pouring grain alcohol over a tincture filtered from rare alpine lichens.

"One moment!" Daelion Fatemaster forbid, if a moment's botched handling spilled a tedious formulation. Months of laborious toil had nearly perfected the curative antidote for the intractable necrosis that cankered a brindled meth snail's venomous sting.

The click of the latchkey let two cats shove through the swing of the strapped-iron door. Verrain trailed their predacious rush to hunt vermin, his more genteel entrance redolent of the draughts exhaled off the bog that infiltrated Methisle Fortress's dank corridors.

Evening had stolen the last of the day, gloom pocked by the fluttering gleam of the spellbinder's pricket candle. Light glanced off the clay crocks and implements scattered over the trestle, sunk in pooled shadow since the tin lamps burned low from her absorbed neglect.

"A meeting's in session," Verrain opened, contrite. "The sudden intrusion's a nuisance, I know. Nonetheless, you might wish to be present."

A suggestion framed with such velvet-gloved tact spelled gravid warning of something amiss. Elaira secured the delicate flask, removed the funnel, and stoppered her decoction with a brusque snap. "If Arithon is the cause, I have the right not to be shielded in ignorance?"

Verrain's smile met her tart quip. "I've placed myself at your disposal accordingly." Stepped forward in his grey robe and frieze cloak, still muddy from beaching his skiff, he caught her elbow and steadied the sharp, upward thrust that jostled the workbench.

Aware more than swift movement had wheeled her dizzy, he added, "Your dry wit is sorely needed, besides, if only to run interference."

"I could guess?" Elaira managed an unforced spark of chagrin, and blotted her hands on skirts stained with olive oil and camphor. "You want a baffle to blunt Kharadmon's caustic temperament."

The Master Spellbinder shed his protective caution and laughed. "Your mettle's infallible." He folded the lady's remarkable strength into his comfortable escort and steered her at a brisk clip towards the vast stair-well built for the horned majesty of centaur guardians. "Are you fortified for a scrap between Fellowship Sorcerers? Within moments, the fortress will be host to four of them."

Unable to bear the admirable surge of her spirited anticipation, Verrain eased her groundless hope gently. "I'm sorry. Ciladis has not returned. He's across the world, still immersed in some project of Davien's at Kathtairr."

"Truly?" Elaira's banter resounded with acidic retort. "Why do I have the intuitive suspicion they're both off to sneak a discreet refuge?"

"I'd do the same," Verrain lamented. "Stuck through the winter chasing the ill doings of Methspawn, who wouldn't?" He pushed open the barred panel at the stairwell's next landing, and grinned. "Though I promise tonight's entertainment won't bore you."

"Do you think?" Elaira suppressed her fraught nerves, grown familiar enough to read deep concern when Verrain's parlour manners resorted to inane gallantry.

Talk lapsed, as they walked, the labyrinthine fortress eerie with echoes from the wind-tossed scrape of maple and willow denuded of foliage. Pale marshlight wisped off the vast bog played across the splotched masonry, to the constant crooned warbles and chittering croaks emitted by Mirthlvain's predators. Splashes pocked the dark water beneath the high walls, until Kharadmon's blustered ranting from the ground floor augmented the amphibious chorus. Racketed off the cavernous, hammer-beam ceiling, his diatribe blew hackled unease through the studded doors to the railed balcony overlooking the main hall.

". . . an abomination! How much of a paltry, bare-fisted effort was needed to toss yon pipsqueak nuisance off a sheer drop? You had the mountain's preference aligned in your favour, plus the boundless advan-tage of gravity. Instead, here you are with the pith sucked clean out of you. Say on? *Exactly* why has the insufferable royal brat not rendered himself expendable?"

Verrain's step quickened, alarmed as Elaira drove ahead through the portal. He flanked her in time for Sethvir's quelling protestation.

"Asandir saw fit to negate the threat by removing Arithon bodily from the vicinity."

From the railing's high vantage, the tableau unreeled, Althain's Warden just emerged through the lofty archway at the front entrance. Marked by his flyaway hair, tangled beard, and air of deceptive frailty, he still trailed the shroud of hazed light from swift transfer via the focus circle sited in the crypt three flights beneath. Nor did he enter alone. His slighter shoulder braced an angular figure upright on unsteady legs. Advanced tenderly, the dragging stride of the larger colleague drew the feline interest of several pairs of lambent, green eyes.

"Asandir?" Verrain gasped, beyond shock. "Maker's mercy!"

A stiff pause ensued, while Kharadmon's swirled cogitation assessed the Warden's enervated burden. Shown the detail fleshed out by his earlier statement, the discorporate Sorcerer devolved to a tight vortex of rapacious interest. "Just how far did you Send the cheeky wee rat?"

Folded into the chair kicked out to receive him, Asandir hooked a lank elbow over the carved back, and delivered his classic, laconic response. "I dispatched him back to his sloop on the southcoast."

A flare of dull silver stirred in the gloom. Black clothes obscured by the pervasive shadow, Traithe leaned forward and amended the bare-bones indictment. "Little Brother's word on the matter said more. The raven gathers you transferred the whole boat, with contents intact, to languish in bluewater on the far side of the planet."

"Dakar went with him," Asandir admitted, discomposed.

Kharadmon's hoot overwhelmed the low whistle Verrain breathed into Elaira's ear. Flabbergasted by the appalling power just expended upon that momentous feat, the Master Spellbinder expounded at an awed whisper. "Two living adults, and the sloop, displaced from salt water, all delivered unharmed *at an instant's notice by naught but bare-knuckled force.* This, in the wake of the step that took Asandir to Rockfell's heights with no other support to receive him. There's *two* raw outlays at scale great enough to dismember a nest of krakens!" Sobered at once by the lady's distress, Mirthlvain's Guardian reverted to sympathy, "We'd better go down."

Their descent of the gallery stair launched the raven roosted on the newel post. Its gliding flight flagged Traithe's attentive regard. He stood stiffly, plagued by the ache of his scars, and yielded his place to Elaira. The tucked cat scarpered from the adjacent seat, displaced as his gimped frame resettled on leather upholstery furred green from the miasmic damp. Silver hair tied at his nape with jet ribbon his only bright aspect, the lame Sorcerer posed a mild question to his fellows.

"Have we fathomed Arithon's motive in full?" Since the black rose had bloomed without the forecast healing of his chronic impairment, the wistful hope ebbed for reprieve from his chronic pain. Although the sheared portion of his essence entrapped with the Mistwraith had no sure path to redemption, he never complained. Only lifted his wrist to receive the raven, which perched, wings folded, and trained an unwinking black stare on impertinent felines too foolish to keep their wise distance.

"I've gathered Asandir put a stop to the assay before Arithon's endeavour breached Rockfell's wards." Traithe pressed on, without pleading. "The release of Desh-thiere could not be risked, beyond question, though perhaps the rash act sought access for a pre-emptive bid to banish the wraiths."

Elaira sat, her graceful acceptance of the lame Sorcerer's kindness as much for his thoughtful analysis of her beloved's indefensible transgression.

"The Teir's'Ffalenn knew the risks!" Kharadmon cracked, annoyed.

Verrain's tacit prompt from the hob where he nursed the tin dipper to replenish the teapot probed the tempestuous quandary. "In fact, was Arithon trying to salvage a redemption for the wraiths sealed in limbo behind the vault's wardings?"

Asandir interrupted Sethvir's ministrations. Still paper white, the creases engraved beneath tired eyes scored to sepia under the candelabra, he refuted ambiguous doubt with clipped brevity. "I'd have been inclined believe that. Except I attended the battle at Ithamon that fought Desh-thiere to incarceration. Kharadmon was there also. His witness can verify. Arithon knew then, as he surely does now: the entities sealed under confinement at Rockfell are still incarnate, sustained within an obdurate body of mist."

Althain Tower's record detailed the insular fog that sheathed Athera's parasitic invaders. The buffer let them mount a sustained attack, which dynamic made the hostile collective by lengths more dangerous.

"A far cry from Arithon's prior experience. He wrought the requite release one by one for the individual free wraiths stripped to their core essence. Not all of them in frontal assault." Kharadmon's distempered roving whisked past the fireplace, the errant sparks sucked into his wake flared up and extinguished to flurried ash. "Disembodied, cut adrift,

Marak's horde were lost spirits, trapped in the invidious, self-imposed loop of their own emotional turbulence."

Elaira understood the precepts of the Masterbard's method of banishment. Her healer's practice parsed exactly how a revenant intelligence spun terrified fear into an opaque cocoon of delusion. The unfounded idea of intractable separation could be dispelled. She had done so, to facilitate the release to dislodge entrenched cases of disease. Dissolve the misguided belief, and the self's endowment of innate awareness recovered the connected source of true Name.

"Much worse, in this instance, Elaira." Sethvir's earth-linked perception corrected the sorrowful gap in her extant knowledge. "We are dealing with a binding invested by necromancy. A sealed barrier that displaces free will in perpetuity also barricades the threshold to natural death. Desh-thiere's matrix of mist imposes an armoured mantle of dominance, purposed as a weapon for lethal annihilation." Harrowed beyond pity, he clarified the short-fall Arithon could not surmount. "Your Masterbard cannot accomplish the feat that let him disarm the invasion from Marak single-handedly. Lysaer's partnership and the combined forces of elemental light and shadow must shear through the substrate of fog to access the natural consciousness suborned under enslavement."

There, the Warden broke off, inexplicably vexed. "Dratted cat!" The diversion deflected the agonized point left unsaid: that a critical fragment of a brave colleague's essence remained captive along with Desh-thiere's stewed wraiths.

While Sethvir bent to spare his hem before frisky claws snagged the embroidery, and the subdued clink of porcelain bespoke Verrain's on-going fuss with the tea service, Traithe himself smoothed over the lapsed explanation tied to his personal stake.

"Destructive intent or altruism on Arithon's part makes no difference, you see. Either way, the upshot of his meddling would have brought disastrous harm to Athera. Your prince scaled Rockfell beyond any doubt aware he could not subdue the Mistwraith's maleficence on his own."

Kharadmon's disparagement huffed mildewed dust from the hall's laddered cobwebs. "Asandir should have disbarred the flip shyster from rank then and there."

"I gave him the benefit of the doubt." Stronger by the moment, the field Sorcerer flexed the capable hand on his knee into a white-knuckled fist. "Arithon's sanction for crown rule has not been revoked, though I took warning steps in precaution. He'll have six months or more to cool his heels at sea, sort his rage, and come to his senses. Wherever he steers to make landfall, I expect his next move will expose his true colours."

Elaira gathered the firm threads of her insight and weighed in at the finish. "Kharadmon implied Rockfell's preference stood at your back." Courageous, now the pinned focus of Asandir's fierce regard, she qualified, "I'd ask whether Arithon adhered to clean form. Did he obtain due permission to set foot on the mountain beforehand?"

Her question met widening silence. Surprise caught Kharadmon, Traithe, and Verrain off centre. Asandir's deadpan mask never flinched.

But Sethvir winced, his sheepish confession like the lapdog caught nipping for treats. "Ath! You noticed the lapse."

Elaira bit down her retort. With patience not to be humoured by platitudes, quite naked before power great enough to quash mortal impertinence to oblivion, she waited with steadfast expectation.

Sethvir's cryptic remark dangled, undefined. Kharadmon's wayward restlessness froze in suspension. Traithe's direct kindness appeared genuine, while the raven resettled on his shoulder kept beady-eyed watch, a stilled sable aspect in service to a far greater entity across the veil.

Asandir's survey neither wavered or softened. Whether his exhaustion preferred to side-step the puzzle behind the egregious incitement, or if the informed stance of his colleagues grappled a wider span of grim implication, Verrain's astute return with the tea tray shattered the tense moment.

Hard against the avoidance raised by that blank wall, the enchantress laid out her opinion. "Arithon is always precise to a fault. All the more when he commits to an action. His defiance at Rockfell can't be a mistake. An imposed term of banishment may buy time, but he won't come around to tender an apology. Don't think he'll change course if he has a reason to avoid sharing his confidence."

Asandir regarded her still, face bleak against the grey rinse of rain against the glass rondels inset above the overhead gallery. "I expect that he won't. But neither has he been handed the quittance from Crown duty he inveigled to gain by means of extreme provocation."

But was that his intent?

Elaira kept her own counsel on that point. Traithe's humane touch of sympathy, in contrast with the raven's stark stare, cautioned her not to broach the perilous quagmire. All along, the motivation that drove Rathain's prince posed the glaring unknown that eluded the Seven's analysis.

Refutation

Dakar loathed many things throughout his long life, though nothing detestable rivalled his virulent hatred of seafaring. Not only for the skinned elbows and banged shins suffered under incessant assault by wave and weather. The glare of harsh sunlight offshore seared his tenderized nerves to perdition, and worse, the slap and splash of salt spray piled miserable punishment on top of brute injury. All dastardly movement attempted on deck demanded agile exertion.

A stout man lacking muscle languished in vile durance, in particular under the wretched after-shock of a long-distance transfer. Cramped at the lee rail, hawking bile, Dakar wondered whether prolonged bouts of dry heaves risked disgorging his liver. Best to clamp his jaws and swallow right quick to shunt his pummelled innards back where they belonged.

Clinging like a limpet, jounced to quivering jelly, he retched while the sloop yawed in irons, the blundering crash of loose tackle pitched this way and that by a helm unattended. Blocks squeaked, slopped and shimmied. Every item not snugged down in the cabin clanged and rattled, while the reel of bare spars gyrated against the burnished arc of blue sky. Sail in the hands of just one able seaman might have steadied the rollicking keel.

But Arithon sprawled unconscious amidships. Without his knowledge of which bit of furled canvas attached to what snarl of rigging, the mystique of skilled mariners eluded the wastrel dumped into the breach. Odds on, Dakar's inept attempt to work *Talliarthe* would sink her forthwith. The barren horizon offered no haven. Asandir's punitive reach would have plonked down the infernal bath-toy bang over some bluewater trench farthest from civilization. Either the spellbinder swam till he drowned, or he broiled to sunstroke until the jerked meat of his carcass got picked to bones by scavenging seabirds.

Dakar glowered at Arithon's inert frame. "Whatever you've done to earn your demise, the Sorcerer might have pitied the innocent sucked willy-nilly into your affairs." Doubled over his thrice-emptied belly, the Mad Prophet moaned. The ordeal imposed by a harsh relocation outstripped the gripes from a shellfish poisoning any day.

Who knew how far his fate had been flung to the four winds and jeopardy? His navigation with charts was disastrous. A cross stave in his fumbling grip was a hen-scratched stick. Trained to read stars and lane flux through mage-sight, Dakar cursed the plenitude of seawater that bollixed the facile use of his refined faculties.

Maliciously peeved, he shoved upright and staggered, the jab toed into Arithon's ribs too enervated to raise a response. His next prod, better aimed, flopped his slack victim over.

Arithon stirred, muttering. "My head's split like a melon and stuffed up with sand."

"More's the pity, and no thanks for the misery," Dakar flared. "What in Sithaer's nine hells did you do to annoy Asandir?"

"Exactly?" Arithon sat up, knuckled his temples, and squeezed his bedazzled eyes shut. "Nothing." He unpinned his cloak and shrugged the winter weight fur off his shoulders. "I climbed a mountain without permission. When asked to leave, I refused."

"You scaled *Rockfell?*" Dakar blanched.

Arithon smiled, tinged a mite green through pasted strands of black hair.

"Nothing." Dakar repeated, thick as he wrestled the horrified cascade of ramifications. "But you convinced Asandir you meant worse."

"You think?" Rebounded enough to notice the sloop's sacrilegious state of neglect, Arithon unlaced his jerkin, loosened his shirt points, and blotted his runnelled neck before musing, "I agree, the implied list of malfeasance is intriguing. Unshackle the Mistwraith? Break wards? *Raise havoc?* I did none of these. Since most of your discomfort stems from a common hangover, why not indulge in the hair of the dog? A frolicsome binge might ease the rude awakening in unsavoury company."

Dakar's regard narrowed. "Your move on Rockfell Peak was a *feint?*"

"Was it?" Bent over to yank off his stout boots, Arithon gasped, "Tut, tut!" the mockery of self-reproach enlivened by sardonic hilarity.

"Don't posture!" Dakar swayed to the next hideous roll, a scrabbled snatch for the pinrail holding him upright, just barely. "I know your tricks! Too well to believe you bothered yourself for a frivolous purpose."

"Well, whatever my reason, the ploy didn't stick." Arithon skinned off his knit hose and stood. Swift assessment of weather, bare spars, and the freshening breeze underran his seamless conclusion. "I'm still stuck in bed with the Fellowship's charter as crown prince." Far too smug for a man lately jolted silly by a forced displacement, he released the flaked canvas on the propped boom and flipped a halyard off the starboard pinrail.

A muscular hoist raised the tanbark mainsail. Thrown into shade while the sloop's wallowing hull rounded to windward, he shed the hot constraint of his jerkin while the whump of taut tackle steadied the keel. Arithon skirted Dakar's wilted stance. He freed the lashed helm, threw down the rudder, and paused, satisfied as his sloop settled into a staid downwind course.

Busied next with the stern vane at the rudder, he deployed the self-steering. A lace nabbed from his cuff let him bundle his unkempt hair into a queue, while his bearing focus tracked the wistful longing stifled behind Dakar's attention.

"Ah, yes, your stashed hoard." A pre-emptive pounce bested the spell-binder's lunge for the aft locker. "We're not going to run out of solace, I see."

Dakar's surge mistimed the pitch of the deck and befouled his panicked reach for the clutch of green bottles stowed in packed straw. The leeward rail saved his headlong skid on leather soles ill suited to fast movement on oiled teak. Too slow to stop Arithon's pilfering hand, he snapped, sulky, "Kharadmon warned me to provision for an apocalypse."

Arithon froze. The ferocious intensity of his return stare routed flesh and bone, unpleasant as any Fellowship Sorcerer's. "Exactly when did you glean that pearl of advice?"

"Ah." Dakar sank onto his hams, pleased to twist the vindictive advantage. "So you weren't aware of the prying shade's presence during your consultation with the Reiyaj Seeress?"

Perspicacity cringed from the silence that gripped blameless air in the scorch of broad daylight.

Arithon would be sifting through memory, dismayed, hindsight frantic to analyse every errant breeze that may, or may not, have been a trifle too chill for the season.

A moment passed, loud with the splash and hiss as the sloop breasted the cross-chop. Then Arithon yanked the cork from the larger flask; not to jettison the precious contents, but to help himself. He did not wince over the eyewatering burn, though Dakar knew the cheap gin bought off the Ithish loggers went down caustic as unfiltered lye.

Relieved that sobriety was off the agenda, Dakar dared the question. "Where are we, anyhow?"

"Precisely?" Arithon lowered the bottle to marvel over their shared predicament. "Somewhere hot. Tropics or southern hemisphere, back side of the world from nightfall on Paravia, since the sun's angle suggests midmorning." A deeper swig, and he hooked a shroud with one elbow to squint aloft. "A noon sight's sure fix will determine a sensible course. Until then, we might as well enjoy the fair weather. Pretty quick, someone's going below to inventory *Talliarthe*'s stores to size up the critical short-falls."

Dakar coloured, sheepish. "The casks are topped up," he volunteered.

"I've got limes and oranges stowed from Sanshevas." Arithon tucked the broached bottle behind his forearm. "Ah, but of course! Unless you've binged on the stash?"

"Erm." The Mad Prophet squirmed. "Surely you laid down more than those two nets strung in the forepeak?"

"No." A ruthless survey of the fat man's girth, then, "You're not apt to perish, I see." Arithon's grin showed wicked teeth. "We'll manage on fish. How many depends upon which archipelago lies closest, by wind and current. You've adequate padding to pay for your gluttony by snaring petrels and netting the bait fry beneath the keel's shadow."

Dakar's steamed language bristled his beard.

Arithon relented and passed over the flask. If his pity was laughable, his temperament stayed strikingly mild. "If I still have a kettle, we'll strain and stew seaweed. Unless you prefer rickets and scurvy? Though take my fair warning, if you topple overboard, I may not bother to mount a quick rescue."

Dakar squeezed his eyes shut, his pudgy fists locked on the bottle. No use, to regret Kharadmon's slick advice. By Dharkaron's short hairs, he hated seafaring. That, and much worse, his cached gin would be gone before sight of land notched the horizon. Without requite from penury, he guzzled neat spirits, and cursed the thrice-damned royal bastard before him. A slim build scarcely sweated in smothering heat, nor bruised from the knocks a more generous frame garnered belowdecks in rough weather. The Mad Prophet nursed his flask, determined to pass out where his bulk would be most inconvenient.

Arithon side-stepped Dakar's petulant rancour.

Barefoot and content in the breeze that ruffled his coal hair, he tidied the sloop's tackle and stowed his discarded clothes in a chest to foil mildew. Nothing about his demeanour seemed stressed by the prospect of a six-month stint under sail.

Dakar stewed over that impervious calm. Whiskey abandoned, he shivered. One forgot at one's peril: Biedar blood on Arithon's distaff side enabled the wily connivance passed down with Dari s'Ahelas's rogue farsight. Asandir's stiff reprisal in all likelihood may have partnered the dance to who knew *what* hectic measure of sabotage.

Esfand's axe whistled down and bit into the log with a savagery better suited for murder than restocking fire-wood. The hewn chip flew through the drab afternoon, the powdered explosion of impact absorbed by a snowdrift.

"Damn the man's secretive doings to Sithaer!" Puffed epithet steamed by the frosty air, he maligned any of several parties driving his exasperation.

Too long on the run, Deshir's clan enclave confronted yet another hostile incursion. War loomed, the might of Lysaer's allied war host positioned to march on Rathain at spring thaw. Strakewood's clan families who had nursed children through bog fever would not bear another summer's retreat in the northern marshes.

Worse, the crown prince's transgressions poked the sharpened stick into the hornet's nest. Dire enough news that formal word came in person: Asandir bided in Laithen's lodge. The chieftain's council assembled, with tonight's acrimonious meet slated to resolve a strategic defence and the terms for a royal arraignment.

"The judgement falls upon you to decide, no one else!" Khadrien's heated loyalty bludgeoned the obvious. Mussed braid doused beneath his furred hood, the proud growth of beard that clashed with his red nose seemed the last colour left in the world.

Stout friendship's encouragement failed to thaw Esfand's cold feet. His next hammered blow chewed into the fuel requisitioned for the clan hall.

"That's difficult." A brute understatement, Esfand fumed, when a grown man bearing Earl Jieret's heritage usurped the ear of the clan elders. His axe bit again. Chips pattered into his stomped patch of snow, muffled as the impatience that dismissed his opinions since his adult investiture. "Tarens spent the past year with our prince. How can I argue that voice of experience? Or deny the conviction our last s'Ffalenn heir has flouted the law and abandoned us."

The momentous delinquency wounded clan spirits deeper than a betrayal, with the scouts' reports of Lysaer's muster unremitting for eighteen months. The enemy stockpile of weapons and supply outfitted the combined campaign to force a claim to the Old Way across Daon Ramon. Take C̄aith-al-Caen, and the hostile advance might wrest passage for mercantile trade over the forbidden pass through the Baiyen.

The log cracked under punishment. "Doesn't help when the grim facts undermine our position." Khadrien swiped pilled ice off his cuffs and planted the next billet upright for splitting. "Though we might slow the invasion with covert forays, our war band gets cut to ribbons."

Sheer numbers must prevail, as brimstone rhetoric from the religion stoked the dedicate zeal for conquest. Town interests might mar Daon Ramon's recovery before the Ilitharis Paravians completed repairs at Alestron and reclaimed their ancient right to rebuild Ithamon.

Esfand's axe blow crashed down. "The lopsided odds aren't my biggest concern." Not while northern cold suppressed logistics, and since Fellowship Sorcerers were law bound to contest a free-wilds trespass at scale. "Who could argue a reasonable case for Arithon after Tarens's eyewitness testimony? Is anyone left unconvinced our rogue prince hasn't broken his oath and integrity?"

Khadrien opened his mouth, gagged into spluttering, tactful restraint by a shower of wet snow whiplashed off the evergreen bough sprung by an unseen arrival. Siantra's habit of stealth became scary, paired with an uncanny insight as wickedly sure as Esfand's hand on the axe. "Your cousin won't need your blowhard opinion."

A grue caused Esfand to set his tool down. "You've Seen something."

"Who hasn't?" Khadrien spat melted snow. Winter long, true dreams had visited everyone with the Sight. Breathless, he loaded the drag sleigh, then tugged on the straps to free the iced runners. "All of the north stirs to arms, and if you don't throw in your weight, we'll be chucking wood till Ithamon's besieged."

Only Siantra noticed the pitched strain beneath Esfand's reticence. "Merciful maker, I'll carry that axe!" she exclaimed, as he yanked the sled's towline from Khadrien's grasp.

Esfand's temper snapped. "Sometimes your talent sees too damned well!" Though he yielded the steel before his recklessness caused someone an injury.

Siantra's sympathetic gaze lingered. "You're up to this, Esfand. Truly."

"Am I?" For his devilsome quandary became redoubled, with Arithon under a six-month decree of punitive exile imposed by the Seven. The prospect that terrified him was his obligation to don the black in royalty's absence. To stand forward as shadow behind Rathain's throne, not in ceremonial oversight, but under Asandir's direct auspice as steward charged with the mantle of crown authority.

Artlessly contrary, Khadrien bulled through the shoals of anxiety. "The bickering's going to drub protocol to broken bones from the shouting match started this morning." Sly forethought centred on his empty belly, he scarpered before the cut wood was unloaded. A shout flung over his shoulder excused the scapegrace defection. "I promise I'll fetch back a bite for you both."

"He won't bother. Cocksure scamp! He knows neither one of us has an appetite." Annoyed by the desertion, Siantra entered the empty lodge tent to help rake the ash from the hearth and rebuild the fire. The chill air still smelled faintly of mice, reminder that last summer's vacancy might for cruel need be repeated.

Esfand shared that foreboding, crouched beside her in quiet, evasive rebuff as he fussed with the kindling.

The great door banged open in time, all the same. Adult oversight brought Laithen with the *caithdein*'s black tabard draped over her forearm. "Up with you. Now. My daughter can manage the fuel on her own." Her bustling fuss, rather than Jalienne's, regaled Cosach's son in formality. Dark as starless night from collar to hem, tradition forbade cloth with ribbon braid or device.

On tiptoe, the careworn woman smoothed the fit over the young man's broad shoulders. Her bundled, seal hair stranded with early grey scarcely topped Esfand's chin. Brown eyes still reflected an unearthly light, distanced near to estrangement since her brush with the mysteries on the Plain of Araithe.

Yet her astute scolding had not changed a whit. "I know you didn't eat. At least scrub the charcoal smudge off your chin. Use the fireside bucket, and hurry if you need a breather to settle your stomach."

Esfand splashed his face and retrieved his antler-bossed belt. The glint of started flame hooded by lowered lashes, he avoided her gaze as he fastened the buckle. "Mother's with Tarens?"

Liathen sighed, prepared for his raw disappointment. "Don't be too hard on her, yes."

Painful bitterness tied Esfand's tongue. Jalienne's contempt for Arithon's delinquency was forgiven more readily than a bereavement that resented her husband's untimely replacement, no matter the blood offspring confirmed as Cosach's successor was her own.

Yet Siantra's eldritch insight saw deeper. "Iyat-thos takes your mother's side because his wife's bearing. The kindhearted spirit lost his birth family. His powerful instinct to protect his own craves stability, almost at any cost, and regard for the widow also aligns with the ancient loss bequeathed to s'Valerient."

That touched a nerve. "Yet he is not Jieret!"

"No." Footfalls approached beyond the closed doors. Siantra diverted Esfand's grievance with a tacit steer towards the dais. "Though I agree, the subjective influence of that past heritage colours Tarens's perception. His townborn outlook yearns to make peace, and the shock incurred by the dead earl's disappointment enforces his impulse to condemn the severance he believes he observed at Ithamon."

Esfand mounted the log stair with pained resignation. "You suggest his opinion's based on flawed conjecture?"

"Nobody has fathomed Arithon's motive!" Swift to support the intuitive ambiguity, Laithen honoured Siantra's retreat by taking her place as head of the council at the young *caithdein's* left hand. "As for Iyat-thos, he has earned due respect. He stood fast with our war band. His honesty holds stature as the prince's upstanding liegeman, yet, Esfand, he cannot overstep your invested office. Right or wrong, you must seize the prerogative and speak for the Crown."

Discussion ended as the hall's double doors opened wide to admit the assembly. The Fellowship's field Sorcerer led, gaunt frame and long strides backed by the brisk wind that flagged his midnight-blue mantle.

Silver braid flickered at hem and collar, a storm-front advance that eclipsed the bunched chieftains behind. Few owned the nerve to crowd Asandir's presence. Latent power sheathed his person, a fiercely kept silence whose depth overwhelmed the coarse scrapes of the incomers jostling for place on the benches. Talk and movement stayed muted as the last arrivals shed their cloaks and settled for business.

Esfand felt exposed in the *caithdein's* high seat, cored naked before a perception that stripped pretence like a scalpel honed by the infinite. Thought raced in dread to imagine how many noteworthy predecessors had been flayed by Asandir's lucent regard.

Rounding the trestle, the tall Sorcerer took pause. "You think you're the wrong choice to be wearing the black?" Large hands roughened by weather spun the heavy, carved chair to Esfand's right with a feather touch. Asandir sat. Cragged features incised by two Ages of care confronted Rathain's *caithdein*, direct beyond quarter.

Esfand lost words under the fathomless weight of those impervious, sheet-silver eyes.

The Sorcerer pursued his broached subject headlong. "Your father Cosach destroyed his prince's confidence in one heated moment atop the Tiendarion. Earl Jieret, also, in his way betrayed the regard of the man who cherished him as a brother."

"Could a true s'Valerient have embraced any higher a calling?" Esfand surmounted the flutter lodged in his gut. "Jieret died to spare his sworn liege."

"Yes, and so saved the royal line for the kingdom." Asandir leaned forward, intent. "Yet that was not Arithon's choice, or his preference. At that moment, he valued the worth of a cherished friend's life above both."

Esfand rose to the challenge, emboldened by the insight he was being served the precious gift of rare counsel. "Inborn s'Ffalenn compassion would have swayed Arithon's judgement to a pernicious degree."

"Do you think so?" Asandir's regard felt like staring into the moon in the etched moment of drowning, a beacon of remote clarity amid a restive, packed room that oddly seemed private between them. "No attuned sovereign granted our Fellowship's sanction is a controlled pawn. None are string-tied by the traits of crown lineage. Arithon is no different in that regard from the forebears who treated for Rathain's weal throughout history. Your prince stands apart from them only in circumstance."

Before Esfand's rapt concentration, Asandir laced his capable hands on the trestle top. Perhaps reluctant, he remarked, "We have all measured Arithon's difficult nature against the same scale." Words plucked as though tendered through thickets of thorn, he qualified with spare sorrow. "At each turn, this duty or that priority claimed precedence and trampled roughshod over his personal directive. You hold the last chance to salvage his trust from the morass where those come before you fell short. Rule wisely and well when your hour arises. Or all of us lose him forever."

Courage resurged before an intimate statement that stunned for the admission of an incomprehensible vulnerability. "Elaira has not broken Arithon's faith in her."

Asandir took pause. Granite strength rent the ambiguous semblance of his complacency. "He has protected her from the crucible, but no longer. Her moment approaches to tread the abyss."

Esfand felt the Sorcerer's entrained focus drill him straight through. Unbidden, the memory surfaced: of the abrasive rebuff dealt by Arithon s'Ffalenn at first sight of a *caithdein* not yet come of age. Liege loyalty would not have crushed young self-esteem with such excruciate cruelty. *But adamant protectiveness might, if the vicious rejection of a boy's obligate oath aimed to thwart the next loss impelled by heroic altruism.*

Response, when Esfand answered, felt like treading over explosive turbulence on an eggshell. "His Grace handled the penalty on his merits when he alone bore the cost. But not when the price in forfeit claimed another. That is where his true nature cried mercy, and also, where Jieret's sacrifice wounded him."

Asandir's smile burst like sunlight through the wear chiselled into his features. "You've clearly read the crux of the matter where Arithon's path will entangle his destiny." Chair angled forward once more, the Sorcerer transferred his attention towards the assembly.

And the gravid interval of suspension snapped, a reverse plunge back into normalcy. The close air again wore the winter taints of damp fur and birch smoke, layered through by the drone of subdued conversation.

Unstudied, the threshold of change lay behind. Somehow the black robe on Esfand's shoulders no longer clothed him as an upstart.

Form demanded his executive opening. Siantra gave him the nod from the bench beside the clan seeress. Tarens had settled with Jalienne at the forefront with the chieftains. Agitation flurried through the back row, a last spasm as Khadrien's tardy arrival elbowed for position amid the standing observers. Chagrined, he met Esfand's glance with a shrug, mouth crammed with the last of his meal.

Esfand's titled prerogative took charge, all opinions weighed by strict procedure until discussion arrived at a compromise. Where contrary viewpoints failed to be reconciled, the *caithdein* resolved discord by arbitration and determined the finalized plan of engagement.

The war band's spokesmen first detailed the tactical strength of Lysaer's reforged coalition. "The enemy has positioned for a concerted assault at frightening scale. Large camps are gathered at Morvain and Narms, with supply and troop rolls drawn from True Sect strongholds in Tysan, and coastal towns across Rathain. More forces by sea, staged from Jaelot, could push westward over the Baiyen by summer."

Margin for reprieve would be narrow, by Asandir's terse assessment. "The banishment we Seven have imposed on your crown prince buys time, but only while salt water and distance slackens the Mistwraith's hold over Lysaer." The renewed provocation when Arithon returned dismantled equivocation. "Bloodshed at Caith-al-Caen would sully the flux and impair the mysteries, a disruption to forestall Riathan fertility, and a defilement of their ancient breeding ground."

The air heated, as pressured argument tussled against clan obligation, with able combatants too sparse to mount a decisive defence.

Scarred elders decried the ruinous stakes. "Our lines will be over-whelmed from the start!"

"Without the surety of Fellowship support, and denied the endowed power of a crowned high king?" Fallowmere's chieftain gripped the hilts of his knives, his objection shrilled through pandemonium. "We'll fall to mass slaughter past question!"

The uproar crashed before Asandir's feet, a hurled gauntlet intercepted by Iyat-thos Tarens.

"Is another armed fight worth the risk of extinction? Given Arithon's defection, allow me to treat with Lysaer!" Arisen to his full height, fist upraised, the fair crofter pleaded with countrybred earnestness. "Send me as your clan representative! I can champion your cause. My birthright understands townbred fear and uncertainty. None better! Aligned with Earl Jieret's historic perspective, who else is equipped to plead in good faith for a sensible reconciliation?" Against strident objection, he pealed,

"True Sect ideology will never bend. The religion's influence throttles dissent to its iron writ with each generation. Fight the guilds' push to ease overland trade, and your people will be shown no mercy. Yet a treaty concession backed by neutrality might buy your bloodlines the grace of survival."

The lodge hall erupted. Explosive noise shook dust from the rafters. Delegates and chieftains clambered erect, shouting to make themselves heard.

A dagger clanged in protest against a bared sword blade. "Why should we stand?"

"What mother, or sister, or wife among us has not lost a son or a brother? How many more must raise weans with no husband?"

From the chieftain's council, with wounded vehemence, "We've scarcely settled our dead since the last battle for Halwythwood! Now we face armed strength fit to flatten us!"

Outrage convulsed the packed seats, the adamant cry to revise charter law rammed against rooted elders exhausted by pain and frayed ragged from centuries of thankless endurance. "Why shed the blood of our young for the wilds, when townfolk enjoy their civilized comforts and sheltered security?"

"We languish in childbirth and weaken for want in the hard years." Jalienne's rebuke shrilled over the clamour. "Why should we hold fast for outdated tradition when our sanctioned prince has abandoned us?"

Esfand stood. Clothed in stark black and bare-fisted courage before the tumultuous wall of cured leather and anger, he gestured for order, crossed forearms raised over his head. Though full authority over a fractious council had seemed beyond his stature the hour before, he felt the Sorcerer's calm at his back. Power sheathed like a banked fire buoyed his self-awareness: Asandir had shown genuine strength could withstand the crisis of doubt through unflinching acceptance of fallibility.

"Prince Arithon did not forsake the field in Daon Ramon when my father's impetuous raid led the war band into fatal jeopardy." The *caithdein*'s rebuttal razed across rank distemper. "All of our warriors who survived owe their safe retreat to his Grace's intervention. Don't forget the price paid for that timely reprieve! Our liege's flight to draw off pursuit led him to a second ordeal in the hands of the Koriathain."

Shame silenced rebuttal. Red-faced contenders shuffled their feet. If not cowed, the most vocal subsided to listen.

"Please, sit." Encouraged by Siantra's cool regard, and Khadrien's reckless excitement, Esfand stayed erect. Through a bristled resistance, the tang of goose grease and steel dense enough to cut with a knife, he continued, "My charge as steward serves you the reminder. Our clans do not fight this incursion alone! The Fellowship has sent Asandir. We also have backing in force by Athera's living Paravians. If ever our role has been subject to question, this is not the moment to fracture the compact!"

Jalienne's resentment refused to be pacified. Tarens's tacit support shaken off, she pushed forward, the ice queen cloaked in ermine. "What about Arithon's venal abdication?"

Esfand met her agitation headlong. "The task to stand shadow is mine! Arithon will be bound for arraignment under the due process of charter law. As your *caithdein*, I will put the s'Ffalenn heir to the question in person either to exonerate or declare him unfit."

Asandir need say nothing. A steward's rightful prerogative lay above any challenger's purview.

Esfand stood tall in the shoes of his forefathers and rendered his unequivocal decision. "Until Arithon's trial, division between us serves nothing. We must hold the free wilds alongside our allies. Clanborn and Fellowship, with the Ilitharis guardians behind us, will maintain the backbone of the defence."

Laithen's crisp interjection stalled the last rumbles of dissent. "Head of council puts the objection to rest."

Since the clan seeress's scryers had garnered no stable pattern of augury, disposition devolved to Rathain's titled steward.

"We honour our committed liaison in full." Esfand appointed Siantra and Khadrien to lead the active war band's contingent to Halwythwood. "Exposure to the upshifted flux must harden our ranks for the test of Paravian contact. Those who pass muster will hold their ground with the Fellowship to forbid an unsanctioned access to the Old Way."

Dusk melted the log rafters into gloom, the hearthfire dimmed from spluttering flame to bedded coals. Youth obscured in low light, Esfand acknowledged that the drawback of the clans' sparse numbers had to be faced. "I have heard your concern for the catastrophic threat to our continuity if failure brings us defeat. Let us come together and formulate a rear-guard plan for survival."

Relieved to redress that priority, the disgruntled chieftains settled to negotiation in earnest. Tarens and Laithen were detailed to assemble

the elders and infants who stayed behind in Deshir. At the families'
discretion, half their members would separate to seek alternate refuge
in Fallowmere.

Laithen closed the discussion forthwith. "We're in accord. On three
counts, against our unforeseen downfall, the established bloodlines stay
divided for safety."

The gathering finished amid murmured talk, the burdened atmosphere
sliced by fresh air as the doors were flung open. Esfand expelled a sigh
of relief, drained to the pith underneath his black tabard.

Startled awareness rattled him, late, that he had forgotten the Sorcerer's
presence beside him. Self-contained with such absolute stillness, Asandir's
forceful quiet had been overlooked until he stirred his angular frame to
depart. "You did well on your merits, Teir's'Valerient."

Esfand regarded grey eyes and gruff features that seemed almost
kindly, beneath the stern temper imposed by harsh service. "Thank you."
Oddly touched, Rathain's young *caithdein* raised hazel eyes and regarded
a being suddenly more frail and human than intimidating despite the
reputation of a near-to-immortal omnipotence. "Are you certain we can't
offer our hospitality and a worthy night's rest for your horse?"

"I would accept," Asandir admitted, ironclad demeanour shaded by
wistful regret. "Unfortunately, updated word from Althain Tower sends
me onwards to Northgate. Aggravation from another pesky infraction
has intensified Sethvir's foreboding."

Malfeasance

The turn of the season unleashed tumultuous change, blown in with the equinox shift in the wind. Where Instrell Bay's deep-water fleet cast off their storm hawsers and began the spring refit for milder air, Rathain's flux currents resounded to the marched drumbeat of war as the allied war host under Lysaer's command rousted its disparate companies from their winter quarters. Drilled to unity, a steel cleaver well sharpened to secure the Old Way through the north verge of Halwythwood assembled to force the east passage across Daon Ramon.

Snowpack yet blanketed the Mathorn foothills, a gleaming tableau of ice foil and white seldom seen through the centuries while the great dam had diverted the Severnir's flow above Darkling. Storm patterns no longer tamed brewed up anvilheads sheared by speared lightning. Scoured by fire, the choked brush brakes and entangling thorn yielded their strangling foothold. The savage splendour of the open wilds unfurled with the budded willows near to the past semblance of forgotten glory.

Once-placid creeks in the low country frothed in raging flood, the trade-road during thaws posed the most sensible place to regroup for rendezvous with the mixed divisions staged out of Morvain.

Northward, the seaports still shucked their grey mantles of ice. The coalition companies stationed there had trained for a year, whetted to their keen edge for conquest. Chafing and crapulous under hard discipline, they bided the fractious wait. Anticipation infused the quivering, strained pause, before hell and slaughter wrapped them in the fecund odours of horse dung and mud, trampled grass, and clashed steel sliced dissonance through the aria of territorial birdsong.

Farthest north, on the desolate shore by the Worldsend Gate, the wintry gale winds howled yet. Turquoise breakers rolled in, shredded to spindrift and scud, frothed crests burst to hurled spray against inhospitable rock cased in rime. The barren slabs gleamed, drenched by turbulent tides, the punishing cold avoided by man and shunned for the bone-chilling damp most detested by dragons.

Sleet rattled and fell through lowered cloud when the fallen Guardian's appointed successor, Ozvowzakrin, trod through the mercury film of the Worldsend Gate. Gold in years, matured to his dazzling prime, he was savage dignity clothed in rife danger, his gait minced like a cat's by disdain for the wet. Sleet struck his hot scales and sizzled to wisped steam. His bellowed annoyance plumed smoke through the azure shimmer of his aroused aura. A hundred spans of sleek muscle and grace, with arched claws head height to a mounted lancer, the dragon stretched his banded, leather wings and refolded the double-layered vanes against his ebon dorsal spines. Then he bent lambent eyes with slit pupils due south.

A league past the range of warm-blooded vision, a despicable fleck trudged across the leaden drab of the coast's weathered ledges. The trespassing human Sethvir's foresight had warned the Protectorate's vigilance to expect, though the field Sorcerer dispatched as messenger had swiftly departed. Distance did not mute the etheric perception of the great drake, whose mailed talons trod the shelved bed-rock that sited the ruin at Penstair. The fourth-lane focus circle in the shattered fortress aligned with the electromagnetic current threaded southward through Caith-al-Caen. As Ozvowzakrin viewed the world's weave, the mighty signature of Asandir's presence now hardened the flux pattern to shield Halwythwood from the gnat swarm of steel-bearing pestilence poised to infiltrate Daon Ramon.

The Guardian wyrm lashed his tail fluke, annoyed. The insectile bothers commanding the Sorcerer's priorities meant little or nothing to a being of dreams, equipped to reorder the aspects of solid existence at whim. Limitations imposed by the Treaty Accord often demanded what seemed an increasingly onerous knot of restrictions. Fresh at his post, too impatient to sort the picayune nuances bequeathed by Chaimistarizog's passing, Ozvowzakrin rumbled in subsonic contempt. He would sooner spit flame and revel in the exuberant savagery of destruction!

A Fellowship Sorcerer bound to ensure Paravian survival should not cavil at wielding brute force to quash such a trivial threat! Finessed restraint seemed a nonsensical waste, since, at the casual flick of a thought, drake dream could erase the aberrant doings of humankind from the planet. Or wield flame to that end: why not indulge for the dire thrill of wrack and ruin seized in satisfaction?

Ozvowzakrin shook his spiked ruff and hissed. He might do as he pleased. Act on his primal impulse, had the Seven's compact with the Paravians not coddled the silly, two-legged mites under irrational protection. Mere anomalies, spun in frivolity by other wyrms' tinkering, fumed the Gatekeeper crouched by fiat on the dank strand while the puny nuisance bent on disrupting his turf neared the Worldsend portal at a snail's pace.

Human sight would have discerned a stout female, swathed in grey wool and stiffened in spirit by savvy determination. Dragonkind interpreted her fork-gaited approach as a swirled vortex of energy, infused by the picture-stream of her thoughts, bundled together by muddles of associative connection. Her sneak's bent for secrecy concealed nothing! Ozvowzakrin's vision dissected the inveigling pretence.

An astonishing *arrogance*, this snip of rife foolishness came to strike a bargain detrimental to Fellowship interests.

Ozvowzakrin peered into the offered incentive to open a negotiation with her superior. The exchange to buy power involved a bribe, sealed into a wrapped chip of quartz. The mineral lattice of offworld origin escaped Sethvir's earth-sense, but not the sensory reach of drake. Direct access through energy sang to Ozvowzakrin's being of malicious intent, cocooned in a meaningless, woven detritus fabricated from worn silk-worms and mulberry leaves. Dragonkind did not comprehend subterfuge. The audacious intruder entrusted as bearer reeked of her smug belief the cached secret remained undetected.

Ozvowzakrin whuffed plumed steam. Even the beacon-bright flame of his Being evaded the figment's pathetic awareness! Such irksome, blind ignorance stickled Drakish pride to acute disdain.

Ozvowzakrin itched to flout courtesy: shift the pathetic mote out of existence, had no imposed word on matter constrained him.

'I entreat your forbearance not to unmake the youngling human's incarnate existence,' the Fellowship's field Sorcerer had negotiated, his impeccable phrases in ringing balance. *'First sight of your glory will drive her to flight. The Protectorate has my avowed surety, with Sethvir's assurance, she will never dare to return.'*

Ozvowzakrin parsed Asandir's exchange yet again. No omission flawed the terms of agreement, or threatened the probity of the Accord. Committed unto boredom, enraged by the discomfort imposed by the icy damp, the dragon settled for spiteful pique. He would merely toy with the stump-footed speck. A trifle was owed in recompense for the insult. Fair game, to offset the colossal affront to his dignity, and a pittance, since dim senses and dullard perceptions were frail and defencelessly simple to dupe.

The Prime Matriarch's directive to her chosen First Senior, Ceynnia, was unequivocal: to carry the bundled crystal to Rathain's northern peninsula in covert secrecy. There, she would unwrap the invested quartz and cast the imprinted record it held through shimmering film of the Worldsend Gate. A contingency plan to abort the attempt sheltered Koriani integrity against mischance or hostile interference.

The order had powerful enemies. Ceynnia grasped the purposeful imperative to abandon her clandestine mission without leaving a trace if her cover drew untoward notice. The precaution seemed a cowardly act, beneath the facile, clever intelligence by which she had bested her rival peers. Ironclad hierarchy ruled the game of advancement. Sly ambition, well played, had delivered her swift elevation to rank. Entrusted to prove herself, Ceynnia had not garnered the Prime's favour only to fail.

Her success within sight, only the last stretch of unpleasant terrain ranged against her, she pressed ahead towards what seemed the bittermost strip of firmament raked by the angry sea. The swept slab of the shingle provided no shelter. Ceynnia huddled into her bunched cloak. Face turned from the sheeted spray off the breakers, she leaned into the gusts and edged onwards, half-blinded by stinging sleet. The icy footing forgave no careless step. She battled each yard of gained ground, with the spired arch of the Worldsend Gate at long last in view, etched against the drab vista ahead. The pitted structure was ancient, an edifice sculpted of stone and black iron, sized to accommodate a mature dragon. Fellowship sorcery the envy of the Koriathain spanned the threshold, an eerie, ephemeral film reactive as shimmering mercury.

Ceynnia repressed her qualm of unease. After all, she need not risk direct contact to fulfil the Prime's bidding.

A rock formation adjacent loomed upwards, a bulked silhouette in the scudded veils of salt spume. The lee side would break the brunt of the blown spindrift, a convenient reprieve to shelter the delicate handling required to unwrap the imprinted quartz. Chin tucked, deafened by the thrummed flap of her skirt, the enchantress laboured ahead. Ten paces away, the icy wind died. Startled by sudden, incongruous heat, Ceynnia dismissed the phenomenon, surely due to a proximal charge radiated by the spelled portal.

Shock withered her foolishness at her next step, the harsh reek of char little warning before the rank blast of a snort flung her backwards. Crashed onto her rump, scalded cheeks seared to blisters by the reeking, singed wool of her hood, she screamed, scared too late by the stupendous error of her misjudgement.

Nose to snout, she confronted a behemoth, golden scales slashed by cavernous nostrils. A serpentine ribbon of forked tongue flickered through glistening rows of bared teeth and stiletto fangs thrice her height.

Electrified terror seized her to paralysis. Soaked by the steamy gush of her voided bladder, aghast, she grappled a horror empowered to eradicate her self-aware grip on existence. Helpless as a wing-plucked fly, she scrabbled backwards, caged on both sides by the mailed talons of a great dragon.

The monster reared tall as a shot tower over her, incomprehensible, immense, gargantuan coils armoured for murder, spiked with horns and brilliantly scaled. The great drake's ferocious presence itself crushed her human identity to a dumb speck.

Yellow as twin suns, slitted pupils midnight black, reptilian eyes surveyed her puniness, burning.

Panic triumphed. Ceynnia scrambled upright and bolted. Sliding, she fled, driven to the mindless, desperate flight of a hunted animal over-whelmed by the need to escape. The bitter air scoured her heaving lungs. Tears of fright stung her scorched cheeks, as unheeded as the sodden slap of her befouled underclothes.

The stumble that skinned her hands and knees bloody upon rock crusted over with barnacles also slammed Ceynnia's gnashed teeth through a bitten lip. Pain jolted her numbed reason and revived the urgency of her directive to obliterate sensitive evidence. No second to spare, she ripped open the purse at her waist and groped with grazed fingers for the silk-swathed crystal she must destroy at all cost.

Ceynnia flung down the incriminating packet, entire. She stamped on the glass-fragile sliver inside, ground the crushed matrix under her heel, then sprinted for her very life.

The pulverized remnants abandoned behind would clear swiftly, rinsed blank by the salt spume whipped off the frothed breakers. No artefact of Lirenda's imprinted content would remain, and no clue but a shred of soaked rag.

Ceynnia ran herself to exhausted collapse. Alive enough to regroup, she shouldered the sour taste of defeat, naught left ahead but the ghastly, long trek to report the demise of her errand to the Prime Matriarch.

Her short-fall at least left no hostile party opposed to the order the wiser. She believed her precautions were adequate. Yet miniscule grains of the particulate quartz left behind sieved through the torn silk. Not quite banished, the pattern presented as bait to snare dragons made unshielded contact with Athera's obdurate, northshore bed-rock.

Spring – Late Spring 5929

Triggers

Flagged by Ozvowzakrin's piqued curiosity, Althain's Warden ponders the fugitive peril sown by the concocted incentive for Lirenda Prime's provocative transaction: the imprint of Arithon's aura offered to dragons in trade for augmented power presented an explosively divisive gambit, irresistible lure for a steadfast Protectorate perhaps sufficient to seek his recruitment, while rogue factions in revolt on Sckaithen Duin would crave the insatiable thrill of live capture for a novel plaything . . .

Lysaer's staged campaign out of Narms to claim the Old Way for commerce becomes thwarted at the Aiyenne Bridge by Asandir's enforced warning: "Woe betide any trespass of Halwythwood to seek lawless occupation of Caith-al-Caen. Set foot in the free wilds south of the river, and your coalition's host will be abandoned to reckon with their sorry fate . . ."

When Arithon's sloop *Talliarthe* makes landfall in a secluded cove on the northwest coast of Vastmark, Nails's shrewd manipulation of Desh-thiere's curse sways Lysaer to redirect his advance eastward down the Mathorn Road: "We camp on the field and stockpile supply until the spring flood subsides, then ford our troops for a frontal strike upon Rathain's heartland at strength . . ."

IX. Violations

The Rockbay ports bustled, on fire with mercantile exchange and transport for Lysaer's coalition encampment in Daon Ramon. Talk embellished the prowess of the regional companies, and tallied with pride the assembly of banners and pavilions pitched in crisp rows at the inland verge of the Mathorn Road. News carried by pigeon confirmed the reports. The yearlong muster at last had called the faithful to arms. True Sect temples hung bunting to honour the divine march to glory to cleanse the Dark-haunted passage through Caith-al-Caen.

"Light's will prevail," the believers remarked in the taverns and streets. Few mentioned the upset delivered at Halwythwood, the intervention of Fellowship Sorcerers declared a Canon anathema.

Guild magnates and practical traders conferred in huddles over the more onerous obstacles: of galleys and goods seized by requisition, and draught teams unhitched from the plough to haul freight for landbound supply. Impositions that stung, insult to injury, atop the already ruinous setbacks imposed on craftfolk and crofters since the wreck of Etarra. The righteous and the powerful smoothed down strained tempers and opined the Old Way promised their future salvation, with naught lost beyond a hard year's depressed profits before seizure of road rights reopened their access across Daon Ramon.

A wayfarer fresh off the dockside at Thirdmark garnered the ominous gist from overheard chatter at the teeming town gate. Dakar and Arithon wove in through the press at midmorning, bent on the next stage of their journey from *Talliarthe*'s sequestered mooring. They slid unremarked off the rancid, baled wool in the shepherd's cart, rolled to a stop by the mud-gravel yard of the horse seller's.

The driver whose favourite provided the ride answered Arithon's courteous thanks in her Vastmark vernacular. "Increase to your tribe, and may guard dogs fend off the yellow-eyed fury of wyverns and Shadow."

The Mad Prophet's envenomed glare darted sidelong as her rattletrap vehicle rumbled away. "Dharkaron strike the priesthood's honeyed words from the oily mouth of a liar!" And damn all straight to vengeance, that no forthright suspicion marked the scruffy, disingenuous creature beside him as the vilified author of consummate evil.

"Well, no one insisted you had to come," Arithon retorted, agreeable.

Dakar staggered abreast on residual sea legs, his erratic course granted the wide berth of a drunkard. Or maybe the ripe whiff of crab trapper's bait repelled the finicky bystanders: hair and unwashed clothes, both of them reeked, debarked from the same skiff that had delivered them from the cragged coastline of South Strait.

"You're not planning to cosy up in this town," the Mad Prophet huffed, broken into a ponderous trot to keep up. Stonewalled by the impassive silence that meant no bath and no mutton stew, Dakar salved his acute disappointment by prying at Arithon's motive, the most scorching irritant tackled forthwith. "Wasn't your manic foray at Rockfell enough? Brainless arrogance won't spare you. No man picks a second-round fight with a Fellowship Sorcerer."

"Speaking from your tepid experience, I'm sure." Nipped through the stable gate, Arithon flagged the head hostler. "I like my feuds on the hot side of fury, and bar nothing, I will put an end to the fracas I've started."

Dakar failed to stare down that bald-faced effrontery. "You'll dive off the brink for the death of one child?"

Thwarted, he fretted, while Arithon dickered over the price to acquire two nags for a journey, destination unspecified. Horses were led up, inspected, passed over. To the thrust and parry of overblown praise and contentiously cheerful disparagement, the reins of two nondescript mounts, with saddles, changed hands.

Dakar resumed his low jab through the chomp of the carrots hand-fed by the cocksure new owner being nosed by two slobbering muzzles. "I have seen you sustain a graceful defeat. You picked up the pieces and carried on after running cold steel into Caolle for his unswerving loyalty as your liegeman."

"My own failure," Arithon shot back, savage. "I alone bear the onus of recourse for my personal short-falls. The burdensome blood spilled at this pass is none of mine! Nor is the innocent's, murdered by the betrayal of my given word at Daenfal. The fist on the sword belonged to the True Sect religion, and the nastier question begs asking. Why isn't the Fellowship quashing that jackal pack of fanatics?"

Dakar nearly stopped short, startled by the abrupt shift, where blame reassigned culpability. Oblivious to the shredded carrot dribbled down his neck by both crowding equines, he chewed over the nuance through the uphill stroll towards the craft-quarter stalls in the market.

Impasse bricked over the preposterous sham, since the Seven brooked no mortal's meddling. The flippant retort chafed all the worse for its niggling sandgrain of truth, for in fact if Arithon craved thirsty revenge, Erdane's dedicates posed the softer target.

"Insufferable maniac!" Dakar elbowed past a street singer, and decried above the backdrop thump of the famed Thirdmark looms weaving herringbone linen and tweeds, "You can't charge off hell-bent to take down Lysaer's zealot believers!"

"Why not?" Arithon laughed, tossed a copper to the vigilant boy at the hitching rail, then tied off their purchased stock and kept walking. "The bedazzled bigots are certainly primed for bear-baiting the clans. Scry and see for yourself. Then convince me they've not entrenched their reserves at East Ward and Cildorn, fortified to reap scalps by more than the usual parcel of headhunting trackers."

Objective argument crushed, Dakar weaselled sidewards to squeeze his girth past a trundling hand-cart. The farmwife he rankled swore at him, loudly, to squawks from the hen also jostled in her osier basket. Heads turned. Rude children pointed. Embarrassed pink, Dakar scrambled ahead and spouted off in exasperation, "I've no mind to attract a diviner's attention, and Sethvir himself couldn't count the biting fleas on my backside in this noisy stew of commotion!"

"Bravo!" Arithon's smile flashed nasty teeth as he ducked an awning and strode into glaring sunshine. "A first-rate excuse for us to stockpile supply and get on our way." He paused at the first stall. From a spread of impractical oddments and glass floats, his brisk selection bartered for canvas, fish twine, and sealing tar.

"*Fish twine?* Are you serious?" Dakar eyed the parcelled items askance. "You're not aiming to haul off to sea with two *horses!*"

"Stay on, you'll find out." Arithon thrust his bundles into the Mad Prophet's convenient arms, then proceeded to the cobbler's for waterproof boots. More equipment piled onto his human mule: sturdy packs, linen nosebags for grain, and two pairs of hobbles lined with felt.

Preparation for landbound travel eased nothing. Dakar disliked the saddle nearly as much, since his meaty, round thighs became torqued to cramps, and short legs chafed to blisters astride. He tacked grimly after his black-haired tormentor. Neck craned to ground teeth over his ungainly load, he watched Arithon acquire a stout satchel, waxed cheese, and salted jerky.

"You aren't going to ditch me so easily this time," Dakar declared in flint warning.

"Tally ho, the sly fox!" Arithon mocked. "Give chase with the rest of the hunt if you can. I'll do you the favour, since you haven't quit. We'll be riding northeast as the crow flies."

Spring melt overflowed the Aiyenne's meandering banks, a roiled brown sheet of riffled current that raked the inundated vegetation. The sun's glint off the herringbone patterns of flattened stems wore ruffled foam at the high-water mark. Stranded bands of suds at the verge marked the moment the river's annual flood subsided at last.

Lysaer's encamped dedicates greeted the slacking crest with exuberance, morale rebounded from the sorcerous setback that had forbidden their direct passage through Halwythwood. Resentment evaporated into high spirits. Rambunctious bluster fomented wagers staked to contentious excess, and the roisterous boasting between rival factions grew more crapulous by the day. Idle men were past weary of the sucking muck trampled between their pitched tents. Of horses with hoof rot, ribs staring on poor fodder, and rusted armour stored under dank canvas. Every gadding torment plucked their wire-strung nerves, the enticement of the green vales across the Aiyenne a mere bowshot away. Rejuvenated by storm-struck fires, the grassland unfurled a bewitching carpet of wildflowers, waist deep, grazed by sleek herds of fulsome deer grown butter-fat and ripe for the pot.

Dace watched the colossal force waken behind the stiff mask of liveried service. Tasked by adversity to maintain a fine gentleman's wardrobe, he fought to keep the master's bed linen crisp, with lye soap grown scarce and space to dry cloth usurped by the practice field, where drilled exercise and galloping horses continually flung up clodded turf. By increments, the high water receded. He lost sleep, overworked, while the slumbering war host shook off its torpor, impatient to arm and break camp.

Swaggering outriders tested the ford. One brash fool drowned. Another lost a good horse, rescued unscathed by his fellows, who emerged caked in black slime and sandy mud. Two more weeks passed to ennui and angst, while the biting flies hatched and nipped flesh to misery. By night, the fumed torches scarcely fended off the pestilent scourge of mosquitoes and swarming gnats.

Dace brewed repellents from bracken and sweetfern, denied the green fuel for torch smoke, while the Seven's adamant warding of Halwythwood made available fire-wood scant. Lysaer made rounds in the cheerless dark, his presence a lit beacon amid the dim tents sunk in shadow by the wan flicker of rushlights.

Whether his Lordship renounced the religion, his shining figure drew worship. He anchored the rallying cry for the True Sect priests, proof on earth of every man's sanctified hope of divinity.

Dace swallowed the bitter fruit of his failure. Silenced by his station, he wrestled the daily sorrow of Lysaer's certain doom with each breath. Cognizant of the appalling risks, he rode the juggernaut of the Light's cause, dread thickened under the waxing heat and the bog taint of drowned vegetation exposed to rot in the sun. The river fell, to the sinister crow of Nails's triumph: the advance scouts finally encountered firm footing on the shoaling gravel that bottomed the Aiyenne's tamed shallows.

Advance parties achieved the far bank without scathe. The whoops of relief from the restive ranks sounded long after dark, the comfort of Lysaer's pavilion a prison from which Dace must bear agonized witness to the death throes of Lysaer's strangled integrity.

Tomorrow, the vanguard would cross over the Aiyenne in brazen defiance of Asandir's edict.

No stopping the war host's surge into Daon Ramon. The True Sect commanders perceived no impediment. Dace minded his duties in smothered despair, while the priest examiner's boastful prayers claimed the arcane enemies would be routed, dispatched to perdition by the sword and the faggots. The valet sickened by that fallacy lit candles and laid out crystal goblets and wine. He folded napkins and arranged brandy-soaked sweetmeats on gilt trays and porcelain plates. The routine tour of duty salved nothing. His moral imperative to stem Lysaer's campaign was toothless against Nails's relentless insinuation. Nothing could stop the juggernaut now. Cozened to bedazzlement on the Light's glory, driven by visions of trade wealth, Mankind's massed companies stoked the fever of venal entitlement to seize their bid for ascendancy.

"At last!" Lysaer's effusive enthusiasm arrived with the patter of sycophants' footsteps. He entered, immaculate in his studded brigandine, his attached entourage crowded by six field captains in half plate, a dedicate commander with a crested helm and gold braid, and Nails, skinny frame furtive as a white weasel in her diviner's regalia. The Light's acclaimed avatar accepted the pre-eminent chair with the tapestried footstool. Blond head turned, still talking, he raised his left leg for the accustomed, prompt service to tend him.

The smirking page was nowhere in evidence.

Trusted to step up, the valet knelt on the rich carpet to unbuckle his liege's chased spurs and remove his soiled boots. On-going, the engaged conversation continued as if his presence was invisible. The subject debated over his bent head involved which companies would march first, and when and where heavy supply wagons might be staged at least risk of bogging their wheels.

No plan respected Asandir's ultimatum. The captains voiced deeper concern over spring traps and forays by clan raiders.

Dace bit back unease and reshod the master in his preferred calfskin slippers. Acknowledged by a nod, he tendered the same courtesy to the officers, and passed their soaked footwear to the shirking page, reappeared while the select conference padded in their stockinged feet to the trestle furnished with tablecloth, currant shortbread and wine.

Bent last before Nails, Dace pulled off her boot with a deft twist, reflexes primed for the vengeful thrust to smear grass stains across his spotless livery. The sardonic smile as Nails stood up mocked the adroit avoidance, an unspoken promise of retaliation in the covert battle between them.

Dace weathered the egregious punches in public, his aplomb faultless under inspection. In private, sometimes, he could react, even counter the diviner's aggressive embarrassments. Twice over, he had maneouvred to thwart the strumpets the sly creature paid to sneak into the master's warmed sheets. But under the eyes of hosted superiors, Dace owned nothing beyond wary vigilance to forestall the petty barrage of snide tricks.

". . . that's plain as tits on a bantling." Laughter applauded the speaker's jest, while Nails sauntered to claim her place.

The hard chair left in reserve by intention was the last open seat. The diviner parked her bony rump, her poisonous glower at the valet scored behind Lysaer's back.

Dace swanned past to refill goblets, prepared for the ankle thrust out to trip him. Since the master's preference decreed each worthy should be refreshed in ranked order, the war host's commander received precedence.

"By glory, we could play the exercise as a contest. First company over the river takes the honour of centre at the front line," the bearded captain from Morvain was saying. Effusive with the bluster from his troop's inspection, he planted his blunt fists on the trestle as a preemptive, territorial stake.

"That's a rife invitation to chaos! Why gift the Dark with divisive rivalry and pointless injuries?" objected the staid senior officer. "A round of drawn lots from a hat would be prudent."

The dedicate commander insisted his temple force deserved the accolade. "Our priests belong at the fore with the drummers to bless and cleanse the ancient taint of Paravian haunts from the unhallowed ground."

Moved to pour the next glass, Dace's peripheral vision snagged on a manic flicker of gemstone: the frenetic tap of the master's ringed finger betrayed the first flaw in his controlled deportment. Porcelain features and straight shoulders maintained the regal countenance of the statesman. But the glitter of frost in fixated blue eyes alerted the valet's keen instinct.

Nails noticed, also. Languid as the stoat primed for mischief, she laced her hands over her Sunwheel tabard, her baleful disdain the practised deception of a plain woman too awkward for male adulation.

Dace listened and watched, every stretched nerve on edge. Somehow, somewhere, a new development fanned the spark of Desh-thiere's curse. Nothing provocative seemed to be evident. The regular problems of logistics and supply steered the on-going discussion, the short-range lists of martial impediments too mundane to have triggered a volatile change.

". . . need an alternate line of support from Daenfal," the dedicate captain insisted. "Word sent by pigeon can coordinate organization through the True Sect temples."

Reference to the south riveted Lysaer's focus. Dace searched for a correlation, stepped aside to replenish a plate of crumbs with fresh pastries.

"Evil spreads with the wind from that direction," Nails offered, the sly prompt a tactical strategy. She held information, likely garnered from a temple source, if not by her sharp aptitude as a diviner.

Hateful temptation, Dace yearned to shower the genteel pastries into her lap. The feral ploy might sideline the disastrous insinuation through distraction, a temporary relief, at best, that would torch his assiduous pretence of servitude.

Cooler wits prevailed. Dace quenched the indulgent cry of raw fury. Kharadmon's warning and Davien's unvarnished language had challenged his nerve to withstand Lysaer's destruction in covert silence. Yet where were the vaunted Fellowship Sorcerers, when the backing of allies was crucial to stem Nails's nasty plot from clinching ascendancy?

That moment, Dace stumbled, not from muscular sabotage by his nemesis, but instead shoved awry by a subtle, cold wind that razed him to the bone. He knew that presence! Puckered to unsubtle gooseflesh, he crashed to his knees halfway under the trestle, accosted in force by a Sorcerer's shade. No breather was given to gape over the pastry tray, neatly salvaged from violent upset on the carpet. Dace's view of cakes and porcelain darkened like spilled ink. Whirled into the involuntary expansion of a Sighted vision, he beheld a slight, black-haired man riding in the company of a plump prophet across the free wilds. By dead reckoning, the pair's travel led them due south of the coalition war host encamped on the Aiyenne.

Cogent fuel for Lysaer to fall prey to the Mistwraith's geas! The Master of Shadow was aligned with the fourth lane, which channelled current engaged Desh-thiere's curse!

Dace's spontaneous clairvoyance dissolved. Restored to his natural senses, whitened knuckles clenched on his tray, he reoriented, appalled by his indecorous lapse before guests in the master's pavilion. Lysaer ignored the gaffe. Censure for clumsiness would come later, in private, since the lackey's untoward spill had discommoded none of his officers. Dace regained his feet, hopeful the late hour might lend him the plausible cover of weariness. Talk resumed around the disruption, except for the predictable backstab of Nails's whetted interest.

Yet hostile divination found naught to detect. Kharadmon's fleeting presence was gone, his ominous message delivered with no moment's grace allotted for grief.

Nothing would thwart Lysaer's course towards disaster, or prevent the curse of Desh-thiere from driving the war host's ill-starred advance.

Around the trestle, risen to toast the morrow's endeavour, the command staff lifted their brimming glasses. "May divine fortune favour the Light!"

"I'll salute the strength of our human resolve," Lysaer snapped in correction. Burnished-gold icon to their adulation, he drained his wine. "Tomorrow we invade the free wilds of Daon Ramon, with sixty days' march between us and our decisive conquest through Caith-al-Caen."

On the morning the war host began fording the Aiyenne, the cool nights of early summer gave way to the first kiss of heat that yellowed the stalks of wild barley. Arithon's unhurried progress astride had dragged Dakar, blistered raw and complaining, across the Radmoore flats. They paused on the trade-road due west of Ganish. An hour's dickering replenished their saddle packs at the Waypoint compound, built where the bridge spanned the north fork of the River Taiffen for the silk caravans en route to the harbour at Rockbay.

News winged by pigeon from distant Rathain had the packed teahouse rumbling with speculation. Trade's avid interest hinged on humanity's seizure of the Old Way across central Rathain.

"You're not helping the cause," the Mad Prophet accused, lounged against the worn bar top. Slit-eyed, he watched Arithon stow his stacked purchases into their dusty satchel.

Clearly, their path never meant to pursue the rhumb-line course northward across Melhalla, but instead bent northeasterly over the wind-swept downs sparsely inhabited by grazing sheep.

Arithon granted the censure his impervious indifference. Black hair noosed in a hide tie, he appeared too cool for a man wearing leathers as he stepped across the planked threshold into the baking glare of noon sunshine.

Dakar tagged behind in short-strided pique, his badgering resentment galled by the hustle to be away from the tap-room's amenities. Hard breathing, he chased Arithon's heels towards the weathered boards of the outriders' post shack, where their snubbed horses idled, switching flies. "I saw last night's sky when I took a piss! Have you checked on the pole star perchance?"

"Do I need to?" Arithon did not untie their hipshot mounts, but pushed through the wedged open door, apparently to negotiate.

Dakar ranted, deaf to the sarcasm. "For all your prowess as a seafaring navigator, the pancake terrain has flummoxed your sense of direction? Keep on," he accused, "and you'll land us bang up to our eyeballs in muck squirming with leeches, huge snakes, and venomous Methspawn."

Since Arithon's silence was not forthcoming, he prodded, "All right, we're deliberately headed for a wretched stint in the middle of nowhere. If that twine you've been tying into a net was made to seine the creeks above Methlas Lake, you should know. Nobody fishes those waters but Verrain, and never to catch anything harmlessly edible."

The rant proved to be wasted. Arithon, unresponsive, engaged the post relay's man, asking whether the senior hostler might sell their two head of horseflesh.

Dakar's incensed yell stalled the polite exchange.

"We won't need mounts if you're bound to stay on," explained Arithon, unperturbed. "Keep yours as you like, although kindness would not loose a blameless, tame beast on the downs to scrounge on poor forage without a caretaker."

The Mad Prophet shut his jaw, fast. Futile hope was extinguished, that Methisle Fortress might be their preferred destination. Though the focus circle sited in the ancient citadel offered a swift, direct passage to Caith-al-Caen, Elaira being in visitor's residence struck that wistful prospect from consideration. The man heart-set on a belated reconciliation did not carry a tar pot and twine mesh to seek amends or pay neglected court to his handfast beloved.

Arithon concluded his horse trade at the post stable, pleased enough by the purse tucked away to allow Dakar's yearning for beer in the tavern.

"No." Sweating with folded arms in the dusty yard, the Mad Prophet viewed the sudden, sweet volte-face askance. "Blandishments won't work to throw me off your tail. I've already guessed. You wouldn't be joining me."

Arithon flashed his untrustworthy grin. "Very well, then. Don't belly-ache over the notion that I never offered. Stay with me if you prefer a boring snooze on the riverbank."

The brief foray downslope to the Taiffen did not involve replenishing water flasks. Arithon hiked a short distance upstream, more interested in the shoaled shallows that bent the river's course into a crook. Lit by sun filtered through the streamered thickets of willow, he drew his sharp knife to trim withies. Dakar fidgeted. Shifting from foot to foot, he settled at last in the shade, lulled by the jewelled flit of dragonflies and the frustration of his brown thoughts.

He never meant to fall asleep. But noon's languid heat soothed his aching back and sapped all inclination to move.

Roused at twilight by the whine of mosquitoes, Dakar rolled over. He gouged out the prickle of the hard-shelled beetle burrowed under his collar, informed by the amphibious croaking from the shallows his immediate surrounds were deserted.

Arithon had departed and left him.

Fury spurred Dakar erect. He stomped upriver, stubbing his toes. Stumbled back onto the rutted dirt road, he crossed the land bridge, ravenous enough to eat tacks, but not tempted by the jocular singing drifted from the tavern behind. Stars burned overhead, brilliant white in a moonless, black sky that favoured initiate senses.

Trained to interpret the flux, Dakar set off tracking Arithon's trail.

The Master of Shadow had not troubled to mask his direction. Left sign of his movement was too obvious. Dakar scratched welted skin in between snarled oaths. Such absence of secrecy bristled sensibility, when he had resigned himself to run down the tough course of a lengthy lead.

Instead of excoriating s'Ffalenn recalcitrance, he picked out the glimmer of Arithon's campfire a stone's throw off the verge. Taunted by the mouthwatering aroma of baked fish and roast coney, he closed the final yards, puffing and puzzled speechless.

Arithon glanced up, at ease in rolled shirtsleeves, legs crossed and his back propped against the supply packs. "You needn't have broken a sweat. I said you had adequate time for a beer and civilized refreshment."

Dakar ground his teeth. He sat down. The maddening note of amiability felt out of place as a whack on the funny bone. Contrary suspicion dawned late, that the man *wanted* a dupe at his side for a witness. "Damned to Dharkaron if you aren't playing me like a jigged frog." Though for what nefarious scheme boggled the imagination.

"Follow on and find out," Arithon invited. The sultry gleam of low firelight spiked his glance as he lifted the spit and pried off a sizzling joint with his knife. "Though if you come, eat and rest while you can. We set off in earnest before daybreak."

Dakar tore into the juicy offering. Not for nothing: the bastard knew how to dress game and forage for a savoury meal in the rough. Stuffed

sufficiently to loosen his waistband, the Mad Prophet loitered at ease
by the fire. When Arithon slept, he rejected the advice to turn in
himself, but instead sought seclusion to engage a scrying to parse what
lay ahead . . .

*The war host trampled south under the proud flutter of coloured banners,
a massed wave of shod horses that broke over clean ground, leaving a
trampled wake of chopped grass and mashed wildflowers. The armed foot
marched behind, company on company ranked in trimmed squares, the
laden creak of their ox-drawn supply wains carving profane ruts across
wilted acres. Horn calls and shouts flushed nesting birds, and milled the
chorus of new life to silence.*

*Other disruptions beyond mortal sight met the eyes of refined perception.
Cacophonic excitement whipped on by rote belief and the lust of insatiable
ambition roiled like storm cloud through the tidal surge of the flux. The
dimmed swathe rolled over the ephemeral, bright imprint of ancient light
kindled since the First Age. The knoll where the Ilitharis Paravians had
spoken the actualized Name of the winter stars shone still, the lit beacon
that jewelled the dazzling crown of Caith-al-Caen's exultant harmonics:
power yet ringing with a purity to stun human senses and strike the voice
dumb. No edifice marred the pristine site where the Riathan Paravians
once danced the annual peal of renewal to the song of the Athlien flutes.
Green grass and wind adorned the wild vales where bed-rock still retained
the memory of dawn that bore witness to Cianor Sunlord's original birth.*

*Where threat advanced now: a steel-clad promise of bloodshed upon
proscribed ground, wanton agony soon to sow the broadscale wreckage to
destabilize the resonant vortex of the mysteries. For the song and light
measure of absolute joy framed the anchor that stayed the dark downfall
to entropy . . .*

Dakar roused in the flannel fog of predawn, soaked by dew and sickened
with dread. No birds chirped. Night blanketed the surrounding flats like
packed felt. The air weighted his lungs down like sodden wool, and the
dull coals of Arithon's fire had extinguished.

The conviction burdened his gut like a stone. He had been left behind,
once again fallen victim to his slipshod failure to pay attention. Except
the flood of panic spiking his pulse had nothing to do with Arithon's
covert departure.

Threat to the mysteries at Caith-al-Caen changed everything!

The urgent scramble to rise and give chase wheeled Dakar's destabilized faculties. Yet his dizzied rush to recoup his lapse stumbled over a campsite still occupied.

Both travel packs were readied to go. Arithon knelt, engaged in his fastidious habit of burying the cookfire's ashes. He finished by smoothing the ambient flux with a cantrip of blessing and thanks likely taken from Ciladis's notes. The small practice cleared and harmonized the left trace of their presence.

While the agitation thrashed up by Dakar's augury swirled and dispersed like whipped wind through static, the eruptive burst wrought by his emotional turmoil was too urgent to quell. "Lysaer's combined war host is marching south from the Aiyenne unopposed. Where are the clan scouts? Esfand's war band? *Why haven't the Fellowship Sorcerers interceded?*"

Within a fortnight, the coalition incursion would violate the heart of Daon Ramon's free wilds. Confronted by Arithon's indifferent silence, Dakar exploded. "By Ath, as Rathain's attuned crown prince, you are oathsworn to care! I can't believe you've forsaken the roots of your nature! If this war host sullies Caith-al-Caen uncontested, your hero's intervention to spare Rathain's war band last time and the round before that went for naught. Worse, your promised settlement to ease Caolle's passing was a fatuous lie."

"Are the Seven so weak they can't back their own grudges?" Too mild to rise to the bait, Arithon sang a clear note to sweeten the dissonance before the fresh ripple of agitation botched up his working. Then he strapped on his sword, shouldered his bundle of withies and the larger supply pack, and thrust the second one into the chest of his fuming companion. "If you're that concerned, why not fare north and attend to the matter yourself?"

"Because I'm not your arse-licking toady!" Knocked backwards a step, Dakar seized hold before the loaded canvas slid and thumped down onto his toes. Since the contents held victuals, he shoved a resigned arm through the strap. Forced to snatch for his stockings and boots, he hopped forward, pulling on footwear, while his dangling burden walloped him breathless. "I won't plod in tow like your bum-basted donkey. Where under sky are we headed?"

"You're the bona fide prophet, and lest you forget, the badgering wit who remarked on the pole star's orientation." Arithon's untrustworthy smile flashed teeth as he settled into his longer stride with impervious confidence. "Stick in your best guess. The geometry's simple. I've kept the same heading since Thirdmark."

Four days later, parked at nightfall on the last westerly stretch of dry ground for nigh onto sixty leagues, Dakar confronted the hideous passage he had dreaded from the ill-omened outset.

Behind, the wind rustled Radmoore's summer grass, cheerful with crickets and nightjars, with nothing alive to fear beyond the owl's silent swoop upon foraging mice. Ahead, noisy screeling, chittering wails, croaking amphibians, and other eruptive, slithering disturbances dwelled in the black pools lapping the hummocks. Mirthlvain Swamp unreeled to the eastern horizon, flounced by the lace-printed crowns of the marsh maples, and wisped mist eerily smeared by the lime-yellow flare of will-o'-the-wisps.

"Sithaer's howling haunts, Arithon!" Dakar exclaimed. "Why here?"

"Why not?" Black head bent over his busied hands, lit carmine by their cookfire's coals, Arithon laced his tied netting on withies, steam-bent earlier into spancel hoops. Hope perished, that ship's tar and green hide had been packed along with them to fashion a coracle. Instead, the two watertight, rope-handled buckets finished and stacked at Arithon's elbow affirmed his unpleasant intent to traverse the mire on foot.

"This isn't Silvermarsh," Dakar continued, rash enough to belabour the obvious. Unwise trespass forgave nothing, where the corrupted spawn of malformed creatures once possessed by *Methuri*, the hate wraiths, had interbred their unnatural horrors for three Ages. "Here the ugly encounter by misadventure is likely to bear fatal consequence."

The deterrent proved futile as rain shed off the oiled quills of a duck.

If the royal attunement to Rathain's threatened wilds troubled Arithon's conscience, if he sensed the disruptive enormity of the war host's intrusion, his clammed silence extended. The poignant recall seemed banished from mind: of the grey pebble once wakened by Asandir, that connected his awareness to the ancient mystery that had danced, living, upon the vales of Caith-al-Caen. No trace of marring sentiment softened Arithon's angular face.

Dakar dozed at last to escape the vicious gnaw of anxiety. Arithon was wakeful when he roused at dawn. Whether or not he had slept, further evidence showed he had kept himself busy. Four stout staves of maple rested beside the packs, the pair with forked ends fashioned as an extended handle for his completed, hooped nets.

Terror choked all inclination to ask after the implements' purpose. Plagued by threats grave enough to seize up rattled nerves, Dakar shoved his bulk upright. Already stiff from poor rest on damp ground, he sucked a breath tainted by sulphurous air and coughed the burr stuck in his throat. "You won't scare me off. Wherever you go, whatever you try, I will dog every execrable step."

The chill promise dangled. Unwelcome or not, the observer would cling by pigheaded necessity to thwart who knew what course of mayhem. The Mad Prophet dared not back down. Despite his better interests, he could not shake off Ciladis's forewarning, foisted upon him amid his muddled retreat in the stews.

Arithon's perverse mood withstood scrutinized censure. He ignored the implied ultimatum. Determined to move on, he strapped his net poles into a yoke for his buckets, then tossed a long stave to Dakar for a hiking stick and retained the last one for himself.

They entered the mire in single file. Squelching steps placed on the hummocks, their careful movement spread quiet before them. Pearl mist rode the dank air, laden with the reek of rot bubbled up from the ooze beneath the shivered surface of the puddles. Strewn bones picked bare under the pallid sun bore no resemblance to the aquatic species seen elsewhere. Wading birds avoided the shallows. Those spotted were hunters, their prey speared in rapacious dives from high perches on the limbs of half-drowned, stunted trees. Twisted stands of red maple and willow shed sickly, limp leaves without a whisper in the breezeless caul of humidity.

Dakar endured, cranked to an apprehension that startled at untoward sounds and peripheral movement. He grew to dread the fat splash of the frogs, and recoiled from the wet slap of the moss draped like grey shrouds over the windfalls sunk amid the speared ranks of the reed beds.

Paused to mop his brow, Dakar ventured, "In case you think we've encountered the worst, the outer verge of the marsh is least threatening."

"If you read the same books in Sethvir's library, I agree." Eyes impervious as sheared emerald, Arithon surveyed the vista ahead, streamered haze fuzzed with the wan glimmer of marshlights against an expanse unremittingly desolate. "The descriptions were hideous." Sweating as profusely, whether from the heat or unsettled regret, he rejected the hint to turn back. "You're under no one's compulsion to follow."

Dakar clamped his jaw. He yanked his sunk stave, the stuck end freed with sucking reluctance. As if any born mortal could resist a request from Ciladis's forthright appeal. Somehow, against evidence, the Sorcerer kept his unshaken faith in the purity of man's better nature.

They spent the first night in the crumbled stone shell of an ancient watchtower, fallen to ruin since the Second Age. Walls and roof were demolished, the rafter beams long since decayed. The silted foundation capped a low mound, shored up by heaved masonry that provided a defensible campsite.

Dakar spent his turn on watch duty brooding. He tried not to listen when the frogs' racket silenced, or hear what screamed in the dark, life and violent death underscored by ferocious splashing. Black water lapped to the stir of inscrutable denizens, scribbled with reflections cast by the stars that burned through the thinned fog at the zenith.

Once built on dry land, before mouldered disuse, such old beacons were minded by a diligent sentinel. A firepan under a top platform's cupola would have been stacked with oiled wood, lit at an instant's notice when dangerous Methspawn surged in migration. Many such tumble-down remnants had succumbed to neglect, or subsided into submersion. The mire's expansion over the centuries left the oak palings and fitted stone redoubts of ancient defences overrun, toppled by the historic quakes that shattered the fault line beneath the Tiriac's jumbled peaks.

Relieved by midnight, Dakar slept poorly. Shaken at sunrise from a muzzy nightmare, he weathered his companion's cranky impatience. The early start failed to ameliorate Arithon's vile mood, perhaps because the Mad Prophet had not succumbed to faint nerve and turned back. Or maybe the oppressive gloom of the swamp frayed the foolhardy royal's mask of braggadocio. Arithon's terse demeanour seemed increasingly brittle the further they pressed into jeopardy. The terrain past the verges became more impenetrable. The sink pools between tussocked islets yawned wider, the meandering pathway relentlessly narrowed. Virid fungus slicked the few exposed rocks, every cautious step treacherous. Their intrepid course continued northeast, the few patches of mushy ground squelching ankle deep, until the mire's puzzle-cut maze of ledes and sunk hammocks extended beyond the limit of Dakar's past excursions in protected company with Fellowship Sorcerers.

Often their footfalls disturbed living things, pursued by scaled predators that launched from the depths with explosive velocity, red eyes lambent and teeth clenched on shuddering prey as they dove splashing beneath roiled waters. The slipped boot sole, the loose tussock, the shin hooked by the razor-edged stalks of bent sedge might cause a trip where movement of any kind drew the arrowed wakes of all manner of horrors, hell-bent to tear flesh in their frenzy to feed.

Two days or four, Dakar lost count, though when asked, Arithon's dead reckoning mapped their steady progress at twenty leagues. "Almost to the outer ring of the second Paravian wall."

"Come back to your senses while you're still whole," Dakar urged, paused to lean on his staff while the murky lagoon that unreeled before them erupted to a diamond-drop blast of flung spray, then subsided to ripples. What serpentine terror sank back to lurk in the impenetrable depths outstripped the bleak boundary of nightmare. "Succumb to some fell creature's viciousness, you'll be sorry. Even Davien's seal of longevity can't restore a mauled limb that's been devoured."

Arithon laughed. "The trained hound, jerked along by the scruff after how many years on the leash? You sound more like Asandir by the moment."

For a cautionary admonition not taken to heart, nonetheless, Arithon tested the ground with his staff at each tentative step. The unstable trail underfoot came and went, the matted, flexible roots where they trod laced over sucking, black ooze. More than once, their chancy progress relied on the rotted hulk of a fallen log. The available, low hillocks to make camp became scarce, until dusk on the day they encountered no dry ground at all.

Arithon felled reeds to shore up the soaked hummocks. Cold wards wrought of Shadow defended their rest, with their watch shifts forced to go fireless. Another night passed, and another, swathed under mist and harrowed by the screelings and racketing wails that marked the relentless demise of the hunted. Filthy and chafed by dank clothing that wicked up stinking moisture from the sodden terrain, Dakar shuffled at Arithon's heels and cursed the hour he turned his back on the civilized outpost at the Taiffen bridge.

Silvery mizzle dimmed visibility when at last they encountered a solid landmark. The notched wall rose from the lapped seethe of the mire, a daunting rampart of moss-crusted stone raised of old by Ilitharis masons. The dry-worked seams showed the scars of repair, patched repeatedly since the Second Age. A massive, carved megalith scribed by the ancients loomed upwards, thatched with unkempt twigs where an owl had nested, fledgling young abandoned or devoured countless seasons before.

"This place is haunted by numinous spirit forms during the full moon." Dakar's low murmur cast unseemly echoes. No matter how hushed, intrusion here posed a desecration. The upright memorial marked the site of Condeleinn's doomed defence, fought to a blood-soaked standstill. Here, his death cry still wailed through the flux. The fraught extremity of his agony and despair echoed yet, for his heroic destruction of the *Methuri* driving the fatal attack had not stemmed the horrendous onslaught. A ravenous horde of the hate wraiths' Methspawn had broken through to rampage unchecked across Shand.

A Masterbard's lore recalled the epic ballad in full, stanzas recounting the Fellowship's intervention, backed by a host raised in the Paravian High King Kidorn Elrienient's reign. Heroic feats and tragic losses had thwarted the escaped spawn from infesting the River Ippash and reaching the sea. The aftermath saw Methisle's Guardian and Asandir labour to eradicate the invasive spill from the Methlas Lake watershed.

The battered wall from that chapter of terror survived, made fast by interlocked wards, with the acres of pools, opaque as sable ink, never since left unguarded.

In the shadow of legend, Dakar surveyed the edifice, mindful of the hitch in Arithon's advance. No awed impulse to pay reverence to the historic dead: the Mad Prophet parsed the reason and sagged, overcome by speechless relief.

The figure he sought loomed through the mist, a quiet presence so patiently still, the encounter almost evaded the rapt notice of mage-trained acuity.

The Master Spellbinder Verrain waited to challenge their foolhardy passage. Russet cloak furled, he held a stout staff of grey ash upright in hands marked by a whitened crosshatch of scars and healed bite marks. "You are not permitted to fare any farther," he informed in an antique, southcoastal accent. "Dangers move abroad during summer that abrogate my protection."

Arithon tossed his yoked bundle of staves and twined mesh over the kerb that rimmed the top edge of the wall. He shed and deposited the weight of his pack. Then he set agile hands to the stone and hoisted his unburdened frame onto the span. "I've requested nobody's guaranteed safety."

Verrain regarded, unmoved, the strapped nets at his feet, with their looped pair of hide buckets, tarred watertight as any fisherman's honest tackle.

"You will not meddle with the meth-spawned creatures laired here. I forbid you to remove any crossbred abomination or sow disturbance beyond the wall." With the disarming culture once admired by women in the ballrooms of royalty, he qualified, "Their ungoverned nature will bring harm to innocents."

"Do tell." Arithon's barbed sarcasm denounced gentility with insult.

Verrain never blinked through the blurred peal of echoes. "You would flout the gravity of my warning? Then you have no concept of the wanton damage such creatures may cause!"

"Any worse than the blighted religion my half brother has sown to cry havoc?" Arithon laced his hands over his tucked-up knees, prepared where he sat to resume his profane stream of disparagement. "What's a savage predator that lusts for warm flesh, before a self-righteous priesthood that peddles the poison of a fear-based ideology? Kill a babe, why not? Destroy a young mother, deaf to her pleas for mercy, then break her neck with less feeling than carrion on the pretext of her redemption in the afterlife? One monster deserves the other, I think. An unprincipled fight for survival as thrilling as pairing riled gamecocks in a pit for barbaric sport and wagers on the outcome."

Overshadowed by Condeleinn's monument, stunned speechless with dread, Dakar stared upwards amid the drawn pause between two stilled powers, while the fraught tension between them stretched deadly as overcranked wire.

Yet Verrain absorbed the barrage of sharp words. "This is no place for a specious argument over philosophy."

"Specious?" Arithon cracked, trained voice vicious with satire. "The True Sect has painted me as their manic image of undilute evil! Let's have a dark force aligned counter to Light and sow fear for the timeworn purpose of binding control on a mass mob of followers. Should I be distressed when the temple gloats at the discovery their Canon's created the nightmare to match the idea so exhaustively preached?"

"Has the priesthood done that, in fact?" Verrain regarded the muddy figure before him, the melting sympathy in his brown eyes acquired through meticulous centuries spent handling all manner of dangerous viciousness. "Take yourself in hand and stand up," he urged gently.

"Leave your half brother's religion to burn itself out on the emptiness of false belief."

"Why should I play the upright puppet for anyone?" Arithon disagreed, not contrite. "A venomous taint of truth to the brew might abscess the pustulous rot to a quicker extinction."

Verrain shifted the grip on his staff and shed his cloak with a calm almost sorrowful with apology. "I cannot allow that."

Dakar detected the ominous change in Arithon's bearing. Flicked by the fallen penumbra before cataclysm, he forgot himself, and cried out, "Have you lost your reason?" Shocked disbelief outpaced his astonishment. This break into fury was too scatheful and raw: a grotesque parody beyond out of character for s'Ffalenn integrity, far less the uncalled-for provocation levelled by a master initiate against an elder peer and a stranger.

"I have lost entirely too much just to keep a half step ahead of being slaughtered like a coursed rabbit!" snapped the Master of Shadow, now risen to his feet on the wall. "Once, I was cursed to destroy Lysaer only. I held to that until I found the means to break free of the Mistwraith's coercion. Aside from the friends lost to my mistakes and failures, I have tolerated, avoided, outfoxed, and left alone where I could, my half brother's armies, his spies, his crazed fanatics, and his zealot priests, whose lies pervert even the innocence of children. No matter how great the enormity of Desh-thiere's grip, Lysaer might have called a halt to the mummery! Well before Valien's execution, he damned well could have mustered the basic morality to lay down the mask! At least try to disperse a horde bent on criminal slaughter, nose-led by the trappings of noble rhetoric and the falsified sop of divine adulation."

"He could not," Verrain pointed out, his steel-clad equanimity a whisper to douse the flux flare of that searing outburst. "Your half brother cannot harness a faith-based religion too fermented in dogma to constrain. Nor can he win the fight to salvage himself. Not while renewed provocation on your part inflames the Mistwraith's directive."

"No," agreed Arithon, matchlessly bitter. "To stand down, he would have to renounce his addiction to vanity and quit the arena!"

"He is not yours to judge," Verrain corrected, his poised balance a warning unsheathed. "Mirthlvain's Methspawn are no weapon to be turned against even the most ruthless war host. Go back. Seek vengeance elsewhere. I forbid you to pass."

The adamant annoyance on Arithon's face chilled Dakar to the heart. Even the mire seemed to hold its foul breath through the gauntlet hurled down in defiance. "By any means, stop me."

Verrain booted the bundled gear off the wall. Net poles and buckets toppled with a splash, scattered ripples the instant attractant for predators aroused in a frothed surge to gorge.

"Now that," declared Arithon, "was impolite." Deceptively indolent, he crouched and extended his walking stave downwards to salvage his jettisoned tackle.

The ill-advised reach for recovery was thwarted. Not by the frenzied thrash of what thirsted for blood in the pool, but by the Master Spellbinder who stood steadfast as the Guardian charged to mind Mirthlvain Swamp.

Verrain spun his staff in a two-handed grip and launched the first whistling blow.

Duel

The knockdown blow to forestall flagrant trespass descended, Verrain's ruthless attack a cobra-swift strike of blurred motion. Arithon's recoil evaded the brunt. The staff grazed his left shoulder and frayed skin through his shirt. Cat quick, mage-trained reflex spun him onto his feet. His stout walking stave double-gripped crosswise, he parried the reverse stroke slashed at his knees. Brute strength met and dispatched his untempered resistance. The flat crack of impact cast echoes across the mire, overlaid and rebounded in ferocious exchange as the hammering sequence of blocked offensive and counterstrike cascaded one into the next.

Dakar backstepped through the suck of grass hummocks, hazed into retreat beyond whistling range of the clattering quarterstaves. The two masters closed in earnest and fought, a sinister dance partnered in relentless focus and light-footed steps that raged up and down the narrow stone buttress.

"Desist!" At risk of a trip on poor footing, Dakar shouted, helpless. "Arithon, stand down. This can't end well!"

The joined battle continued apace. Useless entreaty spared nothing. Unabated, the harsh bash of wood upon wood sustained, then increased the pitiless tempo.

Caught out at the sidelines, the hapless bystander could do little but bear horrified witness. Dakar at least owned the facile perception to call out foul practice. Yet Arithon's wicked aggression thus far adhered to fair play. Neither combatant tried harmful arcana. They wielded bare staves as conventional weapons, clean of crafted enhancement. An empty restraint that yielded no comfort, as feral exchanges engaged with skilled muscle unfolded at frightful speed.

Both aggressors were initiate masters, polished by experience to interpret their surroundings through the ephemeral crosscurrents that patterned the flux. Each informed their hair-trigger responses by charting the half-world potentia of probability. Schooled equals, both reacted to the warning kiss of disturbed air against sensitized skin.

Dakar watched with his fists clenched in petrified terror. Two such powers should never have met in adversity. Pitted against Arithon's early, blindfold training at arms, Mirthlvain's Guardian had honed his reflexes by handling Methspawn, barbed and taloned and unnaturally vicious. Bare-knuckled, Verrain's acuity routinely collared a coiled swamp viper's strike.

The murderous fury of his assaults outstripped reason.

Arithon's shorter stature and reach must yield to the driving onslaught that harried him backwards, then backwards again. Past the opening graze, he managed to stay untouched until the upright memorial looming behind cramped his belaboured shoulders. He sensed the impediment. Defeat should have finished him. All but caught at bay, he effaced a neat turn. His scatheful riposte darted backwards and forced the wrenched stall of Verrain's hammered parry. Staves clashed and slid. The bone-breaking, shed force of collision enabled the agile move that doubled Arithon back. He ducked beneath fatal punishment.

Shuddered by overstretched nerves, Dakar snatched a starved breath through chattering teeth. For how long could such merciless exertion sustain? When, before one or the other combatant took the horrific brunt and fell crippled or dying of injury?

The hairbreadth passage left both determined adversaries unfazed. Neither pleaded to defang hostilities. Stave smacked against stave with the steadfast aim to batter and brutally macerate: smash fingers, break ribs, or bludgeon white head or black to unconsciousness. The fight surged ahead without care for a fall, against ruin to a Masterbard's priceless dexterity. Matched form abrogated exhaustion, unslackened in deadly brilliance and force.

Dakar's scapegrace habit of betting at ringside contests won his admiration for the Master Spellbinder's elegant style. Verrain's exquisite gallantry and court manners may have derived from the cream of society before the overthrow of crown rule. But the young rake of that time also had been a peerless duellist no bravo dared challenge in earnest. In dazzling display against Arithon, that talented offence raised hackles for speed and artistic ingenuity. The madcap pace stepped up, and increased, as the stinging, immaculate sequences foiled and surpassed every devious measure the s'Ffalenn heir attempted by dint of inexhaustible, wicked invention.

Fatigue became the unforgiving impairment. The relentless mire redoubled the hazard, any disturbed fracas a perilous attraction. Increasingly agitated, aroused predators clustered in a fearsome rush to exploit the slipped step, or the moment's fraught inattention.

Dakar wheezed against the lump in his throat. He had seen Arithon renounce caution before, a paired combat as harrowing staged on winter ice against a well-tutored opponent's raw antagonism. The passage at swords against Fionn Areth had begun as a sham to set an arrogant boy in his place, until an inbound threat from armed lancers had burned off restraint. Like scorched wax, the purity of stylized sparring had melted off and turned ugly. Classic thrust and textbook parry discarded, the lick and peal of tempered steel had devolved to vile tricks dispatched in desperation.

No such reserve waited here in the wings. Extreme volatility marked the contorted fight that snaked on, back and forth, up and down the stone wall. Arithon waged today's wicked bid for ascendance with an atavistic ferocity beyond appeal. Perhaps, in fact, he strove for his life. His next, harried backstep skated to the wall's edge and hooked on the drainage notch cut through the curb. Verrain seized the advantage, swung his stave endwise. Lunged full stop, he wielded his staff as a lance. The flexible soles of his suede boots lent firm purchase upon weathered stone familiar as his home ground.

And again, Arithon's stunning agility dropped under the thrust. Saved from the killing blow sliced overhead, he caught his weight on his extended right palm, his freed pole swung left-handed as he rebounded. Upright again, whirled widdershins, he came at Verrain from behind.

But the Master Spellbinder already twisted to counter the riposte aimed to slam his exposed nape. The missed moment of full contact threw Arithon forward. In that second's stayed peril, Verrain pivoted. White hair bound into a tail for quick action whirled outwards and lashed his unbalanced assailant across the face.

No quarter given, features an unrecognizable rictus, Mirthlvain's Guardian hit back in recovery and unleashed the electrical fury of dire conjury.

The attack erupted, a blue-white current of lightning conjured without warning from nothing. Potent enough to cage deadly Methspawn, the crafted offensive spun into a net that laced down the spellbinder's stave with the raised voltage to stun.

Dakar crushed back a full-throated howl, knuckles mashed to clamped teeth. Heart-stricken, he gaped, paralysed by the certainty Arithon's magnificent, maniacal savagery must succumb to flaccid shock in defeat.

Severe cold bit the air. The rank peal in retort, neat shadow wrought from the element crackled back, dense enough to shear pulped flesh to powder.

The shock wave spanged cracks across ancient stone. Moss flash-froze to lace hoarfrost, while the abused atmosphere growled and shivered with muted thunder. Dakar's booted feet seized fast in the muck. Alarmed, he yanked loose before the ice gripped him immobile. Breath puffed through chilled lips, he swore in outraged disbelief. For Verrain was driven into retreat, the fist clenched to his staff blanched as marble under the terrible onslaught.

Panic wrung Dakar weak at the knees. The outcome forepromised evil. More, hostile movement frothed the black mire behind. Predators stung by the arctic blast arrowed in to glut on the windfall bonanza of carrion.

Horror choked the fraught moment as the searing flare of Verrain's next sally collided, counterplayed by flung shadow. The stressed clap of wind in recoil wailed like a derecho.

Light and dark tangled and flickered in primal discord, an eruption of naked force and braw element that sheared chips from the Paravian wall and scoured the named dead graven on Condeleinn's monument clean of moss as though polished. Both combatants remained on their feet.

Yet a shifted dynamic revealed joined opponents no longer evenly squared. Verrain possessed the longevity and trained stamina fit to outlast lesser men.

But Arithon's gift stemmed from primordial nature, a direct expenditure as effortless as breathing reflex.

Light and dark tussled, assaults exchanged with a fleeting intensity
to sow mortal terror. Dizzied by the relentless, hard surge of flux, and
stupefied by the massive draw from raw lane charge tapped by Verrain
to stay erect, Dakar also sensed meth-spawned horrors closing in from
behind. Bent against the gale-force scream of wind, skidding and
battered, he staggered for headway over brittle, glare ice to secure a safe
vantage beyond range. Arm crooked to shelter his face, he banged headlong into stone. The wall loomed above him. Summer humidity razed
from suspension swirled and whipped down, precipitated into blinding
curtains of snowfall. Dakar clawed his way up the Paravian wall. Barked
knuckles skinned raw from the climb, he snatched desperate shelter
behind Condeleinn's memorial.

None too soon: through panting terror, he heard the thrashed water
behind, heels drenched by the smitten-glass shatter of paned ice.
Mirthlvain's aberrations turned one on another, great flailing tussles of
annihilation that churned up scarlet jets and splattered gruesome gobbets
of rent meat.

Before him, the sorcerous challenge raged on, impenetrable to observation. The concatenation of opposed forces broke again and again with
the ferocity to annihilate, each concussive exchange of roiled matter and
fine energies sleeting like needles through nerve, bone and sinew.
Battered half-prostrate, Dakar cried out. Wrung by black despair, he
endured through what felt like the visceral scream that shredded the
marrow from the heartcore of the world.

Awareness returned, stripped of sensation. Dakar blinked. Alive, he
concluded, as vision resurged through the spinning wrench of reorientation. He had passed out, or maybe succumbed to a fit of black-out
derangement. How long, he lacked any measure to guess. Restored to
the semblance of functional reason, sucked faint by incipient nausea, he
gathered he lay prone on dank rock. The sharp air in his nostrils wore
the scent of hard frost, bitter ozone, and sterility.

The shocking stillness that unsettled his nerves in fact was the abrupt
contrast cut by the absence of violent tumult. The place where he
languished was not kindly or safe. The lethal seethe of Mirthlvain's mire
never in memory had been silent or still.

A close splash showered spray, fearful reminder that supine torpor
made him fresh bait, ripe to become chewed to a dismembered carcass.

Dakar groaned. He spat grit. The swarmed cloud of gnats he inhaled gagged his incoherent string of obscenities. Rolled onto his side, distressed and still muzzy, he squinted past Condelainn's marker. Hollowed by dread, cringing, he flinched from the expectation of carnage.

Instead, he spied Verrain. Mirthlvain's Guardian remained upright still in his tattered tunic and scarred leathers, bruised hands clenched on the battered staff that propped his slouched stance. Once sturdy, the ash wood was no longer whole. A black, splintered stump shortened the tip by an arm's length.

Dakar recouped shaken wits and croaked, "What happened to Arithon?"

Verrain stirred and glanced up. A vague elbow gestured leftwards. "Knocked down off the wall." Brown eyes troubled, he surveyed his damaged staff. "At the finish, I had to shove him bodily over the edge."

The Mad Prophet forgot his scuffed bruises and scrambled erect. "*He fell in?*"

"Yes." Verrain's faint smile crooked bloodless lips amid features drawn white with discomfort. "One of us needs to haul him out. Quickly."

"He doesn't deserve clemency!" Teeth clenched, beset by rattled distress, Dakar tottered forward a squelching step. "Forbye, you're not fit to save a drowned mouse."

"Likely you're right." Pained, Verrain inspected his fingers, mottled with purple and blanched milky with frostbite. "Did one of you carry rope in your pack?"

"No." Dakar's denouncement stayed savage. "Just blighted fish twine for nets!" Queasy from precarious equilibrium, he shuffled forward and peered over the inside curb. Arithon sprawled senseless below, a lumped heap of rag submerged to the waist, thighs lapped by jet waters thrashed to roiled spray and the slashed bubbles of sinister wakes.

Swarms of marauders fought and circled, maddened to frenzy to feast on limp flesh.

Dakar resumed his reluctant assessment. Snarled hair masked his view of unconscious features. Arithon's inert torso, hips, and outflung arms had escaped lethal immersion. But the compacted shelf of ice that spared him softened with melt in the absence of shadow. Already the mire claimed its vicious due. Clusters of tiny, brindled crabs scrabbled sidewards on toothpick legs. Other opportunistic shelled predators oozed at a snail's pace from the shallows.

Verrain marked the noisome invasion and sighed. "You don't want to touch any of those ugly critters. They have a mean bite and pack venomous stings. We'll have to scoop yon royal wretch out apace before hungry teeth make a meal of him."

"No more favour than that," allowed Dakar, displeased by the prospect. "The prize fool must survive on his own if he can. His master's initiation at Rauven at least taught him how to transmute deadly toxins."

"Maybe. Few surmount the attempt. Methspawn bites, even from small fry, pack an excruciatingly nasty kick." Verrain kept alert watch as the Mad Prophet scrabbled over the wall's opposite curb. Musing throughout the precarious descent, he added, "Though don't omit the Paravian sword. The advantage is helpful. At least Arithon's wearing his baldric."

"The maniac fought armed with that blade all along?" Startlement slipped Dakar's grip on slick stone. Thumped down on two feet, leery of slick ground and scuttling scavengers, he knelt gingerly and rolled Arithon over. Metal grated. Alithiel's black hilt scuffed a groove in pale frost, secured yet in Davien's handmade scabbard.

"Ath wept for convenience," Dakar remarked, sour. If the pesky crabs fled their unconscious prize, other starved predators surged to replace them. Too bothered to hoist, the Mad Prophet hooked the sword's stout leather harness and dragged Arithon's deadweight like a butcher's quarter of beef.

"Don't look back," remarked Verrain.

Dakar glared upwards. Hastened from behind by a walloping splash, he hauled his benighted parcel of trouble under the vertical wall.

Verrain leaned outwards, a shaky hand offered to help. Dakar grunted, manhandled, and heaved from below until Arithon's inert body overbalanced and flopped onto firm stone. The Guardian extended the sound end of his staff and lent swift assistance to speed the stout prophet's scramble from jeopardy. Then, acute discomfort ignored, Verrain crouched over his salvaged conquest.

"That sword's the luck piece that saved your daft friend," he husked. "Also, what kept you alive in the mire without escort. Did you realize that?"

Puffing, Dakar grunted an expletive.

"I wonder if our swaggering miscreant knew." Verrain flipped his stave endwise and poked something squirmy burrowed into his supine subject's sopped clothing. "Methspawn shy from that sword. Their instincts fear her long history. The major predators with rudimentary intelligence give an Isaervian blade a wide berth."

Nursing damaged fingers, Mirthlvain's Guardian drew his short belt-knife. He slit Arithon's sleeve and despite marred dexterity, dealt the mite nestled within a thorough inspection. "Parasite. Not fatally toxic, thank glory." Survey resumed, Verrain checked the frayed rents shredded through Arithon's breeches. He pried at a wriggling bit with his blade. The shelled critter disturbed from its gory repast squealed and snapped free, serrated mandibles still latched to a gnawed morsel.

Verrain flipped the carnivorous mollusc back into the pool. He scraped away several more, flicked off another snagged onto his sleeve, then wiped his befouled dagger on Arithon's shirt. "What's left are leeches, mostly harmless. They'll leave on their own when they've gorged. Or else perish, dried out, if they overstay their bloodthirsty welcome."

"Leave be, then. You ought to rest." Seated at wise remove, Dakar emptied his waterlogged boots in disgust. "Anyway, I'm not hanging around to count coup on the disgusting banquet. Where's your skiff?"

"Tied up to a mooring, a league down the wall." Weariness burred Verrain's resigned conclusion. "We need only drag Arithon a bit farther. Close by Condeleinn's memorial, the Athlien glyph in the shielding cartouche casts a limited ward of protection."

Dakar peeled off his slimed socks. He stamped puckered toes back into wet leather, too griped for vengeful objections. "Well, stand down and let me shoulder the work. I'd rather be rowing you back to Methisle Fortress straightaway. I need a brandy, and you'll have the benefit of a skilled healing too dangerous to undertake in this dreadful place."

Verrain did not argue. Nor, at this pass, did he waste his reserves to stand straight on his own. Dakar muscled Arithon's slack bulk by himself, the larking idiot dumped by instruction against the splotched pedestal of the Paravian marker. By then, wan sunlight sliced through the vaporous drizzle. Since Verrain languished from pain and exhaustion, Dakar lifted the battered stave, lent his support, and settled the Master Spellbinder's frame against his stooped shoulder.

They walked off, limping southward along the scarred wall, while the screelings and croaks, the whistles and splashes of the deep marsh swelled in racketing chorus behind them.

Arithon lay abandoned in a flaccid heap with the haunts that clustered at the site of Condeleinn's embattled defeat. Unnoticed, through tangled hair, his slitted eyes glinted behind sable lashes. He watched the Fellowship's paired spellbinders labour on their way and leave him in solitude.

Arraignment

Elaira shed the wheedling cluster of cats fixated on the unfinished meal shoved aside by her breakthrough, gestalt awareness of Arithon's egregious transgression. Alarm had her packing waterproof clothing and outdoor supply, before Kharadmon's agitation whirled through her unshuttered workroom and upset the flask utilized as a paperweight. Cats scrambled, chased to fluffed tails as the updraught lofted her piled notes helter-skelter.

One hand clapped to contain her flyaway hair, Elaira braced her rocked balance and tamed the tug of her flapping skirt. "I already know without further warning!"

Three days of exasperation, in fact, had scraped her nerves raw with the pending sense of inchoate catastrophe. The adamant barrier Arithon sustained against her most intimate contact had chafed suddenly thin. By fits and starts, she grasped something dire was amiss. Denied informed relief, she confounded the volte-face reverse, still lacking the detail of a clean connection.

Kharadmon gave her rankled acerbity short shrift. "I'm away, then! Dakar's laggard hand at the oar can't row the skiff back to Methisle fast enough."

"Verrain's hurt, too?" Elaira's distraught snatch for a winnowed page missed. Through the kited flurry of papers, and an errant sheet that muzzled her chin, she declaimed, "Don't let your enthusiasm capsize the occupants."

Arid sarcasm met the shade's pungent derision. "More likely riled Methspawn intent on predation would spill their cockleshell over first. Since they've reached Methlas Lake still afloat, the weather I tinkered to speed their swift passage won't disrupt the boundary ward at the shoreline." Calm marked an arctic pause for inspection, then, "For Verrain, you'll want your best treatments for frostbite."

"From Shadow? *He fought Arithon?*" Horrified, Elaira dared the shocked enquiry. "What happened? Is Verrain's survival endangered?"

"Of course not!" The gyre of Kharadmon's impatient recoil skated the littered folios under the furnishings. "Master Spellbinders are capable. I'm sent to assist because Mirthlvain's Guardian cannot be spared from duty through a prolonged convalescence."

Elaira swallowed. "How bad is he?"

"Laid up enough that he cannot row. And I've stalled for too long." Nailed by her undivided attention, the Sorcerer's clipped tirade changed focus. "Don't shove off after your handfast miscreant, either. Skilled surgery is required of you as Ciladis's apprentice. Then expect to stay on as Rathain's betrothed for an assize quite certain to finish with an arraignment."

"But—"

Kharadmon skewered her cry of revolt. "Sethvir insists. By fiat, he says Arithon's problem can wait." The gusty whisk of the discorporate's exit rattled the leaded panes in the open casement, gone before Elaira shoved her last steamed protest in edgewise.

Sucked off stride by the virulent backdraught, Elaira punched down her billowed skirts, swearing as the unsecured storm shutter banged shut and plunged her upset preparations into gloom. The imposed visitation pumped every dread fear, verified by the nagging, febrile ache arisen from her cross-linked awareness of Arithon's discomfort. No gift of insight suggested what ailed him. His mind and heart remained armoured against her.

Clueless and spurred by corrosive foreboding, Elaira ranted fit to murder, "Shadow be damned to the ninth pit of Sithaer!" What devil-some cause had led the man to wreak harm on a Master Spellbinder? "Ath's tears!"

Verrain's genteel nature deserved no such abuse!

Fuming on vitriol, Elaira tied back her mussed hair and stomped off to ransack her stocked shelves. To the olive oil, camphor, red clover, goosegrass and refined beeswax jammed into her satchel for simples, she added her sharpest knife. After the soft gauze and rolled linen for compresses, she buckled the flap with tedious hours to spare.

The skiff's run to Methisle Fortress could not cross ten leagues before midday, even hastened by Kharadmon's breezy conjury. She took time to change into rugged clothing, don outdoor boots, and thread her belt with a short dagger, game sling, and skinning knives. Girded for the worst and seething in pressurized determination, she folded the Biedar crone's knapped blade inside her two oilcloth cloaks, then a firestarter's sealed batts of greased lint in a corked jar, and wrapped up her unfinished packing.

The boat shed on Methisle's shore threw Elaira's wait into shade when Dakar landed the skiff on the spent curl of foam washed in by an unnatural roller. The flat-bottomed craft scraped aground on gravel sand, the bump jostling Verrain's inert frame on the stern seat. He lay bundled up to the chin in his mantle despite the muggy, noon heat. Elaira surged through the shallows, reached his side, and stripped off the suffocating constriction.

"Kharadmon coaxed wave and weather in our favour," Dakar huffed, defensive as he dragged the blunt prow towards dry land. "Can't blame me for the undue precaution. Not when I mistook Kharadmon's brisk arrival as another attack wrought of shadow."

The prickly shade bridled. "The *bother* you denigrate pushed you nigh onto sixty leagues overnight without taxing your arms beyond steering."

"As if I hadn't worn blisters enough?" Short of sleep from poling day and night through the mire, the nettled prophet sucked up the gumption to martyr himself, muscling the lion's share of his peer's prostrate weight.

Elaira waved off his belaboured assistance. "Verrain's not unconscious."

"Only tranced into a self-induced stupor to manage his intractable pain," Kharadmon interjected, then proceeded to douse the on-going scrap with facetious, bystander's advice. "Kindly bear him up on a litter to avoid waking him."

Still busy with measuring pulse rate and her swift assessment for dehydration, Elaira suggested, "Verrain keeps a high-wheeled hand-cart stored in the shed."

"Not that one!" Dakar ceased his piteous wincing over the galled state of his palms. "The cargo bed reeks."

He was right. Used to shift spawn carcasses for dissection, the vehicle stank like the putrefied dead.

"You've got a better suggestion?" Elaira's tart glance sliced across vacant air and goaded Kharadmon's superior inertia. "Surely your windiness might have the means to banish the smell?"

"That won't be needed." That incisive reprimand arose from behind. Asandir strode down the grassy slope, frowning and out of sorts from the rushed transfer that plucked him away from the catastrophic invasion of Caith-al-Caen.

"You took your sweet time," Kharadmon remarked, rankled. "If you're done saving daisies, and Esfand's come with you, we could put his young brawn to use."

Unfazed by the temperamental critique, the white-headed field Sorcerer side-stepped Dakar's gawping and waded into the lake. His sloshing, long strides rounded the boat's transom. "Rathain's steward stayed in Halwythwood where he belongs. The glaring offence under scrutiny occurred in Melhalla, besides."

Kharadmon's breezy maelstrom nipped the wavelets in Asandir's wake. "You left a *caithdein* just barely invested to stand off a hostile war host fifteen thousand strong?"

Rarely stressed, Asandir matched the shade's lambaste with steel-clad exasperation. "You've usurped Luhaine's place as a nattering fusspot. Kindly back off? I expect to return to enforce Daon Ramon's crucial defence before sundown."

The gaunt Sorcerer scooped Mirthlvain's Guardian out of the skiff, while Kharadmon's rebuff dwindled to huffy concern. Charter law deferred to Melhalla's sovereignty. Jurisdiction ruled first on the outstanding charge, then remanded the formal sentence for Rathain's crown seat to prosecute.

Asandir straightened with his shouldered load, his last word addressed to Elaira as healer with frightening diffidence for one of the world's major powers. "May I suggest we retire Verrain to the warded array in the watch spire? If you'll agree to a working in partnership, I'm prepared to assist."

The rank fool might test Asandir's granite patience to importune for the detail of Arithon's straits. Done was done, and the immediate crisis thrust onto Elaira demanded precedence. She stifled the flash-point anxiety that clouded the engagement of her advanced faculties. Discipline saw her remedies laid out in readiness. She kindled her brazier, while the field Sorcerer installed Verrain on the feather mattress Dakar had hauled like a packhorse up twenty-five courses of stairs proportioned for centaurs.

None disputed the location's urgent necessity. The six-sided chamber atop Methisle's oldest watchtower had been built of white quartzite. Light pierced its wide, airy casements, overlooking the lingering tatters of ground mist tinged blue by the clear sky without. Harnessed from the fifth lane's focus beneath, the refined flux current sang through the warded masonry. A polished-oak floor patterned with silver inlay gleamed like caught lightning, aligned with the compass points. Electromagnetic properties resonated above hearing, tuned to select harmonics. Peace banished distress. Bleak emotion surrendered to calm. The historic array laid down ages past by Ilitharis craft-work sped healing for Mirthlvain's recumbent injured and soothed the ghastly toll of fatalities.

Elaira centred her focus, while the Sorcerer opposite stripped to his shirtsleeves. Unfazed by the steep climb, Asandir commandeered her pannikin. Quarried features serene, he coaxed the water to heat, which freed her to infuse the warmed soak for debridement.

Concentration attended the delicate care that loosened Verrain's crusted dressing and gently unwound the stained wrap of Dakar's clay poultice. The appalling damage laid bare welled disheartened tears in Elaira's eyes. Thaw had ravaged the flash-frozen tissue. Blackened fingers suppurated to rot blighted the swollen, inflamed fissures to seeping lesions.

Agony roused Verrain from his deep trance, the seamed corners of his eyelids pinched by the severity of his suffering.

"Dear man, I'm sorry. You ought to have poppy," Elaira lamented, contrite. "Dakar? Hurry. In my still room, second shelf to the left, the distillate's labelled."

The Mad Prophet winced, prodded sweating from a wilted exhaustion propped up by the doorjamb.

"No need." Asandir knelt instead and cradled the stricken spellbinder's head. "Let Verrain stay clear-minded. I'll manage his pain. You pare away what cannot be salvaged. We'll channel in tandem throughout the subsequent labour of reconstruction."

Elaira steadied her shaken poise for the advanced process of mending in collaboration. The harrowing prospect was not past her depth.

The strength of two Fellowship Sorcerers had guided her acumen before, when Arithon's fatal trauma was halted to save him from an executioner's sword thrust.

Immersive focus replaced the distraction of her external awareness. Attuned to the marvel of Asandir's presence, vast force honed down to a knifepoint of precision far different from Ciladis's subtle, melodic calm, she did not hear Dakar's step in departure. When at length his wheezing effort returned with pillows, a basket of fruit, and a blanket, Verrain's hands wore the tender pink of new skin. Sweetened air held the astringent bite of the salve compounded to numb inflamed nerves, fragranced by the shaved-birch splints fashioned to forestall contraction as natural healing progressed under the restored blood flow.

Elaira soaked gauze in a red-clover infusion, Verrain beside her wide awake and responsive. Dakar slipped a pillow under his head. The kindness earned him a murmured thanks in court phrasing, while Asandir supported the spellbinder's arm for Elaira, dressing each splinted finger. "Can you manage in strapping? You'll be more comfortable if I finish with a padded mitt."

"No bother." Verrain returned a mischievous grin. "Dakar can cook."

Afternoon light slanted through the wide windows. The musk of the freshwater lake and green sedge mingled with the perfume of camphor and beeswax in the replete quiet of aftermath.

Elaira dared the fraught question at last. "What did Arithon actually accomplish on his excursion up Rockfell Peak?"

Asandir maintained his silence, head bent. Verrain kept his peace with closed eyelids. The pause held its breath, while the healer's touch that tended his mauled hand stayed relentlessly steady.

Less reserved in frustration, Dakar plumped down on his ample rear. "I asked the same thing. Arithon stated, directly, exactly nothing, but—"

Elaira interrupted. "Before you run on, I have a significant line of inquiry."

"Save my spirit!" Dakar yanked up the muddied wads of his stockings, tart with offence. "There's a point to be made *after this?*"

The enchantress's quelling glance seared. She tucked down a finished end of waxed gauze, and resumed, without pause embarked on the next dressing. "What did my beloved actually do in his passage through Mirthlvain Swamp?"

"Nothing, either!" the Mad Prophet snapped, fidgeted to annoyance. "He was thwarted!"

But Verrain, brown eyes reopened, surveyed Asandir's stone demeanour and allowed thoughtfully, "Nothing, indeed. Arithon carried two sturdy nets for live capture. His statement concerned an enraged revenge upon the religion for the unjustified death of a child. Inference prompted the reflexive comparison, that Mirthlvain's spawn were as wantonly malicious."

Elaira used cotton padding secured with linen to allow the left thumb's freedom of movement. "As though to pit one monstrosity against the other to inflict their just deserts, I can guess. The ticklish question is, who mentioned the outrageous idea of transplanting pilfered spawn in the first place?"

A cogent silence hung on that subtlety. Dakar buried a violent flush behind stubby hands, while Asandir settled the Guardian's treated wrist, snagged a cushion, and resumed his station on Verrain's opposite side.

"I thought so!" Elaira mopped her finger-tips on a damp towel, stretched briefly, then trailed after the Sorcerer's lead with her salve pot and gauze. "Am I right?" Intent on her work, she kept talking. "You made the connection yourselves and attached the motive implied by appearances. And once you suggested the abomination, naturally, Arithon gamed the indictment to unbalance you."

"Logic spurred our assumptions," Verrain admitted, taken aback if not contrite.

"As Arithon surely meant from the outset." Elaira's asperity devolved to a sigh. "Words are a bard's weapon. How could you miss his line of attack?"

Dakar blinked. "I don't believe his behaviour stemmed from a feint."

Elaira's tender ministration set the next splint. "No? Then what permanent harm ensued from the encounter?"

"Wait, Dakar. She's right." Verrain's savage wounding the issue that inflamed dispute, he remarked as the afflicted victim, "Arithon grasped the range of my capabilities beyond doubt." The prominent collection of Methspawn scars amply affirmed the adept opponent's capacity to surmount a severe injury. "Cast Shadow unleashed to kill does not support the finesse that counterplayed my offensive. I aimed to stun. Arithon parried with the exacting restraint to avoid leaving me crippled to incapacity. We've no clue what he wanted from the exchange. Because I shoved him headlong off the wall, I have likely spoiled our chance to find out."

"You haven't," Elaira declaimed, quick to sympathize. Pitched to wit's end by exasperation, she paused, finally trembling. "Since when has Arithon surrendered to anyone, except by his own design? No one's fathomed his actual motive. He's alienated his friends and burned all his bridges for privacy." Determination stiffened her spine, an invisible line crossed beyond all reproach. "Well, I intend to expose what he's doing!"

Stone still, and so shielded his presence had become overlooked, Asandir glanced up. Sudden and piercing as guarded steel, his stare challenged her declaration. "I don't recommend that."

"Free will!" Elaira blurted with heat. "I will not be stopped. Nor can I stand aside, until I wring honesty out of him. And no! Don't ask me to hold off again. I'll go on my own once Verrain is comfortable, and let no one *think* to prevent me."

The assembly for the assize convened with Sethvir's sundown arrival. Delivered by transit through Methisle's focus, he entered the hall's echoing, vaulted gloom with Melhalla's black-clad *caithdein* in tow, and Queen Ceftwinn of Havish, collected en route. Her cautious step minced, burdened by advanced pregnancy. Sulphurous light from the wrought-iron candelabra sparked off the heraldic gold thread of her scarlet tabard, and woke sullen fire from the Crown Jewels set in the diadem nestled above the realm's plain heirloom circlet. Pale hair and tourmaline eyes like new spring, she carried the dignity of her crowned office with incipient motherhood's long-sighted maturity.

Asandir rose from his carved chair. State solemnity regaled in midnight blue and silver, he saw the Queen seated, then installed Melhalla's *caithdein* at the head of the trestle. The older woman had lustrous, dark hair and blunt features, the swarthy complexion a throw-back strain of ancestry moulded over the square jaw of more recent s'Brydion descent. Verrain perched to her right to give testimony, gaunt cheeks and bruised circles under his eye sockets scarcely lessened by an hour of sleep. A full-sleeved grey robe belted with a russet sash freed his bandaged hands from constriction.

Dakar, as eyewitness, hunched, chewing his nails, sight averted from the piebald cat preening in the vacancy left by Elaira's absence. Short legs swinging in agitation, he had clammed up since the enchantress's diatribe punctured his huffy assumptions.

Queen Ceftwinn's grateful nod to a Fellowship Sorcerer's solicitude preceded the tensioned dialogue with asperity. "This is a dangerous moment to invoke formal proceedings for an infraction."

Asandir's flicked glance quelled the bristle of Melhalla's steward. "Halwythwood's peril is left well in hand."

Sethvir anchored the foot of the table, from nowhere equipped by a toadstool array of balled wool and an immaculate pile of knitting. The busy click of his ebony needles the mild front for who knew what working of powerful conjury, he murmured, "The compact binds our choice on the matter."

The Major Balance was inarguable: Fellowship Sorcerers did not violate free will. While their surety granted Mankind's right to settlement, the provisional interface hinged upon the probity of charter law. Realm sovereigns treated on humanity's behalf in direct liaison with Athera's Paravians; and crown justice executed punitive sentence, where human-kind's freebooting overreach threatened Athera's sacrosanct mysteries.

The Seven withheld from intervention unless a breaking disaster escaped those bounds of mindful restraint.

"We stand at the brink of the abyss," Sethvir allowed. The rapid clack of his craft-work unflagging, he acknowledged Verrain and Dakar. "Please present the account of the standdown in Mirthlvain mire."

The damning details unfolded, tempered towards mediation by the recounted defence of Elaira's perspicacious analysis. Until the reluctant prompt from Sethvir broached the hidden, dark vein of underpinned implications.

Asandir's gravel voice bore the weight of the ages as he outlined the serious complication that shredded all semblance of credibility. "The assault upon Verrain violated my warning, dealt last year after Arithon's trespass at Rockfell. How I wish that were all." Ramrod straight, laced hands locked before him, the Sorcerer wore the dangerous chill of raw power forcefully reined into check. "The problem in question originated ahead of the cursed taint that afflicted the half brothers, the latent seed sown much earlier, during the Mistwraith's subjugation at Ithamon. Wider evidence suggests more than desperation motivated Desh-thiere's intent to foil its defeat."

Dakar's dough face blanched. "You refer to the ambush at nightfall when—"

"Yes." Asandir inclined his head. "That unshielded encounter revealed the Mistwraith's embedded entities are intelligent and self-aware, human shades welded to a singular directive as an instrument of annihilation. Since then, these undead have evolved beyond a blunt force for destruction unleashed on this world by mishandling. The collective amalgamation derives from the exiles expelled beyond Southgate, a sorry sentence we Seven imposed when their insatiable quest for proscribed knowledge challenged the compact. The revenant individuals who identify as Desh-thiere recognized their bane in Lysaer and Arithon's elemental mastery. The cursed enmity they laid on the half brothers may entail more than the obvious, protective bid for self-preservation. Our latent suspicion suggests that the s'Ffalenn heir may have been Desh-thiere's actual long-term target. If Arithon was suborned as the wraiths' covert weapon, the double-blind tactic might one day turn his initiate knowledge against us. How better to breach our guarded defences and enable Athera's final conquest?"

Queen Ceftwinn shattered the riveted quiet, tucked forearms shielding her gravid waistline. "You knew this?"

Her shrill exclamation clashed with the stunned outcry from Melhalla's invested steward. *"Since when?"*

A cough pocked the quiet. "The incidental assault overtook the two princes at Ithamon ahead of Desh-thiere's warded containment." Althain's Warden laid his pale yarns aside.

Stripped of languid reverie, his regard met the scald of the *caithdein*'s speechless, appalled accusation: unthinkable, no, outrageous! that the Seven might nurse such a smouldering spark in a veritable tinderbox of nascent ruin. "You left my forebear, and Melhalla, inexcusably blindered when your prince shouldered Rathain's crown duty to defang the Grey Kralovir!"

"I know," Sethvir grieved gently. "We weighed that risk under provisional oversight, given our dearth of options to thwart Lysaer's allied force from becoming an unparalleled tool for necromantic predation, and also for the long-term chance to stem an apocalyptic disaster imposed by Desh-thiere."

The stark quandaries left unspoken acknowledged her stifled alarm. For the Sorcerers were altogether aware of the unmalleable perils sprung from an attack that once had forced Arithon's hand. The wider scope of today's aggressive predicament palled, darkened past conscience by his subsequent study of the horrific black grimoires sequestered in the annals of Melhalla's history. Before the stark fear, that Arithon owned the same in-depth knowledge expunged from cult practice at harrowing cost, Althain's Warden kept a terrier's grip fastened on Queen Ceftwinn's entitled concern.

"We confess your worst fear is not groundless." Sadness etched Sethvir's weary countenance. "Luhaine exhumed the proof, when he rechecked our defences on Rockfell Pit and encountered an attrition keyed by the purloined awareness of Arithon's mastery."

Verrain grappled the intractable catch. "Then the Master of Shadow's capabilities could have broached the ringed wards on the vault in fact."

"Sithaer's black pit!" Dakar howled. "That hostile stake is still active! You infer an infiltrated catalyst is lurking to poison our best hope of deliverance? Then how dare you trust Arithon in Desh-thiere's close proximity ever again?"

"We didn't," Asandir snapped, dry as acid. "You forgot you spent six months at sea for the purpose?"

Under cavernous gloom scarcely beaten at bay by the fluttered wicks of the candles, none cared to dwell on the malevolence of the scourge pinned in seething confinement: Rockfell's sealed crypt held the frail leash on a muzzled power of inexhaustible fury. Created to sterilize worlds, the Mistwraith bided in cold-cast calculation, from moment to moment poised to seize charge and smother all life until nothing remained.

"Desh-thiere was created by man," Sethvir lamented in finality. "Under charter law, crown justice is charged to keep Mankind's destructive free will in check. Or else our Fellowship sunders the Third-Age Accord, with our obligation in full to revoke the privilege of human inhabitancy."

On the shoulders of princes, Mankind's fate rose or failed.

"What you have is a muddle." Dakar's carping disgust ticked the salient points off his fingers. "Lysaer's about to rip rampant bloodshed through Caith-al-Caen, and Arithon's running amok. That pair's raised enough havoc to upend Athera. Between them, they've punched enough holes in unstable affairs to unravel the integrity of the mysteries."

"The man you name pariah also restored the Paravian presence, retrieved Ciladis, and dislodged the squatters entrenched at Etarra," Sethvir reminded, an absent stroke smoothing the fawning tabby just leaped into his lap. "The signal accomplishments in Arithon's favour lie above all reproach. His sterling probity has halted broadscale wars and replenished the resonant harmony for the Paravian return to Rathain."

"Or his spirit has soured," Queen Ceftwinn put in, the sparkle of her rings tracked from across the trestle by pricked ears and emerald eyes. "The s'Ffalenn scion may be as he's claimed all along, until Davien's inciteful provocation made him unmanageable."

"Facts are not speculation," the *Caithdein* of Melhalla remarked, as yet reserved on the alarming risk posed by Arithon's study of Kralovir necromancy. "By actual count, the concrete harm done is minimal. Innuendo and vicious posturing, maybe. The stark absence of evidence strands us with conjecture, baseless except where defiance of Mirthlvain's Guardian caused bodily harm."

"Only as much as I could sustain," Verrain qualified, not yet against nuanced appeasement. "Whatever Arithon's reason for trespass, I wielded grand conjury first. He matched me with Shadow. If, at all cost, to avoid getting stunned, his defence may adhere to a purpose. An offence that did not exceed my capacity begs a possible plea for restraint."

"That question becomes Esfand's charge to prosecute," Melhalla's *caithdein* corrected. "But a crown-sanctioned royal must be held to an impeccable standard. On one count, verified by Dakar's witness, Rathain's heir has broken integrity. We have a case for a criminal arraignment, laid against a farrago of unanswered questions." She sighed. "Given the damage took place on my turf, my indictment suggests a conviction for wrongful injury. No grounds for expulsion from the compact. Open to reversal, if Elaira's discovery eliminates ill intent, and pending Esfand's right to declare judgement, I recommend a punitive suspension."

The merit behind her analysis met Sethvir's approval. Since Verrain gave no reason for further objection, the Queen of Havish deferred.

Asandir's brisk closure settled the matter. "Consider Arithon's crown sanction revoked. Sethvir will set a star stamp on the document." Further, he tasked Dakar with the prompt recovery of the s'Ffalenn signet ring.

"What about Elaira?" Consternation broke the Mad Prophet's poise. Since the enchantress retained the heirloom in question, the appointed errand must chase her into the mire to retrieve the mettlesome jewel for royal posterity. "She's already gone, and stripped of that emerald, her entitled claim to crown protection lies forfeit!"

Misty gaze more concerned for the fate of his yarn, Sethvir rebuffed the clawed onslaught of feline play as he rendered last word on the verdict. "Handfast connection to Arithon yet bears the potential for a natural s'Ffalenn heir. A pregnancy grants our Fellowship leave to act, provided the lady asks for our help."

Verrain's kindly insight extended that tacit assurance. "Elaira has her own resources, Dakar, besides her years of study with Ath's adepts. Don't underestimate the specialized wisdom instilled by Ciladis's guidance."

"He foresaw this?" Dakar's yelp launched the cats to scrambling flight. "Then why did the Sorcerer abandon her under your roof, and why in Ath's Creation is he not here to edify us at this hearing?"

"Ciladis recused himself due to his personal connection through Torbrand," Asandir said, and, an oddly disingenuous spark to his eye, Sethvir did not contradict him. The unmentioned discomfort between them sat ill, that their authoritative oversight was toothless posturing: *for irrevocably, the crone in Sanpashir had sealed her ironclad claim to Arithon's fate.*

Nor could afterthought rest the disquiet shocked through the gathering's august ranks. Queen Ceftwinn shared Verrain's impenetrable court manners. Melhalla's *caithdein* steamed, clenched jaws fit to chew rocks. Behind Dakar's rumpled frown, anger circled the worrisome gamut of the incontestable accusation.

Chance thwarted the option to weigh dense uncertainties.

"We are unanimous," Sethvir pronounced, for no visible reason shot abruptly erect.

Some unspoken warning exchanged between Sorcerers prompted Asandir's courteous hand, extended to assist Queen Ceftwinn. "Out of time, too. More's the pity, your Grace. The world turns apace. We must take our leave straightaway."

"I am not yet in labour!" Her Majesty cracked, out of sorts.

"No," Althain's Warden smiled sadly, his finished knitting efficiently bundled, and both carved-bone needles tucked through his belt. "Your child's hour of felicity waits." He sighed, fingers preoccupied tidying the last snippets of yarn. "Poor timing that smacks of disaster, I know, but past Northgate, Ozvowzakrin's facing another rogue challenge from the exiled dragons on Sckaithen Duin." Shuffles of jockeying, pack rivalry troubled drakish successions as night followed day. But a duel provoked on the heels of the Koriathain's meddling disturbance demanded the immediacy of direct oversight in the field.

Cast a ripple too wide, and what one great wyrm knew, all others were rapt to discover.

Asandir met the necessity on his feet, the pregnant queen supported on his arm. "Let me also arrange a return for the *Caithdein* of Melhalla by way of Old Tirans en route."

Sethvir was as ruthlessly swift to dispatch the collateral problem ploughed aside by his urgent request. "I'll see word reaches Esfand at Halwythwood myself." The grim possibility of warring dragons by sheer scale eclipsed everything else. Ath show mercy, Lysaer's belligerent crisis in Daon Ramon must be deferred until the ninth hour.

The flux recoil sown by repeated, precipitous departures swept over Methisle Fortress and dwindled to echoed subsidence. Draughts winnowed through the gaped, double doors and streamered the virid cobwebs draped from the great hall's hammerbeam ceiling. While summer's amphibious chorus racketed across the night mire, cautious cats slunk from the recessed corners. Indifferent or wary, they stalked vermin through the taut quiet stretched between the two Master Spellbinders left on their own in the unsettled aftermath.

Fat and thin, clothed in dove grey and drab brown, neither one cared to speak. The ominous tone of the enquiry lingered, explosive revelations floated over the fraught depths of dangerous, ancient connections.

The import stymied all rational projection. The Seven had wrestled unimaginable perils through the lonely course of two Ages. If their guarded discretion was inscrutable, Elaira alone had been positioned by Ciladis to delve into Verrain's knowledge of healing and poisons. The adamant hush shrouding momentous events stayed as opaque as Arithon's intractable circumvention.

What implacable twist in current affairs did the Fellowship Sorcerers anticipate?

Propped in a disheartened slump, Dakar spouted off first. "The Seven grapple with something so terrifying, the undercurrents paralyse sense. Why am I stuck with the gut-hollow feeling Elaira's the only sane person determined to dig for the truth?"

"Go after her," Mirthlvain's Guardian blurted. The neatly bandaged hands in his lap stymied his urge to take action. Fond of the spirited enchantress, he *also* sensed the storm of probability rushing on towards nexus *when he could not row!* "Don't hesitate, Dakar. Take the pirogue. The craft's handier for skimming through shallows, and faster."

"The skiff's bound by a homing spell?" Dakar lifted a face pasty white, the clench of his moist fingers shaking. "You'll recall your spare boat after I overtake her?"

"Cast off anywhere in the open lake and the wind will shepherd the vessel's return." Mirthlvain's Guardian rose, decisive, and fumbled a key from the iron ring at his belt. "Travel outside of the second ringwall."

Dakar's shuffled tread trailing, Verrain moved stiffly ahead. Hampered by his dressed hands, he unlocked the barred closet beside the great doors, still immersed in rapid advice. "You don't want to test the hazards beyond, and as you love life, absolutely avoid the innermost First-Age defences!" Poked into a worn chest of drawers, he hooked out a black-tourmaline amulet strung on a braided collar. "This keepsake may guard your passage, provided you don't stir up excessive trouble."

Dakar side-eyed the offering with offence. "That's a damned talisman wrought for a cat!"

"A strong one!" Verrain protested, stung. "No lactating queen can defend newborn kits without mighty protection in these infested corridors." Too kindly to dwell on chastisement, he added, "The sword Alithiel will stay the worst predators, whether Arithon cares to wield her or not. You may also take this."

He extended his battered grey staff, the stubbed off end splintered and blackened.

The Mad Prophet stepped backwards, appalled. "I could never!"

"Deprive me?" Verrain's quicksilver laughter erupted. "Dakar, it's just a damned stick! But Methspawn don't grasp sentimental attachment. Mistakenly certain I carry a weapon, they are deathly afraid of it."

When Dakar still baulked, Verrain shrugged. "Suit yourself, fellow. I routinely cut and dry saplings for spares, given how often the stoutest wood gets bitten in two."

Liabilities

Quickened dreams lift the tempo of Seshkrozchiel's heartbeat, an ominous sign her deep hibernation ends prematurely, while Sethvir fears the prod linked to that restive change likely stems from the Prime Matriarch's subversive gambit to stoke the rebellious dragons on the splinter world to ungovernable, hostile agitation . . .

Far off in Kathtairr, under the brass glare of a lowering sun, two Sorcerers take pause from their labour to coax desiccate soil and barren rock to extend the tenacious foothold in support of green life; and under the prompt of Davien's regard, Ciladis affirms, "Yes. The assize is over. We're free to return . . ."

At nightfall in Daon Ramon north of the Old Way, light spills from the threshold of Lysaer's war-camp pavilion as a tactical meeting disperses; and knelt to assist the officers with their boots on departure, Dace Morley overhears the imminent mapped plan to unleash the armed conquest of Caith-al-Caen on the morrow . . .

X. Field of Glory

Sunset gave way to summer twilight beneath the canopied eaves of Halwythwood. Eventide dimmed the forest, the verdant profusion of moss and foliage glossed with lucent dew. The pulse of the lane current ran gravid near peak, as the singing band of Athera's electromagnetics streamed near the threshold of visible light. The meteoric splendour of dreams spanned the veil through the shortened nights, when resharpened vision might snatch the glimpse of ephemeral grace in reflection. Ten days ahead of the tidal surge that renewed the mysteries' wellspring at solstice, peace reigned undefiled. In the calm before storm, stars blazed adamantine white and violet, at consummate brilliance in the velvet dark of new moon.

The hour waxed late, the banks of the Willowbrook thrummed with nocturnal frogs and the musical voice of the falls. Esfand roused to an insistent shake that unravelled the ethereal beguilement of flux-bound sleep.

He grumbled and stirred, braced for a scout with bad news. Instead, Siantra's drawn features loomed over him, ghostly in the absence of torchlight. "Wake up! Quick. We've got trouble."

Esfand shrugged off her badgering grip. Clad only in breeches, he shed his blanket and groped shirtless for his weapons. "The Sorcerer's back? High time. Our position won't hold."

Siantra throttled the hopeful expectation. "Asandir hasn't returned."

Sapped to her knees, she faltered, drained by the fresh after-shock of her gifted Sight.

Khadrien steadied her poise from behind, the scapegrace's antics stripped from him. The fact he was here, and not rousting the camp, boded ill.

"What's happened?" Head bent, Esfand buckled his baldric.

"Nothing yet." But Siantra's voice broke.

Khadrien shouldered the brunt in her place. "Sian's scried a warning dispatched by *Sethvir!* The enemy war host will mount their forced march before dawn to claim the Old Way for trade through the Baiyen."

"Dharkaron Avenge!" Leathers flopped over his shoulder for later, Esfand yanked on his soft-soled boots, then reached out to lift the distraught seeress. "How can we help?"

Siantra swallowed, her clammy hand chilled in his grasp. Language failed to grapple the fleeting transmission seared through her sensitive faculties: *that some unforeseen disaster broken past Northgate had caused Sethvir's favourite tea mug to slip through his fingers and smash on the stone stair at Althain Tower.* "Expect the armed vanguard to be ravaging sensitive ground by midmorning, with the resonant stability of Caith-al-Caen despoiled as early as midday." Beyond rattled, she managed, "Asandir's not coming! The on-coming breach appears beyond salvage. We are charged to stand clear and hold Halwythwood."

"Daelion's tears!" Esfand shuddered, aghast. "The Paravian presence cannot help but bear witness. That gross an infraction's hell-bound to seal Mankind's destruction."

"No one else is awake, yet." Khadrien persisted, as though stubborn defiance might wring succour from empty air. "The scout relay has not been informed."

"Scarcely matters." Esfand vented his bitter frustration. "Like spawn in a puddle, we're trapped." Crushed under the frightening burden, he swore. "What sop do I toss to the war band? Ath forbid we shatter their mythical trust that *caithdeinen* know what's to be done."

Khadrien's elbow jabbed into his ribs. "Whip the dead horse we already have! Why rush to stir up useless uproar?"

"That's set to happen on my watch, regardless!" Anguish knotted Esfand's empty fists. "Even before Deshir's drastic losses, we lacked the teeth to defend the free wilds in Rathain."

"That's ragging on before we've grasped the courage to see straight."

Determined, Siantra recovered her nerve. "Let's retire to the great table to parley where we won't be disturbed."

Beyond rowdy bouts of drinking in company, clansfolk avoided the plangent trysting place where Arithon and Elaira had been torn naked from each other's arms: in particular when the dark moon at midsummer respun the emotional artefact branded into the flux. The past imprint indelibly seared by grand confluence resurrected the flare of love's anguish, a shot arrow keen enough to pierce a stone heart.

Khadrien flouted maudlin desperation by stashing an armload of unsplit kindling under the steward's vacated blankets.

"You sleep like a log, anyhow," he needled Esfand through snorted laughter. "Who's likely to notice the difference?"

"The end of the world doesn't kill your lame jokes." But Esfand's ebullience had rebounded enough to shove his cheeky friend off the riverbank into the ankle-deep shallows.

The massive, fallen oak appointed for their refuge had been split by lightning a century after the legendary impression unfurled by the baulked passion of crown-sanctioned royalty. The tree's Name was forgotten, though clan lore recorded the storm, sown by drake war, that caused the forest patriarch's demise. Myth held the bolt sprang from the plaintive, unrequited anguish of the handfast enchantress's cruel separation, while other tales blamed the back-lash on her prince's unreconciled anger.

Truth or fanciful embellishment, the sweat of clan labour had hewed the mighty table from the deadfallen trunk. Age and weather had silvered the wood's exposed grain when Esfand, Siantra, and Khadrien sought their furtive sanctuary under starlight. The superlative vault of live greenery soared overhead, encroaching boughs spanned by the timeless night sky, writ in patience to outlast the ages. Mortal and puny, the trio huddled for solace, where the lilt of the Willowbrook's current seemed too primal to be sullied by the on-coming spectre of ruin.

Irrepressible, Khadrien drew his dagger and scored an irreverent inscription. *'S'Idir loves . . .'*

Siantra slapped down his manic teasing, disgusted. "Fiends plague! Even here? Will you never leave off?"

"Who'll stop me?" Khadrien flashed back his most insolent grin. "While we're hopelessly stymied, doing nothing will scarcely restrain our tenderfoot hotheads in the war band from dying for glory rather than turn tail like whipped dogs scared to bloodless retreat."

Esfand's retort acknowledged the misery. "So help me, I'll force the lot to stand down at sword's point to keep them alive."

The *caithdein's* fury smoked, beyond words. Where were the Seven? How could the insatiable greed of the trade guilds be curbed before cult-driven ambition dismantled the inviolate sureties binding the marrow of compact law? Authority bore down upon uncertain shoulders, the weight of a craven defeat altogether too brutal to bear.

Siantra poked the rebellious spark beneath the smouldering outburst of anger. "Ath wept, Esfand! What are you thinking?"

"If *only* we weren't twenty leagues from the King's Grove!" Rathain's *caithdein* exploded, stung. "I'd risk flagrant trespass and plead on my knees for a direct liaison with the Paravians."

A prospect not only wrongheaded, but unthinkable, and a breach of royal protocol that bludgeoned sense for its breathless audacity.

"Well," Khadrien retorted with heat. "You are charged with the realm's weal by law." No blood prince stood for the designate wilds, not since the clan seeress received Sethvir's confirmed word of the Seven's suspension of Arithon's crown sanction.

"The lunatic notion's quite beyond reach." Siantra declaimed, through a pause that shook firm equilibrium like the subsonic tremor before earthquake.

Khadrien's curiosity ran riot, regardless. "Has any steward on his own merits ever ventured the site appointed for our attuned sovereigns before?"

Siantra puffed out a strand of snagged hair. "Does that matter?" The elder lore mistress, who might have known, was sequestered in Deshir with the mothers for safety. "The seasonal timing is deadly, besides." Crowned heirs of old had synchronized their forays for petition at half-phase, between the peak flux tides at full and dark moon. Never during the maximum crests concurrent with solstice and equinox.

"We made it through Athili," Khadrien scoffed, the wayward simmer of larking mischief agleam behind half-lidded eyes. "Anyhow, given the tinkering brass, who says Torbrand's grove is the only option?"

Siantra stared, blanched. "Save us all!" In fact, they sat a scant league from the forbidden pool at Thembrel's Oak.

"Baylienne's Gyre!" Esfand started and sat, his rigid spine jarred full length against solid oak. "Sian! You're seriously kidding."

"Is she?" Khadrien baited.

Nobody laughed. The feat referenced in legend had engendered a

resounding tragedy, not only for the feckless *caithdein* who had dared
to tread where humanity's disrupting influence was anathema.

Khadrien galloped ahead nonetheless. "My granddame would choke
like she'd gagged on a stick."

Warnings were dunned into clan children from birth: Mankind's
purview stood guard, but never risked the dire hazard of forbidden
ground exclusively reserved for the Paravian presence. The dissonance
of unshielded thought in such places afflicted the resonant harmonic
that upheld the mysteries, with potential to trigger a wanton cascade of
entropic decline beyond mending.

Esfand broke under the strained pitch of his agony. "What choice do
we have? The Paravian seers will hear the commotion. Let them come!
Call down their judgement upon me, and the back-lash would befall the
rampaging townsmen in equal measure." Siantra's caution threshed under
his ice-cold fury, he railed, "The prospect's surely no worse than the
certainty of a broadscale desecration at Caith-al-Caen."

In resolve that scotched Khadrien's sheepish retraction, he said, "We
can't sit on our hands and do nothing! I'm going. Siantra can hold the
vigil for me and keep watch at the verge." Resolute action freed paralysed
nerves. "Cousin? Inform the war band. You're to fill the s'Valerient seat
in my absence."

"That's slapdash nonsense, and the cavalier delegation of your succession's not just premature, but irrelevant." Prudence overruled, Siantra
killed protest. "By morning, the war band's response will be moot. You're
set on this course? Then we go together. Power strengthens by threes,
and our moment rides on the flux crest at midnight."

No footpath crossed the dense thickets of Halwythwood where Mankind's
trespass was prohibited. The deepest, mazed glens kept their secrets,
impenetrable to the tenets of the most gifted scouts' advanced woods
lore. To seek entry, the trio of fast friends bent upon venal intrusion
stripped their clothing down to the skin.

"I hope we're not feasting the midges for nothing." Rueful with
abandon, Khadrien peeled his britches, holed at the knees from mock
sparring with toddlers. He tossed his shucked shirt into a rumpled
heap beside the prim folds of Siantra's cached leathers and blouse.
Esfand, least dressed from the outset, fidgeted empty-handed, yesterday's clan braid tousled from sleep. Barefoot and naked to enhance

sensitivity, the companions pushed forward, steered by the heightened purl of the flux. Alive with the clarity of midnight's approach, the tidal flow of electromagnetics swirled into confluence, amplified by the underground springs that fed the Willowbrook's watercourse.

Tacit signals replaced spoken words. Alert faculties kept their steps silent. Sensitized talents trained for the deep forest, they suppressed their anxiety. Given Esfand's rash quest spurned everything sacred, they courted the historic pall of ruination cast by the s'Valerient ancestor whose disgrace haunted the family name before them.

The destructive course of Baylienne's fate was no fable from the distanced past on this night. She had pioneered the breach opened by Esfand's choice eight and a half centuries before, her desperation likewise birthed from s'Ffalenn royalty's absence when the Mistwraith overran Halwythwood. Grief and tears, earthquake and wreckage had forged the first links in the grim chain of consequence incurred by her violation. The resonant fracture sown at Thembrel's Oak had dimmed the fourth lane and buckled Rathain's etheric web. Steadfast intervention by the last circle of Athlien dancers had retuned the deranged harmonic and salvaged Athera's great mysteries: but not before the instability disrupted a tissue-thin trust, rifting the old order, at terrible cost.

For that decade's strife had hastened the wane of Paravian presence from Athera's free wilds, until the barren winter that Vanomind, third crowned to the lineage of the Ithalivier High Kings, faded and succumbed to despair. His tragic transition by way of Athili coloured the accession of Sestiend First Adaraquend, whose subsequent, failed stand on the field fighting the Mistwraith's conquest at Sanpashir ended in wasted exhaustion. The after-shock of his premature death saw a youthful heir crowned in resentful sorrow over his memorial flame.

Grief's canker was not cleansed by the rites: Parithain Second Adaraquend despised the desolate toll caused by Mankind's desecration. He abandoned the continent, fled into sequestered retreat with the battle-scarred core of the Centaur Legion's survivors. Paravian inscription, penned at Althain Tower, said Parithain broke the sceptre from exile, abjuring his throne on the very hour the last Ilitharis guardian, Tehaval Warden, ceded his post to Sethvir of the Seven.

Charge of Athera's mysteries rested in the hands of the Fellowship Sorcerers thereafter.

Until the fraught hour three friends dared to try the ill-starred course in Baylienne's footsteps: against the egregious pall cast by her failure, in brash hope that Ath's shining gift to the world was not spent, Rathain's *caithdein* defied the repeal of the charter's alliance sundered by Parithain Adaraquend. The companions beside him bid their young lives in solidarity, that the Paravians rebuilding Alestron would not surrender their sovereignty to humankind's depredation.

Here, where the liminal darkness beneath the crowned oaks enriched the registers beyond silence, untoward thought produced tremors that stormed the intrinsic rhythm of harmony. Root and thicket resisted their effort, the tangled way forward deciphered by touch. Coverts of ground laurel scraped their unclothed flesh. If regret woke the unsettled whisper of conscience, the profane imposition of speech smothered the sensible plea to turn back.

The gyre they ventured was untamed, not as the King's Grove, walked by attuned s'Ffalenn royalty for a legitimate summons to liaise with the Paravian presence. No such tempered transition sheltered humanity here, with the spiral into quickened frequency tailored to shepherd incarnate perception into the exalted range of upshifted harmonics. A sanctioned passage would broach the perilous verge, naked vulnerability anchored by an invested *caithdein* fit to stand steadfast vigil.

The volatile interface guarded within the sanctuaries of Ath's hostels saw petitioners escorted by an adept. In contrast, the wild mysteries ran fluid. Long before the core vertex at centre, the speed of reactive response became instantaneous, moulded by the thrust of enlivened consciousness. Contemplation fired conception. Emotional turbulence triggered the kaleidoscopic trajectory of experience, electrified by any active awareness brought into contact.

The extraordinary feat by which Arithon's plea came to banish the Mistwraith's influence had braved such a fraught passage when he fared beyond the King's Grove in Alland. Master initiate, and a sanctioned crown prince also born to Shand's royal lineage, he had stabilized his encounter with the mysteries by main strength and a lifetime's strict discipline.

Three unwise aspirants bound for Thembrel's Oak possessed no such practised control. Sliding through tangled leaves, shivering, soaked by midsummer dew, each grasped the rank scope of their ignorance.

Only legend, passed down through generations by rote described the thresholds to be crossed on the way: the dire portal of challenge that

would mark and measure them, and demand the surrender of unconditional permission. Beyond came the plunge into sensory dissolution,
where the firm limitation of known dimension re-formed into vistas
uncanny and strange, the myriad arc of the etheric template drifted from
the shores of their acquired experience. The innate existence of familiar
plants and animals became *other* – the patriarch tree beheld by Paravian
eyes no longer the native oak given the psychic structure of Mankind's
earthly origin.

Flesh could not withstand passage through the next veil, beyond
which solid form sublimated into pure energy. Corporeal cognition
dissolved, razed through by a sleeting surge of white noise and translated
anew on the virgin carrier wave that sustained the song and light dance
of Creation. Name itself, rebirthed from adept awareness, stabilized the
clarion signature that expressed individuality's patterned frequency.

Athera's titled Masterbards perhaps might command the depth of
endowed talent to traverse the third threshold. Arithon reputably had
done so while surmounting the final challenge imposed by the Maze
of Davien.

Esfand, Khadrien, and Siantra pressed on towards that ephemeral
crossing, unschooled and afraid, fear thundering to the percussive pulse
of rushed blood, and eyes savaged to tears by tingling waves of onrushing,
ecstatic dizziness. None marked the moment they stepped out of darkness,
the unmarked way before them haloed in rarefied light by the glimmering
aura spun off verdant foliage. Together, they burned, a fused star displaced
from the animate envelope of their mortal clay. How far they had come,
whether they had broached the verge and passed the lethal boundary to
sacrosanct ground, no referent between them might measure. Nerve and
sinew no longer recorded location. Bare soles failed to recognize the soil
underfoot amid the sleeting blast of the sonic whirlwind.

Beyond turning back, they could only go forward: through razing
force honed for annihilation and the unknowable terror of abject release.

And there, the impulse to relinquish their Names became arrested,
pulverized by a flare of purified joy too vast to encompass. A pillar of
fire erupted before them, a majestic, unbearable manifestation that unravelled the tenuous thread of conscious identity at close quarters.

Blinded by glory, Siantra cried out. Stunned conviction insisted that
she and the others faced death at Daelion Fatemaster's gate to Athlieria
beyond the veil.

Human eyesight failed. Mortal awareness was too narrow to encompass the immensity of the horned centaur before them. Hearing faltered, struck all but deaf by subsonic vibration as the mighty being addressed them. The lyrical cadence of actualized Paravian ranged through bell tones that resounded, a resplendent music fashioned to span the infinite arc of existence. "Pass no farther! Your appeal in behalf of the threat to Caith-al-Caen has been heard. Teirendaelient Merevalia will answer as Paravia's High Queen Regent. Though heed my warning: her intervention imposes a terrible choice upon Rathain's *caithdein*."

Summoned by Name, embraced by a tenderness matchless beyond compare, Esfand s'Valerient mustered the strength to stand forward. When speech forsook him, the Ilitharis Paravian, Kadarion, once guardian of Caithwood, answered the cry of his heart.

"The unsullied mysteries of Caith-al-Caen might be spared at the price of Lysaer s'Ilessid's destruction." Sorrow's reverberation tolled deep as the abyss, wide as the darkening moment exalted renewal hung trembling at entropy's brink. "Your Fellowship Sorcerers cannot intercede. Lysaer disavowed his burden of accountability in formal hearing before Althain's Warden." For the criminal practice of slavery, and for his arrogant, false claim to divinity, Lysaer had revoked his leave to inhabit Athera. "The severance cast his fate outside of the compact that holds Mankind in shielded protection."

Esfand reeled, undone by the quandary. Without Lysaer's birth-born command of elemental light, the Mistwraith's demise became forfeit. Desh-thiere's threat, unvanquished, laid against catastrophic damage to the shining web that sustained Riathan fertility: either threat imperilled the survival of Ath's living gift to the world.

Siantra contested the cruel conundrum. "May we not plead for a stay in behalf of Lysaer's transgressions?"

"Our power is bound!" Kadarion's grief scored the flux in lament. "Three times before an impeccable witness has Lysaer s'Ilessid disowned his birthright to claim grace! Twice, he turned from the guided release under sanctuary, offered by Ath's white adepts. Third and finally, he rejected my brother Kadierach's appeal for an unconditional redemption on the battlefield in Rathain. Self-imposed separation is not revocable under the Law of the Major Balance. Lysaer cannot be spared against his free will, even from absolute ruin."

"Then we find a deterrent." Khadrien trampled the ethical nicety roughshod. "I'd batter the idiot senseless myself, could I reach him before Halwythwood's wardings spiral into collapse!"

Esfand pursued the impetuous concept. "Is anyone in Lysaer's camp able to act? As Rathain's crown steward, have I the licence to request your help to deliver a warning?"

"One trusted retainer bears Asandir's mark," Kadarion allowed, a sonorous comment that implied hesitation. "Understand clearly, the messenger's passage under my escort by way of the mysteries cannot be accomplished incarnate."

"Esfand, you can't!" Siantra gasped, terrified. "*Caithdein* of the realm, your life is not expendable."

She would volunteer for the sacrifice instead, her hardened resolve betrayed by her outburst.

"I'll go!" Impulse moved Khadrien, first. Before anyone's stunned reaction prevented him, he shoved to the forefront. "Take me there!" he importuned the centaur. "Let me carry the burden myself."

Mortally human and small, the courageous hand reaching upwards accepted the ungloved peril of Kadarion's massive, warm grip. The towering flame of the centaur's presence intensified, a song and light cry that roared aloft. The resonant impact outstripped human consciousness. All referent frame of experience shattered. Exalted ecstasy too rich to withstand slammed the fragmented mind into a sere, bereft silence. Scorched by a hammerfall that smashed the frail spark of awareness, the bystanding pair left behind were plunged into the desolate emptiness of sensory vacuum. Cast adrift without bearing or guidance, Esfand and Siantra spiralled into black-out unconsciousness, oblivious to the chill bed of leaves that received their fallen bodies on forbidden ground.

While Khadrien's meteoric journey was other, a passage through the heart of the mysteries that winnowed pure spirit from breathing flesh. No longer the brash boy who seized Asandir's horse to return a Paravian forged sword to his prince, the young man who chanced the precarious choice to salvage the future did not embrace destiny as the impulsive fool. The action to spare his dearest friends seized the moment in adult conviction both right and true.

Conference in the war host's central pavilion finished after midnight, the finalized plan for advance upon Caith-al-Caen set under sealed orders to start before daybreak. Trim in the panoply of his state dress, a fearful, honed edge to his bearing, Lysaer saw his ranked officers out, their polished appointments and boots attended by his efficient valet. Morvain's grizzled commander, gimping with scars, represented three thousand foot and five companies of light horse. Pert as a ferret behind, the sallow captain from Narms led archers and pikemen eighteen hundred strong. Darkling's garrison captain, a taciturn stickler with matched cohorts of twelve hundred levied from Highscarp and Minderl, was trailed by the True Sect's ordained priest-dedicate, heading a veteran troop of five thousand. After them, with a rankled tread, came Jaelot's commander, his bearded neck thrust like a post from a tabard emblazoned in gold with entwined snakes and lions. His elite three thousand, bolstered by toughened men reassigned from the galleys, would harden the vanguard ranks dispatched at the fore.

Nails swaggered behind, smug as the favourite raptor preened to a pampered gloss on the huntsman's jessed perch.

Dace ducked the creature's dissecting glance, masked indifference pasted overtop of seething rivalry. He refused to throw over the unequal fight. With Lysaer's better nature once again fallen prey to intemperate influence, tonight's contest had been outmatched, the diviner's placed advantage at the officer's trestle unimpaired by the gadfly's attack from the fringes. Nails's strategic remarks and circling tread had wrung Lysaer's nerves long before his brusque dismissal ceded the field to his wary servant.

Nails bowed out in triumphant effrontery at the threshold, too wise to pry into the sanctum of Lysaer's quarters. Cautious instinct shied clear, with her set plan in motion. The master's glittering aura of majesty lidded a friable mood verging on dangerous.

The valet claimed his post. Brave enough to step softly, he closed the privacy curtain. The martial tang of whetted steel, greased hide, and oiled armour fell behind, along with the provocative view of the trestle spread over with tomorrow's tactical maps. The failing candles, used goblets, and untidy furniture thankfully were consigned to the steward's finicky turf.

Dace Morley alone fielded the galled aftermath of Nails's friction, his ironclad discretion and constant, deft handling the sole avenue left to blunt the aggressive thrust of cursed influence. He disrobed the master for bed. Let the soporific fragrance of warm beeswax blend with the fragrance of cedar and cloves, wafted from the clothes-chest propped open to retire the opulent weight of state velvets.

Yet tonight, those subtle palliatives fell short. Lysaer prowled the carpet, an irascible tiger flecked by the actinic flicker of his jewelled rings. Minute to minute, the nerve storm that chafed him rejected sleep, his inherent dignity overridden by burning obsession. A restlessness strung by unnatural influence outlasted the stalker's prod of Nails's needling. Arithon's brief use of shadow, days past, did not quite account for the manic, headstrong commitment to push the assault in defiance of Asandir's warning.

Apprehension pricked Dace to chills for the perilous, ignorant argument driving the overreach. *'The Fellowship Sorcerers are weak! What vacuous priority forbids cutting wood for a cookfire? Why not harvest timber for basic necessities? To save trees! The Seven do nothing but close our useful access to Halwythwood for the baseless enforcement of a frivolous creed . . .'*

Unwilling to bear the exploitive downfall of Lysaer's character, the valet fretted over the friable brittleness that edged his liege's distress. The trim shoulders cranked stiff under his ministrations did not ease as he freed the stud fastenings at collar and cuffs. He might as well be undressing a statue. The brackets creasing the downturned mouth, and the hardened, impervious eyes bypassed him as a stranger: the dread signs were frightening. The short interval left before the predawn call to arms made compounding a mild posset the measure of last resort.

Dace snatched his moment when Lysaer's back was turned. Practised at silence, he slipped through the privacy curtain.

Darkness enveloped the deserted pavilion. The pooled candles had flickered out, the single wick routinely left burning spent under the steward's neglect. That wrongness jarred. The absence of staff suggested late entry to tidy up had been denied. Not the watch captain's lapse: outside activity had wound down as usual, the patrolled encampment shuttered in nocturnal silence. The valet sweated the odd inconvenience, uneasy. By touch, without pilfering noise, he groped for the cartographer's striker. A prowler's activity would raise the alarm. War-camp discipline was unmercifully swift: the sword, before questions, met a sneak thief caught at large by the sentries.

Scared and alone, Dace tasted despair. The name of the vivacious young woman whose loyalty gave rash consent for her plight to a Sorcerer belonged to a ghost. Year upon thankless year, moulded piecemeal, the original person beneath the false skin became alienated beyond recognition.

Anguish had strangled hope, the more often Lysaer's besieged fate slipped restraint. The loss hurt too much, while tenacity broke, forced to watch what remained of the man fray away under Desh-thiere's malevolent hold. Trapped as the insect congealed in amber, Dace threaded the maze of disarranged chairs. He commandeered the cold candle lamp from the trestle, replaced the taper, but kept the wick for the moment unlit. Ruin would not find him complacent. Last card in reserve, Dace played the risk of using his ancestral faculties.

Unbridled, his talent sensitivity sank into the martial tang of greased armour and the cloyed trace of spikenard favoured by the True Sect elite. Eyes closed, immersed, he turned slowly in place and let his heightened awareness map the subtle detail of his surrounds. From the bitter taint of bronze-fitted furnishings, to the fusty wool hangings that gentrified the pervasive miasma of mildewed canvas, naught smelled out of place. Only the earthy scent of bruised grass, and the must of parchment and oak-gall ink, soured by mouldered leather and goosegrease, ingrained wax polish, and the metallic bite of forged steel.

And yet, something untoward niggled. A slight breath of frost wafted from the wooden stand that hung Lysaer's elaborate armour.

Dace shivered. Skin pebbled with sudden gooseflesh, he stepped closer. The mirror polish on his Lordship's gilt helm reflected his shadowy form, the white ostrich plumes at the crest billowed like hovering ghosts in the draught. Nothing looked amiss. But the constriction binding Asandir's spirit mark on his chest did not respond to a phantom. Dace eased nearer, wary. One step, two, and the Sorcerer's craft-work shredded through the seductive beguilement someone's furtive malice had cast to sow misdirection.

Vile language fell short. Braced for unpleasantness, Dace ran questing fingers up and down the scaled gauntlets and mail sleeves. Nothing. He patted down the enamelled breastplate. Nothing, again, until pain like hornet's sting lanced his touch. Nails had sequestered her wicked, spelled amulet behind the jewelled insignia on the ceremonial cross sash.

Dace disentangled the subversive talisman, unwrapped the thin, copper wire, and plucked out the paper strip coiled inside. Darkness smoked off the inked chain of sigils, which manipulative faction at play behind the diviner's allegiance beyond his able grasp to determine. Sulfin Evend's Hanshire background perhaps might have specified the arcana: Koriani in origin, or a temple perversion sourced from Erdane's unsavoury archive. Past question, its malignant purpose invoked the engagement of Desh-thiere's curse.

The vile atrocity forced Dace's hand. He twisted the inked construct into a spill, sparked the striker, and shoved the incriminating enchantment into the catch bowl for wax on the candle lamp. Flame flared. Seized by terror, he shielded the flickering light. Discovery would see him arraigned for dark practice, or worse, since the vile tangle of wire required a banishment dispatched with salt.

The flame spluttered out. Dace ground the sparked embers to ash underfoot, eyes watered by the acrid wisp of spent smoke. Now obliged to ransack the medicinal cabinet for simples stored under lock and key, he cat-footed past the hairline gleam striped beneath the bedchamber curtain.

But the graveyard stillness of the partitioned command post before him was no longer empty.

The apparition of a young man glimmered in the darkness, his pale phosphor form etched into the flux stream by residual animal magnetism. Denied breath to speak, the shade raised an outstretched palm and touched the Sorcerer's mark graven on Dace's chest. Contact snapped off a violet spark. The weak charge that anchored the revenant presence flicked out, vanished like a gale-blown candle.

Dace staggered back, dizzied, internal awareness stunned by the desperate message delivered by the surprise visitation. Khadrien s'Valerient, of Jeynsa's descent, had cast off the mantle of his living flesh as his last resort. Poised at the threshold of manhood, he had forgone his dearest wish for the choice to bear warning in time to turn the coalition war host from Caith-al-Caen.

More than his painful echo of loss overwhelmed the appointed recipient. No field commander, no person of power, the valet entrusted with his fatal entreaty was ill-suited to swerve a liege lord from the lethal directive of Desh-thiere's curse. Dace stood alone at the ghastly crux: *avert the advance of tomorrow's forced march or let Lysaer fall to his destruction and forfeit the power of light essential to the Mistwraith's defeat.*

Dace sank into a chair. Grey head reeling in his cradled hands, he agonized over the price in betrayal required to stem Lysaer's madness. If he wielded the blood tie that forged the dark glamour enabled by Kharadmon's instruction at full strength, perhaps he might sway his liege's fixation. But the intervention demanded a bare-faced exposure at the cost of his last precious foothold for trust.

No honest deterrent existed. No safe harbour for the loyal heart but the shameful perfidy of retreat. Dace smothered the agony. Shrink, and his oath to stand shadow for Lysaer signified nothing. Virtue traded for emptiness, with no worthwhile loophole remaining for salvage, and the wrenching sorrow of Khadrien's last choice passed over death's doorway for naught.

The encampment mustered in the predawn gloom, wakened to voices and the jingle of arms before the watch roster recalled the outlying sentries. Commotion upended routine at the picket lines, neighs from the horses selected for battle shrilling through the seethe of assembly before the advance. Servants scurried through last-minute chores and settled their masters' debts with the camp followers, handily ducking demands from the roustabout labourers caught short-handed in the bustle of packing.

Sleepless through the night, Dace freshened his grooming and brushed the creases from yesterday's livery. He greeted the guards. Unmolested, he completed his daily round to fetch heated water for shaving. His liege's finicky habits supported the pretence of routine. Dace postured through the semblance of the master's rising and dressing, insulated from oversight by rigid adherence to domestic protocol. If normal behaviour prompted no questions, the flimsy charade could not last. The inevitable discovery of last night's transgression must overtake him within the hour.

Lordly preference let Dace pass the guard, cheerful greetings exchanged as he skirted the officers' line at the cook shack. He collected the master's usual breakfast. The tray's contents still steamed, untouched, when the sentries outside the command post dressed arms and admitted the pavilion's first entrant.

Not an arrival of lowly stature: the approaching, firm step lacked the surly, scuffed tread of the page who assisted Lysaer with his equipage. Hag's luck brought Nails instead, with the sharp check to her impatient stride past the armour stand plain enough indication she noticed the absence of her planted talisman.

Yet Nails did not sound the alarm. The discovery of her thwarted ploy to skew Lysaer's judgement checked her no more than an instant. Then she resumed course, transformed on a breath to a stalking predator. Her next hesitation at the curtained threshold of Lysaer's quarters broke

Dace into a cold sweat. Flooded by dread, left nowhere to run, the valet braced for an adversary alerted by the telltale absence of waking activity.

Culpability settled to roost the moment the diviner burst through the flap and beheld the meddlesome, tinkering evidence beyond any hope of concealment. Lysaer sprawled in oblivious, drugged sleep, immaculate as a cut-marble icon under crisp sheets.

"My Lord is not dead." From the stool at the bedside, Dace met savage animosity, quiet hands clamped on his knees. "He asked for valerian to sweeten his rest." Had the page arrived first, youthful ignorance might have swallowed the liar's excuse, that last night's neglected candles and faulty eyesight had caused the botched dosage for a mild soporific. Not the diviner, aware of Dace's expert handling of drugs throughout Lysaer's prolonged convalescence.

Nails measured the fair, shaven features on the pillow at a rapacious glance. The immediate difference was striking, the untoward serenity of his Lordship's repose released from the sway of foul influence. Not hag-ridden, the light of Lysaer's innate character shone through, the quality stamp of s'Ilessid justice pure enough to pierce the heart to the marrow.

A sight Dace himself could not bear to endure, which lent him the backhanded courage to watch the diviner's hard-bitten ambition collide with the altruistic face of its nemesis. Such majestic stature laid out in comatose helplessness gut-punched the unprepared psyche. Whether Nails's shocked pallor stemmed from the impact of vulnerable mortality stripped bare, or if she bridled to find her faith's avatar suborned by callous usage as a servingman's game piece, her unguarded reaction fled as her temple indoctrination rebounded to chill calculation.

"You are not what you seem," the diviner declared, the consonants of atavistic accusation whetted for blood.

Dace huddled by the cot, the steel silence regaled in nondescript livery no longer harmless.

Nails's nasal snort derided the impasse. "Spying weasel, not to have fled when you could. I will have you arraigned. By Canon Law, as an agent of Shadow, a True Sect examiner will tear into your mind and expose your traitorous liaison with Darkness."

Dace stared back, level, through the dangerous pause, as the diviner's righteous antipathy curdled under the murderous, double-edged reckoning: for in fact, any charge of nefarious practice cut both ways between them.

Then Nails dismissed the counterthreat of her corrupt implication. "If anything's left beyond whimpering shreds, you'll be sorry you ever saw birth! Though at my pleasure your suffering must wait. Expect my restitution after your pathetic plot to forestall this morning's advance comes to nothing."

The diviner turned on her heel and ducked out. Her clipped instruction to the pavilion's sentries sent the idle squire for shackles and chain. Dace clung to his position at Lysaer's bedside, numbed by recognition his future was ashes.

But Nails kept the guards ignorant for her own ends, based on their subsequent burst of coarse laughter aimed at the page's expense. "That should scare the tardy brat something proper. A bout at the whipping post should correct his lack of enthusiasm."

"No." Nails poured scorn over the salacious innuendo, her correction without the damning detail. "The rough handling involves a servant's infraction."

One man sniggered. "Whose? That uppity stick of a valet?"

Nails crushed the gossip. "He's a heretic pariah not worth pissed dirt. Canon infractions fall to True Sect authority, besides. No fit taint for your marshal's exertion."

The mention of substitute help from an officer's equerry to assist with Lysaer's armament likewise was sent packing.

"I'll squire for his Lordship myself!" Bent on obfuscation, Nails spoke over her shoulder as she re-entered the pavilion, "If the High First Commander requests consultation, the hour will brook no delay. Tell him the formed ranks march as planned before sunrise. When the delinquent squire returns, hold the shackles for me and send him along to the grooms. Lysaer's mount must be readied to ride with the vanguard."

Brazen creature, Nails snatched the tweaked windfall of her opportunity. She donned Lysaer's splendid, chased armour herself. Sparkling in gold, her imposter's features concealed by the closed visor of the plumed helm, she stepped out and seized charge. None dared to challenge her guise as the master. A curt nod deflected the inquisitive steward. Usurped authority received the restraints, and appended gruff orders muffled behind the chased grille.

"Stand clear of the prisoner. No man's to be spared for the bother." The deferent guard bowed to her hidden spite. "The offender's to languish untouched in my quarters, which will not be dismantled until I see fit to detach a temple escort to take him into custody."

None had reason to question the unscheduled change. Quick-march protocol gave menial labour a full day to decamp the pavilion and relocate at the snail's pace of the baggage train.

Nails's bald-faced bluff carried on, the locked shackles affixed to the stout support post at Lysaer's bedside. Dace submitted without fight. Confined with his recumbent liege, he acknowledged his bittersweet victory, the drugged form on the cot at least sundered from the vulnerable morass of cursed culpability. Come what may, Lysaer would be spared from the coming debacle at Caith-al-Caen.

Love's witness had not forsaken the spirit betrayed for the future's scant hope of salvation.

The cause Nails pursued for her own end behind her brash masquerade only deferred the grim hour of reckoning. "Best pray your perfidious handiwork keeps your liege down while I secure the coalition's greater objective. Plead on your knees for the Light of his mercy should your master recover his wits before then! Swift justice, perhaps, might blast you to cinders before I unravel your secrets and seal your tormented destruction."

A blurred flash of gold armour, Nails spun to depart. She bashed through the curtain, her crisp egress marked at each stride by the brusque jingle of her stolen spurs.

Dace fumed, in hobbles. No more could be done. Nothing. An honest outcry would see him cut dead, while the aimed spearpoint of True Sect ambition and the covert string puppet danced to a more sinister conspiracy paraded untouched on a battlefield laid for disaster. The ill-starred endeavour for Mankind's gain embarked upon conquest, the unholy alliance of greed and blind faith lured to glory by a shining figurehead on a white horse.

The winded horn call blared at the fore. Echoes resounded the length of the assembled columns. The war host surged ahead, the multiplied tramp of fifteen thousand armed foot and pikemen timed by the boom of a hundred drums. In block formation, the companies mowed over dewed grass, the foam-white glimmer of dedicate surcoats interleaved with townborn divisions, proud colours muddled to monotone under the ebbing shadow of night.

Blazoned banners borne upright hung limp in the damp, gleaming chain byrnies and polished helms smothered in gloom as the host tramped beyond the encampment's staked torches. Both wings of light and heavy horsemen spurred restive mounts, tripled ranks of three thousand abreast, a steel-shod avalanche of packed horseflesh that mangled the virgin turf to a chopped pulp of mud and manure.

They left behind the detritus of dismantled camp tents, a gutted grid marked in rows where tensioned canvas caved in slow motion and bellied flat. Nimble boys uprooted stakes, swarming underfoot and chaffed by the wash-women and servants who loaded the stacked hoard of large-scale supply: the grain stores in sacks, the barrels of salt meat and hooped washtubs, the collapsed bricks of the ovens, wreathed in the steam of doused cookfires and the slogging bedlam of wagon teams led to harness.

Ahead, the pristine hills rolled away to the pallid rim of the southern horizon, Halwythwood's scalloped verge of treed canopy beyond view to the west. Eastward, a charcoal sky chalked with false dawn lidded the open expanse of Daon Ramon, for three Ages hallowed as the breeding ground for the Riathan Paravians.

Pearl grey, the crepuscular light snuffed the stars, then gave rise to the red caul of daybreak. Visibility brightened, the damp that fore-promised a swift summer shower enhancing the perfumes of tall grass, of moonvine, bindweed, and wildflower. The vista unfurled beneath burgeoning day wore, unseen, the flux sheen's bewitching, ephemeral resonance.

A delicate pearlescence that dimmed and dissolved, frayed away under clamouring tumult of battle-trained, human incursion. The blight spread, a dusky pall smudged by the armed ranks, the dyed banners of Narms and the velvet purple of Morvain felted to opacity, the scarlet pennons of Etarra's company to mage-sighted awareness less vibrant, dulled as though leached by filmed dust. Early zephyrs riffled the banners, tainted sour with the must of churned earth. Unsoftened yet by the first bloom of haze, the broad, trampled scar carved in rutted mud bisected the jewelled breast of the vales. Bugles shrilled. Drums bruised the air, muffled thunder reprised by the rumble of hooves, the barrage a crescendo of sinew and will bent to seize the Old Way for Mankind's fulsome ascendance.

The mizzle burned off to a cloudless midmorning. Sun blazed the tasselled grass golden, the undulant billow beneath stiffening breeze swooping over bright meadows renowned in the stanzas of legend. Men sang as they marched, the flushed panic of flocking blackbirds and wrens scattered like tumbling scrap cloth before them, until midday heat baked their parched throats to silence.

Their steps plodded, then, flesh scored to blistering misery as pack straps chafed sweaty shoulders. Exertion lathered the gleaming shine of groomed destriers no longer fresh. Flags and standards snapped to the gusts from the west, gilt tassels and blazons burnished in glare. Man and animal, the froth of excitement ebbed, until nothing spoke but the boom of the drums, beating onwards the pebbled, steel tide of armed industry. Vengeful retort for Etarra's demise, the massive host seethed behind the plumed crest of the golden avatar on the white horse.

Yet this fair country lay far from the stony foothills beneath the corniced peaks of the Mathorns. Here, no grant of way rights permitted the exploitive incursion of swaggering feet. On this hour, Mankind's acquisitive arrogance no longer received the benign neglect that had overlooked wanton trespass for centuries.

A deeper note thrummed on the wind from afar.

The sound wakened in counterpoint the treble cry of the bugles calling for battle. Readiness swept the coalition's front ranks. Pennoned lances lowered. Mailed men in trimmed squares levelled pikes and drew steel, fear and bloodlust primed for the charge.

No visible enemy crested the hilltop ahead. No armed force advanced to engage them.

Only the inaugural barrage born of an unworldly magnificence continued, swelled into a mighty crescendo that bloomed into manifest light empowered by focused reverberation. The dragon-spine horn of an Ilitharis guardian ranged the spectrum, above and below, shaking spirit and bone under a rolling crescendo of subsonics. The sonorous cry wakened rock and earth, and rang, shimmering, through the myriad range of aspected creation. A second powerful call joined the first. Redoubled harmonics climbed beyond hearing, compounded yet again as a third centaur winded the black, spiralled horn of antiquity. The trifold tones melded. The clarion summons fused Athera's electromagnetic net into a standing wave of resonant sympathy.

The rarefied burst of vibration soared outwards, a ring-rippled blow that reforged all consciousness caught in its path. Mineral, plant, or red-blooded animal, nothing within range passed unscathed.

Restored to their element, the centaur guardians stepped forth, a majestic presence emerged three abreast through the apex of the fourth-lane circle at Caith-al-Caen. Behind them, haloed in dazzling brilliance, came the sunchildren. Twelve Athlien dancers, male partnered with female in balance, they spiralled, revolving, the piercing, treble melody of their crystal flutes a sweet descant stitched through the sonorous depth of the Ilitharis giants' bass prelude.

A pavane not enacted on Rathain's soil for eight and a half centuries refired the foundational chord, igniting the ambient flux. Light burst, then blazed, adamant as a waxing star as the galvanized elements burgeoned in concert. Unstoppable, the torrential conflagration spilled over, auroric bursts of colour and sound excited to ionic incandescence. Culmination unleashed the fountaining flare that wakened the chord of grand confluence. Too ecstatic for hearing, too pure for sight, the exalted eruption shimmered and pulsed, octave upon pristine octave synchronized to a paean of unbounded magnificence.

A peak event past the scale of mortal tolerance hammered into the clay-footed dross of incarnate human consciousness. Unprepared, snared in the blind caul of their fatal ignorance, the forefront of the coalition war host encountered, full bore, the living Paravian presence. Shieldless, they met the transcendent impact headlong when the gyre of upshifted vibration stormed over their battle-formed lines.

Sinew and steel drilled to unity for the purpose of war became torn asunder by the concatenation.

Drawn weapons ran moulten in nerveless hands. Lancers lost control of mounts gone berserk and pitched like tin dolls from their saddles. Horses left riderless poured like a whirlwind through the stunned rows of the rank-and-file foot, the unfortunate overcome at the forefront crumpled to their knees and struck blind and dumb as their dense bodies blazed incandescent and burned, resistance scorched away by the galvanic force of electromagnetic overload.

The shock of annihilation caused no agony. No mouth screamed, reft of breath. The passion of human endeavour lost relevant meaning, severed at a stroke from coherent sensation. Birth-born identity abandoned connection to memory and sublimated, scoured clean by the primal surge of beatitude. No two-legged spirit withstood the unbearable paradox. No cognizant mind maintained self-awareness. The naked peal of Merevalia Teirendaelient's summons served a unilateral rebuke to eradicate venal intrusion.

The vanguard of the campaign's advance was annihilated outright. Staggered under the shock, the rear-guard reserves were afflicted to reeling derangement when the full-throated vortex that glorified life struck the upshifted frequency inhabited by the Riathan Paravians. Beauty unfurled. The blast of undefiled glory plucked the stunned air into wild harmony. Restored to Rathain by etheric transfer from their sequestered refuge offshore, the unicorns streamed into Caith-al-Caen. They reclaimed the ground forsaken since Desh-thiere's conquest. Burning with the fierce essence of joy too powerfully brilliant to withstand, a torrent like spun moonbeams made flesh, the herd poured across the summer meadow. Golden horns lifted, the silver gossamer of flagged manes and tails whisked over the land with the tender seduction of intoxication. Eyes could not behold Ath's glory, unleashed. Ears could not encompass the resounded cascade of melodic creation, magnified without end, beyond silence.

The unbuffered encounter outstripped the linear plod of incarnate consciousness. Scythed down at the flash point, any left standing who were not the initiate-trained, or the most hardy descendants endowed by latent clanbred resilience, fell prey, hurled into the surge past recall.

Time distorted and slowed at the shimmering crest. Movement hung, suspended. Flensed of separate identity, every born creature overtaken in proximity lost the instinctive reflex to turn away and take flight. Riveted since the first, winded horn call, the rear-guard reserves thralled at the crux were undone, riven asunder and lifted by wave upon breaking wave of explosive ecstasy.

Scythed down where they stood, their strewn bodies sprawled, help-less, lost utterly to the unsustainable surfeit of light when the Riathan Paravian charge sheared through and poured over them.

The potency of the heightened etheric was never fashioned for human endurance. Stripped away from their sensory perspective, none beheld the wild glory: the shimmer of the herd's combined auric flame refracting noon sun into rainbows. Stone sang, through the shattered spectrum of daylight. Emerald eyes with slit pupils of jet beheld all that existed in celebration. Riathan recognized each mote of being unsullied. The hallowed grace of their form, clean as cloud, cast no shadow: solid earth touched by the fleet passage of hooves dissolved into the pearlescent phosphor of supercharged flux.

Contact sparked instantaneous, transformative change. Forged metal for war cooled down, reconstituted to the primal lattice of mineral ore;

lance shafts and woven flax cloth relinquished their former, handcrafted constraints, realigned to the cycle of seed and decay. Tanned leather crumbled, and wooden implements took budded root in the teeming, warm soil.

Over each man fallen senseless, the golden horns dipped. A scything stroke, searing, touched them, newborn and defenceless, and stopped their hearts between beats. Overwrought synapses parted. Spirit winnowed separate from burdensome tissue and bone. Raised to answer the clarion peal of creation, Name rejoiced, reclothed in the full measure of unbounded origin.

Summoned in tenderness too sweet to deny, conscious awareness re-joined the dance that streamed undying throughout the bright realms past the veil.

None survived who bore the brunt of bare-faced witness. No spirit stayed earthbound, where unicorns ran with a beauty that blazed across the wild vales of Daon Ramon.

Summer 5929

Salvage

Dace Morley swore murder, tormented by the excruciate strain on his manacled wrists. The chain snubbed to the pavilion support post permitted him no relief. Crimped by his tethered weight, strangled circulation numbed his bent knees and both ankles to paralysis. The tight confines prevented the leverage required to slide his spine upwards and muscle himself to his feet, which reduced him to the dim prospect of trying to pick the iron lock over his head. Improvisation utilized the only inadequate tool within reach: at present the bent pin on Lysaer's jewelled brooch, knocked off the side table in crowded, close quarters while his captor shackled him in duress. Soft gold lacked the temper to spring him, even as the sharp end jabbed his finger-tips bloody when he applied torque and fumbled his grip.

The closed canvas sweltered under full day, the fetid air stifling. Lysaer streamed sour sweat, inert on his back, the oblivious quietude of his drugged sleep not destined to last. Without an herbal tisane for amelioration, last night's overdose of red poppy would inflict the torment of nightmares, followed by cramping and nausea.

Dace battled the diminished odds of escape, his plight and Lysaer's lost if he failed to win free before Nails returned.

Luck sided against him. The flimsy wire fatigued under stress and snapped off in the keyhole. Dace vented a guttersnipe's expletive that once prompted a cross aunt to slap a small girl on the cheek. Head tipped backwards to rest on the post, the servant disguised as an elderly man surveyed his dearth of alternatives. The blunt spoon lodged beneath the upset basin was too coarse for a probe, and the slender glass stem sheared off a smashed goblet, quite wickedly sharp, was too brittle. Dace repressed tears, his frustration desperate enough to wrench his brutalized shoulders in futile rebellion.

Shouts erupted, outside. A horse screamed in shrill panic and bolted, chased by frantic outcries and running feet. No spurious upset, Dace realized, alerted by the sudden, sharp tingle of Asandir's ward on his chest. Immediate fear for Lysaer saved nothing. Within a split second, the onrushing shift swept the ambient flux to mercurial incandescence. Dace reeled, deranged senses fractured by light. His ingrained spirit mark sang aloud, a note like struck quartz amid muffling darkness. Awareness slipped from him, furled into sealed silence by the Sorcerer's endowed protection.

Dace roused from the fevered dream of oblivion, spiked through the eyes by a smouldering headache. The rest of him sprawled against the toppled support post, heaped under the threshed ruckle of furniture and debris. He stirred amid the wreckage and discovered his shackles had broken away. The forceful, spontaneous demolition of forged steel defied his comprehension, chain and cuffs reduced at a stroke to flaked rust and unsmelted ore.

"Lysaer?" His shaken whisper raised no response.

Dace lifted his head. Thrashed by the incongruous rustle of sprouted leaves, he encountered a live branch and gnarled roots, budded from the demolished wrack of the pavilion's lumber frame. His stinging left wrist wore a livid burn, blistered over the site of Davien's enspelled bracelet. Collapsed canvas bathed him in trapped heat and the orange tinge of filtered sunlight.

Dace bashed the greenery aside and shouldered forward on hands and knees until, groping, he encountered the overturned cot, then the inert, warm body adjacent, still blessedly breathing. Lysaer was not conscious. Dace snagged a torn pillowcase, padded his hand, and salvaged the slivered goblet to jab a rip through the stout cloth overhead.

Fresh air poured through, redolent of crushed grass and the scattered ash of extinguished cookfires. The peephole vantage revealed pandemonium. Untended horses wandered at large through the welter of tumbledown tents and tipped wagons, the dismantled stacks of ordered supply milled to splinters and rags, and flung helter-skelter. Entangled bodies languished in heaps, threshed like flotsam between burst barrels flounced in burgeoning greenery, and flour sacks tufted with oat shoots and sprouted wild barley. A few dishevelled survivors moaned, rocking, their glazed stares vacant with madness. Others gibbered and wept, tearing at their hair, abandoned to desolate grief.

The valet shrank to imagine the fate befallen the advance troops marched at the forefront. He dared not linger, endangered himself if a single sane man in the lot was left standing. Lysaer's condition was bound to deteriorate, hell's deferred payment in recompense once his drugged stupor wore off. Dace sorted his urgent priorities. He firmed his muffled grip on the glass shard and hacked his way through the burdensome canvas with intent to purloin the necessities for a swift escape.

No burden of secrecy hampered Lysaer's extrication from the demolished pavilion. The fusspot steward was nowhere to be seen. A stumbling handful of bewildered staff were too dazed to take notice, and the wit-wandering sentries had forsaken their duty. Dace dragged his unconscious liege from the shambles, bundled him into a blanket, then scavenged at will to acquire provisions. Available transport was his for the taking, abandoned cart teams entangled in their harness, or left saddled and snagged by their trailing reins. Dace soon had a laden wagon under way with a choice string of mounts lashed to the tailboard. He whipped up the rawboned mule in the traces and drove north towards the banks of the Aiyenne, the afternoon sun blotting indigo shade across the dimpled turf of the war host's back trail.

More than evasion spurred his hasty flight. Before the rampant fear spread abroad by fresh news of a cataclysmic disaster, more urgent than vengeful pursuit by diviners, Dace minded the prompt of his ancestral instinct.

Riathan Paravians ranged once again on the free wilds of Daon Ramon. Mankind's illicit incursion was ended, the mysteries of eldritch legend returned. Informed wisdom chose the swift retreat to gain distance from the rampant flux charge shearing through proscribed ground. A safe haven did not exist at the concatenation of forces fast peaking towards crest with the on-coming solstice.

* * *

Far west of the tumultuous flux surge sweeping across Daon Ramon, the echoing footsteps of a Fellowship Sorcerer arrived with alacrity to meet the surge of the whirlwind. Ciladis returned to Althain Tower from Kathtairr, well warned he confronted the turmoil of a pending crisis. How desperately fraught, he failed to anticipate, until his rushed ascent of the spiral stairwell crunched over the porcelain shards of Sethvir's favourite mug. The spilled tea on the stone underneath had gone cold, the puddle yet to evaporate. The vivid impression recorded in water still imprinted the bolt-struck shock that preceded the impact.

The galvanic horror erupted as Sethvir's earth-sense witnessed five unmated, molt dragons defy Ozkvowzakrin's challenge, and dart through the North Worldsend Gate into Athera.

Ciladis surged forward. The cheerful swallows flitting in his wake took alarm, swooped through the arrow slit as he raced at grim speed towards the top-floor library. The Seven knew the striped pattern on those youngling wyrms devolved from a recalcitrant lineage. Get descended from Chesheticax's rebellious clutch, they posed enough devil-some trouble ranging at large on Athera to murder tranquillity. Piled into a knotty hour beset by problems begotten in triplicate, with every fractious Third-Age imbalance already festered for havoc, their truant foray skated into the knife's edge of the Paravian races' return.

Lengthened strides left the telltale fragments behind. Blue-and-white-patterned glaze flickered under the shadow of Ciladis's fleet upwards course, quickly replaced by the winkled reflections of sky shafted through the tower's pervasive gloom.

Atop the last landing, through the oak door, the wide windows let in the slate-grey lour of an inbound storm front. A gaunt silhouette notched the squall line of anvilheads. Sethvir leaned on clenched fists at the opposite rim of the round obsidian table, hair white as fluffed milkweed down screwed into snarls. Such lapsed grooming was nothing unusual on bright days when the air of daft reverie fronted his mild agitation.

Except the wizened, innocuous face of the pixie wore its furrowed frown with a warrior's ferocity.

Ciladis crossed the carpet in sharpened concern, afternoon dust motes stirred to the whispered flap of his wool mantle. "Sethvir?"

The query rang through a pause sealed in silence, until the Sorcerer whose broadscale sight ranged the world turned his head. "I need you. Quickly."

The appeal reverberated, splintered echoes embellished with multif-aceted imagery: of the coalition war host sprawled in lifeless windrows across the vales north of Caith-al-Caen. Like tide wrack, the corpses lay twined in living runners of grass, grazed by loose horses still saddled and trailing the straps of torn bridles. The surrounding air shimmered, burnished yet by the fluorescent sheen of charged flux, rinsed golden by the unicorns' passage. The sonorous chord ranged yet beyond hearing, of Ilitharis guardians' dragon-spine horns winded by threes, and the sweet, bell-tone descant of crystalline flutes played by the Athlien dancers: a calling to spin the wild mysteries to a confluence lost beyond witness for a thousand years.

The quivering imprint of ecstatic resonance sparked a thrill that unstrung Ciladis's poise. Dark features stunned pithless confronted Sethvir, who stood, also stricken mute. Eyes the turquoise tint of spring dawn met and locked with the healer's: no mild glance warmed by serenity, but the fierce, flat yellow of the tiercel emerged in the bind when untenable choices caused wrenching sacrifice.

The stark plunge into sorrow woke a wistful longing for the lost haven of Los Lier's protected peace. Yet the hour's imperative could not be softened. Ciladis greeted his beleaguered colleague, his sonorous baritone a tonic like music upon rampant tension's plucked nerves. "Five fractious molts were never the threat that deferred Asandir's intention to bolster the defences of Halwythwood."

Sethvir prevaricated. "I have Kharadmon tracking them." No easy task: serpents who remade creation at whim might blend seamlessly, anywhere, while they chose not to be found. Reckless, disruptive, the boisterous young were most wild and dangerous at the cusp, before their first mating established their sex at adulthood. The drive to lair in the volcanic seeps where crusted lava flows were the most volatile made them vicious, swift to pick territorial fights. A seasoned discorporate, even with Kharadmon's agile wiles, could do naught but deflect them. Restraint and expulsion back to Sckaithen Duin demanded an incarnate Sorcerer's help in the field.

The intractable reason for Asandir's absence burst from Sethvir in a rush. "The molts slipped through because the Protectorate's Gatekeeper came under attack." No mere challenge by rivals: the Warden's shared image revealed a black expanse of sea under moonlight, waves streaked in reflection by multiple streamers of flame.

"A combined assault!" Ciladis viewed the record of a concerted aerial battle waged with intent to annihilate.

"The Accord Treaty stands yet." Sethvir relinquished the details, his tone gruff with worry. "Ozvowzakrin survived, injured. But Asandir's left holding Northgate alone against the wrath of a gravid female."

Ciladis pulled up a chair and sat down. "She's aligned with the younglings?"

Sethvir shut his eyes, the ink-splotched fingers of the archivist clenched in his sleeve cuffs. "Their matriarch rules them." The brunt saved for last, he exclaimed, "Save us all! She's no less than the vengeance-bent spawn of Chesheticax, damn all to her destructive venom."

Stakes could scarcely be worse, should a great wyrm of that lineage set her next clutch on Athera. She would lay her eggs in the most ancient, geological canker: west of Ettinmere, where the fault line stitched the continent from north to south, and crossed the subduction zone that buckled the active ridge of the Skyshiels. A disruption aimed to upend the ancient Concord's binding peace and seed a drake war of extermination, likely to trigger a massive sundering fit to make a mere pittance of the eruption that sank Mhorovaire beneath the Westland Sea.

"The dastardly timing's deliberate, I fear." Sethvir scrubbed his temples, beyond distraught. "Though bedamned if I care to badger Sanpashir's crone for her answers to pertinent questions."

"She may not know with certainty," Ciladis reflected. For a people whose language regarded all states of being as animate, without distinction between past and future, few might guess, besides, whether the Biedar culture placed value on any one planet of many inhabited through their extended history.

"All outcomes sway in the balance," Sethvir allowed, harried to scraped irony. For the abysmal scope of the drake threat, now rising, shaped a cataclysm to breach the orb of the world and rip the abyssal deeps of the oceans. Quakes might buckle the Paravian continent, gouted magma opened like bleeding wounds as the mashed crucible of plate tectonics convulsed with a violence to reforge the face of Athera. A decisive advantage for the rogue dragons opposed to the Accord: their insatiable thirst to wreak havoc would rejoice to rout Third-Age co-existence by fire and cast down the old races' rightful sovereignty.

Asandir would not swerve or break at the forefront upon Sckaithen

Duin, though his languished affairs past the Gate fell to ruin as the vulnerable breach opened up at his back.

Ciladis triaged the bitter priorities, though his healer's calm felt the rubbed salt in the sores chafed by centuries of stopgap, short-handed choices. "Since Davien's wedded to his own business elsewhere, and Kharadmon's overfaced, hunting molts, should I join forces and drive them at bay, or have you another lapsed problem more urgent?"

Sethvir blinked eyelashes misted with grief, the pending task for his colleague's assignment a sorrow to wring the most steadfast of heartstrings.

Dusk stole over the deep glens of Halwythwood on the hour Ciladis entered the gyre centred by the pool under the ancient crown of Thembrel's Oak. Behind him trailed four gentle horses on lead reins, gathered from the herd abandoned at large past the field of the fallen at Caith-al-Caen. The Sorcerer slipped their bits and left the animals to browse a safe distance from the resonant upshift at the verge of the wild mysteries. The reverent step of his passage turned no moss-crusted stone, where the frequency steepened. He harmed no sprig of quickened greenery. Wild creatures watched him with liquid eyes, not startled to flight. In listening silence profound enough to decipher the language of a forest forbidden to violation, he followed the imprinted trail in the flux left by three steadfast companions the evening before.

Desperate fear and apprehension spoke through the cry of their courage, sprung from tender youth, stainless ideals, and innocent folly. Each one left their individual mark.

Esfand, scoured yet by the shame of his crown prince's brusque dismissal, wore grief's brand overtop a father's death and the recent scars of armed conflict. Maturity's burdens set him at odds with the whispered uncertainty he might fall short of the *caithdein's* mantle thrust on him. No longer care-free, the daring that once had taken the clan holding's green-broken horses at break-neck gallops over the meadows.

Siantra, resilient as willow, wore her tall build gracefully as a sylph, the black flame of the talent seared open since Athili a long-sighted gift almost past her capacity to bear. Quiet truth, and the sterling strength of Sidir's lineage rooted that core of extreme sensitivity. She read auras readily as once she had scented wild beehives and elusive patches of woodland strawberries. Childhood's sweet tooth long since had become self-contained. Armed with cool reason, she braved the turbulent trials of the present behind an immutably grounded reserve.

Of the three, Khadrien's impulsive nature shone the most vivid: thin-skinned and alive with an untamed exuberance that seethed over wiser restraint. Rules checked his behaviour no more than spent smoke. His inner landscape was an open page, but for the one treasure kept private, the tender, hidden vulnerability he guarded dearer than life. Ciladis continued, pierced through by pity. For he knew, oh, he knew: the gyre's upshifted resonance was too powerful for secrecy to withstand. The well-spring of the greater mysteries broke down and subsumed all defensive barriers at the first threshold. More than brash loyalty, Khadrien's undeclared love for Siantra had thrust him forward to claim the honour of sacrifice.

A loss rendered useless if Ciladis did not proceed swiftly. Though the sweet chime of the flux rushed his nerves to beguilement, two other young lives teetered at the precarious verge of the veil. Merciful Ath, the Sorcerer prayed, let him find them before their uplifted awareness strayed beyond reach.

Ciladis pressed onwards, where the scatter of rainbows dissolved into the rarefied range above visible light. The song of unfurled life soaked his being, where Halwythwood's greenery shimmered, leaf and twig dipped in the mercuric sheen of raised flux. Here the cloth of incarnate existence thinned and lightened, earthly senses frayed into the buoyant, unbounded perception of the unfettered spirit.

Apprehension and concern fell away, too dense to withstand the grand harmony that infused the ephemeral octaves. Ciladis set foot at the boundary, where spirit left flesh, and a centaur guardian had challenged for trespass. And there, Esfand s'Valerient, *Caithdein* of Rathain, and Siantra s'Idir sprawled on the mossy ground, naked as birth and entangled in each other's arms.

Ciladis knelt. He laid warm palms on flesh not quite grown cool as the grave. Beneath marble stillness, he clasped each limp wrist and waited for the slowed heartbeat, then the sluggish lift of the rib cage, the reflex to breathe attenuated and shallow. The strength of clan lineage had withstood the exalted shock of Paravian contact, the frayed matrix of human consciousness not yet subsumed by the fever of back-lash derangement. But the heightened experience sustained at close contact had been amplified to near-shattering force at the perilous proximity of the mysteries at Thembrel's Oak. Both spirits, unmoored, were cast adrift.

The Sorcerer worked quickly. His skilled touch stroked inert torsos and knitted the unravelled streamers of life force. He sought the reflex points and stemmed the bleed at the breach, until the faltering stammer of pulse under his finger-tips slowly steadied. As vitality stabilized, and leached skin flushed pink, he hesitated. Complication hindered his effort to coax the strayed spirits back to their incarnate awareness.

Khadrien's impulse to spare his dearest beloved had not leaped off the precipice alone.

Hurled into the bore, beyond incoherent, Siantra's keen instinct had recognized the crossing point of no return. Survivor of Athili, unalterably changed, she could have let go, swept away on the tidal flood of an ecstasy beyond reach of human cognition. Instead, firm survivor, she expended herself to spare Esfand, binding her last scrap of aligned intent to anchor the friend who was Rathain's indispensable *Caithdein*.

"My brave dear," murmured Ciladis, beset. "You saved him, and your-self." But the heroic effort had fused their separate consciousness into a single, merged entity.

No salvage for their condition existed here, where the explosive blaze of heightened electromagnetics ran beyond dangerous. Ciladis shed his grey mantle. He wrapped the limp pair of them with reverent care, thankful his astute forethought had prompted him to bring horses.

For one among many born to a storied lineage, the latest s'Valerient champion lay cold on the ground, never to rise irreverently laughing. Death had parted Khadrien's spirit. Ciladis wept, burdened with bearing the cous-in's body away for mourning. Bitter the price of Lysaer's survival: the brash redhead descended of Jeynsa and Sevrand rested replete, laid out unmarred in his twentieth year by the hallowed hand of the centaur, Kadarion.

Irrepressible youth, Khadrien s'Valerient had forgone his last wish. Parted, never to kiss the black-haired maid long admired in tongue-tied awkwardness from the sidelines. Ciladis paused in his task, overcome by ineffable sadness. Siantra s'Idir might not ever know how desperately Khadrien s'Valerient had cherished her. Inept at affairs of the heart, her deepest admirer had fled courtship to end his petrified fear of rejection. Behind, he left a woman more meaningfully significant to him than any historic accomplishment. He was gone, without thought for the monumental endeavour that enabled the salvage of Caith-al-Caen.

*   *   *

"Siantra."

Name, spoken aloud, rang through sound into light, an imperative cry that pierced like a blade and severed her enthralled awareness. Heat and cold, heaviness and bright anguish wrenched through a distanced awareness loath to return.

"Siantra."

Mandated clarity shattered the caul, broke her away from the consciousness of the friend she had shielded, whose tenacious strength, in his turn, had become her safe harbour under enthrallment.

"Siantra! Awake!"

Tender compassion compelled a response, shaped and matched to the weave of her sundered consciousness.

Siantra s'Idir opened unfocused eyes, shadowed by a dark figure laced like fire with shimmering gold, bright as the thread woven through the jacquard of a fine sarcenet. She felt the breath leave her lungs, thin as spring breeze, then wrenching pain, as though an inseparable part of her had become severed.

"Esfand," she gasped.

A soft touch sealed her lips. "Let him go, as you must. The moment has come for you both to remember yourselves and return to your birth-born heritage."

The impact of speech was raw noise in her ears. Siantra turned her face away from the being whose imperious summons netted her in what felt like the nadir of an unendurable solitude. She closed her eyes, lanced by regret, and shuddered to the well of spilled tears. "Khadrien. Ath wept! He never told me."

Ciladis gathered her close and smoothed her black hair, as her mother had done when she cried with skinned knees as a child. "He could not outrun the reach of your talent."

Siantra said nothing. Words drowned in the surge of bewildered grief that unmoored her like tumbled flotsam.

"Esfand is alive," Ciladis qualified gently. "I am sorry for what may seem needless trauma, but for necessity, the pair of you had to be parted. Not forever. Only until your inner boundaries and auric fields have time to knit back together and heal."

But they would not emerge as the same individuals, who had entered the crucible of Baylienne's Gyre.

Bereft beyond measure, Siantra battled the brutalized onslaught of human sensation: of wind through green leaves, too unbearably loud, and blaring, coarse colours that assaulted her unshielded sight. The wool cloth that enfolded her limbs was abrasive, and weighted her chest to suffocation. Like enveloping lead, her embodied existence felt unresponsive as being buried alive.

Ciladis's patience embraced her raw nerves, his calm through her distress undemanding. Though she wept, distraught, she had enough dignity to stifle her upwelling flood of agonized questions.

"Esfand's recovery continues in Halwythwood." A neat fire burned in the night forest, where the Sorcerer had fashioned a campsite, rich with the near scent of tethered horses, and arched with trees studded by the scintillant spatter of stars.

In darkness, the Sorcerer's form was a shadow draped in pale grey, no longer illumined by the magnificence of his aura. His shielding locked down till he seemed an old man, he volunteered presently, "You may accompany me to meet Traithe in Lanshire, provided you care to accept our invitation to learn the nuance of speaking to dragons." Eyes gold as a wyvern's gleamed, turned her way, folded in crinkles of veiled amusement and the intoxicant promise of wider horizons.

"Why?" Barely intrigued, shackled fast by raw pain, Siantra fastened upon the diversion.

Ciladis took a moment to answer. "Because you have the extreme sensitivity and restraint to master a skill that soon will be needful. Should you grant your consent? I cannot reveal more. A purpose fit to set my colleagues aback must bide in due time for unfoldment."

Siantra closed her unearthly, pale eyes, luminous as a fey pool lit by moonbeams. Already, the splendour of ecstatic dreams faded into a vista of bleak desolation. Sighted talent reeled amok through the interface and grazed against *something* no eavesdropper's perception should have disturbed. Tingled by uncanny dread, she recoiled. Her aghast whisper slipped past constraint. "Who will tell Arithon?"

The stopped movement of the air on her skin recorded Ciladis's sharp stillness. "You've strayed into the morass of a deadly gameboard to be asking me that pointed question."

"You're in league with Sanpashir's crone," Siantra accused, ripped through by another, more violent grue.

"Spit into that gale, come along, and find out." Startled when the seeress under his care did not pressure him for a response, Ciladis tucked the blanket over shoulders too slender and young for the ancient hooks snagging Arithon's fate. "Please, my dear, let everything rest. Acknowledge the triumph your striving's delivered. Because of you and Esfand, and the full measure of Khadrien's selflessness, Caith-al-Caen is yet whole. For today, the balance sustaining the future is stable enough to stage the next round of contention."

Accounting

Mewed up like the jessed hawk in his tower eyrie, Sethvir parsed the extent of the on-coming crisis, stalled but not deflected by the ninth-hour salvage enacted at Caith-al-Caen. His watch gauged the shifted array of fresh impacts, as pressure relieved in one crucial arena transferred strain through the weave of vulnerabilities sited elsewhere. Althain's Warden split pen nibs and stared down the abyss, harrowed by foreboding as the templates of change sped the grim tempo of forerunning probability.

Few moments in history had faced such a gauntlet. The load-bearing axletree sited at Northgate spanned the continent southward to Forthmark, with every thorny snarl of Third-Age entanglement strung taut as cranked wire between. One weakness would snap the frail links of connection. Any slight misstep, and all things hidden that shaped the fair face of Athera would cascade to ashes and entropic ruin. Sethvir brooded, beset. Dread without parallel shaded the offworld storm of the drake war ignited upon Sckaithen Duin.

The night stars blazed above the tower's cracked-open casement, untouched in their remote serenity. Yet Sethvir's entrained focus bent towards the east where twilight darkened the terminator, and summer's eve dawned bejewelled with dew across the wild vales of Daon Ramon. Last night's triumph there set spark to the recoil, the momentous upshift launched by the Paravian return surging towards the peak glory of tomorrow's solstice.

Flux tide kindled the vortex at Caith-al-Caen, harbinger of a grand celebration lost to Athera for desolate centuries. Athlien dancers prepared once again to refire the fourth lane into exalted confluence, a ritual cleanse of residual disharmony to refigure the flame that lifted the undying course of the mysteries to flower.

Today's blight in that setting, the penumbra forerunning latent tribulation snagged on the frayed strand ever poised to unravel the tissue of Mankind's precarious destiny. In collateral impact, the war host's desecrate invasion forced in full the long-deferred call to account: reckoning for expulsion from the compact overtook Lysaer s'Ilessid's cursed fate at long last.

His imminent plight left the Fellowship Sorcerers no legitimate standing. Slim hope of reprieve, and the Mistwraith's defeat, hinged on the fractious gamble of Daliana's initiative.

Lysaer recouped his befuddled awareness, marooned in pitch-darkness between the feverish welter of drug-induced dreams stitched from incandescent colour and noise. His weak effort to stir banged his knees against the rims of hooped casks and planked wood. Uprooted from his accustomed privilege and comforts, he realized his limbs were jammed into a crude conveyance that bumped and jostled and creaked. Pain like dull knives shredded his rational focus. The reason for his straits eluded him. He groaned, spasmed by nausea that threatened to rip him in half. Bile burned his rasped throat. His wracked gut was empty.

Then his sloshed senses spun, wrenched to a halt. Someone gruffly male snapped off an epithet straight from the back-alley stews.

Lysaer retched, helpless.

Evidently not baseborn, the voice resumed in an inflection genteel and Etarran, "I'll be spitted to roast over coals for my trouble." The unseen speaker concluded without rancour, "You likely have fifty fiends' worth of headache splitting your cast-iron skull."

Sick and miserably speechless, Lysaer shut his gritted eyes. The wretched conveyance – a mule cart? – rocked under him. Two hands reeking of oiled harness seized his throbbing head and lifted the tied swathe of rag that blindered his vision.

Daylight splintered through his crusted lashes. Lysaer recoiled, riven by agony that roared through his temples like a smelter's flame.

Someone peeled back his eyelid, not gently enough. Glare scalded his unshielded pupil like a white-hot needle jabbed through to his brain. Perhaps he cried out. Freed by a flinch that cracked both of his elbows, he subsided, too anguished for humiliation.

"You aren't going to die," his tormentor admonished. "The hangover caused by withdrawal is passing, based on the reflexive response of your iris."

A thankless tug slid the crude blind back in place, no favour to his condition.

Lysaer subsided, sweating. Blurred movement above him melted into thumps of disturbance as barrels and bundles around him were ransacked one after the next.

"I'll mix a tisane to settle your ills," his captor explained. "I'm sorry, not warmed. Can't risk a fire even if I dared to pause here."

Glass chinked. Lysaer shrank from the flask pressed to his lips. The sloshed liquid tippled into his mouth overflowed and slopped down his chin: a bitter tea boiled from willowbark, with an extract of peppermint steeped in grain spirits. Swallow, and he was sure to be sick. Hard fingers clamped to his jaw declared otherwise. His nurse-maid seemed determined to hound him, whether or not he owned the inclination to master himself.

The tepid dose reamed his innards with a caustic kick that belted his cramped stomach into surrender, an efficacy that suggested his valet's traitorous touch.

Lysaer lay flat and fumed. Memory resurfaced of the campaign assault, with his order for a predawn march overshot by a damning, blank bout of involuntary unconsciousness. Discomfort eclipsed by dawning, incredulous anger, he husked the imperative question. "Who are we running from?"

Impertinent, Dace evaded the query. "What do you recall?"

The wretched cart creaked under shifted weight, then jerked into forward motion. Milled like chaff in the racketing crush of loose contents, Lysaer lacked the fettle to protest. Shoddily treated as second-rate goods, he weathered the onslaught, wedged in unwashed fetor between barrels and sacks, and the clanking assemblage of tripod and chain secured to a field kitchen's cooking pot.

Lysaer suffered the indignity with steaming resentment, robbed of just recourse as the poppy's lingering influence dulled the sparkling edge from his fury. Satisfaction escaped him. A milder soporific laced into the remedial draught whirled him limp as spent rags and sucked him back into oblivion.

*　*　*

Lysaer resurfaced at length to the rank fust of mildew, spiked by the excruciate discomfort of a stretched bladder. The knotted blindfold was gone. His itchy scalp suggested the same, sour cloth now muffled his untidied hair. The itch of yesterday's stubble offended him, rank as the flecked daylight seeped through the muffling burlap someone's cavalier hand had tossed overtop of him. Everywhere poked and prickled by grass stems, Lysaer sprawled on bare ground amid the cart's emptied goods. The site was uncivilized, the mild slope of an open meadow clogged by noon heat under green, summer air like steamed cotton.

Nausea and his throbbing headache had subsided to bitter thirst, and the sandpaper of a parched throat. The abusive privation scourged him far less than the rifled state of his dignity, beyond frank embarrassment if he failed to answer the urgent means to relieve himself. Primal need confounded his thwarted demand to make sense of his savage predicament.

His gingerly effort to move earned a savage kick on the ankle.

"Stay down!" The whisper rebuked him as though he was common. "We've dodged a southbound supply train, just barely. Patience and luck may deliver us."

That upstart scold galled his stature past bearing. Lysaer flung off the burlap, dazzled to vertigo and hacking oat chaff from his nostrils.

"Damn you!" The insolent valet let fly, propriety sloughed like the skin off a snake. "Can't you park your testy arse for one moment? Now we're stewed! The rear-guard had a slovenly laggard who's reined in and wheeled his mount this direction."

Lysaer's ire exploded, his flare of contempt chipped with consonants. "I will not piss my breeks for the inconvenience." Levered onto his elbow, he shrugged free of the sackcloth and mastered the woozy effort to rise. Pride finished the requisite few tottered steps. Back turned, he seized his urgent relief without toppling into the puddle.

Dauntless under the valet's scorching glare, Lysaer added rancorous, "Why am I skulking from my loyal allies? That outrider's blazoned in Morvain's colours!"

"You're unfit to stand." Exasperated, Dace grabbed Lysaer's forearm and sat him down before his knees buckled under him. "Liege, let me handle this."

Lysaer bridled, sapped by weakness and draped in a dressing robe that made a travesty of state authority. Outrage curdled to imperial ice, he slouched against the jumbled barrels and watched Dace seize the wilful, free rope to hang himself. More times than not, the same tactic brought cagey ambassadors to loose lips and hard downfalls.

Except swimming senses unstrung the incisive subtlety. Lysaer cradled his swaddled head in cupped hands, set aback as his hearing ebbed and resurged through the roar in his ears.

He blacked out momentarily. When the stutter of unreliable faculties again registered nearby movement, restive hooves gouged the bruised turf to his left. Shadow raked over the jumbled supplies, cast by a corpulent rider's rapacious dismount.

Aggressive suspicion scathed through the jingle and ching of rowelled spurs and assorted steel weaponry. "Are you carking daft?" The officious bray of irritation notched upwards. "What skulker's mischief brings a lone wagon this far afield in rough country?"

Dace's mild excuse did not carry, unlike the flash-point retort.

"Do I look dirt stupid? Stick me for a jape! That cock-and-bull story's ripe enough to hatch maggots! No courier, ever, bears the news from command by posted dispatch in single harness. What I see is a rattletrap cart, crammed chock-full of contraband. Dark-bent Shadow's damnation, I've hauled for supply long enough to recognize marked casks and grain sacks tax-branded as troop requisition."

Dace scoffed back, nonplussed. "I don't see the sealed writ for a swaggering hireling to waylay my mission."

"Mission, is it?" The rider's hawked phlegm smacked into dry ground, punctuated by an incredulous guffaw. "That's bollocks from a pilfering sneak! Fancy livery like yours can be had for a bribe, or a tumble flipped on a wink to the laundress."

"My credentials state otherwise," Dace rebutted, crisp. "Disregard what I've said at your peril! The device on the signet I carry outranks the moth-eaten badge on your sleeve."

Ringless, and stunned livid by the discovery, Lysaer stirred. His imperious surge of revolt brought the slap of the valet's driving whip on the barrel that buttressed his back. Astonished to a confrontational pause, Lysaer grasped the outrageous scope of his forcible displacement. Spirited off without senior staff, and no official appointments, he reassessed his appalling position. Under no possible circumstance should his sovereign seal have been removed from his person. That criminal theft usurped the war host's chain of command, with the florid outrider quite unaware.

Lysaer curbed his livid response, braced to render swift judgement as the magnitude of the infringement before him careened on its juggernaut course. Let the valet redeem his good name on his merits, or prove the perfidious case to clinch a traitor's death at the scaffold.

The snitch caught over his head played for bluster. "Who wouldn't've pinched a sapphire setting like that given the chance? Odds on, you're a scumbag deserter who snatched the prize booty to bolt. Rightly ought to haul you in for the corporal's lash and a hanging." The chance to leverage more than the provost's reward for a runaway's capture brightened the gleam of avarice. "Belike you weren't blessed on your way out of camp with four head of prime horseflesh, either. They're mine for the favour of letting you go. And the mule, along with that firkin of spirits I see with the exciseman's stamp out of Morvain."

A weaponless servant should be forced to concede.

Dace gambled instead on the stacked odds against him and dangled a flimsier challenge as bait. "Let's hazard a contest, butty, for who keeps the mule. Thrown daggers, three sets, and your pick of the bull's-eye at thirty paces."

"You, old man?" Derision twisted the horseman's bearded mouth. "There's a joke not worth spit to polish my shoe, never mind the bother to quibble."

"Not even for petty sport at my expense?" Dace showed teeth in what seemed a nervous grin. "Ridicule beats an unskilled match at sword point for bloodletting stakes."

The outrider accepted the gambit, delighted. Witting or not, his marked prospect was meat for his weapons if an upset defaulted the outcome.

Lysaer settled back, his vengeful interest half-lidded. Under the hot sun, stewed in sweat and the cloying scent of bruised grass, the arrangements proceeded. The outrider's handkerchief was tacked to the side of the cart as the target, the distance paced out by the rider's stretched strides, a servile trick of deception exposed by the statement's ruthless assessment. The slight person underneath his lackey's clothes was no meek personality. Whether the outrider saw past appearances, his potbellied swagger flaunted the superior certainty of his advantage. A sneer on his lips, he unsheathed his poignard, while Dace, tone-deaf to contempt, produced a gentleman's eating knife with a pearl handle.

Rank owned the initiative. The horseman threw first. His blade flew straight and thunked into rough slats, the cloth skewered a thumb's width off true.

Dace cast from the shoulder, a practised move bare of artifice. Steel flashed in bright sun, an effortless arc that struck, quivering, at dead centre, and snuffed out the pretence of byplay.

That unforeseen expertise plucked Lysaer to gooseflesh.

The upstaged outrider rammed forward, incredulous. "By the Light's sacred glory! Shadow take you for a slippery cheat!" A piqued wrench freed his knife. "No thieving deserter suckers me as a dupe. I'm taking the horses as forfeit." His irate slash chopped the tethered leads from the cart's tailboard. Hazed off by the gesture, the animals wheeled and scattered, tails flagged at a gallop.

The outrider reached next for the drowsy harness mule, intent on seizure of the cart with the casks. "Be grateful I'm only docking your contraband. The stranding's a pittance, when rightly you should be noosed like a felon and hanged for the carrion crows."

Innate justice offended, Lysaer flung off the burlap. He clawed the concealing rag from gold hair and thrust erect, the iconic carriage of enraged authority burnished by the lordly prerogative of ranked birth-right. "My servant is all that he claims, his covert mission under my assignment." Threat snapped each consonant. "Leave directly, before I place charges."

Bravado withered before that arctic stare, backed in force by s'Ilessid majesty. The deflated shyster snatched his grazing mount's reins. Panicked, he scrambled astride. Loose stirrups clanging against his spurred heels, he belted the ribs of the horse into flight, ripped clods showering behind by his hasty departure.

Obstruction dispatched, Lysaer shifted target to collar his errant valet before the dust settled over the shambles. Firm handling slipped his immediate grasp. Dace doubled up, wheezing, then lost decorum and collapsed to his knees, not undone by relief but whooping with stifled laughter.

"I find no humour in your situation," the Light's avatar said stiffly.

Dace chortled. "No?" Paused to blot streaming eyes on his sleeve, he choked back a snort, then managed, "The wretch could've taken the cart for his pains."

"The casks did not hold refined spirits?" Confounded, Lysaer grappled the astonishment of a nondescript menial forgetting his place.

"Ox manure," Dace confessed, unabashed. "Mixed till it sloshed with swampwater."

"You planned for this!" Scalded red by the heat, light-headed and poleaxed, Lysaer grabbed the rim of the nearest cask for support.

"Surely did." Dace stood. Oblivious to justified censure, he brushed pollen and grass seeds off his smirched livery. "War draws such gormless grifters like flies. The swaggering bully who preys upon servants deserves the comeuppance."

Lysaer pursued his derailed inquisition. "While I'm glad not to be left stranded on foot—"

"Oh, we wouldn't be," Dace interrupted. "Had your aristocrat's bite not put the rascal to rout, the left front lynchpin on that vehicle is sabotaged. The rattletrap won't roll five hundred yards without dropping a wheel."

"Then I'll ride the mule!" Lysaer snapped. "My duty lies south with my troops, a profound obligation unforgivably upset by your treasonous meddling." Yet his brisk snatch for the animal's bridle met gaped jaws and recoiled from bared yellow teeth. "Fiends plague! Hoof rot hound your days to the gates of the afterlife!"

"Insurance," Dace amended with douce satisfaction. "That clever mule won't answer to muscle." Which roughshod cheek spurned the accusation of criminal abduction forthwith. "Embrace defeat, Lysaer. Revise your priority. You're chafing to ask why the devil I've brought you away from your ill-starred campaign for a start."

"Betrayal," Lysaer corrected, crisp as freezing rain. The gall cut like ground glass, that the shield of class etiquette failed to stem the froth of lowbred presumption. "Drop the duplicitous guise of the servant. Which of my enemies owns your first loyalty? Explain for your life's sake, with nothing left out."

"Credit my allegiance to your better interest!" Dace sighed, humour razed to intractable patience. "Stop fooling yourself. Without intervention, you would have fronted the disastrous invasion of Caith-al-Caen."

"Dear me, it's the nurse-maid leading the charge upon loftier principle." Lysaer swiped back with the withering scorn honed to demolish inconvenient detractors. "As the swaddled dependent, I'm meant to be cowed?"

"I didn't expect your humility." Shameless in his mussed shirt and creased breeches, Dace squared off in earnest. "You hate rubbing your nose in your human frailty. The deadly fact is, your judgement was compromised—"

"Supposing it wasn't!" Fury chiselled Lysaer's pinched exasperation. "The fidelity that made you a loyal ally clearly has addled your head. Because this time, you've sullied my moral integrity."

"Desh-thiere's curse flaws your premise. I've exhausted my hand. Destroyed my security in your behalf, just as Talith and Ellaine before me, and yes, let's include Sulfin Evend."

Which personalized skewer jabbed too deeply into the quick. "How dare you!" Cornered in a standoff in desolate surrounds, Lysaer glowered over the festered wound lanced wide open in repudiation. "My past is off-limits, and beyond question, you've ventured far over your head."

"Have I?" Dace crossed his arms, adamant, his familiar, hound's features bruised by the thumbprints of too many sleepless nights. "How long have I known you? Since when have you ever surmounted the prod of Desh-thiere's active curse?"

"At this pass?" Lysaer straightened, all chiselled nobility in the sunlit halo of his disordered hair. "I had to conceal my resolve to defer the dawn call to advance."

"Did you?" The upstart in servant's garb hurled down the gauntlet of doubt. "I parted you from the campaign because you were nowhere near your right mind! Blustered intentions in hindsight are worthless. The war host advanced to its fate, sad to say. Since I could not curb Nails's rabid ambition, she pushed on and accomplished her purpose without you."

Lysaer's bristled fury showed teeth. "Harm to the campaign blackens your hands before hers. But for your untoward plotting, the attack was to be cancelled upon my express orders!"

"No more royal airs and superior rhetoric!" Uncowed, the crass changeling scrapped sense. "You are here, hale and breathing, incensed enough to scapegoat me for your short-falls. Do that! Then run for the comfort of your enthralled sycophants. Salve your torn conceit with the vacuous honey of a gullible crowd's adulation. For I cannot return to face charges. You'll have to surmount your accursed delusion without anyone's volunteer sacrifice prodding you upright."

Lysaer recoiled as though struck in the teeth. No one addressed him this way! None, since the hour he turned his back and repudiated Daliana sen Evend's invasive impertinence.

"Dharkaron Avenge!" he gasped through white lips, stung to critical thought, then to stunned recognition of the effortless style that just pinned a kerchief with a thrown knife. Tripped by his assumptions, Lysaer lost his breath. *How* had he missed the irregular attributes of a valet hell-bent to suborn his autonomy? Few, ever, dared the brazen audacity to breach his personal space and denounce his integrity. Denial bludgeoned into epiphany. The known ancestry, blurred by age, now sprang stark to the eye in Dace Morley's features.

"You!" Sparked to flash point, Lysaer attacked. "Whose vile deception has planted another insufferable sen Evend scion to spy on me?"

"Mine." The untoward speaker approached from behind, an uncanny arrival trailed by an inquisitive bunch of loose horses. Not only the lost animals purloined by the outrider, but several others bridled and saddled. His boots wore the caked dust of hard travel, filmed as his burnt orange leathers and fine shirt cuffs, trimmed and beaded with abalone and onyx. Hatless and weathered, with chestnut-and-white hair tumbled over broad shoulders, he inserted himself into the altercation between master and servant. "Where is the integrity that once claimed the high ground for fairness in a menial's behalf at East Bransing?"

Lysaer found himself raked up and down by an invasive glance that peeled flesh and pierced bone to the marrow.

"Have we met?" he demanded, off-balanced. "I don't recall the invitation to lay open my conscience for a Fellowship Sorcerer's interrogation."

Davien viewed that affronted comment askance, his disinterest composed of ascetic angles and cutting cynicism. "Don't imagine you would have surmounted two years of prolonged convalescence on your own, pinned under the thumb of Erdane's high priesthood. For the selfless rescue that has spared you from the annihilation that destroyed your deluded following, your gratitude is inexcusably lacking."

Lysaer fielded the shattering loss of his war host without impact, the slam of shocked disbelief armoured behind the polish of his practised statesmanship. "The liar's gifts leave a poisonous aftertaste."

"The cockerel's crow of the fool!" Direct as a force of nature, Davien's laconic shrug eviscerated regal pretence. "You have no idea just how far you had plunged into the proverbial abyss. The trigger snare your brave ally disarmed overcame you without even token resistance."

"Show him." For the first time, Dace appeared shaken.

Sorrow flickered, a fleeting glimpse into the fathomless depth of the

Sorcerer's obsidian eyes. "Did you think you possessed the acumen to withstand this?" Davien opened his hand. Light flared from what seemed insignificant as a patterned snarl of floss in his palm. But the effect trapped the mind, the vulnerability forged by Desh-thiere's curse swift and cruel as binding wire.

The distilled flare of hatred sheared Lysaer to his knees, a savage assault that upended sanity, reason demolished by howling rage and the murderous thrust to indulge in red slaughter.

Davien snapped his fist closed. The compulsive tempest died out, vanished into sunlight like a snuffed candle.

Lysaer crouched, trembling and drenched in sweat. Horror flayed him wide open, his charming charisma and resilient composure in shreds.

"Your hope to recall the war host was forfeit," Dace ventured through the shaken pause. "Where Nails fashioned one construct, she would have prepared a replacement to salvage the effort I thwarted. I promise, as a temple agent linked to a Koriani conspiracy, she would have guaranteed your compliant command to advance."

Lysaer groped for the bravado to rise, the desperate redoubt of defensive denial stitched through a self-image shredded to unmanned contrition.

"You will not pluck the rose from the ashes." Davien's remorseless thrust denounced the choked plea for another last-minute reprieve. "The lady who stood as your champion has asked to retire."

"Ath, you knew!" Dace exclaimed to the Sorcerer, jolting Lysaer to startled puzzlement.

"*She?*"

"Of course." Davien's flat rebuff galvanized the stunned pause, his hawk's focus still trained on the careworn servant before him. "My dear, I heard your cry for release from the far side of the world. Tender no apology for what has been brutally obvious for some time."

"Thank you." Dace squared thin shoulders. "But I prefer to declare my own severance." Grime rimmed the nails of the fingers that had bound wounds, emptied night soil, tended finery of velvet and silk, and wielded the razor with patent devotion. That familiar dexterity rolled the cuff from one slender wrist and plucked out the cincture of twisted, black thread embedded in what had seemed aged flesh.

Transformation was instant: in place of an elderly man, Lysaer stared thunderstruck at a young woman with mahogany hair whose slight figure had curves unsuited to the valet's tailored livery that clothed her. Bright, tawny eyes that too piercingly reminded of Talith stared down the jolt of his aghast dismay.

"I once swore not to abandon you to the machinations of Desh-thiere's curse. But the hard years have shown the futility of trying to hold the high ground for someone unwilling to fight. Redemption demands an unswerving commitment, where you have abandoned yourself by the wayside for glory. While your cause is embellished by rabid fanatics, my effort in your behalf is wasted. For your sake, I just burned the last credible bridge to claim innocence against a True Sect arraignment. All I have done would be sacrificed under trial, condemned to the fire and sword by decree of the True Sect Canon."

Davien applauded the bitter denouncement. "Congratulations on the proud accomplishment, to have worn down to nothing the unimpeachable gift of s'Gannley fidelity." Stripped from the rags of false dignity, clad in a wrinkled dressing gown over his nightshirt, s'Ilessid vanity received the Sorcerer's excoriating dismissal. "I've claimed from the start, the sterling character of Sulfin Evend's heir was too good for you."

Lysaer lost words, shorn of wit for the stuttering pretence of a suave recovery.

"Hope dazzled me like a fever," Daliana admitted, unafraid to acknowledge the desolate agony of separation. Nor did Lysaer retreat into cowardice, his stricken regard unwavering as she drove the last nail through his mute plea for forgiveness. "The delusion I clung to is broken, that any spirit alive holds the power to save another from jeopardy. We spin our own webs. Each of us must win free of entanglement. No one's crutch, no matter how earnestly meant, saves anyone from himself. For you, pride must fall before you plumb the flaws that undermine your true strength. Humility founds the honest appeal for anyone's loving support."

No more remained to be said. If she faltered, his wounded beauty would suborn the fierce clarity of her self-acknowledgement.

Davien's burning impatience moved on and whistled for the milling horses. They came at his summons, trailing cut leads and the trampled ends of snapped reins. Methodical, the Sorcerer stripped their tack and freed them. His dispatch of Lysaer's concern for survivors received the same searing economy. "Your supply train cannot stray farther south with too few draught animals willing to bear harness hauling the drays.

Left with the cargo, the handlers won't starve. If they choose the wise course and retreat, the lot may escape the day's blundering impact without further penalty."

"My people deserve better," Lysaer insisted, wooden.

"You don't grasp the ignorant scope of your coalition's defilement, do you!" Davien rebuked. "Your baggage camp broached boundaries forbidden to trespass. Anyone caught in proximity at the threshold of solstice, as well as laggards who have not yet withdrawn to safe distance, will meet their downfall. With scant exception, your invading war host has perished already!"

"*Dead?*" Lysaer reeled, dizzied by stark disbelief. "All of them?" The pain in the moment could not be encompassed. Nor would duty abandon the toll of casualties laid at his feet without verification.

Davien added no more. He pushed off the buckskin that nuzzled his ear, passed its bridle to Daliana, then bent with cupped hands to boost her astride.

While she adjusted her stirrups, the Sorcerer dealt his parting advice to Lysaer s'Ilessid. "You have two choices only. Pursue the guilt that binds you to your troops and face your doom before the Paravians, and you leave the Mistwraith's malice to forfeit Mankind's lawful claim to inhabit Athera. Or else risk a last stand on the pathetic sum of your merits. Own your fate. Take charge and enter Kewar, where no power but yours shapes your destiny."

Lysaer recouped the glacial mask of his poise, deep emotion recoiled to acid disparagement. "My dam's bastard challenged your maze and came through."

Davien's retort pierced the martyr's facade. "Your half brother stood naked before the self-honesty of a master initiate's discipline, where you will engage the unimaginable peril of deceit clothed in no virtue but arrogance." His dismissive toss transferred the lead of a dozy chestnut gelding to Lysaer.

"You must leave proscribed ground." To the vicious spark in blue eyes that forepromised retaliation, the Sorcerer levelled his final remark. "Find a saddle and halter that grey mare as a remount. Then ride hard and fast. Forsake the free wilds for your very life, and if you dare, join the battle for your salvation. Though I frankly doubt you have the guts to endure the full measure earned, far less the bare-knuckled will to surmount the brunt of the unalloyed consequence."

Variables

Thwarted from his course to address the ruin of his armed coalition by the baulky horse underneath him, Lysaer is overtaken near sundown by the ragtag remnant of the host's displaced camp followers: served with their harrowed account of defeat, he firms his resolve to redeem his burden of dead, while news of the disaster wings northward by pigeon to reach the reserve companies stationed north of the Mathorns . . .

Beyond Northgate, as the embattled assault on Ozvowzakrin's succession counts five rivals slain, Asandir sustains his fraught vigil, detained as a sixth combatant rises to contest the Treaty Accord; while Seshkrozchiel stirs to the fresh threat of a drake war, Prime Lirenda and her seniors travel the south road towards the Forthmark sisterhouse for the crowning move behind her deft feint . . .

Ath's adepts attend the reaped fallen that litter the vale above Caith-al-Caen, their task guided not by Lysaer s'Ilessid, but his redheaded son, whose sightless perception sorts the few broken survivors from the strewn thousands of dead: and among the lost handful, inconsolably riven, a woman girded in golden armour is collected for terminal care in the sanctuary at Whitehaven hostel . . .

XI. Rebound

The piercing scream racketed over the misted swamp, diminished to desolate echoes fit to lift hair at the nape under daylight.

"Ath wept, I hope that's not human," Dakar remarked, breathless. Drenched to the knees, greying hair snarled with sweat, he shuddered in trepidation. A fool's choice, to rush into a brangle with a wounded creature, far less entangle himself in the wicked affairs of an initiate mage gone raving mad from a Methspawn poisoning. The pirogue glided on through the cling of wracked bladderwort, while forward momentum yanked the steering pole in his blistered hands from the sucking grip of the mire.

Elaira's silent stance in the prow rebuffed the sensible mention of precautions. Five tormented days since departure from Methisle, she would not be swerved, though what lay ahead defeated imagining. Harrowed through ten nights of suffering agony, a victim able to muster an outcry meant life endured, perhaps with sufficient vitality to surmount the extended delay of their overdue rescue.

Dakar muscled into his labour. The pirogue shot ahead. Her dependable keel knifed the matted scrum of bent stems, the buoyant, fluffed down rubbed off of drowned cattails eddied in her murky wake. Something splashed leftwards, chased by a predacious ripple that slapped against the crook in the Paravian wall. The smeared silhouette of lichen-splotched stone loomed ahead, creped like frayed bunting with moss.

"Not far to go, now," Dakar blurted, unnerved.

The reed bed skimmed under the narrow prow languished, blackened, a killed swathe razed by elemental shadow. Frost-singed scum browned the caked ring at the watermark, and the leaden blanket of summer's humidity bore the stench of corrupted meat. Another lumbering splash laced bubbles across the dark water, sequined in reflection by Verrain's warded talisman, gleaming pale blue at the bow.

Dakar angled their approach for the upcoming turn, anxious to put the horror behind. Past question, he lacked the stomach for the dreadful reckoning mere yards ahead.

Condeleinn's granite marker loomed nine spans above the cracked buttress, an ancient silhouette cut in stark majesty against the hoary thickets of marsh maple.

"Arithon's not there," Elaira remarked, her first observation in days.

"What?" Dakar yanked the mired pole from the muck. "The flux sign states otherwise!"

"I know." Elaira clung to her perch, a rigid figurehead with a scraped elbow clamped over her shoulder-slung satchel. "He left the deliberate impression as a decoy."

"Last I saw, your man was incapable." Dakar veered the pirogue alongside the weathered-stone barrier. "Poisoned senseless with venom, no way Arithon finessed the craft to shape a stable foil with such precision."

"Are you certain?" Elaira laced into the sceptic's denouncement. "You'd bank on the surety he hadn't prepared the fetch with lucid forethought in advance?"

"Perish the idea to the ninth gate of Sithaer!" Dakar swallowed the upended kick of his gut, frightened witless. "Your snake-bitten theory had better be wrong!" Memory was graphic, of the unconscious body left mauled by creatures that gave even Verrain's expertise pause. Dakar persisted, neck turtled into his sweaty collar, "Best if my straightforward assessment is accurate!" Ath wept for grief, a cold-cast gambit premeditated on that scale frankly was too awful to contemplate.

"I'm not mistaken." Elaira fended the pirogue off the vertical bulwark, ripped by a visceral shudder. "This close, my gestalt awareness should feel Arithon's agony directly. Instead, the void where his living awareness should be is deafening."

Dakar stifled his comment, that the lack more likely confirmed a fatality. Chin tucked in his beard, he manoeuvred past the angled jut of the wall, then swung the responsive craft alongside the revetment at the base of Condeleinn's memorial. Leaden streamers of mist veiled a scene eerily smothered by quiet, the mire's cacophony of croaks and screeling wails subdued within warded range of the marker.

The pirogue bumped past the chewed, cartilaginous carcass of something reptilian, the toothed curve of the jawbone tethered by gristle. Verrain's handiest vessel slashed through the slick of emulsified fat and bumped to rest amid the half-submerged mangle of carrion clotted beneath the crumbled masonry.

Dakar coughed, gagged gruff by the putrescent reek. "We'll know soon enough."

Elaira muffled her nose and mouth with her sleeve, while Dakar shoved in reverse and jockeyed the narrow bow clear of obstruction. Nestled into position for Elaira's agile reach upwards, he steadied the thwart as she caught the stone kerb, clambered topside and vanished. Less eager, the Mad Prophet stowed the steering pole. He threaded the painter between the notched scuppers cut into the walkway above, and secured the stern with a half-hitch.

Then he sat, wheezing, loath to survey the fly-blown carnage heaped on the path overhead. Whatever discovery awaited beyond, the site reeked from the gristly remains of what seemed a prolonged and vehement fight.

Elaira's swift return poked the grim spectre behind his unsettled fear. "He's gone. Left behind a blood proxy, most likely as a stopgap diversion to entertain predators."

Dakar straightened, alarmed. Her repressive report side-stepped the unsavoury alternative. Far worse than ravenous Methspawn may have prompted a tactic laid down as a foil. The innocuous complaint of his hollow belly became the lame excuse to duck that gruelling enquiry. "The conniving mountebank took the supplies?"

"Yes." The pirogue rocked and settled to Elaira's weight, the bruised pallor on her deadpan features furrowed with distress.

When Dakar declined her offer to claim the stern for a turn at the pole, she relented, "I found only his fetch, fashioned ten days ago. That, and the shreds of a jettisoned pack."

Incredulous, Dakar forgot to swear murder. "Only one?"

"Yours, of course, by the size of the shoulder straps." Elaira searched Dakar's crestfallen face, beaten numb. "Unless you want to see for yourself, we had better shove off."

"I'm for going, don't worry." Dakar freed the painter and hefted the pole, wincing as his blistered palms took the strain. "Which way? Do you know? If Arithon's gone inside the groin, the line's crossed. I'm not following."

Elaira dealt that statement her mulish forbearance. Then she said, "South, as the crow flies." Anguish masked by grimed fingers, throat choked to a whisper, she pleaded, "The blood trail that's real went that way. Please hurry."

"All right." Dakar spun the pirogue, resigned to starvation. "Though I'm less inclined to forgive, far less trivialize the grim docket of criminal evidence." Ornery and sore, he broached his irksome suspicion headlong. "We're being nose-led by Arithon's design. What benign intent do you imagine drives this round of brutal manipulation?"

The bleak implication withheld at last snapped Elaira's strained temper. "How much did you browbeat him, day after day, harping endlessly over his presumably bankrupt morals? While you badgered him for not sharing confidence, did you care a whit for his human self? Or, tell me straight, do you fear him like everyone else for the potential scope of raw power he owns in restraint?"

Too vengeful to deflect the balefire assault of obstinate, female senti-ment, Dakar picked the fight. "The Fellowship Sorcerers revoked his crown sanction. You insist they've acted in shortsighted error? Then keep on, deny the toll of Arithon's dead. Count them and admit how many came to grief in the tortuous course of his misplayed affairs."

"Everyone closest to him," Elaira agreed. Far past civil exasperation, she unshipped the pirogue's tooth-marked paddle and leaned forward to fend off a snag. "That's the traumatized nerve run through his beating heart! Either Arithon's pushed us off in his desperate need to protect us or, as you perniciously postulate, he is not the same man who mounted the scaffold and near died of his failure to spare a child from wrongful execution." The enchantress reversed her bare-knuckled grip and dug into black water to speed their progress. "I have reason to believe in the former."

Dakar opened his mouth.

She cut him off, ruthless. "Even if your harsh view didn't twist his moral compass too grotesquely far out of true, *nothing* approaches the gruelling measure he endured to surmount Davien's Maze."

Dakar's rooted pessimism faltered, outflanked. He could not, after all, bear to shatter the backbone of Elaira's conviction. Nor could anyone fathom the Fellowship's motive, or second-guess the long-range vision that spanned the complexities that shaped epochs.

The brutal worry that gnawed him was real. "You stake more than our two lives on your premise. The god's gamble in play reaps the counters on who knows *what* secretive gameboard! How long should we cast dice at the bittermost edge in blind habit? There may be no shining thread in the pattern. Nothing to justify the horrendous risk stacked upon who knows what scales of jeopardy."

Any argument but Elaira's ought to have foundered.

"What makes you think Arithon's indestructible?" Unswerved, she doubled down and attacked. "You've all leaned on his strengths for the cause, no matter the taxing wear on his well-being, and yes, the scars he bears on his conscience. Suppose your cankered anxiety is justified? If my beloved has abandoned integrity, what terrifies you to rabid paranoia is the stubborn belief in his total infallibility! Whether he's turned to evil and broken in spirit, or, Ath forbid, still sterling in character, you berate him at every turn with the vicious reflection of your distrust."

"Verrain is more forgiving than I am," Dakar retorted with sting. "Take your wisdom from Asandir. Your man always has made the mighty of Athera more than a trifle nervous."

"Where is the surprise? More than a compliant cipher's required to vanquish the malice imposed by Desh-thiere." Her exasperated reproof dismissed irritation with less fuss than a dog who muddied clean blankets. "Condemned or innocent, what makes you assume Arithon's not prone to mistakes when he's pressured past his human limits?" Elaira stared, owlish, eyes empty of tears, the last colour drained from her cheeks. "Whatever end he pursued at the start, he has badly outstripped the reach of his strength."

Dakar had nothing to say in defence. Conflicted by gormless apprehension, he shoved the pirogue between the shoaled berms of willow and reed beds, and nursed silence as a palliative.

Unaware of the Seven's directive to revoke her possession of Rathain's emerald signet, Elaira mistook the brief standoff as capitulation. Steering paddle laid crosswise, she bent her head and bundled the tumbled mass of her flyaway hair. She secured the braid with the worn cuff tie gleaned from a fisherman's shirt: a plain twill cord, finished at the ends with small pearls. The oddment snagged Dakar's interest, the associative tug of a recalled connection disrupted as Elaira kept speaking.

"Will you hold the benefit of the doubt, or abandon a friend to a summary judgement? I'd plead the forbearance for peace of mind, if only to settle the record."

Dakar clamped his teeth, too breathlessly compromised for the colourful language his hardship deserved. He jammed the pole into submerged sludge and heaved, driving towards a contrary future altogether too opaque to fathom. Whether he went to alleviate his anguished conscience, or for the Seven's greater imperative to salvage the Mistwraith's defeat, he lacked a straight view through the muddle to say.

A day's travel left behind the deepest black pools, and the most dangerous of the mire's large predators. The pirogue skimmed a tortuous course through brackish, brown shallows, scattered with rooster-tail hummocks of sedge and raised knolls ringed with cattails where marsh maple rose from impenetrable thickets of wax myrtle. The pole snagged up leathery pads of water lily, streaming virid webs of algae. Waterbound, a boat's forward passage meandered, where Arithon's track scribed the straight line of a mariner's dead reckoning. Sign deciphered his hardship, the vacated campsites littered with picked bones where Mirthlvain's teeming carnivores had fought and died in pitched fights to devour what seemed easy prey. The scorched rings of spent watchfires and crushed greenery marked the comfortless redoubts, where fevered sleep had been snatched amid harried flight. The distance between, inexorably shortened, recorded the attrition of his resilient vitality.

If the victim screamed, sound died without echo in the oppressive humidity. The flux imprint spoke faintly in the felted damp, the shining harmonic of Alithiel's cry the bright thread stitched through a human anguish coarse as the whine of an arrow's flight, passing.

The fitful overburden of shared gestalt wrung Elaira to haggard exhaustion. She rejected all earnest pleas to seek respite. Dogged, she poled onwards through midday's sweltering heat, while Dakar napped, crammed in the sparse shade of the bow seat. When he roused, she manned the stern yet, a ghost figure napped in the pale scrim of mist as pellucid twilight descended on their third evening of travel due south.

Dakar rubbed crusted eyes and sat up, squinting through the gathered darkness. Will-o'-the-wisps gleamed through the hummocks, the overlapped crescents of scrawled reflections disturbed where sinuous hunters prowled for scuttling prey.

A silvery sheen brightened the dense gloom ahead. No trick of the marshlights, but the fluorescence of excited flux, ringing with an ethereal purity too melodic for the hideous setting.

Hope rushed Dakar's pulse. "That's the proximal halo of Alithiel's ward."

"I know." Elaira's voice cracked to a near sob of relief. Steadfast, the sound-and-light chord that Named the winter stars would scarcely respond in defence of a half-rotted corpse.

Dakar scrambled erect and clambered astern. When he grasped the pole in her trembling hands, she relinquished her grip, grateful for the intervention.

Off the bow, visible through drifting fog and the punched silhouettes of stilled foliage, the tumbledown block of a sentinel tower reared above a flounced petticoat of tangled undergrowth. The pirogue knifed the last yards through muddy shallows, scraped across matted roots, and stalled with a jolt amid the fringed sedge of a shoal.

Elaira launched over the thwart with a splash and burrowed into the thickets headlong, while Dakar dragged the pirogue firmly aground and snatched the stubbed brand from the bow. His awkward weight sunk ankle deep as he puffed up the spongy bank in pursuit.

He found Elaira knelt over a limp figure, crumpled and filthy as an abandoned rag wadded within the stone ring. An outflung hand limned by the flicker of torchlight revealed slack fingers, welted and grazed beyond the semblance of grace that once rendered exquisite music.

Revolted, Dakar averted his face. He could not bear the gut-wrenching ache of a master talent discarded to wretched destruction, far less execute the Fellowship's imperative to reclaim the crown's emerald signet ring.

Elaira's prognosis provided the ready excuse for deferment. "He's alive. Though the man pushed himself recklessly far before he collapsed."

She had not expected to find Arithon conscious. Methspawn venom acted on the nerves. Least harmful effects ranged from disabling numbness to partial paralysis. The most ghastly strains led to rigour and wasting attrition, with intractable agony extending for days before heart and lungs succumbed to fatality. Yet stiffness did not seize the joints under her cautious assessment. The chill, flaccid flesh still reacted to reflex points. The spill of Dakar's held torchlight in fact disclosed a mulish fight for survival.

Arithon had gone down responsive, his struggle inflected by the rifled pack, and the strewn contents ransacked under necessity.

Proof denounced the pithless convenience of surrender, and most ruthlessly voided the platitude that ascribed his vicious acts to unhinged madness.

More than ever, the Mad Prophet was reluctant to measure the damage sprawled under Elaira's diligent attention. "What do you require?"

"That torch, if you please." The enchantress expounded without hesitation, "Then your hip flask. Afterwards, use my blanket to fashion a sling." The paper skin under her touch was wrung dry, the blanched forehead burning with fever. "The marshwort I collected en route to sweat toxins is too rigorous for Arithon's dehydrated condition."

Dakar jammed the cresset between the cracked masonry, unslung his waterskin, and yanked the cork. "You're wanting to move on straightaway?"

"Fast as possible, yes." Elaira stroked tangled black hair away from gaunt features mottled with bruises, and braced Arithon's slack shoulders upright before tippling moisture between his cracked lips. "Best we get him to the lakeshore where firm ground will offer wholesome wood for a fire." Preoccupied, with a thumb laid beside the raced pulse at his neck, she counted off seconds until he swallowed without choking. "If you steer the pirogue, I'll do what I can with infusions and drawing poultices while under way."

Dakar dug in his toes with a steel practicality. "No." The debridement of any putrescent wound promised trouble of the first order. "Blood scent on these waters at night is a lethal attractant. Treat Arithon as best you can where he lies. You need the rest, and we're safer on the defensible ground within these foundations."

No starch left for argument, the Mad Prophet turned on his heel and retraced his steps. He secured the boat, sorted supplies for a meal and a fire, then hefted the load to firm ground in the travel-stained blankets.

Elaira capitulated to the truce, beaten by the relentless demand placed on her deft ministrations. Dakar scraped the soggy moss from a cracked flagstone and laid kindling over fluffed tinder shredded from cattails. Spark struck to new flame, he strangled his squeamish nerves, edged past the roused gleam of Alithiel, and helped to roll Arithon onto dry bedding. The gouge of the empty sheath strapped at his waist squeezed putrefied jets from the cankered bites on his abdomen.

Dakar gagged, reeled nauseous, while Elaira freed the baldric's buckles herself. Snappish, she foisted the noisome tangle of harness into the spellbinder's shrinking grasp. "I'll manage the cleaning and dressing, if you wield the sword's virtue and mind the defences."

Dakar lifted the black blade. The arcane rune inlay blazed up at his touch, the flare of the reconstituted enchantment casting a pearlescent halo through Mirthlvain's obdurate gloom. Something outside the stone foundation took flight. A frantic thrash parted the brush, followed by a splash in the shallows, chased in turn by the frothed water of avid pursuit. Whatever hurtled away in the dark would not have been stalking with benign intent.

"Avert!" The spellbinder wedged the lit blade upright in the cracked wall. He filled the pot with a cloth sieve and a cantrip to strain out impurities, set the water to boil, then resentfully scraped himself raw on the sedge, raising a ward of go hither to discourage predation.

"Dharkaron's Spear take this miserable place! Do your healer's work here through the night. I'll sleep as I can and be up at first light. You can rest by day in the pirogue on my promise to deliver us from the morass by sundown tomorrow."

Elaira stripped off Arithon's boots. Grateful for the foresighted loan of a craft that could travel at speed, single-handed, she drew her knife and set to the grim task of slicing off the crusted tatters of his filthy clothes. Bared skin revealed the puffed lesions of festering bites, criss-crossed with suppurating gashes inflicted by venomous fang and claw. Scored in angry flesh, she charted a toll of suffering more savage than Verrain's clean damage by frostbite.

Anguished, Elaira swiped off tears with the back of her wrist. "What brutal purpose drove you to this? By Ath's mercy," she declared, leaned over the flame to sterilize her fouled steel. "When you wake, I will have my straightforward answer."

The intensive labour of lancing, cleaning, and binding inflamed wounds absorbed the enchantress, night long. Dakar roused between catnaps, lending what meagre assistance he could to the repetitive chore of heating the packed clay infused with herbals for drawing poultices. For each dressing changed, the used rags required boiling. He wrung the strips and draped them to dry between the laborious decoction of recipes for restorative antidotes, which Elaira dabbed in measured doses beneath the invalid's tongue.

Hours passed before Arithon's erratic pulse steadied. The bruised skin stretched over his bones remained fevered, jaundiced as poorly cured parchment. Dakar napped to the murmur of Elaira's voice, threaded through the ethereal, ringing harmonics thrown off by Alithiel's wardings.

Awake at daybreak, the Mad Prophet found the enchantress crumpled with exhaustion. Her snarled bronze plait, looped with yesterday's cord, pasted her wan cheek where she napped, slumped against the broken bulwark. Arithon lay, swaddled unconscious in the grimy bedroll beside her. The forehead under his matted black hair still burned with fever under Dakar's hesitant touch. Yet a flush of streamed sweat soaked his brow. Elaira had won the first round against death. Her mate's sapped resilience turned for the better.

"Ungrateful bastard," Dakar grumbled. Though for his hide's sake, he kept his word, the Paravian sword left unsheathed while he tidied the campsite. He launched the pirogue as the lemon-pale sun speared rays through the misted crowns of the cypress.

Elaira settled in on the floorboards with her shoulders braced against wicker-laced frame of the bow seat, Arithon's head pillowed in her lap. She plied him with remedies and repacked his wounds. Purpled flesh puckered from reduced swelling confirmed her astringent clay compresses had drawn the pus. Weariness felled her by late afternoon.

She slept, oblivious, when the spark of returned awareness gleamed beneath Arithon's cracked eyelids. Febrile consciousness recorded her bent, auburn head lolled against the thwart above him. The wisped braid trailing over her shoulder wore the tie once yanked from his shirt cuff, centuries ago, in the aftermath of a fisher lad's healing in Merior.

Sight of the keepsake struck a blow fit to shatter him, spirit and flesh.

Sunk into the rhythmic stupor of paddling, Dakar missed the invalid's visceral recoil, the fleeting expression on Arithon's face a hammered rictus of horror.

The startled reaction passed by unremarked, while Arithon grappled the enormity of the compromise to his position. He was too weakened to force an escape, sick with lassitude and drugged to depletion by potent remedies. Beyond recourse, he drew upon adamant reflex and reasserted the shreds of his mage-trained control.

Ath above, please to Daelion's last mark on his record, let him be raving, his beloved beside him a phantom born of wishful delirium.

His helpless straits withered hope, the impact of her presence too real, as the cruel claw of farsighted prescience hooked deep in his vitals and twisted. Dream curdled to nightmare, for the craven price paid for his horrendous miscalculation. He did as he must to quiet the beaten outcry of abject surrender. The impervious mask he stiffened at all costs obscured, then obliterated all trace of his naked emotion.

The Mad Prophet fell short of his promise to reach Mirthlvain's verge before sundown. Short sleep and dense heat, with the unforeseen dead ends and detours required to thread the meandering channels between the tasselled reed beds thwarted the pirogue's direct passage. Dusk compounded those hazards to navigation. Rooted hummocks offered no dry place to pause, even as Elaira's supply of ready-made tinctures became depleted.

Full night darkened the puzzle-cut mosaic of drowned landscape when the pirogue at last crossed the standing ward raised at the swamp's southern boundary. Where human awareness perceived no change, mage-sense first noted the profound shift when the craft's gliding course sliced an unseen curtain of force razed through the oppressive air. The gravid burden of threat sheared away like a breath released from blanketing suffocation.

The eerie, racketing wails and shrill peeping of the swamp's denizens diminished behind, replaced by the thrum of croaking of frogs and the scraped song of midsummer crickets. Harrowed nerves met the hollowed absence of peril with stunned disbelief, until the belated acknowledgement dawned that Alithiel's constant hum had fallen mute.

The carved prow above Elaira's hunched form knifed through waters no longer traced by iridescent glimmers of reflection. The indigo gleam of Verrain's charged talisman had winked out in the absence of Methspawn.

Ahead, the benign expanse of Methlas Lake shimmered, scalloped silver by the whispered breeze under starlight. Cold fathoms under the keel, clear as glass, showed the sandy bottom patched with pickerel weed and heaped boulders ploughed up by glacial scour, teeming with wholesome fish.

Dakar beached the pirogue. Undone with relief for the fraught trials behind, he languished on his knees, blistered palms bathed in the lap of the wavelets.

Elaira debarked in the shallows, a touch on his shoulder bestowed in grateful acknowledgement. Arithon's relapsed condition redirected her urgency to kindle a fire. A healer's regimen demanded hot poultices applied in rotation, with willowbark infusions and cold compresses to relieve spiking fever.

Her industry prodded Dakar back upright. He wrung out his wet cuffs and helped shift Arithon ashore, then shoved off to catch bass for a late supper. His return with gutted fish on a string found the tarp laid, and the enchantress seated with her forehead at rest on bent knees and laced arms beside Arithon's bundled prostration.

"He wakened out of his senses in agony. More antidote and my decoction for pain have eased the worst for the moment."

Dakar regarded the unconscious face on the bedroll. Presented with no vulnerable insight to pierce the annoying enigma, he left the enchantress to her wearied vigil, conversation abandoned in favour of peeling green sticks for roasting. The spellbinder scaled his catch. He spitted the fillets and rolled them in biscuit dough before his tentative comment. "You fear you will fail him."

Elaira's sigh emerged ragged. "Sethvir's stark forecast was unforgiving."

Batter dripped into the coals with a hiss, flared up and ignited to sparks and puffed smoke. "As I recall, the burden was equally shared." Dakar sucked a singed finger, too stupidly tired to quash his animosity. "You're not the partner slacking in the traces."

Rigid quiet ensued. Elaira's contrary belief persisted, despite the unsavoury evidence.

Better skilled at the fleshpot arts of seduction than wrangling with female obstinacy, Dakar finished toasting the meal, ate his portion, and turned into his blanket. Sleep granted no respite. Against the grain of hard-won experience, his filled belly delivered bad dreams.

Elaira stayed wakeful, preoccupied by the seethe of her pot and constant measurement of Arithon's vitals. Rewarded at last, she sensed the tide turn: the grip of the venom loosened enough for his mage-trained reflex to seize charge and fight off the residue. The surging fever that followed confirmed his rebound as the body's natural defences sweated out the residual toxins. The necrosed infection yet demanded attention, if not a dollop of summer maggots to forestall the danger of sepsis.

Elaira kept on without letup. She cleaned and rebandaged fouled wounds far into the night, pounding fresh batches of styptic powders, and warming the paste of herbal mashes. When Arithon's curative fever soared higher, she cooled his streaming flesh with soaked blankets. Skin and bone, every part of his body familiar, she did all she could for his comfort.

The lit spark through cracked lashes acknowledged her. No tender regard for his person went unremarked. Dakar had been wrong. Her action in her beloved's behalf never for a moment had been unsupported. The clamped jaw that eased for her next dose of remedies repressed more than the whimpers of bodily pain. Her touch recorded the adamant steel sheathed in prostrate weakness, but driven by will a far cry from infantile helplessness.

Wise instinct nursed needy flesh without pressure, unfooled when subsequent bouts of raving unstrung the mind and let down his adamant barriers. Her tears spilled, when his murmured endearments welcomed her presence, and his teasing response melted into flurried caresses that slid, questing in sensuous pleasure over her skin. The knowing awareness of her within reach fired the responsive poignancy of by far too few cherished memories.

Elaira caught his restless wrists, torn. The fine fingers that struck gold from the lyranthe string were coarsened with callus, the grazed knuckles and ripped nails grimed with peat. She had known those palms, hardened from mallet and adze in the shipyard, and chapped raw during the winter nights spent listening with bardic sensitivity to the deep, tonal secrets embedded in Alestron's fast stone. Nothing as yet matched the aching distress endured through his convalescence at Althain Tower, when those clever, musician's hands had lain still, remote as the carved purity of grain marble.

The contentment of peace through his augmented life span eluded him yet. Her heart addressed his entangled plight without burdensome censure. "You are as you're made. I ask nothing more."

"Best beloved," he murmured, swathed immobile in blankets. "Here again you've retrieved me from the botched coil of my mistakes." Moments passed, while sweat or tears moistened the sable fringe of his lashes. Eloquence born of delirium pleaded with wrenching earnesty for her forgiveness. "Ath's mercy deliver us, I have never deserved the gift of constancy that ruins your happiness."

Detachment where he was concerned was not possible, though Elaira resisted the illusory comfort while raving fever scrambled past and present, and fond sentiment softened his tongue. She knew, beyond certainty: Arithon's locked reserve stayed unbroken. The intractable purpose kept hidden remained in estrangement between them.

She swathed his forehead in compresses. Bathed him, again, in icy water drawn from the lake. She plied Arithon with feverfew, willowbark, and red clover, until his racing pulse settled. When his symptoms subsided, she changed his damp dressings. Ghost lit by the waning gibbous moon, she weathered his ordeal, vised by sorrow as lucid restraint restored his clammed silence.

Patience commanded her, toughened under the inflexible dictates of three antagonistic prime matriarchs. Elaira had surpassed the young woman who first tested her uncertain ground with this man in the tropics at Merior. Then, as now, Arithon's restraint sprang from reactive distrust. He had been hunted and hurled into foreign exile, a mage-schooled prodigy short on experience and wary of his untapped potential. For sound reason he had shied from the reckoning test of himself at full strength.

The resilient innocence of untried ability was beyond him, tonight. Here, Arithon languished under her care, levelled by the emphatic wreckage of his miscalculation. Far from the conflicted world of his birth, his drawn line of battle lay on Athera, in fierce opposition to the inflexible might of the Seven.

Of all impasses, Elaira understood the frightful dynamic of an outmatched defiance of absolute power.

The armed standoff she pressured could not be breached without hurt, where the least misplaced inference might forfeit forgiveness. The blood on her hands since her part on the scaffold at Daenfal could not be redressed: she had backed the Sorcerers' choice to spare his lineage at the cost of Valien's life. Death of an innocent three years of age had cleared the Koriathain's oath of debt to a crown, an exchange repudiated by the vicious adamance of his waking rejection.

Spare her the fury, if he ever learned she might have saddled him with a conception on Glendien in the benighted affray sprung from Dakar's mishandling at Athir!

Elaira respected the knife's edge she trod. Every choice mined with pitfalls, she awaited her moment to brave the excoriating assault of his temper.

The opening initiative evaded her grasp. Infallible, fractious, Arithon's intuitive thought flanked her strategy. She discovered his eyes opened, trained intently upon her: his first acute survey since his reawakening from a near brush with death, three years ago at Althain Tower.

Astute reflex snatched the chance to speak first. "You are alive, still," said Elaira. "Vital enough to maintain the bold front. I've seen through the facade, more's the pity, and thanks to the frailty exposed by high fever." She dared not sustain his direct regard since delirium in fact had not cracked his reserve. The misdirection tried for necessity's sake thumped her pulse and sucked her hollow. "I accept you've forsaken your faith in the Seven. But is this the heritage bequeathed without strings by Halliron's impeccable character?"

She felt the recoil that shoved him erect. The dropped blanket tumbled over her knee, and the tremble to his braced arm bespoke the sapped brunt of infirmity. The graven after-shock framed a betrayal unwitnessed, except by the glitter of the night's constellations.

"I choose the road I walk." His speech, disembodied, desolate, emptied, emerged husked, a gravel hoarseness perhaps due to pain, or else the forceful drive to surmount raw emotion. "Take my grateful quittance and leave. My path is not subject to quibbling."

Elaira reversed the anguished question he had posed to her in the moonlit interval of companioned solitude they once shared in a brief, night encounter on the Scimlade peninsula. "What makes me take your troubles for my own?"

The pause fell with a hitch that may have been hurt, or the hedged thorns of repudiation. She dared not move, or face him to know. Acknowledgement would force the breach, either way. After all, she could not endure the finality of a sealed vault without chink for a key.

Arithon clinched the desolate murder of kindness in any case. "I reject you, your love, and most of all, the inexhaustible freight of your pity."

She held her breath, then forced her seized chest to relax. *Language was his weapon.* Unstrung to the pith, naked and bandaged and felled under blankets, he owned nothing else. Only the blade of a Masterbard's art, exquisitely sharpened to hurt. His attacks were defence; even bleeding inside, she would not rise to the goad. "Nothing's changed. As a girl, I could not leave a tormented dog to die friendless."

The impetuous, childish error that had fouled her wrongside of the law and consigned her to Koriani fosterage was an intimate, shared confidence not lost to him. *Almost*, she heard the ring of distress that pared his response to beaten steel. "Stay, and I promise. You will be left broken, naked, and alone, abandoned on this side of Sithaer's black gate."

Oh, he understood poison! His most exquisite cruelties stemmed from the linebred endowment of his s'Ffalenn empathy. Sensitivity forged the heartcore of him, a two-sided perception blistered with the wounding power to lacerate. Elaira spun the knife back on him, merciless. "I speak, and you are infuriated because the man you are, root and branch, is not dead."

His whiplash response struck to sting. "Shall I prove out the fallacy?"

"No need." Elaira laced her taut fingers to weld the flinch of dissected nerves. "You are pounding both of us bloody to sunder the bars of a cage that does not exist."

Arithon's tempered response was agreeable. "Rather, you are the Fellowship's tether, hounding my conscience to keep their leash on my fate."

Her sigh called his bluff. Sure of her firm ground, Elaira chided him gently. "Then put my given word to the test. When you're not at the wretched end of your wits, try free will. You need only stand upright on your two feet, flex your muscle, and walk away."

The blanket sighed to his studied subsidence. "Had I thrown you over to your tyrannical order," he said, his scraped whisper recumbent, "the string ties on my life would be simplified."

But his extended silence was not resigned. The void shouted aloud through summer's lakeside chorus, the brutalized absence of rapport sunk in stillness profound as a midwinter freeze. Elaira waited, and listened, and somehow forged the bravery to smother her cry for rejoinder. The conversation may not have finished voluntarily. When she yielded to tension and peeked, she found Arithon had outworn his strength.

He slept in abandoned disorder, black hair and stilled features defined by pale skin. The charcoal shadow that scored his fine bones carved a slack form without subterfuge. Exhaustion had claimed him unbidden. Or not: the resurgence of his innate, mage-schooled discipline might have induced a tranced healing. Elaira stayed the intrusive urge to find out, afraid to prod the forlorn indignity of collapse.

Arithon's fever had broken. The life-threatening crisis was past. His even breathing reaffirmed the vital course of a recovery well under way. The last torch flickered out, yawning shadow fallen across the depleted sag of her satchel. Her stores of rootstock and herbals ran low, a need-less lapse in the wild where the meadows were better stocked than a hospice apothecary.

The moon's arc revealed time enough before dawn to harvest select plants and strip cattails for gel to treat Dakar's weeping blisters. Elaira embraced her need for fresh air and gathered her belt-knife and basket.

A final glance assessed Arithon's quietude. His features had lost the pinch of intractable pain. Breeze stirred the tangled hair on his cheek, the tension erased from closed lids in repose.

Ciladis was not present at this time to soften the blunt agony of her uncertainty. Alone, Elaira weighed what had passed. Courage rose to her effort to plumb the lapsed discourse for the full meaning of unspoken nuance. Words were Arithon's last resort, trapped at bay: his shield, and his natural element. He had cast her off. A strict severance *with limits*: he had not lied; never in malice voiced hatred. What he had done was dispatch her loyalty with a savagery that brooked no civil allowance for compromise.

"Ath bless, you are difficult beyond compare!" Exasperation spiked her yearning frustration. She had not managed to fathom his mind. Not yet. Her promised reckoning dangled, unfinished.

A last statement deeper in meaning than words, she parted her collar and withdrew Rathain's emerald signet on its silver chain. The intimate memories once cached there and left in her charge had been restored to Arithon during his convalescence at Althain Tower. Yet the means of shared access remained, keyed by the same lines, thrice affirmed, that linked their inviolate partnership. Elaira sequestered her personal message for him, then slid the ring over the curved crossguard of the Paravian sword.

Arithon distrusted the Fellowship Sorcerers. Should he awaken before her return, she left her sealed vow with the token as proof her commitment to him was detached from formal ties to the Crown of Rathain. Nor did she owe the Biedar crone her allegiance. Not in afterthought, she nestled the flint knife in its deerskin sheath beside the white gold of his forefathers' seal ring.

Her statement verified above question a love that acknowledged no other power. Nothing else but the plain cuff tie once bestowed by his hand in Merior signified the true plight of her troth. "I love you for your faultless gentleness," she whispered, then rose, her sight blurred at last through welled tears. "No matter how viciously guarded."

Her soft step bypassed Dakar, snoring in a heap by the spent coals of the cookfire. The lakeshore lay quiet beyond, the sable prow of Verrain's pirogue a cut silhouette against wavelets lapping against glistening sand. A fish splashed in the shallows. An owl's mournful hoot threaded through the bass thrum of the frogs' uninterrupted serenade.

Elaira donned her damp boots. Scouttrained to traverse the trackless wilds, she slipped unremarked through a ward ring that posed her honed skills no impediment. Three words of permission addressed to the elements mended the spellbinder's circle, and a strand of her plucked hair left spanning the gap rendered her crossing invisible. The campsite's protections unbroken behind, she turned inland and settled into her rhythmic stride through the meandering swale that creased the summer meadow.

The Radmoore flux kept its ancient secrets, a language that sparkled just beyond hearing. Without benefit of Ciladis's lore to distract her, she gleaned what solace she could from the ritual calm tailored to achieve heightened rapport with her surrounds. Twined with the myriad threads of life's tapestry, she sensed the ethereal Song of the Mysteries, burnished with renewed vibrancy where she walked, waist deep through the dew-drenched grasses. Stems nodded in whispered welcome around her, laced by the canes of ripening blackberries, green hazel, thistle, and aster. Her footfall on the breast of the earth disturbed nothing. Crickets wove a virtuoso carpet of sound beneath a sarcenet sky, stitched with stars and the gleam of the moon's fading crescent. Elaira contained the glass edge of her grief, soothed like spun silk by the strictures instilled by the wise. The litany gentled her troubled spirit and harmonized her alignment with the infinite cloth of creation.

'Never take the first plant or the last; not the biggest, the smallest, and never the immature shoot. Accept nothing as given without permission, and leave half untouched, needs met with honour in gratitude for the blessing of bounty received.'

Eased into the quietude of routine collection, Elaira crested a hillock. Dawn loomed to the east, Methlas Lake a gleaming shimmer of beaded silver at the horizon. Her basket wanted only red clover to replenish her needful restoratives.

Upset dashed her plan. A sudden, sharp shock roiled the tranquil flux currents. Her nape bristled, warning of something amiss.

Then like a cast pall, the night insects fell silent.

Poised between steps, Elaira looked up. The stars overhead were eclipsed, knifed across by a sail-shaped shadow. Massive and fast, the airborne predator kited past her location, the whipped vegetation gusted as though raked by a storm front. Sinuous as a cat, alive with the ripple of reptilian scales and abrasive, malevolent insolence, the stalking dragon banked into a curve.

Forty spans from horned head to the dorsal spine on its vaned tail, it alighted, the wicked arch of each taloned foreclaw readily able to skewer an ox.

The molt reared its arched neck and stared down at the two-legged speck in its path, eyes bezeled in armoured lids moulten gold as the sun not yet risen. Restless with rambunctious vigor, immaturity redoubled by the repressed crackle of latent sexual energy, the dragon's interest fired the ambient ether into fluorescent profusion.

Elaira froze, her startlement nailed into frantic suspension. Converse with dragons outmatched her ability. Ciladis's teaching provided the rudimentary measure of precaution, an awareness sufficient to grasp the extent of her danger. She must not show fright. Dared not succumb to emotional panic or flood the inward perception already flung wide open to tap into the subtle nuance of the land in her surrounds. As her discipline stretched to counter the chaos rampaging through the interface, she heard Voice: the young dragon's unruly, excited emanation musing upon its discovery.

'Two-legged, female, this mote did not match the designate pattern of the forepromised, chosen prey. Human, not quite the rich morsel offered to Dragonkind as reward. Yet she wore the trace scent of that dazzling prize on her person.'

Horror swept the enchantress. Pinched in the vice of an alien consciousness too mighty to grapple, she tagged the telltale source of the serpent's attraction: the plain cuff tie with its twinkling seed pearls betrayed her nondescript anonymity. *Arithon* was the treasure dangled in reference to some godless, clandestine bargain. The taint impressed on the dragon's exuberance reeked of sigils wrought by the Koriathain.

The shocked epiphany erupted too late, that she had blundered, heedless, into a trip-wire snare primed with Arithon's life as the bargaining chip.

Faster than thought, the dragon's cocked head snaked down to her level. The golden, slit-pupiled orbs of the monster inspected her. Trained perception consumed by the resonant roar of terrible, eldritch forces, Elaira felt her mindful thought scattered like reeds in a maelstrom. The self-affirmed anchor of her personality became peeled, layers flayed by an annihilating tide of absorption aimed to consume, flesh and spirit unravelled like yarn unreeled from a jerked swatch of knit. *Her existence was nothing.* To a creature dissecting a *figment*, tinkering curiosity would assimilate the quaint sum of her temporal experience.

How to sever the flaying grip of a being whose nature remade natural order at whim? She was the insect entrapped by the firestorm, too slight to escape immolation.

"You will not take me willing, by my Name and birthright!" Elaira screamed in defiance.

Her cry raised the unseen force of a whirlwind. A luminous entity brighter than her unsheathed brazen power, a flaunting ploy to swerve the focus of the creature hell-bent to subsume her. The diversion fractured the young dragon's volatile fascination.

Then Kharadmon's unshielded presence breezed past, a whip's flick at her flank. *'Run!'* exhorted the Fellowship shade, his urgent timbre of terror incomprehensible from one of the Seven. *'Forsake Arithon's side, and for both of your sakes, don't look back at your peril.'* His reckless appearance her decoy, he qualified, *'I will lure the drake molt astray! Bend the flux as you can to muffle your track, and for the love of all you hold dear, pray Dakar's dim-witted practice has engaged something better than slipshod protection behind you.'*

Then the Sorcerer's turbulent visitation was gone. Wing leather unfurled. The downstroke a thunderous gust that scoured the brush, the dragon's launch bashed Elaira onto her knees. The drake uncoiled, a sinuous bolt limned in flared azure that streaked like an arrow's flight into the heavens. A leviathan of shining scales, tucked muscle and ebon claws, it soared overhead, tail vanes carving a buffeted wake in pursuit of the discorporate Sorcerer's gambit.

Elaira thrust upright, spun westward and sprinted. Satchel clapped to her hip, lungs burning, she fled for her life to distance herself from the lakeshore. More than single-minded desperation drove her to seek cover in the deepest wilds of the Radmoore Downs. Past question, Kharadmon's admonishment meant business, given the scope of destructive ambition that bargained with dragons to take down her beloved. Elaira dared not return to Arithon's side, even to warn, lest she should be followed, and he fell prey to the unconscionable plot the reigning Prime Matriarch had unleashed upon him as her nemesis.

Unaware how severely his wards had been tested, Dakar stirred at dawn, bothered by the incessant complaint of his bladder. Birdsong rang too loud in his ears. If the south wind blew clean of the mire's putrid stench, the harbinger foreran the inbound misery of changed weather and torrential squalls. He belched and rolled over. Prodded from basking inertia by necessity's clamour, he tottered erect and shuffled off to relieve himself.

Past the spent fire, beside Arithon's occupied bedding, grey twilight revealed a winkle of white gold left impaled on the black steel of Alithiel's hilt.

"Dame Luck's sweet rosy tits!" Dakar chortled, gloating. For once, the emerald signet of Rathain lay unguarded, with Elaira's watchful presence gone elsewhere and Arithon heedlessly sleeping.

Dakar stumbled into his shameless chance to fulfil the Fellowship Sorcerers' charge without confrontation. Two furtive steps let him reclaim the Crown Jewel, flip the chain over his head, and stuff the emerald signet under his shirtfront. Yawning, he jigged onwards and voided, then burrowed back into his blanket to snatch a last wink.

He woke with the morning sun in his eyes and a vile tongue furred like frog slime. Elaira was absent, along with her knife and satchel. The Mad Prophet sat up and scraped an itch in his beard, annoyed to find the burden of nurse-maid dumped into his lap. But his flare of annoyance encountered no target. The campsite was deserted. Alithiel no longer rested where the invalid's blanket had been.

Arithon had left also, without a word of leave.

"There's thanks for the bother in a rancid nutshell!" Dakar thumped his chest, reassured he still carried Rathain's purloined seal ring. Hungry and disgruntled, he tidied his points, then swore a tirade in ferocious earnest, that rained damnation in triplicate on the s'Ffalenn bastard's twice-royal ancestry. "And, hear my plea, may Dharkaron's Black Spear shear his bollocks in vile and bloody revenge!"

For the sweep of the lakeshore before him showed no sign of Verrain's pirogue. Only the furrowed scrape on the beach left by her keel on departure. The inexcusable theft, for ill grace, left the Mad Prophet stranded fifty desolate leagues from a trade-road, without civilized transport beyond his two feet.

Adversities

Daon Ramon's broad vales offered few landmarks to the man left alone in strange territory. Worse, Lysaer s'Ilessid had never troubled to cultivate facile expertise in the wilds. His reliable sense of direction lost referent under the flat sheet of cloud. If he had salvaged breeches and shirt from the abandoned wagon, no fire had eased his soaked discomfort under a sky spitting drizzle for days. The wide, rolling hills looked alike. Weathered granite split the wind at all quarters, a barren harbour for nothing but lichen. Turned around, doused by the latest brisk storm front, Lysaer cursed his failure to kindle wet fuel, beset by another miserable night.

Sun returned in the morning without fortune's blessing. His spare gelding protested the pinch of the pack harness, yanked backwards, and broke away. What remained of his loosely bundled provisions slid askew on its barrel. Before patience quelled the unfolding disaster, a gust whisked through a burst tie string and billowed the blanket roll. The horse shied, tail flagged, and stomped its looped rein with a jerk that unravelled the last tame nerve it possessed.

Helpless with rage, Lysaer lunged, too late. The nitwit beast wheeled and bolted at a flat gallop over the hillcrest.

The tethered mare snorted. Eyes rolled to the whites, she strained her rope, sidling. The plunge to check her herdbound scramble earned Lysaer a trampled toe. "Brainless meat!"

Sopped supplies jettisoned, he thrust his mashed foot into the dangling stirrup, hopped, one-legged, and clawed astride. Discomposed with no groom to steady the bridle, and annoyed by the inconvenience, he settled into his seat, while the head-shaking equine beneath him pawed turf, and his rope-burned palms tussled with her hard-mouthed fight to kite off in the gelding's wake.

"No, you don't!" snarled Lysaer, and yanked her around.

She baulked, the rank witch. Ears pinned and jaws yawed in protest, the beast humped her spine at the prod of his heels. A thousandweight of intractable muscle, she refused to go southward with a mulish persistence that snapped her rider's frayed temper.

"Gormless ox! Are you jinxed?" Lysaer dug in his heels, jilted by a crowhop. He kicked again, harder, and the mare reared on him, spinning. Spilled from the saddle, he managed to keep his ferocious grip on the reins. Dragged with her snorting panic, Lysaer slid on his belly until she gave up.

The penalty of a flayed palm and torn clothing clinched his distemper. "Damn your worthless hide to the knackers!"

The cursed hack blew at him through a spraddle-legged standoff. Twinged by fresh bruises, Lysaer spat grit from his mouth. Swearing malignant ruin on everything foaled with hooves to the tenth generation, he untwisted the stirrup iron and remounted, too nettled to care if the horse trembled under him. The plight befallen the war host his forsaken command had unforgivably left abandoned found no other available outlet. He lashed out, and the recalcitrant animal exploded. Catapulted by her twisting buck, Lysaer landed hard, banged his head, and passed out.

He woke to a blurred vista of sky, rimmed with grassheads stirred by a sultry breeze. Cumulous cloud piled up to the southwest, not yet flattened into summer anvilheads. Lysaer grimaced and sat up, wincing. Bruised and stiffened like almighty vengeance, he fingered the tender lump on his crown, dislodged a scab, and restarted the bleeding.

Plagued by the murderous throb of his skull, Lysaer tested his equilibrium, shoved erect, and resumed his southbound journey afoot. Sweating hot, he determined to re-join the remnant survivors of his broken company before nightfall. Men lost to the cause could not be returned for death rites to their families. But the reckoning for their fruitless sacrifice required the acknowledgement of his presence. And if a bewildered remnant still breathed, he could do no less than rally them for the march home.

Yet the trackless turf resisted his progress. Shoulder-high grass snagged his ankles, and shed chaff irritated his eyes. Lysaer shouldered onwards, sneezing. He railed at the repressive restrictions on travel imposed by the Seven, and refused to cashier his moral conviction. Mankind deserved liberation from obstructive tyranny. Never would he relinquish that charge, or *ever again* be cozened to lean in treacherous liaison with man or woman. If he failed to master this setback, or wavered from the just cause of free enterprise, he dared not claim the right to fair rule.

Daliana never had grasped the deep-set pain of his culpability.

The dead on the field were his fallen! Did anyone left alive understand the unbearable burden of his responsibility? Better he had ridden with the bannermen at the forefront under the fell influence of Desh-thiere's curse and died in the morning alongside the best and the bravest, than to have been spared by a woman's well-meaning intent to endure such harrowing excoriation. His direct order had sent fifteen thousand to their demise, clothed in the false pretence of a vacuous faith.

What right action could expunge the stain he had unleashed on the honest, hardworking populace of this benighted world?

Empty, rich land unturned by the plough rolled away to blue distance, lidded under the vast bowl of a sky scribed with circling hawks and edged by a darkening storm front. Cheeping finches and insects whirred to startled flight, teeming in the absence of fruitful habitation. Lysaer could not recall his last moment of solitude. Shamed by remorse he flinched to examine, and haunted afresh by the perfidy of Daliana, he cringed to remember the intimate service she had foisted upon him as the Fellowship's spy.

She would live to regret. Weakness purged by Ellaine and Talith before her had toughened the main strength Lysaer needed now to denounce the pitfall of female tenderness. The hurt seared into him by his dam's betrayal might have spared him the trials that left him bereft, had he taken the hard lesson to heart. "Damn all women's wiles to Sithaer's black pit!"

Sunk in maudlin thought, parched and sunburned and furious, Lysaer failed to notice the lone traveller on horseback, halted on the grassland in front of him.

Startled up short, he found himself raked by the stare of a wizened grand dame swathed in black shawls. Breeze ruffled the fringes and flagged her tatty clothes, lending the fleeting, eerie illusion of a black crow perched on her left shoulder. A hood of matte wool cowled her swarthy complexion. The beaked jut of her nose and crimped chin melted into midday shadow, but for the glint of gimlet eyes, deep-set within a skull armature.

Pinned under her brazen inspection, Lysaer's covetous need fastened upon the fine gelding bearing her aged frailty. Ridden bridleless, the rare animal might have been twin to the cherished mount destroyed in the carnage of Etarra's first campaign against the Master of Shadow. Prized stock, bred by the insular drifters who ranged the fells in west Tysan, this gelding's intelligent bearing also reflected the peerless responsiveness of their training.

Lysaer blurted his imperious demand before thought. "I will have your mount, old mother. Either as a gift or by the exigency of the Light's requisition, I must fare south with all speed to attend the disaster inflicted upon the coalition's campaign."

The ancient tipped her cowled head. Her impenetrable regard devoured the daylight and her speech lifted hair like the drawn scrape of steel on a whetstone. "There is no warrior left standing in need of your oversight. The camp's menials at large in the absence of officers are able to fend for themselves."

Lysaer stiffened, incensed by the impertinence. "I will be the judge of their disposition, after I survey their straits and verify the fatalities inflicted upon my front ranks." The welted hand raised with imperial confidence expected unquestioned compliance. "The horse if you please, granddame."

The crone in her tatterdemallion rags scorned his birthright assumption of hierarchy. "You wish to take and give nothing?"

Lysaer bristled, the flush of stung pride whetted by curse-driven antipathy. "Do I seem to have the resource left to pay?" The effrontery scalded, that a brittle, defenceless old stick defied his clear task to shoulder the ruin his own hand had inflicted. "Camp followers, you insist, might look after their own if I did not require their work to attend my mauled companies. In contrast, the dead cannot brook the delay. The casualty list must be tallied in full. Honourable obligation requires their remains to be put to the torch before they are scattered by scavengers."

The ancient peered downwards. Unmoved as mummified stone atop her magnificent horseflesh, she dismissed the peril of his impatience. "Who gives nothing stands for nothing at all."

Erect, gilt hair stirred by the gusty approach of the darkening squall line, Lysaer denounced her toothless senility. "Woman! Take heed. *Do you know who I am?*"

Her cackle of mockery prickled his nape. "No one."

The dismissal pushed Lysaer's abraded vulnerability too far. Fury closed his raised fist. A sharp blast from his gift would topple the shrivelled beldame at his feet, singed bald and weeping in humiliation.

Instead, his wrought light bolt entangled with the shawl the hag flung off her shoulders; or perhaps something else, not loomed fabric at all, but a monstrous crow launched into flight like distilled shadow before him. Uncanny spelled cloth or unnatural bird, the apparition clapped down on Lysaer like starless nightfall and extinguished his conscious awareness without recourse.

The ancient shrouded in her midnight regalia regarded the blond scion of Requiar's descent, dropped in senseless collapse before her gelding's front hooves. Lysaer was, to her eyes, human form without substance, a transparent vessel defined by the nuance of individual character. Her piercing gaze measured his essence and knew keening sorrow for the wilful distortion of a lifetime's noble potential. More than the impetus of Desh-thiere's malice had shaped this spirit's wayward path. The adult man considered women beneath his contempt, never having outgrown a child's resentment for the conflict of principle that had driven the tormented mother's desertion. A seed fallen to poison, brokered on sterile ground, his begetting had shaped an affront to the balance of connected reciprocity. Wounded character suckled upon self-importance cast a blight on the boundless abundance that sustained the myriad world. Lysaer s'Ilessid knew nothing. Learned nothing; refused love's generosity and his faithful servant's advice under the blindfold of venal arrogance. Heart and mind, he lacked respect for the gifts that balanced the hoop of existence.

By Mother Dark's code, a grown being bereft of the empathic humility to seek understanding did not merit help.

The crone took pause only for her greater debt to Davien, whose gruelling service had alienated him from his own and imposed his cruel centuries of solitary exile. The Fellowship Sorcerer had asked her for nothing since the fateful hour she presented her harsh request. No bargain had been demanded or struck in exchange. Today, the ancient chose in her wisdom to grant him the favour he had never begged in return.

"You are no one," she decreed to the son of Requiar's line sprawled inert in the blameless grass. "Be no one."

Her whisper dissolved into a flurry of wings and blurred feathers. The gust of her arcane transformation sheared through flattened greenery, and a deafening drumroll of thunder slammed echoes through the gravid air. Wrapped in tumult before the storm broke, a great owl with black-and-silver-barred plumage soared up and away, leaving vacancy where nothing stood. No horse and no woman remained of the singular presence vanished from the continuum without a trace.

Lysaer roused to the throb of a shattering headache. A soaked rag plastered over his forehead dripped water down his temples and into his ears. The seeped runnel that wet his cracked lips tasted bitter, seasoned by the acidic tang of aged oak from the cask. He lay on the jostling boards of a dray. Discomfort and weakness left him too tender to stir. He drew a breath stilted by his sore ribs, and gagged on the ammoniac reek of cooped chickens. The cacophonic squabbles of hens stuttered through the chatter of female voices.

A lively exchange of frivolous gossip mused on his condition over his head.

". . . must be some officer's fancy boy, d'ye think?"

"Cleaned up? Aye. Dress that build in fine silk, he'd be too gorgeous for an equerry."

"Not a scar on him. No callus. For certain, he never put the parade shine on anyone's helmet and boots."

Blistered by embarrassment, Lysaer flung out an arm. His knuckles collided with somebody's hip, bolstered in opulent flesh and flounced skirts. A piercing squeal of delight creased his eardrums, refrain to the uprush of dizziness that dimmed his cohesive awareness.

"Light bless!" The ponderous shift of weight to his left marked a second hussy, exclaiming. "Dearie oh! Love, be still. You've suffered a dreadful whack on the pate."

Someone else, shrill as brass, posed an unintelligible question.

"Aye, for sure." The stout woman built like a laundress prodded him in the ribs with a fruity chuckle. "He's rousing, all right. Testy fellow!

Here's a shyster's copper against pocket lint, he's a bravo displeased to be flat on his back in our shameless company."

The rag lifted.

Sunlight dazzled his vision. Lysaer shied back from the plump palm that caressed his cheek, an unwise recoil that thumped his spinning head into the wagonbed. What felt like the liquified dregs of his brains sloshed against the tumult banging his cranium. Pain wracked him with nausea, while the presumptuous bawd fussed over his misery. "Lie down, laddie. Your split scalp's got a swell the size of a pigeon's egg."

Lysaer fingered the clotted bruise, winced, and took painful stock. Late day's shadow angled across him, slanted opposite to his preferred course. Elbowed free of patronizing restraint, he let outrage spur his reeling shove to sit upright. "We're going north!"

"O'course, lovey!" The scold's generous, rouged lips framed a smirk. Above rice-powdered cheeks, her kohl-painted eyes sized up his male attributes with the jaded habit of invitation. "Naught's left of the great-folks' campaign to return for. Just wreckage and death and a howling pack of madmen who'd try force before coin for a romp in the blankets. Light's fortune spared you a mugging, since our frisky selves happened along. Plucked you senseless as bundled sticks off the heath from what seems a tumble off the backside of your horse."

Lysaer gritted his jaw. Squinting against the shattering glare, he surveyed the rattletrap flotilla of wagons and beasts, driven or ridden or led in hand by the war host's detritus of camp followers. The doxies, the smiths, the brawny armourers and wheelwrights, the stout laundresses and red-faced cooks, tagged after by their skinny draggle of byblows, who frolicked in raucous play with a lopsided ball. No granddame veiled in black shawls walked among them. No splendid horse twin to the bereft memory of his drifter-bred chestnut. The apparition might have been a figment, shaped in the delirium caused by concussion.

Dream or not, the throb of his pulped skull leached the fire from his irritation. Icily civil, Lysaer enquired, "I missed the finish of the armed assault. Exactly what became of the field troop's advance upon Caith-al-Caen?"

Through the jolting plod of the oxcart, between confounding conjecture and rumour, Lysaer assembled the crushing extent of a defeat beyond comprehension. None who marched with his proud companies survived.

"The religion's priests blessed the dead on what they are calling the Field of Glory. Word goes all of those who perished were taken in raptured bliss. A white pigeon was flown with gold ribbons to East Ward. True Sect witnesses have set seal to their claim the Light's avatar has ascended."

"What!" Eyes hard as cut sapphire widened. "On what evidence does the religion base that preposterous nonsense?"

"Maybe instead the Blessed Lord was damned for corrupted morality," a saucy brunette sneered with a flounce. Strayed faith, after all, funnelled vigorous business to her profession. "Light itself intervened, so they say. A pious reminder that mercantile avarice over way rights overstepped the divine mission decreed by the Canon. The avatar retired to Light, or else he turned apostate and went to his damnation, leaving the greater war against Darkness in mortal hands. The great task of the ages is Mankind's to earn the righteousness of divine redemption."

"The priests in their vaunted temples know nothing," Lysaer snapped, indignant. "I will demonstrate proof." Sore shoulder ignored, he lifted his fist to tap the birth-born wellspring of his gift.

Nothing happened. As though emptied, *his mastery of light did not answer!*

Surprise drained him pale. Speechless, dismayed, he lost his poise. Amid appalled quiet, his plump, painted benefactor patted his knee in sympathy for the mistaken impression he languished in pitiful shock from his injury.

"Suffered a right ghastly ding on the noggin." Else the demise of the patron who kept pretty toys in buttons and bows shook the pampered wits of a bedfellow turned out in a thankless world. "No wonder the poor bereft sweetie's confused."

"Yer welcome to stay on with us to Narms," soothed the battle-scarred matron who muscled the reins of the ox. "Have to harden those hands. Haul slop buckets and pitch tents and work for your board with the roust-abouts." Transfixed by an incensed, blue glare, she slapped her generous bosom and laughed. "Think you've a choice, lad? Then mope off and starve. Nobody gets fed, or rides, or takes up cargo space as a freeloader."

The timber posts for another unsanctioned rope ferry had been sunk by night on the riverbanks above the lowland fork where the Tal Quorin merged into the narrower branch of the Tiethin. Four years since Iyat-thos Tarens had breasted the swifter current upstream, the watercourse here snaked into the eastward bend that stepped in downward cascades from the spring-fed source in the Mathorn foothills. He remembered the Mad Prophet's colourful swearing with reason. Glacial melt ran the shallows ice-cold, even in the dry blaze of late summer.

Earl Jieret's older recollection encompassed the blood hunts for the bounties sought after by scalpers, to the covert ambushes staged for revenge, and loop snares of twine set for hare to line warm clothing for winter. Ages before Mankind's step trod Athera, the pebbled bed of the river had witnessed the sunchild Breienaldien's famed lament for the morass of slaughter by Searduin, and the floated bier, wreathed in flowers, that bore the murdered centaur Rialthan and his wounded beloved towards their last sunset at the scalloped shoreline of Instrell Bay.

Today's gadfly annoyance might not shake the world, or be sung into the annals of history by a Masterbard's grief. But for Tarens, blistered from weeks on patrol, the perpetual thorn stung afresh for the constant assaults imposed by freewheeling commodity.

"Those monstrosities have to come down?" The lithe scout circled in from the flank shed her boots and peeled off dusty leathers, resigned. "More's the pity, your scowl won't lighten the misery."

Rogue traders hauled their ferry logs by yoked oxen across the open grassland with little impediment. They sited their illicit crossings where the spring floods scoured the heaviest overgrowth, ample clearance for the low-slung axles of their lumbering drays. No available timber to mount block and tackle made upending their wretched enterprise harder. Iyat-thos shrugged off his brown thoughts and rounded up the outlying patrol to speed up the excavation.

Whistled in for their muscle, the conscripted band grumbled. "How many of these desecrations have we flattened to flaming wreckage?"

"Three, on my watch. Pointless as pounding rocks into sand! Turn your back, and the coin-grubbing termites just plant their rope anchors all over again."

"Not this time." Tarens wrestled his shirt off sunburned shoulders bulked up by the ploughshare. Before him, the trampled grass at the verge showed the charred remnants of several fires and the flyblown entrails of a poached deer. Senseless waste that offended clanborn sensibility hackled him to white fury, the more so as the heaped manure left by the marauders' trespass varied from bone dry to freshly moist. "More than one caravan's broken this route. We finish the job with a stake pit."

A spike through the foot might sober the two-legged vermin enough to pay better heed.

A deterrent sharpened for retaliation brightened the collective surge towards the river bottom. More scouts arrived. Tarens made disposition: some to stand a perimeter guard, another detail to strip cattail stalks and braid rope, and the lucky pair who drew straws to forage charged to furnish the spit for their supper.

The task of tracking the townbred offenders stayed unassigned, plans for a proper raid on their caravan supplanted by the shriek of a scout's signal arrow loosed from the fringe.

Labour paused, with the canted post partly exhumed and the wicker frame of laid tinder unfinished. Fire would gnaw the sunk wood to live coals, smokeless as a charcoal pit until, top-heavy, the unlawful erection leaned over and toppled.

Half of the relief party sprawled on the Tiethin's east bank, streaming wet from a swim, when the messenger sent from Fallowmere sprinted in under escort from the perimeter. The muddied scouts grubbing up sod by the post joined their idle fellows to hear the urgent dispatch from the west.

Surprised to encounter no hard-ridden horse, Tarens brushed off the black, grasslands loam the born crofter would have rejoiced to till for sown barley. "The relay's come in by foot?"

"Lamed her mare," the laconic runner replied. "Turned the animal loose with a stone bruise to find her way back to the herd." Terse, breathless phrases, pared down the point. "On the run for two days, she's ravenous. I gave her a ration of hardtack and jerky, but fresh meat would be better."

"Deadeye's bow will deliver," a scout quipped from the sidelines. "Pigeon pie on the wing, and plenty of that crisscrossing the region like shuttlecocks."

"Enough!" Tarens killed the loose chatter. "Stow your bid for the roll in her blanket till later."

If the messenger seemed too beaten for flirtatious sport, dirt-caked weariness runnelled in sweat, she still noted the offensive post and its twin, still tamped upright on the opposite bank. "Another? The pests plague us like rats. Once thwarted, they just scuttle sidewise."

An avid admirer, naked and still dripping, thrust an uncorked flask into her hands. "Not water, sweet lass."

She grinned back, tossed off a swallow, then swiped back plastered wisps of brown hair for an appreciative grin. "Don't think to cozen my gratitude, that randy privilege has to be earned."

The provocative challenge raised vivacious laughter.

Tarens deflected the byplay, a lump in his throat. "Report first, if you please." The family man pinched between two incompatible legacies chafed for his pregnant wife, separated with Laithen's band in the far north, since clan custom guarded the threat to her bloodline.

The messenger sobered, her news grave enough to eclipse other concerns. "Lysaer's allied war host is destroyed. The lead companies perished to the last man when the Paravians returned to secure Caith-al-Caen. Additional word from Sethvir sends us warning. Five drake molts range free on Athera. We're to stay low if they're seen, not for any reason to engage them."

"What befell Lysaer?" Desh-thiere's fate hung in the balance, that burden weighting an uncertain future Jieret's terrible sacrifice had yet to secure. "Does anyone know?"

"Sethvir's said he escaped. But the Canon priests have spawned their own myth for the faithful since no body was found." The messenger's sigh exposed crushing weariness. "The Light's record claims the avatar's armour lay empty alongside the dead with the standard-bearers. Given the absence of corrupted flesh, the temple attests the divine miracle of their godhead's incarnate retirement, attached with the righteous caveat. The task of cleansing the world of Shadow and Darkness falls to mortal man in perpetuity."

"And that turkey turd claptrap means what?" sniped a restive scout in disgust.

Only Tarens seized on the appalling transference of power, tailor made to entrench a bellicose ideology. "The religion will strike at the heart of the clans. To suppress the threat of Paravian expansion, the towns' northern reserves will be mustered." The anguish of the farmer's rooted loyalty struck spark to the iron-hard ethic of the *caithdein* and wakened the killer's instinct. Swift deduction measured the scope of the massed opposition – two thousand from Westfen, augmented by the eight thousand rear-guard reserves billeted at Narms and Cildorn. Vengeance for the advance would be swift, hell-bent to wreak merciless havoc on the clan families sheltered in Fallowmere.

"We must pack up the camps and get folk on the move." Earl Jieret's penchant for prescience savaged Tarens to clammy dread. Momentarily, the ground underfoot seemed to ripple, shocked by the tramp of armed troops, while the humid air reeked with the blood stench of fresh violence. "How long do I have to prepare?"

The scout squared off, blunt. "Garrisons from the coasts are marching already, with Perlorn and East Ward to join forces for the first onslaught from the east. Westward, you'll have a narrow delay before the carnage begins in earnest. But only until the temple's dedicate conscripts from Tysan can be staged across Instrell Bay to bolster the offensive."

The snapped question was unequivocally Jieret's. "Numbers?"

"A draw of twelve thousand. Best hope their crack officers with free-wilds experience met their demise at Caith-al-Caen."

Tarens shut his eyes, the clay feet of his practicality harrowed by trouble his countrybred origins never imagined. Remembrance not his own flayed him with the bygone sorrows of tragedy in reprise: of the terror times, when enemies struck for eradication at the threshold of winter. The routed defences counted in lives, fought from cover to cover to hold open the line of retreat. When revered elders died, slaughtered in feints for diversion, while women and children took flight. Harried without shelter or stores, the few hale survivors pushed on without mercy, hollow-eyed at the verge of starvation.

Jieret's sad toll of grief beggared courage. Who remained to count the names of his fallen? The unborn innocents rent in the womb, or the infants found frozen beneath the carcasses of the mothers butchered by the wayside and abandoned for carrion? The fathers cut down in the shocked sight of their sons, and the brained children, cradled limp in the arms of their kin?

Tarens repressed his welled tears for the horror of what lay ahead. How cornered desperation honed the unconscionable measures to ever more ruthless expertise, until league reavers left thrashing in the gore of their death throes spattered the snow, gutted in shattered agony by sprung snares.

For a moment, writ large, the murderous chorus of screams yet to come seemed to echo across the free wilds' skeined rivers and hidden glens. The kind man whose hands had buried two nephews quailed to face the whimpers of frostbitten children, concealed and alone in the silent, white thickets seized at need as a refuge from extirpation.

The crofter in Tarens had endured the pinched hunger ahead of the first milk at spring calving. But Jieret's experience knew the suffering imposed by forced flight when provender in bulk could not be carried, and the bitter pressure of enemy tactics disrupted the game and torched the smoke sheds that cured the autumn hunt's stockpiled meat.

The days of summer's bounty were precious against a looming threat that congealed the hot pulse in his veins.

"Well done." Tarens released the messenger to take her ease, filled his lungs, and shouted brisk orders. "Everyone! These posts come down, double quick! I want stake traps built against worse than merchants, and a sapper's maze sited downriver. Map out the chosen locations by sundown. And call in our best long-range archers. The relay's got to be flagged down by signal arrow to dispatch a swift warning to Strakewood."

Default

The jab of an ox goad in the ribs woke Dakar with a choke that hacked through his rattling snore. Startled half-upright, elbows bashed with a clank on the iron pigs stacked underneath him, he stared nose to eye with the squint of the reinsman whose dray had collected him, destitute, from the muddy verge of the trade-road.

"Dunno how a fat fellow beds down on that jumble. Only a lazybones botched in the pan naps so hard a half dozen pokes in the hide's needed for rousting him."

Too sulky to grouse, Dakar scrubbed his twisted clothing to rights. Worse than bruises and nightmares had soured his sleep. Palms streaked orange by flaked rust stained his scrofulous clothing. Plagued by a nasty crick in his back, he craned to peer over the slatted sides of the cart. "We're here?"

"Ganish town, aye." The pesky ox goad nudged him again, the crimped stare fixed upon him less friendly. "Off you get. Here's the smith's to unload. Move, or be rolled like a lard sack into the street."

Dakar wriggled on his fundament, slid off the tailboard and feetfirst, splashed into a puddle that sieved urine through his swamp-rotted boots. "Here's a wallow befitting Dharkaron's latrine!"

The bustling craft quarter around him received his malingering with indifference, the ungodly clangour of hammers shrill as a sack of squashed cats. Palms clapped to his ears, the vagrant spellbinder dodged a hand-cart wheeled by a brute whose meat thews strained his patched leather apron. Sweltered by the forge at his back, he dripped sweat and surveyed his position.

Ganish town furnished resupply to a trader's route, the board shops of a wheelwright, the sprawled sheds of two smithies, a chandlers' and various coopers and joiners crammed under the mossy ruins of crumbling battlements fallen to decay over centuries. Due diligence no longer manned the old relay of signal towers, once maintained to keep watch for rampaging Methspawn before Verrain's accession as Methisle's Guardian. If lethal invasions had not ravaged the district in memory, above the peaked dormers and through the baking shimmer of hot, tiled roofs, the remanent stone shelters yet wore the crosshatched scars of assault, when deadly swarms from the mire had devastated the countryside. Where the stout beehive towers with their defunct, recessed hinges for siege shutters lent today's populace cool relief from the heat, Dakar found the awning and signpost he sought.

He thumbed the smooth pebble stashed in his pocket, and shoved off, squelching, for civilized refuge in the public tap-room. Penniless and plagued by a perishing thirst, he would sort the onus of his obligations after his comfort was satisfied.

The Mad Prophet stumped into the Fiddler's Rest through the stylish, faced brick that squared up the lopsided entry. A well-polished bar spanned the curved wall ahead, clustered with local layabouts and shirking apprentices. Without a caterwauling musician in evidence, the trestles and benches gleamed with a dented assortment of pewter tankards and plates, bread boards and utensils hard-used by sunburned carters, and merchants plumed in wilted lace. Greybeards hunched over their painted gameboards, unfazed by an idlers' dart game in progress.

Dakar sized up his choice of ripe marks, intent to establish a shell game to wrangle small coin. But his hopeful bid for a meal and a beer imploded as the deeper gloom of the interior revealed the slight, black-haired man perched to the left of the ale tap.

Dakar stalled, skewered in return by a stare better suited to a cornered lynx.

The projected voice of the Masterbard pierced through the background murmur of conversation. *"What are you doing here?"*

Rocked back on his heels, Dakar blinked. "Arithon?"

One forgot at one's peril how quickly the s'Ffalenn bastard moved. Grace primed for murder, he rounded the scarred trestle and clamped a pincered grip on Dakar's upper arm.

"If you're buying a round, I don't need to be manhandled." Steered, skidding on his soaked footwear, the Mad Prophet found himself plonked on a bench. Bemoaning fresh bruises, he cowered, eye to disturbing green eye with the Master of Shadow at his most furious.

"I said, what are you doing here?" Arithon repeated.

Dakar licked dry lips, hope dashed to find the jumbled tankards beside him already emptied.

Arithon pressed, too carefully crisp, "Dare to deny she's not with you."

"Elaira? She isn't." Dakar wrinkled his nostrils, offended by the exhaled reek of beer. "Ath wept, you're drunk!"

The accusation rammed into a wall of deflection. "You let her get past you!" Dismayed, incredulous, Arithon ranted, "How could you fail to stand guard for her life?" Riled past sense, he continued, never mind that the woman was empowered to handle herself on her merits. "At the least, you could have stood by her, if only for her consolation."

"Elaira shoved off on her own," Dakar snapped, stung to defensive frustration. "Her explicit wish said my role was to look after you! What did I get for my thankless support? You stole Verrain's pirogue and left me stranded! If you'd recovered enough to light out, then why, by the torment of Sithaer's blackest hell, did you desert her?"

Aware of turned heads, Arithon muted his argument. "Because the lady only meant to replenish her herb stores."

"Well, in that case, the misery's on your own head. You gave her grim reason enough not to stay as your nurse-maid." Dakar canted sidewards and snagged up a tankard. "If I'm to endure your nasty temper, you can wet my whistle as fair compensation."

The plea brought no joy, only stoked the next round of verbal evisceration. "Did she choose to depart without word?"

Dakar banged the vessel into the board, rude summons to the bar wench draped over the tap cheek by jowl with a swanky skinner.

Arithon's verdict derailed the evasion. "You never shifted your arse to investigate!"

Beard bristled, lips clenched, the spellbinder flipped a leg over the bench. He swivelled, back turned, and hoisted his arm, frantic to flag the lackadaisical service lulled by the slow afternoon.

"You don't know?" Desolate after his whetted aggression, Arithon's rejoinder rang bitter. "Whether she went on her own recognizance, or by the Fatemaster's grief, if anything ugly befell her, the Seven better be swift to enforce the Crown's covenant and spare her from harm by my enemy's design."

The expectant pause lifted hackles and pebbled gooseflesh at Dakar's nape. Riveted by the barmaid's inattention, he broke out in fresh perspiration and loosened his collar points.

"Dharkaron Avenge!" Arithon seized his evasive target by the shirt-front.

Dakar yelped. Jerked face about like bagged game, he squirmed backwards too late. His assailant's hard fingers snaked through parted linen, and hooked the winkle of chain tucked beneath his pouched throat.

"You bear Rathain's signet!" If Arithon's rage had been dicey before, the peril he radiated tightened his fist and twisted the silver links into a garrotte. "Why, Dakar? That ring belongs on Elaira's person!"

"You forget." The Mad Prophet yanked backwards in flustered protest. "Since you no longer bear sovereign entitlement, I was charged by the Fellowship to reclaim the Crown's emerald seal."

Arithon bore down, the crease knifed into the Mad Prophet's dough flesh grown relentless. "Then, Ath above spare us both, why didn't you stay to ascertain her safety?"

Dakar clawed at the irascible chokehold, incredulous. "And leave your crazy devices unwatched?"

The offensive hold on him released as though burned. Arithon sank back down on the bench. Perhaps not quite hale, he propped his tousled head, black hair wicked through his splayed fingers.

Drawn by the scuffle, the barmaid sauntered up, flanked by the two scowling heavies employed to dispose of untoward trouble.

"We're not upset enough to try breaking things." Arithon moved, slipped a knot, and freed the bulging, wash-leather bag slung at his hip. His casual toss struck the trestle with a clink.

Dakar's cobra-quick snatch intercepted the bribe. A shyster's smile parted his beard as he hefted the generous contents: coinweight sufficient to stave off eviction, and more, fill his underserved needs to excess. Gleeful, he ransacked Arithon's stash for a ransomer's sum as placation.

"Well, then, that's better!" Transformed, the wench swanned off to fetch beer, trailed at heel by the animal tread of the tap-room's protection.

No further friction arose. The filched purse apparently not worth dispute, the bystanders' interest slackened to boredom.

Arithon's mild appearance aside, his soft accusations resumed at a pitch no less ferociously dangerous. "She is off to who knows where, under threat, and stripped of her unimpeachable allies!"

Unnerved to distraction, Dakar delved moist fingers into the sack. "You might have given the matter a thought before larking off on your jaunt to insanity." Grubbing excavation arrived at a tally, he groped underneath his mussed shirt to be sure of the intact chain on the signet tucked against his breast. "What threat, forbye?" His inauspicious strait seemed a tad brighter, with the Seven's directive secure without a knockdown fight to retain possession. "Your crafty enchantress owns the sharpened claws to defend herself."

Arithon's features hardened like glass. He confided nothing. Against every conceivable precedent, he withheld the wicked, barbed comment fashioned for hurt to buy distance.

Dakar repressed a prescient shiver. "Not now!" He mouthed underneath his gulped breath. Fortune delivered him, the violent undertow of pending Sight disrupted by the barmaid, sauntered back with a sway of broad hips and a pitcher. She topped up two tankards. Eager to flirt for the prospect of coin, she lingered, while Dakar compiled a stupendous request for victuals to amend the pinch of his belly.

"The sweetening pay was excessive," he allowed, the reaction to his guilty excuse assessed by a swivelled glance sidewards.

But Arithon forbore to comment. The dreadful bent of his introspection instead fastened on the slopped foam that hissed over his wrist, a broody pause he broke without warning. Vessel raised bottoms up, he chugged the sour brew to the dregs. Dakar gaped in awe. All his days, he had never seen beer demolished with such decisive intensity. Curiosity piqued, several bystanders stared also, while the dart players suspended their avid match, and a salacious idler elbowed his neighbour. "How long, for or against, until the nippit stranger's consumption flops him under the trestle?"

Hoots derided the wager.

The next taunt provoked laughter. "Stripling would pass for a maid, trussed in skirts."

"Don't waste yer copper. Lad won't hold a skinful!"

Arithon saluted the untoward slights, leaned forward, and poured a next round.

For a private man averse to outside scrutiny, the non sequitur jolted, as if the bared edge of a lethal threat had been suddenly sheathed. Dakar loosed his pent breath. Too famished for puzzles, he slaked his own thirst, then applied himself, gorging to repletion at the Master of Shadow's expense.

Slantwise, he watched, content not to move, while the contrary creature beside him methodically drank. Vessel followed the next brimming vessel, a flagrant indulgence strikingly rare, even for those few occasions when Arithon had plastered his wits into wilful oblivion. Dakar remembered an evening of grief, the artful release wrought through music following Halliron Masterbard's death, then the close of the torrid affair with a bereaved tribal shepherdess in Vastmark. Years later, the inebriated collapse, foisted upon Arithon by friends in conspiracy to ease a stressful obligation compelled by guest oath in Rathain. Lastly, the wedding celebration of a saucy minx to a virile, young liegeman from Shand, foredoomed by the prescient shadow of murder on the blade of a treacherous ally.

If Dakar counted the knockdown contest to cement loyalty with a prideful, cantankerous shipwright, or the rambunctious merriness aimed to engage a difficult crowd, this bout was different. Arithon applied himself to debauchery with single-minded determination. The continuous flow of hard silver ensured the barmaid's attentiveness. The drained cups were refilled, round upon round, through a focused descent into liquid oblivion.

The rigour of initiate discipline imposed the difficulty of a prodigious capacity. Arithon tackled the challenge, his reflexive conditioning undone with a will to test even Dakar's stone-headed tolerance. The detritus of tankards were turned upside down before his well-beaten path to the privy meandered off the straight track. The midday customers finished their meals, the incredulous scraps over wagers replaced by avid huddles of dicers, whose throws clicked across the nicked boards to the yelps of sore losers. Hungry apprentices and street vendors traipsed through, crowded out at day's end by weary craftsmen, then the caravan outriders bunched up with their drovers, in redolent leathers sifted with dust.

Talk swelled into noise. Whooped laughter and singing grew rowdy. Buried under the din, Arithon's shackled tongue loosened, the incisive satire of his remarks slackened by rounded vowels and blurred consonants. Sundown increased the help at the bar. A younger serving maid with flushed cheeks plonked down more brimming tankards. Arithon raised the nearest, foam slopped from the rim. "For Earl Jieret!" Solemnly drunk, he ploughed on into moribund recollection. "And Caolle. Like thorns in the backside, one daren't forget. Here's to that stickler's pig-iron grit!"

Dakar choked, bumped in mid-swallow by Arithon's ungainly lurch. The contrite possibility dawned a bit late, that a man recently stricken with Methspawn poison may not have recovered his natural wits or his healthy resiliency. Dakar squinted, his belated assessment thwarted by the slovenly drape of his subject's unlaced shirt.

Arithon banged down his tankard. "Another." He sighed. "For Sidir's fierce heart that beats yet in the wicked perception of Laithen s'Idir." A tipsy reach filched Dakar's drink from the board. "Damn all women," declared the Master of Shadow, and drank, without care for collateral hazard.

The Mad Prophet lacked the acumen to plumb the peculiar slide into maundering sentiment. Obliged to stay upright, he ate, and napped, and stuffed his paunch on roast beef through the evening's influx of customers. A second-rate singer supplied entertainment, to hand claps and stamping that swelled into raucous noise. Athera's titled Masterbard withstood the execrable din in his owlish stupor. Lulled into complaisance, Dakar snatched a catnap and woke to a carping shout.

"You wastrels are taking up space!" Broad as a house, with a chin like a spade, the tavern's hired muscle towered above him. "No offence, but a lineup of paying folk are waiting to sit for their supper!"

Dakar peered askance. Arithon slumped upon folded arms, features buried behind rumpled tangles of hair. Sundown's mob of craft-quarter patrons crowded the bar, solicited by nightfall's painted collection of trollops, with standing room packed to capacity.

"Here." Dakar moistened his lips in sly calculation and doled out Arithon's coin to smooth over the impasse. "We'll take two upstairs rooms."

The landlord's impatience stopped short of dishonesty. Appeared with change covering the overcharge, he admitted, "Your besotted friend has rented himself private quarters already."

"Fine." Dakar weighed his obligation to Elaira and cringed. Arithon hated even the most well-meant cosseting. Since his finicky temper objected to oversight with threatening vehemence, Dakar compromised and engaged the paid service of three willing doxies. "Just haul my fine fellow upstairs. Let the ladies wrestle him out of his boots. Three should be sufficient to tuck the testy rooster in bed. After that, they can entertain themselves as they wish. No need to do more through the night than look after him."

The proposed settlement closed with a wink. "You'll be wanting a lissome sprite for yourself?"

"A hot bath alone will do nicely." Satisfied, Dakar cracked into a roasted chicken served hot off the spit. He did not look aside through the strategic indignity as the tavern's strongmen scooped up the bundle of senseless inebriation beside him. Laughing, to cracks that the tosspot was built like a prandey, they hefted their load through the press, mobbed by the magpie chatter of skirted indulgence in triplicate.

Dakar eyed the few coppers in the flattened purse. "Ding me dead out of mercy!" he grumbled, gristle crunched to smithereens between anxious teeth. "The wee man's going to flense me for this!" Unless, powers bless the kick of cheap beer, the hangover ground the bastard to almighty pulp under the wheels of Dharkaron's Black Chariot.

The cry of despair stewed within the stone walls of the craft-quarter tavern in Ganish pierced the shield of protection Elaira maintained in response to Kharadmon's warning. The bolt of rapport wrung her weak at the knees, the surge of her gestalt connection to Arithon flamed to conflagration like a whipped torch. A brief flare, there and gone, but more than sufficient to sear her unquiet nerves to wrecked equilibrium.

Fear shrilled through the after-shocked reverberation unravelled her calm in reactive distress. One moment of Arithon's overset discipline had shredded the buffer welded over her frantic concern for a tenday. Caught on the open plain without cover, she crouched, frozen still as the hunted hare in tall grass.

Yet no drake molts appeared. The sheared whistle of air did not herald disaster, arrived to the thunder of wing leather. An hour passed; two. Naught stirred but mild wind. Her sped pulse steadied as tensioned breathing relaxed. Under locked containment, Elaira raised her tucked head and reopened her refined senses.

Starry night quilted the sky overhead. The steppeland spread tranquil about her, enriched by the passage of hunting owls and the music of nocturnal insects. No emotional outburst resurged to savage her. The enchantress shivered, her stark apprehension too sharp for relief. Arithon also had reasserted his mage-trained control. Her tie to his presence lay sundered, the flux imprint erased without a whispered ripple.

Casualty of his loss of command, smoke roiled over the frugal coals in her firepit. "Damn the man, my dinner has burned!" The game spitted to roast dangled, unturned, and blackened to inedible charcoal.

Elaira buried the carbonized lump in hot ash, then wedged sod overtop to smother the embers. Too riled to sleep, she spread her blanket under a mackerel sky that forepromised an influx of nimbus cloud before daybreak. Before the on-coming rainfall distorted the flux, she engaged a light trance to re-sound the event under the tight scrutiny of skilled observation.

Whatever had triggered Arithon's upset, the stressed impact had passed. His core defences were armoured once more, his opaque motivation swept under impenetrable concealment.

"Oh, beloved," she mused, choked up by throttled exasperation. "What in the world is too dreadful to share?" Estranged from the Fellowship Sorcerers, he had barriered his cross-linked awareness to her behind shields wrought direct from the element.

If she could not plumb his intention directly, her fleeting contact had impressed the peripheral, fragmented detail for speculative deduction. Arithon's resilient health had rebounded. His recovery had embraced the sensible course, gone to ground to recoup his full strength. Her crisp impression of his surrounds revealed the distinctive location. Those curved walls of thick stone were unique to the craft-quarter buildings commandeered from the oldest Paravian construction at Ganish.

Extrapolation sketched Arithon's likely direction of travel, since Waypoint due west, should have offered the closer haven to recoup his depleted reserves. From Ganish, the summertime caravans bound southeastward to Atchaz were plentiful. But traffic by trade galley never resumed their southern ports of call until autumn ended the seasonal fevers. That ruled out a sea passage to Alland's coast. The choice of pause taken for his convalescence more likely suggested Arithon aimed for an overland journey on foot. And if so, the rhumb-line projection scribed across the free wilds by an offshore navigator in a hurry chilled Elaira to inchoate dread. Methlas Lake to Ganish, extended as the crow flew, implied a destination at Forthmark. Or why else reject the comfort of a paid coach east or westward by way of the trade-road?

The riddle's ghastly solution slammed home. "Ath wept! Not the sisterhouse, while the Prime Matriarch's in residence!" Where the Biedar

crone might have cause to rejoice, Elaira reviled the damnable revelation
driving Arithon's likely purpose.

"You are going after Lirenda and the Order of the Koriathain!" The
persistent enemy who had dogged him lifelong, with machinations by
three successive matriarchs responsible for every vicious snare in his
path. Worst of them all, the sisterhood's hand in the priesthood's glove
had slaughtered his ward on the scaffold at Daenfal. The vile puzzle
resolved without seam: Elaira knew her beloved too well for his dark
obfuscation to blind her intuitive certainty. "You would have bided only
until you had severed your oathbound ties, and achieved the fulfilment
of your obligations for Jieret and Caolle's blood sacrifice."

But disaster lurked outside the scope of the vision that shaped her
beloved's design. Koriathain had lost their significant influence, the
decline of their order irreparable since the disastrous break in the Prime's
succession. The Great Waystone's demolition further reduced the
Matriarch's circle of accomplished peeresses. Lirenda's baulked fury
sought vindication. No matter that Arithon carried the Biedar crone's
bidding into the bittermost crux, he walked towards the jaws of a dreadful
trap laid for his annihilation.

He went unaware Koriathain had fashioned their gambit with drake
molts incited to seize him as a toy figment. Dangled as the lustrous
bargaining chip to bait Dragonkind's craving for novelty, he would
encounter such ruinous peril outfaced and unwarned. Stronger spirits
before him had succumbed, shredded alive in pulverized agony amid
the fluid creation of a dragon's experiential reality.

"Though by Ath, not if I get there first!" Terror chilled the life in
warm veins as Elaira abandoned her plan to re-join Ciladis in Lanshire.
Hardened, she weighed her current straits against the obstacles of timing
and distance, compounded by the horrendous gamut of stacked odds.
"Lirenda, damn all to Sithaer's dark pits! Beware, I am coming for you!"

Swift, covert flight due west across Radmoore had brought her southside of the River Sanliet. If she traversed the wilds and rode post on the
trade-road to Thirdmark, she could cross Vastmark at speed and perhaps
reach the Forthmark sisterhouse before Arithon. Determined, she rose
and shook out her blanket. Under the lour of the drifted cloud bank,
she shouldered her satchel and set off to outrace the on-coming storm.

*   *   *

Morning hit Dakar like a brick in the head. Glare streamed through the shutters he had neglected to close in last night's staggered flop on the mattress. The tavern's drink had left him as hard used as the stuffed ticking beneath him, pounded to shapeless hollows and lumps by repetitive fornication. Revolted by the aftertaste of his furred mouth, he hoped the same bout of roughshod retribution played havoc on Arithon's brainpan.

"And may the sweet lovelies have stripped you of valuables down to undignified skin!" the Mad Prophet chortled, and winced. Shrewd experience with hangovers taught him to sleep fully dressed, frowsty clothing the lesser evil beside the discomfort of a tight bladder. Steps padded in stockings, he clutched his holed boots and trundled downstairs to attend the necessity.

Cloudy daylight filtered through the recessed windows blued the tap-room patina of smoky fug. A lanky boy with pimples shoved a mop across the flagstone floor. The languid girl with dark curls by the bar dried the stacked plates. Overnight's billeted carters had gone, along with the boisterous caravan guards. Craftfolk in for breakfast now tended their shops. Last to eat, the pot brats and the cook's staff watched him stumble outside to the privy.

Returned, relieved, Dakar found warmer welcome at the trestle among the establishment's trollops. "Peckish, love?"

The sylph with sloe eyes shoved the egg platter and a basket of muffins across the boards, jostled by tittering rivals who imagined they knew what his wallet was worth.

Dakar admired the luscious assortment of curves. The freckled temptress with flame hair, and the sultry creature who perched adjacent returned his bleared smile like territorial sharks, both recipients of his generous coin to keep his soused companion in check.

Dakar tipped them a grin, snagged the nearest fork and used plate, and dug in with enthusiasm. "I trust you delivered my money's worth?"

"Alas! You wasted good silver." The red-haired tart giggled behind dainty palms. "Too bad."

Her lissome sister waved off the disparagement, quick to soothe the alarm behind his arrested chewing. "Your merry fellow passed out on the drink. We drew straws for his pearl buttons and left Mixie upstairs to manage him."

"He's an ornery viper. Certainly bites." Dakar smirked. "So sorry you drew yourselves the raw lot." Arithon's preference for plain laces and points defanged the gadfly cheek over pilfered studs. "You might have secured the capital prize if he managed to sow you a bastard."

"More's the pity for that." The jade's cynical humour sloughed off regret. "Soused to the gills, your fine lordling was no use to anyone."

"Though, bless daylight," the peppery redhead chimed in, "We got ourselves a night's rest with pay, and the charm for persistence is Mixie's, for trying."

Dakar's complaisance lasted three mouthfuls, before the bedroom heroine's slippered step descended the stair.

"But he wasn't incapable!" A silvery soprano bright with satisfaction denounced the salacious chorus below. "I've teased ones more difficult to rise for the plough!"

Dakar gawped, his headache resurged at full bore. "Ath on earth and Dharkaron's thrice-bloody revenge!" His score with Elaira was already bleak, without packing murder atop the due whiplash of Arithon's temper. "Tell me the mark never kept his coherent wits, or his memory."

The tart twirled the hem of her lace chemise and flitted to an empty seat, smug as the cat caught licking fresh cream. Dakar's sweating pallor earned her desultory moue. "You're worried the stripling has damaged equipment?" She flicked an airy kiss off her finger-tips. "Well! Quit your fretting. A drop too much and a few tender scars are no fuss in the blankets. Not when the wee laddie's affliction stemmed from the heart-sick mizzle of melancholy."

Dakar choked. "What?"

The trollop shrugged, sulky. "Oh, he came to attention all right. When I got a leg over, he cried out aggrieved for his lover. Is she dead, then?"

"Elaira? No!" Dakar shuddered, his unsavoury breakfast suddenly churned to lumped lead in his gut. "Where is he?"

"Upstairs." Rouged fingers plucked the cooled muffin from her stupe-fied patron's plate. "Your pip's spent like rolled-over dough in the sheets. Do you mind I crept out? No thanks for your kinky secondhand prying! I swear I delivered your coin's worth." Hardened to indifference, Mixie snagged the serving knife for the butter and closed the transaction forthwith. "Whatever the williejohn claims when you fetch him, be assured the complaint's beyond refund."

Sleeping dogs on that score were best to let lie. Dakar slumped at the trestle and toyed with his dismembered crumbs, hopeful nobody noticed the terror that murdered his appetite. He mastered his quivering dread in due course. Shoved off for his deferred reconnaissance upstairs, he found the door that concerned him was shut. But not locked: he barged in straightaway, a rat's arse given for Arithon's intimate privacy.

The open window spilled grey light across the extent of his self-made disaster. The wadded bed linen contained nothing beyond the recent trace of left warmth.

"Of course!" Dakar snarled, puffed breathless to find his aggravation had flown. Hands pressed to his ornery headache, he groaned. "What else for my suffering did I expect?"

But the gleam of black metal nestled amid the cast-off wrack of the coverlet dealt the final blow to his hollow stomach.

Alithiel lay abandoned in Davien's sheath, an act of relinquishment that defied the limit of sane credibility.

"Spike my bollocks on the ninth gate of Sithaer!" Dakar roared, forced to take custody of the Paravian weapon. "Wherever you've gone, spawn of mayhem, you deserve every damnable misery and a walloping kick in the bollocks!"

Worse yet, as livid fury rowelled his hangover and pitched him retching to his knees, he was seized by the devilsome double vision that foreran a black-out fit of rogue prescience . . .

. . . Dakar roused to coherence, lying prostrate on floorboards spewed with the heaved dregs of his breakfast. He remembered nothing. Limp under the after-shock sickness bestowed by a prophetic vision, he groaned. His split skull felt packed with parboiled rags. Altogether too viciously queasy, he shrank to take stock, far less face the horrid decision of which divergent trail to pursue: Arithon's, or Elaira's. Ath save him from a justified tour of retribution beyond the torture of Dharkaron's punishment.

Predicaments

Davien breaks his long centuries of exiled silence, "Since my service to the Seven is no longer compromised, you've a few pesky molts to be rounded up?" and dazed yet by the warning dispatched through Dakar's latest Sighted fit, Sethvir gives the prodigal Sorcerer a warm welcome back to Althain Tower, "You're just in time for the crone at Sanpashir to make that dicey trouble more difficult . . ."

"Sparkling daisy! Get off your arse!" The corpulent laundress braces chapped fists on her hips and shouts at the blond whiner slacking off without visible sign of an ailment: "Never seen life from the bottom side up? When I say haul buckets or dig a latrine, you hop to! Else I'll kick your nethers so purple you'll cry for your mam when you're standing . . . !"

Free of his final, obligate ties, and still numb from the maudlin debauchery crafted to cover his tracks, Arithon faces the battle of his life, and long since reconciled to the gruelling odds against his survival, he agonizes over his blindsided failure to swerve Elaira, whose forfeit of Ciladis's protection throws her into jeopardy past his last recourse to salvage . . .

*"Mother Dark's mystery walks in his tracks. But you, Affi'enia,
are the shining Light on the path come before him."*
—*Biedar Eldest, Third Age 5923*

XII. Fugue

Red-and-white hair snatched awry by the gust through the unshuttered casement, Davien placed his offering on the library's ebon table: a plate of cinnamon rolls and fresh butter, and a steaming mug, slid left-handed between the piled books beside Sethvir's inked manuscript. "How long did you negotiate, and what arcane bribe cozened Shehane Althain to permit my reentry?"

Sethvir blinked. Roused from his apparently fuddled reverie, he surveyed the ascetic creature before him, keen intelligence nervy as the caged tiger's behind hatchet-cut grace and gaunt features. Then he laid aside his quill pen. A smile parted his frizzled beard, prompted by the fragrance of his favourite tea leaf cultivated in Shand, and flavoured by Daon Ramon's wild raspberry and the apple smoke used for drying. The thoughtful gift teased a pleased sparkle from half-lidded, turquoise eyes. "You surely knew all along the peace token was unnecessary."

Davien denied nothing. Folded into a seat, averse as killing steel to affected sentiment, he was clothed in provocative style: a saffron shirt stitched with black cord, tastefully matched by a sepia doublet and walnut-dyed breeches. In fact, his self-contained boredom masked the abrasive snap of discomposure.

Sethvir raised his steaming mug in salute. "You endured your agonized trials in solitude by the exemplary grace of free choice." His sip prolonged by enjoyment, he puffed through lightly scalded lips in fond exasperation.

"Pretence serves us no longer." He knew an extreme course of action cultivated in secret had forestalled an untenable lapse that threatened the Seven's integrity. "You carried the crisis of our Fellowship's failure, and averted Mankind's demise at our hands."

"Daelion wept!" Davien's wolfish recoil eddied torpid air that clung like nap on a blanket. "You've seen through my subterfuge all along?"

"Not at first." The crone's citrine ring had masked the gist. "And not everything." A dissembling smile twitched Sethvir's mouth, prelude to the scoured confession, "My shock was sincere when you turned in defiance. I feared more than your death as you broached my sealed threshold on that dreadful day." His horrified shout of alarm had been genuine, when the inquest rebuffed by that fateful step had engaged the punitive might of Althain Tower's defences. *Eyes wide open, Davien had tripped the latch on that warded door. Foreknowing, he had cast himself into discorporate exile, a penury lasting for centuries to defray a horrific calamity staved off by a thread.*

Sethvir suppressed a shudder, harrowed yet by the memory. "Did you know you nearly stopped Ciladis's heart?"

"I dared not disclose my legitimate motive," Davien allowed, his candour unflinching. But inside of these ancient walls, shelved with books, the traumatic echo of raw power that had shredded him, spirit from breathing flesh, spangled sweat on the wrists at rest on the tabletop. *Had his desperation not seized the haven of self-immolation, the restive threat of exposure by his perplexed colleagues would have thrown his frail hope to avert a worldwide holocaust.* Freed at last to seek closure, Davien said, "When did you notice?"

Sethvir's misty gaze veiled a glint of remorse. "I came to suspect." He sipped tea to ease the reluctant admission. "Before the Grey Kralovir's bid to suborn Lysaer forced your hand, the context surrounding Seshkrozchiel's wrath sketched an imprint of the black bargain you struck."

"The crone's warning by way of the Reiyaj Seeress's foresight urged me to dispatch the existential threat posed by the dragon-skull wards." Cynical irony bunched Davien's fists. "I could have declined."

"Indeed. Against certainty we Seven were doomed to exterminate humanity when the drakes discovered the Grey Kralovir's egregious infractions? Our plight by their creed would have named us forsworn." Sethvir's exoneration was tender. "Asandir kept your confidence. He never revealed the burden of dread consequence you assumed in our stead."

"He would give no opinion based on conjecture." Too driven for vanity, Davien unbent and selected a pastry, then drizzled the confection with strawberry jam.

But the gestured attempt to dismiss the solitary torment behind his covert heroics frayed under the Warden's immaculate scrutiny. The unnerved remembrance of panic seared yet from the altercation arisen when Seshkrozchiel's vengeful malice disclosed a partial glimpse of the truth. The subsequent spree of her wroth destruction, that Davien failed to stem, had razed Lysaer's capital at Avenor to ashes, with thousands of guiltless inhabitants cremated outright by drakefire . . .

. . . "You have broken covenant with your kind and mine!" roared the dragon, enraged. The rift into chaos threatened by the death dreams of a clutch stolen and suborned as haunts torched the last, stopgap parlay to salvage diplomacy. "Despoiled! Our pact of alliance by which our Protectorate granted your Fellowship the might to safe-guard this world for Paravian survival."

Davien's valiant protest, extended to mitigate the punitive penalty of total annihilation: for the ghastly abuse visited by Kralovir necromancers upon the skull relicts of four slaughtered hatchlings never should have evaded the Seven's due oversight. "You hold my fast promise to claim retribution. More, I have stayed true to the Concord beyond the delinquency presumed by my colleagues . . . !"

Althain's Warden did not prevaricate. Beneath his daft foibles, fierce insight parsed the worldwide array of thorny connections. Unquiet dangers compounded in reverberation as the great drake's past response rippled into the volatile present: "Then show me Mankind is worth keeping alive! Prove your species is not the festering sore of on-going, mismanaged catastrophe."

Sethvir lowered his drink, grazed the spine of a book, and nipped off a cantrip to stay the slopped contents. Whetted to steely focus, he cracked, "Tell me five rogue molts and Biedar machinations haven't dangled us over the same awful precipice?"

Davien leaned back, licking his teeth, a booted foot propped against the bronze-cast wyrm whose convoluted coils supported the tabletop. "I might resent having been played had the hag's crooked fingers not been busily tweaking the strings from Sanpashir. Her purpose, past

question, runs deeper than ours." Dark eyes pupilled with jet raked the
Warden with sardonic irony. "Given your knack for high-stakes sleight
of hand, how long in advance did you glimpse the pattern beneath her
pre-emptive design?"

Sethvir swirled the dregs of his tea, the crinkle of his testy grimace
evasive. "I relied upon guesswork ridded with holes." Eyes of pale aqua
matched Davien's regard, a warning that all but struck sparks. "No
definitive answer, if you value quietude. I respected your sequestered
retreat, no matter the discord that brangled the rest of us to lost sleep.
Straightaway, this morsel may stick in your craw: I can't let you scratch
your ripe itch to corral drake molts amid the hot crisis posed by the
fracas past Northgate."

"You sent Kharadmon," Davien surmised, the nibbled pastry tossed
aside with a vehemence that scattered crumbs over the incomplete manuscript. "Since a shade can't be tempted to meddle directly, that leaves
the more damnable premise. I can't dispatch the problem myself because
we're confounded by the Biedar's ancestral stake in Arithon's fate?"

Sethvir inclined his rumpled head, sorrowful. "You were ever quick
to taste blood in the water." He peered at his sloshed tea grounds, stymied
for hope by the on-going stream of event: *of the sunchild Merevalia
calling the Paravian Crown Conclave to session as Queen Regent, by
vacancy left to lead the Song of the Mysteries for the dropped sceptre after
Adaraquend; an enchantress on the road south of Thirdmark haggling over
a remount at a wayside stable; a blond aristocrat reduced to a commoner's
lot, damned to self-blindered wretchedness by the fixated belief in his own
inadequacy; where a dragon in Lanshire quickened towards wakeful
dreaming, Siantra s'Idir waged her hard-fought recovery from deranged
catatonia under Ciladis's matchless oversight. While in the fast stillness at
Althain Tower . . .*

. . . with folded fingers stilled as cut marble on an obsidian tabletop,
where melted butter drew summer flies on a plate of uneaten pastry,
Davien spoke, *anguished words crashed like thrown flint through the
juggernaut crisis fomented by feckless drake molts,* "Surety does not exist.
Not without any foothold to steer the cross-grained factions knotting
the endgame." Through a piercing survey of Sethvir's drifty countenance,
"Why have you side-stepped my pertinent question?"

Althain's Warden shuddered, distraught interest torn from a closed
chamber at the Forthmark sisterhouse: *where Lirenda Prime unlocked*

the embossed lid on the warded coffer fetched by a witless assistant. Answer measured, he said, "Elaira's resolved to mount her challenge soonest. If she confronts the Prime Matriarch alone, she'll tip the balance of convergent forces. We've no avenue left to soften the reckoning. Not since Arithon cut all the strings."

Davien stretched out lean legs, unsurprised and without resignation. "I prepared him for the crucible as best I might. Though I fear not enough, if any solution exists to be yanked from the jaws of compounding disaster."

"The long straw was snatched from our grasp since the crone spoke his Name as Requiar's heir." Irked by the dismal prospect of raking up the unbearable toll of smashed pieces, Althain's Warden tossed the milksop of choice to the volatile power returned for the reckoning. ".Where are you most inclined to serve?"

"Arithon bears the Biedar's artefact blade?" Davien's interest showed crocodilian teeth. "Then let me wrangle the gravid drake beyond Northgate."

Startlement pinned Sethvir's maundered wits. "You're sure? Seshkrozchiel's about to awaken."

"I'm remiss to think Luhaine's not stupefied from the nap imposed by the drake's prolonged hibernation?" Davien rubbed the finger unshackled from the crone's citrine ring. "Bless the stuffed virtue in his windy heart, he can pout all he likes from the sidelines. Listening to him saw on in reproach would gall a tortoise to winged flight."

But Sethvir did not chuckle. An impending True Sect war in the north, entangled with Sckaithen Duin's dragons in full-blown revolt, and the crone's meddling with Arithon invited the fall of Dharkaron's Black Spear to bring down Armageddon. The Library's mild scents of oak gall and parchment momentarily bit, overscored by the unnatural reek of fresh brimstone.

Ancient instabilities trod a fractured line. If Seshkrozchiel roused from her torpor too soon, even Althain's Warden lacked the foresight to guess how her rage might impact the future. As ally or saviour or ungovernable enemy, the drake's terrible power could tilt the board and sweep it clean.

Davien broached the garrotted silence at length. "I owe Asandir the reprieve. He can't argue. By strict count of years, I've perfected the knack for blindsiding recalcitrant dragons."

Sethvir was never so easily nose-led. "You think Asandir's the apt choice to advise Daliana!" His swift accusation sheared away pretence. "The lady may not applaud the untoward favour. Provided, of course, we're dicing over the same proposition."

"Why shouldn't the upright stick's fond regard for s'Gannley be allowed to net us the windfall advantage?" Davien's shrug was cryptic as he uncoiled and stood to brew a conciliatory pot of fresh tea. "I left the lady at Traithe's house in Morvain, unsure of her matured direction. She won't thank me for certain. But admit you may never see another benign opportunity."

"By glory, you're back in dead earnest," Sethvir declared in maudlin acquiescence, *while a black-haired man struck southward across the free wilds as the crow flew, as yet unaware of the fatal urgency that narrowed the critical stakes on his destiny.*

Elaira began her furtive entry to the Forthmark sisterhouse at night, with Arithon yet on a lathered horse, trailing six hours behind her. Dismounted, saddle-weary and clad in field leathers, she crossed the southside garden reclaimed from the riotous growth of the old hostel's vineyard. Seeded rows of medicinal herbs had set deep roots since the squatters' claim, extended for centuries under the order's established residency. The limestone scarp loomed ahead under starlight, pierced by the honeycomb cells and pillared loggias repurposed from ruin. Elaira crept through darkness fragrant with flowering comfrey, red clover, and hellebore. Nightshade and foxglove and tangled beds of gentian hedged the coppiced willow and sassafras, and the briar patch trellised for rose hips. Soft loam cushioned her furtive step, tilled and watered by rigid tradition that nurtured the sap of rebellion.

Boy wards hot to tumble the milkmaids, and reckless young novices who craved assignations escaped curfew by way of the drainage culvert from the wing housing the hospice. Qualms gnawed at Elaira's resolve, that her action tonight might see such randy innocents dispossessed. Many were orphans, dedicated to shelter the sick for the charitable branch of the sisterhouse. Until corruption had evolved today's system of barter, and desperation extorted in trade for relief saw the needy recipients indebted to the order. Grey rank sisters gave their selfless service to tyranny, oathbound to superiors of scarlet rank.

Elaira scaled the terraced wall at the boundary, conflicted by familiar bitterness. Forthmark's humanitarian ward was renowned among healers the breadth of Athera, vulnerable to repercussive upset by the rotten core above the fifth tier of initiation. Regardless, she traversed the sloped talus beneath the sheer cliff, careful of the chinking, loose shale between snags of clumped sage and sorrel. The pleated stone rampart reared against sky not yet leached to pallor by daybreak. The recessed aperture she sought was a hoarded secret, located by informed touch.

A sentence of witlessness worse than death for the life-sworn initiate caught on the lam: what price for the defiant deserter, who trespassed to sabotage the Prime's business? Elaira shuddered and shrugged off her satchel, reliant on luck as she probed the grate's fastenings. The loosened pins slid free as they always had, greased with mutton fat pinched from the kitchen. Concealed inside, the rickety ladder fashioned by youthful miscreants still mounted the vertical shaft. Upwards, through stygian darkness made caustic by lye soap, she wormed through the sluice access and emerged in the puddled gloom of the deserted laundry. A torch in the corridor glazed the ceramic vats, backlit steam wisped aloft from the underground hot springs.

Someone's pattered footsteps receded, most likely the infirmary's errand boy sent for clean linens. The store vaults were seldom empty of traffic. A chance-met encounter, or worse, a tripped ward in a passageway would flag her intrusion.

Elaira unwrapped the crystal she partnered in free permission and aligned the matrix to magnify misdirection. The elusive stray noise, or illusory flicker of movement projected to snag an observer's attention let her into the warren of tunnels connecting the sisterhouse cellars. The maze riddled the bed-rock foundation, delved by the vanished adepts. The remnant stamp of their tenancy lingered. Residual traces of etheric harmonics ranged above hearing through the whispered draughts that streamered the cobwebs. Minute, static bursts flicked Elaira's initiate senses and raised errant prickles of gooseflesh. Her prior study at Whitehaven hostel and her apprenticeship under Ciladis exposed the electromagnetic shimmer of subliminal light, an ephemeral flare of translucent violet that sparkled and vanished to nothing. Fear supplanted by wonder, she brushed a questing palm over the derelict symbols graven into the soot-stained walls.

The assumption such markers were directional signposts unravelled at her sounding touch. The array *in fact* channelled an original, contiguous boundary. Not inert, the etheric transmission seemed passive only because responsive power had waned from the site. A containment first shaped to confine the reactive resonance of the adepts' former sanctuary yet remained fully intact.

Few Koriathain, if any, grasped the extensive framework to harness the deep mystery embedded in the foundation under their feet.

Elaira crept ahead, arrived at the fusty annexe stocked to the ceiling with wicker hampers. The old rope and tackle built to lift wine vats had rotted away. But the portal beyond led to the scullery stair, furtive shortcut to the immense, vaulted gallery repurposed for the Prime and her innermost circle.

Always, a posted watch guarded the entrance, a second-degree grey rank too reliable for complacency.

Elaira adjusted her projected glamour. A blanket thrust of quietude strengthened to blunt heightened senses let Elaira whisk past the sister's dulled vigilance. Too easily, perhaps: the suspect qualm made no difference in hindsight. She had come too far to reverse her commitment.

At the portal to the gallery threshold, no subtle working escaped the enduring provenance of natural stone. The adepts' graven ciphers may have been sealed, closed off from the sound-and-light chord of the infinite. The primordial night encountered at hostels elsewhere, sheeted through by coiled power like captive lightning, here had faded into null quiescence for centuries. Yet the carved mineral still carried the exquisite echo of the White Brotherhood's precepts, an obdurate balance that weighted the ambient spectrum towards truth.

Elaira breasted that pillared threshold, knowing her intrusion would raise the alarm. Quite likely had, if her untoward stealth had flagged the lane watcher's notice.

The passage of crossing no longer ignited the mystic's path into transcendent expansion once curated by Ath's adepts. Instead, the strident defence of the sisterhood's sigil quenched the past vestige of that unworldly, dimensional shift. Razed by disharmony, Elaira deflected a lethal assault, shielded without effort by the deft skill the clan hunters engaged to bend flux.

"Let the sisterhood come," she rasped through taut nerves. Against dragons, under the dread apprehension of all she held dear set at risk, she tucked the vulnerable quartz point for safety under her laced linen bodice.

Nothing untoward met her brazen advance. Across the smoke-pale expanse of veined marble, she trod the grit of a mirror finish pitted by weather and time. The historic archive at Althain Tower recorded the exalted release, when the reservoir here had been wrung to immolation by the surge of raw power that launched Mirthlvain's present-day Guardian through his renowned transformation. Verrain himself never broached the particulars, his profound reticence muted by the antique, suave charm of his gallantry.

Whatever brash footnote Elaira's venture might inflict upon Athera's chronicled future, the shell of the sanctuary extended before her, etheric connections silenced by the mighty stays imposed by the departed adepts. Access to the realms past the veil were shut down, the slagged scars that once channelled power repurposed for the aumbries and chests that sequestered the sisterhood's grimoires and crystals.

Cast sigils of guard emanated a wrongness to raise clammy sweat in the smothered air. Entombed behind rows of latched casements, the expansive arches the ancients had built open to sky wore clotted gloom, barred against the evanescence of twilight. The defunct wellspring ahead no longer sang with the melodic shower of virgin water. Shadows crawled in the dry font instead, rippled by the sultry coals in the brazier beneath the matriarch's seat, the order's carved swans a heart-shaped curve spanned by damascened purple upholstery.

Carpets defended by the quadrangle runes of entrained chaos threatened Elaira's approach. Her assay of the copper-thread ciphers seen from the perspective of more advanced knowledge revealed strictures patterned on the rigid theory that *inanimate creation possessed no unique spark of consciousness.* No wonder the Fellowship Sorcerers viewed Koriani workings askance!

Such tinkering ignorance was ugly, unstable, and viciously, dangerously arrogant.

"In for a penny, in for a pound." Enslaved elements retuned to her cause through permission, Elaira drew her steel knife. She knelt, braced for fury, and severed the volatile stay most wont to cry havoc.

The construct exploded, a fountained inferno tinged hellish green by incinerated copper. The glass casements blew out. Sparks and black fumes of singed wool billowed upwards and palled the grandeur of the groined ceiling. Elaira coughed, watered eyesight plunged into gloom as the brazier snuffed, plunging her into darkness. No impediment to mage-sight, she strode through the litter of heated ash and seized the effrontery to claim the Prime's seat.

Her moment of exhilaration was brief.

The Matriarch emerged through the hazed smoke. Mantled in formal violet, and forearmed with the Skyron focus in hand, she brought in tow twelve red-ranked seniors. A mere dozen, where her predecessors had commanded prime circles of twenty-four. That bitter loss must have rankled. Yet Lirenda's sangfroid poise masked the festering lack, malice spiked through her overture for retribution.

"Welcome back." Perfect teeth frosted the consonants of her antagonism. "I see your Master of Shadow keeps a shameless bed for his strumpets. How delightful, he's dealt you the rough quittance your fawning devotion deserved."

No shock to find livid gall towards Arithon still poisoned the Matriarch's outlook.

"Touch him, and I will see you exposed – all your putrid administrative secrets – everything." Mindful that she aggravated a dangerous creature unhinged by obsession, Elaira arose, and declared herself. "I hereby challenge your mandate to rule. For cruelty, for murder, for corruption built on the coercive enslavement of innocents, and not least, for repeated, abusive extortion, meet your hour of reckoning."

"A pretty speech for a stickler's protocol." Lirenda tipped her head, a filigree tiara of diamond and amethyst the strewn sparkle of starlight against her pinned, midnight hair. Her nod dispatched two bonded subordinates to clear the extinguished brazier from her path. Ranked seniors closed in an arc at her back, she engaged the contest with blunt force and glittering malice. "By all means, I require no upstart invitation to enforce due redress for oathbreaking and trespass."

The Prime Matriarch's opening strike in the arena at Forthmark overtook Arithon two leagues away, dismounted atop a windswept knoll to ease his spent horse. The vitriolic assault on his mate reeled him to his knees. No flux-borne recoil: the adepts' ancient strictures embedded on site contained the shock ripple of outside transmission.

The blow instead pierced his shields *from within*, through his heart-tied rapport with Elaira. His initiate reflexes mapped what she faced: the forced blast of a combined Senior Circle, honed through the Skyron aquamarine. The attack spanned four axes, the quadrangle runes enchained for malign chaos spun widdershins with the hooked coil for domination.

Elaira fielded the impact with deft elegance. Her countermeasure, shaped on precepts from Ath's brotherhood, was forged into the shining harmonic alignment taught by Ciladis. A skilled healer's handling of contrary forces deflected the brute slap of crystal-focused hostility, once and again through the exacting phrases tuned to nullify harm.

Yet the breath-taking scope of her mastery fell short. Unsettled, Arithon heard the flawed measure miss the balanced pitch, a sour note's fractional drift that jangled his sensitive ear.

Perhaps brushed by his ephemeral contact, Elaira tightened her core defences. Her stiffened protection broke the flash-point gestalt and severed his spontaneous connection.

Arithon recovered his harrowed faculties, braced against the sweated neck of his horse. Separation knifed him to visceral agony, full contact snuffed by a yawning void that encompassed the very marrow of silence. Hollowed by an estrangement against his straight grain and wrung desolate by exigent necessity, he gripped mane and forced his numbed frame to bear weight.

She was under attack. The self-imposed wound of his absence savaged him. *He could not reach out to her.* However he panicked, he dared not try. Never at the crippling risk of distracting her under the brunt of the Prime's lethal barrage.

Merciful maker, *too late*, and in full, Arithon confronted the drastic price of Dakar's lapsed regard for her safety. Hindsight bought him no forgiveness for the cowardly choice to delegate her well-being. Arithon swore. He had flinched at the crux. Refused the terrible, callous cruelty required to annihilate her loyal partnership. The cost of that lapse became too harsh to bear as his Masterbard's nuanced artistry exposed the poisonous bait in the malice unleashed against her. Elaira fought more than a duel for dominance: firm conviction she acted for *his defence* had enticed her into the jaws of entrapment.

Nothing prepared her for what lay at stake. Lirenda's warped passion, ramped by crystal, revealed the distilled vitriol of an addictive ambition soured into manic desperation by the broken transfer of Prime power. This Matriarch battled to resurrect the order's lost heritage, corroded to envy by her craving for the mature love encountered and coldly denied by Arithon's invidious meddling.

For Lirenda Prime, vengeance was deadly and personal. The consummate joy she could not possess, she would spitefully strive to obliterate.

Elaira dared not forfeit the contest. Lose, and all that she knew, every precept that accessed clean conjury would be plundered to elevate the order's crumbling hierarchy. The unparalleled grace of Ciladis's learning, and the heightened consciousness schooled by Ath's adepts, and not least, the intimate wellspring that shared every aspect of Arithon's mastery would be sullied for domination. A fresh chapter appended to a grifted cache, seized by roughshod appropriation to augment the Koriathain's twisted repertoire.

Healer-trained, Elaira measured nothing by lack. She hoarded no festered resentments. Her resilience of character scarcely could fathom a greed born of acrimony cankered raw by a former prime candidate's ruinous failures.

But Arithon had, in his fight to survive the mad remnants imprisoned within the dark depths of the order's demolished Great Waystone. Terror flensed him to abject despair. He was three hours distant. Too remote to lend help, far less defuse the on-coming calamity.

Too late, he still had to try. The hand Arithon laid on his horse sounded a noble strength already spent. He unbuckled the girth, slipped off saddle and bridle, and freed the dumb beast from a ride to brutalized founder for naught. With nothing beyond the rank clothes on his back and the Biedar crone's hazardous artefact, he set off on foot across the stony duff and baked grass of the Vastmark plain.

The turn of the stars clocked three hours before dawn. The night air in his lungs was thick as warm milk. Arithon shucked his damp shirt, stretched his stride and let the flux currents direct his heading.

He pushed sinew and bone, spurred on by the gruelling pace of the fight. Flickered glimpses of stroke and counterploy jarred through the rhythm of his raced breaths. The deflected complexity of each deadly exchange, layer on layer, spun the fractured recoil of attack and defence across multiple templates. Octave upon octave, dire sigils negated by antipode, the shock-printed back-lash unfolded, livid as the planes of a fan unfurled across dimensions. Elaira surmounted the ciphers for pain, and the shackles of enslavement. She dispersed tracking spells barbed with insidious snares and disarmed subjugation powered through crystal. Versant with her healer's arsenal, she fired the bulwarks of banishment with the wrought strength of unified peace. Silk on oiled water, her neat economy was the skilled surgeon's, a flawless overlay serene and impenetrable as the fortified pearl.

Her adroit competency foreran disaster. A gathered storm held in abeyance, Arithon grasped the impetus driving the Prime's greater strategy. Primal fear ripped him to a visceral outcry, his gestalt apprehension reinforced by Elaira's latent suspicion that her opponent methodically tested the range of her knowledge. Tactical calculation pressured the disclosures, aimed by intent to catalogue esoteric arcana for the sisterhood's benefit.

Long since past the point of retreat, Elaira grappled the first intimation of ruin. The engagement must be won, set and match, before the Prime jettisoned rational limits and resorted to unbridled violence. A cold-struck sigil, leveraged for cataclysmic destruction through quartz, threatened a murderous wave of distortion sufficient to damage the mysteries. Stolen means to access grand conjury, wielded by the order's contempt for conscious balances, threatened to fling wide the gates to disaster.

"Strike first, no warning," Arithon cried aloud. "You cannot flinch! Not even for mercy." His plea crashed against her raised barriers. Elaira was too preoccupied, too determined, or perhaps worse, too deeply wounded by his rebuff. "Break the rules! You must act to salvage a trust far greater than personal integrity. Save yourself!"

Arithon pushed onwards at a gasping sprint. Wind-lashed tears soaked his cheeks. At heart, he acknowledged his impotent dread. His beloved did not own the ugly fibre for ruthlessness, nor ever had. That sterling quality founded the seat of his absolute trust. Always, her kindness had been shelter and haven for the abrasive vulnerability of his compassion.

Elaira shaped her demand with that shining grace, a last chance bestowed to spare an archenemy from a regrettable immolation. "Surrender."

"No." The Prime's amber eyes returned the indifference of a sated serpent. "You have no other choice but to give way to me."

An ultimatum misperceived as groundless defiance, until Lirenda's riposte delivered the cloaked trick withheld in reserve. The bitter defeat forecast by the Biedar crone befell Elaira, unless Arithon re-joined the sundered strand of a reciprocal contact.

His explosive appeal blazed the flux incandescent, a shout that faded, unanswered.

Running fit to burst his lungs and tear heartstrings, Arithon lacked the resource to narrow the distance. Come *too late*, he could do nothing, *nothing at all* to stave off the horror Mother Dark's Aspect had cautioned him to beware of before his reawakening at Althain Tower: *'Do not fall to self-blindness! The threat to all you hold dear has redoubled. The dead prime was cagey. She held more than one rear-guard play up her sleeve . . .'*

Arithon could not influence the outcome. Only rail, as his thwarted awareness seared his Sight with the unbearable, excruciate detail of Elaira's downfall in full . . .

. . . the gravid taint of ozone-laced smoke silted the gloom underneath the vaulted ceiling at Forthmark's usurped sanctuary, swirled by the night breeze through the smashed frames of the casements. Glass splinters glinted, reflections inflected by the remnant echo of charge retained by the fidelity of ancient stone. A punch-cut, stygian silhouette, the Senior Circle buttressed the arc which centred their Prime, who wielded the glacial shimmer of the Skyron aquamarine left-handed. Lirenda's upturned palm gleamed with jewelled rings: amethyst, ruby, and diamond, and a plain sliver of quartz, caged in copper wire that laced the full length of her extended forefinger.

No costly ornament, that commonplace setting seemed displaced, its uncut essence the glimmer of moonstone and dawn at first blush before sunrise. A spark of light Arithon would have recognized anywhere as the weft spirit woven through the warp thread his very self.

Elaira beheld the substance of dread, a copied imprint of the personal quartz she once had worn in partnership under her initiate vows as a Koriathain. A purloined tool subverted for vicious practice before: guidance for an enemy's hunt to hound Arithon to fatal entrapment; and later used to lend credence to the lure fashioned to ensnare him through Vivet. Selectively seeded, the invidious, falsified record had honed the weapon to seal his despair: truthful content edited for the misdirection of a cold-blooded semblance of her betrayal.

A secret third impression retained by the past prime now enabled the trigger for Elaira's demise . . .

. . . the tormented cry wrenched from Arithon's throat crashed against the adamant barrier of Elaira's terrified recoil. No such shielding averted the gut punch of her blindsided shock. The unforeseen vulnerability ambushed her defences through the past tie to her oathbound self.

Lirenda struck in the midst of her stunned hesitation, the quartz rigged as catalyst cross-linked to the enabled matrix of the Skyron aquamarine. The multiplied punch of fused force siphoned from the entrained endowment of the Senior Circle pierced the Prime's targeted prey like a shot arrow. An attack most brutally tailored, and deadly, the razor-point sigil of confusion, rammed through by the rune of relationship entwined contrarywise for compulsion. Those ciphers alone, Elaira could master. But not the impetus compounded by six primal runes of unbinding. Lock on that forged chain, a stayspell empowered to bend time *backwards* completed the snare.

The alignment to Elaira's former self forged the shackle to noose her present-day will in submission. The resonant draw mired her initiate reflex for the fatal instant Lirenda required to launch the most ugly binding of all . . .

. . . running, Arithon's anguished howl shattered the draw of his tortured breath. For he understood at comprehensive, firsthand, exactly how the black conjury had been engineered to take Elaira down.

The premeditated act of unparalleled cruelty seized the amplified imprint of a six-year-old child's oath of lifelong subservience, recorded and sealed in perpetuity by the Skyron's matrix. Through a focus crystal of offworld origin that eluded Sethvir's Sighted reach, the Prime Matriarch enforced the vestigial claim to prerogative and *crushed*: the rune of relationship that seized body, mind, and spirit, slammed home by the imperative demand for absolute obedience.

Elaira screamed.

Ripped, unravelled, and stunned by the power of the Prime's master sigil, she fell prey to the net as though the Fellowship Sorcerers had never released her. Arithon reeled, harrowed witless by empathy. Horrified, he shared her agony as the pitiless prison snapped closed.

His roar of rage would have shaken the earth, had more vital words not demanded priority. "I beg you, Elaira. Allow me to shield you!"

For he knew. *Ath wept, he had sown the insatiable fury that stoked Lirenda's obsessive revenge!*

Yet the sacrosanct power of choice was not his. By inviolate love and birth-born free will, he could not trample her sacred trust. Nor for relief from his unendurable pain could he gainsay the refusal Elaira slammed down against him.

"Do not come! Not for any reason! Arithon, go far away." Her denouncement permitted no ethical grace. She shut him out and cut off his sole avenue to appeal for a rescue.

Arithon could not turn aside. Elaira must realize. Under no terms, while he lived would he suffer her downfall. Or abandon her to an enemy marked for reprisal under his provenance. *'Give me sorrow, give me death, before I become the instrument that seals your utter destruction . . .'*

No chance left, to fathom her cause for rejection, not on top of the fresh laceration imposed by his hostile attempts to distance her from endangerment. Perhaps she might choose the gift of self-sacrifice to spare him from doom in return. No surety silenced that mortal dread.

Worst of all, Arithon grasped in full measure Elaira's hideous predicament. Voiceless to brace her for the on-coming blow, he shattered inside as Lirenda slammed down the insufferable seal. The same ugly binding once wielded on him under the terms of Dakar's sworn debt, made in standing as the Fellowship's agent on behalf of the Crown of Rathain.

Arithon wept for Elaira's drowned spirit. For he could not violate selfhood or help stave off her pain, as, scared and alone, witless, abandoned, he watched as his only beloved plunged into the shackled existence that had caged him for two and a half centuries. He had suffered the stupendous torment of enfoldment; knew the ache of endless despair. As numb suffocation sank the rich texture of incarnate awareness, the throttled spirit cried in vain, diminished to the blank desolation of imprisonment inside of a crystal lattice.

The enchainment swallowed hope beyond solace. With individual remembrance erased, the victim thrashed beyond recourse, deprived of the vivid stimulus of living sensation.

Arithon shouted down the bottomless well that sheared his beloved away. "Anchor yourself!" To a dwindled presence already denuded, he exhorted in abject futility. "Hold your bond to identity and don't think to let go!"

In defiance of fate, he extended a plea sprung from memory: of his hand on the skin over her beating heart, and his reverent touch sliding downwards, a sacred dance wrought on the flesh of his flesh, that broadcast an intimate privacy too sacred for scrutiny. He did not care. Not if he bared the stripped core of his soul to Sethvir's Sighted view, or flung himself in flagrant exhibition before all the world.

"Elaira!" No response answered his frantic agony. "Your body survives this! *Remember.* You must!"

His stricken appeal lost connection as the Prime's ugly working slammed shut, enfolded under the seal for eternity, a triple-coiled snake contorted in the endless act of swallowing its tail.

"Alt!" The closure reverberated, past to present, like the rolling echo of thunder.

Arithon remembered with anguished clarity: the knife's edge of bright panic as that same template had wrought his demise on the spring morning he had walked into jeopardy to play a Masterbard's tribute for Jeynsa's wedding. Keening horror ignited a towering fury that hazed his vision with tears too bitter to bear. Bereft, empty-handed, Arithon ran. He drove nerve and sinew while the creep of on-coming dawn bled the black sky and stars above Vastmark's barren vales to a grey horizon.

The whispered draught fanned by Elaira's collapse sighed to rest in the tepid darkness of the vaulted hall in the Forthmark sisterhouse. There, Lirenda breathed in the fumes of charred wool, trembling with feral elation. Triumph surged, buoyed by the heady release instilled by a Prime Matriarch's work of force-majeure conjury. Skyron aquamarine cradled to her breast, she stood down her drained circle of seniors. The ice-sculpture cast of her patrician features softened to a satisfied smile in the intoxicant moment of victory.

Morriel's shade should applaud the success that anchored the order's redemption.

The bid to restore the Koriathain to pre-eminence hinged on the cipher sprawled at her feet before the ivory seat. Elaira lay limp in her travel-stained leathers, broken consciousness rendered inert as any other initiate brought to heel by the Prime's master sigil.

"Arithon's darling. What use is she now?" Lirenda stroked the chill facets of the heirloom sphere, a routine review of the crystalline lattice due precaution after a focused engagement. Her attention froze with the ritual release uncompleted. The vacancy she sounded in the jewel's active quadrant should have contained her victim's trapped essence.

Annoyance creased Lirenda's brow. Exactly how had her perfected coup-de-grace strayed from her meticulous plan? The upset made no sense! The impermeable nexus of Elaira's confinement should not have detached from the childhood record of her initiate's oath.

Vexed, Lirenda retraced her assessment. The reprise altered nothing. The order's mightiest jewel retained no trace of the caged adversary prisoned inside the closed ring of her construct.

Lirenda stifled a snarl of anger. Shown the face of her baffled uncertainty, her Senior Circle might ask difficult questions. Avaricious as vultures drawn to a weakness, they could rise in challenge and tear out her throat.

"Examine my oathbreaker!" she commanded the seventh-rank enchantress whose critical stare rankled protocol. Her wrath cowed the rest, who scattered remiss, told to clear the littered detritus of the scorched carpet.

Lirenda seized on their flustered preoccupation and pursued the anomaly of the untoward dislocation. Nothing overt seemed to be out of place. The locked sigils of binding were active. No errant drift skewed their precise execution. The wired quartz on her finger vibrated to its imprinted siren song without flaw, the projected copy of Elaira's lost crystal a faithful reflection. Painstaking, the Prime stepped through a sequential review of her enacted conjury.

Her defeated quarry had not eluded her! The sigil for Eternity lay coiled in stasis, the dimensions ruled by time and substance folded inward and frozen by the mineral framework of the major jewel. Oddly, the Skyron sphere retained no further record, no evidence of the crushed spirit pinned into captivity.

The crabbed senior who examined the inert victim confirmed the fidelity of the finished construct. "Your husked rebel is breathing without strain. Her heartbeat is stable. Her bodily life signs are strong."

"Repeat the assay! I must be sure."

Yet the sister's compliant examination only ascertained the stripped absence of Elaira's aura. Her defined personality, reason, and emotion, had been winnowed separate from the animal reflexes driving her vacated flesh.

"The tart did something!" Lirenda clamped back a shriek of pure vitriol. She had risked everything! The consummate sum of the order's future relied on the outcome of tonight's gamble. An unforeseen problem must not throw the reverse to upset her plotted strategy.

The elder senior bent her stiff knees to the floor, wilted before her Prime's scorching displeasure. "An interference may have cross-linked and replaced the spell's intended receptacle if the oathbreaker carried a suitable matrix on her person."

Lirenda glowered at the crumpled trophy heaped at the mercy of her design. "Roll her over and search!" Her burning impatience encompassed the sisters assigned to the drudge's task of clearing the refuse. "You and you! Strip Arithon's trollop down to the skin. Shred her clothes to the seams and find out if she bears a rogue charm, or a hedge witch's talisman."

Swift inspection disclosed the untoward bane. "The enchantress has a quartz point tucked under her bodice."

"The devil!" snapped the Matriarch under her breath, then barked at her hesitant inferiors as if they were stupefied novices. "Go on! Bundle the rogue crystal in silk and bring it to me."

Lirenda stepped down the Skyron's focus, slipcased the quiescent jewel, then beckoned a third subordinate forward to exchange its chill weight for the matrix rifled from Elaira's possession. The immediate bite of the sigil for Eternity and a tingle of constrained power verified the bothersome accident of proximity had diverted her engineered snare. The unintentional receptacle nestled in her gloved palm did not come from the provenant collection brought from offworld by the Koriathain.

The curse escaped the Prime's lips before thought. "Damn the renegade snip to oblivion!"

The hitch rankled. A wild stone with untapped properties never polished or curated under the rigour of arcane assessment now harboured the essence of the order's indispensable, targeted pawn. The blighted inconvenience complicated a secure transfer of the volatile contents to a tame matrix stabilized for reliable service. Inclusions and veils and the rough character of a natural point might resist, even disrupt the pathway for a clean connection. Sound practice must bide with the bothersome flaw. No matter how galling, the trinket in hand held the irreplaceable gambit: adequate leverage to force the last throw to deliver the coveted endgame.

"The irritation can't signify." Soured by the pangs of incipient backlash, Lirenda shrouded her hard-won prize. She swept past the prostrate, drained hulk underfoot and ascended to reclaim the primacy of her ivory seat. Sheathed in purple velvet, crowned with scintillant jewels, she surveyed her subordinates through narrowed eyes. "My working plan will proceed without hindrance. We have captured the requisite lure."

Baited hook for the mate bearing down from the north, and the signal key to impel the Koriathain's ascendance to limitless power.

Breeze through the smashed windows frisked across the veined-marble floor like a promise, forerunning the gathered tempest inbound on the gusts whipped by dragons' wings. "Today at long last we seize our hour to break the Fellowship Sorcerers."

Virtuoso

Where Elaira had crept by stealth through the sisterhouse cellars, Arithon barged through the ancient, inscribed pillars Ath's white adepts had erected to screen petitioners at Forthmark's north gate. The compressed wave of his wrath brushed the residual arcana, a turbulent bow wake of tangible force. He mounted the original carved stair without challenge. Strode beneath the massive, chipped arch of the colonnaded logia at the front entry. Enveloped in gloom, he came shirtless, naked power that walked in plain sight with the scars of his missteps and vulnerabilities blazoned upon him. No space left for reticence, he brought the whirlwind held in check by a thread. Rage fit to seethe Vastmark's shale beds to magma arrived, lawless violence chilled to a quaver of ice that encased a whisper more terrifying.

No initiate sister came forward. None dared. The affront that summoned Arithon's presence was implacable. The Prime Matriarch threw down her gauntlet with the one gambit he would not refuse, and the sole point of leverage between earth and sky with dire potential to break him. Lirenda expected his temper. The gall of repeated experience had hardened her in preparation: no Senior Circle obstructed his path at the risk of annihilation.

Six hours after Elaira's spirit had been crushed into crystalline confinement, the corridor walls still rang with the scream of her pain. Arithon followed, black anger wrung silent, the looming pall of unmanifest shadow a gathered storm front behind him. He need not think. Only feel. Intuition knew which direction to go. Refined masonry gleamed like glazed porcelain before him, yellowed by the flicker of oil lamps. Smoky murk veiled the groined ceiling above, supported by corbels not fashioned by man. The etched lines of old ciphers glimmered in the dark niches, wan remnants of bygone inhabitants chased into hallowed stone.

Lirenda Prime laired up in wait amid the ruined splendour of the white adepts' vacated sanctuary, a deliberate profanity. Placed where dissonant antagonism would chafe a musician's sensitive ear, the strident back-flash of her hatred aimed to rile him into distraction. The strategy failed. Her abrasive aggression was dismissed as rude noise for the quieter theme swirled through the flux. A Masterbard's infallible discernment sifted out only what mattered. The trace signature impressed by Elaira's predawn passage was as familiar to Arithon as his own, inflected by her urgent motive: *she had come to confront Lirenda concerning an unconscionable threat aimed at him!*

Arithon reeled, hammered by the magnitude of his misjudgement. Elaira's endangerment in his behalf, and love's steadfast urge to protect him had perfected the cold-blooded tool to enact the Prime's vengeance. Lirenda used his beloved as the lodestone for her callous ploy to draw him to the net. *For his sake,* Elaira had left Dakar's protection at Methlas Lake. Alone, harried senseless by frantic concern, she had acted on the mistaken assumption she spared a prostrate convalescent from the teeth of a Koriani conspiracy.

Ath's immortal tears! Arithon's stab of regret threatened to unhinge his reason. How his ruse to keep her at a safe distance had gone horribly wrong and blown back in his face! He wrestled an explosive burst of insanity, mage-wise control scarcely able to stem his primal explosion of fury. In that wracked instant, he could have slaughtered bare-handed any hapless sister initiate who crossed his path.

No such foolhardy puppet waylaid his advance.

Expected, *invited,* he strode towards the Prime Matriarch's presence. The very air seemed saturated in darkness, a mutual enmity that spanned nearly three centuries staining the sediment of her repeated failures until the suppurate canker of humiliation seeped into the flux. Spite as entrenched as Lirenda's would not trifle with feints. Such keen thirst for carnage sprang at the throat, claws unsheathed for evisceration.

Arithon crossed an intersecting corridor. Merle stone recast his passage in echoes, light descant to the sonorous, bass chord of earth's

stratified mineral surrounding him. The buttressed arch of the derelict
sanctuary gaped ahead, pallid grey daybreak spilling through the south-
facing casements beyond. The whorled ciphers that flanked the entry
stayed dormant, the ambient power of the departed adepts waned to the
wistful sigh of spent glory. Unlike the energized threshold at Ettin,
Arithon broached an ancient site deadened and sadly bereft. No vast
reservoir of virgin electromagnetics quivered under his wary tread.

Gooseflesh prickled his skin, nonetheless. Quickened mage-sense
noted the ciphers of intact seals fallen mute in the absence of their
founders' function.

The chamber's expanse swallowed his footfalls, dwindled echoes snuffed
by the cavernous silence. That gloved stillness deceived. He was not alone.
Before the smashed mullions and the frosted sparkle of strewn glass, the
Senior Circle waited like shrouded statues behind the Prime Seat. That
eerie state of suspension slaved their lives to the Matriarch's will, a fused
weapon of multiplied might deemed expendable for due cause in a headlong fight. They dreaded their fate, the gelid pool of their stifled fear a
gut-punch deterrent turned without effort against Arithon's empathy.

Lirenda banked on the certainty. Her s'Ffalenn antagonist would hesitate to strike first, his reluctance to wreak lethal harm on the helpless the
softening prelude to the fatal blow tailored for his greatest weakness.

Edged by the sanctuary's electromagnetic propensity, Arithon's
discomfiting survey pierced his antagonist in turn. The bleed-through
taint of Lirenda's jealousy hardened the fortress of ice at her core. Her
solitary obsession eluded his gifts. Of all others that his clarified bardic
perception had redeemed from alienation, he could not excise the root
cause beneath her desire to rend and destroy him. No avenue to her
humanity lent purchase as her hunger tracked his disarmed approach.

Regaled in formal purple, the reigning Matriarch with her coiled ebony
hair and jewelled diadem revelled in her immaculate planning. The select
prey she remembered entered her lair, small frame shirtless and lean as a
wildcat. Rumpled black hair spiked shadow across his distinctive, angular
features, the unremarkable front for a presence that towered: past question,
she prodded pent magma sheathed under blistered restraint. The barbed
satire he wielded for obfuscation was conspicuous for its absence.

Until adversarial rejoinders became rendered moot by the slight,
crumpled figure held hostage. Arithon encountered the ugly reunion
exactingly staged to bring him to his knees. Dropped in the rags of her

rifled clothes, his bronze-haired woman lay limp as death in the concave, barren well, once sourced by the sanctuary's etheric spring.

Lirenda savoured the savage impact as Arithon sighted his fallen beloved. Nothing had prepared him. The horror of her slack, elfin features devoid of verve and intelligence wrenched her stricken mate still.

The Prime might have applauded, had the heart-stopped flare of his anguish not gouged her breathless with envy. Her dropped guard changed nothing. Arithon lacked the spare wits to seize the moment's advantage. The stifled depth of his explosion was the more terrifying without speech. Invisibly deep, something vital inside of him snapped. Broken, he did not lose control. The havoc of his rage remained silent, white lightning contained behind disciplined centuries of ingrained, initiate reflex.

No such restraint blunted his aligned purpose. The sure promise of ruin blazed unquenched behind the wide-lashed storm of agony in his green eyes. Koriathain would fall to wholesale destruction, and damn all to personal consequence.

Joined battle had hooked the game fish on the line. Now the fight in him must be expertly played to ensure he stayed fatally riveted. "Shall we barter for your dearie's release?" mocked Lirenda. "I hold her caged spirit under my thumb." Irresistible gambit, she flaunted the icicle gleam of the crystal point palmed in her velvet-gloved hand. "What will you yield to save Elaira from extended anguish in permanent limbo?"

"Nothing!" One word, incisive as a whipcrack, shaped by a Masterbard's art.

Lirenda toyed with that veneer of bravado, her transcendent confidence eager for the supreme duel with her lifelong nemesis. "Seize your satisfaction before I take mine. *Are you listening?*"

Her ultimatum met the granite of Arithon's exigent, pinned focus.

"Search as you like. You'll find nothing to wrangle for a cagey salvage." Lirenda fondled the crystal point with the careless ferocity to jerk the short leash. "Arithon, you have two choices. Both carry a price. Did you pack Enithen Tuer's primitive artefact along? Then seize the Biedar crone's retribution. My craven murder, if you succeed, would cause a brief setback, but not finish the Order of the Koriathain. Kill me, and the bauble that confines Elaira's spirit will shatter, her life force severed with mine." A brief pause, while that quandary sank in, then, "Or submit to me without condition. Give yourself over and your poppet walks free. On no other terms will I spare her."

"Your rules." Arithon's bitterness scribed the very ether in recoil. "Not mine." He resumed his advance and knelt at Elaira's side. A touch of reverent eloquence set her torn shirt to rights, her desecrate nakedness covered with heartrending tenderness.

"If you prefer the drama of mutual suicide, you might grant her the mercy stroke first." Galled by his immutable disregard, Lirenda taunted, "What principle stands in the absence of love? You tossed me that supercilious advice when your kiss ruined my future on that midwinter night at Jaelot's back postern."

Arithon showed no response. One forgot at one's peril the stubborn persistence he maintained under hostile pressure.

Even now, even here, with his only beloved unstrung before him, defeat found him uncowed. Curdled to irritation bilious as flung acid, the Koriani Prime Matriarch vowed to smash her enemy's self-assurance. She would see the bed-rock of his deep commitment ripped bare and cracked to the quick.

"Where Morriel attacked you as an inconvenience, I have made your downfall my personal affair. All your life, and Elaira's, I've been the tireless instrument hounding you to despair. My design warped Fionn Areth's birth-born destiny through yours. Mine, the grotesque manipulation that shaped your role in Vivet's pathetic demise. How did it feel to bear her sorry death, only to fail to save her orphaned byblow? Poor maligned innocent! Slaughtered on the scaffold in terror and tears for the stain of your criminal reputation."

Arithon made no sound. Her vicious prodding prompted no acknowledgement. But the subliminal crackle of his heightened ire laced through the warded floor underfoot, a thrum transmitted in stone below hearing, galvanic as the crash of a boulder plunged into a stilled pool. The shock riffled through the ambient flux caused two bystanding Seniors to flinch; not his speech, mild as thorn swathed in eiderdown. "May you rue the day."

The threat flicked Lirenda's nerves to disproportionate anger. Few dared to prod that note of constrained temper. Morriel and Selidie both had tested Arithon's mettle and lost. Lirenda shivered, stoked by brazen thrill. She would stop at nothing. The proprietary lever couched in her hand made the vicious temptation irresistible.

"Elaira's betrayal of you was quite real." Lirenda bludgeoned Arithon's steel-clad facade with innuendo, addicted to her desire to rend his unshakable trust. "I don't refer to our former Prime's snare crafted to dispatch you through Vivet. Did your devoted friends ever confide? Were you told of the conspiracy hatched in secret with Dakar? I speak of the pact that set Rathain's royal seal on your miserable centuries of Koriani imprisonment."

Avid thirst slavered with anticipation for the ace card tucked up her sleeve. But her nuanced inference met his insolent rebuff.

Arithon's bent head stymied her dissection of his torment while he surveyed Elaira's condition. Tapered fingers smoothed back her tangled bronze hair and pursued an assay written in the language of tenderness.

When mage-sensed discernment perceived no response, Arithon's careful hands roved onwards. He straightened her tumbled limbs. No harm detected past the bruises from her collapse, his touch moved on and slid under her clothes. Lirenda shivered, engrossed, as Arithon extended his adept knowledge through sinew and bone, with a lover's affinity sounding the signature of Elaira's inert body for damage. Intended or not, the hostel's propensity to sharpen esoteric transmission erased the semblance of chaste intimacy. Cloth hid nothing from the voyeur. The augmented flux currents exposed every eloquent aspect of Arithon's tactile exploration. Lirenda fell prey, beguiled by sympathetic sensation as his deft stroke raised reflexive response from Elaira's naked breasts. The Prime squirmed, her private flesh puckered by quivers that hitched her breathless.

She swallowed panic. Shut her eyes, and battled strained faculties to no avail. Impassive detachment escaped her. The sensory flood torched off in cascade afflicted her suborned coterie of seniors in reflection. The tension compounded by their harnessed consciousnesses multiplied into a drowning wave as the yoke of the master sigil re-echoed the loop of enthrallment. Ill-equipped to weather the tempest, Lirenda gritted her teeth. She would never jettison her hold on prime strength! Nor for the mere blush of heated embarrassment cede her hard-won stake in retreat.

Assuredly, Arithon sought to unnerve her. Unswerving, ruthless, he welded initiate mastery with a Masterbard's command of harmonic penetration, refined artistry sharpened to a shining weapon that quickened the octaves of rarefied light. His palms travelled down Elaira's flank and lingered. The feathered caress of his thumbs wrought subtle magic from the languid spirals that savoured her navel. Dizzied himself by her warmth, he let the wild tumult of his raced pulse drum the flux into concert as heightened awareness guided his finger-tips lower still. He traced the female nexus beneath with matchless finesse, a courtship shaped by poignant knowledge of *her* that affirmed her Name only amid the myriad span of existence.

Lirenda shuddered, quickened past recourse. The plunging swoop hollowed her out, wit and reason milled under by carnal desire that overwhelmed orientation. Captive, she melted to the marrow, transported by worldly bliss that unstrung the celibate boundary of her experience. Her seething flesh ached, a torment at cruel odds with an individual identity keening under the agony of separation. Whirled dizzy, Lirenda groaned, her spirit left stranded in desolation.

Unconsoled loneliness wrenched away meaning and value. Reft of shared affection, her being grappled a tormented starvation that rendered all trappings superfluous.

No platitude eased her stark isolation. No comfort softened the harsh truth. The exalted gift of affection crafted by Arithon's love had never been fashioned for her.

Lirenda bled for the inconsolable irony. Despite her venomous hate and disparagement, no matter the abhorrent stigma of low birth and poverty, a rank deserter of no account had bested her prime privilege for the prize that demolished lofty aspiration. Arithon's priceless regard had gilded not her, but Elaira.

Lashed to furious tears, driven mad and inveigled to mortification by the rank onslaught of secondhand ecstasy, Lirenda suffered the unbearable slight. She trembled, hurled into the abyss of rejection, as Arithon gathered his stricken beloved into his lap. The sweet dance that ravished Lirenda to the abandoned throes of delirium now stretched to reclaim the captive mate caged in crystal. Elaira's cradled body his cherished sounding board, the bard wove the erotic summons to recall the strayed spirit back to the safe harbour of her mortal flesh.

Lirenda swayed, glazed by shock and panting in sweaty arousal. Assaulted, body and mind, through base instinct, she roiled in violate fury as her needy protest drowned in the torrential splendour of sensation. Undone, she burned to eradicate the scourge whose existence hounded her from fullfilled contentment. She fought, raked her wrists with her nails to stave off the ignominious breakdown. Pain spared her from nothing; only heightened the overstrung peak at the precipice of surrender.

All that snatched her from the quivering brink was the flaw that cracked Arithon's sensual immersion. The taut thread he wove snapped at last, frayed at the stricken edge where his utmost effort fell short. His heartfelt cry forged in desperation at the feet of an enemy failed to shake the bonds of Elaira's paralysis.

Arithon's peal of benighted distress shattered the lyric harmonics.

Lirenda crashed, hurled free of breathless entrainment and knocked stupid by proof of her triumph. Amid cruel exposure, in soiled, red shame, she recovered the dropped thread of her purpose. She, not her rival, owned the ace card in the last bid for permanent closure.

The inescapable bond that demolished her quietude *was itself* the scalpel to excise the source of her weakness. From emotional ashes, she would drive Arithon to destruction and seize her rightful empowerment.

The weapon to fissure his unassailable character would wreak devastation, the wedge plied in the salted laceration of Elaira's rejection.

"Did your lover never disclose the venal bargain she struck to recover your life on the sands of Athir?" The Prime taunted the cornered tiger, implacable in her hatred. "Did she never admit that Glendien lent her lascivious flesh as the proxy to bind your strayed spirit? Or that Elaira herself contrived the oath of debt sworn by Dakar for that lusty night's work consummated on your behalf?"

Quiet fell, suspended as etched glass, with the shattering fillip withheld for last.

"You seeded a bastard," Lirenda crowed. "A daughter named Teylia. Born at Althain Tower, raised by Sethvir, the girl was bound over to the Koriathain when she was three years of age. Bartered to our Prime by the Seven, in fact, to defer the sealed forfeit owed on the transaction that spared you."

The violation seemed beneath notice, disregarded as though the gloating punch struck Arithon deaf and mute.

Except the fallen silence went cold, summer's air seized by implacable frost that stilled the ambient flux. No visible impact aroused pain or fury. Not vengeful ruin, or the least whimper of outrage escaped Arithon's rigid expression.

Exhilarated, Lirenda jabbed deeper. "What has your existence been, after all, but a debased charade of deceit?" Smug cruelty spurred her to savage the wound. "You are nothing. Just a Fellowship cipher chained by your ancestor's bleeding compassion. The ethic you milk to nurse your conscience has been tendered in tarnished coin, bought and sold by the sacrifice of helpless children."

Nothing. Victimized hurt granted Lirenda's withering disparagement no satisfaction. Not so much as a flinch yielded notice her vicious dart had stabbed home.

Overpowered male pride perhaps reeled in distress too visceral for rejoinder. Or maybe love-blinded delusion clung to a denial that stunned credibility. Unmasked in betrayal, Arithon's bloodless inertia made a mockery of subjugation.

"Kneel to my demand!" The Matriarch's shrill ultimatum packed venom. "Submit, or I will shred the spirit of the woman you hold dearer than self-preservation."

Arithon did not glance up. Done with glib rejoinder, seated cross-legged on barren marble, he sheltered Elaira's unconscious husk and whispered into her ear, tucked against the support of his shoulder. "The daughter conceived under ritual at Athir was never mine," he admitted. "She belonged to the Biedar tribe in Sanpashir, begotten in ritual by their traditional means to convene with their ancestry."

One protective, spread hand steadied his unconscious beloved through what seemed a pointless statement of release. "Elaira, you were never at fault, though my earthly hand as her sire claims the reckoning for Teylia's death." His unburdened grip drew the crone's flint knife from the deer-hide sheath lodged in his boot cuff.

A ripple shifted the etheric continuum. Seers of all races shuddered to the forerunning back-lash, as Arithon's deft toss reversed the handle. Black flint knapped by the ancients turned inward, he scored the back of his opposite wrist. Descended of Requiar's lineage, his blood primed the tribal blade. No longer the artefact token hoarded with the arcana in Enithen Tuer's fusty attic, ancestral claim consecrated the honed instrument to strike balance for the indebted legacy incurred tens of thousands of years past by Jessian's promise of secrecy.

Dismay shot a pang through the Matriarch's expectation. She brushed off the grue, drunk on the heady foretaste of victory. If a ceremonial instrument's attuned properties might weaken the Prime's master sigil, the late reach for a countermeasure changed nothing. *He would not save Elaira!* Or stave off his wretched defeat. *Koriathain owned him as a bargaining chip,* the convenient pawn played by his heartstrings as the sacrificed gambit to upend the Fellowship's tyranny.

Into the teeth of Lirenda's flushed confidence, Arithon attacked, backed in full by the ranging power of Mother Dark's Aspect. Not to take life or target the Koriani Prime Matriarch directly. Instead, he enacted a delicate stroke in calculated opposition. Precise in form, commanded to exacting alignment by initiate consciousness, he touched the knife to the dry stone basin carved into the floor underneath him. Then wielded what he woke by informed intent, a blade designated to sever without limitation the mightiest of arcane bindings.

Arithon cut the stay laid down by Ath's adepts to seal off the wellspring that centred their defunct sanctuary.

Sethvir's vision captured the whispered invocation Arithon uttered at the signal instant of contact, the hushed moment of upset before the world's mysteries were unleashed to burn.

"For Teylia."

No surprise, to find Arithon s'Ffalenn had known all along of the claim on his life enacted that bleak night at Athir. Damn all to his allies' vain efforts to shield him! That warning, split second's sharp upset overtook the Sorcerer on the spiral steps of Althain Tower's stairwell. Staggered backwards, aghast, he reeled against the rough ledge of an arrow loop. Bristled to expletives in a language long dead, he clung, white-knuckled as the forerunning ripple of shock pealed and shifted the worldwide patterns of probability. Gooseflesh pebbled his skin, raked over by the icy inbreath before the etheric storm front unleashed.

He dispatched terse instructions as the flash-point crest broke: for five colleagues to brace where they stood, then Asandir exhorted *to change course with all speed and return to back Davien's defensive position at Northgate!*

As if any two Sorcerers at their full strength owned the profound resource to stem the whiplash invasion, provoked as the unrest stewed throughout two Ages coalesced to revolt. For the axletree of the crisis at Forthmark threw the dragons' rogue faction their opening to over-throw the Treaty Accord's strict protections. Ath's gift of Athera's Paravians might once again become vulnerable to predation, new-minted drake spawn seeded in malice to upset their precarious return to the continent. Also beyond critical, the swift rise of unstable lane forces *must be deflected!* A pending catastrophe loosed broadscale by itself, without the wyrms' threat of apocalyptic destruction.

Already the flux stream in Lanshire shivered. The spiking quake jabbed a coiled ancient, cocooned in somnolence. The gold eye of a dragon twitched and flicked open. Seshkrozchiel's roused aura flared active and blazed, a crackling, azure corona spun up from quiescence by the blast of ungoverned energy. Her scales shimmered, and her massive, spiked tail fluke stirred and stretched. Flexed muscle burst cracks through the hardened rock shell that nested her long hibernation.

Where no margin existed, Althain's Warden prioritized just one of myriad dreadful choices. He hurled his urgent appeal across distance. *'Ciladis! Do as you must! Stave off Seshkrozchiel's wrath as you can, we are grappling with the breaking calamity of a drake war!'*

Then, all chance for cohesive response swept away, Sethvir bore witness to the epicentric event as the severed stay on the sanctuary's drained wellhead at Forthmark burst wide open in explosive cascade. No longer isolate from the other hostels, the interfaced channels cut free of restraint, disparate equilibrium levelled in reconnection as current gushed from pooled stasis. The unbridled release geysered into the void of the abandoned hostel's emptied receptacle, a millrace of forces boiling in from all quarters, driving a trampling, galvanic cascade of upshifted frequency. The unconstrained flood tapped Athera's gyres and portals and mystical glades. The quiver across the untamed continuum outraced the scope of an immaculate containment as the exalted chord of virgin power from the high registers past the veil fountained through the uncorked breach.

Impact wreaked a vicious cyclone of havoc inside the bounded vault of the Forthmark sanctuary. Every binding established against Ath's Creation and all hindrance made counter to birthright autonomy spanged into dissolution. The blast severed all vows, disrupted the subservient unity of the Senior Circle, and released from constrained service every one of the order's heritage crystals. The sisterhood's proprietary collection of historic records preserved across generations became erased at a stroke, with all oaths of debt under the Prime command annulled in an instant. The Skyron aquamarine relapsed to inert rock in Lirenda's grasp, while the link to her slaved coterie unravelled, the immersive grip of their bonded trance wrenched out of service by the restoration of self-reliance.

The surge ransacked the planet's delicate network of electromagnetics. The web shimmered across the face of Athera, disrupted equilibrium slewed by the wilful puncture opened at Forthmark. The drain raced a flicker like cloud shadow, dimming the reservoirs pent in reserve, as reverberation spilled through the far-flung hostels maintained in devotion by the White Brotherhood . . .

On site at the sanctuary in sisterhood custody, Forthmark's diminished receptacle received the runaway charge like the flash point of grounded lightning.

Torrential power gushed through the ancient spring's unshuttered gateway. Wrapped crystals sequestered inside their warded coffers vibrated and sang, struck to spontaneous resonance by the grand chord that sourced conscious existence. Imposed spells of longevity frayed like whipped floss. The seniors caught out by the surge collapsed where they stood in the puddled folds of their mantles. The frail perished outright. Others gasped in extremis as their aged organs ruptured under the recoil of entropic decay.

Lirenda suffered the dizzying brunt in her ivory seat at the forefront, teeth clenched against spasms of nausea. The endowment of her eighth-rank discipline weathered the harrowing onslaught just barely, as the potent sigils upholding six centuries of youth lost their resilient efficacy. Stretched life span curtailed to decades in an instant, she sought to stem the ebb of unnatural vitality through her personal crystal. The effort to block or reverse the harsh passage lost impetus. The quartz matrix no longer enabled her craft. A scour less violent than the shattering influence of salt had rendered the reliable stone to a worthless blank.

Powerless, emptied, the Prime Matriarch howled. She would not abide! Before loss eradicated the fulcrum to consummate her grand design, she crafted a cantrip to screen the native quartz commandeered as the instrument bonding Elaira's captivity. The sigil back-lashed and singed her gloved hand. Volatile silk ignited. Her frantic reflex to smother the flame jounced the point from her rattled grasp. She fumbled, missed her snatch as the crystal flew airborne. The fragile matrix glanced off her finger-tips, struck the marble floor, and smashed into pieces.

Lirenda shrieked in baulked rage, a wailed dissonance overwhelmed amid the heightened frequency still inexorably climbing. Her antagonist also scrambled to compensate.

Caught in the pressured flood at the basin, knees lapped in electromagnetic charge and the upswell of virgin water, Arithon laboured to salvage his unconscious mate from the fountainhead surge of release.

He shielded Elaira, prepared for the onset of seizures as her displaced awareness grappled the wrench of reunion with her torpid flesh.

"Elaira! I have you. It's safe to wake up!"

Limp in his arms, she stayed unresponsive. Hampered by her flaccid weight, Arithon hauled her bodily from the etheric breach. He pillowed her head in his lap and called her by Name. When a Masterbard's summons of pealing command failed to key an awakening, horror shattered his poise.

Blind and deaf to defeat, he rejected Lirenda's sneer of mockery. Bedamned to the Prime! She could stew in her meaningless malice, crow till she choked on her gloating belief he was finished. Past time the witch earned the comeuppance of her predecessors, undone by their premature expectation he was broken before he lay overcome and knocked senseless.

"Elaira!" No matter what caused her delayed revival, she was not lost. The intimate line of rapport still threaded the heart's gateway between them. Arithon drove his naked appeal once again down that indelible channel.

No movement fluttered her pallid eyelids. His beloved sprawled pale as death in his arms, her strayed spirit inexplicably snatched beyond reach. *She had not crossed the veil.* Not yet. The steady rise and fall of her chest clocked her breath through the comatose warmth laid against him. Terrified, Arithon clothed his summons in song. Full bore, keening through the might of his art, he begged her to acknowledge his plea. For in fact, he may have misstepped in blind faith. Cast her adrift by his desperate, passionate need to distance her from endangerment. Could he have destroyed her unbreakable trust? Driven her off for protection, too selfishly armoured against his own fear to have grappled the price in reciprocal damage?

"No!" She was not so indulgently frail. Not the mate who once mustered the brazen pluck to have rejected his death on the cold strand at Athir. Elaira had not relinquished his life! Not then, at any cost, nor out of fright for the gamut of cruel consequence. She surely must realize the deep, healer's working through Glendien could not have been hers alone, but a Biedar pre-emption of the original framework derived from their ancestral rite. The crone herself authored a daughter's conception out of Requiar's lineage. An obligate sacrifice had branded that unborn spirit, Mother Dark's Aspect summoned to serve ancient justice for a past binding sworn by Requiar under free will.

Lirenda's smug accusation lacked teeth! Elaira herself should have known. Arithon's white fury for Teylia's fate rested at the Biedar crone's feet. Ath knew, the old besom was stubborn. Vengeful as a fiend, and immutable when her notion of balance demanded blood and spent lives to level the score of her debts. A contrary man might break granite bare-handed before bucking the hag's grain of her business.

If forgiveness did not thwart Elaira's recovery, the shattered crystal used to imprison her posed the next likely obstruction. Beyond distraught, Arithon raked up the shards. Shaking as the raced seconds narrowed the margin for recourse, he assayed the fragmented matrix. The remnants bespoke a natural point, uncut, and frosted with inclusions: no brutalized tool of the Koriathain, ground to a featureless polish that sheared away character. Yet the lattice he plumbed for her vital imprint was flushed clean. Emptied, perhaps by the etheric surge unleashed by the crone's knife in his negligent hand.

Whatever the cause, no resonant trace of Elaira's trapped spirit remained. He held nothing to anchor her path for recovery.

Forlorn, forsaken, forsworn beyond conscience, Arithon moaned in anguish.

His grief piqued the Prime Matriarch's vicious delight. "I promised to see you reduced to despair, empty-handed and wretched before me."

Even sorely distraught, Arithon winced. That jarring *wrong note* of supercilious mockery jabbed him to alarm. Lirenda's overweening satisfaction belied the factual evidence her enthroned power as a Koriathain was demolished. Such unshaken confidence scarcely would revel in the wrecked magnitude of the sisterhood's fall: unless such premature gloating celebrated the backhanded thrust of a hidden counterploy cached in reserve.

The Matriarch warmed to her distillate spite. "Elaira was the bait, and you, my staked gambit. White swan no longer, our Koriathain will rise as the phoenix out of the ashes." Lirenda stood for her prudent withdrawal. Attended by the loyal, subservient dregs that remained of her decimated Senior Circle, she exulted as she swept past, "I wonder how long you'll survive to pine over your fruitless regrets?"

For Arithon grasped the mounting scope of his dilemma, placed as he was at the compromised nexus inside the sealed wards that secured the old sanctuary's integrity. Bereft of options, he cradled his dearest beloved, while the untamed currents unleashed by his act streamed through at a pitch to scorch nerves. Linger too long in unshielded exposure, and etheric burnout would sow madness. Experienced, since Los Lier, he recognized the affliction when upscaled frequency neared the threshold to sublimate mortal flesh.

More than the blank crystal's puzzle eluded him. By now, mediation *ought to have arrived!* The breached gateway at Forthmark should have summoned the urgent attendance of Ath's adepts. Yet no shining, robed figures stepped in to take charge. None chastised him for blatant violation. Due authority did not stem the unchecked displacement bleeding the reserves that buffered Athera's mysteries. Help was not forthcoming, no matter the ruin, that Forthmark's disparity would sap the White Brotherhood's curated hostels and destabilize the etheric web . . .

Sethvir sank to his knees on the stairwell's rough stone, crushed pithless as the burden of true vision punched a branched path through the crisis ahead. He, and the elder crone of the Biedar, and the Reiyaj Seeress in her gimballed chair gave Lirenda's glutted satisfaction the correct interpretation.

The bid to seize bare-handed power was hers as her diabolical plotting neared completion.

Fellowship Sorcerers were not exempt from the pitfall of conflicted ethic. Today's hotbed stew of contrary entanglements spawned ruthless exceptions to steadfast prerogatives. Sethvir wrestled, aggrieved, while his merciless overview exposed the horrendous collision of crises, and the helpless bitterness sprung from intractable priorities flayed him raw.

When should upright morality denounce rule of law? Must blood offspring suffer the reaped faults of the forbears, and how long did grief supplant absolution if the inflexible check on disaster unseated the foundation of justice not served? How might the mind burdened as Calum Quaide Kincaid and Warden of Althain steer through the crosswinds of a storm birthed in cataclysm when cultural empires toppled? Which seed and which destined heritage should be first to wither when the concurrent onset of multiplied troubles barraged the sacrosanct cornerstones binding Athera's irreplaceable harmonic existence?

Arithon's fate, and Elaira's, had been wrested beyond Fellowship purview. No pat answer served humanity's case.

The view from the pinnacle assuaged nothing as Sethvir bowed his head, the strength and reach of his office beholden past recourse to the will of Mother Dark's Aspect.

Choice under the stricture of the Major Balance ruled the quandary, as fate's dice, rolling, determined which ironclad obligation to betray, and which must stay inviolate for salvage at all costs, among many tumbled freefall into jeopardy.

For the crux imposed by the Biedar's dire warning arrived.

Doom came on the distant, braked snap of stretched wing leather and whipped eddies spun through broken glass. The hurtling dive of five taloned predators scythed through Forthmark's blown-out casements into the groined vault of the uncapped sanctuary. Jewelled scales the glittering emerald of new grass, the drake molts Lirenda had catastrophically tantalized swooped in and alighted to claim Arithon's aura as their dangled prize.

Late Summer 5929

Aria

Arithon grappled his drastic predicament with no grace for a tailored response. Flight reflex drove him erect, a blindsided stumble as the incredulous scope of his miscalculation settled to roost. Lirenda's backhanded alliance with Dragonkind should not have outflanked him. Informed hindsight had known what she guarded: he had glimpsed the extent of the order's loss in the proscribed records sundered with their Waystone. Her improvident bargain for unbridled power upended his urgent pursuit of Elaira's hung fate. His burdened retreat bore her inert frame from the verge of the etheric spring. Against the volatile peril of the breached vortex, Arithon resorted to shadow. Air shrieked in complaint as his stopgap remedy clapped down, the upwelling surge snap-frozen by a black cold ferocious enough to seize *all* refined current to absolute stillness.

The patch stifled the breach none too soon. Disaster scarcely deflected on one front came under manic assault from the menace barged through the gapped casements. The Koriani Prime and her reduced entourage had fled to refuge in the corridor. No eyewitness lingered in the vaulted chamber when the elemental might sourcing his remedial conjury seared into headlong collision with the inchoate chaos sprung from the reckless excitement of five immature wyrms.

Arithon was the glued subject of their fascination. The choice morsel served up to their savage whim, and Lirenda's trick card to clinch her spoils at the endgame.

The threat saw him outfaced. Dragons by nature were not wont to withdraw. Feckless with youth, contemptuous of superior authority, these fresh subadults did not recognize limitation. Their world was an untested arena for sovereignty. The walloping blast of their interest perceived only a specimen ripe for dissection and assimilation. Heads cocked on cobra necks, they fixated upon the two-legged gambit before them. The scrape of horn talons sized to grapple a horse bore the sinuous, gliding advance of furled leather wings and scaled muscle. Armour patterned in ornate designs, each hide was unique as the laminate ripples forged into tempered steel.

Arithon faced them, Elaira clutched close. He dared not fall back or stir to safe-guard her. Movement excited the drakes' fascination. Retreat would trigger their instinct to kill.

Quietude availed nothing. A wedged skull bristled with spines dipped and snaked level with the marble floor. Two spans of golden eye and slit ebon pupil pinned the toothsome delicacy with the joy of a puppy tossed a fresh marrowbone.

The pressed wave of curiosity rocked Arithon backwards, a hammer strike tolled through the ambient flux as the claimant drake challenged its jostling rivals. '*The figment is mine!*'

The peal trumpeted raw rage and destruction, mighty enough to crush mortal thought and demolish resistance. Except the subject of contention between five rampant wyrms did not succumb. Arithon denounced that shout of fury, his whistled note an incorrigible demand for self-preservation exactingly pitched to dismantle the flare of aggression.

Five serpentine heads swivelled, rapt. Eyes sun-brilliant and tall as a man narrowed to slits to better examine him. Forge-hot breath huffed from scaled nostrils. Arithon could do little but shelter Elaira from the monsters' scrutiny. Her vulnerable flesh clenched in his arms, he tempered the blistering gusts with a discreet screen of shadow.

That subtlety backfired and redoubled the intensity of the molts' fatal attraction. Diverted from their infighting savagery, the dominant bidder coiled backwards. Spiked ruff spread and fanged jaws gaped wide, it reared up, a towering nightmare of predatory malice. A glow deadlier than a lit furnace rouged glistening membranes as the saw-toothed maw gaped like a tunnel to expose its ribbed throat. Then came the tornadic roar as the creature spat fire, a torrential burst to slag stone and crater the impertinent smidgin's rebuff to white ashes.

Arithon countered with shadow at strength. Not just to stave off incineration, horrific consequence obliged him at all costs to shield the etheric well at his back. Give way, cede one inch, and a rupture might spin Athera's deep mysteries into irreversible entropy. The explosive clash of five headstrong molts against human will must be disarmed or endured in the dearth of sound options. Arithon braced himself for the tempest, battered as thrust and counterforce shrieked into hellish recoil. His remedial effort at best deferred ruin. The drake molts might savage him with tooth and claw. Against their mailed talons, he was lost, the imbalanced flux bore he guarded without stable recourse if he died in the critical absence of Ath's adepts.

The fight devolved to a test of survival until the scorching barrage eased and let up. Arithon clung to nothing but hope the brash creatures preferred the thrill of live game for amusement.

He coughed, blurred eyes streaming from the acrid smoke, plumed into an oily fog beneath the groined ceiling. His surroundings were ravaged. The locked chests with their voided collection of crystals, and the carved aumbries crammed with scrolls and rare books, all incinerated to flaked carbon. The Koriathain still standing cowered behind their Prime Matriarch, at remove past the doorway's sealed boundary. Arithon spared them no thought. Ringed by a filmed smut of swirled ash, he attended his most precious asset. Elaira still breathed within his embrace. Unscathed in adversity, he remained upright inside a circular span of gleaming, cool stone.

The astounding rebuttal won him no reprieve: only riveted the molts to obsession. They circled. One after another, they bugled, warbling to vie for territorial primacy. No bloody arena of muscular prowess, this killing field staged an obstinate match to revise existence to their satisfaction.

The trial began as the sated cat might tease a mouse. A menacing foray to unravel form grazed Arithon's self-aware presence. The glancing swipe, deceptively gentle, sought access, tentative prelude to the snagging, sharp jerk to unravel and supplant his shape with another. No illusory phantom, a forced dissolution by dragons was *actual*, material altered by whelming force as the thrust of their thought overwrote Ath's Creation.

Bare-fisted, Arithon defended that native endowment, his own and Elaira's. Falter, and their templates of being would crumple, sucked into collapse. Experience steadied him. A similar trial conquered in Davien's

Maze, and the brutal, etheric attack suffered under rogue shamans at Ettinmere well honed his saving, split-second response. Arithon plied the harmonics that stabilized matter across the four quarters, then strengthened the pattern that underpinned his individuality and his mate's. He knew her essence as his very self. Their two threads twined as one, she the toughened street waif who thrived by her wits, *and* the dauntless healer whose sympathy served the poor and the dispossessed without stint. She was all peerless heart, counterweight for his fractious spirit, and the melody that tempered his lacerated defensiveness with arid humour and laughter. Female to his male, Arithon framed their inseparable partnership, reinforced through his initiate perception and nuanced by his Masterbard's art.

The drake molts encountered a surprise resistance raised from *nothing*, a bulwark sheared whole out of resonant harmony. Annoyed to frustration, they pressured this untoward invention, with auric displays burgeoned to azure fluorescence as their swift counterpunch slammed their recalcitrant prey.

Strike met a retort upstepped to baulk them.

Deterrence inflamed the dragons' thwarted bafflement. *'What is it, why is it, who is it?'* Acquisitive engrossment piqued by the accelerant of defiance, they poked and pried and *twisted* to overwhelm the wayward anomaly before them. What presented as a puny two-legged wisp *did not behave as a trifling figment*. This outlandish phenomenon thwarted their probes with shocking invention! The fathomless quirk prodded the molts to lashed tails, snorted fire, and an incandescent, ungovernable ire. Though squashing the *fleck* of rank irritation spurred them to immolation, they embraced their imperative urge to supplant the upstart *bother* as they pleased.

Arithon received not an instant's reprieve. Stalked by creatures who considered him beneath contempt, he only could field the mauling surge of disintegration rained down upon him. Such ferocity outstripped an exuberant conquest, scour and scourge aimed by force to dismantle structure and sow the ravenous maw of the void.

Yet the contrary, two-legged conundrum withstood the scorched fury of the molts' assault. Arithon's resiliency now posed them an affront that demanded destruction, the concept of negotiation and compromise beyond any molt's comprehension.

Their push for annihilation stormed down, an auger's stab of undilute chaos to shatter the ordered continuum. Arithon extended his

song in thought, in spirit, and through the flexible conduit of his voice.
He clothed all he was, and the woman he cherished, into the purified
essence of melody. To the outer edge of his aura, he shaped harmony
sprung from bright sound, within range of hearing and into the ephemeral registers octaves beyond. The raised chord to tame the wild
elements met the onslaught, a silver-toned cry for peace. His wrought
defence sustained, carried through the maelstrom without flaw and
without sign of breaking.

The precise intonation left Arithon no resource to spare.

Slip, and raw antipathy would unmake his Named essence. If he was
subsumed, Elaira's frail hold on survival died with him. The dragons
would seize charge of all that he knew. A master's trained provenance,
wrested from his structured ethic, could warp his talented resource to
shape who knew what vile spawn, an *otherness* beyond his most dreadful
imagining. An unhallowed desecration not to be borne, no matter the
bittermost price paid in consequence.

Wrung out of choices, Arithon extended his range far past the limit
of Halliron's teaching to supplant the drakes' savage unbinding. He
sounded the deep registers. Wielded as his weapon the harmonic vibration to redefine beingness. Clear reverence rescribed the inflected
subtleties of personality – his own, and more cherished, Elaira's. Her
peril was his fault, fallen to him to preserve on his limited merits.

The drakes tore at his adamant composition. His ringing counterpoint
wrangled them into a blockade, textured nothing like Fellowship
conjury. Tail flukes slashed in tantrum. Stymied, the molts grappled
what could not be deciphered. Their flummoxed, blind rage became
reft of impetus, stalled by a strength forged in steel by a whisper. Arithon
sang. His heartfelt peal fused the essence of stone and laced the air with
subsonics. Line by song line, he braided the flux into a paean of unimpeachable exaltation.

The creation of dragons knew nothing of selfless affection. Their
hierarchical grasp of existence had no language for compassionate partnership. Braw molts, green with youth, eschewed patience as well.
Insatiable wrath inflamed their assault, scope expanded to obliterate
the historic site that once had ignited the miracle of Verrain's transformative deliverance.

Frail stay on catastrophe run amok, the ancient ciphers laid down by
the high art of Ath's white adepts: their remnant working had been

crafted to stem the ranging force of virgin power. Yet a breach of their bounded containment from inside would level the cliffs overhead. Demolish the hostel, its warren of storerooms and corridors, and kill every soul in the south wing that sheltered the world's most renowned infirmary, should Arithon's harmonic reinforcement fail to secure the old sanctuary built at the wellspring. Alone, he conducted a countermeasure anchored by sheer concentration. Exhaust that limit, and the last option of self-immolation, even through the rune of unbinding, became untenable. The reprehensible malpractice once engaged to unmake the substance of a crossbow bolt at Tal Quorin could not be tried here, where the upstepped effects would reverberate past the veil and tear ruination through the core of Athera's deep mysteries.

Arithon railed, allowed no escape from the terminus of human stamina. He was never invincible. The ghastly memory scarred still from his effort to repulse the hostile fiend plague that had beset Feylind's brig. Against that lesser storm, his frailty nearly had seen *Evenstar's* gallant crew lost at sea. Teive's lesson from that dreadful day remained valid: his precocious resource was brutally finite. A man overstretched would break beyond recourse, to the destruction of all he defended.

At this pass, outfaced, Arithon bowed his head. Without pride, in abject humility, he pitched his cry through his matrilineal heritage, an appeal he had no given right to express invoked by a tenuous thread. On Forthmark soil, upon Shand's sovereign ground, he pleaded through Dari s'Ahelas's ancestral bloodline for help to strengthen the melodic score upholding his stand. Spoken aloud, past retraction, he extended his call by Name in petition to Athera's Paravian Queen Regent. The debt to her mercy was his to acknowledge: her gift of release from Desh-thiere's curse in the King's Grove once had granted a reprieve beyond his earnest means to repay.

The last obligation could not be forsworn. Given his salvation then to spare innocent lives from the slaughter clinched amid the siege at Alestron, Arithon surrendered himself yet again for the cause of Paravian survival. Not to Lirenda; never to the dragons' brash arrogance, but to a shining entity more perilous: *"A'Daelient Merevalia! I pledge to do anything in my power, whatever you ask, if you will defend what is not mine to yield through the course of my blunder. My word, set under seal by Ath's light, under surety of Dharkaron's Redress, do with me as you must to secure the continuity of Athera's mysteries."*

If she acted, if she raised the Athlien dancers to extend his song line through adversity, Arithon understood he would be flayed in the crosswind of upstepped harmonics. A sunchild's power unleashed would incinerate breathing flesh. He might surmount the course as a self-realized entity; but Athera's dimensional spectrum could no longer contain him.

Yet no whispered response arose to spark his anguished sacrifice. Disappointment near strangled his art. Wounded by setback, Arithon salvaged the presence to steady the pitch. If not rejected, then too likely, his extreme appeal had not pierced the white adepts' seal of restriction.

Bare-handed, afraid, Arithon withstood the wracking strain by dint of grim strength and endurance. Exhaustion must not sap his peak effort before the molt dragons tired of mauling him. The fool's wish damned faith, that he might wear down a drake's contemptuous prowess for self-made creation. Nothing other *existed* for them past the absolute prerogative of their supremacy. To the molt wyrm, he became the eccentric pitched against that cocksure belief. The tussle to squash the usurper's exception posed them nothing more than an outrageous taunt. The contest could not be retired. Never, until crushed, overpowered and erased, no wisp of his upstart defiance remained. Only a deconstructed idea for Dragonkind's wilful analysis: Lirenda's unique plaything delivered as promised, tossed into the game as a bargaining chip.

Arithon muscled despair beyond his mortal depth. No inadequacy grieved him more than the burden of harm to the woman held dearer to him than all else.

He shaped his last stanzas in her behalf.

"Elaira, beloved! Take heed! You must." At the end, he sang *love* as his final, honed weapon. Arithon fired the octaves that bloomed into light above audible hearing. The ringing chord summoned through heart and mind reforged his indelible cry for her forgiveness. "If I've broken your trust, at least save yourself. Awaken, Elaira! I beg you. If you don't reintegrate with your flesh, I cannot deliver the protection required to let you walk out of this whole."

Elaira's reft spirit failed to respond because her essence was no longer confined by the Prime Matriarch's sigils of entrapment. An infallible working applied through a tamed crystal of known provenance never had been tailored to seal an Atheran matrix plucked from a wild vein in the Skyshiels. The natural stone mistakenly cross-fired as her receptacle retained its unique provenance. Inclusions and impurities mazed its lattice with quirks that retarded the crushing finality of her imprisonment. Hazed as the restrictive spell coil narrowed, Elaira's pinned consciousness darted in cornered flight through the natural maze of plumed veils and rainbow refractions. Her hope of last refuge seized in desperation stemmed from the surprise visitation once conferred upon her by one of the wise from Ath's brotherhood. A winter night's counsel, sent at Sethvir's request, had breached her locked, attic room through that gateway. Graphic recall of the uncanny encounter drove Elaira's agonized flight.

She sought and found the ephemeral gleam of refined light left imprinted by the white adept's exalted passage. The trace led to the portal, a bright beacon punched through the dark caul suffocating her spirit. Elaira plunged through. As a fluttering moth drawn heedless towards flame, her adrift being tracked the infallible path etched through the etheric web.

The calm, twilit haven where she emerged was a place of bewitching beauty no whit less perilous. Her tread scattered dew in a hidden dell, fine grasses and sweet wildflowers bejewelled with the cellophane flutter of disturbed insects. Stars pricked through a canopy of magnificent trees, clothed in grandiloquent silence. Beneath, the shimmer of a shallow pool lapped against a ring of white stones. The latent air of serenity prickled her bemusement to sudden unease. Elaira realized where her unwary foray had led. The hallowed glades spun from virgin power by the White Brotherhood were wellsprings of mystery, maintained at the sacrosanct heart of the hostels anchored by their devotional rites. Which active site she had broached scarcely mattered. She was far removed from her body at Forthmark, and more: her entry disturbed a conductive interface where the ephemeral octaves above sound and light expressed the actualized patterns of thought and desire.

Elaira had encountered that dread verge before. Alive to her danger, she knew her magnificent surrounds were beyond deadly and volatile. Each exquisite bloom, the peridot leaves and lush ivy that wreathed the massive boughs overhead – all the fine-grained, surreal perfection that detailed her perception was self-made – a reflection cast by her individual presence. The dappled deer grazing, each glistening frog and iridescent mayfly seemed more than superlatively real, their fearlessness quickened by the reactive charge of her living consciousness. She intruded where imbalanced emotion and strident opinions posed a dire hazard for the unwary. Ignorant impulses sparked misadventure for those who strayed here unattended.

Elaira froze between steps, too late to stem the whispered deflection sown by her trepidation. Ominous eddies rustled the foliage. Puckered wavelets dimmed the well's limpid surface. A rabbit ceased nibbling. Head raised in alarm and ears perked by the gust that flattened the grasses, it thumped a warning hind leg and bolted. A torn leaf whickered down, followed by another, scything through fireflies winnowed like sparks chased aloft by an on-coming storm.

Initiate healer, Elaira seized hold of lapsed discipline. The drilled ethic to avert harm invoked by trained reflex, she grounded and centred her equilibrium. As her impulsive panic subsided, the turbulent burst gentled to a cat's-paw of breeze, and resettled into quiescence. The owl startled on the wing circled back onto its perch, then folded barred wings and regarded her with coin-yellow eyes. The timid hare crept from cover, unafraid of the hunting cat just padded like poured oil from the shadowy undergrowth.

Elaira knelt and righted the painted tortoise overturned at her feet. Through a breath-taken pause, she measured the quandary of her predicament. She had no ready plea to excuse the importunate damage caused by her unforeseen trespass.

"Escape from oppression incurs no offence." The white-robed speaker stepped from the wood, male to balance her female orientation. Not a prior acquaintance, this dark-skinned elder had the spare bones and elegant hands of Biedar descent.

"I'm so sorry!" Elaira exclaimed, contrite with relief for his guided oversight. "Please forgive my unwitting disturbance."

"Be welcome, lady." The adept caught the last, drifting shred of torn greenery between his cupped palms. "Your beloved, not you, wrought the greater share of the momentary imbalance."

"Arithon?" Severed from linked rapport, Elaira tempered her rattled astonishment. "How?"

The adept bowed his hooded head and breathed on the leaf, which transformed. A violet butterfly fluttered through his lean fingers and flew, trailing pale gold phosphorescence. "Your mate left no inventive measure untried to spare you from the sisterhood's trap." Shown a patience that

did not badger him for reassurance, he applauded her wisdom and qualified. "Arithon wielded the Biedar's flint knife and severed the stay we
imposed to seal off the dry wellspring in the Forthmark sanctuary. Since
our brotherhood vacated the site over nine centuries ago, for safety, no
active link connected that site to the mysteries."

Elaira stifled a gasp, rocked by the appalling scope of entrained
consequence. The torrent erupted when the defunct conduit was
reopened to the etheric web would have levelled the imbalanced deficit,
sweeping asunder all ties that hindered the grand chord of harmonic
alignment. "The flash-point surge would annihilate every resistance
caught in the breach!"

Koriathain derived power through coerced enslavement, amplified
through crystal resonance. Their moribund transmission would have
collapsed at one stroke, every harnessed chain of ciphers swept to dissolution. "Forced expansion would have imposed merry havoc on the
hierarchy of compulsion." A blow to dismantle far more than the order,
Elaira mused, inwardly overawed. "My mate has courted disaster of a
proportion far surpassing the sisterhood's grasping interests."

"Quite." The adept returned a startling smile, brown eyes not without
sympathy for the ranging gut punch of ramifications. "Except the breached
gateway tapped the full bore of the mysteries only for a fleeting instant."

"Of course, Arithon would have curbed the cascade just shy of explosive calamity." Elaira folded her jellied legs and sat down, forehead pleated
in thought. "Ath wept! On a good day, his bent for terrifying tactics
wrecks even the Fellowship's sturdy digestion. I'll guess he cracked the
seal for the burst to denude the Koriathain of their suborned power?
When cornered, he's apt to innovate and flatten the opposition with
disruptive efficiency."

"He accomplished that much," The white adept admitted in wry
admonishment, "Also, by the one stroke he could take, your beloved
dispatched you beyond reach of jeopardy."

Elaira shivered, unnerved to be reminded of her state of discarnate
separation. "At what price?"

"Short of broadscale apocalypse?" Her escort's subtle influence
tempered the shimmering ripple her spiked unease chased across the
purity of the spring. "Your man capped the fountainhead surge with
hard shadow. A stay potent enough to seize flux transmission to absolute
stillness and arrest vibrational resonance. Forthmark's gateway is blocked,

and the free quartz point that delivered your consciousness outside of time became shattered by mishap soon after you left."

"Arithon could not have realized I'd secured my escape." Dismayed, Elaira measured the unforeseen consequence sown by the Atheran crystal seized as the stopgap vessel for her imprisonment. "The upshot strands me in a touchy position," she supposed. Though she could not reunite with her body at Forthmark by way of the original portal, she had ridden the etheric winds through discorporate trances before.

The adept let her hopeful assessment down gently. "You would not survive passage as unclothed spirit where the flux transmission is ravaged to chaos by warring dragons. Arithon battles the molts for his life."

The bleak shock of Elaira's despair defied words.

"You are not impaired," the adept was swift to point out. "Form does not dictate or limit your consciousness. Whole in spirit, you command the grace of your being. As healer, you understand the greater frame of existence does not reside in the flesh."

"Transcendence? You suggest crossing the veil is my only path to requital?" Courageous, Elaira argued the immaculate choice of an immediate, escorted transition. "Once, through your brethren's truthful advice, I breached the sealed wards of Davien's Maze to reach my beloved as he walked the abyss."

"Connection by way of the etheric bridge wrought through dream? Then you are the only being alive who may claim that means of direct access. Love freely shared opens the gateway through the human heart." The adept offered counsel, inexplicably saddened. "Yet to what end, lady? Try that route at the risk of destruction by Arithon's side. Do you grasp the fullest extent of your danger? More than the body might fall to the whirlwind as Dragonkind seeks his immolation."

The grove's peace abruptly acquired the stillness of cottonwool suffocation. "But—"

The adept's raised palm forestalled her rash impulse. "My dear, at least know what you're facing. With due permission?"

His tap on her forehead was purely ephemeral, all bodily form an etheric construct wrought from the sanctuary's sensitive interface. The vantage of the white adepts extended perception, an exalted connection through spirit that parted the veil. Elaira's awareness unfolded to a shared view of Arithon's straits at Forthmark . . .

*   *   *

. . . where naked song shaped by a Masterbard's art waged a doomed battle, all that stayed the wavefront of dissolution unfurled by five furious drake molts. Bent on absolute conquest, the creatures pursued without stint the incomparable trophy promised by Lirenda Prime. Arithon fought back for more than the woman sheltered in his arms. Cede the field, and the Koriathain gained Dragonkind's expansive power as their coveted prize. Direct access to outstrip the limitations of crystal would unbridle their thwarted ambition, their aim to supplant the Fellowship's protective custody of Athera's assets seized at one stroke . . .

"Whatever should come, we would be together," Elaira protested in favour of joining her mate. "And what else is left?" *His past statement indelible as a vow endured since the hour Arithon first broached his undying affection: 'Give me torture and loss, give me death, before I become the instrument that seals your utter destruction. Of all the atrocities I have done in my past, or may commit in the future, that one I could never survive!'*

Elaira swallowed back tears, unstrung by the grief she might leave him as legacy, sundered amid his belief he had failed her if they should be parted untimely. "I cannot leave him abandoned!"

The molts posed the existential threat if he faltered. The whiplash of their destructive triumph would wreck the tenuous bulwarks that stemmed humanity's ham-fisted rise to ascendancy: everything beautiful in Athera, and all the exalted glory bestowed by the shining grace of the Paravians would become swept away. Diminished to entropy along with ascendant wisdom's demise, the mystical sanctuaries tended by Ath's brotherhood would wither as well.

The adept sent to advise her must acquiesce, despite stakes too dreadful for compromise. Their precepts honoured the birthright of free will. For thousands of years, their restraint had eschewed the temptation to deflect the course of the world. Yet core knowledge that embraced the blinding expanse of the infinite understood the imperfect mind could never encompass the limitless grandeur of all that existed.

Elaira hung her plea upon love and thin air. "Your brotherhood taught me the future has not been written, besides."

The adept bowed before her stated truth. "We choose our own destiny, sourced from the range of *all* creative probability. Your course is yours to mould as you wish, even where the ethic of clear guidance forbids me to endorse your destruction."

Prompt or warning, Elaira gave rein to her fear. "Then please lend me your counsel under advisement."

Shown the unwavering face of commitment, the White Brother indulged her request. "Just as you entered Kewar's maze, your spirit must embark on a passage beyond our directive. Then, as now, the ebb and flow of Athera's electromagnetic transmission will open the way through what lies in your heart. But the volatile currents you traverse will be turbulent. Conflict in the north is distorting the lane tides, compounded by the stresses at Forthmark likely to flare out of control."

Elaira sighed, wrung by the sharp qualm that feathered her skin into gooseflesh. "I promise to swerve neither right nor left, and hold fast to my purpose."

"Resolve alone may not weather this storm." Discouragement coloured the adept's reserve. Since the journey outmatched the supplicant's experience, he addressed her peril unflinchingly. "Your spirit could become irretrievably lost past the verge, where the fluid awareness of imagination supplants the cardinal referents of navigation. More, the bias of alignment is critical. The tangential energies polarized by Athera must rise to match the resonant stream that unlocks the dimensional gateways. Mistime your crossing, and you might wander the realm of extemporal dream beyond recourse."

"How long must I wait?" The tonic perfume of flowers and grass, and the sweet tang of evergreen cloyed the impetuous flame of her anxious impatience.

The adept broke the worst with gentle reluctance. "The designate moment lies two days hence." Before his departure left her to the volatile interface of the active sanctuary, he bestowed a last warning. "Once you embark, you cannot return. The body in Forthmark will ground your spirit into Athera's continuum. Incarnate once more, you must meet an adversarial fate under mortal free will. Go in grace, *Aff'enia*. Know whatever befalls, the greater mercy that weaves Ath's Creation walks with you, and firms the path under your feet."

Elaira bowed in gratitude for the honest counsel. Undeterred, she stood on her own, by claim of personal sovereignty entrusted with the eerie power steered by her tensioned presence. Amid liminal twilight, she nurtured the patience to endure until Athera's planetary alignment matched the correct aspect of the quarter moon.

The brutal wait taxed more than her solitary endurance. Arithon must stay the course meanwhile, his steadfast nerve sustained beyond sight of reprieve. Everything hinged on the strength of blind trust: that he would not forsake his innate character, never to give in or succumb to despair without fight, no matter how hopeless the task laid against him.

He could not hear her plea for encouragement. Abandoned to the custody of her limp body, he subsisted upon nothing but the desolate adamance of his protection.

Elaira spoke anyway, eyes closed against the distraction love's ripple scribed into reactive surrounds entrained by her patent desire. "Trust me, Arithon, be assured I will come. Beyond all bounds of reason or sanity, nothing will keep me away!" He must rely on her, as firmly as once she had sold herself out for his resourceful invention to spare Fionn Areth. Or else all partnership would fail, the frayed bonds of covenant destroyed between them. He had his given right to abandon her, since Valien's death bought the opening for her intervention. She had betrayed him before, spared his life at Athir through the fell pact commandeered by a crown's obligate usage. Once and twice over, the compassionate empathy that founded Arithon's nature recouped the space for forgiveness.

Or not.

No surety existed, no unblindered path through the pitfalls of faith. Amid the soft silence by the silvered pool, Elaira owned nothing but words gifted by the Biedar tribe's eldest under night stars in Sanpashir: 'Mother Dark's mercy walks even where no light appears to be found. The grace of the heart is not subject to boundaries, and witness is made and sealed by the moment . . . Arrogance does not admit to its weaknesses. But love does, respectful for fear of love's absence.'

Salvation hung on the moment the pathway through dreams opened conscious access to the mysteries. Firm bridge for the crossing between her and her handfast mate demanded the unshakeable commitment to span the abyss and access the gateway through Arithon's living heart.

Counterpoints

Packed into the Light's temple with the foundered war host's jetsam of camp followers, Lysaer fumes in clamped fury, forced to kneel for a sham creed of his own invention, while a painted bawd elbows his ribs: "Whether priestly flummery makes you puke, best pray like the pious, because handsome won't save your unbelief from an examiner's charge of apostasy . . . !"

As Elaira bides for the propitious alignment, and Lirenda Prime fidgets through the protracted throes of Arithon's foredoomed contest, Ath's adepts complete their transcendent escort for Nails, last of the afflicted to perish from Riathan Paravian exposure at Caith-al-Caen; while elsewhere, a besotted prophet slinks out of Ganish bearing a black sword and a signet ring he would give all of his damaged joy to consign to oblivion . . .

At Scarpdale to temper Seshkrozchiel's awakening, Ciladis senses the violent surge of a molt's incipient death throes, fast followed by another etheric quake that drops Siantra unconscious at his feet; and his cry of dismay blends with Luhaine's exclamation, all three of them swept up at the forefront as the great drake explodes into flight. "Ath's glory preserve us, that expansive ripple of change was *nothing* released on the world by a dragon . . . !"

XIII. Concerto

Diplomacy with a maddened dragon was dicey as juggling knives, a torrential flood of quicksilver peril wont to test the most agile Sorcerer's heightened awareness. Bound to Seshkrozchiel's flight out of Scarpdale, Luhaine dreaded the process. His tedious preference for thoroughness already was stressed past due diligence by reckless haste. The beat of Seshkrozchiel's wings thundered upwards, the arrowed course of her launch hurled past corniced ice and scoured rock. Two dozen strokes, and the crackle of her auric field broke the bow wave of temporal space. The diminished tapestry of the Storlains spread like crumpled foil beneath, dropped behind in the wink of an eye and replaced through the soaring pause on stretched leather and splayed bone. Below, fleeted past at a dizzying rush, the parched expanse of the Havistock plain unrolled like seamed burlap.

The dragon's speed skated the verge of disaster.

If hurry nettled Luhaine's staid nature, few things quickened a dragon's wrath like the violent death of an immature wyrm. When a youngling's demise occurred on dry land, the fatality sparked into the driest of tinder: the rife altercation at Forthmark raced towards the frightful precursor to a full-blown, vengeful revenant. Any fresh haunt unconstrained by the barriered flux of a grimward seeded a gyre of relentless destruction.

Murder of young undercut the grounds for mitigation, whether or not diplomacy existed to assuage a mature drake stung to rampant aggression.

Taxed in the flesh, Luhaine would have paced, flustered hands clasped at his girth. As the volunteer wraith doomed to uphold Davien's most execrable bargain, he shrank to the inertia of prevarication.

The port town of Spire passed under Seshkrozchiel's shadow, a diminished jumble of child's blocks pinked by crenelled towers, and roof peaks of dull lead and terra-cotta. Lane flux curdled by her feral anger radiated from her burnished scales, the scald of draconian emanation spitting outbursts of ozone-laced static. Cindered bellows, her breath exhaled white flame, streamered sheets sizzling through the crystal cirrus at rarefied altitude. The azure blaze shed from her dorsal spines flaunted a might to dismantle the firmament under her rampaging path.

Shown Mankind's tinkering thumbs in the breach, the great drake would not dally to sort whose inveigling business started the provocation.

Hamstrung as the arbiter wedged in the avalanche, Luhaine quashed a rare spate of foul language: for one wyrm's excited discovery kindled the riptide of widespread emotion. Dragonkind elsewhere sensed the whirlwind of magnified force in aware synchronicity. The conundrum stymied Luhaine's stilted personality. Kharadmon would have laughed at his pedantic addiction to sequential order. Davien's sardonic genius made shreds of persnickety logic; and even, by Ath, Asandir's pragmatic temperament was better suited to parry the bolt-lightning strike of Seshkrozchiel's ire!

Urgent demand impelled direct action. Or shuddering rifts in the continuum threatened a breakthrough to inflame the exiled wyrms in rebellion on the splinter world of Sckaithen Duin. All of today's woeful consequence compounded the incipient fracture of the Northgate Accord.

Luhaine tiptoed into the fraught dialogue, his meticulous phrases weighted and countermatched. 'The Master of Shadow is not to be killed on impulse for *satisfaction*. No enemy of Dragonkind, he is not a threat. His gifted talent for *music* incinerated to *scorched meat* in misplayed reprisal would destabilize the precarious seal of wrought shadow holding the breached well at Forthmark in check.'

'Mistake beyond folly!' For a Sorcerer standing enfleshed, Seshkrozchiel would have levelled her head, the glaring disk of one monstrous eye fixated in contempt. Her scornful retort to an embedded spirit flayed courage with still more disconcerting ferocity. "The two-legged Dark-binding *tidbit blood-sack* was the select gambit for temptation! *Puny human grub,* but in *grudging admission,* one with better sense than to slay an *impetuous snail-witted youngling* clumsy as a hatchling slimed from the egg sac."

Luhaine had no throat to clear in surprise. 'He,' *reference to the sable-haired, murderous packet of human insolence,* 'was not the culprit? Then given his *brash* innocence, let misappraised fault for the plotter's offence be acknowledged.' As a fleck tucked behind the dragon's left pupil, the Fellowship shade winced over a protest that seemed absurd, pompous even to his stiff-necked rectitude. 'One must not rush to swallow the *unsavoury* taste where the pith of whole fruit includes both rind and seed.' Luhaine poked onwards with tight-lipped suspicion: Arithon's damnable motives never trod the straightforward path. 'Bloodshed *killing's* involved. The man's *scheming* may not be the only sharp stick behind the *disruptive* agitation.'

Seshkrozchiel snorted, the eddy of belched fire and ice a vicious disparagement. 'You credit that *insignificant mayfly* twolegs' misdoing? Not for this brangle! Fool molts turned on their hatch mates. They fight one another, a match of brainless sibling jealousy.' A whipped streamer of smoke shredded away on the buffeting whoosh of the next wing stroke. 'Your singer strives by his puny *harmony* to shape a reconciliation. An insect's buzz! Scarcely *fierce enough* to swat down teeth and talons and *might* unsheathed for annihilation.'

The snuffed thought fragment sliced into the formless void, that a two-legs *mortal construct* dared the *hubris* to requite a raging haunt bled into the throes of a death spiral.

'Athera's titled *Masterbard,*' Luhaine corrected Seshkrozchiel's windy huff. 'Polite wisdom *suggests* we might turn around and seek backing *strength* from my colleague, Ciladis.'

'Too late.' A drakish rumble of reptilian humour, then, "I have already dispatched him ahead of us. And, by insistent audacity, a *stowaway* mediator also has inserted her presence and come along for the journey—"

Startled aghast, Luhaine forgot prudence. 'What! — ? — '

Seshkrozchiel flicked her spined tail. A shed wisp of blue light from her aura stalled the actualized recoil thrashed up by the Sorcerer's unconstrained startlement. The adamance jolted by the exchange peppered the dragon's refusal to tender a satisfactory explanation. 'No return for a trespassing *speck's interference* hopped along for the *thrill ride*! Unless you prefer *several* dead molts and a pocked crater that smashes the *ant heap* of Forthmark's walled town into rubble.'

'I require more detail.' Luhaine crammed his jagged upset back hand. 'What *headstrong* mortal trespasser whose vainglorious *impertinence* do you speak of?'

'This.' An image returned, of a black-haired young woman, slight as a willow, but with steely grey eyes, and the unimpeachable insight stamped through Sidir's lineage.

'*Siantra is with you?*' Luhaine curbed blossoming horror, his bastion of stuffy sensibility unravelled. 'Fey girl, wise of insight, yet bereft of sane sense and *impetuous.*'

'She's lodged in my right eye,' Seshkrozchiel confessed through the scream of the gale carved through cloud by her stretched wing leather. 'By her own *rock-hard* insistence, she declared her *importunate notion was needful.* Her *adamance* believed someone ought to stand forward as your *outfaced* singer's ambassador.'

Luhaine lapsed into sour silence, aggrieved, and brooding over the convolute gaps drakish logic mined through the sorrowful complication. Whatever imperative drove Siantra's rash move, the girl owned the dread scope of a seer's unbound vision, one foot set over the veil into Athili tenderly young. That narrow escape from dissolution compounded by the near-fatal encounter with a centaur guardian at Baylienne's Gyre, she had been too long and too deeply winnowed by the unworldly stream of the etheric. Now embedded, unshielded, in the tempest of a dragon's torrential flux, she might snuff the last, frail attachment to her humanity. Fate would chart the penalty exacted for an impulsive moment of suicidal free choice.

'Wyrm castings!' Seshkrozchiel's insults were ever succinct. 'The shifting of *inconsequential* gobbets of meat!' – a dismissive twitch of a tail fluke – 'has been rearranged. The packet of your mote's *animal carcass* has been reinscribed in displacement to Vastmark *now/later.*'

Luhaine flinched, slammed twice over by Seshkrozchiel's naked contempt, that, '*Ciladis, as well, has translocated to the locus of the molt rumpus ahead of us.*' The flicked vision returned, of the Forthmark infirmary, implied the Sorcerer's talent as healer had meaningful interest in the outcome.

Though how anything might be left standing for salvage in the wake of the molts' rampage seemed a moot point to a pessimist.

'Too late to signify?' Seshkrozchiel's rumination twitched a rattle of scales, snapped off by the percussive clash of bared teeth. 'Perhapsssss.'

The ferocity of her agitation outstripped Luhaine's vantage. All of Dragonkind accessed the protective assault of the gravid female whose rank confrontation with Asandir and Davien unfolded apace beyond Northgate. The fanned seethe of her outrage fed the rogue faction's disgruntled revolt, and ignited the cataclysmic instability on Athera. Which unified stew of reciprocal hostilities cascaded directly from Lirenda's flagrant bargain for power, whipped on by brash molts plunged into redoubled frenzy.

'Your Masterbard's aura is the dangled bait at the root cause of disturbance!' Seshkrozchiel fumed. 'A sparkly bauble of *unique* enticement traded from the Forthmark sister-nest *by an eggless female two-legs,* who coveted the empowerment our eldest wyrm granted to Fellowship Sorcerers under the Protectorate Concord.'

Dragons bored silly for novelty were easily prone to blandishments. 'Scatter-brained molts are the most fecklessly tempted of all.' Drakish wrath over humanity's gall scattered reason. 'An *offensive mistake* to allow such a *brazen* two-legged infraction's existence! Far less to leave the ill-spawned *pip* at liberty for a sister-nest's pawn to sow mayhem! Your *nearsighted* Fellowship has been remiss! What human mote of any stripe could be worth an upset to befoul Athera's mysteries?'

Luhaine projected an uneasy, stilted neutrality, too gutted to contemplate how an adult drake might respond at first hand to Arithon s'Ffalenn, hereby referenced as an expendable blandishment. Ath wept! For good reason, Althain's Warden had nursed that fateful prospect in clamp-jawed dread.

A feint ventured in hopeful distraction, the Sorcerer's shade paired to the dragon demurred, 'The High Queen Regent of Paravia might share your intolerance on that score.'

His worry referenced the galvanic ripple lately unleashed through the flux, a crested wave of harmonic compression racing towards convergency with the engaged crisis at Forthmark. The comment whiplashed Seshkrozchiel's vaned tail. Her auric flare exploded into azure streamers of perturbation. 'Your freeloading *mote* Siantra insists Merevalia Teirendaelient has not staked her involvement.'

Luhaine shuddered, walloped by an unknown inference that upset his finicky reliance on precedent. "If not the Paravian Queen Regent, then whose colossal gamble would play Mankind's fate to the brink of collapse behind a smoke screen of catastrophe?"

Seshkrozchiel sheared down her next wing stroke, preoccupied. The answer that defied imagining came from the young mystic herself, derived through her uncanny affinity. Siantra Saw, wide open to the arc of unformed probability in the eerie half world past the veil. 'The on-coming cry through the elements is being summoned by Elaira herself.'

Silence pocked a riveted gap through an already-shocked conversation. Luhaine suspended his stunned disbelief, while Seshkrozchiel rumbled, soaring on taut vanes through the thermals that threshed the baked air above the furrowed valleys of Vastmark.

The roar of concussion funnelled in from the vale past the sanctuary's arched facade battered vibration through the marble floor under Arithon's feet. Dust and clotted spiderwebs shaken loose from above brushed like ghost fingers down his sweat-drenched cheek. The groined structure of the vault overhead had not yet collapsed under punishment, a tribute to the unparalleled mastery of Ath's departed adepts. The opaque seals crafted to shield the reactive, raw power pooled under their provenance continued to buffer the walls from dissolute entropy. The lasting effect stayed impervious, still fit to surmount the quicksand abrasion of Dragonkind's shapeshifting flux, else Arithon's stand would be ended. Yet the toehold advantage of trustworthy stone did not lessen the gravity of his peril.

Drakeflame lashed and licked past the wrack of smelted glass and charred mullions blown from the wide casements. Two infighting wyrm molts rampaging over the one fallen, outside, left the last pair intent on the on-going fight to demolish his ebbing resistance. Arithon gripped the frayed threads of his concentration, mage-sight riven by the sparkle and flash of incipient overextension.

Prime Lirenda had not quit the arena. She and the few shaken seniors left living lurked yet beyond the warded threshold, rapt vultures avid to witness his collapse, or loyal sycophants vying for the scrap favours their Prime might bestow for unshaken devotion.

Arithon nursed the pulverized dregs of his strength, by increments backed against the carved, ivory bulk of the Matriarch's vacated chair. Concession to his flagging support, he propped Elaira's inert form in the cushioned seat, his protective right hand draped over her collarbone.

Smoke coiled off the singed upholstery, rank with the taint of scorched wool, and the burnt-copper reek of the stitched sigils smelted down by the flint knife's unbinding. Beyond, frigid shadow deeper than the nadir of night sealed the breached wellhead of the adepts' etheric spring. Close proximity feathered a ring of white hoarfrost across a limited patch of unscathed stone floor.

The drake molts had learned not to trifle with that dire cold. Their skittish tread minced, as they circled. Arithon watched, slit-eyed, mind and mastery twined into the song that countermanded their unravelling assault. Through tempered harmonics, he locked the surrounding flux to stability, while keen observation wrestled through his muddled wits strove to interpret the irked dialogue evoked by their movement. The brash creatures knew he could match flame with shadow. They were not averse to test him anew or ambush his pressed span of attention.

The beasts' sinuous length counterbalanced the momentum of their sudden movement. The lash of a finned fluke telegraphed the dart of a horned head and the snap of fanged jaws. A scythed flick of the tail dealt the split-second warning before the flared aura kindled the forces of ruin.

Taut readiness afforded scant grace for the strikes that slammed down, invisible. The *wave* hammered his stance as a raw blast of dissonance, chaos pitched to unstring his bardic concentration and refabricate his hold upon solid existence. Arithon captured the tones to remediate, scalded vision nearly caught blindside by *flame!* spat from the dragon ranged opposite.

The maelstrom barraged his beleaguered redoubt, a crackling holocaust dammed by a curtain wall of hard shadow slapped up scarcely in time. Coughing on vile smoke, Arithon kept his head. He steadied the register of his melodic defence through the tempered poise of relentless practice. Too often, the chamber's focused acoustics amplified his strategic edge for the worse. The fractional wrong note became unforgiving when the wyrm molts acted in concert against him. Attack on the continuum, coupled with a fireburst from behind, threatened him through Elaira's vulnerability. The temperamental conflagration he had swatted down early on was too dangerous to be met with complacency.

More gouted flame loosed against him in frontal assault, a feint to distract from the pressed movement of air hackling Arithon's nape. He kicked over the chair. Caged Elaira beneath his prone body as shield, and narrowly escaped the sideswipe of the talon lashed out to cleave him in two.

He rolled, skidding the chair along with him. The evasion thwarted the drake's reverse thrust, followed up by a pounce, ebon claws splayed like knives to impale him. Knees skinned, bruised elbows smarting, Arithon cowered behind flimsy ivory struts that lent no semblance of adequate cover. Hard-pressed, he reforged the dropped skein of his melody, steadied the strained harmonics before the song lines diminished past salvage. Alithiel's defence at this pass might have helped. But the heirloom blade rightly left in Dakar's charge foiled a covetous appropriation by the Koriathain.

Into that frenetic second of recoil, Lirenda haggled for terms from her safe redoubt at the sidelines. "Surrender and I promise, Elaira goes free. Once my bargain with the dragons is closed, our order has no further use for her."

The gutless appeasement merited no reply. Clamped teeth bit back the temptation. Arithon did not rise, or let spiteful irritation threaten his focus. His love was too precious to become dangled bait, mauled to and fro by untrustworthy interests to leverage the restive ambition of enemy factions.

Defeat the molts, or perish in the attempt, and Lirenda's abusive posturing was defanged. Arithon regrouped at the brink, left with the strained threads of his intellect. Seamless finesse lay beyond him. No convincing illusion might decoy a dragon. The bare bones of human endeavour must swerve the drakes' riveted fascination. All he valued in life, he still owned in full measure. At the end of invention, Halliron's example had schooled him to listen. *'Hear only what's there, and you cannot fail to expose the theme to unlock the next passage.'*

The flux informed Arithon, at deafening volume, exactly what the molts lacked that he possessed in abundance. Before naked, brute might, courage showed him the colourful depth of his own extended lifetime's personal experience.

Arithon snapped the carved swan's head off the Prime's Seat. Lungs poisoned by a greasy roil of fumes, he awaited his opening. If he succumbed, he would go self-possessed. To whatever end, he defied the grim odds with every last attribute he held in hand. For as long as he could, Elaira's trust would be kept undefiled by his short-fallen mistakes.

The molts jockeyed for position, a slithering tussle that chinked broken glass, and the scored gouge of scales across the marred floor. Arithon snatched his moment and shied the ivory finial. The throw's low-slung trajectory skipped and bounced, clattering, the scattered acoustics off the groined ceiling a re-echoed welter of misdirection.

The molts ceased their shouldering, spiked heads reared aloft and wedged muzzles swivelled in diversion. Arithon shifted his tuned harmonics. Atop the clean construct that anchored his natural form and Elaira's, he augmented the pattern of defined personality with a counterpoint swell of amplified emotion.

Dragons grasped rage. They revelled in jealous rivalry that glorified contentious challenge. The raw flush of mating established their adult sexuality by the climactic thrill of dominant victory. Yet their copycat style of creation by force sprang from blunt will without nuance.

Masterbard, Sorcerer, Arithon wielded the exquisite, trained skill to upset fixed belief and instil the expansive insight for epiphany. Art fashioned and forged in the flame of adversity translated passion, sound carved into rapture fit to raise fire and storm. As the veteran survivor beset by hundreds of thousands of free wraiths, he owned the steel discipline to surpass his undoing. In his dire despair, he plumbed the dark for the heartcore of light thrown to jeopardy by the spectre of horrific failure.

Arrogance denounced his puny retort. Hit with what seemed nonsensical garble, the drakes wrought *destruction* in force. Their vehemence roared at a volume to smash the noisy anomaly entangled like thorn in their path. Stubborn fury crashed and broke against Arithon's *adamance*. The bellowing bluster of *Dragons!* met *patience*, a clinging rebuttal that strangled the permeable stature of wyrm-cast existence. The contrary notion of *permanence* planted into a fluid dynamic, rebuilt and torn down, and rebuilt again, seemed a wasteful fuss made in futile denial.

The dragons recoiled, stymied. 'What flimsy *figment* would bother to fight a useless stance on impossible ground?'

'Mortals!' The bard drove the wedge into their disbelief. 'Unto the last breath, we will meet the inevitability of a pointless death with stringent rejection.' To a dragon's loss, that grasped naught beyond the cold fury of dispossession, Arithon detailed the indelible burden of *grief*. He recounted the stigma of unending *hurt* imposed by that irreversible severance:

the intricate, irreplaceable puzzle that shattered when the precious link called *relationship* parted, and singular joy torn from the world of experience became reft beyond reach forever.

Drakes acknowledged no right to claimed sovereignty. Irrational synergy stumbled against the grain of their straightforward power to replicate. 'Not possible!'

Arithon served the dragons' flat *'no!'* and their shove to obliterate with *'not ever!'* a cry that denounced the immutable principle of surrender.

He magnified *sorrow* at scale that slammed across octaves in reverberation.

The molts recoiled, stung. This triflesome plaything was no longer *amusement,* but a mad desecration to battle in earnest. They reverted to *fury!* How *dare* a mere figment, *a mote!* seize the bald-faced effrontery to upset the prerogative of drake-spawned creation? Animate creatures were wrought fabrications, like *insects* and *iyats,* constructions endowed with *movement for sport,* and a *busyness* without consequence. The wyrms' wrathful rebuttal remanded *this!* rebellious, wisped fragment to an instantaneous, total *unmaking.* They struck in vicious partnership, a shout of exponential adamance against which *no* such frailty might stand.

The *nuisance* before them rejected erasure. His *not mote!* rebuke in flagrant retort asserted a genuine *Name!* and far more: the collective complexity of two-legged *cognition* unreeled a whole tapestry alien to the most *arrogant* drake's experience. Nor was its preposterous claim to independence without self-actualized teeth.

Arithon s'Ffalenn had survived Davien's Maze. He had owned the anguished impact of every individual death inflicted by force of arms or through Desh-thiere's cursed influence. He recalled, bone and nerve, the plunder of true meaning. In stark depth, he had suffered the tragedy thrust upon bereft kinfolk and children. No two crossings out of breathing life were the same. None alike, on a roll call of ruin that encompassed tens of thousands of wrecked aspirations.

The wyrm molts belittled, ignored, then attempted to bypass that unpleasant comeuppance.

Arithon fired back with irrefutable proof drawn at first hand from centuries of dissociate captivity. When, day upon day, he had plumbed the warped derangement that barred Marak's free wraiths from natural death. He held the memories of their damnation, forged in sorrow and pain beyond measure; had unravelled the hatreds and murderous self-revilement of millions of tormented shades strangled alive by the Mistwraith's conquest of the splinter world beyond Southgate. He had not flagged under the trials of salvage. Not until every sundered, lost spirit among them regained the plundered humanity of their existence.

The molts writhed like pinned moths thralled to flame as the enriched gamut of human emotion dismantled their dismissive prejudice. *'Not mote!'* was a truth to demolish delusion and quench the protest of ignorant certainty.

Arithon allowed the drakes no reprieve, no mercy to side-step their wailing confusion. His ferocity savaged the bastions of their belief: his existence *never had been* less than meaningless, nor any whimsical byproduct of a serpent's dream of creation. Measure upon measure, he shaped a flux surge that shredded Dragonkind's egocentric identity. From scouring misery, he loosed the dark themes, retreading the twisted thicket of thorn out of leaden despair towards the rekindled hope that brought healing. Endowed since his birth with s'Ffalenn compassion and the royal farsight of s'Ahelas, he had grown adept at transmuting tragedy. In his hands, the keys to repeal raised a force to wring salt tears from the dead. He had carried, relentless, a freight of human remorse to wrest an uncaring world to its knees.

That harrowing course, retuned for redemption, slammed into the wracked interface hounding him towards dissolution. Arithon had passed beyond intimidation. He once surmounted a morass of fear that loomed larger than life; before this, had interpreted graphic terrors and insipid ennui looped into a refrain that unravelled sentient reason. He had wept for the shattering joy of relief achieved by a requite deliverance, transported by the exultant cry that unfurled when conscious being transcended the agony of separation. His forged song knew the endless, rich themes to reprise the ecstatic reunion encountered when spirit merged into the arc of the infinite.

Stone rang underfoot in resonant sympathy as, unwithered by doubt, he stood fast on conviction: self-aware personality made indelible on the myriad loom of experience had *meaning* to outlast the false coin of defeat.

A clawed talon swiped to bowl him aside. Arithon rolled, Elaira dragged clear in his clenched embrace. He jabbed back, wielding the raw cost in consequence when such wanton, untimely destruction cut *any* one life span short.

To the roar of *'Not dragon!'* he delivered *child starving in snow,* refracted in manyfold variation. He compounded that pain with *the distilled agony of extremis, of men, brothers, husbands, and fathers bled out by the excruciate savagery of an arrow struck deep into vitals.* He served up *drownings,* and *more cherished fallen milled to smashed bones in a shale slide,* compounded by others more piteous still. Arithon knew, *oh, he knew!* every desolate cry of abandonment, unto *the aged cripple spoon-fed in poverty by a mate deprived of support.* He told over such wretchedness in rending detail: the war price rendered, again and again, upon wounded survivors, their river of anguish passed on to blight the following generations.

Before such *tragedy* as drakish *pretention* dismissed, those benighted, crushed spirits had known joy. Their humour kindled laughter, the wide range of excitement and purpose enriched by ties of friendship and family. The gamut of human feeling was *real,* each moment unique to existence.

And lest brash denial should justify wanton desecration as stock-in-trade to sate a Prime Matriarch's disaffection, Arithon recounted in full the adulterated coinage reaped from bargains with Koriathain: the betrayed innocence of Fionn Areth, compounded by Valien's death, and the vicious confusion of Vivet's abuse, fashioned under compulsion through the obligate theft enabled by the sisterhood's oathbound enslavement. No choice remained to him. He must keep the molts intellectually stymied, deafen and disrupt the slipstream of their inimical manifestation lest by main strength they resorted to tooth and claw, and rent him to destruction . . .

The last historic crisis that paired Asandir with Davien had joined their resource to resolve a cataclysmic dispute between packs of rogue dragons. The titanic conflagration levelled three snowclad peaks in the Skyshiels, the crag that founded Highscarp overlooking the sheared face laddered into the present day's mountain range. The Third-Age town perched on the site by Mankind's inveterate industry loomed like an eyrie above the inundated crater pocked into the Eltair Bay shoreline. Ejected debris now sheltered the deep-water harbour, the scarred flanks of two barren, unstable slopes since repurposed as a quarry. Other damage remained. Shorn trees fanned across the northward expanse towards Ithilt saw the heartwood of Taernond still riven, the truncated forest laid waste below the south riverbank of the Falhench.

Three feral dragons safely put down, their mouldered, dead bones quenched to a requite grave in salt water, were no match for the insane ferocity of today's gravid female hell-bent to breach Northgate. One whose challenge flouted her exile at wroth strength against the Fellowship's two most agile defenders. Her attack battered the landscape, yet held at remove on the splinter world of Sckaithen Duin.

If her reckless offensive broke through to Athera in Ozvowzakrin's delinquent absence, the gargantuan scar gouged in the Second-Age rising sown by the False Treaty of Ithilt would pale to a toddler's tantrum by comparison. Her disruptive rampage might raze a swathe through the northern free wilds, threat to the deepest groves guarded in Strakewood where the Song of the Mysteries yet flourished, unsullied and true, since the vortex at Athili illumined the dawning of the First Age.

Davien apparently lacked the spare resource to acknowledge the timely relief of staunch backing.

Asandir took pause one stride beyond the shimmering span of the Worldsend Gate. Beaten tired, his lean face creased as worn leather, he breathed in the reek of stirred sulphur, ozone, and hot flint, tanged by steel freshly quenched from the forge fire. His grim survey mapped changes that defeated speech, the burdensome warning dispatched by Sethvir far too urgently brief to encompass the ravaged panorama before him. The brass dunes and shimmering desert recalled from his recent departure were gone, swept away like flung milk by the broadscale ferocity of drakish invention.

The Gate's threshold now overlooked a jagged rock shingle necklaced in froth, battered by towering, purple-grey breakers that knuckled over into dousing banners of back-fallen spume. Hurled spray melted without seam into rainfall, grainy daylight smothered in dismal mist that veiled the horizon. The dragon had amassed herself a winged escort. Friendly, or curious, or latently hostile, their serpentine silhouettes wove and dove in her wake, animate shuttlecocks that spat sultry winkles of flame through the oppressive mizzle.

Davien's presence eluded the eye, a vacancy belied by the concurrent evidence the Worldsend Gate's access to Athera remained unbreached.

More dragons clustered, engrossed in combative displays atop the jutted spur of a distant headland. Asandir counted eight by the flare of spined jowls as long necks snaked and darted and struck, fangs extended. The scrap involved tearing an unknown, spiny sea creature's carcass to gory dismemberment. Other drakes strafed what seemed an inert boulder, oblivious to another, innocuous rock nestled amid the glassine rivulets painting the waves' ebb from the shingle.

Asandir bent his particular interest on that one. Cued by the ozone taint wafted on the landward breeze, he surmised Davien's forays to Kathtairr had lent him the space to perfect his command of the shape-shifter's craft first begun in close contact with Seshkrozchiel. The result showed a skilled execution to shame Sethvir's dissembling touch for avian impersonation.

"Ciladis provided a great deal of help." The twitch of a suppressed shrug marked Davien's comment as his lean presence reappeared at Asandir's shoulder. Control of the dragon's difficult legacy indeed had required a wide latitude for mistakes, where collateral damage left the least impact. Unmussed by the wind and unscored by the cinder burns spotting his colleague's saddle-worn leathers, he added, "I gather Sethvir noticed the gross tilt on the odds?"

Asandir side-eyed his colleague's flamboyant dress, the doublet of sienna velvet and cream shirt adorned with jet embroidery, also unnat-urally dry. An exquisite illusion worthy of Kharadmon's vanity, down to the white-and-chestnut hair tumbled over immaculate shoulders: while the suspect stone also remained, too flagrantly ordinary for the faint, indigo halo too refined for a dragon's roused aura.

The field Sorcerer remarked on his colleague's acumen with the edge that eviscerated dissembling. "Since you wouldn't make Kharadmon jealous for show, what's the nasty detail left unspoken?"

Davien's answer sprang, sourceless, from the howling, churned air, desiccate with sardonic humour. "Althain's Warden skipped over the appalling gist? As you see, our opposition has multiplied. The Prime Matriarch's agitation at Forthmark spreads disaffection like the wicked gleam of false gold to the serpent."

Asandir caught the frenetic note of exhaustion. The hours of travel that delayed his return had tested and tried the deft invention of the Seven's most ingenious spirit. The sensitive, unmentioned facet of his grievance implied an affection Luhaine's upright pretention would have discredited. "You laid the groundwork for the advanced training that's probably keeping your s'Ffalenn protégé alive."

"Protégé, loose weapon, or a colossal miscarriage of judgement," Davien allowed. "Polite reference hasn't determined the verdict." Wary irony acknowledged the shared inflection of trepidation. "This can't be your circumspect apology for the dethronement forced on you despite Verrain's astute judgement during the assize at Methisle Fortress?"

Cued reference to Arithon's flagrant transgressions met Asandir's unflinching response. "The man wanted no ties, no outstanding attachments. Be certain of that much." Desolation chilled the short pause, while drab atmosphere scribed moist reflections on the field Sorcerer's metallic-grey eyes. "Your wild falcon's insistent behaviour made sure we Seven had no other choice but to cut the jesses and cast him off the glove."

Davien withheld comment.

At distance, one dragon launched off the disputed carcass. Sped aloft like a javelin, it scattered the clustered pack weaving around the airborne female. Her trumpeted bellow slammed over slate waters, roiling up tattered steam and spindled waterspouts. The contentious muddle of her cohorts wheeled and regrouped, turned on their fresh rival with redoubled ferocity. Before the impending shock ripple destabilized the flooded landscape, Asandir said, "You and Arithon are much alike."

Davien's snort was derogatory. "No provocation aimed to run roughshod over due process without moral cause? Pity Ciladis. He must be tearing his robes to frayed threads!" The incongruous, dandiprat construct vanished, discourse over Arithon's straits eclipsed as two other, mature platinum wyrms joined the fray. Their plunging ambush pinwheeled the flocked males into flustered confusion, and drove the scrappers to flight off the stranded carrion.

"Fifteen!" Asandir snapped, annoyed.

A punched glimmer of blue sky shafted sun through the overcast, prelude to scrimmage as the radical shake-up reordered wyrmkind's mercuric alliances. The Sorcerers seized the inauspicious moment as respite, while gyrating formations embedded in mist altered course and split off, paired into aggressive aerobatics to re-establish a dominant hierarchy. Elder dragons with their scaled armour bleached silver sliced like scimitars through the tumbling melee. Bowled head over tails, the younger adults flurried and regrouped, green-and-gold coachwhips of sinuous murder iridescent as festival sequins tossed into a gale. Wind slammed and cracked to the thunder of wing leather, rickled with static discharge.

Distance obscured individual markings. The chaotic display suggested the uncertainty of unaffiliate independents. Fellowship observers had scant means to determine which dragons were rogues, embittered with ancient rebellion, and which might be staunch proponents of the Accord, allied with the Protectorate. The two Sorcerers outwaited the unsettled lull, braced for the moment the reshuffled factions renewed their concerted assault on the Worldsend Gate and hurled a fresh round of disruption against the sliver of firm shoreline where they stood.

Davien's monosyllabic alert marked the second the stalemate broke. "Duck!"

The next instant delivered the compressed, deadly shear of the inbound flux wave aligned for destruction. Asandir checked the onslaught. His shield ring at strength warded the Gate's permeable interface and bound substance and air within close proximity into protected stasis. No relief, before the shattering roar of the female's baulked fury slapped against his adamant perimeter. Solid ground shimmered as the surrounding strata of bed-rock transmitted the pulverizing vibration. Her invasive passage ripped shadow through the scalded elements, the roiling crash of ocean breakers against shingle whiplashed into the sequential flash points of multiple rapid-fire transformations. Snowclad peaks became a forest aflame, razed the next moment to cinders and smoke that birthed in turn bitter cold and shining rills of striated jasper, drilled with arches that keyholed a cobalt sky. Davien's planted boulder withstood the radical shifts, flagrant target for the doubled-back, whistling dive that cleaved the heavens directly above. The great wyrm was a behemoth, ninety spans from her fanged incisors to the horn spur on her slashing tail fluke. The etheric tirade she rained down upon Davien's redoubt immolated all material form in her path into auroric curtains pale aqua as gas flame.

But the token that received her wrathful demolition was no longer present, or mineral. Sleight-of-hand finesse had transferred Davien's consciousness elsewhere.

Asandir adjusted his defences and blinked, then with casual tact skirted the frightening conversation. "Your affinity with Seshkrozchiel has enlarged your scope of perception." A taut pause, as a gust buffeted his crafted shield, and the frigid temperature flipped on an inbreath to blistering heat. "Sethvir's hair must be standing on end." Punctuated by exasperation, he finished, "Can you seriously be eavesdropping on Dragonkind's feuds with impunity?"

Davien did not laugh. "Not by any such measure of implied subtlety," he qualified, the tart admission delivered in spoken words by flesh-and-bone substance, now *inside* of Asandir's construct. Never mind *that* feat should not have been possible without prior notice or preparation. "Let's hope to survive without lasting regret. Or Althain's Warden might be obliged to remand me to an extended exile all over again."

The force shield overhead rippled again, a rival faction's failed sally to displace the barren vista of stone, while an impending sunset stained the sky lurid mauve above bruised swathes of lengthening shadow.

Asandir kept his strained focus, the shuttlecock weave of winged peril aloft too intense for a dumbfounded glance at the colleague who stood, relocated in nonchalant readiness alongside him. The spare comment he managed scorched for dry irony. "Time, also, I see, now bends at the whim of your insolent purview?"

"Sometimes." Davien's laconic mockery rang a tad flat under stress. "Just now, because we need to track what's on-coming from the Atheran side of the Gate."

"You have a synchronized contact? From here?" Unflapped by astonishments, one after the next, Asandir narrowed his probe past his penumbral protections, where some crackpot invention of Davien's had scattered the bunched flight of the most persistent antagonists. Wads of compacted snow, condensed on the fly and hurled into the dragons' formation, might seem a whimsical act of indulgence. Except wyrms hated water and cold worse than cats, and the disordered flurry that recoiled through the male coalition's combatants was bound to redouble their furious spite.

"Distraction," Davien confessed, not contrite, then admitted the feat of communication across the void between worlds lay beyond him. "But I do hear the drakes when their communal awareness spans the black deep. An incident on Athera has thrown Sckaithen Duin's dragons into agitation. I arranged to disrupt their focus for a critical moment. While the tactic shows merit, the impact in progress elsewhere may yet strike here like Dharkaron's fell Spear and sow havoc."

Asandir coughed back laughter. "Sethvir implied Elaira had not quit the field."

A breath-taken gap evinced Davien's startlement. "I was not privy to that development." Then, in afterthought sprung from an urgent review, "No ploy of the lady's for certain! This upheaval bears the undilute stamp of Arithon's making. Be ready! The brunt will sow upset on the grand scale, and you'll want to stiffen your bastion."

The female dragon screamed, shrilled to a murderous rage that cracked air like taut canvas gale-whipped to tatters. She reared overhead. The smacked force of her wing beats lashed up dust devils that sand-blasted grit across the barren waste of red orange jasper. The two silvered males flanked her, neither aligned with the Protectorate. Asandir recognized the scars on one monster's snarling snout, and a talon lopped off the forelimb of the other. The Seven had outfaced both opponents before, in recalcitrant confrontation.

"Merry hell!" Davien's oath met the resonant blast as it struck.

For what one dragon knew, amplified at scale by distress, others could share simultaneously. Distance was no obstacle. For one seized moment, the continuum across time and space shivered like struck crystal as Arithon's song at Forthmark overran, then supplanted, the immature consciousness of the drake molts ranged against him. The clear-cut measure of consummate art, ruled fair by his mastery, locked the synchronous beat of a standing wave, multiplied by harmonics. Octave upon octave, the mighty ripple expanded across the contiguous arc of the electromagnetic spectrum.

The crest thrummed through the reactive span of the North Worldsend Gate and slammed like fell fury into the wyrm swarm upon Sckaithen Duin. Tempered force broke over resistance and struck, a concatenation of aligned focus no dragon had faced in any past era of history. Their species possessed no ready defence. The patterned impression spun from Athera slid like honed steel through the cross-chop of energetic contention: a unified frequency, tuned to an indelible imperative by Arithon's command of pitched sound. The refined composition threshed chaos to order, a clarion cry that razed through the collective muddle of Dragonkind's etheric emanation. The heightened effect walloped into a heated contest for dominant conquest, spearheaded by the unstoppable might of a clutch-bearing female.

Dissonance shattered under the onslaught. The exponential vibration chorused by the aligned psyches of four suborned molts took charge and prevailed: and human intent wrought by Athera's Masterbard struck registers outside the compass of any great drake's living experience. The flash point escaped their inherent containment. The impact commandeered, in midstream at full bore, the very nexus of conscious creation.

Yet the manifest structure now exponentially empowered by fifteen adult wyrms was *not dragon*, but wholly human. Their serpentine grasp of form and event became overset by incomprehensible emotion that smashed limitation and revised the gamut of cold-blooded imagining. From Forthmark, unadulterated, came the searing riptide of remorse drawn from the gristly carnage of myriad battlefields. Arithon's pristine rendition delivered, intact, the agony of the fallen undone by his star-crossed, cursed fate. Each voiced outcry reprised the raw wound, individual as the lives filled with promise at birth and shortened by violent death come untimely.

The rendition delivered in full measure the nerve-stripped impact of Kewar's maze. Experience endured under merciless vision torn open to mage-sighted sensitivity found Dragonkind without defences. No shield existed against such a wound, scalpel-cut through the heart by the scald of intimate empathy, branded by s'Ffalenn compassion. Wyrmkind's conceptual reality shifted, remoulded in the furnace blast of the crucible. Lost forever, their embedded concept that a *mote* owned no claim to self-aware existence: to the last Name, the least human possessed individuality beyond reach of a dragon's wildest turn of invention.

Davien released the fabricated shape of his boulder, warm flesh and bone beaten ragged. Asandir stood erect at his side, whipped hair singed, and his crusted leathers ringed with salt sweat and blown spray. From the perspective of ages, grown wise since their human redemption from the unilateral carnage unleashed by Calum Quaide Kincaid's mighty weapon, the paired Sorcerers beheld a realized vista *not dragon*. Before them unfolded the composite memory dredged up from the blood-soaked fields of Vastmark, Tal Quorin, Daon Ramon, and Lanshire. Inspired in fraught re-creation, they surveyed a triumph of outrage against barbarous slaughter for no worthwhile cause. Death inflicted in flesh by pierced arrows, butchery by the sword, and the wholesale maceration of lives pulped under the hurled boulders of trebuchet and catapult: mass horror was presented barefaced and raw, without mercy, without quarter, without reprieve. No softened facet argued for virtue. The storied cloak of martyrdom and the false cloth of the poets became ripped threadbare by truth, that any cause underwritten by murderous carnage offended the gift of creative sentience.

An ordeal once impelled by a blood-bound imperative to survive should have snapped the fibre of Arithon's determination, the sheer course of inflicted anguish akin to the historic burden surmounted by the Fellowship Sorcerers. The day's measure, by rights, should have flattened resistance. Yet the spirit harrowed by s'Ffalenn empathy had not buckled to raving madness.

Asandir swiped filmed grit from his blistered face. He did not ease his ward guarding Northgate. The demonstrative candour that interpreted Davien's expelled breath instead prompted his ragged words. "Arithon co-opted the singular power of *twenty great drakes!* Dharkaron's Black Vengeance, we've just witnessed a tectonic shift in perspective to alter the course of the ages."

The irrefutable evidence unfolded before them, pricked by the stars of an alien twilight seized into ashen quiet. Stunned out of flight, the rogue dragons minced and paced in wing-folded disarray, too perturbed to take charge and dismiss the epiphany unreeled before them. Flight and rivalry displaced, the knit of their dream became sundered. Humankind in fact were *not motes at all!* Each singular one was a whole being with aware intelligence, born to the unparalleled experience of singular consciousness.

From that shocked discovery, amid blank disbelief, Davien's cool observation crumbled the foundation forerunning the slide to disaster. "I don't find the signature of Seshkrozchiel's consciousness anywhere in the weave."

Which signal omission meant Arithon had forged this working alone, without the augmented power of another dragon acting in concert.

"Merciful maker!" Asandir hardened his nerve in the staring eye of a compounded crisis. The affray sown at Forthmark by the Prime's meddling had turned for the worse in a manner never envisioned by Sethvir himself. For the acknowledgement of conscious independence, established by human merit, raised Mankind's status in the mind of the serpent: no more the odd curiosity dismissed as beneath contempt, Athera's Masterbard had staked out a claim Dragonkind would deem worthy of challenge.

Time was not to be given for grace.

The gravid female raised her horned head. A bugled roar marshalled her rattled escort for an immediate clash to reclaim the threatened apex of their supremacy.

"Best roll up your sleeves," Davien remarked, piqued to madcap joy by the unexpected. "Our situation's about to get messy."

"Whenever not?" Asandir's mouth flexed into a grim line that might have been a suppressed smile. "Ere we're done, you may wish yourself back at Kewar, holed up with your fell collection of dangerous books."

"If I have a library left," Davien snapped, terse rejoinder clipped by necessity. "The upshot hell-bound to take roost on Athera will warp Dharkaron's nightmarish vengeance into a pittance."

Duet

Across the continent from the desolate strand at Northgate, a world removed from Sckaithen Duin where two Sorcerers engaged in defence of the Treaty Accord deflected predation by restive dragons, quiet shrouded the shocked aftermath of Forthmark's provocative tumult. Afternoon sunlight shafted the sifted dust wafted through the hostel's blown casements. The clogged air in the gloom reeked of the abattoir, the stench of excrement and let blood tanged by the metallic taint of steel weaponry. Mass carnage respun from the mangle of dead reaped from three centuries' forgotten battlefields lay piled in manifest nightmare across the stained floor: human casualties long since mouldered to bones, gravesites shrouded in verdant overgrowth through the passage of years.

This rampant horror reclothed from the past was the graphic creation of two rogue molts overwhelmed by the Masterbard's song line.

Arithon had yet to rise from the ordeal. Brought to his knees, dazed by incipient back-lash and overexertion, he tallied his tattered assets. The dry well at his back remained seized to inertia under his stopgap freeze of wrought shadow. Unconscious, Elaira still breathed in his arms. Had anything else mattered, he might have stumbled erect, moved on his own merits to acknowledge the inadvertent impact imposed by his hard-fought defence. Clueless as yet, he never imagined how far his talented conjury had spilled beyond the ancient containment bonded by Ath's departed adepts.

He feared to stir, though the grisly wrack that surrounded him revolted his nerves. Not alone in adversity, he dared not trust his shaken balance to bear up Elaira's slack weight, or risk an erosive lapse of attentive focus that might trigger renewed provocation. The heightened resonance raised by his bard's working diminished. Unsustained, the harmonic registers subsided back into the ambient stream of the flux. Arithon's riveted gaze tracked the restive molts just fought to a traumatized standoff, while the wrenching change sown at large by the strength of his besieged faculties swept outwards apace. He had no spare thought left to recognize, far less encompass, the gestalt awakening hurled onwards with the ranging force to afflict Dragonkind across dimensional space.

The immediate shock ripple had fractured the fracas of three-way rivalry beyond the sanctuary's battered arches. The wounded molt ripped out of flight by its fellows lay gasping in the extremis of broken defeat. Both upright antagonists caught in haughty contention faced off, befuddled and panting in stymied confusion. No concept existed to span a divide that upended everything their species once understood. All their brash arrogance shrivelled, self-importunate aggression threshed to dust in the trampled collapse of their stupefied faculties. The bard's artistry had suborned their invention. His recombinant influence had recarved and transformed their arena into a vista of materialized carnage. The strewn corpses and violent death of his making also fouled Vastmark's vales with the horrific slaughter of war.

Over that savage hellscape, through the recoil of uprooted perception reforged by the blunt impact of human tragedy, Seshkrozchiel swooped down from the stratosphere. She arrived without banking in braked descent. Amid the backwinded clap of taut wing leather, she was dry thunder wrapped in a cyclone.

The bow wake of her palpable fury slapped more than the air with fell vengeance. Mature power sheared into the breach and banished from the landscape the putrescent atrocity of human massacre. The tingling blast of Seshkrozchiel's auric flare cauterized the hostel's defiled grounds to clean stone, then cratered the scoured expanse with the mineral gleam of a volcanic salt pool. Earth shook to her juggernaut landing. Taloned claws bit through hot bed-rock and scored jagged grooves to the lash of her tail. The raked whip of scaled muscle spined with black horn tumbled the gasping, maimed molt from its throes like chaff bashed by a flail. Cowed and thrashing, it rolled over and plunged to a requite death in the saline sump engineered as a gravesite.

The walloping splash of immersion sent both hissing opponents scrambling into retreat. Not fast enough to evade adult wrath: their disordered flight met the whistling hammer of Seshkrozchiel's fluke. Her blow hurled them head over wing tips in squalling distress. A blast of white flame chased their slithered recovery and singed them aloft in flapped panic. Her bellow shook loosened shale from the peaks and dispatched the younglings in shame back to their eyrie in exile past Northgate.

Seshkrozchiel glared after their chastened disgrace, snorting fumaroles of cinders and smoke. She erased the rime pit from existence with a casual flicker of afterthought. Her sinuous stalk trod the steaming, sheened slag repaved over the demolished miscreant's mausoleum. Around her, the ambient flux currents boiled. The unfurled display of her cobalt aura needled the ether in daylight to the gaslight shine of a polar aurora. Matter quivered and quailed before *Dragon!* Vicious in temper too bristled to cross, she dealt Luhaine's tentative query her savage retort, that Ciladis had retired to the hostel infirmary with Siantra's *gut-sack of meat* in his diligent care. Undamaged due to the Sorcerer's presence, that portion of the historic edifice had withstood the ravaging brunt of the turmoil.

Few powers alive would have challenged the wrathful advance for this hour of reckoning. Not with Dragonkind's equilibrium seized in duress and overturned for the worse, while the preposterous concatenation of forces incited the splinter world's rogue conspiracy to destabilize the Second-Age treaty founded under the Protectorate's Concord with the Paravians.

Seshkrozchiel huffed. She flicked her forked tongue, tasting murder. Luhaine's sober plea for her temperance lacked any foothold for purview: Arithon's crown sanction had been rendered forfeit, a fact Dragonkind grasped to a faretheewell: their silver-scaled ancients had been party to Fellowship business *long and long!* before Mankind's fraught plea for safe harbour had wheedled the upstart boon of settlement in Third Age Year One.

The crone in Sanpashir, who might have claimed influence, by fathomless silence kept her own counsel.

Last flimsy checkrein, the White Brotherhood's vacated residence posed the dragon's behemoth entry small impediment. Whether their old bonded ciphers retained virtue sufficient to withstand her roused might, or to clap her wild fury under containment, no residual force, and no authority chose to argue. Seshkrozchiel reared rampant. Latched onto the vertical cliff by clenched talons, she topped the pillared sill of the sanctuary. The gold eye aligned with the casements peered through the felted gloom and surveyed the abomination inside.

The other two molts caught in stunned disarray from Arithon's song line hissed in startlement, raised tail flukes curled over their spiny, humped backs in submissive recoil. Seshkrozchiel's snarl belled subsonic vibration throughout the stone vault. Her bass growl of warning pitched the young into scuttling disorder. Quick as singed lizards, they darted and fled. Their trampling claws mauled the rag-piled corpses kept manifest by the hallowed seal on the inner sanctuary. No such arcane stay barred the bolt-holes. The molts slithered over the nearest open-air sill and shot into frantic flight hard after their vanished fellows.

Sun-gold iris an annular ring around the distended, jet well of her pupil, Seshkrozchiel regarded the puny two-legged culprit crouched with his unconscious mate in his arms.

Terror ought to have paralysed: *dead* dragons' dreams spun the dread forces to gyres secured at laborious cost under the dire protections of grimwards. *Living*, Seshkrozchiel's flaunted might had the reach to reknit the fabric of the known world. She recalled the stormed chaos from the centuries of legend: when Athera's great wyrms had reigned supreme, and the primeval proliferation of their drake spawn had scourged the Paravians through two Ages of near-to-catastrophic, ravening slaughter.

The bard pinned by her gaze had nowhere to run. Fear itself became futile, a naked babe's whimper before peril that crushed courage and liquefied human bowels to water.

Cross-grained perversity only remained.

Green eyes met the dragon's presence in turn with resistant defiance that shouted, 'Arithon!' and 'not mote!' with damn all to Sithaer's bleakest pit for the draconic threat of fell consequence! That resolute vehemence filled the stowaway witness of Siantra's disembodied, fey presence with dread, and stung Luhaine's rapt shade to a sucker-punched flinch.

The *worst move* for a mortal confronted in challenge by dragons was to declare contentious autonomy, all the more with blunt insolence that spat into the teeth of such overpowering might.

Seshkrozchiel's snort pitted a furrow of magma down the ruin's weathered facade. Her furious, crackled wave of affront without effort enlarged the pillared archway. She thrust her massive, horned head through the gap, then distended the groined ceiling above like blown glass. The adepts' craft-work held: access for her winged bulk left their ciphered seals of etheric restriction intact. But the dragon stepped through unimpeded. Stone quaked beneath her stupendous, lithe bulk, and the clawed joints of furled wing tips scuffed grooved scratches in the far wall.

The threshed corpses heaped in her path succumbed first to her blast of distaste. Fire streamed from her nostrils and raked across the despoiled chamber, the charred kindling of furniture and the reconstituted detritus of armoured carcasses immolated in an instant. The scour swept the veined-marble surface and restored a mirror finish not seen for a thousand years. Except for the dull patch, where the impudent blot of humanity wove shadow, and the bitter, black freeze, unrelenting, yet capped the etheric well.

Arithon beheld in full glory the gleaming magnificence of Seshkrozchiel in the shimmering gilt of her prime. Outmatched and exhausted, he measured her sinuous tonnage uncowed because he had no other option. His neutral, listening poise reflected no shred of regret: not for his monumental achievement as Masterbard that hurled Dragonkind into the crucible of permanent change, nor for the spark unleashed into cascade from the torment of his personal battlefields. Shieldless, with Elaira's slack form precious deadweight in his embrace, he tipped his chin upwards. Tangled black hair and scuffed bruises bare-faced, he met, stare for stare, the primordial creature whose horned crest scraped the ceiling groins twenty-five spans overhead.

Whether from sobered foresight, or enervated weariness, his motionless posture invited the dragon's aggressive inspection in turn. Neither contender spared a glance for the overawed enchantresses lurking in arrested suspense past the door at the sidelines.

Lirenda observed the encounter, thrilled ragged with terror and satisfaction. Throughout her tormented life, she had longed to see Arithon run to the end of his clever resistance. Rue the day, his conniving failed him at last with the honeyed wine of her requital tainted by unforeseen helplessness. A savourless victory, come with the bitter ignominy that tumbled the pinnacle of her due triumph. Arithon's downfall, achieved through hard-won power, had been sapped to nothing at a single stroke.

Sithaer's damnation and curse the flint blade of the Biedar crone's knife! If prior matriarchs had ever suspected the existence of a shamanic talisman endowed for a unilateral unbinding, the criminal negligence of their secrecy had suppressed the appalling pitfall unto ruination. Blindsided *again*, Lirenda silenced her quaking seniors' importunate pleas for retreat.

"Be still!" The last card in her ransacked hand must be played, or leave Mankind's rightful potential forever lost to posterity. She would snatch her opening to salvage redress though everything burned. Embrace disaster at all cost, before fading away into gormless obscurity. Win or lose, the ascendant continuance of the Koriathain hung on the contest with her captive male gambit dangled as the incentive to tempt the vengeful, primordial serpent.

Seshkrozchiel snaked around Arithon's crude redoubt, a tempestuous whirlwind of sizzling rage with the blunt-force capacity to annihilate. Arctic cold wafted off the capped wellhead did not faze the hot blood sheathed in the razor-edged glitter of her scaled supremacy. Two spans high, her ochre talons and curved claws could impale a grown bullock with ease. Man and woman could be swatted to pulp with less fuss than the flick to dispatch a scurrying ant.

Spined snout lowered, Seshkrozchiel fixed her slit-pupilled left eye on the miniscule nuisance before her. A glowering orb, fearsome and deep, topped his erect height by a span. "You are gifted, born foolish, and your presumptuous *autonomy* is *dangerous* beyond measure."

"The venomous snake, the sea urchin, and the sting of the wasp trouble nothing while their purposeful enterprise stays unmolested." Gravel burred Arithon's voice, hoarse under the strained effort to strike a note that projected reason. "Licence is not given to dragons to declare themselves arbiter of my fate."

"A molt *perished* for the vacuous fact you *exist*! Rogue wyrms beyond Northgate are stirred to revolt. The Treaty Accord has ensured the Paravian races' survival for nearly nineteen thousand returns of the sun! Until the day's reckless *whistle* on your *two-legs!* initiative has rocked the foundation that safe-guards Athera. Your meddling alone tips the scales towards chaos and unbridled jeopardy!"

"Is self-defence not a legitimate cause?" Arithon tempered his tone with exquisite care, petrified by the stricture that every phrase must balance creation and destruction with consummate symmetry. Fear of the dragon's umbrage was real: his surrounds could evaporate at the blink of that titanic eye, all solid structure altered at whim to who knew what unknown frame of expression. "Show me a dragon content to lie down with bared throat before enemies bent upon murder."

"Enemiessss?" Seshkrozchiel's drilling stare narrowed beneath the notched jut of her browridge. She huffed. Refutation billowed fumes through her bared teeth, serrated daggers of ivory glistening two cloth yards in length. "You, whining *gnat!* came here to do battle on your own merits."

"Choice brought me under threat to my mate." Strained by overextension, his access to music impaired, nonetheless Arithon denounced with a Masterbard's diction. "More, my answer for outstanding claim to redress has defanged the irresponsible plotter's aggression."

Seshkrozchiel's snort riffled steam in disparagement. "At what cost to the peace?" Since the breached seal on the adepts' defunct well undercut Arithon's flimsy argument, the dragon dismissed him forthwith. "You were not dragged here under duress. Your rash intervention has invoked an unconscionable *risk*, and threatened the wider world for the sake of the *shell* of the mate you're protecting."

"I agree!" If Lirenda's bold interjection rang shrill, she had naught to lose but her stake. "This man poses a danger to material order that should not have leave to exist. Matriarchs in our Prime Seat before me felt the same. For sound cause, my arrangement has disarmed the culprit and rendered him helpless. Peril that he is to the weal of young drakes, and a demonstrable weapon to unravel the Protectorate's Accord, I have delivered him for summary judgement and disposal. In exchange, grant my closure to replace the obsolete terms of crown law."

"*Egglesssss!*" Seshkrozchiel's hiss withered audacity with smoking contempt. "For what reason do sister-nest *vermin* stain the air with pithless complaint in my presence? A mettlesome craving for power to rival the Fellowship Sorcerers serves no meaningful purpose. Seven only were summoned by *our* call from Corith at the conclave of dreaming. Our treaty predated *two-legs'* chartered right to infest Athera's turf. You dabbling upstarts with your *squeaky* mineral *trinkets* were not the ones tasked to stand guard for Paravian survival in perpetuity!"

"A charge your vaunted Fellowship's royal prodigies have failed repeatedly to support." State jewels and purple-silk regalia smutched with stirred ash, Lirenda stepped forward with bald-faced authority and finished her arid denouncement. "The Sorcerers themselves are red-handed destroyers, glutted to sick insanity upon the picked bones of wrecked civilizations. They cater to a weakened tradition, their policy of free-wilds oversight corrupted before the uprising threw down the crown seats. Wanton slaughter among Mankind continues unchecked. For senile sentiment, why bother to establish a restoration? My evidence lies undisputed in the unprincipled royal submitted before you." All or nothing, Lirenda hurled down her ultimatum. "Meet my price. Reassign provenance of town rule to Koriathain. Empower my sisterhood to steward Mankind's destiny, and I promise: no such exotic threat will arise to sow barbaric ruin again."

Arithon broke in, snapped to flint by astonishment. "You think to usurp the Fellowship's standing and supplant the law of the compact?"

"Oh, please!" Lirenda stifled superior laughter. "Have you not spent your resource lifelong to evade your obligation to uphold Rathain's charter?" She crossed the inner threshold and swept into the sanctuary, from the indignant rustle of skirts to the sparkling diadem in coiled hair the patrician image of injured entitlement. "What's left to choose between you and me? Your record at large has stained the impervious shine of the Fellowship's favour. You have no integrity as the rogue prince. Whereas I head the ranks of an established order, steered through thousands of years by unerring discipline."

The dragon settled like a cat, spiked tail a curled flourish around her crouched forelimbs. If her rage appeared dampened in favour of interest, the bent of her thought outstripped the horizon of mortal experience.

Deportment alone suppressed Lirenda's trembling. Emboldened by the fact she had not been flamed outright, she pressed her case like a barrister. "What has the Seven's darling to show for himself but a history of feckless caprice, bought and sold for the sorry demise of a molt, and a wild, irresponsible song of destruction? Let Dragonkind choose between us by our merits. I am willing to yield my claim to Arithon's fate and receive the award of our order's prerogative under fair arbitration."

If no dragon alive could resist piquant challenge, the serpentine mind expanded the lethal exchange beyond rational boundaries at shattering speed.

"*Rules!* Two-leg *posturing!*" The earsplitting bellow shook the Forthmark escarpment. "Why tolerate scurrying humans at all?" Quarrelsome, Seshkrozchiel skewered debate. Her demand echoed Davien's historic deflection at the razor's edge of fatal diplomacy on the hour Grey Kralovir's abominable theft of an unhatched clutch had used necromancy to craft the dragon-skull wards. "You dare speak of infractions that murder our young. Show me Mankind is worth keeping alive! Prove humanity's penchant for tinkering madness is not the botched blemish of chance."

"Unprincipled licence enshrines such ineptitude," Lirenda was swift to agree. "Cull the strangling weed and cleanse the entrenched rot. Blameless folk suffer at large due to the Seven's absolute oversight." Expounding on her reckless initiative, she gestured towards her living proof. "Scion of two royal houses, and an initiate master trained from the cradle – despite every advantage of lineage and schooling – what has handpicked crown succession to show but an insatiable talent for strife and the incorrigible rejection of principle?" Her nod referenced the etheric well shrouded in elemental shadow. "Tell me Arithon hasn't exceeded contempt and wounded the web of the mysteries. I daresay his criminal havoc might require a dragon's remedial fire to cauterize the menace and salvage stability."

. . . Far off at Althain Tower, Sethvir held his breath. Luhaine, entwined on site with Seshkrozchiel's consciousness, had no grounds to venture an intercession: not over the Biedar crone's obligate claim through Requiar's ancestral prerogative. As if any statement by Fellowship auspice might excuse the bard's callous revision of drakish priorities, or settle the rogue dissent seething on Sckaithen Duin to topple decreed exile under the Treaty Accord.

Nothing prepared Arithon for the role thrust upon him as spokesman for Mankind's reprieve.

The weight of the ages hung on the inbreath of fate. Embedded in the dragon's-eye view, both of humanity's advocate witnesses garnered no sign the small, dark-haired man on his knees still possessed the aggressive reserve to be dangerous. By Luhaine's critical assessment, Arithon had seldom appeared so thoroughly beaten. Pressed on foot across country, sleepless and spent by exertion, he reeled from the stringent focus required to anchor his faculties. Incipient back-lash rifted his vision and flawed his masterful access to grand conjury. Shirtless, crouched at bay with Elaira dependent, he held no weapon but a discharged knife of knapped flint, worthless as a toothpick against the scaled hide of the dragon before him. Left his affinity for primordial shadow, he lacked the finesse for aught but a ham-handed, foredoomed assault pitched for murder.

Of all his crass failures, the woman sheltered in his clasped arms was the icon that mattered. Sethvir had time to recall Dakar's question, seared to anguish by the volatile misery sprung from the thwarted, past tryst in Halwythwood: *'You love her that much that the whole world should burn?'* and Arithon's response, *'You don't. The world has stayed whole. Everyone else can rejoice for the fact. But not me.'*

The same ferocious measure of risk had pushed Rathain's forsworn prince to shoulder the Biedar crone's debt: for unconscionable slaughter of an innocent child, and for the abuse of a sacrosanct love turned against him as a weapon . . .

Slant sun through the arch snicked gilt highlights that blazed as Seshkrozchiel unfurled her restive coils, stood up, and slithered towards Arithon. Spined head raised and eyes torch-brilliant, she was the monster stepped out of legend, the primal epitome of ungoverned force. Lirenda's rapt malice infected the standoff with sadistic anticipation . . .

The foretaste of her incipient triumph broke across Sethvir's anguished presence, where he poised over his unfinished manuscript, seamed features masked behind tensioned fingers. He seemed the carved monument to age-old sorrows, the fast endurance of Althain Tower cased in the cold stillness of a sealed tomb. This trial, gone wrong, would reduce the Fellowship's compact to the exhaustive labour of futility. What hung by a filament at Forthmark defied grief . . .

. . . as, outfaced at the ragged end of his faculties, Arithon stared down judgement for humanity's sake under a great dragon's caprice. No turning back, he confronted the cross-roads thrust on him, a cruel culmination brewed to explosion by fraught conflict and centuries of fermented malice.

Words failed the bard. Song died in his throat. Subterfuge abandoned the duplicitous trickster, the glib games of his desperate, historic defences stripped like dross as quick wit and invention fell by the wayside. Only the mulish spark of resistance smouldered unquenched at the close of all measures.

Arithon held fast to Elaira, no matter her fate lay past the dregs of his fallible resource to save. Her warm flesh, so long parted from longing embrace, and the auburn plait in mussed need of a comb, plucked his heartstrings to savage regret. The fine skin bronzed by weather in hardy contrast to the moonbeam satin of her tender breast: misery stabbed like edged glass to the quick, that he might never savour the pleasure of her aware humour again. Insupportable, that his agony on her behalf was destined to perish, too brief.

No eulogy marked the finish. No farewell kiss and no sound beyond the cavernous draw of Seshkrozchiel's breath. The backlit casement cast the diminutive mortal antagonists under the doom of the dragon's shadow: the Prime, in her costly, ornamental regalia seemed reduced to a porcelain doll, and Arithon empty-handed and pinned by the ruthless commitment he had smashed an inviolate trust to preserve.

Now his life, and Elaira's, and the Matriarch's downfall, and Mankind's bid for continuance teetered, subject to the behemoth looming above him . . .

Where Davien's razor-sharp intellect might have dared the bold comment, Luhaine's stickling penchant for detail paralysed his loquacious tongue. Siantra waited, isolate in the uncanny stillness of the patient seer . . .

Seshkrozchiel's ferocity focused on the upstart man, hapless vermin at the mercy of her wicked, flexed talons. "You do not plead."

"For what is already mine by born right?" Arithon's stare rebutted the dismissal that weighed him up as flecked dust. "I am not a cipher at Lirenda's disposal! Nor will I become the willing scapegoat diced in cold blood on the chopping block for Mankind's shortsighted faults." Dragonkind dared to regard him lightly, that Seshkrozchiel's arrogant, impetuous wrath could extinguish all that he was, and Elaira as well, with less thought than the swat dealt to a biting insect.

Ire jabbed Arithon beyond reason, dark as the gathered storm laced by the lightning of outrage. He and his beloved together were *more*! Let the dragon be shown in full what such impoverished disdain would destroy. He hurled the gauntlet. "To beg for a stay implies my consent, which I will not yield! Commit to my ruin, and hear my last word. I will lay bare what is taken by murder through each moment I still breathe and to my last spark of consciousness."

That instant, from nowhere, *something* beyond vast, *far more* than the echo of his ultimatum touched the electromagnetic sheen of the flux . . .

*   *   *

The surge welled beneath the seized tension, an inbound swell of pearlescent luminosity that ruffled Sethvir to gooseflesh at Althain Tower. The dissociate mirror of Siantra's awareness grasped also the forerunning ripple. Beyond sensitive, her Sighted gift shimmered to a whisper of rapture that quivered the etheric web. Her outcry inflected the precarious instant the conflict within Forthmark's hostel ignited. "Now!"

Gaze locked to Seshkrozchiel, defiant of her contempt at the last, Arithon let down his shielded barriers. Naked candour laid bare the rare joy he had found and risked all to save at the penalty of an inconsolable personal loss. The keening grief of his effort gone wrong, his most scrupulous protective strategy foundered upon the resilience of Elaira's unshakable loyalty: she had not relinquished him. Could not, no matter how wounding his provocation, and never for his vulnerable need, beyond life itself to secure her safety.

Wide-eyed and beyond all regret, Arithon released the core tenderness held from within. In thought and with the frayed rags of his presence, he surrounded his mate with his own living light, the irreplaceable cloth of his deepest regard for her, body and spirit.

He was hers, as no other. Together, the glory of their unique partnership had fired the highest registers of the land's flux to pealing exaltation. They had lifted each other: raised the ringing, struck peal of a harmony octaves beyond a drake's nature to fathom. Their nurture surmounted the plunge through adversities, spiralled like the phoenix through renewal by a soaring compassion wyrmkind had never dreamed. To the embodied theme of *himself and Elaira,* Arithon released the cascade of longing sprung from the nadir of unalloyed agony: the drowning void birthed from individuality's legacy of intractable separation.

The torrent of feeling wrenched open the vault of Arithon's privacy. As an emptied vessel, benighted, he faced Seshkrozchiel's lowered head. The massive, burning eye brought level with his, scoured his innermost heart. He met and matched the reflection of his utter insignificance unflinching, but for the burning shout of commitment, forged to ameliorate harm beyond mending to the world's greater mysteries.

He had a plea to declare, after all. One imperative obligation yet dangled unfinished, if the breached wellspring battened down under shadow should be left unsecured by his passing. "I would not break a promise made to Merevalia Teirendaelient without the grace of her answer."

Seshkrozchiel slashed her spiked tail fluke, the wafted gust of sulphurous heat a testament to her impatience. "And what incomplete obligation could stem your fate in reprieve?"

"I have not yielded a plea for deliverance!" Arithon cracked, not so easily tricked to surrender by the ancient serpent's sly semantics. "My hold over elemental shadow will fail at the end of my strength. Lirenda Prime was remiss not to mention my placed appeal to the Paravian Queen Regent. Kill me ahead of her dispensation, and Dragonkind breaches the Concord and owns the disaster posed by the etheric well's damaged seal."

The glint of gilt scales and gold eyes gleamed through the hazed smoke expelled from Seshkrozchiel's flared, scarlet nostrils.

"Empty words!" Lirenda scoffed from the sidelines. "Too little, spoken too late for a problem imposed upon sisterhouse turf! Leave the Forthmark hostel to me. Koriathain will curb the uncapped breach through the empowerment granted to us by the prearranged terms of our settlement. The burden devolves to our new order, once the Fellowship's pawn is dispatched."

Seshkrozchiel's glower remained locked on the man, presented as the scapegrace sacrifice.

"I beg to differ," Arithon insisted, and recited the vow lately spoken. *'A'Daelient Merevalia! I pledge to do anything in my power, whatever you ask, if you will defend what is not mine to yield through the course of this crisis. My word, set under seal by Ath's light, and by the surety of Dharkaron's Redress, do with me as you must to secure the containment and safe-guard Athera's mysteries.'*

Arithon tipped his head back and glared up at the dragon, a gesture equal to the boon seared into an epitaph of scorching irony. "If the Paravian Queen Regent withholds her acceptance, the third statement is final. I task Seshkrozchiel under the same formal terms to seal the breached well if the means to serve the world's balance becomes wrested from me."

Lirenda's scorn curdled that sombre entreaty. "What use, to recant the same wanton crime that brought you to this pass in the first place?"

Dorsal spines bristled, Seshkrozchiel pronounced her sentence. "Thrice is final." Cobalt as arctic sky, her auric field flared. A bright, sheeting brilliance cast stygian shadow as she lowered her massive jowls over the Prime's offered gambit.

Eyes shut before the inevitable, Arithon shaped his final thought in
defiance: love, absolute, for Elaira and his piercing sorrow to be the
flawed instrument to have let her down and caused her destruction.
Wherever her absent spirit had wandered, by whatever foul trick of
entrapment the Matriarch had waylaid her, he could accomplish no
more. The faint hope persisted that he might seek her ahead of his
passage across the veil. The lifeline of his connected rapport yet existed.
Since a fisher lad's healing in Merior, he still harboured the shining cord
strung through his beating heart.

Arithon flung wide that inviolate gateway. Last intent, as the breath
of the dragon blistered his face, he aimed to trace his beloved's lost spirit
before death negated his incarnate will.

That instant, Elaira's presence poured through him.

From nowhere, impossibly, improbably, her spirit *re-joined his awareness.* The current of her being surged through, dashed like the rush of
sea tide until the bleak void of his desolation brimmed over. His cry of
affection rang through the scarred marble beneath him. Female to his
male, two became one, tightly laced as the stitched silk of a tapestry.
Together, they framed a wholeness unattainable, a balance in motion
forever unfinished as the loving dynamic of their mortal partnership
struck a flame just shy of exalted perfection.

Ever and always, they had been two halves, indivisible. Gateway
through the heart, Arithon embraced the essence of her, ephemeral dawn
and moonlight and tenderness that accepted him without condition. He
acknowledged Elaira's true Name, never less than a part of him, just as
the whorled tip of the dragon's frontal horn lowered and touched the
crown of his head.

Contact shattered his human awareness. Light sheared the continuum
of known sensation. A thousand smashed shards of mirrored brilliance
blasted cohesive vision to bedazzled blindness. The burning immersion
of Seshkrozchiel's dream leveraged the impossible into the shaped reach
of the probable, a fluid act of creation wrought and forged under the
peal of love that rang like struck iron through the vaulted sanctuary.

What one dragon knew, all others shared in the blink of an instant.
Perception cast in the absence of empathy underwent a radical realignment, wyrmkind's frame of egocentric perspective uprooted forever after.

While, for Arithon, and Elaira twined in his embrace, the rainbow
shimmer of Seshkrozchiel's influence buckled the conscious measure of

all that he was and ever would be, man and woman together were hurled through the tempest of dissolution that set them adrift without substance. Arithon clung to his Name and Elaira's as absolute force sucked the sum of his being into a turbulent gyre. Plummeted through the great serpent's slit eye that blazed like the core of the sun, he shook to the drum of a heartbeat that stopped, paused, then resumed, slammed through the explosive shock of rebirth as the warp thread of true being, his and Elaira's, laced through the bright weft of Seshkrozchiel's making. Nothing became *something* at dizzying speed. Sparked through every electrified nerve, transformation thrummed through sinew and bone smelted down and recast white-hot from the crucible. Seized by drake magic that also had forged seven human beings before him into the mages who comprised the Fellowship, paired entwined figures of incarnate flesh grounded the colossal charge and returned to existence, no longer mortal.

Arithon lost his grip. Flooded by a rush of exponential expansion, he felt like the hollowed-out vessel abruptly brimmed full, then stretched and extended past brittle capacity. Panic trampled his wits. The black-out rush smothered his imperative priority to know whether Elaira survived. No shred of awareness remained. None, to anchor his stopgap stay of wrought shadow. He lacked means to grapple the terrible cost if his patch on the breached wellspring was sundered. No space left to grieve, if the torrential burst of unleashed flux had ripped loose to wreak irreversible, worldwide havoc.

Above his collapse, dimmed beyond sight, Seshkrozchiel reared rampant. The bellows swell of her cavernous lungs mounted the wroth prelude to obliterate the desecrate sanctuary and everything it contained. Moulten magma would flow in the blast of her flame. The etheric vortex and all structure within its surrounds would become destroyed, utterly.

Luhaine's cry became swallowed up, a flung rag of sorrow whipped away by the drake's inbreath. Connected across distance by earth-sensed awareness, Sethvir clung to poise by a thread, pummelled as the flux deluge rocked the axis of change. He sat, transfixed, his pen stalled between lines of manuscript in the warded silence of Althain Tower.

In the dragon's right eye, Siantra's exhortation alone pocked the onrushing course of the cataclysm. *"Wait!"*

Pause seized the dynamic.

Within the closed circle of Arithon's arms, Elaira's eyes fluttered open. The stopped second before the titanic implosion overwhelmed her return to seated consciousness, every bystanding witness trained on the event centred at the Forthmark hostel shared the dawn of a wonder beyond credibility.

For she who had been named *Fferedon'li* by the seers and *Affi'enia* by Ath's white adepts had forged her pathway back to her beloved, unerring. Her passage across the etheric abyss steered by way of a beacon kept burning only for her, she emerged through the portal of Arithon's heart, guided home by the star of his being.

Yet she had not reached her safe harbour alone.

Anthem

Lirenda regarded the entangled couple dropped limp on the floor under the great drake's shadow. Man and woman, both dead, if not immediately, then soon enough at Seshkrozchiel's ruthless discretion. A fire-breathing wyrm stung to rage scarcely deigned to deliberate over particulars. Lirenda shivered in visceral release. Sifted dust raised a tickling cough or a laugh from her sigh of replete satisfaction. Her eyes were not damp. No regretful echo haunted her conscience for the appalling ache of worthless sentiment. No looking back at what she had traded for access to ultimate power at all cost.

A pretty picture, brought together at last: the thrice-accursed junior rival and the inveterate, male nemesis whose hindrances disrupted two prior Matriarchs' aims and galled her to lifelong torment. Put to rest, Arithon's dark hair fanned over Elaira's stilled cheek, nestled into the hollow of his shoulder where he lay crumpled, her slackened weight twined within his embrace. Delivered, as promised, the human coin to complete the bold arrangement brokered for the Koriathain's ascendant destiny. From the prongs of defeat, at the nadir of ruin and the compounded losses of her mistakes, Lirenda strode forward, jewelled diadem glittering against her midnight hair. Imperious, she moved to collect on her radical gamble. Let Dharkaron's Black Vengeance trample to dust the Fellowship's coddled Paravians! She would raise from today's ashes the unchained archive of Mankind's age-old, suppressed heritage.

Athera became her justified fiefdom. The limitless worlds in the heavens one day would be ruled as her order's rightful domain.

Lirenda spoke, grateful her poise did not break with elation for a deliverance claimed on straw hope at the final draw. "I expect my acknowledgement in satisfaction."

Seshkrozchiel did not turn her head. No sideward glance of those glaring, gold eyes acknowledged the debt brought to closure. Until the dragon actualized her elevation, Lirenda could do naught but rely on deduction drawn from skilled observation. The aggravation stung with surprising virulence, to fall back upon discipline blunted without the groomed augmentation of a crystal matrix. Eighth-rank attributes irremediably dulled by that deficit leaned upon settled assurance she had won the day.

Arithon's stubborn influence expired, the fight in him fordone. Lirenda felt the arctic chill cap on the breached wellhead dissolve under the volcanic heat of Seshkrozchiel's presence.

Yet the dragon's implacable bulk remained still. Her banked fires did not immolate the upstart bard whose rank trespass had usurped the manifest stream of Dragonkind's sovereign awareness.

Motionless as cast metal, the great drake maintained her stance, while the air in the released spring's proximity riffled to a shimmer subdued as the winking shine of a drowned sequin. The phenomenon swelled, brightened to blinding intensity, until the stone declivity at the etheric aperture fractured, sheared into hazed rainbows as the element binding the mysteries in check sublimated away.

Preternatural quiet gripped the bowl-shaped depression. A pause soft as the echo of a stopped breath seized poised senses to eerie suspension.

Veined marble lost its mineral opacity, infused by a milky translucence that cleared to glass before the pearlescent blaze of a waxing star. Then that pinpoint light lit to incandescence, emerged through the tapped source of the adepts' ancient spring. The flare brightened to a punch-cut brilliance that dazzled, precursor to an on-coming presence that torched the flux to torrential radiance vast as an aurora. The flood fountained and climbed. Upwards, the bright curtain slashed through the overhead vault, a vertical ray like a sword's edge that keened, lifted into a heightened vibration that pierced the domed zenith. The rush of connection beyond time and space made the ancient hostel ring as though struck to resonance by a carillon of crystalline chimes.

Glory incarnate emerged through the gap, living force that recharged the etheric web once curated by Ath's departed adepts. Had mortal vision withstood the deluge, the delicate head, silk-floss mane, and golden, spired horn of the Riathan Paravian radiated a naked beauty that seared with the ferocity to sublimate flesh.

Joy ignited to rapture where the living bridge connected the earthly realm to the prime source. Ath Creator's gift to illumine Athera arrived on the moonbeam glimmer white, and the mother-of-pearl gleam of cloven hooves. Exalted grace pealed a clarion cry of release that unravelled the illusory gauze of fixed boundaries.

Lirenda covered her face and cried out, overset. Shame scalded through her self-importance, past bearing. Sundered by ecstasy too poignant for resistance, she lost her rigid grip on identity. The benchmark trappings of her achievements dissolved like dank fog under a risen sun. She had no thought to spare. Not for the fate of the dragon, nor for the man and the woman once envied until sour hatred warped her passion to enmity. All concerns fled before a living wonder that shattered her mortal foundations. No marvel of Mankind's invention held substance. No world-spanning empire in recorded history spoke with the eloquence to thaw the frozen solace pursued in the vice grip of logic and reason. Swept away, reft asunder, she buckled, razed clean, as the dross of her mind peeled away and exposed the dimmed vault of a petty existence.

Under the lens of diamantine purity, she beheld her poverty and wept: for a loss beyond reach, and a scouring grief that exposed the self-made prison of her aspirations.

Broken in shivering pieces, she howled, fractured by remorse she could never ameliorate. Her obsessed pursuit of ambition bequeathed emptiness. The least speck of sand had more meaningful purpose. She gasped for the pain, that she had achieved nothing. Done nothing. Loved nothing. Only laid waste to priceless happiness, hers and others', for all her born days. Privilege and perfection shucked away and left her a starved husk, hollowed by failure that choked every valid claim to fulfilment.

Her worship of prime power had done naught but strangle the untamed exuberance of free will.

One fleeting moment allowed recognition before human frailty succumbed. The last of her postured barriers crumbled, dashed under as joy beyond hope overwhelmed the piercing surfeit of excoriation.

Then darkness clapped down, silent as the deep. Tears and terror and exultation were lost. Absolute night inundated the frenetic spark of Lirenda's consciousness.

Elaira resurfaced from the limitless peace of the void to a shattering cacophony of dissociate noise. Light through cracked eyelids stabbed her pummelled sockets like an auger reamed into her brain. She whimpered, unable to sort the chaotic assault. Her bruised mind floundered, faculties too deranged to calibrate the jumbled barrage of stimulus. Sensory overload flinched at the pressure of air upon skin. She struggled for breath, seized under the crushing weight of her mortal flesh.

The shock of her bodily distress piled into the battering surge of emotion. Grief beyond spoken words to encompass savaged her beleaguered awareness. A loss beyond bearing spiralled her into unending despair, cold and dark as the primal abyss.

A warm hand cupped her brow. "Rest easy. Relax." Inchoate noise parted. Kind fingers eased a damp compress over her tormented eyes. Then the whiskey-grained music of a Sorcerer's voice steadied her dizzied bewilderment.

The nauseous tumble of confusion subsided, soothed into a fragile semblance of calm.

Elaira released a shuddering sigh, quieted by the familiar blend of lavender, gentian, and iodine. She recognized where she lay abed. The healer's wing at Forthmark hostel had sheltered her acute suffering once before, when the cruel course of Koriani longevity imposed by her Prime had become transmuted by Luhaine's intervention. The scent of crisp linen, and the soft, summer breeze through the open-air arch wafted the sun-drenched, earthy fragrance of green herbs from the infirmary garden.

Her dissociate blur of past into present raised the nearby rustle of cloth. The slipped compress was tidied by a tender touch. Leashed power contained by immaculate shields gentled her wracked nerves, and a different Sorcerer grounded her unmoored perception. "This is not a disjointed dream from your youth."

Solidified proof that her oathbound servitude had ended, a man's intimate presence flanked her repose. His lean wrist cupped her ribs in protective abandon underneath the shared drape of the coverlet. He also wore nothing, his languid, muscled form stretched at full length in relaxation beside her.

"Asleep from exhaustion," Ciladis responded before the spurred pulse of her surprise careened into untoward concern. Calm restraint checked her reeling effort to rise. "Be still. Arithon has not slept beyond catnaps for days, and the forces he brought to bear through the Biedar crone's reckoning tested him to his breaking point."

Elaira subsided, unstrung by the spin of stressed senses. "What haven't you told me?"

She battled the backslide towards velvet darkness, made sharply aware the reliable frame of her cognizance had become radically altered. Through the cloth compress and despite her shut eyelids, she clearly discerned the Sorcerer's kindly, black features and hawk's stare trained upon her. As if the continuity of her vision had not vaulted beyond the spectrum of normality, Ciladis's lips turned with solemn amusement.

"Sleep is the best remedy for you both." His smile illumined the tender moment of quiet. "Arithon will be here when you wake up, and your questions in earnest can wait."

She wanted to protest. The etheric pathways flung wide open through the veils of dream tumbled her into a ranging morass of expanded avenues and chartless uncertainty. Where perils spawned from self-made terror and panic preyed on the estranged spirit, Elaira shrank in defence-less fear from the volatile quagmire of threat sprung from nightmares. The long-sought reunion achieved at such cost was altogether too preciously tenuous.

Fighting drowsy oblivion, she managed a whisper that grated like gravel against her tenderized ears. "This is truly real?"

Ciladis leaned forward. A presence too mighty to be sheathed in flesh, his gentle contact felt too credibly human as he guided her clasp over the fit sinew under the blanket beside her. Animate warmth and strong pulse affirmed the solid contact. Alive, and together with her beloved, she turned her fevered cheek and inhaled a tickle of sable hair. Relief came too fast. Tears and joy crumbled the wreckage of dignity. Arithon lay next to her, constant as the daylight streaming through the compress Ciladis tucked back over her burning, flushed forehead.

Sleep claimed her again, Elaira thought for a short while, until her eyes opened. Candleflame burned on the nightstand adjacent. Stars pricked the night sky beyond the arched window of the cloistered room, where summer's chorus of insects scraped through the smack of some-one's vigorous mastication.

Not Ciladis; the rotund, grey-robed figure in the bedside chair slouched on a bent elbow, licking the short fingers that crammed whiskered cheeks with a buttered muffin. Elaira knew him. No mistaking the terrible presence swathed beneath a pudgy girth and scholarly trappings. What walked on two feet, clothed in sumptuous flesh, was the Fellowship Sorcerer who had visited her as a shade to restructure a crystal-based course of longevity.

As if memory spoke, his chewing arrested. Dark-lashed eyes bright as beads under bristled brows swivelled from the plate of baked delicacies by the pricket.

Caught staring under that peeling regard, Elaira blushed pink.

Luhaine swallowed. His broad forehead thoughtfully creased. Unoffended, he seemed more embarrassed, caught out while indulging his appetite. He admitted, a sonorous, bass apology at odds with his frightening stature, "Unlike Kharadmon, who relishes life as a flit, I found being collared for errands at Sethvir's beck and call unrewardingly tiresome."

Elaira snuggled into Arithon's settled warmth at her back. "The dragon released you from Davien's wearisome terms?"

Never enamoured of Ciladis's spare quiet, Luhaine delighted in pontification above his craving for pastry. "Actually, that was your Masterbard's doing." He dusted off sprinkled crumbs, sniffed in disapproval, then expounded, "Arithon's working disabused the wyrms of their ideological arrogance. Shown another being not actually authored by the singular cloth of a drake's fabrication, Seshkrozchiel renounced her two-legged partnerships like hot iron shot from a catapult. Evidence convinced her our kind were not dispensable figments, which irked her finicky preference for single-minded autonomy."

"She did not release your Fellowship from the binding terms of the Protectorate Concord?" Reckless in the surfeit of drugged rest, Elaira pressed her inquisitive enquiry. "The same argument would seem to apply."

Luhaine fidgeted. As though his broad belt pinched his belly, he waved a vague hand, round features puckered over his waterfall beard as he dredged up a bare-knuckled admission. "The dreamers at Corith did not create our Fellowship at the close of the First Age. Rather, what Dragonkind willed to occur matched our extant being with ruthless precision. The resonant pulse intercepted our fate, a summons dispersed across time and space that selectively plucked the web of creation.

Sympathetic alignment made us manifest here on Athera. Before the Paravians bestowed our redemption, we Seven seeded a course of red-handed destruction without parallel across worlds engrossed in contention elsewhere. Wanton power framed us for our transformation. We were the answer called at need for defence to end the predation and slaughter perpetrated upon the blessed races by drake spawn."

Comprehension struck a ripple, rushed into sudden expansion that leaped the floodgates of memory. Plunged back into disorientation, Elaira cried out, shocked to agony by an imposed separation that yearned for a grace scribed in gossamer moonbeams and light. The lost echo of transcendent ecstasy consumed her psyche like a wisp ignited to flame. Immolation beckoned, the promise of painless release a wild tonic that rushed her dulled nerves like the incense sweet blast of an updraught.

Leaden flesh choked her expansive flight. Yanked short, crashed back into muffling dark, she wept bitter tears for the sting of unrequite lacer- ation. The desperate flex of her mage-trained reflexes pulverized her slipped perception. Wing-broken, she tumbled, dragged earthward by the intractable prison of gravity.

"Steady. Don't panic. You're going to recover." Luhaine's broad palm enveloped her hand, an anchor of bed-rock peace that gentled and steadied her.

Elaira shivered, savaged by grief. Bereft of the unicorn's presence and bound to a drained existence suffocating as an entombment, she gasped. "Is Arithon beset also? Why are we still breathing?" Riven by shaking sobs fit to burst her seized chest, she fought an onset of sorrow beyond description. "I'd heard Lysaer's war host perished to the last man, struck down by the insupportable exultation of an unshielded exposure to the Riathan Paravians."

Questions splintered to echoes and multiplied, scattered unto infin- itude by a whiplashed explosion of sparked probabilities that outpaced her quickened comprehension.

Luhaine cradled Elaira's damp nape, the stone weight of her head supported while he pressed a cup to her lips. Coaxed to swallow, she tasted a pungent decoction that flooded fragrance like liquefied flowers over her tongue.

"Better?" The word bloomed the flux to a pearlescent shimmer.

Distracted, senses swimming, she managed a nod.

The fat Sorcerer set the emptied vessel aside, cloaked in the patience of ages until her erratic perception ceased its bewildered stuttering and took hold.

Shaken spirit and flesh, Elaira tried speech and again tripped her destabilized equilibrium. Sucked back towards derangement, she expelled a frustrated cry, touched quiet as Luhaine's feather touch cupped her crown. The slight pressure tethered her orientation, and gentled her like a kite played on silk string in skilled hands. She let go her strained breath. Her balance stopped spinning.

"Hush. Be still." Through the recoil of her queasy reaction, the Sorcerer's deep voice resumed. "What you have experienced lies past the pale of your mortal experience. Too much heightened resonance, undertaken too fast, has torched your faculties like an accelerant. You need time. Rest will let you catch up and assimilate." The wooden chair creaked beneath his stowed bulk through the reach for the pitcher to replenish the goblet. "Drink, if you can. The infusion will help."

Elaira accepted the draught, potent with the sweet tang of herbals: starflower and ginger root for grounding; alder to ease back-lash fever, blended with a dash of valerian to quell her racing anxiety.

Someone's hushed query murmured, close by.

"She's into recovery." Luhaine's placid assurance answered a bright figure hazed by a gold aura not cast by the flame on the candlestand.

Pensive thought furrowed Elaira's expression. "Ath's brotherhood has reclaimed their residence at Forthmark hostel?" Misted eyesight picked out the soft-spoken arrival, hooded in a mantle agleam with the twined ciphers of a white adept. Adrift in bemusement, she rambled ahead, "Then the unicorn's presence as the living bridge to the prime source recharged the drained spring and staved off a catastrophic collapse of the mysteries?" One burden less upon Arithon's conscience raised a hope too scaldingly bright. "Am I hallucinating?"

Luhaine blinked. "Not at all, and no salvage of Arithon's doing!"

The shimmering visitor bypassed the Sorcerer's querulous exasperation, came forward, and knelt at her bedside.

"Your credit alone, *Affi'enia*." Dark face smiling amid dazzling light, the adept bowed to her. "The Riathan followed the steadfast beacon your love traced across the etheric web. She stepped through the breached portal of her own accord, the blessing of the well's restoration the exalted gift laid at your feet."

"Not mine only, I think." Elaira blinked through welled moisture. "I heard the gist of the solemn promise Arithon made to the Paravian Queen Regent."

Luhaine coughed, belly quaking to the deep, throaty chuckle that rumbled his chest. "The Riathan came to your virtue alone, lady. Though what Arithon wrought under a dragon's eyewitness has transformed your legacy also."

Elaira could not deny the overwhelming recollection: of the unnerving, torrential implosion that broke down all known perception, then rebuilt the foundation of power from particulate packets of polarized charge to cosmic scale on an instant. She had crossed the heart's gateway to join her beloved, and encountered far greater than the expected, incarnate reunion.

"What happened?" She remembered Arithon's embrace. Also the terrifying, monstrous wedge of Seshkrozchiel's scaled head reared above their entwined figures on the cold marble floor. Something linked to the unforeseen change had upended the Koriathain's attempt to supplant the Fellowship's compact. "What else thwarted Lirenda's treachery and granted us our last-minute reprieve?"

Luhaine darted an uneasy glance sidewards, loath to mention the reason he wore a grey robe in subdued respect. Hurt could scarcely encompass the selfless courage of the other, small voice in the dark: the whisper that had checked the dragon's fire at the bittermost brink of a drastic annihilation. The lone plea that stayed the wellspring's total destruction and the human lives trapped in the breach. Conversation filtered in from the outer corridor filled a discomfited pause, while the Sorcerer stowed the drained goblet on the bedside tray.

Reticence passed the prerogative to Ath's adept. "You survived because the beacon of love between you and your handfast mate ignited a catalyst that altered everything."

"Fate's Forger, Dascen Elur's mages Named Arithon. A choice of uncanny foresight." Luhaine leaned back, the sparkle restored to dark eyes by his stuffy enthusiasm for lecturing. "Throughout two epochs, Dragonkind dreamed and altered the fabric of whatever they pleased, a wilful rambunctiousness that riddled Athera with the noxious gamut of drake spawn. Creation in the absence of love led to horrific bloodshed without remorse, an outlook perpetrated by pigeonholed power, ranked by contention into rigid hierarchy." Warmed to his subject, the

Sorcerer expounded, "The Koriani Prime Matriarch sought leverage on the same principle. She gambled for absolute reign over human destiny, a mad venture with dragons aimed to upset the pre-eminent directive the Protectorate laid on our Fellowship of Seven."

Elaira gasped under the lagged punch of epiphany. "You're implying Lirenda's fulfilment was slighted?"

Luhaine laced a pudgy clasp over his paunch. "A statement of fact. Great drakes do not ever renege on a promise."

The truth fit. Looking inward, she *knew:* the electrical shock and the wrench that reforged her being before she blacked out from the Riathan's arrival had been *everything* dragon: a frightening, terrible lagged second as her heartbeat stopped, re-formed, and restarted, all that she was and *much more* drawn like shining floss through the eye of an uncharted initiation. Her Named spirit was left sacrosanct: Dragonkind now recognized the human right to autonomy. But the thread of an augmented existence, *hers and Arithon's*, had been respun on the loom of Seshkrozchiel's making.

"Wyrms measure and weigh their obligations by mean strength," the Sorcerer allowed with sly irony. "Balance and counterforce level the scales inconsistent with recognized order. Bargains with them are declarations of challenge, and Arithon tilted the contest."

The momentous spark that had deflected disaster sprang from the forge fire of human love, and a cry of loyalty pure enough to have summoned a unicorn's visitation. The Riathan's presence disrupted the arc of probability. Dragonkind's fixated prerogative had been overturned, shattered forever by the discovery they were not the sole arbiters of existence.

The adept tucked Elaira's chilled fingers into his firm clasp and brushed off the tear that sparkled on her fevered cheek. "Your beloved's song broke the shackled belief held by drakes that they alone possessed valid consciousness. But you, *Affi'enia*, were the steadfast light that brought the Riathan and woke the great serpents to their dawning awareness of love."

What Seshkrozchiel experienced in the scald of emotion, all her kindred absorbed in the moment. The blunt force of her species' inventive creation must carve a different track through the ages, henceforward.

"Dragons don't forgive a meddler's incitement involving the death of their young," said Elaira, a touch tart with accusation.

"They don't, in their way." The White Brother smiled and stood. "As you'll see."

His benign departure ceded Luhaine the delight to explain, gruff with ironic bemusement. "Callous ambition was the base incentive that lured an immature molt to destruction. Seshkrozchiel's sensible closure of terms therefore did not elevate the Koriathain."

The drastic pause stunned, thought and motion arrested.

"Dharkaron and Daelion Fatemaster wept for mercy!" Elaira exclaimed presently, her consternation emphatic enough to stir the sleeper tucked in beside her.

Luhaine's smile peeped through his white beard, ferociously pleased. "Oh, yes! You and Arithon were granted the receipts in full measure! Though I declare, from personal expertise, you'll both need time and practice to assimilate the drastic reach of a dragon's bequeathed inheritance."

The same power bestowed on the Fellowship Sorcerers now sang through her veins, a vast gift that extended far into the deep, beyond grasp of all mortal awareness. Elaira wept then in earnest, curled against her beloved's spare warmth, altogether too clearly aware of the possessive arm wrapped around her. "Arithon's going to hate this! If the burden means we owe service to Athera's dragons in perpetuity, brace for an apocalypse when he wakes up."

"Oh, my dear!" Luhaine's laughter boomed outright. "You and your man were not bound in that way! Seshkrozchiel bestowed the raw gift of her magic at scale, but without condition. The blood rite the wyrms laid over we Seven is what binds our fate to the Protectorate's side of the Concord."

Movement rumpled the bedclothes.

"You are not tied by anyone's strings, mine least of any." Arithon's rueful confession tickled the sensitive ear he caressed with a kiss. "For the penalty of my loose tongue, the debt I must own is held by another."

The stout Sorcerer peered down his snub nose and nodded in solemn salute. "Her High Grace will collect on her due when she wills." Shown Elaira's confusion, he clarified with his habitual, stilted formality, "Your man's promise, undertaken in free will, is owed to the Paravian Queen Regent, Merevalia."

Arithon ducked the onslaught of Luhaine's windy remonstrance, more intent on the pursuit of sensual pleasure. His tightened embrace snugged Elaira against him, no breath wasted in pointless apology for the precocious gift of her survival. "I'll see you're not entangled by my idiot folly."

Elaira leaned into him, a delight no longer hampered by need for a warded sword on the mattress beside them. She said through the languor of bone-deep contentment, "Try to keep me away." Of all things, he had failed at that signal task. Let him try again at his peril.

Luhaine shut his dropped jaw, pending diatribe deflated. Indeed, back-lash fever and resonant derangement had more satisfactory cures than tiresome possets and invalid bed rest. Unnoticed, he dabbed the sleeve smeared with butter and heaved his commodious bulk upright. The emptied plate collected as he left, he eased from the room and abandoned the oblivious couple to their well-deserved privacy.

Another less felicitous concern hastened his stumpy stride down the hostel's open-air corridor. His sombre mien did not brighten, despite the starry sky and clean summer breeze that ruffled the scholarly pleats of his robe. Another casualty under his charge had yet to mend from the storm at the forefront of Seshkrozchiel's encounter.

Luhaine crossed the threshold of the lamplit chamber where Siantra s'Idir lay unconscious. Too still, her combed hair fanned a swathe of obsidian against the infirmary's bleached linen. Her tenuous hold on survival flickered from moment to moment, uncertain. The Sorcerer's scuffed tread raised no response. Stilled lids and closed eyelashes, she still seemed the willowy sylph, fast asleep, until closer survey revealed the disturbing anomalies. The whorled nubs of three jet spikes defaced her pale brow. The faint imprint of azure hexagons inked her youthful skin, a glancing sheen of reflections caught by the gleam of translucent scales. The five-fingered hands on the coverlet were not human, narrowed digits transformed to armoured talons tipped with reptilian claws.

Two White Brothers sat in constant attendance, one placed at Siantra's head, and the other installed on a physician's stool at the foot of her bed. The adept not immersed in a healer's trance turned back his hood at the Sorcerer's entrance.

"How is she?" Luhaine parked the useless plate on the side table, right thumb hooked in the ox-hide belt girthed at his barrel waist.

"Less dragon today, but from hour to hour, her orientation continues to fluctuate." No record existed to determine whether the young woman's hybrid condition could stabilize.

Human or wyrm, Siantra might never recover her natural faculties. Mage-sighted awareness mapped the grim truth: she was a being long since frayed thin by her repeated ethereal exposures. The Paravian encounter at Baylienne's Gyre had further eroded her fragile identity. She had never been stable or grounded enough to withstand the torrential ferocity at the nexus of Seshkrozchiel's dreaming.

Whether Siantra regained her original birthright, or if she became other, or crossed the veil in transcendence, her eventual fate exceeded the experienced wisdom of Ath's adepts.

Luhaine knelt at her side, humbled afresh by the scope of her sacrifice.

"We owe you the world," he murmured in homage. Self-indulgent lament would but demean the brilliant depth of her insight. No plea on his Fellowship's part would restrict her choice to determine her destiny.

Her words of restraint at the fulcrum of crisis had been worth any cost by the hard measure of the Seven's priorities. The brave stay that staved off a collapse of the mysteries, and salvaged Arithon and Elaira from the volatile nexus of the Biedar tribe's debt, had impelled the Koriathain to their final defeat. The Dragon Protectorate as yet withstood the tumultuous threat of the drake war past Northgate. Hope endured for the future closure of a service that spanned the blood and sorrow of two Ages.

On that score, Luhaine's practical pessimism forbore to puncture the verve of Sethvir's elation: '*We may yet see that day, for what happened here.*'

Dragonkind for two Epochs had dreamed and created with the fractious chaos of wanton destruction. Who might have guessed Mankind's nearsighted bumbling would shake the great wyrms to compassionate conscience? The provenance of Athera ceded to the Paravian races faced one less dire threat in perpetuity. Provided, of course, Desh-thiere's fell directive did not prevail to wreak the disaster that laid waste to the splinter world of Marak.

Luhaine chewed over his maudlin deliberation, nettled by the chill draught as Kharadmon whisked in and bestowed a plucked rose on Siantra's pillow.

Admission came dear, that the shade's flippant gesture was apt: the moment was too preciously raw, and the taste of reprieve altogether too blessedly sweet. Arithon and Elaira must surmount the trial imposed by Seshkrozchiel's capricious augmentation. Exponential expansion would force them to anneal an unruly, fresh power far past their trained scope to assimilate. Lysaer had yet to meet his deferred reckoning as outcast from the sheltered terms of the compact.

"Feckless ghost," Luhaine grumbled, hair and beard snagged on end by his turbulent colleague's breezy departure. "Can you not keep the peace undisturbed by your antic buffoonery for a single day?"

Grace Notes

Seshkrozchiel alights on the splinter world of Sckaithen Duin past the North Worldsend Gate, where Davien maintains his on-going, crucial watch, for as lightning on thunderbolt, the redoubled recoil of galvanic upset shifts the contour of drakish priorities: an uncertain new order bought at harrowing risk and high cost, trembles still at the precipice of consummate risk . . .

Transformed by the grace of the Riathan presence, Lirenda emerges from back-lash derangement in the ward at Forthmark hostel, and in chastened humility answers a taciturn visitor of tribal descent: "Koriathain are finished. Given my choice? No more vows of enslavement. If any grey sisters remain devoted to charitable service, let me study the healer's art under them until the last of my days . . ."

Assured by the Reiyaj Seeress that the ancestral rites twisted into perversion for power by Koriathain are expunged, Sethvir petitions the Biedar crone concerning the burden of Requiar's lineage: "The order's defanged, all oath-shorn sisters subject to our Fellowship's lawful purview. Since we will stamp out any tinkering relicts, why not release Arithon's blood obligation back to us against Desh-thiere's captive malice within Rockfell Peak . . . ?"

XIV. Solo

Rain chapped the glass of the diamond-paned casements latched tight against the dank winds of autumn. For centuries, the stately, snug town house in Morvain had withstood the seasonal storms that punched salt-laden gusts off Instrell Bay. The verdigris bronze caps on the dormered slate roof remained weather tight. Brick walls laid in herringbone patterns retained warmth to ease the bone-deep ache of the owner's crippling scars.

The house kept no hired servants to maintain its immaculate upkeep, though proliferate Canon priests and their zealot examiners had deterred Traithe's seasonal residence for years. Stepped from the carriage shed with a two-penny candle lamp guttered to pooled wax late at night, the tenant by loan anticipated her customary dark homecoming. Not the gleam of the firelit window that nicked carmine glints on the puddles.

Surprise stopped her short in the lash of the rain, amid the rattled stems of the sere garden. None dared broach the door to this house, far less try the threshold without a Fellowship Sorcerer's invitation. Daliana sen Evend shivered. The fact the stable sheltered no additional hack tickled her nerves. She splashed down the flagged path, steeled for an encounter with another legitimate guest, and cracked the kitchen's back door. Dripping and pungently smelling of horse, she slipped through on the gust that snuffed her spent lantern.

The log blaze laid in the generous hearth had crumbled to bedded coals. Cheery warmth in soft light, Traithe's crockery plates lay strewn with crumbs on the worn trestle table.

The arrival who had eaten his fill was a gangling, lean ancient with chapped hands and prominent knuckles. Silvered hair and a gruff profile weathered as teak notched an erect silhouette, installed in the spoked wooden armchair. Eyes closed, in field leathers musked by wild bracken, he seemed to have drifted to sleep.

Daliana crept forward and eased her hot lamp onto the slate slab by the drain board.

Not quietly enough: imbued with a Sorcerer's frightening presence, the stilled figure addressed her unspoken thought. "Lysaer s'Ilessid is insinuated at Narms with the ragtag dregs of the war host's camp followers."

"I don't care," she snapped, stung to vehemence by her own naïve folly.

"Well, that's a frank relief." Asandir opened grey eyes, formidable as north-facing rime on a cliff. Lysaer's prop on the crutch of tender-hearted forbearance should have ended long since. "Martyred charisma will take its hard knocks under poverty's rude awakening."

"The shorn apron strings hurt?" Daliana snorted the plastered lock of hair off her face with determined goodwill. "High time he got over skinned knees and stood up on both feet."

Chastened by experience, she did not ask what brought Fellowship interests under Traithe's roof. War against Shadow had rocked the mercantile port since the demise of the coalition host at Caith-al-Caen. Requisition commandeered Morvain's famed looms, white silk manufactured for the priests and broadcloth and canvas for the bursar's outfitters. Galleys flying Sunwheel pendants lay snubbed three deep to the wharves, swarmed by burdened stevedores, and supply drays jammed bayside streets seething with couriers, conscripted recruits, and increasingly testy officials.

Folk squeezed by raised tithes voiced complaint to the clink of scant coin, short-changed by the temple for provender and beer, the sacked flour, the raw plate levied from the armourers. No trip to the market evaded the clamour, stymied trade caught in the teeth of armed press gangs sent to stem the desertion of faith bleeding the troop rolls.

While vengeance-bent obsession regrouped for conquest to carve a new passage through Rathain's northern wilds, Asandir's preoccupied reticence ranged farther afield. From gaunt wrists tucked into singed cuffs from a dragons' revolt barely checked on the splinter world beyond Northgate, to the difficult transit from Halwythwood, where flux bloom sheared by the Riathan Paravians forced vengeance-bent clansfolk into migration, he looked towards a hasty crossing to Tysan, and urgent priorities sent from Sethvir. Lane fluctuations played havoc with critical wards: Khadrim at Teal's Gap were excited to violent predation, stirred restive by the riot of their greater kin, and a danger without periodic Fellowship oversight.

Dread quashed false bravado. Daliana broke the Sorcerer's granite introspection. "Don't expect me to pick up the broken pieces again and salvage your prince from his cursed delusions."

"No." Asandir's sigh was not wistful. "I'm afraid Lysaer's fate has run out the slack string, with no avenue left to recover our protective custody under the compact. You were our best chance to try, and in truth, the Mistwraith's design sabotaged that hope from the start." More than a forsaken chill bled the heart for the entrenched fracture grown worse: fanaticism cemented the failure to unseat the fundamentalist canker of Canon doctrine.

Asandir leaned forward. Before Daliana shivered in damp clothes, his long reach and deft forethought ransacked the woodbox and built up the flagging fire. "That's not why I wanted the grace of a hearing."

His phrasing a gentle request for permission, he waited, while Daliana shed and hung her dripping mantle, hedging to defer a commitment.

"You warned me the last time, clearly enough." Wiser to the pitfalls, she determined to try him. Pick his lofty phrasing apart until nuance disclosed the beggar's lint in his pockets.

Asandir laughed aloud. Not insulted, patient as rock, he approved her acerbic resolve, content to honour her preferences.

Shadows seamed his gruff features, etched by a calm hard-used enough to intimidate. That such vast strength, capable of manhandling the forces of cataclysm, should seek her audience in a cosy kitchen revealed all the cracks: of sorrows riven through a dauntless persistence by two Ages of service. In close quarters, mortality flinched to contemplate how far Asandir's endeavour had ventured, blown in with raw weather between feats that leached human marrow to contemplate.

Not to be rushed, Daliana eased the awkward gulf of disparity as best she could. She hung the teapot on the hob, then piled a spalt-maple tray with biscuits and cheese, dried apples, and a bowl of shelled nuts and raisins.

Asandir obliged the diversion, his query devolved to the enterprise that had smirched her bodice with chewed shreds of grass.

Daliana dug into a string pouch at her cincture, and tossed the dog-eared pack of playing cards on the trestle. "Gaming for horseflesh, aside from my upkeep. Skirts and petticoats," she admitted, her vixen's grin rueful. "I fancy a draught team and carriage for the day I'm inclined to move on."

The insinuation struck a cruel point: of a home at Etarra demolished to restore the Paravians to Daon Ramon, and an estranged family left scattered. Asandir did not wince but tacitly laid the foundation for her lasting quietude.

"Your selfless service enabled more than you know. The Koriathain's last redoubts are being dismantled since the free-choice vows that bound their initiates have been annulled. The stolen knowledge maligned to suborn Lysaer's cursed affliction will be purged from the sisterhood's remaining libraries forever by Kharadmon's diligent sweep. The religion inspired by false worship of light has lost tangible credence without its self-styled avatar." Asandir wielded the paring knife to slice bread and cheese, focused beyond small consolation. "Dogma won't wither on the vine straightaway. But in time, sound rule can stamp out the wrongful practice of burning condemned talent."

The teakettle boiled. For a candle-lit interval, across steaming mugs, the snacks were consumed to the last morsel. Asandir watched Daliana, relaxed and replete, then resumed his lapsed conversation.

"Paravian presence returns to the continent, and the day will arrive to restore the full measure of charter law." Come at last to his purpose, he broached his appeal. "When that hour is ripe, I'd like you to travel beyond the West Worldsend gate in my company to select the next heir for the crown seat in Tysan."

Daliana smothered a gasp, jolted to a start that jostled her cards over the table's edge. Implication suggested *Lysaer would be dead*, or much worse, too far lost in the sway of his poisoned narrative to excise the warped stamp he might leave on his progeny. The acknowledgement stung in the harsh light of tragedy, with his curse-blighted obsession to seek righteousness perhaps too sharp a tool for manipulation.

Asandir's voice arrested her plunge into self-laceration. "The posited end for Lysaer is not written. Sethvir's vision cannot foretell the sentence Paravian judgement must impose. Only that the allowance for his deferred penalty is nearly spent."

There was more. Daliana felt the Sorcerer's piercing regard, unrelenting in the felted quiet. "You want me along. Why?" Her hoyden's pose useless to deflect his deep scrutiny, she attacked first. "Does your request imply Tysan's royal lineage has failed? Has the virtue of s'Ilessid in contentious straits proved too fallible to corruption by grandiose principle?"

"Did you know the ancient history of your ancestry?" Asandir lowered his gaze. As intimidating, the cragged features quarried by sorrows beyond mortal compass. Large, weathered hands that should have seemed awkward embodied the salt of earthbound competence.

Habitual flippancy shielded her vulnerable fear. "I'd heard I'm the descended offshoot of a pillaging Hanshire aristocrat's abduction."

Amusement crinkled the corners of Asandir's eyes. He did not look up. "Diarin s'Gannley had sharper mettle than that, and her famously irregular marriage forged more than your family history retains."

Desperation pounced on the salacious feint. "You knew her?"

"I referred instead to her Third-Age linebearer." The Sorcerer pressed onwards, "My preference at the founding of the royal lines was Halduin s'Ilessid for *caithdein*, with choice for the attribute to anchor the crown the unshakable rock of tenacious loyalty." He added, nonplussed, "No light matter, as you have experienced under a brutal test of sound character. Your primogenital forebear Iamine s'Gannley refused the request."

Daliana bent and recovered her scattered cards, no longer perturbed when she straightened. "You have a *caithdein* to take up the reins for as long as your heirship is vacant."

Asandir watched her tap the flimsies into alignment and shuffle them with curt expertise. "Saroic's branch has been tempered by centuries of defensive flight under hunted oppression. Critical qualities to sustain survival, but not what is needed to anneal the sword of crown justice and back the fourfold attunement for full-contact negotiation with the Paravians."

Daliana realized like a thump to the chest the loaded import of this roundabout conversation. Before the Sorcerer phrased the question, she let accusation outleap prudent sense. "You've picked your desired candidate for the s'Gannley succession."

"Yes." He glanced up, grey eyes bright as sheared steel, and a flattened hand raised to quell her evasion. "Take your time, Daliana. We'll say nothing more now. But the subject will arise at the cross-roads when the determinant question for Tysan's restoration begs answer."

Kingmaker, Sorcerer of the Seven, he arose, broad shoulders bearing the weight of the world all too poignantly human. Daliana felt devastated, that relentless demand denied him the ease of casual company. "You can't at least linger for a dry roof and a restful night's sleep?"

Asandir's smile showed regret as he crossed to the fireplace. "War is building, and loose troubles aplenty must be curbed before the next crisis upends the peace."

He shook out his dried storm cape. Tall frame bundled, he stepped out to the whispered click of the latch, his ghost step down the path swallowed up by the drumming downpour.

"Dharkaron's immortal arse and Black Chariot!" Daliana swore in stunned after-shock.

The Sorcerer's brief presence seemed unreal. A phantom visitation faded as a remnant of dream, but for the used mugs, the cored apples, and cheese rind that littered the plates on the table.

Day dawned on the hour the Light's Canon rewrote sanctioned history to elevate the ranks lost to glory at Caith-al-Caen. Lysaer s'Ilessid's divine ascension was documented, formalized under ribbon and seal as an immaculate apotheosis. Commemoration flourished the occasion with lavish pomp and ceremony to awe the faithful.

At Narms, sea fog and mizzle wilted the golden banners and swagged bunting lining the streets. Sodden mobs packed the shop fronts to cheer the procession of priests and armed dedicates, parade ranks brightened by trilling bells and the burnished glitter of weaponry. People screamed adulation and tossed white-silk lilies, which pelted the polished honour guard on cream horses escorting the vacated suit of gilt armour. Incense wreathed the chosen anointed bearing the sainted artefact's canopied litter.

Sun did not shine on them, despite the rayed halo of citrines and diamonds added to the plumed helm last worn by the Divine presence on earth. Autumn's drab overcast nicked a leaden sheen on the black bullocks yoked to the studded iron cart bedecked with Shadow's effigy, trailing the Light's sainted radiance. Evil leered at the crowd with demonic green eyes, skewered by the executioner's sword venerated and blessed as the relic that dispatched the infant Spawn of Darkness at Daenfal.

Fervour chose to ignore the same dazzling panoply enacted in other towns under the beneficence of the Canon. Swathed in its drenched flags and finery, Narms bore up under the onerous burden of martial transformation. Crofts on the outskirts hosted muddied encampments of billeted troops, a flesh-and-blood validation of temple defence welcomed by a guild port without revetted walls. Garrison men in burnished accoutrements oversaw the tossed coin for largesse, while a soprano choir performed from the bell tower's balcony. If the adulation rang a trifle too shrill, folk denied the fresh fear behind the show of extravagance. Trade fed the veins of commerce at Narms. The brocaded officials wore their jocular, pasted smiles, feverish desperation alarmed by lost profits since the lethal setback at Caith-al-Caen.

Displaced from the avatar's exalted pedestal, Lysaer s'Ilessid subsisted, alive, in the filth of his mortal condition. Temple scripture disavowed his survival. The man stripped of godhood kept no illusions. Jealous doctrine did murder to salve its prestige: his Talith was assassinated by cold calculation before the stain of her adultery sullied the faith.

Too vividly marked by his fair colouring, Lysaer learned to grovel, in the pinched straits of his anonymity.

At present, he spat grit through a bleeding lip, crushed prone underneath the hobnailed boot on his back. "Think you're the Light's blessed come back from the dead?"

Reviled by the bystanders' laughter, he endured the pustulent rant of the squire above him. "Serves you scum right to have got in my way!"

A gob of spittle splashed Lysaer's nape. Jaw clenched, he swallowed his fury. Such bullies usually succumbed to boredom, once their sneering onlookers accepted their failure to bait a picked fight. The raw lesson came hardest, not to strike back. Fisticuffs tagged a wretch without rank as fair game, to be collared past nightfall and matched in the pit, where roughneck bouts staged for off-duty bets provided the idle troops with their sordid amusement.

Officers ignored what occurred out of sight. Or they placed illicit wagers themselves through an intermediary. The underbelly of a billeted war camp vented its crapulous nerves through brutality, excess, and licence.

Lysaer hunched to hide his resentment and retrieved the lyme sack dropped in the fracas. En route to the latrine pits, he quashed the rash

impulse to hurry, wary of lurking informants who might view the avoidance of temple festivities with side-eyed suspicion. The devout fervour
of a dedicate company mauled by defeat did not rest. Bounties rewarded
the righteous who helped the diviners ferret out heretics. The examiner's
inquests spared no torment to expose the suspect taint of talent.

Lysaer shifted his burden, exhausted by rage, and not foolish enough
to dare the effrontery to enlist. Only his downtrodden station forestalled
his chance-met risk of recognition. Head down, he trudged to the
reeking trench and dumped his load into the puddled sewage and
feces. Then, eyes burning from the caustic plume of billowed lye, he
stumbled to shoulder the next vile task, while the bleak afternoon
stretched before him. Unskilled at mean labour, he avoided the scrutiny
invoked by an admission of literacy. No trustworthy hire engaged
scribes without references.

Day upon day, scrimping, he earned his bread with the camp following
as a roustabout, elbowing for whatever brute work required a human
packhorse. Bearded, rough, and unwashed, he barked his knuckles
fetching stacked wood for the ovens, the officers' pavilions, or the
armourers. He avoided unloading provisions, excoriated by the uproar
when the straight grain of s'Ilessid justice ran him afoul of his fellows.

"What's wrong with you," disparaged a brute branded for felony on
the left cheek. "O' course we filch and skim what we can! How else to
grift for warm clothing to spare yer cullions from shrivelling frostbite?"

Laughter scorned any prospect for better employment. "And where
will you go? Can't survive over winter picking the fleas off yer crackernut
scrotum!"

"Bucko, there's no cushy job. Unless you prefer to bag a few back-alley
brats for sellin' to leaguesmen?"

Hostile glares had not braced Lysaer for that horror. Not until the
morning he awakened to screams and witnessed the headhunters training
their pack dogs. "Maul their barbarian weans, and you get the tactical
shot to put an arrow into the adults. Works a trick, and shortens the
time to line a silk purse for retirement."

The terrified, ragged urchins caged next to the kennel pens prompted
the unwanted memory: of underfed children in an Etarran back alley,
sold to dismember carcasses for the horse knackers. Lysaer shivered,
sickened anew by recall of the abuse once exposed by the bastard half
brother *who was not yet dead!*

Lysaer folded his arms across his seized chest. The immutable lacer-ation of Desh-thiere's curse blighted reason, until naked truth drove him mad. He acknowledged that he clung to this execrable misery in the warcamp because the Light's cause alone satiated his drive to pursue his half brother's destruction.

His need to drown himself in oblivion sought a tavern, that ejected him at the door. Even the vendors peddling yesterday's crusts denounced his shiftless appearance. "Get along, cheat! Take your thieving mitts elsewhere!"

Destitute, he refused to stoop with the lowest and pilfer. Ruled fair by his conscience, Lysaer dragged sacks of fodder for the grooms, warned off with pitchforks to keep clear of the horses, or even thinking to borrow a tool. The rare copper sometimes rewarded the removal of offal from the slaughter pens, or worse, stinking corpses perished of sickness or wounds, muscled on planks from the surgeons' tent.

Petty robbery taught Lysaer to cache his windfalls in a hidey hole after dark. He took the beatings, found empty-handed when the priests' acolytes made absolution rounds with their batons, dunning the sinful. Saviours of nothing, they did their rough work to shrieks and foul-mouthed abuse from the whores they accosted.

"Was your mam diddled by ten rutting goats?" Through smudged paint and tears, the trollop they pinioned kicked and struggled, arms twisted behind her.

"I say yon frigger was starved at the tit!" yelled the madam shaken down to torn laces. "Ravening greed as he's got from the first would've chewed bloodied milk from the nipple!"

"Cock-suckler!" A rowdy hoot, from the buxom brunette rousted nude from a client's sweaty embrace. "How long d'ya suppose these louts pray on their knees with their jacks in wet fists, squeaking the pip till 'e whimpers!"

Lysaer cringed, scalded red. How had he failed to notice the cruelty inspired by his lofty rhetoric? No experience prepared him. Not for the sorry coffles of recruits culled from countryfolk whose blighted harvests left them no means to pay tithes at year's end. Young girls, aunts, and daughters, trafficked for usage as prostitutes, and stouter matrons for cooks and laundresses, seized by war-bond conscription. Their plights galled his upright principles to impotent fury. The high command never paused to imagine the burdens endured by the common folk, or question the Canon's spiritual fist knuckled over their lowly destinies.

Wakeful in the wee hours, Lysaer wrestled his galled conscience. *When had such shameful practices become the acceptable standard?* How long and how far had Desh-thiere's pressured choices let this war host degrade the forthright ethic Sulfin Evend had shaped from the crack troops of bygone summer musters?

The days waned. Lysaer endured, dispirited, his precious knit mittens stolen by a drunk sergeant who staggered in from the shoreside stews. From the paucity of his reviled existence, he nursed the bruised outrage, without friends or the safe comfort of fellowship. Then the cold came, relentless. The glaze ice on the puddles lingered past daybreak, and raking storms off the bay chapped his skin to raw sores.

Since the pox-raddled whores occupied the dry beds, Lysaer bunked on dank ground, or scrapped for shelter beneath the parked drays to escape the wet coastal snowfall. He weathered the squalor, too curse-ridden to beg, or fall in with the cast-off scum who gleaned the middens. Before braving the innkeepers' mastiffs for kitchen scraps, Lysaer made himself useful cleaning for the page boys from good family denied privilege for servants until they earned rank. A wretch who volunteered could get warm, tending their kit after dark. He blacked rows of soiled boots for inspection until his chilblained fingers cracked and bled. Painful remembrance stung all the worse: Daliana had shouldered such degrading tasks while keeping his warped instincts in check. He hurt for her loss, until resurgent obsession overrode sympathy. *Her damnable interference in fact had seen him shackled to these benighted straits in the first place!*

Mantled in gloom behind the long benches in the officers' tent, Lysaer scraped caked manure and mud with a bristle brush, then waxed scuffed leather, while the off-duty idlers gossiped over his head.

The Paravian incursion into Daon Ramon made armed forays south of the Mathorns perilous business. "We'll march north, come the spring. Mark my word, there's pickings aplenty. The forest redoubts spawn old-blood talent by the clutch."

"Nasty work," a veteran demurred, thumb licked to sweeten his luck for the dice. Through the rolling clatter of his next throw, he complained of the casualties taken by snares. "Disembowel a man, then yank him upside down, spilling out guts like a butcher's cut. Unholy atrocity, to leave someone dangling, screaming until they bleed out."

Vile traps with trip strings released swinging logs. "Brains the horse out from under a lancer, with sharpened stakes turfed in mulched leaves to pierce armour after a fall."

Victims died of wound fever, ghastly punctures seeping rank pus. Lysaer had tossed more than one impaled carcass into the lyme pits, as longer nights prioritized the stockpiled fuel in the woodsheds. The barbarian reavers' gristly work was not new. The same bloody horrors had harrowed the summer campaigns from Etarra, run cheek by jowl with the headhunter's league.

While winter ice closed the northcoast passage, vengeful talk turned towards planning to flush out the clan hunters and haze the game off the Plain of Araithe.

"Starve out the slinking devils from cover! They'll be weakened and desperate by thaws." Family bands driven deep into hiding became bunched pickings for a mass target.

"Mark my word, we'll have plucked geese for the taking when our host marches to join the reserves and we mount the offensive in earnest."

Lysaer listened, huddled in crawling shadows beneath the low lamps. Luck might let him nap in his dry corner, unnoticed, though any such stolen respite was brief. The provosts' men barged through before dawn, irritable from chasing down the night's crop of deserters.

A riding whip, or a boot thrashed a layabout caught under canvas. "Lowlife vermin! Piss off and wheedle for charity from the priests!"

Yet the temple was the last place Lysaer dared to seek a poor man's relief. His likeness was ubiquitous: stamped into votive candles and shadow-banes, embellished with gems upon painted icons and carved into statues. He had been the godhead depicted in friezes above True Sect altars across the continent. A flesh-and-blood threat to the hallowed divine would see him strangled in secret by Canon examiners, if not torn limb from limb by a mob. A terrible end had befallen the sharp-eyed informant who brashly made claim to a sighting. The hapless bloke had been arraigned for the scaffold under a Canon charge of false worship.

Lysaer swathed his bearded face behind rags, in petrified dread of self-disclosure with no power of light to defend himself.

Winter nights lent momentum to the frenzied fear sown in the after-math of the massive defeat in Daon Ramon. Panicked authorities locked horns behind the barred doors of the trade guilds, while the new crop of recruits trained under streamed torches on the iced fields after twilight.

The solstice ceremony for the year's honoured dead brought the veiled widows for the Light's requiem. Priests offered prayer and deliverance for the sacrificed fallen at Caith-al-Caen. Pennons and black bunting shrouded the temple's tiered bell towers, a display of toothless solemnity. Pomp could not replenish the measure emptied by loss, or ease keening grief, with no revered bodies interred with the stone-faced solace of heroes' memorials. The sainted instead lay unshrouded, unsung under sky where they languished, bones picked by ravens and weather. Their remains could never be brought home to rest. Not while the Athlien dancers with their crystal flutes called down the great mysteries for renewal upon proscribed turf.

Lysaer had no gold to soften the plight of the mourners. No balm of largesse to feed their gaunt, orphaned children. For the first time since birth, he was powerless to render assistance or uplift the benighted. Spring planting would suffer the shortage of labour, yesteryear's field hands reforged into shining ranks to march under flags down the same, beaten path to a premature end and false glory.

What had the Light's blessed accomplished through three centuries of battle against darkness and sorcery?

Another spring would green winter's sere earth, and dry out the roads for campaigning. The next host would depart under banners and prayer, fresh with resolve and starry-eyed purpose. The white-and-gold priesthood would count offerings and praise the Light, mouthing rote blessings along with the promise of sweet bliss in the afterlife for the anguish and death spent against entrenched evil. Slaughter of the clan enclaves in northern Rathain posed the soft target to revive hope the old races might be suppressed, turned back, or banished in favour of human progress.

Lysaer emptied slop. He hauled wood and sanitized the latrine pits, chained to an existence that fed upon ruin. The curse of Desh-thiere sucked him into despair, the veil of his vaunted purpose undone as he grappled the poisonous groundswell: his trumpeted principles now fashioned the lethal weapon for brokered power and acquisitive commerce.

The oppression trussed up in righteous faith was untenable. Too many lives in the past had been claimed, with more yet to be reaped for a vacuous creed sugared over venal corruption. Lysaer cowered in helpless regret, humbled down to the marrow. He had no agency. No claim to influence left to paste over the pretence of altruistic self-sacrifice. Wretchedness swallowed him, heart and spirit, for the wanton waste his life's work had established. Addiction to adulation had rotted all of his fruitful choices. At rock bottom, as nobody, self-deceit found no grandiose cause and no susceptible party to shoulder the blame. Nor might he do aught to amend the on-going damage sown at large by his influence.

Desh-thiere's curse owned him. The last, fragile stay of cesspit anonymity framed the sole check on his charismatic misuse of leadership. Ever since his depraved assault upon Daliana, he most feared to become the Mistwraith's finest instrument for annihilation.

Northern gales drove the blizzards, gusting drifted snow and dire cold that whistled and flayed like knives through the Mathorn ranges. Stars burned in white splendour on the moonless nights, guidance for the remnant clan war band sent packing from Halwythwood's glens since the flux tides' crest over solstice. Hush shrouded the wilds. Deeper than the absence of trade, the wound stillness strained the gap of anticipation before the plucked note shattered quietude. For change had arrived with Athera's Paravians, the ancient resurgence of forgotten joy conflicted by Mankind's tensioned dread.

Riathan ran wild again on the downs by the River Severnir. For the first time since the Adaraquend abdication, Athlien dancers sparked the renewal of Athera's great mysteries. The wave of grand confluence spun from Rathain's heartland rippled across the refounded etheric web. At peak surge, the quickening for centuries held in abeyance charged the lane current in Daon Ramon, the shimmer of prepotent flux beyond the capacity of most human minds to withstand.

The clan scouts assigned to the rear-guard through migration threaded the pass at Leynsgap amid the harsh freeze of midwinter, more concerned by wolves and starvation than pursuit from headhunting diviners. They brought updated word from Ciladis, installed as liaison to the High Queen Regent, Merevalia. Also Esfand s'Valerient, dazed yet from his ordeal within Baylienne's Gyre.

Iyat-thos Tarens met the northbound band on the open plain in thin snow, trail leathers stiffened to chafing discomfort in the frigid conditions. Glare creased fair skin to a squint beneath his fur hood, the cropped hair he preferred greyed with rime, and his broken, scarred nose peeled red by the elements.

The backslap he dealt the lead scout raised a roar that flurried the ice silted into thick clothing. "You look a drastic sight worse than I do!"

"Beet purple and thin as boiled string?" The bluff woman laughed. "Sithaer's black gate, man! When are you going to rub off that appalling town accent?"

Greetings were boisterous, through snorts of plumed breath, no reunion taken for granted in these harrowed months, where frostbite purpled toes in wet boots overnight, and the starved predators scavenged the backcountry hollows for weakened prey. The brusque jokes and camaraderie heightened by stark hardship made Esfand's subdued quiet stand out.

The young man was unshaven, verging on unkempt. Squared jaw averted, he stayed withdrawn, his glazed introspection unlike the thoughtful, vibrant *caithdein* departed from Deshir last spring.

"Esfand?"

Tarens's tacit query raised no response. The feral scout who took notice shortened a farsighted gaze resharpened from crossing the peaks. "Looks to be wit wandering again. He's touched in the head. Been that way since his venture onto proscribed ground. Ath spare us if others lose their firm bearings from a living encounter with a centaur guardian."

The vacancy caused by Arithon's abdication hung bitter on the frigid pause. Loss of a sound candidate for crown liaison, coupled with Khadrien's death, left a dearth of choice and a young, untried brother in line for the steward's succession. No softening overture could console Jalienne for her oldest son's altered condition.

Admiration burnished an irreparable tragedy none owned the stout bravery to countenance. "Stood in for sanctioned royalty, true to a *caithdein*'s charged office. Sad luck, that Caith-al-Caen's jeopardy demanded an unshielded contact beyond mortal reckoning."

"Ciladis couldn't say whether Esfand might recover." The scout shrugged, fatalistic. "We're for taking him back to his family. If he can't settle with time, or uphold his appointment, the council will bind a match for his offspring to salvage the bloodline."

Tarens clamped back a heated retort, his crofter's outlook shaken afresh by the sere practicality of clan tradition. The import of Siantra's intractable convalescence at Forthmark tightened his chest and choked words. Someone must bear the hard news to Laithen s'Idir, a sufficient excuse to duck Jalienne's wrath, not counting the onslaught of Khadrien's bereaved younger brother, his quarrelsome cousins, and the scrappy flint of the s'Valerient granddame.

"I'll go on to Fallowmere," Tarens offered, his galled temper better off blunted by sorrow. He craved the solitude, wearied and sick at heart as he was from teaching the youngsters Jieret's murderous tricks with a spring trap. "I'd re-join my wife with time to spare before she lies in for childbed."

The scouts yielded, quick to surrender the hardship. Seventy-five leagues of overland travel exchanged for the snug comfort of Strakewood's redoubts, they tossed Tarens their pack pony's reins and veered west the moment he had their dispatched news committed to memory.

Arrived off the Plain of Araithe past midseason, still mildly euphoric from the confluent surge of blue light spun off the old centaur markers, Tarens was intercepted by the scout sentries at Drimwood. Their escort led him into the covert encampment, where a welcome stilted by wrenching privation met his solo arrival. Quite a few hunters limped: whether from frostbite or chilblains or last summer's wounds, nothing lessened the heartache. Others nursed livid scars from the bountymen's sorties to bag their last autumn's human trophies. Tarens measured gaunt features pinched from lean rations, and the shadowed eyes sunk beneath muffling furs. He ached for the short-fall. His pack pony carried no cloth goods and needles to lighten fraught spirits, and no sweets to cheer the small children.

The young piled into him anyway, free as larks at slack season when the leaguesmen retired to shelter in town. Noisy, they clamped onto his legs like limpets. Others tussled to seize his gloved fingers, pleading for a rambunctious spin.

"Tadpole pests!" Tarens bowled them off, shrieking with laughter, their boisterous energy bundled in hide and laced leggings, the few quilted linings among them cut from Sunwheel surcoats and horse barding gleaned off the battlefield as practical spoils.

He saluted the tiny girl sucking her mittens, and ruffled the heads of the toddlers, and failed to swallow the lump in his throat. His dead nephews by now would have been young adults, shaving new beards and wrangling for their first kiss. With his own precious firstborn still in the womb, the troubled report he carried weighed like a stone in his breast.

Over the raucous tumble of exuberant clan innocence, Tarens placed his request to see Laithen.

"She's in closed council with Fallowmere's chief," said the woman bent over a sledge stacked with flayed hides. "Can't pry her away. Got spokesmen in from the named lineages, and for days they've been at it like stoats in a screeching match. Your news can't wait?" His stiff silence met the woman's resigned shrug. "Very well. Go softly nosing into that brangle."

The inauspicious precaution brought Tarens into the steaming, dark warmth of the lodge with the muddied ice from the river course still melting from his boots. His broad-shouldered frame cast no shadow ahead, the tent's entry flaps at his back overlapped to cut draughts and to muffle the chance gleam of firelight from hostile notice.

Stepped blinking from daylight, he encountered a volleyed exchange, his quiet arrival gone unremarked between the locked horns of yelling combatants.

". . . and that's windy with arse gas enough to float shite!"

"How else can we test which family lines have attenuated and grown weak?"

"Waste too long fuddling without resolve, we'll be trophy scalps on a saddlecloth for some swaggering townborn's claim to salvation."

"Forget league predation! If the Paravians migrate northward from Daon Ramon, we'll have the wave of glory upon us, fit to winnow our own, and the Light's armies, like so much chaff on the wind."

". . . no use if half of our able adults fall to the throes of back-lash madness!"

Tarens coughed.

Conversation rocked to a halt. Walled silence absorbed his intrusive reception. He was offered no food. The atmosphere of scalded impatience gave him no chance to request the seemly privacy to break sensitive word of Siantra's precarious prognosis.

The assembled council fixed him with inimical glares, a row of stiff faces distorted by the streamed flames of staked prickets. The stifled setting warred with the breath of fresh air wafted off his calf-length outdoor mantle. Written on him, head to foot, the long weeks of sun glare and dazzling snow, and the bitter, black nights spent in shivering cover on the frozen heath.

"Iyat-thos Tarens?" Laithen beckoned him forward, small-boned and tough in sepia leathers worn to patches. Fallowmere's clan chieftain perched to her right, a wiry man of middle years, deep brown hair threaded grey, and bland features the disarming front for an overbearing intelligence.

The rangy, cragged loremaster leaned back beside him, arms folded, the frumpy bulk of the seeress perched opposite, while the quick, ferret's strides of the war band's strategist ceased pacing, his restless stance bristled behind. Keen expectancy cut like a knife, where harsh news arrived with the regularity to snuff the guttered embers of hope.

Laithen's survey pierced through traveller's exhaustion and broached the interruption through the stiff atmosphere. "Whatever has prompted you to leave Strakewood, the reason had better justify the potential cost of your absence."

She expected catastrophic bad news, Tarens realized. Come into the light, he paid her due deference with crossed wrists and opened with the mild reassurance of a formal greeting. "Deshir's outposts are holding, intact. We've received the war band back from Daon Ramon." Regretful, he added, "I have updated words for Laithen in person."

Pert as a sparrow, the Teiren s'Idir gave him inflexible steel. "Concerning my daughter? If she's languished or dead, I'll hear what's befallen. Our stock has withstood the effects of Paravian presence, or endured the failures since the time of the founders. Speak directly. Earl Jieret's experience would bear up, and Fallowmere's council stands witness."

Tarens cried, caught aback, "I don't bring a condolence!" Upset under need to defend his decision, and dismayed that an early reunion before his mate's pending childbirth saddled him with an unforeseen censure, he wrestled for a composure hard-set against the gentle grain of his character. Merciful decency should not be forced to unburden any mother's trials in public.

Yet Laithen's demand rejected the kindness.

Tarens quashed his reluctance and recounted Siantra's condition, a comatose affliction unknown to the Sorcerers and beyond the wisdom of Ath's white adepts at Forthmark hostel. "She still breathes. But her body undergoes an unknown alteration, without guidance or means to determine the outcome. Her case has no precedent and no cure."

Laithen made no sound.

The seeress alone displayed anguish, having been the young woman's mentor. "I never foresaw this!" Shaken to remorse, she clenched her gnarled hands. "Had we grasped that girl's peril, I could not have sanctioned her venture to Halwythwood!"

"You dishonour free will!" snapped Fallowmere's chieftain, gruff before untoward lamentation. "Are we grown so timid we dismiss out of hand the harsh choices that blindside the Sighted? Ruled by prescient talent, she did as she must! Honour the bravery of Siantra's named heritage."

Laithen sat, deathly still and rammed upright. She might have been carved out of wood, but for the dark eyes spilled over with tears. Unblinking beneath the unbearable, she endured, while the war band's strategist slammed the board and laced into Tarens for his shameless dereliction.

"All the worse you've deserted your post. Not only for the enclave placed under your care, the free wilds require the most stringent protection with the Paravian presence at large!" His gesture chopped protest. "You've seen the evidence of our straits!" Falwood's clans had withstood incessant attack, harried by relentless armed forays from the companies based at East Ward. "The moment the pack ice breaks off the northcoast, we'll have galleys sheltered behind Crescent Isle landing more dedicate troops."

The east had strategic liabilities enough. Tarens, as war captain stationed in Deshir, had no business leaving the territory and the people under his charge through the buildup of the temple forces amassing at Narms and Morvain. "The war host will march before equinox. If Esfand stays unfit to lead, Khadrien's brother is too fecklessly young. That leaves you with Earl Jieret's knowledge to stand firm and protect Rathain's mysteries in place of crowned sovereignty."

Which was too cruel, thrown into the teeth of Laithen's intractable pain. Tarens broke under the wave of raw fury, that grief by the callous dictates of duty lent no compassionate slack for the fate of a daughter in jeopardy.

"Just keep dying off under the enshrined ways of your ancestors!" Tarens ploughed into the aghast silence, goaded sick by the endless, evasive measures of life snatched on the run under vicious predation. "If not this season, then within five years, the True Sect will rebuild and expand on their gutted campaign. In a decade, two at best, you'll have suffered too many irreplaceable losses."

Did they not see? Panic sown by the Paravian incursion would recruit by the *thousands* the next wave of fanatical reavers.

"What is left, beyond year upon year of retreat?" Tarens ranted, past stopping. "I don't want my children brought up in the fens!" For as long as he lived, he refused to lose sleep, gadded by whining mosquitoes when the cattail punks smouldered out. Nor could he bear to anoint the tender skin of an infant with the caustic repellent of swamp-cabbage oil.

"I would sue for a treaty while we still have the numbers to negotiate terms in our favour."

Laithen stared him down, her streaked cheeks drained white. "You speak out of turn here."

The council ranged against him, unanimous. Given the Paravian presence, and no Teir's'Ffalenn to curb the exploitation that threatened the mysteries, a departure from form for chancy diplomacy brooked no discussion.

"Take this route, and you will divide us!" warned Laithen. "I for one will never abandon the charter that binds our given commitment!"

Fallowmere's chieftain closed the council forthwith. Final disposition granted Iyat-thos leave to stay only until his gravid wife delivered her child.

Tarens received his firstborn from the midwife, a tiny daughter perfectly formed, and glistening wet from the womb. She was a lively snip, cradled in his chapped hands, tiny red feet beating the air while she screamed in earsplitting fury. Choked up, overset with awe and love for the miracle of her new life, he bent and kissed his wife's florid cheek, beyond words. The husband's lot imposed by Earl Jieret's legacy jammed like thorn in the heart.

Morning saw him gone, precious time with his dear ones shortened by circumstance beyond his purview to change. Laithen's courage exemplified the tragic necessity. The plight of the clans rode the perilous precipice. No fight in generations had faced such a war, unsupported by Arithon's shadow, or sorcerous backing from Dakar's feats of illusion. Outside the ravines of Tal Quorin's watershed, Deshir offered no advantageous terrain to stage an effective, small-scale defence.

The refreshed, armed campaigns against Rathain's clans would converge when the weather broke in the spring.

Tarens reined his pony towards the open plain, confronted by a thirty-day trek through rough country, alone with the frigid sting of the wind. Provisioned with jerked meat and dried berries, and loop snares for game slung from his belt, he ached for the comforts of Aunt Saffie's kitchen, and the ease of an eiderdown mattress.

"Cosach, my friend," he gasped through the unbearable wrench of leaving his newborn and wife in a canvas hovel. "*Caithdein*, I believe you had your brash priorities straight all along." Subsistence in the free wilds was too harsh to bear, and thankless service for steadfast centuries of due diligence deserved better than the blood prince who had turned his back and forsaken his oath. Earl Jieret's voice was rendered silent, the appalled devastation inflicted by that wound past the pale of the champion who once had sacrificed all for the realm, and true fellowship. The unendurable blow of Arithon's defection surpassed contempt. Death grant the kindness of ambivalence, that Red-beard's selfless end in behalf of his liege had finished, so sorely betrayed.

For the hour when Rathain's crown legacy was most needed, her protectors were left with an empty throne and a lineage effectively ended.

Tarens raged, embittered by the burdensome yoke. For Khadrien, harebrained hero, gone far too young, and for Esfand, halfway unmoored from the world, and for Siantra's limbo of blurred identity, perhaps the last gift in his power to give might forge a changed stake for the future. Then the dual legacy driving his tormented anguish might not have seen his kinfolk in Kelsing abandoned for nothing.

Roundelay

Lysaer s'Ilessid did not march in fine trappings ahead of the dedicate war host leaving Narms. Augmented by the forces overwintered at Morvain, and the High Temple's new divisions transported by galley from Tysan, the assembled advance on Deshir from the west numbered a scant fifteen thousand. They departed to fanfares and snapping banners as spring thaw patched the sere, rounded flanks of the hills flanking Instrell Bay. Ranks freshly recruited since Glory had taken the fallen at Caith-al-Caen, they were commanded by greybeard veterans recalled to field service by mandate.

Supply lines by ship and by cart trains supported the mild first leg of their progress, where sprouted grass greened the meadows and geese flew above the solid, shored stone of the trade-road crossing the flats. Men sang their praise to the Light, in step with the beat of the drums. For duty and righteous reward in the afterlife, they maintained sharp formation, squares dressed into columns across the low grades where the remnant spine of the Mathorns narrowed the way. Past equinox, the downs northward wore burgeoning mantles of wildflowers. The segmented companies snaked downhill, warm sun on their backs, while meltwater roared in frothed cataracts from the heights towards the Tal Quorin basin.

Before the spent flood shoaled the riverbed, and firm footing opened the free wilds of Strakewood and the Plain of Araithe, a lone rider bearing the white flag for parley met the armed vanguard in the roadway.

Twenty leagues south of the ancient stone bridge that spanned the spate at the river mouth, he had reined up, garbed in the drab cloak and patched leathers of a forest clansman.

The Light's first commander halted the march. Flanked by the aggregate company banners snapping in the brisk gusts, he detailed two reliable officers, and a squad of ten men-at-arms to take charge and secure the irregular horseman by force. "Don't be swayed. If the setup's a ploy, you'll be facing the decoy."

A seasoned man on campaign sniffed for rats: barbarian tricks were too ugly, and merciless for the savage, swift strike primed for bloodshed.

Whatever proposition came with the flagged spokesman, the plains gelding he rode was cut out from under him without any civilized over- ture. Yanked from the saddle, he was roughly disarmed, then strapped with bent elbows to his own flagpole by his dead mount's bridle reins. No counterstrike troubled his hostile reception.

Either side of the roadway, the brush tossed in the breeze spiked with salt taint off the bay. No concealed war band erupted from the clumped meadow grass when the armoured escort dragged the prisoner up and threw him facedown before front-ranked authority. No cloud marred the zenith, no harbinger yet of the gathering storm as the Light's first commander surveyed his catch. A suspicious glance measured the fringed buckskin jacket for the concealed seam that might hide a wire garrotte. Rough inspection probed for the hidden knife sheathed in the boot cuff, but found nothing.

The big, fair-haired fellow with the smashed nose met the inimical scrutiny with earnest blue eyes and the forbearance of a dirt-born farmer. Speech packaged in town accents claimed harmless goodwill, then opened the peacekeeper's plea for a treaty, smashed short by the mailed fist of the Light's pugnacious sergeant.

Bait for a laid ambush, or a lying, mad dog: the puzzle earned the commander's dismissive contempt. Countrybred recruits in their grov- elling thousands had shown how readily they hardened under the rigours of training. One fallen in with barbarians would be as quick to assume their sly ways.

A swindling liar of any stripe met short shrift, with forward progress stalled at midday under the onset of fickle weather. "Put chains on the wretch. Then hand him off to the temple's examiner. A True Sect inquest will sort the wickedness out of him."

Horns blared. The drumbeat resumed the timed pace. The massed columns shuddered back into motion, while afternoon blew in mare's tail cloud, and until evening's loured overcast forced the halt to pitch camp ahead of the squall line.

The first Lysaer knew of the man taken prisoner was the ragged scream shrilled through rising gusts after nightfall. Such graphic unpleasantness outpaced sped rumour: the Canon's tribunal had a victim under sorcerous interrogation again. For sound reason, the camp followers steered clear of the tents blazoned with the Sunwheel of the religion. Even glimpsed at second hand, the cruel process inflicted unnatural agony. Nausea and helpless disorientation savaged the subject as, layer by layer, the mind became ransacked and stripped.

The wind blew hard enough to stagger a man hauling a bundle of split wood on his back. Lysaer plodded, half-bent, a safe distance removed, as wave upon wave, the piteous cries racketed through the darkness. The ghastly ordeal knotted qualms in the gut. Men blunted their livid unease as they could. Unrelenting, the shrieks sawed on through their whoops and raucous laughter as queasy nerves piled them into the heaving, hot flesh of the trollops, or roughhouse banter vented their edgy hysteria.

Lysaer cringed all the worse, having once interrupted a True Sect trial up close. His rescue of Dace from such a probe in an East Bransing sailor's dive still revisited his bleakest nightmares. The after-shock's illness had wracked the poor valet for days, with back-lash fevers broken by cold sweats and gruelling hallucinations. Cries such as these had spun vicious dread through the years spent in crippled confinement, locked under guard in the High Temple's bell tower at Erdane.

A sudden grip clapped on Lysaer's shoulder from behind, the steel bite of a dedicate's gauntlet unmistakable. "You!" Impatient authority waylaid him. "That fuel goes elsewhere, with ten more loads wherever it came from. Priests want a stacked pyre for a heretic's roast before the Shadows damned sky opens up and soaks everything."

The wretch under inquest was already condemned, his suffering destined to be extinguished as soon as the Canon examiner cracked his innermost secrets. Few lasted the gristly course for an hour. Grace willing, tonight's luckless subject would break soon. Lysaer emptied his burdened sling at the post, forced to endure the unpleasantness until the laid faggots were oiled in readiness.

Fortune forsook his intent to steer clear when a hooded acolyte singled him out. "Leave your task to another!"

Collared, Lysaer followed, reluctant steps led through the buffeting gusts to the temple pavilion where the gruesome tribunal was in progress. Inside, the glued warmth of red coals in a terra-cotta firepan breathed char through the sickly astringence of camphor. Paned oil lamps tossed, hooked overhead, the gyrating of welter shadows flitted over spread rugs and costly furnishings. Vomit soured the draughts beneath the billowed canvas, wafted from the cerecloth tarp spread for catchment of the splashed effluvia from the examiner's workbench.

Lysaer shrank, hollowed by dread. Past the acolyte, embedded between four burly armed guards, the tormented offender languished in cuffs, stretched on a plank punched by ring bolts that anchored stout chain. A large man, well muscled, his stripped body glistened with sweat. The examiner loomed like a bleached vulture over him, pendulous sleeves turned back and palms cupping the shorn thatch of his quarry's blond hair.

No empanelled jury attended, although the bronze-cornered wardrobes for priestly vestments had been ploughed aside to make space for a clerk's trestle and stool. A field secretary's lap desk, opened for business, suggested an official transcription. Yet the weighted papers were blank, and the pared quill, unused beside the horn inkwell, plunged in and out of the haloed glare cast by the swing of the overhead lamp.

The acolyte thrust his bull's-eye lantern into Lysaer's charge with a steering shove, slurred instructions mumbled through a capacious yawn. "Steady the light for the exalted's dictation. A scribe's on the way."

Lysaer did as bidden, cowed subservience his best cover before an examiner in the rapt pursuit of an arcane entrainment.

The accused thrashed under the on-going punishment, the fair skin of his contorted face welted by old scars from a broken nose. His ragged screams sprayed blood through split lips, gravelled hoarse by relentless anguish. The guards weathered their duty, cringing discomfort suppressed behind their professional poise and glazed stares. The stench of bile pervaded the air, fused with the sweet fetor of funerary oils, blessed and stored in stoppered clay jars to anoint the sainted fallen.

Nerves threatened Lysaer's stomach to revolt as the arcane practitioner sustained the assault, crest upon crest of mindbent agony prying the battered shreds of will for subjugate access. Pressured by inexorable force, the victim's resistance crumbled apace. Moans gave way to the first broken words, wrested through peeled-back lips in defiant Paravian.

Lysaer shivered, jolted alert by a blistering courage he had witnessed before. Jieret Red-beard's fatal torment under the loyal handling of his former war commander, Sulfin Evend, still scoured his waking conscience.

Frayed impatient by the subject's slurred obfuscation, the Canon examiner snapped, "Where's that laggard scribe? He's had time aplenty to fetch the leaguesmen's interpreter."

The upbraided guard fidgeted. "Eminence, the expertise you demand may not be available."

"What?" The priest looked up, incensed. "We have linguists aplenty! Dog trackers keep half a dozen on hire to interrogate their bagged clansfolk!"

"They do." The dedicate guard coughed, his shining helm and immaculate white plume tipped in hesitant defence. "With respect, eminence, the detail's been assigned to the scout's outriders sent on patrol. Top-down orders. If this busy fellow had saboteurs backing him, brass wants the barbaric lot rounded up, roped captive, or dead before sunrise."

The derisive glare raised by secular priority flicked sidewards at the approach of splashed footsteps sprinting through the cloudburst outside. The flap cracked back. A raw gust needled with wet delivered two puffing, soaked figures.

The scribe flapped his sopped cuffs, swore, and squelched to claim his stool. The weathered translator in caped cerecloth behind paused and dripped, nose distastefully wrinkled.

Tirade deflated, the examiner reverted to his singular purpose. The secretary directed the trackers' man to knuckle down quick, pay attention, and render dictation fit for the pen.

Lysaer minded the lamp in precarious need to stay inconspicuous. The grotesque interrogation resumed to the scrape of the quill recording in common tongue. Names, dates, locations, numbers, the list of extracted facts slowly lengthened. The content of the exhaustive entries prickled Lysaer to redoubled uneasiness. Had the blatant inconsistencies flagged the Canon examiner's awareness? For the painstaking responses wrested from the captive were two and a half centuries out of date.

Soon enough the oddity chafed. The examiner's fist cracked into the board beside the prisoner's head. "Damnation curse sorceries to the nethermost pit! This is a Dark-spawned case of possession, aimed by fell design to baffle my inquiry!"

The translator shuffled his feet and demurred. "Information's not worthless. Most patterns of migration and old redoubts are still used. Matched against recent lines of defence, some won't have changed over the years." His gesture encompassed the scribe, pen laid aside to stretch his cramped fingers. "Permission's requested to deliver the compiled notes to our captain at once."

The examiner stroked his tucked chin, his flushed exhilaration undampened by the violent weather shaking the pavilion. His narrowed regard surveyed the stretched meat on his board, puddled in leaked urine and rendered slack-jawed beneath the bruising that ringed bloodshot eyes. "Very well," he allowed, mellowed to complaisancy since the subdued client was physically spent. "Take a guardsman with you to corroborate. The other dedicates and the scribe have my leave for relief."

If an overlaid personality obfuscated his inquiry, he had coarser methods to dig deeper. The assay to strip the core spirit to its birth-born identity was best undertaken without squeamish distractions.

The parties released in dismissal filed out, crowding elbows in their haste to escape the unsavoury particulars. When the flap slapped shut at their heels, Lysaer found himself beckoned forward.

Pulverized by fear of discovery, he hunched into his overgrown beard and kept his lowered gaze fixed on the carpet.

"Bring that lamp over here!" The summons followed the temple examiner's stalking tread into the jumble of storage chests and stacked furnishings. While the squall's fury sheeted over pegged canvas, his pampered hands ferreted out a particular jewelled coffer. He unlocked the lid, removed a weighty, bagged item, then waved at the grisly, stained plank. "Shine that light in the minion's eyes."

Lysaer did as required in vexed desperation, undone past reprieve if the temple talent glanced up. But the Canon's robed priest had eyes for nothing else but unveiling the heavy gold maul just retrieved from his consecrated paraphernalia. Not a relic for ceremonial display: the encrusted glitter of jewels and the graven Sunwheel of the religion embellished a torturer's implement.

Lamp and bearer ignored, the inquisition proceeded. The prisoner moaned, strained throat cracked by an earsplitting scream as the next probe pierced his mind and re-established a psychic connection. "I want your true name!" the examiner intoned.

The subject retched, a Paravian oath ejected through foamed lips. His second cry shrilled and trailed off, ripped by a shudder of helpless agony before he ground out a reluctant response. "Jieret. Red-beard. S'Valerient."

Impossible! Lysaer flinched, the lantern flame juddered by his appalled start.

The talent priest hissed at the lapse, too immersed to divide his attention. Wedded to the Light's glory, he must not realize his victim had claimed the identity of a dead man! *An ancient ghost, tortured to his destruction then run through by the sword and burned as a corpse by Lysaer s'Ilessid's own hand:* the unconscionable atrocity exhumed under torment stemmed from the winter campaign in Daon Ramon Barrens two hundred and sixty years in the past!

Oblivious to the resurrected echo of that nightmare incident, the examiner dogged his objective, unswerving. "No more lies and evasion! I'll have the name bestowed by your natural mother at birth!"

He bore in, drilling through his captive's deflection with a savagery that creaked joints and quivered overstrung muscle. Rapine of the mind wrung a harrowing cry, wrenched from crushed hope and demolished resistance. And still, the gasped reply stayed insistent. "Dania named me!"

"Truly? No. Surely not." The priest changed his approach and slammed down the mallet. The blow thudded into the prisoner's stretched wrist. The sharp crunch of bone raised the inhuman, shrilled cry of an animal dragged down and flayed under the knife.

Lysaer squeezed his eyes shut, riven by nausea. He could not escape. Could not block his hearing, as in broken phrases jerked through seizures, the chained man on the plank yielded his natural identity.

The bravest effort undone at the last, a wretch put to the question by a Canon examiner would betray his own children and family. Born a crofter in Kelsing, once wanted for killing a vested Sunwheel diviner, the broken husk shivered and wept, his fragmented secrets laid open to ransack. Like Earl Jieret before him, the tormented fellow wished for the good sense to die before beaten flesh saw his ethic undone. The base drive for survival robbed preference instead. The pitiless glare of Lysaer's lamp exposed all of his savaged dignity, while the True Sect examiner rummaged at will through his violated identity.

The next query struck, excruciate, pure fire that razed into the tormented man's temples. He lost breath to scream, the dregs of gasped air expelled from his seized lungs wrenched to nerve-stunned paralysis.

"I'll have the rest from you before the end!" The Light's examiner reversed his jewelled mallet. Drunk on cruelty, he jammed the spiked handle into the pulped mangle of the man's shackled wrist. "You, Tarens, are the corrupt associate of the Spinner of Darkness!" Spittle flew from the priest's moistened lips, as he shouted, "Tell me where the world's accursed evil has nested! Give me Arithon, called Master of Shadow."

That name, spoken by a trained talent with forceful intent to impose domination, struck like a tolled bell with the focused impetus to wake Desh-thiere's curse. Lysaer had no chance to shy from the impact. Lashed by the geas, full face, he stared down at the tortured supplicant chained to the plank. Blue eyes ablaze with unnatural hatred met the unhinged gaze of the victim suborned under an arcane inquiry: and the imperative probe of the True Sect talent entangled them both. One galvanic instant of naked exposure shredded the tissue of Iyat-thos Tarens's destabilized identity and impelled the disastrous recoil of recognition.

"*You!*" The horrified exclamation arose from *Earl Jieret's* graphic recall. Coercion would not betray his absent liege. Instead, his next word would identify the scruffy roustabout who assisted the priest with the lamp.

Lysaer reacted, first. Spurred by self-preservation, he spun and smashed his lantern into the tranced face of the True Sect examiner. Heated panes shattered. The florid man shrieked. Blinded by spattered oil and fragmented glass, he staggered backwards, tripped up, and toppled into the welter of displaced baggage. His nape cracked against a brass-cornered trunk. Unconscious or stunned, he sprawled inert amid crumpled silk vestments.

Curse-driven, Lysaer gave rein to murder and grabbed the fallen grip of the Light's blessed mallet. His vicious blow crunched through skull and soft tissue, then hammered until the pulped hulk of the priest thrashed in fatal seizures, never to rise.

Lysaer snatched the keys from the brained corpse's belt. Seconds before the kicked wrath of the hornets' nest, he knocked over the pyramid of crockery urns. Funerary herbs cloyed the air, spread by the gurgling flood of spilled oil. Lysaer hurled the lamp. Open flame spattered across the wool carpet. As the wicked fuel spluttered and ignited, Lysaer rifled the priest's embroidered stole. He twisted the silk for desecrate use as a rag and bound Tarens's mouth. "You can't scream, understand?"

Then he bundled the befouled tarp over the manacled captive, hauled the laden plank off the trestles, and manoeuvred his ungainly trophy to the pavilion's rear wall. The scribe's stolen penknife rent the tough seam. Burst through parted canvas, Lysaer dragged Tarens bodily into the black, windy night and the blinding drench of cold rain.

Foul weather had harried the sentries to shelter and doused the camp's outlying torches to sullen coals. Gusts plucked the last feeble, guttering flames. Half-glimpsed under downpour and wheeling shadow, a swathed corpse with a roustabout scarcely merited questions. Far less a butcher's carcass consigned for disposal from an examiner's inquiry perhaps miscalled on an innocent.

Lysaer hastened, head down, past the officers' tents. Too cautious to run, he skidded through skinned grass and splashed mud, avoiding the socketed banners and the hindrance of tent stakes looped with guy lines. Circumstance favoured him. A night camp on the march wasted no labour on lyme pits. Expediency dumped the dead of least conse-quence on the wild heath and abandoned them to the vermin. Lysaer bypassed the darkened cook shack without challenge. He skirted the steaming, soaked fires, half-roasted joints left sodden on the spits in the driving downpour. Slackened oversight let him steal a lamb shank. The few scurrying figures paid little notice to a pilferer's salvage, shoved into the bundled tarp on the lam.

The provost's inspectors, who should have cared, preferred to stay huddled under dry cover. Only one bothered to poke at the canvas.

"Mind the puke!" ribbed his fellow.

Laughter followed, the disgusted man swearing over the vile taint on the glove raised to swipe streaming wet from eyes.

"Get gone!" snapped their sergeant, drawn by the complaint.

Lysaer heaved his ungainly load forward. Beyond the horse lines, he slewed through the latrine ditch and threaded the gauntlet of the perim-eter sentries. Past sight of their vigilance, he broke into a sprint and plunged into the pitch-black scrub beyond.

Shouts erupted behind, raised as the temple pavilion caught fire and hurled the camp into confusion. Sleepers kicked from their blankets formed bucket brigades, while the examiner's guardsmen found away from their active duty scrambled under sharp questions to frame their excuses.

"Shadows-damned captive was a clan spokesman, put to the question for likely possession." The damning conclusion rang bitter in review. "Light's ruin upon him, that white flag of truce planted us with a Dark-spawned Sorcerer!"

The examiner's bones were raked from the steamed coals, with the devilsome search for the absconded minion foisted into the lap of the high command's cross-grained watch officer.

"No sense giving chase in the dark. Slippery clan weasels just vanish like smoke. Let the Leagues' dogs unravel the trail when the storm breaks, then follow up with armed patrols to sweep the thickets and leave nothing standing."

Drenched to the skin, and freezing with anger, the rankled commander pivoted into collision with the talent diviner who sidled up at his flank. Disentangled, swearing, he backstepped as the creature's uncanny focus hackled him to raking chills. "Clear my way!" Prepared to shove past, he heard the fellow's insistent response despite the impetuous prod of his irritation.

"Want help? The late examiner's inquest cracked the riddle behind the clansfolks' barbaric abilities. By turning their hunter's tactics against them, I might narrow the fugitive's lead on your dogs a bit faster . . ."

Earl Jieret s'Valerient had endured the excruciate horror, hauled wounded and blind off a winter battlefield, in Lysaer's hands under Desh-thiere's cursed influence. Tarens confronted the same ugly fate. Jounced in chains on a plank, he spluttered, half-drowned by the torrential downpour. Shattering agony thrashed him incoherent. Forced to endure, he gained no relief. The escape of unconsciousness eluded him. His mangled wrist, and a head reamed by the fiery after-shock of an arcane inquisition wracked him dizzy. The sodden gag forced between his bitten lips muffled his moans, while inherited memory inflamed a torment made worse by his desperate helplessness. He was not born to Jieret's stern fibre; had not sustained the cruel inquisition without spilling his guts.

Arithon's rescue would not spare him this time. He had strayed too far from clanbred tradition, and farther still from his family in Kelsing.

Tears or rain, his face streamed. Sobered hindsight made a travesty of his remorse. Cry mercy, how Laithen s'Idir would come to rue her intervention that day, when she had checked Cosach's hasty sword for his escort, that saw Esfand and Siantra home by way of the Arwent Gorge.

All the good and the bad impelled by his choices led him to this brutal crux. Tarens ached. How by any measure of loyalty had he come to betray everyone and *everything* dear to him? If threat to Kerelie and Efflin's well-being had died with him under a Canon trial at Kelsing, today's immeasurably greater forfeiture might have been averted. Jieret's antique knowledge of terrain and clan redoubts yet supported the backbone of old-blood survival. Tonight's confession seized under duress would inform the Light's next campaign in appalling detail.

The lives of his wife and infant daughter in Fallowmere thrown to risk for the barking-mad notion he might, in vain arrogance, have brokered the prospect of peace.

Now in the custody of Lysaer s'Ilessid, his fate met disaster. Tarens gagged on bile and bleak consolation, that disclosure of Efflin and Kerelie's names at least had perished with the slain examiner. Now, his plight mirrored Jieret's, retained as the key to bait Arithon to his destruction. No matter that goodwill between them had ended in sore words and ill will at Ithamon. Tarens had cut off a friend, then torched the last bridge in hot temper for nothing.

The plank banged over a rock. Slewed to shooting pain by the grate of smashed bone, Tarens throttled a shriek that scarcely pierced the gush of hard rainfall. Uphill or down, the punishment jounced onwards. He seized, retching, unmoored by spun senses. Jieret's excoriating remembrance mapped the relentless predicament imposed upon Tarens as hostage. Ready weapon against the vulnerability of s'Ffalenn compassion, his survival yielded a leverage as powerful as Valien's slaughtered innocence.

Gasping and sick, Tarens reeled in despair, shivering and soaked in the black, roaring wind, and strung in agony over the abyss. Lysaer would not be twice cozened to let a crucial captive slip through his grasp. Clever, cursed, and beyond ruthlessly murderous, the man pressured his inhuman stamina past quarter.

The only frayed thread in common between them was the fugitive's priority to outrun the True Sect pursuit.

Tarens suffered the course, chills burned away by the back-lash fever of after-shock. Delirium spiralled his suffering into nightmares, riddled by the gamut of terror and remorse.

Night passed. The rain lessened. Flat terrain dimpled with vernal bogs gave way to rolling foothills clothed in pin oak and gorse. The gouging, raw scrape of the plank, towed and bumped over granite punched through Tarens's wheeling disorientation. Lysaer laboured up the knife-cut crest of a steepening scarp, half-lit by the grey gleam of an overcast dawn when at length his staggered strides faltered. He tripped. The board slewed, jerked from his white-knuckled grip.

Tarens slammed into damp ground, broken wrist savaged by the attached shackle as he tumbled downslope. The gag strangled his scream. Wracked breathless, he whimpered as his abused body tumbled to rest. He lay strapped on his back, spilled from the shed tarp, his side gouged by the singed joint of filched meat.

Patched vision returned. The sky brightened above him. Alarmed instinct woke to the immediate threat posed by leaguesmen set on their back trail. Flight would take them no farther. Lysaer sat, streaming sweat. Shoulders heaving, wind spent, he cradled his head on the wrists draped across his drawn-up knees.

Small use to crow for the irony, that Tarens recouped so pathetic an edge for advantage. Still at risk of Canon retribution, beyond terrified of their diviners, he tested the gag with his jaw. The soaked knots were intractable. But refined, soggy silk, worked against his set teeth, might be frayed under stress.

The sky lightened. Ravens flew like soot ash in the vale below, a raucous, excitable flock likely mobbing a predator. A fox, or a wildcat, Tarens prayed, unstrung by grief beyond measure. His small band of scouts had parted his company under orders not to involve themselves in his insane venture. Ath grant his plea, that stubborn clan loyalty had not enticed them to linger. Their skills in the wilds sustained their concealment. But if they broke from cover with armed searchers abroad, any foolhardy attempt at his rescue would end on the thirsty knives of the scalpers.

Full daylight coloured the soaked vegetation when the shredded gag gave at last under punishment.

Perhaps warned by his prisoner's marginal triumph, Lysaer lifted his head. "We'll have to eat and move on straightaway." He arose, movement stiffened from overexertion, and retrieved the congealed mutton shank from the ground.

"Food won't matter," Tarens croaked, "unless we throw off the hounds. That haunch, some plucked hair, and several green twigs should suffice. You have a knife? Then cut a few finger-length sticks. Notch both ends and sharpen the tips into points."

Frost blue, Lysaer's eyes, as the winter zenith. "Filthy barbarian traps?"

"For dogs." Tarens coughed, lids pinched against misery. "Other means are preferred to deflect armoured men." Jabbed by the warning unease, as if closing pursuit harrowed the backcountry too swiftly, he resumed his hoarse advice. "Bend the sticks. Use the hair strand to bind the bowed ends together. Wrap them in meat. The tracker's pack will gobble them whole. Digestion will break down the hair in their stomachs, and the twig—"

"Springs straight from inside and impales them, I see. A gruesome technique for expedient slaughter." Lysaer scrubbed his bearded face with chapped hands. Weary past artifice, the statesman's mask slipped. His own straits evidently required an expedient distance from the dedicates' reach. "I presume you also know how to snare game?"

Tarens twitched his sound arm to a metallic clink. "Not while I'm in chains. Can't carve a snare either, one-handed, or fashion the means to waylay the league scalpers."

"Since I can't drag you farther, you'll walk on two feet." Lysaer stood, in guarded possession of the priest's key for the shackles. "Don't imagine I'm setting you free."

Grey on grey, the furtive suggestion of movement flickered between the backlit brush rimming the skyline. Tarens glimpsed the moth flit of what might be a hooded shadow, or several, at the edge of peripheral vision. The same covert presence had stalked him four years ago on a barren slope in the Skyshiels en route to Darkling.

The fool's risk seemed worth taking, with nothing to lose.

He pulled a strained breath, chanced the hunch he brokered with more than a figment, and forced a plaintive appeal through his skinned throat. "You only want me alive as your wretched hostage to hunt down and kill Arithon s'Ffalenn."

Eight silent shadows rose out of the ground. Tarens spared his curse-bent adversary no warning as the Biedar dartmen raised their slim blowpipes and let fly on Lysaer from behind.

Fallen

Beyond Iyat-thos Tarens as eyewitness, other signal powers on Athera observed the drugged darts let fly by the Biedar warriors in northern Rathain. Paravian visionaries of the *dient haylios* took quiet stock from their eyrie vantages at Alestron, Caith-al-Caen, and ancient Ithamon. The Reiyaj Seeress, enthroned on her gimballed chair, watched in lock-step as the southern sun dipped her tower vantage in gold at the advent of sunrise. Ath's adepts sensed the tremor in the etheric web, not moved in reaction to worldly event but aware of the precarious flicker of change riffled between past and future. Lodged at Atchaz in a silk-spinner's loft, a slack prophet sweating amid muddled bedclothes tossed and turned in fell dreams, unawakened.

Of those who Saw, only two responded.

Fast as a ricochet, while the curse-driven target just punctured folded to his knees and sprawled unconscious in the Mathorn foothills, a request from the Warden at Althain Tower touched she who was Mother Dark's Shadow, incarnate as eldest crone in Sanpashir.

A bristled appeal for her audience had been expected long before her dartmen struck down the blood scion of s'Ahelas called Lysaer s'Ilessid.

She would not be summoned from her underground shrine, carved deep into bed-rock beneath the volcanic sands of the southern desert. Sheathed in her black veils, seated cross-legged within the interlaced circles of serpentine carvings, the ancient opened her seamed eyelids.

The whorled symbols sewn into her hems seemed alive in the dance of cast flame light. Glass-and-bone fetishes clinked on her wrist as she raised her upturned palm, the gesture a grant of permission. The Sorcerer's appeal for her consultation brooked answer, provided Sethvir left his station to meet upon her sovereign ground.

Such was his urgency, he did not decline.

Breeze stirred the air in the round chamber, where no natural wind deigned to venture. A whispered sigh trembled through sacrosanct silence, broken but faintly by the distanced plink of water from a buried seep. The velvet quiet lay textured with the moist smells of earth and hot oil, ingrained by the dusky smoke of smouldered ceremonial herbs. The disturbance unfurled by the arcane arrival ceased as though snuffed at the instant of manifestation.

Sethvir, Warden of Althain, stood upright before her Aspected presence, his formal maroon robe cuffed with jet-braid interlace traced in carmine and shadow by the shimmer of birch embers laid in the coal pot before her.

Effectively blind beyond direct mage-sight, Sethvir bowed. His linked earth-sense did not connect in this place, a hazard that spiked his uneasiness. Nothing might shake the pending anxiety that lurked just past the dimmed range of the probable. Nonetheless, without hurry, he bestowed the due courtesy of his respect. "Manyfold blessing, Ancestral Grandmother of the Tribes."

Within her laired presence, whatever reached him came by her design, tendered through her uncanny wisdom, or by her partnered vision through the sun-scalded eyes of the Reiyaj Seeress. Here, Fellowship Sorcerers knew to walk softly. In particular Sethvir, whose justified plea for a boon had received naught in return. His call for the return of Arithon's fate had been met by a seven-month span of blank silence.

The entangled heritage invoked by Requiar's descent inflected the airless quiet between two elder entities whose interests throughout Athera's Third Age had sometimes aligned, and other times tussled, diametrically opposed.

"Starborn." The Biedar eldest inclined her mantled head. Charms chinked in the gloom as she folded her wrinkled, linked hands in her lap. She waited, unlikely to volunteer speech past the scope of any petitioner's asking.

Sethvir phrased his opening with utmost care. "Permit me to say what I know from the standpoint of my observation."

The shrouded figure relented a fraction. "You may sit. Tea will be brought. Hospitality is sacred, and goodwill is earned for the grace of the Seven's restraint. No small feat was accomplished at Forthmark by way of your colleagues' courageous forbearance."

Sethvir withheld his sharp censure. The Biedar debt rendered against Koriathain may have levelled one ancient score. But closure on that count yet exacted a frightening, unresolved price: the abrupt acquisition of revised values imposed upon Dragonkind roiled the unquiet aftermath, and saddled the Seven with an unpredictable array of forthcoming consequence. Davien's rapt vigil on the splinter world past Northgate sifted the disrupted patterns of hierarchy, hampered without the Protectorate's counsel while Ozvowzakrin's absence extended throughout his wounded recovery.

The radiant embers offset the pervasive, dank chill of the sequestered cavern. Sethvir seated himself on the stone floor, engraved with eldritch ciphers that fooled static vision, shifting with movement like blended views stitched through time and parallel, alternate space. To focus too long on the templates that altered vibration caused disorientation that beckoned the mind towards madness. No longer quite mortal, Sethvir averted his sight from the maze nonetheless, while a cat-footed young woman delivered a brass tray with a clay pot and two wooden saucers. Through twining steam, and the murk of her veils, the crone's black eyes glinted like gimlets couched in the seamed sills of dark eyelids.

"Arithon triumphed, but I gather he is not freed of Requiar's blood obligation." Sethvir accepted the refreshment he was handed, raised the filled vessel in grave salute, then savoured a first sip as the invited guest.

None but a rank fool broke the pause before the crone lifted her face cloth and drank in turn.

When she set her bowl down, he continued. "You did not release him back to our charge, although Kharadmon has been faithful to the letter of our given word. The Koriathain's records and books with the spell-crafted sigils for necromancy and forced domination now are purged from Athera."

Yet the Biedar's ancestral grandmother yielded credit only where credit was due. "Three cults of necromancy took root on this world, branched from the sisterhood's theft of our ancient rites. Two will pass out of living memory with time, if covenant is kept by your Fellowship. Although they are destined to perish, extinct, one last form yet remains to be conquered."

Sethvir swallowed more tea, a syrup-thick blend of rootstock and steeped leaves whose robust bitterness was gilded with wild honey. "Desh-thiere is our doom, and Mankind's, to answer." The captive, trapped spirits embedded in mist under Rockfell Peak yet posed a virile threat to the mysteries vital to Paravian continuity.

The pixie's pucker of mischief erased from his wrinkled features, Sethvir ploughed ahead. "Last year, Arithon ventured to Alestron and received a hearing with Tehaval Warden. I know he pleaded for an intervention on behalf of Lysaer s'Ilessid, declared outcast from our Fellowship's bonded protection under the compact. Arithon begged for a stay upon grounds of kinship, that Paravian judgement not befall his half brother before his attempt to facilitate a redemption."

"Tehaval refused," the crone allowed. Two stripped words, unequivocal, acknowledged his tact: Sethvir forbore to disclose a private confidence not under his purview to share. Bone and glass clinked as the eldest stirred. Her open hand, yet again, yielded courteous acknowledgement of the Sorcerer's need for elaboration in detail.

"Arithon went on to ascend Rockfell Peak. Asandir and Davien were led to believe he meant to meddle, likely to remove himself from we Seven's good graces and force the terms of our severance from royal inheritance." Sethvir's effusive pause met blank silence. Then he said, "When that tactic apparently failed, Arithon provoked Verrain's challenge at Mirthlvain, which accomplished his aim. Asandir revoked his sanction as crown prince of Rathain."

The crone verified the nuance withheld. "Your prince insisted upon the clean ethic, that Requiar's obligation laid on him might cross the grain of his oath of feal service."

Sethvir sighed, come at last to his purpose. "Yet now I suspect that abdication was the lesser motivation behind Arithon's extreme actions. Today I fear to insist I know why."

Speech failed, after all, to state the implication: *because if Tehaval's stay upon Lysaer's case already had been granted to another party beforehand, Arithon's foray to Rockfell hinged on a deeper intent.*

Strong drink did nothing for Sethvir's parched throat. While the eldritch, carved patterns whispered into the void suctioned out by the stifled span of his greater earth-sense, he ploughed through his painful reluctance. "Arithon braved a visit to the Reiyaj Seeress in desperation to ascertain whether his awful deduction was wrong. She confirmed to the contrary."

The crone's gravid stillness swelled the enclosed space, the vast tonnage of earth and rock overhead a force crushed under felted silence. Sethvir placed his enquiry. "I am here as the Fellowship's spokesman to clarify that you were the party who laid prior claim to Lysaer's stay from Tehaval Warden. I dare say this morning your dartmen were sent to collect."

"Lysaer s'Ilessid is Requiar's issue, out of s'Ahelas through Meiglin s'Dieneval." The crone's reedy response held the timbre of sorrow. "We mark and measure the worthy by character. Just as your s'Ffalenn prince was tested, and likewise, Elaira, his mate, Lysaer s'Ilessid has been weighed as well. On his hour of trial he was twice found wanting. Third on the balance determines his fate."

The naked truth cut. Sethvir owned no solid ground for defence. Earth-sense confirmed that Desh-thiere's geas alone had spared Tarens his life: firstly, lest Lysaer s'Ilessid's exposure reveal his identity to the priests, and secondly, for his worth as a hostage to engineer Arithon's betrayal. No moral grace had answered the royal drive to seek justice. The ex-crofter's rescue had been anything but a principled act to defend blameless innocence.

Only Sulfin Evend had surmounted his liege's cursed instincts during the siege of Alestron. None since had surmounted the thankless endeavour. Davien's timely intervention alone had spared Daliana from retribution upon the dark hour her love was cast off.

"Why?" Sethvir pressed the last point through his tight apprehension. "Or have you not just laid claim to a man proven fatally flawed as the catalyst for your preferred instrument?"

"You have not guessed?" The crone spoke aloud to affirm the logic behind the conundrum. "The last bastion of necromancy on Athera must fall, both for Biedar debt and Requiar's sworn burden of ancestral accountability. You Seven must stand in defence of Athera's mysteries. Davien believed the last path to atonement for Lysaer ran through the maze under Kewar, and past question, the man lacks the ethical strength to survive the attempt. There is one other way. That path crosses through the Mistwraith's prison in Rockfell Pit."

Sethvir shut his eyes, blistered to the heart. For he *had Seen* the thread of the crone's binding unfold in the preternatural fullness of terrible clarity. She would toss Lysaer's lot to Desh-thiere's consumption, and Arithon, by the compassionate drive of his ancestry, would strive by free choice to recover him.

The crone's judgement on the outcome was ice. "Kewar's maze promised failure. You knew this well before Lysaer's injured rejection cast off
the gift of Daliana's immaculate loyalty. With his salvation entangled by
the Mistwraith's design, Biedar obligation seeks closure. Your Fellowship's
only chance remains open thereby. Athera's weal and Paravian sovereignty
may survive Mankind's failures."

Which absolute purpose ruled the Seven's response, cemented under
the binding bestowed by the dragons: no gift of consolation at all. None.
Sethvir felt swallowed up within Mother Dark's lair. The hag had the
Sorcerers' interests collared. They had to stand firm. Just as Arithon
before them, after his forlorn plea to the Reiyaj Seeress, the Fellowship
must stride forward in step on the glimmer of hope proffered by the
crone's frightful gambit. Take the informed stand at the forefront and
stare into the darkness unflinching, or cave in to retreat, wide awake to
the truth: only one way embraced mastery.

Set under the crucible, strength and flaws were two sides of the same
spinning coin. Choice, not chance, would determine the outcome.

Sethvir finished his tea. Severed moment to moment from his
earth-link to Athera, he dared not dally while events moved apace beyond
his keen oversight. While the chamber's web of strung silence thrummed
at plucked nerves that felt slack as a damp string, he gave thanks in
tribute, then requested his leave with implacable patience.

The Biedar ancient tendered her gracious dismissal. Ever and always,
her favours were edged. She gave him the posited trial of agony and
defeat, laid against the tenuous glimmer of light that might wrest back
a precarious victory. Not only the doom of two royal half brothers, but
Traithe's hale recovery, and Athera's intact mysteries hung on the
Mistwraith's requited banishment.

Aside from the wounding tangle of sentiment, the Biedar eldest's directive and the long-term aim of the Fellowship Sorcerers were one and the
same. Means never justified the moral end. Yet the crone in her wise way
had been merciful. She had lifted the inconsolable, unconscionable weight
and ensured Arithon would shoulder his half brother's cause on his own.
He would act to free Lysaer and rise to the necessity without the unbearable, cruel obligation binding the Seven to undertake the exigent request.

Sethvir was not too mean, nor lacking in the generous spirit to grant
his acknowledgement as he rose to depart. "Count on our Fellowship
to stand behind your ancestral cause to the end."

The crone inclined her head, then paid him a tribute, eldritch bracelets chiming as she turned back her sable veils. Low light traced the
liquid tracks of the tears streaming down her seamed cheeks. "Be wary,
old friend. Guard your back every step."

Sethvir bowed to her. Better than any, he understood the import of
her cryptic warning. More than his dire memory of the perils invoked
by the vile practice of necromancy haunted him: a scar as long as his
arm crossed his groin, past horror scored into his living flesh by the
darkest rite of foul perversion.

Tarens opened his crusted eyes, sight speared by the jewel-toned sparkle
of midday sun off the wet scrub. The unbudded vegetation of early spring
fell away, a tangled, brown mat patched pale yellow downslope where
new grass speared through the sere folds of the Mathorn foothills. The
calm wore the lingering nip of night's chill. He must not have languished
unconscious for long. Sodden ground where he sprawled had dampened
his clothes. Puddles silvered the pocketed hollows from the departed
storm's drenching downpour.

Nothing moved on the heights beyond the brisk wind, chasing the
shadows of broken clouds across the untenanted vales. No hounds bayed
in excited pursuit, not yet. Only birdsong sliced the expansive quiet, the
flit of small sparrows dispersed by the gusts that whined over lichened
rock and riffled the tossed clumps of furze.

Tarens took cautious stock, muddled under the after-shock of abuse
that knitted pain through his stiffened sinews. The examiner's art had
kicked his innards to pulp, and jabbed needles and tongs through a
ringing skull that felt packed with boiled flannel. Tarens shivered, teeth
clenched through a spasm of nausea. Whether he had been darted by
Biedar warriors, or if their eerie tricks had foisted an enspelled sleep
upon him mattered little.

Lysaer s'Ilessid seemed nowhere in evidence. Presumably the man
had been removed by the same tribal hands that had sprung his locked
shackles. Past alliance with Arithon counted for something, apparently.
A field splint bound Tarens's crushed wrist, the dull throb of injury
expertly dressed and treated with an herbal compress.

Tarens tried to sit up. The wracked breath he drew to steady his rushed
dizziness delivered the smoke taint of fire and cooked meat. Whatever
his trials, the tribesmen had not abandoned him to languish from hunger.

"My work," corrected a deep voice like burled granite in response to the plucked stream of his unspoken thought. "The dartmen have gone. Eat while you can. This is no place to linger."

Recognition compounded Tarens's unease. No one met Asandir of the Fellowship under felicitous circumstance.

The Sorcerer's step paused nearly on top of him. Tarens's pained effort to rise met the hard, callused grip that steadied him upright. His battered flesh received the touch like a tonic. Lifted from the dull glaze of malaise and exhaustion, Tarens realized the Sorcerer had been present for some time. The uncanny black stallion grazed at large, stripped of tack, coat rubbed down to ebony silk. A small, smokeless fire built of dry brush roasted neat cuts of snared game. Also the embarrassment embedded in coals: the charred lump of the haunch never sliced into bait for the snares aimed to foul the headhunters' tracking dogs.

"I have other means to waylay blameless mastiffs," Asandir said, a straightforward reproof stemming from sadness for the mishandled usage of four-footed creatures.

Tarens feared to ask what brought a Fellowship presence to wait on his forsaken straits. Even one clad for the field in tough leathers, cloaked in a travel-worn mantle redolent of horse sweat, crushed grass, and birch smoke.

Asandir was not forthcoming. Glass hard, his stark survey throttled discussion until the spare explanation surfaced, unasked. "I need a messenger to Rathain's northern clan enclaves with my urgent warning to relocate." The hindrance posed by a mauled wrist caught short shrift. "May I? The Biedar are skilled healers, but the damage you suffer cannot be properly set. You have pulverized splinters of bone that will fuse the joint without prompt intervention."

Tarens yielded his bandaged infirmity into a clasp ephemeral as the brush of a moth's wing. Dread diverted into nervous speech, he enquired, "Lysaer's no longer here?"

"He's with Sanpashir's people, his fate taken outside of my purview." Asandir bent his head, silver hair whipped by the freshening breeze across the jut of cragged features. Brief quiet, then a spoken phrase in actualized Paravian unleashed an electrical surge through Tarens's maimed arm. He cried out, flushed by heat and rocked by a rush of tingling, vibrant sensation. Shaken and terrified, he screwed his eyes shut.

Yet the limb released back to his provenance was whole, the tentative flex of five fingers restored by a power beyond comprehension.

Past patience for marvels, Asandir visited his trim cookfire and fetched the skinned sapling used for a spit. He snapped the stick to split the portions of his jointed hare and passed half to Tarens. Then he folded long legs, parked on a boulder, and tucked into his share.

Common sense overcame hesitation. Tarens perched shoulder to shoulder and ate, conversation suspended throughout the efficient consumption of the rough fare. When the stripped bones had been tossed for the foxes, and the cookfire snuffed, the black horse came at some unseen cue to be saddled and bridled.

Asandir spoke, large hands busy with buckles. "You'll ride, also. This country is no longer safe."

Tarens glanced where his cryptic gesture directed. A rough-coated bay gelding with pricked ears wandered at large up the slope. A marred blessing, the animal came equipped with a clan hackamore and surcingle strapped with a fallen scout's bedroll. Tarens caught its trailing reins with a pang, distressed for the dead friend whose belongings he recognized. The earlier scrimmage of squabbling ravens had not flocked to animal carrion in the lowlands thickets. "Dharkaron Avenge! My band should have been secure under their skilled talent this far into the free wilds."

"I am sorry." Astride his black stud, Asandir faced forward, his graven profile hewn out of rock. "I arrived too late to turn the armed patrol, even had the plight of your scouts brooked the time for delay." The admission masked grief, not apology. The Sorcerer rendered no judgement for those needlessly lost. Nor did he excoriate Tarens's culpability, or soften the bitter disclosure, that their demise had sprung from the ill-gotten insight handed on to the temple's diviner. "The re-establishment of heightened resonance eventually would have enabled townbred talent to manipulate flux as the clan hunters do, in any event."

Tarens vaulted astride, left to wrestle his guilt for the lapse on his merits. Past question, he lamented the misguided hope that had lured him astray for the straw hope of treating with townborn. "I ought not to have overstepped clan tradition. Laithen was right."

"Was she?" Asandir's oblique glance showed surprising acceptance. "Desh-thiere's invasion has extracted a toll beyond the most steadfast commitment. Fellowship strength has fallen short many times, with clanblood shed to salvage the deficit."

The admission broached tragedy too grievous to bear. Tarens winced for the unspoken referent to the alliance war host that once inflicted Earl Jieret's horrific demise. *That historic invasion of Daon Ramon should have been forestalled by charter right, had the Sorcerers not been too sorely beset for a remedial response.*

Tarens owned too much heart to find fault or lay blame. Had he faced the past high earl's forsaken dilemma, he never could have shouldered the battle plan Arithon had devised against odds to stave off a sweeping defeat. The bitter sacrifice that had claimed the lives of Jieret and his Companions resounded yet from the stanzas of legend.

Asandir carried his sorrows unflinching, his endurance past the pale of regret as sparrows winged from the budding scrub, and the black stud picked a downhill path through rough footing. "The hero whose memories became your inheritance paid in full for our breach of trust. The Seven's lasting debt to him cannot be reconciled. The choice was forced on us. Because our dwindled number bypassed his crown prince's need, we met our priority to preserve the grand conduit driving the mysteries."

Shamed by a might that bowed to sad necessity, Tarens stiffened the nerve hollowed out by last night's wracking ordeal. "What does the land's need require of me?"

Asandir's smile resurged like spring sunlight through cloud. "I need you to ride! Go at speed to Deshir with my urgent directive to lead Rathain's people to Fallowmere. Take them to ground within Drimwood's glens farthest north of the trade-road and enjoy the summer's respite with your wife and child."

Tarens stared. The bottom dropped out of his gut. This call for an urgent withdrawal was not the mandated recoil from an advance by the Light's western war host. Nor any graceful request to clear the Plain of Araithe for a scheduled return of Athera's Paravians.

Disquieted by what seemed an inexplicable reticence, Tarens queried at a hoarse whisper. "What does your Fellowship fear?"

The field Sorcerer's hard-set regard never wavered, the rebirth of life on the greening vales a fragile reflection in mirror-grey eyes. Upright as steel in the black stallion's saddle, with phrases that seared for blunt honesty, he divulged Sethvir's word regarding the end that awaited Lysaer at the hands of the Biedar. "The posited surety follows, that Arithon will challenge the Mistwraith's possession at Rockfell Pit. He will try to salvage his half brother's fate, no matter the cost paid in consequence."

And anguish chiselled those obdurate, creased features for that burden, since the royal gift of compassion driving that confrontation was Fellowship given. Culpability lay with the Seven, whatever befell the man who would set forth alone against Desh-thiere's wraiths at the crux.

"Merciful Ath, I should never have left him!" cried Tarens, the Sorcerer's desolation momentarily shared.

Asandir shook his head. "There was no path forward from Ithamon, for any of us, when the walls at Etarra came down."

The grate of shod hooves, and the sparkle of dew on damp grasses filled a pause incongruous as a desecration.

"I will defend the free-wilds interface, meantime." Asandir reined up for his parting remark. "If the affray at Rockfell goes awry, at least your clansfolk need not fret over an immediate attack from the Light's false religion."

Tarens swallowed, overcome by simpler needs. "Thank you for all you have done."

"My blessing on your lady and newborn daughter." The Sorcerer gave the black rein and fared on his way, while clean sunlight striped the fresh, growing earth, and birds sang as though nothing troublesome lurked in the on-coming shadow of unformed potential.

Asandir left Iyat-thos Tarens to the cross-chop of his split loyalties with nothing more ominous said. Little help would be gained had he spoken his mind, or admitted his deepest concern. If Sethvir's long-range foreboding took root, the five kingdoms across the continent stood to go up in flames, with two Ages of labour and tribulation gone for naught but wrack, brutal slaughter and ruin.

Lysaer opened his eyes to spinning dizziness under the open sky of a starry night at high altitude. He lay on his back atop a mountain ridge. The cold, barren stone underneath him gouged his pinned limbs to discomfort, bound as he was at his wrists and ankles. The restraints were primitive: braided cord twined from tough grass or peeled vine. The vicious knots did not give to his struggles. They tightened to his flexed effort instead, and garrotted his circulation to tingling protest.

His throat was parched. Numbness deadened his nerves where the blow-darts had punctured, the loss of tactile sensation progressed to an intractable paralysis down his left side. The points likely were poisoned, or worse, primed with spellcraft that gapped his vision and stunned his reflexes.

His sluggish tongue attempted slurred speech. "What do you want with me?"

The question floundered into immutable silence. No touch but the wind stirred his hair beneath the remote glint of starlight.

For a panicky second, Lysaer believed he was alone, abandoned to a cruel, slow death by exposure. Dread squeezed his vitals, chased by heated rage, that all he was and ever hoped to become should perish, with nothing left beyond morbid carrion scavenged to gristle and bone by buzzards and kites.

Time to dwell on regretful complaint was denied him. Grey-clad figures circled his helpless position. Hooded features melted into deep shadow, the whites of dark eyes against sable skin furtive as the gleam on chipped ivory. Biedar desert folk, they said nothing. Scholars claimed their kind acknowledged no tongue beyond their obscure tribal dialect. Older legend suggested they spoke without language. Lysaer heard only the faint scrape of their sandals, and the rustle of robes as they settled cross-legged around him.

None responded to his hoarse questions. Uncanny, motionless, their quiet presence blended into their surrounds until the remote summit seemed uninhabited.

Chill harrowed Lysaer, not sprung from the cold. Primal fear lanced through him, a pervasive dread without definition. Terror beyond his worldly reckoning disrupted his warm-blooded impulse to scream.

Past question, he centred a ritual array, aligned to the major and minor points of the compass. Then the eight eldritch figures started to sing, male voices woven into an intricate counterpoint that overturned the firm semblance of orientation. Their eerie incantation spun self-awareness away, until mindful thought was devoured by sleeting bursts of static.

Lysaer wheeled, seized past recourse by the sucking plunge as his consciousness swooped out of his immobilized flesh. Time and sensation faded, swallowed whole by a whirlpool of dissociation that erased the familiar boundaries of his known world. He saw serpents. Gnarled and knotted, they ringed him, carved from what seemed the jet nadir of the void. Studded scales glinted like interlaced braid, his caged being entrapped in the monstrous, perpetual cycle of form devouring itself, head to tail. The blended male song line was augmented at length by female overtones in ringing balance. Then all voices faded from hearing but one, the solo melody sustained by the scraped tremolo of a crone. Her summoning soared and fired the resonant octaves past hearing, then harnessed the rarefied stream of ephemeral light beyond time and space.

Lost to himself, Lysaer could not weep or cry out. The breath whipped from his vanished lungs left him airless. Adrift, he was harrowed by forces beyond his control, surely damned beyond reach of redemption.

The aged woman laid claim to his consciousness. The blood in Lysaer's veins possessed no other heartbeat but *hers*; no grounded existence, except through the inflexible tether that haltered him. By some fickle trick, her eldritch heritage laid claim through a blood tie laced into his ancestry. He smelled earth, a closed space run red as the womb centred by a clay pot of birch coals. Momentarily, he thought he lay on his back, swaddled in wool spun from goat's hair. The stopped instant encompassed the dense impression of an enquiry, a moment's overlaid torrent compressed into simultaneity, punch cut at the finish by a piercing question.

A choice was demanded.

Terror laced his response.

Then those fleeting impressions forsook him. Formless colours came unstrung by the treble shimmer of glass chimes, or bone. Lysaer's being dissolved into a whirl of kaleidoscopic upheaval that shifted and blazed and re-formed, black on foil, to the knife-point peak of a mountain pierced like hammered iron through a vista of cloud. Carved stone gargoyles regarded him in his nakedness. Under the ruby flare of their warded eyes, the mark and measure of him was pared down by swift judgement.

The trial hearing that might have spared him was forfeit. He had squandered his plea for forgiveness. No grace in reprieve set him free. The release, without warning, dropped Lysaer through what felt like a hole in the world, a plummeting fall down a fathomless pit that enveloped him in utter darkness.

He passed through layer upon layer of strong wardings that burned. Heard a whisper of forgotten, ethereal singing accompanied by the faint echoes of crystalline flutes.

Then the bottom ripped out of cohesive experience, and he spun like a mote plunged through absolute silence.

Cold air and enveloping darkness returned. He was not alone. The creeping, unpleasant suspicion of something aware coiled around him. He felt no sensation, no connection through his banished flesh. Yet the hostile chill of an unseen, questing horde of *otherness* fingered him over, tunnelled into, and through him.

Disembodied and voiceless, he could not scream. Past mercy, he found himself shieldless.

The malevolence twined into him and clamped down, a piercing that shredded and minced his violate selfhood like an infinite dissection by brutal knives. Sieved piecemeal, he drowned. Consumed by the essence of insatiable *hate* beyond all recollection of sanity, naught existed but malice that snuffed outside hope of a requite end.

Lysaer writhed, mute, within Rockfell Pit, while Desh-thiere's wraiths devoured all that he was and all that he might have become. Forsaken by love, he languished in limitless, suffering agony, until, mobbed past birthright memory of self, he became one with the core directive the Biedar crone's sentence of penury tasked him to break.

What seethed here harrowed the concept of mercy, sequestered in the depths beyond reach of sunlight and air. Amid the Mistwraith's multitude of trapped entities, the hidden mandate remained embedded by Desh-thiere's original makers.

The Mistwraith had been crafted as a weapon at scale for the express purpose of the conquest of worlds. One Sorcerer had come forward and thwarted the thrust of its voracious design. Alone, Traithe had checked the full-scale incursion, his desperate closure of the South Worldsend Gate averting Athera's destruction. Entrapped at the forefront of the initial assault, he had staved off the crisis of possession by shearing off the part of himself suborned under attack.

But that fragmented sliver abandoned to assimilation in turn granted the wraiths an intimate knowledge of the Seven, whose sentence had banished them into penurious exile on Marak. *The cursed fate subsequently imposed on two half brothers in fact had preserved Desh-thiere's teeming entities intact for the moment their primary bane could be lured back within reach.* Absorbed by the collective, at one with its will, the insatiable drive to wreak bitter vengeance became absolute: wield the key to suborn Traithe completely, and the spiteful, revenant horde could demolish the Fellowship Sorcerers from within their own ranks.

Descants

A messenger pigeon from the Light's armed command bears orders for revised tactics: since the Fellowship Sorcerer's line baulks the advance on Deshir from the west, galleys from Cildorn will transport the thwarted companies southward for a quick march over the Mathorns through Leynsgap, the new prowess to thwart the vigilance of clan sentries aimed to back the combined assault under way from Rathain's northern coast . . .

At Althain Tower, despite irksome concern for the True Sect's changed strategy while Asandir is preoccupied at Penstair, Sethvir maps Dakar's movement with the black sword, Alithiel, then ties a crystal tagged with a ciphered note to the raven perched on his tower windowsill: "Fly, little brother. Tell Traithe, at long last, the time's come upon us . . ."

On the Plain of Araithe bound for Fallowmere, Esfand is retrieved yet again by his keepers, repeatedly driven to wandering off with ever more determined persistence; while southward at Forthmark, Siantra opens eyes no longer grey, but gold as the sun with vertical pupils inhuman, midnight-black slits . . .

XV. Chorus

Sea trade stalled off the northern coast of Rathain. Where the lingering, unseasonable chill gripped the grey, heaving swells, the suck and swirl of treacherous, frothed currents muddled the calved icebergs into clusters. Threat of mangled timbers and drowning kept the boldest of captains in port. Howls from thwarted merchants over their delayed cargoes clashed in chorus with officialdom's vituperative complaint. Neither faction prevailed. Galleymen held hostage by weather stayed deaf to bribes and temple requisition alike. Troops denied transport to bolster the Light's planned campaign in the east languished, crapulous as flocks of scrapping gulls, while the goods stacked in limbo beneath mildewed tarps suffered spoilage on the crowded wharves.

The racketing clamour lit tempers into midsummer as fickle directives from the dedicate high command extended the rankling wait. Malcontent suspicion blamed the Fellowship's invasive tinkering to spare Fallowmere's clans from predation. Yet the dissent bandied by rumour in fact overlooked the Seven's most critical focus.

At present, the hitch in their broadscale affairs bounced discordant echoes upslope towards the stark pinnacle of Rockfell Peak. Kharadmon and Luhaine bickered throughout the ascent, the former a miffed snap of breeze and the latter, a belaboured corpulent figure, puffing condensation like fumaroles in the frigid climb past the timberline.

"The muckle bother's insane!" Kharadmon's remonstrance spun off cracked ice, showered chips consigned willy-nilly to gravity. "Why stump along on two legs, sacked in lard? After nine centuries discorporate, who's missed the bother of spit, teeth, and a tongue? Lack of such apparatus did nothing to put the gag on your lecturing twaddle."

"Perhaps because the short straw saddled me with your excruciate nattering." Unswerved from picking the gnawed bones of pessimism, Luhaine resumed his dissection of Arithon's dearth of experience. "He's a liability, thrown into a shocking expansion by the great wyrm at Forthmark. Oh, he may have sounded the flawless notes to redeem the wraith swarm set on us from Marak. But such glib expertise cannot compensate for the profound upset to his perception. His quickened faculties are not yet stabilized! The prodigious endowment's too fresh."

"And we Seven knew any better, pray tell? Omit the lugubrious lesson, Luhaine! We were pea green with ignorance when Dragonkind's summons waylaid us in flight from our past. I daresay a master's initiation under the High Mage at Rauven has allotted Arithon the sounder foundation. Or were we not running flat out for our lives from the genocide sprung from the fruits of our egotistical intellects?"

Luhaine's retort whistled, the near-vertical pitch of Davien's stair no boon to short wind and his ample girth.

Kharadmon frisked capped snow off the glower of a horned gargoyle. "And you're welcome to the ripe nuisance of flesh. Don't whine when you have to unbutton and piss. This is Rockfell, where nature's cross-grained caprice blows back spray from undignified acts of necessity!"

"Your gasbag insolence is just as likely to blame!" Luhaine sniffed with offence. "Or hasn't your prank for bending the weather put the blight on the True Sect campaign?"

"You think steering the drift of Stormwell Gulf's icebergs is a fair-weather picnic?" Kharadmon blew a raspberry. A briar sprig laden with fruit winnowed downwards and snagged on his colleague's ear. "Let Sethvir foist that assignment on you, I'd be thrilled to reward your upholstered travail with a twine net and a paddle!"

"Vacuous jape!" Luhaine's tart wave flipped off the prickly construct, bald crown breasting the rim of the ledge atop the high-altitude staircase. Domed forehead furrowed to bristled brows over his apple-round cheeks and snub nose, he paused, his martyred squint widened.

Against the searing glare thrown off the sunlit snow-fields, three prior arrivals gazed back at him, agreeably parked on the shaded outcrop notched into the cliff face. Traithe lounged, legs extended to relieve his scars, his black clothing accented by his cropped white hair and broad-brimmed felt hat with a silver band. Beside him, as starkly attired, Arithon's slighter form sat cross-legged, sable head bare to the elements. Elaira snuggled beneath his draped arm, tucked in for shared warmth under the ornate cloak gifted to him by Davien. Like her mate, she wore leathers for the rough wilds, bronze hair bound into a sensible plait.

"Wicked ghost!" Betrayal pounced, scathing, upon the discorporate Sorcerer's sardonic omission. "You knew we've had eavesdroppers here all along!"

Kharadmon snorted. "You might have noticed had you laid off carping." Whisked across the scarred groove of fused slag from the averted lane upset once brokered by the Koriathain, he added, "Last time you brangled with me in this place, you weren't oblivious to the eavesdropping diligence of Davien's markers." A zephyr swiped at his colleague's beard muffled the lips parted for the next incensed retort. "Not my task to curb your gushing gossip, or spare you from the flaming embarrassment when you don't listen."

"Feckless shade!" Luhaine spat out his inhaled hair, shouldered off a looped strap, and lofted his satchel ahead of his ungainly scramble to gain the high ground. "I've brought victuals." Food offered in place of a gruff apology, he insisted, "We'll have time to eat."

"Thanks be to Dakar for that." Kharadmon's boredom flicked a kindlier kink in the gusts blasting off the snowclad peak. "He's trailing at least an hour behind, sweating off a green hangover."

Traithe chuckled. Delight sparked into a grin, he presented his open palm towards Arithon. "Five royals. Luhaine bested your prophet, I said so."

Arithon relinquished his wash-leather purse, content to pay up on the wager without counting the change. "Coin won't be any use where I'm bound."

The prospect he faced was no topic for levity. Kharadmon's teasing humour went cold, viced into a patience by lengths more unnerving, while Luhaine plunked himself on his haunches and divvied ham and hard cheese into portions. Traithe nibbled, his share largely pilfered by the raven swooped down to perch on his shoulder.

The drunken indulgence behind Dakar's tardiness stemmed in fact from fainthearted dread of Arithon's censure, foot-dragging reluctance redoubled by the recurrent nightmares left over from his prior stint in Fellowship service upon Rockfell Peak. Choice would have brought him nowhere near the benighted spellcraft that secured the Mistwraith's confinement. Once divested of the Paravian sword foisted on him, he meant to be gone fast as his short legs would carry him.

"Soonest started," he groused through jittery nerves, the last clumsy yards of his journey betrayed by a clatter of pebbles scuffed over the brink.

Arithon met him, as he had feared. Dodgy avoidance could not mistake the eldritch, silver embroidery that patterned a distinctive black cloak, or bypass the field boots planted before him.

Dakar shrank as though bitten from the lean hand extended to steady his balance. "I'm not staying." The squirmed effort to shuck his unwanted baggage spurred his craven rush to retreat. "Survival, if not better sense, wouldn't bother to rake your leavings out of coal-fed fires. Like tempting the wheels of Dharkaron's Chariot, everyone's fingers but yours end up burned."

"Dakar." The bard's tensile grip clamped the baldric's snagged strap and tugged the baulky spellbinder upwards and over the lip of the precipice.

Mulish heels dug in, the Mad Prophet let fly. "You can't pin the blame on my sorry hide! That maudlin binge was your fault on the night you drowned your misery in the tap-room at Ganish!"

Beyond shame, and despite the excoriating interest of his mate within earshot, Arithon laughed. "Dakar! After three centuries lived mage-wise, did you honestly think I could drink myself to dissipation?"

Dakar blinked, flummoxed. Cowled like a tortoise in his tatty collar, he sucked a vexed breath through pinched nostrils. Be coldcocked and damned, before he mentioned the doxies, far less Mixie's insolent claim to his bounty as prize for a royal conception.

Arithon's reproof merely reclaimed Alithiel. The adjustment of buckles his tactful kindness to relieve the spellbinder's stilted embarrassment, he added, contrite, "Honestly, I expected not to survive the Prime Matriarch's horrid pitfall at Forthmark. Therefore, my earnest promise made to Caolle's memory, and Jieret's, as their sworn liege became obligate."

When the perplexed frown stayed furrowed into the Mad Prophet's dough features, Arithon regarded him, faintly exasperated. "Exactly how could I have done otherwise?"

The Mad Prophet flushed scarlet. If a crown heir for Rathain had been intentional, in dead earnest, culpability roosted squarely on his inept watch. Handed the penalty for his lapsed charge to safe-guard Elaira, Dakar flinched to acknowledge how far Arithon's innate prefer-ence had been ripped from his capable grasp.

"Daelion's grief, Dakar! You're foundered on guilt?" Arithon's frustration gave way to hilarity. "Then I'll spell it out quickly. The whore and the drink were to frame your excuse! My botched effort to let you off the hook with Elaira if I wound up killed for an ancestral pledge. At least, in your boots, I wouldn't have relished that confrontation with her over my grave site."

"With your backhanded slap at the Fellowship as the wicked double entendre?" The Mad Prophet coughed. "There's a plea to butcher all credibility. Don't deny the freight of sly malice crammed into your offered glove of reconciliation."

Abruptly serious, Arithon cradled the Paravian sword just restored to his possession. "Hoist a flagon for me, fellow, if after today, I can't make amends to you properly. Or brood eggs on your festering grudge all you like. If years and distance don't mellow the sting, Ath knows, you have reason enough to nurse rancour. Caught up in my wake, all my staunch friends have suffered the whipping post. Go with my blessing, whatever you choose. And if I've harnessed the Seven with offspring, have somebody able make sure the poor bastard's not raised to sow merry hell in my footsteps."

Hurled off his bearings, Dakar lost the knack of forbearance through banter. Far less could he bear to meet halfway the changed creature before him: the self-same spirit his callous abandonment had left to challenge Lirenda alone. Arithon had survived her vitriolic assault and five drake molts, then stared down the wrath of Seshkrozchiel, unsup-ported. Pique aside, the spellbinder found himself gutted in brutalized sympathy. Mere *thought* of the shock suffered during a grand augmen-tation imposed on mortal flesh by a dragon scared him spitless: just one *day* of trauma spent mantled in Kharadmon's extended awareness nearly had broken his mind beyond realignment. That Arithon and his mate walked upright in the bolt-struck wake of an incomprehensibly vast expansion smashed human credulity.

Luhaine's gloomy assessment held merit. The magnitude of the shift was too dreadfully recent to bridle. How the Seven themselves sustained the hectic barrage that outpaced linear thought defied reason: perception

that extended past time and space, in duality, bridged the veil and tapped
into the well of a greater unknown beyond sanity. Dakar cringed from
the memory. Wide awake, his recall of one glancing encounter drove
him to shuddering cold sweats. He refused to look up. Lacked the
dauntless nerve to meet Arithon's gaze, far less brave a relentless attentiveness that could pluck the harrowing gist of his personal regrets.
Sorrow quailed to measure the gulf, or endure the loss of the friend,
transformed to the stranger recast in that terrible crucible.

"I am not staying!" Dakar repeated, fixated on his scuffed boots.

"I know." Arithon placed his last request lightly. "Send word through
Tarens should my debt to Earl Jieret's legacy and Caolle's score be fulfilled.
Laithen s'Idir must be told if an heir to Rathain's lineage is born living."

Dakar winced, that a newborn sown through his scapegrace machinations yet again might grow up fatherless at Althain Tower. His lame
protest was sorry. "You don't have to fail here!"

His awkward remorse earned Arithon's smile, forthright as few ever
witnessed. "No one's eager to reckon my odds. You, more than any,
should be less inclined to discount my say on the matter."

Reft of his obligation to linger, Dakar could not find adequate words
of farewell, or choke a flimsy wish for good luck past the lump in his
paralysed throat. *He knew what was coming,* as Arithon could not: the
dire forces that imprisoned Rockfell's captive contents outpaced every
imaginable horror. His cowardly need for avoidance made way, as was
right: Arithon's final moments belonged to Elaira.

The clinging embrace was never her style. Resolute as she claimed
her place at his side, her wind-burnished colour drawn pale, she gently
leaned into the warmth of his presence. The steady beat of his heart and
the leashed pace of his breathing bespoke the exerted strength of his
discipline. No place, now, to stress that finite stamina with her savage
flood of emotion. Anchored by her steadfast consent to embark on the
arduous course firmly chosen, he acknowledged her gift of restraint, his
eloquent kiss bestowed on the crown of her head. "We are ready."

Such ringing confidence made Dakar flinch. He was not twice the
fool to stay within range through the opening of Rockfell's defences. His
bungling scramble as he quit the ledge became blurred by welled tears
as he seized his retreat to safe distance.

Others lacked the option to leave. Traithe tossed the importunate raven
off his wrist. The aspected bird took wing in the bitter wind, punch-cut

night against the azure zenith. Scars stiffened, the crippled Sorcerer stood, empty-handed, while Luhaine chewed and swallowed the last bite of ham stuffed into pouched cheeks. He dusted the crumbs and lumbered erect, his more ponderous anxiety distilled into wheezy, last-minute instructions to Arithon. "Advanced sight will trip you, no matter how thoroughly Ciladis spoke in forewarning. Don't let the templates of alienated perception throw you, or lose your centre in alternate streams of experience. If you slip, remember. Re-frame your human perception before your ungrounded referent expands past recovery."

"Oh, do quit blowing off redundant steam and get along while we're still wakeful!" Kharadmon's presence whistled across the polished, black glass of the face that concealed Rockfell's primary threshold. "Talk without action will kick any hero's bravado to death."

Stout fibre quailed, nonetheless. No one engaged in dialogue with Rockfell Peak without profound reservations.

Luhaine initiated the formal greeting, flattened palms laid on blank stone. He stated his name and purpose with immaculate humility, a stretched pause appended to listen.

The mountain answered. The stately language of mineral reverberated in subsonics, tender patience at distinctive remove from the pattering tempo of red-blooded consciousness. Rockfell's sonority evoked the grand weight of the ages, every day and each second's detail retained with nuanced accuracy. Mankind could but weep before the noble scale of such exactitude. Rockfell grasped the peril its core integrity guarded, the potential downfall to disaster past prevarication. If the frailty of flesh joined into partnership faltered, a staunch watch maintained above reproach across centuries might be squandered in a moment.

"Arithon s'Ffalenn, are you committed to carry the risk?" Luhaine demanded in the mountain's behalf.

"With my life and beyond, under Ath's Light." His hammered calm wrung Elaira and three Fellowship Sorcerers to grief for the absolute need to endorse his free-will obligation. "The burden is mine at the penalty of Dharkaron's Vengeance."

Rockfell accepted, trust granted with ponderous gravity: for heart-rock might come to bear untold sorrows forever if today's bonded endeavour should fail.

Arithon bore up as the weight of finality settled upon him, assurance founded on what seemed puny bluster. No turning back: a whining snap triggered a release made irrevocable as Luhaine's and Kharadmon's work in tandem disarmed the lethal array of primary counterwards. The rapid-fire onslaught pulsed an ache through the marrow, until Luhaine stepped clear for the sequenced unbinding. White lightning flared over the exposed cliff face as Kharadmon severed the linkages of the fused mineral. Runes flickered over polished stone, flared bright, and vanished, while power sheared updraughts that towered the clouds and fanned anvilheads above the knife-point summit. At first hand, protections wrought at such scale crushed reason and sapped the pith of intelligent resolve.

Then all tumult faded. The backwash of grand conjury relapsed into air currents curdled by the storm scent of ozone. The threshold into the mountain lay open. An oblong portal cut into lightless dark, where moments before the glassine wall had been seamless.

Never had the bracing bite of glacial ice smelled as sweet, or glorious colour been so unbearably vivid. No smirch marred the cobalt sky, saturated through wisps of disbanded cloud. Cotton billows masked the vales far below, furrowed slopes and bare scarp and stunt fir banished from memory as a remnant dream.

The insupportable pang defied endurance, as Arithon turned his back on the view, squared his shoulders, and stepped into gloom. Elaira shifted her stance at his heels.

"You don't have to do this," Luhaine blurted, impulsively plucking at her sleeve.

Delivered on tiptoe, her kiss brushed his plump, bearded cheek. "I appreciate your concern, but I must."

Pale in the cerulean glare off the snow-fields, she entered Rockfell. Her steps cast faint echoes, smothered under the pressure of an implacable stillness. Dry air stirred with metallic traces of dust as Kharadmon's ranging chill flowed in behind. Luhaine followed, trailed by the hitched scrape of Traithe's limp. The raven watched from aloft as the Sorcerer crossed over the threshold into the upper vault. Parted from fast companionship, the bird circled the peak once in salute, then soared free of a service shared for nine centuries.

The smooth floor past the entry was featureless granite, yet no creature trod over the covered shaft at the centre. Even shielded, the secondary ring of defences reamed flesh and bone, a vicious coil of unseen currents spiked by chill that harrowed up gooseflesh. The ward's daunting magnitude defied challenge, and yet: signal exception, the Biedar crone's frightful, long reach had cast Lysaer's condemned spirit to languish with the fell horror imprisoned inside. How her eldritch endowment accomplished the feat, the mountain itself shrouded her secret.

"Our intact seals show no trace of a breach!" Luhaine muttered, confounded as he grappled the paradox.

Kharadmon's nettled gyre flipped off in retort, "We could stump ourselves over that question until the sun collapses to cinders." His gusty exasperation nipped at his colleague's ample backside to enact the next course of deconstruction.

"Best not to watch." Traithe cautioned, even before his impairment chary of the drastic forces his colleagues mustered to deploy.

Arithon and Elaira huddled against the far wall, turned away and by no means prepared for the savagery of the event as the interlocked conjury laid down and swathed under convoluted inversions underwent the staged process of diffusion. No surface assay garnered from Arithon's climb braced him for the perilous impact when Kharadmon and Luhaine in concert unravelled the intricate puzzle, layer after tuned layer meshed in triplicate. The explosive recoil struck in bone-hurting waves, flares hot enough to vaporize flesh chased by the flash freeze of punishing cold. The intensity battered averted awareness, and taxed Luhaine to streaming sweat. Closure shuddered through bed-rock as the unveiled capstone emerged in untrammelled relief.

"Your turn for brute muscle," remarked Kharadmon, to a glower from his flushed colleague. "More than welcome by my lights for the pulped fingers I'll never miss."

Arithon and Traithe lent assistance, the massive slab pried up and dragged clear of the well underneath. The uncanny borehole sunk by Davien fell away, black as the void, sliced by the unlikely wood of a narrow ladder. Kharadmon's flighty presence flowed in, while Luhaine, complaining, entrusted his bulk to the frail, silvered rungs for the arduous descent.

The wait topside frayed nerves as the tertiary ward rings were undone, far below. Morning faded to late afternoon. The oblate gleam of the outside light sheened the interior walls, nicked in ruled lines with ciphers that evaded the eye and resisted translation. Speech seemed an intrusion. The eldritch silence felt boxed in paned glass, crawling with indefinable vibration. Pooled air lay rancoured by indefinable currents that raked tingles across naked skin.

Kharadmon's brisk return eddied into crackles of static, the pervasive scent of electrical charge vented into the sterile granite enclosure. "The wards are disbanded," he announced, out of temper.

Traithe surveyed his bristled colleague, touched thoughtful. "You think the crone's byplay with Lysaer may frame a sneak trick beyond the free-will imperative to bind Arithon to her timing?"

"Sethvir himself avoided that worrisome question," snapped the Fellowship shade. "Who knows? Damn her infernal, wayward interference to the torments past Sithaer's ninth gate!" Confirmed proof the sealed flask sequestered below was inviolate salved none of his agitation. "The vessel we crafted atop Kieling Tower at Ithamon still secures Desh-thiere's confinement. But the Biedar's ancestral granddame left us her pissing mark! The pit floor's inscribed with her serpent, devouring itself head to tail."

Returned puffing by ladder, Luhaine shed prim restraint, wrung white by the visceral tenderness shrouded beneath his humourless outlook. "Reconsider," he begged, while Elaira watched stricken. "No man should be asked to shoulder this test."

Arithon rebuffed the outburst of sympathy. "I must. Else the sovereign charge of charter law fails, and we bequeath Mankind's future an unfinished reckoning with no path for hope."

The scalpel's edge of that courage killed protest. Luhaine hardened his desperate care and wagged a schoolmasterish finger. "Do not rest on your laurels. Although you brought Marak's invasive swarm to requital, the revenant intelligence you sounded encountered you, one on one, as a stranger. This pass will be different." Lysaer as precursor granted the Mistwraith's rife malice forewarning. "You enter the arena as the known enemy." Desh-thiere was a cohesive, hostile collective, nourished by a smothering mist fashioned as a lethal weapon.

Arithon acknowledged his peril. "Don't forget my prior encounter at Ithamon." Eyes like sheared tourmaline rejected equivocation. "I have met attack from Desh-thiere's bound souls in their pure state of malice before." His matured capability had been seasoned since. "The wraiths will expect the youthful initiate I was at the time."

Not the opponent of consummate might reforged by the dragons at Forthmark.

Luhaine was not one whit reassured. "That makes your position more dangerous!" If fresh strength fit to rival a Fellowship Sorcerer's should be overwhelmed and hooked into possession, Arithon himself could become the forged instrument to destroy Athera's viability. "You stake far more than your personal fate. One error will call down a disaster past our able recourse to stem."

"I was not prepared at Forthmark, either." Arithon's resolute touch soothed Elaira. "Let us not cede the field to uncertainty."

Luhaine cleared his throat. "Then we rise or fall by your fallible merits."

An unconscionable truth, should aught go amiss. Arithon might not withstand the arduous course. A misstep could strand him, discorporate.

Shaken, Luhaine pursed nervous lips. "You could be entrapped for all time in the pit as a threat to the world without remedy."

"I will not be gainsaid." Kin-right to reclaim a lost sibling curtailed the argument. Buffeted by Kharadmon's taciturn impatience, and braced by Traithe's kindly reserve, Arithon s'Ffalenn bade farewell to Elaira. "Forgive me, beloved. We've not had enough time."

Tears gilded her smile through his parting embrace. "It was always enough, even if forever."

Traithe's halted step flanked his final approach to the pit. "Ath's mercy go with you, and every bright strength of protection."

Arithon clasped the crippled Sorcerer's wrist, salute to the first casualty in a fight now reliant on him for a long-sought deliverance. Then he swung onto the ladder alone. His descent into darkness swallowed him whole, perhaps never to see sky or sunlight again, or share living warmth with his dearest beloved. From the Fellowship, he carried a crystal imbued by Sethvir with a repertoire of sealed knowledge. From the Athera's Paravians, he bore the Second-Age sword Alithiel, forged by the storied skill of a centaur armourer and endowed by the exalted virtues of Athlien and Riathan. To his own birthright gift of elemental shadow, he brought Rauven's initiate mastery and the exquisite command of music nurtured by Halliron. Of the Biedar, he had only Requiar's blood heritage, thus far no boon but a burden that steered him time and again into jeopardy.

Poignancy strangled all dismissive platitudes. The relentless parting broke dignity down. Elaira's hands shuttered her grief-stricken face. Three Sorcerers endured, as they must, while hurt scoured the unbearable, widening silence as distance muted the rustle and scrape of Arithon's steady descent. No recourse for mitigation remained. Only the brutalized drive of necessity to set ruthless safe-guards against the on-coming storm.

Luhaine and Traithe wrestled the capstone back into place. The booming report as stone settled on stone resounded with the graven finality of a closed tomb.

Restraint crumbled, outmatched. Elaira swayed, shattered by a fierce stab of agony nothing alive might assuage.

Traithe steered her aside before her knees buckled. His support cushioned her through the drastic steps of engagement as Kharadmon and Luhaine restored the dire wards over Rockfell's prison after her mate.

No palliative relieved the onslaught of misery. Arithon would endure this trial alone, sealed in the mountain's fast depths beyond respite. Sethvir's visionary forecasts made no difference. No remedy known to the wise could wrestle a quandary spun beyond quarter: dragon-wrought power come to bear at the scale Arithon owned was not malleable. Such a wild force was too mighty to curb should the Mistwraith's corruption breach his integrity. No surety existed. Every concern raised at the crown assize at Methisle held a posited grain of validity. Rockfell's stringent protections stood guard for Athera if mischance tilted the finishing throw and bad odds rolled the dice of calamity.

For Elaira, the harsh measure felt like an abandonment: far worse now, as she confronted her upcoming part in the sacrifice. The hard moment hung on her voluntary consent to surrender her person to the inflexible, cold wards of extended stasis. Kharadmon reined in his searing impatience as the painful finality of her decision harrowed her loyal commitment.

"You need not put yourself through this." Traithe's empathy sprang from understanding: he must undertake the ritual himself if the shorn fragments of his damaged spirit were to find salvage. He chafed her damp wrist, saddened that no one alive might provide her with humane solace. Not even the sterling assurance he would share her travail, spun down to a state of oblivious suspension: a work of grand conjury quite unforgiving, engineered to extend for an unknown duration.

Her worst fears were not groundless. The risk to her last, hale bid for survival carved a precipice too vicious to contemplate. "Arithon would pardon your sound choice to turn back."

Elaira's emphatic refusal belied her unsteady voice. "Sunder my linked rapport with my beloved? No. I will not abandon my faith in him, or leave him alone come what may." The connection between them could frame his salvation as readily as drag her to damnation in shared liability.

"Besides, I've spent too many centuries of waiting without him." Bravery, before calm, stiffened her tremulous poise. "Don't imagine I could endure that awful uncertainty ever again."

Minutes fled past, the precious sensation of breathing far too poignantly sweet. She lay down on cold stone, bolstered by Traithe's steady warmth at her side. The last disposition in place, past regret, Kharadmon marked the circles of limitation and raised the ciphers to cocoon them forthwith. The wrought seals stopped time, a working far beyond the crude, ceremonial ritual once staged in the open for Earl Jieret's extended spiritwalk. Painstaking and thorough, Luhaine constructed these mighty seals of preservation to withstand millennia. The Seven endorsed the decisive precaution. No risk was acceptable, however slight. If the Mistwraith seized charge and took Arithon in conquest, the hazard posed by Traithe's tie to Desh-thiere, and Elaira's connected rapport with her mate, might mount the leverage to fracture the mysteries and hurl Athera's grace into entropy.

Heavy of heart, Luhaine fussed through his meticulous closure. Kharadmon quietly tidied the energetic loose ends. Last departure, the pair cleared the vault with scant latitude. Whipped by bitter wind off the ice, they resecured the outside entrance. The red-golden glory of alpenglow rinsed the black-iron summit when the dire wards over Rockfell's threshold stood fast to the utmost reach of their industry.

At the finish, three living spirits and countless trapped entities were left sealed in utter darkness below. Perhaps forever: Sethvir himself might not hazard a guess on the precarious outcome. Ill-omened harbinger, Traithe's raven had not returned to perch on the cornice. Most faithful companion, the incarnate aspect of the greater archetype had not stayed to keep vigil.

Truth shadowed the hour, beyond unremitting.

Arithon had but a scant handful of days to surmount the challenge before him. After the short-falls of breathing flesh failed him, he might seize a discorporate transition, at best leaving Elaira stranded and living. At worst, a fall to possession and assimilation would anneal her shared stake in his destiny.

The paired Sorcerers rested their labour with the solid stone at the entry restored to its former immaculate polish. As sundown scalded the ice fields in carmine and lavender, the remote beauty of the Skyshiels surrounding them seemed an untouched violation. Behind mirror-smooth stone that gently slept, Rockfast's dedicated endurance resumed its fell charge under the last seal of closure. Neither Fellowship Sorcerer doubted the cruel necessity.

"That does not make me feel any less like a murderer," Luhaine lamented. Weary and sunk into gloom, he resigned himself to a hurried descent to take shelter before the grey dusk of high-altitude twilight dimmed into nightfall.

This once drained of verve, Kharadmon forbore to sharpen snide wits on his colleague's disheartenment.

Arithon's resolute descent of the ladder within Rockfell's capped depths extended for time beyond measure, except as the staid perception of bed-rock recorded the magnetic flow of the seasons. No star song penetrated the Fellowship's tiered array of obdurate wards. Isolation was total, without sound but the whisper of his steady movement, his drummed pulse and each susurrant breath. The dry air was chill, the temperature constant. Small respite granted by his heightened faculties, he did not fare downwards in darkness. Hypersensitized, his refined mage-sight unveiled the strata of the mountain, layered splendour laced through with the metallic sparkle of ore and veins of crystallized mineral. The upshifted glory of earth's latent beauty bewitched his inner eye, secrets clenched in the hush of dense silence.

Best not to dwell upon what lay ahead, or fret over the narrow, available margin to resolve a dangerous contest freighted with catastrophic complexity. Three lives and uncounted tortured, lost entities relied upon his facile wits. Not least of the spirits ensnared were the sundered fragments of Traithe. And his half brother's devoured consciousness, blighted by curse-driven enmity.

Fear could saturate confidence and suck the mind dumb.

Arithon redirected his crushing anxiety, told over instead his prior appeal, made to High Queen Regent Merevalia: *'Teach me the flute song you played for the Athlien dancers to unshackle my fate from the Mistwraith's directive.'*

'I cannot.' Her mellifluous sorrow had wounded the heart and flayed hope, that the trial before him evaded her illumined guidance. *'Falyrionient – Masterbard – our working made in your behalf required your willing spirit stripped naked to claim the undefiled essence of your true Name sourced by Ath Creator. Our singers danced the pattern strained*

*through the Song of the Mysteries. Exalted harmonics countermanded
what did not stem from your birthright until the dissonant notes of coercion dwindled and faded away.'*

Her wisdom confirmed the intricate template to key wholeness was unique to each individual. A matched solution for Lysaer required her unconditional access for a composition beyond secondhand means to bestow. Mage-wise talent grasped that basic stricture. Nonetheless, Arithon's insistent ethic had petitioned her High Grace for the certainty.

'You'll not leave empty-handed.' Black hair studded with shimmering jewels, the Queen Regent had tilted her pert head and regarded him. Complexion radiant as new pearl and verdant spring in her emerald eyes, she allowed, *'I can gift you intact our memory of your own deliverance.'* The small disposition within her reach tinged the tender sorrow of her regret. "But for your half brother, you must find the melody and forge the keys for requital yourself."

The daunting prospect haemorrhaged pity.

Each step down the endless succession of rungs, Arithon resurveyed the facets of knowledge amassed throughout his extended lifetime. Rauven's teaching, enhanced by learned healing drawn from Elaira's experience in the field; study of volumes sequestered in Davien's library and Ciladis's journals cached on Los Lier; shadow mastery and tenets of Paravian lore he had snatched from the desperate straits of past crisis – no knowing what scrap of leverage might lend him advantage, caught up in the clinch.

Descended to the core of the mountain, he set foot at last in the five-sided vault at the base of the shaft. Another come before him had branded the site. Symbol of eternity, the snake devouring itself ringed his stance on arrival. The crone's making in queer, carved relief presented the surface impression of null resonance, *or else harboured other*: a worked power of appalling quiescence locked under the absolute seal of infinitude.

Small use to ponder the vexatious enigma, where even the expansive Sight bestowed by Seshkrozchiel lacked the naked insight to penetrate.

"Death's hand on Fate's Wheel!" Arithon swore, ever chary of Mother Dark's riddles.

By contrast, the sheer walls with their pentagonal angles were solid, the incised array of the Fellowship's ciphers and convolute, spiralled lattices now discharged of residual power. The inert script was picked out by the faint, phosphene halo cast by the last ward field yet active. Asandir's original working surrounded the sequestered flask, infused with Kharadmon's wicked flourish, and the borrowed elegance of Ithamon's Paravian history. Its shimmer unsettled the naked eye, flickered between the eerie black of the void, and shuttling flecks of light that traced geometric mazes through the mineral structure of moulded stone. The effect cast a deadly corona that skewed the initiate mind towards madness. Arithon assayed the laced interface of a grandeur that commanded the weave of creation, and in merciless paradox, ripped the splendour of natural order to chaos that lashed him to visceral terror.

By configured inversion, the array shouted warning. The wraiths trapped within were peril distilled: entities mechanically stripped from the flesh by perversion invoked through the aberrant practice of necromancy.

Ath lend him strength, he grasped what he faced in the bowels of a pit where grace and clean sun did not shine! Offered a second chance for reprieve, Arithon would have moved sky and earth to be anywhere else. Sane wisdom flinched from a repeat entanglement with an undilute evil, evolved like a cancer from the maleficent source behind the Grey Kralovir's grimoires. The prospect siphoned Arithon hollow, and ripped puckered flesh clammy with fear.

Yet the venture to subdue Desh-thiere's murderous ill found no anti-dote in the arsenal of docile strategies. The wraiths must be sprung to make progress. First imperative, he must extinguish the wan comfort of Asandir's protective geometry. Deconstruction deepened the penumbra of gloom, fast reduced to featureless darkness as Arithon unravelled the rigorous wards safe-guarding the stoppered flask. He proceeded on tuned instinct and delicate touch, in dread of the menace he tempted.

The conjury's sinister intricacy itself bespoke terrors that stalked in broad daylight. No salvation existed within Rockfell Pit. No help stood at Arithon's back, no informed counsel to warn off a misstep. Once the foundational defences dispersed, the residual harmony of Kieling Tower's virtue alone sustained Desh-thiere's captivity.

Arithon poised, listening to that frail stay, the peeled sensitivity of his heightened faculties stunned by the wistful traces of ancient Paravian harmony. A bard could but weep, lacerated to heartache, made witness to the expression of undefiled rapture put to such hideous use: Athlien flutes twined in exaltation with the pure registers of Ath's adepts, a replete whisper drawn from the thundering chord that ignited the mysteries as yet undiminished throughout Athera's bygone ages.

Shattered to the heart, Arithon resisted the bewitching enthrallment. Delay shaved his narrow margin for survival. Enclosed without supply and fresh air, he could succumb through inertia.

Spurious haste would kill him by overreach. Volatile, unacclimatized power eroded constraint and inflated the simplest cantrip. Elementary ciphers outpaced his control, unruly as the splash of flung mercury. Limitation demanded the most onerous strictures, as second to precarious second, he caught back and stayed a torrential endowment sped beyond his practised experience.

Worse, Lysaer's entrapped awareness would react to his presence. The instant he breached the stone flask, ferocious attack would be instantaneous. Within fatal proximity, the adversity of Desh-thiere's curse provided his only reliable footing. Self-defence and Alithiel's virtue must wait. His initial contact would be unshielded, the brunt wave at the forefront engaged bare-handed to draw his half brother's essence from the ravening pack. Arithon gauged his straits, stripped of false confidence. Lose himself, and he would be suborned by the wraiths beyond salvage.

Against ominous stakes, he could only go forward. Last thought of Elaira at this menacing crux only sapped his momentum and leached his resolve. Rockfell's defences excised her precious rapport, she and Traithe isolated and sealed under stasis. No more stringent precaution could brace him for the baleful impact.

Teeth gritted, Arithon yanked the stone stopper.

Released, the rank fog boiled into the vault. A plume dense as gaseous lead, Desh-thiere's sentient rancour enveloped him. Unimaginable, that this fresh contact could be any worse than the abomination battled to a standstill upon Kieling Tower. Past question, the corrosive malice that cursed him had not dimmed throughout centuries of captivity. Slammed by the nightmare echo of his first defeat in the crowded square at Etarra, Arithon clung to beleaguered awareness. The snare that had hobbled and unstrung him then found no purchase. Twice and three times since, he had claimed in full measure the sourced autonomy of his true Name.

The crucible of Davien's Maze, the evil rites of the Grey Kralovir, and most exhaustive of all, the unconstrained might of riled drake molts had not sundered him. The false foothold to overturn self-awareness and lay claim to him pried at the roots of a strength too profound to dislodge.

The malignant wraiths tested and tried him, unswerved, their piteous clamour tailored to engage him through sympathy, then snatch access by the reflexive response of his birth-born s'Ffalenn empathy. Arithon countered that weakness, strikes met in riposte by the song imbued by the High Queen Regent. Bright harmonics upshifted far past the veil permeated his being and wove a deflection against the sneak bid for coercive influence. When that shining armour proved unassailable, the Mistwraith's offensive raged on with blunt force to tax mortal stamina and wear Arithon down.

Time edged the tactical impetus against him.

He was one against many, as incarnate flesh, vulnerable on all quarters, with his reflexes hampered by the unruly leap of quickened faculties. Desh-thiere's wraiths suffered no such impediment. Fluid at simultaneous coordination, they laid siege in earnest. Arithon staggered, clawed by raking, incessant blows that grappled his balance off centre. At reckless need, he torched his reserves to fend off subjugation

The hilt of Alithiel lit and moaned while still sheathed, an unbidden response not witnessed since the gruelling past ambush sprung on him at nightfall in Lysaer's company at Ithamon. The smothered gleam of the Paravian starspell tinged the billowed mist, a nacreous shroud teeming with writhing shades. Contorted faces gnashed teeth and leered with inhuman ferocity. Translucent, clawed fingers plucked at his essence, seeking to rend his vitality. Arithon stared down the epitome of voracious hunger, starved and ridden by craving to outlast eternity.

Then as now, the ghastly phenomenon of stretched contact lagged into temporal distortion. The same eerie subterfuge had stymied the Seven, before the aggressive assault had impelled Desh-thiere's entities to exposure. Arithon stood them off, barely, at this pass equipped with the structure of Asandir's counterward. The compensation he now required to harness his accelerated proficiency intensified his concentration, while he was plagued a thousandfold to distraction by raving voices, keen as blades and relentlessly multiplied.

'Join join join join with us! Embrace immortality and share our purpose purpose purpose to feed feed feed upon life until our insatiable want consumes all that lives . . .'

The wraiths begged. They whined. Against his besieged defences, they wheedled with sugared promises in temptation. Arithon had withstood that savage litany before: folly and ruin to listen. Adamant in resistance, he knew every twist the invasive host drawn from Marak employed to prey upon human fears. Yet this was no contest against shades winnowed separate. The tidal cascade turned to murderous threats, an onslaught that undercut self-conviction as fiercely as undertow in a riptide.

'We know you you you you! We have tasted the measure of your blood blood blood blood heritage and we are the essence of manyfold vengeance vengeance vengeance returned.'

Rathain's chartered history supported due cause to revile his ancestry: countless s'Ffalenn forebears had upheld crown justice across generations and indicted these malcontents for their lawless infractions. Arraignments for the rogue pursuit of proscribed hazards to Paravia's etheric web had imposed the Fellowship's exile to the splinter world beyond Southgate. Desh-thiere *was* the retaliate essence contrived by the incorrigible offenders dispatched to Marak.

The shades of those outcasts swarmed in thirsty revenge to supplant the Sorcerers' mandate. Deathless persistence envenomed their spite. 'Paravians die die die die die of lost hope. Where we who are dispossessed have none none none, we wreak destruction in kind for our despair and perpetual suffering.'

Yet the secondary trials within Davien's Maze hardened Arithon for the importunate horde that beset him. Mobbed by assailants that gouged for fell conquest, he did battle, flayed raw and trampled by his innate empathy. He had not succumbed then, though tears rendered him blind. Seared as though branded, cut to ribbons, he bled for the lost fragments of Traithe, swallowed into the rapacious maelstrom. Yet pathos for the Sorcerer's piecemeal torment must not sway him at any cost. Hesitate, and all causes were forfeit.

Of the ravening throng that bombarded him, Arithon challenged but one in fullest command and with singular focus: his rebuttal addressed his half brother's suborned spirit at the exacting pitch to spark incendiary flame.

The adamantine cry called down in fused fury the scald of the Mistwraith's curse. Lysaer's discorporate consciousness lashed back, a sally intensified by the sirens' chorus of Desh-thiere's amalgamate wraiths.

Arithon retorted with shadow, a honed blast of bittermost cold to ice the invasive mist ragged. His bulwark repulsed the embedded entities, starved them to depletion as thoroughly as the subduction of swarming *iyats*. Beaten into recoil, this stunned mass kept cohesion.

Inextricably embedded within, Lysaer's possessed consciousness could not be cut free. Provocation fashioned the method to trigger him, until induced rage subsumed his control, and the stigma of his curse-driven passion mangled the wraiths' unified alignment.

Arithon closed the battle forearmed. His half brother's most intimate, personal imprint set into crystal by Sethvir provided the arsenal.

Three women had fractured Lysaer's trust. There lay the foundational wounding beneath his flawed character. Arithon's strike battered that weakness first with the offensive illusion wielded before: Avar and their mother Talera, twined into the rapture of carnal embrace. Aggravating the festered hurt of a three-year-old child's desertion, Arithon blistered his half brother's profound insecurity, gouging into the later, mistaken suspicion of the primal betrayal that never occurred. He reprised the ugly unforgivable lie: of Lysaer's cherished wife Talith and himself in the perfidy of an adulterous liaison.

Then, past reprieve, Arithon tormented Lysaer's cankered pain with Daliana's abandonment. Where the scalpel's edge of his adept awareness laid open the man's true regard for her, bardic intuition twisted the knife. Arithon salted the festering sore, then savaged raw hurt to violation. Remorseless, he vivisected the brutal fact that curse-bent compulsion had treated with her as a threat, until her indelible faith in him perished.

The tragedy flayed bleeding remorse beyond bearing. Daliana had lacked Sulfin Evend's main strength, unable to muscle Lysaer by force to beat sense and sanity into him.

Emotion fashioned the Mistwraith's tool of enslavement. The victimized script of self-justification, warped by insidious deception, fanned the psyche to curse-driven combustion; also, double-edged, the same channel was most readily wielded by a Masterbard's art to disrupt the fell grip of geas-bent fury in turn.

Arithon seized the ruthless opening, bore down, and struck to the core without mercy. "Your mother, your women, your son – all deserted you!"

Lysaer's inflamed roar smashed all frames of identity. Distilled rage consumed him. "You seduced Talith from me!"

"Did I? The factual record says otherwise." Arithon slashed through with absolute proof, shields flattened for the irrefutable veracity anchored by his own recollection. "Your lady deserted you first for your obnoxious obsession. She punctured your pride because she cut you down to size, kicked you off your inflated pedestal, and shoved your nose into the noxious excrement of your delusion."

Over and over, unto ruination, Lysaer had denounced the cloth of true character. Desh-thiere's malice twisted his clouded will, chewed at the festered scars of his rejection to denounce its most powerful threat. The curse stole the matured gift of reciprocal love, and replaced the vacuous lack with excuses and blame, until self-driven revilement skinned every traumatized nerve ending desperately raw.

Arithon compounded his half brother's agony. He pitched the exacting, steely harmonics that rifled the soul. Ever more merciless lines of themed dissonance stropped privacy and dissected Lysaer's hidden heart.

"Come on, brother!" Past forgiveness, Arithon dug in with excruciate adamance. "All that you stand for, I have destroyed." The dark side of the healer's inspiration claimed every foul avenue to crystallize torment and cement immutable hatred. "For Talith, for Ellaine, for your faithless mother, call me to account!"

And the terrible moment arrived.

Lysaer's adulterated persona snapped into alignment. The stunted affection despoiled to loathing eclipsed in full measure the glimmer of his birth-born value. Incandescent with hatred, the fanned flame of his personal consciousness coalesced, distinct from Desh-thiere's conglomerate morass of nameless wraiths.

Arithon spun wards. Shadow braided with surgical finesse sheared into the surging mass at the torn breach, until freezing darkness wrought direct from the element stunned all active charge to paralysed inertia. Then, selectively, he extended his own core protection and spun Lysaer's haltered spirit inside.

Paired, now faced off in sealed opposition before the goaded fury of his cursed nemesis, Arithon baited the face of annihilation. Shieldless, no refuge between them, Avar's bastard and Amroth's disowned prince stared down the maw of mutual calamity.

Blind and shackled by crippling enmity, Lysaer's spirit raged beyond quarter. Dispossessed as he was, and consumed by primal ferocity, he had no purpose. Only the naked commitment to shred his profane torturer to oblivion.

Arithon unsheathed the black sword Alithiel as his half brother sprang.

Song and light flared into explosion. The star song's quintessential harmony hammered into Lysaer's feral animosity with the sundering shock of an avalanche. Fixation shattered. Adamantine beauty blasted to rags the flux torrent of anger, spite and despair cut away at a stroke. Ecstatic hope pealed into exaltation, a clarion summons that disrupted the entrenched viciousness of implacable conflict.

Lysaer screamed, consciousness shredded piecemeal by the insupportable dichotomy.

Amid that rent gap, Arithon wielded the blade spell-forged by the Paravians for healing through transcendent change.

Veracity spoke in the song of Alithiel. Grace resounded with purified clarity *only* for the true cause.

Murder strangled on the unstrung pause. Against the thundering might of the chord sung to Name the winter stars, the latched grip of Desh-thiere's possession relinquished the birth gift of justice instilled in the s'Ilessid royal line.

The shackling coils binding Lysaer to the Mistwraith's collective sundered and snapped. Too fast to assimilate, the unequivocal severance hurled his individual awareness free of coercive obsession.

Adversaries

Lysaer recouped his suborned identity, threshed separate from the morass that had crushed him down beyond hope of release. Traumatized, shocked into brutalized recoil, he found himself bodiless. Powerless. Shorn of flesh as the wraiths whose deathless stew of malevolence had terrorized and devoured him. Panic consumed him. Mangled and mauled, Lysaer clung to a salvaged existence, spiked through by primal panic.

His fragile autonomy was utterly tenuous. No safe harbour existed. Lysaer knew the sound-and-light chord whose ranged resonance bought his salvation: the same reprieve offered once before at the harrowing brink had let Sulfin Evend talk him down from the throes of insanity. But that precious instant of relief had not lasted. The harmonic cry shining with grace had snuffed out and stranded him beyond recourse. The ghastly plunge backwards into the coils of curse-bound hostility had strangled him, a cruelty rendered intolerable by the brief breath of freedom.

The bitter loss of independence burned still.

Nothing stood between him and the reprise of eternal nightmare but the starspelled vibration of Alithiel's drawn blade, a weapon wielded by the unreliable caprice of an inveterate enemy. Lysaer had no personal initiative left. Desh-thiere's ravenous entities choked his defended surrounds, a desolate tumult absent of mercy. Gnashed teeth and glittering, bottomless hunger shrieked and gibbered, slavering for the prey reft away from the seethe of undying, demented animosity. His straits in their hold promised him a fate uglier than oblivion. Excruciate desolation would seize him forever if he was retaken. The abyss had no end. Horror that exceeded his bleakest imagining froze pride and destroyed the demolished shreds of denuded self-respect.

"Don't let me fall!" Empty-handed and desperate, Lysaer had to beg. A whipped dog cringing at bay would have snarled. Not cowered and wept, worthlessness stripped to indignity for a deliverance that bent the knee without condition.

"Don't look, brother." Arithon's entreaty was meaningless.

Lysaer saw himself, broken. Wrecked past catharsis, he wore the branding scourge of defeat, never again secure in self-command since his trampled will had been turned to attack Daliana. Not inwardly whole since his mother's adulterous defection, nor his own master after Rauven's high mage had consigned him to exile in retaliation, he had no path forward. Debased, he had reviled himself: tempted fate to receive the anonymity of the grave, only to fall time and again to the scourge of Desh-thiere's cursed hatred.

Even then, the callous repudiation of his own nature had failed. The Biedar crone had rejected his wish for death. Her piercing sight too clearly discerned the craven purpose behind his suicidal provocation. *'The blood in your veins was not bred to run.'*

Yet shame ceased to matter after the voracious despair of Desh-thiere's enslavement. Dread embraced shrinking cowardice. Unravelled to uselessness by abject fear, Lysaer was unmanned enough to sell out, no coin too abased to buy him another scant moment of surcease.

"Lysaer," said his nemesis, a tender address surely false. "I guarantee the Mistwraith does not have my leave to reclaim you."

Foolish braggadocio, even if true, void of surety or reassurance. Lysaer had slaked on the horrors that lurked in the dark: the mist's revenant horde *knew* the s'Ffalenn antagonist came to baulk them! Desh-thiere's murderous, teeming spite slavered for long-sought revenge. Before terror and madness to liquefy bowels, Lysaer shrank, a stripped wisp of consciousness doomed to tumble, subsumed to purgatory among them.

He was lost beyond help. Whether or not his bastard half brother toyed with him, the grandiose mask of his denial had been ripped away during Alestron's benighted siege. The peacock's ploy of false causes and glib rhetoric no longer cloaked the insidious entrapment that lured his inborn bent for fair-minded rule into the weeds of self-sacrifice. Delusion was threadbare. The merciless rebound, inevitable, had twisted self-hatred into revulsion since the pivotal hour the crone had unmasked the latent weapon, sequestered within him.

Unforgiven, condemned, Lysaer rued his stained hands, red with the premeditated slaughter of *thousands* and burdened by wreckage that spanned generations. Fine statesmanship, warped to depravity, already had cost too much.

He dared not risk worse!

For the crone's condemnation of him had been warranted. He carried the blighted seed that would tip the scales. His treacherous secret, the horrendous perversion the Seven's keen insight and Daliana and Sulfin Evend's unstinted devotion had yet to discern. The half brother whose mercy excoriated him *did not grasp the buried atrocity entangled with his predicament!* Straddled over the precipice, lacerated to agony on the thorns of dichotomy between total damnation and Alithiel's cry for harmonic completion, Lysaer faced the unbearable temptation. He could not be saved. Yet the tenuous, frail promise of unlikely redemption honeyed the poison of absolute ruin.

The only acceptable endgame condemned him. Consumed by rank cowardice, Lysaer shrank from the wicked, unconscionable choice lodged within the unsprung pitfall before him.

Rockfell's vault was impenetrable, an adamant stay built at scale to imprison aberrant monstrosities older than the raving voracity of Desh-thiere's wraiths. Outnumbered, untrained, now indelibly spirit-marked by the latent germ of retaliation instilled through Traithe's purloined knowledge, Lysaer understood with finality: the seductive, last prospect to defeat the Mistwraith's primary directive risked the certainty of his total destruction. A mistake would receive no appeal in this place. No fair enchantment might stave off the honed weapon fashioned by cunning to wreak Athera's demise.

"I am not your enemy," Arithon insisted, blind yet to the Mistwraith's ultimate ambush.

"What other than wretchedness lies before me?" Three centuries of bloodshed abrogated forgiveness. Lysaer's fraught whisper sluiced through a river of tears. "You don't know me!"

"Perhaps not." The bard's tender commiseration resumed, implacable in compassion. "But I daresay there are others who do, and who have, Sulfin Evend foremost among them."

"At what cost?" Lysaer's mauling anguish scalded too deep to share even tenuous confidence. "Everyone I cared for, or needed, I left destroyed in my wake." Nor had anyone beyond the Biedar eldest grasped the dire scope of the danger he harboured.

Arithon denounced his half brother's pain. "No, Lysaer." Forthright, he blocked what he believed was nothing worse than the next venal cry for escape. "You are no more the flawed puppet than anyone else! We are never the saviours of others. Only the tool Desh-thiere intends if you step back and forsake your authority."

How the wider truth lanced the pustule of hidden malice unknown to Athera's defenders! "The monster cannot be reconciled," Lysaer said, afraid beyond words to broach the laid snare of entrapment already unwittingly triggered. "Trust is forfeit. What other than wretchedness lies before me?"

"Shoulder the work in the present." Arithon gestured towards the mercuric pall of baulked wraiths, repulsed in their frenzied thousands by the resonant stay of Alithiel's harmony. "Help me redeem them."

"How?" Lysaer spread his spectral fingers and laughed. "The basic resource no longer exists. Even if the crone restored my access to light when she rendered my being discarnate, I cannot channel the volatile element in this state! The attempt would incinerate consciousness."

"We change places," Arithon said.

"What?" Lysaer wavered, afraid. The wretched, unlikely glimmer of hope surely played the last straw of his vulnerability to the Mistwraith's advantage.

Wry encouragement breezed through the inflexible strategy that placed Arithon at reciprocal risk. "Elaira once replicated the Biedar ritual that enables a consensual loan of the body." Proof in theory existed. The same craft-work used to break through his incurable coma at Athir founded the sober proposal. "You will borrow my form, with our mutual safety ensured by the warded field of Alithiel."

"To what guarantee?" Apprehension harrowed Lysaer's distress. "My birthright power might not respond after transfer."

"Then we take that risk," Arithon insisted. "My experience with the Biedar suggests the crone's gift of a lesson does not countenance punishment. She never acts to no purpose, and my act of conjury originates with her people. I have the mage-trained experience to spiritwalk while you take my body and engage your light to carve down the mist. The free wraiths that remain can be accessed for healing, once pared from the buffered substrate that suspends them."

"Which makes them more dangerous!" Lysaer objected. Suspicious of magic, he regarded the half brother before him. Immaculate self-possession coupled with a cat's fit resilience, Arithon wore his sincerity without prevarication.

Yet slippery deceit could take many forms. Lysaer had bittermost cause to question the blandishment. "If aught goes amiss, I lack your initiate learning. Nothing to stand my firm ground against revenants loosed without boundary."

"I have handled that volatile peril before." The depths of Arithon's green eyes were a Sorcerer's, direct but unfathomable in their reticence. "Alithiel's virtue would expose the shades by true Name. Shielded from them by that active power, even while discorporate, I can compose their songs for requital without undue risk of becoming suborned. Once the collective's passed beyond the veil, your personal autonomy under free will ensures you a natural transition."

"To what end?" Lysaer weighed the unsettling prospect, one body between them, with his dearth of adept awareness no less than pathetically mortal. "Just how long will your detached existence stay viable?" Echoes rang off impervious rock, the warded mineral enclosure without exit, while the yawling entities crammed into the encircling mist leered and capered, implacable in their hunger for conquest.

Since Arithon made no pretence of denial, Lysaer voiced the obvious. "You surely knew you were doomed from the outset."

"Not unless you abandon the contest," Arithon allowed, unflinching. "We are both undone if we can't stand together."

Reason argued for hope, run hard against the defensive resistance that feared to lean on fraternity. "What if I fumble or fall short too soon?" Lysaer pressured for surety, cognizant of the horrific, unequivocal harm poised to roost through a premature failure. "You'd become stranded in harm's way, alone, with Desh-thiere's replete banishment left unfulfilled."

"Then you'd take my death, brother. I did not come this far to abandon your fate." Master initiate, Arithon faced the worst prospect, prepared. "No perverted abomination will rise if I immolate my corrupted husk with white mage-fire. A bard's true ear for sound can, and will, shape the song for your spirit's intact release. I'll survive discorporate and finish the Mistwraith's reduction, defended to the end by Alithiel's resplendent endowment."

The coal of embedded resentment still smouldered, for Rauven's advanced training denied to the grandson sired by s'Ilessid. Unprepared at this final, forsaken pass, when arcane secrets prized from Fellowship knowledge saw him forged as a hapless decoy, Lysaer measured the poison: of his cashiered autonomy wagered against the slim margin for a clean escape. The Biedar crone's warning never had warranted the safe haven of his reprieve.

Nerve quailed before the relentless alternative. The vault's granite walls enclosed a warded prison, churning with unreconciled, circling wraiths: worse than a tomb, consecrated to bind aware consciousness captive indefinitely.

"Daelion wept!" Birth-born justice rammed headlong against the chill of aghast epiphany. "Arithon, swear to me!" Lysaer blurted, appalled. "You can't have come down here at the price of your own survival!"

The stiff silence burned, through the song of a sword that decried the sorrow of discord.

The half brother strapped beyond recourse recoiled, his cruel straits already proscribed. Since the yawning pitfall of his father's rejection, his predicament had been unmalleable. Now, by voluntary consent, Arithon assumed the fatal consequence. Straddled between abject damnation and the unbearable, siren cry of whole harmony, both of them faced the dread plunge from the brink. Ensnared sanity snatched the silk strand of reprieve. Fragile calm in the storm's eye clung to elusive hope: the last, tenuous chance to slip the covert knot baiting the noose of redemption.

Reason insisted, left with nothing to lose. Rockfell's vault must fail in the course of the ages. At scale, no stone fixture and no contrived stay might contain the raving voracity of Desh-thiere's wraiths. Not forever.

Outnumbered, unschooled, and indelibly spirit-marked by a latent perversion warped into him during the Mistwraith's possession, Lysaer had no alternate recourse. He could not save himself, or disentangle his compromised being from the insidious, embedded directive. No possible avenue qualified him to subdue an inimical collective, wedded together by necromancy for annihilation and conquest.

Choice set against an unbearable quandary disemboweled all virtue but pity.

Lysaer outlined the terms of uncertain alliance. "My epitaph written, and clean death for us both as the brightest available outcome?"

"Free will," stated Arithon. "I've committed myself."

Helpless regret stabbed Lysaer to the quick. He was more lost than anyone knew. Bleeding need had forced him to reject Daliana, a moral sacrifice more profound than he ever dared to admit.

"Sunlight on Athera endures for posterity, a worthy end come what may." Lysaer's spirit form blazed, his corrosive sarcasm scoured by recrimination. "It's a thankless endeavour. Your moral high ground leaves me a dastardly burden on Daelion Fatemaster's ledger."

"Are heroic appearances worth all that much?" Arithon withheld judgement, transparently strained. "No one else dies, brother. Innocents outside of Rockfell's protections will not suffer the torment of unending terror. Take your deliverance on my given word. Or languish and cede your last, honest fight. We have only this moment to break the Mistwraith's bonded enslavement."

Born royal, raised from childhood to uplift the many, Lysaer yielded, resigned. Without access to tears, he could not weep. Every shining dream cracked by his last unseen flaw, he weighed the final line of his perfidy. The penalty if he shrank stripped him bare and scorched the tinsel of honour to ashes. Personal need in the end did not signify. Vainglory stripped, Lysaer counted the toll for a precarious passage yet to be paid.

Justice spoke in Alithiel's radiance, an immaculate song for a purposeful cause that was true. Illumined by an ecstasy that torched human falsehood, the wormwood of personal short-falls found no cranny to hide. Tysan's crown lineage could but rise with the blistering courage to answer.

Having never lived, never loved, never laughed for himself, Lysaer confronted the unimpeachable ethic that demanded of him the excoriate, counterfeit coin. For the dice throw to unbind the Mistwraith's malevolence, he knew, *Ath forsake him for his unshed tears, how sorely he knew!* At the last, he must author his half brother's betrayal to salvage the loophole for triumph.

"I have suffered the terror of Desh-thier's imprisonment," Lysaer s'Ilessid said, shorn by grief. "Let nothing and no one else ever suffocate, consumed by that fell darkness again."

*   *   *

"So be it." Granted his sibling's clear word of permission, Arithon knelt. One-handedly awkward, hampered by the active sword in his grasp, he unfastened and shed Davien's black mantle. Silver embroidery gleamed like flicked mercury as he spread the cloth on cold stone. "Take position over my head, if you will."

Lysaer's spirit form drifted above, as with spare economy, Arithon laid down the ceremonial stays for the old Biedar ritual. He sketched the requisite ciphers at the four quarters, then, focus unswerving, steadied himself for the weightless suspension of transfer. His aligned focus resisted the sideward glance; ignored the crawling gooseflesh that suggested the crone's uncanny, carved serpents looked on with jet eyes. Such arcane observation should not have surprised him, lent the long sleeve through his enactment of her tribal practice.

Arithon consecrated the placed markers. Poised for an initiate's launch into spiritwalk, with Alithiel's ward his sole stay against the Mistwraith's undying malice, he assumed his stance on the outspread cloak. Lysaer's essence must be sequestered within his borrowed flesh in seamless form, with no moral stricture omitted.

He must not slip, while the leading edge of honed faculties quickened his laggard reflex. Concentration absolute, he let go, uncoupled from the envelope of his warm flesh. Activation of his preset intent drew Lysaer's unmoored self into the flash point of transfer. Faith ruled the tenuous, free-will exchange, his inner barriers openly vulnerable, and his dedication nakedly blind to the split-second backstab arriving without warning.

Arithon never foresaw the wild turn of event as the pivotal crux overtook him. Nor did he perceive his half brother's need, driving Daelion's fist on Fate's Wheel. On assumption that his quickened faculties had outpaced his painstaking restraints, he grappled in vain to brake what he *thought* was his own, runaway talent. As well attempt to stay magma with kindling: the explosive cascade sparked *too fast and too powerfully*, the unbridled forces in motion outstripped his control . . .

The chain-lightning transition from ephemeral spirit to an unfamiliar, compact body stunned Lysaer's orientation barely an instant. Spun down into the gravid sensation of flesh, he recorded the ungainly weight of the sword sliding through the grasp of slackening fingers. Light dimmed from the blade. Alithiel's ranging song dwindled, fast strangled by deso-

late silence. Terrified of the bottomless plunge into the dread pall of the
dark abyss, Lysaer screamed.

No option remained. No escape, to delay the unforgiveable, premeditated calumny aimed to force Arithon's unwary hand. Lysaer acted, as
he must. The split second before the Mistwraith closed its ravenous rush
to consume, he invested all that he owned beyond recall. He released
his birth gift of light to subsume the wraiths' calyx of mist. Immolation
hurled him past the point of return. At the parted threshold of the veil,
his dissolution disgorged the aberrant blight of the curse sequestered
within his birth matrix. Also, more sinister, the wicked brew not of his
making: the nefarious knot gleaned from the husked fragment of Traithe's
suborned consciousness unfurled, free to wreak its fell sabotage.

The Biedar crone had forewarned him of the irreversible catastrophe
should the latent peril he carried break loose. The informed knowledge
that enabled the wraiths to warp time, coupled with the long past, proven
access to penetrate Arithon's shields, now launched the impetus for a
greater conquest: the might of his half brother's exquisite, trained acumen
redirected into a weapon.

"*I cannot grant you death,*" the Biedar ancient had told Lysaer on the
hour her dartmen snatched him away. '*Wound into your current incar-
nation, you bear the insidious spring for the trap to destroy the Fellowship
Sorcerers. Desh-thiere's vengeance, dispatched by Marak's exiles, plotted
the Seven's demise under guise of the curse that pressed you to murder
your half brother. There is one way, only one, to disarm the blight set upon
both of your fates. Do you own the strength to make the attempt? Walk
into that hazard, and everything in the world's balance crosses the shadow
of jeopardy.*'

The dread crux foreseen by her wisdom came due.

Lysaer gave himself, willing. He torched every spark of his mortal
reserve into his birth-gifted channel, *which answered*, and unleashed the
element. The concatenation of torrential force razed him through, spirit
and borrowed flesh. Continuity perished. Married to abject annihilation,
the blast of his release smashed a wave of untempered light against walls
of immutable stone. The concussive shock slammed through the five-
sided vault, the brute force of explosion hammered to thunderous echoes
in the confined space.

No moment was given to know whether Arithon's discorporate presence owned the adroit skill to field the unchained brunt in the aftermath.

No grace, before the impact razed Lysaer's sundered awareness beyond cohesion. Consumed wholly by violent immolation, he could not tell if his half brother's overset straits survived the withering blast with the shreds of cohesive reflex intact.

Perhaps the raging eruption itself overwhelmed the dropped thread of aligned possibility. Or, left unpartnered, maybe the wild cascade unstrung the future, both brothers charged with the Mistwraith's demise consigned into a damnation beyond the cleanse of white mage-fire.

Lysaer knew nothing else. Black oblivion robbed his final thought and extinguished the spark of awareness.

Arithon survived the shattering burst on the preconditioned foundation of his initiate training. Lofted by turbulent shock and cast into an untethered spiritwalk, the spark of his consciousness tumbled. Discorporate, deafened, and blinded, he fended off panic and crammed his disorientation back into centred awareness. Mage-sight measured the damage. Stark evidence confirmed the irrevocable price of his half brother's suicidal deliverance: the crumpled body on loan as a willing receptacle had vanished, gone without so much as a trace of wisped smoke. No ashes winnowed through the roiled air. Davien's spread cloak lay vacated, midnight velvet picked out by the sheen of silver embroidery and the liminal silhouette of the dropped sword. The blade's shining runes swiftly dimmed, steel dulled to polished black glass as the opaline shimmer of the Paravian starspell failed in the absence of just cause and animate contact.

Danger stalked, unchained amid falling darkness. The substrate holding the mist was destroyed, scoured off by Lysaer's torched reserves. Yet the banishment granted no victory.

Reduced to a shade, Arithon confronted his peril redoubled. The after-slam of the setback just triggered exposed his naked essence to the horrific bindings that shackled Desh-thiere's remnant horde. Caught out, defenceless, on the wrong side of the veil, he encountered the disastrous strait his worst nightmare had never foreseen: the hideous perversion of Traithe's suborned fragments, turned hostile against him.

Time slowed, stretched and warped into ghastly distortion. Entrapped along with him, the Mistwraith's collective swarmed at large in their ravening thousands. Unleashed upon him as free wraiths, their perversion was more deadly than the invasive spirits escaped from Marak. Not only spawned by the insidious atrocity derived from the practice of necromancy, these debased entities twisted the cached theft of Fellowship knowledge to wreak harm far beyond Arithon's personal downfall.

Worse, the augmentation lately bestowed by the dragon compounded that lethal danger. The immanent, perilous reckoning dawned late, that Desh-thiere's vengeful strategy devolved from the fateful ambush, years past, when he and his half brother had been caught undefended by night in Ithamon. Intelligent, insatiable, the revenants had shaped fell directives that violated them both: for Lysaer, the immediate seed of the curse that engendered armed conflict to fracture the compact, and for Arithon, long-range seizure of the perfected tool to take down Athera's defenders.

Here and now, stripped of shielding before them, a power to rival the Fellowship's might would deliver Traithe's sullied essence and forge the ultimate hostile partnership in coalition against them. A catastrophic stroke of deceit, but one narrow step short of completion, and prelude to an act of treachery without parallel. Arithon's perverse role would drive home Desh-thiere's incontestable victory.

The adverse throng had their selected prey isolated.

Cede this conflict, and the undying mysteries perished, all the shining grace of Ath's gifted glory snuffed out. Traithe's and Elaira's fates foundered along with him, Athera's Masterbard stared down the inflexible stakes. All he had laboured for might go for naught, the sterling integrity of a lifetime's initiate triumph and wisdom undone. The substance of Luhaine's gloomy forewarnings, recast, were utterly unforgiving. Fall here, inducted and suborned, and all that Arithon was would become the destructive instrument forged to spearhead the ruin of all things.

No bolt-hole existed within this dread place. At best, he and his beloved, and Traithe, would stay sealed within Rockfell as a peril to life and the world's weal beyond remedy.

Set at bay against an intractable impasse, Arithon seized on the only solution within his immediate grasp. While decision hung weightless, execution was lead. Given one sorry, sad moment to impose his free will, he embraced the grievous, inviolate course left before him without hesitation.

Rearrangement

In the predawn darkness five days after Luhaine and Kharadmon completed the impervious, grand conjury sealing off access to Rockfell Pit's threshold, Dakar the Mad Prophet rolled out of his blankets, rumpled and chilled from a restive night spent thrashing in sleepless distress. The whiskey that thumped his muzzy head with the waning pangs of a hangover was drained, his last wistful toast to oblivion gone with the dregs. Saddled with a damp beard, an evil, furred tongue and a sand-papered gullet, he tottered erect. Fumbled on his stiff boots and belaboured the fact his discomfort should have been worse.

The dulled aftermath of his binge left him stranded, far short of the stupor to obliviate his dismal spirits. High altitude rankled his throbbing temples and chased gooseflesh over his clammy skin. Dakar lurched the deadweight of his carcass into a quest for dry fire-wood. The scrub forest clawed him at wrist and knee, diabolical punishment for a man with a paunch, whose messy regrets roiled in conflict. He bashed through needled boughs, swearing and stumbling on the roots grappled into the steep, rocky slope.

"Dharkaron's Black Spear gaff the gizzard of fate!" he snapped, testy expletive steaming in the frigid air. "And crap on the doings of disbarred royal bastards, and the lockjawed teeth of s'Ffalenn ethic, too, for that matter!"

Day upon day, Arithon's margin for survival expired, without means to know whether he had achieved his half brother's salvation, or if his pitched stand against Desh-thiere's wraiths had battered him to damnation. Althain's Warden himself could not scry through Rockfell's raised defences. Bad feeling above the pinch of earned guilt fretted Dakar's incipient dread. His gutless cowardice wanted a fire, the hotter the better. Flailing over the skeletons of last winter's snags, he barked shins and skinned knuckles gathering seasoned branches until, tipsy under his armload of kindling, he ambled back towards the hollow that sheltered his camp.

He managed three paces without mishap before the forsaken seer's fit overtook him. Sucked into the velvet caul of catatonia, the curse on his lips unravelled to gibberish. He crashed forward. Joints loosened, clubbed as he succumbed by his own scavenged wood, he languished in a sprawl as the throes of involuntary prophecy seized hold and savaged him as a blank instrument.

Dakar woke, nauseous, to bad weather past dawn. He had bitten his tongue. The coppery tang of let blood soured his mouth, with the last, ringing words in stunned ears his own voice, sliced through the sluiced drum of rainfall, *'of dragons past Northgate transfixed by madness . . .'*

Cramped sickness curled him into a knot. Forehead pillowed on drenched billets of wood, he shivered, spasmed by dry heaves. Best not to move, far less try to think. As useless to wonder how long the brute seizure had felled him. Until the aftermath misery passed, he could do nothing but cower and retch. His overset faculties yet ran amok, when the claws of hag's luck fouled his recovery. Another surge of vision ran riot and savaged his consciousness. Skewered by his ungoverned talent, his inward eye cartwheeled into a tumultuous view of salt air and seawater churned into chaos . . .

. . . where a screaming roar of monstrous rage spewed flame across starry sky, a solid, shingle abutment dissolved, plunging Davien into the shocking cold swirl of rip currents. Half-drowned, he clawed through the maelstrom and surfaced. On the splinter world of Sckaithen Duin, purple waters shoaled into lucent turquoise shallows, turbulent with blowholes and back-splashed spray jetted off ramparts of glacial ice. Overhead, maddened dragons wove and darted in duelling packs. The blue shimmer of their auric charge roiled a flux stream transformed by their dreaming. Contrary gusts cracked off their leathered wings, and explosive, shed static sparked the face of the deep, spawning gargantuan whirlpools as incompatible forces whipped into collision. Entangled in sodden garments, the Sorcerer hurled into immersion bobbed and spun like a hapless cork.

His shouted directive to water and air framed an urgent appeal, cadenced in actualized Paravian . . .

Slapped off by the shearing might of the distant incantation, Dakar snapped out of tranced vision. Shaken and gasping in puddled clothes, he opened his eyes to the grey chill of dusk. Plastered hair runnelled icy rain in his eyes, mingled with tears. The appalling sense of on-coming calamity rattled the breath in his throat.

Whether prescient warning, or concurrent vision, dragons gone raving mad anywhere in existence commanded destructive forces sufficient to savage an embodied Fellowship Sorcerer. Given wyrmkind's fraught penchant for gestalt awareness, the potential for wider-scale impact stared down the maw of a breaking disaster.

A frigid shudder of panic reamed Dakar, spirit and flesh.

The mere *chance* mature drakes might become sundered from reasoned intelligence defied contemplation. Far worse, if the resonant trauma sparked their species to mass conflagration on both sides of the Worldsend Gate. Davien knew dragons. None better, he might withstand a deranged attack. But to hold the aggressive, firm ground to check the quaking upheaval of a cross-world outbreak required backing in full by the Protectorate's designate gate watcher.

Where was Ozvowzakrin? However that urgent question begged answer, the imperative for an immediate scrying was thwarted. The storm had rinsed away the recent flux imprint mirrored in stone, the best access past his seer's reach to parse the import of his black-out prophecy.

Dakar rolled to his knees and tottered upright, despite brutalized faculties forced to seek wiser counsel. But the scared, shaken glance he cast upslope towards Rockfell's heights to locate his nearest ally swept the blank silhouette of a mountainside swathed in veiled cloud.

The pinpoint, orange glimmer of Luhaine's cookfire was gone. No Sorcerer kept the vigil to back Arithon's trial within the sealed depths of the pit.

If Dakar had been afraid before, dread sucked the pith from his bones. "I should have walked away care-free while I had a chance to cling to the pretence of ignorance."

The abandonment wrenched, and not only for the fates resigned to Traithe and Elaira. *'Raise a tankard for me,'* the black-haired bastard had said, a poor gesture to distance the lancing hurt caused by a terrible parting's ineptitude.

Since Dakar had dismissed that earnest advice, he was wretched, coughing up bile alone in the most desolate vale on the continent. Naught could be done but collect his damp kindling, spark a fire, and dry out, then snare something gamey for the needful sustenance to stabilize his shocked wits. Or else suffer the course of a miserable night, flayed raw by anxiety for a massive upset he lacked the resource to put right.

Dakar steadied himself at the jagged edge of an ugly predicament. Midnight came and went, before he recovered the acumen to appeal for a direct contact with Sethvir.

The star at the zenith he tapped for his crafted connection with Althain's Warden instead raised the centaur awareness of Tehaval at Ithamon. Dakar slammed into recoil, not quickly enough. The back-lash surge from the Paravian contact overset him all over again. Hurled prostate, weeping, he could not shake the dread Sight: *of Seshkrozchiel, her scaled coils strangled around Althain Tower, while streamered smoke rolled off the downs of Atainia, the historic vista laid to waste yet again by the scouring flame of her amok fury . . .*

Whatever had hurtled the world's course awry, the prescient glimpse of the elder dragon who treated for the Protectorate on Athera embroiled in such a crazed assault well might wake another elder power of major proportion. The centaur spirit of Shehane Althain, whose dedicate shade guarded that ancient foundation, was unforgiving of violent trespass: two legendary forces locked into vicious antipathy posed a recipe for ruin beyond compare.

Dakar mewled, beset. Past question, the hag's wind of ill luck landed bad news in batches.

Before dawn, further delving confirmed his worst fear. No Fellowship presence remained on Athera. Asandir had vacated his attendance upon the restive Khadrim in Tornir Peaks, his signature on the stays at the Sorcerers' Preserve put aside in patched haste. At Forthmark, Ciladis no longer oversaw Siantra's healing. Sethvir did not hold his posted station at Althain Tower, and Kharadmon's elusive shade evaded the reach of the spellbinder's talent.

Dakar slumped on his hams, shaken witless. No catastrophe in his knowledge of historical record raised the penumbral spectre cast by today's brutal gamut. He had no place to turn. None, beyond the last beacon: the sole, titled authority born human who upheld the compact was Verrain, stationed as Guardian of Methisle Fortress to mind the drake-spawned aberrations at Mirthlvain Swamp.

Dakar set off on foot as the crow flew and crossed over the Skyshiel divide. Travel through that rough country was slow at the turn of the season, the ash trees at altitude changing summer's mantle from green to gold. He asked due permission of a sturdy, straight sapling and cut a stave to brace the mincing limp caused by raw blisters. Down to the flats, he ploughed through softened ground, where the scythed wheat stood up in bound shocks and the scream of flocked birds wheeled over the stubbled rows, gleaning. He reached Tharidor in the lingering warmth of the shortened days before autumn's storms broke the calm and brought frost. Sunburned and gaunt as a rail, he paid dear, and booked a fast passage by galley. A dodgy seal on a counterfeit requisition convinced the ship's master to land him on the untenanted shore near the old way crossing the east fringe of Atwood. Too harried to pause, he placated clan sentries as worried as he, and pressed southward to reach the Paravian focus in the ruin at Old Tirans.

Transfer on the lane's crest delivered him on his last legs to Methisle Fortress. He buckled to his knees on arrival, propped by the straight stave brought along to replace the one with the scorched tip, borrowed under expedience from Verrain.

"You're a desperate sight for sore eyes," the Master Spellbinder exclaimed. "Though by Daelion's witness, you've lost flesh. A walking shambles of picked bones, the Fatemaster would be hard-pressed to recognize you for the unfinished score of your misdeeds in the hereafter."

Dakar clasped the extended hand offered and swayed erect. "I brought you a new ash stick. Your original sank, chewed to splinters in the bog by something with hideous teeth I didn't stop to identify." Mangled by grief, all but incoherent, he blurted his burdensome nightmare aloud. "Where are the Seven? They've as good as left them entombed alive within Rockfell Peak!"

Verrain's self-contained calm was less comfort than the iron-shod mask of practicality. "Elaira and Traithe will not suffer, cocooned as they are in oblivious stasis."

"And Arithon?" Dakar's dammed anguish broke. By now, if the man had survived the encounter, he would persist as a shade. "Should the Masterbard not be subsumed as a wraith, he's to languish until someone resolves the Fellowship's lapsed promise to free him?" Dodging the fearful topic of dragons, Dakar retorted on a tremor of exhausted hysteria, "Provided he doesn't go stark raving mad, exposed to the blunt-force horror of those wards in the dark! Nothing conscious deserves that ghastly fate. When I catch up with Kharadmon, I will curse the whirlwind flit's fecklessness to Dharkaron's everlasting torment!"

"Kharadmon stands off a greater problem, just now." Verrain's regret implied sorrows beyond the horizon of woes besetting Athera.

"Then we're left without recourse! Confluent stress between drakes has diverted the Fellowship past Northgate to Sckaithen Duin?" Aghast, Dakar realized his glimpsed vision of Seshkrozchiel's insane assault upon Althain Tower already had outpaced the grim shadow of prescience.

"If you want consolation," said Verrain, "bless your timely fit. That blind prophecy you delivered at Rockfell Vale dealt the Seven their fair warning to act, or they would have been caught unprepared."

Alarmed afresh by Dakar's stricken pallor, Mirthlvain's Guardian snatched the stick's sliding fall from the slackened grip of his peer's nerveless hand. He braced the distraught spellbinder upright and steered his stumbling steps towards the spiral stair. "Straightaway, let's mend the wear from hard travel. You'll want to be seated with a stiff restorative before hearing the brunt in detail."

Late-morning sunbeams from the upstairs gallery shafted golden light through the pervasive gloom in the cavernous chamber built for the stature of centaurs. Verrain stood to receive his harried guest, whose thumping commotion descended down the cobwebbed stair. Dakar swiped back dripping hair from his hasty bath, his echoing complaints punched through by the shuffled scuff of his boots.

"If our Fellowship shade's not inclined to bestir his windy arse, we'll need copper rods to take the initiative." A snatched pause for breath, and his tirade uncorked in earnest. "Placed at strategic locations on Rockfell Peak, grounded lightning unleashed by the equinox storms will erode the integrity of the outer wards. Correct placement to best advantage should lend us adequate leverage to breach the defences on the upper vault."

Verrain's tucked frown evinced disapproval, though the courtier's manner ingrained since his birth remained mild as he tipped off a lounging tabby to clear a chair at the trestle.

The Mad Prophet plonked down in the wadded sag of loose clothes, to a lofted tempest of shed cat fur as the cushion beneath him deflated. "We must hurry before—"

Verrain interrupted, sliding a tray across the scarred planks, piled with autumn's plain fare of nuts, cheese, boiled eggs, and hard bread. "Dakar. Thirty five days have passed since Arithon made his descent into Rockfell. That unpleasant tragedy is written and sealed. If he's survived unimpaired by possession, he must carry on as a discorporate being. Since we can't determine whether or not Desh-thiere's malice is safely subdued, the Masterbard must complete that dire work as he can. *Salvation for his plight and the Mistwraith's lost entities cannot signify!* Not if we don't surmount the hot crisis that's disrupted the Fellowship's custody of Athera's straits first!"

Dakar thumped his bearded chin on propped palms. Stalled in mid-rant, he blinked troubled brown eyes, reinflated his lungs, and glared at the untouched food without appetite. "What's happened? I caught the snatched Sight of an upheaval by dragons, with Davien beset on Sckaithen Duin."

"We have that, and worse thrust upon us right here." Verrain dropped the news, a terse blow fit to shake the foundations of Methisle Fortress. "The untoward stimulation of human perspective infiltrated the psyche of Dragonkind through Seshkrozchiel, after Davien and Asandir salvaged the Scarpdale grimward. The attractant curiosity restoked the old rebellion against the Protectorate, aggravated again by the emphatic breakthrough incurred by Arithon's brisk handling of the molts at Forthmark. The compounded excitement has caught fire since, and plunged the species' stability over the brink."

Dakar stared appalled. "Ath's tears, Siantra!"

Verrain shrugged, destitute. "Perhaps. I don't know! She may have become the inadvertent catalyst, immersed into unshielded rapport with Seshkrozchiel. Likely or not, the taint of human emotion has bled through in force and altered Dragonkind's behavioural instincts."

Dakar digested the unpleasant development. Dragons were a partially unified consciousness, the intensity of an individual's perspective often shared between them as a common experience. Minds that manifested creation straddled a dynamic nexus: a conceptual thought stream, impetus and counterforce precisely matched in a perpetual dance of delicate balance. But humanity's ungoverned feelings adhered to no such frame of restraint. The radical influx of unbridled passion incited a runaway reaction: unstoppable, explosive destruction, with no curb to brake the cascade.

"We are facing the brutal consequence alone," Verrain affirmed in quiet despair.

The watchful, emerald eyes of the cats gleamed from the dimmed corners as Dakar ruminated on the conclusion. "You imply the combined result may inflame more than Seshkrozchiel to unreconciled madness?"

"That's happened, I fear." Verrain's strained features showed a desolation seen only in the guarded privacy of his annual visit to the Paravian marker raised in tribute to his long-lost beloved. "That knotty turmoil has risen to reap the whirlwind. Or else the rogue factions' revolt has united against the Protectorate. Ozvowzakrin may not have the hardened experience to put down the nexus of conflict. Cause or effect, the Worldsend Gate's keeper has failed to blunt the concerted attack. The Seven themselves were called to avert a unilateral upset spilling through to Athera."

A wracked pause ensued as Athera's two Master Spellbinders sorted the daunting ramifications. Lose Ozvowzakrin, and no elder dragon on Sckaithen Duin held the authority to bind the breach in the treatied alliance.

At drawn length, Verrain said, "All four corporate Sorcerers raced for the grand circle at Penstair. They passed through Northgate to back Davien and stem the fracture ahead of the Accord's collapse. Against the greater threat of chaotic invasion, they broke the worldsend conjury behind them. Sckaithen Duin's access is sealed, with Kharadmon assigned to hold fast at Althain Tower."

Which stopgap precedent defied credibility, since no discorporate spirit might endure the shredding wave at the forefront of a dragon's interactive creation. Should Kharadmon venture to try, he would be thrashed into dissolution.

"You aren't finished?" Dakar stabbed distraught fingers through his tangled beard. "Sweet life, don't say my vision of Seshkrozchiel on the rampage was not latent prescience, but true Sight of an unhinged assault!"

"I'm sorry." Verrain massaged his temples, grey under his weathered tan as he resumed his frayed summary. "To all appearance, the ancient wyrm has succumbed to severe derangement along with the rest of her kin."

Dakar clutched at the last, flimsy straw. "We're not bereft of a Fellowship presence, given a transit point through the Paravian focus in the tower dungeon."

Verrain sighed. "Yes, if the Sorcerer dared to leave his current station. Right now, I assume his placating presence is too busy keeping the dedicate shade of Shehane Althain from unfurling a full-scale defence."

"Sithaer's fiery gates!" Dakar gasped. A clash of titanic power on that scale would wreak Atainia's galvanic destruction, and worse, a fatality befallen Seshkrozchiel could raise the spectral horror of a new grimward. "Someone might have bothered to keep me informed."

"You were knocked flat and unresponsive," Verrain allowed. "Forbye, the Sorcerers had only moments to muster themselves for departure."

"I don't have to like the demeaning excuse," Dakar groused. "Though I still find it damnably hard to forgive the abandonment, with four souls condemned to perpetual imprisonment in Rockfell's sealed vault."

"You imagine Kharadmon's pleased with his lot? Five colleagues are cut off, until Seshkrozchiel's wrath is contained." Asandir, Luhaine, Ciladis, Davien, and Sethvir were entrenched in the throes of a drake war, denied any straightforward route to return until Kharadmon could be extricated from his besieged redoubt at Althain Tower.

"We are on our own," Dakar surmised, crushed. Without a discorporate Sorcerer to rethread the path through the void, the onerous process to anchor the geometry for transit between stars involved consummate danger. The conjury to span a worldsend gate exposed an incarnate colleague to the fraught risk of an extended spiritwalk.

"At best, we face a disastrous lag." Verrain voiced the inflexible summary, fighting despondency. "We might be forced to uphold the compact through the next century, provided Northgate's riven portal can be safely restored."

"Mankind's affairs will pitch us to havoc long before then." By spring thaw, the baulked line of the True Sect assault was hell-bound to press Fallowmere's remnant clans into precarious refuge at Ithilt. "What can be done?" Dakar banged the trestle in anguish, to the shrill clank of jounced cutlery. "We're stuck holding the reins, while a religious bloodbath is poised to disrupt the tenuous foothold of the Paravians' return to the mainland!"

Defeat in Rathain further jeopardized Mankind's destiny, with naught but two spellbinders and a Fellowship shade to answer the lapsed terms of the compact.

"You cannot leave Methisle unguarded." Dakar rolled his eyes to the whites, saddled with the bad lot as the only free agent. "Ath, I'm not ready to wear Asandir's boots. Nor you, to shoulder Sethvir's role as Warden stuffed in the bleeding breach!" Hedged by the dearth of alternatives, the Mad Prophet slouched in his chair, too distraught to notice the growl of his empty belly. "Exactly what would you have me do?"

Verrain visibly gathered stripped nerves. "Eat, first of all. Then pack winter clothes. You'll fare onwards to Fallowmere and warn the clans they'll be facing a war to protect the northern territory on their own merits. Then snag Esfand. You'll have to use his poor, broken mind as your link to track down Siantra."

"She's gone feral as well?" Dakar spluttered, chewing by rote as he crammed sustenance into his cheeks.

"She slipped the adepts' custody at the Forthmark hostel a month past, gone who knows where on the lam. Whether her acute restlessness stemmed from the dragons, or worse—"

"You believe she exacerbated the drakes' derangement?" Dust silted down from the rafters, sun-caught flecks winking like gilt through the appalled quiet. "Glory preserve," Dakar cracked. "I can't be the benighted sod sent to dispatch her!"

"Precisely our wretched verdict to face." Verrain's legendary gallantry gave way to anguish. "If she's the flash-point impetus driving the wyrms, we must handle the unpleasant consequence. The adepts by their code won't take a life, and Ciladis stayed his hand for a reason but left no word on the matter. Since he did not condemn her, we stand at the crux. The hard question of choice could be moot. Hesitate to apprehend her, and she's likely to become arraigned for a True Sect execution."

The prospect of her traumatic death well might provoke an emotional chain reaction at scale, if not throw the ugly potential of an unrequited haunt into the deadly, unstable mix.

"Siantra s'Idir is drake spawn, in fact," Verrain ground on in vexed sorrow. Human stock altered beyond recognition, in possession of who *knew* what ruinous range of untapped, latent faculties. Mirthlvain's Guardian

668 J A N N Y   W U R T S

wore his torn heart on his sleeve, wrung by sympathy for the vicious, ungovernable creatures his post obliged him to eradicate. "The young woman was permitted to live on the Fellowship's sufferance, despite the unparalleled potential for danger." Debt owed her the chance to surmount her fate after her courageous initiative at Caith-al-Caen, and for the insight that salvaged the lives thrown into the crucible of Seshkrozchiel's reckoning at Forthmark. "No guessing how far her innate strength of character may hold sway over the hybrid intelligence she has inherited."

The impact of Arithon's foray with the drake molts had seeded the gamut of today's vicious coil. Unrelenting, Dakar shared the anguish of mourning the regrettable tangents in hindsight. "You imply we were premature to count the Koriathain's collapse as a victory?"

"Who knows?" Though Siantra's demeanour had not seemed aggressive, she had been shiftless enough to forsake the adepts' compassionate oversight. "Dakar, I'm sorry." Verrain's apology poured ice water over the sting of abrasive apprehension. "We have little margin. Without the sound counsel to know if Seshkrozchiel's agitation may be linked to Siantra's cross-grained influence, no plausible chance of salvage exists unless you overtake her."

The Mad Prophet gorged himself on sliced cheese, morose. "Fate wept! To think I used to lie sleepless, paralysed by my pitiful fear Elaira might one day rip me to shreds over Arithon's drunken dalliance at Ganish!"

For the grotesque horror overshadowed all else, that drake wars spun off uncontrolled lines of consequence. Beyond the damaging, past alterations cratered into Athera's terrain, live beings caught up in the weave at the interface revived the hideous peril of resurgent Methurien. Such hate wraiths foreran Mirthlvain's lethal predators, and bred the endlessly vicious array of today's recombinant monstrosities.

The ghastly stakes were unmalleable, should a fresh cycle of drake spawn emerge to savage the world in the Fellowship's absence.

Variations

Footsore and heartsick, Dakar steps off the Paravian focus at ruined Penstair and embarks on the hundred-league journey to Fallowmere, a fool's errand pursued without means to renew Kharadmon's hold on the pack ice that stalls the war host supply through the northshore harbours, or to remedy the foresighted need to waylay a True Sect advance in the south from sneak access through Leynsgap behind Asandir's line of protection . . .

Besieged by the maddened dragon wrapped around Althain Tower, Kharadmon quells Shehane Althain's defences, cut off from the raging drake war besetting his colleagues on Sckaithen Duin, and denied insight to penetrate Rockfell Pit to determined the status of Arithon's shade, under Desh-thiere's assault with no safe-guard should the virtue of Alithiel's song be extinguished . . .

Winter solstice dawns: to a raven's flight across Rathain's free wilds; to the aching, pure strains of crystalline flutes as Athlien Paravians dance to invoke the grand confluence; to Rathain's displaced clan council mapping the furtive routes to send families to emergency haven in Melhalla, while debate compiles the grim list of names for a war band too scant to defy the upcoming overthrow of the free wilds . . .

XVI. Discord

Desperation convulsed Fallowmere's clan council, just handed the death knell of hope with the spellbinder's grim packet of news. The overtaxed bearer weathered the bitter arguments, sidelined throughout four contentious days. Dakar tried without stature to shout down the panic as reason frayed into hysteria. Better than any, he knew the razor-edged quandary before them outstripped sober compromise to ameliorate. No solution salved the spectre of anguish. Only bad choices, leading to worse, each beset by a hideous gamut of drawbacks. A Master Spellbinder lacked the authority to quell the inimical cross fire, while harried chieftains butted heads and slammed down ultimatums too paltry to amend their disastrous straits. Man and woman, they grasped to a fare-thee-well how ill-prepared Dakar was to assume the burden that walked in a Fellowship Sorcerer's shoes. Heard through the tumult by dint of a fist repeatedly gavelled to bruises, he fielded the bickering, derisive complaints until he was pummelled to hoarse exhaustion.

The last hour before daybreak, he packed to press onwards. Still gimping from several fortnights of harsh travel, a man rued the penalty imposed by every slack century spent in fleshpot dalliance on a feather mattress.

Austerity sat awkwardly on his stout frame. Dakar tightened a belt notched ragged with holes to take up the slack as rolled fat melted off his starved flanks. The loose end tongued through the tinker's brass buckle dangled to his calves as he stamped on dank boots and hefted his blanket roll. Outside, the weathered lodge tent glittered with hoarfrost in the liminal dark that shrouded the clan enclave. The crabbed evergreens of Drimwood creaked and soughed under the pillowed upholstery of last night's snowfall. Cold air socked his lungs like a punch to the chest. Dakar swore, drained of venom. A hundred leagues afoot across the northern wilds had worn the blithe hedonist in him to gristle and string.

Chilblained and chapped, he picked his course through weltered movement, the shuddering fall of downed tents, and the purposeful, hurried figures already abroad in the predawn gloom. Clanborn efficiency became a rife bother for a late riser wanting quiet to void his bladder.

"Scorch virtue off the Fatemaster's list!" Like the hunched storm crow, Dakar clenched his jaw and breasted the seethed industry dismantling the refuge at speed.

The ungainly obstruction, between terse talk and bustle, he stumped past the fretful wail of a newborn, tacked past a laden sledge, and cursed the impediments of slacked ropes and rolled hides and provisions. No apology sugared the taint on the messenger whose frantic tidings impelled the swift exodus.

Dakar slouched in his mantle, not yet seasoned enough to learn Asandir's preference for solitude. Paid in reckoning for a few nights' hospitality, a looming figure bundled in bearskin flanked his furtive retreat.

"You're leaving," observed Tarens, his blunt disparagement scored by the scrape of his scabbarded knives.

"As soon as I've collected Esfand, I must." Dakar's sigh repressed pity he dared not admit, lest breaking sorrow unmanned him. Shoved way over his head, he was the bit player trapped in the lead role as an imposter. He dared not tinker with Fallowmere's markers for warded protection without the Paravian presence. Limitation narrowed his ethical choices to salvage humanity's right to Atheran inhabitance, a short-fall that foisted the hideous brunt on the scattered descendants of Rathain's clan lineages. "You've drawn the short straw to stay on for defence?"

"To captain the handpicked war band?" Tarens skirted a woman yoked with bundled arrows, his longer stride clipped to match pace. "Ironic, forbye. Since my fumbled debacle last spring, the bad lot was plucked for me by fiat. The advantage of Earl Jieret's knowledge has appointed me to carry the torch."

Death's vulture perched on the heroic assignment, hooded with gimlet-eyed certainty. False glory fooled no one. Pitched against the armed ranks of a replenished war host, fed, trained, and resplendently outfitted, the most ruthless party of handpicked scouts presented a suicidal inconvenience. Sent abroad to be swatted like biting flies before the onslaught of the inevitable, Tarens's stoic acceptance looked tired, the faithful hound tossed a marrow bone instead of a beating. "Laithen's wrangling throttled the gnashing of teeth. My skin's not flayed, but geld me before I'd make her an enemy! She clapped the naysayers and their bilious spleen like nettled squirrels in a gunnysack."

Although banter camouflaged the mortified sting, Dakar seized on the costive gut hidebound by the gripe of tradition. "Your failed suit for peace never mattered." Preference had spared trueborn s'Valerient blood and selected the most vigorous scouts to lead the young families to seek sanctuary in Melhalla.

"My own go among them," Tarens allowed, wooden. Two nephews dead of fever filled his thoughtful pause, grief compounded by anguish for the decree forcing his tiny daughter's relinquishment. Burred gruff, he added, "That bargained concession was the choke point that bristled the snarling objections all night." The children and parents were staged to leave in small groups, their covert safety hung by a thread, snatched under the drastic rigour of midwinter travel. "They'll journey upcountry and slip through the ranges to dodge the league trackers who scour the lowlands."

Dakar guessed the conclusion: the s'Valerient granddame would put forward her sister's son, Evrand, as acting *caithdein*, a stopgap substitution to be reassessed when Khadrien's younger brother reached his majority. Provided any hale man among them lived to celebrate their next year.

Blunt-force practicality drove the anxious tension, more than one kinsman's clamped quiet forerunning the desperate hour of parting. Families soon to be sundered quashed their shortened tempers, none with more poignancy than Tarens, whose wife's year-old babe was but recently reunited with her doting father. Nerves scalded raw amid the roiled flux, Dakar struggled to dredge up inadequate words of condolence.

Tarens spared the lame effort. "My place is here, beyond question. If aught can be done on the field to hold Mankind's tenancy for posterity, Jieret's spirit will carry me through."

"Don't sell your sterling loyalty short!" The generous crofter who had outfaced the horror of a Sunwheel inquisition to spare his own never would be reconciled with the Canon's ossified screed. No matter how futile, the strength of his defence would contest the True Sect's expansion.

Brute cost already paid to the butcher, the once-kindly crofter had worn granite hard, his easy smile and ready laughter overwritten by the chiselled mask of the killer. More than an examiner's cruelty stretched the difficult pause, before Tarens expressed his stilted reluctance. "The favour I ask concerns my wee daughter. Dakar, she is half-bred!"

The Mad Prophet detested his plaintive response, where his Fellowship master's stern nature ever had eased awkward anguish in response to a heartsore request. "You fear your wean may mature lacking her mother's endowment?"

Tarens nodded, relieved. Children with reduced chance of inherited talent might fail under trial, more susceptible to dissociative madness from exposure to the Paravian presence.

"My father and siblings are living in Kelsing." At pained odds with an indomitable stature studded with the gleam of edged weapons, Tarens qualified with spread hands. "Let them know I'm a father if I cannot. Please, Dakar! Promise my little girl is raised aware she has townborn kin and a dual heritage."

"She'll do fine." Dakar coughed, chafed by gormless unease. "You don't think every parent bound south to Melhalla sweats through the same tender concern for their offspring?"

Yet the blandishment rang false in the cold, woodland dark. No westlands crofter ever conceived had borne the hard legacy Tarens staked his lifeblood to defend. Consolation was empty for a man brought to the code of clan birthright by mischance.

"You'll tell them yourself." Dakar blinked moistened eyes. Gutted, he returned a mealy-mouthed mumble unfit to gild hope from a vista of ashes. "If not, I'll rope Arithon down. The bastard will be made to shoulder the delinquent debt owed for your service."

"From Rockfell Pit?" Tarens clapped the spellbinder's cringing back and shrugged, humour restored as the temperate realist. "He's paid up in Daelion's black currency, I should think. And you'd better piss quick, or surrender the chance. Here's Laithen, nipped on the raw to harangue you. Mercy on fire can't singe the pluck off that mothering lioness."

"She's unsheathed all her claws," Dakar agreed, chilled as the wind-break of Tarens's bulk shifted.

The nervy small woman bore in without shame, her spry frame

burdened with a trail pack. "Blazes, she's not bent to tag along with me!" The Mad Prophet's grab to stay Tarens's avoidance swiped air, his own cowardly sidle thwarted by youngsters who swarmed to uproot tent stakes and reel slack guylines.

"Damn all to the red spear of Dharkaron's Vengeance!" yelped Dakar as the diminutive harpy collared him. "Woman, you try me! I've barely scuffed the rimed ice off my boots, far less picked out the gravel stuck in my socks from my last stint on shank's mare."

"You're going to pound the wash and clean Esfand's soiled linen?" Laithen snorted a laugh, her sparkling effrontery the white puff of breath through a weasel's bared teeth. "Ath ding me dead, I thought not!" Her grin levelled Dakar's punctured deflation, the tousled mop of his greying hair frisked by the breeze as nearby canvas collapsed and whumped flat. "Don't bank on your shyster's luck, Prophet. We'll draw lots for the laundry on alternate days, and don't fib! Sticks for bones, I'd suggest inept snares have grossly shorted your rations." Advantaged by the spellbinder's dumbstruck annoyance, she quashed his hag-ridden protest outright. "Siantra's my daughter! What did you expect?"

Dakar cringed, still the unkempt, muddied spaniel wreathed in a wisped beard uncombed for three fortnights. "Daelion Fatemaster's almighty bollocks! By those terms, I'll be hobbled with escort for Lady Jalienne's baggage as well!"

Laithen's struck silence might have sheared air, the frown cleft between her sable brows precise as a glass cutter's stylus.

Scarlet under his windburned scruff, Dakar ground his molars, embarrassed for the oafish remark astute forethought might have kept muzzled. Past question, Cosach's spiteful widow would fly south with her youngest daughter, half-grown. For the sake of the child yet unmarked by the bittermost obligation of Cosach's bequest, the son's fate abandoned would be the grown heir's, caught up in the breach between warring dragons.

Liathen's jabbing censure against him like daggers, Dakar bit his tongue. Scouts twice his stature ducked her picked fights. In particular, while the Seven's relentless straits demanded the exigent sacrifice: Mankind's rampant avarice too often wounded the charter's selfless defenders past reason.

The blistering impasse stayed mercifully brief. Esfand approached, a figure of diminished docility clad for the rigorous trial lying ahead. He was brought through the tumultuous activity, not by the pale hair and cold, regal poise of Lady Jalienne, but a rawboned, stern woman who led her charge without sentiment as the older half sister sired during Cosach's first marriage. At her heels tagged the cur pack of boisterous toddlers too little to be tasked, breaking camp.

The mites swooped in like swallows on blustered spring air. Chattering, they fell upon Laithen. "You're going!" piped one.

"Will you see a dragon?"

"Are there Paravians on the Plain of Araithe?"

Rocked under the onslaught of exuberant affection, Laithen ruffled heads. She cupped rosy cheeks not yet pared gaunt from privation. "I wouldn't know, pea pod. We're not headed south."

"We're not?" Ambushed by the four-year-old latched to his leg, Dakar staggered. "Pests!" He shooed, distracted, at the screaming imps who gleefully jostled to pile on him if he toppled. "Off you go! Or I'll change the lot of you into worm castings."

Children squealed and scattered.

Except for the sprite clinging to the adult half sister caught up in the buffeting rout. "You'll be reliant upon Esfand's lead?" Eyes suspiciously bright, she prodded to break off the youngster's embrace, then relinquished Esfand to Laithen's care. "For weeks, his footloose impulse pulls him due west." She added, "Be watchful. He mutters in uncouth tongues before his attempts to slip custody."

Horrified epiphany drained Dakar white. "Do you tell me the lad speaks in Drakish?"

"A barking jumble of croaks, mixed with hissing?" The woman shrugged her strapping shoulders and sighed. "Could be. Don't shine off my warning the hard way."

Dakar's stiletto glance skewered Laithen's bland calm. "What else haven't you told me?"

The small woman denounced the accusative enquiry, at ease in a belt looped with skinning knife, tinderbox, recurve bow, and long dagger. "That I don't speak Drakish." Rugged sylph, her doeskin boots scarcely left tracks. "Do you?"

"Not here," Dakar snapped, galled to flash-point resentment. Apprehension fit to rattle Sethvir sucked him hollow, atop the griped bowels calcified by aghast dread. The late misery of his journey from Penstair became a vicious pittance before the omissions armoured behind Laithen's silence.

Chary to try her, Dakar bowed to the browbeaten prompt of hard-won male experience. "Best hope you're fully aware what's at risk."

"If my daughter's become a threat to the world, I'd be present to witness her fate." Sorrow freighted that statement far worse than a poisoned gaff to the heart.

"Shave Dharkaron himself!" Dakar exploded, unravelled before the benighted quandary laid on him. If no grace might reprieve the mother's commitment, the rank fool might venture to say so. Not to a woman tough as forged nails, who had endured offspring lost to miscarriage, the last one conceived by a cherished husband fallen under the knives of league bountymen.

Anguish brooded instead across deadlocked silence. Neither combatant cared to broach the collateral impact should the on-coming glut of martial carnage sully the fifth lane's harmonic flowing through the Paravian megaliths on the Plain of Araithe. Mankind and whose inno-cent children survived could be moot. If Esfand's hell-bent course was connected to the disaster that yawned behind Seshkrozchiel's hostile entrenchment at Althain Tower, the imperative of Siantra's swift inter-ception became fatally urgent. The prophet turned Master Spellbinder shuddered, strapped beyond his capacity. He courted the wrath of a maddened drake, powerless, with no viable path for retreat.

Alone, he would have spun about-face and fled with naught but the clothes on his back.

"For more than my child," Laithen prodded, agreeable. The clear eye for truth bestowed by her ancestry mined setback for the windfall advan-tage. "A route west might skirt the foothills of the Mathorns to reach Leynsgap before spring. If you have arcane means, close off the notch. That tactical gain may forestall the enemy's access from the south."

"Presupposing I could!" Dakar snapped with heat. "I am not Asandir." Ath forfend, he was unfit to take up the reins of the compact, or avert the breakaway slide towards disaster.

No person was safe if humanity's bellicose folly called down the dragons' retribution. Least of all the stalwart clansfolk who managed the exodus from the encampment. Esfand and Laithen were bound out of Fallowmere with him, perhaps not to return. The throes of leave-taking commanded the moment, as kinfolk and lifelong friends gathered round to embrace their own in farewell. Effusive love and quiet grief surrounded Esfand's estranged silence. Come to see him away, the young woman he had courted before war in Daon Ramon settled the mantle of Cosach's deathbed legacy upon him. The children he had taught to ride and to hunt, and the scamps he had cozened for assignment to the water brigade, then the solemn, blood cousins of Khadrien, inwardly raw and yet grieving. Laithen found herself smothered by the clan's granddames, then clapped on the back by the scouts who had shared the tedium of countless watch posts beside her.

Red dawn rinsed the sky through the trees, then brightened to orange. Daylight spattered gold dollops through black limbs like new coin, before the three forlorn travellers were relinquished and set on their way. They struck out across the free wilds towards Deshir, elongated shadows spilled blue across the pristine snow sheeted under Drimwood's ancient trees.

Early departure spared them the stoic trauma to separate parent and child, family and friend, and brother from sister. The next hour saw the encampment split into efficient, tight groups, then the first batches of vulnerable fugitives dispatched for the stealthy flight to seek safety. Last of all, the backbone of the war band fell in with Tarens, honed weapons muffled beneath winter furs, and spare conversation lapsed into taciturn silence. Long before the purpled quiet of dusk, the rumpled snow in the forest glen lay emptied of Rathain's clanborn inhabitants. Nothing remained. The dimpled impressions of the struck tents were swept clean, the wistful, last trace of the lodge fire erased by the rear-guard's diligent scouts.

Crossing northern Rathain on foot posed rough hardship at best, beset by the ferocity of midwinter's freeze, and needled by gales whipped down from the Stormwell coast. White-out blizzards buried all but the prominent landmarks in drifts. The party of three travelled light, huddled under the lee of stone ledges, or crammed for shelter against the undercut bluffs carved by meandering streambanks. Stockings singed by the small, smokeless blaze Laithen nursed from brush and dry grasses, Dakar discovered why Asandir seldom leaned upon wielded power for comfort.

Exhaustive priority demanded the starspells, contact with Verrain at Methisle his lifeline to stay abreast of distant events. A loss of Sethvir's broadscale vision fit to tax even Fellowship stewardship piled a crippling handicap on two isolate spellbinders skirting the jaws of disaster. Dakar stood sentinel during the fair-weather lulls, terrified by the inadequate oversight guarding the compact's integrity.

How many times had Asandir crossed and recrossed these swept plains, beset by crisis and harrowed by setback? Had any crux faced by the Seven matched the gruelling stakes thrown upon such scanty recourse? Hag-ridden past guessing how many of the world's major perils might be fallen dangerously into arrears, Dakar tramped through day upon worrisome day under Laithen's relentless perception.

Their pace, even pressed, proved disastrously slow. Fail, and he lost the moment for a crafted deterrent to bar the notch through the Mathorns at Leynsgap, ready bolt-hole for the enemy to slip a rear-guard incursion behind Asandir's outdated defences. Time and hardship befouled swift passage as short supply forced pauses, with seasonal forage grown scarce. Effortful progress suffered as well from Esfand's moody recalcitrance, whiplashed to incomprehensible extremes and resistant to pressure. Laithen's legendary patience showed cracks. The weary need to stand watch against his fitful bouts of wanderlust sapped rest through the moonlit nights too bitter for heedless exposure.

Laithen paced through the wee hours to stay wakeful and warm. Exhaustion tempted the drowsy haven of sleep until the bleak cold lulled flesh to surrender, bewitched, to the grave caul of hypothermia.

Dakar wielded the strictures of Asandir's discipline as never before. Emerged from deep trances, time and again, he beat circulation into his wooden limbs, disturbed by the uncanny impression of movement beyond the stretched range of his faculties.

Like a step onto thinned ice over current, he could not finger the itch that ruffled his instincts. Until dawn, when a creeping chill caused the Mad Prophet to glance over his shoulder. Regarding him from behind, Esfand watched with a stalker's intensity. Who *knew* whether the spawned creature merely shared his unease, or created the upset to quake human nerves. Dakar grappled the conundrum, clueless to sort whether Seshkrozchiel's transformation of Siantra had seeded an ally or created Mankind's potential, inveterate enemy. Prescient prophecy sealed his chapped lips, stubbornly mute on the question.

Neither was Laithen's tuned perception blind to the ominous portents. Inscrutably quiet, she withheld her remark over Esfand's failure to fasten his jacket. His irregular behaviour accompanied unnatural surges of flushed heat, marked by the ground thawed to mud underneath his spread blanket roll. Constant hunting kept Laithen preoccupied, the heavy demand on her pressured by Esfand's sullen temperament. The bleed-through spun from his link to Siantra could not be sidetracked with blandishments. The watchful handling required to tame the edge of his petulant ferocity chafed

sensible equilibrium, interspersed by periods of impervious, near hibernation, when no roughhouse measures might roust him.

Bitten during a tantrum one morning, Dakar bound a slashed thumb
and harangued, "Why am I the soft target mauled to drawn blood!"

"Because you've never salved the skinned knees of small boys." Laithen
grinned, her pack roll secured with the enviable, deft knots of woodwise
experience. "Maybe try not to corner him?"

The Mad Prophet tussled with his strapped belongings one-handed,
with dismal results. "You would nourish a snake!"

"I surely have." Laithen's retort bested Arithon's for snide sympathy.
"Once, to upset a prank staged by my randy cousins. The other, by
Siantra's request. She was three."

Dakar coughed back gruff laughter, eyes slitted like pips and gaunt
cheeks thatched in his wire-sprung beard. The hard-bitten woman before
him likely had been ancient at birth, her tart sagacity too self-possessed
for escapades and skinned knees. "Next time your scaly charge tries to
bolt, you'll be my volunteer to collar and leash him."

Westward, they fared at a tortuous crawl, while the days inexorably
lengthened. Bitter wind tumbled loose crystals of ice, and the stars
burned, bright as adamant, garnet, and diamond through the harsh
nights, until sunrise speared light across the sparkling snow, and new
morning tinted the zenith deep cobalt. Dazzled, they ploughed through
drifts like lit shards, one mired leg plodding after the next until dusk
shaded the undulant vales in violet and cerulean.

Cloud brought in the storm fronts, keening gales that roared down
and beset them, hunkered down under inadequate cover. Laithen nursed
the small fires. She melted goosefat for chilblains, and compounded the
stinging ointments that hardened split blisters and fended off frostbite.
Her skilled archery fed them on stringy, lean hare, while Esfand's reflexes
sharpened like a feral cat's, and his tensile nature took umbrage for no
reason, daily more viciously testy. The snatch of his nails shredded
clothing, if stray noise or quick movement surprised him.

His changeling stare bristled Dakar's nape, and disturbed his deep
scrying. Rebuke died, as the glancing flicker of firelight raised the translucent sheen of ephemeral scales on his cadaverous cheeks. Alarm drove
the breath from the spellbinder's lungs. The stare fixed upon him was
no longer human, the half-lidded eyes flared ruby red and bisected
vertically by slit pupils.

Teeth clenched in paralysed fear, Dakar stilled for the predator's spring that never came.

Days passed before he overtook Laithen alone by the throaty gurgle of a swift-running brook. A poised huntress sharpened by winter's privation, she crouched, fishing with a pointed stick through the lede at the edge of a trout pool paned in black ice. "How long were you planning to wait before telling me Esfand's birth-born pattern's destabilized?"

The spear angled to skewer aquatic flesh might have been nailed into place. "Would my opinion have put a dent in your thinking?"

"Maybe." Dakar shuddered, mulish stance undermined by the slippery slope as sapped courage loosened his knees. "You don't speak Drakish," he snapped. "But I do."

Laithen struck. An expert thrust from the shoulder shafted her target, unerring. "Then you've known the young man is still bound to my daughter, his plight past our means to reverse." The water scarcely broke more than a ring ripple until, calm shattered by an explosive splash, her flopping, silvery catch was yanked bloody and thrashing onto the ice. Laithen's knife sliced the spine at the gills, prey dispatched with reverent mercy. Then, "You won't be putting him down on my watch."

"Dharkaron avenge! Best do more than hope not." That too-competent blade was a statement of threat, staked over the precarious pitfall. Verrain's candid concerns gave Dakar palpitations. "Keep your errant charge under containment!"

For the Seven's reticence had stranded the case without counsel, either to mend or condemn the affliction imposed on Siantra. The bleak precipice yawned into the unknown chasm of doubt: *either the Sorcerers understood the hybrid shift was intractable, or Daelion Fatemaster forfend! Some dire reason had prompted Athera's most versant healers to choose restraint and abide her drake-spawned transformation.*

The clanswoman flensing cold fish with keen steel was too facile. Transfixed by her rapacious insight, Dakar shrank from the bitter predicament she soon must grasp quite as emphatically as he had: Esfand's hale recovery, if not his return to humanity, might require a severance from the linked consciousness incurred during transit of Baylienne's Gyre. Dakar shied from the ugly necessity himself, loath to shoulder the unconscionable anguish of her child's blood on his hands.

Laithen's glower gutted his reticent quiet as though his wretched thought was transparent. "Esfand's mind and my daughter's are one. What grants you the leave to enact your uninformed judgement and part them?"

"You're twice the pest, curse your ornery ancestry!" Dakar grumbled. Murder, before mayhem, might drive a stumped man to seek refuge at Sithaer's black gate. Give him a spat with a whore any day! Brangles with motherhood baffled him.

Laithen demolished the subject forthwith. "We'll cook half of this catch. Three days taken to smoke the remainder can't bungle our straits any worse."

"You might have saved the bad news for tomorrow," Dakar retorted, bent out of sorts. Her confounded nose for disaster was right: they had crossed the Valsteyn three days too late to outpace the True Sect advance. His jabbed toe dimpled the granular slush underfoot, grey rime softened under afternoon sun. "Who knew Asandir's prior ward over Strakewood would bind us for yesterday's purpose too well?"

The enemy's fallback campaign ran against them. Within weeks, the high plain would be riddled with troops. Their benighted flight to the coast for a swift crossing of Instrell Bay might be moot, with Esfand's strengthened link to Siantra become ripened bait for league trackers and Sunwheel diviners.

Forest-bred to the bone, Laithen shrugged in contempt. "Whining won't bring back Sethvir any faster."

"No." Dakar curbed his furious urge to stomp on thin ice and cause her a ducking. "We'll just muddle on. Squeezing whey from the shrivelled dugs of Dame Fortune long since milked dry!"

Cowardice smothered the obvious argument that human mortality feared to address. Athera did not lack for vigilant oversight: The centaur Warden, Tehaval, at Ithamon, possessed effortless means to weigh the gravity of their predicament. Dakar quailed to petition that mystical contact. Help asked from that quarter delved into affairs past the compass of Mankind's viable interests. Verrain's access to the ancient library at Methisle ascertained the fathomless purpose of the Paravians was altogether too perilous without a Fellowship intermediary.

Prod that proverbial kraken, and two Ages of coexistence might go for naught, futility sprung from misinformed arrogance and the tinsel-thin mask over reckless bravado.

Dakar's grumble was snatched from his teeth by the wind, whining like the down swing of a sword's edge. "Past question, these dicey problems are fathoms over my head."

His forlorn scrying at midnight congealed the fish dinner in his queasy belly. Unfolding, the scope of recent developments ripped his optimal planning to shreds. Confronted, befuddled and sleepless at dawn, Dakar careened into Laithen's clear-eyed assessment.

"The True Sect dedicates not only will reach Leynsgap ahead of us, we'll have to change course or run like flushed hares into the front lines of their east flank's advance."

"What?" Dakar's stilted reticence snapped the dammed torrent of his frustration. "We have no choice but take to the high ground to evade them. I have scaled the Mathorn divide by stealth before this." The same, precarious footpath had concealed his desperate flight to prevent Arithon's forecast execution by the Light's priests at Daenfal.

Laithen disparaged his suggested evasion with the enthusiasm of rigour mortis. "Try that hazardous route through the rim under snowpack, hear my promise. If not avalanche, the landslides as the seeps melt will finish us."

She was wrong. How far wrong, the seer's vision shrank to contemplate. Spared as the bite of the wind mashed his hood against his blanched pallor, Dakar lost his nerve. Voiced failed him before the vistas of ruin reeled through his prescient talent.

Disclosure would but canker the dregs of morale. Angry and helpless, Dakar shoved off Laithen's enquiry, gutted beyond the naked effrontery to lie under the flint eye of her bent for truth sense. "Milled to flinders by rocks might be counted a kindness!"

Not then could he mention what else he had Seen. Relentless as tide, his unbridled visions too often vaulted the shadowed array of near possibility and launched him into sick bouts of rogue prophecy. Far-flung futures he lacked the perspective to sort harangued him to muddled decisions.

While the days fleeted past, a clan scout's awareness measured the sun's angle rising. Liathen's adamance never countenanced falsehood. She knew, keenly as Dakar, their dawdling progress ran out the margin before the weakened ice held by Kharadmon's conjury faded. The spring tides that would reopen shipping drew nigh. The shortening span of each subsequent night saturated his dreams with the movement of stars, clogged by scents of incipient thaw and warm weather. Firmed glimpses heralded the flux-borne tremor of marching troops on the trade routes, both northward and south. Birdsong counterpointed the horns of the officers, and melted ice breaking upon swollen streams bespoke waters thrashed white by oared galleys. Transport and supply clogged the ports and the trade-road, mired and gashed by the wheels of ox drays to soupy puddles and mud. But not for much longer.

When the leeway for kindly ambivalence ended, Dakar's laboured wards to deflect the inquisitive probes of the Light's talent diviners stretched thin, after nightfall scarcely sufficient to dampen the rippled disturbances broadcast by Esfand's bestial tantrums. More frequent outbreaks increased in ferocity, with painstaking attempts at remedial reason thrashed into eclipse.

By morning, Dakar bent to smother the coals of a cookfire that should not have smouldered past daybreak. Laithen's hand on his collar jerked him away. He stumbled, tripped up. Flung onto sharp stone, swearing murder, he nursed his scraped palms and belatedly realized she had yanked him clear of a slashing blow that almost cost him a kidney.

Sore with a wrenched neck and bruised knees, he raked his skewed hood off his rumpled brows and confronted the predatory danger he coddled: the vicious yellow-eyed glare of a territorial instinct more dragon's than man's. "That creature's a menace! I'm deaf if you try to plead otherwise."

Laithen's brown eyes blistered skin for the tactless reproach. "Did you never imagine Esfand's temper might reflect the disturbed mind of Seshkrozchiel? Siantra may be the victim as well."

"If so, I've not seen it." But, then, how would anyone, with Esfand's uncanny havoc unseating the stays that framed a reliable scrying? The disruption frayed more than tired wits ragged. Dakar rose to his feet. Scourged by knit mittens embedded with gravel, and peeved over the newest rip in his trousers, he vented the vitriol jammed in his craw. "Don't let me be the naïf who tried the tranced assay and got himself eviscerated to find out!"

Swollen buds on the willows heralded a mild spring breaking early, scried sessions grown ominous with the whispered rumour snatched over a foot soldiers' campfire farther south: of a devil-spawned girl, wanted target under pursuit for the Temple's talent examiners. And again, as though his unquiet alarm was transparent, Dakar felt Esfand's glance burning like a coal brand at his back. As if he needed the rowelled spur on the riddle behind the fraught stakes tipping the world's greater balance. No pat solution existed to stem the red war in Rathain, with the Fellowship Sorcerers gone beyond the unknown, and the inscrutable well of Rockfell Pit's wards shuttered over the horror of Arithon's fate.

Dakar wrestled necessity, squatted to eject the lodged pebble worked inside the split seam of his boot. "Our route to the west is not viable. By tonight, we'll have an enemy encampment a thousand strong pitched between us and the coast."

He proposed they veer south towards the ranges for cover. Laithen's preference argued against, the better strategy for evasion secured by the skilled stealth of her clanbred experience.

"I've seen sign disturbing the ground on our flank where none should be!" she admitted. "Perish the idea an intrusion may have slipped past our mountain patrol keeping skeleton watch. More unsettling, the flux currents off the ranges did not carry the distinctive imprint of the untoward trespass."

"Then turn back!" Dakar stamped his galled foot and winced, mouth crimped like a clam in his grey, tufted beard. As never before, he sympathized with Arithon's snappish efforts to send his liege-sworn packing for safe-guard. Cruelty scourged the spirit left bankrupt by the many who had not come home. Pain spoke to defer the next loyal sacrifice, and the burdensome anguish thrust upon the beholden survivor.

Worse, when true integrity held its staunch ground. Thin-skinned to a fault, Dakar lacked the iron stomach to use hurt as the whip to serve urgency. At the crux, he could not emulate Arithon, the tragedy of Laithen's losses torqued into the weapon to crumble the impasse between them.

Dakar admired the tenacity of her lineage. Sidir's conduct throughout the horrors of Tal Quorin and the siege at Alestron had dismissed sensible argument by the same impeccable creed. The overstepped victim ripped hair to bald roots quite in vain. Set on the offensive for bed-rock integrity, Laithen s'Idir was a demon.

Today, perhaps tired, she softened her mettle and compromised her resistance. Pushed off in anger to reconnoitre the furrowed dell that snaked into the track to the Mathorn heights, she verified her vexing report before noon. "These town intruders were outlying reconnaissance, perhaps for a larger force coming behind. I suggest the league trackers may have gained someone's untoward arcane assistance."

"Here?" Dakar rolled his eyes beneath fringed, ginger lashes. "The lane current says otherwise." Scathing before her imperious calm, he scoffed at her hackled suspicion. "I've detected nothing else within leagues but denned animals and small birds pitched to terrified flight from Esfand's habit of stalking them!"

Laithen stared him down, whipcord lean in worn leathers, a tensioned fist clasped on her sheathed knife. The uncomfortable, mystical depth to her silence packed an edge in rebound since her brush with the resonant upshift Arithon had raised westward of the ancient marker stones. "We must strike for the coast."

"I am listening." Dakar shook off the sudden, incipient chill of a ghost trampled over his grave site. "But to run an armed gauntlet equipped with diviners? I need more than a hunch to accept your demand."

"Proof, then?" Her ready laugh rang through the fir-scented air. "Hindmost buys the spiked cider, fellow. Just watch Esfand until I get back."

"I will string the best wards." Dakar kept his promise. He snitched the plucked strand of hair he required and spun the refined boundary to quell the changeling's broadcast noise before Laithen's departure.

Her second foray extended all day. Pinned down and fretted by the adroit handling required to curb Esfand's agitation, the spellbinder smothered his testy concern. By nightfall, the onus of the Fatemaster's ransom fell due for his feckless dismissal. Past question, the lapsed hours spelled trouble the longer Laithen failed to return.

Esfand lay curled in one of his bouts of intractable sleep. Dakar clipped a second hair from the young man's head, unable to bear the sight of those peaceful, closed eyes. Unreliably human, the pacified face in repose jerked the heartstrings and savaged the long-sighted directive of Fellowship priorities. That such bleeding pity might not be misplaced did not lessen the deadly pitfall of sentiment. Dakar redoubled the ward circles shrouding the flux. Then, through the fallen dark, with his mage-sense tuned fine enough to hear winter sap sunk into dormancy, he set off to trace Laithen's cold trail.

The black night was windless around him, the bare branches of birch and maple like pale thread basted through the swatched tangles of fir. Dakar ploughed through the pristine silence where the voles hunted by ermine printed furtive tracks under the stealthy flight of the owl. Scout fashion, Laithen had dusted her footsteps, evinced by the pen-stroke needles of shed balsam. He followed her ephemeral trace on the ridge-tops, zigzagged across the windswept striations of fieldstone and cracked boulders. Under the slatted, pitch shadows at moonrise, he skirted the deep, drifted hollows, clouded in his puffed breaths.

Dawn came. Brightened under full daylight, he encountered the chopped trail of armed horsemen. Evidence, beyond question, the Light's war host encroached behind the drawn line of Asandir's warding. Auxiliary troops infiltrated the backcountry through Leynsgap, with no scout sentry's signal arrow, and no runner to sound the alarm. Rathain's mysteries well might founder in the dearth of Sethvir's vigilant guidance. Dedicates marched on the northern wilds in force from the south. Surely as fire and thundering storm, Laithen's heightened acuity had found them.

Or they had found her. The notion pulverized quietude.

"Damn all to Sithaer!" Dakar snarled, beset. He scented the copper-sharp taint on the air. Sick fear dismembered the last of his courage. Wrenched by dry heaves, he succumbed to sapped nerve until his revolted gut emptied. Too late, he reeled erect and pressed onwards, into snapped branches and rumpled snow where the armed ambush broke Laithen's cover. No subtlety to the site where rabid pursuit had closed on her craft-wise lead and overwhelmed her canny expertise.

The spellbinder swallowed the rasped burn of heaved bile. "Ath's pity! Not this!" A man could weep forever, gagged on the wormwood of hasty words and regret. Her despoiled body, couched in bloodied rags, rested amid the thrashed evidence of a resistance fought with a wild animal's cornered ferocity.

Dakar sank to his knees. Around him, rendered brilliant in dazzling sunlight, the crumpled, defiled epitaph to her struggle spread scarlet and diamond white, smudged and trampled by hobnailed footprints. Scuffed depressions revealed where her enemy fallen had lain. Wounded or dead, Laithen's toll of casualties had been borne away, secured from the depredation of carrion crows startled, indignantly flapping, from their grisly repast.

By knife and by bow, the clan huntress had taken her savage due. Gone down fighting, the record of her fraught ending carved the thickets of scrub fir, graven with the splashed afterimage of violent carnage. Forced at bay, her last seconds were a desecration thrashed across the remote hollow where pack numbers had surrounded and overwhelmed her desperate, doomed stand.

Her gored assailants had sated their fury. Slashed and twisted, her wracked leathers cradled a picked mangle of bones, savaged to ruin well before scavengers had tussled over her cooling remains. The eggshell of her scalped skull lay jawless, denuded of the glossy brown clan braid hacked off as a bountyman's trophy. Harvested, for two venal coinweight in gold paid out by the True Sect Temple.

Gutted, Dakar hunched under the glittering stares of perched crows. Indifferent to the fluttered descent of the single bold raven, just settled, he choked on his shattered composure.

"I am sorry," he grated, strangled to a whisper. Death condemned the rank cowardice of his soft heart. He had never been ruthless. Not quickened by the enabling fear to meet this moment's hideous reckoning. Broken by Asandir's vacancy, he lacked the command sprung from Arithon's depth of compassion. No anguished awareness of on-going consequence had stiffened his will to enforce the hard measure thrust upon him by painful necessity. Had he listened, or acted, or shrank less from harsh expedience, Laithen s'Idir would be alive. Her maternal fallacy ought to have been crushed long since for the obdurate fate of a daughter turned rogue by a dragon.

The revenant imprint of Laithen's passing condemned his craven mercy, the vivid agony of her extremis seared into the ambient flux and bare stone. Dakar's traumatized senses delivered the cry of her last bequest: a wounding of conscience resounded from beyond the grave. *'Trust my daughter! Lend your assistance to Siantra before everything!'*

"Ath's grief! Dharkaron's Spear would be kinder!" Shredded piecemeal, Dakar stared down the terrible choice between a human spirit corrupted as drake spawn and the tangled entrapment befallen Rathain's young *caithdein*. The incompatible legacy writ large in Laithen's let blood could never be reconciled. For Esfand to rise and bear the steward's black when the realm's people most sorely needed him, no other recourse remained but to destroy Siantra as the source of his feral perversion.

"Curse the day to Dharkaron!" Dakar ground his knuckles into swollen lids. "And crap on the doings of both deposed princes and their bull-headed ethic as well, while I think of it!"

Whatever befell, he was driven to act: first to trample the lacerate wound of remorse, then to address the imperative Laithen s'Idir had died to pursue. Fixed under the ghoulish hunger of crows, Dakar took shelter out of the wind. He laid down exhaustive protections. Then, by careful measure, he wielded his Sight to scry out how the blindsided skills of a trail-wise talent had succumbed to a league tracker's ambush. Amid the reactive, free-wilds flux, why had an enemy foray skulking through these foothills broadcast no sign of unsanctioned disturbance?

Noon came and went. Time's passage distorted under deep trance. Disbelief hazed the assay, confounded as discovery unfolded the vulnerable breach that Laithen's clan practice had never seen reason to guard.

Somehow, somewhere, an astute temple initiate among the Light's faithful had unlocked the artistry to blend the flux patterns into resonant favour. The same technique the accomplished clan hunters employed to read sign and stalk game had masked the disruptive imprint of this incursion. Laithen's trail had been read by a hostile townsman whose arcane innovation had become enabled by the restoration of Rathain's upstepped resonance.

Dakar stared full bore at the seed of disaster. The Light's northern war host advanced on the Plain of Araithe, backed by a second force marched over Leynsgap to strike from the rear. Masked by the rogue bent of this talent diviner, the two-pronged assault would close in undetected, a surprise to outflank the short-handed strategy, fashioned threadbare, for the stopgap delay to evacuate Falwood.

Horrified dread left the spellbinder reeling. Tarens's covert war band at the forefront faced slaughter, cut down unaware. The deaf ear and short shrift dealt to Laithen's sound instincts had botched Dakar's option to dispatch her with urgent warning.

Threat posed by the dragons commanded priority. Dakar choked off his tears. Will he or nil he, the Fellowship Sorcerers' jeopardized interests brooked no delay. No quarter squandered in guilt for his short-falls, he dared not swerve now. Not for a dead mother's sentiment, or the decency of a burial. Laithen's hardened spirit bore him no grudge for the dearth of last rites. Clansfolk had abandoned their slain as they lay for survival across generations.

Dakar cursed the crows and did as he must. He tripled down on his wary defences, then turned his back and retraced his steps in hurried descent lest another graphic encounter ravage the campsite before his return.

Yet no True Sect butchery swept down in his absence for a repeat round of carnage. Far worse, Dakar found his ward ring broken through and left vacant. Esfand had awakened and bolted already. Gone who knew where, driven by some unimaginable purpose, with Sithaer's drastic brew of hell-spawned mayhem slipped along with him through the breach. The broadscale potential for trouble outpaced the pale of catastrophe. Come too late, the spellbinder chased the next untoward upset before fresh incitement catapulted Dragonkind to the cataclysmic throes of en-masse gestalt.

Dakar swore murder for the irreparable setback. The trail he pursued was past ten hours old, with no kind option allowed for s'Idir's dying plea to support her lost daughter. Had pity not catered to her tender faith, he should have crossed Instrell Bay and reached Althain Tower in better time. The magnificence of motherhood's courage bedamned! His vital mission had been hobbled, when sound forethought might have dispatched the aberrant drake spawn for the best, with Arithon's defeat of the Prime Matriarch's plot at Forthmark left standing as a historic victory.

Alone with his excoriating mistakes and the anguished hindrance of failure, Dakar reclaimed his blanket roll and set off, every artful faculty he possessed engaged to outstrip the invasion through Leynsgap and sprint headlong for the coast. Though he died trying, whether Laithen's unquiet shade haunted his backtrail, he must cross Instrell Bay to Atainia and reach Althain Tower before Seshkrozchiel's torched wrath tripped the avalanche to disaster.

If he met a bad end in the clutches of the True Sect's tracking diviner, Dharkaron's excoriate vengeance would snuff the agony of his ineptitude. Never before had he been forced to admit the painful penalty incurred by his years spent in scapegrace avoidance: protracted centuries of novice apprenticeship frittered away to side-step the onerous gift of his talent.

He had wasted the greater part of his life!

Repeatedly gorged himself on self-indulgence, while years of unparalleled opportunity slipped away unregarded. Until Arithon's intolerant, brisk handling had rattled complacence and booted him towards a matured perspective, he had shirked accountable action with clownish enthusiasm. Again and again, ditched the serious learning at his fingertips under an adept of exemplary competence. He had played the smirking craven, while the master mage who apprenticed him for raw potential reproached him, but never forbade his incorrigible ways. Dakar had no excuse left for inconstancy. Reprobate excesses and crapulous drinking had displaced applied study.

Now the Fatemaster's judgement for that lapse came due with Dharkaron's deathless, black vengeance.

Today, with the weight of all things in his hands, Dakar met eye to eye the cumulative sorrow of his unregenerate faults. A blown-glass shell, frailty subject to shatter, he was no substitute for a Fellowship Sorcerer's deep wisdom. Lessons learned too late flayed his callous foolery. Had he applied his intelligence to the utmost and managed an honest effort when his role mattered most, he could have been ready. Perhaps, even, shouldered the gravity of Asandir's burden, and if not, should he miss the extreme demand in the moment, he might have faced the critical hour prepared to the best of his able potential.

Requiem

Past equinox, the last, fragile stay holding Kharadmon's weather dispersed. The iron-hard grasp of the deepened frost faded to patched swathes of greening earth. The northern downlands warmed early to a mild spring, loud with honking geese streaming in straggled formations black as knotted crepe against pellucid blue sky. The season's turbulent, grey rain clouds bellied like carded wool as breeze from the west combed the vales. Blackbirds scattered, flocks peppered to wheeling flights that resettled to glean upon the open ground not yet teeming with grubs and insects.

Yet keen senses quivered in the freshened air, dusted golden with pollen, and sweet with the renewal of burgeoning life. Cat-footed, the spectre of on-coming death cast no shadow across the stainless light of new morning. Talent sight rejoiced to the rainbow flare of the land's restored flux, studded bright with clinging sparkles of dew.

Burdened with the defence of Rathain's northern free wilds on short strength and inadequate resource, Tarens savoured the rare moment of calm before the appalling dread that yawned like a chasm under his feet. Doubts aplenty pressured this outlying sweep for security, shared between a rapt detachment of scouts.

His sappers were done staking out deadfalls and pit traps on the old trade routes from East Ward to Anglefen, and fly-by-night sabotage had undermined the timbered, span bridges to break under load. The seasoned war band of five hundred settled in wait to the north, a hand-picked roster of older veterans and spry grandfathers, the crack archers among them tough women past their fertile years, or volunteers with grown offspring.

The frail strategy to slow the enemy advance relied on the spring thaw, while frost heave yet softened the soil and the fresh melt muddied the bottomland. Intimate knowledge utilized the deep wilds terrain to funnel the True Sect invasion into a frontal engagement upon select ground at the marsh springs, welled from the rill at the Callowswale's headwaters. There, strict timing and wily tactics might lend a small force the hairbreadth advantage.

The mightier Lithuamir flowed deepest towards Stormwell Gulf as the shrinking snow-fields northside of the Mathorns swelled the river course to frothing spate. Near equinox, the risen flux sang in concert, threaded like floss with the spectral shimmer of bygone history, quickened in the channelled arc of the First-Age marker stones.

Tarens counted the critical days. Stall too long, and the Light's war host might spurn the laid track, content to stake out and camp until the shoaling fords became passable. Once the mired ground firmed, and the warming sun dried the vernal pools and parched the high grass, the odds laid against his defenders turned sour. The clan war band could be mowed down, mauled in red slaughter for the desperate margin to save the scattered, fugitive families who fled into refuge. Break the frail line of his stand in the wilds, and Fallowmere's proscribed territory lay open to exploitation without any Fellowship presence to enforce the boundaries established by charter law.

A fortnight before the crucial sway in the balance shaped the final engagement, Iyat-thos Tarens lounged on a propped elbow amid verdant grass, relaxed in the rare moment of respite. His stealth squad of twenty catnapped on the damp ground, the wakeful few busied with routing the pervasive rust from their weapons.

"You look fashed, and for what?" rumbled his second, an imposing hulk in layered buckskin, sprawled with chin rested on folded arms at his side. Marsh mud crusted his breeks to the knees, and a frown pinched weathered features streaked for concealment. "No sign of hog-footed townsmen. Not yet."

The dismissive comment raised sparks. "Soon enough, we'll be clapped tight as dreams in a lovesick maid's blanket. Ding me dead, if our handful of field bows and this dastard batch of scaled knives scares the Light's horde to shy off from the fight."

A bald-headed companion returned a wry snort, stripped to his clout with an awl to stitch a patch on worn leathers. "I'll be clad in naught beyond blisters and short hairs if we're culling more saplings for spring traps. We're already plucking our own braids for the triggers, and bad cess to the nob come cutting for scalps to cash out the bounty."

The glum remark incited no laughter.

None faced their hard prospects self-blinded. Three massive, armed hosts marched upon proscribed ground. Naught remained but to strive and fare onwards as clanblood had done for arduous centuries before them. Such whistling banter acknowledged, bold-faced, their benighted position. The fact no definitive trace had been sighted strung taut nerves to unease before confidence.

The massed force pitched against them was no elusive phantom.

"Shift our front line by a fraction," muttered the woman who nipped off the thread end of a refurbished bowstring, "and someone taking a piss in the brush should be wetting the feet of the prayer-mongering faithful's advance patrols."

A scoff, from the companion who glanced sidelong from the hawk's feather being trimmed up for fletching. "Poke our nebs up their pious backsides, more like! Puling prayers over sacrilege won't stop an arrow, nor banish the haunts from the flare at the full moon's crest tide."

Tarens rubbed stinging eyes, abashed by the show of steel heart: would another hour, or a day, or a week shift the course of a vicious struggle foredoomed from the outset? At what point did hope cave to crushing futility, ground down by the tonnage of a zealot's cause whipped on by superior numbers? More than humanity's collective fate trembled at the brink if the on-coming blow unravelled the mysteries. Light and dark, warp and weft, the expansion of Athera's Paravians dangled at the abyss on the outcome.

Tarens bolstered fragile morale with straight kindness. "Better stow the useless carping and snack while you can!" Tall frame and broad shoulders furled in bearskin, he cut as incisive a figure as ever Earl Jieret had under trial before him. "We'll be sharp on the move by tonight, soon as the dark falls past moonset."

No longer the uninformed crofter, Tarens grasped the meaningful scope of the energetic overlay laced through the land. He discerned the ephemeral shimmer beyond eyesight that showed *why* the thoughtless, small cooking fire here was not inconsequential, or harmless. He listened through subtle awareness and knew which trees to spare from the axe, and which hollows pooled the flux current to the staid calm that softened the tumultuous hunt to take sustenance.

No argument challenged the cry of exigency. Wary as foxes, scouts versant with the patterned stream of the world's greater mysteries walked lightly, their tight-knit patrol skirting the verge where the pristine resonance of sensitive ground opened vistas too reactive for disturbance. Risk attended their passage, past regard for due cause if the harmonic threshold was inadvertently crossed, and heightened frequency exceeded the range of incarnate tolerance. Passage to the far side of the veil enveloped the unwary, and beckoned them into the shining realms of Athlieria that began with the ecstatic slide into bewitching enthrallment.

None fared carelessly near the tuned arc of the marker stones while the shadow of war crept upon them. Soon enough, the day's last light bled to grey. When the afterglow quenched after sundown, the faint, orange nimbus cast by the enemy host's ordered campfires outlined the black silhouette of the hills. The encroachment of the advance swarmed the vales a scant league away.

Hush swallowed the badinage till the crescent moon sank, and the moment came to pull out.

Tarens and his furtive range patrol went, flanked by keen talent scouts with their entrained senses wide open. Through budding brush, over marsh and the reed banks of the stippled streamlets, they prowled like wolves at home in their setting. The flux currents ran strong, clarified since the levelled bulwarks at Etarra unsnarled the obstructive disharmony clogging the fifth lane's transmission through the Mathorn Pass.

Cautionary protocol maintained in immaculate silence, by hand signal, the returning squad dispatched two fresh scouts to relieve the pairs assigned at right and left flanks.

Pale dawn broke, the gold sky before sunrise unfurled in glory when Tarens crested the next rise. No whispered sign foreran the view unfolded in front of him. The vale below was crammed with armed dedicates, a massed company flying the standard, pennoned with the temple seal of a talent diviner. Rough count at first glimpse, the troop numbered a thousand mounted and foot, just breaking camp, with their straggling pack train of mules halfway harnessed and laden. Pikemen and archers assembled to march out, led off by four double-file lines of light horsemen in mail, and a caparisoned cohort of fifty lancers.

Grouped divisions bore the subordinate devices of Cildorn and Narms, two flagged as league headhunters with mute dogs and scout trackers. Attached for the wild country as guides, their wily picket of outer sentries sprang alert at the first, suspect movement etched against brightening sky. Their shouts raised swift notice. The horn blast of an officer shrilled urgent alarm.

Tarens was caught in the open, exposed. But not his companions, sheltered beyond sight in covert ascent just behind. No second remained for shocked surprise to unriddle the lack of etheric disturbance. No thought explained how an armed force at such strength had breached proscribed terrain, undetected.

"Run!" The desperate, hurried whisper flung backwards spelled disaster, most likely too late. "Turn back! Go to ground!" Already marked, Tarens rose to full height. He bolted over the hilltop like flushed game to buy what precious time might be seized in diversion.

First light of the sun lit his flaxen hair like a beacon, and dipped his drawn sword in dazzling flame. Tarens barrelled downslope towards the enemy with a berserker's yell impelled by fear and feral adrenaline.

The lancers coalesced. Reined around, spurred to a thundering charge, they surged on their massive horses upslope, levelled points driving straight towards him.

Tarens sprinted, the wind in his face heady with the sweetness of spring. A fit ending truly. Perhaps the overdue payment in kind for the diviner jabbed through the heart with a poker in the flash-point heat of protective ferocity. Far behind him, today, his close family and the cottage stair back in Kelsing. Danger seemed unreal as dream, and regret insubstantial as death thundered towards him over terrain never turned by the blade of a plough. Such black soil had cushioned his step as a child, ripe for the nurture of crops yet uncut by the roads that brought sweat and toil to wring wealth from covetous industry.

The honest crofter caught in the breach could not shed the rough dirt of his origins. As relentless, the heritage of s'Valerient perception unravelled the simplistic perspective and carved a remorseless division drenched in misaligned strife and centuries of bloodshed.

Who lived and who died made no sense, wrapped in causes and flags and the dog-pack fear that cemented religion. A better world should have been possible. Rathain's clansfolk were not going to survive to shepherd Mankind's chance for the privilege. Tarens ached. The steep slope sped his downhill plunge, fuelled by dwindled hope that the infant daughter in his wife's arms might evade the mailed fist of True Sect persecution.

Pennons snapped, rushing forward to meet him. The coloured silk tassels danced against the velour coats of the horses, chestnut, and grey, and deep sable. The riders were faceless, behind visored helms. Impersonal killers whose kinfolk, like his, were a wistful thought separated by distance.

The phosphor gleam of the ambient flux current expressed no ripple of pending violence. Tarens ran, jolted suddenly by the icy, queer grue of *wrongness*. Earl Jieret's clanborn instincts clamoured amid the peculiar, *unnatural quiet,* as if some untoward influence stifled the responsive flow of the free wilds' etheric web.

Too late! Tarens woke to the wider spectre of ruin pitched against the clan war band. Poisoned fruit of the examiner's interrogation, these Sunwheel's devotees had deciphered the specialized art of talent concealment. Against Canon precedent, informed use of clan lore masked a martial incursion against the last enclave of old-blood descent for their purposeful manifest of extinction.

The war band's five hundred positioned for the precarious stand to stall the advance at the forefront were poised to engage, unaware of a second, combined force at their rear. The chosen ground staged to slow the invasion would see them entrapped in a bottleneck, with no avenue open to stage a retreat.

No use to lament, or dwell on the bitter disclosure gleaned from his capture that crafted their doom. Tarens stumbled into the lancers' charge at full stride as their impetus thundered on top of him. He met the leading lance with his last parry. The deflected point missed his heart, glanced off and rammed home with a thud that pierced his right shoulder. The next rider's weapon struck him in the chest. Then a third speared into his solar plexus.

Spiked through, he grunted, but did not go down. The momentum of the armoured rider and horse drove his impaled body stumbling backwards. The burdened shafts unbalanced and dipped under load. Tarens rammed into the spongy turf, battered faceup as he fell by shod hooves that tumbled and milled him to maceration. Pulped bloody, he lay, shocked in shuddering extremis, while the following horses swerved and thudded around him, whipped past as blurred shadows against citrine sky. Pelted by the punched scallops of gouged turf, dizzied and drowning in gushed fluid, Tarens gasped, laboured by seizing agony. Vision darkened. Thought scattered, throttled by suffocation. All he knew and loved in the world spiralled away: a beloved wife and her infant daughter, an estranged sister and brother in Kelsing, and the father a forlorn boy had barely known, until nothing remained but the burning regret of the abandoned clan war band's doomed plight.

"No!" Denial rejected the absence of hope. The ferocious grip of true loyalty behind his plea flung against the tide's ebb, Tarens raged into the fast-falling dark before consciousness faded. *"Grace spare me, no!"*

The seized hush fallen over his languished spirit was stark black upon infinite black. A dense night without stars, yet not empty: uncanny wings whispered in descent, spiked by the beaded jet eye of a Raven.

"Tarens?"

Unseen, the speaker's tender address resumed in the lilted cadence of ancient Paravian. *T'cuelan e'caithdein s'Rathain i'tier, Iyat-thos!'* Translation belonged to another man's heritage, sworn to as hard a service before him: *the kingdom's crown steward attends you.*

Which declaration made little sense. The voice was not Arithon's; nor Esfand's, invested in formality as shadow behind Rathain's vacated throne.

Tarens battled the spinning whirl of drowned senses. Stopped pulse congealed the blood in his veins. His limbs were poured lead. If a bounty-man ransacked his inert frame for a trophy, his nerves were divorced from sensation.

Feathers rustled, instead. The stir of coal pinions resounded like thunder unleashed in the void, followed by the uncanny suggestion of movement. Then a spark of light kindled a liminal gleam that strengthened and dissolved like pearlescent, white flame the dense caul shrouding awareness.

"You are not alone." Tall, sturdy, and more vital than life, a red-bearded visitation surveyed his plight, dark brows drawn over aventurine eyes. None else but Earl Jieret, the shade declared, "My brother in spirit, lay your striving to rest. Your full measure of suffering is ended."

Tarens found in dismay his reply came too easily. "The dead cannot salve the mistakes of the living."

"You are in transit," Jieret responded in gentle correction. "Not yet crossed Fate's Wheel, burdened still by the sorrows you cannot find the requite grace to lay down. At the verge of the veil, after all you have done for Rathain, did you think I would not be at hand to receive you?"

"But I failed at every meaningful action that mattered!" Not only the benighted attempt to seek truce that delivered a True Sect talent's access to clan knowledge, or the unchecked threat of armed conflict poised to savage the site of the centaur markers. Yet the anguished burst of self-condemnation cast no pall of doubt over Jieret's luminous patience.

"Why are you of all spirits supremely untroubled?" Tarens gouged back in distress. "I could not avert your liege's defection! Deny that your vaunted crown prince deserted your people in their gravest hour of need."

"Aye, for sure!" Jieret agreed. "You'll say dying is meant to be serious business, and isn't Arithon the stickling bastard! Obstinate to the bone and stubbornly vengeful as Skyshiel granite!" Perverse laughter cracked by fond hilarity, the *caithdein*'s shade shrugged. "Doesn't he just jab his verbal stings under the most vulnerable patch of chafed skin! Makes you forget, doesn't he? That, sure's frost, we've both seen him grunt, squatting bare-arsed in the broom to drop steaming shite same as everyone else."

"Dharkaron Avenge!" Tarens cried, indignant. "Is this baiting sarcasm or a contrary spat in ribald philosophy?" Did the renowned vision of the s'Valerient farseers not know? He had personally stood before Rathain's council to deliver the word of Arithon's abdication, later confirmed by the indictment of the Fellowship's refutation as the realm's disenfranchised crown prince. "Have you no qualm that your Teir's'Ffalenn broke the covenant sworn on his knees before his *caithdein*, your father?"

"Did his Grace abandon his sovereign oath, in fact?" Jieret grinned, his merry demeanour unruffled by the accusation. "Oh, for certain, I know what you *think* has occurred." Sly amusement laced into badgering debate. "But you never parsed the heart's core of my liege. Not as I have. Else you may have seen his Grace led you astray. How he played your uncertainty and inflamed your doubts until, gadded to rage, you deserted him. Arithon reveals *nothing* to anyone freely. Never, when his obligate risks could drag someone he cares for into harm's way."

Yet the jammed bone stayed lodged in the craw, and for worse than the wholesale destruction wreaked out of hand on the unsuspecting folk at Etarra. "You still insist Arithon's not forsworn?" Astonishment gouged

Tarens to anger. "Tomorrow's razed dead might forgive the renouncement
that left them on the field, dispossessed. I can't, if the best of them might
have been saved." Sympathy foundered. Hurt for a betrayed friendship
scalded too deeply for platitudes. "Right or wrong, all I sought to accomplish since I left Kelsing amounted to naught!"

Humour melted like wax before Jieret's objection. "The fate of the
world held two paths on the morning you sheltered the vagabond
encountered on your way to market in Kelsing. Because you spared my
liege from recapture by the Koriathain, we stand here at the cross-roads.
I say this again. Arithon s'Ffalenn failed nothing and no one. And neither
have you."

"He attacked Verrain in trespass at Mirthlvain mire!" Tarens's baffled
frustration exploded. "And worse, he trespassed at Rockfell Peak with a
madman's intent to meddle. The assize concluded he meant to test his
straight power against the Seven's defence wards! What possible justification exists to have threatened the Mistwraith's incarceration?"

"On the contrary," Jieret denounced. "Did it never occur my liege
went for an assay to ascertain the protections defending Desh-thiere's
confinement were strong enough?"

"I have your assumption in trust against a state arraignment sealed
by the Fellowship?" Tarens bristled, astonished. "You may have acquitted
your liege for the enemy's knife that maimed you to secure his escape.
But the man who survived the executioner's sword at Daenfal no longer
honours the accolade of your sacrifice."

The offensive rebuke should have rent civilized equanimity. Yet Jieret
absorbed the personal sting, subdued only by reflective sadness. "Ciladis
perceived Arithon's probity, surely. And I'd hazard also, Davien."

"Then why in the name of Dharkaron's Redress did neither one lift a
finger to speak for your prince?" Gadded past measured debate, Tarens
fumed, "Honesty doesn't taunt danger for subterfuge. Why, if reason
existed, should any adept power endorse the disbarment of Arithon's
crown sanction?"

"Because, under the auspice of charter law, the Sorcerers grasped our
liege's sterling intent." Jieret qualified gently. "Arithon cast off the ties of
royal connection. He wanted no lawful standing left to compel the Seven's
duty-bound pledge of support."

Shown Tarens's perplexity, the shade of the High Earl succumbed to
impatience. "Ath on earth, fellow! You rammed a fire iron through a

Canon diviner to spare your family from charges of heresy! Did Arithon's rescue snatch you from the balefires of hazard and teach you *nothing*? Of course his true character repudiated the Seven! In the event he might fail to salvage his brother and sunder the Mistwraith's malevolence, he relieved the Fellowship's disastrous obligation to attempt his rescue from the Pit. More, his gadding provocation ensured the most stringent safeguard against mishap of all! When Kharadmon and Luhaine rebuilt Rockfell's wards, their inflamed suspicion guaranteed their wrought seals with cantrips specifically tuned to antipathy under his Name. Arithon braved his descent in the dark on the airtight reassurance he possessed no possible means to break free. If he lost his way and succumbed to possession, the revenant horde could not twist him and wrest the key to effect their release."

Horror in recoil struck like a gut punch. *Arithon had entombed himself beyond reach of reprieve.*

"We abandoned him. All of us." Too late for tears, Tarens reeled under the resharpened agony of remorse.

"Rathain had the gift of him only on loan," Jieret admitted in aggrieved sympathy. "His Grace's talent ever belonged to the crone, his destiny born and shaped to spearhead the fight to eradicate necromancy. He enabled your parting. Forced your dauntless loyalty to let him go, that you might weave your own thread in the larger web for posterity."

"Pray, for what earthly good?" Tarens railed at the spirit glimmering at the cusp of the crossing before him. "Since my legacy's sealed on the Fatemaster's list, what have I left but a fatherless child and a wife bereaved to no purpose?"

"Your last act." Jieret's ghost bent his head and smiled in salute. "Choice only empowers the present."

Too late for salvage, Tarens acknowledged the wheeling tug as the tide ebbed. Past question, his reckless generosity had cost more than his birth family's future. Grief could not spare the clan survivors left at risk of True Sect persecution, or bestow comfort to his cherished widow, or the daughter forsaken without any certainty of maturity. Nor might he amend the desertion that bequeathed Arithon to a cruel travail, sealed in a vault rendered proof against the ravening malice of Desh-thiere's unrequited collective.

Thinned to blown phosphor in the fathomless twilight of the liminal deep, Earl Jieret had no condolence to relieve the undying stab of regret.

"Living or lost, our liege languishes still. Or be certain, he would be here in spirit to share your last passage beside you."

"Then what have I been but the pawn caught in the mangle between deadlocked factions?" Release promised no quietude. Not for Tarens, with the war band's doomed effort to spare the free wilds thrown into the maw of disaster.

"Life does not always deliver our triumph the way we envision." Jieret's shade offered an unblemished hand, warm as flame. "Do you truly crave peace? Then commit your decision. Arise with a glad heart and be done."

Nothing left but surrender, Tarens yielded his substanceless grasp to a melting clasp, spun from gossamer. Contact uplifted him beyond anguish, a surge quickened by the susurrant beat of Raven's wings in soaring flight. Obsidian feathers sliced the unrelieved darkness and evoked an explosion of burgeoning light. Smelted into the core of the mysteries, Tarens gazed downwards and retraced the forged path of Jieret's enlightened transcendence. Yet not quite: this moment of galvanic creation was unique, entirely his very own.

The land unreeled beneath like a dream, the grey pockmarks smudged by the bloodshed of men flecked amid the silvery sheen of the flux. The interlocked stress points of conflict diminished as the greater Plain of Araithe spread outwards in aerial vantage. Inviolate country, bracketed by the sparkling watersheds of two rivers, and the vast arc of a diadem gem-studded by the liminal glow of five Second-Age marker stones. The consecrate array erected in concert with Fellowship sorcery and Ilitharis masons yet combed the fifth lane's electromagnetic transmission into harmonic alignment. Arithon's working and Etarra's obstructive demise had enhanced the focal point to a beacon.

There, like a promise, an emergent flare of unearthly light sheared through the palled colours of dawn. The wracked throes of war lost relevance as the fierce emanation waxed brighter and blazed. Radiant as a star come to earth, the emergent visitation charged the pearlescent flux to the shattering dazzle of sun flashed off a flawless mirror.

This august arrival outstripped mortal reckoning, a presence befitted to stun the extended range of initiate sight. At the verge of the veil, raised into expansion past mortal awareness, Tarens beheld the wonder in full. Unshielded by limiting flesh, he witnessed the blinding glory as the Tiendar Shayn'd, Cianor Moonlord, emerged from the lane focus and set foot upon free-wilds turf.

Strife and discord dissolved before his advance. Grief, death, and heartache unravelled, rendered meaningless as the pristine torrent of joy surged through the resonant web.

From tined antlers to the feathered gleam of his hooves, the manifest centaur of elder legend loomed fifteen spans high at the shoulder. His dappled coat shimmered like sea foam and abalone, tail and mane stainless as newfallen snow. His breastplate and bracers were inlaid with moonstone and opal. The twelve-stranded plait at his crown streamed thick as rope down his back, tied and tasselled with midnight velvet. A sable mantle and caparison draped his muscled frame, ivy patterned with stitched seed pearls and diamond. The illustrious trappings from three Ages of history armed the prowess of his person.

Sheathed at his side, the black sword Darisain, of the twelve blades forged at Isaer and wielded on the Paravian front line at the first binding of the Great Gethorn. The culmination of Ffereton's unique forging was augmented by the arts of Athlien and Riathan, the star song of midsummer writ into chased runes of fire opal and woven light.

Slung behind the broad shoulder of the storied Reborn, the ebony spear that had blooded the First-Age scourge of sea pillagers and slain the monstrous terror of the greater kraken. The mighty weapon was twelve spans in length, banded in the blued sheen of Mhorovian steel, its leaf-shaped point knapped from obsidian glass imbued with the indigo glimmer of deadly enchantment. On the cross-belted strap at his chest, the Moonlord carried the massive, whorled trumpet fashioned from the dorsal spine of the dragon Skenivarichiel, whose winded note at the Reprieve of the Horns had forced marauding drake spawn to furious standoff. The mouthpiece and rim of carved alabaster shed a cerulean corona instilled by the remnant echo of the wyrm's aura.

"Cianor Moonlord has answered your call," Jieret ventured with a reverence beyond knowing. "You are the first who left your origins without the incentive of talent perception. More than once since that moment, you risked your life to preserve the free wilds' mysteries."

The world greeted Cianor's regal tread cloaked in hush. The peridot grass stems bowed before him, with nary a trembling, strung droplet of dew disturbed by his passage. No bird's melodic song cracked the quiet. Nothing moved. Spring's verdant air poised, the stilled breeze a held breath, while the greatest Ilitharis of legend closed his gauntleted fist on the black horn at his hip. Then he lifted his antlered head, listening.

Tarens beheld the foremost Paravian champion, stunned mute.

Yet, in the exalted way of all things at the verge of life and death, his heart acknowledged why the centaur of ancient renown had come forward: *because of a vagabond spared on a desolate road, and an execution thwarted in courage on Daenfal's scaffold, the flower sprung from a Masterbard's art had wrought the restoration of Rathain's etheric web.* And because of the last signal thread, not least in significance, the counsel of Jieret's shade need not interpret the culmination scribed into the Fatemaster's record. *Due to a plainspoken crofter's defence, undertaken without hope in the absence of Fellowship backing, a clan war band today mounted Mankind's doomed stand to defend the northern free wilds.* Unbroken, still honoured, the terms of the compact that permitted humanity's settlement, no matter the armed force of the unsanctioned trespass invading the Plain of Araithe.

Mankind's acquisitive aspiration did not centre this world. Athera was not, and never had been, humanity's birth-born inheritance. Yet on this hour, a fallen man's selfless loyalty framed the tenuous foothold laid down for cooperative citizenship. Cianor's salute vouchsafed the seed of the dream, sketched in potential through Fellowship auspice when Mankind's rootless population received their stay of refuge under Paravian sovereignty. An inhabitance yet to be won fair upon merit, claimed by right through human autonomy.

Tarens yielded in grace to the centaur's salute, a bittersweet deliverance authored from the blood coin of impending tragedy. He could do nothing else. Embraced in tender care by the infinite, he heard the rolling, sweet thunder of Cianor Moonlord's imperative summons.

'Dientli'ient s'Athera i'tier, Iyat-thos!' The mighty of Athera appealed for his release: an imperative call, made in triumph and tribute, though an ocean of tears lent no salve for the reckoning.

Life or death, for the scouts set on the run before the Light's lancers at his departure; and brute slaughter for the outmatched clan war band gathered northward on the field, whose courage stood forth with no earthly means at hand to prevail. Ending or beginning, their fate ceased to matter. Taren's earthbound thread was complete, the rising song of expansion his clarion cry of rebirth in renewal.

The spread wings of Raven received his embrace. The twined spirits of a steadfast *caithdein*, and the family man, born to a Kelsing crofter, whose part knit the unfinished tapestry another stitch nearer completion, rose upwards together, welcomed home by true Name in bright glory forever.

Magnificat

The recalcitrant fisherman glowered at the scruffy traveller, the distaste on seamed features flushed purple by gin, and jaws clamped like a stranded clam raked into a shell-fisher's basket. "No." Predawn gloom inked him in disreputable shadow, marked out by the whites of his shifty eyes. "Flense me liver for bait and jabber into me lugs all ye like. I'm deaf! Takes a lubber's dunnage o'coin afore my fickle wind shifts in yer favour. True Sect's pinched every bilge-raddled keel for supply, and the unrighteous butty who stows wrongful passengers gets hauled aground on arraignment for heresy."

"Light everlasting, whyever didn't you say so?" Dakar huffed a vexed breath from his whiskered cheeks. Pegged as a Sunwheel deserter for the heavy, troop-issue crossbow slung from his shoulder, he elbowed the stolen weapon aside and caved to extortion. Dug into his satchel, before the prickle of incipient prescience saw him branded and cashiered as an unsanctioned prophet.

Five coinweight gold smoothed over his undue haste and squelched further need to negotiate.

Waved onto a rickety gangway with a shark's toothy grin and a wink, Dakar boarded a slovenly, black-marketeer's tub bespattered by the scavenger gulls roosted in fluffed rows aloft. Slack in her stays, her weedy hull listed, crewed by a laconic knave napping openmouthed on his backside in a bight of frayed rope.

Dakar did not care. Oars or sail, he would brave any plank heap afloat. His persistent onslaughts of clairvoyant vision could not salve Rathain's miserable plight. Dogged by the pending horrors of a war he was power-less to avert, he could not shed the onus of his talent Sight to seasick dissolution quickly enough.

The captain's boot roused the stupefied deckhand. "Crack on! We're running due west on the rhumbline, slick as a spit shine on brass."

Docklines were cast off the wharf's bollards. Dakar stowed himself midship, maligned by the pith of bluewater invective as halyards were cleared and hoisted canvas slatted and banged taut overhead. Tidal bore sucked the lugger from the log pier, the rickety snaggle of smug-glers' shacks lining the remote cove fallen astern. Dakar sagged in relief, too beaten to rue his ransacked purse. The exhaustive checkpoints imposed by martial occupation should have braced him for the jacked price of an illicit passage. Bound across Instrell Bay to Atainia's coastal wilds without a stamped pass, and no questions, guaranteed he would be sold out to the next avid bidder. One step from the gaol, the Mad Prophet exchanged his fussed anxiety over inquisitive diviners for the bruising indignities of salt water. Whitecaps and salt spray at least dampened the prescient surges sparked off by the resonant flare of impending violence. He might snatch a night's rest despite his green penchant for seasickness.

That expectation turned hag-ridden soon after Dakar closed his eyes. Against the barrage of peaking event, cold fathoms of brine lent his taxed nerves no buffer. In the black hours before daybreak, the graphic onslaught of vision stormed into stretched faculties too long shuttered in guarded defence . . .

Day already brightened the heartland of Rathain's free wilds far eastward, yesterday's showers blown through to clear air and a citrine sunrise. The clan war band confronted the onset of ruin, their meagre line strung across the wide vale selected for their chosen battleground. Huddled in redoubts dug into dank earth, or crouched behind flimsy hidings of thatched grasses and woven brush, they faced their last battle, snarling wolves backed at bay for the bittermost fight that would see every terrible inch of precious ground dearly lost. The surrounding countryside wore its gem-studded mantle of dew. The air hummed with foraging bees, tickling nectar from the riotous blooms of laurel and wildflowers. The hawk's cry above, and the cheeps of nesting wrens bespoke life, the anthem of nature's prosperity untouched by the clash of discord and desecration.

Spring gilded Rathain's northern territory in sunlight, the exuberance of mellifluous flux song restored by the clarified harmonic of the fifth lane. Impending defeat seemed unreal, remote as a jewel-toned dream too exquisitely vital to dim under a nightmare invasion of unbridled arrogance.

Violence executed for protection seemed a misplaced jape, a bit player's script written for mockery's absence of true-sighted vision. The clan fighters braced in opposition for their last hour of token resistance endured the hush, seized by regret, that perhaps, surely, some better choice in the past might have turned the tide and prevented the True Sect host staged against them.

The Sunwheel banner and the fervent belief in a Canon writ, carried forward by men's faith, aligned for a disastrous victory to sunset Mankind's chartered right to inhabit Athera. This definitive battle would seal that sad end through an insane inversion of sacred priority. Trade would stockpile its wealth in needless excess, seized at the plundering price of honed steel that respected no boundary.

The clanblood at the verge of today's killing field understood they would die under arms for Rathain, to the waste of their sanctioned crown prince's endeavour, that had brought the hard-won return of the Paravians. If title to the free wilds fell to conquest, the reaped toll would reverberate elsewhere. Future generations might lose their privilege to savour the heady exhilaration that invigorated the change of seasons amid the grandeur of an unspoiled landscape.

High ground granted the war band full view of their doom.

Dull blight crept across the mottled green vales and the budded riot of vivid colour, the True Sect host trampled over the tender carpet of early wildflowers. Stilled air quivered to the distant beat of their drums, the fitful, stirred whisper of forerunning breeze clipped by the frenetic, shrill crotchets of the officers' bugles. The Light's dedicate companies advanced in trimmed ranks, the seethe of their righteous commitment glued to unified purpose at ten thousand strong. They came on, arrayed in oblong formations, mounted companies and foot aligned block after block, drilled and groomed and sanctified by temple prayer for righteousness and the Light's glory. A thousand armoured lancers hove from the west, helms streamered and crested in gaudy town colours beneath the Canon's tasselled standards of dazzling gold. Light horse armed with sabres pranced at the flanks, centred by dedicate foot troops from Miralt and Erdane in snow-white surcoats blazoned with gilt, then their rear-guard swelled beyond three thousand strong by the auxiliary town garrisons from Narms, Cildorn, and Westfen.

Silk pennants snapped in the risen breeze, many-coloured and gaudy with fringes. Polished helms and forged breastplates from Castle Point's forges gleamed in the glare, while the synchronized tramp of hobnailed boots ground the soft turf to mud. The metallic timbre of steel and the thud of shod hooves muttered in counterpoint to the shrill rattle of snares and the whump of the kettledrums. The mixed reserves trailed across the chopped swale, more glittering lancers and bristles of pikemen and short swordsmen with long, rectangular shields, shipped over by galley and marched in stages from the northcoast seaports. Archers and skirmishers deployed, fanned out for attack, movement sliced by the banners of Jaelot, Highscarp, and Whitehold, with mailed lancers in cavalcade behind the lines trailed by the ox-drawn hulks of the surgeons' drays, stacked high with boxed medicines and baled linen for bandages battened under roped tarps.

Before that mauling threat of massed tonnage and might, a strung arc of frail flesh clad in leathers and brigandines, the clan defenders waited in covert ambush with their tough, recurve bows, and bearing the wrapped hilts of long sword, steel dagger, and cross-laced javelin. Past the brief advantage of terrain, they were fodder ripe for the shredding charge that would deliver annihilation.

No song would be sung. No footnote accolade rewarded the dry-mouthed, sapped nerve vised in place by cheerless duty and dauntless bravery. In Sethvir's absence, the annals at Althain Tower would bequeath a blank page on their record. Outmatched fifty to one, the clan bowmen nocked their readied arrows. The uncounted nameless poised here to defy the loomed fabric of history braced for the charge. Few expected to live to see how their unremarkable stand came to matter. None realized, in the cold sweat of fear and fraught anguish, that if any frail link in their chain was removed, the events of an age would unravel.

For the war band's focus on the spread vantage before them spared no thought for the untoward calm that muffled the flux stream at their backs. Eyes ahead, tension riveted, they measured the war host laid out for their carnage.

Tin notes across distance, the first bugle sounded, a treble flourish bright as scrolled bronze carried against the stiffening breeze.

The enemy lines shuddered to a brief halt. Then the commander's horn sounded the charge, and the packed wall of lancers jostled under the spur and surged forward. The rumble of a thousand heavy horse shook the vale, hammered to a gallop that rushed the low ground, and bogged in the softened spring soil.

The clan archers loosed into the weltered mass. The swift volleys sleeted into the armoured fore like fell vengeance, horses and men picked off by marksmen drilled lifelong to strike down small-game targets. The damage inflicted could not stop the attack. The toll of those first fallen deterred nothing. Deaths in their front ranks only inflamed the ardour of the skirmishers, backed by the light horsemen and foot troops whose secondary advance engulfed the churned ground, swarmed up the rise, and surged into the clan war band's strategic retreat. Half fell, cut down before their sheaves of arrows were spent. More battled the swarm, surrounded by threshing steel, spitted and slashed in the merciless mill of destruction.

Down the far slope, the pitched battle raged, with escape for the nimble cut off by the readied strike in retaliation. The surprise assault waiting for the clan defenders found them unprepared, harried as the covert lance company chewed into their rout from behind. Caught in the vice by the unforeseen charge, the startled survivors encountered their doom. Unwarned and unwary, they locked weapons and died: butchered as handily as Tarens's slaughtered patrol, whose sodden braids hacked as trophies swung in grisly triumph from the finials of the league hunters' banners sweeping to finish their brethren.

Skewering clan prey like vermin in flight, the townborn dedicates surrounded the melee, hell-bent in pursuit of their massacre. Milled under hooves, minced by the sword, spitted by pole arms and arrows, the desecrate dead littered the turf, crushed grasses and matted, pulped flowers soaked scarlet, while the rank scent of blood drew, like black rags swept by a noxious wind, the flocks of raucous carrion crows, the ravens and circling vultures.

The scattered few still upright sprinted for their lives, soon under pursuit by the mounted lancers, who would run them down until the last man and woman became overtaken . . .

Dakar aroused shivering and disoriented. The hissed friction of wet lines and the rattle of tackle snapped short to the whump of taut canvas aloft. His slack frame rolled by the jolt on the deck of the lugger, just sheeted close hauled on port tack. Ploughed spray and the cut of the wind through doused clothing compounded his misery, fetched up short by the midship rail. For a halfpenny bet and simplicity, he would have tumbled overboard and let the foaming wake swallow his wretched despair.

Rathain's war band broken and the cruelty of their fate recast his intent to relieve Kharadmon at Althain Tower as an exercise in futility. Outfaced from the start, Dakar wrestled his recumbent nausea.

At what point did the relentless toll of botched charges become too heavy for the mauled heart to withstand? The red end to the morning's debacle on the Plain of Araithe would tear open the core of Rathain's free wilds to Mankind's rapacious expansion. Gone for naught, the brave war band's doomed stand in the breach. The aftermath consequence bought no reprieve from an epitaph graven by tragedy.

The unleashed cascade tipped the scales straight to havoc as the sundering of charter law revoked the compact's surety for human residence on Athera. Curdled ash on the tongue, Dakar forecast no path through the bitter avalanche of cause to consequence. Should he surmount the dreadful, long odds, if the destruction of Siantra's influence defused Seshkrozchiel's intractable madness, the restoration of Fellowship oversight spared nothing. On the contrary, the Seven's primary directive itself forged the lynchpin spinning the unchecked plunge to catastrophe.

Grief and tears, Dakar swore through gut-wrenched malaise. Lift the siege that locked Shehane Althain's defences, and the compact's warrant of surety then must be called to account.

Kharadmon's freedom to act would yoke him with the obligate horror of routing out Mankind's tenancy from the planet, root and branch, till no vestige remained to seed a recurrence.

Or else the slide into entropy would fray the fabric of renewal binding the mysteries. The magnificence of Paravian survival would fall to humankind's egregious lust for wealth and the ignorant, unchecked pursuit of consumptive commerce.

The weal of the world come undone shattered nerve and savaged the spirit for more than this day's toll of losses.

How had Arithon s'Ffalenn mustered the mulish defiance to shoulder his descent into Rockfell Pit? His fate in the sealed dark with the Mistwraith's malice tore an already-unbearable grief to the lacerate

marrow, beyond all sorrow to contemplate. Dakar cradled his forehead
in clammy palms, eaten raw by cankerous doubt. His own role demanded
the same blindfold measure of courage, plumbed from an uncharted
depth he had never possessed.

Tarens had exceeded himself and somehow embraced selfless sacrifice and died for his scout companions and a clan war band he had no
earthly power to save. Not all men rose to the calling of fate. Some
threads snapped under load. If one flawed vessel failed in the flesh,
must the whole cloth tear asunder? Did the stumble to ruin destroy the
future for all generations? Dakar's initiate training yielded no answers.
Hope was a persistent caprice, an insane ferocity that defied the ruled
stasis of logic. Maundering thought foundered to impasse against the
shoals of human limitation, until the seer's tortured lot devolved to the
onus of putting one foot in front of the next.

The seedy lugger ploughed through a wave. Sunlight sparkled off
jetted bursts of white spray, shearwaters skimming ahead like black
shuttlecocks over the glistening crests. As oblivious to the encroaching
blight elsewhere, and the storm's shadow of crowding disaster, the
deckhand tripped over Dakar's wedged bulk in his barefoot rush to
ease sheetlines.

"Griped, eh? Heave over the rail, or get tossed yerself. Nobody's
mopping your leavings if you sick up."

The jibe raised a laugh from the master at the helm, followed by a
lewd anecdote about curing hiccoughs. Dakar neither heard the derisive
taunt nor succumbed to his upset digestion. The trauma churning the
lateral channels of the flux ripped through his talent faculties and
upended his awareness into a fit of black-out prostration . . .

Under the midday horror of battle, beset clansman chased down by the
True Sect lancers were murdered in flight, or flushed from cover to be
swarmed and butchered in dog-pack frenzy under the blades of vengeful
dedicates long savaged by spring traps and covert ambush. Combatants
locked in lethal contest raged over the death throes of their strewn
casualties. The war band's few standing survivors fought their annihilation, the talent reach of their refined perception shut down where the
ambient flux shuddered in poisoned recoil. The shed emanation of animal
magnetism lashed up in the path of lethal engagement blighted their
surrounds in the after-shock recoil of unfettered violence.

Agony and hard-pressed exhaustion nailed their fixed concentration, until the reflexive response to clashed steel upon clotted weaponry and the uncertain, slipped step on the gore-soaked ground dulled the visceral screams of the stricken.

No combatant swerved from the bloodbath when the centaur, Cianor Moonlord, breasted the hill's crest above, the horned majesty of his immense silhouette reared rampant against an etched backdrop of sky. Muscles rippled like oiled steel, the Tiendar Shayn'd, Ilitharis legend reborn into flesh, surveyed the throes of the carnage that sullied Rathain's northern turf. Aggrieved, he acknowledged the viciously outmatched defenders whose sacrifice failed to stem the appalling tide of armoured steel bent upon desecration. The cry of his sorrow spoke on the wind, a whisper unheard through the strife of spurred horseflesh and crossed blades, and the piteous groans of the dying.

Cianor lifted his head. He raised the mighty, spired horn to his lips, that had spoken on battlefields more brutal and tragic than this one over the passage of Ages. His winded note overwrote the engorged tumult and spoke in the register of hallowed silence. The call resounded over the land, echoed and re-echoed in building vibration that wakened the mysteries. Bed-rock trembled underfoot in bass counterpoint, then sang aloud. The expansive, tolled sound exploded across the continuum, seen and unseen, a blow that disrupted the entrained flux patterns and pulverized all embedded transmission like smashed crystal and cymbals. The rolling wave of reverberation ranged forth, an imperative summons not heard in the world since the mythic battles fought against ravening drake spawn wreaked slaughter and havoc in the Second Age.

The clarion call to arms raised its implacable answer. Light flowered, silver as mist streamed from the focal point of the great arc at the standing array of ancient stone markers. The burst speared through the fabric of known existence, split into rays, and from them emerged the glittering ranks of the Ilitharis Legion. A thousand strong, their tined antlers steel-capped for war, they came: four-footed giants armoured and jewelled and caparisoned in ruby and emerald and sapphire. Magnificence outfitted with spear, ebon bow, and the crescent curve of the honed axe, the weapons brandished in Paravian hands were storied in myth; of their swords, four more borne with them onto the field were originals forged by Ffereton at Isaer. When Cianor lowered his horn and raised aloft the bared blade named Darisain, others worn by their bearers were unsheathed in concert.

The commensurate burst of unmuzzled song raised a shout of unbridled bliss that beggared reason and shattered the resonant grip of despair. Imbued by Riathan with the exquisite purity of star song, and aligned by Athlien enchanters to the elemental properties of fire, water, and air, the combined chord's harmonic had not been heard as one voice since the powers of Sorcerers, high kings, and Paravians beset at the forefront had contested the Mistwraith's invasion.

Lightning unleashed in burning white sheets, the undying celebration of sound and light that ignited creation brought to earth the release of a pearlescent flood that flushed through the lane tides. Living bridge to Ath's glory, the charge thundered down on the warfront and spilled over stained ground churned to bloodied muck and heaped with the tangled fallen. The rarefied force cleaved into the knot of slaughter and death where a war host of thousands even yet scythed down the beleaguered clan war band's exhausted defenders.

The clap of Cianor Moonlord's momentous reprieve exceeded the threshold of mortal awareness. No animate human who marched on the Plain of Araithe possessed the upstepped perception to encompass the unadulterated impact of the living mystery made incarnate. Animate flesh caught at the cusp encountered the presence: a deep thrum of vibration rolled through the ground as a subsonic, bass tone that built and burgeoned and waxed upwards into a bone-shaking blast of audible sound. Skin and viscera shuddered to thrills, rushed through like a tonic by etheric momentum as the flux lines crested into resplendent confluence.

Clan tradition grasped the significance. Gifted scouts shielded their etheric awareness. They dropped swords, knives, and weapons, their foes irrelevant before the urgency of unfolding consequence. Instinct prompted the imperative drive to seek centre, mask their eyes and lie flat, grounded to the rooted stasis of bed-rock before the onrushing comber of charge shredded the framework of embodied cognizance.

The Light's faithful engaged in the throes of raw combat fell prey, overwhelmed in the heedless gulf of their ignorance. Long since lost to history, the known measures forgotten, they never grasped the appalling extent of their peril. Talent diviners caught unawares crumpled at the knees, clubbed insensate. Few officers noticed their abrupt demise, and

fewer responded to the shocking, sharp break in the rampant fury of
the clan resistance. Dedicates caught on the killing field flinched from
the warning crackle of static snapped off their steel armour and weaponry. Lances and swords dropped from their slackened fingers. Men
cried out, hurled in shock off their feet, overcome by a joy that disallowed
hatred. They clawed off crested helms. Wept, while their fellows astride
vainly wrestled the reins as their seasoned mounts bolted, overset by
the feral urge to run free. Drilled order unravelled. Weltered chaos
destroyed the momentous advance as upended equilibrium sent the
rear-guard companies staggering in disorientation.

The reserves come behind lost their purposeful way. Terror drowned
reasoned intellect as they beheld the uncanny vision sweeping down
the standing war host before them like scythed windrows of ripened
wheat. The disruptive force winnowed through man and beast, before
which the hindmost broke and fled, tumbled as sheared leaves as the
best and the bravest clawed down and trampled their stunned fellows,
paralysed in slack-jawed derangement.

Front, centre, and flanks, the armed host peeled away, stampeded by
galvanized panic. Flight failed them as the last semblance of unmoored
sensation evaporated, the hesitant and the stalwarts toppled full length.
The foolish who stared were struck dumb and blind, cohesive memory
scattered before the deluge of unbearable light. Hearing frayed, deafened.
Forged metal tempered for war keened aloud, hammer-struck by the
electromagnetic flood that rolled through at full bore, until the wild vale
thrummed under centaur hooves like a sounding-board resonated by a
thousand plucked strings.

The harmonic wave sown by their passage sliced the defined edges
of substance and form into rainbows, the textured contour of the natural
landscape doused under the shimmering web. Ambient flux excited to
fluorescence scattered and burned a pearlescent haze through the air.
Scintillant as the sheen of moonlight distilled, the phenomenon poured
the glimmer of argent through the glare of unrefined daylight.

The pealing note of the dragon-spine horn and the rarefied chime
of five Isaervian swords altered and lifted the threshold of audible
frequency. The bass vibration sent ringing through turf and the buried
strata of Athera's mantle rove outwards, immersive resonance extended
farther by wind, striking off collateral ripples throughout the substance
of the perceived world. The peal raised bell-tone reverberation and

treble harmonics that ranged octave upon octave into the ephemeral realms of the unseen. The carrier wave of impact fell upon mortal awareness like a blow, stunned nerves sparked and ignited to dizzying ecstasy.

The impact left no spirit standing on two legs. Arrested at a stroke, the armed might of the Light's war host languished, blunted, riven unconscious and pulped to the marrow by the grand chord of the mysteries brought to full flower. The injured and dying were lifted beyond pain. Unhurt townborn still breathing perished of stopped hearts. Others survived, catatonic or witless, minds scalded to dissociate raving. None among the clanborn who wakened to sanity retained living memory of an encounter outside the pale of mortal endurance . . .

. . . stunned insensate on the wallowing deck of the lugger, Dakar rode the spiral of his tranced awareness into the expanded throes of seer's vision illumined by the confluent, mercury shimmer spun off the heightened aftermath: of five hundred fighters in the clan war band, a third slain by wounds on the field lay amid the entangled wrack of townborn fallen. From a battleground swept by the mysteries unleashed by Cianor's charge, few of the Light's faithful shocked senseless would rise. The rare handful who recouped their sanity would desert the cause for their loved ones, never to bear weapons by mandate for the True Sect Canon again.

The marked cohort of clan-blood survivors who sustained the unshielded impact of the Paravian presence attended their casualties and laid their hacked dead to rest. Tried and confirmed in the forge flame of their obdurate heritage, they saluted the hallowed gift of late victory and walked away, grieving. For their honoured losses, and in tribute for Tarens's unparalleled sacrifice, the ancient free wilds of Rathain were once more defended by the Ilitharis guardians of old. Past question, henceforward, the realm's proscribed ground was no longer ripe for Mankind's acquisitive desecration.

Triplet

Prodded awake and debarked through the salt shallows onto the wild coast of Atainia, Dakar finds the etheric chaos thrashed up by Seshkrozchiel's unhinged assault has roiled the third lane, foreclosing direct contact with Kharadmon through Isaer's Great Circle focus, and disrupting his forlorn bid for a last consultation with Verrain at Methisle . . .

Tied up wharfside at Lorn by night, a trade galley from Cildorn waits for the exciseman's early-morning inspection before unlading her cargo, and the port's assigned guard asleep at his post misses the stowaway no longer quite human, who leaps over the landward rail and slinks furtively into the dark . . .

While the Biedar crone harkens to the keened register of star song in the rooted deeps of Rockfell Pit, the Reiyaj Seeress faces sunwards, her marble orbs on the shifting reflections spanning the fates of two worlds: one threatened by whiplash and hung by a thread, and the other flogged into unstable tatters by rogue dragons whose aspected creativity manifests the incomprehensible torrent inflicted upon them by the galvanic welter of human emotion . . .

XVII. Transpositions

O n the splinter world of Sckaithen Duin, called Fortress of Dragons, atop the warded hillock where the worldsend portal once had enabled the transit to Athera, only wind spoke through the susurrant rustle of leaves. An unlikely orchard coaxed to take root by enchantment bore apples, pears, fragrant peaches, and a smatter of oranges, surrounded by towering hickories and spread canopies of moss-bearded live oak. The grove sheltered a small, sun-drenched clearing where glossy hares grazed on strawberry leaves, and a flock of speckled hens pecked for iridescent insects in lush grass. There also, the Fellowship Sorcerer Sethvir knelt in the turf, tending a vegetable patch run riot, herbs and peas, tubers and melon vines laden with blossoms and mature fruit. At his elbow, a tea bush grew out of its element, fair testament to Ciladis's mystical touch.

Thatched in shade several yards from the haphazard plot's straggled stakes and the cant of a bee skep gone wild, a granite archway carved with interlaced serpents spanned empty sky. The glittering, salt grain of incised runes crafted by Davien's genius wore flecked dollops of light, cold-struck ciphers inert, the pearlescent sheen of a new interface through the black void yet to be forged.

That day, and for the unforeseen future, the drake war that sundered the Protectorate's Accord raged on unabated, years and resolute patience away from a brokered resolve. Where mounded dunes lapped the verge of an opaline lake, Luhaine's defences sheared a fractious boundary between warded calm and restive air. Conjury that voided a rending assault by dragons protected the isolate knoll. Proof against vicious spats waged with tooth and claw, and gouted fire that seared rock to magma, and far worse, the whiplash of dreamed thought wont to pulverize surrounds and firmament, the very substance of life itself shaped and reshaped in violent recoil. Mighty collisions of compressed energy splashed the barrier like flung acid, shed to the quivering, backwash distortion of a soap bubble snagged in a gale.

No hour passed without tensioned vigilance; no moment slackened the imminent threat. Even a Sorcerer's discipline chafed under such relentless peril. Yet the overture to set the stage for a stand down demanded the utmost exactitude.

Ciladis's encroaching escort of sparrows flicked shadows over turned earth and sprouts, cultivated in untidy jumbles as haphazard as the books and manuscripts left heaped in the library at Althain Tower.

Equally content in the dirt, the Warden plucked a stray spider out of his sleeve. Sunburned nose smutched with soil, he acknowledged the ebon elegance of the hunter just returned from another outlying patrol. "Bass again?"

Ciladis flourished his string of fresh fish, then unburdened the driftwood tucked under his arm. "The creatures are willing and plentiful." He knelt, drew his knife, and set to cleaning and scaling his catch. "I've corrected the planetary wobble incurred during yesterday's full-on attack." Met by a dearth of comment, he added, "I'm sorry. This morning's alignment did not favour my effort to reach through to check on Siantra." Amber eyes keen as a tiercel's analysed his colleague's nearsighted squint. "Your attempt did not fare any better?"

"No." Stickling brevity, or evasively reticent, Sethvir sighed. The distortions spun off by wroth dragons clouded his extended vision, even at the opportune moment Athera's distant star crossed Sckaithen Duin's azimuth meridian. "Siantra left Forthmark. She's crossed the continent and bypassed the ruin at Isaer without mishap. I have nothing more."

No momentous harbingers, although Seshkrozchiel's rampage scrambled the ambient flux in Tysan enough to blur his reliable view of the probable outcomes. Sethvir was loath to dwell upon bitter uncertainties. Stirred to lay the cookfire, he withheld his forbidding unease, that Imaury Riddler's restive shade might yet stir from quiescence at Mainmere.

Unlike Asandir, who confronted the Warden's dissembling outright, Ciladis more tactfully bent to the chore of roasting their meal. But his humble patience broke off unrewarded, any further pursuit of the deadlocked subject disrupted by a seismic tremor.

Then the islet shuddered, lurched by a quake that tumbled the spitted fillets into the flames.

"Ward breach!" Shot to his feet without blotting his fingers, Ciladis sprinted from the forested knoll towards the open shoreline. Sethvir pelted a spry step behind, staggered off stride as a thunderous crack slapped through a tranquil setting no longer innocuous.

A finger of magma slashed from the lake bed and ripped through the sandy shallows. Water scalded to a boil erupted, shrieking steam through the billowing ink of volcanic fumes seething down like a storm front.

"*Allessiadient!*" Sethvir's shout for peace in actualized Paravian clapped the geothermal incursion to a halt, barely shy of their stabilized haven.

Ciladis leaped the crusted swathe of congealed rock. Unfazed by the geysered plume of hot water, he splashed forward barefoot, in time, and caught Luhaine's stumbling bulk on arrival.

"A piddling spark to ignite a great fire, damn all to the plaguing curiosity of irascible drakes!" Singed and streaming sparks from his hair, Luhaine shucked his colleague's supportive grip. A gimped step sieved sand through burned holes in his boots. Scatological invective more Kharadmon's style met Sethvir's owl-eyed bemusement, until the stout Sorcerer recovered his straight-laced aplomb. "Davien's backed Ozvowzakrin at bay. Finally!"

"We've gathered the Gatekeeper's complicit, and not under muzzled coercion?" Sethvir's astute deduction devolved into woolgathering as he dusted flaked ash from his palms. Several green dragonflies winnowed out of his cuffs, back-splashed artifacts affected by his incantation. "Rejoice in the bright side. The rough consequence at least defanged the Koriathain. One less aggravation to fester during our absence."

Luhaine heaved a cavernous sigh. A side eye on Ciladis ascertained his gapped ward was being properly stitched before he unloaded his persnickety summary. "We're past negotiation. Whatever blandishment Davien proposed, the ornery wyrm picked a fight. At least we've cornered the provocative reason behind Ozvowzakrin's defection."

"Dare I guess?" Sethvir pinched an ember smouldering in his beard, and forestalled the incipient lecture. "Our Protectorate allies neglect the Accord because the infiltration of humankind's mischief has rattled the scales of the ancients."

"The drakes consider our probity forfeit." Luhaine heaved a martyred sigh. "They have reason. If humanity's freebooting licence has not yet supplanted Paravian sovereignty, the fine line's become a close call." Paused to cement Ciladis's closure with a fussy flourish, he tucked his splayed fingers into his belt and rumbled on in glum afterthought. "We won't be finished here anytime soon. Unless you have better news, and the hopeful work begun with Siantra brings the chance of diplomacy to bear on the crisis besetting Athera?"

"No way to tell. Not with certainty." Sethvir poked at the scorched remains of a meal thrifty habit inclined him to salvage. "Siantra had not fully mastered her transformation when she left the oversight of Ath's adepts." No guessing how far her blended faculties may have progressed, or whether the rift in her consciousness still hampered a logical framework of comprehension. "Our posited supposition won't matter if Asandir and Davien can't offset the impact of Ozvowzakrin's rebuttal."

Luhaine conceded, too stuffy to wallow in hangdog apology. "They are inbound, hard-pressed. I came ahead to stiffen our guard against a spin-off incursion of drake spawn."

Sethvir scrapped the diversion of kindling and fish. "How pressed?" He shot erect. Alerted by the striking chill permeating Ciladis's calm, he shared the Sight of an ominous pall about to engulf the horizon. "Luhaine? Exactly which drake spawn?"

Too agitated for long-winded indulgence, the corpulent Sorcerer threw up his hands. "I wasn't inclined to look back to find out!"

The barrage sown by the dragons' wrath barrelled down, a black morass of boiling cloud, shot through by actinic tangles of lightning and towering, spindled waterspouts. The pressurized wavefront blown off in concatenation threshed up battering wind, raised to a shriek as the clash of deconstructive creation jumbled land and sea into tectonic upheaval and change. Mountain ranges erupted from nothing, then drummed through an incredulous, abrupt transition into walled glaciers, pounded by tidal waves webbed with froth and back-fallen spindrift. A vista no sooner formed, than reenactment rove a surreal replacement, the jewel-toned fathoms of oceanic expanse melted into sere desert, furrowed with canyons mottled purple as an angry bruise.

Narrowly leading that irruptive cusp, the rag-doll figures of Asandir and Davien raced like scuttled twigs flung ahead of a hurricane. Yet no manic, two-legged sprint might outpace the event bearing down at the flash-point interface of dreamed thought.

Asandir's faint shout ruled the split second before his power unfurled, a blue-white halo centred by a star that waxed to a dazzling burst of argent fire. The report punched the air, a thunderous blast that eclipsed sight of Davien, a scant half pace behind.

Then the dragon's instantaneous retort raised a serrated cliff, vertical ramparts sheared into jet spires that glittered like honed knives under a burning, blue sun. The site where the paired Sorcerers fled was inundated, slagged from existence with tornadic ferocity.

Sethvir uttered a mild expletive, more intrigued than alarmed. Luhaine's apple cheeks crinkled with reproof for the bothersome need to reconfigure the ward field his proprietary care had just mended. "Twice in an hour is outright excessive."

The obsidian scarp abruptly disintegrated. Searing rays speared like fanned blades through flying shards of split rock, followed by the rumbling ground shock transmitted by the avalanche of incompatible forces. The two Sorcerers momentarily engulfed reemerged, dodging the back-fallen rain of debris, then the reverberate slam as a crevassed tundra opened up underneath them. Other sinuous nightmares gave chase in pursuit, angry and living, with taloned claws and ravening teeth.

Ciladis sighed. His lilted phrase in actualized Paravian shifted the tumbling boulders and horrific predators in mid-descent to a harmless flock of petrels and a rainbow shower of flip-flopping fish.

"Efficient," Sethvir mused in appreciation, "if we weren't bored silly with aquatic fare on the menu."

The roar of the baulked dragon soaring behind should have boiled the lake to parched dust, had Davien's riposte not scythed up a chill that precipitated a blizzard of dry ice from the stress-heated, turbulent air. The flakes struck the churned water, each pocked impact spitting fogged tendrils of sublimation.

The drake's bellowed fury shocked sky and earth. Belched flame raked the vista. Scythed curtains of red gold showered cinders through billows of caustic fumes. The roiling cloud enveloped both Sorcerers, their fuzzed silhouettes rinsed by an actinic flare that splashed into a starburst of iridescence. Flecked discharge streamered down and dispersed, flayed by a stinging gust reeking of ozone.

Asandir broke away, emerged at a flat run down a slate causeway made manifest by a masterful feat of transformative sorcery. He reached Luhaine's sheltering wards and plunged through, one leading step before stark dissolution unmade the pavement beneath him. His work of firm conjury unravelled, superseded by a carmine tongue of sprayed magma that became devoured in turn by the pummelling suck of a whirlpool.

Luhaine's staid tread waded in and tidied the back-lash arrowed in by Asandir's wake. Ever thorough, his neat cantrips and entrained strings of banishments sliced like flung cleavers across the unsettled continuum. The miasmic heave of spawned monsters dispersed. Insoluble chaos heaved and unravelled. The spewed rumble of moulten mineral subsided to liquescent sludge, the after-slap of debris combed clean by a wave of residual charge that sloshed, hissing, into repelled subsidence from the sandy shore of the Fellowship's patch of dry land.

"Welcome back!" Sethvir's cheerful greeting from the high ground acknowledged the colleague, emerged ragged and singed as a refugee from the tumult. "Davien?"

"Still behind me." Not winded, but attenuated as frayed string from the sharp expenditure of raw power, Asandir plucked a wriggling minnow from his hair, passed on without thought to Ciladis.

The healer's touch cupped the stranded mite. A soft phrase entreated its displaced creaturehood for permission. Ciladis blew gently on his hands and released the misfortunate being, harmlessly transformed for retreat to the gentler refuge of air as a butterfly.

That arrested figment of drake spawn dispatched on the flutter of iridescent wings, four Sorcerers regarded the on-coming maelstrom, raging untamed. The rift wall of impenetrable chaos howled with Sithaer's indomitable fury, Davien still beset in the cyclonic core as the tempest crashed down on their warded position.

"At least we're spared Kharadmon's crackpot remarks," Luhaine grumbled. "The collateral uproar's exciting enough without his baggage of skeletons. I have to admit I didn't miss Davien's manic addiction to tweaking the tail of colossal risk."

Asandir's emphatic head shake demurred. "I'll hazard his collaboration with Seshkrozchiel lends him the precision to finesse the line of drastic peril he treads."

Controlled risk or not, the incursion closed upon Luhaine's defence matrix at relentless velocity. Inundated, the impeccable protection responded, a magnesium pulse of immaculate light that quenched the assault's unravelling brunt with an earsplitting crackle. Then buoyant resistance achieved compensation, and haltered the runaway impetus. Past the gelid backdrop of opposed forces mauled into distortion, the black storm of the dragons' volatile interface crumped overhead. Screaming wind followed. The snap and sizzle of static cracked off of splayed vanes and taut wing leather, shedding excess electrical discharge across the unmuzzled maw of the void. The translucent shimmer of the Sorcerers' barrier alone spared their besieged knoll from immolation.

A sunburst shafted the murk overhead, raw gold trailing a comet tail swathe of cobalt. Nearly the same tint as the azure flame snagged off a live dragon's aura, the phenomenon unravelled. A spitting flare of sparked ball lightning unfurled and disgorged the spread wings of an eagle. Sable feathers trailing streamered light, the avian construct stooped like a dropped anvil, snapped through Luhaine's ward without shearing a seam, and glided to a crisp landing.

No longer winged, the upright form of Davien strode out of the shimmer of discharge that was *dragon!* still flaring the queasy ripple of transient creation shape-shifted at whim. "We'll see Sithaer's cauldron of past Methspawn brewed up, and worse! Savage recombinants shaped for the full spectrum of tooth-and-claw murder if this drake war runs rampant much longer."

Sethvir translated the glance exchanged with the two Sorcerers just returned through the maelstrom, Asandir deadpan, and Davien's ascetic contempt wracked with distaste. "I gather Ozvowzakrin's not inclined to negotiate."

"Not on any terms we dare to recognize." Asandir sidelined the irrelevant particulars and applied his assistance to Luhaine's harried effort to stiffen the challenged weave of his barrier. More dragons scythed past. Again, the outside surrounds past the ward flexed into radical alteration. Slight improvement, the smothering atmosphere thinned. Red-shifted sunlight hazed a film of sulphurous murk, streamered with poisonous gas bubbled from the foamed acid of caustic waters. The benign, sandy beach anchored under the Fellowship's stay overlooked a headland transformed, volcanic pumice thrashed by hissing current knifed across by jagged reefs. Hurled spume jetted over the stranded hulk of a gigantic beast with spurred tentacles. The beaked gape of jaws needled with glass-edged teeth suggested a horrific, unknown permutation derived from a greater kraken.

"Yon's as graphic a warning as we've ever faced." Luhaine mopped his bald head, morose. "Since the drakes are tossing up the nightmare remnants of monsters subdued since the Second Age, what forsaken kernel of wickedness has swayed Ozvowzakrin's allegiance?"

"Asandir failed to confide on the matter in detail?" Davien resettled his mussed clothes, gaunt shoulders ruffled as a raptor with soaked feathers. "The cross-grained distortion of human emotion has twisted the wyrms to imbalance. They cannot reconcile contradictory impulses that are unmalleable to reason. As we feared, the evolving blend is intractable."

"A pestilent predicament growing worse by the hour!" Luhaine retorted. "Stop gloating. You cautioned us. Long before you meddled with Arithon, you said the leap from the fat of humanity's frying pan would toss us neck deep into hellfire's boiling pot."

"Ah, well. For once, we're agreed the outlook's not rosy." Davien shrugged, unappeased. "Asandir has the priorities straight. His late invocation overlaid upon yours realigned three more layered barriers against a reincarnate resurgence of Methurien."

Luhaine pursed his lips, a sour eye swivelled to measure the field Sorcerer's reinforcement of his base construct. "I see we'd better prepare in advance for revived packs of Searduin, if not the fell gamut of drake spawn reborn like the radical plagues that left scars from the Era of Destruction."

"Something like." Davien, agreeable, struck a note to raise hackles. "We might wish for the pick of the enhanced weapons stored in Althain Tower's armoury if we cannot wrest Ozvowzakrin's interest out of collusion. Has Kharadmon's situation steadied enough to consider retuning the Worldsend Gate? If so, I suggest we weigh in upon cutting our losses. Mind Athera, and leave the wild dragons in exile here to their insane devices."

Sethvir blinked, unperturbed. "That won't curtail the threat of a mass gestalt." Leaned against the vacant archway's foundation, he let the pause hang on the inferences, then finished his bleak deduction. "A retreat from Sckaithen Duin would forfeit Seshkrozchiel's stake in the Concord binding the Protectorate's interests, besides."

Asandir fielded the probable hitch. "A break in the treaty annuls the restrictions on Dragonkind's destructive access to Athera, and at least one of you hasn't been forthright. Just how severely has Seshkrozchiel's mind become compromised?"

The impasse resounded through Sethvir's bleak silence.

"Force our obligate surety to eradicate humanity, and you have the raw gist of Ozvowzakrin's demand to broker the peace." Davien's caustic sarcasm ebbed to bare honesty. "Drakish revenge, I venture, for the curse of emotions their kind have never evolved or required the primal endowment to process."

"Well, then," Sethvir temporized, sunburned hands stroking his frizzled beard, and his daft regard glittering, "Since our stay in these trying conditions might extend for some time, thank goodness Rathain's unrest has resolved under the reins of Paravian rule."

A spiked second followed that stunning news, while Ciladis's tawny gaze matched his colleague's reticence, inflected with accusation. "You insisted your meridian star sight was unclear."

"I did." Sethvir stared back, blithe as a toddler with a pilfering fist shoved into the cookie jar.

The blunt standoff broke before Asandir's laughter. "Sethvir! You devious cheat." To the mystified pique of three colleagues, he added, "The conniving scribbler's had a clean contact with Tehaval Warden for weeks! He never mentioned the pebble I brought with us? Because he was given the one I found lodged in my boot after our whirlwind departure from Penstair."

"I was saving that bit to relieve the scrum of bothersome news." Althain's Warden stared skyward and ticked points off his fingers. "Provided your wee bit of slate's a true touchstone. And if the centaur's breadth of vision has projected Athera's messy cross-chop of affairs without smug omissions the size of the clandestine refuge pocketed on Los Lier. Everything left under Kharadmon's charge pivots on the axis surrounding Seshkrozchiel at Althain Tower."

A world removed, cheerlessly situated at the convergent fulcrum of crisis, Dakar crawled on hands and knees through wet scrub. The obscured battle past the hilltop he scaled scared him to jellied paralysis. Showered by moisture from recent rainfall, and snagged bloody on the briar canes lacing the downs of Atainia, he need not choke on the smut of scorched ash to take stringent precautions. Nerve quailed, despite talent faculties damped down to minimize the whiplashing chaos as geysered flux savaged the third lane's transmission. No travellers ventured the trade-road to Lorn, their desertion grim proof that Seshkrozchiel's rampage continued apace.

The ungoverned impact lifted his hair. Past his vantage, the distortion field thrown off the far vale rippled skyward like heat-waves, shredding the blanket of overcast and scattering rainbows off the slabbed bed-rock rammed through the moistened turf. Dissonant bursts puckered skin already clammy with terror. Dakar shuddered under the warmth of full sunlight. The elder dragon was raving insane. Static discharge from her agitation spiked through his wet clothes. Prudence made him shrink to behold a strait dire enough to destabilize Althain Tower.

Initiate faculties should have forewarned him. Ruptured flares of elec-tromagnetics had mauled his awareness across latitude for leagues, undampened despite the dispersal of salt water while crossing Instrell Bay. Close at hand, the disruption set an ache to the bone and poured icy dread through clenched viscera. The crazed taint unfurled over longi-tude with a virulence to rattle Queen Ceftwinn's crown seat in Havish.

"I'm not fit for this," Dakar snarled through chattering teeth. Sensibility insisted he ought to turn tail, fast and far as hale muscle could run. Instead, the fat fool cursed his rampant stupidity, scrambling on hands and knees. Scraped through thickets of rowan, bashed on lichened rocks, the spellbinder dropped flat and wormed belly down. Prickled to rash through clumped gorse, with the ungainly crossbow gouging his ribs, he hauled himself yard by yard up the slope and peered, trembling, over the crest.

Nothing had prepared him for the sight of the great wyrm in the fulsome torment of her madness. Past compare, the stark tragedy of such power contorted by agony into helpless knots. Seshkrozchiel's coils wrapped the bleak spire of Althain Tower from the foundation to the slate roof. Without parallel, her sullen, serpentine grace: from slant snout to the lash of her massive, fluked tail the untamed epitome of indomitable strength, she was everlasting, a living sculpture wrought of shining, gold scales, ebon claws, and armoured prowess. The roaring torch of the auric charge spun off the spiralled horn of her dorsal spikes sheared upwards like an aurora: a column of shimmering cobalt flame that excited her surrounds to fluorescence.

Dakar had expected to feel overawed, even scared. Not poleaxed by terror that melted his spine and pulverized every moral resolve to the annihilation of conscience. Least of all, at the brunt of his distilled dread, he had not forecast the blunt-force sorrow of his human pity.

Such monumental vigor, torqued in on itself and strained to convulsions, defied imagination. Seshkrozchiel's adamant pain unstrung her intelligence, reduced her magnificence to bestial savagery married to no purpose but ruin. She vented her torment in blasts of flame. Roaring sheets repeatedly crisped the tower's surrounds to slag and white ash. The scour whipped up scattered wind devils, black and swirling with gritted carbon. Speared through the raw violence of her mindless fury, the ancient Paravian keep stood like a vertical shaft, timeless and immutable. Shehane Althain's active defences resisted demolition with a steadfast, sheer glory that narrowed mortality's perception to insignificance.

To mage-sight, the actinic halo of forces threshed outwards from the wakened awareness of the tower's primordial stone. Needles of naked, inviolate power chained the dragon into what seemed an interlocked cycle of endless combat. Dakar's twinge of unease compelled the mindful oversight of an in-depth reassessment. More than bound to a straightforward engagement, the great wyrm writhed and bellowed, thrashing in the throes of an incessant struggle that engrossed her vast consciousness beyond quarter. She was as the pinned moth, transfixed in the cruel glare of daylight. Her outcry shattered merciful thought. Echoes rebounded off a ravaged landscape long since broken to desolation, spliced into the overlay of bygone history, and haunted times over by the resonant wail of past trauma and the deep imprint of Paravian grief.

The daunting scale of the present day's problem dwarfed Dakar's meagre capacity. To try Althain Tower's arcane bulwarks and reach Kharadmon begged the certainty of his destruction. As if any Master Spellbinder's effrontery *could* surmount the stupendous trial of separating the engaged combatants, or survive long enough to frame the attempt to lure the maddened dragon away. The mere prospect thwarted consideration on a supercharged field of forces too friable to engage, far less to cross unsupported. Venture too near the perimeter, even under stout wards, a mage would find himself pulverized to dissolution for interference.

If not a silver-scaled ancient, Seshkrozchiel wore the scintillant gold of an elder dragon at peak maturity. Her lifetime encompassed the strife compounded through ages, rooted in prehistory's Era of Destruction. She had survived the death of her mate Haspastion, tasted fire and blood at the wasting of Kathtairr, and had flown the skies through the horrendous cataclysm of the First Sundering, and the Second, at the subsidence that sank Mhorovaire beneath the waves. Among the founders of the Dragon Protectorate, she had known the conjoined dream summoned in appeal to Ath Creator. Her witness had seen the hallows that sourced Athili's vortex and the dance of the An'Tieni who begat the first Spirits of Light, progenitors of the Paravians. Her remembrance encompassed the dawn when the third dance birthed Shehane Althain, first among the Dace'am Ilitharis.

Less than a millisecond's afterthought before that freight of renown, Dakar shrank, crushed prostrate by the picayune inflection of his insignificance. Trepidation plundered the dregs of initiative. Cut off from learned counsel, he needed more time, at least for sounding the means to unravel this deranged entanglement. The titanic struggle itself made no sense! An overwrought upset by a handful of molts never should have triggered Seshkrozchiel into a frenzy. Nor caused her betrayal against the unimpeachable shade of Althain Tower's dedicate guardian. As one of three dragon allies in residence on Athera to anchor Dragonkind's Concord with the Paravians, Seshkrozchiel must be curbed here and now, or not at all. Loosed at large on the world, her rampage might resurrect the likes of the vanquished Methurien. Or havoc much worse, she could disrupt the warded hibernation of silver-scaled Vuccarimaish, Queen Dreamer and her mate Zaynackshish: wyrm ancients whose poison deceits owned the naked hatred to shatter the continent.

The unmalleable challenge thrust upon Dakar's discretion too easily might raise Imaury Riddler's shade from the fast stones of Mainmere to herald the world's final combat. An impossible task, to stay the clinch of disaster, unless the human hybrid herself was the irritant cause. Siantra might be the weak link and the only remedy within able reach. Dakar peered through the etheric cross-chop of distortion. Eyes narrowed, he sought the diminutive point of the maddened dragon's fixation.

There: he located a frail figure at the core of the maelstrom, unscathed beneath the horned wedge of Seshkrozchiel's serpentine head. Siantra s'Idir braved the tumultuous turmoil with upraised palms, for good or ill mesmerized into rapport, or hell-bent on inciteful communion.

'Trust my daughter!'

The echo of Laithen's last plea tore the heartstrings, a dangerous pall of sentiment clouding the steel of mindful commitment. Barring irrefutable proof, the unshakable faith of maternal love could not sanction the horrendous risk. Not where the altered creature under sway of a monster was drake spawn, by no means anything human.

Dakar tightened his grip on the crossbow. Braced for cold-blooded murder, he spanned the cable and slotted the four-bladed, razor-sharp quarrel, blinking through upwelling moisture. Whether he fought anguished tears or the abrasive sting of blown smoke did not signify. Steadied for the lethal execution of mercy, he propped the cocked weapon, took aim, and choked.

The creature squared in his sights had been a gifted young woman, barely two years past her majority. Descended of Sidir's proud lineage, she was by her birthright bound under crown justice, subject to the sovereign law of Rathain. Dakar squeezed his flooded eyes shut. Overwhelmed, he shouldered the weight of a death Arithon s'Ffalenn never would have condoned: not absent the clear-sighted burden of surety. Yet on this brutal second's decision rested the viable weight of the world. Uncertainty must not override harsh necessity. The vanishing chance of a regretful mistake dared not shy from the terrible price a decisive choice could avert.

Dakar levelled the bow, gnawed sick with regret. Arithon might risk the fraught balance to mercy. But in his place, *would Asandir*?

Debate ended, past remedy, he levelled the stock. Surprise overtook him instead from behind, batted him in the nape, and clobbered him senseless.

The Mad Prophet groaned. Wakened to a splitting head and the copper taste of a bitten tongue, he struggled to rise and encountered the bite of rawhide knotted at his wrists and ankles. Strapped helpless, he swore, crooked his neck, and peered upwards. Squinted eyesight revealed a malformed silhouette stamped against the noon glare. Not just one captor. Spined and scaled, both drake-spawned anomalies stared him down with inimical, slit-pupilled eyes.

Terrified, Dakar cowered from the excruciate certainty his next breath would end with disembowelment by razor-sharp claws.

"We need you alive," declared Esfand, unblinking.

Socked through the ground by the thunderous tremors of Seshkrozchiel's tempestuous bellows, Dakar squeezed his crusted lids shut in sarcastic forbearance. "Unless you think slitting my throat in ritual sacrifice will mollify Shehane Althain, I can't imagine what sorry use you may have for my trussed carcass."

"Siantra insists the drake and the guardian shade are not fighting," Esfand corrected, the growl that mangled his tortuous speech no assurance of friendly intentions. His inhuman, hot glare no encouragement, he amended, "She doesn't talk. Not in language with words."

Incisive, Siantra's impatient retort flicked out a jet claw and severed the ties on the spellbinder's wrists.

Dakar flinched, cringing fright masked by the semblance of a shrug. With panicked care, he sat up, a shaken assessment snatched as he chafed circulation back into his tingling limbs. The spanned crossbow had been confiscated, along with the pathetic, dulled steel of his eating knife. As the morsel pinned in ripe straits for predation, he vented his jangled anxiety. "If either of you have better insight to offer, best say what you know before Seshkrozchiel's fit tears this hilltop asunder and wrecks the memory of our existence."

Siantra tossed her triple-horned head. The spurt of auric flame off her knurled spines granted stinging, short shrift for his bungled attempt at assassination.

"Save us all!" Esfand snarled, caught in the breach as ambassador. "You've miscalled everything and flipped the situation upside down. Shehane Althain happens to be the last force of restraint keeping that dragon in check. Seshkrozchiel *knows* the surfeit of human emotion imposed on her psyche cannot be balanced. She is trapped in a cycle of runaway creation, without seasoned experience to buffer the impact. Althain Tower's defending shade is her *ally*, you fool! The sole force with the power to spare her."

Dakar opened his mouth.

Esfand squelched protest. "Much more, the wyrm has repeatedly seared everything within her active radius to sterilized ash. She's had to suppress the irruptive expression of a new crop of Methurien and thwart the recurrent bloom of fertile drake spawn!"

"The devil!" Frazzled headache and fright grilled over by livid exasperation, Dakar revised a drastic list of priorities that collapsed the last shim of reassurance. Tactful reason was useless, set against a remedial defence that razed everything to desolation. Shown the wrack of a killing field fit to bankrupt invention, he railed, "Exactly what nonsensical miracle am I being asked to pull from my tattered sleeve?"

"A difficult prospect, uncertain at best. We are pleading for your backing in partnership." Prompted by s'Idir's impetuous glare, Esfand made haste and explained. "Ciladis was teaching Siantra how to balance the flow of reactive creation, in concert with Ath's white adepts. She was to gain mastery of her human-born passion, then transmit the offer of her mindful knowledge to evolve the awareness of Dragonkind. But the dynamic to stabilize her altered nature and learn restraint took too long. Her training remains incomplete."

Dakar scrubbed at his throbbing temples. "Then why did she bolt? Why not stay at Forthmark under the brotherhood's mentorship?"

"Because we're out of time! The Fellowship Sorcerers will be overwhelmed by the drake war on Sckaithen Duin! Five set against multiple wild packs in rebellion cannot hold their firm line on the splinter world. Their restraint has to break, and while Athera has Shehane Althain's defence keeping the leash on Seshkrozchiel, the bleedthrough gestalt from the rogue factions elsewhere will drive her beyond containment."

"Ath's tears, you believe I have a solution? Some crazy plan to swerve catastrophe on the grand scale?" Dakar flopped over backwards, jabbed to a yelp by prickly vegetation. "Don't even dare to suggest we should try killing that dragon! We'd provoke our destruction, or worse, somehow against nature succeed, only to sow the fresh hell of a grimward!"

Siantra's stinging, steam-kettle hiss rattled Esfand's awkward effort to juggle the interface of his linked consciousness. Pressed to translate the alien stream of her concepts, he said, "Dakar, we want your help to construct a dampening field to suppress excessive emotion."

"What! Have you gone barking mad?" The Mad Prophet jammed sweaty fingers through his snarled hair, at the end of his wits. "Davien tangled with Shehane Althain just once and got himself rendered discorporate! Sethvir complains to this day the scream left embedded in the King's-Chamber threshold is resistant to ritual cleansing." Socked prone with his beard jutted skyward, the deflated spellbinder clutched his tender forehead. "Show me an alternative I can survive."

"Unless you've got a more brilliant idea?" If reptilian features could smirk, Esfand's scowl certainly qualified. "There is none."

"You don't know what you're asking!" Dakar shivered, sapped to parboiled whey.

Two pairs of slit-pupilled, gold eyes stared him down.

How to admit the shocking depth of his short-falls? Dakar threw up his hands. His most dogged struggle with excessive emotion made him a persistent magnet for *iyats*. That posed an inveterate problem, since dragons and the gamut of their spawned creations were sensitive to the imbalance. However small, susceptibility inflamed their inter-actions, a disastrous flaw amid a fraught circumstance too precariously tilted for ruin.

"The ward you imagine doesn't exist," Dakar lamented.

Siantra snarled.

Esfand echoed her, adamant, "Seshkrozchiel obtained a rudimentary grasp of humanity's passion while she melded with Davien. Lent the added foothold to recoup her shocked balance, we believe she could find her recovery. If you can reconfigure the shielding Asandir once used to enable our safe passage from Athili, Siantra can blend her awareness with Seshkrozchiel and try to impart the structural concept into Dragonkind's greater consciousness."

"The Creator's portal at Athili!" Dakar exclaimed. Courage forsook him. A Sorcerer's escort to salvage three strays from the unconstrained font of the mysteries had demanded an impervious, warded defence. *One that seamlessly dampened thought and emotion, then stripped out the deflections of uncontained resonance from the stream of prime flux and annulled the impact of extreme reactivity.* "To checkrein a wyrm's inflamed emanation, your premise is basically sound. Except, I don't possess the innate strength! Far less the advanced grasp of conjury to fashion an immaculate construct at such magnitude."

"But Kharadmon does." Esfand prodded Dakar's ribs, too unpleasantly reasonable. "Siantra says you collaborated with the Sorcerer before. Or did you not share his past labour to avert a catastrophic lane surge at Rockfell Peak?"

"Damned if we do, dead if we don't." Defeated by that unvarnished truth, Dakar stirred upright with grudging reluctance and plucked the slackened cords off his ankles. "I haven't any more promising strategy." Forget the caveat that ritual transference of an idea between species had never been tried, by his reckoning. "Though bedamned to eternity's chaos if I'll weigh the ridiculous plan while I'm arse deep in gorse with a tight bladder and an empty belly."

The Fellowship Sorcerers' evolved effort to dispatch the drake war raging upon Sckaithen Duin moved apace, the live capture of a wyrm at the height of maturity the first, dicey throw in a countermeasure to surmount the reverse of Ozvowzakrin's defection.

"A hazard to spiral us to destruction, if not wring a demise to sour our restful idyll in the afterlife," Luhaine rumbled, contrarian doom and gloom at the forefront.

"You never did enjoy flirting with madness," Davien agreed, stimulated by suspect enjoyment.

Snare a drake too young, and the impact of the individual would lack the exigent power. The riveted nexus of command required to wrest the advantage back into the Protectorate's favour might be dismissed en masse by the combatants. Capture an elder platinum with age, and the wily subtleties of long experience twisted their promises, sly principles, and apparently straightforward influence ever riddled with pitfalls.

"Our chance of surprise will be forfeit, besides." Set aback by contentious terrain subject to change without notice, Luhaine's lugubrious nature craved plodding convention above flighty, mental gymnastics. His carping hitched by huffing exertion, he minced across an exposed tidal reef, pocketed with salt pools and ridged coral, fragrantly stubbled with barnacles and rotted seaweed. "We are buzzing insects, pitted against a living arsenal of armoured weaponry, equipped with the murderous cunning to devour scaled rivals eras before Mankind clambered erect to throw rocks at vermin!"

In the lead, Asandir took rough field work in stride with his penchant for taciturn silence.

Not Davien, who relished the blood sport of traps primed with innocuous bait. "You don't fancy jigging the fly to hook trout?"

"Game fish don't alter creation at whim, or charbroil their morsels before shredding the flinders with eighty-eight teeth!" Plagued by his flat feet and generous girth, Luhaine windmilled for balance against a buffeting change in the wind. "Forbye, I volunteered."

In fact, Ciladis was best suited to stay in reserve with Sethvir and countervail harm to the planet, and no feat under threat of endangerment received better rear-guard support than Asandir and Davien could provide. "Were you planning to share your strategic design before setting me up as the gullible lure?"

Asandir masked a gruff cough.

Davien preferred flippant deflection. "Why? For a windbag debate? We've beaten discussion to death from the outset, past all borrowed time to prevaricate."

"We've come far enough." Paused with boots awash in the back-fallen roar of a breaker, Asandir gestured. "That outcrop suits our purpose."

Slid to an ungainly halt, Luhaine surveyed the raised promontory
wedged in a seethed froth of petticoats against the treacherous roil of
tide. A narrow spit whipped by lashed spindrift spanned the rough
channel between, drenched rock and sheets of lofted spray a natural
deterrent for Dragonkind's abhorrent distaste for immersion.

"We might push the pace," Luhaine grumbled, "before the incoming
flood sees us stranded. Spare me the bother of taming the sea with a
nettled dragon in tow." Since Asandir waded ahead without consultation,
he voiced his stiff-lipped concern to Davien. "You know the ways of
Dragonkind best. More experience than mine to manage the forefront
with the most devious invention between us."

They angled to engage a single wyrm, after all. Not the combative rogue
pack, stirred to rife odds and hell-bent upon indiscriminate slaughter.

"You're up to the task." Asandir's mindful focus stayed absorbed by
the suck and shove of strong current over pitfalls glossed over by
submerged footing. "Careful, unflapped, and trusty enough to brangle
with chaos without budging an inch."

"Just park up there and look ornamental," Davien agreed, dark eyes
lit to wicked mirth as the slap of the rip crashed and foamed into sucking
eddies around them. "Tie on the douce gambit. We'll settle the lines for
containment."

Luhaine's steamed comment through plastered hair dealt a reproach
to flay skin. "A misplaced relief, to depend on your flamboyant genius."

"Asandir's not flamboyant." Davien laughed at the steel glare his austere
colleague flashed sidewards. "Like the toothpicks stuck into the slippery
slope, our flit-brained reflexes will have your back."

Luhaine resettled his rucked belt, reproof quashed behind the prim
resignation shown to dolts who dog-eared the pages of books. Since
haste rankled a perfectionist, he parted company and set off, a methodical beetle scaling the naked flank of the cornice. Seamless partnership,
evolved over centuries, obviated the need to glance backwards, or verify
the difficult, unpleasant work, as Asandir and Davien threaded immaculate boundaries over uncertain terrain, impermeable to more than the
contrary properties of wind, wave, and brine.

At remove from the active forefront at the promontory, Ciladis paced
the tranquil shoreline surrounding the islet's warded refuge. His gaze
raked the cobalt zenith, a warrior's vigilance pitched to detect the flecks

of hostile dragons blue-lit by the auric flame of their ungoverned rage. The incessant assault to unseat the Sorcerers' foothold beset their entrenchment at all hours, each hammered strike an etheric battering ram wrapped in fire, bashed against upstepped defences with the naked force to annihilate.

Harried as well by the collateral sorties mounted by drake spawn, Ciladis swept the current, saltwater horizon for the thrashed wakes of incoming krakens. He listened through his bare soles, alert for tremors from burrowing worms, and searched the arrhythmic curl of breaking surf for the scuttle of pincered, aquatic scorpions. The nuisance to repel such unnatural monsters taxed his intuitive faculties and fragmented his incessant sweep of the splinter world's fractious existence.

Retreat was no option. The Fellowship's embattled commitment to salvage the Treaty Accord trod a delicate course, the certainty of unilateral ruin juggled on precarious terms without Ozvowzakrin's reciprocal alliance.

All morning, the narrow prints carved by Ciladis's feet rutted the sand at the tide mark. Swept by his gaunt shadow, passing, Sethvir sat with tucked knees, his maroon robe flecked with bits of shell and minced kelp, and the veiled gleam of languorous eyes fixed on nothing. As if Sckaithen Duin's perilous firmament was not transitory, the reliable contours of land and sea as friable as cobweb strung in a gale, he seemed a woolgathering daydreamer nodding off for a nap.

Reverie had absorbed him for hours with no latent sign of unease. Yet an unbidden gravity to his stillness wrenched Ciladis to a sharp pause. Astute healer, he dissected the stamp of Sethvir's entrained perception: razor keen as a hawk's underneath the innocuous glaze of distraction. Weathered lines and sunburn darkened bruised sockets pouched to exhaustion. Althain's Warden might appear rudderless, the worn poet displaced from his comfortable clutter of books and cached oddments of esoteric antiquity.

Yet the draw on his resource commanded the scope of events threading the precarious fate of two worlds. Sethvir's Sight spanned the yawning abyss, stitched through the relentless throes of a drake war their intrepid resource was losing. The clarity of his observer's role required an incomprehensible discipline, sustained in detachment more taxing than the brute demand of direct action. Across distance, moment to moment, the Sorcerer sorted Tehaval Warden's broadscale awareness of Athera; while tracking in tandem the refined chains of spellcraft knitted in seasoned partnership by three colleagues on site.

Flaw in the drifty semblance of tranquillity, a furrow pinched Sethvir's bristled eyebrows.

"What's amiss?" Ciladis asked softly, loath to unseat that tranced focus. Sethvir's unresponsive quiet stabbed nerves to a chill in hot sunlight. Ciladis extended his subtle probe and ever so gently eased into rapport.

Engaged vision revealed the jagged notch of the seabound promontory where, in bold strokes like interlocked ribbon, Asandir and Davien had anchored an arrayed construct deep into the core bed-rock beneath. Lateral tendrils spun for stability fanned outwards across the ocean floor. Six leagues in circumference, the edifice carved by their arcane foundation was capped off and crowned by the delicate, whorled spindle of Luhaine's framed lure. The poised net would snap shut, hair-triggered by an embedded spring set in resonant balance.

The minutiae revealed a snagged whisper of discord. An intrusive darkening tugged the construct's immaculate symmetry into distortion. Surely that nascent wrongness had tensioned the patterns of Sethvir's prescient Sight. Ciladis surveyed an interference by dragons that tugged the tight weave of the three-pronged spellcraft awry.

Hackled by the shared prick of unease, Sethvir broke his immersed silence. "If so, the drake at fault is not present upon Sckaithen Duin." His opened left hand cradled the pebble from Penstair's distant strand, frail talisman by which he parsed the overlaid stream of impressions in simultaneity. The confounding, stretched span of his conscious reach destroyed utterly his appearance of daft senility.

The pantherish pounce of Ciladis's regard pierced through that rapt stillness, his strident concern graphic as midnight's fallen shadow amid the brass glare of daylight. "Ath on earth!"

The hitch surged past remedy. Already three winged flecks soared over the promontory primed as an attractant. Not the isolate drake drawn by Luhaine's intent, but several, circling in the contentious posture of rivals. "We may be sabotaged by an assault stirred up by event *from Athera*?"

A cogent setback, given Dragonkind's consciousness leaped temporal dimension. Excited to heightened emanation, drakish influence held the potency to exceed the threshold of the veil. Above the rigid boundary of matter, one dragon's evocative experience blended with others in synchronicity.

Sethvir stirred. "Not a posited fear for much longer."

Ciladis restrained the intrusive urge to peel through his colleague's vagary. "What's pitched to go wrong?"

"Or right. There's the devilish paradox." Althain's exiled Warden scribed a circle in the sand with his right forefinger. A mild request coaxed his palmed pebble to acknowledge his need for a collaborative link to Athera. When he straightened, his visionary awareness tapped into the mineral's Name beyond time and flooded his sketched figure with the holistic image pulled across the void from the wild heath of Atainia . . .

. . . where Siantra positioned herself at the spearhead of a desperate strategy. The frailty of her exposed stance defied sense, the ferocious courage of her birth lineage and the duality of her altered nature undertook a stunning attempt to leverage an intervention. She pitched her cry in the harsh cadence of dragonsong to the great drake Seshkrozchiel, whose aggression contorted her entwined coils around the warded edifice of Althain Tower. The mad effort aimed to pierce through the confluent power of Shehane Althain's active defences. A puny summons, most certainly doomed, strove to swerve the maddened serpent's mired attention: a distraction that might interrupt for one moment the titanic clash of two ancient powers' locked conflict . . .

Ciladis parsed the snap-frozen gist at a glimpse. Lensed through the stream of Esfand's linked presence, his assessment mapped Siantra's intent to quell Althain Tower's guardian shade long enough for seized access to contact Kharadmon. The appalling endeavour all but unmanned the Fellowship's steadfast healer. "Siantra, Ath wept! She cannot possibly muster the gravity to stem that dragon's amok rampage!"

"She can, to our sorrow." The swipe of Sethvir's palm banished the disturbing development. "She has. By re-creating the imprinted memory of Haspastion's mating song, she is hell-bound to succeed."

Ciladis went grey. Unwitting, with no grasp of her naked peril, Siantra's unschooled prompt could trigger Seshkrozchiel into an actualized dream of reliving, empowered by the reactive charge to return the great drake's dead mate *as reanimate drake spawn!* "Ath's tears and Daelion forfend, that ill-starred notion is tempting the havoc of total disaster!"

Catapulted into the cross-contaminant seethe of volatile human passion, the shaping calamity became inevitable.

"Why?" Ciladis whirled in palpable distress. "Siantra was nowhere near mastery of the template to secure her mental control! Pure folly, if she tries to bridle the bearing influence of Seshkrozchiel's explosive imbalance alone!"

"Give me a moment." Sethvir shut his eyes, tapped the nugget of stone, then impressed a luminous pattern of geometry for projection by way of the air. Like strands, the figure compacted the extant forces and factors in play. Ciladis interpreted the hacked-out plan under way in Atainia, Siantra's ploy backed by Dakar's desperately cobbled attempt to replicate a null field of influence: the same stay Asandir had once wielded to salvage three runaways from the grand portal at Athili. The intricate construct, based on sound principle, indeed held the potential to capture, contain, and smother the reactive burst of Seshkrozchiel's upset. Yet the spellbinder's command fell impossibly short, a tinker's inept measure to wring stopgap relief for the critical moment to stall the arc of destiny worldwide.

"Delay only," Sethvir surmised. "Yet an opening to bring Kharadmon's knowledge to bear, provided Shehane Althain's aroused protection can be curbed for the keyhole instant to free his hand."

"Merciful glory!" Ciladis gasped, appalled. "They are striking the same template we are working ourselves." Hence the skewed influence, fore-running event, that accelerated the measured construct in train at the promontory.

The five Sorcerers on Sckaithen Duin confronted the resonant ruin of both workings in parallel, snarled under the bleed-through of concurrent sympathy.

"The flawed influence cannot be halted from here," Sethvir affirmed, desolate for the remedial conclusion he had to try, nonetheless. "We're dealt the benighted odds of a forced hand."

Ciladis stared, appalled, as the Warden tested the durability of the touchstone birthed from sedimentary origins on Athera. Yet his outlying hope of effecting a bridge to warn Kharadmon above the vibration of temporal space became dashed straightaway. Overmatched, the willing beach pebble from Penstair spalled to flinders in Sethvir's clenched hand.

Ciladis gasped. "Ath avert!" Last throw on an emptied board of defeat, no emergency crossing through the upper dimensional register could surmount the loss of direct contact at an instant's notice. The forces unleashed by the inadequate talent on Athera spun into motion, meanwhile, past the Fellowship's starcraft to recall.

Fingers gouged bloody by fragmented mineral, the Warden raised his head, wide-opened eyes trained into distance. "Kharadmon cannot intercede outside of the tower on the ground in Atainia." The raw currents spun by Shehane Althain's engagement would shred a discorporate piecemeal at the boundary. Sethvir's distraught regard locked onto Ciladis with the frantic clarity of a man drowning. "We've run out of time! Nor can we muzzle this crisis with anything near measured caution or subtle approach."

"We'll have to back Siantra's attempt," Ciladis perceived in sharp summary. What other choice remained but surrender? Dakar lacked the main strength and the instantaneous reflexes of tried prowess. He *would* fall short if he sought to facilitate a working of such magnitude from green inexperience. Moreover, Kharadmon could not be set at risk. Sethvir's handful of pulverized slate was inadequate to anchor the channel for refounding a Worldsend Gate.

"No option's left," Sethvir agreed. The scope of the onrushing concatenation would blast both worlds to cinders if any one of them flinched. "Will we, or nil we, to whatever end, we must shoulder the brunt from our stance here and now upon Sckaithen Duin."

A wild-card run, all or nothing, to propel the incomplete pattern threaded through the tenuous, untried connection forged between Siantra and Seshkrozchiel. One chancy throw to cure the rift that unhinged the great dragons, with naught left to mitigate failure if the concurrent blending of their mismatched resource fell short.

"Luhaine is going to be furious," Ciladis admitted, tawny eyes fierce with dismay for the conglomerate mess of loose ends.

Then he dropped his close rapport with Sethvir. The gentle healer exchanged for the warrior, Ciladis faced the beach where incoming breakers creamed over white sand with deceptively fragile tranquillity. He strode into the backsliding, lace sheets of foam. Without space for regret, and no fear, he raised his hand and sent summons to Asandir with an actualized demand for immediate transfer.

"Reach!"

Concussion

Asandir responded to the frantic appeal from a windy ledge splashed by flung surf. Extended to receive, his callused grip closed over his distanced colleague's warm hand. Contact bridged the void and anchored the arcane transference. Ciladis's lank form emerged through the turbulent air, grounded in the flesh as his footstep came down on the rocky shelf at the base of the promontory. The precipitate storm of information brought with him reframed the Fellowship's priorities, the markers laid into painstaking alignment revised and reset on the flash-fired spark of an instant.

Asandir's astute eye parsed the critical gist, his grasp of sweeping change amid breaking crisis surpassed only by Davien's perverse enjoyment of the scorching irony.

"Welcome to the crucible." Mane of red-and-white hair flung back, ascetic features flushed, the Sorcerer once called Betrayer laughed outright and clapped Ciladis on the back. "Broth's spilled into the bonfire, I see, with Luhaine's fusspot sensibilities torched to a crisp."

"We cannot hesitate for an explanation!" Asandir wrestled the unmalleable facts, the narrow margin left for response run too brutally short, far less for a nitpicking debate in deliberation.

"Luhaine's preference for caution cannot signify." Ciladis appraised the extant work of conjury strung into exquisite perfection. Inflected geometry mapped at a glance, he solidified the requisite expansion of intent in harmonic concert.

For the Seven owned in strict form the directive to act in Athera's defence, the substance of permission established by repudiation of the Accord. The Protectorate's sealed terms granted Dragonkind's right to a noncompliant haven on Sckaithen Duin, provided the exiled drakes abrogated their primal claim to disrupt continuity on Athera: and Seshkrozchiel's distress was a bleed-through event, causation rooted in the ravening savagery driving Sckaithen Duin's intemperate factions.

While Sethvir could not sustain his earth-link to Athera in concurrent force, the rogue dragons themselves posed the last sure connection to address a disaster fused into broad-reaching simultaneity. All or nothing, the incumbent action to uphold the Treaty hurled both worlds into the breach.

Luhaine's huffy indignance must be harnessed for impetus, the changed thrust sprung on him retrenched for resharpened resolve.

Fair grist for the mill, to Davien's wicked delight. "All the more blistering torque for the catalyst."

"Provided Dakar finds the brass bollocks to handle the fulcrum on impact." Asandir set his grip on the conjured reins without flinching, surety hardened with no prudent check to look back.

Bridled potential became actual *now*!

Ungloved force set in motion shot into engagement, a recombinant work wrought on the fly, accomplished without forethought or speech. After millennia spent in tight partnership, the Sorcerers knew each others' attributes. They had laboured in seamless coordination, performed under the repeated, blistering stresses of disparate perils throughout two Ages. Asandir's augured strength and endurance linked to Davien's mercuric invention, rectified by Ciladis's exquisite grasp of harmony, and adjusted for Luhaine's reflexive response, that would calibrate with exacting precision demanded by infinitesimal detail.

Sethvir's peerless touch for channelling earth-sense locked and maintained the planetary integrity of Sckaithen Duin. Single-handed, he stabilized the shock wave of collateral impact as the galvanic surge of the precipitate shift refigured the Fellowship conjury's base alignment.

Luhaine caught the surprise slam of upshifted transition, wide awake at his post, and under murderous scrutiny by a swarm of inimical dragons. The ripple of his startlement was seized by Ciladis, rebraided into resonant alignment, and streamed into the explosive point of release.

Luhaine gasped a scorched expletive, rallied his wits, and rose like a champion to meet the necessity.

The actinic blast hurtled outwards, the unified power of five Sorcerers melded into a hackled, dissonant shout expressly pitched to stun Dragonkind and *provoke*!

Slammed into recoil, the minds of all wyrms upon Sckaithen Duin wrenched into joined conflagration. Combined reflex ignited their dreaming and sounded the singular note whetted for unilateral destruction.

The magnified blow hammered the firmament, a flaying concussion that swept over the splinter world at full bore: and hit the forged anvil of Sethvir's adamant protection with the ringing impact of mallet-struck iron. *Unstoppable force!* met *immutable shield!* and unleashed an explosive gestalt that annealed all of Dragonkind into matched resonance. Shared experience, engaged at peak intensity in the smelted instant, viced the Dream into crystalline clarity. The shock unleashed, vaulted through the expanse of the void in the flash-point leap of amalgamate, mass consciousness.

"Now!" Sethvir shouted across time and space.

Into the torrential rankle of chaos, the five Sorcerers on Sckaithen Duin launched their preshaped wards across the continuum. The template of absolute stability that froze thought and emotion slapped down, a decisive blow that haltered the disunified emanation of every last dragon alive and seized their raging turmoil utterly *still*!

The Fellowship's tuned chord raised the antiphonal resonance to cancel all motion, a piercing shaft of white light thrust into the weltered nerve storm of wyrmkind's joined consciousness. Insanity bent for unbridled havoc became shafted, nailed, and conflated into the null stillness steadfast enough to support the immaculate balance of Ath's grace before the liminal dawn of Creation. Light and dark, all the interim shades of potential, *and none*, became swept at a stroke into breathless suspension. And in the hung moment reeled to profound silence, the Sorcerers flung the keys to curb unchecked emotion magnified, en masse, to run rampant.

Synchronicity welded Dragonkind's collective awareness in the crackling beat of a millisecond. Not with the stately elegance of their prior plan, staged to quell the rogue combatants upon Sckaithen Duin. Instead, the single walloping throw loosed a percussive explosion, rendered at scale. A gambled detonation that could not do other than fire the requisite catalyst, with Seshkrozchiel on Athera centred as the touchstone for all of the great drakes at large. She would capture the chiselled template hurled in force across the abyss, the species-wide impact brought to gestalt shared in collateral fusion with Dakar, two drake-spawned humans, and one Fellowship discorporate pinned down in the adamant whirlwind of Shehane Althain's defences . . .

The resonant charge blown off Seshkrozchiel's dorsal spines flung Dakar backwards ten yards. He landed with a bone-jarring smack on his arse. The mangling jolt bashed the wind from his chest. Momentarily blind, rendered deaf and near paralysed, he fought to recoup jangled senses. Dazed vision cleared before his ringing ears registered the continual roar that rattled the ground like drummed ironware under him. The silvered flare of reactive power still enveloped Althain Tower. The centaur shade's protective might stayed engaged, unabated, with Kharadmon's discorporate spirit mewed up like a firefly in a jar.

The sheet flame crackle of the dragon's raw fury obscured mage-sighted perception and obliterated his view of Siantra or Esfand. Yet the pattern that roared through the wyrm's aura, intact, was delivered in gestalt phenomenon triggered at distance by the focused conjury imposed by the Fellowship through the rogue factions from Sckaithen Duin.

Not without unforeseen collateral: as hearing recovered from the flash-bang assault, Dakar picked out a gravel-rough human voice. Someone's shouting pierced through the howling maelstrom in Drakish. Esfand, whose barrage of screamed insults damned wyrmkind by the clutch, scale and claw reviled unto the shells of their hatched, rotten eggs.

The vernacular might have prompted hysterical laughter, had the young man not been baiting the dragon to salvage Siantra's predicament. She lay undone in collapse at his feet, her engaged rapport with Seshkrozchiel's consciousness back-lashed in the brunt at the forefront, before her immersive attempt broke all the way through the dragon's entangled conflict with the tower's guardian.

The Mad Prophet groaned. He sat up, shocked wits pressured to juggle the runaway gamut. No question, he was overfaced in the pinch of two firestorms seized in a flux tempest of annihilation.

A breath before ruin, the paired weal of two worlds lay at stake. While Seshkrozchiel's tempest faltered and reengaged, Shehane Althain's abrasive influence was fast eroding the strained cloth of the Fellowship's counterward past functional recognition.

One glance deflated the spellbinder's prowess. The remedial pattern dispatched by the Sorcerers from the splinter world was too vast, far beyond Dakar's able power to reinforce. He could not command the resourceful scope to impel the template into rapt closure. Only for Laithen, he might spare Siantra.

The pathetic expertise sharpened by practice made him a dab hand at scapegrace ruses spun for evasive subterfuge. Dakar worked the common creature comforts he understood best to try turning Seshkrozchiel's attention. Immersed in her raging tempest for weeks, she ought to be hungry. Lent sufficient enticement, the dragon might be tricked into arcane sympathy through animal instinct.

Dakar wrought his smoke screen of temptation with panache, expertise honed by the throes of privation. The irresistible construct he cast, of fat beef on the hoof, should have wrung inert stone to salivation.

The dragon's head whipped towards the suggested movement of prey. Not one whit captivated, she ignored the piquant reek of fake cattle, embellished with alarmed snorts and stamped hooves. Almost lazy, she unwound her golden coils from the tower. Riveted, furious, Seshkrozchiel unfurled her vaned wings, foretalons unsheathed to pounce on the nattering arrogance of the illusionist.

Dakar shouted, stricken all over again, at the unshielded edge of the dragon's electrified field of projection. He collapsed as the wave of adamant energy rolled over him, laced yet by the stamp of the Fellowship's laid construct to smother runaway emotion. A crafted counterward, scaled to tame the uncontrolled madness of a *great drake* and enforce a null state of neutrality, razed through the raging interface of the dragon's interactive dreaming. The punch hit with the cataclysmic, brute might to paralyse hope and disintegrate reason. Dakar faced the annihilation of consciousness. A puny mote threshed under siege, he grappled an influx too massive to flee. Past all help, at wit's end, he had less than a fractional second before his being shredded asunder. Also one fleeting instant, before the pattern dispatched at high cost from the Seven decayed beyond reach of recovery.

Willy-nilly, stripped to bare reflex for survival, the Mad Prophet poured all of his constrained talent and pithless fear into a focused mirror. That desperate shield founded his last recourse to spin the onslaught back in deflection. The extravagant flourish of cattle unravelled, subsumed by his instinctive response. Falling, Dakar crumpled in shock, bowled head over heels as vectored power blasted headlong into his desperate, passive construct. He landed with the force to smash bone.

While collision hurled back on the dragon, full blown, the cyclonic ferocity of her supercharged aura. Onrushing, unstoppable, the reverse impact crashed into her dreaming. Hate and insanity murderously distilled, *also torqued in the weave by the Fellowship Sorcerers' impressed working:* a template magnified and exponentially impelled by the concatenation fused into gestalt by Sckaithen Duin's rebellious dragons.

Parity redoubled that blindsided stroke. The explosion struck off a standing wave that overscored Seshkrozchiel's rampage and belted Dakar flat senseless.

The Mad Prophet cracked open gummed eyelids to Kharadmon's shade, berating him with a hovering, fussy concern that compounded the excruciate ache in his head. "You've the devilsome luck not to be crispy and dead, with naught beyond ash for a burial."

Dakar groaned. He spat the grit fouling his teeth, and croaked, "The dirt I swallowed made me think I was cursed to reincarnation as an earthworm."

"Scarcely the reward due the consummate hero." Done with inflicting his chilly presence as the replacement for stopgap restoratives, Kharadmon backed off, inconsiderate comments withheld as the prostrate spellbinder regrouped his pummelled composure, rolled over, and stood.

"Hero? You're kidding!" Dakar sneezed, caught aback by the belated assurance the shade's nagging presence was no wishful figment. Indeed, Shehane Althain's might had stood down, the tower's active defences subsided into quiescence. The shade's irritable slap that puffed dust from his clothes made him cough, red-faced from bashful embarrassment. "This implies my bumbler's reaction spared a bit more than your lame ghost and my sorry hide?"

"A mirror spell of redoubled reflection, pitched back at a rampant dragon? Quite!" Kharadmon's acrid snort spun a wind devil that speared sunlight through thinning tatters of dispersed smoke. "The upshot dropped Seshkrozchiel square in her tracks."

Dakar peered, blinking against the sudden, sharp glare of daylight. In fact, the hulked lump he discerned in his path was no spiny hill raised amid the scorched coal of a ravaged landscape, but a scaled monster curled like a cat in wing-folded repose.

"She's asleep," Kharadmon confirmed, "and dreaming in a safe register that allows her to assimilate the packeted imprint dispatched by the Seven."

Dakar rubbed streaming eyes, and forced the rough question past the lump in his throat. "Siantra? Esfand?"

"Knocked down with their lights out." Kharadmon's shade flicked up an impertinent pebble with the precise aim to sting flesh. "Which is why I need you on your feet."

"Dharkaron Avenge!" Dakar's taxed comprehension curdled to dismay. "Don't say they were cross-linked in rapport with Seshkrozchiel!" The stupendous smackdown of the construct to curb rampant emotion would have levelled more than Dragonkind's collective consciousness.

"They're alive enough to require your help!" The breeze scoured up by Kharadmon's irritation arrowed ahead. "While I could, I have stabilized their survival. I can mend shattered bones, well enough. But my capability does not include shifting hulks of inert muscle efficiently."

Dakar's knees buckled. He folded and sat. Crumpled, wheezing, his head propped upon his grimed palms, he cowered behind tousled tangles of dusty, singed hair. "I can't do this." Above packing two comatose parties to bed rest, he foresaw the tasked import Kharadmon's next demand would lay on him.

"Oh, yes, my fat prophet! Since you've salvaged the day, and saved our Fellowship's bacon, we have the renewed obligation to shoulder the future." Kharadmon's gusty tempest nailed the smug gist. "If Athera's to regain the Seven's backing at strength, I'll be away soonest to rescue my incarnate colleagues from the penury of their exile." Past question, a shade was best equipped to surmount the long path through the airless deep. A crossing between stars was required to restore the access portal for transit.

"But you'll be gone for decades!" Dakar yanked the frayed ends of his beard in dismay. "Who's minding the compact while you refound the North Worldsend Gate?"

"Verrain cannot leave his posted watch at Methisle," the discorporate Sorcerer ran on to point out, his impeccable logic tweaked by amusement. "My fine fellow, the obvious prize for your victory leaves you on station here, and not only to nurse two human drake spawn to health. You might weigh the wisdom of establishing a relationship with Tehaval Warden, if your yellow belly can stomach advice."

"Ath spare me the misery! You can't leave me with the appointment to shoulder the vacancy at Althain Tower." Dakar squirmed helplessly as a gaffed fish, then staggered under the whiplash retort of the shade's breezy slap on his shoulder.

"The conundrum at Rockfell cannot be addressed otherwise. Forbye, your tour of duty ought to be light!" Delighted by the stupefied worry that clouded the spellbinder's countenance, Kharadmon scoffed. "Glory day! Luhaine will be poleaxed when he returns. Asandir wins the take on a very long wager if after all, *finally*, you've exhausted your gormless libido and kicked your addiction to drink."

Teeth snapped shut on his tongue, Dakar yelped, swiped at air, then scrambled erect in bristled offence. "By the Fatemaster's nightmare, what possessed me to accept a Fellowship apprenticeship in the first place?"

"Brainless ignorance?" Yet in fact, the discorporate Sorcerer's laconic impudence was not frivolous.

Siantra and Esfand had survived the crucible, well set upon the mature course to help anchor the faulted liaison with Athera's great dragons. Queen Ceftwinn's reign maintained Havish under the stable precepts of charter law. If Tysan was hobbled by the True Sect Canon, Rathain reclaimed under Paravian sovereignty halted the reach of religious expansion. A *caithdein* remained in firm charge of the free wilds in Melhalla, and the crone's ensconced presence in Shand posed the formidable deterrence that steadied the high earl's seat as steward in Selkwood.

"If today hasn't earned my just deserts with a wineskin," Dakar grumbled, then stalled, abandoned, as Kharadmon whisked off and vacated the planet ahead of him.

Elegy

Nineteen years since the older brother condemned by a True Sect arraignment left home in chains to stand trial for an execution by fire and sword, Kerelie finished the short days by candlelight, tidying up before she closed her fashionable dress shop on Shuttlecock Lane. Upstairs, the muffled voices of children wove through the bass remonstrance of Efflin, disturbed at his books by their antics. The ebullience of Father's gruff laughter rumbled through the counterpoint clink of crockery in the kitchen. The knock from outside repeated, interrupting her as she raked the snipped ends of thread and cloth scraps into the dust bin.

Not a late customer: upright clientele did not chap at the back-alley door like a flunky dispatched for delivery.

Kerelie kept a stout broomstick to hand. Crossing the storeroom, she snatched the lit pricket and, in added precaution, palmed a steel hat-pin from the bin on the counter. Wary, not quite alarmed, she slipped the bar, lifted the latch, and cracked open the door. Cold flowed in on the draught. The spiked scent of frost displaced the musk of fine fabric and traces of the faint, floral fragrances worn by genteel patrons as she cautiously peered outside.

Stark against the evening's fallen gloom, a stilled figure in a pale mantle dipped a cowled head in respectful greeting. The sliced light from her fluttered candle flared over the entwined, gold-thread ciphers stitched into the brow band of a stainless, white hood.

Kerelie's timid start prompted an immediate assurance. "I am no Canon priest, or a temple enforcer sent to accost you for heresy. On the contrary, matron." The man pushed back his mantle and bared kindly features. "You have nothing to fear from a white adept of Ath's Brotherhood."

The radiant quiet he projected soothed the reflexive leap of unease. Kerelie released her hitched breath, calmed enough to recall times in Tysan were changing. Her close family were no longer at risk of arraignment. Not since reinstatement of the realm's steward had begun to reform due process under the precepts of charter law. The True Sect's unquestioned authority waned, credibility undercut since the disastrous, mass apostasy consumed their invasive campaigns in Daon Ramon. The whiplash of doctrine now branded arcane knowledge as a liability to the faith. Banishment damned the unrighteous who risked the perilous taint of Paravian exposure, and persecution for heretical practice faced indictment as the realm's *caithdein* restored crown justice.

"You have no grounds for anxiety, matron." As if the persistence of lingering dread shadowed the clear air between them, the adept smiled gently and qualified. "The last of the temple's examiners are deceased, or thralled to the Song of the Mysteries, and the handful of diviners who kept their wits have been expelled from the priesthood."

"I'm sorry." Kerelie shivered, a visceral reaction to white raiment of any kind after the sweating terror ingrained by a forced bout of interrogation. "Distrust is a habit not easily shed." She widened the door, enough to discern two additional figures cast into eclipse by the uncanny shimmer that hazed the adept's presence.

No mere talent expressed the sheen of golden light that defied credible vision. "At the behest of Fellowship business, I've provided an escort for these folk from the Master Spellbinder at Althain Tower. The matter bears on a promise Dakar made to the dead concerning blood ties to you and your family."

Cold air puckered Kerelie's scarred cheek. Not easily warmed to visitors, in particular ones who imposed after hours, she softened enough to acknowledge the unpleasant chill freezing her ankles. She stepped back and admitted the party of three into shelter from the bitter cold.

Hat pin stuck in her sleeve cuff and broom cocked at the ready, she mulled over the memory of the last eldritch caller come to her door, unannounced: a rakish old man clad in unseasonal velvets, met at the threshold by the hurled weight of the doorstop she pitched at his head. Shame still raised her embarrassed flush, despite the understandable jolt to her nerves. When her flung brick passed straight through the unruffled, dapper apparition, she had keeled over in a silly faint. Awakened by the solicitous shade, who named himself as a Fellowship Sorcerer, she had perched on the embroidered stool used to take the measure of her female clients. Nursing a bruised elbow, she had listened, agog, while the spirit's breezy diction related the account of Tarens's heroic death on the Plain of Araithe.

Hard to credit the tale, that her beefy, rock-headed brother had achieved such lofty renown. Her pursed lips still evinced disbelief, short shrift given to the Sorcerer's testament of a *caithdein*'s shared legacy, claimed in transcendent glory from beyond the grave.

Yet this evening's visitation brought no astonishing stories of distant lands and deeds graven into Athera's history. His charge delivered instead two strangers of flesh and blood, cloaked in rugged, barbarian dress. The sturdy, weathered woman in leathers paced over the waxed, wooden floor with the uneasy, fit tread of a wildcat. Latched to her sinewed hand, bringing with her the woodsy scents of balsam and birch smoke, came a half-grown little girl. She was rawboned, the baby fat melted off rosy cheeks. Perhaps eleven years of age, she had tawny hair plaited in an elaborate pattern, topped by a brindled fur cap. The hide jacket on her squared shoulders and her cross-laced, sturdy boots belonged to no mite raised in cosseted comfort beneath a town roof.

The frank stare that eschewed manners was caught short, remiss, as the woman crossed her arms at her breast in clan-styled salute.

"Mistress Kerelie?" Formal greeting in the crisp accent of the deep wilds, the arrival declared herself. "I am Kyrwen s'Iyat-thos, by our custom sister-kin through marriage to your brother, Tarens." Her lean hand guided the girl child forward, her straight stance reserved, but not shy. "And this is Kyra Elie, named by her father's wish after us both. His willed choice further entreated our people to let our daughter spend time in fosterage under your roof. Given your acceptance, he wished her to experience the blood-right of townborn education, and awareness of her dual heritage."

The fur hat, shoved back, revealed a strong, earnest face, wrenching in likeness to Tarens. Level blue eyes inspected the knotted scar on Kerelie's face without flinching. Then, darted sidewards, the girl's glance swept over the pine-topped counters and ceiling-high shelves. She gasped, entranced by the rainbow hues of fine silks and bolt velvets, the beaded trim and gleaming sarcenets, pinned and laid out to be sewn in the smart order of a superlative craftshop.

Stunned speechless by wonder in turn, Kerelie relinquished the broom handle. Melted, she blinked, overcome. Then her welled-up vision helplessly blurred. Brimmed lids spilled over and streamed unabashed tears down her cheeks. "Oh, my dear! You have packets of cousins your own age, did you know?"

Joyously weeping, Kerelie dropped to her knees. She welcomed the youngster – *a lost brother's beautiful daughter* – with wide-open arms. Then, civil restraint overturned, she shouted upstairs for the rest of the family to share tonight's gift of a precious, unlooked-for reunion.

"Kyrwen," she said past the lump in her throat. "Meet your kin-brother, Efflin. We're croft folk, scarcely refined, as you'll see. Pray to grace, the rest of my relations don't terrify you or trample your forestborn dignity with their rowdy happiness."

Heedless of clumping noise, the pack piled down the wooden stair, a father and an elder brother, a cherished husband who partnered her only for love, then the pert enthusiasm of Efflin's plump wife, who chivvied between them the effusive excitement of their combined offspring.

Verified by the benevolent witness of Ath's adept, family from two disparate backgrounds crowded together to share surprised introductions and hugs. The closed circle of destiny laid a first foundation for a tenuous bridge across cultures, enabled by Iyat-thos Tarens's prodigious courage and irrepressible generosity.

Autumn 6022 – Spring 6085

Tributes

Restoration of the North Worldsend Gate to Athera returns five Fellowship Sorcerers from their sojourn to quell the unrest of the rogue drake war and enforce the Protectorate's Accord binding the peace, but their subsequent inquiry at Rockfell Peak denies them permission to unseal the wards imposed to check Desh-thiere's malice: dire indication that Arithon's effort is not yet resolved with a decisive banishment . . .

In transit across the Plain of Araithe, Asandir dismounts in homage at the hallowed site where a sixth standing stone added to the tuned array by the Ilitharis masons sings in resonant harmonics the Name of Iyat-thos Tarens, the rare honour bestowed for a plain-spoken crofter's transcendence twined through Rathain's mysteries in perpetuity . . .

In the same year the Biedar tribe relinquishes their Third-Age residence in Sanpashir, there and gone without trace in secretive quiet, Ciladis completes the training of two dragon-spawn, once human-born: a mated pair, first of their kind, Siantra and Esfand take charge as the Gatekeepers to broker Athera's interface with the wild dragons on the splinter world of Sckaithen Duin . . .

XVIII. Mystery

Enshrouded in spellcraft under deep stasis, Elaira embraced the insensate haven as a blessing, cut off as she was from rapport with her beloved for the duration of his trial in Rockfell Pit. Arithon's destiny and hers were entwined, inextricably bound through the throes of locked contest as he matched his initiate wits against Desh-thiere's naked malice. His failure might bequeath her that lonely reprieve in perpetuity, sealed into entrapment with him as an existential threat to the world. Victory alone would see them both freed, the Fellowship Sorcerers become their immutable arbiters.

Elaira had expected to drift in a null state of suspension beyond conscious awareness, and yet the blanket of timeless repose she experienced was not sterile, or silent as the dreamless void. Rockfell's steadfast presence cradled her being. An unbreakable patience beyond animate knowing bled through and altered the scales of cognizant value. Stone broadcast the exquisite, refined harmonics as the sound-and-light chord of Alithiel's cry resonated through the bed-rock strata of the mountain. The bliss of that current, sustained, had wrapped her spirit in star song, until the dread moment the ringing exaltation unfurled by the warded blade dwindled and fell quiet.

The vacuum of joy that followed was terrible.

Sheathed in the eiderdown of isolation, deafened hearing and shrouded senses strained against the staid temperance of Rockfell's vast being for the least whisper of familiar relief. As though forever, Elaira listened to dust adrift on the eddyless air. She heard the language of mineral, expressed in the subsonic rhythm of epochs, parsed by the rigid cadences ruled by crystalline geometry. Myriad voices, peculiar and strange, posed a stilted contrast to the virtuoso clarity of translated impressions learned in her partnerships with refined quartz. These dissociate registers cloaked her starved awareness. Lulled her insatiable restlessness and her frenetic, bright pain, the pall of stark madness driven at bay until, exhausted, the stream of her consciousness spiralled down and down, slowed to the placid, bell-tone vibration that anchored Rockfell's intrepid strength.

A second might have passed, unremarked, or a day, or the millennia that compiled an age. Elaira existed, unmoored from the warm-blooded heartbeat's measure of time.

In the intrusive moment her seated consciousness surfaced from the deeps of immersive stasis, the unrippled pool of voided sensation reawakened to a drawn breath. Bitter awareness crashed through her false peace. *Arithon was not there.* Her linked rapport with him had been sundered. The absence of constancy where his spirit *was not* left a vacuum she had withstood and survived twice before.

Yet this brutal vacancy was different.

"Elaira?"

Someone's brisk hand chafed her wrists. The touch flooded her with the overwhelming surge of animate restoration. Her eyelids fluttered. Glued lashes parted. Sluggish focus revealed Asandir's cragged features, chiselled in white glare above her. The air smelled of ice and wet mineral, traced with the pungency of ozone and horse sweat ingrained in the Sorcerer's mantle.

Elaira blinked through upwelling tears, while his gruff effort at consolation voiced what she already knew.

"For good or ill, the long travail is over. Kharadmon and Davien are dismantling the wards."

Her rusted whisper emerged, fraught with anguish. "And Traithe?"

"Ciladis attends him." Asandir steadied her onslaught of dizziness through the shock of disorientation as she stirred torpid limbs and sat up. "We're agreed you deserve to descend the shaft and bear witness when the last defences in the vault are dispelled."

"Desh-thiere's wraiths are banished?" Flushed by a shudder as her dormant flesh quickened, Elaira shied from the unbearable clamour of personal enquiry.

"We act upon the well-founded assurance the threat imposed by the Mistwraith is annulled." Features beaten to aggrieved furrows by the terrible burden not broached, Asandir qualified, "The misuse sprung from the theft of the Biedar's ancestral knowledge has been expunged. No further enclave of necromancy exists. We know for certain because the crone and her people have abandoned Sanpashir, their obligate residence withdrawn from Athera." Since nerves strung on false hope feared to ask, the Sorcerer eschewed cruel delay and addressed Elaira's devastation directly. "Arithon's triumph exacted a price. Rockfell's shaft has stayed sealed for one hundred and fifty-five years."

Beyond hope, any chance of his incarnate survival. No embodied initiate master could withstand that prolonged duration alone. Informed she might face her beloved's demise, or worse, a haunt deranged and left wretched with madness, Elaira stiffened her spine. Crushed to devastation, she flexed wooden joints and managed to stand. A guttersnipe's childhood spent in threadbare poverty had instilled the harsh lesson early: nothing else mattered but life in the moment. Whatever sorrow awaited her, she would shoulder the brunt in Rockfell Pit at full face, before tearing herself ragged or breaking beforetime.

Arrived at Asandir's shoulder, the loomed contour of a broad-brimmed black hat marked the revived person of Traithe. His scarred grip enfolded Elaira's clenched hand and gentled her rocked balance. "Sweet lady, I will be at your back, no matter what awaits us below."

Elaira leaned into the disabled Sorcerer's presence, speechless with gratitude. Brown eyes softened by the stoic endurance of suffering met and matched hers, the fresh tint of dawn sky flecked with the forged gleam of ferocious tenacity. Whatever they found, she faced only loss. Traithe's urgent need overshadowed her own, the wound to his truncated spirit come at last to the prospect of wholeness. He had traded the fullness of Name to stave off the Mistwraith's invasion, the arc of his fate thrown to intractable risk for the world's weal without hesitation.

Today's undemonstrative calm seemed inconceivable. Trained sight was not fooled by that semblance of quietude. The maimed Sorcerer looked forlorn in his unrelieved black, his stooped shoulder pronounced without a perched raven's quirky companionship. Separation from the aspected bird perhaps signalled the end of his handicapped need, or might instead be the ill-starred harbinger of a disconsolate abandonment.

"When you're up to the challenge, my dear?" Traithe squeezed her fingers in cheerful salute, crinkled laugh lines enlivened by irony. As if crippling impairment did not task him as sorely as her ravaged heart-strings, he stepped aside and made way in salute for her generosity. The sacrifice that endorsed her beloved's free choice had been great as his own, to let Arithon brave the descent on his merits.

Elaira released Traithe's support. Her clipped nod acknowledged the gratitude no earthly language held words to express. She strode between the fathomless depth of Ciladis's limpid regard, and the hard-leashed might behind Asandir's admiration. At the knife-cut rim of the shaft, wracked as sorely in trepidation as the cherished mate gone before her, she set her trembling hands and entrusted her foot to the rungs of the narrow ladder. Committed, she embarked on the prolonged descent that imposed far too much empty space for morbid reflection.

The fond memories resurfaced in flash-point succession: of Arithon, laughing, ink hair mussed by a sea breeze under scalding tropical sunlight, where once, barefoot in knee breeches and shirt, he had guided the plane over new pine for two tow-headed brats on the sand spit at Merior. Elaira recalled him, naked and vital beside her in the herb-scented privacy of the citadel's guest tower: way too brief, those tender interludes of stolen bliss, wrapped in the unearthly harmonics of Alithiel's song and secured by warded walls under siege at Alestron. She ached anew for the spilled blood that had failed to spare a fatherless child, and again, shared the shocked fury and grievous despair on the stark instant before cold steel on Daenfal's scaffold pierced his body. In life, in extremis, in unfettered joy, always Arithon shielded his innermost heart; but never from her. Their first meeting had forged an unquenchable bond. The pent rage that resisted an imposed crown had not sullied the matchless touch that once brushed the snagged straw from her hair. His compassion had shone like a beacon of flame in the fust of the stable hayloft seized as a haven from a headhunting mob.

Painful remembrance lanced unmercifully deep. Benighted longing jellied her viscera. Elaira wrestled the incomprehensible disbelief in rebellion, that the forlorn centuries she had suffered without him might finish here. Bereft, she approached the bottom of a stone well where he would have endured his last hours of excruciate solitude, denied fresh air and sunlight.

Despair's sickly whisper spoke in the dark. Had Arithon perished of thirst, or died by degrees in weakened starvation? Or had he gone down fighting in swift immolation, spirit reft from the flesh in an instant?

Elaira muffled the cry wedged in her throat. She deflected the horror, recall fixed instead on the piercing focus of Arithon's rapt attention, his sly wit, and the rare, fragile gift of his spontaneous smile. The exquisite aliveness and satirical barbs lifted the sputtering torch of her courage, until robbed by the grinding toll on sapped strength, she fought the quiver of tired muscle and shortened breath. Relentless exertion sapped her reserves, and the frayed thread of exhausted thought faltered.

The long shaft struck downwards, sliced through Rockfell's layered bed-rock, the polished surface that enclosed stifled air sheared to glass by Davien's unparalleled craft-work. A pinpoint flare of light sparked in the night depths below, where he and Kharadmon partnered the arduous task of unbinding the wards at the base of the pit. Wheeling rays burned by harsh resonance flared in dazzling relief, the knife-edged swathes of cast shadows speared in flickering sheets up the shaft at each soundless retort of etheric release.

Elaira descended, seized body and mind by inchoate dread.

Fear plucked her hollow. Here, she confronted the memorial rendered by Arithon's last act, with who knew what toll of merciless penalty written in epitaph. Choice befitting the brilliance of his matured talent, his life's course had made him a spirit increasingly lightly contained by the flesh, repeatedly set ablaze by incendiary exposure to the rarefied octaves of transcendent resonance.

Elaira crept downwards, rung after rung, on a wooden ladder whose very existence screamed spellcraft that unsettled the limitations of natural law. How much harder, for Traithe, the taxing descent into the abyss, the same wretched uncertainty strung through the arduous strain to surmount his chronic debility? Hearing recorded the asymmetrical rhythm of his scraped movements above, stiffened joints plagued by the ache of old scars. Pity stripped the marrow of enterprise, that no coveted reprieve might await him. His extreme fortitude, past and present, promised him no guarantees. Hope of healing for his maimed faculties might leave him empty-handed, with no choice going forward but to bear the ascent back into the world for a half-life existence beyond repair.

Elaira tried not to anticipate, or thrash through the thorny thickets of analysis: in fact, the terms of Dakar's Black Rose Prophecy remained unfulfilled. The Seven's seal upon Arithon's abdication as yet kept Rathain's crown title vacant.

Traithe's voice winnowed downwards, as if he shared the timbre of Elaira's unspoken distress. "Two Ages of weighty experience has taught me the effort can signify just as much as the outcome. Desh-thiere's banishment means nothing Arithon did went for naught."

Yet the tacit, unspoken rebuke bit bone deep. Without Traithe's heroic closure of South Gate, the Paravian presence would have been lost. The immaculate grace of Ath's gift to the world had been restored to the continent, the free wilds required for them to flourish sustained still by the rule of the compact.

"Our hope and our anguish express who we are," Traithe allowed. "How you feel in response is unselfish."

The compass of intent steered each subsequent action. Whatever result the endeavour delivered, the framing defined all that mattered. Arithon had seized the primary initiative. He had entered the pit, and confronted a cursed half brother's hatred entangled with Desh-thiere's stewed malice. Elaira could do naught but follow his path and endure what befell at the finish.

The oppressive gloom brightened as she neared the base of the well. Rinsed by the flare of raised mage light, Elaira blinked, dazzled. Unprepared for the sudden break in monotony, she set foot off the last rung, jarred by the firm stone at the floor of the vault.

Someone's thoughtful hand steadied her balance. Davien's, the contrary warmth of his contact displaced where the autumn tones of his hair and clothes seemed bled colourless, the cold-struck flood of sorcerous illumination frosting his form in stark black and white. Flanked by the chill vortex of Kharadmon's shade, Elaira squinted against the actinic glare and picked out the confines of a pentangular chamber. Sheer walls were engraved with intricate, parallel lines of runes, sooted with a flash-burned patina of carbon. The dry air held no scent, devoid of the fust of ancient rot exuded from withered remains. No mouldered bones lay wrapped in decay amid crumpled clothing: nothing. No impression or sign of Arithon's person, living or dead.

The enclosed pit before her was swept clean of taint.

Unmarked mineral retained no etheric stamp, no lingering fragment of record. Elaira's tuned assay through mage-sense parsed only the unpleasant, resonant trace of the dire wards just dispersed by the signature power of Fellowship sorcery. Yet the enclosed space she surveyed was not empty. The ancient symbol for Mother Dark's eternity ringed the artefact objects left untouched at the centre.

If death had visited, no corpus affirmed proof.

Afraid to delve further, Elaira regarded the crone's serpent. Scaled coils entwined into sinuous knots with fanged head devouring its tail, the working's sculpted relief had been rendered in preternatural detail, sinuous curves picked out in glinted reflections and inked shadow. Perhaps the eldritch carving was inert. Or else she beheld a gravid cipher, brim full of quiescent forces locked under the Fatemaster's seal of infinitude.

A symbol whose veiled attributes had been incised by no Sorcerer's hand.

"Not ours," Davien confirmed, as though flicked by the unease of her introspection. "But we already knew the Biedar eldest intervened when her will consigned Lysaer's fate to the crucible."

Sethvir himself might not fathom the untamed might tribal interest had poked into the breach. Elaira quailed, chilled and unsettled by Kharadmon's stark quiet. Here stood the violate evidence of a craft that, *by no means and no measure, should have crossed the triplicate seals of the Fellowship's adamant defences.*

"Extant danger, if any existed, has passed." Davien stirred, his rustled movement re-echoed in susurrant whispers. "You may cross inside without harm. What charge the figure retained is long spent."

"Then you have ascertained Desh-thiere's wraiths are banished from Athera's continuum?" Embarrassment tensioned the strain past Elaira's acumen to suppress.

"Apparently, yes." Davien's mercuric restlessness snapped through restraint. Tagged by his scythed shadow, he paced. Awash in the stewed eddies slapped off the close walls, he vented the seethe of his frustrated intellect. "No inflection lingers from the sundered spirits' human malice bound into penury. The captive entities are gone. We're confounded because the resonant marker inscribed by their requite departure or their abject destruction has been excised."

"That is the crone's doing!" Kharadmon bristled, glittering hoarfrost fanned beneath the gyre of his peevish restlessness. "Past question, the hag would have scoured the lot in snide quittance for her past grievance."

"Fair play," cracked Davien. "Not to mention the favour that spared us the thankless bother of closure on our part." The acrimonious, past argument kept its envenomed sting, that off-loading Mankind's misfit meddlers to the splinter world beyond South Gate had dealt the Seven the wretched reprise of a bad call.

Since, above question, the malignant, mechanical tinkering on Marak derived from the debased tenets usurped from the Biedar, a tribal sentence imposed on the revenant horde would have rendered Traithe's toll of damage irreparably permanent. A damning indictment not yet refuted: the sparkle and flash strung through Davien's clamped fist confirmed the receptacle purposefully endowed by Sethvir to sequester the reprieved fragments for Traithe's recovery had been stripped. The quartz point carried here at unthinkable cost had been retrieved as a useless blank.

"We found the jewel and chain strewn on the floor," Kharadmon qualified for Elaira's benefit. "Though our immediate disappointment may not bear the final word on the matter."

Cankered regret weighed the hardest upon Davien's conscience, the excoriating burden laid on him beyond a lamed colleague's tragic predicament. Belated acknowledgement forced the due nod of respect for the meticulous hours he had spent training the unique talent come to his gloved fist under tribulation at Kewar. Grief scored the glass edge of a sorrow too heavy to bear for the mate now standing bereft at the forefront.

Past Elaira, stamped into the ambient gloom by the harsh gleam of light and crisp shadow, the relics left at large by Arithon's travail sprang stark to the eye, encircled by the enigma of the Biedar crone's chiselled cipher.

There, the cylindrical stone flask fashioned for Desh-thiere's containment rested upright, denuded of the Fellowship's stringent wards. The jasper wrought from the Paravian masonry of Kieling Tower still carried the faint song of Ilitharis workmanship. The plug stopper, removed and laid aside, had released its prisoned content. But the neck of the vessel had not been left open. Refined vision detected a seamless closure, yet intact: the signature harmonic repurposed to set the broached container under a delicate seal.

Arithon's talent spoke through the weave, fashioned on the tenets of resonant sound with a spare, vibrant eloquence untouched by the rigorous cleanse. One remembered, in witness: that Athera's titled bard had mastered a unique command, blending the myriad strands of arcane tradition from Athera's full spectrum of mystical endowment.

Elaira's entrained focus took wrenching pause. She swallowed, mustered frayed nerves, then moved on. And there, black on midnight nicked with starred reflections off silvered embroidery, her assay discerned the velvet folds of the cloak once gifted by Davien, cast off in a rumpled heap. Nestled on top, the dark sword Alithiel gleamed unsheathed, the blade forged by the centaur armourer Ffereton ruled fair by the gleam the Athlien artisans' inlaid runes.

The chord that named the winter stars raised no ranging cry in the darkness. Quiescent, the Paravian weapon lay cold and dimmed and inert.

Stricken numb by an acute pang of mourning, Elaira steeled herself to endure what could not be borne. She stumbled, checked short by a grip on her forearm.

"Dear lady," Davien said, his entreaty terrifying for an uncharacteristic mildness. "Touch nothing without care!"

Yet no warning was needed. As Arithon's beloved, Elaira knew: Alithiel had been the selected receptacle to secure his naked spirit before. The same refuge, seized here at the crux of raw need, would have sheltered his discorporate integrity from assault and the horror of Desh-thiere's possession. Tears brimmed for the certainty. "He wove his music through the active song of the sword and rendered the requite severance to free his half brother. Then, of course, he laboured onwards and composed the exalted release for every last captive wraith."

The signature pattern of Arithon's spirit, imbued in spelled steel, yet held his Named essence. A precarious haven unsecured in the open, with naught but the spread cloak between the grounding contact of stone. The volatile stasis endured against brutal odds and attrition, that one heedless touch would unravel.

Sorrow rendered the discovery beyond words. The long years Elaira had passed in repose had been filled with the transcendent melody transmitted through Rockfell's vast matrix. Adamance like cut diamond, paired with rugged tenacity to defy entropy, framed the pristine shield of Alithiel's grand conjury. The song of the winter stars imbued by the Athlien enchanters, through which Arithon had seized his defence, had sustained to completion his exhaustive, meticulous execution of a Masterbard's healing tones that lifted each wraith to requital.

Crushed by a deed to resound through the ages, Elaira fell back on her strengths. Annealed by her most harrowing tests of adversity, she reached outside herself: bought the balm of distance in familiar refuge through sincere concern for another. "Traithe?"

"If Arithon achieved a clean remedy for his fragmentation, the answer can wait a bit longer." Caustic insight disallowed the ache to lend sympathy.

Davien withheld the shallow consolation that would have unstrung Elaira's brave equilibrium. "We felt you should be first to venture inside the Biedar crone's cipher."

The eternal serpent, which assuredly had configured the portal of access which delivered Lysaer s'Ilessid to his reckoning with Arithon, and the resolution of Desh-thiere's curse.

Elaira dredged up her tattered courage. Paralysed wits could be unlocked by determination, if she smothered the turmoil of distraught emotion. She felt nothing, heard nothing, as she stepped into the serpent's closed coil. She knew only the unwritten score in the silence of absence, while rote movement brought her to her knees before the dropped cloak. Ath wept for the necessity, her hands did not shake. She surmounted the flawless office required and shrouded the naked steel of Alithiel in dark velvet and glittering argent embroidery. Sorrow could be harnessed by purpose. A mind savaged by desolate grief could rely on the spine of trained discipline. The same expert restraint that had handled charged crystals let Elaira fold the Paravian blade with its precious, etheric burden into buffered protection. With the tie tugged from her braid, still warm, she laced the bundled sword under the ritual knots to secure the ephemeral essence of her best beloved.

She stood upright at length, the weight of cold metal cradled like death at her breast. The tears she had dammed behind iron control spilled over, then. Davien's steady regard, and Kharadmon's hushed presence gave time to remember the abject care with which Arithon had guarded his friendships. *Almost*, she sensed the caustic sting of the inventive retort he had been wont to voice when cornered by trying sentiment.

Distance won no reprieve. No sober tribute could encompass the loss of his melting talent on the lyranthe, flexibly turned to ease suffering, and unbridled joy to bring merriness beyond measure. No balm existed to ease the remembrance of his tender caress. Nothing ameliorated the severance of a loving partnership that should rightfully bless a full lifetime.

The future bequeathed to posterity remained: in the legacy of the Paravians, and in the brighter prospect of Traithe's relief from the affliction of painful impairment. Healer trained, Elaira reached as though drowning for that spar of comfort amid the bleak sea of her desolation.

"Elaira?" Davien broke through her fog of bereavement. "Our wild falcon is discorporate. Not crossed past the veil."

The enchantress nodded, seized beyond speech. The excruciate quandary had not escaped her. In her hands rested the irreversible decision to be made in her beloved's behalf: whether to release him to his final passage, or to risk the consummate, empathic pity that might bind him to her side, his existence prolonged as a discarnate shade. The double-edged gift of indefinite mortality, granted to them both by the transformative power bestowed by the dragon at the fount of rebirth engendered at Forthmark.

However forsaken, Elaira was not left stranded to anguish. The hitched scrape of Traithe's descent from the shaft brought him to the base of the ladder. Blanched with discomfort, he paused, brown eyes softened. His halted step reached Elaira. His enduring sympathy parsed the swathed sword. Then he bundled her and her wrapped burden into his generous embrace.

"Not for nothing," he murmured. "Never for no purpose. Don't waver or fall to the cynic's belief in futility."

Elaira smiled through tears and returned the warm clasp of his earnest encouragement. "You have been my example since the priceless counsel shared with me in our long-ago meeting at Narms." Sensitive to his need, she stepped back. Retired alongside Kharadmon's turbulent shade, she braced herself to bear witness to the last with his expectant colleagues.

Davien and Traithe pressed forward together and broached the protective seal on the jasper flask. The moment hung, while frail hope ignited the flame of a long-sought reprieve. Then, winnowed free, the sundered wisps of Traithe's spirit emerged, sequestered in safety for salvage.

A profound release, for the Fellowship Sorcerers: indescribable celebration infused their combined presence as the fire of wholeness restored the rifts stitched through Traithe's damaged aura. Sweet remission was swift, as his lost access to unbridled power resurged. The light-and-sound clap of spontaneous regeneration infused his battered frame, easing the stoop of intractable pain and lifting the hindrance of drawn scars. Against untold hardship, the signature kindness of his mild features shone through restored flesh and bone like a torch. The inexhaustible dignity forged upon an anvil of indescribable suffering illumined tenfold Traithe's return to hale strength.

His soft laughter, inflected by his puckish whimsy, embraced the two colleagues poised speechless before him. "I see Davien's struggle to mask his relief. Don't tell me which one of you Seven lost the coin toss for the bother of lugging my broken hulk to the surface."

"Luhaine, of course," Kharadmon interjected. "Dependable as the sunrise, he takes the champion's fall as the pessimist."

The Mistwraith's fell grip on the world had been sundered. Athera might thrive, exalted by the splendour of the Paravians, and the Seven rejoice with ebullient verve as Traithe emerged from the black deeps of Rockfell whole in body and spirit.

Only for Elaira, the price paid for Arithon's deliverance of Desh-thiere's predation came by far too bitterly dear.

Late-afternoon shade purpled the napped furrows of Rockfell's forested vale, the gorges sliced by silver floss where the River Avast's unreeled falls snaked beneath powder-puff combers of drifting cloud. The notched summits above shimmered yet, dipped in gilt, the iron-black spike of the peak overhead damascened in sunlit pockets of summer snow. Three Fellowship colleagues had parted ways, dispatched to other arenas tasked by Sethvir.

Ciladis lingered. The cold breeze whining over sheer cornice and ice knifed through his white hair, snapped by the eddies that buffeted his stance before the sealed access to the vault's upper chamber. Davien's wry remark, that the mountain's dignified isolation resented the intrusive clamour of warm-blooded visitors seemed displaced by the sweeping serenity settled in the day's aftermath. The sough of lofted snowflakes swirled with a lilt, perhaps moved to joy by the Sorcerer's presence.

Dark profile turned in stamped silhouette against the enamel brilliance of indigo sky at high altitude, he addressed his tacit query to the diminutive person muffled for travel beside him. "Where will you go from this cross-roads?"

The pause stretched, filled by the thin, plaintive cry of an eagle, circling on the thermals below. At length, Elaira mustered the wry presence to answer. "I expect I'd be unwise to attempt an appeal to Seshkrozchiel."

Ciladis's tender letdown came gentled by sadness. "A great drake's dreaming capacity can remake the flesh, but not without the intimate template to frame an actualized concept of full-bodied form in the moment. For Arithon, not subject to the blood binding imposed on our Fellowship, Seshkrozchiel's might cannot amend the deficit."

Elaira cradled the dormant, cloaked bundle against her breast. "He was not resigned." Memory replayed the indelible moment when Arithon had been with her, alive, before he had turned from the last kiss of daylight and faced the black threshold cut into the mountain. Her fleeting glimpse had captured his face, as he left her side and believed no one watched. Whether through connected rapport, or by her acute intuition, or some other prompt dredged from her innermost self, she had seen the fracture as his expression had slipped.

White to the bone, Arithon had looked utterly terrified as he steeled himself for the ordeal ahead.

She had shelved the certainty then, desperate under hindsight's denial. For surely she realized he had gone with the prescient awareness of his fate in the pit.

Now she held him, a spirit bound mute by cold steel in her arms, and the future before her tormented her conscience.

Ciladis was not deaf to the clamour that harrowed her beyond peace. "Arithon trusted you, always. You will not fail him, as the blood and the marrow of his true self, however unquiet the choice you resolve through deliberation."

Rockfell's vast presence affirmed Arithon's own indelible statement, left to her in perpetuity: *'You only, beloved.'*

But Alithiel's haven now fashioned his prison, with herself the untrustworthy gaoler. Release would leave Arithon stranded, discorporate. Masterbard and beloved, reft of his vibrant expression in flesh, what joyless existence would she bequeath to him? To dismantle the sword's sterile containment was to saddle him with the excruciate decision in turn: to stay on as an ephemeral shade in companionship for her sake, or tear her asunder and pass across the veil, her path abandoned by his willed choice to refurnish a separate life after parting.

The Fellowship Sorcerers had no guidance to offer. Their precepts were met by the Mistwraith's demise, and the Paravians' return prioritized their fulfilment of several crown vacancies under the covenant ruled by the compact. They held no stake in the course of her outcome. Their vested interest in Arithon's bloodline was spent, beyond wistful regret and aggrieved consolation.

Shared sorrow rooted Ciladis's vigil beside her. Or perhaps the intrinsic balm of the healer extended his undemanding support. Love without condition lent her the quietude to sort through the pitfalls shredding the raw wound of her anguish.

The abyss left to tread lay riddled with severances, Requiar's ancestral debt brought to a verified closure by the Biedar people's departure. Whose tenuous thread of wisdom remained to offer sure counsel? Not the tribal crone, but perhaps her mystical ally, the Reiyaj Seeress entrained at the sentinel's seat in the tower northwest of Ithish.

Kindly ambivalence fled. Amber eyes on her fierce as the warrior's, Ciladis settled her unvoiced query directly. "The Seeress still communes with the sun. Her pact with the tribe's eldest may yet have a say in the matter."

Summer's warmth lingered into the dry days of autumn, where the baked grass bowed and tasselled with ripened seed cloaked the rolling vales that sloped down to the southcoast harbour at Ithish. The Seeress's spire of yellow sandstone snagged the pale sky, notched by the narrow, outside stair carved into the curved wall that fell sheer to the ground with no railing. The climber's vantage unrolled beneath, sun-drenched gold patched in shade by the ancient clusters of live oaks, distorted through the late season's ripple of heat-waves.

Mated spirit to the one come before, she who had been called by *Affi'enia* and *Fferedon-li* arrived to place her petition. The oracle's attendants bowed to her polite request and permitted her access. Long since, her arrival had been expected.

A step tempered to fitness by Elaira's journey across Melhalla's free wilds made almost no sound in ascent, though the burden strapped to her shoulder weighed on her progress. Atop the swept height, she knelt, unspeaking, before the high chair that enthroned the withered oracle. Impervious as baked leather, the elder's skeletal frame lay veiled in sheer azure silk, the wizened, carved bone of her features creased bronze from relentless seasons of weather and sun.

Elaira's brought offering of late-blooming asters whispered in the wind, imprinted still with the flyaway dust of streamed pollen, the delicate wingbeats of butterflies, and the hum of foraging insects. Schooled to the etiquette that respected old power, the bronze-haired supplicant did not speak. She laid down her gift, then rendered her appeal by placing the bundled sword flat before the oracle's gimballed seat.

The Reiyaj Seeress was a law unto herself. She would respond, or else lend the stern counsel of her unbroken silence.

Daylight glanced through the jewelled-horn combs at her crown, while the wheeled mechanism beneath her high seat shifted and clunked the geared counterweight that kept her eggshell-white orbs entrained sunwards. The breeze itself stilled as if listening, while the scourging brilliance of noon stamped the knots that secured the furled midnight cloak with its cryptic border of silver embroidery.

Then the oracle said, "Choice may not be yours alone to determine."

Truth answered Elaira's petition as querant. Arithon's promise to the Teirendaelient Merevalia had not been met. Content with the gifted word of affirmation, she assumed personal charge of unravelling the complication.

Yet the Seeress delivered one further counsel before her cryptic quiet signalled dismissal. "Your answer lies in the one place this world's earth-linked visionaries cannot see. You must venture the site where, even yet, no Fellowship Sorcerer dares to tread uninvited."

The Biedar crone's lair in the cave warrens of Sanpashir was the only such known location.

Elaira gathered the wrapped sword and bowed with the bundle hugged to her breast. Thanks on her part were superfluous. The jewelled sparkle of the single, salt tear spilled in gratitude before the oracle's slippered feet exceeded the gravity of all words.

The underground warren in Sanpashir sloped downwards beneath the black desert's sands. Layered level on level into the earth, a maze of footpaths had been delved by hand through damp bed-rock, linked to other natural, meandering channels and caves carved by seeps and virgin springs. Elaira breathed the cool air of a place that was barren, void of presence, and seemingly empty of all but the echoes cast by her intrusive exploration.

The fulfilled circle of Biedar purpose had achieved completion with the defeat of the last holdout of necromancy. Nothing remained. The imprinted record in stone of their peoples' six thousand one hundred years of inhabitancy had been wiped clean from the face of Athera.

Yet the caves were not energetically dead. Elaira's patient assay of the flux currents, waxing and waning, had led her down to the deepest vault in the labyrinth. Emptiness met her at the narrows before the last threshold. The velvet darkness ahead of her hung dense as the expanse. She breathed in stilled air thick with mineral dust, but not stagnant. The ascending octaves of frequency that had guided her downward steps slackened into an unquiet silence. She stared into a vacancy of such stringent adamance, the hair prickled erect at her nape.

Unseen and unheard, the whisper of *nothing* bespoke the heart of Mother Dark's Mystery. The null point of power, untouched by creation, fraught with the unborn promise that seeded all myriad imprints of possibility. Infinity slept here. No mystical guidance was needed to warn the initiate mind of the seeker. The gravity of trespass in violation would destroy the intruder arrived without cause. Forces guarding the entrance combed through Elaira's being like ghost fingers brushed through her aura.

All that she was, and would be, was sieved through. Keen as a knife blade slid under the skin, no private part of her passed unseen. She had been weighed and measured, her purpose laid bare. Her next choice by free will came at her peril, her own to complete or abandon.

In trust, the Reiyaj Seeress's counsel had bestowed a semblance of due permission, Elaira knelt, a reverence to Biedar culture made awkward by her laden satchel and the bundled sword slung on her back. She sorted her burdens, unpacked and kindled the coal pot she carried, then sprinkled the sweet-oiled tinder with an offering of cedar and incense salts. Twined smoke caught and flared blue, tendrils wafted upwards like silver-grey marbling swirled upon ink. The pungent fragrance upended her heightened senses, until *almost* she heard the struck notes of music, otherworldly and strange.

The crone's lair before her unveiled its fast secret in the uncertain, flickering light. The circular chamber beyond had been carved with spiral patterns, the convergent array of eldritch tribal symbols centred by the interlaced snake carved in the perpetual act of devouring its tail. Elaira beheld the twin to the figure impressed into the vault beneath Rockfell Pit.

Yet here, the crone's cipher was not inert, and for cold certainty, not harmless to the outsider's footstep treading within.

Entry would surrender her being to occult forces beyond knowing. Yet the hollow left to her by Arithon's absence drove a commitment as irreversible as direct action. Elaira laid the coal pot aside, stood erect, and steadied her fierce apprehension. She had not travelled this far to turn back, or languish with the misery of uncertainty.

"Forgive my ignorance, should I plead wrongly." Voice firm, she defined her intent. "As handfast to Arithon, of Requiar's descent, I beg the Biedar tribe for the grace of ancestral counsel."

Eyes closed, fingers clenched on the cross-strapped sword, she dared the gyre and stepped into the cipher, coiled and scaled, which symbolized Mother Dark's infinite arc and the limitless span of eternity.

Her footfall came down and unleashed black lightning. The explosion that consumed her being was vast, a vortex untamed, primordial, and utterly terrifying. Upended by forces that cancelled sensation, Elaira swung untethered over the abyss. Then she became seized, body, mind, and spirit, by an awareness that *knew* her most intimate self. That exquisitely tender consciousness Named her, and claimed her, intact from the deeps and thrust her in rebirth from the womb of the vacuum.

Elaira broke through the featureless darkness and surfaced to arid air and dazzling light. No place on Athera: the ambient flux stream where she emerged rushed through her initiate faculties. A spate thundering with the roared might of a waterfall inundated her trained awareness. The dance with the torrent that steered her delivery, a circle of singers fell silent around her. Robed figures with desert-tribe features, surrounded by a vista otherworldly and strange. A cave mouth yawned in the high ledge beyond them, scraped from the rough pumice of a volcanic scarp. Other crags thrust upwards above, stacked pinnacles twisted at drunken angles. The alien range towered against a greenish blue sky wisped with sulphurous cloud. The breeze smelled of baked mineral, the unfamiliar alkali tang fragranced by the astringent scents of exotic plant life.

Elaira wrestled astonishment through the dizzy, jarred shock of disorientation. Transferred who knew where by unknown means for the gift of this audience, she bent her head in respect, held to patience, and waited.

Hearing would be granted by Biedar leave; or not. The protocol guarding access to their Eldest would not have changed since her past encounter under night stars in Sanpashir. This time, come without escort, she might well be disowned for trespass.

One of the male singers broke from his fellows with no visible signal exchanged. His gesture directed her into the cavern, where she met their tribal crone seated cross-legged, swathed as before in layered veils and embroidered black skirts. A crabbed hand that clinked with elaborate, carved talismans beckoned the visitor forward to share tea, poured steaming hot in two earthenware cups without handles.

Careful of her balance, Elaira approached. The potency of the natural flux stream reamed through her, a deafening tumult that transmitted thought as clearly as spoken words. *'Eldest, by grace of your hospitality, where am I?'*

The ancient lifted her face cloth, rapacious visage wizened as a walnut. Speech like the rustle of windblown leaves stamped a clarion imprint upon Elaira's awareness. "This is Scathac, the living world our Biedar people revere as our preferred residence." A sweeping gesture of welcome honoured the rugged surroundings, then conveyed the invitation to sit.

Elaira accepted, settled through a hospitable interval to savour the proffered drink. Aromatic and strong, invigorated with strange spices, sweet butter. and honey, the brew had no discernible narcotic properties to augment the range of her faculties. The flux tide's galvanic stream roared unchecked through her refined senses, more potent than Athera's innate song, and a tonic that stretched the threshold of her initiate tolerance.

Amid the cool shade, after both cups were emptied, the Biedar eldest deigned to comment. "Jessian Oathkeeper stood where you are now. By our custom of gratitude, you have earned the right."

Elaira slipped the strapped scabbard from her shoulder and laid down the blade swathed in Davien's gifted cloak on the ground at the elder's mantled knees.

"Have you come here for closure or reckoning?" The crone stirred. Bracelets melodic with bone-and-glass fetishes quieted as she laid her wrinkled palm overtop the swaddled sword.

Whether the contact effected an assay, or imparted a reverent caress, the swelled ripple of flux charge raised the fine hair at Elaira's nape. Beyond question, Arithon's sequestered spirit responded, aware of the eldest's informed touch.

"Your choice, *Affi'enia*," the ancient resumed, her desiccate voice neutral steel. "Whether your beloved stays here with the hallowed of Mother Dark's people, and the line-bearer's ancestry sprung from Requiar, or if he is reclaimed for a fate that bequeaths him to Athera."

Elaira weighed the decision, not without a shiver of trepidation. While the anguish of unbirthed probability thickened the pause grown dense as a blanket around her, she refined her commitment and spoke. "Arithon once made a sealed promise to the Teirendaelient Merevalia, Queen Regent of the Paravians. Whatever I think, that obligation may not be mine to leave forfeit."

The crone inclined her head, the delicate rustle of her midnight garments stirred by the sough of the draught through the cavern.

"Then, called by *Fferdon-li*, take care what you ask. Frame the intentions of your appeal wisely."

Elaira yielded to the solemn tug of a smile. Schooled by Ciladis, and blessed often by the counsel of master initiates, she measured her need by the precepts bestowed by Ath's white adepts. *How did she feel? What belief did she serve, and where did her heart's whisper steer her?*

Clarity sang upon Scathac's uncanny flux, reinforced by the sure guidance bestowed on a starry night's audience once held on the sable sands at Sanpashir. "I would have the weave between us complete." Still, the bottom dropped out of her gut. The courage required to do right by her love came with welled tears and a wrench at the heart that near broke her. "Free will leaves the initiative in Arithon's hands. If need be, I will answer in person for his lapsed charge of the Teirendaelient's obligation."

"You are sure?" Black eyes, black skin, midnight cloth, the ancient lowered her embroidered veils. "Said is done, then."

Elaira bowed her head in acceptance. Relieved of the dread burden that had harrowed every moment since her descent into Rockfell, she did not feel lighter. Nor did she catch the glint sparked alight in hooded eyes, or the enigmatic smile on the crone's features.

The last word of the Biedar melded into Scathac's streamed flux as a shout that upended perception. "Go in grace to Requiar's reward."

Elaira recovered her senses, sprawled on the carved stone that floored the dim cavern in Sanpashir. The lit coals in her offering pot glimmered orange, the feeble glow muted by whiskered, grey ash curtained in encroaching shadow. Dust, and the scent of charred herbs and fresh ozone pervaded the afterclap of the momentous charge that had restored her, alive, to Athera.

Alone, she presumed, as she gathered her shaken nerve, grounded her wrenched equilibrium, and stirred upright. Her elbow grazed fabric. Davien's mantle, surely, returned with the Paravian sword that rightfully belonged at Althain Tower with the heirlooms held in trust for the next confirmed s'Ffalenn heir.

Yet the acute discernment of mage-sight showed otherwise. Davien's cloak and the sword rested at her left side, the black blade with its white rune inlay unshrouded. The spirit sheltered within would have fled, bared to casual touch. Whether to a swift transcendence and a named place with the Biedar ancestry on Scathac remained under question. To her right, Elaira encountered a sarcophagus, fashioned from felted goat hair and stitched with Mother Dark's cipher of stasis. The seams had been secured with ritual knots of guard and protection, matched precisely to the ones she had employed to bundle the sword in the deeps of Rockfell Pit.

Residual power no longer thrummed through the silence. The crone's interest appeared to have achieved completion, the long reach of her finger withdrawn from Athera's orbit. The coiled serpent that patterned her shrine was spent, inert as the intertwined carving impressed within Rockfell's vault. A tomb befitting Requiar's issue, ashes to dust consigned to Athera, or by Arithon's will, a new path just beginning.

Elaira had to know, if only for closure. She lifted Alithiel's icy weight, turned the edge, and snipped the ties on the sarcophagus. Fingers shaking, she parted the cloth, tingled by a surge of charge sprung from the severed pattern under her hand. An expelled riffle of breath puffed the gauze silk of a winding sheet. Heart racing, she tore the caul through and touched flesh, vibrant and warm, and quite naked.

Rapport with her beloved resurged, clear as water welled from a dry spring. Freed from the parted cling of spelled fabric, she beheld familiar features, fronded in tousled black hair, spare angles cherished by her as no other. Green eyes opened, fathoms deeper than she remembered. Rapt vision had seen what no man imagined, and yet, the sensitive, questing intelligence regarding her was unchanged.

"You only," declaimed the Masterbard gently. "If I'm pleased by the dearth of clothes in your presence, whose idea was the damnable prickly swaddling?"

Elaira gasped, laughing. "Please to Ath! Arithon! Let us never endure the like of such cruel separation again!" Then she collapsed, wrung pithless by joy as Arithon stirred from recumbent repose, freed his arms, and swept her into a ferocious embrace, by intent never to let her go.

Restoration

The windblown traveller in a dark cloak and worn leathers reined up for a rendezvous on the causeway that stitched the lowland flats at the trade-road's terminus by the town of West End. No mere sable stallion, the mount bearing him had a ghost eye and the uncanny aura of a creature touched by the magic of dragons. "Are you ready to hold the *caithdein*'s black through one final service to Tysan?"

Daliana s'Evend regarded the Sorcerer come to claim his request for her counsel on his mission through Westgate to Dascen Elur for the selection of two royal heirs to accede to the crown attunements for s'Ilessid and s'Ahelas. Grey eyes as intimidating as ever, and a face stern as hammered steel awaited her pleasure with the relentless patience of ages.

"Who's left?" she challenged, combative verve undiminished by the passing years as she closed petite hands gloved in calfskin on the bridle of a mare gentle enough to forgive her unease in the saddle. "Most everyone's aged or dead, who remembers this realm's royal line in the flesh."

Saroic had been laid to rest over a century ago, having stood shadow for an empty throne through the trials of war, the outpost rebuilt at Orlan his accomplished reward for a service that spanned fifty-five winters. Three generations since, his great-grandnephew's son was the heir designate, named to assume the black after Daliana's retirement.

Asandir inclined his bare head, white hair nipped in a cord against the fresh breeze. "Step down now, if you truly wish. But this time, I promise you won't come to regret the adventure."

The referent name dangled unspoken between them: Lysaer's fate at the hands of the Biedar crone lost under Rockfell's sealed wards in the final battle to subdue the Mistwraith. Daliana's inquiries since had been stonewalled, the Seven reluctant to answer. Sethvir's word on the matter had been as cryptic when she pressed her request to ascertain his destiny for the kingdom's historical record. "Your liege is not on Athera."

Outcast from the compact, never presented before the High Queen Regent Merevalia for Paravian judgement, Lysaer's forfeited right to inhabit the planet never had been lifted.

Daliana set determined heels to her mount, faced ahead as she reined off the roadway. Pleased by her choice, Asandir urged his black into step, bearing cross-country due south. Her accusation packed sting when she tried his complacency. "Say honestly you didn't expect my agreement from the hour you first proposed the favour in question."

Asandir's alert ear picked up the suppressed note of bitterness no effort on her part might tame. If he felt remiss for the extended years her request to share Lysaer's prolonged longevity might leave her stranded, then as now, he withheld his counsel. Perhaps he understood her tolerant acceptance stemmed from ennui, as the lengthened perspective of her experience outstripped, then discomfited, the diminished handful of latecoming friendships and ever increasingly youthful associates.

"Honestly?" The rich baritone of Asandir's laugh warmed like wine aged in the cask. "Your right was earned, truly. But given your fettlesome nature? I had no idea."

"Huh!" Daliana yanked loose her pert snood. A toss freed her luxuriant coil of mahogany hair to stream in the breeze. "Say that to Davien and keep a straight face!" Still the minx, she kicked her mare to a gallop and made the Sorcerer stretch the black's stride through the trackless broom to catch up.

Shortly the overgrowth gave way to wilder woodland, threaded by game trails. Asandir's guidance retraced the unmarked way once trodden through a rainy night to recover two royal exiles cast destitute into Athera. So began a new journey through Westgate to the splinter world of Racinne Pasy. Delivered onto the desiccate sand amid the abandoned stone ruins of Mearth, Daliana surveyed tumbledown walls and toppled pillars, strewn like battered shells on an oceanless vista of sere hardpan and vacant, purple sky. The pooled shade in the crannies harboured none of the fell scraps of enspelled darkness that had wrought the demise of antiquity's inhabitants. Almost, Lysaer and his bastard half brother had succumbed, geas-bent by compulsion to the madness that once drove the s'Ellestrion heir, raving, to suicide.

Touched by the atmosphere of desolation, Daliana broke the stultified quiet with the tinny sound of her own voice. "No bane lingers from legend?"

"Davien cleared that trouble ahead of us, never fear." Asandir's notched profile stayed trained forward. "His engaged craft-work was the original defence to deter ignorant meddlers from the Five Centuries Fountain. The regrettable tragedy happened in error when he was rendered discorporate. He never fashioned such horror to run at large and cause injury."

Nothing moved now across Mearth's banked sand but baked wind through the blasted blocks of cracked masonry. No sound disturbed their passage astride but the chink of horseshoes and bits, echoed off broken facades and the pedestals of tumbled statues, warm with the trapped pall of the day's glaring heat.

As if to fill the stark emptiness, or to repel the benighted remembrance of a once-thriving town packed with the bustle of gemcutters' industry, Asandir volunteered conversation. "The waterborne spell crafted for extended life is dismantled, though for a whim, Davien left the well intact as an oasis for travellers."

Mounted, the horses fresh under them, Athera's delegation of two fared west across the barren waste where Arithon and Lysaer had once striven footbound as beset enemies partnered in exile. The low, orange ball of today's winter sun did not broil the desert to the cruel furnace endured by two half brothers stressed to the verge of survival. Cloaked against the fierce chill of the wind, cast under the shadowed crests of the dunes tipped moulten scarlet by fading sundown, Sorcerer and *caithdein* reached the ancient archway of the far Worldsend Gate, flaked iron polished clean of splotched rust, and the wide span between no longer empty or dead.

Luhaine's and Kharadmon's recent labour had restored the silvered sheen of the spelled matrix for transit.

The horses, led through, breathed the textured damp of salt air, brisk with spindrift flung off ocean whitecaps. Seabirds wove and shrieked overhead, scrap white and grey against a seaside cliff ruffled by the lace petticoats of Dascen Elur's curled combers. Two square rigged ships rode at anchor in the sheltered cove, standing well off the gravel reef that firmed past the tidemark into a sandy beach. Delivered to a handkerchief patch of greensward on the outskirts of the splinter world gate's remote islet, Daliana caught her breath, stunned at first sight by the royal banners that streamed from their mastheads: familiar, the gold star and crown on the azure field of Tysan, and the crisp chevrons, gold and purple, of the adjunct kingdom of Shand. A device soon to revert to the prior falcon and crescent moon, Daliana reflected, once the Paravian presence reclaimed from secession the free-wilds territory on the southwestern peninsula.

"You didn't expect we would be met in state?" Asandir remarked, arid amusement thrust through her reverie as he slipped the stud's girth and removed saddle and bridle. "You might free your horse. The leeside vale has plentiful fodder for grazing and a sweet spring."

The animals could take their ease and frolic at will, given a fortnight's leave to themselves in the absence of human oversight.

The squeal of ships' davits echoed over the water, both vessels in the seafarer's process of lowering longboats. Daliana shouldered her share with the tack, unfastening buckles, until the Sorcerer prompted her to don the black tabard of an office she had handled through the radical, contentious change imposed during the difficult decades of the interregnum. Before she had smoothed her formal clothing to rights, the Sorcerer gestured towards the leading oared tender, thrust through the billow of the backsliding breakers.

"My dear?" Asandir said, "I could not be sure of the welcome beforehand. But you might want to glance up."

The longboat grounded upon shoaling sand, wet looms raised by her crew, while the plain-clothed man in the bow leaped the thwart and splashed into the shallows. He bore no badge of rank. No honours set him apart from the rough-cut sailhands behind him. Immersed in his role to steady the craft against the tug of the surf, he seemed nondescript, except for his bearing. A fit stature, imbued with an unconscious majesty seperated him from his fellows. Fair in colouring, his burnished hair caught the sunlight. The sight galvanized a recognition that struck Daliana's heart like a hammerblow.

Beyond real, alive, Lysaer s'Ilessid hauled the longboat's keel to firm ground on the shingle.

Almost, she wished she dared the effrontery to smack Asandir. "You knew!" she accused. "Why didn't you tell me?"

The field Sorcerer's burning gaze remained fixed on the lordly person, whose brisk strides outpaced the first fanfare declaring the official delegation's approach. "Sethvir insisted the man was not ready to face you." Asandir turned his regard on her, then. Cragged features scoured by centuries of harsh weather crinkled with his reserved humour. "Did the years pass with such difficulty? We Seven made sure you had plenty to occupy the ferocious loyalty of your ancestral line."

"I may not be inclined to greet anyone without indulging my impulse to rip for the jugular."

Asandir's laughter was free as the breeze. "I trust he'll have some explaining to do, and the weightier penance of mending torn fences."

Then Lysaer reached them, tall and vibrant, but embarrassed and hesitant as none on Athera had ever seen him. Without trappings, no longer invested with title, he still owned the presence of a born prince. What had changed, the metal beneath was recast to a temperance that wore gut-wrenching diffidence in plain sight.

Asandir granted him grace, and the moment to unwind strung nerves and speak. "We know," he said gently.

Then, quietly, the Sorcerer addressed Daliana, with no small measure of poignant regret. "Not everything happened as you might suppose. More occurred on that hour of reckoning in the bowels of Rockfell Pit." A respectful nod towards Lysaer, and Asandir added, "The path to delivery from Desh-thiere's curse was more fraught with pitfalls than the wisest of us ever imagined. Let the survivor tell you himself. Allow him the slack to find his equilibrium and explain when he's ready."

Ashamed by the abusive wreckage lodged in the history between them, Lysaer regarded the woman who had given his hope for redemption more than all she had owned in the world. The impact of his charisma still savaged her heart, an innate endowment that forced him to carry the shame and face the harsh toll of the reckoning. Her confusion and dismay were not lost on him, or the sudden, sharp pain of the wounds reopened as an awkward reunion brought them together.

"You have outlived your peers, as I have," he managed, a lame effort to spare her from the deeper emotion he felt he had forfeited his privilege to share. "I alone will remember and be here for you when you've lost connection to others with firsthand experience."

"You can never leave Dascen Elur," Asandir confirmed. "Your banishment from Athera is permanent, and outside of our Fellowship's purview to revoke."

"I know." Lysaer's direct regard on the Sorcerer never wavered under that stark acknowledgement. But the ruthless, entrained focus owned by the Seven caught the flicker of suppressed longing that shied from an exposure too intimate to bear under scrutiny. "The crone gave me the choice at the last. Lifelong exile, or transcendent passage beyond the veil under the sentence of Tehaval's judgement."

Asandir softened. "But the lady is under no such constraint." Her term of service as Tysan's steward would finish at Avenor, once the sanctioned crown heir was enthroned, and beyond further need of her counsel. The *caithdein*'s charge would be passed to another, with Davien's given longevity yet to extend through the course of another century. "She could, as she chooses, return here of her own accord, by free will."

"I have friends!" Daliana interjected, too proud to give over her spirited independence. Gone were the days when she would devalue her endowments. Hard earned self-worth refused the young girl's heady impulse to chase after a man to rectify his entrenched short-falls, far less bother to launder the self-imposed arrogance of his mistakes.

Lysaer's smile burst through, wry with the rare honesty she treasured yet in remembrance. "I have time on my hands to be patient." Then chaffing, perhaps to shield the spark of his vulnerable aspiration, "May I write?"

Asandir's stern demeanour cracked before that fresh bent for humility. "Address your letters by name to Sethvir. He hears what directly concerns him." Obliged to accompany Tysan's *caithdein* and acknowledge two kingdoms' delegations coming ashore, the field Sorcerer finished the statement over his shoulder. "Althain's Warden has a nosy, sharp knack for transcription, and a fair hand with a very long reach. Be sure he'll see your words are delivered wherever Daliana decides to go next."

Late Spring – Early Summer 6086

Finale

On the morning Arithon s'Ffalenn returned through Daon Ramon's free wilds to fulfil his promise to High Queen Regent Merevalia, he entered Ithamon with Elaira at his side. The ambient flux current upon his arrival no longer sang the resonant harmonic of desolation. Framed once again by the backdrop of golden vales, the tiered walls had been lifted from ruin. The soaring splendour of magnificent artistry renewed a wonder once thought lost to the world, except in the record of bygone history.

Paravian masons had restored the main gate arch in granite block. Flecked mica and veined pyrite sparkled in full sun against spring's azure sky. The names a sanctioned crown prince once vowed to honour were inscribed there by chisel and mallet at the behest of Tehaval's archivists. Their meticulous care had failed none of their memories. Shaken, Arithon ran his hands over the graven tribute: Steiven and Dania, Caolle and Earl Jieret's; a mountain trapper who had died faithful; Feylind and Teive, Dhirken and Tarens, Cosach and Khadrien, Siantra and Esfand, with a shining wisp of melody appended in commemoration for the master mentor, Halliron sen Al'Duin. The roll call included too many more: the unforgotten ghosts of his past who had lifted him, selfless, to stand here, where the reclaimed Song of the Mysteries endowed the heart of Rathain's hallowed ground.

Dark head bent, Arithon laced his arm around Elaira, silenced by gratitude for the accolade granted to his cherished dead. Then, together, he and his mate acknowledged their difficult trials and stepped through.

Deserted no longer, the avenue leading upwards to Ithamon's eyrie overlook rang with the plink of the stone workers' mallets. Warm air bore the scent of sheared mineral. The mercuric shimmer of heightened flux mantled the transformation wrought by skilled centaur workmanship. Mossed over footings refashioned in marble jetted with fountains and lapped ripples to the playful breeze, or shone, mirror still, in graceful placement as reflecting pools. Gardens and flowering vines and carved marker stones led the traveller upwards, layer on level, the vertical scarp tiered like a cliff swallows' colony with dwellings for the diminutive Athlien.

The sparkle and flash of the Severnir girdled the hypocaust of the old bath, now reclothed in rich earth and tended with the blossomed seedlings of nut trees and orchards. Atop the high crag, the Compass Point Towers sheared upwards, centred by the incomplete spire of the King's keep arisen, halfway rebuilt on the ancient foundation. Surrounded by the shy bustle of sunchildren's industry, and the grind of the sledges hauling uncut block, pulled on stout ropes to the rhythmic chant that unified centaur muscle, only the deafened might not pause to linger, undone, by the fifth lane's resurgent harmony.

The stone stair leading upwards switched back, dizzy height unfolding the broadscale view of Daon Ramon, vales strung one on the next in an ocean of grassland dotted with rowan and cedar. Riathan frisked in the distance, the effusive joy unleashed in their proximity flaring the excited flux incandescent.

Elaira trembled in Arithon's arms, paused for a breath-taken moment to marvel upon the profound expansion bestowed by their altered perception. The blinding light of the Paravian presence no longer unbalanced them. Pure impact, the undilute surge of ecstasy, did not blind their once-mortal senses. The crucible of initiate experience had been annealed into their flesh by the legacy of the dragons.

The poignant moment pierced the unguarded heart and seared the dross off worn spirits. For the triumphant journey had left them blessed beyond the measure of their human birthright.

Rushed giddy by the tug of beguilement, Arithon swept his beloved into a kiss, broken short by her tender remonstrance. "We have an appointment to be met in state. Remember?"

Equinox would not wait on their dalliance, nor was their privacy sacrosanct. Above the next landing, the Centaur Legion turned out in parade arms to meet them in glittering ceremony, chased armour and jewelled caparisons storied in three Ages of legend and history. Cianor Moonlord Reborn fell in step with a double-file escort, leading them into the open-air court, circled by high, pillared arches clothed in rustling ivy and drenched in the fragrance of flowering roses.

There, amid dappled shade, the Paravian Conclave waited in solemn assembly. Above the steps of a circular dais, Merevalia held the regent's seat on a winged, carved chair. Her exquisite grace was clothed in dazzling raiment, velvet deep as moonless midnight spattered with radiant stars and adorned at hemline and cuffs with small birds worked in peridot and gleaming embroidery. To her right hand, upon taloned feet, reared the black edifice of the Paravian throne, incised with the triplicate spirals symbolic of Athera's great mysteries. The tasselled cushion of velvet lay vacant, but for a simple, twined circlet of silver set with three cabochon emeralds.

Arithon drew Elaira forward. Bareheaded, with Alithiel sheathed at his hip, he came before the august congress whose wisdom guided the unity of the Concord that allied the Dragon Protectorate. He wore only commonplace field leathers musked with the wild briar and sweetgrass ingrained by cross-country travel. In humility that assumed nothing, with Elaira steadfast at his shoulder, he bent his knee before those gathered as the supplicant with naught to offer beyond his empty hands. "I am come to fill the vow of service made to your High Grace at Forthmark."

To his dismay, the High Queen Regent arose. She descended the dais. Stepped into full sunlight, shining, she bowed before both of them, the feathered shell ornaments and pearls twined through her jet hair chiming like ethereal bells. "Welcome, Falyrionient."

Arithon gasped. His shocked cry of protest, and Elaira's surprise, raised the silvery peal of the sunchild's laughter. "My regency ends here. Had you not guessed? The high seat at Ithamon shall stand empty no longer. Arithon, accept the accolade and take up the Crown of Paravia."

Arithon flinched as though kicked in the chest. "Lady, High Grace, I am at your disposal, but of all things under Ath's glory asked of me, please, I beg for your mercy, not this!" He had finished his obligate tie to Rathain; had striven mightily hard to be quit of the onus of imperial rule. The feal charge too often had strapped him with bitter regrets, inflicted at punishing cost.

Yet his debt to the Teirendalient Merevalia bound him. He would not be forsworn, though the gilded cage of her obligation hobbled his happiness and collared him, body and spirit.

"My brave, sweet Masterbard!" Merevalia's smile was moonlight and pearl beneath the midnight coil of hair, ablaze with a constellation of miniature gemstones. "Your service yielded to Athera is not punishment." The gossamer sheen of her being stirred rippled harmonics, breathing the fragrance of honeysuckle. She took his hand in tiny fingers, perfect and gleaming with exquisite jade rings. "You have misappraised the purpose that founds the Paravian throne. Our sovereigns do not hold governing sway over others! Quite the contrary. They are equal among us, the voice given to translate the mysteries and the appointed keepers of natural harmony. They are the picked cream of our most gifted healers, and the master musicians whose exalted art leads the dance. You and your lady are welcomed among us with peerless delight. Did the Seven not tell you? The office that awaits you, and that of your mate, is never given, but claimed."

Arithon Teirient'Daelient, First Falyrionient allowed the fairest beloved of the elder sunchildren to raise him. Dark head bent in reverence, he kissed Merevalia's hand and lent solemn voice to his gratitude.

For a suspended moment, the song and the glory of Ithamon's restored flux flamed around him. Since taking altruistic leave of his grandsire to rebuild an impoverished realm on a splinter world's islet, he had conquered regret. The reconciled gifts of music and talent, perfected, had brought him finally home. Not alone, never without the constant lodestar at every step on his path, Arithon had forged his way always by Elaira's light come before him.

More than his fleeting smile acknowledged his beloved, in partnered agency at his side.

"Very well." Sparked by a glimmer of mischief, the first human being to be acknowledged for the Paravian accession gave the High Queen Regent's abdication his attentive rebuke. "But only until our gifts are surpassed."

"Have you neglected history?" Merevalia chaffed him, amused as she threaded an arm through Elaira's and drew them up the stair to applause, and the bone-shaking, thunderous fanfare as the Centaur Legion winded the hundredfold voice of their dragon-spine horns. "The traditional term of high office dictates the terms of succession. The royal seat is passed down for three generations, and only through your wedded mate's direct progeny."

* * *

In the top-floor library at Althain Tower, Sethvir set down his dipped quill. Misty, turquoise eyes glazed with distance strayed from his penned page of manuscript a moment before the thumped step echoed upwards from the turnpike stair. Delivered onto the landing at length, the rumpled, puffing commotion took pause for a muffled knock at his door.

Sethvir stifled a chuckle behind a pensive fist. "Come ahead."

Dakar the Mad Prophet shuffled over his threshold. Wheezing, more than usually pink in the face, he blurted, "I came back because I wish to study in residence here."

Sethvir's stare became owlish, his untidy hair fine as cobweb under the shafted light through the casement.

Dakar sniffed. Nerves rattled, he advanced his persistent appeal, shuffled steps paused before the ebon-stone table. He managed to sit without stubbing his toe, or banging a maladroit shin on the carved snout of the coiled dragon pedestal. The antique chair creaked under his replete bulk. He had eaten well in the aftermath of the strained hour three spirits he valued had seen their deliverance from Rockfell Pit.

A Fellowship Sorcerer's silence gave him nothing by way of encouragement.

Master Spellbinder, expected to place his appeal on his own, Dakar clasped clammy palms to subdue his impulse to fidget. He ploughed on, contrite, but determined, "I am too portly for field work, unsuited to the rigours of travel and hardship. Asandir's tired of being held up by my blundering, and I love my comforts too much." On a deep breath, sweating, he plunged into the gist. "I thought I might ask. To apply for the chance to know if my seer's gift is suitable for expansion under your guidance. Perhaps as the prelude foundation to develop the access for broadscale vision."

Sethvir twiddled his goose quill, his creased, pixie features not astonished. "You wish the inaugural study to access Athera through simultaneous probability and planetwide vision?"

"I could learn." Dakar cleared his throat behind a plump fist. "Apply myself seriously." Brown eyes direct, he straightened his shoulders, and added, "You Seven have earned a reprieve, now the Mistwraith is banished, and Mankind has stepped up to shoulder their responsible share of world citizenship."

Sethvir snorted, ink-spotted fingers tickled by the frizzled spill of his beard. "Partly true." The Falyrionient had claimed the Paravian succession, in fact. And Seshkrozchiel's tutelage steered Siantra and Esfand to serve as the Gatekeeper's liaison to uphold the Treaty Accord that reined the wild drakes upon Sckaithen Duin into check. "Though humanity as a whole is not *quite* yet evolved to assume their proficient partnership as Athera's fourth race."

"I suppose," Dakar allowed, intimidated more than a little by the Sorcerers' long-range aspiration. "The Light's temples aren't going to fall down on their own."

Sethvir's mouth twitched. "Won't they?" Teeth flashed, split into a devilsome smile. "Paravian presence is waking the mysteries. Stone itself may decide to cease the cooperative support that upholds their unhallowed foundations. I might suggest, in a century, the True Sect may become an untenable order. Roofless, impoverished, and reft of their cause for a pretentious war, they are parasites. Do you imagine their priests can sustain themselves in righteous pomp on the trumped-up charity of the faithful?"

"I would live for the day to see the exploitive penchant for dogma collapse. The overburden placed on the Fellowship's provenance will grow lighter. You may have idle time." Paused to squirm, then caved to his nerves, Dakar pleaded, "You might wish extra hands to help mind the housekeeping here whenever things get a bit rough."

In fact, the initiate mind's need for solitude grew to miss the old tower's relentless wards and fast silence. The place had become home more than anywhere else Dakar had hunkered down through the centuries. His fondness for the wild sweep of Atainia had grown through the decades during the Sorcerer's absence. Verrain had his outpost at Methisle. Dakar ached as never before with the urge to set down lasting roots.

"I daresay," Sethvir allowed at due length. The knotted affairs of the towns were ripe for shake-up and strife, as Athera's resonant mysteries unfurled at full bore through the scope of the upcoming shift in the balance of power. "Be sure we've not seen every parcel of mischief Mankind will require our diligent guard to dismantle."

The Khadrim and Mirthlvain's monsters between them brewed up incidents like sown teeth. Other drake spawn bound under restraint required deathless vigilance, as well as a blacksmith's child born of Torbrand's descent at Ganish, with as wicked a temperament. Through the years he matured and fathered offspring in lineal descent, perhaps one would be suited for royal sanction and the attunements of Rathain's human crown.

Sethvir tidied his thatched piles of manuscript, then ploughed a space between his cached books, by habit indulging his inclination to brew tea. Nonchalant, he said as he exhumed his mug, "Is this an application to succeed me as Warden? Would you undertake an earth-linked aware-ness for curbing Mankind's shortsighted excesses?"

Dakar choked. "Ath wept!" Beet red, he composed himself. "What better candidate could you select? Who else but someone who outgrew his grave flaws could apprehend the short-falls of his imperfect fellows?"

"You'll have to conquer your aversion to direct interaction with Tehaval Warden and obtain his grant of permission." Althain's resident Sorcerer appointed with critical oversight of the earth-link stood up and rummaged after his battered pot and the pitcher kept filled with fresh water. "Do that, and for certain, I'm ready to listen."

The statement was near as Sethvir ever came to the finality of a commitment.

The tea caddy lurked in the aumbry, located by the fragrance of its past contents. Dakar fetched and carried, scrounged and wiped down two spoons, corking the opened inkwells he salvaged from the library's clutter en route. "One day, Mankind's maturity will bring your Fellowship's task to completion. When the dragons grant you their leave to abdicate, will you Sorcerers depart from Athera?"

Sethvir stopped, the opened jar of honey cupped in hand forgotten in wistful distraction. "Some of us, maybe." A gaze misted with distance perhaps parsed the long shadows cast across multiplied tracks of many thousandfold probable futures. "Don't you think we Seven love this world well enough to stay on awhile and enjoy the sweet fruits of our labour?"

Three Towers

Atop the lofty spire in south Shand, blind eyes fixed on the sun's disk at high noon, the ancient form of the Reiyaj Seeress crumbles to dust in her chair, her remains ceded to the wind and the elements; and released with her spirit, her vessel of service: the Mad Prophet's black-out seizures from absolute forevision never recur . . . .

Partnered with Elaira atop the Tower Kieling in Ithamon, High King Falyrionient, Athera's titled Masterbard, plays the heirloom lyranthe earned from Halliron sen Al'Duin, and art brought to full flower leads the Paravian dance to raise midsummer's grand confluence; and while the blazed peal of renewal unfurls, unicorn dams quicken with foal on Daon Ramon for the first time since the Mistwraith's invasion . . .

Seated beside Ciladis while midnight's stars turn above Althain Tower, and the resplendent song of Athera's mysteries, cresting, thrums through bone and flesh, Dakar reflects on the master musician he nearly had dismissed as a criminal: "How much did you Seven see from the start?" which prompts the dark Sorcerer's secretive smile, "Free will or destiny? Study long enough under Sethvir, and find out."

Epilogue

Time blurs the imperfect stamp of event. Layman's writ diverged over the question of Lysaer s'Ilessid's divinity. Eastern text states the godhead forsook the avatar as a fallen vessel under the influence of Paravian contact. Contrary views assert his corruption instead stemmed from deviant magecraft. Enshrined Canon insists their Lord of Light transcended death. Past exception, the stain of apostasy branded the faithful who took arms and strayed into Shadow in Daon Ramon. All sects agree the Religion of Light banned arcane pursuit as anathema thereafter.

The Master of Shadow and the name of Arithon s'Ffalenn vanished from human history, his fate after descent into Rockfell to vanquish the Mistwraith unknown. Althain Tower's archive claims with authority the First Falyrionient's accession as Paravia's High King spanned the threshold of Mankind's evolved partnership with the mysteries and cohabitation with Athera's exalted races. The recovered account confirms they were the same man.

Of the good and the evil, the Seventh-Age sages suggest that intent might inspire right action or error. Let the reader's perspective discern which distortions alter the framework of truth.

Glossary

ADRUIN—fortified coastal town in East Halla, Melhalla.

    pronounced: add ruin

    root meaning: *adruinne* – to block, or obstruct

AFFI'ENIA—name given to Elaira by an adept, meaning dancer in Biedar dialect, with the mystical connotation of 'water dancer', the wisewoman steering the ritual of rebirth, celebrated at spring equinox.

    pronounced: affee-yen-yah

    root meaning: *affi'enia* – dancer

AIYENNE RIVER—flows through Daon Ramon, Rathain, from an underground spring in the Mathorn Mountains, and emerges south of the Mathorn Road. Site of battle between Earl Jieret's war band and an Alliance host under Sulfin Evend, which enabled Arithon's escape in Third Age 5670.

    pronounced: eye-an

    root meaning: *ai'an* – hidden one

ALATHWYR TOWER—one of five towers raised by Paravians at Ithamon in the First Age, oriented at north, white-jasper walls bear the warded virtue of Wisdom.

    pronounced: ah-lath-weer

    root meaning: *alath* – to know; *wyr* – all, sum

ALESSIADIENT—command for absolute peace in actualized Paravian.

    pronounced: ah-less-ee-yad-ee-ent

    root meaning: *a'lessiad* – feminine prefix/balance; *ient* – suffix for 'the most' or 'the highest' form, the demand for absolute balance between all things

ALESTRON—town in Midhalla, Melhalla, built by Paravians with warded defences. Once seat of the s'Brydion earls, until entailment by the Fellowship Sorcerers closed the siege in Third Age 5672.

    pronounced: ah-less-tron

    root meaning: *alesstair* – stubborn; *an* – one

ALITHIEL—one of twelve Blades of Isaer, forged by centaur Ffereton s'Darian from a meteorite, inlaid by Athlien with arcane endowment for transcendent change, and infused by Riathan with the chord that Named the winter stars, which powers ignite only for a just cause. In Paravian possession, acquired the secondary name Dael-Farenn, or Kingmaker, as wielders often succeeded the change to a royal line.

Eventually awarded to Kamridian s'Ffalenn for valour in defence of the
Princess Taliennse, early Third Age, and passed down through his heirs.

    pronounced: ah-lith-ee-el

    root meaning: *alith* – star; *iel* – light/ray

ALLAND—principality in southeastern Shand, ruled by High Earl and
Caithdein of Shand.

    pronounced: all-and

    root meaning: *a'lind* – pine glen

ALTHAIN TOWER—spire built at the edge of the Bittern Desert, early
Second Age, to house antiquities and Paravian histories. Third Age,
archived the records after the rebellion, overseen by the Fellowship
Sorcerer, Sethvir, named Warden since Third Age 5100. Guarded by
the Ilitharis Paravian spirit of Shehane Althain.

    pronounced: all-thay-in

    root meaning: *alt* – last; *thein* – tower, sanctuary

    original Paravian pronunciation: alt-thein

AMROTH—kingdom ruled by s'Ilessid descendants sent to safety on
the splinter world Dascen Elur past west Worldsend Gate to spare
the royal bloodline from the rebellion in Third Age 5018.

    pronounced: am-roth

    root meaning: *am* – to exist, to be; *roth* – brother

AN'TIENI—trifold gift of Ath Creator, beings from Athili, the First
Dancers who awakened the mysteries in the First Age, some remained
as spirit consciousness, others became the Spirits of Light, the An'Ami,
the first Elders and progenitors of the three Paravian races.

    pronounced: ahn-tee-en-ee

    root meaning: *an* – one, first; *tien* – spirits

ANGLEFEN—large mire in northern Deshir, Rathain.

    pronounced: angle-fen

ANSHLIEN'YA—name given to Meiglin s'Dieneval by the Biedar tribe,
prior to her conception of Dari s'Ahelas, crown heir of Shand, bearer
of the rogue talent for farsighted vision.

    pronounced: ahn-shlee-yen-yah

    root meaning: *anshlien'ya* – dawn, idiom for hope, ancient Biedar
    dialect

ARAETHURA—grass plains in southwest Rathain; principality inhabited
by Riathan Paravians in the Second Age. Third Age, used as pasture-
land by nomadic shepherds.

pronounced: ar-eye-thoo-rah

root meaning: *araeth* – grass; *era* – place, land

ARAITHE—plain north of the trade city of Etarra, in the principality of Fallowmere, Rathain.

pronounced: a-ray-th-e, the final e being nearly subliminal

root meaning: *araithe* – to disperse, or send/properties of standing stones that temper the lane currents which once flowed unimpaired before Mankind settled the notch at Etarra.

ARITHON—son of Avar, Prince of Rathain, 1,504th Teir's'Ffalenn after founder of the line, Torbrand in Third Age Year One. Also Master of Shadow, the Bane of Desh-thiere, and Halliron Masterbard's successor. First among Mankind to tap the transcendent powers of the sword, Alithiel, and also responsible for the final defeat of the Grey Kralovir necromancers. Held captive by Koriathain from Third Age 5674 until his escape in 5922, condemned to death under a crown oath of debt, with a stay on his life bought by Fellowship intercession for the purpose of utilizing his Masterbard's title to subdue the free wraiths from Marak, and left to survive on his own merits under Asandir's oath of nonintervention.

pronounced: ar-i-thon

root meaning: *arithon* – fate-forger; one who is visionary

ARWENT GORGE—river in Araethura, Rathain, that flows from Daenfal Lake through Halwythwood to empty in Instrell Bay.

pronounced: are-went

root meaning: *arwient* – swiftest

ASANDIR—Fellowship Sorcerer. Secondary name, Kingmaker, since his hand crowned every high king of Men to rule in the Age of Mankind (Third Age). After the Mistwraith's conquest, acting field agent for Fellowship affairs across the continent. Also called Fiend-quencher for his reputation for quelling *iyats*; Storm-breaker and Change-bringer for his past actions when humanity first arrived upon Athera.

pronounced: ah-san-deer

root meaning: *asan* – heart; *dir* – stone "heart rock"

ATAINIA—northeastern principality of Tysan.

pronounced: ah-tay-nee-ah

root meaning: *itain* – the third; *ia* – suffix for "third domain" original Paravian, *itainia*

ATCHAZ—town in Alland, Shand, famed for silk.

pronounced: at-chaz

root meaning: *atchias* – silk

ATH CREATOR—prime vibration, force behind all life.

pronounced: ath

root meaning: *ath* – prime, first (as opposed to an, one)

ATH'S ADEPTS—initiate masters of the White Brotherhood who have achieved a state of transcendence.

ATHERA—name for the world which holds the Five High Kingdoms; four Worldsend Gates; formerly inhabited by dragons and current home of the Paravian races.

pronounced: ath-air-ah

root meaning: *ath* – prime force; *era* – place "Ath's world"

ATHILI—proscribed region at the border of Havish and Rathain, between the principalities of Lanshire and Araethura, site of the etheric portal created by Ath Creator to manifest the Paravian presence in the world.

pronounced: ah-thill-lee

root meaning: *ath* – prime force; *i'li* – a state of self-aware exaltation.

ATHIR—Second-Age ruin of a Paravian stronghold in Ithilt, Rathain, site of a seventh-lane power focus. There Arithon Teir's'Ffalenn swore a blood oath to survive to the Fellowship Sorcerer, Asandir. Location of Teylia's conception and Dakar's swearing Oath of Debt in behalf of Rathain's crown, to Koriathain under Fellowship auspices in Third Age 5671.

pronounced: ath-ear

root meaning: *ath* – prime; *i'er* – the line, or edge

ATHLIEN PARAVIANS—sunchildren, dancers of the crystal flutes. Race of semi-mortals, pixie-like, but possessed of great wisdom/keepers of the grand mystery.

pronounced: ath-lee-en

root meaning: *ath* – prime force; *lien* – to love "Ath-beloved"

ATHLIERIA—a dimension removed from physical time/space, or the exalted that lies past the veil.

pronounced: ath-lee-air-ee-ah

root meaning: *ath* – prime force; *li'eria* – exalted place, with suffix for 'beyond the veil'

ATTIN RIVER—northern branch of Isaer River, sourced from highlands in northern Atania, Tysan.

pronounced: ah-tin

root meaning: *a'tiend* – female dreamer

AVAR s'FFALENN—historic pirate King of Karthan on splinter world Dascen Elur through west Worldsend Gate, deceased in Third Age 5637, father of Arithon s'Ffalenn.

> pronounced: ah-var
>
> root meaning: *avar* – past thought or memory

AVAST RIVER—sourced in Rockfell Vale, flows southward into the Daenfal outflow's river route to Shipsport.

> pronounced: ah-vast
>
> root meaning: *a'vhast* – brown with female prefix

AVENOR—Second-Age ruin of a Paravian stronghold in Korias, Tysan. Traditional seat of the s'Ilessid High Kings. Restored in Third Age 5644 by the Alliance of Light. Destroyed by the wrath of Seshkrozchiel's drakefire for misuse of hatchling skulls in Third Age 5671.

> pronounced: ah-ven-or
>
> root meaning: *avie* – stag; *norh* – grove

AVILEFFIN—Ilitharis Paravian, greatest of the Second-Age master ship-wrights.

> pronounced: av-ill-eff-fin
>
> root meaning: *avie* – stag; *lieffen* – pale yellow hair

BAIYEN GAP—causeway and trail through the Skyshiel Mountains built by centaur guardians in First Age 198, connects Eltair coast with Daon Ramon Barrens. Twice the site of drake battles. Old right of way not sanctioned for Mankind's use.

> pronounced: bye-yen
>
> root meaning: *bayien* – slag

BARACH—former Earl of the North, second son of Jieret s'Valerient and older brother of Jeynsa; presided over Eriegal's trial for betrayal; brokered a peace treaty with Mayor Lysaer s'Ilessid in Third Age 5688; died Third Age 5712; forebear of Cosach s'Valerient and Esfand.

> pronounced: bar-ack
>
> root meaning: *baraich* – linchpin

BARRIS ETARRA—rogue squatter who took advantage of Charter Law's waning oversight in Third Age 4994 and rebuilt the fortified stockade in the Mathorn Pass dismantled by King Kamridian's edict 835 years prior. Charged illicit tolls for trade passage until settlement's expansion founded the walled town of Etarra on the site.

pronounced: bar-ris ee-tar-ah

root meaning: *bar* – half; *ris* – way; *e'* – prefix for small; *taria* – knots

BAYLIENNE'S GYRE—Baylienne s'Valerient, *Caithdein* of Riathan succumbed to grief in Third Age 5064 when the Mistwraith's advance darkened Halwythwood. In desperation, she dared to walk the gyre into the forbidden glade at Thembrel's Oak to plead for an intercession. Folly saw her emotional upset tear rifts in the resonant flux that sustained the mysteries upon sacred ground. Athlien dancers righted the imbalance, but in consequence, the Paravian High King, Vanomind Third Ithalivier, lost heart to despair at Mankind's desecrations, and retreated from Athera by immolation through the vortex at Athili.

pronounced: bay-lee-en

root meaning: *baie* – to snap or stress past a breaking point; *lien* – to love

BIEDAR—Tribal people living in Sanpashir, Shand, known as the Keepers of the Prophecy. Their sacred weaving at the well initiated the conception of Dari s'Ahelas, crossing the old *caithdein's* lineage of s'Dieneval, of half-bred descent from Requiar, with the s'Ahelas royal line, adding Biedar blood and the gift of prophetic clairvoyance to the Fellowship-endowed penchant for farsight.

pronounced: bee-dar

root meaning: *biehdahrr* – ancient desert dialect for "lore keepers"

BREIENALDIEN—Athlien bard whose lament in First Age 132 sung the barge bearing the Ilitharis Rialthan and his wounded beloved to their death rite beside Instrell Bay. The centaurs were attacked in the ecstasy of *abrend'aia* by resurgent Searduin, which wanton violence spurred the rogue dragons against the Dragon Protectorate's guardianship to mass spawn packs in assault at the Great Stand at Bittern Field in First Age 140.

pronounced: bre-ee-en-all-dee-en

root meaning: *breien* – patterner, creator of origin ; *aldien* – poet

BITTERN DESERT—waste in Atainia, Tysan, north of Althain Tower. Site of a First-Age battle between the great drakes and Searduin, permanently destroyed by dragon fire.

pronounced: bittern

root meaning: *bityern* – to sear or char

CAILCALLOW—herb brewed as an infusion for colds and congestion.
   pronounced: kale-callow
   root meaning: *cail* – leaf; *calliew* – balm

CAITH-AL-CAEN—vale at a major intersection of lane and flux
   currents, where Riathan Paravians celebrated equinox and solstice to
   renew the *athael*, or life-destiny of the world, and where the Paravians
   Named the winter stars—or encompassed their vibrational essence
   into actualized language. Birthplace of Cianor Sunlord.
   pronounced: cay-ith-all-cay-in
   root meaning: *caith* – shadow; *al* – over; *caen* – vale, or vale of
   shadow

CAITHDEIN—(alternate spelling *caith'd'ein*, plural form *caithdeinen*)
   Paravian name for a high king's first counsellor, charged with oversight
   and integrity of crowned royalty's fitness to rule; also would stand as
   regent, or steward, in the absence of the sanctioned sovereign.
   pronounced: kay-ith-day-in
   root meaning: *caith* – shadow; *d'ein* – behind the chair "shadow
   behind the throne"

CAITHWOOD—free-wilds forest in Taerlin, southeast principality of Tysan.
   pronounced: kay-ith-wood
   root meaning: *caith* – shadow – shadowed wood

CALLOWSWALE RIVER—flows west to east in Fallowmere, Rathain,
   seaward delta at East Ward.
   pronounced: cal-low-swale
   root meaning: *calliew* – balm; *swael* – gutter

CALUM QUAIDE KINCAID—headed the research team who developed
   enhanced fusion, basis for the great weapon of war that destroyed
   humanity's starfaring civilizations and sparked the refugee exodus
   that led to Mankind's settlement on Athera under the compact in
   Third Age Year One.

CAMRIS—north-central principality of Tysan. Original ruling seat at
   Erdane.
   pronounced: cam-ris
   root meaning: *caim* – cross; *ris* – way "cross-roads"

CANON LAW—doctrine of the True Sect, faction of the Religion of
   Light split away from the Alliance at the Great Schism in Third Age
   5673, when Lysaer denounced the High Temple at Miralt and returned
   to rule the mayor's seat at Etarra.

CAOLLE—past war captain of the clans of Deshir, Rathain. First raised, then served under, Lord Steiven, Earl of the North and *Caithdein* of Rathain. Captained the campaign at Vastmark and Dier Kenton Vale for the Master of Shadow. Served Jieret Red-beard, sworn as liegeman to Arithon of Rathain; died of a wound dealt by his prince while thwarting a Koriani plot to entrap his liege in Third Age 5653.

    pronounced: kay-all-eh, with the "e" nearly subliminal

    root meaning: *caille* – stubborn

CARITHWYR—principality in Havish, ancient breeding ground for Riathan Paravians.

    pronounced: car-ith-ear

    root meaning: *ci'arithiren* – forgers of the link with prime power, colloquialism for unicorn.

CEFTWINN s'LORNMEIN—High Queen of Havish, crowned by Asandir in Third Age 5923, after her brother Gestry died in the Battle of Lithmarin, defeating the True Sect invasion led by the Hatchet.

    pronounced: kef-twin slorn-main

    root meaning: *kef* – jasper; *tuinne* – rose; *liernmein* – to centre or bring into balance

CENTAUR GUARDIANS—Ilitharis Paravians ritually bound to the land to protect and anchor high-resonance sites on Athera. The connection transcended time and space, with the suffix *erach*, appended to their names, denoting their root to that place.

CEYNNIA—a promising young initiate of the Koriathain.

    pronounced: say-nee-ah

    root meaning: *cian* – spark; *i'on* – a line of fate/destiny

CHAIMISTARIZOG—Elder dragon in standing as Guardian of Northgate to enforce the Treaty Accord banishing the factions of drakes who dissented with the Dragons' Protectorate to exile on the splinter world of Sckaithen Duin, called Fortress of Dragons.

    pronounced: shay-mist-tar-ee-zog

    root meaning: *chaimistarizog* – Drakish for fire gate keeper

CHESHETICAX—dragon matriarch, mate of rogue king, Syfeshkazion, hatched in turn from Tachymirizhen and Bechashimol's clutch of four, historically called 'Scourge of Mhorovaire'; her vengeful offspring align with the rogue factions upon Sckaithen Duin against the Treaty Accord.

    pronounced: chess-shet-ee-cacks

    root meaning: *chesheticax* – Drakish for rage-poison

CIANOR SUNLORD/CIANOR MOONLORD—centaur of legend born at Caith-al-Caen, First Age 615. Crowned High King of Athera in Second Age 2545, until his death in Second Age 3651. He is the only Paravian in history to rebirth in spirit, a *tiendar'shayn'd* or "reborn". Cianor Moonlord, reincarnate at the darkest hour of the Second Age, was present in Third Age Year One when the Fellowship Sorcerers wrote the Compact that enabled Mankind's settlement. His hand bestowed the sword Alithiel on Kamridian s'Ffalenn for valour. Bearer of the Isaervian sword Darisain, and the dragon-spine horn of Skenivarichel.

> pronounced: key-ah-nor
>
> root meaning: *cianor* – to shine

CILADIS—Fellowship Sorcerer who vanished in Third Age 5462 . Gone to stabilize the Paravian races in refuge on Los Lier after Mankind's upheaval caused their exodus, he fell prey to his own enchantment awaiting the Mistwraith's defeat, wakened by Arithon in Third Age 5925, and returned to Althain Tower in 5926.

> pronounced: kill-ah-dis
>
> root meaning: *cael* – leaf; *adeis* – whisper, compound; *cael'adeis*, "gentleness that abides"

CILDEIN OCEAN—blue water off the east coast of the continent of Paravia.

> pronounced: kill-dine
>
> root meaning: *cailde* – salty; *an* – one

CILDORN—a Paravian holdfast, now a trade town in Deshir, Rathain, famed for woven carpets.

> pronounced: kill-dorn
>
> root meaning: *cieal* – thread; *dorn* – net, 'tapestry'

CONCORD—Alliance formed by the Paravian Crown Conclave and the Dragon Protectorate that summoned the Fellowship Sorcerers and quelled dispute with the rogue factions by the Treaty Accord exiling those dragons who rejected Paravian sovereignty on Athera to Sckaithen Duin.

CONDELEINN—centaur guardian whose doomed stand against Seardluin at Mirthlvain's Second Wall in Second Age 6280 failed to stem a disastrous outbreak of Methspawn during the reign of High King Kidorn First Elrienient. The memorial megalith bearing his name marks the site where he fell in defence.

> pronounced: kon-de-lay-yin
>
> root meaning: *cond'e'leinn* – loves small argument/contentious

CORDAYA s'VALERIENT—daughter of High Earl Cosach and Jalienne, sister of Esfand, born in Third Age 5923.

>pronounced: kor-day-aa sval-er-ee-ent

>root meaning: *kordi-a* – newborn; *val* – straight; *erient* – spear

CORITH—ruin on the isle of Caincyr in the Westland Sea, site of a drake lair and a First-Age ruin, last remnant of the sunken continent of Mhorovaire, main keep of the Eliathe principality after the fall of Dalghaire, and the fortress where the Paravian Conclave assembled while under siege by drake spawn, allied with the Dragon Protectorate for the Great Dreaming which summoned the Fellowship of Seven to Athera.

>pronounced: core-ith

>root meaning: *cori* – ships, vessels; *itha* – five, for the five harbours

COSACH s'VALERIENT—Earl of the North and *Caithdein* of Rathain, husband of Jalienne, father of Esfand and Cordaya, died in Third Age 5924 fighting an armed incursion in Daon Ramon Barrens.

>pronounced: co-sack s-val-er-ee-ent

>root meaning: *cosak* – bluster; *val* – straight; *erient* – spear

DACE MARLEY—alias of Daliana sen Evend, in service as valet to Lysaer s'Ilessid.

>pronounced: days mar-lee

>root meaning: *dace* – two; *marle* – quartz rock

DACE'AM—the sires and dams quickened in the Second Dance, sprung from the An'tieni, 'Beings of Light', Ath's gift of consciousness sent to Athera through Athili as progenitors of the Paravians.

>pronounced: dack-e-am

>root meaning: *dace'am* – second being

DAELION FATEMASTER—"entity" formed by mortal beliefs, which determines the fate of the spirit after death. If Ath is the prime vibration, or life force, Daelion governs the manifestations of free will.

>pronounced: day-el-ee-on

>root meaning: *dael* – king, or lord; *i'on* – of fate

DAELION'S WHEEL—cycle of life and crossing point at the transition into death.

>pronounced: day-el-ee-on

>root meaning: *dael* – king or lord; *i'on* – of fate

DAELTHAIN—King's Tower, fifth keep raised by centaurs in Ithamon, binding virtue was Justice, fell to ruin on the eve of High King Marin Eliathe's death in Second Age 1542 at the hand of an assassin possessed by Methuri. The remnant foundation is the site of a Paravian focus circle.

> pronounced: day-el-thay-in
>
> root meaning: *dael* – king, lord; *thein* – tower, sanctuary

DAENFAL—lake and town on the northern lakeshore that bounds the southern edge of Daon Ramon Barrens in Rathain. Site of Arwent ferry, and also the ancient necropolis where Paravians once honoured their dead. Site of Arithon and Valien's execution by True Sect priesthood.

> pronounced: dye-en-fall
>
> root meaning: *daen* – clay; *fal* – red

DAKAR THE MAD PROPHET—apprentice to Fellowship Sorcerer, Asandir, during the Third Age after the Conquest of the Mistwraith. Master Spellbinder and gifted seer, Dakar forecast the fall of the Kings of Havish allowing Fellowship intervention to save the heir. His Prophecy of Westgate predicted the Mistwraith's Bane, and the Black Rose Prophecy, which foresaw reunification of the Seven.

> pronounced: dah-kar
>
> root meaning: *dakiar* – clumsy

DALIANA sen EVEND—descendant of Sulfin Evend, Asandir's chosen heir to the s'Gannley lineage.

> pronounced: dah-lee-ahn-a sen-ev-and
>
> root meaning: *dal* – fair; *lien* – harmony; *a* – feminine suffix; *sen* – descended of; *eiavend* – diamond

DANIA—mother of Jieret s'Valerient, wife of Steiven, *Caithdein* of Rathain, massacred at Tal Quorin in Third Age 5638.

> pronounced: da-nee-ah
>
> root meaning: *deinia* – sparrow

DAON RAMON BARRENS—central principality of Rathain and ancient breeding ground for Riathan Paravians. Barrens appended after the Mistwraith's conquest, when Mankind's diversion of the River Severnir at Darkling dried the fertile plain. Battlefield where Lysaer's Sunwheel war host cornered the Master of Shadow and met their defeat by clan war bands and Jieret s'Valerient's transcendence in 5670.

> pronounced: day-on-rah-mon
>
> root meaning: *daon* – gold; *ramon* – hills/downs

DARI s'AHELAS—crown heir of Shand sent through Westgate after the uprising. Daughter of the last Crown Prince of Shand born to Meiglin, descendant of the s'Dieneval line of seers, and the second *caithdein* lineage of Melhalla of half-breed Biedar blood and Requiar's descent, she was raised and taught by Sethvir to manage the rogue talent of a dual inheritance.

    pronounced: dar-ee sa-hell-as

    root meaning: *daer* – to cut; *ahelas* – mage-gifted

DARISAIN—Isaervian blade, of the twelve forged by Ffereton s'Darian, endowed with the element Fire and the song of the midsummer stars, wielded by Cianor Sunlord at the binding of the Great Gethorn in Second Age 618. Currently borne by Cianor Moonlord Reborn.

    pronounced: dar-is-ay-en

    root meaning: *daer'isain* – black flame, light that cleaves above the visible spectrum.

DARKLING DAM—built by Mankind in Third Age 5063, diverted the Severnir River's flow eastward across the Skyshiel divide, leaving Daon Ramon's lush grassland a barrens, and driving the Paravian presence from the most fertile Riathan breeding ground.

    pronounced: dark-ling

    root meaning: *dierk-linng* – drake eyrie

DASCEN ELUR—splinter world linked through the West Worldsend Gate, connected to Mearth; primarily ocean, that harbours the lesser kraken, with scattered archipelagos inhabited by the kingdoms of Amroth, Rauven, and Karthan, birthplace of Lysaer s'Ilessid and Arithon s'Ffalenn.

    pronounced: dass-sen ell-ur

    root meaning: *dacsen* – ocean; *e'lier* – small land

DAVIEN THE BETRAYER—Fellowship Sorcerer responsible for provoking the great uprising in Third Age 5018, which resulted in the fall of the high kings after Desh-thiere's conquest. Rendered discorporate by the Shehane Althain's judgement in Third Age 5129. Exiled since, by personal choice. Davien's works included the Five Centuries Fountain near Mearth on the splinter world of the Red Desert through West Gate; the shaft at Rockfell Peak, used by the Sorcerers to imprison harmful entities; the Stair on Rockfell Peak; and also, Kewar Tunnel in the Mathorn Mountains. Restored as a corporate being through Asandir's interaction with the Great Drake, Seshkrozchiel during banishment of the Scarpdale grimward in Third Age 5671. Bound to the dragon's service until Luhaine took his place when the dragon went into hibernation in Third Age 5923.

pronounced: dah-vee-en

root meaning: *dahvi* – fool; *an* – one "mistaken one"

DESHIR—northwestern principality of Rathain.

pronounced: desh-eer

root meaning: *deshir* – misty

DESH-THIERE—Mistwraith that invaded Athera from the splinter worlds through Southgate in Third Age 4993. Access cut off by Fellowship Sorcerer, Traithe. Battled and contained in West Shand for twenty-five years, until a town rebellion splintered the peace, forcing the high kings to withdraw their defence in Third Age 5018. Imprisoned by Lysaer s'Ilessid's gift of light and Arithon s'Ffalenn's gift of shadow in Third Age 5638, and contained under wards in the shaft of Rockfell Pit.

pronounced: desh-thee-air-e (last "e" mostly subliminal)

root meaning: *desh* – mist; *thiere* – ghost or wraith

DHARKARON AVENGER—mythical entity called Ath's Avenging Angel, drives a chariot drawn by five horses to convey the guilty to Sithaer. Dharkaron as defined by Ath's white adepts is the dark thread mortal men weave with the prime vibration, that creates self-punishment, or unreconciled guilt.

pronounced: dark-air-on

root meaning: *dhar* – evil; *khiaron* – one who stands in judgement

DHIRKEN—lady captain of contraband brig, Black Drake, killed by Lysaer's allies for a business liaison with Arithon s'Ffalenn in Third Age 5647.

pronounced: dur-kin

root meaning: *dierk* – tough; *an* – one

DIARIN s'GANNLEY—daughter of *caithdein*'s lineage of Tysan, handfast to a Westwood clan chieftain, but wedded to the Mayor of Hanshire by abduction. Ancestor of Sulfin Evend and Daliana.

pronounced: die-are-in

root meaning: *diarin* – a precious or coveted object

DIENT HAYLIOS—the high circle of Paravian seers.

pronounced: dee-yent hay-lee-ohs

root meaning: *dient* – greatest, highest; *halios* – visionaries, seers, scribes of white light

DIRENTIR—Second-Age ruin with a Paravian focus circle in Deshir, Rathain.

    pronounced: deer-en-teer

    root meaning: *dir* – stone; *era* – place; *tir* – hold

DRAGON-SKULL WARDS—dark practice artefacts created in Third Age 5010 from skulls of hatchling dragons, decanted alive from stolen eggs and ritually killed, then inset with rubies and ebony. Wielded at the four quarters, the constructs shielded acts of black necromancy from Athera's visionary seers, concealing the alliance between Grey Kralovir, Koriathain, and Hanshire's mayor that fomented the uprising to unseat the thrones in Third Age 5018. Destroyed by Seshkrozchiel's drakefire, a vengeful retaliation that consumed Lysaer's capital at Avenor in Third Age 5671.

DRAKE SPAWN—life created, or altered in form, by the dreaming of Dragonkind.

DRIMWOOD—free-wilds forest in Fallowmere, Rathain.

    pronounced: drim-wood

    root meaning: *driem* – fir tree

DURN—trade town in Orvandir, Shand. Birthplace of Meiglin s'Dieneval.

    pronounced: dern

    root meaning: *diern* – a flat plain

DYSHENT—trade port known for timber on the coast of Instrell Bay, Tysan.

    pronounced: dye-shent

    root meaning: *dyshient* – cedar

EAST BRANSING—town on the coast of Instrell Bay in Tysan.

    pronounced: bran-sing

    root meaning: *brienseng* – at the base, at the bottom

EAST HALLA—principality in Melhalla

    pronounced: east hall-ah

    root meaning: *hal'lia* – white light

EASTWALL—trade town in Skyshiel Mountains, Rathain.

EFFLIN—born a croft holder near Kelsing, and older brother of Tarens and Kerelie.

    pronounced: eff-lin

    root meaning: *e* – prefix for small; *ffael* – dark; *en* – suffix for 'more'; *effaelin* – a dark mood

ELAIRA—initiate enchantress of the Koriathain, healer who served the order as a wandering independent until the Seven released her vows. Began as a street child, fell afoul of the law, and inducted by the sisterhood at Morvain at six years of age. Arithon's beloved, handfast to Rathain in Third Age 5672.

> pronounced: ee-layer-ah
>
> root meaning: *e* – prefix, diminutive for small; *laere* – grace

ELLAINE—daughter of the Lord Mayor of Erdane, once Princess of Avenor by marriage to Lysaer s'Ilessid, and mother of Kevor s'Ilessid, who became an adept of Ath's Brotherhood.

> pronounced: el-lane

ELRIENIENT—Paravian dynasty founded by the Athlien, Kidorn Elrien. Ruled the high seat at Ithamon unto the third generation from Second Age 5126 to 10,560, uncrowned heirs carried the Isaervian sword Iaimon.

> pronounced: el-ree-en-ee-ent
>
> root meaning: *el* – short; *rien* – stride or step ; *ient* – suffix for highest, most

ELSHIAN—Athlien Paravian bard and master luthier who crafted the prized instrument held by Athera's titled Masterbard.

> pronounced: el-shee-an
>
> root meaning: *e'alshian* – small wonder, or miracle

ELSSINE—port town in Alland, Shand, renowned for superb steel, ship's ballast, and granite.

> pronounced: el-seen
>
> root meaning: *elssien* – small pit

ELTAIR BAY—body of water on the east shore of Rathain.

> pronounced: el-tay-er
>
> root meaning: *dascen al'tieri* – ocean of steel

ENITHEN TUER—sisterhood's name for Biedar Audua Sedjii An Teshua, lastborn of Hasidii's lineage. Stole the artefact knife from her tribe, joined the Order of the Koriathain but failed to eradicate her ancestral knowledge from the order. Released from her oath by Asandir of the Fellowship, resided as a seeress in Erdane and guested the s'Ilessid and s'Ffalenn princes of Requiar's lineage in Third Age 5637. Died after she released the Biedar knife to Sulfin Evend to free Lysaer s'Ilessid from necromancy in Third Age 5670.

> pronounced: en-ith-en too-er
>
> root meaning: *en'wethen* – farsighted; *tuer* – crone

ERDANE—Paravian site given over to Mankind's rule; seat of the old
Princes of Camris and the s'Gannley bloodline until the uprising in
Third Age 5018 hastened Desh-thiere's conquest. Became an iniquitous
nest of necromancy in the years following, then sited the True Sect High
Temple of the Light since the Great Schism in 5683, when the Light's
priests signed the First Book of Canon Law into doctrine in 5691.

> pronounced: er-day-na with the last syllable almost subliminal
>
> root meaning: *er'deinia* – long walls

ESFAND s'VALERIENT—*Caithdein* of Rathain's heir designate in Third
Age 5922, son of Cosach s'Valerient and Jalienne.

> pronounced: es-fand s'val-er-ee-ent
>
> root meaning: *esfan* – iron; *d* – suffix for behind; *val* – straight;
> *erient* – spear

ETARRA—trade town built in the Mathorn Pass after the revolt that over-
threw the High King of Rathain at Ithamon. Nest of corruption and
intrigue, and shaped policy for the North. Lysaer s'Ilessid was ratified as
mayor upon Morfett's death in Third Age 5667. Site where Arithon defeated
the Kralovir necromancers in Third Age 5671. Seat of the Alliance armed
forces, under Lysaer s'Ilessid, since the Great Schism in Third Age 5683,
until True Sect priests usurped the Mayor's authority in Third Age 5923.

> pronounced: ee-tar-ah
>
> root meaning: *e* – prefix for small; *taria* – knots

ETTIN—White Brotherhood hostel in the Storlain Mountains, Ghent,
Havish, commandeered by secession by shamans, and restored to
purview of Ath's adepts, Third Age 5925.

> pronounced: et-tin
>
> root meaning: *ettend'era* – slow place

ETTINMERE SETTLEMENT—insular village in the Storlain Mountains
in Ghent, Havish.

> pronounced: et-tin-meer
>
> root meaning: *etennd'miere* – a place that parted ways, slowed down
> and went separate

EVENSTAR—brig captained by Feylind, destroyed in the siege of
Alestron in Third Age 5671.

EVRAND—sister's son of Khadrien s'Valerient's granddame, heir designate *Caithdein* of Rathain.

> pronounced: ev-rand
>
> root meaning: *evrand* – eight

FALHENCH RIVER—flows east into Eltair Bay from Ithilt, Rathain.
  pronounced: fall-hensh
  root meaning: *fal* – red; *hench* – sand
FALLOWMERE—principality in northern Rathain.
  pronounced: fall-oh-meer
  root meaning: *fal'ei'miere* – 'the place of perfect trees'
FALWOOD—free-wilds forest in West Shand.
  pronounced: fall-wood
  root meaning: *fal* – red
FALYRIONIENT—name given to Arithon by the Paravian High Queen Regent.
  pronounced: fal-ee-ree-on-ee-ent
  root meaning: *ffael'lyrionient* – dark master bard
FARL ROCKS—First Age 218 watchpoint and beacon, standing stones erected in Daon Ramon Barrens, Rathain, also channelled the flux crest raised by the Paravian dancers at equinox and solstice.
  pronounced: far-l
  root meaning: *ffael* – dark
FEITHAN—wife of Jieret s'Valerient, mother of Jeynsa, widowed in Third Age 5670, remarried to Rathain's liegeman Sidir, founders of the named clan lineage s'Idir, talented with truth sense.
  pronounced: fay-than
  root meaning: *feiathen* – ivy
FATE'S WHEEL—see Daelion's Wheel.
FELLOWSHIP OF SEVEN—Sorcerers bound to Athera by the summoning dream of the Dragon Protectorate and charged to secure the mysteries that enable Paravian survival. Achieved their redemption from Cianor Sunlord, under the Law of the Major Balance in Second Age Year One. Originators and keepers of the covenant of the compact allowing Mankind's provisional settlement on Athera in Third Age Year One. Their authority backs charter law, upheld by crown justice and clan oversight of the free wilds.
FFEREDON'LI—ancient Paravian healer, 'bringer of grace' – name given to Elaira by an Araethurian seer at the birth of the child Fionn Areth Caid-an, Third Age 5647.
  pronounced: fair-eh-dun-lee
  root meaning: *ffaraton* – maker; *li* – exalted grace

FFERETON s'DARIAN—centaur armourer of legend who forged the
twelve Blades of Isaer to fight drake spawn in Second Age 391.
>pronounced: fer-et-on s'dar-ee-on
>root meaning: *ffereton* – craftsman, maker; *s'darian* – descendant
>of the first cutter

FIONN ARETH CAID'AN—born in Araethura in Third Age 5647,
shape-changed as Arithon's double by Koriathain as bait for an
entrapment, rescued from execution for Arithon's crimes in Jaelot
Third Age 5660–70, died fighting in the Siege of Alestron in Third
Age 5671.
>pronounced: fee-on ar-reth cay-dan
>root meaning: *fionne arith caid'an* – one who brings choice

FIRST AGE—began when the dragons formed the Guardian Protectorate,
and their appeal to the Creator brought Ath's gift to the world, the
An'ami, progenitors of the Paravians through Athili. Ended 827 years
later, when the Paravian council and the dreaming of Dragons at
Corith summoned the Fellowship Sorcerers to Athera.

FIRSTMARK—trade town in Vastmark, Shand.

FIVE CENTURIES FOUNTAIN—a well in the Red Desert of Rasinne
Pasy built and endowed by Davien, as a test of Mankind's wisdom,
specifically to determine whether men were fitted for long-term rule,
its properties bestow five hundred years of longevity upon anyone
who partakes of the water.

FORTHMARK—city in Vastmark, Shand. Once the site of a hostel of
Ath's Brotherhood. By Third Age 5320, the site was abandoned and
taken over by the Koriani Order as a healer's hospice.

GANISH—trade town south of Methlas Lake in Orvandir, Shand.
>pronounced: ga-nish
>root meaning: *gianish* – halfway point, stopping place

GLENDIEN—a Shandian clanswoman, wife to Kyrialt s'Taleyn, who was
formerly the heir designate of the High Earl of Alland; mother to
Arithon's bastard daughter, Teylia, conceived in the confluence at
Athir in Third Age 5672.
>pronounced: glen-dee-en
>root meaning: *glyen* – sultry; *dien* – object of beauty

GREAT GETHORN—deadliest winged predator, semi aquatic, had a
dreamer's ability to twist time, spawned in Mirthlvain mire in First

Age 800, when Methuri possessed a dragon clutch. Hatched out what became the worst scourge to Paravian civilization. Maddened in molt in First Age 812, the monster damaged, then broke free of the warded wall to ravage Melhalla. Great Drake Sharchekaz wounded fighting it to spare the Protectorate, duelled the Gethorn until wing torn and grounded, to be slaughtered by Seardluin in First Age 826. Gethorn led the greater drake spawn besieging Ithamon, and roosted in the ruin after the second fall in First Age 827, with Cianor Sunlord left crippled in defence until his healing in Second Age Year One. When the Gethorn's predation slew the Paravian High King Enastir Third Perehedral, Cianor and Isaervian sword Darisain bound the marauding creature at Rockfell in Second Age 617, where it remained imprisoned until escape during the Third Sundering in Second Age 3668. Flew free and slaughtered until the last hunt, where Paravians and Fellowship Sorcerers hounded the creature across Myrkavia to its requite death in Second Age 4072.

> pronounced: great get-thorn
>
> root meaning: *gaet-thorn* – monster, terror or perversion that slaughters

GREY KRALOVIR—see Kralovir.

GREAT WAYSTONE—see entry for Waystone.

GRIMWARD—mighty spells of Paravian making that seal and isolate the dire dreams of dragon haunts, a force with the potential for mass destruction. With the disappearance of the old races, the defences are maintained by embodied Sorcerers of the Fellowship of Seven. Of seventeen separate sites listed at Althain Tower, thirteen remain active.

HALDUIN s'ILESSID—founder of the s'Ilessid royal lineage in Third Age Year One, bearing the gifted attribute of justice.

> pronounced: hal-dwin sill-ess-id
>
> root meaning: *hal* – white; *duinne* – hand; *liessiad* – balance

HALLIRON SEN AL'DUIN—Masterbard of Athera, succeeded Murchiel for the title in Third Age 5597. Son of Al'Duin, mentor of Arithon s'Ffalenn, who assumed the title as Masterbard in 5644.

> pronounced: hal-leer-on sen-al-doo-win
>
> root meaning: *hal* – white; *lyron* – singer; *sen* – denotes paternal descent; *alduin* – scribe

HALWYTHWOOD—forest in Araethura, Rathain, preferred site of the
caithdein's lodge.
>   pronounced: hall-with-wood
>   root meaning: *hal* – white; *wythe* – vista

HANSHIRE—port town on the Westland Sea, Tysan; birthplace of Sulfin
Evend; mayors historically opposed to royal rule which seated a hotbed
of unrest in the rebellion, also maintain an ancient alliance with the
Koriathain.
>   pronounced: han-sheer
>   root meaning: *hansh* – sand; *era* – place

HASIDII—lineage of the Biedar tribes, taken captive as a family and
coerced by Koriathain for theft of their ancestral lineage.
>   pronounced: has-sid-ee
>   root meaning: *hai shidi* – stigma, Biedar dialect

HASPASTION—ghost of the dragon grimwarded in Radmoore, and
Seshkrozchiel's mate.
>   pronounced: has-pass-tee-on
>   root meaning: *hashpashdion* – Drakish for black thunder.

HAVISH—one of the Five High Kingdoms of Athera founded under
charter law by the Fellowship of Seven. Ruled by Queen Ceftwinn,
who succeeded Gestry s'Lornmein. Crown heritage: temperance.
Device: gold hawk on red field.
>   pronounced: hav-ish
>   root meaning: *havieshe* – hawk

HAVISTOK—principality in Havish.
>   pronounced: ha-vi-stock
>   root meaning: *haviesha* – hawk; *tiok* – roost

HENNISHE—ruling Prime Matriarch of the Koriathain when Mankind
settled on Athera.
>   pronounced: hen-ish-shee

HIGHSCARP—town and stone quarries on the coast of the Bay of Eltair,
in Daon Ramon, Rathain. Also a sisterhouse of the Koriani Order.

IAMINE s'GANNLEY—woman who founded the caithdein's lineage for
Tysan.
>   pronounced: ee-ahm-meen-e sgan-lee
>   root meaning: *iamine* – amethyst; *gaen* – guide; *li* – exalted or in
>   harmony

ILITHARIS PARAVIANS—centaurs, of Athera's three semi-mortal old races; defenders and guardians of the earth's mysteries who dwindled after the Mistwraith's conquest, departed the continent to take sanctuary on the Isle of Los Lier by Third Age 5100.

    pronounced: i-li-thar-is

    root meaning: *i'lith'earis* – the keeper/preserver of mystery

IMAURY RIDDLER—Dace'am centaur guardian who enspelled the Second-Age foundation of the ruined keep beside Mainmere; legend holds the stones will sing aloud on the hour of Athera's greatest peril.

    pronounced: ah-more-ee

    root meaning: *imauri* – riddle

INSHIDIK EN VAYAR—cavern in Sanpashir with a fissure open to sky, where Arithon recovered his resiliency following his ordeal banishing the Grey Kralovir cult of necromancers. Biedar call it by the name of the Air, and it is known by Paravians as the 'Great Crack in the World'.

    pronounced: in-shi-deek-en-va-yar

    root meaning: *inshidik en vayar* – Biedar ceremonial/sacred word for Name of Air.

INSTRELL BAY—waters off the Gulf of Stormwell between Atainia, Tysan, and Deshir, Rathain.

    pronounced: in-strell

    root meaning: *arin'streal* – strong wind

IPPASH RIVER—source in the Kelhorns, flowing south through Shand to Innish at Southsea.

    pronounced: ip-ash

    root meaning: *ipeish* – crescent

ISAER—major power focus built at an etheric node in the First Age in Atainia, Tysan, by the Ilitharis Paravians, to source the defence works of the Paravian keep of the same name.

    pronounced: i-say-er

    root meaning: *i'saer* – the circle

ISAERVIAN BLADES—twelve swords forged from a meteorite by centaur Fferedon s'Darian at Isaer in Second Age 391–404, each blade endowed with master wardings and elemental virtues by Athlien and Riathan enchanters. The weapons were created to fight drake spawn. Five are held by the Ilitharis, six by Athlien, and one in Mankind's charge, all renowned in legend.

pronounced: is-say-er-vee-en

root meaning: *i'saer* – the circle

ISCHARIVOTH—dragon who incited revolt against the Protectorate/ Concord alliance, sought to level Althain Tower and died in the Bittern Waste, unrequited haunt grimwarded in Atainia in Second Age 144.

pronounced: iss-char-ee-voth

root meaning: *issskarreevoth* – Drakish for sundering fury

ISHLIR—town on the east shore of Orvandir, Shand.

pronounced: ish-leer

root meaning: *ieshlier* – sheltered place

ITHALIVIER—Paravian dynasty that succeeded Evalia, lineage held the sceptre from Third Age 1228 until Vanomind Third's retreat to Athili in Third Age 5064 bestowed the succession to the First Adaraquend.

pronounced: ith-ah-li-vee-er

root meaning: *itha* – fifth; *li'vier* – keeper or guardian of grace

ITHAMON—royal seat loaned to the s'Ffalenn high kings, built at the etheric node on the fifth lane in Daon Ramon, Rathain. Ruin was a Paravian keep, location of the Compass Point Towers, and site of the Mistwraith's captivity, enacted by Lysaer s'Ilessid, Arithon s'Ffalenn, and the Fellowship in Third Age 5638.

pronounced: ith-a-mon

root meaning: *itha* – five; *mon* – needle, spire

ITHILT—principality in eastern Rathain, and the peninsula dividing Eltair and Instrell Bay.

pronounced: ith-ilt

root meaning: *ith* – five; *ealt* – a narrows

ITHISH—port in Vastmark, southcoast of Shand, where the tribal herders ship their wool fleece.

pronounced: ith-ish

root meaning: *ithish* – fleece or fluffy

IYAT—energy sprite, and minor drake spawn, invisible to the eye, wont to seize temporary possession of objects. Feeds upon energy sourced by fire, breaking waves, lightning, and excess emotion where humans are in conflict and disharmony.

pronounced: ee-at

root meaning: *iyat* – to break

IYAT-THOS—clan dialect name, see Tarens.
  pronounced: ee-at thoss
  root meaning: *iyat* – broken; *thos* – nose

JAELOT—port on Eltair Bay at the southern border of the Kingdom
  of Rathain. Originally a Second-Age keep, repurposed by wealthy
  merchants known for excess. Third Age 5643, Arithon s'Ffalenn
  played his eulogy for Halliron Masterbard, charging the Paravian
  focus circle beneath the mayor's palace and waking resonant
  harmonics that damaged buildings, watch keeps, and walls, not in
  alignment.
  pronounced: jay-lot
  root meaning: *jielot* – affectation
JALIENNE—wife of Cosach s'Valerient, *Caithdein* of Rathain. Mother
  of Esfand and Cordaya.
  pronounced: jah-lee-en
  root meaning: *jia* – binding, tie together, intertwine ; *lien* – to love
JESSIAN OATHKEEPER—historical sister of the Koriathain, prior to
  settlement on Athera, when the order was a secret society, sent to
  the planet Scathac to treat with the Biedar, and witnessed the tribal
  rite that averted ruin by Calum Kincaid's Great Weapon. Sworn to
  secrecy, she subsequently was tried and imprisoned when she refused
  to reveal the tribal rite she had observed. Executed for her silence,
  her courage sent the sisterhood to widen their search, until the
  coercive disclosure of Hasidii resulted in Koriani theft of the Biedar
  ancestral knowledge.
  pronounced: jess-ee-an
JEYNSA s'VALERIENT—daughter of Jieret s'Valerient and Feithan, born
  Third Age 5653; Seven's appointed successor as *Caithdein* of Rathain,
  married Sevrand s'Brydion, as Khadrien's forebears.
  pronounced: jay-in-sa
  root meaning: *jieyensa* – garnet
JIERET s'VALERIENT—former Earl of the North, clan chief of Deshir;
  Caithdein of Rathain, liegeman of Prince Arithon s'Ffalenn. Also
  son and heir of Lord Steiven, blood pacted to Arithon by Sorcerer's
  oath prior to the battle of Strakewood Forest. Known by headhunters as Jieret Red-beard. Father of Jeynsa and Barach. First
  husband of Feithan. Died by Lysaer s'Ilessid's hand in Daon Ramon

Barrens, Third Age 5670. Bequeathed his memories to Iyat-thos Tarens in Third Age 5923.

    pronounced: jeer-et sval-er-ee-ent

    root meaning: *jieret* – thorn; *val* – straight; *erient* – spear

KADARION—Ilitharis Paravian, or centaur guardian, living brother of Kadierach.

    pronounced: kad-ar-ee-on

    root meaning: *kad'i'ria'en* – to quicken etherically, to blossom under the masterful touch of refined awareness

KADIERACH—Ilitharis Paravian, brother of Kadarion, also centaur guardian of Rathain, summoned by High Earl Jieret during his transcendent passage in Third Age 5670, also appeared for Arithon's requital in Kewar's maze.

    pronounced: kad-ee-er-ack

    root meaning: *kad'i* – to quicken etherically; *era'ch* – suffix for rooted to a place

KALESH—port town at the mouth of the inlet from the Cildein Ocean, in East Halla, Melhalla.

    pronounced: cal-esh

    root meaning: *caille'iesh* – stubborn hold

KAMRIDIAN s'FFALENN—crowned High King of Rathain, called flower of his line and bearer of the Paravian sword Alithiel. Compassionate conscience brought his death in Davien's Maze at Kewar in Third Age 4151.

    pronounced: kam-rid-ee-en sfall-en

    root meaning: *kaim'riadien* – thread cut short; *ffael* – dark, *an* – one

KARTHAN—island realm on the splinter world of Dascen Elur, through the west Worldsend Gate, once ruled by s'Ffalenn pirate kings descended from an exiled prince from Athera.

    pronounced: karth-an

    root meaning: *kar'eth'an* – pirate

KATHTAIRR—barren continent in the southern ocean, across the world from Paravia, left barren by Dragonkind after destruction by Cathukodar's flame during the Third Age of Nightmare, Era of Destruction in the Age of Dragons.

    pronounced: kath-tay-er

    root meaning: *kait-th'era* – empty place

KELSING—town south of Erdane on the trade-road in Camris, Tysan.
  pronounced: kel-sing
  root meaning: *kel* – hidden; *seng* – cave
KERELIE—sister of Tarens and Efflin.
  pronounced: care-ah-lee
KEWAR TUNNEL—cavern built beneath the Mathorn Mountains by
  Davien the Betrayer; secures the library records too dark to house
  with the Paravian record at Althain Tower, also holds the maze of
  conscience built to test the strength of the royal lines; caused High
  King Kamridian s'Ffalenn's death. Arithon Teir's'Ffalenn successfully
  completed the challenge in Third Age 5670.
  pronounced: key-wahr
  root meaning: *kewiar* – a weighing of conscience
KHADRIEN s'VALERIENT—clanborn second cousin to Esfand s'Valerient, friend of Siantra s'Idir, descendant of Jeynsa s'Valerient and
  Sevrand s'Brydion.
  pronounced: cad-ree-en sval-er-ee-ent
  root meaning: *khadrien* – mercuric; *val* – straight; *erient* – spear
KHADRIM—winged, fire-breathing drake spawn, intelligent, vicious,
  and a scourge that slaughtered Paravians. Confined to a warded
  preserve in the volcanic mountains near Teal's Gap in north Tysan
  by the Fellowship Sorcerers in the Third Age.
  pronounced: kaa-drim
  root meaning: *khadrim* – dragon
KHARADMON—Sorcerer of the Fellowship of Seven; discorporate since
  attack by Khadrim and Seardluin levelled the Paravian stronghold at
  Ithamon in Second Age 3651. Kharadmon's intervention secured the
  fifth-lane focus for the surviving defenders' retreat.
  pronounced: kah-rad-mun
  root meaning: *kar'riad en mon* – 'twisted thread on the needle' or
  'knotted entanglement.'
KHETIENN—spotted wildcat found in the northern wilds' symbol on
  Rathain's royal blazon.
  pronounced: ket-yen
  root meaning: *kietienn* – small leopard
KIDORN ELRIENIENT—legendary Athlien Paravian, First Elrienient
  High King, held the Paravian sceptre from Second Age 5126 until
  death in Second Age 7915 during the campaign to end Seardluin

predation on the mainland. Bearer of the Isaervian blade Iaimon until his crown accession.

pronounced: kid-oorn el-ree-en-ee-ent

root meaning: *ki* – broad; *dorn* – net; *el* – short; *rien* – stride; *ient* – suffix for highest, most

KIELING TOWER—one of the Sun Towers, built of jasper by Ilitharis at Ithamon, Daon Ramon, Rathain, virtue binding the stone is Compassion, from which the Fellowship Sorcerers fashioned the cylinder flask to secure the captive essence of Desh-thiere.

pronounced: kee-el-ing

root meaning: *kiel'ien* – compassion

KORIANI—possessive and singular form of 'Koriathain'; see entry.

pronounced: kor-ee-ah-nee

KORIATHAIN—female order of enchantresses headed by a Senior Circle, ruled by the absolute will of a Prime Matriarch. Selective talent is acquired from orphaned children, or from daughters dedicated to service by their parents, with ranked initiation and a vow of consent that shackles the spirit to a crystal keyed to the Prime's control.

pronounced: kor-ee-ah-thain – to rhyme with "main"

root meaning: *koriath* – order; *ain* – belonging to

KRAKENS—greater and lesser aquatic drake spawn, emerged during the Second Sundering in First Age 774, crossbred from the Loessim, sirens, and the Morkhadrim, water lizards. These terrors of the deep rose up to attack and scourge Avenor. Paravians and Fellowship Sorcerers battled them through the Wars of the Kraken, to the ruin of the keep of Sadiera in the Second Rising saw their defeat in Second Age 4484. Peace followed under the Westgate Accord, which exiled the lesser krakens to the splinter world of Dascen Elur, through the Worldsend Gate, provided they ceased predation upon land and shipping in perpetuity.

KRALOVIR—grey cult, sect of necromancers destroyed by Arithon in Third Age 5671.

pronounced: kray-low-veer

root meaning: *krial* – name for the rune of crossing; *oveir* – abomination

KYRA ELIE—youngest daughter of Kyrwen, clanswoman from Rathain.

pronounced: kee-ra

root meaning: *kier* – perfect; *elie* – bud

KYRWEN—clan woman of Rathain, widowed after the birth of her first children.
> pronounced: keer-wen
> root meaning: *kier* – perfect; *wen* – kindness

LAERIENT—emphatic form denoting homage and respect.
> pronounced: lay-er-ee-ent
> root meaning: *laereient* – the highest state of grace/appreciation

LAITHEN s'IDIR—clanborn woman from Fallowmere of Sidir's lineage, mother of Siantra s'Idir.
> pronounced: lay-then see-deer
> root meaning: *laerethien* – pillar or tower of grace; *s'* – of the lineage; *i'id'ier* – almost lost

LANSHIRE—northernmost principality in the Kingdom of Havish. Name taken from the wastes at Scarpdale, site of First-Age battles with Seardluin that blasted the soil to slag.
> pronounced: lahn-sheer-e
> root meaning: *lan'hansh'era* – place of hot sands

LAW OF THE MAJOR BALANCE—primary tenet of the Fellowship of Seven: no force of nature shall be applied without conscious free-will consent.

LEYNSGAP—narrow pass in the Mathorn Mountains, Rathain, where clan Companion Braggen in Third Age 5670 single-handedly fought a troop of Sunwheel soldiers in pursuit of Arithon.
> pronounced: lay-ens-gap
> root meaning: *liyond* – corridor

LIFFSEY RIVER—flows from the Plain of Araithe to the northern coast of Rathain.
> pronounced: liff-see
> root meaning: *lieffesi* – to laugh

LIRENDA—demoted First Senior Enchantress of the Koriani Order; failed her assignment to capture Arithon s'Ffalenn, slaved as a passive mute under her Matriarch's sentence of punishment in Third Age 5670, and claimant to the Prime Seat by irregular succession upon Selidie's death in Third Age 5924.
> pronounced: leer-end-ah
> root meaning: *lyron* – singer; *di-ia* – a dissonance – the hyphen denotes a glottal stop

LITHUAMIR RIVER—flows northward across Fallowmere, Rathain, to the sea at Anglefen.
> pronounced: lith-oo-a-meer
> root meaning: *lieth* – flow; *mieren* – mirror

LORN—town on the northcoast of Atainia, Tysan.
> pronounced: lorn
> root meaning: *loern* – an Atheran fish.

LOS LIER—archipelago in the Cildein Ocean
> pronounced: loss lee-er
> root meaning: *lios* – to designate, scribe or write; *l'iera* – exalted place

LUHAINE—Sorcerer of the Fellowship of Seven, discorporate since Telmandir's fall in Third Age 5018, when the insurgents overwhelmed him while in deep trance to secure the infant royal heir's escape.
> pronounced: loo-hay-ne
> root meaning: *luirhainon* – defender

LYRANTHE—instrument with fourteen strings, tuned in courses to seven tones: two drone strings' set to octaves, and five melody strings, the lower three courses pitched octaves, and the upper two in unison.
> pronounced: leer-anth-e (last "e" being nearly subliminal)
> root meaning: *lyr* – song, *anthe* – box

LYSAER s'ILESSID—prince of Tysan, 1497th in succession since Halduin founded the line in Third Age Year One. Gifted at birth to wield elemental Light, known as Bane of Desh-thiere and Blessed Prince, self-styled as divine avatar for the Alliance of Light. Elected Mayor of Etarra in 5667. Declared apostate by the Light's priests at the Great Schism in Third Age 5683, retired to rule at Etarra, and signed a Treaty of Law with Rathain's clans in Third Age 5688.
> pronounced: lie-say-er sill-ess-id
> root meaning: *lia* – blond, yellow or light; *saer* – circle; *liessiad* – balance

MAENALLE s'GANNLEY—*Caithdein* of Tysan, met Lysaer s'Ilessid's return, executed by his decree under town law in Third Age 5645 for raiding his cavalcade in the Pass of Orlan.
> pronounced: may-noll-e s'gann-lee
> root meaning: *maeni* – to fall, disrupt; *alli* – to save or preserve

MAINMERE—town at the head of Valenford River in Taerlin, Tysan, north of the ancient ruin where Imaury Riddler's dedicate spirit keeps watch.

    pronounced: main-meer-e

    root meaning: *maeni* – to interrupt; *miere* – reflection

MARAK—splinter world accessed by South Worldsend Gate, origin of the Mistwraith developed by exiles expelled from Athera for breaking terms of the Fellowship's compact.

    pronounced: mar-rack

    root meaning: *m'era'ki* – a place held separate

MARIN ELIATHE—Paravian High King murdered by an assassin possessed by Methuri in Second Age 1542, which brought the King's Tower at Ithamon to ruin.

    pronounced: mahr-in el-ee-ah-the

    root meaning: *marin* – happening; *e'li* – in harmony with; *ath* – prime life force

MATHIELL GATE—Twin keeps guarding the inner citadel at Alestron, housing for the great winches that anchored the span of the chain bridge to the Wyntok Keeps on the landward side.

    pronounced: math-ee-el

    root meaning: *mon'thiellen* – sky spires

MATHORN MOUNTAINS—range that bisects the Kingdom of Rathain east to west.

    pronounced: math-orn

    root meaning: *mathien* – massive

MATHORN ROAD—trade-road running south of the Mathorn Mountains.

    pronounced: math-orn

    root meaning: *mathien* – massive

MEARTH—ruin in the Red Desert, splinter world of Rasinne Pasy, beyond the West Worldsend Gate. Destroyed when Davien was rendered discorporate, as the elemental working protecting his Five Centuries Fountain escaped containment. Called the Shadows of Mearth, the geas haunts the site, trapping the mind to repeat the worst experience held in memory until the victim achieves self-release, or succumbs to madness.

    pronounced: me-arth

    root meaning: *mearth* – empty

MEIGLIN s'DIENEVAL—daughter born to the widow of Egan s'Dieneval in Third Age 5019, after his death defending his King in Third Age 5018. Heart's love of the last High King of Shand for one night, prior to his demise fighting the Mistwraith. A weaving by the Biedar of Sanpashir, done at the behest of the last centaur guardian, ensured the union's conception of Dari's'Ahelas. Named Anshlien'ya, 'dawn of hope' in tribal dialect for the out-cross of Requiar's ancestral blood with the royal line of Shand.

> pronounced: mee-glin s-dee-in-ee-vahl
>
> root meaning: *meiglin* – passion; *dien* – large; *eval* – endowment, gifted talent

MELHALLA—High Kingdom once ruled by s'Ellestrion lineage, held by the steward's line of s'Callient after the linebearer perished in the Red Desert past West Gate.

> pronounced: mel-hal-la
>
> root meaning: *maelhallia* – grand meadows, or open space

MEREVALIA—see Teirendaelient Merevalia – Paravian High Queen, Second Evalia; stepped up as Queen Regent after Third Adaraquend broke the sceptre in fury over Mankind's transgressions.

MERIOR—fishing village on Scimlade Tip in Alland, Shand, site of Arithon's shipworks in Third Age 5644.

> pronounced: mare-ee-or
>
> root meaning: *merioren* – cottages

META-VERIARCH—off world, prehistory, funded scientific research, most notably Calum Quaide Kincaid's team specializing in molecular architecture and accelerated fusion, enabling the great weapon that destroyed worlds and caused Mankind's refugee exodus and settlement on Athera.

> pronounced: met-ah vary-arch

METHISLE FORTRESS—oldest Paravian keep and fifth-lane focus circle on the island in Methlas Lake, Melhalla, etheric foundation mapped in First Age 87, later expanded and fortified by Ilitharis masons Abercaer and Faradir in First Age 208, then maintained by the first centaur guardian, Bainhalt to suppress drake spawn: venomous eels, flenser fish, and *methtiend*, demon spirits that fed upon animal magnetism, the etheric release caused by violent slaughter. Third Age guardian in residence is Verrain, Master Spellbinder.

> pronounced: meth-eye-el
>
> root meaning: *meth* – hate

METHLAS LAKE—fresh-water lake in Radmoore, Melhalla, adjacent
to Mirthlvain Swamp.

    pronounced: meth-lass

    root meaning: *meth'liass'an* – the drowned or sunken ones

METHSPAWN/METHURIEN—drake-spawned parasitic entity, related to
iyats, but with a malevolent intelligence that once infested and warped
live host animals. Extinct by the Third Age, though their mutated
offspring birth dangerous crossbreeds that flourish in Mirthlvain Swamp.

    pronounced: meth-yoor-ee-en

    root meaning: *meth* – hate; *thiere* – wraith

MHOROVAIRE/MHOROVAIN—western continent coveted by warring
dragons, until First Age 164 brought the first landing of Paravians.
Eamonier Eliathe and Avileffin found a lush paradise, beset still by
lingering perils from The Era of Destruction, Ages of Dragons.
Bechasimol's haunt, and Kurithazich's haunt, whose curse poisoned
his rival were grimwarded on the high ground. Torianor Eliathe
founded his princedom, and ruled the Westland crown seat, until
Mhorovaire and Paravia united under High King Elriath First
Perehedral in First Age 512 to subdue malevolent drake spawn. A
dragon revolt under Chavenomic, 'Scourge of Mhorovaire', dreamed
havoc in the Great Slaughter of First Age 596. Much of the Westland
was scorched waste in First Age 601 in war against drake-spawned
Khadrienient, recorded by Athlien Masterbard Ammach's Great
Lament for Mhorovaire. Dragon battles and spawn attacks, and Greater
Krakens besieged mainland Tysan from Mhorovaire, until Requinishar's
fall into the sea destroyed the Khadrim horde and restored ascendancy
to the Protectorate. Paravians repopulated in Third Age 710, Marin
Eliathe born to Mhorovain Princess Duindalia restored a brief golden
age until the subsidence at the Second Sundering sank the continent.
Last remnant above water, the Lost Islets of Min Pierens, and the keep
at Corith, site of the Second Dreaming that summoned the Fellowship
Sorcerers to Athera at the close of First Age Year 827.

    pronounced: mhor-oh-vay-er

    root meaning: *mhorent* – treasure hoard; *vaerer* – keeper

MINDERL BAY—north of the Ithilt peninsula, inside of Crescent Isle,
west shore of Rathain.

    pronounced: mind-erl

    root meaning: *minderl* – anvil

MIRALT—port town on the northcoast of Tysan, became a stronghold
of the True Sect faith.
>   pronounced: meer-alt
>   root meaning: *m'ier* – shore; *alt* – last

MIRTHLVAIN—bog with an ancient Paravian stronghold in Midhalla,
Melhalla; infested with dangerous crossbreeds created by
drake-spawned Methurien, continuously guarded by the Master
Spellbinder, Verrain, Guardian of Methisle.
>   pronounced: mirth-el-vain
>   root meaning: *myrthl* – noxious; *vain* – bog.

MISTWRAITH—see Desh-thiere.

MIXIE—a prostitute from Ganish.

MORNOS—port town on west shore of Lithmere, Havish, housed the
remnants of Telmandir's libraries salvaged from the uprising in Third
Age 5018, archive later relocated to Los Mar.
>   pronounced: more-nos
>   root meaning: *moarnosh* – a coffer to hoard valuables

MORRIEL—Prime Matriarch of the Koriathain, invested in Third Age
4212, she upset the planetary electromagnetic lanes to mask her covert
possession of novice initiate Selidie's body in Third Age 5667; the
death of her flesh during the ritual created an irregular succession.
>   pronounced: more-real
>   root meaning: *moar* – greed; *riel* – silver.

MORVAIN—port in the principality of Araethura, Rathain, on the west
coast of Instrell Bay. Elaira's birthplace.
>   pronounced: mor-vain
>   root meaning: *morvain* – swindler's market

MOTHER DARK—tribal name for the all-knowing, all-encompassing
stillness of the void that is untapped, virgin power, the latent and
limitless state of potential that precedes the imprinted act of
Creation.

MOLTS—young dragons who have left the nest, immature and sexless
until they mate as adults.

MYRKAVIA—island in Rockbay Harbour off northcoast of Havistok,
Havish.
>   pronounced: meer-kay-vee-ah
>   root meaning: *miere* – reflection; *kavia* – spruce tree

NAILS—nickname for a True Sect diviner influential with the Light's war hosts.

NARMS—port town on Instrell Bay, founded by Men in the early Third Age, famed for dye works.

    pronounced: narms

    root meaning: *narms* – colour

NEW TIRANS—trade town in East Halla, Melhalla.

    pronounced: tee-rans

    root meaning: *tier* – to hold fast, to keep, to covet.

NORTHGATE—Worldsend Gate above the Ruins of Penstair in Deshir, Rathain, connects splinter world Sckaithen Duin, designated domain of dragons who disagreed with the abdication of Athera to Paravian sovereignty, Chaimistarizog appointed as Gatekeeper.

ORLAN—pass in the Thaldein Mountains in Tysan, site of the clan seat and hidden outpost.

    pronounced: or-lan

    root meaning: *irlan* – ledge

OZVOWZAKRIN—heir apparent to Chaimistarizog, Guardian of the Northgate and keeper of the Treaty Accord between the Dragon Protectorate and wild drakes exiled on the splinter world, Sckaithen Duin.

    pronounced: oz-vow-zack-rin

    root meaning: *ozvowzakrin* – Drakish, to fracture or tear asunder

PARAVIA—continent originally inhabited by Paravians, and locale of the Five Kingdoms.

    pronounced: par-ay-vee-ah

    root meaning: *para* – great; *i'a* – suffix denoting entityship, and raised to the feminine aspect, which translates as 'place inclusive of, or holding the aspect for greatness'

PARAVIAN—continent and name for three semi-mortal races inhabiting Athera before Mankind. Centaurs, sunchildren, and unicorns embody the world's channel, or direct connection, to Ath Creator.

    pronounced: par-ai-vee-ans

    root meaning: *para* – great; *i'on* – fate or great mystery

PARITHAIN SECOND ADARAQUEND—succeeded Sestiend First, killed in the Mistwraith's conquest at San Pashir, Third Age 5095; Parithain Second despised Mankind's desecration, abandoned the continent for refuge in Los Lier, then broke the crown sceptre in Third Age 5100. Tehaval

Warden then ceded Althain Tower to Sethvir of the Fellowship. High
Queen Regent Merevalia assumed Paravian sovereignty in interregnum.

   pronounced: par-i-thay-in ah-dahr-a-kwend

   root meaning: *parat* – great; *thein* – tower; *a'dariquen'd* – see past
   evil, unmask deception

PELLAIN—trade town between East and West Halla, Melhalla.

   pronounced: pell-ayn

   root meaning: *peil* – odd; *ai'an* – hidden one

PEREHEDRAL—the Athlien crown lineage charged to rule east and
   west in the First Age, assumed united rule of Paravia under Eriathan
   First Perehedral, until the lineage ended with Enastir Third Perehedral's
   death in Second Age 617.

   pronounced: per-e-hee-drahl

   root meaning: *para* – great; *hedreal* – oak

PERLORN—trade town en route to Werpoint and Etarra in Fallowmere,
   Rathain.

   pronounced: pur-lorn

   root meaning: *perlorn* – midpoint

PRANDEY—Shandian term for gelded pleasure boy.

   pronounced: pran-dee

PRIME MATRIARCH—head of the Order of the Koriathain by ninth-
   rank initiation.

PROTECTORATE—elder dragons rallied from defeat at close of the First
   Age to defend Paravian sovereignty from Dragonkind's murderous creation of drake spawn and Methurien, allied with the Paravian Concord
   to stabilize peace, and arbitrators of the Treaty Accord exiling wild rogues
   to the splinter world of Sckaithen Duin past Northgate. Engendered the
   Second Dreaming at Corith that bound the Fellowship Sorcerers.

RACINNE PASY—splinter world of the Red Desert, accessed by West
   Worldsend Gate.

   pronounced: rah-sin-pah-see

   root meaning: *racinne* – orange; *pash'era* – place of grit or gravel/wasteland

RADMOORE DOWNS—meadowland in Midhalla, Melhalla.

   pronounced: rad-more

   root meaning: *riad* – thread; *mour* – carpet, rug

RATHAIN—High Kingdom of Athera ruled by descendants of Torbrand
   s'Ffalenn since Third Age Year One. Device: black-and-silver leopard

on green field. Arithon Teir's'Ffalenn sanctioned as crown prince by the Fellowship Sorcerers, in Third Age 5638.
pronounced: rath-ayn
root meaning: *roth* – brother; *thein* – tower, sanctuary

RAUVEN TOWER—residence of the s'Ahelas mages on the splinter world of Dascen Elur, through Westgate, where Arithon trained for initiate mastery.
pronounced: raw-ven
root meaning: *rauven* – invocation

REQUIAR—Biedar man of Lassiver's heritage, sworn to surety for Jessian Oathkeeper's integrity.
pronounced: reck-wee-ar
root meaning: *requiar* – a binding commitment, Biedar dialect

REIYAJ SEERESS—titled seeress sequestered in a tower in Shand, near Ithish, whose oracular visions derive from meditative communion with the energy gateway marked and measured by Athera's sun. Born sighted, until practice of her art causes blindness, her tradition stems from the mystical practice of the Biedar tribe in the Sanpashir desert.
pronounced: ree-yahj
root meaning: *ria'ieajn* – to touch the forbidden

RIATHAN PARAVIANS—unicorns, the living bridge whose undilute connection to Ath Creator channels the prime vibration through the horn.
pronounced: ree-ah-than
root meaning: *ria* – to touch; *ath* – prime life force; *an* – one

RIVERTON—port town in Korias on Tysan's south shore.

ROCKBAY HARBOUR—on the southcoast, between Shand and West Shand.

ROCKFELL PEAK—mountain in West Halla, Melhalla, holds Rockfell Pit, prison for harmful entities throughout three Ages, and warded containment for the Mistwraith, Desh-thiere.
pronounced: rock-fell

ROCKFELL PIT—shaft drilled into Rockfell Peak by the Sorcerer Davien, augmented the original Paravian enclosure to contain harmful entities; sequesters the Mistwraith, Desh-thiere.

s'AHELAS—royal line appointed by the Fellowship Sorcerers in Third Age Year One to oversee the High Kingdom of Shand. Gifted geas: farsight, with latent rogue talent for prophecy introduced when the *caithdein*'s lineage of s'Dieneval, whose Biedar descent from Requiar in Third Age 5036, birthed Dari in 5037.

> pronounced: s'ah-hell-as
> root meaning: *ahelas* – mage-gifted

SAFFIE—deceased aunt of Tarens, Efflin, and Kerelie, mother of Paolin and Chan.

> pronounced: saf-fee

SANLIET RIVER—flows west into Rockbay Harbour from Thirdmark, Shand.

> pronounced: sahn-lee-et
> root meaning: *san* – black; *lieth* – flow

SANPASHIR—desert on the southcoast of Shand, home to the Biedar tribe.

> pronounced: sahn-pash-eer
> root meaning: *san* – black or dark; *pash'era* – place of grit or gravel/ wasteland

SAROIC s'GANNLEY—heir designate by Asandir, sworn *Caithdein* of Tysan in Third Age 5923.

> pronounced: sa-row-ic
> root meaning: *sae* – circle; *roic* – to finish, or complete; *gaen* – guide; *li* – exalted, in harmony

SCARPDALE—waste in Lanshire, Havish, sown by a First-Age war with Seardluin. Site of dragon Charshaimkul's grimwarded haunt, since banished by Seshkrozchiel in Third Age 5671.

> pronounced: scarp-dale

SCATHAC—one of the historic home planets settled by the Biedar Tribes.

> pronounced: skath-ack
> root meaning: *scathac* – Biedar dialect for 'home haven'.

SCIMLADE TIP—peninsula in Alland, Shand.

> pronounced: skim-laid
> root meaning: *scimlait* – scythe

SCKAITHEN DUIN—called Fortress of Dragons, splinter world accessed by the North Worldsend Gate, where dissident dragons against Paravian sovereignty of Athera are in exile under the Dragon Protectorate's Treaty Accord.

> pronounced: skay-i-then doo-win
> root meaning: *s'caithen duin* – 'from the shadow tail', or the unseen truth behind the story.

s'DIENEVAL—past lineage of the *caithdeinen* of Melhalla, until Egan's death beside his high king in battle to subdue the Mistwraith. The bloodline's heritage and exceptional talent for prophecy stemmed from an out-cross of Biedar ancestral descent from Requiar. Egan's pregnant wife escaped the sack of Tirans in Third Age 5018, birthed a surviving daughter, Meiglin, mother of Dari s'Ahelas, crown heir of Shand.

    pronounced: s-dee-in-ee-vahl

    root meaning: *dien* – large; *eval* – endowment, gifted talent

SEARDLUIN—drake-spawned predator, first dreamed as slayers to prey upon rival drakes' clutches for territorial enforcement in the Era of Destruction. When ungovernable bloodlust spurred their thirst for etheric death, they turned to rogue slaughter in vicious packs. In the Age of Nightmare, they killed drakes in hibernation, evolving the imperative to cocoon in stone for safety. Hunted to suppression by the Dragon Protectorate, resurgent outbreaks occurred through resonant concordance on Paravia and Mhorovaire, until they were battled to extinction, costing death to High King Kidorn First Elrienient in the Second Age 7915.

    pronounced: seerd-loo-win

    root meaning: *seard* – bearded; *luin* – feline

SECOND AGE—Marked by the Fellowship of Seven's arrival at Crater Lake, and their bound provenance to fight the drake spawn and secure viability for the Paravians on Athera.

SELIDIE—young initiate appointed First Senior by Morriel Prime as a candidate in training, acceded as Prime Matriarch in Third Age 5670, through an unprincipled act of possession by which her predecessor usurped her body to keep the sisterhood's legacy intact.

    pronounced: sell-ih-dee

    root meaning: *selyadi* – air sprite

SELKWOOD—forest in Alland, Shand.

    pronounced: selk-wood

    root meaning: *selk* – pattern

SESHKROZCHIEL—female dragon once mated to Haspastion. Forged the black bargain with Davien, for the loan of her powers during her hibernation in exchange for his term of indefinite service. Her wakening in Third Age 5671 incurred the debt, assumed by Luhaine in Davien's behalf, since he was reincarnate and at risk of death when she returned to hibernation in Third Age 5923.

    pronounced: sesh-crows-chee-ell

    root meaning: *seshkrozchiel* – Drakish for blue lightning

SESTIEND FIRST ADARAQUEND—High King who took the Paravian sceptre after Vanomind Third Ithalivier despaired and passed into Athili. He perished of exhaustion at the Mistwraith's final conquest of Athera in Sanpashir in Third Age 5095, leaving the crown to his heir designate, Parithain Second, who darkened to despair, retreated to refuge in Los Lier, and broke the succession by abdication.

    pronounced: sess-tee-end ah-dar-ah-kwend

    root meaning: *ses* – seventh; *tiend* – spirit; *a'dari-quen'd* – to see past evil, unmask deception

SETHVIR—Sorcerer of the Fellowship of Seven, allotted the earth-link and appointed Warden of Althain in Third Age 5100, when the last centaur guardian Tehaval withdrew after the Mistwraith's conquest.

    pronounced: seth-veer

    root meaning: *seth* – fact; *vaer* – keep

SEVERNIR RIVER—dry riverbed in Daon Ramon, Rathain, dammed and diverted at the source to flow east into Eltair Bay after the Mistwraith's conquest.

    pronounced: sev-er-neer

    root meaning: *sevaer* – to travel; *nir* – south

SEVRAND s'BRYDION—son of Duke Bransian s'Brydion, heir designate until Alestron was entailed by the Fellowship Sorcerers in Third Age 5671; married Jeynsa s'Valerient, forebear of Khadrien.

    pronounced: sev-rand sbry-dee-on

    root meaning: *sevaer'an'd* – one who travels behind, a follower; *baridien* – tenacity

s'FFALENN—royal line appointed by the Fellowship Sorcerers in Third Age Year One to keep charter law the High Kingdom of Rathain. Gifted geas: compassion/empathy.

    pronounced: s-fal-en

    root meaning: *ffael* – dark, *an* – one

s'GANNLEY—lineage of the Earls of the West, once princes in Camris, now bearing the titled heritage of *Caithdein* of Tysan. Iamine s'Gannley, the woman founder, declined the crown to stand shadow.

pronounced: sgan-lee

root meaning: *gaen* – guide; *li* – exalted or in harmony

SHAND—southeastern kingdom on the continent of Paravia, assumed charge of the Paravian adjunct of West Shand after the old races' exodus in Second Age 5100, overseen by s'Ahelas crown rule, incorporated device the purple-and-gold chevrons, from West Shand's original falcon and crescent moon.

pronounced: shaynd

root meaning: *shayn* or *shiand* – two or a pair

SHADOWS OF MEARTH—elemental working of Davien's, see Five Centuries Fountain.

SHEHANE ALTHAIN—dedicate spirit of the Ilitharis Paravian who defends and guards Althain Tower, and whose power rendered Davien discorporate in Third Age 5129.

pronounced: shee-hayne all-thayn

root meaning: *shiehai'en* – to give for the greatest good; *alt* – last; *thain* – tower

SHIPSPORT—town on the shore of Eltair Bay in West Halla, Melhalla.

SIANTRA s'IDIR—clanborn daughter of Laithen s'Idir, of Sidir's lineage. A talented seer whose gift was enhanced by her encounter with the resonant forces in Ath's vortex at Athili in Third Age 5923.

pronounced: see-an-tra see-deer

root meaning: *sian* – spark; *tier* – to hold fast; *a* – feminine diminutive; *i'sid'i'er*—one who has stood at the verge of being lost.

SIDIR—one of fourteen Companions, boy survivors of the massacre at Tal Quorin in Third Age 5638. Served Arithon at the Battle of Dier Kenton Vale and the Havens in 5647, and at the siege of Alestron in 5671. Commanded Earl Jieret's war band, married Jieret's widow, Feithan, in 5672, founding the lineage of s'Idir, with a second descendant branch derived from a youthful liaison with a clan woman from Fallowmere.

pronounced: see-deer

root meaning: *i'sid'i'er*—one who has stood at the verge of being lost

s'ILESSID—royal line appointed by the Fellowship Sorcerers in Third Age Year One to keep charter law in the High Kingdom of Tysan. Gifted geas: justice.

pronounced: s-ill-ess-id

root meaning: *liessiad* – balance

SILVERMARSH—large bog south of Daenfal Lake, in West Halla, Melhalla.

SITHAER—mythological concept of hell, halls of Dharkaron Avenger's judgement; according to Ath's adepts, a state of being where the prime vibration is not recognized.

    pronounced: sith-air

    root meaning: *sid* – lost; *thiere* – wraith/spirit

SKENIVARICHIEL—renowned Great Dragon, queen at the founding of the First Dragon Protectorate in First Age Year One, whose grant of the dorsal spine sundered in battle against krakens fashioned the horn carried by Cianor Sunlord, the winded note at the Reprieve of the Horns in First Age 805 that forced marauding drake spawn to back off. The dragon oversaw the founding of the citadel at Alestron in Second Age 3004–6, with new walls impervious to dragon fire. Duelled Great Gethorn, after Cianor's fall, and died enabling the Paravian retreat from Ithamon's ruin in Second Age 3651. Sung into legend by Athlien as she flew, fatally wounded, to her requite death in Eltair Bay.

    pronounced: sken-ee-var-ee-chel

    root meaning: *skenivarichel* – Drakish for challenge cry

SKYRON FOCUS—aquamarine sphere employed as a primary focus for major craft-work by the Koriani Senior Circle after the loss of their Great Waystone during the rebellion in Third Age 5018.

    pronounced: sky-run

    root meaning: *skyron* – colloquialism for shackle; *s'kyr'i'on* – literally "sorrowful fate"

SKYSHIEL MOUNTAINS—range running north and south along the eastern coast of Rathain.

    pronounced: sky-shee-ells

    root meaning: *skyshia* – to pierce through; *iel* – ray

s'LORNMEIN—royal lineage of Havish, founded by Bwin Evoc s'Lornmein in Third Age Year One. Gifted geas: temperance.

    pronounced: slorn-main

    root meaning: *liernmein* – to centre, restrain, bring into balance.

SOUTHGATE—Worldsend Gate in West Shand, closed off access to the splinter world of Marak by Traithe's effort to stem the Mistwraith's invasion of Athera in Third Age 4993.

SOUTHSHIRE—town on the southcoast of Alland, Shand, known for shipbuilding.

    pronounced: south-shire

SPIRE—port town in Havistok, Rockbay Harbour also the active site of a White Brotherhood hostel.

STARBORN—Biedar name for the Fellowship Sorcerers.

STEIVEN s'VALERIENT—Earl of the North and *Caithdein* of Rathain until death in the Tal Quorin massacre in Third Age 3658, husband of Dania, and Jieret's sire.

> pronounced: stay-vin
>
> root meaning: steiven – *stag*

STORLAIN MOUNTAINS—range running north and south, dividing the Kingdom of Havish.

> pronounced: store-lanes
>
> root meaning: *storlient* – largest summit, highest divide

STORMWELL GULF—salt water off the northcoast of Tysan and Rathain.

STRAKEWOOD—forest in Deshir, Rathain, and free-wilds seat of the *caithdein*.

> pronounced: strayk-wood
>
> root meaning: *streik* – to quicken, to seed

SULFIN EVEND—son of the Mayor of Hanshire, titled as war host Alliance Lord Commander under Lysaer s'Ilessid. Arranged the rite sparing his liege from dark binding by Kralovir Necromancers, which wakened the talent heritage of his out-bred, s'Gannley descent, through Diarin, once abducted by his great-grandsire. His bargain with Enithen Tuer to acquire the ceremonial knowledge and Biedar knife used to sever the etheric cords the cult bound for enslavement required him to swear a *caithdein's* oath to serve the land in Fellowship standing at Althain Tower in Third Age 5670. Named Heretic Betrayer by the True Sect Canon for belief he corrupted the divine avatar and caused the Great Schism in Third Age 5683, he became the forebear of Daliana sen Evend.

> pronounced: sool-finn ev-end
>
> root meaning: *suilfinn eiavend* – colloquialism, diamond mind "one who is persistent"

SUNCHILDREN—common name for Athlien Paravians, see entry.

SUNWHEEL SQUARE—site of Sunwheel Shrine in Avenor, destroyed by drakefire in Third Age 5671.

SUNWHEEL—heraldic symbol for the religion of Light, and the device of the True Sect.

s'VALERIENT—family line of the Earls of the North, *caithdeinen* serving the High Kings of Rathain.
    pronounced: val-er-ee-ent
    root meaning: *val* – straight; *erient* – spear

TAERNOND—free-wilds forest in Ithilt, Rathain.
    pronounced: tay-er-nond
    root meaning: *taer* – calm; *nond* – thicket, copse

TAIFFEN RIVER—flows northward from Vastmark to Methlas Lake in Shand.
    pronounced: tay-if-en
    root meaning: *tayiffen* – sinuous

TAL QUORIN—river and canyon ravine in Deshir, Rathain, flows west into Instrell Bay, and site of the massacre of the clan war band in Strakewood by Etarra's war host in Third Age 5638.
    pronounced: tall-quoor-in
    root meaning: *tal* – branch; *quorin* – canyon

TAL'S CROSSING—town in Deshir en route from Englewood and the Plain of Araithe to Etarra.
    pronounced: tall's crossing
    root meaning: *tal* – branch

TALERA—s'Ahelas princess and daughter of the High Mage of Rauven, from the splinter world of Dascen Elur, married Demar s'Ilessid King of Amroth, mother of Lysaer and Arithon.
    pronounced: tall-er-a
    root meaning: *talera* – branch or fork in a path

TALITH—Etarran princess; former wife of Lysaer s'Ilessid, estranged and incarcerated on charges of consorting with the Master of Shadow. Murdered by conspiracy, when the Sunwheel Alliance and Avenor's crown council staged her fatal fall from Avenor's tower of state in Third Age 5653.
    pronounced: tal-ith – to rhyme with "gal with"
    root meaning: *tal* – branch; *lith* – to keep/nurture

TALLIARTHE—pleasure sloop built by Arithon s'Ffalenn in Third Age 5644, named after the mythical Paravian sea sprite who spirits away maidens who stray near the tidemark at twilight.
    pronounced: tal-ee-arth-e
    root meaning: *tal* branch; *li* – exalted; *araithe* – to disperse or to send

TALVISH—clan liegeman born to s'Brydion fealty in Alestron, granted to Arithon's service in Third Age 5654 in redress to resolve a debt of injury, and later claimed in life protection by crown debt for the criminal offence against Jeynsa s'Valerient. Died honorably, loyal to Rathain.

> pronounced: tal-vish
>
> root meaning: *talvesh* – reed

TAL QUORIN—river sourced in the confluent of watershed in Deshir, Rathain, where traps laid for Etarra's war host opened the battle of Strakewood Forest, ending in the rape and massacre of Deshir's clans-women and children by Lysaer and league headhunters under Pesquil's command in Third Age 5638.

> pronounced: tal quar-in
>
> root meaning: *tal* – branch; *quorin* – canyons

TARENS—townborn crofter from Kelsing, brother of Efflin and Kerelie. Liegeman to Prince Arithon, and recipient of *Caithdein*, High Earl Jieret's bequeathed memories in Third Age 5923, also named Iyat-thos Tarens by the clans.

> pronounced: tar-ens
>
> root meaning: *tirans* – *tier'ain* – protect

TEHAVAL WARDEN—last centaur guardian to leave the continent at the Paravian withdrawal, Keeper of the Records and Warden of Althain Tower, bestowed the gift of earth-link and transferred his post to Sethvir in Third Age 5100.

> pronounced: tay-have-all
>
> root meaning: *tehav* – tell, speak; *val* – straight

TEIRENDAELIENT MEREVALIA—High Queen Regent of Paravia, sunchild who granted Arithon Teir's'Ffalenn's request to be freed of Desh-thiere's Curse in Third Age 5671.

> pronounced: tee-er-en-dee-er-el mer-e-vah-lee-a
>
> root meaning: *tieren* – female successor to power; *daelient* – queen; *miere* – reflection; *val* – straight; *ia* – suffix for 'the third domain' (three octaves of vibration)

TEIVE—first mate of merchant brig *Evenstar*, father of Feylind's children, died in Third Age 5671 running resupply to Alestron during the siege.

> pronounced: tee-ev
>
> root meaning: *tierve* – reliable

TEYLIA—a *tiendar'shaynd*, ancestral soul of Biedar tribal origin, reincarnated

as the bastard daughter of Arithon Teir's'Ffalenn and Glendien, widow
of Kyrialt. Born in Third Age 5672, entered the Order of the Koriathain
by free will at three years of age and stayed throughout Arithon's incarceration until his release freed the last wraith from Marak. Considered
intractable, she facilitated his escape in Third Age 5922, then perished
foiling the death spell aimed at her sire by the Prime Matriarch.
>   pronounced: tay-lee-ah
>   root meaning: *tien* – dream; *li* – note struck in harmony; *a* – female
>   diminutive

THARIDOR—port town in eastern Melhalla on the coast of Eltair Bay.
>   pronounced: tha-rid-oor
>   root meaning: *tier'id'dur* – keep of stone

THEMBREL'S OAK—patriarch tree at the site of the sacred spring in
Halwythwood, heart of the mysteries where Athlien dancers enacted
rites of renewal, and centre of Baylienne's Gyre, forbidden to trespass
by Mankind.
>   pronounced: them-brel
>   root meaning: *thembrel* – acorn

THIRD AGE—marked by Mankind's refugee settlement on Athera under
the compact.

THUNDER RIDGE—see Tiendarion.

TIENDAR SHAYN'D—name given to Cianor reborn, see Cianor Moonlord.
>   pronounced: tee-en-dar shay-end
>   root meaning: *tiendar* – spirit and flesh; *shayn'd* – second time/
>   second born

TIENDARION—Paravian name for Thunder Ridge, a subduction ridge
forming the backbone of the Storlain Mountains in Ghent, Havish.
>   pronounced: tee-end-are-ee-on
>   root meaning: etheric connection between sky and earth: *tiend* –
>   spirit; *darion* – tie, with suffix for the emphatic

TIETHIN RIVER—flows from the Mathorn range, northwest into the
Tal Quorin in Deshir, Rathain.
>   pronounced: tee-ah-thin
>   root meaning: *tieahn* – dream; *theinn* – to bear, carry or ride

TIRANS—Second-Age ruin with a Paravian focus in Atwood, East Halla,
Melhalla.
>   pronounced: tee-rans
>   root meaning: *tier* – to hold fast

TIRIAC MOUNTAINS—range north of Mirthlvain Swamp in Midhalla, Melhalla.

    pronounced: tee-ree-ack

    root meaning: *tierach* – alloy of metals

TORBRAND s'FFALENN—founder of the s'Ffalenn royal line charged by the Fellowship of Seven in Third Age Year One to maintain charter law the High Kingdom of Rathain.

    pronounced: tor-brand sfall-en

    root meaning: *tor* – sharp, keen; *brand* – temper; *ffael* – dark, an – one

TORNIR PEAKS—mountain range west of Camris, Tysan.

    pronounced: tor-neer

    root meaning: *tor* – sharp; *nier* – tooth

TORWENT—fishing town and smuggler's haven on the coast of Lanshire, Havish, just south of the border. Many outbred clan descendants settled there to escape persecution under the pretender, Lysaer s'Ilessid, in Third Age 5653.

    pronounced: tore-went

    root meaning: *tor* – sharp; *wient* – bend

TRAITHE—Sorcerer of the Fellowship of Seven, single-handedly closed Southgate to curtail the Mistwraith's invasion in Third Age 4993, at the crippling loss of his greater faculties. Since impairment prevents his transfer to discorporate existence, he has suffered the scarred state of body and mind.

    pronounced: tray-the

    root meaning: *traithe* – gentleness

TREATY ACCORD—agreement forged by the Fellowship Sorcerers, and the Dragon Protectorate that binds the exile of drakes who refused to honour the Concord granting sovereignty of Athera to the Paravians. The factions in dissent reside on Sckaithen Duin, the splinter world beyond Northgate, bound under law not to threaten harm to Athera or damage the weal of the mysteries.

TRUE SECT—branch faith of the Religion of Light reformed by the Great Schism, when the Light's divine avatar turned apostate to Canon doctrine in Third Age 5683.

TYSAN—one of the Five High Kingdoms of Athera designated by charter law and maintained under Fellowship auspice by the s'Ilessid royal line. Device: gold star on blue field.

pronounced: tie-san

root meaning: *tiasen* – rich

VALIEN—Vivet Daldari's son by an unnamed trapper, born at Ettinmere Settlement in Third Age 5924, claimed as ward under child-right by Arithon s'Ffalenn, condemned to fire and sword, and executed as Spawn of Shadow by the True Sect priesthood in Third Age 5925.

pronounced: val-ee-en

root meaning: *val* – straight; *lien* – to love

VALLEYGAP—a narrow vale where the trade-road threads the notch between Etarra and Werpoint at the north end of the Skyshiel Mountains, where leaguesman Pesquil died in Jieret Red-beard's ambush as the Light's war host marched on campaign to Werpoint in Third Age 5645.

VALSTEYN RIVER—flows north across the Plain of Araithe in Rathain to the shore at North Ward.

pronounced: val-stayn

root meaning: *valsteyn* – to meander or wind

VANOMIND THIRD ITHALIVIER—High King of Paravia worn to loss of hope by Desh-thiere's invasion, then succumbed to despair when Baylienne, *Caithdein* of Rathain, trespassed the gyre at Thembrel's Oak in her mistaken effort to stem loss of sunlight. Though her damage of the resonant current sustaining the mysteries was mended by Athlien dancers, Vanomind Third despaired of Mankind and perished of self-immolation in the vortex at Athili in Third Age 5064.

pronounced: van-oh-mind i-tha-liv-ee-er

root meaning: *van o min'd* – behind the purple; *itha* – five; *li'vier* – to gentle by exaltation

VASTMARK—principality in southwestern Shand, ruggedly mountainous, with treacherous coasts renowned for shipwrecks. Inhabited by nomadic shepherds and wyverns, non–fire-breathing, smaller relatives of khadrim, and the site of the grand massacre of Lysaer's war host of forty thousand in Third Age 5647.

pronounced: vast-mark

root meaning: *vhast* – bare; *mheark* – valley

VERRAIN—Lisianne's beloved, reprieved from afflicted madness at Forthmark Sanctuary, which drained the adepts' reservoir, apprenticed to Luhaine to curb Methspawn; achieved Master Spellbinder and charged as Guardian of Mirthlvain by the Ilitharis Paravians after the Mistwraith's conquest.

pronounced: ver-rain

root meaning: *ver* – keep; *ria* – touch; *an* – one

original Paravian: *verriaan*

VHALZEIN—port in West Shand, west side of Rockbay Harbour, near Havish's border, famed for black-lacquer furniture inlayed with mother of pearl.

pronounced: val-zeen

root meaning: from Drakish, *vhchalzckeen* – white sands

VISSONCHARIZEL—rogue dragon whose fire and storm by drake spawn besieged Ithamon and forced Paravian evacuation and retreat during Esinivier Second Perehedral's reign in First Age 827.

pronounced: vee-son-char-i-zel

root meaning: *veesssonsharizel* – Drakish for murder storm

VIVET DALDARI—woman from Ettinmere Settlement, ran away and swore oath to Koriathain at Deal, then was crafted as bait for the Prime's trap to take Arithon. Gave birth to a trapper's son, Valien, and was killed by a True Sect Examiner at Daenfal, with her child condemned to execution as Spawn of Darkness.

pronounced: vee-vet dahl-dar-ee

root meaning: *vivet* – bait; *dal* – fair *diere* – life

VUCCARIMAISH—dragon, silver ancient Eldest Dragon, and Queen Dreamer, alive since the Era of Creation, signal influence in the Age of Dream, and progenitor of Seshkrozchiel.

pronounced: voo-car-i-may-ish

root meaning: *vuccarimaish* – Drakish for revered eldest.

WARDEN OF ALTHAIN—title held by the Fellowship Sorcerer, Sethvir, granted earth-linked Sight and charged with custody of Althain Tower by the last centaur guardian, Tehaval, in Third Age 5100.

WAYPOINT—small trade-road inn with a riverside post station in Melhalla, west of Methlas Lake.

WAYSTONE—faceted amethyst sphere, and the most powerful focus in the possession of the Koriathain, lost during the Third Age rebellion in 5018, until recovery from Fellowship custody by Lirenda in Third

Age 5647. Remapped, after sabotage infiltrated a stray *iyat* into the stone's matrix in 5671, the stone became shattered while entrained to subjugate Arithon s'Ffalenn in Third Age 5924.

WERPOINT—port on the west coast of Rathain above Minderl Bay.

　　pronounced: where-point

　　root meaning: *wyr* – all

WESTFEN—port town on the east shore of Deshir, Rathain.

WESTGATE—Worldsend Gate in Tysan, accesses splinter worlds Racinne Pasy and Dascen Elur.

WEST HALLA—principality in Melhalla.

　　pronounced: hall-ah

　　poot meaning: *hal'lia* – white light

WESTLANDS—originally a term for the western kingdoms of Tysan, Havish, and West Shand. Evolved to mean a specific set of mannered customs mostly practised in Tysan after the great uprising that threw down the high kings in Third Age 5018.

WESTLAND SEA—ocean west of Paravia, named after the tragic inundation of the Paravian Kingdom on Mhorovaire.

WEST SHAND—The adjunct territory including the free wilds of Falwood, exclusive to the Paravians in the Third Age, and traditionally guarded from Mankind's encroachment by Shand's heirs apparent. Annexed to the High Kingship of Shand when the old races forsook the continent in Third Age 5100.

　　pronounced: rhymes with 'hand'

　　root meaning: *shayn* or *shiand* – pair or partner

WHITE BROTHERHOOD—see Ath's adepts

WHITEHAVEN—hostel of Ath's adepts in the Skyshiel Mountains, near Eastwall, Rathain, where Elaira received advanced training as a healer, outside of Koriani precepts.

WHITEHOLD—town with a Koriani sisterhouse on the shore of Eltair Bay in East Halla, Melhalla.

WILLOWBROOK—stream in Halwythwood, Rathain, sited near the Gyre of Thembrel's Oak, where Arithon and Elaira's tryst once incited a grand confluence.

WORLDSEND GATES—four energetic portals set at the compass points on the continent of Paravia, constructed by Fellowship Sorcerers, and leading to splinter worlds held in reserve to arbitrate incompatible conflicts.

WYNTOK GATE—twin keeps that guarded the wooden span bridge over the tidal moat at Alestron, destroyed by Lysaer's attack in the siege, Third Age 5671, left in ruins since the s'Brydion entailment by the Fellowship Sorcerers.

pronounced: win-tock

root meaning: *wuinn* – vulture; *tiok* – roost

WYVERN—lesser drake spawn endemic to Vastmark, winged, and non-fire-breathing, mate for life.

ZAYNACKSHISH—silver-scaled ancient birthed in the Era of Creation, powerful enough to break the backbone of the continent; mate of Queen Dreamer Vuccarimaish, and sire of Seshkrozchiel.

pronounced: zay-nack-sheesh

root meaning: *zaynaksheesh* – Drakish for ice cloud

Masterbard's Lament for the Widows of Dier Kenton Vale

If tears were hardened stone to carve
    a monument to grief,
would we let loss and trouble starve
    our spirits for belief?
Our men have gone from home and hearth
    and faith has made us weep!

If feet that marched the earth to war
    could count their wounds by steel,
and blood that scorched clean ground in gore
    could speak in words that feel,
the cry would ring forevermore
    for mercy and repeal!

If song could hold sharp edge to fight
    through distrust, rage and fears,
and hope blaze up as blinding light
    to burn through pain and tears,
if heart touched mind, and eyes held sight,
    would blight and blame not clear?

If vengeful shouts towards mercy bent,
    and care unstopped deaf ears,

would every spirit not transcend
    to bind up hurts and heal?
Would every voice not cry to end
    the sorrows of the years?

If tears were hardened stone to carve
    inscribe my cry for life:
let no man raise his unsheathed sword,
    may no man draw his knife,
that this, our sore and grieving land
    waste no more hearts to strife.

No cause is scribed in fire and star –
    then whose truth must we heed?
Why bind the will and blind the heart
    more lives to rend and bleed?
Our men have gone from home and hearth,
    and hate has made us weep!

Arithon Teir's'Ffalenn
Third Age Year 5649